W9-CCD-617

"I have long admired Jane Kirkpatrick's rich historical fiction, and *Something Worth Doing* is well worth reading! Oregonian Abigail Duniway is a vibrant, fiercely passionate, and determined activist who fought for women's suffrage. Women of today have cause to respect and admire her—as well as the loving, patient, and supportive husband who encouraged her to continue 'the silent hunt.'"

Francine Rivers, author of *Redeeming Love*

"On the trail to Oregon, young Jenny Scott lost her beloved mother and little brother and learned that no matter what, she must persist until she reaches her goal. Remembering her mother's words—'a woman's life is so hard'—the young woman who became Abigail Scott Duniway came to understand through observation and experience that law and custom favored men. The author brings alive Abigail's struggles as frontier wife and mother turned newspaper publisher, prolific writer, and activist in her lifelong battle to win the vote and other rights for women in Oregon and beyond. Jane Kirkpatrick's story of this persistent, passionate, and bold Oregon icon is indeed *Something Worth Doing*!"

Susan G. Butruille, author of *Women's Voices from the Oregon Trail*, now in the 25th anniversary edition

Praise for *One More River to Cross*

"Based on true events, Jane Kirkpatrick's *One More River to Cross* (Revell, 2019) is the remarkable tale of a wagon train's attempt to cross the Sierra Nevada during winter."

World Magazine

"Jane Kirkpatrick has turned a scrap of history into a story of courageous women strong enough to meet the challenges of nature—and of men. Starting with a footnote about a group of 1844 pioneers caught in snows of the California Sierra, Kirkpatrick weaves a tale of extraordinary women (oh, and a few men too) who fight blizzards and starvation to save those they love."

Sandra Dallas, *New York Times* bestselling author

"What an incredible journey this novel is! Without ever trivializing or sentimentalizing the harshness of the circumstances, Kirkpatrick centers her novel on the bonds of community, family, and friendship that sustained these strong, complicated women through a harrowing winter trapped in the Sierra Nevada. There's not a false note in this book. It's moving and beautifully told, and I absolutely loved it."

Molly Gloss, award-winning author of *The Jump-Off Creek* and *The Hearts of Horses*

"I can wholeheartedly recommend the book. Jane gets the facts as right as they can be got out of the stories of the various participants in the experience of the winter of 1844–45 in the Sierra Nevada of California. Anyone can tell you what it was like—dirty and hungry and cold and lonely. Jane puts the heart-pounding, breath-taking, adrenaline-soaked feelings into the thoughts and the mouths of the people who lived the experience as real-time commentary on the events. The thoughts and words may not be exactly what those folks were thinking and feeling, but I believe in my heart they could be."

Stafford Hazelett, editor of *Wagons to the Willamette*

"Award-winning western writer Jane Kirkpatrick tells the remarkable story of survival of the Murphy-Stephens-Townsend Overland Party of 1845, the first to bring wagons through the Sierra Nevada into California. Unlike the great loss of life suffered by the tragic Donner Party the following year, all fifty members of the party survived, despite harrowing ordeals in mountain snows, often with nothing to eat but tree bark. As with so many of Jane's books, she tells the story of the women who are so often ignored in western histories—giving birth along the trail; enduring their own illnesses to comfort near-starving children; taking charge in emergencies, such as helping rescue a drowning man or a stranded horse; and resisting men who try to shout them down when they insist on being heard. And don't overlook Jane's acknowledgments at the end where she says she hopes this story 'might celebrate the honor of self-sacrifice, the wisdom of working together, and the power of persevering through community and faith.' This wonderful new book accomplishes this, and more."

R. Gregory Nokes, author, former editor for the *Oregonian*

Something Worth Doing

Also by Jane Kirkpatrick

One More River to Cross
Everything She Didn't Say
All She Left Behind
This Road We Traveled
The Memory Weaver
A Light in the Wilderness
One Glorious Ambition
The Daughter's Walk
Where Lilacs Still Bloom
A Mending at the Edge
A Tendering in the Storm
A Clearing in the Wild
Barcelona Calling
An Absence So Great
A Flickering Light
A Land of Sheltered Promise
Hold Tight the Thread
Every Fixed Star
A Name of Her Own
What Once We Loved
No Eye Can See
All Together in One Place
Mystic Sweet Communion
A Gathering of Finches
Love to Water My Soul
A Sweetness to the Soul

Novella Collections

Sincerely Yours
Log Cabin Christmas
The American Dream

Nonfiction

Promises of Hope for Difficult Times
Aurora: An American Experience in Quilt, Community, and Craft
A Simple Gift of Comfort
A Burden Shared
Homestead: A Memoir

Something Worth Doing

A Novel of an Early Suffragist

JANE KIRKPATRICK

Revell
a division of Baker Publishing Group
Grand Rapids, Michigan

© 2020 by Jane Kirkpatrick

Published by Revell
a division of Baker Publishing Group
PO Box 6287, Grand Rapids, MI 49516-6287
www.revellbooks.com

Printed in the United States of America

All rights reserved. No part of this publication may be reproduced, stored in a retrieval system, or transmitted in any form or by any means—for example, electronic, photocopy, recording—without the prior written permission of the publisher. The only exception is brief quotations in printed reviews.

Library of Congress Cataloging-in-Publication Data
Names: Kirkpatrick, Jane, 1946– author.
Title: Something worth doing : a novel of an early suffragist / Jane Kirkpatrick.
Description: Grand Rapids, Michigan : Revell, a division of Baker Publishing Group, [2020]
Identifiers: LCCN 2020004897 | ISBN 9780800736118 (paperback) | ISBN 9780800739249 (hardcover)
Subjects: GSAFD: Historical fiction. | Christian fiction.
Classification: LCC PS3561.I712 S66 2020 | DDC 813/.54—dc23
LC record available at https://lccn.loc.gov/2020004897

Scripture used in this book, whether quoted or paraphrased by the characters, is taken from the King James Version of the Bible.

This book is a work of historical fiction based closely on real people and events. Details that cannot be historically verified are purely products of the author's imagination.

Published in association with Joyce Hart of the Hartline Literary Agency, LLC.

20 21 22 23 24 25 26 7 6 5 4 3 2 1

Dedicated to the ever hopeful,
especially Jerry

A storm was coming
But that's not what she felt.
It was adventure on the wind
And it shivered down her spine.

ATTICUS, THE POET

Character List

Abigail Jane (Jenny) Scott Duniway—daughter, wife, mother, farmer, teacher, milliner, novelist, owner/editor of *The New Northwest*, nationally known suffragist

Benjamin Duniway—husband of Abigail, horse trainer, farmer

Abigail's siblings

- **Mary Francis**—Fanny
- **Margaret**—Maggie
- **Harvey**
- **Catherine**—Kate
- **Harriet**
- **John Henry**—Little Toot, Jerry
- **Sarah Maria**—Maria

Mary Gibson—Ben's sister

***Shirley Ellis**—friend of Abigail, wife, mother, divorcee, suffragist

John Tucker Scott—Patriarch of the Scott family

Susan B. Anthony—friend of Abigail, president of National American Woman Suffrage Association (NAWSA)

Children of Abigail and Ben Duniway

- **Clara Belle**
- **Willis**

Hubert

Wilkie

Clyde

Ralph

***Harold Bunter**—suitor and nemesis of Abigail

***Eloi Vasquez**—second husband of Shirley Ellis, California attorney

Sarah Wallace—member of Stephens-Murphy-Townsend wagon train and president of California suffragist association

*fully imagined characters

Prologue

June 1852

Her dreams of late had been of books with maps of unknown places. Jenny Scott wished she were dreaming now instead of sitting here beside the family wagon, a gushing stream to serenade them. They'd left Illinois two months previous—2 April 1852. She had written the date in the family journal she'd been assigned to keep as they crossed the continent. Since that first roll-out of wagons toward the west, Jenny traveled without maps. She needed them to help her reduce the fear and anxiety of the unknown; but she did not have them. Though only seventeen, she'd already learned that living required coming to terms with uncertainty—not that she did that well. She had lost another kind of map as well—the map of her mother.

A different kind of pain awaited this June afternoon.

"The agony will be worth it." Jenny spoke with conviction as she eyed the fat needle her new friend blackened in the flame. Then, "Won't it?"

"It does have a sting," Shirley Ellis said. "Fair warning."

Jenny lifted the dark curls to hold them behind her ears. She thought of her hair as unruly with its thickness and natural twists that made morning brushing a chore. She envied her brothers who kept their hair short, curls under control.

Kate, Jenny's twelve-year-old sister, patted Jenny's shoulder while Shirley continued. "Shakespeare had this done and even biblical Jacob gave a pair to Rachel way back when. The pain has to come before the glory."

"Ha," Jenny said.

"I'm here to comfort you," Kate said, "but I don't understand why you want to hurt yourself for fashion."

Ignoring her sister, Jenny took a deep breath. She sat on a three-legged stool they used to milk the cow. The stool did double duty as a seat for medical ministrations. Jenny squeezed her eyes shut. "Go ahead. Do it."

Kate pinched her sister's earlobe as hard as she could, then said to Shirley, "Now."

The pain of the needle seared. Her sister's pinching simply wasn't enough to dull the agony. But at least Jenny felt misery for something physical instead of the heartache she'd carried since the deaths. *Did I know that physical pain could distract from emotional hurting?*

She felt the blood trickle down her neck as Shirley pulled the needle out. "It's a good thing I have a strong stomach," Jenny said. Kate dabbed at Jenny's bleeding earlobe. They'd have to soak the handkerchief to rid it of the red. "Are you certain that Jacob gave Rachel a pair of earrings? What chapter and verse?"

"I don't really remember," Shirley said. She had thick, naturally arched eyebrows that framed her blue eyes. "It's too late for second thoughts, though if you don't put the pin through, it'll grow new flesh right over the hole." Shirley dabbed at Jenny's ear with a clean handkerchief, then wiped the needle, and now rolled it in the flame again until blackened.

"Ready," Jenny said.

She straightened her back. Kate pinched the other ear and Jenny closed her eyes. The second piercing commenced. Her older sister Fanny, standing to the side, winced. It took a team.

"Finished. And you didn't even faint," Shirley said.

Kate dabbed at the blood on Jenny's cheek, then held out the tourmaline-studded gold rings. "I'll put them in for you."

Jenny felt the metal push into her ears, surprised again at the sting and pain.

"You'll have to twirl them a few times a day until they heal," Shirley warned. "You don't want the skin to attach itself to the rings." She eyed the earrings now adorning Jenny's ears. "They're really pretty with that one gold gem in the middle of the disc. A good size too. Won't draw too much attraction."

"Isn't attraction the point though?" Kate said.

"The point," Jenny corrected, "is not adornment but memorializing. Momma loved these. She got them from Grandma who received them from her mother, and she left them to me."

"I thought one of the stones like those we covered Momma's grave with was your memorial keepsake. You insisted to Papa that you had to put that rock in the wagon." Fanny dabbed Jenny's other ear with a bit of whiskey kept only for medicinal purposes.

"You can't have too many mementos, I say." Shirley wiped the needle with the liquor, then put it back into her fabric sewing kit attached to her bodice.

"It's more than a memento. Earrings and rocks and a cut of hair, they're all ephemera, items of the historical record that are neither documents nor maps," Jenny said. She touched her ear and winced.

"I'm sorry." Kate leaned in.

"What's a little smarting in memory of our momma who endured so much bringing us into the world, and then had to leave it so prematurely? She didn't want to leave Illinois, you know. I heard her tell Papa that they'd always lived on a frontier, and now civilization was catching up to them so couldn't they stay and enjoy it. Papa said no." Tears welled in her eyes while her stomach clenched with anger. It wasn't fair, it just wasn't.

"Will you take some item for . . . your friend too?" Fanny asked. Her voice was gentle. A boy Jenny had met on the trail had drowned not long after their mother's death.

"One earring for Momma and the other for him. And then no more." She took the mirror Shirley handed her, turned her head from side to side to admire the earrings. "No more sadness. I've had enough." She stood and with conviction declared, "I will control it."

Their brother Harvey sauntered by as Jenny made her declaration of sending grief away. Harvey, with his good looks and opinions, walked backward away from them then, saying, "You can't control anything, you females. Not a thing. Lucky for you us men protect you."

"Ha!" Jenny shouted after him as he turned his back to them, striding off as though he owned the land, the stream—his future. "No one knows what they can accomplish until they undertake it." Fanny, Shirley, and Kate nodded agreement.

And so Abigail Jane "Jenny" Scott set forth to do the best she could to prove her brother—and all men—wrong. Girls had power too. One day, she'd show them.

PART 1

The things nearby, not the things afar,
Not what we seem, but what we are,
These are the things that make or break,
That give the heart its joy or ache.

Inscription in autograph booklet

ONE

Making Her Own Map

April 1853
Willamette Valley, Oregon Territory

A spring rain pattered on the shake roof of the schoolhouse near the little settlement of Cincinnati, six miles south of Salem. To Jenny, it sounded like the clapping of children's gloved hands connecting in a steady, soothing rhythm. Jenny shook her thick curls of the mist she'd ridden through to get to the structure before her students arrived. Her first day of teaching had begun with fixing meals for boarders at her father's inn, then riding several miles warmed by the congratulations of her sisters. Despite less than a year of formal schooling back in Illinois, she'd passed the teacher's test and been hired. She'd board out with a district family who paid their child's fees by offering a bed and meals to the teacher during the week. She'd ride home on Friday to help again at the inn.

Her mother would be proud. It had been her mother's snippets of wisdom offered through the years while cornbread baked or she stitched a pantaloon that created Jenny's educational foundation. Either due to illness or her need to be home as the third oldest child, Jenny had been less than a year inside an Illinois schoolhouse. It was her parents' love of reading, the many books and newspapers available to peruse, and her mother's conveying facts and figures through stories that had prepared Jenny for this day. Some of the newspapers, like the *Lily* that promoted women's issues or Horace Greely's *New York Tribune* that railed against slavery, were considered unusual for their frontier family to acquire, but the Scott children had all been allowed to read them as soon as they were able.

For Jenny, education was critical for boys and girls to grow to make good choices and be wise citizens too. This schoolhouse was her arena to awaken minds to the possibilities of their lives even when others appeared to control their destiny. She controlled what would happen here, the minds she'd affect, yes, but personally, this job granted her a chance to draw her own independent map. It gave her a level of freedom she never saw her mother have. Anne Scott had birthed twelve children, lived to bury two, and once told Jenny she was sorry she had brought girls into the world, as their lot was harder than the boys and would always be. It had been a warning. As a respected teacher, Jennie would chart her own course. It was one of the few professions allowed a woman outside of the home. Operating a boardinghouse or a millinery made up the only other two. That *Lily* editor had risked more than her design of the bloomer costume by running a newspaper. Jenny was grateful her father let that broadsheet into their house, or perhaps he didn't realize a woman was at its head. But her mother did and she'd made sure Jenny knew it. Another snippet of sagacity perhaps.

A chill in the air moved Jenny to set the kindling to fire in the little stove. She was grateful that someone had not only chopped and stacked wood outside but had tented dry sticks over bits of pine needles and forest duff so the flame took without effort. Part of her teaching contract was that from now on, she would split the wood and stack it, start the fires, and remove the ashes as well as maintain the inside and the surrounding grounds outside, sweeping pine needles from the stairs and even the roof if necessary. Cobwebs drifted from the corners, and she grabbed the straw broom and swept them and the floors. As she worked, she remembered the interview with the board of education. She'd kept her tongue when one of the farmers asked her if she had a beau or was using this opportunity to find a husband—as though that were the only goal of a woman's life.

None of your business, she'd wanted to say but smiled instead. "With one woman for every one hundred men in this Territory, I doubt I'd need a schoolhouse full of other men's—and women's—children to attract a husband. No, I'm delighted to teach little minds and to have a few coins to call my own." She thought her mother would be proud of her for controlling her sometimes intemperate tongue. Truth was, she was torn about marriage. She liked the idea of falling in love, being swept away, but only wished to marry a man who saw value in a partner and not just be a "hand" in the drudgery of women's work that took so many women's lives at such a young age. Her parents had loved each other, she felt sure—but she'd wished her father had paid more attention to her mother's needs and waited a little longer before remarrying after her death. But he ruled the roost, as her mother often said. And because she'd let him, she accepted their journey west and it had taken her life.

Marriage could wait. Jenny had brushed off a few offers already, determined that they were more land-based than promising love. If an Oregon man married within a year of reaching the territory, his new wife could bring 160 acres into the marriage in her own name. Of course, as soon as she married, the control of it became her husband's. But it did expand the spouse's holdings. She made light of most of the proposals, encouraging them to seek a less willful mate. She didn't want to offend, but she certainly wasn't interested in expanding a man's wealth without at least a little love to go with it.

Dawn pushed its way into darkness, announcing she had time yet to scan the lessons she'd prepared using the one primer she'd snuck along on the journey west. Her father had restricted what the women could bring—including books and dishes—and never knew until they arrived that her sister's beau had bought their auctioned dishes—a set of Spode—and given them back to Fanny before they left. With tears, Fanny, her oldest sister, had sewed the butter plates, dishes, and cups into a feather bed so their father never knew that he slept on them. Jenny's book had survived, buried in the barrel of corn meal. A woman needed a little piece of home. At least their father hadn't broken the dishes when he discovered they'd defied his orders, as she'd heard some men had. He hadn't complained about the schoolbook, either.

Jenny rubbed her hands to warm them at the flame, reset the combs in her hair to control the curls. She counted the slates piled on the crude table that served as her desk. There were six, so if all the children attended, they'd have to share. With her first paycheck she'd buy two more. She'd have the students work on writing their names today so she could learn who they were and assess their skills. She planned to tell them stories and weave the lessons into them to hold their attention. It worked for her siblings. It had worked for her.

The sound of stomping boots on the pine stairs took her from the primer. *Must be an older student.* She straightened her back, ignoring the pain that lived in her spine.

She expected twelve students. At least that's what the board had told her she'd be responsible for, though she remembered one man's caveat. "Some days you might have more, if they bring a little brother or sister usually too young, but maybe their ma is sick and there's no one to look after them at home. Can you adapt?"

"I've six younger siblings—no, only five now." She swallowed. Willie had died in the Blue Mountains the year before. "Like any good western woman, I can corral them without a rope."

Today she'd see if that was true. If students arrived this early, she'd have to rise at 4:00 a.m. to stay ahead of them in their lessons.

"Welcome," she said as the door opened. Now she'd see what a day in her domain would hold and what kind of a creative map she could draw.

TWO

Courting or Confrontation

"Harold Bunter," the man said. He hadn't removed his hat. "I come to press my case to you, Missy."

Rigid as a fence post, he was a big man, well over six feet tall, with a ruddy face and a broken front tooth. He stood too close and she backed up. "Excuse me?"

"Time's a-wasting, Missy. I've got until December to find my bride, and I hear you're a hard worker helping at your father's inn. He don't serve spirits, only beer and wine, so I guess you're a teetotaler, which is good for me. And you must have common sense or the board wouldn't have hired ya. So I'll court ya proper-like, but we both know the end result. Glad to see you're punctual too, getting here long before the babes arrive. I think an August wedding would be fine, don't you?"

"Mr. Bunter, I am working here. I'm sure you understand the need for my full attention to be given to preparing for my students. Your offer is generous, of course, but I can't entertain it today and likely not tomorrow or the next day either."

"I'll give you time. Until August, like I said."

"I'm barely of age, Mr. Bunter." *Holy cow chips. What was the man thinking?*

"You're almost nineteen. Many a girl at fourteen is marrying in these parts."

It bothered her that he knew her age. It was true that young girls were being handed over by their parents to willing men to help expand their farms and be extra hands. She prayed that some of those girls found love in the process. "You've done your homework, Mr. Bunter."

"I know how to woo a woman." When he grinned, that broken tooth gaped at her.

"Oh, I see another early bird may have arrived." She looked beyond him to the misty dawn. "If you'll excuse me, I must get to work and make my students welcome." She'd looked out through the open door and hadn't seen anyone but hoped she had distracted Mr. Bunter enough for him to at least stop talking about marriage.

"I'll come back after class and we can confer more," he said. "That's a good educated word, isn't it—'confer'? My farm's not too far away, so I can get here easy. I know all the board members. They can vouch for me. I'll let 'em know they'll need to be looking for a new schoolmarm, as they won't let a married woman work out, you know. A woman's place is in the house."

She turned back to him. "Mr. Bunter, I'm sure you're a very fine citizen and your farm is very fine too. But I'm new to the territory, I've just begun my job, and I really can't think about marriage at this time. With you or anyone. So please don't speak for me to the board."

"Now, don't get too frazzled, Missy. I can wait. I got 'til December for my year to be up. Only April now."

"Mr. Bunter, you're not listening to me." *Am I being too rude? No, I must be firm.* "I am not interested in marriage—to anyone at this time. So please, spread your charms to another missy, as you'll be wasting your time with this one."

He took a step closer, inhaled deeply through his nose like he was trying to inhale her. She moved back. Her heart pounded like a butter churn. He was big and could hurt her if he chose to. She shouldn't give him any fuel for his fire by suggesting they would discuss it later. That would only lead him on. But she couldn't think of anything else to do. "Let's talk about it over the weekend," she said. "I'll do my homework too. And find out about you."

"Good for you, Missy. I'll come by your father's inn on Saturday. We can confer then. I'll be sure to tell the board about what a loyal teacher you are, not wanting to mix pleasure with work." He grinned, showing a mouth of tobacco-stained teeth, touched his hat brim, turned his back to her, and clomped down the steps.

She'd deal with him on Saturday. She couldn't think about it now. She took a deep breath, inhaling the new-lumber scent of the building and the desks.

Before she'd returned to her chair, more step noise, and a man's voice, singing. "Holy cow chips," she said out loud. She stood to confront Mr. Bunter once again.

But instead a small child appeared, holding the hand of a tall man with sky-blue eyes and curly hair that matched the child's, with just a hint of ginger to the brown. He'd been the singer. He removed his hat and nodded to her. "Ben Duniway, ma'am."

"And this is . . . ?"

"Josie. It's her first day."

"Welcome, Josie. I'm Miss Scott. How old are you, sweetie?"

"I'm six. We're having a sister or brother. Momma said she could tell me which it is when I got home. I guess she went to town to pick it up."

"That's lovely."

"Her mother would have brought her, but she's, uh, feeling poorly today."

"Yes, I can see how she might be." To the child, she said, "Would you like to put your lunch pail on the entry shelf?"

"Uncle Ben bringed me. He and Momma are sister and brother. Like I'm gonna be."

"Ah," Jenny said.

"I see you've already met Harold," Ben said. "Courting, is he?"

Jenny felt her face grow warm. "He might call it that. I wouldn't."

"Discouraging him could be a full-time occupation. He's made many a proposal, and I hear he's getting desperate to find a wife before his year is up." He let Josie's hand loose, and the child stood beside him, a thumb in her mouth, lunch pail in her other hand, her eyes moving back and forth between the adults. "I brought a slate for Josie. Figured you might be short."

"Thank you, Mr. Duniway."

He removed the chalkboard from his loose shirt.

"I appreciate that thoughtfulness. Josie, would you like to pick one of the front desks? You'll sit with another student, but since you're early, you get first choice. After you put your pail away."

"Yes, ma'am. Thank you, ma'am." She scampered to the entry.

"If you need a rescuer from Harold, let me know," Ben said. "He can be as cantankerous as a green broke horse. And for the record, not that you've asked, I've got my 320 acres and didn't need a woman's 160 acres to make it so. When I come courting, it'll be for the woman's heart and not her land."

"You're right, I didn't ask."

"But you don't mind knowing, now do you?" His grin slid across his attractive face, and she felt a glow inside.

I believe he's flirting. She'd keep this professional. "I'm an educator, Mr. Duniway, a seeker of information for its own sake," she said. "One never knows when one will need it to advance a cause or carve a path forward."

He grinned as he put his hat back on. "I'll be back at three to bring you home, Josie. You be good now and mind Miss Scott."

"I will." The child reached up to him, and he squatted down to let her wrap her arms around his neck. *Children like him.* And he bent to them, didn't stand above them. That was a good sign. "Bye, Unc," Josie said.

"Don't forget to sing when you leave to go outside," Ben told her as he stood and brushed the top of her head with his wide hands. Two honey-colored pigtails poked out on either side of her head.

"I won't," she said.

He turned back to Jenny. "Singing when they face the world is a good way to calm the stomach wiggles. There's lots of them when you're a child."

"And when you're a grown-up too," Jenny said.

"Indeed."

He replaced his hat and headed out, singing a song Jenny didn't recognize, about "seeing Nellie home." It was a happy tune, and Josie giggled as she skipped her way past Jenny and found a front desk. Jenny watched as the man patted her horse's neck and checked her grain bag. Jenny had her mount at the hitching post where other children's ponies would soon be tied. Her horse nickered to him. *Animals and children like him.* He turned and waved at her and she blushed. He had known she'd be watching, the scamp.

She witnessed horses and their child riders coming up the trail, dismounting and tying their animals to the post, filling grain bags, then walking up the stairs.

She was the queen of her domain here, and as she greeted each child, she felt a lifting of her spirit. She didn't know if her joy came from this being her first day as a teacher or if the meeting of Ben Duniway played a part. She couldn't be sure. She just hoped he wasn't a diversion on her map to independence.

THREE

The Hesitating Heart

Ben Duniway had returned to pick up his niece and continued to bring her back and forth the entire week.

"This is the longest child-birthing in history," Jenny had joked to him on Friday.

"I figured she told you she has a little brother. I'm still helping my sister out. And I'm hoping we might have a conversation longer than a blink one day. Perhaps while riding to the dance at Lafayette this Saturday night. Would you consider going with me?"

Her independent self was a bit annoyed that she was so easily swayed by those blue eyes looking right into her heart and the way he listened without interrupting when she spoke. The man asked questions and didn't give orders, though they had only short opportunities with her students her priority. "I'd be pleased. Of course, my sisters would need to come along."

"Understood. I wouldn't want to tarnish your fine reputation."

Thoughts of knowing she'd be seeing him twice a day distracted her studies, and she had to force herself to concentrate on reading and arithmetic rather than his warming smile. She wasn't ready for love. She had too much to prove about taking care of herself and being there for her sisters and youngest brother, Little Toot. Her brother Harvey seemed well able to care for himself. She wasn't sure she could trust Ben's courting kindness, either. People changed. Husbands became domineering once they'd won over their wives. Ben's presence gave her comfort now, but would he always? Her heart hesitated. Back to her lessons. When in doubt, work.

* * *

"Put the creamer on the table," Fanny told Jenny. "I'll get the biscuits. You'd think there was a wedding going on with all the people here today." She winced at her own words.

"Travelers," her father said. "Though a good wedding would be in order. Right, Fanny?" He held the door open so Jenny could use both hands to carry the heavy ironstone pitcher to the table.

"It's too heavy, Papa. Let's put it into two smaller jugs."

"Ah, you're right. Give it here, Jenny." He turned to the pantry to make the exchange, and Fanny mouthed "Thank you."

Jenny had wanted to rescue her sister from any wedding discussions. Fanny had been forced to leave the love of her life behind in Illinois. He'd proposed but had an ill mother he needed to care for, and then John Tucker Scott—the family patriarch—said his entire family was heading west, true love left behind. Fanny still reeled from the heartache she carried from their arrival last fall. Work at the inn had not taken the pain away. The tavern, as inns were often called, had been operated by an uncle looking to farm instead, so Tucker Scott had taken over the duties. It provided a good space for his children and his new wife and her two young ones. For Jenny and Fanny, his remarriage seemed hasty, not giving much grieving time to their mother and little brother who had died on the trail. And his new wife was already with child. That their father had also insisted that Fannie consider marrying a well-known man in the territory twenty years older than she was had added to the family strain. "I want you girls married and safe so there are no reputational issues. Unmarried women can be the heart of scorn without even trying. Safety is when you're under the roof of a husband."

Jenny wasn't so certain of that. She had argued that if she married, she wouldn't be able to teach and there'd be fewer coins to help meet the family's needs. They'd left Illinois with a cache of money, but it had been stolen on the trail, the culprit never found nor confessed to it. Jenny had decided she needed an untarnished reputation, and she'd do that by focusing on slates and schoolwork. When she thought of introducing Ben to the family, she found her stomach hurt the tiniest little bit. The feelings she had for him had deepened in such a short time and they'd never even been alone. She hadn't spoken to her father yet about the dance, but she'd told her sisters and they were ready to chaperone.

Ben's introduction would come later—if he even showed up. And how would she feel about that if he didn't? She set her mind on cooking, serving, splashing suds on plates, and scrubbing linens for the guests who had spent the night.

She'd just swirled her skirts through the dining room door to bring out a platter of ham and eggs when she saw Harold Bunter standing at a table. She made a quick turn back into the heat of the kitchen where she told Fanny, "You need to rescue *me* now. That farmer I told you about is out there."

"The handsome one?"

"No, that first-day one who proposed marriage so he could get his 160 acres. I forgot I told him I'd do my homework and we could talk on Saturday. I wanted him to go away."

"Well, let's see. I'll take the platter out and treat him like he's here to eat and nothing more."

"What'll you say when he asks to see me? Or worse, Papa?"

"I'll say . . . that you're not here. That you've . . . stepped out. Go." Fanny shooed her out the back. "Stand on the porch steps so I'm not lying."

River mist rose off the Willamette as Jenny pulled her shawl around her and shivered on the back porch. Why had she told him to come here? How had she forgotten it? Ben, of course. She'd been distracted by his company. Still, this wasn't right, her hovering like a scared rabbit, forcing her sister to speak for her. She needed to let Mr. Bunter know she was not interested before he talked to her father and the two of them came up with some scheme to marry her off.

She took in a deep breath and walked back into the kitchen, then through the door into the dining area, where her heart sank. Her father was already talking to him.

"Jenny. Mr. Bunter here is asking for your hand in marriage." Her father said it loud enough for other guests to hear, and she felt her face grow hot and her palms get sticky wet. "Said you told him to come by today and speak to me."

"She's quite the missy."

A general murmur of approval came from the diners, with a couple of the men actually applauding.

She nodded to Mr. Bunter, then said, "Papa, may I speak with you? Alone?"

"Now, don't you go all shy," Bunter said. "We're going to be family, so you can say whatever you want in front of me."

"We're not family—yet," Jenny said. "Papa? Please."

Why she had to gain the approval of her father to make such intimate decisions was a frustration. Men always seemed to have the upper hand in a woman's life. But it was the way it was and no changing it at the moment. "Please. If Momma was here, she'd want you to talk with me about this privately. You know she would."

Her father nodded. "We'll be back in a moment, Harold. You enjoy a meal now, on the house."

"Oh, well, that'd be good then." He took a seat and asked for the platter to be passed to him while Jenny turned on her heel and headed to the kitchen, her father behind her.

"Did you direct him to come by today and talk with me?"

"I told him to stop here, yes, to get him out the door. He came early to the school that first morning, didn't want to leave, and I said I'd do some asking around about him and we could discuss it on Saturday. But I totally forgot because, Papa, I have met someone else. A young man."

"You've been off on your own, have you?"

"No. No. He brought his niece to school, and we've barely had a conversation what with the children there. He's Ben Duniway. He's already got a farm and wouldn't qualify for my 160 acres because he's been here since 1850. He's from Illinois." She took a deep breath. "I'm not even sure about him, but I enjoy his company and he's coming by to take me and Mary Francis and Catherine to the dance. With your approval. I haven't had time to ask you. But I know I'm not interested in Mr. Bunter's proposal. He's only interested in the land I'd bring to him. He even sent me a letter of proposal. It's embarrassing, Papa. I did nothing to warrant his attention."

"I see."

"And I do have a little more information about him. Mr. Duniway said he'd made a number of proposals already and been turned down."

"If you don't want to accept his proposal, you have to let the man know. I won't do that for you."

She clasped his elbow in gratitude. "Oh, Father, thank you so much."

"You got everything settled then?" Harold had walked right into the kitchen. Fanny stood behind him, signaling that she'd been unable to stop him. "We can set the date then?"

Jenny swallowed. "I'm glad you've come." This way he wouldn't be humiliated by her refusal being witnessed by a room full of guests. "I must decline your proposal."

"What? You leading me on and then saying no?"

"I didn't intend to lead you on. I simply needed time to consider, and now I have, and I am not interested in your marriage proposal."

"What do you want? Pretties? I can buy you some nice things to flatter you. Consider it wedding presents. Not something to expect often though."

She could see that she had created her own problem by not putting a stop to it that day in the school. But she'd done what she did to protect herself from him. Instead she'd given him fuel to make the decision an affront to him rather than honoring her own right to her choices. She'd remember this. Don't make excuses or put someone off. Face the music. Hook your corset and stand tall.

"Mr. Bunter, I know you mean well and your offer will be accepted one day, I feel certain. But not by me. I'm sorry I led you to believe a little time to consider would change my mind, but I did tell you I wasn't interested in marriage. And I'm not. Now. Or ever, with you."

"I won't give up. I'll come a-courting."

"Then you'll be wasting time better spent seeking another."

He looked around. The color drained from Fanny's face, turning it white as her starched apron, and fourteen-year-old Catherine—the most beautiful of the Scott girls, at least in Jenny's mind—backed out the door into the dining room, her blue eyes wide as biscuits.

"Court other than a Scott girl," her father said. "My daughter has spoken, Bunter. And I back her."

Jenny felt a warmth of gratitude toward her father for his defense.

"She leading you by a nose ring, is she, Tucker?"

Her father bristled, and Jenny reached to put her hand over his. "It is a woman's right to make her own choices," she said. "Men's laws give that God-given right to other men—their fathers and sons, brothers sometimes—and certainly to husbands once the vows are said. I happen to have a father who believes a woman can make some decisions on her own, and this is one of them." She thought of another argument. "I'm actually saving you from a life of misery with me. We'd be at constant odds."

"I'd break you."

"No, you wouldn't."

He arched his back, looked down at everyone in the room, his eyes landing on Jenny. "I wouldn't want you anyway, though breaking you from a wild filly into a steady mare could be a worthy effort. But not worth it for 160 acres. Woe to the man who does win you. He'll never get a word in and be henpecked for certain."

Don't defend. Don't add fuel to his fire. "I hope you enjoyed your meal," Jenny said. "Now if you'll excuse me, I need to see if the chickens have given up any more eggs."

She spoke a prayer of thanksgiving as the door closed behind her and she heard Mr. Bunter say to her father, "I don't envy you trying to find a mate for that missy. You got yourself a spinster on your hands."

And what would be so bad about that?

FOUR

The Timing of Love

The quartet walked. Sisters Maggie and Kate trailed Jenny and Ben to the dance, meandering a discreet distance behind. At the last minute, her father had told Fanny she needed to remain behind to tend the inn and spend time with her father's choice of beau for her, Amos Cook. *Poor Fanny.*

Jenny's younger sisters giggled behind them, and Jenny found herself apologizing for their silliness, even as she remembered the intensity of the confrontation with Mr. Bunter. He'd frightened her with his bluster, and while she was grateful her father had stood up for her, it also troubled her. Would she always need a man to buttress her decisions before they'd be taken seriously? And how fortunate she was that her father supported her, though he'd done the opposite for Fanny's preferred suitor. How unfair to Fanny.

"Giggling girls is a happy sound to me, so long as they aren't giggling at me," Ben said, bringing Jenny back to the moment.

"They're happy. We've had such grief in the past year with Momma's and little Willie's deaths. It seems happiness has escaped us." She put her arm through his, and he patted her gloved hand.

Maggie said in her still childlike voice, "Be careful up there." Maggie was her pious sister.

She turned around and put her finger to her lips to signal silence adding, "I'm eighteen, Maggie."

"A body has to come up for air in a world where there are always floods and fires and family feuds," Jenny told Ben as she turned back, her elbow securely attached to his. "That's one reason I like teaching so much. If I ever run a school of my own, I'll call it Hope School, because that's what I think education does for people—gives them hope to get them through the hard times, to try for higher things. Some things are worth doing regardless of how they turn out. That's my thinking. What do you say to that, Mr. Duniway?"

"Good thought. I headed to the gold fields in Southern Oregon a few months after I arrived in Oregon. I hoped I'd become rich. Instead I mined enough to buy a donation land claim but not enough to operate it like a manor boss. It's hard work but worthy work. It'd be more fun to have a wife and family to share it with. Not the work so much, but the outcome of it."

She didn't feed his fire, either. She wasn't certain about a married life, and a week of courting ought not take her there. Risky decisions should be made with caution.

They reached the dance hall, and Ben helped her step up the stairs to the music flowing out the open door. It was a balmy evening. Ben motioned her sisters to come ahead, the chaperoning now reversed with Ben and Jenny looking after them in this jubilant crowd. He directed them toward the punch bowl beyond the coatroom.

"Got my little flock to look after," he said.

"We Scott girls can look after ourselves," Kate said. "Can't we, Jenny?"

"I think it's proper to have a man watch out for our welfare." Maggie spoke up.

"Let me get you all a cup of punch while you nestle yourselves by the wall there."

"He's nice," Kate said, as Ben drifted to the refreshments, stopping on the way to talk with friends.

"And handsome." Maggie settled herself on a higher chair and swung her legs back and forth.

"It is nice to be waited on, isn't it?" Jenny said. "We do our share of serving at the inn. I wish Fanny had joined us."

"It's a woman's place to serve," Maggie said. "Scripture admonishes us."

"Scripture also shows us we should learn at another's feet and not always be working." Jenny recalled the verses about Mary and Martha. She tended to behave like Martha but wished to be able to rest and learn like Mary.

Ben brought the drinks back and sat beside her. "So you want to open your own school one day?"

"Possibly. I want to be able to support myself or contribute to a family if I have one. But I like having coins I get to spend the way I want. I can do that now, after giving some over to Papa, of course."

"That seems reasonable." Ben took a sip of his drink, wiped his mouth with the back of his hand. He waved at someone across the floor, returned his attention to Jenny. "I think a wife ought to have a say in how monies are spent, though when in doubt, it's the man's duty to make the final decision."

"Hmm. What if it turns out he made the wrong decision?"

"Might teach him to listen more closely to his wife. But then, we all make mistakes. Can't let the count of them hammer too long and hard at your chest, or it'll break your heart. Won't go far with a broken heart. You'll have to find a way to mend it or be miserable for life." He took another sip. "I'm good at fixing things. You might give me a chance."

"This is getting too profound," Jenny said. "Are you fixin' to dance with me?"

"If you'll have me."

Jenny took another sip of her drink. It had a fizz to it. From the sassafras, she imagined. She let Ben lift the cup from her fingers, set both of their cups on their chairs as though to hold their place, and they took to the cornmeal-polished wooden floor. Jenny thought she might not be able to breathe, his gentle touch, the way he held her eyes as they moved around the room. *Of course, the man can dance.* He could sing, and the rhythms moved casual as a lazy stream through his lanky body. Jenny lost touch with what was happening around them, could only see those blue eyes holding hers. She felt herself lifted—not physically, but like she'd been carried to a mountaintop where the air was thin and she had trouble catching her breath.

Then she did have trouble catching her breath.

It might have been the activity or perhaps the heat of the room, but she lost her balance and found herself sagging into Ben, who put his wide hand around her waist and glided her from the floor to their chairs. The girls quickly picked up the cups to let them sit.

"What happened?" Maggie asked. "Are you all right?"

"I'm fine, really. Holy cow chips, it's nothing." She didn't want to bring attention to herself.

"First time I ever literally swept a woman off her feet. Let me get you a little water."

"I'm glad of that," Jenny told Ben. "I just need a moment's rest."

Ben settled her on the chair, frowned, but succumbed to her suggestion that he dance with her sisters. Watching them ease across the floor, she thought it must have been the passion of the day that weakened her. She'd gone from anticipation to confrontation to Ben's kind ministration, all leaving her reeling. It was happening too quickly. She wasn't ready to fall in love. *I wonder if this is how it happened for Momma.*

Then it was time to leave. Papa had been strict about when they had to be back. He would have come himself, except that his wife was pregnant and it wouldn't do to have her there nor to leave her home alone. And he had to chaperone Fanny, after all, left behind with her not-chosen beau.

On the way back, Ben suggested the girls walk in front of them, and they concurred. The moon lit their way. He held Jenny's hand, spoke softly. "I'd like to do this every Saturday night with you. Even midweek. Or every single day."

That shortness of breath caught her again. Her legs ached, her back hurt. Only her fingers wrapped by his were warm as though she held them before a fire.

"Take your time, Miss Jenny," Ben said. "But my mind's made up. And I don't think you'll find anyone who could love you more."

"You barely know me. I have a caustic tongue at times. I can be officious, bossy as a herd cow. Aspirations drive me, call me forward, for opportunities my mother never had because she was pregnant nearly all the time and had to endure both hard births and too-soon deaths. It broke her." Jenny remembered her mother's tears once when she learned she was pregnant again. "She was so kind, so gifted, and so tired all the time. I don't want that."

"But you'd like a babe or two?"

"Or three or four. One day. I want to be able to raise them in safety, without worry over debt or illness we couldn't afford to get a doctor for."

He shouted to the girls ahead. "Not so far out there. Your pa will shoot me if you fall in a puddle or worse." To Jenny he said, "I like the 'we' word you used."

"I'd want a marriage to be a team."

"Good thought. I train horses to work as a team."

"Are you comparing us to horses?" She laughed as she said it.

"Might be a few factors in common, most important is that they're certain they're headed in the same direction." He cleared his throat. "May I speak to your father? We wouldn't have to marry right away. Take our time."

She liked the idea of taking time to see how their walking side by side might work—and she'd have time to savor her independence before giving it up for love. "Let's wait until after the school term is over. You might change your mind the more time you spend with me and my family."

"Not likely. But I can wait. Just don't let ol' Harold slip in and steal you away." He had a deep voice he raised when he teased, although she didn't think what he said was totally in jest.

"There'll be no chance of that. My father has affirmed my interest in another." She squeezed his fingers. "Once Papa decides, it's pretty much a baked pie." She could only hope that a life with Ben Duniway was the sweetness to the soul she wanted.

* * *

Spring brought its high step to the region, buds bursting, the fragrance of wild roses perfuming the air. Jenny still rode to the school early, leaving the family she boarded with before dawn each day. They were a kind couple with one young child, who paid the school fee by providing room and board for the teacher. Ben no longer brought Josie to school. That child rode her own horse. Instead, Ben joined the Scott family each weekend, went to church with her, and they became a pleasant gossip whisper long before Ben spoke to Tucker Scott about his daughter Jenny's hand. She found not seeing him all week long was a greater distraction than looking forward to a morning and afternoon short visit at the school chaperoned by children. *Is this what I want?* She posed the question to herself a dozen times a day when thoughts of Ben interrupted a math lesson where the children measured their desks or shared a biscuit to figure out fractions. She was just getting started with her profession and believed her work was important. But so was the work of a wife and mother. At least Ben wasn't pressuring her. He waited for Jenny to set the timing.

As sometimes happens, though, timing is often taken from us.

FIVE

The Vagaries of Choice

"It's this way. I'm sorry, but you girls cannot remain under my roof with . . . my wife's indiscretion. Fanny, you must marry Amos and you two can take over the inn. Maggie and Harriet can remain with you, as can Kate and Sarah. Jenny, is it Ben, or are you wanting me to find you someone else? There's always Harold."

"You can't stay married to her, Pa," Harvey said. "She dishonored you."

It was June, the summer heat beginning its rise in the Willamette Valley. They sat in the parlor, the coolest room of the inn, darkened by shades that made Jenny think they were at a wake. Perhaps they were. They all spoke as though Jenny's stepmother wasn't even present, but she was, sobbing with a broken heart. Her remorse was genuine, Jenny could see that. But they'd all recently learned of her indiscretion before she ever married their father; the child she now carried was not Tucker Scott's. If word got out that the child wasn't her father's, it would be worse than the divorce he was contemplating. Either way, it would be scandalous for marriage-aged daughters to be living in the same home as a fallen woman or a divorced father.

Jenny was torn. His wife had made a poor decision, but she shouldn't have to have her life destroyed by gossip and rumor when the man who caused it had no repercussions. And a divorce—such an act would spill down on all of them like water over a ridge, splattering everything below it. All the girls were in the splatter. She supposed her brothers were too, but they'd at least be able to decide for themselves whether to stay with their father or go live with one of their married sisters—as soon as the girls found husbands.

Her stepmother had written a letter at her father's request where she apologized and revealed how she'd been duped by a previous proposal following the death of her husband. Widowed and desperate, she'd accepted the man's word of marriage and succumbed to his advances. But she hadn't known she carried a child when the man abandoned her, and she met Tucker Scott and fell genuinely in love with him. She begged for forgiveness, and why shouldn't she have it? Wasn't that what Christian compassion was all about, making space for healing from the hardness of life?

"Jenny!" Her father barked her name to bring her back to the tension of the room. "Ben hasn't officially asked me for your hand. I imagine you've told him not to."

She nodded. *And he's honored that request.*

She had wanted the decision about marriage to be hers and Ben's alone. She could stay on at the inn with Fanny if her sister was forced to marry Amos. Or try to rent a room somewhere. She couldn't go with her father, with her stepmother's mistake becoming known. Her father's indecision about divorcing her—she could see he still loved the woman—caught them all off guard. It was the close of the school term, when she planned to take on more sewing in her spare time, help at the inn, and get to know Ben. It was all a swirl, and her growing feelings for Ben were in the middle.

If only her father had waited to remarry! If only she'd had more time to pursue her profession. If only Ben's farm were closer to civilization so she could consider a fee school operated out of their home. *If only.* The most useless words in the English language.

"I asked him not to talk with you until I was ready," Jenny told her father. "I'm still not sure I am prepared." She didn't add how dismayed she was that despite her father having made the decision to marry so quickly, it was all the women who would pay the highest price for having choices rushed or made for them.

"Not much time to spare," her father warned.

"Yes, time's a-wasting and we with it," Jenny said. "I'll advise him to seek your permission." As had happened for her mother, John Tucker had taken a choice from her.

* * *

Jenny and Ben married on August 2, 1853, in the town of Lafayette. She wore a dress the color of daffodils, with a white bow that trailed down her back and showed off her tiny waist. She'd sewed the dress in between making one for Fanny too, who two weeks later married Amos Cook, a well-regarded pioneer of the Territory but still twenty years older than his new wife.

"It isn't fair," Jenny told her sister as she pulled the curling iron from the coals, tested it with her spit to make sure it cooled enough to not singe her sister's hair.

"Some things aren't." Fanny dabbed at her eyes with the blueberry-dyed handkerchief.

"But Papa married whom he wanted. Men get better choices not because they're wiser—but because they're men." She thought of Harold Bunter and the law that aided him if he found a wife in time. "And because they make the rules. Why is that?"

"Oh, Jenny. You'll frustrate yourself wishing it weren't so. We're girls. Men aren't. We have to make the best of it."

There didn't seem any other option but to accept. Still, Jenny's tears as her sister spoke her vows came from both sadness and guilt—because Jenny at least had the luxury of love. Fanny had to learn to love her husband if she could.

* * *

At Fanny and Amos's wedding, Harold Bunter showed up. "Holy cow chips," she told Ben when she saw his brooding scowl as he dismounted and tied his horse to the rail. Oddly he said nothing perverse to Jenny or Ben nor anyone else. He stood at the edge of the crowd, spitting his tobacco juice into a cup, while he stared at Jenny.

"Don't worry," Ben said. "I'll always protect you."

She nodded, took her serving platter of beef dodgers, and set them on the sawhorse table between the vases of wildflowers dotting the crisp white tablecloth. Fanny had served the same foods—beef dodgers and beans, blueberries, and pies of various nature—at Ben and Jenny's wedding. Jenny had waited for Harold to show up on that day and decided, when he hadn't, that a woman could waste a lot of time in worry. Better to think of what to do if trouble did appear and have a plan of action for then but otherwise focus on the moment. At Fanny's wedding he was less imposing to her with a husband by her side. He did nothing but stare, and Jenny could abide that. She turned her back to him, welcoming Ben's assurance that he'd be there to take care of her should the need arise. Many husbands weren't so protective of their wives and daughters—her father included—but she had hope in Ben.

* * *

The yo-yo of "yes or no" about Jenny marrying or not had ceased, and there was relief in that. The vows—for better or for worse—rang true. This was a lifelong commitment, and having made it, she prayed their union would be blessed and gave herself wholeheartedly to loving Ben.

Little Josie attended their nuptials, along with her parents and new brother, and Jenny met all Ben's family for the first time that August day. She heard stories about his growing up in Illinois, about his waddling to the barn and petting the nose of a big draft horse shortly after his first birthday. "Horses were his first love," his father told her. "But I'd say he's found their match in you."

"Come here, my new wife." Ben held out his hand to her and asked her to sit before the gathering on a rocking chair brought to the outside from the inn. "I've a little present for my bride." He strummed the guitar strings. "I wrote this myself." Jenny blushed at his attention and that of the guests. The words of his song praised "a girl with the eyes of kindness and a heart of hope" and went on to tell a story of a strong-minded woman who ultimately "determined she'd fall in love and marry." She applauded and the crowd with her. *I should have written a poem for him.* She'd do that, she decided, and read it to him in the privacy of their cabin she had yet to see.

They spent their first night at the inn and rode to Ben's ranch the morning after, the sweet scent of honeysuckle bursting in the air. They stopped to pick blackberries, filling a basket, laughing as they fed each other the warm, plump fruit that stained their fingers and lips.

"I couldn't be happier, Jenny," Ben said, his naturally white teeth a faded blue.

"It's a good day, Ben Duniway." And so it was. Perhaps not the sweeping romantic fantasy she'd thought of when she read those novels her mother slipped into the house, but sweet and safe nonetheless. This man beside her loved her, and while she wasn't sure what love was, she knew that when he touched her hand to help her from the wagon, then held her to his chest, she felt warm and wanted, and worries over the past and of the future sank like the sunset, slow and easy from their view. Surely if that was not love, it was close.

* * *

"I'll think of it as *our* claim." Ben swept his arm before them. He tried to see what Jenny did: tall firs thick as weeds covering the vast expanse except where he'd worked so hard to clear ground. Would she see the potential? He'd built a small cabin and acquired horses for breeding and riding. He had two cows, chickens, and sheep for wool and mutton.

Ben thought of it as "their claim," even though he'd farmed it an entire year before he even met Jenny. Besotted, his own father had said of him, and Ben guessed he was. Her acceptance of his offer of marriage sent him spinning his hat to the wind in gratitude. He suspected he loved her more than she him, but he was a persuasive man and he'd convince her in time that no man would ever love her more. She would come to love him deeper. He knew that she cared for him but also that he was a good way out of a bad situation in her family. He'd appreciated her honesty in her acceptance.

Today, he walked behind the mule plowing the rock-peppered earth. John Henry, her little brother—the Scotts called him "Little Toot"—picked up rocks and made cairns of them beside the field. Ben knew it was hard land and he might have made a better purchase, but it was his. It was also beautiful and green, though as Jenny pointed out once or twice, it wasn't as good a cropland as farther west in the valley. He hated to hear disappointment in her voice, but most of that land had been already claimed by the earlier arrivals of the 1840s. Still, this farm was much better than the Boonsboro land of Kentucky, or Pike County country of Illinois where his family came from.

Ben had managed to bring his father west in '51, a year after his own footsteps onto Oregon soil by way of California. With earnings from the gold field, he'd paid his father's way out west and operated his own farm from those gold nuggets too. He'd made some lucky strikes but preferred farming to mining any day. Shoot, if he hadn't come to Oregon, he never would have met Jenny, and what a great loss that would have been.

The jerk of the shoulder harness as he split the earth brought him back to the field, but his mind soon wandered to Jenny. He'd first seen her as part of a relief team sent out to meet the wagon trains in the fall of '52. Locals had heard several Illinoisans were headed that way, and like his father's company of '51, by the time they reached the Willamette Valley, people had slim pickings for food and other provisions. Ben had helped organize rescue parties.

Well, relief parties. People liked that term better and were more willing to accept the beans and bacon and blankets the settlers had brought with them. He'd seen but a glimpse of the slender brown-haired beauty. She was sitting on a rock beside a stream, writing in a book, waiting for others to get their beans and bacon before her. Something about her made Ben look longer than a stranger should have, and she raised her baby blues to him, he guessed because she felt him staring.

He tapped his fingers to his hat, nodded. She stared back, didn't acknowledge him at all, and soon returned to her book. Ben turned his horse away, not wishing to interrupt the lady, and looked instead for someone to tell him who she was. He couldn't see who her family might be, as she was off by herself, and when she wandered back to the cluster of folks, he noticed her handing out biscuits to anyone who came along. He guessed she saw everyone as her responsibility—once she set her scribbling down.

Then one day in the rainy winter of that year, Ben learned about a new schoolteacher in Cincinnati, a little burg in the Oregon valley. She was boarding out—what teachers did, living with parents of students a month or term at a time. One of Ben's neighbors said she was a popular guest at parties, well-chaperoned by her father and sisters, and a sought-after sweetheart, though she turned most suitors away. "Her tongue's got acid on it, so be wary," one of Ben's friends said, punching him on his shoulder. He'd taken the courting from there and didn't mind, when he later told her, that she had no memory of that gaze exchanged back on the trail. Now here they were, man and wife. God was good.

A late-afternoon breeze dried some of Ben's sweat. He felt he had a few virtues to offer. His hardscrabble farm, for one, with its tall timber and horses. He trained them to ride, gentled them rather than broke them, and they'd taken to the harness too, with his whispering words to their twitching ears. He'd even worked a few to tricks and sold a pair for circus horses. He'd begun a breeding program and hoped for matched white teams one day or a pair of trained pintos to prance at Fourth of July celebrations. For now he'd limited his breeding to help farmers needing animals ready for harness. He had a good reputation for hard work and won loyal friends, and his word meant something. He offered Jenny that.

And he could read. That was a virtue, though he wasn't prone to it. Words didn't hold the same reverence that they did to his wife. She'd even insisted on leaving the word "obey" out of the marriage vows. He'd gotten a kick out of that and how she'd talked down the Methodist minister's objections. Ben preferred to sing and play guitar and talk to friends or work beside them if they had a need. Giving was an important virtue in this young country, and Ben knew how to do that.

Ben had had a gal or two say he was good-looking, and he'd never been in a fist fight. He hadn't had to defend himself, because no one wanted to take him on, being six feet by the time he was twelve. Hard work had filled him out.

Another virtue was his desire to be a matched team with his wife, not one pulling in different directions, so he didn't tell her what to do and she didn't direct him. At least that's what they'd agreed to that day in August. And though they were newly wedded, he hadn't minded a whit having her ten-year-old brother John Henry move in with them after two weeks. The boy liked the horses and the hardscrabble place too, though he was of slight build and tired as easily as Jenny. Her back hurt her often "from an old injury," she'd told him without her usual detail.

Ben unharnessed the plow mule and led him out to pasture. He washed up at the pump, taking water from a shallow well. He wiped his tanned arms as he surveyed his land. Their land. God had been good to them, bringing them together and to this place, an area bordered by split rails to fence the mule and horses in without having to be hobbled. Ben was a good rail splitter too. Another of his attributes along with being a bit intuitive when it came to women's needs, he hoped.

They'd been married a little over two months. It had been an ongoing education. He walked to the log house, stopped at the garden to pull an October carrot. He'd planted these vegetables, but next year, with Jenny here, they'd have a better garden with potatoes and pumpkins and maybe even a little popped corn.

He kissed Jenny and inhaled the scent of supper on the table he'd built. He tried to remember to call her "Abigail." She said a married woman ought to give up any childhood nickname—but it wasn't easy. She'd always be Jenny to him. He took the platter she handed him, set it on the table, then lifted his leg over the back of the chair to sit. Little Toot, not yet ten, was already there, smiling.

"What are you grinning about," Ben said. The boy swung his legs beneath the bench. Ben reached for the fresh bread. Heavens, he loved this married life. How blessed he was and more to come, once they began their family. "Come on, Jenny. I mean, Abigail. I'll say grace over the food for the three of us."

"Make that four," she said as she took her seat.

"Who's coming for supper?" He put the steaming bowl of potatoes she handed him on the table as she sat. "Should we wait?"

"Already here." She patted her abdomen. "He—or she—will be joining us in May in person."

"Well, I'll be. She tell you first, Little Toot? That why you're grinning big as a canyon?"

"Yes, sir, she did. I'm gonna be an uncle."

Ben rose and took Jenny in his arms. "Thought I couldn't be happier with getting you as my wife and now this. All that laboring not in vain."

She laughed and pushed against his chest, but not before he kissed her. "We have children present," she cautioned.

"More than one. I'm happy for us, Jenny."

"I am too, though I'd have liked a little more time to get this cabin into shape, perk up the chickens into better layers, and make and sell more butter. A baby's going to cost, Ben."

"That I know, but it'll also give back twice its weight in joy."

"I hope it's a boy," she said after Ben had spoken a table grace.

"Do you? A daughter would be grand."

"Yes, but she'll have a harder life than you boys have. Girls just do."

"We'll love her like a son, then," Ben said. "And do all we can to make it easier on her. And on you too. What can I do to help?"

"Me too," Little Toot said.

"Well, aren't you versatile men," Jenny said.

"But another of our many virtues," Ben said. "Just know, I doubt I'll ever learn to cook, so give me something else to commandeer."

"Laundry," Jenny said. "It's more work than planting corn and twice as arduous. A babe will bring on more."

SIX

Early Storms

1853 TO 1856

She hadn't remembered the winter being so drippy and dark. So much had happened their first months in the Territory—her teaching, her father's marriage, the work at the inn, the dances, her sisters always present—she guessed she hadn't noticed the heavy downpours, broken now and then by shards of sun. "Sun breaks," the locals called the half hour or so when the rains stopped long enough so a girl could jump the puddles and head to the privy without getting wet. Maybe it was a wetter winter. Or perhaps the weather wore on her without the joy of her sisters' voices or the children from her school to invigorate. Morning sickness didn't help.

It was just the three of them at Hardscrabble, as Jenny thought of their 320 acres. Ben often rode off to drum up potential breeding contracts or sales. Little Toot would go with him, so she had hours alone, never hearing another voice while she mended torn pants or churned butter she put in molds to sell. The chickens gave in to winter and ate more than they gave back in eggs. "We're both gaining weight," she told them as she reached beneath their warm plumage seeking one or two eggs instead of their usual four or five.

She'd sewed festive curtains from the feed bags, embroidering flowers onto the gray material in the evenings by candlelight when she'd rather be reading or even writing, but she needed color to brighten the rainy days.

When her "boys" were gone, she spoke to their child, thinking of the baby as a boy, and she told him stories about how to treat a lady. "When your poor momma says she needs a little help with the chickens, you come running," or "You consult your momma and later your wife about big decisions, like where to move to or what to buy. You remember that, now." She spoke as much to advise as to hear a feminine voice.

When the afternoon waned, she would pull out her foolscap paper and write. She thought it a luxury she might not have, once the baby arrived, and since Ben was off doing what he loved, and furthering their livelihood as well, she'd take the time to advance her own. While she stitched, she thought of words to write down, starting with poems that had a hint of humor to them.

> There once was a farmer's wife.
> Who worked hard to avoid marital strife.
> She kept her tongue still
> When handed a due bill . . .

"What's a good last line?" Jenny asked her baby as she picked dried eggs from the dishes. Later, while spinning carded wool, she tried to come up with that final line. "I'll give up writing limericks," she said, or not write poetry that needs something to rhyme with "wife." Still, the effort filled her days and she found when resentment over Ben's absence or, worse, when he brought his single friends home in time for her to add a plate to the supper table, that word-seeking was a good way to keep her tongue in check. At least until their "guests" had gone. Then she'd spill a few thoughts to Ben about the extra work his "generosity" brought her.

"I'll help with cleaning up," he said.

"As though that's the only effort." She slammed a frying pan down a little harder than intended, and Little Toot jumped.

"I'll help too, Sister," the boy said and shot from the stool, swirling around looking to see what he could do. "Polish the lamp? See to the pigs?"

"Good idea," Ben told him. "I'll check on the chicks." At the door, he turned and said, "You can out-argue me anytime, Jenny. But you'll never out-love me."

They both scurried out of her way then, which wasn't what she wanted. She wanted them to ease her loneliness. And, like Ben, to be able to love fully. She didn't know what held her back.

There once was a farmer's wife.
Who worked hard to avoid marital strife.
She kept her tongue still
When handed a due bill . . .

Knowing payments are a part of life.

She'd settle on that last line , though her hope for humor had escaped her.

* * *

Spring arrived along with labor pains. Ben patted Jenny's hand. "I'll get my sister. Will you be all right while I'm gone? Should I leave? Oh Jenny."

"I'll be fine." Jenny said. "Just go." But as soon as he was gone, she wished he were still with her. Little Toot stared. "I'm all right," she told him. *I have to be brave for my brother.* "Having a baby. Women do it all the time."

"What can I do?"

She laughed. "I don't know. We're two lost pups, aren't we? Oh, oh, oh!" Another contraction. *Pain. Good pain.* "Bring in kindling," she directed. He was panting along with her and would pass out if she didn't give him tasks. She wished she'd had Kate come, at least. But her sister-in-law Mary had delivered two children and would know what to do. Jenny had been there for her siblings' births, but now that it was her body bringing forth a babe, it was as though she couldn't remember the sequence of events. She waddled around the room, stopped to pant with each contraction. Urged Little Toot to read his book. In between the pains, she filled and heated up water in the cast iron pot. *What do we need hot water for? Bathe the baby maybe?* She gathered up cloths she'd set aside. She walked to the barn, inhaled the wild roses growing next to the log structure, and her brother helped her haul in the old feather mattress so as not to stain their good one. She had covered it with a pieced quilt, made ready for this glorious May day. She didn't much care what happened to the cover; she wasn't much of a quilter, knowing her big stitches would never rival her sister Maggie's tiny ones. Besides, quilting hurt her fingers while writing did not. *I can write about this.*

But she couldn't. "Holy cow chips," she said to the log walls. She was an emotional train rushing forward with no way to stop.

She lay on the quilt, panting through the pains, sending Little Toot out to get the eggs. *Where is Ben?* "Go feed the chickens, check on the sheep too."

"I already did, Sister."

"Do it again."

"They'll be awful fat chickens," he mumbled as he opened the door.

Anything to get him away so she could groan at the pain and not alarm him, all the while wishing Ben were there for her to yell at and at the same time wanting his hand to squeeze.

Am I strong enough for this? Will this baby be all right? Can I do this?

She remembered her mother saying, "Women have been doing this for centuries," and yet it was her first time and she wasn't sure she could. *I have to.*

* * *

"Everything will be all right," Ben told her.

"Thank God you're back."

"You've everything ready, I see," Mary Gibson said. She was tall, like Ben, but more commanding. It was the first woman's voice she had heard since New Year's Day.

Ben remained in the room, holding her hand while she snapped at him, silencing his utter joy at what was about to happen while she groaned in misery. "It'll be over soon, Jenny, it will. You're doing great."

"Easy for you to say."

"Push now," her sister-in-law said. She had a high-pitched voice that had once annoyed Jenny, but now her words gave her strength. "You can wail to the moon. Go ahead."

Jenny took her advice and shouted, though she didn't remember her mother ever doing so. But Jenny did, and then the child arrived, ripping its way into the world with a pain nearly as great as the labor pains.

"I'll stitch in a minute," she heard her sister-in-law say. "Ben, you cut the cord. We have to wait for the afterbirth."

"Oh, help me," Ben said, his words a prayer. "My hands are shaking."

"Is he all right?" Jenny tried to sit up as Mary placed the wet weight onto her belly.

"She's perfect," Ben said. "It's a girl, Jen. A beautiful baby girl. We made a girl."

"A girl." She sighed and gentled her hand on the still wet crown of her child's head. *A girl.*

She felt another contraction-like movement. *The afterbirth.* All was as it should be.

But it wasn't.

"This is going to hurt. You've torn quite a bit. Take this laudanum. It'll ease the pain." Her sister-in-law picked up the needle and thread Jenny had laid out. "Think of something else. Do you have a name?"

"We don't," Ben said. "Well, not one we agreed on."

"I was sure it would be a boy." Jenny's words barely passed her lips before she felt herself drifting. *A girl. We have a daughter.* She looked at Ben and saw his tears matched hers. "We'll go with your choice," she told Ben, and then she faded.

* * *

Clara Belle joined their lives. Yes, a girl's life would be hard. Yes, her mother had been correct in that, and yet to see the tiny lips, the fingers small as new carrots reaching for her, to nourish this child's body from her own, to imagine a future chattering and exploring with this girl, brought joys she'd never known. She loved her in an instant. In the beginning, she had wondered if she loved Ben as much as he loved her. She had grown to care more for him in the nine months of their marriage. But with Clara Belle, there was no doubt to the depth of her emotion. With the first look into those baby eyes, she was in love. This was unconditional love that only grew deeper in the following days. Clara Belle's presence eased the loneliness, and Jenny vowed she'd do all she could to make this girl's life better and maybe other girls' lives richer too. She didn't know how, but she was committed to educating her, giving her all the advantages that their small farm could bring. She'd teach her about the joy of the landscape, towering trees with needles ever green, help her notice the soft rains turning their log cabin rooftop moss the perfect shade of jade. Clara Belle would see what devoted parents looked like.

When she found herself mumbling at the doughboy, kneading bread while Ben and his bachelor chums waited for her to serve up biscuits, she vowed to see their presence not as intrusions but as opportunities for her daughter to see how men could rest while women worked and how one day, working together, women might change that. She didn't know how. "We need rest too," she told the intense blue eyes of her daughter in the cradle. "Your father works hard, he does. But so does your momma."

She envied the men in her life, that was the truth of it. Ben found a way toward ease that escaped her. He refreshed with the laughter and guitar-playing and singing to his daughter. She'd never learned to rest—she had no practice. Maybe playing with Clara Belle in the middle of the day would bring such pleasure, but there was always work to be done. Eggs to collect. Cream to churn. Butter to place into molds and sell. Laundry.

Still, as Clara Belle grew, Jenny could imagine standing her on her mother's slippers as she shuffled a dance away from the stove and into the higher chair Ben had built her or blowing on her belly while she changed her. Those would be small moments she could savor with her child. Her mother must have had those moments, hadn't she?

Today, that kindred binding would have to wait. Jenny sighed. Washing a mountain of dirty diapers was the immediate future of this mother and her girl.

* * *

"Everything will be all right." It was Ben's mantra, and sometimes Jenny resented Ben when he said it. If she expressed concerns about her isolation or how much her bones ached or that their larder needed filling and there were no coins nor eggs to trade, he'd say "Everything will be all right." It felt like he dismissed her concerns. Things didn't always turn out all right. It was what she was thinking as she milked their small herd of three cows while Clara Belle lay in the cradle chewing on a bit of dough Jenny had tied on a piece of string around her toe so her jerky feet would keep her from swallowing it. Chickens cackled, wanting out of their coop. Jenny pressed her head into the side of a cow while she stripped the teats of their white gold. The butter and egg sales were their only income many months. Ben was once again gone to try to sign a breeding contract. He'd taken Little Toot with him. Clara Belle cooed. Jenny loved that sound.

She felt a cooling come across the timber, and the wind picked up enough to move the harness hanging on the hook beside the open door. The barn darkened. Birds had stopped chirping, and the cow's tail twitched and she began to prance. Jenny looked outside. A black cloud had moved in. Her heart pounded as she swooped Clara into her arms. She raced to the cabin door as rain poured and she witnessed the shape of a funnel drop down into the timbers, the wind threatening at the leather hinges of their door as she pushed into the cabin. She threw the slide bar across the opening and raced to the back of the cabin as she heard the roar. Deafening.

Jenny fell to the floor, her baby beneath her as she pushed them both to a corner where they huddled, her baby against her breast. And she prayed, oh how she prayed that they'd survive this tempest, that Ben was all right and Little Toot, too, out in this cyclone. Her words flew to the wind, the clacking of hail against the roof, and then she heard the wrench of logs as the ceiling timbers tore from the walls as easily as an ax splits kindling.

Jenny hovered over Clara as the hail ground onto them, no protection, no roof. Pellets of ice, some the size of new potatoes; more like popped corn but rough as rocks. They shredded the bed linen, tore at the table, cupboards, the stove. Jenny's hands were bloodied, held over Clara's crown; her own head pierced with pain from the ice.

And then a stillness though the rain poured down, the moss-covered roof, gone.

Jenny stood. She shook and looked around her. Trees like children's toys scattered in all directions. She could see them through the missing walls. Fences, gone. Cattle, dead. A timber driven into the side of the house as though it were a peg to hold the clothes of giants. Her teeth chattered in the cold. The barn flattened with timbers sticking up through logs, and a first cutting of grass hay a mass that looked like drenched salad greens. A strip of field crops, vanished. She began crying then, clinging to her daughter.

What if Ben's caught up in this? What if—

She couldn't let herself think the worst. "We'll go to Mary's. We'll go to Mary's."

She grabbed a rag and wiped Clara's face, her own, and her bloodied hands. Rain pelted them. "We'll go to Mary's." She repeated the mantra, a promise of an action she could take. It brought her strange resolve.

The three miles to her in-laws took what seemed like hours through the mud. When she saw Ben's horse and Little Toot's at the trough, she started to cry. They were all right.

She cried out, "Ben! Ben! Oh, you're safe."

Her husband stepped out onto the porch, beginning to welcome her with a question on his face. Then she saw him race toward her, taking two porch steps at a time, catching her as she collapsed. She was so weak, but she had protected Clara Belle. That was all that mattered.

Ben pulled his daughter from Jenny, ran his big hands over the child before handing the crying Clara Belle to Little Toot, who stood behind him. Bruises had formed on the back of the child's palms. "What's happened?"

"I did the best I could. The farm is gone. It's all gone. Wind. Hail. No roof."

"It's barely raining here." Ben sounded confused.

"Hail, the size of river rocks. I tried to cover us."

Her in-laws came out onto the porch, heard her.

"Shh, shh. Hush now." Ben held her in his arms, his warmth a comfort as he helped her forward. Clara had quieted as Mary held her.

"You're bleeding," Ben said.

"You won't recognize . . ." Jenny's words drifted.

"Bring them inside. Goodness. You poor thing." Ben's sister helped her stand.

"It can't be as bad as all that," Ben said, helping her up the porch steps. "You're here in front of me. You're safe and Clara is too. Everything will be all right."

"It isn't."

"Did you walk down the creek? You're muddy as the pig sty." He tried to make a joke.

She collapsed on Mary Gibson's bed, and the men were shooed out so she could be stripped of the wet clothes by her sister-in-law.

"They'll dry out. You rest now," Mary said. Little Josie had followed them in. "You've had quite a scare, I can see."

"I couldn't make it stop. I tried to cover Clara Belle, but her hands are bruised." Tears welled. She couldn't stop shaking.

"Don't you worry." Mary directed her daughter to get Clara Belle a little hat and her brother's night shirt. "They'll be big on 'er." To Jenny she said. "You're safe now. You're through the worst."

"I'll ride home and check on things," Ben shouted behind the closed door.

"No! Wait. Don't go." She felt exposed as a newborn kitten. She rose, pulled open the door. "Please. Stay. We'll go back together."

Ben patted her shoulder.

And so they did. Theirs was the only farm in the area that had been hit, the destruction stunning. "We can re-roof the barn easiest, live there until the cabin can be readied."

The rebuilding will take months. Jenny watched Ben wander through the debris. "I was so scared," she said, holding her fussing daughter close. She felt herself shiver, made herself calm for Clara's sake.

"But you did everything right. Looked after Clara and yourself. I wish I'd been here to help. But no matter. You took care of things. Everything will be alright." He patted her shoulder as they surveyed the wreckage.

Ben's brother-in-law and neighbors, her father and Harvey and her sisters would come to help with rebuilding, the days of work and sharing food a blend of sorrow and delight. And during it, Jenny began her push for them to sell the farm, to find a place closer to their neighbors where a woman could have a cup of tea now and again to ease the troubled times of women's lives.

"It's a campaign, Ben," she told him. "To get you to change your mind about this acreage. Let's sell it to a man with sons who can run it while we find a place more suitable."

"But we've put so much work into it."

"I miss being closer to my sisters. Let's find a place where Clara Belle can one day go to school. Let's consider it at least."

"We'll get more for the farm if we rebuild."

"And be further from where we want to be because we took the time. Let someone else replant it as they'd want. Re-roof the house so it's livable, but then let's find a place we can both love."

"Sometimes one has to cut one's losses. Is that what you're saying?" Ben said.

"Yes." Was it a failure to leave a challenge? Or wisdom to face another? Was that the reason her father had moved west, even against her mother's wishes?

SEVEN

A Clearing in the Fog

1856

Ben patted his hat down, mounted his big bay gelding, and rode into the fog. It wasn't that he didn't want to go for the doctor. It was that doing so meant leaving Jenny in a bad place. He trusted his sister and the women who had arrived for the birth of this second child, but ever since the tornado, he'd been worried about her. She was more fragile than he'd seen her be, jumping at small sounds, jerking away when he touched her shoulder from behind without first announcing his presence. She was short with Clara Belle too, snapped or sighed in frustration. He hoped it was the child-carrying attitude of easy annoyance and impatience. He didn't want to think her irritation was because they still lived at Hardscrabble Farm and, now with a second child, might find it even harder to afford to leave it, even if he did find a good place for them.

He felt a chill and pulled his wolfskin coat around him. Jenny had sewed the coat for him from the hides he'd brought in. He'd gotten a bounty—which helped their finances—but she'd insisted that he hold enough hides back for his coat. In this kind of weather, he was glad for it.

He realized he had ridden beside the barn when he thought he'd headed out toward the trail to the main road. It was still daylight, nearly dusk he guessed, but the fog made everything unfamiliar. He kept his eyes on the trail now and found the main pathway toward Needy and the doctor.

She was larger this time than with Clara, even he could see that. And his sister wasn't one to rush to worry, so her insisting that they needed a doctor wasn't just a plan to get him out of the way. A second child in less than three years of their marriage. Maybe they were pushing it. He felt her urgency, even if Jenny had minimized it. He did know she'd like having womenfolk around. He'd thought he'd be enough, but she missed her sisters and other women. He guessed he could have taken her along when he headed out to neighbors. But women's work never quit, as Jenny was fond of reminding him. Farms gave the ladies no rest. His lady. Truth was, he didn't want to move. They owned this land, had built it up together. One day she'd understand.

He started singing to keep himself company and to set a pace that would get him to Needy. "Camptown Races" and its line "gwine to run all night" was a favorite tune, and the sound of his voice in the fog echoed with a deep resonance. He crooned out "Home Sweet Home" and "Old Susanna" before belting out the "Alphabet Song," a move that made him laugh and think of Clara, whom Jenny sang it to as much as he did. Then the fog lifted and he pulled up Biscuit's reins. The treetops were still misted, but he wasn't on any trail. "Where are we?"

He felt a clenching in his gut. "How can a man who lives on horseback and knows this country right and left not be sure where he is?" The horse shook his head, jangling the bit and bridle rings. "Yeah, I don't know the answer to that either." He'd have to pick a direction and hope to intersect the trail or come upon the town or another farm or something familiar. He pressed his knees against

Biscuit's sides and reined him to the right. They rode through the timber for an hour or more, easing around treefalls and deadwood. Ben watched in despair as the fog descended again and he could barely see his horse's ears. He'd been gone at least two hours, and he wasn't anywhere near the doctor. He didn't know where he was. He heard a wolf howl and hoped it wouldn't be answered by a pack. As long as he could take another step, he'd be all right, but the best thing he could do would be to sit tight, build a fire and stay until the fog lifted. But how would he explain to Jenny or his sister that he sat by the fire while she suffered and maybe . . .

Women died. Jenny told him that childbirth was the greatest cause of death for women. The plight of women was her favorite topic.

No, he'd have to keep going, even if it was like riding inside a duck.

* * *

Blood everywhere on the bedclothes despite the women's efforts. "He must weigh ten pounds," she heard Mary say. *So, a boy.* She also heard her son cry, and the women oohing that he was healthy as they washed him and laid him on her breast. But they didn't leave him there long, needing to tend to the hemorrhaging. Anticipating possible problems, Jenny had made a mustard pack and directed Mary to it. She could hear Little Toot talking softly with Clara under the lean-to roof, entertaining her on the child's feather bed. Their voices soothed her, though they came from a distant shore.

"It'll be better after the placenta comes, surely." One of the neighbor women massaged her abdomen to release the afterbirth, while Mary placed the mustard pack, then removed it with the rush of blood and tissue.

"You should sew me up." Jenny panted. "I know I tore. Again."

She saw the women look at each other. "I'll do it," Mary said.

"I've done the sewing before," one of the midwives said. "It's a very large tear. The doctor would be so much better. And he'd have something . . . for pain."

"We don't have a doctor." Jenny's breath carried worry over what could have happened to Ben. He'd been gone for hours. She kept her mind from racing to all the possible tragedies, like accidents or wolves or who knew what all. Hadn't they had a miserable past year with the storm and rebuilding? Prices for wheat and apples were down. Miners in Jacksonville and California were less dependent on Oregon goods. And the Duniways had fewer goods to sell. *Why does my mind go to money worries? It's stitching up I need.* "Just sew. There's laudanum on top the pie chest. I wish I had chloroform."

"Or that laughing gas," Mary said. She had a kerchief tied at the back of her neck, holding her thick hair in check as she ministered to Jenny. "I saw it used at a forum once. Ten boys volunteered. They didn't remember a thing afterwards, they said, even when the host poked a needle into their fingers and drew blood."

"Not the image I'm needing right now," Jenny moaned. "Give me a small dose of the laudanum and then sew quickly. I want to be able to nurse that boy. Willis, we'll call him. After my little brother William who died on the trail. He even looks like him a little."

The conversation depleted her. Mary dipped the tincture onto Jenny's tongue. The neighbor put a rag in her mouth to bite on, and the older midwife began to sew within seconds. Jenny remembered little after that. She woke hours later to Ben, looking haggard, leaning over her.

"What happened to you?"

"I—the fog was so dense that I got lost. I . . . I still can't believe it. I finally gave Biscuit his head and the gelding brought us home, though hours it took. I'm so sorry. I—" He knelt beside the bed.

"Did you meet our son?"

"I did. And massive he is."

Jenny winced. "I'm still bleeding."

"Not as much, though it's likely to continue." The midwife didn't look at Jenny when she spoke. She fiddled with her instruments she'd placed in the pan of water no longer boiling. "It's a clean wound, but there'll be seepage and you must stay down. No heavy work at all or the bleeding will begin again in earnest."

"When the fog lifts, I'll go fetch your sisters."

"Until then," Mary said, "I'll stay." She saw another look pass between Ben and his sister.

I am worse than I thought. She patted Ben's hand. "Kate will come and Harriet. Neither have seen the rebuilt cabin."

Her sisters would laugh together and tell stories, which is what they did in a week, when March brought on the Willamette Valley spring and the doctor arrived too. He pronounced the sewing a fine stitching. "Any number of folks got discombobulated in that fog, Ben. You shouldn't feel bad about it."

"The outcome was all right," Ben told him. "I'd never have forgiven myself if Jenny had . . ." His voice caught and he couldn't finish.

"Bad things happen to the best of men," the doctor said. "Things work out."

"And sometimes they don't," Jenny said.

She had survived another birthing, but this child left his impression. Jenny spent weeks propped up in bed, frustrated with not being able to do the work that needed doing. After her sisters returned to their homes, Ben served as a good nurse and not a bad cook either, despite his having said he wouldn't be.

"My father didn't lend a kitchen-hand with babies around," Jenny said. She'd never seen her father pour hot water onto oats for his children to eat nor cut up venison for stew.

Ben washed their dishes. "He'd be missing out."

"You think so?" Household chores were mundane, repetitive, even though she knew they were essential tasks. "I haven't minded not being able to sweep or scrub."

"That's because you're destined for bigger things," he told her. He handed Clara Belle a tin plate. "Wipe it like this." He showed the child, and the toddler beamed.

"I help," she said.

"Yup, you do."

Jenny pondered Ben's offhand remark. "Destined for bigger things?" *Such nonsense.*

"It's true. You've got the kind of mind that thinks past the moment," he said. "Once you come out of this post-baby fog you've been in, you'll be pondering again. You're always ponderin' on something, mostly about women you don't even know."

"You've as good a mind as mine."

"Don't think so. Mine is content to brush a horse or scrape dried eggs from the pan." They turned together toward a crying Willis, lying in his cradle. "I'll leave it to you to change the world. I'll just change his diaper."

* * *

Writing helped ease Jenny's healing, but what she couldn't seem to regain after Willis's birth was her sense of hopefulness, that as Ben said, things really would work out all right. He'd point to how the children thrived, how neighbors had helped them recover, how she healed—though she still bled, often grabbed the table corner, and placed chairs equal-distant so she always had something to hold on to as she moved around the house. *Will this be my life now?*

"It'll get even better once you're able to let go of all the way stations," Ben said. "And can join in the neighborhood doings. Go to the horse races, pie fests. You know, participate."

"I haven't felt much like being out. Besides, we need new farm equipment, and I'd love a labor-saving device for washing clothes. And we could use an addition built onto this cabin if we're going to stay here. We stumble over ourselves. Besides, I've no energy for neighboring."

"Sure, you do. Being around people feeds you, rubs away some of your cranky edges."

"I'm not cranky without reason," Jenny said.

"Not arguing that." Ben held his hands up to ward off her sharp words that could rise as quick as a wind change. "I'm merely seeking a way to buff it into something that restores your high spirits."

He'd persisted in his gentle way, and on a Saturday when Willis was a few months old, the Duniways took the buggy to Needy, past the little school Jenny had taught at. They stopped by the Aurora Colony where the communal colonists played music on Saturday afternoon and there were stores the general public could buy from. It was said they had their names on ledger sheets recording what they brought or bought but didn't need to bring cash or trade. And that women were taught Greek and Latin like the men.

It was a glorious day in early October and hop harvests were in full swing in the valley, the air fragrant and leaves magically turning green to vermillion. Jenny ran into friends who commented on how well she looked (*Do I?*) or how they'd missed hearing her side of issues in the cloakroom while men discussed potential statehood at the local schoolhouse. She had to admit, she missed those conversations too, especially when they spoke of subjects of import and not only about the value of packaged yeast over sourdough starter.

Heading home with a bit more grit, she realized Ben had been right about her getting out. She did appreciate the compliments about the children looking well and healthy, and she liked hearing Ben's laughter as the men exchanged stories of horseflesh or hunting. There was life beyond the cabin walls harboring wet diapers and the daily drudge of churning. She breathed in the soapy smell of Clara's hair as the child leaned against her on the buckboard seat. Willis reached out to pat his older sister's arm and rocked himself back and forth as he sat on Jenny's lap. "Gentle," she cautioned.

She wondered if all women in fact found sustenance not only from things nearby, like the hug of a child, but also from things outside the domestic realm. Both near and far were necessary to withstand daily demands, she supposed, and vowed that evening to write about it, to continue to fill up on a day that had reminded her of her resilience. And friends. The future wasn't so bleak after all.

Ben chirped the team forward as dusk settled onto the roadway. Jenny leaned her head onto her husband's shoulder.

"That was a good idea, Ben, to get out."

"I have a few now and then."

"That you do." She needed to remember that.

After the inspiring day, they drove the wagon up the last incline, and Ben held the team back as they started down the grade. He sniffed the air. Jenny did too. *Smoke.*

EIGHT

Brooms of the World

1857

Their cabin was a pile of burnt timbers and black rubble.

Things don't always turn out well. "Now we have to move," she said.

Jenny was insistent, and so they moved—temporarily—into the barn.

After locating the andirons, arranging for how they'd cook and sleep, and while she nursed Willis, Jenny gave her requirements to what a new farm would need. "Within a mile—no more than two—of some kind of village where I can sell eggs and butter, take in some sewing. And horrors be, laundry."

"I'd suggest land with fruit tree possibilities," Ben said. "A place for the sheep and horses of course." Ben's requirements were of the soil, the land, Jenny's of connection, family.

"And a southern exposure," Jenny said. "I need sun whenever it appears."

"I have your list branded in my brain," Ben told her.

"When you've found one, come get me before you make any offer, all right?"

"Agreed."

He had found a farm in Yamhill County, and when Jenny and the children rode up to the gate in the wagon, her spirits lifted. The sun shone on the cleared fields, and at the top of the hill, a two-story frame house with a covered porch beckoned them to this harbor on the hillside. She named it Sunny Hillside Farm and it was all she'd ever dreamed of, she told Ben.

Moving day arrived and her sisters—minus Maggie, who had delivered her second child on the Oregon coast—arrived to assist. Even her brother Harvey came. He drove one of the teams and a wagon to the new farm about twenty miles distant from their old one. Harvey had enlisted to fight in the Yakima Wars and would leave soon. She was grateful Ben hadn't decided to go with him. The danger seemed far away and he was needed closer to home.

"Two moves are as good as a fire," Fanny told Jenny. The sisters raked up ashes, seeking anything of value that might remain. Ben had determined that it was a spark from the hearth that caused it—who knew what had been left close enough to catch aflame. The stone memorializing Jenny's mother was black as tar pitch.

Several brass buttons appeared through the swept ashes. A pair of earrings—not the ones Shirley Ellis had helped push through Jenny's ears on the trail, thank goodness. Those Jenny had worn the day of the fire. Her *Primer*, the book she'd managed to sneak along on the trip west despite her father's wishes, was stored in a trunk in the barn along with pages of a manuscript she'd been working on. When they'd arrived to what was left that day, she went into the barn to make certain the trunk was there. She pressed two poems to her breast from it, pieces she'd written during her convalescence after Willis's arrival. She'd stored old newspapers there too, including an issue of the *Argus*, an agricultural paper that she thought could use a woman's touch. She had a poem in mind to send the editor. There must be other women who suffered loss and struggled, who might find comfort in her words.

Writing something for publication caused a small conflict for her, which had kept her from submitting her poems. Her words in print would make her both a public and a private woman. She hadn't yet shared that concern with anyone, including Ben. Writing had become a balm, different from being a reader. Hadn't she found solace and been challenged by Shakespeare or that *Lily* woman, Amelia Bloomer? Amelia also edited a newspaper, something a bit scandalous for a woman to do. Yet when Jenny was a child learning to read, her parents took subscriptions to such newspapers. And the world had become more than simply a home on the frontier.

At the same time, her father had impressed upon her that respectable women ought to keep themselves from public display. "A woman's reputation is all she has," he said. *And a man can ruin his without consequence because he is accepted in the public arena.* Her father had cautioned all his daughters about avoiding public spheres. Women were to be unnoticeable, subservient. She'd carried that attitude like a proper platter served up for herself and younger sisters on how they ought to best behave. What would happen if she wrote something controversial, not that she was intending that. Just a little poem. Yet words put into the open could arrive as something unintended by the poet.

But when she watched Clara Belle prance around the room, singing, she wondered why such joy should be kept only in the kitchen or in a church choir. Why were women with gifts not allowed to show them? And she could hear that her daughter had a gifted singing voice.

"It's good that Ben found a claim so quickly, one with a frame house bigger than your log cabin was anyway." Kate's words brought Jenny back to the cabin ruins. Kate removed her work gloves. The women all wore wrappers to protect their day dresses. The Scott girls liked color, and each wrapper was dyed differently: yellow from daffodils, blue from berries, red from blood, and if Maggie had been with them, bleached white as a baby's tooth with embroidery around the edges.

"It's the perfect time of year to move," Kate continued. April daffodils dotted the pathway between the barn and their former house, and Kate had dug up the bulbs for planting at the Duniways' new farm.

"Take a few for yourself," Jenny said. She entered what was left of the house, swept the old hearth once more. "You can plant them in pots until you know where you and John will settle." Kate planned to marry a steamboat captain in June.

"Give yourself time before you start your family," Fanny advised her. "It'll be easier on you, believe me."

"Believe her," Jenny added. "Any news, Harriet?"

"We want to wait." Harriet had married her own sweetheart.

"It's good you and William are of one accord with that," Kate said. "John and I have discussed it." She blushed. "And he doesn't want to interfere with nature."

"That's my Ben too," Jenny said. "What they don't realize is how repeated pregnancies deplete a woman's body and interfere with nature too. Look at Momma."

"Twelve of us. And there'd have been more if she had lived," Fanny said. "Father being who he is." She wiped Eda's face. The child always had a runny nose and a frequent cough, especially in the spring. Fanny inhaled. "How does a mother survive the death of a child? At least she didn't live to witness William's lonely grave on the trail."

"Birth and death. It's a woman's lot to mark her world by those bookends." Jenny sighed. "But," she perked up. "I think we've done all the damage we can do to what's left here. The wagon's ready as soon as Ben and the men return with the teams. Let's have a cup of tea."

Harriet found the tea tin and lifted the pot from the iron over the outdoor fire they'd built. "I'm glad you found Clara's silver spoon though. Momma snuck that along."

"I could write a poem about all the things we brought that Papa never knew about." Jenny laughed.

"Do that," Fanny said. "I managed to bring needles, right out in the open. Father never said a word."

"He knew you'd need them to patch his pants," Kate said.

Copies of the *Argus* Jenny had stacked and tied were ready to be put into the wagon.

"Are you saving all those issues?" Sarah Maria, the youngest sister, asked.

"They can be cut up for dress patterns. And they'll be useful if I ever teach again," Jenny said. "The *Argus* deals with hide prices and women's recipes, so the men think we can't get into too much trouble reading it. But the articles that stimulate the mind is what people need, even farm wives. At least I do. So I read *News of the World* and the *Spectator* too. I just don't accept everything as gospel." She lifted her eyes in time to watch a breeze flutter across the field, brushing bachelor buttons, grasses, the movement easing toward them like an invisible wave until it reached the girls and cooled Jenny's face. She looked up at the sky. No sign of a storm. "Did you see that?"

"See what?" Sarah Maria asked.

"The way you can watch weather change. All was quiet, and then with barely a flutter, the entire field began to wave and carried the breeze right here."

Kate—the beautiful sister, as Jenny thought of her—stared at the timbers.

"Never mind," Jenny said. "I suppose I'm twisted as an old oak, finding metaphors where no one else does. It's that change happens so invisibly at times, one hardly notices. Like Clara Belle. One day she was babbling as though she carried on a conversation with inflections and bursts of sounds that made no sense, and then within a day, voilà! She said, 'Where's Pa?'"

"Your teaching gifts are showing then," Kate said.

"Maybe. Time is moving. The world is moving."

Jenny kept her gaze at the field where all the foliage whispered and aspen leaves fluttered. She decided then to write something down about what she'd seen, how change crept up on people when not expected, how the language of the landscape spoke as loudly as words sometimes.

Jenny shook ash from the straw broom. She'd swept through this mess soon after the fire, and they hoped the spring rains might have washed up other treasures. But she thought they had taken all they could from this hardscrabble place.

"Do you want to keep that?" Sarah Maria reached for the broom. She had celebrated her tenth birthday and looked up to her older sisters, whom she didn't get to see much as she lived with Fanny and Amos. She appeared to relish being brought this time to help out. Jenny watched her grasp that broom, a woman's tool, and stand the way men held rifles in studio photographs as though they were a defense as well as a stabilizer.

"An ode to the broom," Jenny said, using her teacher's voice. "It sweeps up dirt, then gets put back into the closet until the next mess. Not unlike a woman. Brooms of the world we are."

"We all have something of Momma's, I think," Fanny said. She shifted baby Eda to her other hip. Eda had her mother's deep-set eyes and looked sober and wise beyond her almost three years. And she had full, arched eyebrows like Sarah's. She looked pale, Jenny thought.

"I've got Momma's thimble," Kate said. "And you've got the spoon and her stories."

"Being sickly kept me inside a lot, so she talked to me. But I also saw how hard she worked, how tired she was, all the time." Jenny saved the tea leaves in a small linen bag. She stuck it in her apron pocket. There might be another cup inside it.

"Having children every other year didn't help."

"Let that be a lesson to us all." Harriet said. "I have a twist of her hair I wove into my bridal veil."

"I remember that. It was lovely," Kate said.

"If you want to wear it, you can. It can be your something borrowed."

"Or something old," Fanny added.

"It's nice you've had time to plan for your wedding, Kate." Jenny sounded wistful and she knew she shouldn't. She'd made the choice to marry Ben as soon as she had. It wasn't like there was a mass of suitors. Well, that one—Bunter—who had written her a letter and acted like he was doing her a favor in proposing. He'd since written letters to the *Argus* editor about strident women and how he was as eligible a bachelor as any and the government made it hard on him to compete with other landed gents who could snatch up an Oregon woman who brought land with her. Land was all that man had wanted. Ben had wanted something more, and she was grateful for that. If she hadn't loved him to begin with, how would she have endured these past years as they struggled together?

"It has been fun to be courted by a captain over time. But he's quite certain of his preferences," Kate said. "He picked out our house with little say from me. Not like your Sunny Hillside Farm you and Ben chose together. I like the name you gave it. It has a happy tone to it."

"Near beautiful Lafayette. The French would be so pleased," Jenny said. "It is a good part of the valley. Orchards abound." Lafayette was the county seat, so stores were but a few miles from the farm. "Maybe it won't be so lonely during the rainy season. We women can get together now and then, even in the rain."

Ben and her brother Harvey and others brought the teams and empty wagons back and chatted to her sisters while Ben harnessed the horses to the wagon the women had loaded.

"It's a good place, Jenny," Harvey said. "You'll thrive there."

"Women thrive wherever we're planted," Jenny said. But she knew the soil, the tending, and the exposure to the sun made all the difference in how well one flourished.

She turned back one last time to look at the burned-out carcass, witness the rebuilt barn and fences after the tornado and all that had happened at this hardscrabble place. She wished the new owners good fortune. They had a nice barn and fresh-peeled logs for their cabin to begin with anyway. She hoped for better things at Sunny Hillside Farm. Give the neighbors something good to gossip about the Duniways now, instead of clucking their pitying tongues at their tragedies.

She faced forward on the seat and watched the wagons ahead, carrying harnesses, shovels, forks. "Wait! Let's take the broom."

"I'll get you a new one," Ben said.

"No. That one is my symbol of endurance."

Ben pulled up the team. "Little Toot, ride back and get your sister's old broom. Where'd you leave it?"

"Leaned it up against the hearthstones." Jenny pointed.

"I'll have it for you in a minute, Sister."

Little Toot kneed his mount and rode back to bring her symbol of a woman's work—and maybe of her life. Old brooms swept away dust and disappointment, but both came back.

NINE

Ora et Labora

November 1857

"They published it. *The Burning Forest Tree* by Jenny Glen." Jenny put the newspaper on the table while Ben drank his morning coffee. "What do you think?"

The sun had peeked its nose above the horizon, casting long shadows over the green. It promised to be a pretty day, fluffy clouds pushing November gray away. The babies slept, a moment of reprieve. Little Toot had grown into "Jerry." After Harvey returned from the war, Jerry, now a wisp-of-whiskers teen starting to shave, had gone off to live with their father and stepmother, helping his father farm and work at the sawmill near Forest Grove. Jenny had resisted Jerry's leaving, but the appeal of his being able to go to school in Tualatin Academy won her over. Education was critical for all people. Harvey was right about that but wrong that he thought it less critical for girls, and that if someone wanted schooling for their children past the eighth grade, they should pay for it and not expect the government to do it. Her argument—exchanged over the meal the evening of Harvey's celebratory return—was that it was in the country's best interest to have educated, critical thinkers, and providing for it for free with all citizens helping to pay for it, for as long as someone gained from it, made sense to her. Their siblings present had groaned at the rising level of voices, and it was Jerry who had eased the temperature down and said, "Let's just eat."

Harvey worked now too for their father in the sawmill and took college preparatory classes—that he paid for himself, he reminded them all. He'd been hardened by the war, living in harsh conditions, and didn't have much room for looking after those Jenny saw as less fortunate through no fault of their own. She knew firsthand how a storm or a fire could set a family back. Jenny watched her youngest brother eat. Thin as a bird he was. He'd lost weight since leaving Sunny Hillside. Like her, he tended to frailness, and like her, he would push himself to exhaustion to prove he could. She knew he dreamed of becoming a lawyer, taking on cases to help others. She'd do everything she could to help make that happen. She knew about dreams.

She'd burned the midnight oil to write that poem and had overcome her fears by taking it to the *Argus* editor. He'd accepted it.

"Abigail Duniway. That's how it'll be attributed," the editor said.

"Oh. No." *What will people think? If they don't like it, it'll bring ill repute onto Ben.* She should have thought of that before. "No. Ah, let's say Jenny Glen wrote it." Her pen name. The editor had shrugged and wrote it on the copy she'd presented.

"You're Jenny Glen?" Ben's blue eyes gazed up at her, held surprise. He read the poem again. "I like the part where you talk about the air being like no other. And 'I feel no loneliness.' I like that best." He handed the *Argus* back to her. "I don't want you to be lonely. That's why I invite friends over. But why didn't you use Jenny Duniway. Or Abigail Duniway? Are you—"

"No, no. I thought it might bring negative attention to you if people don't like it. To us."

"Naw. It's a little poem. The womenfolk will like it. Well done, Wife." He changed the subject. "We finished planting those five acres. Apples soon. This land is perfect for it." He stood, tipping back the chair as he lifted his leg up and over on his way to grab his hat, kiss Jenny, then head out the door.

"My moment of glory," she said as she lifted Ben's chair back up and pushed it under the table. "Your father did like it though," she told Clara Belle. "Now we'll see if anyone else does." Willis woke and she soon lost thoughts of poetry as she washed his face of mush and took him from the high chair. Clara made her way out the door to wave at her father in the fields and sing a little song to him. "Later I might show your father my column they call 'The Farmer's Wife.' They published it anonymously." Willis looked back at her with inquisitive brown eyes. "Pretty soon people will be talking about that, if not my poem."

She had begun with the anonymous letters to the editor and did a little jig around the wooden floors when she saw the first one in print. She'd signed it *The Farmer's Wife.* It recounted an episode when Ben had offered to help her with the laundry that turned into a tale of stumble and trouble, resulting in more work than either of them planned. She made light of Ben's awkwardness—she referred to him as "the Farmer"—and yes, he was the misery of the episode, but she had wanted to show that a woman's work took coordination and effort and could be as complicated as that of planting a field of straight rows or operating a sawmill safely.

* * *

After supper, Ben picked up the paper. "Did you read this, Jenny? The Farmer's Wife is quite a cutup. Looks like we weren't the only ones who had a bad washday, though she makes it funnier than ours was."

Jenny remained silent, her heart pounding.

"Say." He looked up at her. "Did you write this?"

"I did. Are you upset?"

"Me? No. It makes hay out of straw." He laughed, tapped his finger on the page. "I bet you get some letters though."

And she did. People said they liked the Farmer's Wife and hoped she'd continue her stories. During the long rainy months, she'd written of isolation and how their being closer to a town had made the showery days less dreary, knowing once a week they could traverse the muddy roads to go to church, if not to market. She planned to slip in a few words about the value of women's work and such—if the editor allowed it. The copyeditor started putting a block around Jenny's letters, to make them stand out, as though they were a column.

She speaks my heart, a reader wrote. It was then Jenny knew that words had power. Her words, at least, got others to respond. Wasn't that the purpose of words—to get movement, to share the burdens and even joys?

She got braver. She wrote not about who visited whom or of church events. She left those topics to others. Jenny's subjects pushed toward the fate of women, how hard they worked, how some men took better care of their horses than of their wives and daughters. She charged that once men gained wealth to hire workers, they never thought to bring such hired help to their mates (Kate's husband John's hiring help excluded) and how they acted like they didn't want to tax a woman's constitution by allowing her to attend public events with men. And certainly many men did not want women to vote—heaven forbid, and a few men thought heaven did actually forbid a woman's vote—but it was fine to treat a woman like a beast of burden.

"The Farmer's Wife is a peevish, ill-natured, irritable, fault-finding common scold." The letter wasn't signed. She wasn't surprised. She didn't mind being called a scold, but a common one? She was better than that, and she wrote as much in her follow-up letter to "anonymous upset reader."

> *Who is the Farmer's Wife, advising men how to treat their families? She should stop her malicious babbling at once.*
>
> *Her husband needs to set her down and teach her a thing or two.*

Most responses were anonymous, but Mr. Bunter had written that such a witchery point of view had no place in a family press and he was canceling his subscription.

She'd purposely not shown Ben those letters nor the responses the newspaper had printed either. Ben didn't read all that much, and some comments made her cheeks burn when she saw them referring to her as that "common scold" and even a "hag."

Those words stung, but they also fueled. How could simply pointing out the importance of treating women like people and not beasts of burden create such an uproar? She wasn't sure what they'd say once she got her novel published, and she would. But whether she'd use her own name or not, she wasn't sure. How far could she go using words as brooms to sweep up trouble and even stir up more trouble that needed stirring up? She'd taken a risk and now would have to face the consequences.

* * *

When Jenny wasn't finding respite in writing, she worked and often mused of what other women did to overcome the drudgery of their days. How did they build their spirits up? She'd think of loftier things, but then the daily regimen would take over.

It being Monday, that included laundry. "Why Monday?" she told Clara, who chased Willis around the table as the toddler squealed in delight. "Why not do laundry on Saturday when clean clothes can be worn on Sunday, the very next day," she told her children. And when the following day a woman could have respite in the pews, laundry being the hardest of labors. *Ora et labora.* Prayer and work. Harvey had given her that Latin phrase. He was teaching himself Latin and Greek. *How fortunate for him he has the nights to study.*

At least today it wasn't raining, so as she moved between their frame house and the laundry cottage at the farm, she wouldn't get doused and the clothes would dry faster.

She heated the water on the cookstove, lamenting that she

didn't have the strength to lift the heavier cast-iron pots and instead had to dip pitchers into the scalding water, then carry them to the big wooden tubs where she'd add the lye soap and stir the sheets and mud-stained jeans with a stick as wide as an oar. Then into a second tub of rinse water before hanging them with split pegs on the line. Before the children were born, Ben built fires beneath the cauldrons so she didn't have to carry the water, but she'd heard tales of children falling into the tubs or tripping into the fire. Twice in her own childhood she'd rescued both Kate and Harvey from laundry fires. *I must remind Harvey that I once saved his life.*

At least here she stoked the cookstove, feeding it kindling, and it took the chill off the laundry cottage in the fall and winter; heated it to a misery in the summers. Despite the work it took—and how Monday always ended with her joints aching worse than any other day—she preferred this safer method. In the distance, she could see Ben and his workers planting apple trees and wished she had help as she pegged the sheets.

The truth, she told herself, was that she'd rather be teaching or writing, almost anything except laundry or other "domestic arts." Her sisters were so much better at them than she was. Fanny could whip up a meal for a dozen with hardly a second thought, even with her Eda's runny nose and Lillian's weepy eyes. "Something in the air bothers them," Fanny had written in her latest letter. Maggie had two children as well, but her boat-house-store dodging in and out of ports on the coast was still as tidy as her quilt stitches. "Clean house, clean heart," she said. "You only need what's functional."

"I'll decide later about the clutter," Jenny had told Maggie. "The children don't mind and the floors are clean. Cobwebs grow overnight. Can't be helped. Spiders get free rides inside on the logs."

She supposed it was some small comfort knowing that all of her sisters—and women everywhere—were washing clothes on this day of the week as she was. Kate would be doing laundry too, but John had hired help for her, and it was only the two of them! Such a small basket of dirty clothes. Envy stuck out its tongue.

Laundry was such a thankless task having to be done over and over. She'd told Harriet's inventive husband that he ought to come up with some way to make laundry easier and not just spend his inventive mind on doodads like punched patterns in tin lanterns. She'd told Ben that too, and he'd said, as he often did to her suggestions, "I'll think over it."

When she wasn't composing poems or articles while she spun wool or churned cream, she worried over money. Teaching had once given her currency to call her own. Ben listened to Jenny at least. He still thought though that men were entitled to hunt and fish and "jaw" and visit and offer undiminished hospitality as respite from their labor no matter the season nor their income. Women had no such hope to interrupt their daily demands. He didn't always know how inventive she had to get to spread their cash or trade in ways that kept the family—and the many friends Ben brought around—fed.

He let her save a little of her egg-and-butter money for her books, papers, and lead, and she had proposed they buy a small house in town where they might spend winter months so the children could attend school. "A man should be responsible for financial matters," he'd said, but he went along with the Lafayette house purchase. "It's how we look after our women, protect you." But what of those men as she imagined Mr. Bunter was? Who protects those wives? And widows? A woman needed control over her income, but laws would have to be remade to make that so. And men made all the laws. How would that ever change?

Her hands were chapped by the harsh lye soap she used to launder clothes. Jenny prayed while she folded the "underlings," as her mother had called the unmentionables. She wished she could find peace in the everyday work instead of resentment of its dailyness, its weekly-ness, its constant-ness. The domestic arts did not make her thrive. Instead, they were bars on a window women had to look through to accomplish anything. She stood and pressed both hands on her lower back. She'd need to stop and prepare a noon meal for Ben and his helpers. She walked toward the house, checking the line to see if those clothes were dry enough to remove and she could prepare to hang up others after the cleanup from the noon break. She felt a trickle between her legs. She still bled, especially on Mondays.

* * *

Jenny finished the laundry as the day waned, bringing evening cooling. She rested her body on a bench Ben had built outside the laundry cottage. Clara's clear voice belted out the alphabet song to Willis, who tried the same but babbled an up-and-down rhythm instead. "Clara, you have your daddy's voice, and poor Willis, you got mine."

Why she pondered women's labor so much, she wasn't certain, but women spent so much time in work, praying for ease. Except for childbirth, she'd had no time to lie and rest. There was always something more to do. She had written that ode to the broom, singing its praises as a sign of what women were—laborers in the never-ending fields.

"A woman should get paid for her housework." She said it out loud to Ben.

"How would that work?" Ben asked. He settled on the bench beside her.

"If her husband paid her, she could hire others who liked to sweep and clean and tend, women who did that well. And she could do what she was called to. That would allow a woman to take on work more meaningful to her, like asking questions. Why couldn't a woman make her way doing what she liked to do as much as a man? Why shouldn't she get land in her own name even without a husband? The Farmer's Wife might need to take on that subject."

"I hope it doesn't become too obvious who the Farmer's Wife is, Jenny."

She turned to him. "Does that worry you?" She didn't want

to make his life complicated nor somehow tarnish the Duniway name.

He was thoughtful. "I suppose not. Must be a sign of a wise farmer if he can allow his wife to speak her mind. At least you're not up on some stage like I hear those Eastern women sometimes do."

"Yes, public speaking is the realm of men. My father always says that." She watched the sunset turn the world a rosy hue. "But something might be so important that it would be worth risking a woman's reputation to speak her voice in public, as a man can, don't you think?"

Ben sat silent. "I'll think over it."

TEN

Life, Death, and What Is Sure

1858

They'd endured more than celebrated the Christmas holidays. Her niece, the sickly Eda, had passed. For Jenny, the very thought of the death of Clara or Willis caused such heartache that she sometimes couldn't catch her breath. Her mother had grieved her firstborn, and then another son died when Jenny was eleven and the boy only one month old, followed by their sister Alice, born and died the same day, the autumn before they left Illinois. The work hadn't stopped for her mother with any of those deaths, and it wouldn't for Fanny either. But neighbors helped. Families brought food and talked softly while preparing Eda for burial, putting all the hopes and dreams for her gentled into the wooden casket that the Lafayette furniture maker crafted. There was nothing more forlorn, Jenny decided, than an empty child-size casket being brought into the house—except one holding a child when it was taken back out.

It made Jenny want to grab up her two children and set them inside a fleece-lined basket and hold them there, prevent death from reaching its greedy fingers into their lives. But of course, living held risk, the very act of breathing meant another step into the unknown. How one took those steps would shape the character of those around you—Fanny's other children, her husband, Amos. Men had their own struggles with such a loss. Women suffered differently. Jenny vowed to visit Fanny often, help her with the daily tasks that must go on, and put her own struggles and fatigue aside when she was with her. And she wouldn't mention a word about the restrictions placed on women to mourn in silence and not too long, as though there were a timeline for grief to close the cracks in a family's foundation.

She must also include such loss in her novels—for any frontier reader would relate. There wasn't a single family who hadn't experienced a death of some kind. She would attempt to capture life inside her stories . . . give new meaning to the tragedies they couldn't control.

* * *

"It's something you're good at, Fanny. It will give you a sense of accomplishment, when right now you likely can't feel much of anything except anguish."

Fanny sighed. "I have no skills. I couldn't even keep my girl alive."

"You did everything you could for her. Illness . . . there's so much we don't control, Fanny. Only how we respond to what life hands us. And you have a talent I desperately need. Please."

Jenny had opened Hope School in the Lafayette house. She'd thought of the idea while washing clothes and wondered if mundane tasks might indeed be the catalyst for creativity. She got Ben's agreement with the promise she'd be back on Sunny Hillside each weekend with the children and all summer long.

"Not much of a married life though." Ben had chewed on his pipe stem. He never put tobacco in the bowl.

"Men go off to the mines. Or they work large ranches East and leave their families to operate their farms. It's what people have to do. I'll make up stews, and you can fix potatoes and bacon easy enough. You'll have plenty of eggs. I'll still make butter to sell."

She could out-argue him, and he'd agreed, so Jenny had her subscription school she called Hope, and now Fanny was enlisted to help with the school's Christmas pageant.

Jenny admitted to herself that she liked the drama, the rehearsals, hearing children read the lines she wrote telling a story of a lost present and how it had been magically found and everyone lived happily. And then the grand performance. She had actors for the Bible story, and each student had a part. After all, the Christmas story was for everyone. She dressed Willis up in a fleece, and he moaned "Baaa! Baaa!" even when he wasn't supposed to. Clara sang. One of the tallest boys was Joseph, and her youngest sister with the beautiful eyebrows, Sarah Maria, acted as Mary, who had to shout above the bleating sheep. The others were either shepherds or angels, and they had more than three wise men, who also had to yell above the bleating ram. Everyone laughed, even Fanny and Amos, grieving parents finding comfort in the family and friends who walked beside them as they were reminded of the story of Christ's birth and promise.

Jenny accepted the congratulations from her students' parents and that night sank into bed happy.

Her best work had been convincing Fanny that her labor was worthy and that there was life after grief. She loved seeing Fanny enjoy herself. As she told Ben, "She accepted my few coins to reimburse her for her stitching too."

"Always working to honor women's labor," Ben said. "Well done, Wife."

* * *

Spring was approaching, and Jenny knew she'd have to close the school down and be available for the farm work, especially cooking for all the men. Ben had enjoyed the winter, coming into Lafayette midweek and fixing meals so Jenny had more time for lesson preparations. He told of ways that other families adjusted to the challenges of frontier finance.

"There are gold strikes in Idaho." Ben turned the bacon and the aroma filled the large kitchen. Jenny sat at a day desk he'd built for her. "I was thinking this fall I might go there and make a strike like I did in Jacksonville before I met you."

"We'd be separated even more than this past winter." She looked up from her foolscap.

"If I made a strike, you wouldn't have to have the school. We'd have enough with the farm."

He doesn't see how much I love the teaching, having a part in contributing to the family through more than just laundry.

He smiled at Clara, who sat waiting for the bacon. "I'd miss my pumpkins, that's sure."

"I'm no pumpkin, Pa," Clara said. "But Willis is a squash."

"Am not."

"Are so."

"Children." Jenny's voice stopped the fracas. Ben did enjoy his time with Clara and Willis. He was a good husband, despite his tendency to visit and bring back friends—at his leisure—for her to serve them supper. And he didn't mind cooking for the family, which was a boon to her, though she couldn't imagine him frying potatoes for his guests or hired men.

Once they'd had a row over how his "guests" were treated. Two of his bachelor friends had stopped by Sunny Hillside Farm after the supper hour when Ben wasn't home. Jenny had been quilting—not her most favorite activity—and she kept on as the men chatted with each other about whether Oregon would become a state, how they'd lose their autonomy as a territory able to make their own laws once Oregon joined the union. They talked around her, didn't ask her opinion. Eventually realizing there would be no food forthcoming, they made some comment about it.

"Oh, were you waiting to be fed? Had I known that's what you stopped by for, I could have told you an hour ago and you could have made your way back to your own kitchen." Which they then did and later told Ben about it. He'd been livid.

"You provide when you can, knowing that someday someone will help you," he had told her, his voice raised. "Hospitality is the bedrock of this country."

"No. Work is the bedrock, and I was working, but not to prepare their suppers. You get them married off so they can eat at home." *Poor souls who accept those proposals seeking stomach-soothing over love.* "I'd say I'm not alone in my feelings about this. Why should women be expected to take care of everyone? It was the end of a long day, and they expected me to wait on them just because I was a woman."

"They're neighbors."

"Who should eat at home or when invited." Silence. Then, "The Farmer's Wife might have words to say about such frontier hospitality. It's the pioneer women who are expected to be hospitable while you men make the rules about what that looks like."

"As it should be," Ben said.

"Maybe one day it'll be different. Ouch." She had poked the needle into her finger, sucked on it. Her Farmer's Wife gave her an outlet to express her upset, but it didn't change anything for the lives of women and that had been her intent and still was.

Her finger bled.

"Let me kiss that and make it better," Ben said.

She let him. He said he understood that women got little rest and that she especially didn't seem to know how to play.

"We women have no time to play."

"You need to laugh a little more," he'd told her and kissed her hand again. "Try to be a little more accommodating."

"Holy cow chips. One more task to put on my list." She had sighed. "I'll think on it."

"Good. Now let me hold you and kiss that pain away. I hate arguing with you."

"Because I almost always win."

He had grinned at that, and she let him pull her close.

Come spring, they were expecting another Duniway.

ELEVEN

Surety

January 1859

Jenny listened. She'd been busy stuffing duck feathers for comforters while frying potatoes for their supper. She was as big as a washtub, carrying this third child, and her belly bumped against the table, so her back hurt as she stretched to fill the comforter. She wasn't sure how she felt about another child so soon, but Ben wanted a big family. She blew feathers from her nose as she heard Ben say to yet another guest in their living room something about "surety." *Ben is offering to secure something?* When she later recalled this day, it would be with the scent of bacon swirling around the house, children chattering, and her hands inside the softness of feathers, while her mind pondered uncertainty.

She didn't know well the man who'd be staying for supper. He'd stopped by and talked apple markets with Ben previously, as she remembered. Since the time she hadn't been hospitable to two of Ben's bachelor friends, she rarely said anything about the surprise meals (as she called them) that she had to serve.

She peered into the room and saw something legal-looking in

three folds lying on the slab table in front of them. *This is not good.* She put the feathers aside, sneezed—as she often did around duck feathers—and moved the frying pan off the burner with a scraping sound, then entered the room where Ben watched the children and "jawed" with Mr. Markham. *Yes, that's his name. Bob Markham.*

"What high finance is happening in our living room?" She kept her voice light. "I heard the word 'surety.' We can't afford a cosigned note, Ben."

"Like good Oregonians, we look after each other," Ben said. His eyebrow twitched. *He's nervous about my interfering.* "We're helping Bob here make his investment in the field. Don't you like my pun, Wife?" Ben beamed.

He's trying to distract. Her heart started pounding a little faster. She reached for Willis and plopped him on her hip. He squirmed. Her belly got in the way, so she let him down.

"And how are we helping Bob, here, become outstanding in his field?" She heard the sarcasm in her voice and saw Ben frown.

"Shouldn't your little lady be protected from thoughts of business and investments?" Jenny heard the challenge to Ben's "head of household" status in those words.

"I'm signing a note at two percent per month, Abigail."

He's called me Abigail!

"They'll be compounded semiannually until paid, but Bob can then get his loan. He's good for it. You'll manage your money well, won't you, Bob?"

"No question about it."

She could feel bile rise beneath the baby she carried. "That's a hefty interest rate." She turned to Ben. "If Bob"—she emphasized his name—"fails to pay, we could be ruined meeting that kind of obligation in his stead."

"Now, Jenny, let's not air our underlings in public."

He's offended that I bring up a concern? She was offended that he hadn't.

"You'll always be protected, don't you worry now. Is supper

ready? I think I smell that bacon frying but no rasher of potatoes as yet." He used his fingers to gesture her back into the kitchen the way she clucked at the chickens. She forced a smile, returned to the kitchen, helping three-year-old Willis onto the bench. "Clara, sit. I'll serve you now." She banged the pans on the stove, prepared the children's plates, fed them, and cleaned their faces, and when the men came in, she served them but chose not to sit with them while they ate, going to her bedroom to write and await Bob's departure. She was as frightened as when Ben got lost in the fog.

Ben signed three notes for Bob. And they argued, fear fueling her words until Ben yelled, actually shouted at her. "Cease, woman. I can take no more. It's done."

Their words led to nothing but them curled with their backs away from each other—after Jenny bathed the children and Ben read to them, followed by Jenny cleaning up the table and the kitchen. What could she do? *I'm powerless.*

"It's a lot of money, Ben," she said in the morning, not wanting to challenge him nor return the argument to its burning state.

"He's good for it. Don't you worry. Apple markets are excellent. Wheat is too. Remember that proverb. 'He who waters will himself be watered.'"

She considered that. "I'm not sure watering our neighbor's field means we should risk our own supplies though, and just expect God to deliver our water from somewhere else."

Ben patted her crossed hands as they sat at the table. "You worry over much," he said. "Haven't we done well here on Sunny Hillside Farm. And your Lafayette school, in season? Everything is turning out fine."

"And I'm grateful. But my egg-and-butter money is our only cash until fall. And Californians are planting again, so not buying our wheat. Several of our neighbors have opted out for schooling, lacking the cash for tuition, they say. It's worrisome. Something is happening all around us. It makes me nervous. I feel . . . vulnerable and—"

"You're oversensitive. It'll be better when the baby comes. Work on your story. You always do better when you've had a time to write—even those farmer's letters."

"I get to blow off steam like our kettle," she said. "Writing helps turn the heat down. But it doesn't ease my worries."

"You'll always be sheltered," he assured her. Then added, "First lamb was born last night. We need to start the watch."

"So much for my writing," she said, though she'd get a few lines in—memorizing them—while she huddled in the lambing shed awaiting the arrival of lambs whose mothers often needed help. All mothers did. She would trust Ben. What else could she do?

* * *

Oregon's status changed from territory to statehood on Valentine's Day 1859. In March, Hubert arrived. He was a smaller baby than Willis had been, and though she bled again, the doctor had been there and stitched her up. "Three babies," she'd cooed to the round face. He was a plump child. "My best delivery yet. Don't tell the others." His eyes followed hers.

A month later, Jenny made another delivery—her book. *Captain Gray's Company or Crossing the Plains and Living in Oregon* was published.

"I did it, Ben." She handed him the book. "Turns out it's the first published novel in the newest state. Will you read it?"

"I'll think on it," he teased, then realized she couldn't decide if he jested. "Of course I will. I'm married to an author. How about that?" She beamed. "Not right now. But I will read it."

That night she watched him while he turned the pages, then left him to put the children in their beds. She sang to them one verse, then stopped, saying, "Singing's not my talent, is it?"

Clara Belle answered with her own sweet notes. "We all have our gifts, Momma. You always say that."

"Singing is one of yours."

"And you write, Momma."

"Yes, I do. I hope your father likes my story."

"Is Papa in it?" Willis asked.

"Hmm. Maybe a little of him is. As are each of you. It's hard not to include the ones we love in a story." She lowered her voice, whispered, "There's a villain too."

"What's that?" Willis tucked the quilt around him so Clara Belle, lying next to him in the featherbed, wouldn't touch him. "What's a 'vill in'?"

"Someone the heroine of the story has to fight against. It wouldn't be much of a story if she didn't have someone to fight against to win her cause."

"So it's good when Willis and I fight? It makes a better story?"

"Not all tales need arguments." She kissed their foreheads. "And sisters and brothers should never fight. They should look after each other. Now get some rest."

Her sisters applauded when she handed a copy to them at a family gathering after church. She hoped to be invited to the Presbyterian academy, though novels weren't exactly a preference of the literary crowd.

"Congratulations," Harvey told her. "After I read it, I'll place a copy in the school library. If it's suitable."

"Why, thank you. I think."

"There are few novels in the collection. They're somewhat of an anomaly, more of a curiosity than anything learned, of course."

"Are they checked out?"

"Oh, of course. By students studying fiction as a format. And by what I call simpering women who are somehow engaged by such. They have to make sure it's suitable for our students."

"I would expect nothing less. If you reject it, of course, as not good enough, I'll have to take an ad out in the paper and mention that it's banned. That'll make my sales go up." *Might they reject it? Could it be so bad?*

He grunted.

Jenny waited for the reviews, but no one wrote a one. Except for her family, it appeared that her book landed like a stone in a pond, making no waves at all.

Her father told her the family back in Illinois would love it, as it was a story of the Scott crossing with the sadness of the widow's death, "being your mother's, I assume" and poor "Effie—I guess that's you? Having to work so hard once they arrive."

"It's not me, Papa. It's a novel."

Her sisters said little after they'd had time to read it. She'd sent a copy to Shirley Ellis in Sacramento and hadn't heard back from her friend, either.

Ben had deemed it "interesting," and then added, "You'll get your saddle under you with the next one."

"So it's not appealing?"

He shrugged. "What do I know about novels and such? And firstfruits aren't always the best."

Then the reviews came, and she knew why her sisters and friends hadn't known what to say. Newspaper editors did. "Bad taste" and "slang language"—"simplistic plot full of sickening love stories." Tears seeped from her eyes as she read them. Harold Bunter wrote a scathing letter lamenting "Poor Mr. Duniway" married to such a wretched writer. *Poor Ben!*

The *Argus*, that had sold more advertisements and increased subscriptions from the letters from her "Farmer's Wife," wrote nothing at all. Not a single word of praise or piercing. They simply carried the ad and the price. It was the first commercially published book in the new state, and the *Argus* didn't even do a story about that?

Ben stroked her arm as they sat side by side on the divan while she nursed Hubert. "Maybe it was your strident letters about men and their treatment of their women where you used your own name now and then, maybe that's why people haven't taken to the book."

She wanted to blame someone for the disappointing response. *I hate to hear what Harvey thinks, if he even reads it.* "But my characters, at least one of them, is the proper wife, the one who wouldn't speak in public or challenge her domineering employer, and eventually the lovers find each other again and marry. It's a happy story. The husband's not the villain, the employer is."

"But the men don't come out so well."

"She has failures too. And her brother sends her to school. Some of the men are good." She cried now—for the wasted hours writing, for the time away from the children and from Ben, and for what? "It's all rubbish."

"Jenny, Jenny." He pulled her closer. "Celebrate that you not only delivered a child, a 'little man,' a future voter in the cradle as you put what mothers do—"

"That might have been too forceful," Jenny said. "About women making voters and not just giving birth. My last 'Farmer's Wife' might have turned some readers away."

"I think you write better about real things than imagined ones. You birthed a book while teaching and taking care of the little ones and me. That's quite an accomplishment, Mrs. Duniway. Quite amazing indeed."

"Everything didn't turn out all right, now did it?"

"It's what comes after that matters," Ben said. He thumbed her lashes and brushed her cheeks of tears. "Best thing to do when you're bucked off a horse is to get back on. Ride another one."

"You think so?"

"I do. You found satisfaction in the work, didn't you? Isn't that part of your scribbling? It can't be all about how others like it or don't. You'll learn from this."

She wiped her eyes. The pain ached, made her wince as she took a deep breath. "Will I learn something from this?" The scathing reviews cut like a knife, but the wounds would heal and she'd see what she could do differently in the next novel. She might have to publish it herself and anonymously write a good review. But first she'd read those rotten rejections to glean what she could learn from them. *Yes. That's one way to make things turn out better. Learn.* It was the only surety she could count on.

TWELVE

The Farmer

1860

Sunshine warmed the earth, and early plantings ensued throughout the region. Abigail—since the publication of her novel she went by her official name, Abigail Duniway—loved her view on Sunny Hillside and only wished she had more time to sit and enjoy it. Or had a chair that felt better on her back. Or didn't have the morning sickness. Again. This child would be due next February. Abigail wrote now too for the *Oregon Farmer.* Her essays included information about the economics of the area, advised women to "buy local," and took on California merchants who had complained about Oregon butter costs. She proposed a union for women who "do the work and get little of the profits." She advocated for hired help for farmers' wives; urged women—and men—to save; and preached about the value of staying out of debt. She winced when she wrote those words, knowing that Ben had signed those notes. She still signed her columns "The Farmer's Wife" and often gave examples of what "the Farmer" himself had been up to, personalizing her pieces. She was paid small amounts for her articles, whose topics continued to garner interest both from the ladies of the region and also at men's gatherings. *Words have power*, she told herself more than once. But did they really have the power to change a woman's lot?

The extra money, though, felt good in her teapot bank, so words were changing their financial lot. It wasn't much, but if disaster struck, she would have a next step to take and a little money to make it.

Her sister Kate gave birth "with ease," she told Abigail. John was an attentive husband, and Kate's life seemed more sublime than Abigail's. She was happy for her sister but a bit wishful for those hours Kate had to read or simply sit and spend time with her baby. "You have time too," Kate told her when she commented.

"Holy cow chips, when?"

"Early morning. But I suspect you're writing then."

"I am. And during school days, I'm preparing lessons."

"We all make our choices."

"Yes, we do." Writing was one of Abigail's. Becoming financially secure was another.

The summer eased its way into their lives with daily toils. Maybe Kate was right and she wouldn't know a moment's leisure if it washed her with warm water in a copper tub. Work consumed, though she did find joy in attending meetings at the Butte Creek Store, startling the men when she and a few stalwart women showed up not to speak, mind you, but to listen to the conversation about the fall election when a Republican had a chance to become president—an Illinoisan whom they had known as a lawyer from their small town back east.

Their wheat harvest that year was abundant, filling the warehouses along the Willamette River so ships could take their goods afar. Ben was happy and Abigail was too when America did elect its first Republican president in Abraham Lincoln. Abigail hoped he could stop the spread of slavery. All people should be free, in Abigail's mind. Regardless of race—or sex.

Close to home, Sunny Hillside Farm proved productive too. Abigail thought there might be enough to buy a few household conveniences like a self-propelled butter churn and decent chairs, but Ben informed her that he'd spent $500 on the purchase of an adjoining farm. "We wouldn't want someone else to come in under our noses and take that good property."

"I could have used a new wringer. And I've read that a carpet sweeper has been patented. I'd like to have such a thing. Honestly, Ben, the hardest housework I do is sweeping. It agonizes my back no end. Couldn't the needs of the farmer's wife get a little attention?"

"Your back is likely worse now because you're expecting."

"Whatever the reason, it's hard labor sweeping the carpets and floors with a broom."

"I'll sweep for you."

"And where will you be when I'm gathering crumbs from beneath the table? You'll be out on that additional farm with your paid helpers while I'm in here preparing food for them."

"Now, Jenny. It's in our best interest."

"Our best interest would be to get out of those notes, to be able to set aside money. We're paying interest and I haven't seen Bob around reimbursing us." She grunted at Ben's silence and returned to her churn.

* * *

Wilke arrived February 13, 1861, the day before Oregon's birthday—and right after six more states seceded from the Union. Abigail worried there would be war, but there was nothing she could do about it. Instead she delivered another boy for Ben to cuddle as he loved to do. Clara, at seven, was old enough to help by looking after Willis and Hubert the way that Abigail—as an older sister—had looked after her siblings while her mother gave birth. Clara, with her dark curls and puppy-dog eyes, big and brown and round, followed Abigail's directions, then got out of the way when the midwife arrived.

"Good girl, Clara. Momma will be all right." Abigail prayed even as she held her newborn in her arms that all her children would grow up healthy and able to spread their wings toward safety and goodness.

A few days after Wilke's birth, Ben brought in the mail, including a large envelope with no return address. "This was in our postal box."

"What is it?"

"A valentine perhaps?"

She looked to see if Ben had a glimmer of tease in his eyes.

He brushed at his copper-tinted hair, then bopped his forehead with the back of his hand. "I totally forgot. You give me another son for a valentine, and I get you nothing. I am a clod of a spouse."

He bent to kiss her while she opened the envelope, not sure if he was the conveyor of the missive or its originator.

Looking inside, she knew. It was a drawing of a hen-pecked man with children crawling all over him, crying, clinging; and a disheveled woman, snaggletoothed and worn, holding a rolling pin like a weapon over the man's head. The handwritten words were "Fiend, devil's imp or what you will / you surely your poor man will kill / with luckless days and sleepless nights / haranguing him with women's rights."

"You . . . you gave me this?"

"What is it?" He stared. "Never. Jenny, no. Forget it."

The sobs were as deep as they'd been when she'd read the horrible book reviews. "Have I ever given you reason to say such a thing?"

"I didn't send that card to you, and if I'd realized that you'd take it seriously, I wouldn't have brought it home. It's from one of those 'Farmer's Wife' readers. Bunter maybe."

"Bunter. No, it's too creative for him." She paced. It scared her that everyone knew who the Farmer's Wife was. "There are others out there, Ben, men who hate me, who besmirch you. I . . . I'm so sorry." She set Hubert in his cradle. *Will they threaten my children?*

Like the reviews, the image was difficult to set aside. She didn't want people thinking Ben was hen-pecked just because he loved his children or because his wife had opinions. Perhaps she should be a little less strident in her columns. Maybe back off from some of her suggestions, even though there were other writers—men—who advocated paid household help for farmers' wives, and others—men—who wrote of women's health and the depletion that came with too many children too close together. Even the *Oregon Farmer* carried articles now about family planning, they called it, and wrote discreetly of contraception. The economists—men—recognized the role of farmers' wives in the successful weathering of the vagaries of markets. The moneymen saw how women marshalled attacks against everyday challenges of cooking, cleaning, and laundry. Of course, laundry.

Ben had told her of a man seeking a loan to build a bigger barn, and the lender had said unless he improved the condition of the house first, they wouldn't make the loan. "A happy woman can make all the difference to the success of a farm. The lender said that."

"Smart man," she said.

She'd have to build stronger armor and not let such things as a mean-spirited valentine set her eyes to sprouting wells. Maybe having delivered a "new voter" to his cradle, she was oversensitive. Yes, she'd pony-up, as Ben told her when he wanted her to ride with him and go forward, forgetting past disasters.

At least she didn't have the fate of the nation to deal with. Poor Mr. Lincoln would be inaugurated in March while a Confederate government had already installed its own. *What do I have control over? Think on that.* It became her new mantra.

* * *

War news dominated the summer. Harvey had had his fill of combat from the regional conflict, and he now slept in a tent in Forest Grove so he could attend the university there. Heavy snows fell early that winter in the Cascade mountains, and once or twice a foot or more at the valley floor.

"It'll be good for the soil," Ben said, though tromping the snowy mud through the house did little for their hardwood floors. More scrubbing on hands and knees ensued. More meditation with the broom.

Then it turned cold. Bitter cold. Rivers that had never frozen did. Cattle died for lack of feed in the eastern part of the state. Even in Lafayette, ice in water troughs had to be broken daily.

Abigail shivered as she rolled out egg noodles, looking with longing at the teapot, hoping she wouldn't ever need the money inside to see them through.

At first when the warm rains came that November, people were relieved to have the snow melt. But it kept raining, for days, weeks, then months, off and on, through Christmas holidays and all of January 1862, pouring on them harder than any could remember. "Ark Rain," the old-timers called it. Sheets of silver so dense Abigail couldn't even see the fruit trees from the window. What should have been more snow in the mountains turned out to be early snow melt, the heavy snowfall in the Cascades earlier in November now swelling rivers and streams. The news from California and Nevada, too, reported heavier rains than usual and flooding. Rivers swamped the storehouses on the Willamette, carrying buildings and trees and bloated animals all the way to Astoria and the sea. The Duniway home stood above the waters with no risk of flooding—but getting across bridges to town proved a challenge, so eggs and butter remained unsold; letters for her column couldn't be sent; no one was able to attend school; apples failed to reach their California or Chinese markets.

Abigail learned that the little town of Canemah—where her sister nursed her baby—had four feet of water running through the streets. People climbed to their rooftops, and John Coburn, Kate's husband, was one of many ship captains and crew sent to rescue overwhelmed settlers onto steamships. Abigail hoped Kate was on one of those ships and not waiting in her attic for rescue. Towns that were a part of Oregon's young history, like Champoeg where the vote to become a part of America one day and not Britain had taken place, were washed away with nothing to show for what had been there except the memories of the survivors.

And Lafayette's new warehouse holding 80,000 bushels of wheat—including the Duniways' bumper harvest—was washed away, along with Amos and Fanny's store and much of the business district. Abigail sent word when she learned of it, and communication resumed that the Coburns and Cooks—Amos and Fanny—should come to Sunny Hillside where they'd welcome them high above flooding streams.

The warehouse loss devastated the area, but Ben had already lost on the sale of his wheat when he was forced to sell it before the flood for fifty cents a bushel. It was less than the going market rate. But he had to pay that surety debt at 2 percent interest. Abigail wrote of it in her 'Farmer's Wife' column, though she never mentioned Ben by name. The subject was always "the Farmer." She wrote that the merchant who had purchased the Farmer's wheat at a bargain price (because the Farmer had a debt to pay) hoped to resell and make a profit. That merchant had lost now too—to the flood. In her column, she wrote of the devastation, how people lost cattle and how surging waters kept them all from beginning repairs. Water. Flooding. Waiting. That was the real force of nature, worse than tornados or fires, because after those, one could begin cleanup and start over without having to wait and obsess about what one would do in the aftermath and what might be salvaged or lost.

They called it the Great Oregon Flood of 1861–62, but Abigail's trail friend, Shirley Ellis, wrote that a boat was required on K Street in Sacramento and that people had died, washed away, their bodies never found for burial. It was more than an Oregon flood.

"Such a tragedy," Shirley had written.

"In so many ways," Abigail wrote back, and didn't even mention wondering if her novel had ever arrived.

Abigail became even more specific in her next column. She told her readers that the Farmer's debt amounted to $240 a year and his farm only earned $500 on a good year, so there was little left to support his family. She also complained that the typesetter had made many errors in a previous column but added that "My husband says I ought not to complain about the printer, because he probably couldn't read my scratchings. I advise the Farmer that people often compliment me when they watch me write before them. He says, 'They're looking at your handwriting upside down.' Perhaps he's right," she conceded and hoped the interchange between the Farmer and the Farmer's Wife brought a bit of joyful relief as people came out of their badger holes to assess what had happened to their landscapes and their lives.

"That last column was a little too personal," Ben told her. "You ought not mention our debts, and so specifically." They had put the children to bed, and Abigail worked on another piece to submit to the paper.

"I want people to see that they aren't alone." She looked up at him.

"And poke your thumb in my eye?"

Was that why I was specific? "Details give authenticity to a writer's work."

He grunted. "A little less truthfulness at my expense could be pleasant."

She did consider whether she was being unfair or not and decided that she wasn't.

"It shows that the Farmers, the men, are in charge, and they make the deals, for good or bad." Abigail said. "Every man and woman can relate to that."

* * *

The flooding aftermath attacked the economy. Jobs disappeared, households split, forest trees fell over roadways, their roots loosened by inundated soils, blocking transports and deliveries.

Steamships on the Willamette maneuvered through waterways clogged with debris and changed channels. The school where Jerry and Harvey attended closed down for the term as it tried to recover. Everything wasn't working out all right. Harvey's camping site had been swilled away by the greedy river. Damaged sawmills like her father's hindered rebuilding, both getting logs to the mill and out to building sites. Abigail's little house in Lafayette had water to the third step leading to the porch but hadn't been washed away. Her sisters' families could stay there while they rebuilt.

"At least no water in the basement like there would be back in Illinois," Abigail said.

"No basements in Oregon," Ben said. "Another western innovation."

It was a few weeks into March when her brother Harvey rode up the hillside to the house through a field of daffodils at dusk, a drizzle of rain dripping off his hat.

"You're not bringing bad news? Jerry and Father are all right?"

"No bad news. Nothing you haven't already heard," he said.

"Come on in. Get yourself dry. I'll tend your horse." Ben spoke, motioned for Harvey to dismount while his brother-in-law led his mount to their barn. Abigail heard him talking to the animal on the way, then start singing a little tune.

"I read that 'the Farmer's Wife' gave her permission for 'the Farmer' to head to Idaho," Harvey said as Ben returned and put Wilkie in the high chair, his one-year-old legs sticking out like little stumps. His hands reached out to pat his father's cheeks as he bent to the boy. The men took their seats with Clara, Willis, and two-year-old Hubert perched on a bench side by side. "The Farmer is you, right, Ben?" Harvey took the bowl of beans Abigail handed him. She kept ahold of it just a second longer than she needed, making him pay attention to her and not talk about her as though she weren't there. Harvey gave her eye contact, said, "Thanks, Sister," then to Ben he said, "Does it bother you that she's always putting private things out there for the world to read about in her column?"

"I don't mind it much," Ben said. He moved his peas around the plate, didn't look at Harvey. "It gives Jenny respite, as she calls it, to scribble."

"Still, a little delicacy wouldn't hurt. Or a letter informing the rest of the family of the Duniway-doings before we have to read of it in the paper."

"I never write about you," Abigail said. "Are you envious?" She set a platter of rice and a chicken she'd butchered onto the table. She cooked it up with dried herbs that Harriet had given her the last time they were together.

Harvey snorted. "At least your farm wasn't damaged." He forked a chicken thigh. And 'the Farmer' managed to pay his debts."

Ben winced then. "The Farmer will pay his debts," Ben said. "Why I'm heading to Idaho to the mines."

"I wondered if that was true, what the Farmer's Wife said."

"The Farmer's Wife always writes true things," she said.

"Just not always factual."

Before Abigail could object, Harvey continued. "I thought I might go with you to Idaho. I'm not taken by the war effort. I think those Southern states have made a mistake, but I don't think dying to end slavery is the right answer. Negotiations makes more sense. But I thought I'd take a year while the school gets back on its feet and students can return to create needed capital so I can go through the university without having to work at the sawmill."

"Will you study law?" Ben asked. He passed the platter to Abigail, who had at last sat down.

"Maybe. First a general degree in economics. Then math, English, the usual advanced courses."

"A woman wouldn't know 'usual' when it comes to the higher education she's deprived of."

"Not now, Jenny," Ben said.

She sighed. No need to be strident at the table. There'd be time for her and Harvey to wrestle over issues later—if either had the energy for it.

Ben said he'd be glad for the company in the mines, though he worried about leaving Abigail with the children, and hired workers to run the farm.

"Send the money," Abigail said. "We'll be all right, though missing you more than all the water in the Willamette."

"I'll miss you more than all the water in the ocean, Pa," Clara said.

"Where are you going, Papa?" Willis asked.

"On an adventure, Son." Ben squeezed his daughter's shoulder and made his voice light for his children.

For the first time since they'd made the decision for Ben to leave, Abigail realized how much the children would miss him, and they didn't have the luxury of knowing why he was leaving, sacrificing home and hearth in order to help them all, and yes, make amends for his poor judgment. She let herself feel the pain of the coming separation, then vowed that she couldn't let those feelings intrude or she would be a puddle when he left and that would upset the children even more. In the same way that she brushed by little joys that she didn't think she deserved, she tamped down sadness by getting to work.

"Finish up now," she told the children. "Take your bowls to the sink."

While Abigail washed the dishes and Clara dried, Harvey caught them up on the news and told tales of daring rescues during the flooding, stories of people helping neighbors, free blacks and Asians helping whites and vice versa, the vitriol of race and politics diminished for a time.

"Disasters bring out the best in us," Abigail said. "It's that pioneering spirit, how we have to try new ways when the circumstances force us into different channels."

"And give a man permission to make mistakes," Ben said. "I'm told by my carpenter friends that the mark of a true craftsman isn't that he makes no errors but how well he covers them up so no one notices, that's the key."

"A little difficult to do when the carpenter's wife spreads the error in the newspaper," Harvey said.

He held a teasing voice, but Abigail noticed Ben's bearded face turned a little redder, and she thought in the future she ought to increase the good tales she told of the Farmer. Surely his sacrifice of leaving home would be worthy of a column. Maybe even two.

THIRTEEN

Going On

1862

Abigail sent Ben off in March, hopeful for the benefit of this needed separation. But with him gone, she realized how much she relied on him, even when he merely sat and jawed with friends in the other room. Buttressing in a relationship, she realized, came in many shapes and sizes. He'd never complained about the Farmer stories she wrote, except that one time when she'd harped about the loan. But maybe Harvey was correct, and flapping the Duniway "underlings" in the newspaper winds wasn't the best use of her time. She'd write of less personal things or use those personal events to be symbols of wider concerns. She penned a column in the spring about the death of someone "dear" and how alcoholism had shredded the promise of his life. It was an uncle she worried over, and she used the occasion of his downfall to urge Oregonians to wage war on King Alcohol who is "if possible, a worse enemy to progress than the dire hallucination of secession."

She wrote about missing her farmer. Anonymous said she'd driven him away. She penned a sad tale of her children crying for their farmer-father. Anonymous said she was a poor mother to let her children suffer so. Without Ben to put the nasty reply letters into perspective, she dwelt overmuch on negativity rather than on hope. One needed others to nurture optimism, or at least she was finding that she did.

So far there'd been no gold strike in Idaho, and her Hope School hadn't restarted due to the regional flooding aftermath. Ben wrote of his longing to be home and encouraged her that if she had some idea for income that would bring him home, she should pursue it. So she did.

"*Forty dollars a month,*" she wrote to Ben, "*is at least a sure thing.*" She'd taken a position teaching in a private school. "*Some people still have capital to pay tuition, but it's a relief to not have to manage the collection of funds and just take my salary at month's end. Clara and Willis can attend for free, so there is that added bonus. Soon you'll strike it rich, God willing, and I can buy new shoes for the boys who are so badly in need.*"

Like the two tracks of a wagon wheel through tall grass, she sent him dual messages: shared stories of how much the children missed him, next to expressed concerns about their fragile pecuniary state. Her letters gave him details, too, of the spring at Sunny Hillside and the glorious blooms on the apple trees, a blanket of white fluffs floating on a sea of green. "*I wish you could see it, Ben. The farm is so beautiful.*" Then she'd consider striking out those very words, writing a new page, not wanting him to feel homesick. "*Save these letters, Mr. Duniway, that I might draw upon them one day when I have time to work on another* improved *novel or two. They'll help me remember what was happening for us during this* temporary *separation.*"

She decided to hire a bit of help for herself and put a small portion of her income toward a woman to care for the children while she taught. "*It puts money into the economy so don't say I'm wasting it.*" She wished Jerry still lived with them. He'd lend both happiness and help, but schooling was more important. She knew that.

Clara Belle had taken an interest in the piano, and Abigail traded laundry work for her lessons. One day she'd buy a piano for her, she would. She gave Willis the task of sweeping every day, told three-year-old Hubert he had the important work of watching fifteen-month-old Wilkie while she soaked the more well-to-do neighbors' duds. While the clothes dried, she worked the spinning wheel, turning their sheep's wool into thread she could mend with or sell. She had to remind herself to relax her shoulders, take little pauses in her labor, because Ben wasn't there to remind her. She read to the children before bedtime, though she could barely stay awake. And each evening when she fell onto her own feather comfort, she longed for Ben, prepared a celebration for when he'd come home, and prayed for a bountiful harvest in the fall on Sunny Hillside Farm. And each evening she turned questions over in her mind. *What do I have control over? How can I make everything be all right?*

* * *

"It's Jerry. He's very ill and he's asking for you."

"The flu?"

"We don't know . . . he collapsed at the mill." Jenny's stepmother's voice caught and anguish flooded her face. "Tucker's with him. He may not make it through the day. Come. I have the carriage to bring you back."

"No. You take the children to Fanny's. Let her know what's happened and to bring them and her own." Abigail turned to the children's nanny. "Please let the school know I won't be there, and catch Clara and Willis and bring them back."

"Of course."

Abigail raced to the paddock behind the house where they kept one mare. The breeding stock and other animals stayed at Sunny Hillside. The horse recognized Abigail and came trotting across the field to get her treat. "We've a twenty-mile ride, Bonnie. I hope you've eaten your breakfast. Poor Jerry's down." The tears came as she saddled and mounted up.

Anger and frustration were the reins she held as she kneed Bonnie toward Forest Grove. Why did her father make Jerry work so hard at the mill? At nineteen, he was still a frail young man, competing with Harvey. She chastised herself for not having found a way to have Jerry stay with them instead of being under her father's thumb. She should have insisted he remain with them. Shearing sheep was tiring work but seasonal. The sawmill was heavy, demanding, year-round labor. Wind dried her tears as she pushed the mare, slowing only when she felt the horse might falter if she didn't.

In the end, it didn't matter. By the time Abigail reached Forest Grove and dismounted a lathered horse, her father stepped out of the house. His face told her everything she didn't want to know. She'd never missed Ben more.

* * *

Abigail rinsed the cloth she'd used to wipe Jerry's eyelids, his thin face. "No way to avoid it," Abigail said, answering Fanny's longing to sweep away grief as so large a part of their daily lives. "We have to plow through."

"You're always so strong, Abigail," their stepmother said. Their hands touched when Abigail gave her a wet cloth.

"Strong? No. I've found a way to push the pain under. Get angry at the world, at . . ." She started to spit blaming words toward her father, but she didn't.

"May you never lose a child," her father said as he leaned against the doorframe, shoulders drooped, watching the women. What they did was women's work.

It might ease his grief to participate. Why couldn't men perform such ministrations as women did?

"Love helps," his wife said. She left Jerry's body to go to their father and stroke his crossed arms. "Love always helps."

Her father held her hand as she leaned her face against his shoulder. The shared grief was visible to Abigail, and she felt a new appreciation for Ruth as the woman returned to rub Jerry's body with fragrant oils.

Perhaps, Abigail thought, love is the only real balm to pain. Perhaps that was why her father had remarried so quickly. They could say "time heals all wounds," but it wasn't time, it was courage. It was being willing to risk love, after love had disappeared, after sorrow for whatever reason caught the heart up short and pierced it like an arrow. Her stepmother grieved Jerry's death too. He'd been her stepchild, but she had loved him, done his laundry, cared for him, fed him. And Ruth's mistake those years before had happened after her own husband died and she sought comfort, thought she'd found it in an irresponsible man but had encountered only fleeting warmth. Love had come into her life again through Abigail's father. Abigail thought of Ben and how fortunate she was to have someone who loved her so very much.

She vowed to love her children more deeply, to give up her insistence to work so hard, to *make* things happen as she wanted, to change the world quickly. She knew that vow might not last long, but it was still good to make the promise to her children, to herself. And to Ben. She would write to him and Harvey of this terrible grief and how the Scott descendants would once more gather at a grave.

And she prayed that she would never have to learn what her father knew: how to go on after the death of a child. For him, Jerry was the fourth.

FOURTEEN

Refresher

1862

"You are a godsend, Captain John. And where did you learn how to shear sheep?" Abigail handed her brother-in-law a jug of water.

"Not on board a steamship, I can assure you." John Coburn had agreed to help the hired man, Sam, shear the animals at Sunny Hillside.

"It's good physical work, and Sam's a good instructor," Abigail said.

"Even without my chew," Sam grumbled. The hand was testy that day because Abigail had told him she didn't have the money to buy his tobacco.

Kate watched the children with Clara's help and waddled as she walked, expecting the Coburns' second child in September, a month away. "He's a good sport about so many things," Kate said.

"Yes, that laundry help he hired for you is an envy of many, including me," Abigail said.

"Hold 'er tight," Sam said. "They like to squirm on ye."

The ewes were in good shape, had dropped their lambs in the

spring. The hired hand and Abigail had shared the long night hours watching to make sure the ewes didn't by mistake roll onto their babies or reject them as though they had no idea such a thing had come from their bodies. Some ewes needed assistance in letting the lambs suck, and more than one baby sat warming by the cookstove at the house. Now they were being sheared and separated, and the bleating was incessant.

"It reminds me of Willis at our Christmas pageant," Abigail said to Kate. It would be a long day with the women preparing meals in between stomping down the fleeces. Canvas bags hung down from a platform like giant hummingbirds' nests. The fleece was dropped down into the bags around the women who stepped into the canvas, allowing new fleeces to fall in beside them and be pressed into tight bales. The women grew closer to the top as the bags filled and stepped back onto the platform while the men tied the canvas bales. Men below unhooked the packed fleece and carried them off on their shoulders to the wagons for transport.

"You'd better not stomp, Kate," Abigail said. "And be careful of the wood floors. They get slippery from the lanolin."

In all, they had several bags the hired hand would take to the market. "It might be enough to buy coffee," Abigail said, lamenting the poor harvest.

"More than that, surely." Kate fanned herself with her fingers.

"At least the chickens are laying well and there's the butter money and my ever-optimistic hope that Ben will return healthy, wealthy, and wise. Refreshed, perhaps, but with emphasis on the wealthy."

"Oh, Abigail. It can't be as bad as that, is it?"

"You know about those notes Ben signed? I told you, didn't I?"

"Not directly. The Farmer's Wife did, though."

"I don't know if we'll make the payment this year. It scares me to death. I've been trying to confer with Dear Bob, but he's nowhere to be found."

"Maggie says the Lord never gives us more than we can handle," Kate said.

"Then the Lord has to work on his estimation of my capacities. I'm reaching the end of my already frayed rope."

"You're missing Ben."

"That I am. I told him in my last letter how the children wake with 'Pa' on their breaths and how Clara sleeps with me now and moans 'Pa' in her dreams and how I think I will surely die if he doesn't come home soon, that I'd rather have him here healthy more than wealthy. I miss him terribly."

Kate patted Abigail's hands. "That lanolin really makes hands soft, doesn't it?"

It was Kate's way of saying she'd heard enough of Abigail's laments. May as well speak of hand care than of longing, homesickness, and worry. She'd just have to wait for Ben to return for things to get better.

At dusk, John took Kate home, and then Abigail saw their wagon stop just at the corner at the end of the lane. *What's wrong now?*

It was nothing wrong; all was right. Ben had come home.

The children climbed all over him; Abigail hugged him tight. She didn't care that he hadn't written her of his homecoming. He'd read between her lines and come back to them all.

"I'm sorry I'm not bringing bags of gold," he said.

"You're my bag of gold."

"I'll remind you of that when things get tough," he said.

She held him close all through the night.

Harvest went easier with Ben there, directing the hired men, conferring with them about tobacco costs and whether such was included in their wage. She didn't even mind cooking for the crew or the extra visitors Ben brought home with him. Her eyes would catch that now-empty teapot, but she imagined putting egg money into it again someday. She still taught at her private school, but with Ben back, she handed her wages to him. At least they talked about how to spend them. Abigail knew other wives who handed over their laundry wages or brought resources into the marriage and then their husbands drank up any profit at the local tavern. Her life was so much better than that. Best of all, he was home. Safe.

In the evenings, they talked about public things—the war, the commissioning of the 1st Oregon Cavalry and whether Ben might join them.

"No. You're needed here," Abigail insisted. "Don't even think about going off again."

It was pleasant to have a sarsaparilla while they watched the sun set and shared opinions about the area's rate of recovery from the floods. She was grateful they had similar views about slavery and how the state appeared conflicted, having entered the union as a free state but having an exclusion clause in its constitution meant to keep out free-black people. She didn't see many of that race, but they had hired one or two, and they'd been good workers, pleasant to the children when they sat together at the table for their noon meal.

Yes, she loved having Ben back, but when he rode off to spend an evening with his friends, or when he bought a new hay rake with money she'd earned, she realized how much she missed the singular command she'd had while he was gone. And he'd insisted she let the hired woman go as soon as school ended for the term.

"Hazel could have helped with the housework," Abigail pointed out. "She was also very good at getting the children to make their beds and pick up after themselves."

"You're their mother and I'm their father. We can sway their behavior better than an outsider."

"Perhaps."

"Don't you worry." He tapped his pipe, tidily cleaned the bowl. He'd begun to smoke it now. "You're a wise mother."

"It isn't my wisdom I need help imparting. It's saving my back and body so my mind can work."

"You know I can help."

"When you're not otherwise occupied."

"I can take care of them—and you. It's what husbands do, Wife." He smiled, looking at her with those big blue eyes that had won her over those years before. "Trust me."

They'd left the conversation there. It was a woman's role to step back and let herself be taken care of. Abigail had grown up with her mother imparting such wisdom. There were roles men and women played that kept society in order and moving forward. Still, when she remembered her mother's reluctance to go west and what not challenging her husband's wishes had cost her, she wondered if some roles didn't just need to be changed. She glanced at the teapot while Ben smoked his pipe, a habit taken up in Idaho. It had been her mother's china pot; one *her* mother had given her with the birth of the last of her mother's twelve children. Something to celebrate, she supposed, was that she wasn't expecting another baby. And she had another idea for making money. She had to run it past Ben.

* * *

In the spring of 1863, they attended Harvey's graduation in Forest Grove—the first graduating class of Pacific University founded by that feisty Tabitha Moffat Brown. Harvey was the single student receiving his degree. Mrs. Brown had broken the rules of roles for men and women, Abigail thought as her brother received his diploma. *I should think about going to the university.* She'd let her character in her novel go on to school and even start a magazine. But that was fiction. Besides, what would such a degree give her that she wasn't already able to do with her teaching certificate? Garner a bit more respect? Or disdain that she was moving too far outside her expected lane? Harvey had been successful in teaching himself Latin and Greek, and while she wasn't sure if those languages had gotten him the job as a librarian in Portland, at least it had earned him employment where he would use his mind instead of his back. She envied him that he wouldn't need to help slaughter a pig or ever again have to plow a field as they had back in Illinois. But no amount of advanced education would enable a woman to rid herself of backbreaking laundry. It was a woman's fate.

Later, back at Sunny Hillside Farm, with Ben off making arrangements for their stud to travel to a nearby homestead, she mused that momentous events seemed to happen at dusk, when one was already tired and had not yet time for the contemplative evening prayer, the *labora*—work as prayer—having filled the day. It ought to be a time of calm, recounting the successes of the day. Instead, bad news took the whole day to arrive, it seemed.

She had heard a coyote howl near the sheep pen and started down the lane to yell at it to protect her sheep. Ben had been away the whole day. They'd acquired a dog—Hubert had named it Buffy—and she told the dog to "Stay!" She thought when Hubert named him, he was trying to say "Fluffy," as the mixed breed of black and white with a roly-poly body and long tail looked like a ball of wool when they'd gotten him as a puppy a few months back.

"You stay back there, Clara. Hold Buffy. I don't want him to get called out by the coyote."

That task finished, she returned to the house, when she heard a horse clopping at the front. She recognized the sheriff as he dismounted, and her first thought was that something had happened to Ben. She felt a weight in her stomach. "Everything all right with Mr. Duniway?"

"Yes, ma'am. After a fact." He didn't meet her eyes, pulled a folded document from his pack. "I've this summons to give you, Mrs. Duniway."

"Summons? For what?"

"For nonpayment of your notes."

"My husband's notes." Her heart pounded harder now with Ben safe somewhere but her having to bear this catastrophic news. Alone.

"Your notes too, missus. The law sees you as responsible too."

"Even though when he signed it, I had no say. Ah, yes, justice is a man's name."

"Sorry, Mrs. Duniway. You've missed the last payments."

Are you really sorry? Enforcing laws that turn people's worlds upside down? The Duniway state of being was known, of course, in part because of "The Farmer's Wife" columns. But she hadn't known that Ben had missed the last payments. She noticed he was gone more often but thought his absences were because he was making money with his horse breeding, a task that took "jawing" and politicking to get potential customers ready to pay the stud fees. He hadn't shown her the books. But she as well as he was now responsible.

She didn't invite the sheriff in. He went on his way as she read the word "Sale," her stomach churning. She slammed the frying pan against the stove, wanted to lift the stovetop and throw the summons into it but couldn't. She'd had no say in Ben's decision. She warned him and he patronized her, assuring her that Dear Bob was good for the money, that pioneer hospitality meant helping out a friend. Who would help them? Her face felt warm. She rehearsed what she'd say to him and wondered if this was what her mother felt when her father had to file bankruptcy back in Illinois. He too had signed a note for another man who had failed to pay. Had that been the real impetus that sent the Scott family traveling west?

"Why are you crying, Momma?" Willis asked.

"Just a little sadness. I'm fine." She forced a smile. "Have you finished your work page? Arithmetic is important to learn, you know." *Especially for a male child.* "Though it seems your father could use a refresher."

"What's a refresher?" Clara said.

Wilkie started to climb up onto his chair. "Not yet," she told him. "Wait until Pa comes home. Then we'll eat." Then to Clara she said, "A refresher means breathing new life into something forgotten." She changed her mind. "We'll eat now," she said. "Let me get the potatoes on. Willis, put aside your papers and get the ham from the smokehouse, please." *If he's like his father, he'll need a math refresher before he turns fifteen.* Why make the children wait on their father's timing? It was something she could do—feed her offspring. At least for the moment.

Vulnerable. That was how she felt as she waited for Ben to come home. Harvey had told her once that the word *vulnerable* came from the Latin word meaning "wound." And what healed a wound? She wasn't sure.

The day waned into darkness. She fed the hired hands and sent them off. While she served the children their ham and washed the dishes in the pan, she stewed. While she read their bedtime story and listened to their prayers, she fumed, waiting, planning all she'd say to Ben when he finally got home, beginning with "I told you so." She'd remind him of the thousand times she'd scolded him about their financial worries, how he needed to take them seriously and not always brush her concerns aside, and now it was too late. They would have to sell the farm, have to. *Sheriff's sale.* It would be in the newspapers, the shame of it for all to read. And whoever bought it would know that they were forced to do so, and the Duniways would be required to take whatever high bid was offered, even if it was lower than a sow's belly. The bulk of any profit—if there was any—would go to pay the notes. She had no idea what might be left, or once off the farm, what on earth they would do to support the family.

Ben arrived. He took one look at her. "What is it? One of the children?"

"No. They're safe, thank goodness." She took in a deep breath. "The sheriff came by." She slapped the summons in his hand and started her rehearsed spiel. But his face turned pale as he read. He sank onto the divan, folded up like a broken ladder. She saw tears in his eyes when he lifted them from the paper.

"What will we do?" Ben's words came out as a whisper.

"Sell Sunny Hillside. It's all we can do, and hope there's enough left to, I don't know, find another way to make a living." She'd been pondering that. "I'll have to do something more than take a teacher's salary. You . . . your horse breeding, well, without a farm—" She opened her hands in dismay.

He hung his head. "You're right, of course. You've been right all along. I'm . . . I'm so sorry."

"Of course I'm right. And of course you're sorry, after the fact. That's always the case. You always feel badly. It's never your intention." *Of course. Always. Never.* Acidic insults, nails for her hammer. He deserved them, didn't he? Righteous outrage fueled more words. She had more to spit out, but she watched his face—pale and grief stricken—and the disdain drained from her. She suspected anger wouldn't long stay away, that with every dish she packed she'd resent him—but she could see his remorse in that nearby moment; could almost feel his humiliation, not from her words, but from what he told himself.

Anger had always been a secondary emotion anyway. That's what her mother had once told her, that fury rode on a fast horse charging through a relationship, trampling right over loss, disappointment, and grief. And if one wasn't careful, wrath crushed love too. *"Pay attention to those forgotten feelings when you lose your temper, Jenny. Those are the trio of emotions that if not recognized and dealt with, will surely bring a soul down and make ire the driving force in your days. Wounds must grow new flesh."*

Jenny rose from her rocking chair and went to Ben, his shoulders hunched over the trifold document he held in his trembling hands. She sat on the wide arm of the divan, slightly above him. She put her arm around his shoulder, and he gentled his head into her side, the summons falling from his fingers. She felt his body shudder as he tried to hide his sobs. She'd never seen him cry before.

She felt the disappointment and the loss, but he felt it too. Perhaps more. "We'll weather this storm," she told him. "Take a refresher course in how to start over. And we'll make it."

He nodded. "I'll do better."

"It'll all turn out all right."

It was a prayer as much as a promise.

FIFTEEN

Moving and Moving Forward

1864

"Hang that linen a little closer," Abigail told Ben. "We want to get as many girls in here as we can but still give them a sense of privacy."

"Yes, Jenny—Abigail."

She heard him trying to accommodate her request to not be called by her nickname, one of many adaptations he'd made. Ben didn't go very far from home these days, no visiting his bachelor friends. At least they had a roof over their heads because Abigail had invested in the Lafayette property, and now the attic was finished and would be a dormitory bedroom for boarders. Ben built a pen behind the house for the chickens so that they still might have egg money. They kept a cow. The dog had stayed with the farm and she missed him. But he would have disheveled the house with his bulk. Another sacrifice they had to make.

Ben gave up the breeding stock, selling his beloved stallions he'd been building a solid bloodline behind. He did so without a word of protest. *Penance. Self-imposed.* She chastised herself when she snapped at him. She found she liked living in Lafayette full-time, closer to family, finding new ways to make money, relieved of the heavy farm work or chasing coyotes from sheep pens. But oh, how she missed the view!

Ben had managed to find a buyer, so they didn't have to file bankruptcy to settle the claim. Millard Lownsdale, the son of a man who had brought apples to the Oregon Territory and had made a fortune because of it, bought Sunny Hillside. He planned to expand the orchard and had the capital to do so. Abigail was glad that the land would be nurtured but resented that some had the means to prosper at the expense of those working hard every day who lived on the edge and by some small mistake could fall to ruin.

"If not for you, we'd be there too, Abigail. Penniless. You work so hard."

She thought to encourage him by saying that the farm brought as much as it did because of his work, his vision of the orchard he'd begun. That she knew he'd sacrificed by going to the mines and that he too had lost dreams along with the farm. But she kept silent, perhaps sending her anger at despicable men, which at that moment included her husband.

Withholding comfort now and then was better than being strident. Even Clara had said once when Abigail snarled at her spouse, "Don't be mad at Pa. He's doing the best he can." Abigail knew he was, and she chastised herself for her attitude, hoped the husband-bashing and self-lashing would not last. She didn't much like herself for her reluctance to prop him up, but she hadn't yet learned that not forgiving Ben hurt her as much as him.

* * *

"I've been working on something." Ben stared at the egg noodles he swirled on his supper plate, not at Abigail. It was months since they'd moved and life had taken on new patterns. Ben was gone often in the afternoons, and Abigail assumed he was once again visiting with his friends. That was good. She hoped he'd start singing again too. He cleared his throat. "Something that could help with the laundry."

"One of those Thor washing machines would be handy to have, but we can't afford it."

"I've made a better one and enough different with the wringer attached and two rinse tubs that Capt John thinks it could be patented." Ben's words were tentative.

"Don't forget to scrub that noddle pan, Clara." Then to Ben, Abigail said, "So that's what you've been doing. Why, that's wonderful." *It is!*

"I apprenticed with a cooper back in Illinois. Did I tell you that?" She shook her head that he hadn't. "I'm ready to give it a try here. If you approve, of course."

"Why would you even wonder. Anything to make laundry easier, though saving for one of those newfangled Thors might have been quicker."

"Mine has features." He looked up at her now.

She reached across the table and took his hand not engaged in noodle-shifting. "If you designed it, I'm sure it will be superior to anything on the market. Bring it home. Let me see those features."

"Thank you."

Ben pulled his hand from beneath hers, stood, and carried his dishes to the soapy water in the dishpan. "Are you ready for your story, Wilkie?" he asked their youngest. The child nodded his head. He'd been slower to pick up language, though Abigail wasn't worried. Yet. "You are? Good. I'll read. You turn the pages."

"We do it together. You sing, Pa?"

"Maybe." He smiled at Abigail, kissed the top of her head as he walked by.

* * *

"Well, I never," Abigail said. "It works . . . fine, Ben. Yes, it does."

"You say it as though you doubted it would." He'd filled the tubs with water, and a pump heated it so Abigail didn't have to lift steaming pots of water. She still had to swirl the clothes with a stick, but the heavy lifting was gone. Dirty water drained into a bucket he could carry for watering the garden.

"No. I didn't doubt you." *But I did, shame on me.*

"I'll eventually work out some kind of trough so you can do laundry in the kitchen instead of outside or in the laundry house. We can put the wastewater on the garden." He showed her how the rinse tub worked.

"I won't make much on the sale of each one, but it'll bring in something now and then."

She kissed his cheek, dabbed sweat from his forehead with a towel, then wiped her own. "A labor-saving device. It's wonderful, Ben. I'm proud of you."

It looked like he might cry.

* * *

Abigail rose at 4:00 a.m. in order to prepare the day's lessons, staying one step ahead of the learners. Ben watched their children too young to attend school, and he'd taken over preparing much of the larger meal of the day. The boarders were fed breakfast and supper. It was a cooperative effort.

"If I'm honest with myself," Abigail told her sister Kate, "It's all been good. I love running the school and the bustle of the boarders and having the children know of current events and giving them wise counsel. My counsel, of course." She clacked her knitting needles, making winter socks.

"A chance to pontificate," Kate said. "Your forte." The two sat on the Coburns' porch while Ben and Captain John smoked, leaning over the back rail.

"It is my *métier*." Abigail grinned. "And Ben is such a help with the children and the housework. He doesn't bat an eye at that broom. And he's invented a washing machine. It actually is quite useful."

"I hope you've let him know how much you appreciate him."

"In my way," Abigail said.

"Ha! I know your ways."

Kate rose from her rocking chair where she'd nursed her youngest, placed her baby in the cradle where a lace coverlet draped nearly to the floor. "You've turned your loss into something full of gain, Jenny. Perhaps you'll worry less now, enjoy your teaching more. And Ben's assistance. He doesn't appear as sad about the farm sale."

She'd noticed that too. He sighed less and even joked with her now and then, when she let him make her laugh. Perhaps inventing something took him from his cellar of sorrow the way writing worked for her.

"I've another novel rising in the doughboy."

"I don't know when you find the time."

"Ben helps, as you note."

To herself, Abigail acknowledged that despite the loss of Sunny Hillside, she was more invigorated now than she'd ever been, stood straighter, and had less pain in her joints, even found time to work on that next novel—when she woke at 3:00 a.m. and gave herself that hour to indulge in pure writing without regard to lesson preparation or boarder breakfasts.

Ben had undertaken the laundry, and she said not a word when she had to replace a button torn off in the wringer because of how he'd fed the contraption that squeezed water from the cloth. He'd even taken out a patent, with her assistance.

She thought about how one of the worst moments of her life—that wretched sheriff's visit and the sale of that beloved farm—could have resulted in this time of respite. Maggie would have quoted her Scripture, maybe Romans 8:28 about God working for good for those who follow him. Maggie used that verse often enough, even with a brother's or niece's death, events so sad Abigail couldn't imagine how anything good could come of them. But might it mean that even in sorrow, one wasn't alone. Abigail found Scripture beautiful as a language but never held it to be predictive the way Maggie did, she who could spout its words to support whatever view she held, whatever pain she had to bear. But for this day, in this moment, Abigail would admit that something good had come from the disaster of the farm loss.

As they drove back to Lafayette after visiting Kate and the Captain, Ben said, "Capt John's offered to loan me use of acreage he's purchased that I might take up horse training again." Anticipating her protest, he raised his voice. "I could work out some during the day, help farmers with haying, and still have an hour or two to work breeding stock. I've been checking around. Experienced farm hands are sought after."

How hard it must be for him to think of working for others when once he owned his own place.

"There's a market for matched white circus horses. You know I'm good with training." He kept his eyes forward, gave her time to think.

She thought about how he wouldn't be as available to help with *her* ventures if he was gone working horses and forking hay all day.

"Are you up to that?"

"Absolutely. I can still fix breakfasts while you study your lessons and be there for supper too. Willkie's three already. He could sit in on your classes, couldn't he? I sold another of my washing machines, so we could bring in a helper."

"Squeeze another bed into the attic?"

"Something like that. Or I could fix up that small room behind the kitchen stove." He kept his eyes on the road ahead, reins loose in his hands, while the children chattered to each other behind them in the wagon box.

Abigail thought of Kate's words and the good that had come from the sale. Ben was entitled to a bit of goodness too. "I know that working with horses gives you great pleasure." *And he loves to gab. He needs people around. He doesn't ask for much.* "You've earned that, Ben. We're moving forward in this westering place. We can make it happen."

PART 2

In those simple relationships of loving husband and wife, affectionate sisters, children and grandmother, there are innumerable shades of sweetness and anguish which make up the pattern of our lives day by day . . . These secret accords and antipathies which lie hidden under our everyday behavior . . . more than any outward events make our lives happy or unhappy.

Willa Cather, Not Under Forty

SIXTEEN

The Direction of Light

1864

The next year found Ben doing what he loved. He kept a garden at the Lafayette house, nurturing the tomatoes and marveling over the lettuce sprouts unfolding as delicate as a baby's tongue. He spent hours away with horses and farmers while Abigail hired a Chinese cook and housekeeper so he could. In the early evenings, Ben and eight-year-old Willis wielded a saw and hammer and wooden pegs, contributing to the cabinets Ben made to furnish the school. He joked with men who came to him for his advice on horses and found "pleasantness," as he called it, when he worked his young colts, forming teams.

Abigail continued her teaching, but she knew it wasn't enough. Contentedness wasn't a part of who she was, she decided. She began making a few loans to women in need. She didn't always confer about them with Ben, thinking that he didn't run every detail of his days by her, either. She wanted to help them get back on their feet. She'd made a loan to a divorced woman to help her buy furniture to start a boardinghouse to support her children.

As soon as she had the chairs and table and beds to replace what her former husband had taken in the divorce, he returned and gathered up what she'd bought and sold them out from under her.

"Can you imagine?" She told Ben as they sat at the table while Clara and Willis cleared the plates and squabbled at the dishpan over who would wash and who would dry. Hubert played with Wilkie. An advantage of having more than one child—they could look after each other. The boarding girls had already gone upstairs for the evening.

"Tragic," Ben said.

"Yes. Tragic and perfectly legal. What was hers, was his. Even after the divorce, he could trot right into that house and take what he wished. She had no say. And now she's in debt, and you can bet no law will make him pay it. She'll be liable for it and still without a pot to sit on. It's so unfair."

She didn't tell Ben that the money the woman owed was to the Duniways. Instead, she wrote a scathing letter to the editor describing the need for changes in property laws so women would have more choices when deserted by unscrupulous men—some of whom were husbands. She wrote letters to help women, supporting changes dealing with unfair practices, like a neighbor having to pay off a debt incurred by a deceased husband, a debt he had before the couple even married.

"What I need," she told Ben one evening while she added a patch to a thinning shirt elbow, "is a wider reach."

"The paper publishes your letters every week now." He drew on his pipe, the breathy air the only sound she could hear above the crickets. "And you and your 'flamboyant' friends attended an open meeting. That sent some tongues to wagging. We men let you."

"But the reporters barely mentioned it. There is no reason women can't attend public meetings and even speak at them. We'll go again. The editor will have to do an article about such a commotion. Editors have total control in deciding what goes in and what doesn't."

"Advertisers influence that, I suspect. There has to be a balance or they'll lose subscribers."

"If I ever run a newspaper, I'll find supporters willing to fund my perspectives. Balance won't be a part of it, because the scales are already tipped toward papers that celebrate men, protect their interests, not their wives or even mothers."

Ben sucked on his pipe again. He'd been giving up actual smoking, just used the pipe stem to chew on in the evening again. Abigail said she didn't like the taste of tobacco on her lips, and she kissed him more since he didn't fill the bowl. He held a sleeping Wilkie in his arm.

"I had no idea you hankered after running a newspaper. When did that happen?"

"Susan B. Anthony owns one, and the *Lily* has a long history. Both are women's rags, and they celebrate how life needs to change and offer ways to do it. Anne Royall ran one in the '30s, and though she was tried as a scold for being so outspoken, she supported herself with it and made a difference fighting corruption and taking on religious leaders who had forgotten that Christians are to be loving souls. My little letters barely scratch the surface to do what that Royall woman did with her paper." She put the thimble down and grinned. "Besides, with a newspaper I could get my novels printed. Serialize them, then bind and sell them later. I certainly haven't had any luck finding a real publisher since my first . . . fiasco."

"You learned from it."

"I hope so, but until the books are in the hands of others with reviews, I'll never really know."

"Oh, you know. You never let a lesson pass you by." He set his pipe aside and motioned for her to put her mending away. "I'll put Wilkie to bed, then let's take a look at the garden. We've a full moon. You can almost see the melons grow."

She shook her head. "I've got a lesson to plan."

"You're giving up a good moment, Mrs. Duniway." His voice had teasing to it, and for an instant she thought she might succumb, allow affection to soothe the tension in her shoulders, the racing of her mind.

"Those melons will grow without my admiration. And the moon will shine as bright. But if I'm not ready to stimulate those young minds in the morning, who knows what ideas they might walk away with." She saw the frown on his handsome face. "I'll only take an hour," she said.

He grunted. "I know your hour. I'll be long asleep by the time you notice you're still working at midnight."

She rose, bent to kiss him and Wilkie too. "Good night, Ben."

And so, she gave up tenderness, let it slip away, turned to thoughts of commerce. She didn't let herself wonder why.

* * *

It was late in the year, the children napped, and Abigail sat on the floor, a rare moment of pause as her back leaned against the couch. She'd bought a rag rug from a woman with arthritic hands, marveled at how that widow persevered to feed her family. Abigail ran her palm over the wool braids.

Ben sat above her reading an agricultural magazine.

"I've been battling the unfairness of a woman's life ever since I watched Momma go along with Father's decisions that failed. I hear these stories of women suffering through no fault of their own but from laws that mistreat them—as they mistreat our free-black and Chinese neighbors. It's the laws that have to change."

"You'll have to get men to vote the changes in."

"Fat chance of that." She crossed her arms. *Maybe I could start a cooperative where women sold their work and encouraged each other at the same time.* She sighed. "I thought the West would be a vibrant place for women's rights. Women work right beside their men. But here we are, still chattel."

"You should write about the importance of women securing the vote," Ben said. "It may be that the only thing that will really make a difference in a woman's life is her having a chance to make her mark at the ballot box. Men will have to grant that permission, and our lives might be made easier if we do, though we're a stubborn lot." He set his magazine down, stroked her hair. Tender. "It'll take good wisdom to create that end in Oregon. You could make the case better than anyone I know, if you find the right way to ride that horse."

"Do you really think so?" She turned to him. "I want women to have so much more control over their lives, so many more options to excel with their talents, their economic progress, their education. Removing barriers to either gender's excelling would help both sexes. Why can't men see that?"

"You'll have to show us. Become a suffragist." He smiled.

She turned back to stare at the mirror on the far wall. It reflected her mother's portrait behind the divan. "I never saw myself as being one of those kinds of 'Hurrah' suffrage women."

"Much as I hate to say this, perhaps you've been hiding your light under a bushel." Ben patted her shoulder.

"But back east . . . they hold parades and bang kettles on the streets and are so . . . strident. I don't see that going over well here. I don't want to compromise a woman's reputation. I want to expand it by showing that she can make good decisions, as a man can."

"Perhaps try another tactic."

What might that be?

Ben added, "They could vote out taxes they now have to pay."

"Yes. Women have taxation without representation. I believe the founding fathers had something to say about that. Not to mention the founding mothers. Bless Abigail Adams. But she couldn't get the word 'woman' added in either, though we all thought 'man' meant 'mankind' and not just the sex bearing whiskers."

"Expand that meaning. You can do it."

"I wish I knew for certain this was the best path to take. And I so wish we had a map to get us there."

"There's little certainty in the world, Jenny. Except attitude and effort."

A beam of light came through the window then as they sat together, the shaft illuminating a circle on the carpet's burgundy-shaded cloth. Abigail's whole body warmed, whether from having the luxury of a husband who understood and supported her or from that light pouring through the window like a period at the end of a most meaningful sentence. And then she did know.

"Do you see that light, Ben? You'll think me foolish, but I think that's God sending me a sign." Maggie, her faithful sister, would say that too. "In women's suffrage lies the answer to women's liberty. I don't know why I never saw that light before."

SEVENTEEN

Misfortune's Middle Name

1865

Abigail's next novel started the morning after that suffrage conversation. It took on the message of freedom for women by building the case for a woman's right to vote. Women were capable of birthing citizens in a cradle and raising them up, so they ought to be hardy and smart enough to vote about a school board position or who ought to be president. She planned to work such arguments into a plot. She was invigorated and gave Ben's sage advice and that directional beam of light the credit.

She felt a new energy in her classroom lessons. She chatted longer with the parents of her students, especially the women, to get a feel for how her arguments landed on men's and women's heads. She started wearing a white silk scarf held at her bodice with a fancy pin to offset the dark clothes she wore. She felt in constant mourning, so black linsey-woolsey made sense, but the dark colors also weathered the tendering in the wash tubs better than the bleached cloth the hot summer sun forced her to don. She posted a sign about her sewing abilities, deciding that stitching other than quilts would be a good way to earn extra cash—but also give her time with women, a chance to listen to their interests to better incorporate a strategy for how to secure them the vote. The idea of a newspaper would stay a pipe dream.

She used her editor letters to start her campaign. Spoke with her next-door neighbor, carefully bringing up the subject of suffrage, and found there were others like herself, contented wives who wished for more. Oh, yes, she had a hundred ideas now that the focus of her energy was so clear. She loved the organizing, the idea-generating, pulse-driving joy of knowing where she was headed and having a path forward, even if she had to push the boulders out of the way herself. Ben's temperament, too, had lightened with his work with his horses again. There was singing in the house. His occasional sales of both washing machines and matched teams took her farther from her fears of poverty. She felt secure for the first time in years.

* * *

Through the opening in the glass door, she watched the sheriff walk up the steps. "What now?" she asked. She often made the sheriff a villain in the drafts of her novels. The one she worked on now had such a character.

"There's been an accident, Mrs. Duniway." Abigail's eyes scanned the room: all children were present and accounted for.

"Ben? My sisters?"

"Ben." He held his hat in his hand and didn't look at her.

"Where? What happened. Children. Class dismissed." She reached for Wilkie, who had been playing quietly in the back of the classroom, something he did when Ben was either in his workshop or at the farm with the horses, which was where he should have been and was now. *Why when things are going so well does disaster always strike?*

"I'll take you to the doctor."

She swallowed the lump in her throat. "Clara. Watch them all."

Abigail rushed through the house, jammed a hat on her head, grabbed her purse, and went through the door the sheriff held open for her. She pressed the silk scarf at her throat, gaining small comfort from the softness. She waited to pepper the sheriff for answers until they were in the carriage. Spring birds chirped.

"Best I know, missus, is he was tossed from a wagon when a team he was working broke loose. They trampled him, the wagon straight across his back. Soft earth from the spring rains might have saved his life."

She breathed her prayers, trying not to chastise a God who allowed these tragedies, over and over. Financial strain. Ben's depression. Her own physical depletion, the joint aches the doctors named rheumatoid arthritis. Now this, when they were moving forward, had found a good routine and rhythm. *At least he's alive. At least he's alive.*

"Broken back," the doctor said. "I've given him laudanum for the pain. He'll need to be kept quiet. Fortunately, there doesn't appear to be any organ damage, just broken vertebrae from what I can determine by the feel of his spine."

"Just broken vertebrae." Her sarcasm appeared lost on the doctor. "Can he . . . will he walk?"

"Time will tell. Healing takes time." The doctor patted her hand as she sat beside Ben's bed at the doctor's office, the distant clank of instruments on metal punctuations to her rushing heartbeat and the patter of his retreating shoes leaving them alone.

"Oh, Ben." His eyes claimed hers.

"Sorry, Jenny."

"I know you are." She brushed hair from his forehead, watched the bruising spread before her eyes on his cheeks, even his hands. He forced a weak smile. She could only imagine what his back looked like.

"What'll we do?" Ben whispered through the laudanum haze.

"Right now, you'll heal. We'll pray your spine will hold you up again and you'll be back fit as a fiddle. I'm sure of it." *No, I'm not.*

But she knew that he drew from her confidence. "You rest now. We'll be fine." She put all thoughts of the future aside and laid her head down on the bedside, breathed a prayer of gratitude that he was alive. They'd find a way to work things out, God willing. At least they didn't have Sunny Hillside Farm to take care of.

* * *

Ben's pain was like an uninvited guest who came to dinner, had to be accommodated, then stayed well past the promised departure time. In fact, Abigail began to wonder if there would be a departure time. He was a good patient, asked to be allowed to lift hand irons so he wouldn't lose arm strength. He let the nurses help him stand. He joked with them and made them laugh. Then when they left, he sighed to Abigail, leaned on her. "Will I ever walk again?"

She wanted time with that cheerful Ben who made the nurses and doctors grin with his stories. Instead she got needy Ben. Then she chastised herself for even lamenting her frustrations when he was dealing with broken bones and who knew what he might not be able to ever do again. He'd lost—at least temporarily—what he cherished: time with his horses and tossing Wilkie in the air to catch him. He could look forward to . . . what? Neither of them knew.

"John and Harvey have moved a bed into the parlor downstairs. I kept the piano in there so Clara can practice and soothe you with music at the same time. She's quite good. I think we can stop the lessons. She can even *give* them."

"Hopefully we won't need a disrupted house for long. I'll be up. Lincoln's won reelection. The war is over. Hope is in the air."

"That's the Ben I married." She kissed him. "The doctors say you can come home any time we're ready. There's a chair with wheels to get you around, and John and Amos installed a board nicely smoothed by the boys you can pull on to get you upright and taking those steps."

"I'll miss the nurses offering aid." He smiled at her.

"I'm sure you will. The children can help and I will. When I can." She straightened his bedsheets, smoothed the pillowcase above his head. "I've been thinking, Ben. Albany's a larger city than Lafayette, and with the war ending, business will boom. Albany's got a steamboat stop from both north on the Willamette and south at Corvallis and the Calapooia. Bigger things are happening there. The Presbyterians have started a college and we could live right next door to the Fosters. You remember them? They had a house in Lafayette. And my sister Harriet lives in Albany now too, you remember."

He looked thoughtfully at her. "I've got my friends where we are. When I'm better, I'd have to find a farm to work the horses instead of being able to use Capt John's. Albany's farther away."

She didn't correct him but thought if he ever worked horses again it would be a miracle—if not a terrible mistake.

"There's a Union-leaning newspaper in Albany, giving the southern Democrats a run for their money. They already accepted a couple of my letters."

"Ah," Ben said.

"And we can purchase a bigger house there." She pulled a chair up beside him. The room smelled of disinfectant. "I've been thinking."

"No doubt."

"If we sell the school now, we'll make a profit. I've been looking over the figures. Plus, the extra room at this newer house I've found could be used for a retail operation, and there's . . . a bedroom on the main floor, to accommodate you. Us."

"You've located a house? When did you ever find the time? Oh. Sure. I've been here and you've been, well, carrying on."

"Didn't you expect me to?"

"No. Yes. Of course. It's what you do, thank goodness."

"I hand-delivered my letter to the paper a few weeks back and had time to talk with an agent." She looked away. "The house is perfect, Ben. A much bigger attic space. We could take in six boarders."

"And the retail idea?"

"I've a plan."

"You usually do. But leave Lafayette and our friends? Couldn't your plan involve where we are now?"

"You'll make new friends. You're good at that. Kate says I don't praise you enough for your many gifts."

"Bless Kate."

"I do. You do make friends easily and you keep them. Yes, they take advantage of you—at times." She added that last when he began to protest. "But your goodwill softens my shrill."

"Goodwill over shrill. I'll remember that."

"It'll serve you well in Albany. And we have to do some things differently now, Ben. You won't be able to . . . add to the teapot. At least for a time. We have to take advantage of the market. We must hire a nurse to help. Someone for you to flirt with when your old wifey is busy."

"You're the only one I want to help me walk again."

"I know."

He lifted her hand and kissed it. "Go ahead and get your house. You probably already have."

* * *

The teapot was the last of the items Abigail packed as the Scott sisters and their husbands helped the Duniways move. Again. The teapot sat proudly on the mantel over the fireplace in their new Albany home. It had coins in it again.

She might have exaggerated to Ben in a small way. The profit wasn't much from the sale of the school but sufficient to get them started. They'd still have to pinch their pennies, but she wanted to continue her newspaper subscriptions. She needed to see how the rest of the country was working on women's suffrage and how Oregon's campaigns would be different. But in Albany she could have conversations with the instructors at the college. She could debate with friends as well as those who saw the world differently than she did. She did love the intellectual pursuit. She might not have a Pacific University education like her brother, but she could go head-to-head with Harvey on current events around the world as well as at home, she was certain of that. He might have an advantage as he studied law now, too, in addition to having access to every book in that Portland library collection. She wished Ben liked to read more, but his was an oral tradition, telling stories rather than reading them.

Perhaps the move was more for her than for the rest of the family, though the extra space did help Ben move more easily, first with the wheeled chair and then with canes. The children would adjust. They had Scott blood in them and knew how to persevere. The Duniway side seemed a bit more fragile. She had to remember that as she watched Ben sigh when he looked over the financial sheets she'd showed him and told him of loose boards in the attic. The house's foundation was sound, but the roof would need buttressing.

* * *

Abigail hired men to fix rafters, put old newspapers for insulation in the walls, readied the attic for additional boarders while she drew out on paper how she wanted the largest room on the first floor converted. "We'll put the glass case here, where one can stand behind it and take out the beaded purses from the back.

"I can build those cases."

"Can you?" She hadn't thought he could do such work. "That would be wonderful, Ben."

"It'll take me a little time." Ben stood steadied by two canes. "Willis can help. And Hubert. I can sit."

"Then we'll have clothes trees along that back wall where we can shape wires to hold the ready-made dresses. They'll be hung rather than folded, giving a better view of the handiwork from the moment people come into the store. Fortunately, there's a separate entrance, so people won't need to tromp through the house."

"I can twist wires into round shapes to hold the hats." Clara showed her parents one she'd made.

"That's perfect. They can be bookends on the glass cases. We need to make the counters wide enough to accommodate the hat stands but also allow people to look down through to see the wares for sale." She kissed the top of Clara's head and gently touched the cascade of curls that fell to her nearly twelve-year-old shoulders. *She's beautiful. We need to be sure she finishes school and make suitors wait.* "My creative daughter."

"I can sew too, Momma."

"Better than me, that's for certain. But I want to hire out seamstresses, give Albany women money for their work. With the war over, we'll have a booming business. Women like to have other women do the fitting and stitching. When you're older." She saw the disappointment. "You'll do well behind the counters, Clara. You could knit a purse or two. That would add to the stock."

"What stock?" Ben said.

"My kind of stock is going to come from my teapot nest egg. I'm taking my thirty dollars and heading on the steamboat to Portland to meet with Jacob Mayer. He's that retail genius in Portland where things are booming too. I'm going to ask for a loan, then head to San Francisco and get the latest frocks and unmentionables, needles and threads, and felted hats."

"A loan."

"Yes. I can show him how I can repay him. I've got the numbers all worked out. You're making progress. It won't be long, and you'll be contributing better than you did before. The pain is less, isn't it?"

"It comes and goes. The laudanum helps."

"At least there's something." She didn't like him taking the liquid because it made him so sleepy. But life was a balance. Without it he suffered; with it, more often than not, he lay in the shadows.

"You're leaving me behind, Mrs. Duniway."

"No, I'm not. I'm moving *us* forward. You're right with me. You checked the figures. I'll build up a way to push for suffrage—my way. No parades or crazy-marching women holding signs. My way is a 'still hunt.' Quiet coercion of men in power and men in general to be less frightened by women. I need capital to do that. I think Jacob Mayer has a nose for investments, and I want ours to be his next. But I can't do it without your approval."

He shook his head. "You can. I wish I could help more. You won't need me in the end."

A flash of anger surged through her. *Why do I have to prop you up? Don't I have enough to do?*

"I'll always need you, Ben. You're my rock. You keep me out of trouble. Well, sometimes. People love you. They tolerate me."

"You're strong enough not to care."

"Oh, I care. But I can't let it deter me from my task."

"Being the breadwinner. Yes. I know. I'm so sorry."

"Making a difference for women, Ben. That's the task. And you help with that by progressing, being there for the children and letting me be me despite the boulders I uncover on this journey we're on. Now, you work on your exercises while I head to Portland. And say a prayer that Mr. Mayer will have the vision to support Albany's newest millinery."

EIGHTEEN

The Stars and Spoils

Abigail loved the bustle of Portland. The clatter of harness and hames—even the smell of horse droppings in the streets near the still unpulled tree stumps—didn't offend her. Good walkways bordered the shops. She might even stop by and see Harvey at the library if things went well with Mr. Mayer. The merchant had begun a new business, Fleishner, Mayer and Co., with two brothers from Albany—of late and earlier from Germany. The Albany dry goods store had closed, and the men partnered in Portland now. Abigail could see why. This was the city of Oregon's future. But for now, she hoped to capitalize on the customers they'd left behind.

Mr. Mayer was a smallish man with bright brown eyes and hair slicked back over a beginning-to-bald pate. She started to introduce herself, but he interrupted. "I know who you are, Mrs. Duniway. I read the papers up and down the valley. You've quite a poison pen—when it calls for. I approve of your support of the downtrodden and the Jews as well."

"I guess I ought not be surprised that you'd reviewed my history, knowing I came to ask you for money. I didn't think my political proclivities would enter into the discussion."

"A man doesn't want to do business with someone he wouldn't introduce to his wife or family."

"I'd be honored to meet your family one day." She was pleased he wasn't put off by her columns that sometimes pushed aside a woman's role as demonstrating solely decorum and a family focus. "For now, I have a solid business plan I want to share with you."

She watched him read her documents. She was glad she'd dressed in her finest black dress worn over the larger bustle that the wind-down of the war allowed. She was up-to-date and as fashionable as any *Godey's Lady's Book* model.

He laughed and she swallowed bile. "Thirty dollars, Mrs. Duniway?"

"Is it—I thought it a reasonable amount."

"No, I won't loan you that."

"I'm good for it." Her face felt hot with embarrassment.

"Your reputation says as much. No, I won't loan you thirty dollars." He adjusted his glasses. "But I will loan you twelve hundred dollars to buy stock in San Francisco."

"That's . . . stunning. Thank you for your confidence in me."

"And why not. You've a good business head, Mrs. Duniway, and you can see what women are interested in, now that the war is over and it's safe to spend again. Prosperity. Yes, I think you are right at the cusp of it, and I'm happy to be of assistance."

She barely remembered the steamship ride back. She told Ben that evening and his proud grin pleased her no end. "Oh Ben, he believed in me."

"Smart man."

"I'll head south tomorrow and make my purchases. I've already paid for an ad in next week's paper. Clara's ready to stand behind the counter."

"And I can too," Ben said. "I'll wear my best coat and collar."

"It won't tire you?"

"Got myself a stool to sit on, but I'm taking steps with only one cane."

She hugged him. "That's so good, Ben."

When she started to break away, he kept his arms around her. "I only want to hold you close for a moment. Kiss my happy retail magnate." He did kiss her then, and she let herself sink into his arms.

"I'm not a magnate yet." She pushed herself away, though he still linked his arms around her waist. "Only on the journey. I hope. One I need to pack for."

"Just so long as I'm on the voyage with you."

"You always will be. Not literally, of course. You're not up to a steamship ride yet." She patted his vested chest. *He always takes such good care of his person. Tidy.* "I'm not sure I could do any of this without you."

She wished his progress made her as giddy as her success with Jacob Mayer, but she was genuinely pleased he wanted to help and pushed himself to do it. They were a team, though not one exactly matched.

* * *

Abigail made the trip to San Francisco, bought her twelve hundred dollars' worth of baubles and beads, fabrics and finery, and returned to sell them. She paid Mr. Mayer back within three weeks and returned to California with a three-thousand-dollar advance from the financier and came back to sell those items too. She'd been at the front of a buying boom and was in the right town to make that happen. Only Lincoln's assassination had slowed things as the country mourned.

"Did you read Harvey's essay about Lincoln published in the *Oregonian*?" Kate asked. "It's quite moving."

Even Abigail had to admit to the passion and the expression of grief brother Harvey so beautifully conveyed.

Then Maggie, their faith-loving sister, died that fall, and Abigail was back to wearing black.

They'd taken in eight-year-old Annie, as Maggie's children were brought into their aunts' folds. Harvey, with more means than any of them, had not taken on his nieces or nephews as wards. *Where is his generous Scott heart?*

"That husband of hers," Abigail complained to Ben as she packed for yet another buying trip to California. "He took Maggie on that swampy boat in and out of coastal ports selling bread and basics, putting her right in the path of consumption. And then did nothing to help her when she became ill. He didn't even let us know. Just allowed her to suffer." She sat at the edge of the bed, noticed a sock stuck between the mattress and the footboard, and grabbed for it. "She hadn't wanted to go with him to the coast in the first place. How I wish she'd stood up to him."

"She believed a woman must listen to her husband. A God-given requirement of a good wife. You know that."

"But there are other ways to interpret that Scripture. We are all made in God's image, so we are all equal, though different. There's that message too. Her word means as much as his, it does. More, because frankly she's smarter than George Fearnside. Was smarter." Her death was one more on the heels of Lincoln's assassination. It was nearly too much to bear.

But then, Maggie's children were now under the spell of their aunts, away from their father's influence. Maybe it was good that women would have more to say over the little girls and not have them exposed to the restrictive views of women's roles that their father held. Or that Harvey did. Harvey had told sister Fanny that he didn't approve of Abigail traveling so much for business, that it wasn't a woman's place. She'd confront him at some point, but it was so like him to complain to another sister rather than speak to her directly. He wouldn't like at all her decision to have another woman present at the store while she traveled—a woman who would also share the financial load. With Ben's consent, she'd taken on a female partner.

"A prominent family," Ben commented. He straightened a small area of men's hats that Abigail had decided to purchase to see if they would sell in a woman's shop.

"They're good Republicans," she said. "She's operated a millinery out of their parlor on Elm Street so knows that trail all right. She has the social contacts, and as you know, my social skills aren't always the best."

Ben laughed. He sat behind a glass case, his body filling out again as he became more mobile and active and didn't need the medication so much. Nor the canes. But the pain came and went, ebbing and flowing like the tide. He'd wince bending to pull a carrot from the garden. That could put him down for hours.

"With a partner, I can be away from here now and then with fewer worries."

"But the children are devoted to you and really like your being around more. I want to start training again, Abigail. I don't want the accident to keep me from getting 'back on that horse,' so to speak."

Abigail was grateful Ben had improved, but it also meant he had more ideas and sought greater independence that forced her into new arguments to get him to accept her "plans."

She resented the weight of responsibility of being the primary supporter, but she also liked holding the reins. As he got better, he'd have to make different accommodations. "I suppose we could use the extra income if you're successful. But it's risky too. You could get hurt again."

"And you could get hurt traveling so much, alone as you do. I should go with you."

"One of us has to stay with the children. And I'm only gone for a few days at a time." She reset a feathered hat on one of Clara's wire head mounts. "All right, let's give it a try. Maybe a day or so a week?"

"Aunt Abigail, can I help in the store?" Annie's voice broke into their discussion.

"May you help," Abigail corrected. "Of course. What would you like to do?"

"I can draw pictures to put in the window." She pointed to the glass behind a sitting area where friends could wait during a fitting. She showed her aunt a drawing she'd done.

"Very good, Annie. Let's see what you can do for a newspaper ad. Would you like to try that? Clara, can you find lead and wrapping paper?"

"I would." Annie danced her way out of the room, the first time Abigail had seen the girl smile since her mother's death.

"Training needs to be daily," Ben said.

"What? Oh, yes, we were speaking of your getting back on that horse, so to speak."

"I'll spend the mornings."

"Yes. All right. Mornings."

The new partner would increase sales. She would share the costs—but also any profits. Business or personal, there would be a price to pay. Relationships were so unpredictable, and she longed for certainty—certainty she could control.

* * *

The family gathered to attend Harvey's wedding at the end of October to Elizabeth, a quiet soul who adored him as she gazed at him with admiration in her eyes. He was quite a catch, Abigail decided, though his domineering opinions about everything meant Elizabeth might have a difficult time expressing hers—especially if they differed. The woman didn't say much, so the sisters weren't sure what she thought about issues of the day. Still, she knew Latin, which probably attracted Harvey to her in the first place. She did say she found it quite remarkable that Abigail traveled so much when she had young children still at home. *I wonder where she heard that?* "Steamships are so full of . . . strangers." Elizabeth dabbed at her full lips with her napkin. "What if something should happen?"

"I find travel quite invigorating," Abigail told her. They were at the breakfast Abigail hosted for the couple at the Albany Hotel when they returned from their honeymoon. Abigail was rather pleased they had the finances to put on such an elegant breakfast for them. She was as prosperous as Harvey was. In a way. At least she wanted him to conclude that.

Rain fell, but it didn't prevent Kate and John from arriving from Canemah. Fanny and Amos sat at the far end of the table, ferns behind them moving gently as the servers passed by. Harriet and William sat across from the Captain and Kate, while eighteen-year-old sister Sarah sat next to Ben. It was the first time they'd gathered since Maggie's death, as Fanny hadn't been able to make Harvey's wedding. She'd been struggling with morning sickness.

"One simply has to let go of having total control when traveling," Abigail said. "There are opportunities for serendipitous moments on a steamship or even a stagecoach."

"I never thought of you as liking the unpredictable," Harvey said.

"I'm quite adaptable."

Harvey coughed and raised his eyebrows toward Ben.

"One has to be," Abigail continued. "That's what wives and mothers do, adjust to the whims and fortunes of their men. Let that be a warning to you, Elizabeth." She raised her fork to emphasize her point.

"Seems to me you do more than adjust." Harvey leaned back to allow the server to place bacon strips onto his plate. "I see you planning the destination, setting the sails, and if the captain would let you, organizing the wheelhouse." Harvey smiled at her, more indulgent than critical, but she took afront anyway.

"I prefer to be the captain, it's true. But I know how to be a good crew member too."

"She runs a tight ship." Ben passed the rolls around. "And she's the hardest working woman I know of. Fingers in lots of pies."

"A sign of a life with misplaced purpose perhaps. Being a dutiful wife and mother is a higher calling than indulging in the business world, rushing off to San Francisco, writing letters to the editor exposing yourself to public criticism, leaving poor Ben to manage the home fires you ought to be tending."

"Poor Ben does fine," Abigail said. "Don't you, Ben."

"That I do. I've got a matched team ready for sale. Not the pair that got away from me. Someone else finished them. Wish I could have."

"You're back at doing what you love. Good for you, Ben." Harvey turned to his new wife. "He talked of little else when we were at the mines together. Well, horses were second—to Abigail and the children. He both loved and loathed your lengthy letters, Sister."

"Loathed?" She looked at Ben.

His cheeks above his reddish beard had turned a shade of pink. She had been hard on him at times, begging him to come home but not until he struck gold; telling him stories of how the children missed him while listing needs they had and hoped he could meet.

"I told him to overlook your punctuation," Harvey said. His usual downturned lips lifted in his moment of jest—at someone else's expense, Abigail noted.

"It was missing you all," Ben said. "Your letters made me sad and glad at the same time."

"Well," Abigail said. "Words have power. I won't apologize for that. Nor should anyone who writes of truth and heart, even with bad punctuation. Some of us had the benefit of early education, and some of us were sickly and worked our fingers to the bone."

"Have you settled into your Portland home, Elizabeth?" Kate said. "It's a lovely area of the city."

Catherine, ever the diplomat.

"Yes. We have. And it's so much closer now to Harvey's new appointment."

"What's that, Brother?" Sarah asked.

"I've been named the editor of the *Oregonian*. Mr. Pittock liked my essay on Lincoln so much he made the offer. And I accepted." He beamed.

"You're the editor?" Harriet said. "Congratulations. That's quite a feat."

"It is indeed," Ben said. Congratulations were sent across the table.

Abigail bit off her biscuit, staring at Harvey, who smirked at her. She didn't see a newly examined lawyer, head of the Portland library, and now editor of the *Oregonian*. She saw her little brother putting himself above her just because he'd been born a boy.

"If I'd had primary schooling and a college education, I'd have been a newspaper editor by the time I was twenty-one, not waited until I was twenty-seven."

"Abigail," Fanny chastened.

"I didn't realize you aspired to be a newspaper editor," Harvey said.

"I do. And I will be one day." She took a deep breath. "But congratulations anyway, Harvey. You've done the Scott name proud. And who knows, you might be publishing one of my essays one of these days."

"I look forward to that. Make sure you double-check your punctuation."

NINETEEN

An Editorial Option

1866

Abigail waited at the landing called Steamboat Point in San Francisco, her ship having rattled by swamps still visible in a city infused with gold and silver riches. Porters carried trunks off, and others dragged luggage and who knew what all on board, followed by passengers dressed in the finery Abigail hoped to find duplicates of and purchase. She was anxious to do her buying, read the *News of the World* and other local newspapers, and be treated to supper in the ladies' dining room of the Cosmopolitan Hotel. A porter called a cab for her—drawn by a white horse that made her think of Ben—and when the porter helped her up, she saw that another passenger waited inside.

"Jenny Scott? Can that be you?"

"Shirley Ellis? Oh, what a wonder!" Her mind flashed back to the girl who had pierced her ears. A slender young woman smiled back at her, though with eyes that showed more strain than the sparkle she'd been known for on the trail across.

"Jenny Duniway, I mean. What are you doing here?"

"I'm on a buying mission. Dress trimmings, threads, the latest in hats."

"Of course you are. I remember you writing about your millinery. What a gift our paths should pass in person once again. Let me look at those earrings."

Abigail turned her head.

"Still look fine."

"They're my favorite, though I've a dozen pair now."

"How's Ben? Your children?"

"Thriving. What are you doing in San Francisco?"

"I moved here from Sacramento. I'm teaching and just took a friend to the ship. You'll stay with me, won't you? We've so much to catch up on."

For a moment Abigail longed for that quiet supper at the hotel. She liked solitary times when her thinking became clearer, and after supper, she'd enjoy the time to write, free of distractions. Still, seeing Shirley again reminded her of good times the girl—the woman—had brought during hard trials. And she had yet to hear what Shirley thought about the novel she'd sent her.

"Yes. I'd be pleased."

Shirley hugged Abigail as she settled onto the leather seat. She was surprised to feel tears in her eyes. Shirley's presence brought back memories of her mother, the journey across the continent, and her youngest brother's death too. Shirley had helped them all out of their sorrows, made her and her sisters laugh despite themselves. She was also reminded of how glorious it was to have an old friend. They chatted and caught up, and it was as though no time had ever separated them.

"You're limping," Shirley said when they stepped out of the cab.

"Sometimes. After sitting a long time. It's my joints and the strain of childbirth. I think the latter is passed now." She smiled. "Too busy supporting the family to have time to make it larger."

"I'd love to meet your children. And Ben."

"Come and visit but wait until spring or summer. The rains are wretched, the only thing I dislike about Oregon."

"We have our share too." A wet December fog near the Bay had them pull out their umbrellas when they reached the brownstone building where the driver stopped. "I don't suppose the rains do anything to soothe your bones either. Here we are." They climbed the stairs to the third floor. Shirley opened and closed her umbrella to knock the rain off, then unlocked her door, and they entered the tiny apartment, nicely furnished. The umbrellas were popped into the stand.

"It's lovely." And it was, with no clutter, no children's toys lying about, no business dealings mixed in with family. Abigail set her carpetbag down. She loved tidiness but couldn't seem to manage it in her own life. A wreath of grapevines with peacock feathers accented with burgundy bows hung over the fireplace. "That's gorgeous. Did you make it?"

"Oh, no. There's a collective, a group of women who make crafts to sell, to support themselves and their children. My women's group helps them. Will you buy Christmas items this trip?"

"Most seasonal items were commissioned before September. But if there are more of those, I might take a few back. They look so festive. Your entire apartment does."

"It's big enough for our women's gatherings. Now that the war is over, we can put our hearts and hands into being able to manage our own money, gaining property rights for women, achieving custody of our children."

"And voting."

"Oh, yes, the franchise. You wait. California will be the leader in the West getting women's suffrage. We're organizing. Maybe your next trip you can attend a meeting. There's strength in numbers." A daguerreotype of Shirley holding an infant sat on the sideboard. Shirley paused to look at it before she stepped into the galley kitchen. "Our efforts won't be taken well by the men of

California, and yet we have to win them over to get our way. We're tightrope walkers balancing on a swinging rope."

"Is that . . . ?" Abigail turned to Shirley, holding the photograph.

Shirley looked at the picture in its cast-iron frame. "It's a sad story. My husband brought her here to San Francisco when he divorced me after only a year. I don't know how I chose so poorly." She sighed. "He told the court he could care for her better, and I've rarely been allowed to even see her. If he knew I was involved with women's advocacy, he'd cut off even those few visits."

"I didn't know."

"Shame has a way of silencing people."

"But why should you be ashamed? You didn't do anything wrong."

"I never should have married him. My parents warned me against him. I didn't listen. They worry over my women's meetings too, but I have to put my heartache somewhere, make a difference for my daughter's future life. The friend I told you about from Roseburg, she's divorced with a child too and has endured rebuke because of it. Fortunately her parents supported her decision, as well they should have. They married her off when she was fourteen, and the man was abusive. He's moved to San Francisco. She's hoping to gain custody of their son."

"There must be a few men who share our hopes. Ben does. I'm so grateful for that." Abigail pulled the pins from her hat, removed it. She realized how much Ben's support meant to her, his goodness and how despite letter-writing attacks on her, he never suggested she was anything more than a dutiful wife and mother. She wondered if she'd have the strength to pursue her frank letters, push to be accepted in places that barred women, if she didn't have the confidence that Ben offered.

"There's the *Pioneer*." Shirley pointed to a newspaper lying on her table. "Sit and read while I fix us tea." She heated water while Abigail scanned the single sheet. "Have you officially organized your group? Tried to vote or anything like Susan B. Anthony did back east?"

"We're starting to gather. It's so much easier with pals. The hardest is getting the word out so women know they aren't alone."

"That it is." She turned to the backside of the *Pioneer*, read the masthead. "It has a woman editor."

"Yes. One of the first on the West Coast."

"A woman editor." She thought of Harvey and his editorial against free secondary education, leaving the masses without hope of advancing themselves unless they had money. He'd influence voters with his opinions that were now able to go out across the West—if not back east. "It would take quite a bit to finance a newspaper. I've done some figuring. That's why moneymen are the ones who do it."

"The *Pioneer* has backers, I'm sure. You could meet with her on your next trip."

"I'd like that."

She might be able to submit some of her essays and articles to the *Pioneer* and gain a wider audience.

"Along with taking back fabric, I think you've given me something else to return with," she said as Shirley filled the teapot with steaming water. "A newspaper, one that speaks for women's needs and desires and encourages women and girls. That's what Oregon needs."

Yes, she would write for newspapers that advocated a better life for women and children, her children and Maggie's and all girls. Perhaps operate a publishing company. It would be her new method to achieve that most important goal of freedom for women. It could give Harvey's *Oregonian* a run for his money. But first she had to plan it out, figure out the financing, and get Ben behind it. Because it would mean a move. They'd have to live in Portland, the fastest-growing city in the region. And of course, where Harvey presided. She'd take her silent hunt right into the king's forest.

* * *

There was no move to Portland and no newspaper either. Life got in the way. Harvey's wife gave birth to a baby boy, but the family soon grieved when the child failed to thrive and died before reaching two months. Abigail sent a condolence letter, her words as tender as any she had exchanged with Harvey. No room for anything but compassion.

"Stay a little," Ben told her one February morning in 1866. Ben had been down—to use a term for horses foundering—from his having twisted strangely while lifting a leather collar over a pinto's neck. He'd done it a hundred times without issue, but this time he'd been brought home by a neighbor who had heard his shout while passing by where Ben rented land to work his teams. "Rest," the doctor had told them. This day, she'd picked up Ben's noontime food tray and what was left of the ham sandwich and the crusts of bread Chen had freshly made. Ben didn't like the crusts.

"You're always so busy." Ben patted the bed. "Come. Sit."

"If I sat down now, I'd fall asleep in seconds."

"Would that be so bad?"

"It would. I have to finish the order, among other things. Just rest as the doctor said. Or read." She heard the edge to her voice and the twinge of resentment that seeped in when he did foolish things that he knew could result in a recurrence of his back strain, forcing days in bed, leaving her to wonder if this was the incident that would seal his life as an invalid. Their lives, with him once again barely able to walk. "What I wouldn't give to have the time to reread *The Woman in White* or dig into my shelf of books I have only read once."

"You work too hard." He winced as he moved over to make room for her. "Put the tray down. Lie beside me. Let me hold you. You do so much."

She sighed and rested her head on the pillow, facing him. He stroked her arm. In seconds she was asleep.

"Jenny? Jenny."

"How long was I out?"

"Only fifteen minutes. I knew you'd never nap beside me again if I let you sleep until you awoke on your own."

"That would have been tonight at 10:00 p.m." She yawned. "I

would have harangued you when I saw the wasted time if you'd let me sleep on. There's too much to do. I've got three dresses to finish."

"You can slow down a bit. Wouldn't hurt you."

"Don't, Ben. I don't want to argue with you now about my pace or schedule."

"Me neither." He kissed her nose, started to kiss her lips but stopped. His voice lightened. "Go on. Tend to business. Maybe I'll get you tomorrow for another catnap if you see I can let you go, even when I'd rather keep you here." He flashed that smile at her, the one that had won her heart those years before.

"I hope that by tomorrow you'll feel able to get up again."

"I'm sure of it. But if not, watching my wife slumber is one of the rare pleasures to come from this . . . spine with a life of its own." He touched her elbow as though to help her sit. "Would you put my name on tomorrow's dance card?"

"Sleep card, more like it." She sat up, straightened her hair combs as he rubbed her back.

"Off with you," he said.

Maybe I should stay. The snooze had refreshed her, and he had awakened her and was letting her go, when she could tell he wanted the comfort of her presence. Maybe more. *And would it be so bad to let your husband love you?* "'The things nearby, not the things afar,'" she quoted.

"What's that?"

"Just thinking. I hope you've no need to rest tomorrow, but if you do, I'll see if you want to have an old tired woman take a lie-down beside you."

"It's a deal, though you're far from a tired old woman."

* * *

In March of 1866 Abigail discovered she was pregnant. There was joy, yes, but angst too. She was thirty-two years old, had already given birth to four children, with only one arriving without much trouble. Months abed followed the delivery and to have both her and Ben foundering wouldn't do.

Ben was delighted. "You'll have to stay at home more."

"This is the last one now. It has to be." She'd have to read more about timing births. There were ways to do that.

"Whatever you say." He grinned.

"I imagine you can hardly wait to let your horse friends know."

"I'm back in the saddle," Ben joked while Abigail blushed.

* * *

It was probably the mood swings caused by the pregnancy, but she found herself annoyed by the children more, by Ben—even though he was up and only occasionally using his cane as the summer progressed. Even Mrs. Jackson, her partner, irritated her with her constant fluttering over the books, "questioning her judgment," rather than merely inquiring over an entry she had made. Mrs. Jackson didn't think they should branch out into dry goods, such as the wreaths Abigail had brought back from San Francisco. Such items were seasonal and no competition for the Jackson store, so Abigail didn't see the problem. Nothing irked her more than having someone question her competence or judgment. Mrs. Jackson also made noises that Abigail should pull back her letter-writing to the newspaper. But Abigail believed that in this time of government turmoil—a new president, the war ended—people were most likely to consider change. *People*, being men who had all the power over the vote. Mrs. Jackson had made noises about Abigail being a tad too strident in her letters before.

"It's time," she told Ben.

"But she's a huge help to you."

"Trying to be diplomatic is not my forte, as you well know. It takes more energy to hold my tongue than to live with a little business uncertainty."

She arranged to buy her partner out, settling the split on good terms, as she didn't want bad feelings to filter onto the customers Mrs. Jackson had brought to the millinery.

The newspaper idea would have to wait, as would the organizing of women, until after Abigail gave birth that November.

* * *

"Another voter in the cradle." Abigail smiled at Clyde, whose delivery had gone surprisingly well. He was a sweet baby who curled into her arms and gazed at her with eyes that seemed to bore right through her. As with Clara who was her first, Clyde was to be special—as their last child.

"No more babies," she told Ben.

"Of course," he'd agreed. *Why wouldn't he? He doesn't have to bear the morning sickness.*

And like her, he loved his children, whose personalities blossomed. Willis, a boy who could declaim on any number of subjects from the Constitution to the life cycle of a butterfly and who enjoyed his lessons, always finishing first. Hubert was her outdoor child, his father's helper in the garden—except when he joined Ben in his woodshop—and who knew the name of every tree and plant on their street. Wilke loved to play games like Tiddlywinks, garnering stacks of colored winks, always urging a little competition especially with his older brother. It was a popular game. She interrupted the boys when they teased Clara Belle as she practiced scales, or pulled on cousin Annie's pigtails just because they could. The girls held a special place in her heart, and it pleased her that neither of them had blisters or backaches from the heavy work of farming or even laundry.

The work of family life had been spread out, and if it wasn't for Ben's intermittent bouts of increased pain and decreased ability to hold his own for weeks at a time, life would have gone on without major worries. Money in the teapot brought her closer to that newspaper. And she almost believed everything would turn out all right.

TWENTY

Tend and Befriend

1868

Abigail hated missing her annual trip to San Francisco in November to review spring fashions. She wired money to Shirley, who made the purchases, and Abigail paid her a commission for her work. Shirley used the money for legal fees, she told Abigail, still seeking more time with her daughter. Shirley told her one of her attorneys, Eloi Vasquez, had taken an interest in her case—and her. *"He's of Spanish descent with cocoa skin and dark eyes and I think I'm falling in love,"* Shirley had written. *"Perhaps that verse about all things coming together for good was speaking to me all the time."*

"Maybe that's so for me too," Abigail had written back.

Travel stimulated Abigail's thinking. She was challenged by dealing with new people, had no fear of disagreeing with those who saw the world differently. Their perspectives gave her ideas for her novel. She liked seeing how another state intervened in the suffrage fight. But alas, mothering kept her close to home, working in the millinery and being a seamstress. She didn't see much stimulation in that work.

Then a mother brought her fifteen-year-old daughter in for a fitting of a dress. The girl had a waist the size of an embroidery hoop, with skin as white as a baby's first tooth. *Listless* was the word Abigail used to describe her as she pinned the dress the mother had sewed. The woman hadn't been satisfied with her own efforts and so had hired Abigail to make alterations. The child's corset trussed her already ample breasts and tiny middle into an abnormally curvy shape.

"Do you like the way the dress fits you?" Abigail asked the girl, who had shrugged her shoulders.

"What does it matter if she likes it or not," the mother said. "Fix the gap between her small midriff and her bodice. The dress needs to make her look . . . inviting."

"What is she inviting?" Abigail loosened the pins and let out the material so the bodice wasn't pushing upward in such a stark fashion.

"She's of marriage age. What else?"

"Yes, she is. But many girls are waiting." Abigail kept her voice light, as though she gossiped about the latest news rather than promoting an obvious contrast to the mother's view. "Girls are going to school and finding interests, in addition to traditional roles." She fussed at the sleeves but returned to loosening the waistline. *We have to do something about the corset.* "Some of the latest fashions from San Francisco—where I've been going on buying trips—are designed to have a little fuller waistline. Just as we are all free from the war, our bodies are seeking freedoms too. Our corsets might be squeezing the life from us women. There'd be less fainting or need for smelling salts if we could take deeper breaths." She smiled, engaging the mother while she let out the dress seams.

"She does faint often. I assumed it was her weak nature—which makes her less appealing to the opposite sex, of course, and means I must do everything I can to affect that."

"Let's loosen those stays, shall we?" Abigail raised the girl's arms and did the deed before the mother could protest. "Doesn't that feel better?"

"Yes, ma'am, it does." The girl's eyes sparkled. She inhaled and let a long breath escape. *She's relieved.*

"After she's done her religious duty and married and had children, she can think about taking deeper breaths."

"The frock will fit better if it's looser," Abigail said. "And give her room to eat a bit more. Robust is invitational too." *Healthy is the finest aphrodisiac of all.* "My own Clara Belle has found less corset and more carrots give her energy, and she can sing better too."

"Really?" It was the first time the mother seemed intrigued by Abigail's words.

"Are you a singer?" Abigail asked the girl.

"She's a lead in the church choir. The young music director has shown an interest in her voice."

"You see? Let her natural talent loose and who knows what joys the Lord might bring into her life."

The mother harrumphed but gave Abigail the go-ahead to loosen the whalebone stays a bit more. The dress fit much better and made the girl look less like a wicker mannequin and more like a young woman.

"You're a fine seamstress," Abigail told the mother. "This was an easy fix. We have to pay more attention to our God-created forms and not let fashion force us into . . . unintended shapes. I'll finish this up and you can return for a final fitting next week. Will that work?"

"I hope we haven't ruined her invitational design," her mother said.

"Ah, enticements come in many forms. Natural being the best of all."

The girl smiled and her cheeks held color for the first time since she'd arrived.

That day Abigail realized she could affect a girl's future right at home. The satisfaction surprised her. Perhaps those words in the intimacy of a fitting room were part of a "still hunt." She'd make sure Clara Belle knew that her own corset fittings had influenced another young girl's future. Sway could happen any place where one paid attention, one conversion at a time.

* * *

"We have to have a specific plan for the newspaper," Abigail decided.

The entire family sat around the table. Ben ground coffee beans as Abigail urged how they might all get involved in starting a newspaper. Clara's musical talents were advanced enough that she began giving music lessons for actual pay rather than trading for beef or pork. The boys could contribute to the Duniway finances by shooting sparrows to sell to the local butcher—the ones the Duniways didn't eat themselves. Ben, back working with the horses, taking only small doses of laudanum that kept the pain from spiking, also helped.

Abigail speculated on a piece of property near the dock after a day she'd taken a brisk walk and saw the potential there. The property wasn't yet for sale but should have been. She located the owner, made an offer, and it was the Duniways'—who sold it two weeks later at double the price when a steamship operator decided it was the perfect site for his expansion. *Just as I thought.* She'd figured that out before he had.

Ben had put his name to the purchase and the sale as required. But he resisted her suggestion that they speculate on Portland property. "It'll never be as big a place as Albany," he'd said.

But off and on he bought land that she told him would be good investments in towns throughout the state. She put a portion each week of millinery income into the teapot for her newspaper.

She used old *Argus* issues to cut out dress patterns she'd seen in *Godey's Lady's Book.* She could spy a dress photograph and remake the design. She hadn't thought of it as unusual, but her sisters all brought ads to her to reproduce the patterns. She did that while she spoke with Ben. "Harvey's buying Portland property and selling like we did here in Albany. At a profit." She considered asking Harvey to make a purchase or two for her, but he'd never agree to such a thing without Ben's approval. "We'll rue the day we let land on Front Street slip by us. I could be a very rich woman if not for hesitation of the male sex."

When she wasn't working in the millinery, making patterns, dusting the plate rail in the parlor, directing the children and breaking up skirmishes between the boys, and potty training her toddler, she was imagining plot lines. If she could sell more novels, she could add to the money in the teapot and they would one day have that newspaper. *Judith Reid* consumed her days. She wrote the novel as though she were Judith, a woman who had loved an artist who disappeared. Judith, the lead character, is then taken to Oregon from Missouri, where her mother dies. Judith must care for her siblings and is forced to work in her father's sawmill. She makes the audacious decision to defy her father, resist the "invitation" of a reckless man whom her father chose for her to marry, and returns to Missouri where she rediscovers her long-lost artist, and both live happily ever after. She read her book out loud to Ben.

"I always like a happy ending," he said. "But why do the men always have to be such scoundrels. And is the first love always the best? I mean, it was for me with you, but I wonder if it was for you with me?"

He pulled his starched collar from his neck and put it in the box on the dresser top. They'd returned from church, lunched, and had the afternoon for a quiet time and so she'd read to him.

"It's not about you, Ben, or me. It's fiction. Listen to what *Putnam's Weekly* says about the novel." She picked up the popular magazine. "'Novels are one of the features of our age. We know not what we would do without them. . . . Do you wish to instruct, to convince, to please? Write a novel! Have you a system of religion or politics or manners or social life to inculcate? Write a novel!' See, a story is the perfect way to convince women of what's possible.

Readers expect to be entertained, but there has to be tension and struggle as there is in life. They wouldn't read it if it didn't have something the characters are trying to accomplish and the reader given to wonder if they'll ever achieve it."

"The women always come out smelling like roses though."

"It's the only place where we can be assured of roses. Real life promises us thorns."

"Not always." He looked at Clyde turning pages in a book as he sat on the horsehair-covered chair.

"True. But enough encounters to leave us bleeding. I write so women know there are other ways of living, especially if we stand firm and don't marry the first man who asks us. Or don't assume an early marriage is a requirement of womanhood. Just see where I'd be if I'd fallen into Mr. Bunter's trap."

"Your timing was excellent, Mrs. Duniway," Ben teased.

Except when it comes to having babies. Clyde really must be our last. "Well, you had a big part in when we got married, as did my father's poor decision."

"But everything worked out." Ben kissed her neck. "Didn't it?"

"Yes, it has. But there's so much more to do, Ben."

"There always is, with you."

* * *

"I'll have to sell," Kate said.

"Probably let the help go?"

"We shouldn't have had so many children so close together."

"What's done is done, Catherine. Regrets will weigh you down. Let's think of the options you have."

There'd been an accident, an explosion on board the steamship, and Captain John was dead. It wasn't fair. So much of life wasn't. Abigail helped her sister through the funeral and the reading of the will several weeks later. Kate received the house, a small savings that would last the year perhaps, and the steamship company gave her one month of John's salary. Nothing else.

Kate's youngest slept on her breast. She stroked the child's forehead with the back of her finger. "I've been so spoiled. We could have saved the money we paid for help. I should have done my own laundry."

"Stop. Think of what you can do." Abigail put on her pragmatic hat.

Kate sighed. Even in grief, she looked coiffed and held together, her shoulders straight, not hunched over in sadness. "I guess I could teach. I know what they paid the male teacher last year, and he left for greener pastures. With that salary, I could maintain the house, maybe have enough for a nanny."

"Let's see if Sarah Maria might like to live here instead of with Fanny. She could help with the children."

"She would be of assistance. But Fanny needs her too." She sighed. "John was only thirty-eight years old. We had our whole life ahead of us." She brushed tears from her cheeks.

Abigail patted her sister's hand. "It's the way it is now. Tragedy happens. I'm not dismissing the hole in your heart." She didn't want to think of what her life would be without Ben in it. "John would want you to go on, to make the best of it. Why don't you talk to the school board? That's a good idea. You're certified and would make a fabulous teacher for Canemah's sprouts."

"It's one of the few respectable things a widow can do. Or remarry. Your old suitor has been by."

"Bunter? Oh, that man! You're not that desperate. We'll help as we can. Harvey will too, if we ask. Please don't, you know, marry just for safety. Because in the end, there is no guarantee. We women have to protect ourselves."

"I have you all," Kate said.

"Now, what will you wear to your interview? And who is on your local board? We'll see if we can politic them."

Kate smiled. "Discreetly, of course."

"That's my sister. We'll get you through."

It was what they *had* to do a week later when Kate learned she had the job, but it would pay half the salary of the man who had left.

"Outrageous," Abigail said. "I'm going to write a letter to the editor about such unfairness."

"Can they do that?" Sarah Maria, the youngest Scott sister, had come to live with and help Kate out.

"They said it was the law."

"That doesn't surprise me. But they make the school board laws, or at least they can fudge them," Abigail said. "They could change it if they wanted to. I'll go talk with them."

"No. Don't. Please. It's a good job, one I can do. And I can sew in the evenings. Maybe Harvey needs someone at the *Oregonian* to copyedit. I'm good with details."

"Yes, you are. And a better writer than he is, if I might say so." *Better than me.* "I can use another to crochet reticules. They're popular now. At least you won't have to marry someone you don't wish to."

"Yes. Bunter has been by again. He seems to like Scott girls." They both turned to Sarah Maria.

"Don't let that man near you," Abigail said.

"I won't."

"Good. We will tend and befriend each other. That's what women can do."

Abigail's newspaper would have to wait. Family needs came first.

TWENTY-ONE

Building the Ladder

1869

In late February, in the last year of the decade, Abigail learned she was pregnant again. "Oh, Ben. I . . ."

"It's the Lord's doing," Ben said.

"No, it isn't. It's our doing." She sighed. "Six children? How will we manage? I don't mean to demean, but the matched teams—you haven't sold one all last year and you're getting older too, like me. You can't do that heavy haying or picking apples at our old place forever."

"We'll do fine."

"I've got to find something else I can do to bring in money."

"Abigail . . . what you have to do is take care of yourself now."

"At least I'll be carrying through the summer when there are fresh fruits and vegetables. Let's see if we can get more chickens. We can sell the eggs."

"We might have to dip into the teapot." He said it quietly.

"No. That's the newspaper money. We'll think of something else."

"Or God will," Ben said. "You underestimate him."

"God put us here so we'd take care of his earth and make good decisions. Tripling or quadrupling ourselves, I'm not sure that's wise at all."

"'Be fruitful, and multiply,'" Ben said, his voice a tease.

"That would be the Scripture you'd quote."

"We men memorize certain ones." He took her in his arms. "It'll be fine, Abigail."

"It isn't always, Ben. Maggie died. John died. You were injured. Bad things do happen."

"And people overcome them. My worst worry is over your health. You've got to take fewer buying trips, let Shirley do that for you."

"I still have to pay her. Oh, Ben, I'm worried. If business falls off, what'll we do?"

"Don't wear future worries. Dress for today." He patted her back, and she let herself sink into his chest if only for a moment. "I have confidence. Something will come our way. It always has."

"Yes, but what has come has often been more misery than amusement."

* * *

Abigail wrote an essay on equal pay for women and asked Harvey to publish it. He declined, he said, because it wasn't up to the *Oregonian* standards. She fumed as she told Ben. "He said it was 'florid with female emotion' and needed better punctuation. 'Florid with female emotion,'" she sputtered. "How would he know about female emotion? That's called 'passion for a subject.' Yes, I could use a little polish with my paragraphs and exclamation points, but he's an editor, for goodness' sake. Why didn't he edit it? No, he didn't like the conclusion, and my arguments were strong. He knew if he published it, I'd change minds. One day I'll publish it in my own newspaper. And I'll write articles promoting women having the right to vote. See what Harvey says about that."

She'd forgotten in the three years since Clyde's pregnancy that the condition increased her anxiety, and she spent days in bed where she worried over fluctuations in the fashion industry and the costs of changes to her business and how they'd survive taking care of six children. Women now wanted bustles instead of crinolines. Dresses took scads more materials, and women liked the brighter synthetic dyes over those of plants. Silks and satins weighed more than linen or cotton, and women's corsets had to be reinforced to deal with the extra load. Loops of materials called panniers swooped as overskirts, emphasizing smaller waists by the many layers of fabric. Abigail lay awake at night obsessing over purchases. At least men's fashions kept to the grey, brown, and black shades, with changes in tie length the only real upgrade. Women's fashions changed so quickly that by the time she got the dresses back for fittings, the design had to be altered too. She'd sewed Sarah Maria's wedding dress, the color of cream frosting. Her sister had married a lawman. *I'll have to temper my villains now.* Sarah Kelty was the epitome of innocence and an advertisement for the latest fashion.

For Abigail, the wedding was a nostalgic time. All the Scott girls now married off to men they either loved when they began or, like Fanny, learned to love. They all thought of Maggie, wishing she could have been there. Pregnancy made Abigail teary. She'd forgotten about that too.

Since she wasn't traveling, Abigail and two other Albany women started the first suffrage association in the state in Albany. "We'll tend and befriend more women to join us," she'd declared, and her cohorts had agreed, talking with a neighbor while sweeping a back porch or sharing conversations while helping a friend peg laundry to the line. Abigail took more time with her clients, who told her stories of their trials, of a woman's "teapot" money set aside for her daughter's Easter coat, only to have her husband take it to buy himself a racehorse. Not long after that, Abigail learned that woman had died in childbirth, and the editor of the *Democrat* paper wrote condolences to the husband for being "left with the obligations of a family."

"He has a racehorse to comfort him," Abigail told Ben as she read aloud the editorial.

She wrote a letter to the local editor about 172 New Jersey women having voted for the presidency with ballots in a separate box. Of course their preferences hadn't been added to the totals, but just the idea of women making their mark like that, imagining a female with head held high, acting like the citizen she was, offered Abigail hope. Wyoming had scheduled a vote in December to grant women's suffrage. Still, the Fourteenth Amendment recently ratified had once again claimed a "citizen" and "vote" had to be male.

She put her essay rejected by Harvey in a drawer, intending one day to rewrite it. She'd ask Kate to review it before she delivered it to Harvey again. Right then, she had another kind of delivery to worry over.

* * *

The pain frightened her. It was different, more like with Willis's wretched birth when Ben had gotten lost in the fog and hadn't found the doctor. And it shouldn't have been happening yet. With the first splintering contractions, she told Ben to seek the doctor. Now. And he had. Her labor went on for hours, maybe days. She lost track of time, felt herself in and out of consciousness at times, fatigued beyond anything she'd ever experienced. Kate was there. Clara Belle's sixteen-year-old frightened eyes leaned over her with a cool rag to soothe her forehead.

Then finally—Ralph Roelofson was born. November 7, a month before he was due. Abigail was exhausted and bleeding and still in excruciating pain when they placed him on her breast while the midwife assisted in cutting the umbilical cord. But Abigail was grateful Ralph came early and was smaller than her other babies, because if he'd been full term and larger, both he and Abigail might well have died.

This child surely had to be her last. The bleeding stopped, but something was still very wrong, and she wrote to Shirley to ask if progressive San Francisco doctors might have new devices to assist women with "prolapsed uteruses" and could she find that out? "*There must be something,*" she said. "*I can't afford to be even a semi-invalid and yet that's what my body is advising me to do. The pain when I walk is almost unbearable and I leak. Ben says horses suffer from this too. Imagine. All those years before, I wrote of some women being treated as workhorses by their fathers and husbands and now, I find we can have similar ailments.*"

She used Ben's cane for a time. And purchased the intimate articles that kept parts of her body in place. And she and Ben had the conversation that meant their physical relationship would need to change.

"We won't have a loveless marriage," she said. "It's never been so." They lay beside each other, she on her back and Ben on his side with his arm across her abdomen, resting on the patchwork quilt she'd tucked around her like a mummy. Ralph was asleep in his cradle beside their bed. It was early morning and the dawn seeped through the window to ease across the tin-pressed ceiling.

"I've mostly wanted the affection of your attention," Ben said. He was tearful, but he'd suffered with the delivery of Ralph, had made bargains with God, he'd told her, that if she survived, how he would never put her through such a pregnancy again. That she came to speak of it first was the way it was with them, her pragmatism preceding both his disappointment and his understanding before he could speak of either. They'd come to terms on how to proceed.

It was a new phase in the Duniway days, another adaptation they'd have to make. That too was the way of marriage and, Ben reminded her, of life.

"Just don't say 'it'll all work out.'"

"I won't," Ben said. "But it will."

* * *

"Would you look at this." Ben snapped the *Oregonian* and pointed to a short entry on the front page. "'Editor Harvey Scott has resigned his post of this fine newspaper to assume the position of Collector of Customs in Portland. This distinguished federal appointment could not be bestowed upon another with as exceptional credentials as our Harvey Scott. We regret to see him depart but wish him well.' There's an opening, Abigail."

"Phooey. Pittock wouldn't let a woman through the door to assume such a position."

"I wonder why Harvey gave up such a post."

"Collector of Customs is a lucrative job, carrying prestige and a salary no woman could ever hope to achieve. I bet he wrote that announcement himself." Harvey would have more money to invest in his Portland properties, in addition to gaining commercial connections from around the world. She guessed their friend Senator Baker had made that happen for him. "Still, it might be worth the uproar to see how the new editor would cover my effort to apply." Abigail grinned at her husband. "And my rejection as a qualified candidate—except for my gender." *I could write about it.*

"You'd make it a story, all right." Ben put the paper down, drank his coffee.

She should apply. What could it hurt? But she didn't need the disappointment. *Why torture myself?*

"I'm having a pretty good morning. I think I'll ride out to the farm and work the team of pintos I started. Poor things need everyday adventures that I don't seem to be able to give. Maybe Harvey could get me on at the customs house."

"We'd have to live in Portland."

"I was only jesting." He backpedaled. "Our business is here. The millinery. Our boarding the working girls. The school. We're established in Albany."

"And I'm meeting with the Marthas this afternoon. Yes, Albany is home now." One Martha was a neighbor and the other a music teacher from Portland. "I've been talking with them about a newspaper. The *Revolution*, the paper Susan B. and Elizabeth Stanton operate, has increased its subscribers, I've heard. We need that Northwest newspaper." There'd been activity back east with a National Woman Suffrage Association formed and then an American Woman Suffrage Association, the former with a desire for a constitutional amendment to get women the vote, and the latter dedicated to suffrage for all, regardless of gender or race. The groups had righteous arguments covered by the *Revolution*, but campaigns for people in the Northwest would be different. Women here, as in Wyoming, worked beside their men more often than in the industrialized East. They struggled on farms and small businesses so men could see the competence of their wives and daughters, and many, like Ben, were sympathetic to women achieving more rights. They didn't like the strident "Hurrah" features of some of the promoters carrying banners, going in to men's clubs only to be asked to leave. Abigail had to watch her step in that regard. She didn't want that kind of bad publicity.

Could I become the editor of the Oregonian*?* No. Converting that newspaper would not be possible. It had a New England snobbishness that Harvey fit right into and advanced. Moneymen, some Democrats who wanted nothing to do with the new Republican party of Lincoln or the progressive ideas toward rights for men of color and for women. Any newspaper that didn't carry the Pittock party line would face fierce competition. But she was up to it.

Abigail's "Marthas" were not.

"It's too large of an undertaking, Abigail." The fledgling Albany association brought reality to her dreams. "We're neophytes in this."

Abigail patted baby Ralph, resting on her shoulder.

"Starting up will take hundreds of dollars. Printing presses. A place to rent. Subscribing agents, how will we pay them? And the work itself of writing and typesetting and getting the papers on the streets."

"I have children." Abigail put Ralph into his cradle. She poured tea for her friends and colleagues. "I can employ them for some of the work. As for capital to begin, I might approach Jacob Mayer for a loan. Or perhaps sell the millinery."

"But that's it. You have too many activities already. And there's your health."

"Let's see what the new year brings." Abigail tapped her hand against her cane in a nervous gesture. "We'll get through the holidays, which are always lucrative for the millinery. Meanwhile let's find new recruits. There is strength in numbers. It's a chicken-and-egg question: does the newspaper get us more recruits, or do more recruits help support the paper and broaden our cause?"

"There has to be a way," she told Ben that evening. How she would have loved to be in the position Harvey was in—able to leave behind a career she envied, step into social settings she could only hope to look at through windows of the finest hotels. Why, he'd even been given a ticket on the maiden voyage of the steamship *Oriflamme* between Portland and San Francisco. She only imagined the grandeur. If she ever booked passage on the ship, she'd be sleeping in steerage. If only she'd been given an education, she too could climb the rungs of that ladder out of the depths of a ship to the captain's table and the successful men and women who dined there. She would have to build her own ladder, find the lumber for it, and climb up. She imagined she'd be doing it herself, but Ben might have other options. He was a builder at heart.

TWENTY-TWO

The California Connection

1870

It would be my humble pleasure to serve as a delegate to the California suffrage association meeting in San Francisco in December on behalf of the Salem Equal Suffrage Association. I will be in the city for my millinery business and will, with humility and shared purpose, represent both your fine organization and the State Equal Suffrage Association of Albany in this cause that calls us all.

Sincerely yours,
Mrs. A S Duniway

Abigail finished her letter and paused, only half hoping the Salem group would allow her to add their weight to her presence at the California convention that serendipitously coincided with her buying trip. If they appointed her, they might even allow a small grant of expenses. They were a bigger chapter in the cause than Albany. She financed most of the Albany group she'd helped start, feeling ever guilty for spending family money. But then she'd advise herself that she had worked hard in the past year since Ralph's birth to get herself back on healthy feet.

She sent the letter and prepared her millinery order, always leaving herself open to discovering new items. In a previous visit she'd picked up hosiery and false hair additions, sorted through jewelry pieces, and even added a few toys she thought might sell, especially at Christmastime. And she looked forward to seeing Shirley.

"I wish you didn't have to go this time of year." Ben was having a down day, as they'd come to call the episodes of increased pain, back spasms, and debilitation from the laudanum. "The stage from Albany to Portland is unpredictable in the rainy season and neither does much for your aches." Clara Belle played the piano while Ben rested on the daybed they still kept in the parlor.

"The weather is hard on my bones if I'm at home too, and at least this way I have a little time to myself." She hung the boarders' dresses. They had three living in the attic.

"Yes, there's that. You do enjoy your time to yourself."

"And see here." She held up the mail she'd picked up on her way back from the classroom. "Here's a reply from my request to be a delegate for the Salem crowd. And look what they granted me. Not only a delegate status but a pass on the rail line from Albany to Portland and a steamship ticket to San Francisco. I won't have to take the stage. I'll be rolling in luxury. I've never been on a train."

"You should take me with you, Momma." Clara Belle stopped her playing. "Then you wouldn't be alone at Christmas."

"Oh, that would be fun, but this time I can save good money by riding on Salem's ticket. I'll bring you back something special. And what would Annie do if you weren't here for the holiday?" Maggie's daughter still lived with them.

Clara Belle returned to the piano in silence.

"What's that you're playing? 'Toll the Bell Mournfully'?"

"No. It's one I've composed. 'Bring Me Home Oh Distant Ship.' I wrote it for you."

"It's lovely."

Her seventeen-year-old daughter twisted so she could smile at her mother, and Abigail's heart clutched. She was such a help and so kind and unassuming, generous. Abigail often overlooked Clara Belle, who was especially good with her cousin and with Clyde and Ralph as he tottered around the furniture, just learning to walk. The boys brought attention to themselves, but Clara Belle was content to serve in the shadows. Maybe she should take her along to California. But the cost . . . no. She'd pay more attention to her. "You must play that at our next meeting, would you do that?"

"I would."

Abigail vowed that in her effort to help all women rise to their potential, she not neglect the feminine presence beneath her own roof. It would be something to remind the California mothers too. The married women and mothers working in the cause bore an extra burden to make sure their own daughters weren't set aside for the larger effort. Advocacy had its price, even with occasional privileges.

* * *

The trip couldn't have gone better. She spent Christmas Day at the home of an abolitionist and her husband and met Sarah Wallis, who had been named president of the 1870 conference. She was famous in her own right, having been a part of the Stephens-Townsend-Murphy company of 1844, the first to bring wagons into California through the Sierra Nevada. Sarah was a woman who landed on her feet, as Abigail thought of her perseverance and rise. She'd been abandoned by her husband a few years after reaching California, following a harrowing winter of near starvation. Then she married a second time, only to discover that *that* husband was a bigamist from whom she got legal custody of their son, extracted a settlement for her pain that she used to start a boardinghouse and speculate in land. She later married a judge who became a state senator, and together they supported women's suffrage and were working to allow women to be admitted to the bar. At the reception for the delegates the night before, Abigail garnered up her courage to introduce herself to Mrs. Wallis.

"I've heard so many—I mean much about your—I mean about you, Mrs. Wallis." Abigail found herself stumbling over her words upon meeting the famous woman.

"And I you. I've admired reading some of your letters to the editor."

"In our little agricultural papers? You read them?"

"They're often reprinted in Emily Stevens's *Pioneer.*"

"I wasn't aware."

"You've such a way with words, Mrs. Duniway."

"Please. Call me Abigail."

"And I'm Sarah. I didn't learn to read until my journey west in 1844 and '45 as an already married woman. Educating girls is a top priority of my efforts, along with the vote, of course."

"There are so many threads to our freedom cloak," Abigail said. "Education, ratifying amendments granting Negro men the vote, temperance without prohibition—at least that's my position. I don't wish a sip of wine, but I decry anyone's right to tell me I can't have it. And I so hope we don't bring prohibition into the suffrage cause, because men will never grant us the vote if they think we'll take away their liquor."

"California is pushing the vote by showing what kind of community goodness we can bring, beautifying cities, operating immigrant shelters for women and families, representing the arts. It's wonderful to have you able to join us. Perhaps we can meet later. I'd love to hear about what's happening in Oregon."

"That'll be a quiet conversation," Abigail said. "We Oregonians favor the still hunt, pressing prominent legislative men to bring the vote to the people, without flamboyance or efforts that might suggest we'd neglect our duties as wives and mothers."

"There's always that pressure, isn't there? Your husband is encouraging, obviously, or you wouldn't be here."

"He is." She hesitated, then, "Do you get support from the national organizations?"

"We do, but we raise most of our own funds for our activities and to publicize our efforts."

Abigail nodded. *I shouldn't advance our work at our family's expense, even though Ben approves.* "I hope to learn things from being a delegate."

The women exchanged addresses and circulated to other parts of the gathering. Abigail loved meeting these men and women. There were eastern representatives and advocates of legal reforms and women who edited regional newspapers; and there were working women, eastern-trained female physicians, one of whom advised Abigail not to let her ailments hold her back. "Our best hope of avoiding invalidism is to declare ourselves engaged in the wider world. It's a much better elixir for health than laudanum or even rest. You're fortunate you're young, Mrs. Duniway. You have much life ahead of you, now that your child-bearing years are behind you."

It surprised Abigail that she was willing to express her personal concerns to women she had only met. It was as though she'd known them her whole life, like they were sisters she didn't know she had. They were as open to her as her sisters—perhaps more. She made copious notes of other speakers and her own observations of the bustling city and formed them as articles she would submit to the *Oregonian*, not that she had any assurance they'd be printed unless she paid for it. Harvey held no sway there now with his customhouse work. News was happening here, and those righteous editors needed to cover it. There were no journalists assigned to this event. But she was here, and she'd have stories for a dozen letters to the editor. And a feature article or two—on the famous Mrs. Wallis or the editor of the *Chicago Legal News*, who'd been refused entry to the Illinois bar despite her stellar reputation as a legal journalist. Oh, yes, she had stories to tell.

This network of women mattered never more so than when Mrs. Wallis surprised her a day after Christmas with an invitation. "Will you grace us with a rhetorical presentation on New Year's Eve?"

"Speak? The way Susan B. Anthony does? Oh, I'm not sure—that wouldn't be wise." Public speaking was still considered risqué and unladylike. "Poor Susan B. Anthony had tomatoes thrown at her. I've never spoken about women's issues in public. Or any issue, really." A lecture at her schoolhouse to parents hardly counted. Abigail had addressed Fourth of July schoolhouse rallies, introducing the children before their presentations, but she had never orated to a crowd, on a subject that mattered to her deeply, from her heart. "I . . . I'm not sure my husband would approve."

"You're here over the holidays. He must trust your judgment greatly. It's safe here, Mrs. Duniway. You won't be risking your reputation among this body. We women have voices God gave us. We mustn't shy away from using them."

She's right.

Now, on New Year's Eve of 1870, Abigail's heart fluttered behind the curtains at the hotel stage. She twisted her mother's earrings. *Am I honoring her? Would Ben approve?* There was no time to send a telegram to ask. *There is time. I don't want him to say no.* Her fingers shook as she held the velvet drape and peeked out to see several hundred women and some supportive men in the audience, their feet shuffling on the polished floor, the wooden chairs creaking as they settled beneath the hum of chatter. A chandelier cast streams of speckled light over them. She'd spent the two previous evenings writing out what she wished to say but knew she did not want to be tied to reading her words, given the poor lighting.

"Are you nervous?" Shirley asked.

"Yes." She twisted her earrings again.

"Didn't you orate to your younger siblings when you were a child?"

"And to the mules and cows when they'd listen, those big eyes looking up at me while they chewed their cuds." She smiled. "Speaking is different from writing or even twisting a man's arm about a subject one-on-one." By instinct, she knew she had to be fully present at the moment to give a speech and not somehow translate words from paper to tongue. She needed to see what was happening in front of her, whether people were getting restless or whether someone had dozed off. At least she imagined she needed to see those things—and more—to make what she was saying relevant to her immediate audience. To move people, she had to give herself wholeheartedly to where she was on the stage, reaching out to the minds and hearts of those before her and not to the script on the podium with a fern set before it.

"I'll say a prayer for you," Shirley said.

The offer brought a surprising calm.

She heard her introduction, then stepped out onstage. In seconds, she would see in front of her whether she had moved people or lost them. She took a sip of water and a deep breath. Then using the voice that got the attention of her sons and their friends when they rattled through the house with swords and saunter, she began.

She was humble. Thankful to those who had invited her. She told stories. She made her audience laugh, and she brought them to tears with her own vulnerability that she saw as demonstrating strength to those before her. She spoke things she hadn't written at all, quoted Scripture she wove into the struggle of women's lives. And she appealed to them as western pioneers, people who had come from somewhere else, had chosen to live with the uncertainty of a journey with promise but without the assurance of success. She invoked Sarah's story of survival more than her own that endeared her to her California audience, most of whom were pioneers themselves, having come across a challenging landscape or survived a ship's crossing. They had lived on a frontier, made do, innovated, worked side by side with men, and come together in community to help a neighbor regardless of their race or religious or political beliefs. People applauded mid-speech, feeding her spirit. Abigail reminded them of their own pioneering moments.

And then she spoke of the American revolution. "That is the basis on which we press for women's rights. We work toward the nation's ideals rather than on what the nation might gain from women achieving the vote. It is to advance the cause of democracy, of freedom. This great nation did not intend to leave women out." Thunderous applause followed that line, as it did with her closing when she charged the audience to go forth and do great things. "Ours is a cause worth doing regardless of how long it takes or how it turns out."

She perspired as she sat down, the heavy curls wet against her neck, and at first didn't see Sarah Wallis urging her to stand back up, for the audience had done just that. The applause was music, almost as beautiful as Clara Belle's composition. By speaking, Abigail knew she'd tapped into something inside her that she had not known was waiting to escape.

* * *

Gave public lecture. Newspapers praise. Stop. Offered salary and speaking tour of California. Stop. $800. Stop. Must extend time away. Stop. Seek your blessing. Abigail.

It was happening so fast. She'd been asked to be the Portland editor of the *Pioneer*, to go on a lecture tour of California, perhaps beyond, to inspire. *Ben has to approve!* She'd sent the telegram. Surely the money would make him say yes.

Ben's return telegram was swift and short.

Come Home Immediately. Your presence required.

"What could it be?" Shirley helped Abigail toss her clothes into her trunk, made sure the invoices for her purchases were in order and ready to ship.

"I have no idea. I've a housekeeper and manager for the store while I'm gone. Surely, he would have said if one of the children was ill, wouldn't you think?"

"It would seem so."

"I hate to see that eight-hundred-dollar salary disappear down the latrine." Abigail supposed they would have another speaker they could send, but what a joy it would have been! She couldn't think about that now. She boarded the weekly steamer to Portland and, on the way, wrote an announcement for the *Oregonian* she hoped they'd publish.

Arriving in Albany, she rushed home to find out what the crisis was. Ben wasn't there. He was at the farm with his pintos.

"Everything fine, Mrs. D. You worry things no good?" Chen seemed confused by her opening question of what was wrong.

"The children? They're all right?"

"All good. Like all time, good."

She picked Ralph up, hugged him, kissed his fingers sticky from a summer jam he'd poked into. Clara Belle put her arms around her. "You're home, Momma. I missed you. We all missed you."

"Is everything all right at the millinery?"

"Yes, fine. Why do you ask?"

Her sons came in stomping their rubber boots of the rain. "Pa's at the farm. Did he know you were coming in on the steamer today?" Willis asked.

She felt like she'd been riding in a hot air balloon and someone had turned off the fire, bringing it crashing to the ground.

* * *

Abagail telegrammed her brief article to the Portland *Oregonian*, adding a final sentence she hadn't written while on board ship.

> Mrs. A. S. Duniway of Albany arrived in this city yesterday morning to ascertain what interest can be raised here in behalf of the removal of the *Pioneer* newspaper from San Francisco to that city.

She hesitated before writing the next announcement, but she'd already made the decision weeks ago. Ben could read it in the paper as well as the next person.

In anticipation of success, she will remove shortly to this city. We have little doubt that she will find encouragement enough, unless she entrusts the canvassing business to some blockhead of a man. When women go for their own rights, they generally get them.

She considered the reference to some "blockhead of a man." *I should leave that out.* But she didn't.

* * *

"I thought you should come home," Ben said when she challenged him after supper. "The children need you. I need you. You were gone over a month."

"But it was eight hundred dollars, Ben. We could have used that money."

"We're doing fine."

"No, we aren't. We live hand to mouth, week to week. That money would have given us a breather, and we could have made gains on the newspaper fund."

"But no breather for you. You'd have worn yourself to a frazzle traveling around California on a stage. Not to mention your lecturing, in public. Who knows what sort of danger you'd be in."

"It was not your call to make, Ben Duniway."

"I guess you could have ignored me."

She glared at him. "And risk the public humiliation of your telling people not of my wonderful welcome in California but of a wife who defies her husband's orders?"

"That was your choice." He cleared his throat. "Did you bring back something special for Clara Belle? She's hopeful."

"Did you expect me to forget?" *I almost did.* "A silk scarf and a summer bonnet, so when she wears it in June, she'll know I was thinking of her in the off season as well as at Christmas, that I have her interests at heart even when she's not in front of me." She felt defensive and irritated and angry about the limitations life placed on women and Ben's restriction on hers. She took in a deep breath. "I'm back. At least the California *Pioneer* thinks I might make a go of expanding their paper to Portland. I'll never have one of my own." She lifted her carpetbag to the bed.

"Not that it's worthy of publication," Ben said, "but I thought you might want to know that I saw your brother Harvey this week."

"My wealthy, lucky, highly educated brother? Where did you run into him?" She had her back to Ben, had opened the wooden handles on her paisley bag, pulled out soiled clothes she'd need to launder. At least she had Ben's machine to make it easier.

"At the customhouse in Portland. Where I asked for a job. And got it."

Abigail twirled to face him. "You took a job? In Portland? But how—"

"How else will I get you to consider staying closer to home? I decided to follow up on my instincts of some time ago, about working in Portland and giving us a steady income so you could get the paper going. I know it's what you want. And I want to support you in it. And in life, Jenny." His face turned a shade of pink over his sparse beard. "It'll pay thirteen hundred a year."

"Oh my goodness, Ben." She sat down, the dirty laundry in her hands. "That's . . . but you'll have to give up the horse training, the thing you love? And will your back pain allow you? And we'll have to move to Portland."

"Yes, but I can work a few animals on the weekends if I'm up to it. And yes, Harvey knows I might have some difficulties, but he's prepared for that. We'll find a place to live close to where I'll work. You probably already have a house picked out, if I know you. A 'wish' house with room for a printing press." He chuckled as she nodded. "I couldn't let you take a position that would take you traveling around California when you'll be needed here to set up your own new venture. Our new venture. Duniway Publishing Company."

"Oh, Ben." It wasn't the name of the newspaper she'd had in mind. But no matter. She stood and he held her, kissed her, and she felt the warmth of his tender hands at the back of her head. He was making a huge sacrifice for her . . . for them. She had to make this paper a success. She had to use it to advance the cause of suffrage. "It'll be a wonderful thing for women, move us closer to getting the vote, I just know it. And we'll do it together, won't we?"

"Like a matched team of circus horses."

"It'll be a circus all right."

"I'll let you have the lead."

"And I'll take it. A newspaper—well, I'll be learning something new every day. But I want to call the paper the *New Northwest* because that's what we'll be advancing, the Duniway Publishing Company will be advancing it."

"Name the paper what you like," Ben said. "I signed the incorporation papers. Your task is to find us a place to live and to sell the businesses here to raise the rest of the capital we'll need. I had to get you to come home to do all that. And I wanted it to be a surprise."

"You are the surprising man," she said.

His arms squeezed her a little tighter. "You're taking me along on the ride of our lives, I suspect." His throat caught, and when she stepped back to look into his eyes, she saw tears in them. "But we're doing it together. It's all I ever wanted."

What is that little verse someone had written in Willis's schoolbook?

> The things nearby, not the things afar
> Not what we seem but what we are
> These are the things that make or break
> that give the heart its joy or ache.

She was entering a new era. She'd bring Ben along if he would come. *How unkind of me, after all he's done.* She and Ben together were beginning something special. It had been his support in the first place that told her that getting women the vote was the only thing that would change women's lives for the better. She'd remind him of that. The newspaper would be the vehicle. They'd still be a matched team if she had anything to say about it. *And I usually do.*

PART 3

Hope is an orientation of spirit, an orientation of the heart. It's the ability to begin something not just because it has a chance to succeed but because it's a good thing to do. . . . It's not the certainty that something will turn out well but the certainty that something is worth doing regardless of how it turns out.

Vaclav Havel, Disturbing the Peace

TWENTY-THREE

Getting Ducks in Order

1871

She loved the smell of the ink that prickled the nose hairs and its viscosity, the consistency of Johnny cake batter. Willis spread the ink across the wooden tubes, preparing the presses. Abigail admired the tiny type raised in the wood that eleven-year-old Hubert's little fingers set into the box where the ink would highlight and transfer to the paper. He was an excellent speller and didn't seem fazed by the typeface being backward so it would print correctly on the stock. She loved the feel of the paper—she used good quality so people would be willing to pay money in expectation of getting something worthy that was easy to read. Even the crispness of the paper cuts, it all appealed to her. The rumble of the presses, rattling the chandelier on the first floor while the presses rolled the newspaper out on the second.

She'd rented a house on First and Washington with room for the family downstairs (along with a millinery that Clara would manage). She'd hired a foreman to help them learn the printing business, borrowed $3000 from Jacob Mayer to be paid back over time. He didn't charge her interest and she never sent him a bill for his ads.

On May 5, 1871, Abigail and Ben together turned the handle for the first edition. Like magic, the words appeared on paper, her words, the first newspaper a sort of memoir of how "we" had come to write a paper, how "we" began scribbling while as a farmer's wife, and about the business failures (she wrote that her novel had been a failure) and the successes (teaching, boarding, and dressmaking—and hopefully, newspapering). She editorialized that it was women's lack of political and consequent "pecuniary and moral responsibility" that resulted in the public being opposed to "strong-minded women," as she had once been herself. But now, she saw—and hoped her readers would see—that society kept "half the population overtaxed and underpaid, struggling, while another group of women acted frivolous, were idle and expensive." Both conditions, she contended, were "wrong," and the goal of the paper was "to elevate women, that thereby herself and son and brother man may be benefited and the world made better, purer, and happier, is the aim of this publication."

It was a lofty goal, she knew that. And they'd risked all they had and went into debt for this cause. But it was what her heart had told her, what that beam of light had illuminated about her life's mission being not only to be a good wife and mother but to advance women's God-given gifts and talents in addition to household roles. Abigail had managed so far to keep her dignity and the love of her family while being willing to be mocked and chastised for stepping out. If she could do it, she hoped other women and men would see how each would benefit by the advancing of women. Or at least not standing in a woman's way.

She watched Clara Belle speaking to a customer purchasing a reticule at the millinery. Such a gorgeous daughter, so charming and without a vitriolic bone in her body. How had Abigail raised such a gentle soul when she was such a torrent? *It's Ben's influence.* Thank goodness for Ben.

"When you've finished, come join us," Abigail told her daughter. "The first press run is finished, and I want you to be there when we lift them up and get them on the streets. I've had six months of selling subscriptions ahead of time, and today they'll be delivered." Even southern Oregon would be getting papers, as Bethenia Owens, her millinery friend from Roseburg, had been promoting the paper, readying people for this grand adventure.

"Coming, Momma." Clara Belle locked the outside millinery door to join the family upstairs.

They had to wait until the ink dried. Meanwhile, using turpentine to remove stains from their fingers, the boys gathered up the pages, Ben spoke a prayer over the venture, and Abigail felt tears form in her eyes as she watched her family head out their Portland door to sell the *New Northwest* on the street. Even nine-year-old Wilkie could charm a dime from a grumpy man looking for someone to blame for his bad day. He held the hand of his older brother to cross the street and join the business of the Duniway Publishing Company.

Abigail found invigoration in this newspapering thing, and yes, she told herself, in the assurance of Ben's steady income that surprisingly took strain from her days. It was all in the family sphere, not unlike farming had been, but with less physical pain. Ben's sacrifice and job had made the difference in her constant chasing away the demons of foreclosure and debtor's prison. Ben had been right. Something always did come along in the end . . . she just had to trust that if she was on the right path, doing what needed to be done, they'd be all right. How ironic that it was Harvey who turned out to be a part of that answer to a prayer.

* * *

A Journal for the People
Devoted to the Interests of Humanity
Independent in Politics and Religion
Alive to all Live Issues and Thoroughly

Radical in Opposing and Exposing the
Wrongs of the Masses.

Abigail capitalized every other word, used language like "Live Issues." Kate had said it was a bit flamboyant, but it was also her style. It was the masthead, at least for now, reminding people of what the *New Northwest* was about. She showed it to Ben. "I want people to see it as a different kind of newspaper, because it is. I sent Susan B. Anthony a copy and she's pleased. And Ben, I boldly asked her to come west to do a speaking tour." They'd been in production for three months.

"Abigail—"

"Now, I would only arrange the performances, introduce her, collect the donations, et cetera. We'll split the income after expenses. I wouldn't be speaking beyond that." When Ben had called her back from California, she had assumed it was to speak of his new job, but she hadn't actually asked if he would have approved her speaking. *Maybe I don't want to know.* "I'd try to book us at the Oregon State Fair. We could all camp out together. That's very suitable. Families back east are camping all the time. The fashion industry has even introduced clothing that keeps women proper, of course, but a little freer to hike and take in the sunshine."

"You two women are not going to camp out across Oregon."

"No, no. I just meant at the fair. We'll stay in respectable hotels or at the homes of like-minded women on the tour. Think of the good copy such an adventure would offer my readers and encourage women starved for entertainment in the rural areas. I think she's quite a remarkable woman. I can pluck her thoughts about newspapering as we ride in the stage or walk a few miles."

Ben sighed. "I've come this far. I guess it's not much farther to have both a newspapering wife and a public-speaking one. I'll be busy at the customhouse, so you'll have to tend the home fires. I like a good campout now and then." He stretched his back, winced. "Besides, working inside a building all day long, I'll need some nights out in a tent for my sanity."

"At least you aren't suggesting that I'm the one challenging your sanity."

"I was being diplomatic." Ben grinned. "Something I need to be in the customhouse."

"One of us should be," Abigail said, and kissed him. "Lord knows I'm a lost cause when it comes to that. Perhaps our travel from here to Victoria, British Columbia, and east to Idaho will give me lessons in discretion."

Ben smiled. "We can hope."

* * *

"Hubert, put that straw over there, against that tent side. Ben, do we have the carpet ready to roll out? Oh, isn't this grand!" Abigail fluttered about the tent at the Oregon State Fair. It was October, one of the most glorious months in the Willamette Valley, with harvested fields golden next to maples and oaks flashing their reds and greens, flirting with pure blue skies. The evenings were cool, the days hot but dry.

The family—most of it, along with sister Sarah Maria and her husband and of course the guest of honor, Susan B. Anthony—would spend the week at the fair. It was the end of the grand tour the women had made to Washington, Idaho, British Columbia, and throughout Oregon. Aunt Susan, as Abigail referred to her, had been a warrior in the wilds. For the first half of the tour, Clara Belle joined them to sing and, if a piano was present, to play music as people gathered. Then Abigail gave the introduction, which amounted to a speech of her own. She couldn't help herself. She loved the audience responses to her presentations, often saying, "I never imagined when I first declaimed to my father's grazing mules that, one day, I'd be asked to speak to legislators, which Miss Anthony and I did last week." Then she'd add: "Not such a very different audience, regardless of whether those mules in the pasture were looking toward me or away." There'd be a pause and then the crowd would laugh. Jokes at legislators' expense seemed to go over well with the masses, Abigail decided.

At the fair, they'd be competing with men hawking games that gents could play to earn trinkets for their mates. Musicians and ventriloquists along with banjo-playing farmers would perform on an outdoor stage next to them. People would wander by, heading to the tent restaurant that the Aurora Colony men and women operated, to the delight of the Duniways and others who could purchase food right on site and not have to pack for a week.

Best of all, the Duniway family enjoyed the company of the famous suffragist.

Susan B. Anthony was a tall woman, slender, who had deliberate movements, including settling down onto the straw bed in the fair-tent like a stork slowly clucking over her eggs. Abigail, on the other hand, would just plop, which she did, wincing as she sat next to her famous friend. "Clara Belle, dear, are you going to sing for us as the opening tonight? We should have a big crowd."

"Yes, Momma. In fact, I think I'll find a quiet place to practice. It is getting stuffy in here."

Abigail hesitated. "Be careful out there. There are scoundrels."

"I'll come with you. See if I can find James." Sarah Maria's husband was a law officer on duty looking for pickpockets and inebriates. "He can protect two damsels if we get in distress."

"Sing your way out into the world, now." Ben started up—a routine he'd taught his children from the time they were little. Ben sang and Maria grabbed Clara Belle's hand and pulled her toward the opening, voices brimming with good cheer. The younger boys were all that were left of the children, and Ben said he'd take them to the restaurant if the women needed some privacy to prepare for their presentation that evening.

"Won't you remember this western trip for the rest of your life?" Abigail nudged Aunt Susan. Abigail poked her with her elbow as the girls left.

"It's my first and I suspect my last camping experience. We're stuffed in here like herrings."

"I know. Isn't it cozy? No need to shout to express thoughts or share a story."

"I confess, I prefer your Chemeketa House and the Oregon Supreme Court as audiences, though you Duniways I suspect are better to sleep with."

Abigail laughed with her. She'd grown quite fond of the eastern suffragist and her ability to adapt to the primitive conditions she'd been exposed to. They'd been heckled out of hotels with their ideas. They'd been asked to leave a home where they'd been invited when the woman's husband chastised his wife in front of them for failing to seek approval before extending the invitation. Out they went. Churches were often closed to them—pool halls and saloons, open, mostly to mock any presentations they made outside them. But in Pendleton, in a light rain, they had hesitated.

"Ben will be dismayed if it's reported that we spoke inside a saloon," Abigail said.

"No one ever made any gains without ruffling a few feathers."

"I know, but being married—"

"It's why I never did. I have enough to manage myself without the additional weight of family."

"They aren't exactly a burden. Do I make it sound that way? It's that I have to consider them in what I do, Ben especially. I never want to lose his support."

"From what I see, that wouldn't be possible. He adores you."

"Yes. He does." *But he might have his limits.* "Let's not speak in the saloon. Let's make our presentation outside it. We might gain more votes one day that way than forcing ourselves into the bar. And women on the streets can hear us. Our umbrellas and our ideas will give us something to share with our audience."

They collected money for their expenses and sometimes shared the take with those who needed it, leaving them barely able to cover their meals and hotel lodging when they couldn't secure a bed from a sympathetic suffragist in Olympia, Washington, or in a tiny frontier town like Umatilla, Oregon. In every village, Abigail sold subscriptions to her *New Northwest*, and at every rest stop, sharing beds with children or with Aunt Susan, Abigail wrote, telegramming her reports from the field for the paper to Kate, whom she'd contracted to do the layout. Sometimes they were in an actual field when she prepared her articles. She also wrote chapters for a long poem she serialized and created a rhythm for corresponding while on the road, her arthritic fingers scribbling away well into the night. She was writing with a purpose, covering their trip and experiences and advancing a cause.

She'd feel depleted by a short and interrupted night's sleep, exhausted by the stage or wagon box that took them to the next town, frustrated by changes in where they'd be allowed to speak once they arrived, at times a little frightened by the vitriol spewed by both men and women who were threatened by what they stood for: change.

But once they stood onstage, Abigail would feel something coming to her from the crowd. Her spine would tingle as she stood before a mass of mostly women who hungered for the hope Abigail and Aunt Susan's presence inspired.

Abigail was counting on this evening of the fair being a grand finale to the tour. She'd had posters printed and the boys handed them out. She hoped they'd get a couple of hundred people to attend that evening. She wanted the tour to do Oregon proud for her eastern friend. Of all the Northwest states, she hoped Oregon women would be the first to vote, and she saw this canvasing in the Northwest and her newspaper as in service to that goal. This event at the fair was to be the crown on their royal trip.

* * *

"How many do you think were there, Ben?" Abigail shook the quilts, then placed them back over straw to freshen the beds. It had been a long but satisfying evening.

"Over a thousand, easily."

"We sold a lot of subscriptions to the paper," Willis said. At fourteen, he towered over his mother and stood nearly head to head with Ben.

"Imagine having a thousand people hear about the importance of freedom and the vote for women." Abigail placed a shawl around Susan Anthony's bony shoulders as the night had chilled. Musicians played in the background, and one could still hear the murmuring of fairgoers chattering as they made their way toward the exits. "Could you ever have imagined a crowd like this when I was writing my 'Farmer's Wife' letters?"

Ben nodded. "I knew you were destined for bigger things the day I met you."

"Your invitation to speak to the Oregon legislature as the first woman to do so may take the cause further than our presentation this evening," Susan said. "That's quite an accomplishment. And you quadrupled the influence by being able to write about it in your paper."

"Five hundred subscribers and climbing. My Clara and Willis and even Hubert are quite the newsboys. News-people." She ruffled eleven-year-old Hubert's curls. "Who can refuse that smile."

"Your paper probably has a wider audience, but flesh and blood coming out to hear, that word of mouth will bring you more readers than smiling sons, good hawkers that they are," Susan said.

"The anti-suffrage crowd was out too." Clara heated up tea on their little camp stove. "But I think they only had forty or so attend. I slipped in the back just to check. You and Aunt Susan are the novelty." Her sister Sarah Maria had started a suffrage group in Forest Grove where James was the sheriff and Kate taught school. And the sisters also acted as agents for subscriptions or ad sales, working from Albany or Forest Grove or wherever they lived. Even relatives back in Illinois had been conscripted to read the *New Northwest* and find new subscribers.

"Women of many persuasions are being allowed to speak in

public," Susan said. "And that is an advancement as well. We cannot push the rights of some women. We must work for all, even those who resist our efforts to improve their lives."

"That is a paradox, isn't it? To have women not want more freedoms?" Sarah Maria shook her head.

"They think they'll be taken care of by their husbands and fathers, and many will. But they'll never know what they might have been able to accomplish if they had the opportunity."

"One can be both a good wife and a promoter of a worthy cause," Abigail said. "Somehow, in our writings we must make the case for issues other than the vote. It's a means to an end, not the end itself, that's the story that matters."

"Well spoken, Abigail. If we can advocate for improved property rights, for legal protections for women, the journey to those reforms will be the underpinnings of the suffrage fight and perhaps keep our organizations from tromping in the mud over issues like temperance and prohibition." Susan sounded like she was still on the platform. She stopped herself, then added, "I think you may be right, my friend, about not having our eastern groups come into Oregon with a campaign. The Northwest is unique. You can promote that singularity in your newspaper and your 'still hunt' attitude. We have to employ a number of methods to reach our goal. And we have a huge roadblock before us." She cleared her throat and this time did pontificate as though on a stage. "The Supreme Court just wrote this: 'The paramount destiny and mission of women are to fulfill the noble and benign offices of wife and mother. This is the law of the Creator.'"

"So if we operate outside that, we are defying God's laws?" Even Sarah Maria sounded aghast.

"So the court has ruled."

Abigail thought of the verse in Jeremiah about God having plans for everyone's life. Shouldn't a woman discover what her own destiny and mission were in order to be in step with Scripture, even if that meant stepping outside of her home?

"We can challenge that in the newspaper, mine and yours."

Susan blinked several times. "Did I not tell you? I had to close *Revolution*. My newspaper has, as they say in the West, 'bit the dust.'"

"I didn't know."

"It was one of the reasons I undertook the tour, to make a little money to dissolve my debt."

A bitter taste of reality made Abigail swallow. She was entering in to risk larger than what Ben had put them in by signing the notes those years before. He had done it to help a friend. *If I'm doing it for something greater than myself, will that guarantee that all will turn out well?* She didn't say those words out loud. Instead she said, "And still you gave more than half your share of the gate in Olympia for the victims of the Chicago fire."

"'Give, and it shall be given unto you,' as Scripture says." Susan sighed. "It hasn't failed me yet. Look here what luxury has come my way since I gave away my take: friends to share tea and shelter with and a straw bed on which to lay my head."

Abigail exchanged a glance with Ben, wondering if he might be thinking what she was. If the famous Susan B. Anthony couldn't succeed with a newspaper with the large subscription base in the populous East, a newspaper that captured the action of the political capital of the country, with renewals easy to come by, however would her little paper make it in the West, where horses and cattle far outmatched readers living in sparsely settled areas. To move forward, she'd have to believe that something was worth doing no matter how it turned out.

TWENTY-FOUR

Shaping

1876

Purposefulness: Abigail hadn't realized how important having a goal was in keeping one balanced and able to pick back up after challenges and change. The first half of the seventies whizzed by, with Abigail helping found the Oregon State Women's Suffrage Association and hiring Kate full time to be the editor of her paper so she could travel, interview, investigate, and write and send back news. She missed the buying trips to see Shirley Ellis in San Francisco, but Clara Belle traveled alone for purchasing stock and also managed the millinery. Abigail sometimes took the youngest boys with her to remind everyone that she was a "strong-minded mother" and not just a "risk-taking, outspoken businesswoman," as some detractors wrote.

In 1876 she set out to visit New York City and be in Philadelphia for Centennial Day, where the national suffrage association had numerous plans to present women voter proclamations to the president. She'd said her goodbyes to her children and boarded a stage heading east. The venture cost money, yes, but she'd have ample copy for several issues of *NNW* (as she often abbreviated her newspaper now), and she was touring and speaking in Idaho, Utah, Iowa, and her home state of Illinois on the way.

"I'm hesitant to have you up on stages so far away," Ben told her as he carried her carpetbag to the carriage.

"You know there'll be like-minded men with their wives and sisters at the meeting houses. I'll be fine." She kissed him discreetly as he helped lift her up and gently settled her on the leather seat. He handed her the cane she used, a piece of bone for the head he'd attached to it, smooth in her hand. "I'll imagine you on the sideline."

"I'll be praying for you anyway."

"I know."

Public speaking invigorated, and she'd managed to convince Ben that such an activity was necessary in these times to both extend the cause of women's rights and to increase subscriptions and gain renewals. "Those poor women out there selling the paper see my speaking as both a stimulation and reward for their efforts. I can't let them down."

Her first event in Idaho challenged her position. Mid introduction to her speech, she felt a thump on her chest scarf and then another on her jaw. Audience shouts interrupted, and she realized she'd been egged by angry women who felt she was overstepping her domestic bounds.

Shouts and "Calm down" and "Shame" from both sides of the aisle rose up. She lifted her hands as though giving a benediction and said, "Let them speak. Then I will." She heard the hecklers out, then said, "My commitment as wife and mother are not strained or impaired by my presentations here. I'm the mother of six, remember, and have a daughter who has waited to marry if she ever does, choosing instead to give music lessons and to operate a millinery. I've not hurt my family one iota."

Several men began to escort the egg throwers out, but Abigail urged them to wait. She wiped her chin and neck of the scum, hoping not to ruin the hand-crocheted edging on the handkerchief she used. Clara Belle had done the fine needlework. "My husband approves and supports my efforts, for he sees that women and girls are kept in bondage by the laws preventing them from voting, from helping them define their own destinies—as well as how domestic duties can prevent men and women from moving forward. He has always helped with laundry, for example, inventing a washing machine any number of men here might purchase for their wives and mothers."

"Here! Here!" she heard a man shout out. Several applauded.

"But more, his willingness to let me be the woman I feel God created me to be is one of the greatest acts of love anyone can show another. I am first and foremost—as are each of you—a created being. 'Do not hide your light under a basket' speaks to each of us. Mister Duniway has been the reflector of that light for me, illuminating the path I believe has been chosen for me, and that having the right to vote will only make that light brighter. For each of us. Now, let me tell you about why I'm heading to Philadelphia," she said. The egg-ers sat down and the women selling papers had a bonus night after the loud applause following her speech.

She loved the countryside of Idaho and kept pictures in her mind of its scissor-sharpened mountain peaks, the artist's palette of colors as fall approached, the sounds of raging streams that cut through deep canyons. She'd regale Ben with the pictures of the Pahsimeroi River when she returned. The landscape would be perfect as the backdrop in a new novel she had brewing in her head.

As she moved east, though, flooding spread through the country. Trains she'd planned to pick up were delayed. She rode in stagecoaches around flooded tracks and had been gone four months already when she finally reached New York City where she hugged Aunt Susan B.

"Your book, it's selling well here in the East," Susan told her. *David and Anna Matson*, her long poem, had gotten published, and the reviews continued to be good ones.

"I can learn from my mistakes," she said, still embarrassed by the negative comments that first book had brought her.

"A necessary skill for any successful woman," Susan told her. The women attended the Exposition together, applauded at the Women's Convention where she heard inspiring speeches, and then visited the Women's Pavilion, outside the exposition area, as women's inventions were not deemed worthy to be inside the main center. She picked up a self-heating iron to hold and imagined owning one. Interlocking bricks and a frame for lace curtains fascinated her. An odd traveling typewriter was featured too. She could use one of those. Each had been invented by an enterprising woman.

"These are wonderful. Oh, and there's a dish-washing machine." She would write about it and her adventures, along with her tasting something called Heinz ketchup and drinking Hires Root Beer, but those latter were offerings inside the exposition, as they'd been inspired by men.

Susan B. Anthony was scheduled to present to the vice president a proclamation on women's voting rights, but instead President Hayes was there to receive it. Abigail felt proud to be in the room where women were willing to put forth laws to advance the citizenship of women.

Her telegrams to Kate for the *New Northwest* served as teasers of stories she'd write on her return. So much she wanted to share. But her journey home was interrupted in Illinois with a terrible cough and a weakness she'd never known. For weeks she was tended by relatives and did recuperate, having lost ten pounds before she finally headed back to Oregon in the spring.

When she arrived in Portland at the stage stop—ten months after she'd left—Ben greeted her with open arms. "You will never be gone so long again," he said as he kissed her.

"I agree." *Home.* The Oregon air never felt so fine.

Ben lifted her carpetbag into the family carriage as he shared news about the paper. The boys had done a good job in her absence, and Kate was invaluable as an editor. His own health had been good, mostly, he answered when she asked. "I lost a few days of work in December. I think the cold rains get inside my back bones and twitch there until I lie on the carpet in front of the fireplace and ferret them out."

"I'm sorry I wasn't here to look after you. I've never been so sick as I was in December."

"Clara Belle was a good nurse." He hesitated, but Abigail didn't notice, chattering like a squirrel to him as he drove her back, laughing when she did, shaking his head at all the marvels she'd seen. "I'm glad you're healthy now," he said.

"Oh, I am. I can take on those prohibitionists and anti-suffrage voices with new vigor."

They pulled up to the house. And Ben put his hand on her wrist, urging her to wait. "I've been authorized to prepare you, so you can gear yourself up for the shock—"

"What shock?" She grabbed his arm. "The children, they're all right? You would have telegrammed."

"Everyone is fine. However—" He put out his hands as though to shush her. "Clara Belle is now Mrs. Donald Stearns."

"She's who?"

"The wife of Donald Stearns. They eloped in December."

"And you never told me? Why wouldn't you have told me?"

"There was nothing you could do about it. You'd have tried to come back, and you were ill in Illinois. You said so yourself. Besides, bad news is better handled in the spring than in the rage of winter."

"Aren't you the philosopher." *Don Stearns.* "He's a losing newspaperman, starting that evening rag last year. How could you let this happen, Ben?"

"She's her mother's daughter with a mind of her own, Jenny. As we've raised her. Don's all right. Young. Allowed to make mistakes as we did when we were newlyweds. And you gave them the idea in the first place, musing about starting an evening edition. He decided to do it. And he has a wise partner who knows a little about newspapering, so she can help him."

"This is awful." Abigail had jumped out of the carriage before he could help her and had stomped up the stairs. She turned to him. "Are they in there?"

"All your children await your arrival."

"She got her brothers to defend her. Oh, Clara." She raised her voice to the sky. "Why didn't you wait? You could have gone on the stage with your voice, your musical talent."

"She still can, she'd say to you," Ben said. "She'd say you taught her how to be both a wife and mother and a businesswoman." He opened the door to the cheering of her children.

* * *

"You were gone so long, Momma."

"Working on behalf of women and girls. For you, my daughter."

"And yourself," Don Stearns said. He was tall and skinny as a split rail. *Weak.*

"Oh, dander," Willis said. "You're in for it now, Stearns."

"He's right, Momma." Clara Belle stepped closer to her husband. "You do work for girls and women, but you also do it because you love it. And no one begrudges you that—we don't, even though we miss you terribly. Ten months you've been gone, and we've carried on without you. But we have to do things that move our lives forward too. And then you got ill and I didn't want to worry you."

"But I praised you for not marrying young, for waiting for the right man."

"And I did. Momma. Mother, please, your face is getting all red and you look like you're going to faint. Please—"

Abigail growled, her fury uncontained, her face a dark cloud of rage. She knew it. Could stop it.

Clara Belle sank to the floor.

Don Stearns dropped beside her, held her head in his lap. He glared at Abigail. "See what you've done?"

"It's what *you* did, eloping with my daughter." Abigail shook as she reached for the smelling salts to revive Clara Belle.

"Stop it now," Ben said as he moved Abigail aside. "What's done is done." He and Don Stearns bent over the awakening Clara Belle, who with woozy eyes blinked.

"Am I all right?" she asked.

"Yes, you are," Ben told her. "Stearns, take your wife home. We'll have breakfast in the morning and plan the reception to invite our friends to celebrate. Won't we, Abigail?"

"You two don't live here? You have your own house?"

"They're on their own, Abigail. Let them be."

* * *

"No small feat," Ben said later. "A man who stands up for his wife against a tyrant—"

"I wasn't a tyrant." Abigail plopped on the side of their bed.

"You were. Your daughter fainted, she was so upset."

"I am sorry about that. But holy cow chips, she shocked me. And you could have told me earlier."

"They're happy, Jenny. No man would have been good enough for Clara Belle, from your point of view. They've had four months together to gird themselves before seeing you. It's too late for you to even think about an annulment, and besides, she's twenty-three years old, well able to make her own decisions."

"I hoped she wouldn't marry young like I did."

"Hey," Ben said. "Has it been so bad? Your marrying at eighteen—almost nineteen." His words choked.

I've wounded him. "No, it hasn't." She patted his arm.

"What haven't you done that you might have done if you'd waited to marry or perhaps never married at all?"

"Nothing. And more, likely because you've been there to support me—us."

"And haven't you said the greatest joy of your life are your children? Would you deprive your daughter of that same great joy?"

"You're right. Of course. We'll have a reception for them. I'll announce it in the paper." She unhooked her high-button shoes. "But Stearns is a competitor, Ben."

"Competitors make us better."

"I suppose they do in the end."

"By the way, while you were gone, Harvey returned as the editor of the *Oregonian.* New administration—he lost his customs post. He's bought a controlling interest in that paper, so if you want to focus on a competitor to rail against, choose him and let Don Stearns and Clara Belle make their own way. Return to your purpose—using the *New Northwest* to get women the vote."

"You're absolutely right. We'll win Harvey over and get Oregon to be the first of the Pacific coast states where women can cast their coveted ballot. There's a purpose I can work toward." One didn't have control over much—certainly not one's children—but she could control what mattered and have the courage to act on that.

TWENTY-FIVE

First Hurdle

1877

"I'm riding through quicksand with the temperance issue," Abigail told Kate as she hovered over her latest article. "I don't want to raise the ire of Portland's liquor interests who will pour money against suffrage if they think women will vote in prohibition. I support the lack of drink, but no one should advise anyone else what decisions they should make about their personal lives. I won't touch wine, but I decry anyone who will tell me that I can't. If I can only get that across."

"You do better when your articles explore those issues indirectly," Kate said. "The story when you visited the asylum or that trip with Clyde, seeing things through the eyes of a ten-year-old, people can find themselves in that kind of piece. You're pursuing something worthwhile and can still be a good mother and wife and friend to those in need. And you give legitimacy to widows trying new things, like me. Even single women who otherwise would be forced to be nannies for their nieces and nephews. Some of them can now be inventors."

"But those stories don't really advance the cause of voting. I'll keep writing about quilting bees and barn raisings, but something is missing. I've had the paper for more than five years, and we're no closer to even getting the legislature to bring up the issue."

"You had a nice response when you told of Willis leaving the nest and heading to San Francisco to make his own career as a printer elsewhere."

"I suppose all families undergo changes. I hate to see ours experiencing it this way."

Her chicks were leaving the flock and she still hadn't accomplished what she'd wanted, even with their efforts as part of the newspaper. Women still didn't control the ballot. She and two of her suffrage friends had actually attempted to vote in '72, but there'd barely been a mention of it in the *Oregonian*. Harvey gave not the slightest copy to anything that sniffed of suffrage action except to oppose it. "We have to clarify our purpose," she said. "Set a singular goal. That's how we got the paper. Now we have to use that same strategy to get the vote."

* * *

"We'll have to do it ourselves." Abigail spoke to the Portland chapter of the National Woman Suffrage Association. "We must set a specific target, a date by which we will have the legislature refer women's suffrage to the male voters of the state, and my newspaper will tout that until it happens."

A chorus of voices agreed. Abigail was the president, and her vice president added, "It will have to be 1884 for the vote. That requires that we convince both houses of the legislature to agree to refer it first in 1880 and then in 1882."

"Such a cumbersome law, making a change in the constitution go through two consecutive legislative sessions before it can be voted on by men, especially when they only meet every other year." Abigail stated what the women already knew.

"We knock down the first hurdle of 1880 and push until the

next session—1882—and if it passes again, which it must, then in 1884 they will refer it to the voters. That gives us four years to make our push." The vice-chairman drew out the timeline on the blackboard. They were meeting at the neighborhood school, and it smelled of chalk dust and old books.

"They don't make it easy," someone said.

"It's the challenge that will inspire us," Abigail said. "Now let's start breaking this down. How much do we want National involved? I say very little, but I'm open to hearing your ideas."

She was open to it, but she'd already decided: they would do this the Oregon way, without visits by national suffragists—though it would be helpful if National sent them a little cash for flyers and posters and paid for ads in the *Oregonian.* Harvey might not support suffrage, but he likely wouldn't turn down ad revenue. He wouldn't run them for free as a public service the way the *New Northwest* would.

"But we might engage younger women if we had more national involvement," another member said.

"No. They don't understand us here in the West."

Another member offered, "But I've been in the East, and they'd be willing to let us do it our way. I've spoken— "

"No." Abigail said. "They'll want something for it. We have to do it the Oregon way. Now, let's move on. How will we sustain public events to educate women and their voting men?"

Abigail was aware of the silence and that she'd cut off conversation. But they didn't realize what she did. She'd given her life for this cause, and she wasn't ready to let younger, ill-informed women threaten the campaign. The real work was in the legislature, meeting with men while in session, showing them how it might be to their advantage to have women able to vote, and National could not do that. Yes, a few legislators had been impressed when Susan B. Anthony and Abigail had met with them during their tour, but Susan B. was an oddity to the men then. Now, they were wary of women talking about voting. Abigail didn't believe that women would be somehow better voters than men, more moral or noble. Rather, she thought that the domestic lives of men and women would be better if women were seen as equal citizens and could contribute fully their talents to society at large. *I should treat my suffrage sisters as more equal by listening to them more. But we haven't time. We must persist. Without National.*

The conversation went back and forth about the role of "outsiders," with Abigail standing firm. Eventually Kate pointed out that Oregon men might resent Eastern women having a say in their activities, flashing their VOTE FOR WOMEN banners in their faces. Oregon would do it one by one. Quietly, like the moon rising, something inevitable, though at times it might seem to disappear. They would be steady, if not noisy.

"Then it's decided, at last," Abigail said. "We begin our still hunt meeting with legislators, let those eastern Hurrah women go their way—away from here. Those of you with contacts, let's make a list. And don't forget neighboring states. If one of them decides on the franchise, that'll influence Oregon men. They'll not want to be left behind. We help our sisters to the south, north, and east."

"And they'll see that good men in the West understand that women deserve the vote," another chapter member said.

"Take your husbands with you when you go to visit legislators," Abigail said. "Or fathers, to show them men support us."

"Or brothers," another woman said. "Abigail and Kate, yours is the biggest effort. To try to get Mr. *Oregonian* himself to endorse us."

"That's been a lifelong campaign, to no avail."

"Yet," Kate said.

All the Scott girls were in favor of suffrage. Making it a family affair would be the most important "still hunt" the Scott girls could pursue.

"We sisters will do our part with Harvey. If the *Oregonian* supported it statewide, that could make all the difference. Meanwhile, the *New Northwest* will begin a fresh campaign. My book is finished and published and well received, this time." Scattered applause followed. She cleared her throat. "And the newspaper debt is but one hundred six dollars." *Am I bragging? Yes.* "We can show that women are successful. And we must report back after any legislator meeting to assure ourselves that we know all of the objections and make plans to address them."

"We're aware of the argument," someone said, "that voting will bring disrepute onto women who don't belong in the dirtiness of politics. Women are to be protected from such things." She counted on her fingers. "I've heard my women friends say the same thing."

"But we do fine in the dirtiness of cleaning horse stalls," someone said, and the women laughed.

"There are other points of opposition out there. We need to address each of them. But we also need to make a list of what pushes this idea forward. Those are two different strategies," Abigail warned. "We have to manage both what pushes us forward and what holds us back."

"Do you think we can win Harvey over?" Kate asked as they walked back to the Duniway home.

"It's worth the effort. He did give Ben his job and didn't change his mind after he realized we'd be able to start the paper because of it. Of course, he wasn't at the *Oregonian* then. He may feel differently now. He also bought a steamship ticket for me when I went to San Francisco that time. Maybe he didn't realize I'd be attending the suffrage events."

"That has to be our campaign then. Both a still hunt for legislators and a family hunt for Harvey."

* * *

"You've earned a level of prominence so legislators are listening, that's certain," Ben agreed. "I'm not sure they've even noticed the formation of the Women's Christian Temperance Union."

"Oh, they've noticed." Abigail had come from a suffrage meeting where reports were worrisome about how the temperance ladies were wildly—in Abigail's opinion—entering the saloons with their umbrellas, sometimes smashing glasses and shouting at the men imbibing there, "hurrahing" their philosophy. They wanted the suffrage movement to come on board their wild ride against liquor. It saddened Abigail that even Susan B. felt the groups should join up, but doing so in the West meant women's votes would be doomed.

"Joining could affect the German vote," Ben agreed. "They like their beer, and the brewers have both financial and political influence. Republican influence. With Harvey's paper too. We won't want them against our suffrage."

She'd been more concerned about temperance supporters swilling with prohibitionists, an alliance that would put those seeking the vote in opposite camps. She'd listened to too many speeches opposing women's suffrage that began and ended with "if women get the vote, they'll bring in prohibition and men will never have another legal drop of liquor available in the streets of Portland." That was hard to imagine with a saloon on every corner. But she'd have to separate temperance and prohibition and suffrage in people's minds. That was another task of a newspaper editor—to bring clarity to busy people and help reformers see how their efforts might be received differently than intended.

Confederate-leaning newspapers had been curtailed by Oregon's Republican legislature that convinced the postal service not to distribute "abusive and treasonous" papers. They considered those who reported with sympathy to the South and with antipathy to reconstruction efforts, like getting Negroes the right to vote, as "abusive." No one wanted the *New Northwest* to somehow end up as an illegal paper. But the tabloids would change their names or hand-distribute until discovered and be put out of business again, only to start up under another banner. That was politics and she was on the right side of it. Now. The *New Northwest* had subscribers as far north as British Columbia and as far east as New

Hampshire. She'd made readers into "agents" who were free to sell subscriptions for a small commission. That expansive coverage was a feather in Abigail's newly felted hat. The *New Northwest* was still pretty small, though, which for now kept her from being the target of the *Oregonian.* And opened the door for her campaign.

* * *

Abigail had taken the steamship to San Francisco to confer with California suffragists and to spend time with Shirley Ellis. She never wanted to be too far from the daily demands on women while she worked in the loftier climes of legislative action. Shirley's struggle over child custody was yet another avenue of what drove Abigail toward more freedom for women. Her friend in San Francisco had remarried but kept her first husband's name so it would be the same as her daughter's.

"Has marrying Eloi made your time with your daughter more difficult to negotiate?" The women walked arm in arm down the main street of San Francisco, past dry good stores and shops with dresses modeled by women standing in the window still as stone.

"I'm hoping not. I told the judge that when she's with me now, she'll have two parents to look after her, while being with her father, she only has one. Eloi suggested it as an argument. His being a lawyer helps. Truth is, I was looking for a reason to marry him beyond loving him." Shirley blushed.

"You're entitled to happiness. We women have a way of discounting that. Yet even our Lord said he came to give us an abundant life. All beings, not just men."

They spoke of the Club Women campaigns in California to push for women's rights and the growing threat of dissension between factions of temperance and prohibitionists and suffragists. It was the same in Oregon. "We've done some direct things, like putting ads on streetcars and held a few rallies, but mostly we're pushing what good things women can do for communities. We're trying to downplay temperance issues."

Back in Portland, Abigail told Shirley, the temperance bug showed up in congregations led by "boy preachers," she called them, who sent "singers and prayers" around wherever Abigail was trying to speak about her view of temperance. She felt compelled to argue on behalf of people's rights to make their own choices about alcohol consumption or any personal decisions. Besides, she couldn't imagine how the sheriffs would enforce prohibition. She wished that Portland's religious community could see how her work was Christlike. Even her father, stern as he was, served also as a Cumberland Presbyterian elder, and he approved women's suffrage. But in Portland, only one pastor—Thomas Eliot—had welcomed the Duniways when they'd arrived. That reverend agreed with Abigail that prayer and works went hand in hand. The man's congregation worked on behalf of poor children and animals, forming a humane society. He also saw the arts—music, literature, paintings—as important to spiritual growth, spurring intellectual thought. Best of all, he supported a woman's right to vote, affirming his intelligence, according to Abigail.

"Once I stood up in the temperance meeting to speak and the reverends ordered my ejection. They knew what I was going to say, and the little choir group stood up to sing me into silence."

"Oh, Abigail," Shirley said. "You endure so many insults. I don't know how you do it."

"Kate and Ben say I invite some of those insults because of my 'acerbic tongue,' they call it."

"What did you do when they started to sing you out?"

"Well, I was hit with a thunderbolt of insight, and I shouted, 'Let us pray!' then led a half-hour prayer asking God to enlighten us all, to encourage liberty in his followers, to help us all have an abundant life by knowing him and granting freedom to all God's children, men and women, black or white. Oh, those 'boy preachers,' they were too stunned to know how to shut down the prayer."

"From the tongue of an intemperate woman." Shirley smiled

and shook her head. "I could never be so bold. How is Clara Belle? Does she still sing at the meetings?"

"Sometimes. They have that new baby, and Stearns talks about moving them to the swamps of Washougal."

"You're a grandmother? How wonderful."

"Is it? A sign of my aging. I do like the little tyke, though. But there's little medical help in that Washington burg should she need it. The baby is sickly, it seems to me. And they don't have the income to bring in help. Ben and I gave her one of his washing machines, but it's still hard labor in the laundry."

"Will getting the vote mitigate those hardships, do you think? I sometimes wonder," Shirley said.

"At least it will allow women to help pass laws that let her keep the income she makes from eggs and butter and stitchery instead of having to hand it over to some man—unless, of course, she wants to do that. It's about choices." She sighed. "It has to make a difference, doesn't it? Otherwise, is this effort all for nothing?"

"Don't you get discouraged, Abigail. Or we'll all lose hope. We're working to expand women's opportunities. We all have gifts differing, isn't that what St. Paul wrote to his followers, both men and women, I might add. You do what you can do, push for legal changes, quietly but faithfully gather women to organize."

"And urge my brother to remain quiet in his opposition as he'll never support us. Then we'll have a fighting chance."

TWENTY-SIX

The Moving World

1880

The meetings were endless and not always productive, the smell of tobacco lingering on her jacket for hours after a discussion with a senator or house member. She'd come home, rub lavender on the cloth as it hung on the outside porch to air, reviewing what she'd said, how she'd managed the interview. Sometimes she thought she'd had a legislator's vote, only to learn by the grapevine that he hadn't committed at all. Other times she'd left the offices thick with memorabilia of photographs and family and the man's special interests—horses, dogs, a brewery he stood in front of—thinking she had failed to have him even entertain the idea, when a woman at a meeting would report, "He's seriously considering backing us."

She wondered.

She hated the unpredictable nature of this still hunt, but it carried more hope than the rallies and parades. Somehow eye to eye carried weight. Even Shirley had said that she thought Oregon with its pioneering ways would be the first to get passage.

Abigail found greater satisfaction in writing about the encounters.

Once she told of an exchange not with a legislator but a potential voter that ended with the man saying his wife had long wanted a subscription to the *New Northwest* so she could read it at home, but she "hadn't had the money." He'd crowed that as a generous husband, he'd given the delivered paper to his wife as a gift and wasn't that grand? Abigail agreed it was, adding that "if women had the vote and control over their money, your wife might one day use *her* money to buy you a special gift. Perhaps a ticket to a pugilistic event or even a new pipe."

"You've a point there, missus," the new subscriber had said. "Something to consider."

That's all she could hope for with a new conquest: that the man would consider the possibility that suffrage might have an advantage to him. At the same time, she showed her readers how diplomacy and humor could turn a patronizing man into a subscriber, while highlighting how women were still dependent on men in order to accomplish the simplest of wishes.

It was how she had to manage legislators too. Gently, soothing their egos, always trying to find a way to show the advantage suffrage would be for them. A few listened and agreed because they believed in equality. But the women had to win over those most opposed in order to get sufficient backing. And in 1880, they did. The legislature agreed to refer to the voters the question of giving Oregon women the right to vote. The governor signed it. The first hurdle had been crossed. Now the second legislative session had to agree. "Onward to '82" became the new motto.

* * *

A spatter of rain hit the tin bucket sitting on the front porch. Otherwise Abigail wouldn't have been aware that an April freshet washed the streets of Portland, matting the leaves, turning the day to darkness. Abigail was deep in reading the latest issue of her *New Northwest.*

Kate had brought onto the paper's pages excerpts from Mark Twain and writer Bret Hart; letters from Aunt Susan and local authors too. She'd even recommended a couple of pieces written by Willis. Abigail liked seeing young writers get into print, remembering how difficult it had been for her all those years before. Frances Fuller Victor, a prominent Oregon writer, had her works appear in San Francisco's *Overland Monthly* and now Abigail's *New Northwest.* Abigail's own serialized novels appeared weekly, sometimes written in great haste. She was grateful Kate was there to give them polish, though she didn't like changes beyond improved grammar. No discussion of characterization or plot ever resulted in a pleasant sisterly conversation. Letters to the editor often spoke of the novels and how they had moved readers, reassuring Abigail that words had power to change people. Her words could do that, both with her factual, journalistic pieces and with her fiction.

Her women readers still wanted entertainment and a chance to dream of another life they might have had, one not so burdened with hard labor. Her novels served that purpose. Sometimes, when she wrote late at night with Ben snoring softly, she understood she too dreamed of another life, when a hero would have swept her off her feet—as Ben had—but who also took care of her—as Ben had not always. She put those longings into her characters and gave them courage to take risks, seeking happiness but always "doing good" and finding ways to forgive themselves for mistakes they made. She created hopeful endings, if not always happy ones. That gave her stories realism, she felt, and she resented the preachers who described her novels as both frivolous and spiritually harmful. Her poor readers were described as sinful. There were certainly greater affronts to God they might have railed against, including real men, not fictional ones, abandoning their wives and children.

It was true, she did write of girls who became entangled with men and moralized about the tragedy of girls becoming pregnant without marriage. She could understand how such mistakes could happen—hadn't her family been involved in that through her father's wife? But such shenanigans meant a lack of discipline on the part of the woman and the man. Her novels emphasized how devastating the consequences could be when a girl didn't wait until marriage. She wanted her children to read those stories—especially her sons.

* * *

In between writing, she found herself attending more local meetings, balancing the politics between the Temperance Union's wanting to pass their reforms and Abigail's fear that the liquor industry would block suffrage efforts if the temperance ladies were successful. Abigail had good friends and supporters in the Jewish community led by Jacob Mayer, who had funded her millinery venture. She placed his ads for free, and he supported women's suffrage and said he would work on his associates in the legislature. She wrote articles defending the Chinese and how it was a Chinese man who went into his store to bring out chairs for the comfort of the women when they protested an injustice. She noted that the people she was closest to were considered outsiders, Republicans, but working folks, not moving in the circles of her brother or the wives of investors. She didn't mind being an outcast, but both Ben and Kate pointed out that she ought not to agitate those powers that be.

"How else can we take them on but through the press. We can't *only* be about the vote. Otherwise they don't even see us, and what they do see they dimish."

"It cuts into our subscriptions," Kate said.

"And gives us bad press," Wilkie had agreed.

Not a week later, someone had written in the Albany paper that when she traveled, Abigail drank and entertained men in her hotel rooms. Abigail had defended herself against one Mr. Bunter, while at the same time saying if the original accuser didn't want a slander suit, he might get the editor to retract his accusations or she'd get witnesses to some of the rumors she'd heard about him. "That should show him at last. The man has been a burr under my saddle for decades," she told Kate.

The Duniways thought all had died down, when another report appeared in the *Portland Sunday Welcome*, and Willis—back at the *New Northwest*—and Hubert decided to cane that editor, a level of force that stunned Abigail. *How I have failed them.*

"Words," she told them, tears in her eyes. "Not violence. Not ever."

The boys were arrested for assault and battery, and now letters addressed how the famous suffragist was unable to manage her own children. "See what comes of such activity," wrote Mr. Bunter.

"They're grown men," Abigail defended. "It's a sorry day when a mother's sons have to defend her."

A few of her minister friends came to her defense, and even Harvey wrote an editorial, taking to task any editor who would question the name of a "good and faithful mother." She was as shocked at his support as she'd been with the ferocity of her sons' defense of her.

"I'm not much of a mother if my children disobey or act with cruelty before I could even make a written response."

Ben whittled on a block of wood, nodded at her outrage. He put it up and set the tea kettle on to heat. "At least the jury found the boys innocent and the editor admitted it was a ficticious story."

"Bunter never apologized."

"He never will. He's a lost cause, Jenny. He'll never vote for yours. Let's hope the story winds down."

"You know it won't. It'll be a filler in the *Walla Walla Union.* Or front page of the *Statesman.*" She fumed, then sighed. "Advocating for rights requires a balance between notoriety and publicity." Abigail shook her head. "A couple of the suffrage women have suggested I lower my celebrity for a time." *Could they be right?*

"We could use a little break in the financial drain your cause is taking."

"That's the very fact of things. I could be a millionaire if I'd have invested in land instead of the paper and this important work, but what would I have in the end? I'd have money but at the expense of bettering a woman's life. A man's too, if they'd ever admit it. At least the bill to allow women to have control over their own property and money passed. Tiny gains."

"You're on target to get the '82 legislative vote."

"That we are." She had to find moments of hope in the midst of this powerless swamp of old nemeses who took her to task and sons whose methods of confrontation startled her with their vehemence. She was grateful they wished to defend her good name. What mother wouldn't be. But chastened that they thought aggression would be the proper proportion of response. *Maybe they've learned that from me*? She could get strident and perhaps "caned" with words no differently at times than the actual hickory sticks they'd used.

* * *

The Woman Suffrage Amendment was proposed in the United States Congress, a sure sign of progress nationwide. It added to the hopefulness of the individual meetings Abigail scheduled with legislators, old men sucking on their pipes and cigars. "I'm not sure why they send grown men who are not yet weaned to make laws for women," she told Ben after one visit to the Washington legislature.

"I hope you didn't say that."

"Not to their faces, but it's a good line and I'll find a time to use it."

"Not while you're trying to win them over, Jenny."

"You're right. I'm grumpy. We were making such gains and then Kate's leaving—" Her voice caught and she felt tears come. "What did I do?"

"Nothing." Ben patted her shoulder.

They'd gone to the old farm where Ben had once trained horses and saddled two calm mares. Ben had insisted that she get some sunshine and do something she once loved. She had loved the wind on her face riding a fast horse. There'd be no racing, what with her prolapsed uterus and Ben's back. But side by side with

Ben, the control of the horse by the reins in her hands, the brace of breeze on this April day was invigorating. She needed that now.

Yes, they'd made good advances, first with the passage of a bill to allow women—and men—to vote in all school elections. Abigail had promoted such action in her newspaper and spoke of it at various meetings. If a woman was capable of teaching young men, she ought to be able to vote about what they should be taught. The legislature had agreed. The same year, women were granted freedom to manage their own property, own it without spousal consent.

"I need to rejoice with these new laws, but they add to Harvey's editorials as yet another reason why suffrage *isn't* needed. 'Men are taking care of women, so women need not lower themselves to the legislative floor in order to gain rights.'" She mocked her brother with a fake voice, pontificating as he did at family gatherings. He'd gotten even more pompous with their father's death and his being the head of the Scott clan. He'd also gotten more odious in his objection to the woman's vote. Until their father's death in 1880, Abigail hadn't realized that her father had been a mitigating force on the suffrage issue between his daughters and his one surviving son.

Still, it had been Kate's leaving the *New Northwest* that had hurt her the most. She had always thought it would be Harvey who betrayed her.

"The *Daily Bee* gives her a chance to lead the team. She can write more too. And it helps Don and Clara Belle as well."

"But it's an inferior paper. He gives it away for free, Ben! No wonder those children live hand-to-mouth. How can he make any money giving a paper away?"

"They aren't children. And Kate tells me he prints invitations and posters—for a fee, of course. And he sells ads. People love free things, you know that."

Why did it seem that things could go smoothly on a trail only for a short time but that rugged roads went on forever?

"It's time," Kate had said that morning in February when she told of her taking the new position, leaving Abigail on a boulder-strewn road just when things were looking up with the legislature. "And he offered me more money than you can afford, not that that's the best reason to do anything. You have to make cuts somewhere, and Abigail, you're a fine editor."

She was a *fine* editor, but Kate had given the paper polish and shine, freeing Abigail to travel and lecture. She'd need to do more of that, not less, with the hope to get a bill before the legislature by 1884 and continue to support the Duniway Publishing enterprise, not to mention her efforts to encourage Washington's, California's, and Idaho's voting campaigns.

"But he's a competitor," Abigail said. "And he took my Clara Belle away and now you too." She rolled her lower lip out in a pout.

"You could be pleased that your daughter married into the news business and that your sister, too, will be an editor of another paper that could promote our cause." Kate's curls cascaded down the side of her face, perfectly coiffed, and she pushed them from her cheek.

She has to get up early to have her person look so together. Abigail touched her own hair, tucked in stray strands. She planned to try the new bob look, smooth at the sides, the way Susan B. wore her hair. But Ben loved brushing her long hair for her.

"We're in the same business, Jenny, and yes, competing, but that competition keeps us sharp." Kate's eyes softened, and Abigail saw in them sympathy. And kindness. "I'll be closer to Clara Belle too. And little Earl."

"She brings the baby to work?"

"As her forward-thinking mother did."

Kate picked up her personal things, her special pen and ink set, and her teaching certificate she'd had framed and hung on the wall. "I won't stop working for the vote. You know that."

"You've cut my feathers, though."

"You can blame me for keeping you home a little more." She

sneezed then, and Abigail worried for her health. "Just the dust," Kate had said.

Abigail's horse shook its head and blew through its nose and brought her back to this glorious spring day. She pulled up and turned toward Ben. "I hope she'll carry suffrage articles in the *Bee*, maybe reprint a few of my pieces." She sighed. Was there nothing she could do about this? "The world is moving and women are moving with it. That's what I told her, Ben."

"She'll use that saying as a filler."

"Just so she credits it to her older sister. Let's go back." They turned the horses on the dirt trail. Apple trees had leafed out and promised blooms. "She told me that the *Daily Bee* will be a Republican paper, so I can rest easy that we have another voice in our fight. She said she was glad I'd talked her into leaving teaching to become a newspaper editor, that I'd paid her well and treated her fairly, that we are still working together. But it doesn't feel that way. I probably took her for granted." *Do I take everyone I love for granted?*

"You're still on the same team, Jenny."

"I hope so. I don't need any more editorials complaining about my strident voice. Kate helped temper my tone." She wiped at the tears on her cheek. *Who will do that now?* The world was changing and women with it. She'd have to change too.

TWENTY-SEVEN

Drawing Closer

1882

Abigail had accepted with pleasure the invitation to speak at the Idaho statehood planning convention. It took her to a new landscape. Her stagecoaches rolled across the trails, with canvas window coverings rolled down to hold out at least a portion of the dust. But when they stopped to change horse teams, or she rose in the early morning to catch the dawn, she stood in awe at the vistas. Mountains like purple lace circled the prairies, and she was always imbued with a hopefulness, an inevitability that progress would happen for women, that such a landscape not only promised it but helped shape it. At one stage stop, she met Carrie Strahorn, another writer and wife of a railroad promoter, her husband an author as well. They laughed at the terrible coffee as they looked out across sagebrush dipped in sunrise. They spoke of women's rights. The air was crisp, and they parted as sisters in the cause, each taking a stage in a different direction.

Idaho wasn't so grand as Oregon's panoramas, Abigail didn't think. Oregon could claim the ocean's blue and the mighty Columbia as well, though Idaho had the Snake River and its massive canyons. This might be a place to live after her suffrage work was finished and women had the vote, when children were off and married and she and Ben had a quiet place for him to brush his horses and deliberate in small-town liveries about the merits of the latest leather harness or breeding stock; and for her to write.

She'd imagine that quiet life, but then she'd be in the throes of statehood or suffrage with the mix of men and women and she would see how her words inspired, celebrated the local heroes while singing the praises of Thomas Jefferson and reciting the preamble to the constitution, something she'd required every student to know when she taught school. The words refreshed, and who could deny their call that "all men are created equal"? She merely had to get the legislative men to think loftier, more expansively, that man in this instance meant human. She wrote out her speech for the paper, infused with the goodness of the Idaho landscape and her men and women. But once written down, Abigail never looked at the paper on the podium when she gave her speeches. Instead, she let the words from her heart inspire the efforts of the suffrage men and women. Then she'd be back in Oregon, pushing her still hunt, the landscape in the background—legislative corridors at the front.

* * *

Clara Belle's husband had sold his *Bee*, and Kate, instead of returning to the *New Northwest* as Abigail encouraged, took instead a position editing the *Evening Telegram*.

"It's Pittock's paper. He owns Harvey's press. Why—"

"Abigail, it isn't personal," Kate said. "You're still on a hummingbird's budget in an eagle's flight path. You can't afford me. And Pittock asked me to stay on. He's changed the name. Don will manage and sell subscriptions, but he has other interests. I'll have total editorial control. I rather like that idea."

"What are Stearns's other interests?" She got most of her news about Clara Belle through Kate. She hoped that wouldn't stop.

She wanted to visit Clara Belle, but . . . she still couldn't forgive her, that was the truth. And then there was Abigail's schedule, always pulling at her.

"He's hoping for his land speculation to be productive. The prune orchard."

"In Washougal? He's finally moved them there to the middle of nowhere." She remembered the hardscrabble farm and the terrible loneliness. "We'll be fortunate if Clara Belle and Earl can get through the winter without pneumonia."

Kate sat across a large desk, tidy as always. "Clara Belle seems excited about the move. She is so optimistic, that girl. She loves little things. Her music. Stitching. She always looks so fashionable too. She's an attentive mother."

"So was I."

"It wasn't a criticism, Jenny. Merely an observation."

Abigail stepped over her defensiveness. "What does she know about pioneering in remote places? She has no idea how much work it's going to be in that undeveloped land." Abigail remembered how the little girl had hung on to her skirts in their log home, sometimes standing on her mother's toes, the two pretending to be an elephant thumping around the wide room, bonded together as one. Abigail had made it fun despite her own pain and debilitation, especially after Willis's delivery. Maybe she should have made it harder—as her own childhood had been—to better prepare her daughter for the realities of life. Then Clara Belle might not have married for love but for pragmatics.

"Perhaps she likes the idea of pioneering the way her parents did it." Kate left the desk and sat in the chair next to Abigail. "You advance that spirit in your speeches. We're going to reprint the one you have in the Idaho Territory."

"We can all relate to pioneering. It's a romantic period in people's lives. And it calls up our forefathers, so it brings into their minds and hearts, I hope, the idea of liberty and the inevitability of it, if we pursue the goal. The world keeps moving—"

"And women are moving with it. I know. I'm glad your trip went well."

"And now the road takes us to the legislative session. Cross your fingers."

"I'll do that."

They spoke of Kate's children, talked of her daughter's engagement to a doctor in town, but conversation came back to Clara Belle. "She is helping to support him. I do know that," Kate said.

"And who will she give music lessons to in that swamp?"

"The paper will pay her for some correspondence. The area is growing. They have a new dock, and a farm produce boat leaves at seven in the morning and returns by 2:00 p.m., so Clara and Earl could visit. Or you could go and spend the night."

"Not with that man. No. I'll send my prayers for her. Are they taking her piano? I hope so."

"Try to see her before they move completely."

"I will. Ben will make sure we do."

"He already has. While you were off in Idaho."

"I enjoy that territory. I even thought Ben might like it too. When we get old. We could live in a lodge in the wilderness." She made her voice light.

"It's always good to have a place to think of final settling, but I thought you had left log cabins behind."

"I said a lodge, not a log cabin. I'll want a little luxury in my old age. If I can keep the paper going and get a little money for my speaking. Once we get suffrage, we can sell the paper. Until then, I have much to do until all the West's women have the vote."

"You'll always be a reformer. I just wish for your sake you'd take more time for being a grandmother and a wife. I get wistful sometimes, seeing you leave Ben as you go off. Makes me miss John so much." Kate cleared her throat. "And I'm sad for you that you're passing up moments you'll never have again, experiences I so wish I still could have."

Kate was right, of course. But Abigail couldn't see her way to memorialize the pleasures, let alone permit them to take precedence over the cause that drove her life, even if that cause kept her from enjoying it.

"Give Clara Belle my regards. And tell her I'll come see her. I will."

And she fully intended to do so.

* * *

She was invited to speak to the Oregon senate on behalf of Resolution 2. The associations had been working toward making this happen for ten years. Abigail had been given twenty minutes to speak to SR2, and Ben and Willis sat in the gallery. Abigail hoped her son was proud of her. He was quite an orator himself, and she hoped he'd speak well of whatever she had to say.

The resolution giving Oregon women the vote would have to pass the senate. Then be introduced in the house and passed there. Another resolution, related to prohibition, had also been proposed, and she clearly wanted the two separated so didn't speak to it at all. She spoke to what united men and women with this proposed law, but more, using her most ceremonial speech, she appealed to the men as husbands and fathers, reminding them that the Negro had been given the right this resolution called for now for Oregon's women. "Ought not your mothers and sisters and daughters have the same freedom?" Wasn't this the very end those who died in the Revolutionary War had given their lives for? She used a term, "aristocracy of sex," that had resonated when she'd spoken to the Illinois Legislature.

Abigail had to appeal to these senators, not through the mundane of referring the resolution to the men of Oregon for a vote two years in the future, but to the larger issue of liberty. And she'd loved it that she was introduced by Senator Hirsch, whom she'd known since the days when his partner, Jacob Mayer, had loaned her money for her millinery. And Willis saw it all.

The next day, the women in the gallery watched as the SR2

passed 21–9. Applause broke out but quickly turned to the flashing of white handkerchiefs the way Chautauqua audiences expressed their glee. The women were pleased beyond words and wanted the senate to know it but didn't want their noise to get them removed for lack of decorum. The following day, Abigail was asked to speak to the same resolution in the Oregon house where there'd been a more lively and disunifying debate. She held her tongue and said only that she felt the resolution spoke for itself but that passage would put them all on a winning track for women and for themselves. It passed 29–25. White handkerchiefs fluttered the air.

A grand celebration at the Salem Opera House followed. Men and women of the cause sang the praises of the supporting legislators, and Willis gave a rousing speech. She was so grateful Ben and her sons were behind her. She wished Clara Belle had been there.

"You've done your part, Ma," Willis said as they rode in the coach back to Portland. "You birthed five votes and Pa's is the sixth from the Duniway house. The beginning of a precinct."

"Not the recommended way to achieve votes. Better to win them over from another mother's womb." She patted his hand. "But I'm glad you've taken up the cause."

Harvey's *Oregonian* published her senate address the day after the house passage; *New Northwest* carried the senate speech the day before the *Oregonian*. Harvey had made no editorial comment against the passage, for which Abigail was pleased, though she wished he'd find a way to support her life's effort.

* * *

"Harriet, we've one battle left." Abigail spoke to the vice president of the Oregon State Women's Suffrage Association after the vote. Abigail called Harriet Loughary the "Patrick Henry of the new dispensation" and knew this mother of nine could have made as strong a case as Abigail had. Harriet was a fine speaker with a teacher-husband who, like Ben, was a partner who supported the cause. "I should let her present more," Abigail told Ben. But she hated letting loose of the limelight.

The first two steps were climbed. The resolution had passed in two consecutive sessions. It would now go to the vote in 1884.

"We must work even harder to educate the public, praise the legislature, and try to hold the arguments about prohibition as far from suffrage as brew masters are from coffee grinders." Abigail expounded to the association gathering.

"We might take a moment to applaud our efforts," her vice-chair said. "And some of us take a well-deserved rest."

"If you're speaking about me," Abigail countered, "never you mind. This effort is my lifeblood. If I stopped now, well, I'm not sure but that my blood would stop flowing."

"Perhaps you Scott sisters could focus on your dear brother and silence his opposition."

"We'll do better than that," Abigail said. "We'll get him to support us."

Kate gasped. "Jenny," she whispered when Abigail sat back down. "That's so unlikely."

"Nothing is impossible. Who but us could make this happen? I'll schedule an appointment with Harvey next week."

But later, lying awake with sleep escaping her like the wayward sheep of Sunny Hillside Farm, she wondered if she hadn't pushed too far, promised too much in response to the vice-chair's assertion that Abigail rest a bit. *Am I so strident to the cause? No. I'm the very reason we have come this far.* They could push Harvey to their side. After all, the legislature—his colleagues and friends—had seen the light and voted for the referral. His sisters would bring a little sunshine to his countenance. They just had to find the correct lamp.

* * *

Abigail saw her opening with her brother and how the *New Northwest* could assist. It had to do with Harvey's alma mater,

Pacific University in Forest Grove. She named the woman in her article, Bridget Gallagher, and told of her story, of how as a young girl, she'd been taken advantage of by a married man. She'd given birth to a child out of wedlock. Few means of support were available to this young woman tending her child as best she could. She became a woman of "negotiable affections," Abigail called it. Eventually, the woman became a madam of an ill-reputed house. She made donations to the community, gave loans to young girls so they didn't have to resort to her "profession" which men kept possible. She wanted more for her son and had sent him to live in Forest Grove, a town founded by Congregationalists, Abigail made sure to note, where she attempted to enroll him in Harvey's alma mater.

> She was coolly informed by a professor that the child of such a mother could not be received in their ranks! And yet this school is a noted asylum for Alaskan, Japanese, and Chinese pupils, and is just now preparing to receive in its Christian fold a reinforcement of fifty young Indians of both sexes. Who checks to see if their mothers are all chaste and of the highest reputation? No wonder there are infidels in the land. No wonder they are multiplying in Forest Grove. Ah me! A.S.D.

Harvey sent her a note suggesting that she did her woman's cause no good deed by consorting with prostitutes. She replied that since the men of the state had relegated all women to the class of idiots and prostitutes in their inability to vote that she saw no harm in attempting to aid the *son* of such a woman in gaining an education. Kate had wondered if she might have gone too far in bringing up their brother's educational institution.

"I'm going to appeal to his Christian nature in this. He asked me to publish a series he'd written on religion and I agreed. It's fitting for us to have this discussion."

"But it doesn't help us get him behind the vote."

"It can't hurt."

"Yes, it can, Jenny."

But she'd gone to visit him anyway, praying she could hold her intemperate tongue.

"It's your alma mater, Harvey. You ought to stand for its motto to educate and to perform its Christian duty to the same." His office walls were covered in wood so polished she could almost see her reflection in them. Tall, narrow windows brought in summer light. It was the office of a legislator-in-waiting and it reeked of power. She inhaled. She would not be intimidated. "And I hope you can see that this is one of the very reasons women should be allowed the vote. So they'd have a say about fair treatment, be able to make their own way when men destroy their reputation, without resorting to prostitution."

"The woman is a prostitute."

"Yet even our Lord consorted with such women, seeing into their souls and past a tarnished reputation. As a full citizen, with rights to vote, she might well have made different decisions. Perhaps she could have taken the child's father to court, gotten him to provide for *their* child. Perhaps she could have gotten a loan and started a boardinghouse? She'd surely have had more options. For now, she wants the best for her son." Abigail looked at a portrait on the wall. Of Harvey. *That would have cost a fortune.* "How can your school deprive him of that when it's said to be a Christian academy? Are we not charged to look after widows and orphans?"

"This child you speak of is neither."

"He might well be with his mother a nonentity in the public eye or, worse, the lowest of women. That did not stop our Lord."

He was quiet, so she knew she'd hit a nerve. He sat, fingers made into tents, his forehead wrinkles deep and familiar in their groves.

"One day you might run for public office," Abigail said. "Might it not be wise to be able to show that you have compassion for all your constituents? In this instance, you'd be educating a voter."

"I can see the value in educating the lad."

She remained silent.

"I'll write to the professors."

"And urge them to allow him into school? Not just be tutored privately somewhere?"

"Yes. I'll urge that."

"Good, because I've had a fair number of letters from supporters, including other professors. You'll want to be on the winning side of this one, Mister Scott. Editor Scott. And am I assuming too much, perhaps one day, Senator Scott?"

Harvey's face turned tomato-red above his dark beard.

And with his revealing countenance, she saw her suffrage argument, the one her sisters could make with their brother.

* * *

"He'll want to be with winners. We simply have to convince him that the referral will pass. Because it will, I know it." Abigail reported to her sisters taking tea at the Duniway house. "And that women will vote for reasonable, good men."

"I don't know," Fanny said. "I think if we can keep him from writing editorials against the vote, we'll be doing good. To get him to write one in favor? That's an enormous task."

"But one we have before us."

"*You* put it before us, Jenny." Sarah Maria crocheted as she spoke. "You might have gone too far."

"Nonsense. We have less than two years, but we'll canvass the state, get a show of hands at every meeting, monitor the numbers coming out for the presentations, count our *yes* legislators, and spend time in their districts."

"We can give out little premiums when people come to the events."

"All right. But no parades," Abigail said. "No flashing banners or taking over saloons."

"I wasn't proposing that. Small reminders, pins to wear, that show they are supporters. Quietly, but that might open up discussions for them while they shop or get a dress fitted. We'll give them things to say." Sarah Maria held up the baby bib she'd been working on. "I could perhaps stitch in *Votes for Women.*"

Her sisters laughed, but Abigail tapped her finger to her lower lip. "You might have something there, but an opposing man will surely say that babies spit up on the very idea of a woman voting. No, our biggest task is to give supporters words to counter negative conversations. And to convince Harvey that it will pass and that those same women who get the vote will want to vote for a man like Harvey—educated, wise, and a supporter of women's rights—when he runs for Senate."

"Do you think he wants to do that?"

"I'd bet my life on it."

TWENTY-EIGHT

Thirty Years and Counting

June 1883

They returned home from the Annual Pioneer Association gathering on a beautiful June day. Ben had come with her, and she'd planned to simply mingle with old friends and mention face-to-face the constitutional amendment that was the referral for the 1884 vote. She wore a green ribbon with words "Votes for Women" written in black over a white backing. She would speak one-on-one and listen to any new arguments in opposition so she could address them. But the main speaker—a man—had gotten ill and she'd been asked to read his presentation. Which she did, joking that here was an example of a "woman representing a man" and soon women would have the vote and a woman might represent a man in the legislature. People had chuckled. Abigail never lost a chance to mention the vote. There was nothing controversial in her saying so.

When she finished reading the missing speaker's manuscript, she spoke for thirty minutes more, quoting words of a revered pioneer named Jesse Applegate, who had said how he wished his wife—now deceased—had shared liberty with him in her lifetime. Everyone in the Pioneer Association loved Cynthia Applegate, and Abigail built on that shared regard to remind the men that Cynthia Applegate was the example of the kind of wise women Oregon cherished and it was only right that such women be permitted to share liberty with men. "Next year, you men have a chance to make that happen for your wives and daughters." Polite applause followed.

"I think that went well, don't you, Ben?" Abigail removed her hat, lifted her thick curls from her neck, and fanned herself, then went into the kitchen to slice the loaf of bread she'd brought back from the picnic. Both Ralph and Clyde had joined them. She wasn't sure where the older boys had spent the afternoon.

Ben followed her into the kitchen, chewing on his pipe stem. "I didn't know you were going to lecture today."

"I wasn't scheduled to. It was because their speaker became ill. I told you, remember?"

"Oh. Yes. I do now. I always like it when you mention this Oregon country, all its beauty and that line about there being 'lessons of liberty in the rock-rimmed mountains that pierce our blue horizons with their snow-crowned heads' and on like that."

"Do you? I'm impressed you remember that line, word for word."

"You've said it before, and I always have an image of the view from our Sunny Hillside farm." Ben pulled a chair out from the table and sat. The family still congregated in the kitchen area, despite their having turned the old millinery into a large-gathering living room where suffrage meetings were often held.

"Oregon pioneers relate to the expansiveness of this country, at least most men do. I try to equate our land with the effort of the men and women drawn to it and help make them take that leap that, in such a country with its wide expanse, men must open their arms to women's spirit too, to our capabilities to make right decisions. I mean, the law allows drunkards and wife-beaters to vote, why not wonderful women like Cynthia Applegate or widows like Kate who have no man to represent them?"

"You don't need to convince me, Jenny."

She smiled. "I do go on, don't I?" She patted his shoulder as she moved behind him to open the larder. *Is he getting thinner?* "I know I ruffle feathers. Often." *I'd like to be revered like Cynthia Applegate is.*

"It's your way. But you also give us good pictures in our heads of how liberty and rimrock ridges join hands."

Back at the table, she sliced ham and cut chunks of cheese. The younger boys waited patiently. "And that's my calling. Our calling, to make waves for liberty." She held the knife up as though it was a torch.

"Momma." Fourteen-year-old Ralph stepped back out of her way.

"Ma's pontificating," Clyde said. He sat at the table, having gotten the mayonnaise from the icebox. He had whipped it up himself with eggs and oil and spread it on the sliced bread.

"She does that a lot," Ben said. "But seldom with a knife." The men in her life laughed.

"My words are my weapons." She smiled and finished cutting the bread for their light supper. Chen, the Chinese cook, had taken the day off.

They ate and chattered, and the boys told of overhearing suffrage conversations that spoke well of passage in the vote the following year. But Ben's forgetting that her presentation hadn't been planned concerned her. She was sure she'd told him that. Lately, he had been surprised at things she'd told him of—where she was going, when she'd be back. She made sure Willis and Wilke knew, so that if she needed to be reached, she could be. They were so close to achieving this goal, together. She didn't want to think about Ben's not being able to remember how important it all was and his part in it.

* * *

The associations, national and local, had been doing their educating, writing, speaking, forming new local suffrage groups, attempting to force the liquor industry from going against the franchise. Abigail traveled too, but she also stayed a little closer to home, paying attention to Ben. She didn't want to ask how his work was going. Maybe it was routine enough that his memory lapses wouldn't be obvious. Tuition for the youngest boys meant they could use every dime that came in.

On one of those days at home, Clara Belle visited, bringing four-year-old Earl with her. He seemed listless, but Clara was in high spirits, exclaiming about their log home. "I've found work in Washington Territory sewing for a new hotel in Washougal. The Columbia River is so majestic, Momma. And you can see Mount Hood from our cabin. It's beautiful country. And growing. I made all the window curtains for the hotel, crocheting each edge. Come visit us and we'll take supper there."

"You're having to sew? What's that Don doing that you're compelled to work?"

"Momma, you still stitch in the evenings. You even talk about it in your speeches, how you have to sew and pay your own expenses half the time."

"I do it because I like to."

"You do not like to sew." Clara Belle laughed. She had the most engaging giggle, Abigail thought. "You grumble all the time you're threading the needle. We children just learned to overlook it."

Abigail harrumphed. "How are things with the battle for the ballot in the Washington Territory?"

"You know as well as any of us, Momma. There are good rumblings that this year we'll see passage. A year before Oregon."

"That's all right. It'll push Oregon legislators to see their neighboring men make a sound decision."

"They almost passed women's suffrage in 1854, but it lost by one vote. I hope we don't miss that close this time," Clara Belle said.

"Surely those legislators have learned their lesson. Oh, this law-promoting is worse than sausage-making."

Clara Belle laughed again. "Remember that time we had to catch up the hog to butcher? Papa was away and Uncle John helped out."

"You were so young. I'm surprised you remember that."

"You hooted after you got cleaned up from the muck. I don't see you laugh much, so I guess it stayed in my memory as special."

Abigail hadn't thought she didn't snigger and chortle all that often, but perhaps Clara Belle was right. "Are you laughing much yourself these days?"

Clara Belle looked away. "Don's working a lot." Her daughter nodded at the scraps of cloth Abigail had cut out and were spread across the table. "Are you making something for the fair?"

"I had to. I wrote about how dreadful I thought it was that women were relegated to spending precious time on stitchery at the end of their hardworking days, only to earn a few coins as fair premiums. They could be taking needed rests or promoting the vote. I suggested we women were meant for bigger things, bigger inventions like those I saw at the exhibition in '76. Well, I got some letters about that."

Clara Belle picked up the cloth pieces, rubbed them between her fingers. "It's very soothing, quilt-making and stitching. And I end up with something beautiful and warm for my family. Some items I sell but that feels good too. I've met other women that way, made friends and been inspired. Maybe you ought not to disparage the domestic arts, Momma. Artists need a community."

"I don't think my quilting will ever be considered art. A couple of letter-writers challenged me to make a quilt. I wrote—foolishly perhaps—that any fool can make a quilt. After making so many through the years, only a fool would spend so much time cutting and stitching back together those little pieces. I started this one after Ralph was born. Anyway, I've been charged with making a patchwork quilt out of silk and satin. Terrible material to work with. Not unlike suffrage having to take scraps of ideas, shape them to fit the men who will vote, and somehow come up with a glorious result we want. After the fair, we'll sell it to raise money for suffrage."

"You see, stitching does have a higher purpose."

"I suppose. Where's Don traveling to? Has he gotten you help?" Abigail gave Earl a book she'd gotten, filled with sketches of horses and simple words he might recognize if Clara Belle had been teaching him.

"I miss my husband, the way you missed Papa when he was in the mines."

"I hope you're not having to work *that* hard, so hard as I did then."

"I can do it. Earl takes long naps." She leaned over as he pointed to a word. "Dressage. It's a special kind of riding people do back east." Then to her mother she continued. "I thought I had enough wood chopped for the whole year, but it's cool near the river and it looks like I'll have to store up a few more cords." She flexed her muscles. "Now my arms are as strong as my piano-playing fingers."

"At least you have the piano." Later Abigail would remember that Clara had not confirmed this statement. Abigail went on to express a warning instead. "Chopping wood by yourself is not a good idea. What if you drop the ax or cut yourself, all alone out there? I'll send your brothers up to ready you for the winter. Your father will want to go too."

"Women have been chopping wood and building fires for generations, Momma. It's work that makes us stronger, helps define who we are. You did it yourself. And when we left the farm, you brought that old broom along, as a symbol, remember?"

"Humph." *Can it be that the years on the Illinois farm, the years on Hardscrabble have shaped me more than I realize?*

"We can make a party of it," Clara continued. "I'd like to show you my home, Momma. You'll come, won't you, if you send the men out to rescue me?" She grinned.

"I'll see what my schedule allows."

She saw the frown across her daughter's face. *There it is again, this avoidance of a happy potential.* "A family gathering would be a good get-together. We'll see what we can arrange." Maybe Kate was right about her aversion to things that could touch the tenderness of her own heart, that gaining the vote had robbed her of the very things that might bring her joy in a battle that had already taken thirty years of her time. She could not let it matter. This suffrage work was worth doing, no matter how long it took or whom it took from.

* * *

"You take that businessman." Abigail pointed to the list of men they'd need to nurture through this final phase. "I'll take these. You know the routine. Curry and comb, pamper and praise. I will personally be on my best behavior."

The members of the association chuckled. Abigail on her "best behavior" could still bring a stinging rebuke if she thought it necessary.

When she was invited to speak to the Washington Territorial Legislature and celebrated with them the passage of women's suffrage, she traveled to Olympia at nearly her own expense. The organizations had been unable to secure stable financing, and Abigail had reported in her role as president of the Oregon association that she'd neglected this year to prepare or tabulate a statement of receipts and expenditures. "I tried it for two months, and the balance on the wrong side of the ledger became so large that I feared to keep it up, lest the unpleasant reflection over statistics would so discourage me that I would not have the heart to carry the work to completion." That confession, or perhaps chastisement, had resulted in a small reimbursement for her expenses, but her vice-chair had also told her that the treasurer would want an accounting. She'd have to ask Ben to help—if he could.

On her way back from her speech-making, she had taken the

steamship to Washougal. With directions at the landing—people had heard of the Stearns place—Abigail tromped along the path into the thickness of trees and brambles, blackberries, and bushes that someone had cut back from the roadway for the main path. But the side path she'd been told to take to Clara Belle's house wasn't so neatly cleared.

Ben, Willis, and Wilkie had chopped wood for the Stearnses. Ben had supervised, he assured Abigail, had not strained his spine. He'd reported back on the conditions. "Pretty primitive," he'd said. She had not joined them. Too many duties. "But our Clara Belle has turned that hut into a home. The way you did at Hardscrabble. You two have more in common than you might want to admit."

"Is she eating all right? Is Earl well? He looked so thin when they were here last."

Ben shrugged. "I didn't go through their cupboard. Earl is growing, though he is a skinny boy, but then Don is tall and lanky. And Clara Belle is willowy too. He sings like an angel. I wouldn't worry over their food supply."

"I'm glad you took some hams with you, anyway."

"She seemed grateful." He paused. "She asked after you, said she knew from her suffrage group that you'd be visiting the Territorial Legislature and hoped you might stop by. She read your association report saying you'd given 296 speeches last year and figured one of them should have brought you near Washougal and that your invitation to Olympia would."

"That swamp is a far pace from Olympia."

Why do I still hold an affront to their long-ago elopement? It was the reason she had not joined the men for the work party. She felt a failure that, after all this effort on behalf of women, she had not protected her daughter from the very hardships she'd had to endure as a young wife. Ben told her that letting go of past pains wasn't hard. He'd had lots of practice and could show her how it was done. Abigail wondered if he was being sarcastic, but that wasn't like him.

Now, here she was, at her daughter's home. She saw the stack of cordwood first, nearly as tall as the roofline. Her brothers had done well by Clara Belle. Their grandfather would have been proud to see his sons stand up for their only sister. She missed her father.

A dog barked, noticing her arrival, and she took in a deep breath as she put her hand out to its nose, let it sniff, then scurry back beneath the porch where Abigail heard the sound of squealing puppies. A dog would be a good companion if she ever stayed home long enough to make a friend of it.

Abigail stepped up onto the porch. A single rocking chair with a colorful patched pillow was tucked into the side. *Only one chair.* She lifted her gloved knuckles, prepared to knock on the door, when she saw a knothole not filled in. She could look right into the house. Clara Belle lay on a cot, Earl beside her on the floor stacking blocks. Clara Belle lay so still. *Is she dead? Did that man kill her?* Abigail didn't knock but lifted the latch and stepped right in. Earl looked up at her, startled.

"Hi, Earl. I'm your grandmomma. Do you remember me?" He shook his head no. "I'm going to wake your momma."

"She sleeps quiet," he said. A splatter of freckles crossed his nose.

Abigail squatted down, patted his shoulder, then touched Clara Belle's, expecting her body to be cold, swallowing back the tears, then brushing them away with anger directed toward the child's father. "Clara Belle?"

The girl opened her eyes.

Abigail leaned back. "Wake up, baby. It's your momma."

"Oh, Momma." She sat up, looked frantic. "You've caught me napping. I didn't know you were coming." She brushed at her hair, smoothed her sleep-wrinkled dress.

"I was afraid it was worse than napping in the day. Are you well?"

"Just tired. I'm fine. I really am."

"You scared me half to death, lying like that."

"I'm sorry. I . . . I was . . . weary. We dried apples."

Abigail scanned the room and saw the strings of apples hanging from the rafters. She also saw a sparsely furnished house. Except for Clara Belle's stitchery on the windows, a crocheted doily on the back of a narrow couch, the room didn't have much to say for itself. It looked stripped of any grandeur.

"Where's the piano?"

Clara Belle kept her voice light, forced, in Abigail's mind. "It wouldn't stay tuned in all this moisture. Don . . . we sold it. Another child will have the chance to play it with parents who can afford to bring the tuner in from Vancouver."

"He sold your piano. Your pride and joy."

"Earl is my pride and joy. I can still sing."

"Now will you admit your marriage was a mistake?"

"Momma. I have a son. I eat regularly. I have a fine roof over my head and friends not far away. There's even a church here now where I can sing. What more could I need?"

"A husband who looks after you in the style you deserve."

"He's doing the best he can."

"Where is he, by the way? I saw no evidence of prune orchards or whatever it is he said he'd cleared land for."

"It's further away from here." She stood up. "He's sold it anyway. Let's get you a little bite to eat. Earl, I bet you're hungry too."

"I'm always hungry," he said.

"Me too." Abigail brushed the boy's curls with her gloved hand. *But it's for more than. I'm hungry for a better life for my daughter and her son.*

TWENTY-NINE

Victory or Defeat?

November 1883

Autumn foilage had splattered the roadways, colored the grass beneath like a patchwork quilt. November arrived, with a few maple and elm leaves holding tight to their branches. Abigail sometimes thought of herself as like those tenacious fronds, clinging, refusing to let go. The campaign was seven months away from the momentous vote. With her sisters, she'd proposed a plan to bring Harvey to their side.

Abigail had sent letters to her brother thanking him for remaining quiet about the suffrage question, for allowing the "good citizens of Oregon to make up their own minds." And the *Oregonian* had not spoken about the referral at all as yet. They'd kept him neutral. Now they needed to turn him to their way.

"The *Oregonian* will have to take a position before long," Abigail said. All the living Scott sisters met at the Duniway house, preparing the final stage of their plan. "Kate has gotten us a meeting with him, at his home, so he'll see this as a family issue." They agreed to let Fanny and Kate do most of the talking in his ornate parlor.

Something burned between Abigail and Harvey. She was the older sister and he the fair-haired baby boy, and perhaps it happened with all siblings that way, between older sisters and loving younger brothers, both longing for the same approval to witness in their parents' eyes—and each other's. Her parents never knew of their arguments out in the field, the anger they could arouse in each other. Once, Harvey was so infuriated with her that he took a stick to Abigail, beating her back. Barely able to walk back to the house, she withheld her tears, wouldn't give him the satisfaction. She couldn't even remember what it had been about now, but sometimes, with the raise of an eyebrow or the grimace on his mustached face, she felt her stomach clench. It was the visage he'd chosen just before he struck. It became a warning sign, like the rattle of a snake. She didn't want to provoke him.

The sad thing was that she did love him, had rescued him from a laundry fire, admired his accomplishments while still being envious. He had everything she'd ever hoped for. So why he was so oppositional to her still escaped her. But then, she was oppositional to him as well.

She would keep her words to herself. He knew where she stood and the arguments in favor of suffrage. She would let her sisters make the case with him.

"So that's our hope, that before the actual election in June, you might see yourself writing an editorial promoting the referral." Kate had concluded her presentation.

Harvey adjusted his glasses. "You know my concern about women getting the vote and then ushering in prohibition, something I oppose."

"We know," Fanny said. "We oppose prohibition too, not because we think control of liquor would be a bad thing, especially on the streets of Portland, but because, like you, we believe in individual freedom. People ought to make their own choices of whether to sip wine or not."

"You'll have to work hard to assure the powers that be that

enfranchised women are not of that persuasion. The liquor industry has already placed ads opposed to your referral based on that assumption."

"Which is why your opinion is so crucial, dear Brother." Abigail kept her voice calm. She sank back in her chair with Fanny's grimace at her.

"My own wife does not share your views. I'll be inviting dissension in my household, to do what you ask."

"Ah, but a man is still the master of his castle, is that not so?" Abigail leaned forward. She wondered if they ought to be courting Mary rather than Harvey. It surprised her that he would even acknowledge his second wife's opposition. He'd been widowed eleven years when he met his wealthy second wife. Not only had he landed wonderful jobs, but he had wooed an intelligent (though misguided when it came to suffrage) partner as well. *He wants to show us how generous he is in going against his wife in order to satisfy his sisters.*

"Master, indeed." Harvey tapped his finger on the blotting pad.

"The most important thing, Harvey," Sarah Maria said, "is that in our canvassing, we believe the resolution will pass. You wouldn't want to be on the wrong side."

"Your electoral instincts will be up for scrutiny," Abigail said. "There are rumors of your interest in a Senate run."

He jerked his head toward her. "No decision has been made." He tapped again. "It's your judgment that there is support for the referral?"

"Yes." Harriet said. "Southern Oregon, Eastern Oregon, we hear nothing but positive words. When Abigail speaks, men come to her events and applaud."

"Do they now?"

"The legislature is simply following their constituents, as good lawmakers should. That's why the referral passed last session and why men are going to the polls to vote for the very first time on this momentous occasion," Kate said.

"The *Oregonian* needs to be on the winning side." Abigail said the last with a fist punch to the air.

"I'll think about it. I have to maintain my integrity. And I do have an editorial board I need to respond to. I can't do this simply because you ask."

"You could do it for Papa," Sarah Maria said. She had a childlike voice. "He supported the cause."

"He did. Well, he had a house full of smart women." A small grin leaked beneath his bushy mustache. "But I have to think of the man who lives with a shrew or a scold or an idiot. Who will speak for him if I don't?"

"Let him speak for himself," Abigail said. "He already has the right to vote."

She watched to see that raised eyebrow. It did not come. But the frown returned, and she vowed to keep her distance from Harvey until the vote.

* * *

Six weeks after the sisters met with him, Harvey posted his editorial. It was written in response to an *Oregonian* reader who had objected to Washington's passage of women's suffrage.

Harvey started by saying the reader noted objections raised by those who hadn't really thought through the issue. He didn't say that ignorance was the cause of opposition, but he implied it. "And listen to this, Ben." Abigail read from the paper, her hands shaking. "'And is any man really prepared to claim that his wife, mother and sisters'—he said sisters, Ben—'are inferior to his own judgment, in patriotism, in love of good government.'" He went on to note that they weren't disqualified from getting the vote as people who might not perform certain citizen functions like building roads or serving on a jury or fighting in wars, because "half the citizen men avoid doing these things too."

Harvey concluded with words Abigail breathed in. He had heard them. He was behind them. "'A woman is capable of exerting an influence in public affairs which the state needs, and this influence can be made effective only through suffrage. Prejudice may for a while prevent it, but no argument can stand for a moment in its way."

"Holy cow chips, he's done it! He's supporting us! The referral is ours!"

She sent a note to Harvey expressing her thanks, valuing his influence, calling on their father's memory to say how he would be so pleased, "looking down upon us and using his influence from that sphere—along with our mother's—to bring about this outcome that the Scott women had so long proffered." It was the culmination of a lifetime of work. She just knew the referral would pass.

* * *

A certain giddiness prevailed in the Duniway household. Abigail sang with Ben as she packed her carpetbag for travels to speak and support the effort. She found herself smiling on the stagecoach for no reason at all. *Harvey has come through.* Back in Oregon, suffrage women and their groups spent hours at small gatherings in agreeable churches, courting women whom they urged to convert their husbands toward the cause or support the men who already furthered their campaign. Letters went to newspapers throughout the state. Abigail wrote editorials quoting her brother and serialized novels that sang the praises of women who had to be capable because of the poor decisions by their men. She celebrated the legislators who had the referral voted in, and she wrote of how a woman could govern herself and her family, so why wouldn't one expect her to govern her fellow citizens with wisdom and grace. The women hung posters and they wrote songs of suffrage—Abigail wrote one that she wished Clara Belle was available to sing—and their meetings rallied the faithful with the hope that they won a few converts to their cause.

Around April, with barely a lamppost free of a "Votes for Women" poster, Abigail swallowed hard when she saw that the *Oregonian* had published letters both in support of suffrage and in opposition. The paper itself had not repeated Harvey's earlier stand.

"I'm surprised Harvey hasn't come out in favor as he did last November," Abigail said. She and Kate stood in the dappled sunlight beneath an elm tree after worship one May Sunday. "Other papers have made their opinions known. You'd think the mighty *Oregonian* would have too."

"I haven't wanted to ask Harvey," Kate said. "He's built a moat around his newspaper castle where family isn't supposed to cross."

"So, no inside information about when they'll take their stand. It's getting close to the election." Abigail turned slightly to avoid the bright sunshine streaking through the trees.

"I haven't wanted to say, but he's scheduled to be back east on election day. He leaves a week before."

"Will he post an editorial? Has he done that in the past?"

Kate shrugged her shoulders.

"But he does support us, right? We are so close. His November editorial sang the highest suffrage note."

The night before the vote, Abigail lay awake. She thought of how her life's work had been shaped by her mother's words, wishing she'd had sons because a girl's life was so hard. She considered the decision to marry Ben, which had been hers and came from love, but with a tinge of resentment that it had to be so rushed because of her father's own wish to marry again. And the losses—of Sunny Hillside, but more, of her sister's death from following her husband to the wilds of the Oregon coast where she'd died of tuberculosis, having no other choice but to do his bidding. And Clara Belle's decision. At least she now lived in a territory where she had the vote. Abigail had put so much of her life into this effort. And tomorrow would be the culmination.

She woke Ben. "What if it fails?"

"Not likely. And if it does, you'll begin again. You won't have to wonder what you'll do with your time." He punched the pillow and went back to sleep.

It has to pass or all our work—all my efforts—will have been for naught. "It must pass," she said to her sleeping husband. "It was divinely inspired. How could it not?"

She read every issue of the *Oregonian*, looking for encouraging words, supportive editorials, a repeat of Harvey's fine deliberations. Nothing. Not a single word in favor—and none against. He chose a neutral stand. *The coward.* He kept his his light under a bushel. She'd have thought better of him if he had openly changed his mind. *Maybe not.* But the euphoria of that November editorial had sunk like a rock in the river.

The vote was held June 2, 1884, but it took three weeks to tally the ballots that had to come from hither and yon over the mountains and through the canyons of this massive state. Still, Abigail could see from the first reports in the Portland precincts that it was going down. "*It does not look well,*" she wrote in her June 5th editorial. The sisters stayed on pins and needles, planning the celebration yet fearful of jinxing it by assuming too much. Abigail could hardly write her articles for the paper. She sketched out another novel, a shorter story. She tried to pay attention to Hubert's wedding plans. It would be such a year of merriment, and yet the foreboding of that spring night crept over her like a heavy fog rolling in from the river, holding her hostage.

Then the tally was counted and reported. They were defeated: 28,176 opposed to 11,223 in favor.

* * *

It was as though she'd lost a child. She didn't say that out loud at the suffrage meeting, for with her sat her niece and her sister Fanny, who had lost children, but the depth of Abigail's grief took her to that tearful trail. When at last the vote was complete and the numbers available for posting at the capital for publication in the newspapers across the country, it was Abigail who had to tell her sisters and then the state and nation that the referral had failed. Her *New Northwest* carried the story. She added in the announcement "*We are not defeated,*" even though she felt they were.

THIRTY

Postmortem

How could the vote have been so strongly opposed when their face-to-face discussions had nearly always ended with words of support? How could such a worthy cause, an inevitable hope, something so worth doing, have lost? Negroes had the vote, a race many men thought inferior in every way but who now began to be seen as equals, as citizens at least. Equal in their ability to vote, though she had read of poll taxes and other encumberments local jurisdictions flaunted against those people. Still, they had the right. It had to happen for women, too, and even Harvey had supported it. What had gone wrong?

"We'll have to analyze what precincts we won and where we lost," Kate noted. They had gathered at what Abigail called the "postmortem" to take apart the body politic.

"It appears we won in the countryside." Sarah Maria looked at the tiny marks recorded on the clerk's report. "Those farmers and ranchers know we women are no threat but rather help-mates. It's in the cities where we lost. Actually, it was Portland who voted against us." She turned to her youngest child, a four-year-old daughter, who leaned into her side. "We'll get you the vote yet."

"It was the liquor industry." Harriet crocheted while they sorted through the embers of defeat. "Washington Territory's women voters have been blamed for stricter liquor laws, and Portlanders likely saw empty glasses in their future."

Abigail had written that Washington women were at risk to lose the vote because of the heavy spending by San Francisco and Portland liquor interests funding a repeal of the women's suffrage there.

"We Washington voters have passed prohibition kinds of legislation," Clara Belle said. She had taken the produce boat to offer solace to her mother. "And they don't like it that women are on juries, and we might find for plaintiffs against corrupt liquor industries. Did you know they pay three dollars for jury duty? One woman told me it was better than a trip to San Francisco, that she got a day of rest, her family was still there when she returned home, and she had money to put aside for a rainy day."

"I'll write about that," Abigail said. *But how will I write about this defeat?*

Earl played with a cousin in the yard. Children's chatter was a wind chime sounding through the open windows, lightening the timbre in the room.

"Even the brewers turned against us." Fanny sighed.

"And they said as much in those German newspapers that reach most of Portland, despite your newspaper's efforts to counter them, Abigail." The vice-chair of the association shook her head. "We worked so hard. Maybe we should have brought National in."

"No. Oregon's men would have their backs up if we had brought in eastern women," Abigail said. She had to defend their tactics and yet, her strategy had not won them the vote. "Though we could have used more of their money returned from our dues, that's certain."

"They weren't keen on being asked to stay out while we requested funds," Kate said. "But I agree, Oregon flies with her own wings, as our state motto reads. When Aunt Susan's group said they should 'leave Oregon severely alone,' she was right."

At least she'd helped those Washington women get the vote. But here in this blessed state, she'd failed. Perhaps she should have come out for prohibition, but people ought to make their own decisions about the morality of drinking. And supporting it, she knew, would bring the liquor industry down upon them.

"What a waste of our effort." Another young reformer spoke up. "All those posters and meetings and—"

"We had nearly twelve thousand men who understood and voted for us," Fanny said. "Next time, we'll double that. We must refocus our efforts in Portland before the next referral."

"The next referral." Abigail's despair dropped into the room like a horse stepping on a woman's toes. "With biennial legislative sessions, that means getting passage again in the '86 session, '88 session, too, with a hope for a referral vote in 1890. Or later. It's another long walk toward uncertainty."

"There's a move to permit citizen initiatives, where with a certain number of signatures, ordinary people can make proposals for a general vote. We can move faster if that passes." This from a younger member.

"Maybe the men are right. Do they know something we don't know?" said another member.

Still another acolyte to the cause raised her voice. "Perhaps we should go back to our kitchens and parlors and bring up our sons so when they are men, they will grant their mothers the vote, if not their sisters and wives."

The young woman's comments held merit for Abigail. She was tired. Maybe staying home, spoiling Earl, and waiting on other grandchildren, writing her novels, tending to Ben, perhaps that is what she should be doing with the rest of her life. She'd be fifty years old this October and her bones felt it. She could lay down the sword of truth and righteousness, having witnessed her daughter be able to vote in Washington. They could sell the paper, the Portland home, and move to Idaho, where Ben had fallen in love with land near Hailey. *Why not?* That beam of light that had led her to spend her days promoting this cause, maybe it was only sunshine coming through the window. If it had truly been God's work, wouldn't the referral have passed? They'd misunderstood, she and Ben. And she'd led her brother down the primrose path, telling him they would win. And he'd supported them—safely, months before the vote. He probably wouldn't ever talk with her again. But then, she wasn't sure she ever wanted to speak with him again either.

* * *

"You told me it would pass. I believed you." Harvey paced his office where Abigail had gone to lament that they'd both lost something that mattered.

"I . . . I had reason, strong reason, to believe it would pass. In the rural areas, it did."

Harvey harrumphed. "What do they know out there. Do they even read the newspapers, find out what's happening around the world?"

"Perhaps if they had free high school education, more would be better informed."

"Don't go there, Abigail." Harvey pointed his finger at her. Rage filled his eyes.

He's frightening me. "I'm more distressed than you are. To spend my whole life on something and have it defeated? You can still run for the Senate whenever you want. But our work means slogging through two more sessions if we are to continue the fight. Maybe I'll move to Washington. It's a big territory. Did I tell you they invited me to run for governor?"

He guffawed. "That'll be retracted when they realize how inept you are in understanding the electorate. They'll likely repeal the woman vote anyway."

"Why didn't you repeat your support? Your November editorial made my heart sing, made all suffragists celebrate. You have so much influence."

He glared at her. "Do you have any idea how many letters the paper received after that . . . that . . . lapse on my part?"

"Lapse? But the argument was well written, wise. When women do get the vote, and we will one day, they'd vote for you when you run." She saw a flash of pain cross his eyes, his own political career careening out of his control. "We Scotts don't like to lose, do we?"

"This vote was not *my* loss."

"No. It's mine. I'm devastated. But I am grateful that your *Oregonian*—you—supported it, once. I just didn't understand why you stayed neutral at the eve of the election, printing as many negative letters as those in support. Yes, I counted. The greatest newspaper in the Northwest stayed neutral." She sighed. "I came to thank you for that early support and ask for it again as we move forward."

"It will never happen again, dear Sister. Never. Ever. Ever. From here on in, I stand with the majority of men in this state and never, do you hear me, will I write an editorial in support of the woman vote. In fact, I will confess my error and write editorials to defeat any future attempt. If you continue this fight, you will do so without my backing, and I will do everything I can do to defeat it." He spoke to the window, then turned to face her. "I had to convince my board. And now, I have to wear my shame. Now go. I don't want to see your face here again begging for my support for anything. Ever."

Her steps from Harvey's office were heavy. She was grateful for a cab close by to take her home. Old confetti from the anti-suffrage crowd scattered in the streets. Her life's work, ended. Her relationship, such as it was with her brother, broken like a cane. She thought she could go no lower.

* * *

"We can't sell the paper," Ben said. "It's our livelihood. We have children employed by it." Their three oldest sons were engaged in some aspect of the business and the younger boys hoping for professions that would require they attend eastern schools. The paper was needed to support them. And Ben's job was here in Portland. The cause that defined her life, it was here. No, there was no rest ahead in Idaho.

She thought of other times of despair. When her mother had died. When her brother had passed. When her father had the crisis of marriage. She had gotten up from those days realizing that when fatigue settled in, the worst thing one could do was to take a nap. Better was to increase her curiosity, expand her effort, multiply the time she spent in educating both men and women to the importance of the climb toward the peak of justice. It was what she'd done when Ben signed the notes and they'd lost the farm. It was that disaster that had spurred them on to new things: she'd begun the school, the millinery, and found suffrage as a life's mission.

"The only thing to displace the bitterness of defeat is the taste of victory." Abigail heard herself say those words even though she wasn't sure she believed them anymore. "We begin again. Grief cannot hold us back. We are wiser but not worn down. Let us ponder what we know, and come next week with new strategies that might very well mean putting a wolf in sheep's clothing into Harvey Scott's shed."

"Rather than a wolf," Kate said, "we need a shepherd."

"With a shepherd's staff to gently, diplomatically, bring in the fold," Fanny added. She winked at her sister.

"That leaves me out," Abigail said to the knowing laughter of her siblings.

But she was also out of this campaign. She was tired. She would use her words to inspire, to further the cause in her newspaper, but perhaps it was time for her to step aside. Her heart wasn't in it anymore.

* * *

The women began again with letter campaigns and meetings, speeches and sparring, without Abigail's enthusiasm. She worked on her novel, meddled a little in her sons' lives—Hubert had fallen for one of the boardinghouse girls but had proposed to another. She hovered over Ben, who suggested when she was asked, that she make the trip back east through the snows of the spring of '85. "It'll do you good. You'll come back ready to take up the mantle."

"I'm still carrying it."

"You are. But you're not meeting with legislators, pressing your still hunt. Maybe you should be."

She made the trip meant to negotiate a truce between warring factions of associations working toward suffrage passage and seeing—with horror—the growing influence of prohibitionists attaching themselves to suffrage. It pleased her that she was asked to be the diplomat. Even Susan B. Anthony felt the causes must join hands, the position causing the two old friends to disagree. But in Abigail's fifteen hundred miles of travel and forty-nine speeches given nationally, she could see that linking these two great causes would doom them both.

What she also found was that she came alive with the challenge; doing something worthy beyond her own life and family invigorated. She loved the travel. Oh, the coaches were uncomfortable and the trains cold as winter through the mountains at night. And the porters weren't always quick to pick up her bags, even when they saw she used her cane. The Washington, DC, hotel she stayed in often had mice, and the different foods in Philadelphia made her stomach queasy. But in both places, she felt the stirrings of liberty, of what must have driven the Founding Fathers to risk everything for a new nation. Her writing was better from these places, and her words soared when she spoke in the churches and halls, bringing news of the forward-thinking West—Washington Territory's advancement especially—to the burdened East. She never doubted on those days that she was doing the Lord's work, lifting the downtrodden, visiting women in jails, freeing the spirits of all beings of God's creation. She gained fuel for the fight when she traveled. Returning, she felt the old stirring. Things didn't always turn out well, as Ben proposed, but some things were worth doing, regardless. There was another campaign to wage.

THIRTY-ONE

The Things That Sustain

1885

"A little old age, Ma," Willis had said.

"How old is he?" Hubert's wife asked.

"Barely fifty-five," Abigail said. "He worries me."

"He seems to know details of the past." Wilke bit a radish, crunched it.

"Yes, but what he did yesterday or even a moment ago escapes him." Abigail sighed. "The other day, he stood right next to me when Clara Belle was here telling us that she and Don and Earl were considering moving back to Oregon."

"I wonder why they'd do that?" Hubert said.

"We chatted about it. Little Earl didn't look well, if you ask me, but she said it had to do with Don's work, whatever that is. The man is so elusive. Ben was there, heard it all. Clara Belle walked away, and I said to him, 'Won't that be lovely if Clara Belle and Earl come back home?' and he said, 'Clara Belle's moving home? Why didn't I know about that?' I mean, he had been listening to the conversation. Not thirty seconds had passed."

Into the silence that followed, Hubert said, "That is concerning. But he's no trouble, really, is he, Ma? He takes care of his needs. And it's only temporary. It's just a quirk, maybe. Of old age."

"He's tidy about his person, as always. Dignified in that." She felt torn between a growing interest in getting back into the arena while watching Ben wane. "I worry that he might get lost if he goes out alone. And there's his job. How long will he be able to keep it? And he asks me repeated questions. I'm not much for patience, you know."

"You might have to stay home a little more, Ma."

A leaf falling from a tree to the forest floor would have been louder than the silence that followed Willis's observation.

"You might have to sell a few more subscriptions," she snapped back. Inside, Abigail felt her throat close. *How can I be so unloving as to fear more time with Ben? And why does suffrage work offer more sustenance than caring for a loving man?* She used the travel to escape; she could see that now. Ben had recognized it before she had. And he'd encouraged it. He knew her better than she knew herself.

* * *

He had treated it with hot lemon. For months. Don Stearns had seen the symptoms, he told Ben and Abigail, and thought that it was a deep cold from the vapors off Lake Camus where he'd moved his little family.

"But you're still living in that swamp. If you had but told me, we would have gotten a doctor there or brought you all here. Sooner. How could you not see it was consumption?"

She had to find someone to blame. Had to. Her daughter was dying and there was nothing she could do about it.

She picked up doilies from the back of the horsehair couch, smoothed them, moved them, her fingers hopelessly busy over nothing. This inability to make things happen—to improve Ben's memory, protect her daughter, gain the vote for women after all her effort, sacrifice, and yes, time away from family—her life was as useless as these doilies.

"Maybe I'll recover, Momma." Clara Belle hacked out the words, the act of talking bringing on a wracking cough that brought pain to Clara's face and to Abigail's heart.

"Of course you will. You must. If only we'd known. We could have found a mountain place with pure air to bring you healing. Why didn't you write, Clara?" She turned to her son-in-law. "Why didn't you?" She ignored the tears he brushed from his cheeks, didn't give him a chance to defend. "You . . . you need to go, Don. I can barely stand the sight of you. Earl will stay here. He needs to be close to his mother now, emotionally, if not able to touch and hold her."

"It would be better if he came home with me. He's my son."

"No. We need to watch for symptoms for him. It's clear your diagnostic abilities are lacking."

"As are your mothering aptitudes," he choked out.

Abigail gasped. "How dare—"

"Jenny . . ." Ben reached for her hand.

"I brought Clara here at her insistence, but I'll not give up Earl."

"Please." Clara Belle coughed. She turned her eyes toward her father. "Don't let them argue." Her lips tinted blue with the effort to stay her shallow breath.

Ben was having one of his good days. "Jenny, Clara Belle doesn't need any more troubling." He sat on a chair beside the daybed she lay on, the very one he'd rested on after the horse accident while they all listened to her playing the piano. *No more.* "What would please you, Daughter? To have Earl here?" She nodded yes. "And Don?" She hesitated but nodded yes to that as well. "Son, you are welcome to stay."

"Ben."

He raised his hand to silence Abigail. To the Stearns family members, he said, "Jenny's grieving. She has a sharp tongue sometimes, but it's how she plugs the hole of pain. If you want to be here with Clara Belle, you're welcome. No need to separate the family."

Abigail snorted, but she saw the pleading look upon her daughter's face, and she inhaled. "You can remain. Of course. All of you."

Don's eyes were on Clara Belle. "I fear our feuding would bring you stress. I'll come often. I promise."

Abigail couldn't let Don be the better person. "Ben's right. What matters now is Clara's peace and healing. We can pray and hope," she said. "You're welcome here, Don."

"Then we'll stay for you, Clara Belle."

A feeble smile crossed her daughter's face. She pressed her hands in prayer and nodded to him, her mother, and then to her father. Speaking was simply too tiring. Abigail could see that, and she'd need to remember it, not upset her daughter. It only made her weaker.

And yet her outrage at Don for not calling a doctor, for waiting so long, for taking her away from them those years before and the piercing sorrow of such an imminent loss as a child's death would not be enough to caution her every time. She would rail at this man who, like Maggie's husband, had ignored the signs of illness until too late. The very sight of him would bring out the worst in her.

"I've got to make that meeting back east," Abigail told Ben that evening.

"You can't leave. Not now."

"You're a greater comfort to her than I am. You and the boys. She said to me, 'You have a mission, Ma.' She understands."

"Not just for her sake, Abigail. But for yours, you should be here. You could read your latest novels to her. She'll enjoy hearing Hubert's wife giving piano lessons, just as she once did, and you can enjoy the music too."

"I feel helpless here, and frankly, the very sight of Don . . ."

Ben patted her back, then took her into his arms. "My Jenny. How you miss the things nearby. Can't you see there is no real joy in the things afar?"

"You're remembering that little autograph book poem. The second line though is 'Not what we seem, but what we are.' I'm not the loving parent that you are, Ben. I'm a demanding, domineering, controlling—"

"Stop. Don't punish yourself that way. Who you are is a devoted, benevolent, and loving mother who pushes grief away. Didn't you read to me what Shakespeare wrote, that one should give sorrow words?"

She nodded, tears dampening his shirt.

"It was something about if you don't speak what your heart feels, it will break. Silence isn't always a good thing, if I recall it."

"Yes. *Macbeth.* But when I speak, it comes out stinging. I'm better to be away, Ben. You're here. You'll comfort her. The things afar will bring me consolation in the end."

"No. They won't."

Abigail packed her bags while Ben sang old songs to Clara Belle. Earl watched as Abigail folded her dresses, put her curling iron, powders, and perfume into the burgundy bag she had carried with her through the years. "You look after your grandpa now, you hear? Make sure he doesn't go outside without his coat. Evenings can get cold. Will you remember that?"

Earl nodded. She hugged him, his thin little shoulders like a bird's frame. She would fatten him up when she came back. She knew when she returned, all would be different, but she would do all she could to keep Earl with them. She had to. His father lacked the proper judgment to raise a child. Anyone could see that. It would comfort Clara Belle in the hereafter to know that her son was safe. She had already begun that campaign by letting Don and Earl remain and removing herself as a point of contention so her daughter wasn't disturbed in the last days of her life. One had to begin a campaign for change long before one thought one should.

* * *

Abigail found little peace in this latest trip back east. The division between temperance and suffrage and prohibition swirled around the eastern cities and in the halls of women gathering. When asked to speak, she sounded defensive, she knew, but she'd been accused of taking money from the liquor industry—she hadn't. Her having championed the plight of a brewer's widow in Walla Walla, Washington, a story she'd told in her speech, had gotten her labeled as a traitor to the cause of controlling the blight of alcohol, betraying the temperance movement. Her colleagues couldn't seem to understand that she cared about the property rights of women too, not only their right to vote. She supported even widows of brewers who'd been left with debt by a brewer husband. Abigail advocated helping the woman turn the brewery into a cannery or develop another kind of business that would help the community and this woman. But no, because she was associated with hops and foam, Abigail was labeled as a traitor.

She penned a letter to Shirley.

The hardest thing is that I'm supposed to be a communicator, someone who, with written and spoken word, can express difficult perspectives facing us. But I am failing at this. I can't seem to find the handle of this pot so that I can remove it from the heat. I fear Washington Territory will repeal the vote for women because our fair sex are indeed voting for prohibition.

I am lonely here in this eastern city of government, sitting on a park bench beneath a canopy of trees. I am misunderstood and I begin to see that it is my own fault. But I lack the wisdom, my dear friend, to know what to do about it. And my usual rebirth is clouded with grief for Clara Belle's impending death, for all I didn't do and might have and now it's too late. I can only pray that one day I will find a way to be understood, by myself, if not by those around me.

* * *

It happened that Abigail was home when Clara Belle breathed her last; Don wasn't there. He'd gone back to Washougal to tend to business, and so on that late January day in 1886, Abigail sat stern-faced as Ben sang "Rock of Ages" to his daughter. Clara Belle's eyes were closed with the smallest flutter of her eyelids now and then to suggest that she heard. And then the certainty of it caught Abigail by the throat, her sob swallowed so as not to have Clara hear it. She held her daughter's hand, rubbed her palm, and prayed, oh she prayed! Her brothers sat around the bed, heads bowed, hands clasped between their knees. Hubert's wife accompanied Ben's singing, and he looked strong beside Clara and her labored breathing, and Abigail prayed that her daughter's suffering would end soon, as the pain of watching, listening, of powerlessness wore upon them as the coming of a heavy storm.

She had thought once that losing the vote had been like losing a child. It was nothing like it. Outliving the flesh of one's flesh was a grief like no other. There was no map to follow, no way to get over the pain, only try to find a way through. She and Ben and the mothers and fathers of deceased children walked in a wilderness, far away from any promised land.

* * *

"I'm going to visit Shirley," she told Ben. "The air in San Francisco will perk me up. Should I take Earl with me?"

"Leave him be. He's getting into a routine here. And he's a good help to me. Reminds me of things."

She felt a tinge of guilt but slipped over it. Clara Belle had been buried, and Don had returned to Washougal, reluctantly leaving Earl behind.

"It's nothing out of the ordinary, Don." Abigail had tugged at her black neck scarf. "We've had nieces and nephews and the sons of friends stay with us for a time. You'd have to hire a nanny or someone to look after him. Visit anytime."

Defeated, Don had left his son behind.

"I asked Earl to remind you to put your coat on in the evening." Abigail washed an ink stain from her fingers as she spoke to Ben. A dove cooed in the elm tree.

"Oh, yes, he does that. But he also notices if I've already eaten a bowl of mush when I ask Chen why he hasn't gotten breakfast out for us yet." Ben chuckled. "Craziest thing." He shook his head. "I guess food doesn't taste all that good if I can't remember that I just ate it."

* * *

Shirley welcomed her, and Abigail felt the greatest comfort in the arms of an old friend who had lived a lifetime with another kind of lost child. She and her husband Eloi had children together, but her eldest daughter—now grown with children of her own—was still the heart-child. That girl, taken from her by the legal system, had given Shirley direction toward helping women seek their rights in divorces they had not wanted and been unjustly granted. Eloi, with his dark hair and gentle eyes, would put his arm around Shirley as they talked, a gesture of protection.

"Clara Belle's last words were that I needed to get back into the fight. She said she was going on ahead and that I had work to do here. But I'm not sure how to do it now."

"It'll come to you, Jenny. You're in an understandable slump. Such a disappointment to you—Clara Belle's death, losing that vote."

"It was. But I snapped back, or so I thought. And then encountered the tension back east that doesn't appear to be going away. I seem to be the crux of the contention. My outspoken views at the conventions about us not lining up with prohibitionists. And then my writings."

"Maybe you should do what you always wanted to do and just write your poems and novels."

"I can't support myself on that."

"You could sell the *New Northwest*."

She stood thoughtful, the waning sun sending glittering reddish light across the bay. "But how would I carry on the mission that Clara Belle wanted for me?"

"Edit someone else's newspaper. Kate's doing that. Write for someone else, earn a salary."

"Oh my, who would hire this outspoken old woman?" The friends laughed.

"You're not old."

"But I am outspoken."

"It's who you are. You're a reformer, Jenny. An activist. You see injustice and must act on that. The way you do it can change through the years. With less stress from the newspaper, you could give more time to your speaking and even publish a collection of your speeches, to inspire others to keep the faith. What is it you always say—'the world is moving and women are moving with it'? We just move differently, to adapt to the times."

Shirley's words formed a knot at the end of a thread that Abigail could imagine pulling through a new cloth.

"I'd have to talk to the boys. And Ben, of course. He talks about Idaho and the Lost Valley. It is beautiful country, and with water, we might grow crops. I convinced him that if I could write in a dusty stagecoach stop, I could surely write in a cabin shadowed by mountains while streams rushed nearby." She'd even thought it might become a gathering place for campaigns. Perhaps offer refuge for women and children in need, but she didn't think Ben would go for that. *Is that the way my mission to elevate women will take now? I'll advance the place of women in public life by retreating into a wilderness?* Her prayers asked for guidance.

* * *

She called a family gathering as soon as she returned to Portland. "What would you do, Ma?"

"Why, find a ranch in Idaho, as you boys and Ben have been touting for some time now. We could all move there. I'd find my little 'lodge in the wilderness' and write. I could be a correspondent to the new buyer, and Idaho still doesn't have the vote. Yet. They could use me. And of course, I can travel back here, stay with Kate or Harriet or Fanny or Sarah Maria. Goodness, what's the benefit of all those sisters if one can't impose upon them from time to time—not to mention nieces and nephews."

"Earl would like it, though I doubt Stearns would," Hubert said.

"Should we tell her, Pa?" Clyde asked. Her second youngest son was sixteen already. He had a beard. How had her boys grown up without her noticing?

"Tell me what?"

"We've already found a place that Pa likes. I like it too," Ralph told her. "Hubert took him last week."

So that's why the Idaho images were so readily available to Ben.

"We were trying to figure out how to buy it, but now, if we sell the paper, we could do that." Hubert added, "We boys made a down payment on it."

"You bought something without my even agreeing to it? Not knowing if you could pay for it?" *Encumbering me?* "Ben?" *What has happened to our partnership?* "When were you going to let me know?"

"I quit the customhouse, Jenny. It was time. I couldn't . . . well, I forgot important things."

Like telling me you'd resigned.

"Earl and Hubert and me, we went to Idaho. You were traveling like you do." He grinned. "I didn't take your teapot money, Jenny."

Shame washed over her. She hadn't been aware that Ben's problems had become severe enough that he had recognized his need to quit work. They hadn't even discussed it. As usual, she had been so involved in her own world afar that she hadn't seen what was happening nearby.

Yes, Clara Belle's death had come during that time, and travel had been a way of her grieving. But Ben grieved too.

"Oh, Ben. I . . . you could have telegraphed me at Shirley's. I would have come home."

"You needed your time there. You always come back with new ideas. And it happened." He looked around the room at their sons and Earl. "Where's Cora? She always fixes my evening cocoa."

"It's not night yet, Grandpa." Earl eased up beside Ben.

They've moved on without me.

* * *

The swirl of getting the books in order filled her time: deciding whether to sell the presses separately or give a credit knowing new ones might be warranted. Deciding whether to put the house on the market too, how to let subscribers know about the changes. When she'd had any second thoughts about the sale of her work for the past sixteen years, the enthusiasm with which her sons were willing to divest of it kept her from being tearful. Even changes that resulted in things one wished for could carry heartbreak, she decided. At least Clara Belle didn't have to see that her beloved Washington had repealed the woman's vote when the Territorial Legislature found it unconstitutional. What had Shirley said when she pierced Abigail's ears? "Pain comes before the glory." She'd felt that when they left Hardscrabble Farm and when she sold the school and millinery. As with her other losses, she would grieve in time. And maybe these back-to-back devastations with Clara's passing and the voting loss, perhaps in order to move forward, one needed things so upending.

With Ben, Wilke, Earl, and Hubert, they traveled to the Wood River district, east to Idaho. The land the boys had found for Ben had a large log cabin on it, with several bedrooms and a wide porch that wrapped around the house, offering a vista of green and snowcapped mountains they called the Lost River Range. It was in the Pashimeroi Valley. They'd made a good purchase. The expanse caused her to take in deep breaths. This would be a healing place; she could feel it.

"What would you say about using the bunkhouse to house women and children in need? We could perhaps start a utopian community like the Aurora colony, where all are equal and—"

"Ma. No," Wilke said. He put his hand up to stop her. "This is our place, not the whole world's."

Yes, this would be a space to get away from the world, to stop rehashing the arguments at National, put away the sting of the charges made against her as being in the hands of the liquor industry. Breaking with Aunt Susan had been painful. She hated being misunderstood. Here, she could be heard again, write with more clarity. She had written a letter to Shirley about the planned move but also pouring out the anguish of Clara's loss and her trouble with National. *"I will die as I have lived, misunderstood by those I love best and serve most."*

She sat on the porch steps while Ben smoked his pipe from a rocking chair downwind of her. *Can I really give it all up to come here?* Her stomach tightened at the uncertainty that clutched at her. She felt most in control when she drew her own map, and this move had only vapors of that. She remembered asking her students once to define *powerful*, giving her definition first. "I think it's a word that means one can set a goal and then figure out how to make it happen." That was being powerful.

But her students had told her no, it was wealth. Another boy said, "No, when you're big and strong like Mr. Duniway, that's powerful." But it had been the smallest child, the quiet one, who had taken her breath away.

"I think powerful is when you want to quit but you keep going."

Maybe there'd be enough with the sale to pay for the ranch and still have a small house in Portland, permit her to "keep going." The winters might be brutal in this valley, and having a refuge among the association women of Portland could be her escape—if she found she needed it. A meadowlark flitted from a shrub. She'd have to learn the name of the plants and trees, and she'd become familiar with the sound of their dry leaves crinkling in the fall and discover how the Pashimeroi Valley got its name and what were the weather and the ways of this place. A neighboring rancher stopped by to explain a sound that was like horses crossing a creek. "Salmon spawning," he'd told her. "Slapping the water as they splash over each other."

"Imagine," Abigail had said.

She rose and found her foolscap paper. They'd brought personal things with them on this trip. The "lodge in the wilderness," as she began to call it, had come furnished with beds and linens and dishes and even a dog. They'd have to hire a cook and a housekeeper. She'd want time to write.

September 2, 1886. Blanche Le Clerq, a Tale of the Mountain Mines. It would be a novel about a wealthy mineowner who falls in love with Blanche, who refuses to marry him unless he accepts her passion for the stage and realizes that women can be public and wise and chaste and willing to rule *with* him and not *over* him.

"I've started another novel, Ben," she called out to him after a time.

"I thought you owned a newspaper."

"We did." *How many things will I need to repeat?* "And I have another story to serialize for it. I'll mail it from Ellis, Idaho, so Willis can get the first chapter into the next edition. He's staying to help the new owner."

Ben nodded and smiled at her. "This is good, Jenny. We'll get horses once we move. We can do that, can't we?"

We are moved. "Of course."

He sighed. "I'll have my two loves back again: you and my pintos."

At least he put me first in the lineup of his loves. That was what she needed to do for him now too. Put him first. The vote for women would follow, surely, as inevitably as the mountains that rose before them. She'd spent her life doing something worth doing. She'd continue but in a new way from a new place. It was how the world moved and women with it.

THIRTY-TWO

No Worry in the World

1893–96

Abigail adjusted her hat. At least the fashion now allowed for the brim to be flattened at the back so a woman could lean against the stagecoach leather without worrying about smashing the brim or removing her hat to hold in her lap—if alone in the carriage. Dusty as it was, the trip was the balm she needed. She'd been spending summers at the lodge, looking after Ben. At least helping the boys look after him. Clyde was home from Cornell for the summer, and Ralph helped as well, so she was free to take the call. She lowered the canvas window to prevent the dust from rolling in. She'd be in Boise by evening, geared up, as they said about harnessed horses, to work.

Come at once. The Women's Christian Temperance Union is spoiling everything. They've arranged for a hearing before the convention, in advance of ours, asking for a clause in the new Constitution to prohibit liquor traffic. They won't get it, of course, but they will prohibit us from getting a Woman's Suffrage plank, if you don't come.

Eighty miles she'd traveled by train after nearly two hundred miles by stage. She'd been in remote Blackfoot when the letter reached her. Still, she'd arrived on time.

"Oh, thank goodness you're here." The head of the local suffrage association met her. They hoped they could insert women's right to vote into the proposed statehood constitution.

"It's the prohibitionists that'll kill us," Abigail said. She felt a kinship with those women fighting the opposition to suffrage, making the cause her own no matter what state or territory she might be in. "And the women who support temperance, they'll be our death too if we let them."

Abigail brushed dust from her skirt, grateful once again that hoops had gone out of style. Her added weight wasn't complemented by the new hourglass jackets over skirts, but seeing her reflection in the full-length mirror as she entered the hotel made her decide she looked "formidable." Just what a woman needed these days to take on the politicians. "I'm beginning to think that the hops growers are the ones promoting temperance and prohibition, in the background of course. They know the very idea that women will vote to take away the average man's access to liquor will keep them from voting yes with their pens."

"You never tire," her colleague said. She set Abigail's dusty carpetbag on the floor in front of the desk at the Boise hotel. "I thought you might like the quiet time in your room before tomorrow's speech at the legislature. Otherwise I'd be so pleased to have you stay at my home."

"Very thoughtful," Abigail told the younger woman, though she wondered if her reputation for late-night talks of a woman's plight—and sometimes a bit too much of her own—might have influenced where she stayed. She actually would have liked the give-and-take of civic conversation. It fed her, got her dander up so she was fiery in her presentations. Her sons tired of her constant talk of suffrage, and Ben . . . well, Ben didn't talk much at all anymore, occasionally of simple things: how the dog loved to jump into the stock tank on hot days, or the smell of sagebrush wafted by a gentle breeze. He was aware of what was right in front of him, the present moment, but carried little interest in politics or even how well the boys were doing or how well Earl, Clara Belle's son and their only grandson, had taken to ranching.

At least that was one good thing that had happened from their land purchase—Earl had found an interest. The boy was also the one to write long letters to her when she was in Portland and had become a stable caretaker to Ben. She found him to be a better letter-writer than talker when she was with him, though.

The invitation came on behalf of women getting the vote. She could promote her cause and add a side dish of comradery she now missed inside her own home.

"I'll see you in the morning. Thank you for welcoming me."

"This is the great Abigail Scott Duniway," the woman told the hotel agent. "We've reserved the best room for her."

Outwardly, Abigail brushed away the compliment, but she took it inside, let it fill her up.

* * *

The presentation went so well that Abigail found herself beaming as she boarded the stage to return home, savoring her own words. The July heat brought out her fan, and she wasn't looking forward to the journey, but she could bask in the accolades of how creatively she'd organized her presentation. She had pointed out—the legislators having just heard from a temperance promoter—that they were witness to how women were able to hold different views and weren't all of one mix. The observation served her argument that this was what the framers wanted when they created this American idea, that moving toward freedom and the vote for all would simply bring out stronger discourse, more rational ideas for discussion from all citizens.

They'd applauded politely as they had for the temperance folk. But she'd felt hopeful that they'd include a separate plank in their state constitution. She'd travel back to support it if needed. It was what she did.

* * *

"I have become a magnet for opposition, it seems," she told Ben. They rode side by side on the path that followed the stream running through their Lost River property. Ben's mind was clearer after their rides, she'd noticed, though she didn't know why. She could hear the stream. Water, too, had become a point of contention, with their neighbors disagreeing about a diversion dam they'd placed to irrigate their fields being seen as interrupting the water needs of downstream neighbors. *Is there nothing in my life that doesn't carry controversy?*

The dog they'd inherited, Champ was his name, followed along behind. No one had any idea how old the mutt was, but she guessed he was ten or more. He didn't bound about like a puppy. His long hair easily matted if she or Ben or Earl forgot to brush him. As with her, middle age had set in to Champ.

"The magnet is in the barn," Ben said. "What did you need it for?"

"Nothing. Sorry I mentioned it." She wished she had someone to talk over her frustrations with, someone to bounce her ideas off. Earl chattered of cattle raising. She wrote to Clyde, who responded, but he was busy at class—he had transferred to Harvard. It would be as good as or better than Harvey's legal degree. The other boys, minus Hubert, lived at the Clay house in Portland and did not write often. Ralph was a full-fledged lawyer now, and Wilkie worked as a proofreader for the *Evening Telegram*. Willis stayed in the printing business too as a proofreader for Harvey's dreaded *Oregonian.* Hubert and Cora had gone to New York to make their mark brokering lumber from the West. Children, scattered to the winds like maple leaves. Their lodge-in-the-wilderness ranch had simply not been enough to support them all, with wheat and cattle prices plummeting. Abigail would rather be in Portland herself, but Ben did so much better here, especially in the summer months. And right now, suffrage action was in Idaho. She hoped she'd be invited to give a rousing speech and find someone to talk politics with afterward.

"The magnet's right where I put it," Ben said. "I haven't misplaced it."

She patted his arm. "I know, Ben. It's fine. Let's head back to the house. Earl's coming later."

"Earl? Where did he go?"

"He's working some of his own cattle now, Ben. And he's teamed up with another rancher. We've had to sell our cows, remember?" Ben didn't. What people were calling "the panic" had hit them too. She'd wanted to sell the ranch when the market was still good, but the property wasn't even in her name! How Ben had managed that and how there was still $4000 owing stung her. The boys must have known but had not invited her into the decision when they'd expanded the boundaries, buying new property just as the economy was toppling.

"I remember now," Ben said. "He's a good cowboy. Did you see the way he lobbed that rope around the calf? Wouldn't be without him for the branding."

We won't be branding here again.

She turned him toward the ranch house. Geraniums bloomed in large pots on either side of the porch steps. The one plant she could keep from dying, it seemed. They were cheery, and their presence lifted her spirits, though not high enough. She sighed.

"What's the matter, Jenny? Are you sad?"

"Weary. Nothing for you to worry over."

"I don't have a worry in the world, Jen." Ben took her hand, kissed the palm. "Everything always turns out all right."

As they watched the sun set, she repeated her hoped-for words of a wonderful outcome. She hadn't gotten everything she wanted—most importantly the woman's vote. But oh, didn't she have an amazing story to leave behind? Daughter, wife, mother, grandmother, teacher, milliner, businesswoman, writer, poet, newspaper owner, public speaker, activist—a new word people were using for those who sought change for worthy causes. And now rancher. And all along, friend. Ben had been right. Things had turned out all right. They had weathered great disappointments and great loss. The world was changing and women were changing with it. She'd be so grateful for that. As she thought of her ever-hopeful and adventurous life, a shiver ran up her spine.

* * *

The letter asking her to speak to the Columbian Exposition in Chicago brought a welcome change. Here was a prime opportunity to once again be on the national stage. And they would pay her and cover her expenses. It was to celebrate the quadricentennial of Columbus's discovery of the Americas, and she would use that idea of discovery to frame her entire speech. She wrote on the porch table at the lodge, Ben rocking in the chair beside her.

"Ben, I've come up with a doozy of a speech." The dog thumped his tail on the boards at the sound of her voice. Ben said nothing so she spoke to Champ. "I'm going to invite them to think what exploration would have looked like if Columbus had landed on the West Coast instead of the East. We'd have an entirely different country. We'd all have pioneering spirits pushing us east, creating not only geographic explorations but economic, social, moral, and intellectual discoveries with a different cast. I'll show them that men and women would have been seen as equal, discovering 'with' each other. Don't you think that sounds like a good approach?"

Champ lifted his head, his tongue hanging out, responding to the enthusiasm in her voice.

"The dog gets it." She spoke to Ben's silence.

Her speech was innovative, and she could encourage the idea that there were new opportunities in the West. Women could homestead and become property owners. There were new possibilities in this rugged mountain landscape, just as there'd been for her. The energy of her having thought of such an inventive approach kept her mind spinning with new metaphors and imagery that she thought the largely eastern audience would find compelling. This was the fervor she'd been missing. Even when she'd written *The Coming Century—Journal of Progress and Reform* and gotten it published through '91 and '92, she hadn't felt the zest and zeal of knowing she'd be speaking to a large crowd with an inventive presentation. Spoken words had power too. They could help people look at things in different ways, and that was worthy work, even if how people chose to act because of those words weren't her ways.

She took Ben back to Portland and headed east for the speech. It was a marvel of a time for her, despite her need of the cane and her female parts causing pain.

"Such a wonderful speech, Mrs. Duniway." "Thank you for coming so far and at such a physical cost to you."

Abigail soaked in the praise, even though she knew accolades shouldn't fall on her but for the cause. Still, she wrote to Shirley and her sisters about the excitement of the exposition. *"Maybe Oregon will do something like it for the 100th anniversary of the exploration of Lewis and Clark in 1905."* Of course, Harvey had been selected to chair that event. Maybe by then they'd be successful with the vote and he'd have to recognize the reality of women's suffrage whether he liked it or not. There was a new campaign set for 1900. She would be involved. She'd already designed the banner.

* * *

She had lost the Ben she'd known and loved years before. The boys said the same thing, that the Pa they'd adored and tended wasn't the man they said their final goodbyes to in October of '96.

Ben had witnessed the three weddings of '94 when Clyde, Willis, and Wilke all found their life mates and married. And while he likely didn't realize it, Idaho passed women's suffrage in a statewide election with every county except Custer—the one they lived in—voting yes. It was good Ben didn't know about that. Abigail was sure it was over that water argument they'd waged with neighbors.

They'd sold the ranch, not getting nearly enough for it, but back in Portland, she and Ben had found a quiet life. She wrote her novels. More than nineteen, the last one in two parts, completed before Ben's death. She noted that she'd been most productive during the years she had the newspaper, as though having a dozen brands in the flames gave her impetus and order. She wasn't writing articles much, except copies of her speeches. The buyer of the *New Northwest* had gone under less than two years after the purchase. She learned later that it was a friend of Harvey's who had bought it, and she wondered if perhaps he deliberately ran it into the ground. But her sons assured her that without major investors like the *Oregonian* attracted, a newspaper's success depended on a commitment like hers that carried the charge ever forward as she had. The boys had withdrawn their shares of the business and moved on to new lives, first the ranch in Idaho and then later, when it was sold, on to legal work, university presidencies, and becoming the state's printer. It was as it should have been.

But she missed Ben. Missed his calm and wisdom and shared understandings, especially about Mr. Bunter, who continued until his own death the following year, still a bachelor, complaining about strong-minded women.

Most importantly, Ben was now in a place where he truly didn't have a worry in the world. Her worries were pecuniary ones. She badgered the boys into setting up a trust they paid into, giving her a small monthly income. Not enough to hobnob with the women's club members in Portland, though she had founded that club, but someone had paid her dues. She thought it might have been her daughters-in-law. She liked the work they were doing for Portland's beautification, but she yearned for the fight for the vote. For all the confidence she exuded when on the stage or in the fight, it was Ben's assurance she was doing something worthwhile that had sustained her. She had resented him at times during the marriage—the notes he'd signed, leaving her off the ranch title, his need for care when they had so little funds and she needed care herself—but when he told her not to worry and to do what she knew well, she'd carried on. It was what women did.

THIRTY-THREE

Abigail Scott Duniway Day

1905

Shirley came to the Clay Street house to retrieve Abigail. A spring rain served as prelude to a warming sun, both bringing out the smells of pine trees and lifting Abigail's spirits. Kate settled the pins in Abigail's hat, held the mirror for her to assess the look. It was the week of the big 1905 Lewis and Clark Exposition, and the National American Woman Suffrage Association convention had been meeting for several days now in Portland, their activities wrapped into the exhibits. Her brother Harvey, chairing the exposition, had surprised her by inviting the association to meet as part of the events in Portland. She'd been wary but hoped perhaps he had come to his senses and would support the suffrage amendment on the ballot for 1906. Abigail had read an opening speech, "Centennial Ode," her voice a bit shaky as she still struggled with her rheumatism and the aftereffects of having two toes amputated when the infections wouldn't heal.

"I hope I'm up to the day's events," Abigail said. "I've wanted my eastern colleagues to enjoy Oregon hospitality, but I haven't been up to much of it myself."

"Your minions have taken care of things." Kate tied the hat bow beneath Abigail's chin. A banner reading "Votes for Women" flapped from the porch railing.

"Don't get the strings caught in my double chins." *I've put on so much weight just sitting around.* "I need to leave those morning donuts alone."

"If Maria was still here, she'd have rustled up precious knitted gifts or made sure everyone went out to see Multnomah Falls," Kate said.

Abigail lamented not being able to organize everything as she had in the old days.

"Your youngest sister, Maria, right?" Shirley clarified.

Abigail nodded. "Died in '01. The year after we failed yet another vote. I think it broke her heart. At least she wasn't alive to see the '03 defeat too. That was another tough loss. Miss that girl. Miss dear Ben too."

Abigail held the mirror. Gone were the long curls. Her hair was smoothed beneath her hat, a bun snuggled in at the back of her neck.

Shirley nodded approval. "California still doesn't have suffrage either, so don't be too hard on yourselves."

"That's two of our dear sisters who made the Oregon Trail journey, gone to be with Momma and Papa." Kate sighed.

"Not sure what good I'll do you or the cause today," Abigail said. "I haven't yet, it seems." They walked out toward the landau Harvey had sent Shirley in to retrieve Abigail. Another surprising generosity of her brother. *After all these yearsm does he feel guilty?*

"I wouldn't be here today without you, Abigail," Shirley said.

"Me? What did I have to do with it?"

"You've been a kaleidoscope of goodness in my life—and that of hundreds of women. Specifically, don't you remember what you said when Clara died? That it was the nearby, not the faraway, that mattered in life, that you wished you'd have moved right next door to her when her husband took her to the wilds of Washougal."

"I did wish I'd done that."

"I did do that when our Mary and Walter bought their land in Idaho."

"I don't think I realized that was why you and Eloi left San Francisco."

"Well, it was. And you were a part of that."

"Not my ranch. Ben's gone and so is that land with a river named Pahsimeroi running through it. *Pa-simmer-eye.* I love the sound of that Shoshone word."

"You've always loved words," Shirley said. "It was what drew me to you on the trail, when you read from the journal you kept. You were a map for me."

"Isn't that strange. I remember dreaming of maps after Momma died. Life doesn't give us one, does it?"

"We do what we see to do and trust there'll be a light to guide our way in the dark times." Abigail hoisted herself into the carriage, and Kate slipped in beside her. Shirley did the same from the other side.

She could hear the *clop-clop* of the horses' hooves on the cobblestones. "Now whatever good I can do, I'll do right here in Oregon," Abigail said. "But I'm afraid some of the NAWSA members would say I've done more harm than good, Harvey and I have. He wrote the most scathing editorial opposed to us before the 1900 and 1903 vote, and I suspect he'll do the same in '06. Look at this noggin." She patted the hat on her head. "Bumps everywhere from this suffrage work. What do you suppose Harvey's up to, being so nice to the association? Such work we have to do."

"But pleasure too, Sister," Kate said.

Shirley laughed, then turned to face her friend, hands over Abigail's gloved ones resting in her lap. "You never really knew your influence, Jenny. It wasn't in the big campaigning or even the novels and newspapers. It was in the everyday living that you did, writing your own map for how to proceed from tragedy and trials, disappointment and defeat. You cared for and about others and learned lessons in your still hunt."

"Some took me awhile. Like holding my tongue."

"Oh, you're still working on that one," Kate said.

"You did all that without even knowing it, I suspect, how you brought hope to our lives." Shirley had tears in her eyes.

Kate said, "A fierce love for justice and liberty for all of us. That's your legacy."

"A passion, I'd say, for anything you put your heart toward. Even when things didn't pan out," Shirley said. "When no gold sank to the bottom, you never begrudged the effort of looking for it and helping others swirl the waters in their seeking." Shirley put her arm through Abigail's.

"If you only knew," Abigail said. She thought of Ben, Clara, her other children too. There were regrets. But Ben would be the first to tell her not to worry over the past. "I didn't know I needed to hear such good words. Thank you, Shirley, Kate.

"I am so excited about this day," Shirley said. "Your children are already at the pavilion, along with Eloi and Fanny and all the nieces and nephews."

"My children? Aren't we just having a little tea to encourage campaigners?"

"We are doing that, too, with you, dear Abigail, as the sweetener," Shirley said.

Abigail guffawed and the horse's ears twitched to the sound. "Sweet has never been a moniker given to me."

"It only takes a pinch to stir up a little joy," Kate said.

The driver chirped at the team and the horses pulled forward a little faster. The breeze cooled her face.

"Today," Kate said, "we're also celebrating the Abigail Scott Duniway Day."

"We are?"

"Your brother Harvey arranged for it. The entire day is about you, Abigail." Shirley blinked back tears.

"Harvey organized it?"

"He'll be there for the photograph taking, with you and Susan B. in the front row."

"I'm . . . speechless."

Both Shirley and Kate laughed. "That's something for the woman who gave more than, what, fifteen hundred speeches? I can hardly wait to hear what you don't say today," Kate said. "The woman who spoke up for liberty. That's you. The woman who stays the course, even when there are boulders in the road."

Epilogue

1912

Abigail

Well, it finally happened. Oregon women finally earned the right to vote. I lived to see it! My brother Harvey did not. He was far away in Maryland when he passed three years ago, unexpectedly, but then is death ever expected? Even with an illness it comes as a shock. He needed emergency surgery, and it ended badly. He left his family well-off, his wife a millionaire, but she earned it having to live with him all those years. Oh, I should let it go now. I've had my life as rich as his, and we found a truce before the end, despite his editorials at each campaign urging defeat. And he had his own defeat when he ran for the Senate.

Oregon went through six suffrage campaigns before the vote arrived. Washington women got their say—again—in 1910. California beat us too, voting it in last fall. I suspect Harvey's opposition had something to do with Oregon's delay, and perhaps my own fractious ways contributed as well. Kate notes that. I can take criticism from her.

I have time now to write my autobiography. I've already begun, and the title will be *Path Breaking: An Autobiographical History of the Equal Suffrage Movement in Oregon.* I'll write of the struggles but also the triumphs. We had them both, but that is what passion is about, is it not? The ups and downs, being in the thick of things and then wasting away at times in the thin of them. Women were appointed to public posts even before they could vote. Oregon had a female public health officer, and Lola Baldwin became the first woman detective in the entire nation. She served right here in Portland. Even a female market inspector happened before we had the vote, and why not? Who better than a woman to know about pork and health and, yes, enforcing the laws that we had no say in making but can recognize justice when it's needed?

I'll write too of my greatest achievement and greatest assets—my children. I love them so, and they are coming here for this big occasion. I wish Sarah Maria and Maggie had lived to see this day and Little Toot. And Ben. And Clara Belle, who sang at those suffrage meetings and gave me permission to continue on even while she breathed her last. Both she and Ben had those glorious voices. Ben thought I didn't notice and perhaps I might not have said so as often as I should have, but I heard them and take comfort in those little things remembered, the things nearby.

There are photographers arriving soon to take my picture with Governor Oswald West while I sign the proclamation affirming Oregon's women have the right to vote. He's coming right here to my Clay Street home, and I'll sign it on the library table where I've written so many of my books and speeches. I've a finely tanned hide from our Idaho ranch (Earl, my grandson, tanned it) to spread across the tabletop. Shirley and her precious Eloi are here too. And other suffrage leaders. Now I hope to live to actually vote in 1914, the first elections when we'll be allowed. But even if I don't, it will be a life well lived—for all my mistakes.

Our past president, Mr. Roosevelt, gave a speech about citizenship while we here in Oregon were fighting our fifth campaign for the vote, and I remember feeling the most defeated after that 1910 disaster. But I read the president's speech, and he said something I cling to still. That the men to be celebrated are those in the arena, fighting the big battles even if they end in defeat. Well, he said "the man in the arena" is the one to be praised for being there, but I'm sure he would see the merit in putting women in that arena too. We too can fail deeply, but we fail by daring greatly. And that is how I hope to be remembered, that I dared greatly and so shall never be known as "those cold and timid souls who neither know victory nor defeat."

Oh, the governor's here. The world is moving and women are moving with it. Isn't that grand! Now where's my best hat? I must look festive for the occasion that celebrates something truly worth doing.

Author's Notes and Acknowledgments

Abigail Scott Duniway is one of only six women whose names are written in the halls of Oregon's government chambers, but she is perhaps the most known for her forty decades of working for women's suffrage and for the famous rivalry with her younger brother, Harvey Scott, editor of the *Oregonian* newspaper. Until I began research about her, I didn't know that Abigail also owned and edited a newspaper, quite a feat for a woman in any century. Her suffrage work through so many years without success speaks to the continued efforts today in seeking justice and liberty for women. We remember the one hundredth anniversary of the ratification of the Nineteenth Amendment to the Constitution passed in 1919 that granted women the right to vote. Abigail's hard-fought victory epitomizes the need for a vision and the persistence to bring it to fruition. As was said generations ago, "Women's work is never done."

Dozens of scholars and historians, sociologists, and genealogists found Abigail's life and work of utmost importance. I am deeply indebted to them and to descendants whom I was able to confer with. The intricacies of the suffrage fight between National and American suffrage organizations, the vitriol of temperance and prohibition workers, and Oregon's own path toward the vote are not detailed in this novel. But references will direct those who want more about those battles. The Library of Congress hosts a website of the National American Woman Suffrage Association collection. It includes a timeline *One Hundred Years toward Suffrage: An Overview* compiled by E. Susan Barber.

My interest was in Abigail the woman, wife, mother, sister, friend, novelist, newspaperwoman, overcomer, in addition to her decades as a champion of women's rights.

She was a complex woman. Despite the laws working against women, Abigail became one of those rare beings, a woman who was the editor/owner of the *New Northwest*. Her brother Harvey Scott edited and was later co-owner of the *Oregonian*, a competitive paper with the potential to support or denigrate suffrage. While their feud is legendary and written about, I was interested in other relationships, too, including parents and other siblings including sister Kate, who also worked as an editor for both papers and the Duniways' son-in-law's paper. Abigail's husband, Ben, has been portrayed through letters Abigail wrote in later life to her sons, as being less involved in his wife's advocacy. But he did go to the mines with Harvey, had the terrible accident, cosigned the notes. He held the customs job for fifteen years following his injury, and that provided financial security. They did move from Albany and later to Portland and began the paper about the same time. He invented the washing machine and trained horses, and their six children suggest they were a team until Ben's later years with his deteriorating health condition. Abigail's superior intellect; her unceasing drive on behalf of women; her extraordinary production of twenty-two novels, poems, song lyrics, and essays; her giving over fifteen hundred speeches at a time when women were not encouraged to be public; and her being one of the elite women who owned and operated a newspaper in America who still kept her dignity and national reputation—those were avenues I wanted to explore in this novel.

This novel is based on facts. There were so many facts to sort! Abigail did teach in little Cincinnati, Oregon, and Needy, near the communal society of Aurora; she ran Hope School and the Union School, named so all would know that the Duniways supported the North in the Civil War. They sold Hardscrabble after the disasters, bought and lost Sunny Hillside Farm, moved to Lafayette and later to Albany. Abigail opened her millinery and successfully negotiated with Jacob Mayer to help her advance her business. She took in boarders to help finance her efforts and contribute to the family's support. In 1870, Abigail went to California to give a speech at the women's suffrage meeting there and likely would have met the California president at the time, Sarah Montgomery Wallis of my *One More River to Cross*. She was offered the *Pioneer* editing role and $800 for her tour, and Ben sent the telegram ordering her to come home when, like a good wife of the time, she had asked his permission. I speculated that he had news of his own job at the customhouse to share with her, but he may well have told her no for other reasons. Nevertheless, it was after that that the family moved to Portland and Abigail borrowed $3000—we don't know from where. And she did indeed start a newspaper, the first edition being May 5, 1871. Copies of the *New Northwest* are available online. The entire family was involved in the Duniway Publishing Company for sixteen years. The sale came the year after their only daughter's death.

Clara Belle's elopement and move to what Abigail called "the swamps of Washougal" did happen. Today, it's a very fine community where my granddaughter and her family live.

Schools are named for Abigail, parks and other public entities honor her passion and persistence, despite the fact that Oregon had six campaigns to win women the right to vote—more than any other state. Perhaps it was Abigail's clarity of purpose and her ability to overcome the setbacks during forty years that makes her so remarkable. Her powerful brother opposed all her public efforts, though the occasional support he gave her by buying steamship tickets or sponsoring Abigail Scott Duniway Day is documented and adds to the complexity of their relationship. He did indeed write an editorial of support in late 1883. But before the 1884 vote, he left town and was neutral in that election. The 1883 editorial was the only time he supported women's suffrage, and he wrote scathing opposing editorials ever after. The fact is that Oregon did not pass women's suffrage until after the death of Harvey Scott. Oregon was the seventh state in the nation to approve the woman's vote, eight years before the national amendment. Surrounding states passed suffrage before Oregon. Washington in 1883, repealed in 1887 and renewed in 1888 and also repealed. It was finally passed in 1910. Idaho in 1896. California in 1910. Abigail wasn't able to travel much to support the 1912 effort that did pass. Her health had continued to deteriorate, but she hung banners proclaiming "Votes for Women" and dispatched messages of encouragement to suffrage supporters.

In 2016, an Oregon commission met to choose possible new statues for the National Statuary Hall in Washington, DC. Abigail was chosen as the first woman for such an honor, which has not yet been carried out. She was also the first woman nominated from Oregon for the National Women's Hall of Fame.

Most of the incidents in this story are based on actual events. The status of women—having no say in business dealings but being responsible for a father's or husband's bad debts; lack of control over their own earnings; the inability to offer opinions at public discussion without scandal; the agony of unwanted divorces and custody battles favoring the father regardless of his capacity to care for the children; and more—these were all part of the struggle women faced in pioneering territories of the West that often left women destitute and without influence over much of their lives.

Abigail's father's scandal in the early chapter did occur and strained the siblings. Ben and his injury and his affable character are all documented. The tornado and fires; Ben's fine singing voice and being a househusband, going to the Idaho mines, receiving the customs job from Harvey; Abigail's millinery success; the boarders; Abigail's property speculations; the 1861–62 flood's impact on the Duniways; the deaths; and even some of the strains recorded in letters kept are a part of the true aspects of this story.

Susan B. Anthony did come to Oregon, and the two women toured the Northwest, camped out at the Oregon State Fair along with several of the Duniways including Ben. Abigail was present at the Centennial celebration in Pennsylvania when Susan B. (whom she sometimes referred to as Aunt Susan) presented the women's proclamation to President Ulysses S. Grant. (The vice president had been scheduled to receive it, but that office was vacant the entire year of 1876. That's another story!) The Nineteenth Amendment to the US Constitution used the same wording proclaiming women nationally now had the right to vote. Oregon was the twenty-fifth state to ratify this amendment in January of 1920, but by then, Oregon women had been voting for six years.

Abigail did live to register to vote in Multnomah County, Oregon. She also served on a jury and wrote her autobiography before dying a few weeks before her eighty-first birthday. An infection in her toe that would not heal ended this extraordinary woman's life, a woman who traveled far and wide on behalf of raising the quality of life for all women and, she believed, for men as well.

But fiction is the realm of emotion in addition to history, and exploring how Abigail felt about her life and effort is what intrigued me.

I did not dwell on the intense debates between the suffrage groups and the temperance and prohibition forces, nor Abigail's arguments with certain religious forces (because she did not support prohibition, believing people needed freedom to make their own choices in all things). I was interested more in the personal relationships and how Abigail's family dealt with her national persona at a time when women were not public beings and risked scorn for using their voices. An 1829 trial of another outspoken woman/writer/newspaper editor, Anne Royall, in Washington,

DC, for being a "common scold," might well have been Abigail's fate but for her image as a faithful wife and mother (*The Trials of a Scold, The Incredible True Story of Writer Anne Royall,* by Jeff Biggers [Thomas Dunne Books]). What did Abigail's passion for women's liberty cost her?

Only three characters are "fully imagined": one is Mr. Bunter (though there was a rejected suitor who found ways to complain about strong-minded women through the local press, and that person may have been the sender of the valentine that upset Abigail so); Shirley Ellis and Eloi Vasquez are also imagined characters. Shirley became a composite for the many friends Abigail would have had. As part of an auction in a First Presbyterian Church Bend fundraiser, Jan Tetzlaff bought the right to name a character in one of my books. Shirley Ellis was Jan's dear friend who died too young, and a part of her compassion and care for others I hope lives on in my Shirley. Eloi Vasquez is another character honoring a friend of Rory Johnston who bought the right to name a character by helping an Oregon literacy program called SMART (Start Making a Reader Today). Mr. Johnston chose his deceased friend Eloi Vasquez, a good, kind Californian, whose name and memory fit perfectly as a wise attorney and second husband of Shirley.

It could take an entire book to acknowledge those many souls who assisted me in sharing this story—some do not even know. I was heavily dependent on *Rebel for Rights: Abigail Scott Duniway*, a premier biography of Abigail written by Ruth Barnes Moynihan. The book's pages are thumbed and marked, and I am grateful for her scholarly and engaging work. A second book, equally marked up, is *Yours for Liberty: Selections from Abigail Scott Duniway's Suffrage Newspaper*, edited by Jean M. Ward and Elaine A. Maveety. This research, in addition to online access to copies of the *New Northwest*, proved invaluable. Another significant online source, "She Flies with Her Own Wings" (http://asduniway.org/) is a site of many of Abigail's speeches (including the Columbia Exposition speech) with introductions to each by USC professor Randall A.

Lake. Dr. Lake graciously corresponded with me about her public speaking life and directed me to his chapter about her in *Women Public Speakers in the United States, 1800–1925: A Bio-Critical Sourcebook*, edited by Karlyn Kohrs Campbell (Greenwood Press). Librarians at the Knight Library at the University of Oregon and at the Oregon Historical Society offered exceptional help, and I'm grateful. An article by Judge Susan P. Graber, United States Circuit Judge for the Ninth Circuit Court of Appeals, titled "The Long Oregon Trail to Women's Suffrage," proved invaluable. In 2019, I was honored to be a part of a panel celebrating Pioneer Courthouse in Portland, where Judge Graber and professor and historian Tracy J. Prince and I spoke about the passage of the Nineteenth Amendment. The courthouse was the site of the customs office, though it was built after Harvey Scott would have served in that role.

When publisher, writer, and editor Steve Forrester of EO Media invited me to write a chapter for a book he is publishing called *Eminent Oregonians* (forthcoming), he couldn't have known that I had already considered Abigail for my next novel. His interest as I worked on that chapter helped frame questions to answer for this novel, and I'm grateful. He also provided me with a book by Debra Shein, *Abigail Scott Duniway*, Western Writers Series #151, whose survey, analysis, and insights of Abigail's novel writing gave support for characterizing her fictional efforts. I am also grateful to Marianne Keddington-Lang, whose editorial queries for that chapter expanded my understanding of Abigail's journey. Abigail's own writings were also accessed. She was prolific and active into her eighties. A writer friend once told me that writing was a good profession because one could do it into one's old age, as Abigail showed.

Once again, my research friend CarolAnne Tsai located resources I might never have discovered. I am deeply indebted to her for reading early drafts as well. Robert and Kate Speckham, descendants of Abigail's youngest sister, Sarah Maria Kelty, spent a morning sharing their extensive collection of photographs, ephemera, and documents, including a copy of John Tucker Scott's tear-stained letter sending Sarah Maria to live with her older sister Fanny because of the consternation with his second-marriage circumstances. Bob's contributions to Find a Grave websites introduced me to him, and his willingness to share family documents and stories tenderly kept is deeply appreciated. He also had an extra copy of the 1997 *Oregon Historical Quarterly* special issue about the famed rivalry between Abigail and Harvey, written by Lee Nash, then a professor of history at George Fox University in Oregon. It referenced the one editorial written by Harvey in support of suffrage that he later retracted—to Abigail's great disappointment. Janet Meranda again lent her copyediting expertise to assist me. I am grateful for that and for her information about the DAR chapter named for Abigail.

I'm grateful to two special endorsers, Francine Rivers and Susan Butruille, both writers and students of suffrage history. Susan pointed out important corrections in the manuscript for which I'm very grateful and clarified the importance of referring to these hardworking women as *suffragists* and not the dismissive term *suffragette*. Abigail was definitely a suffragist.

I lifted the phrase "holy cow chips" from a writer colleague Randi Samuelson-Brown, who used the exclamation while we sat around a table in San Antonio talking about stories. I told her if I ever used that cheerful phrase, I'd mention her name with gratitude. I gave it to Abigail to use, and it seems fitting.

The Bend chapter of the American Association of University Women introduced me to *Reflecting Freedom: How Fashion Mirrored the Struggle for Women's Rights* by Eileen Gose and Kathy DeHerrera (self-published) that posed ways Abigail and her millinery work might have both informed and advanced her interest in women's liberty. Other authors' works that assisted me were Oregonian Sheri King, *Oregon's Abigail and Her Lafayette Debut*; *Covered Wagon Women Diaries & Letters from the Western Trails,*

1852 (edited and compiled by Kenneth L. Holmes & David C. Duniway*)* and an edition with an introduction by professor Glenda Riley. Abigail's own *Path Breaking: An Autobiographical History of the Equal Suffrage Movement in Pacific Coast States* (Shocken Paper Back Series); *Abigail Scott Duniway and Susan B. Anthony in Oregon: Hesitate No Longer* by Jennifer Chambers (History Press); Elinor Richey, author of "Abigail Scott Duniway: Up from Hardscrabble," in *Eminent Women of the West* (Howell-North).

To my Revell team, a humble thank-you. Editors Andrea Doering and Barb Barnes, their cadre of copyeditors extraordinaire, terrific publicist Karen Steele, marketing guru Michele Misiak and her team of cover designers, and the sales staff . . . every one of you. It couldn't be a book without you.

My agent of nearly thirty years, Joyce Hart of Hartline Literary Agency has been a gift beyond description. I am grateful for her prayers, wisdom, and good humor. Thank you is hardly enough.

Friends and family both near and far gave sustenance and encouragement. My brother and sister-in-law; Jerry's children Matt and Melissa Kirkpatrick and Kathleen and Joe Larsen sustained us through Jerry's ongoing treatment so I could concentrate on Abigail. Webmaster Paul Schumacher (I've spelled his name correctly this time!) and my prayer team of Judy Schumacher, Gabby Sprenger, Carol Tedder, Susan Parrish, Loris Webb, Judy Card, and significant others who held us in their prayers and hearts, including Mike and Marea Stone, Sue Kopp, Sandy Maynard, Kay and Don Krall, Dennis and Sherrie Gant, Laurie Vanderbeek, Karen and Tim Zacharias, Ken and Nancy Tedder, Jack and Carol Tedder, Maggie Hanson, Deb and Jim Barnes, Sarah Douglas, and other family and friends who brought special love during the writing of this book while we faced the death of a dear nephew and Jerry's diagnosis and treatments. You know who you are. I thank God for you. Thank you as well to the prayer team at First Presbyterian Bend and the ministerial staff.

Champion of support is my husband of forty-four years, Jerry, who at ninety (when this book is released) and with thirteen compressed vertebrae, and beating three cancers, and now fighting another, nevertheless in this book helped me understand what Ben might have endured physically as well as the challenge of living with what Mr. Bunter would call a "strong-minded woman." He offers what every writer seeks: kindness, no matter the place in the writing process, where failure seems inevitable; encouragement to get up and write again. That is what love looks like. I'm humbled and grateful.

And to readers: Madeleine L'Engle once wrote that when we create, we co-create. We co-create with Spirit and with readers. Thank you all for your co-creation, taking these stories and making them your own. You have made my literary life. Thank you.

Jane at jkbooks.com

Discussion Questions

1. What influence did the journey on the Oregon Trail have on the life work of Abigail "Jenny" Scott Duniway? Have you made a long journey to arrive where you are? What has influenced you as you travel without a map?
2. Early on, Jenny worried about not bringing disrepute onto Ben or her family. Was she successful in her life? What changed her attitude to make her more outspoken? What role did writing play in how she changed?
3. How did the landscapes of the Northwest inspire and challenge Abigail's view of the role of women in public life? Are there landscapes that you turn to for inspiration, respite, or escape?
4. Biographies of Abigail paint a picture of a single-minded woman who traveled far and wide, was a prolific writer, outspoken and often acerbic in her interactions with others as she fought for justice for women and ran her businesses. This author focused on the vulnerable side of Abigail; her need for support from her family, especially from Ben, and her uncertainty at times. Which Abigail rings true, or are both reasonable explorations of a complicated woman? How are our own complexities mirrored in this activist's story?

5. What part did the loneliness and isolation of Hardscrabble Farm have on Abigail's future endeavors? Have there been times when you've felt alone in a struggle? What helped you through it?
6. Abigail was the descendant of Cumberland Presbyterian ministers from Illinois. Her father was an elder in Oregon. How did Abigail's nurturing in the faith affect her efforts on behalf of women? Why did religious communities oppose women's right to vote? Were Abigail's strategies to address their worries successful?
7. How did fashion affect the women's movement? How did it influence Abigail's activist life?
8. Abigail grieved her daughter's illness by traveling, going somewhere not so close to the pain, giving herself to work. How might her absence have been seen during that time? How does grief affect a life's mission? What, if anything, did Abigail learn from grieving so many deaths in her life?
9. Was Abigail the most successful suffragist in the West even though Oregon did not get the vote until 1912? After the defeat of 1884, how did Abigail keep going? Are there lessons for us in this century when we face uncertainty and defeat?
10. Has your perspective on suffrage changed as a result of reading this woman's story? If so, how?
11. The author was once denied (in 1968) a public library card unless her husband signed for her to have it. Have you experienced the impact of a woman not having equal rights? How did it make you feel and what did you do about it?

Sign up for Jane's *Story Sparks* newsletter at jkbooks.com and follow her on Facebook and BookBub.

Jane Kirkpatrick is the *New York Times* and CBA bestselling and award-winning author of more than thirty books, including *One More River to Cross*, *Everything She Didn't Say*, *All She Left Behind*, *A Light in the Wilderness*, *The Memory Weaver*, *This Road We Traveled*, and *A Sweetness to the Soul*, which won the prestigious Wrangler Award from the Western Heritage Center. Her works have won the WILLA Literary Award, the Carol Award for Historical Fiction, and the 2016 Will Rogers Gold Medallion Award. Jane and her husband, Jerry, divide their time between Bend, Oregon, and Rancho Mirage, California, with their Cavalier King Charles Spaniel, Caesar. Learn more and sign up for her monthly *Story Sparks* newsletter at www.jkbooks.com.

Jane Kirkpatrick

WEAVING THE STORIES OF OUR LIVES

Get to know Jane at

JKBooks.com

Sign up for the *Story Sparks* newsletter

Read the blogs

Learn about upcoming events

Adversity can squelch the human spirit
. . . or it can help us discover strength we
NEVER KNEW WE HAD.

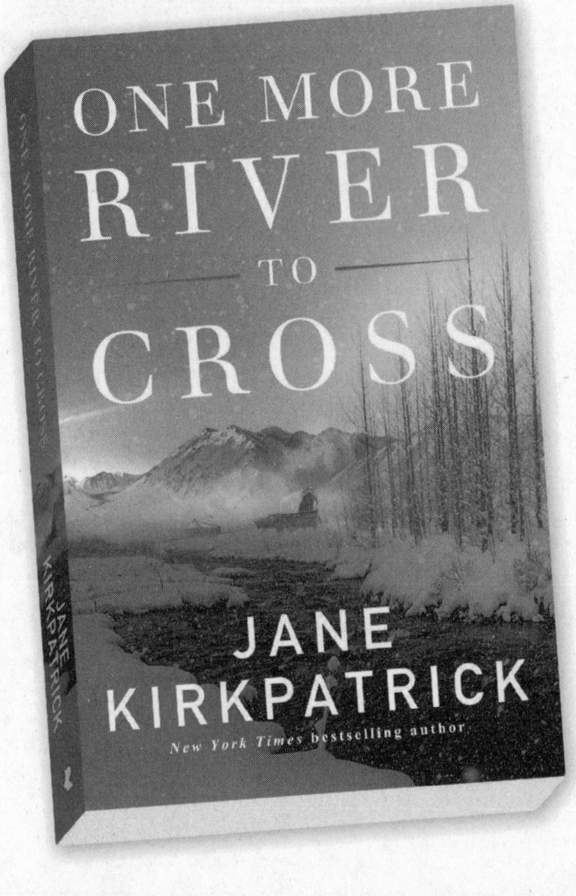

Based on true events, this compelling survival story by award-winning novelist Jane Kirkpatrick is full of grit and endurance. Beset by storms, bad timing, and desperate decisions, 8 women, 17 children, and 1 man must outlast winter in the middle of the Sierra Nevada in 1844.

Revell
a division of Baker Publishing Group
www.RevellBooks.com

Available wherever books and ebooks are sold.

There is more than one way

TO TELL A STORY...

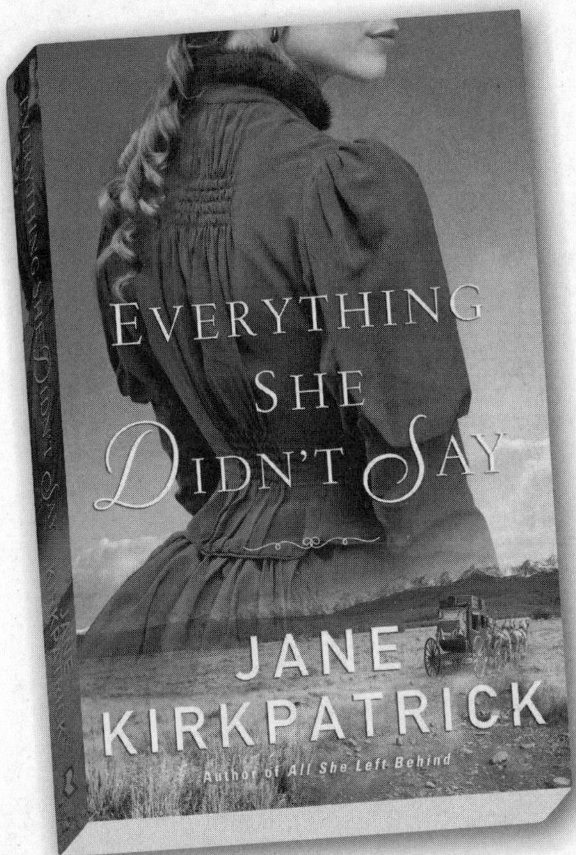

In Carrie Strahorn's life, there are two versions of everything: the one she'll share with others and the one she actually lives. As she follows her husband through the American West, her journey takes her through heartache, disappointment, and a life of unparalleled adventure.

Revell
a division of Baker Publishing Group
www.RevellBooks.com

Available wherever books and ebooks are sold.

"Once again, Jane Kirkpatrick creates a bold and inspiring woman out of the dust of history. Jennie's triumph, in the skilled hands of one of the West's most beloved writers, leaves its mark on your heart."

—Sandra Dallas, *New York Times* bestselling author

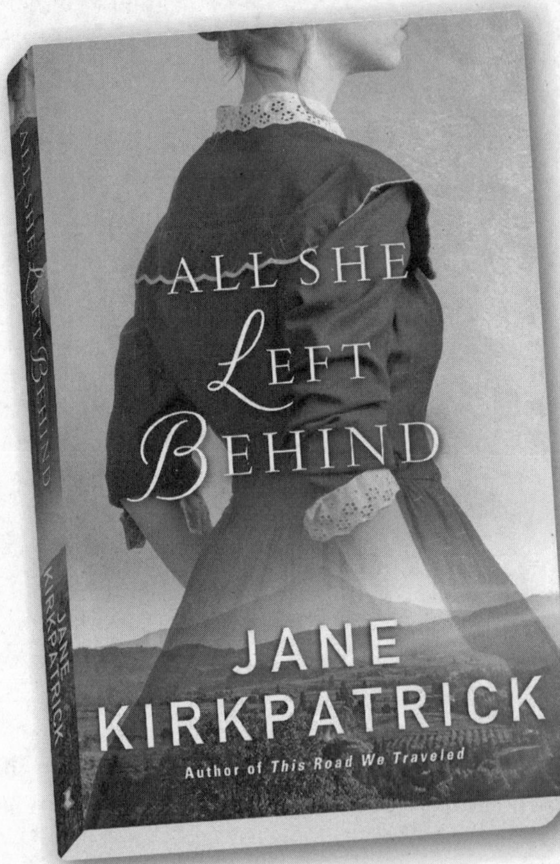

Revell
a division of Baker Publishing Group
www.RevellBooks.com

Available wherever books and ebooks are sold.

Jane Kirkpatrick

Inspires the Pioneer in All of Us . . .

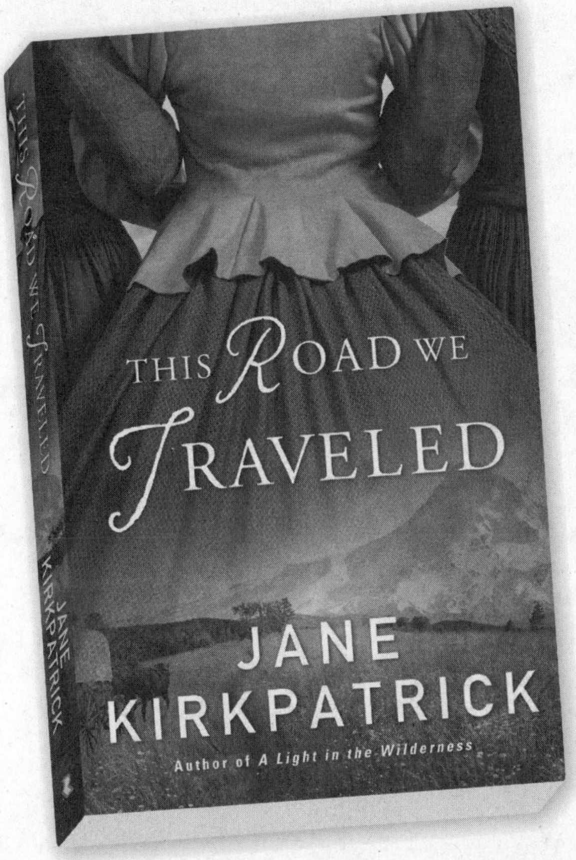

Three generations of the Brown women travel west together on the Oregon Trail, but each seeks something different. The challenges faced will form the character of one woman—and impact the future for many more.

Revell
a division of Baker Publishing Group
www.RevellBooks.com

Available wherever books and ebooks are sold.

W9-AQE-801

WRITING RESOURCES IN *Backpack Literature*

"WRITING EFFECTIVELY" FEATURES IN MAJOR CHAPTERS

Writing Advice ■ focused, practical tips
Writing Checklist ■ easy-to-use list of key points
Topics for Writing ■ paper topics on the chapter's theme or selections

Chapter 30
WRITING ABOUT LITERATURE

Read Actively
Plan Your Essay
Prewriting: Generate Ideas and Issues
Develop Your Argument:
- Purpose
- Audience
- Topic
- Thesis
- Appeals
- Organization

Format of Finished Paper
Rhetorical Appeals
Draft Your Argument
Revise Your Argument

Chapter 31
WRITING A RESEARCH PAPER

Choose a Topic
Begin Your Research: Print and Online
Evaluate Sources
Visual Images
Organize Your Research
Maintain Academic Integrity
Acknowledge All Sources
Document Sources Using MLA Style

REFERENCE GUIDE FOR MLA CITATIONS, P. 1220

Handy "how to" guide for works-cited lists.

SAMPLE STUDENT WRITING

Works in progress and finished essays show how to move from discovering ideas to a completed paper.

7 Student Papers
Drafts and Works in Progress

Brainstorming Techniques:
On Frost's "Nothing Gold Can Stay," p. 1152

Rough Paper Draft:
On Frost's "Nothing Gold Can Stay," p. 1161

Analysis Papers:
On Bishop's "The Fish," p. 1180
On Shakespeare's *Othello*, p. 1184

Argument Paper:
On Frost's "Nothing Gold Can Stay," p. 1169

Comparison and Contrast Paper:
On Faulkner's "A Rose for Emily" and Mansfield's "Miss Brill," p. 1190

Explication Papers:
On Poe's "The Tell-Tale Heart," p. 1173
On Frost's "Design," p. 1177

Response Paper:
On O'Brien's "The Things They Carried," p. 1193

BACKPACK LITERATURE

An Introduction to Fiction, Poetry, Drama, and Writing

SIXTH EDITION

X. J. Kennedy

Dana Gioia
University of Southern California

Dan Stone

Pearson

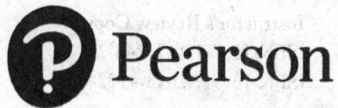

Executive Portfolio Manager: Aron Keesbury
Content Producer: Barbara Cappuccio
Content Developer: Elizabeth Farrell
Portfolio Manager Assistant: Christa Cottone
Senior Product Marketing Manager: Michael Coons
Product Marketing Manager: Nicholas Bolt
Content Producer Manager: Ken Volcjak
Managing Editor: Cynthia Cox
Designer: Alisha Webber
Digital Studio Course Producer: Elizabeth Bravo
Full-Service Project Management: Lois Lombardo, Cenveo® Publisher Services
Printer/Binder: LSC Communications, Inc.
Cover Printer: Phoenix Color/Hagerstown
Senior Art Director: Cate Barr
Cover Design: Cadence Design Studio
Cover Illustration: Robert Kennedy

Acknowledgements of third party content appear on pages 1229–1242, which constitute an extension of this copyright page.

Copyright © 2020, 2016, 2013 by X. J. Kennedy, Dana Goia, and Dan Stone. All Rights Reserved. Printed in the United States of America. This publication is protected by copyright, and permission should be obtained from the publisher prior to any prohibited reproduction, storage in a retrieval system, or transmission in any form or by any means, electronic, mechanical, photocopying, recording, or otherwise. For information regarding permissions, request forms and the appropriate contacts within the Pearson Education Global Rights & Permissions department, please visit www.pearsoned.com/permissions/.

PEARSON, ALWAYS LEARNING, and Revel are exclusive trademarks in the United States and/or other countries owned by Pearson Education, Inc. or its affiliates.

Unless otherwise indicated herein, any third-party trademarks that may appear in this work are the property of their respective owners and any references to third-party trademarks, logos or other trade dress are for demonstrative or descriptive purposes only. Such references are not intended to imply any sponsorship, endorsement, authorization, or promotion of Pearson's products by the owners of such marks, or any relationship between the owner and Pearson Education, Inc. or its affiliates, authors, licensees or distributors.

Library of Congress Cataloging-in-Publication Data
Names: Kennedy, X. J., editor. | Gioia, Dana, editor. | Stone, Dan, editor.
Title: Backpack literature : an introduction to fiction, poetry, drama, and writing / X.J. Kennedy, Dana Gioia, Dan Stone.
Description: Sixth edition. | Boston : Pearson, [2020] | Includes bibliographical references and indexes.
Identifiers: LCCN 2018042232 | ISBN 9780134756790 | ISBN 0134756797 | ISBN 9780134756790 (Student edition) | ISBN 0134756797 (Student edition) | ISBN 9780134772486 (Instructor's review copy) | ISBN 0134772482 (Instructor's review copy)
Subjects: LCSH: Literature—Collections.
Classification: LCC PN6014 .B26 2020 | DDC 808.8—dc23
LC record available at https://lccn.loc.gov/2018042232

Rental Edition
ISBN-10: 0-13-475679-7
ISBN-13: 978-0-13-475679-0
Instructor's Review Copy
ISBN-10: 0-13-477248-2
ISBN-13: 978-0-13-477248-6

Pearson

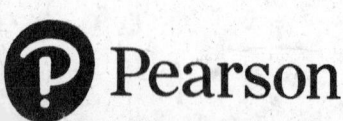

CONTENTS

Preface xxix
About the Authors xxxviii

FICTION

TALKING WITH *Amy Tan* 2

1 READING A STORY 5

THE ART OF FICTION 5

TYPES OF SHORT FICTION 6

Sufi Legend, Death Has an Appointment in Samarra 6
A student tries to flee from Death in this brief, sardonic fable.

Aesop, The Fox and the Grapes 7
Ever wonder where the phrase "sour grapes" comes from? Find out in this classic fable.

Bidpai, The Camel and His Friends 9
With friends like these, you can guess what the camel doesn't need.

Chuang Tzu, Independence 11
The Prince of Ch'u asks the philosopher Chuang Tzu to become his advisor and gets a surprising reply in this classic Chinese fable.

Jakob and Wilhelm Grimm, Godfather Death 13
Neither God nor the Devil came to the christening. In this stark folktale, a young man receives magical powers with a string attached.

PLOT 15

THE SHORT STORY 17

John Updike, A & P 18
In walk three girls in nothing but bathing suits, and Sammy finds himself no longer an aproned checkout clerk but an armored knight.

WRITING EFFECTIVELY 24

THINKING ABOUT PLOT 24

CHECKLIST: Writing About Plot 25
TOPICS FOR WRITING ON PLOT 25
TERMS FOR REVIEW 26

2 POINT OF VIEW 28

IDENTIFYING POINT OF VIEW 28

TYPES OF NARRATORS 29

HOW MUCH DOES A NARRATOR KNOW? 29

STREAM OF CONSCIOUSNESS 31

William Faulkner, A Rose for Emily 32

Proud, imperious Emily Grierson defies the town from the fortress of her mansion. Who could have guessed the secret that lay within?

Edgar Allan Poe, The Tell-Tale Heart 40

The smoldering eye at last extinguished, a murderer finds that, despite all his attempts at a cover-up, his victim will be heard.

Eudora Welty, A Worn Path 45

When the man says to Phoenix, "You must be a hundred years old, and scared of nothing," he might be exaggerating, but not by much.

Flannery O'Connor, A Good Man Is Hard to Find 52

Wanted: The Misfit, a cold-blooded killer. An ordinary family vacation leads to horror—and one moment of redeeming grace.

WRITING EFFECTIVELY 66
THINKING ABOUT POINT OF VIEW 66
CHECKLIST: Writing About Point of View 66
TOPICS FOR WRITING ON POINT OF VIEW 67
TERMS FOR REVIEW 67

3 CHARACTER 69

CHARACTERIZATION 70

MOTIVATION 71

Tobias Wolff, Bullet in the Brain 72

Anders is in line when armed robbers enter the bank, and he can't help but get involved.

Joyce Carol Oates, Where Are You Going, Where Have You Been? 77

Alone in the house, Connie finds herself helpless before the advances of Arnold Friend, a spellbinding imitation teenager.

Toni Morrison, Recitatif 91

Over many decades, two women's lives continue to collide, as they find that their relationship is complicated by the challenges of race, class, and circumstance.

Raymond Carver, Cathedral 107

He never expected to find himself trying to describe a cathedral to a blind man. He hadn't even wanted to meet this odd, old friend of his wife.

WRITING EFFECTIVELY 120

THINKING ABOUT CHARACTER 120

CHECKLIST: Writing About Character 120

TOPICS FOR WRITING ON CHARACTER 121

TERMS FOR REVIEW 122

4 SETTING 123

ELEMENTS OF SETTING 123

HISTORICAL FICTION 124

REGIONALISM 125

NATURALISM 125

HOW SETTING CAN HARMONIZE WITH OTHER ELEMENTS OF A STORY 125

Kate Chopin, The Storm 126

Even with her husband away, Calixta feels happily, securely married. Why then should she not shelter an old admirer from the rain?

Jack London, To Build a Fire 131

Seventy-five degrees below zero. Alone except for one mistrustful wolf dog, a man finds himself battling a relentless force.

Jorge Luis Borges, The Gospel According to Mark 144

A young man from Buenos Aires is trapped by a flood on an isolated ranch. To pass the time, he reads the Gospel to a family with unforeseen results.

Amy Tan, A Pair of Tickets 149

A young woman flies with her father to China to meet two half sisters she never knew existed.

WRITING EFFECTIVELY 165
THINKING ABOUT SETTING 165
CHECKLIST: Writing About Setting 166
TOPICS FOR WRITING ON SETTING 166
TERMS FOR REVIEW 167

5 TONE AND STYLE 168

TONE 168
STYLE 169
DICTION 169

Ernest Hemingway, A Clean, Well-Lighted Place 171
All by himself each night, the old man lingers in the bright café. What does he need more than brandy?

William Faulkner, Barn Burning 176
This time when Ab Snopes wields his blazing torch, his son Sarty faces a dilemma: whether to obey or defy the vengeful old man.

IRONY 190

O. Henry, The Gift of the Magi 192
A young husband and wife find ingenious ways to buy each other Christmas presents, in the classic story that defines the word "irony."

Margaret Atwood, Happy Endings 197
John and Mary meet. What happens next? This witty experimental story offers five different outcomes.

WRITING EFFECTIVELY 200
THINKING ABOUT TONE AND STYLE 200
CHECKLIST: Writing About Tone and Style 201
TOPICS FOR WRITING ON TONE AND STYLE 201
TERMS FOR REVIEW 202

6 THEME 203

PLOT VERSUS THEME 203
SUMMARIZING THE THEME 204
FINDING THE THEME 205

Tim O'Brien, The Things They Carried 206

What each soldier carries into the combat zone is largely determined by necessity, but each man's necessities differ.

Sandra Cisneros, Barbie-Q 220

The trouble with buying Barbie dolls is that you want all the clothes, companions, and accessories. But in this neighborhood things suddenly change.

Luke, The Parable of the Prodigal Son 223

A father has two sons. One demands his inheritance now and leaves to spend it with ruinous results.

Kurt Vonnegut Jr., Harrison Bergeron 225

Are you handsome? Then off with your eyebrows! Are you brainy? Then a transmitter will sound thought-shattering beeps inside your ear.

WRITING EFFECTIVELY 231

THINKING ABOUT THEME 231

CHECKLIST: Writing About Theme 231

TOPICS FOR WRITING ON THEME 232

TERMS FOR REVIEW 232

7 SYMBOL 233

ALLEGORY 233

SYMBOLS 234

RECOGNIZING SYMBOLS 235

John Steinbeck, The Chrysanthemums 236

Fenced-in Elisa feels emotionally starved—then her life promises to blossom with the arrival of the scissors-grinding man.

Charlotte Perkins Gilman, The Yellow Wallpaper 245

A doctor prescribes a "rest cure" for his wife after the birth of their child. The new mother tries to settle in to life in the isolated and mysterious country house they have rented for the summer. The cure proves worse than the disease in this Gothic classic.

Ursula K. Le Guin, The Ones Who Walk Away from Omelas 259

Omelas is the perfect city. All of its inhabitants are happy. But everyone's prosperity depends on a hidden evil.

Shirley Jackson, The Lottery 265

Splintered and faded, the sinister black box has worked its annual terror for longer than anyone in town can remember.

WRITING EFFECTIVELY 273
THINKING ABOUT SYMBOLS 273
CHECKLIST: Writing About Symbols 274
TOPICS FOR WRITING ON SYMBOLS 274
TERMS FOR REVIEW 275

8 GALLERY OF INTERNATIONAL VOICES 276

NIGERIA: Chinua Achebe, Dead Men's Path 277
The new headmaster of the village school is determined to fight superstition, but the villagers do not agree.

MEXICO: Inés Arredondo, The Shunammite 280
When Luisa visits her dying uncle, she has no idea that her life is about to change forever.

COLUMBIA: Gabriel García Márquez, The Handsomest Drowned Man in the World 289
Even in death, a mysterious stranger has a profound effect on all of the people in the village.

CHINA: Ha Jin, Saboteur 294
When the police unfairly arrest Mr. Chiu, he hopes for justice. After witnessing their brutality, he quietly plans revenge.

ANTIGUA: Jamaica Kincaid, Girl 303
"Try to walk like a lady, and not like the slut you are so bent on becoming." An old-fashioned mother tells her daughter how to live.

EGYPT: Naguib Mahfouz, The Lawsuit 305
He thought he'd seen the last of his late father's second wife, but now she's back to trouble his peaceful existence.

INDIA: Bharati Mukherjee, Saints 309
Shawn wanders around his neighborhood at night, imagining an existence other than the sad, confusing, and often frightening home life dominated by the unwelcome presence of his mom's boyfriend, Wayne.

9 STORIES FOR FURTHER READING 318

Sherman Alexie, This Is What It Means to Say Phoenix, Arizona 318
The only one who can help Victor when his father dies is a childhood friend he's been avoiding for years.

T. Coraghessan Boyle, Greasy Lake 328

Murky and strewn with beer cans, the lake appears to be a wasteland. One grim night on its shore, three "dangerous characters" learn a lesson.

Ray Bradbury, A Sound of Thunder 337

In 2055, you can go on a Time Safari to hunt dinosaurs 60 million years ago. But put one foot wrong, and suddenly the future's not what it used to be.

Kate Chopin, The Story of an Hour 347

"There was something coming to her and she was waiting for it, fearfully. What was it? She did not know; it was too subtle and elusive to name."

Neil Gaiman, How to Talk to Girls at Parties 350

Two teenage boys try to navigate a party filled with exotic, mysterious girls.

Nathanial Hawthorne, Young Goodman Brown 360

Urged on through deepening woods, a young Puritan sees—or dreams he sees—good villagers hasten toward a diabolic rite.

Zora Neale Hurston, Sweat 372

Delia's hard work paid for her small house. Now her drunken husband Sykes has promised it to another woman.

James Joyce, Araby 382

If only he can find her a token, she might love him in return. As night falls, a Dublin boy hurries to make his dream come true.

Franz Kafka, Before the Law 387

A man from the country comes in search of the Law. He never guesses what will prevent him from finding it, in this modern parable.

Katherine Mansfield, Miss Brill 389

Sundays had long brought joy to solitary Miss Brill, until one fateful day when she happens to share a bench with two lovers in the park.

Alice Walker, Everyday Use 393

When successful Dee visits from the city, she has changed her name to reflect her African roots. Her mother and sister notice other things have changed, too.

Virginia Woolf, A Haunted House 401

Whatever hour you wake, a door is shutting. From room to room the ghostly couple walks, hand in hand.

POETRY

TALKING WITH *Kay Ryan* 406

10 READING A POEM 409

POETRY OR VERSE 409

HOW TO READ A POEM 410

PARAPHRASE 410

William Butler Yeats, The Lake Isle of Innisfree 411

LYRIC POETRY 413

Robert Hayden, Those Winter Sundays 414
Adrienne Rich, Aunt Jennifer's Tigers 414

NARRATIVE POETRY 415

Anonymous, Sir Patrick Spence 415
Robert Frost, "Out, Out—" 417

DRAMATIC POETRY 418

Robert Browning, My Last Duchess 419

DIDACTIC POETRY 420

WRITING EFFECTIVELY 421

THINKING ABOUT PARAPHRASING 421
William Stafford, Ask Me 422
William Stafford, A Paraphrase of "Ask Me" 422
CHECKLIST: Writing a Paraphrase 423
TOPICS FOR WRITING ON PARAPHRASING 423
TERMS FOR REVIEW 423

11 LISTENING TO A VOICE 425

TONE 425
Theodore Roethke, My Papa's Waltz 426
Stephen Crane, The Wayfarer 427
Rhina Espaillat, Bilingual/*Bilingüe* 427
Franz Wright, Alcohol 428
Weldon Kees, For My Daughter 429

THE SPEAKER IN THE POEM 430
Natasha Trethewey, White Lies 430
Edwin Arlington Robinson, Luke Havergal 432
Anonymous, Dog Haiku 433
Langston Hughes, Theme for English B 434
Karen An-Hwei Lee, Rainfall 435
William Carlos Williams, The Red Wheelbarrow 435

IRONY 436
Robert Creeley, Oh No 436
W. H. Auden, The Unknown Citizen 437
Sharon Olds, Rite of Passage 439
Edna St. Vincent Millay, Second Fig 439
Thomas Hardy, The Workbox 440

FOR REVIEW AND FURTHER STUDY 441
William Blake, The Chimney Sweeper 441
Richard Lovelace, To Lucasta 442
Wilfred Owen, Dulce et Decorum Est 442

WRITING EFFECTIVELY 443
THINKING ABOUT TONE 443
CHECKLIST: Writing About Tone 444
TOPICS FOR WRITING ON TONE 444
TERMS FOR REVIEW 445

12 WORDS 446

LITERAL MEANING: WHAT A POEM SAYS FIRST 446
William Carlos Williams, This Is Just to Say 447

DICTION 447
John Masefield, Cargoes 448
John Donne, Batter my heart, three-personed God, for You 449

THE VALUE OF A DICTIONARY 449
Henry Wadsworth Longfellow, Aftermath 450
J. V. Cunningham, Friend, on this scaffold Thomas More lies dead 452
Samuel Menashe, Bread 452
Carl Sandburg, Grass 452

WORD CHOICE AND WORD ORDER 453
Robert Herrick, Upon Julia's Clothes 454
Kay Ryan, Blandeur 455

Thomas Hardy, The Ruined Maid 456
Julie Larios, What Bee Did 457

FOR REVIEW AND FURTHER STUDY 457

E. E. Cummings, anyone lived in a pretty how town 457
Sarah Cortez, Adam 458
Anonymous, Carnation Milk 460
Gina Valdés, English con Salsa 460
William Wordsworth, My heart leaps up when I behold 461
William Wordsworth, Mutability 461
Lewis Carroll, Jabberwocky 462

WRITING EFFECTIVELY 463

THINKING ABOUT DICTION 463
CHECKLIST: Writing About Diction 464
TOPICS FOR WRITING ON WORD CHOICE 464
TERMS FOR REVIEW 465

13 SAYING AND SUGGESTING 466

DENOTATION AND CONNOTATION 466

William Blake, London 467
Wallace Stevens, Disillusionment of Ten O'Clock 469
Robert Frost, Fire and Ice 470
Timothy Steele, Epitaph 470
Hieu Minh Nguyen, Arranged 470
H.D., Sea Rose 471
Alfred, Lord Tennyson, Tears, Idle Tears 472
Richard Wilbur, Love Calls Us to the Things of This World 472

WRITING EFFECTIVELY 474

THINKING ABOUT DENOTATION AND CONNOTATION 474
CHECKLIST: Writing About What a Poem Says and Suggests 475
TOPICS FOR WRITING ON DENOTATION AND CONNOTATION 475
TERMS FOR REVIEW 475

14 IMAGERY 476

Ezra Pound, In a Station of the Metro 476
Taniguchi Buson, The piercing chill I feel 476

IMAGERY 477

T. S. Eliot, The winter evening settles down 477
Theodore Roethke, Root Cellar 478
Elizabeth Bishop, The Fish 478
Emily Dickinson, A Route of Evanescence 480
Jean Toomer, Reapers 481
Gerard Manley Hopkins, Pied Beauty 481

ABOUT HAIKU 482

Arakida Moritake, The falling flower 482
Matsuo Basho, Heat-lightning streak 483
Matsuo Basho, In the old stone pool 483
Taniguchi Buson, On the one-ton temple bell 483
Taniguchi Buson, Moonrise on mudflats 483
Kobayashi Issa, only one guy 483
Kobayashi Issa, Cricket 483

HAIKU FROM JAPANESE INTERNMENT CAMPS 484

Suiko Matsushita, Cosmos in bloom 484
Hakuro Wada, Even the croaking of frogs 484

CONTEMPORARY HAIKU 484

Nick Virgilio, The Old Neighborhood 484
Adelle Foley, Learning to Shave 484

FOR REVIEW AND FURTHER STUDY 485

John Keats, Bright star, would I were steadfast as thou art 485
William Carlos Williams, El Hombre 485
Gary Snyder, Mid-August at Sourdough Mountain Lookout 486
Angela Alaimo O'Donnell, Tattoo 486
Stevie Smith, Not Waving but Drowning 487
Robert Bly, Driving to Town Late to Mail a Letter 487

WRITING EFFECTIVELY 487

THINKING ABOUT IMAGERY 487
CHECKLIST: Writing About Imagery 488
TOPICS FOR WRITING ON IMAGERY 489
TERMS FOR REVIEW 489

15 FIGURES OF SPEECH 490

WHY SPEAK FIGURATIVELY? 490

Alfred, Lord Tennyson, The Eagle 490
William Shakespeare, Shall I compare thee to a summer's day? 491
Howard Moss, Shall I Compare Thee to a Summer's Day? 492

METAPHOR AND SIMILE 492

Emily Dickinson, My Life had stood – a Loaded Gun 494
Alfred, Lord Tennyson, Flower in the Crannied Wall 495
William Blake, To see a world in a grain of sand 495
Sylvia Plath, Metaphors 495
N. Scott Momaday, Simile 496
Jill Alexander Essbaum, The Heart 496
Cody Walker, I'm Like 497

OTHER FIGURES OF SPEECH 498

James Stephens, The Wind 498
Robinson Jeffers, Hands 499
Dana Gioia, Money 501
Carl Sandburg, Fog 501

FOR REVIEW AND FURTHER STUDY 502

Robert Frost, A Patch of Old Snow 502
Kay Ryan, Turtle 502
Emily Brontë, Love and Friendship 502
John Keats, Ode on a Grecian Urn 503

WRITING EFFECTIVELY 504

THINKING ABOUT METAPHORS 504
CHECKLIST: Writing About Metaphors 505
TOPICS FOR WRITING ON FIGURES OF SPEECH 505
TERMS FOR REVIEW 506

16 SOUND 507

SOUND AS MEANING 507

William Butler Yeats, Who Goes with Fergus? 509
Edgar Allan Poe, *from* Ulalume 510
William Wordsworth, A Slumber Did My Spirit Seal 510

ALLITERATION AND ASSONANCE 510

Frances Cornford, The Watch 511
Alfred, Lord Tennyson, The splendor falls on castle walls 511

RIME 512

Hilaire Belloc, The Hippopotamus 514
Bob Kaufman, No More Jazz at Alcatraz 515
David Barber, Aria 515
Gerard Manley Hopkins, God's Grandeur 516

HOW TO READ A POEM ALOUD 517

Gerard Manley Hopkins, Spring and Fall 518
Michael Stillman, In Memoriam John Coltrane 518

WRITING EFFECTIVELY 519

THINKING ABOUT A POEM'S SOUND 519
CHECKLIST: Writing About a Poem's Sound 519
TOPICS FOR WRITING ON SOUND 520
TERMS FOR REVIEW 520

17 RHYTHM 521

STRESSES AND PAUSES 521
STRESS AND MEANING 522

LINE ENDINGS 524

Gwendolyn Brooks, We Real Cool 525
Alfred, Lord Tennyson, Break, Break, Break 526
Dorothy Parker, Résumé 526

METER 527

Edith Sitwell, Mariner Man 531
A. E. Housman, When I was one-and-twenty 531
Edgar Allan Poe, Annabel Lee 531
Walt Whitman, Beat! Beat! Drums! 533

WRITING EFFECTIVELY 533

THINKING ABOUT RHYTHM 533
CHECKLIST: Scanning a Poem 534
TOPICS FOR WRITING ON RHYTHM 535
TERMS FOR REVIEW 535

18 CLOSED FORM 537

THE VALUE OF FORM 538

FORMAL PATTERNS 538

Ernest Dowson, Days of wine and roses 540
John Donne, Song ("Go and catch a falling star") 540

BALLADS 541

Anonymous, Bonny Barbara Allan 541
Dudley Randall, Ballad of Birmingham 544

THE SONNET 545

William Shakespeare, Let me not to the marriage of true minds 545
Edna St. Vincent Millay, What lips my lips have kissed, and where, and why 546
Robert Frost, Acquainted with the Night 547
Kim Addonizio, First Poem for You 548
R. S. Gwynn, Shakespearean Sonnet 548
Sherman Alexie, The Facebook Sonnet 549

THE EPIGRAM 549

Sir John Harrington, Of Treason 550
Anonymous, Epitaph on a Dentist 550
Wendy Videlock, If Not for the Dark 550

OTHER FORMS 550

Dylan Thomas, Do not go gentle into that good night 550
Paul Laurence Dunbar, We Wear the Mask 551
Elizabeth Bishop, Sestina 552

WRITING EFFECTIVELY 553

THINKING ABOUT A SONNET 553
CHECKLIST: Writing About a Sonnet 554
TOPICS FOR WRITING ON CLOSED FORM 554
TERMS FOR REVIEW 555

19 OPEN FORM 557

Denise Levertov, Ancient Stairway 557

FREE VERSE 558

E. E. Cummings, Buffalo Bill 's 560
William Carlos Williams, The Dance 561
Stephen Crane, The Heart 562
Walt Whitman, I Hear America Singing 562
Wallace Stevens, Thirteen Ways of Looking at a Blackbird 563

FOR REVIEW AND FURTHER STUDY 566

E. E. Cummings, in Just- 566
Langston Hughes, I, Too 567
Francisco X. Alarcón, Frontera / Border 567
Carole Satyamurti, I Shall Paint My Nails Red 568

WRITING EFFECTIVELY 568

THINKING ABOUT FREE VERSE 568
CHECKLIST: Writing About Line Breaks 569
TOPICS FOR WRITING ON OPEN FORM 569
TERMS FOR REVIEW 569

20 SYMBOL 570

THE MEANINGS OF A SYMBOL 570

T. S. Eliot, The *Boston Evening Transcript* 571
Emily Dickinson, The Lightning is a yellow Fork 572

IDENTIFYING SYMBOLS 572

Thomas Hardy, Neutral Tones 574
Yusef Komunyakaa, Facing It 574
William Butler Yeats, He wishes for the Cloths of Heaven 575

ALLEGORY 576

Matthew, The Parable of the Good Seed 576
George Herbert, Redemption 577
Edwin Markham, Outwitted 577
Suji Kwock Kim, Occupation 578
Antonio Machado, Proverbios y Cantares (XXIX) 579
Translated by Michael Ortiz, Traveler 579
Robert Frost, The Road Not Taken 579
Christina Rossetti, Up-Hill 580

FOR REVIEW AND FURTHER STUDY 581

Mary Oliver, Wild Geese 581
Emma Lazarus, The New Colossus 581
Karen Holden, Bats in a Box 582
Lorine Niedecker, Popcorn-can cover 582
Tami Haaland, Lipstick 583
Wallace Stevens, Anecdote of the Jar 583

WRITING EFFECTIVELY 584

THINKING ABOUT SYMBOLS 584
CHECKLIST: Writing About Symbols 584
TOPICS FOR WRITING ON SYMBOLISM 585
TERMS FOR REVIEW 585

21 MYTH 586

THE SUBJECTS AND USES OF MYTH 586

Robert Frost, Nothing Gold Can Stay 587
William Wordsworth, The world is too much with us 587
H.D., Helen 588

ARCHETYPE 589
Louise Bogan, Medusa 590
John Keats, La Belle Dame sans Merci 590
A. E. Stallings, First Love: A Quiz 592

PERSONAL MYTH 593
William Butler Yeats, The Second Coming 594
Diane Thiel, Memento Mori in Middle School 595
Sylvia Plath, Lady Lazarus 596

MYTH AND POPULAR CULTURE 599
Aimee Nezhukumatathil, What I Learned from the Incredible Hulk 600

FOR REVIEW AND FURTHER STUDY 601
Alfred, Lord Tennyson, Ulysses 601

WRITING EFFECTIVELY 603
THINKING ABOUT MYTH 603
CHECKLIST: Writing About Myth 603
TOPICS FOR WRITING ON MYTH 603
TERMS FOR REVIEW 604

22 WHAT IS POETRY? 605

Dante, Samuel Taylor Coleridge, William Wordsworth, Thomas Hardy, Robert Frost, Wallace Stevens, Mina Loy, W. H. Auden, José Garcia Villa, Christopher Fry, Elizabeth Bishop, Joy Harjo, Octavio Paz, Lucille Clifton, Charles Simic, Some Definitions of Poetry 605–606

23 POEMS FOR FURTHER READING 607

Aaron Abeyta, thirteen ways of looking at a tortilla 607
Francisco X. Alarcón, The X in My Name 609
Anonymous (Navajo chant), Last Words of the Prophet 609
Matthew Arnold, Dover Beach 609
W. H. Auden, Musée des Beaux Arts 611
Elizabeth Bishop, One Art 611
William Blake, The Tyger 613
Gwendolyn Brooks, the mother 614
Elizabeth Barrett Browning, How Do I Love Thee? Let Me Count the Ways 615
Charles Bukowski, Dostoevsky 615

25 TRAGEDY AND COMEDY 689

TRAGEDY 689

Christopher Marlowe, *Scene from* Doctor Faustus 692

In this scene from the classic drama, a brilliant scholar sells his soul to the devil. How smart is that?

COMEDY 698

Oscar Wilde, *Scene from* The Importance of Being Earnest 700

Lady Bracknell is no softie when interviewing a potential future son-in-law.

David Ives, Sure Thing 704

Bill wants to pick up Betty in a cafe, but he makes every mistake in the book. Luckily, he not only gets a second chance, but a third and a fourth as well.

WRITING EFFECTIVELY 715

THINKING ABOUT COMEDY 715

CHECKLIST: Writing About Comedy 716

TOPICS FOR WRITING ABOUT TRAGEDY 716

TOPICS FOR WRITING ABOUT COMEDY 716

TERMS FOR REVIEW 717

26 THE THEATER OF SOPHOCLES 718

THEATER IN ANCIENT GREECE 718

THE CIVIC ROLE OF GREEK DRAMA 720

ARISTOTLE'S CONCEPT OF TRAGEDY 721

SOPHOCLES 723

THE ORIGINS OF *OEDIPUS THE KING* 724

Sophocles, Oedipus the King ***(Translated by David Grene)*** 725

The dark story of Oedipus is considered by many to be the greatest example of classical Greek tragedy.

WRITING EFFECTIVELY 768

THINKING ABOUT GREEK TRAGEDY 768

CHECKLIST: Writing About Greek Drama 769

TOPICS FOR WRITING ON SOPHOCLES 769

TERMS FOR REVIEW 769

27 THE THEATER OF SHAKESPEARE 771

WILLIAM SHAKESPEARE 774

A NOTE ON *OTHELLO* 774

PICTURING *OTHELLO* 776

William Shakespeare, Othello, the Moor of Venice 778

Here is a story of jealousy, that "green-eyed monster which doth mock / The meat it feeds on"—of a passionate, suspicious man and his blameless wife, of a serpent masked as a friend.

WRITING EFFECTIVELY 891

UNDERSTANDING SHAKESPEARE 891

CHECKLIST: Writing About Shakespeare 891

TOPICS FOR WRITING ON SHAKESPEARE 892

28 THE MODERN THEATER 893

REALISM 893

Lorraine Hansberry, A Raisin in the Sun 895

In this Civil Rights–era classic, a poor family from Chicago's South Side tries to cope with the forces of poverty, external challenges, and internal conflict.

Henrik Ibsen, A Doll's House ***(Translated by R. Farquharson Sharp, revised by Viktoria Michelsen)*** 973

The founder of modern drama portrays a troubled marriage. Helmer, the bank manager, regards his wife Nora as a "little featherbrain"—not knowing the truth may shatter his smug world.

EXPERIMENTAL DRAMA 1036

Milcha Sanchez-Scott, The Cuban Swimmer 1036

Nineteen-year-old Margarita Suárez wants to win a Southern California distance swimming race. Is her family behind her? Quite literally!

DOCUMENTARY DRAMA 1051

Anna Deavere Smith, *Scenes from* Twilight: Los Angeles, 1992 1051

The violence that tore apart a city, in the words of those who were there.

WRITING EFFECTIVELY 1060

THINKING ABOUT DRAMATIC REALISM 1060

CHECKLIST: Writing About a Realist Play 1061

TOPICS FOR WRITING ON REALISM 1061

TERMS FOR REVIEW 1062

29 PLAYS FOR FURTHER READING 1063

Sharon E. Cooper, Mistaken Identity 1063

An odd couple tries to find common ground in an English pub.

David Henry Hwang, The Sound of a Voice 1068

A strange man arrives at a solitary woman's home in the remote countryside. As they fall in love, they discover disturbing secrets about one another's past.

Brighde Mullins, Click 1084

A long-distance phone call leads to darkly comic misunderstandings between a man and woman.

August Wilson, Fences 1087

A proud man's love for his family is choked by his rigidity and self-righteousness, in this powerful drama by one of the great American playwrights of our time.

WRITING

30 WRITING ABOUT LITERATURE 1147

READ ACTIVELY 1147

Robert Frost, Nothing Gold Can Stay 1148

THINK ABOUT THE READING 1150

PLAN YOUR ESSAY 1151

PREWRITING: GENERATE IDEAS AND ISSUES 1152

Sample Student Prewriting Exercises 1152–1155

DEVELOP YOUR ARGUMENT 1156

STRENGTHEN YOUR ARGUMENT: RHETORICAL APPEALS 1157

Logical Argumentation: Evidence and Organization 1157

Emotional Argumentation 1158
Credibility: Tone and Balance 1159
CHECKLIST: Developing an Argument 1160

DRAFT YOUR ARGUMENT 1160
Sample Student Paper, Rough Draft 1161

REVISE YOUR ARGUMENT 1163
CHECKLIST: Revising Your Argument 1167

SOME FINAL ADVICE ON REWRITING 1167
Sample Student Paper, Revised Draft 1169

WHAT'S YOUR PURPOSE? COMMON APPROACHES TO WRITING ABOUT LITERATURE 1172

Explication 1172
Sample Student Paper, Fiction Explication 1173
Robert Frost, Design 1176
Sample Student Paper, Poetry Explication 1177

Analysis 1180
Sample Student Paper, Poetry Analysis 1180
Sample Student Paper, Drama Analysis 1184

Comparison and Contrast 1188
Sample Student Paper, Fiction Comparison and Contrast 1190

Response Paper 1192
Sample Student Paper, Fiction Response 1193

THE FORM OF YOUR FINISHED PAPER 1195

TOPICS FOR WRITING 1196

31 WRITING A RESEARCH PAPER 1201

BROWSE THE RESEARCH 1201

CHOOSE A TOPIC: FORMULATE YOUR ARGUMENT 1202

BEGIN YOUR RESEARCH 1202

Reliable Web Sources 1202
Print Resources 1203

Online Databases 1204
CHECKLIST: Finding Reliable Sources 1205
Visual Images 1205
CHECKLIST: Using Visual Images 1206

EVALUATE YOUR SOURCES 1207

CHECKLIST: Evaluating Your Sources 1208

ORGANIZE YOUR RESEARCH 1208

ORGANIZE YOUR PAPER 1210

MAINTAIN ACADEMIC INTEGRITY 1210

ACKNOWLEDGE ALL SOURCES 1211

Using Quotations 1211
Citing Ideas 1212

DOCUMENT SOURCES USING MLA STYLE 1213

Keep a List of Sources 1213
Use Parenthetical References 1213
Create a Works-Cited List 1214
Cite Sources in MLA Style 1214

CONCLUDING THOUGHTS 1219

REFERENCE GUIDE FOR MLA CITATIONS 1220–1227

Literary Credits 1229
Photo Credits 1241
Index of Authors and Titles 1243
Index of Literary Terms 1252

PREFACE

This is the sixth edition of *Backpack Literature*, a specially condensed version of *Literature: An Introduction to Fiction, Poetry, Drama, and Writing*. The primary aim of the book is to introduce college students to the appreciation and experience of literature in its major forms. The book also seeks to develop students' abilities to think critically and to communicate effectively through writing.

All three editors of this volume are writers. We believe that textbooks should not only be informative and accurate but also lively, accessible, and engaging. Our intent has always been to create a book that students will read with enjoyment and which will inspire them to take their own writing more seriously.

Backpack Literature offers selections and apparatus especially suited for instructors teaching a one-quarter or one-semester introductory class. It includes the core selections of our larger *Literature* books and much of the pedagogical material, particularly in the area of student writing. The book offers an alternative to the more extensive selections and critical coverage in the larger editions of *Literature*. Our purpose is to provide the introductory student a smaller, more portable, less expensive book.

Backpack Literature tries to help readers develop sensitivity to language, culture, and identity to lead them beyond the boundaries of their own selves and see the world through the eyes of others. This book is built on our conviction that great literature can enrich and enlarge the lives it touches. The edition's features are detailed below.

WHAT'S NEW IN THE SIXTH EDITION?

- **New stories**—twelve new stories, including Toni Morrison's "Recitatif," Sandra Cisneros's "Barbie-Q," T. Coraghessan's "Greasy Lake," Eudora Welty's "A Worn Path," Ray Bradbury's "A Sound of Thunder," and Neil Gaiman's "How to Talk to Girls at Parties," as well as new fables by Aesop and Bidpai.
- **New chapter on international voices in fiction**—presenting powerful stories from Nigeria, Mexico, Columbia, China, Antigua, Egypt, and India.
- **New poems**—thirty-nine new poems appear in this edition, ranging from classic selections by Wallace Stevens, William Carlos Williams, Claude McKay, Edith Sitwell, Emma Lazarus, and Robert Frost to fresh contemporary works by Kay Ryan, Franz Wright, Karen An-Hwei Lee, Sarah Cortez, and Suji Kwock Kim.
- **New plays**—three new plays provide greater flexibility in studying diverse contemporary trends in a crowded curriculum. The new works include David Ives's *Sure Thing*, Sharon E. Cooper's *Mistaken Identity*, and Lorraine Hansberry's Civil Rights–era classic *A Raisin in the Sun*.

- **New writing assignments**—new writing topics have been introduced in many chapters.
- **Updated MLA Coverage of the 8th edition of the MLA *Handbook***—the Reference Guide for Citations has been expanded and updated to reflect the latest MLA guidelines.

KEY FEATURES OF *BACKPACK LITERATURE*

The new edition contains a wide and varied selection of works that both students and instructors have found appealing and accessible. These include:

- **Diverse and exciting stories—49 stories** from familiar classics to contemporary works from around the globe.
- **Great poems old and new—235 poems**, mixing traditional favorites with exciting contemporary work.
- **A rich array of drama—14 plays and scenes** from classical tragedy to Shakespeare to contemporary work by August Wilson.
- **Exclusive conversations between editor Dana Gioia and celebrated fiction writer Amy Tan, former US Poet Laureate Kay Ryan, and beloved playwright David Ives**—offer an insider's look into the importance of literature and reading in the lives of three modern masters.
- **Illustrated version of William Shakespeare's *Othello***—includes production photos of key scenes.
- **Audio version of Susan Glaspell's *Trifles***—specially created for this book.
- **Complete writing coverage** (detailed below).
- **"Terms for Review" feature at the end of every major chapter**—provides a simple study guide to go over key concepts and terms in each chapter.

COMPLETE WRITING COVERAGE

- **Writing coverage in every major chapter**—comprehensive introduction to composition and critical thinking, including easy-to-use checklists, exercises, and practical advice.
- **Topics for writing in every major chapter**—provide a rich source of ideas for writing papers.
- **Dedicated chapters on composition process and research process**—concise, step-by-step coverage of the writing and research processes, amply illustrated with student writing examples.
- **Reference Guide for MLA Citations**—handy "how to" guide for works-cited lists.
- **Student writing**—6 papers by students with annotations, plus prewriting exercises and rough drafts, provide credible examples of how to write about literature. Includes
  - Explication Papers
  - Analysis Papers

- Comparison/Contrast Paper
- Response Paper

TEXTS AND DATES

Every effort has been made to supply each selection in its most accurate text and (where necessary) in a lively, faithful translation. For the reader who wishes to know when a work was written, at the right of each title appears the date of its first publication in book form. If a work was composed much earlier than its first book publication, parentheses have been added around its date.

RESOURCES FOR STUDENTS AND INSTRUCTORS

For Students

Audio Production of Trifles

So many students today have limited experience attending live theater that we offer a complete audio version of our opening play, Susan Glaspell's *Trifles*, which we use to teach the elements of drama. The audio version was produced especially for this edition by the celebrated L.A. Theatre Works. It includes an introduction and commentary by Dana Gioia.

Handbook of Literary Terms

Handbook of Literary Terms by X. J. Kennedy, Dana Gioia, and Mark Bauerlein is a user-friendly primer of more than 350 critical terms brought to life with literary examples, pronunciation guides, and scholarly yet accessible explanations. Aimed at undergraduates getting their first taste of serious literary study, the volume will help students engage with the humanities canon and become critical readers and writers ready to experience the insights and joys of great fiction, poetry, and drama.

For Instructors

Make more time for your students with instructor resources that offer effective learning assessments and classroom engagement. Pearson's partnership with educators does not end with the delivery of course materials; Pearson is there with you on the first day of class and beyond. A dedicated team of local Pearson representatives will work with you to not only choose course materials but also integrate them into your class and assess their effectiveness. Our goal is your goal—to improve instruction with each semester.

Pearson is pleased to offer the following resource to qualified adopters of *Backpack Literature*, Sixth Edition. This supplement is available to download from the Instructor Resource Center (IRC). To register for access, please visit the IRC at www.pearson.com/us.

- **Instructor's Resource Manual** Create a comprehensive roadmap for teaching classroom, online, or hybrid courses. Designed for new and experienced instructors, the Instructor's Resource Manual includes learning objectives, lecture and discussion suggestions, activities for in or out of class, research activities, participation activities, and suggested readings, series, and films. Available on the IRC.

THANKS

The collaboration necessary to create this new edition goes far beyond the partnership of its three editors. *Backpack Literature: An Introduction to Fiction, Poetry, Drama, and Writing* has once again been revised, corrected, and shaped by wisdom and advice from instructors who actually put it to the test—and also from a number who, in teaching literature, preferred other textbooks to it, but who generously criticized this book anyway and made suggestions for it. Deep thanks to the following individuals:

John Allen, Milwaukee Area Technical College
Alvaro Aleman, University of Florida
Jonathan Alexander, University of Southern Colorado
Ann P. Allen, Salisbury State University
Karla Alwes, SUNY Cortland
Brian Anderson, Central Piedmont Community College
Kimberly Green Angel, Georgia State University
Carmela A. Arnoldt, Glendale Community College
Herman Asarnow, University of Portland
Susan Austin, Johnston Community College
Beverly Bailey, Seminole Community College
Carolyn Baker, San Antonio College
Rosemary Baker, SUNY Morrisville
Lee Barnes, Community College of Southern Nevada, Las Vegas
Sandra Barnhill, South Plains College
Bob Baron, Mesa Community College
Melinda Barth, El Camino Community College
Robin Barrow, University of Iowa
Joseph Bathanti, Mitchell Community College
Judith Baumel, Adelphi University
Anis Bawarski, University of Kansas
Bruce Beckum, Colorado Mountain College
Elaine Bender, El Camino Community College
Pamela Benson, Tarrant County Junior College
Jennifer Black, McLennan Community College
Brian Blackley, North Carolina State University
Debbie Borchers, Pueblo Community College
Alan Braden, Tacoma Community College
Glenda Bryant, South Plains College
Paul Buchanan, Biola University
David Budinger, Broward College
Andrew Burke, University of Georgia
Jolayne Call, Utah Valley State College
Stasia Callan, Monroe Community College
Uzzie T. Cannon, University of North Carolina at Greensboro
Al Capovilla, Folsom Lake Community College

Juliana Cardenas, Grossmont College
Eleanor Carducci, Sussex County Community College
Thomas Carper, University of Southern Maine
Jean W. Cash, James Madison University
Michael Cass, Mercer University
Patricia Cearley, South Plains College
Fred Chancey, Chemeketa Community College
Kitty Chen, Nassau Community College
Edward M. Cifelli, County College of Morris
Marc Cirigliano, Empire State College
Bruce Clary, McPherson College
Maria Clayton, Middle Tennessee State University
Cheryl Clements, Blinn College
Jerry Coats, Tarrant County Community College
Peggy Cole, Arapahoe Community College
Doris Colter, Henry Ford Community College
Dean Cooledge, University of Maryland Eastern Shore
Patricia Connors, University of Memphis
Steve Cooper, California State University, Long Beach
Cynthia Cornell, DePauw University
Ruth Corson, Norwalk Community Technical College, Norwalk
James Finn Cotter, Mount St. Mary College
Dessa Crawford, Delaware Community College
Janis Adams Crowe, Furman University
Allison M. Cummings, University of Wisconsin, Madison
Elizabeth Curtin, Salisbury State University
Hal Daniels, Broward College
Robert Darling, Keuka College
Denise David, Niagara County Community College
Alan Davis, Moorhead State University
Michael Degen, Jesuit College Preparatory School, Dallas
Kathleen De Grave, Pittsburgh State University
Apryl Denny, Viterbo University
Johanna Denzin, Columbia College
Fred Dings, University of South Carolina
Leo Doobad, Stetson University
Stephanie Dowdle, Salt Lake Community College
Dennis Driewald, Laredo Community College
David Driscoll, Benedictine College
John Drury, University of Cincinnati
Tony D'Souza, Shasta College
Denise Dube, Hill College
Victoria Duckworth, Santa Rosa Junior College
Ellen Dugan-Barrette, Brescia University
Dixie Durman, Chapman University
Bill Dynes, University of Indianapolis
Justin Eatmon, Wake Technical Community College
Janet Eber, County College of Morris
Terry Ehret, Santa Rosa Junior College
George Ellenbogen, Bentley College
Peggy Ellsberg, Barnard College
Toni Empringham, El Camino Community College
Lin Enger, Moorhead State University
Alexina Fagan, Virginia Commonwealth University
Lynn Fauth, Oxnard College
Karen Feldman, Seminole State College of Florida
Annie Finch, University of Southern Maine
Katie Fischer, Clarke College
Steven Fischer, Harper College
Susan Fitzgerald, University of Memphis
Juliann Fleenor, Harper College
Richard Flynn, Georgia Southern University
Billy Fontenot, Louisiana State University at Eunice
Deborah Ford, University of Southern Mississippi
Doug Ford, Manatee Community College
James E. Ford, University of Nebraska, Lincoln
Peter Fortunato, Ithaca College
Ray Foster, Scottsdale Community College
Maryanne Garbowsky, County College of Morris
John Gery, University of New Orleans
Mary Frances Gibbons, Richland College
Julie Gibson, Greenville Technical College
Maggie Gordon, University of Mississippi
Joseph Green, Lower Columbia College
William E. Gruber, Emory University

Huey Guagliardo, Louisiana State University
R. S. Gwynn, Lamar University
Steven K. Hale, DeKalb College
Renée Harlow, Southern Connecticut State University
David Harper, Chesapeake College
John Harper, Seminole Community College
Iris Rose Hart, Santa Fe Community College
Karen Hatch, California State University, Chico
Jim Hauser, William Patterson College
Sandra Havriluk, Gwinnett Technical College
Lance Hawvermale, Ranger College
Kevin Hayes, Essex County College
Jennifer Heller, Johnson County Community College
Hal Hellwig, Idaho State University
K. L. Henderson, Northwestern State University
Gillian Hettinger, William Paterson University
Mary Piering Hiltbrand, University of Southern Colorado
Martha Hixon, Middle Tennessee State University
Jan Hodge, Morningside College
David E. Hoffman, Averett University
Sylvia Holladay, Hillsborough Community College
Mary Huffer, Lake-Sumter Community College
Patricia Hymson, Delaware County Community College
Carol Ireland, Joliet Junior College
Jenifer Jackson, Austin Peay State University
Alan Jacobs, Wheaton College
Ann Jagoe, North Central Texas College
Kimberlie Johnson, Seminole Community College
Peter Johnson, Providence College
Ted E. Johnston, El Paso Community College
Jacqueline Jones, Francis Marion University
Mark Jordan, Odessa College
Cris Karmas, Graceland University
Tammy Kearn, Riverside City College
William Kelly, Bristol Community College
Howard Kerner, Polk Community College
Lynn Kerr, Baltimore City Community College
John Kivari, Erie Community College
D. S. Koelling, Northwest College
Damien Kortum, Laramie County Community College
Dennis Kriewald, Laredo Community College
Paul Lake, Arkansas Technical University
Patricia Landy, Laramie County Community College
Susan Lang, Southern Illinois University
Greg LaPointe, Elmira College
Tracy Lassiter, Eastern Arizona College
Helen Lewis, Western Iowa Tech Community College
Sherry Little, San Diego State University
Alfred Guy Litton, Texas Woman's University
Heather Lobban-Viravong, Grinnell College
Karen Locke, Lane Community College
Eric Loring, Scottsdale Community College
Deborah Louvar, Seminole State College
Gerald Luboff, County College of Morris
Susan Popkin Mach, UCLA
Samuel Maio, California State University, San Jose
Jim Martin, Mount Ida College
Paul Marx, University of New Haven
David Mason, Colorado College
Mike Matthews, Tarrant County Junior College
Beth Maxfield, Henderson State University
Janet McCann, Texas A&M University
Susan McClure, Indiana University of Pennsylvania
Kim McCollum-Clark, Millersville University
David McCracken, Texas A&M University
Nellie McCrory, Gaston College
William McGee, Jr., Joliet Junior College
Barbara McGregor, Tarleton State University
Kerri McKeand, Joliet Junior College
Robert McPhillips, Iona College
Jim McWilliams, Dickinson State University
Elizabeth Meador, Wayne Community College
Trista Merrill, Finger Lakes Community College
Brett Mertins, Metropolitan Community College
Bruce Meyer, Laurentian University
Shawn Miller, Francis Marion University
Tom Miller, University of Arizona

Joseph Mills, University of California at Davis
Cindy Milwe, Santa Monica High School
Dorothy Minor, Tulsa Community College
Alan Mitnick, Passaic County Community College
Mary Alice Morgan, Mercer University
Samantha Morgan, University of Tennessee
Bernard Morris, Modesto Junior College
Brian T. Murphy, Burlington Community College
Carrie Myers, Lehigh Carbon Community College
William Myers, University of Colorado at Colorado Springs
Madeleine Mysko, Johns Hopkins University
Jennifer Myskowski, Lehigh Carbon Community College
Kevin Nebergall, Kirkwood Community College
Diorah Nelson, Hillsborough Community College
Eric Nelson, Georgia Southern University
Margaret Nelson Rodriguez, El Paso Community College–Valle Verde Campus
Jeff Newberry, University of West Florida
Marsha Nourse, Dean College
Hillary Nunn, University of Akron
James Obertino, Central Missouri State University
Julia O'Brien, Meredith College
Sally O'Friel, John Carroll University
Elizabeth Oness, Viterbo College
Regina B. Oost, Wesleyan College
Mike Osborne, Central Piedmont Community College
James Ortego II, Troy University–Dothan
Jim Owen, Columbus State University
Jeannette Palmer, Motlow State Community College
Mark Palmer, Tacoma Community College
Paige Paquette, Troy University
Carol Pearson, West Georgia Technical College, Carroll Campus
Dianne Peich, Delaware County Community College
Betty Jo Peters, Morehead State University
Timothy Peters, Boston University
Norm Peterson, County College of Morris
Susan Petit, College of San Mateo
Louis Phillips, School of Visual Arts
Robert Phillips, University of Houston
Jason Pickavance, Salt Lake Community College
Teresa Point, Emory University
Sally Polito, Cape Cod Community College
Deborah Prickett, Jacksonville State University
John Prince, North Carolina Central University
William Provost, University of Georgia
Wyatt Prunty, University of the South, Sewanee
Allen Ramsey, Central Missouri State University
Ron Rash, Tri-County Technical College
Michael W. Raymond, Stetson University
Mary Anne Reiss, Elizabethtown Community College
Barbara Rhodes, Central Missouri State University
Diane Richard-Alludya, Lynn University
Gary Richardson, Mercer University
Jennifer Riske, Northeast Lakeview College
Fred Robbins, Southern Illinois University
Doulgas Robillard Jr., University of Arkansas at Pine Bluff
Daniel Robinson, Colorado State University
Dawn Rodrigues, University of Texas, Brownsville
Linda C. Rollins, Motlow State Community College
Mark Rollins, Ohio University
Laura Ross, Seminole Community College
Jude Roy, Madisonville Community College
Lillian Ruiz, Greenfield Community College
M. Runyon, Saddleback College
Mark Sanders, College of the Mainland
Kay Satre, Carroll College
Ben Sattersfield, Mercer University
SueAnn Schatz, University of New Mexico
Roy Scheele, Doane College
Bill Schmidt, Seminole Community College
Beverly Schneller, Millersville University
Meg Schoerke, San Francisco State University
Janet Schwarzkopf, Western Kentucky University
William Scurrah, Pima Community College

Susan Semrow, Northeastern State University
Tom Sexton, University of Alaska, Anchorage
Chenliang Sheng, Northern Kentucky University
Roger Silver, University of Maryland–Asian Division
Josh Simpson, Sullivan University
Phillip Skaar, Texas A&M University
Michael Slaughter, Illinois Central College
Martha K. Smith, University of Southern Indiana
Matthew Snyder, Moreno Valley College
Chrishawn Speller, Seminole State College of Florida
Richard Spiese, California State, Long Beach
Wes Spratlin, Motlow State Community College
Lisa S. Starks, Texas A&M University
John R. Stephenson, Lake Superior State University
Jack Stewart, East Georgia College
Dabney Stuart, Washington and Lee University
David Sudol, Arizona State University
Stan Sulkes, Raymond Walters College
Gerald Sullivan, Savio Preparatory School
Henry Taylor, American University
Jean Tobin, University of Wisconsin Center, Sheboygan County
Linda Travers, University of Massachusetts, Amherst
Tom Treffinger, Greenville Technical College
Michelle Trim, University of New Haven
Pamela Turley, Community College of Allegheny County
Peter Ulisse, Housatonia Community College
Leslie Umschweis, Broward College
Lee Upton, Lafayette College
Rex Veeder, St. Cloud University
Michelle Veenstra, Francis Marion University
Deborah Viles, University of Colorado, Boulder
Melanie Wagner, Lake Sumter State College
Joyce Walker, Southern Illinois University–Carbondale
Sue Walker, University of South Alabama
Irene Ward, Kansas State University
Penelope Warren, Laredo Community College
Barbara Wenner, University of Cincinnati
Terry Witek, Stetson University
Sallie Wolf, Arapahoe Community College
Beth Rapp Young, University of Alabama
William Zander, Fairleigh Dickinson University
Tom Zaniello, Northern Kentucky University
Guanping Zeng, Pensacola Junior College
John Zheng, Mississippi Valley State University

Ongoing thanks go to our friends and colleagues who helped with earlier editions: Michael Palma, who scrupulously examined and updated every chapter of the previous edition; Diane Thiel of the University of New Mexico, who originally helped develop the Latin American poetry chapter; Susan Balée of Temple University, who contributed to the chapter on writing a research paper; April Lindner of Saint Joseph's University in Philadelphia, Pennsylvania, who served as associate editor for the writing sections; Mark Bernier of Blinn College in Brenham, Texas, who helped improve the writing material; Joseph Aimone of Santa Clara University, who helped integrate web-based materials and research techniques; John Swensson of De Anza College, who provided excellent practical suggestions from the classroom; and Neil Aitken of the University of Southern California, who helped update the chapter on writing a research paper.

On the publisher's staff, Aron Keesbury, Rachel Harbour, Tom Stover, Betsy Farrell, and Cynthia Cox made many contributions to the development and revision of the new edition. Thanks to Joseph Croscup for handling the very difficult responsibility of securing hundreds of reprint permissions. Carmen Altes oversaw the art and image production. Lois Lombardo directed the complex job of managing the production of the book in all of its many versions from the manuscript to the final printed form. And lastly, we would like to thank our excellent copyeditor, Stephanie Magean.

Mary Gioia was involved in every stage of planning, editing, and execution. Not only could the book not have been done without her capable hand and careful eye, but her expert guidance made every chapter better.

Past debts that will never be repaid are outstanding to hundreds of instructors named in prefaces past and to the late and dearly missed Dorothy M. Kennedy.

X. J. K., D. G., AND D. S.

ABOUT THE AUTHORS

X. J. KENNEDY, after graduation from Seton Hall and Columbia, became a journalist second class in the Navy ("Actually, I was pretty eighth class"). His poems, some published in the *New Yorker*, were first collected in *Nude Descending a Staircase* (1961). Since then he has published seven more collections, including a volume of new and selected poems in 2007, several widely adopted literature and writing textbooks, and seventeen books for children, including two novels. He has taught at Michigan, North Carolina (Greensboro), California (Irvine), Wellesley, Tufts, and Leeds. Cited in *Bartlett's Familiar Quotations* and reprinted in some 200 anthologies, his verse has brought him a Guggenheim fellowship, a Lamont Award, a Los Angeles Times Book Prize, an award from the American Academy and Institute of Arts and Letters, an Aiken-Taylor prize, and the Award for Poetry for Children from the National Council of Teachers of English. He lives in Peabody, Massachusetts.

DANA GIOIA is a poet, critic, and teacher. Born in Los Angeles of Italian and Mexican ancestry, he attended Stanford and Harvard before taking a detour into business. ("Not many poets have a Stanford M.B.A., thank goodness!") After years of writing and reading late in the evenings after work, he quit a vice presidency to write and teach. He has published four collections of poetry, *Daily Horoscope* (1986), *The Gods of Winter* (1991), *Interrogations at Noon* (2001), which won the American Book Award, and *Pity the Beautiful* (2012); and three critical volumes, including *Can Poetry Matter?* (1992), an influential study of poetry's place in contemporary America. Gioia has taught at Johns Hopkins, Sarah Lawrence, Wesleyan (Connecticut), Mercer, and Colorado College. From 2003 to 2009 he served as the Chairman of the National Endowment for the Arts. At the NEA he created the largest literary programs in federal history, including Shakespeare in American Communities and Poetry Out Loud, the national high school poetry recitation contest. He also led the campaign to restore active literary reading by creating the Big Read, which helped reverse a quarter century of decline in reading in the United States. He is currently the Judge Widney Professor of Poetry and Public Culture at the University of Southern California.

(The surname Gioia is pronounced JÓY-A. As some of you may have already guessed, *gioia* is the Italian word for "joy.")

DAN STONE worked for many years as a program manager and documentary producer at the National Endowment for the Arts, during which time he wrote, recorded, and produced nearly thirty radio documentaries on classic American novels for the Big Read, interviewing more than 200 prominent writers, actors, artists, musicians, and public figures. While at the NEA, Stone helped create Poetry Out Loud, the popular national high school recitation contest, and he produced educational and audio programming for the initiatives Shakespeare in American Communities and NEA Jazz Masters. He studied poetry at Colorado College and received an MFA in fiction from Boston University, and he has taught middle school, high school, and college. With Dana Gioia, Stone edited Penguin's *100 Great Poets of the English Language*. His most recent book, *How Money Became Dangerous*, is about the modern evolution of Wall Street and the financial services industry. He is the founder and editor-in-chief of *Radio Silence*, a magazine of literature and rock 'n' roll. For City Arts & Lectures and NPR, he has conducted lengthy stage conversations with Bruce Springsteen, Patti Smith, George Saunders, and Elvis Costello. Stone owns an establishment near his home in Oakland, California, called North Light, which serves as a bookstore, record store, restaurant, and café.

Amy Tan in Chinatown, San Francisco, 1989.

FICTION

TALKING WITH *Amy Tan*

"Life Is Larger Than We Think"

Dana Gioia Interviews Amy Tan

Q: You were born in Oakland to a family in which both parents had come from China. Were you raised bilingually?

AMY TAN: Until the age of five, my parents spoke to me in Chinese or a combination of Chinese and English, but they didn't force me to speak Mandarin. In retrospect, this was sad, because they believed that my chance of doing well in America hinged on my fluency in English. Later, as an adult, I wanted to learn Chinese. Now I make an effort when I am with my sisters, who don't speak English well.

Amy Tan with her mother.

Q: What books do you remember reading early in your childhood?

AMY TAN: I read every fairy tale I could lay my hands on at the public library. It was a wonderful world to escape to. I say "escape" deliberately, because I look back and I feel that my childhood was filled with a lot of tensions in the house, and I was able to go to another place. These stories were also filled with their own kinds of dangers and tensions, but they weren't mine. And they were usually solved in the end. This was something satisfying. You could go through these things and then, suddenly, you would have some kind of ending. I think that every lonely kid loves to escape through stories. And what kids never thought that they were lonely at some point in their life?

Q: Your mother—to put it mildly—did not approve of your ambition to be a writer.

AMY TAN: My mother and father were immigrants and they were practical people. They wanted us to do well in the new country. They didn't want us to be starving artists. Going into the arts was considered a luxury—that was something you did if you were born to wealth. When my mother found out that I had switched from pre-med to English literature, she imagined that I would lead this life of poverty, that this was a dream that couldn't possibly lead to anything. I didn't know what it would lead to. It just occurred to me I could finally make a choice when I was in college. I didn't have to follow what my parents had set out for me from the age of six—to become a doctor.

Q: What did your mother think of *The Joy Luck Club*?

AMY TAN: Well, by the time I wrote *The Joy Luck Club*, she had changed her opinion. I was making a very good living as a business writer, enough to buy a house for her to live in. When you can do that for your parents, they think you're doing ...ly well. That was the goal, to become a doctor and be able to make enough money to take care of my mother in her old age. Because I was able to do that as a business writer, she thought it was great. When I decided to write fiction and I said I needed to interview her for stories from her past, she thought that was even better. Then when I got published, and it became a success, she said, "I always knew she was going to be a writer, because she had a wild imagination."

Q: *The Joy Luck Club* is a book of enormous importance, because it brought the complex history of Chinese immigration into the mainstream of American literature. Writing this book, did you have any sense that you were opening up a whole new territory?

AMY TAN: No, I had no idea this was going to be anything but weird stories about a weird family that was unique to us. To think that they would apply to other people who would find similarities to their own families or conflicts was beyond my imagination, and I have a very good imagination.

I wanted to write this book for very personal reasons. One of them, of course, was to learn the craft of writing. The other reason was to understand myself, to figure out who I was. A lot of writers use writing as a way of finding their own personal meaning. I wrote out of total chaos and personal history, which did not seem like something that would ever be used by other people as a way of understanding their lives.

Q: Did you have any literary models in writing your short stories or putting them together as a book? Or did you just do it on intuition?

AMY TAN: I look back, and there were unconscious models—fairy tales, the Bible, especially the cadence of the Bible. There was a book called *Little House in the Big Woods*, by Laura Ingalls Wilder. Wilder wrote this fictional story based on her life as a lonely little girl, moving from place to place. She lived 100 years ago, but that was my life.

The other major influence was my parents. My father wrote sermons and he read them aloud to me, as his test audience. They were not the kind of hell and brimstone sermons. They were stories about himself and his doubts, what he wanted and how he tried to do it.

Then, of course, there was my mother, who told stories as though they were happening right in front of her. She would remember what happened to her in life and act them out in front of me. That's oral storytelling at its best.

Q: Is there anything else that you'd like to say?

AMY TAN: I think reading is really important. It provided for me a refuge, especially during difficult times. It provided me with the notion that I could find an ending that was different from what was happening to me at the time. When you read about the lives of other people, people of different circumstances or similar circumstances, you are part of their lives for that moment. You inhabit their lives, and you feel what they're feeling, and that is compassion.

Life is larger than we think it is. Certain events can happen that we don't understand. We can take it as faith or as superstition or as a fairy tale. The possibilities are wide open as to how we look at them.

It's a wonderful part of life to come to a situation and think that it can offer all kinds of possibilities and you get to choose them. I look at what's happened to me as a published writer, and sometimes I think it's a fairy tale.

Here is a story, one of the shortest ever written and one of the most difficult to forget:

> A woman is sitting in her old, shuttered house. She knows that she is alone in the whole world; every other thing is dead.
>
> The doorbell rings.

In a brief space this small tale of terror, credited to Thomas Bailey Aldrich, makes itself memorable. It sets a promising scene—is this a haunted house?—introduces a character, and places her in a strange and intriguing situation. Although in reading a story that is over so quickly we don't come to know the character well, for a moment we enter her thoughts and begin to share her feelings. Then something amazing happens. The story leaves us to wonder: who or what rang that bell?

Like many richer, longer, more complicated stories, this one, in its few words, engages the imagination. Evidently, how much a story contains and suggests doesn't depend on its size. In the opening chapter of this book, we will look first at other brief stories—examples of three ancient kinds of fiction: a fable, a parable, and a tale—and then at a contemporary short story. We will consider the elements of fiction one after another. By seeing a few short stories broken into their parts, you will come to a keener sense of how a story is put together. Not all stories are short, of course; later in the book, you will find a chapter on reading long stories and novels.

Here follows a wide variety of stories—with many traditional favorites along with some surprising contemporary selections. Among them, may you find at least a few you'll enjoy and care to remember.

1 READING A STORY

What You Will Learn in This Chapter

- To define *fiction*
- To identify the major types of short fiction
- To explain the elements of plot and key narrative techniques
- To identify the protagonist and antagonist in a literary work

After the shipwreck that marooned him on a desert island, Robinson Crusoe, in Daniel Defoe's novel, stood gazing over the water where pieces of cargo from his ship were floating by. Along came "two shoes, not mates." It is the qualification *not mates* that makes the detail memorable. We could well believe that a thing so striking and odd must have been seen, and not invented. But in truth Defoe, like other masters of the art of fiction, had the power to make us believe his imaginings. Borne along by the art of the storyteller, we trust what we are told, even though the story may be sheer fantasy.

THE ART OF FICTION

Fiction (from the Latin *fictio*, "a shaping, a counterfeiting") is a name for stories not entirely factual, but at least partially shaped, made up, imagined. It is true that in some fiction, such as a historical novel, a writer draws on factual information in presenting scenes, events, and characters. But the factual information in a historical novel, unlike that in a history book, is of secondary importance.

Many firsthand accounts of the American Civil War were written by men who had fought in it, but few eyewitnesses give us so keen a sense of actual life on the battlefront as the author of *The Red Badge of Courage*, Stephen Crane, who was born after the war was over. In fiction, the "facts" may or may not be true, and a story is none the worse for their being entirely imaginary. We expect from fiction a sense of how people act, not an authentic chronicle of how, at some past time, a few people acted.

Human beings love stories. We put them everywhere—not only in books, films, and plays, but also in songs, news articles, cartoons, and video games. There seems to be a general human curiosity about how other lives, both real and imaginary, take shape and unfold. Some stories provide simple and predictable pleasures according to a conventional plan. Each episode of *CSI* or *New Girl*, for instance, follows a roughly similar structure, so that regular viewers feel comfortably engaged and entertained. But other stories may seek to challenge rather than comfort us, by finding new and exciting ways to tell a tale, or by delving deeper into the mysteries of human nature, or by doing both.

Literary Fiction

Literary fiction calls for close attention. Reading a short story by Ernest Hemingway instead of watching an episode of *Grey's Anatomy* is a little like playing chess rather than checkers. It isn't that Hemingway isn't entertaining. Great literature provides deep and genuine pleasures. But it also requires close attention and skilled engagement from the reader. We are not necessarily led on by the promise of thrills; we do not keep reading mainly to find out what happens next. Indeed, a literary story might even disclose in its opening lines everything that happened, and then spend the rest of its length revealing what that happening meant.

Reading literary fiction is not merely a passive activity, but it is one that demands both attention and insight-lending participation. In return, it offers rewards. In some works of literary fiction we see more deeply into the minds and hearts of the characters than we ever see into those of our families, our close friends, our lovers—or even ourselves.

TYPES OF SHORT FICTION

Modern literary fiction in English has been dominated by two forms: the novel and the short story. The two have many elements in common. Perhaps we will be able to define the short story more meaningfully if first, for comparison, we consider some related varieties of fiction: the fable, the parable, and the tale. These ancient forms, whose origins date back to the time of word-of-mouth storytelling, are relatively simple in structure; in them we can plainly see elements also found in the short story (and in the novel).

Fable

The **fable** is a brief, typically humorous narrative told to illustrate a moral. The characters in a fable are often animals who embody specific human qualities. An ant, for example, may represent a hardworking type of person, or a lion may represent nobility. But fables can also include human characters. To begin, here is a celebrated Sufi fable, which has been told and retold by many writers, most notably ninth-century Muslim writer Al-Fudhayl bin 'Iyyadh. (Samarra, by the way, is a city sixty miles from Baghdad.)

Sufi Legend

Death Has an Appointment in Samarra c. 800

Translated by Virgil Abadi

One day in Baghdad a man, a student of Sufi, was sitting in the corner of an inn when he happened to hear two people talking. From their conversation, the man realized that one of the figures was the Angel of Death.

"For the next few weeks," Death told his companion, "I'm gathering people in Baghdad." As he said this, Death looked over at the man in the corner.

Terrified, the man fled from the tavern and tried to plan some way to escape Death. He decided that the best course was to leave Baghdad at once and travel as far away as possible. He hired a fast horse and rode to the town of Samarra.

Meanwhile Death met the man's teacher, who was an old friend. As they talked about various acquaintances, Death asked the Sufi master about his student.

"Where is your disciple?" Death asked.

"He is here in Baghdad, busy with his studies," replied the teacher. "Why do you ask?"

"I was surprised to see him here," Death responded. "I have an appointment to take him next week, but it is over in Samarra."

Elements of Fable

That brief story seems practically all skin and bones; that is, it contains little decoration. For in a fable everything leads directly to the **moral**, or message, sometimes stated at the end (moral: "Haste makes waste"). In "Death Has an Appointment in Samarra" the moral isn't stated outright; it is merely implied. How would you state it in your own words?

You are probably acquainted with some of the fables credited to the Greek slave Aesop (about 620–560 B.C.), whose stories seem designed to teach lessons about human life. Such is the fable of "The Goose That Laid the Golden Eggs," in which the owner of this marvelous creature slaughters her to get at the great treasure that he thinks is inside her, but finds nothing (implied moral: "Be content with what you have"). Another is the fable of "The Tortoise and the Hare" (implied moral: "Slow, steady plodding wins the race"). The characters in a fable may be talking animals (as in many of Aesop's fables), inanimate objects, or people and supernatural beings (as in "Death Has an Appointment in Samarra"). Whoever they may be, these characters are merely sketched, not greatly developed. Evidently, it would not have helped the fable to make its point if it had portrayed the teacher, the student, and Death in fuller detail. A more elaborate description of the tavern would not have improved the story. Probably, such a description would strike us as unnecessary and distracting. By its very bareness and simplicity, a fable fixes itself—and its message—in memory.

Aesop

The Fox and the Grapes

6th century B.C

Translated by V. S. Vernon Jones

Very little is known with certainty about the man called Aesop, but several accounts and many traditions survive from antiquity. According to the Greek historian Herodotus, Aesop was a slave on the island of Samos. He gained great fame from his fables, but he somehow met his death at the hands of the people of Delphi. According to one tradition, Aesop was an ugly and misshapen man who charmed and amused people with his stories. No one knows if Aesop himself wrote down any of his fables, but they circulated widely in ancient Greece and were praised by Plato, Aristotle, and many other authors. His short and witty tales with their incisive morals have remained constantly popular and influenced innumerable later writers.

A hungry fox saw some fine bunches of grapes hanging from a vine that was trained along a high trellis, and did his best to reach them by jumping as high as he could into the air. But it was all in vain, for they were just out of reach: so he gave up trying, and walked away with an air of dignity and unconcern, remarking, "I thought those grapes were ripe, but I see now they are quite sour."

Moral: It is easy to despise what you cannot get.

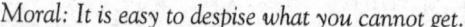

Woodcut by William Caxton, from his 1484 edition of Aesop's fables, the first English translation.

Questions

1. In fables, the fox is usually clever and frequently successful. Is that the case here?
2. The original Greek word for the fox's description of the grapes is *omphakes*, which more precisely means "unripe." Does the translator's use of the word "sour" add any further level of meaning to the fable?
3. How well does the closing moral fit the fable?

We are so accustomed to the phrase *Aesop's fables* that we might almost start to think the two words inseparable, but in fact there have been fabulists (creators or writers of fables) in virtually every culture throughout recorded history. Here is another fable from many centuries ago, this time from India.

Bidpai

The Camel and His Friends

c. 4th century

Retold in English by Arundhati Khanwalkar

The Panchatantra *(Pañca-tantra), a collection of beast fables from India, is attributed to its narrator, a sage named Bidpai, who is a legendary figure about whom almost nothing is known for certain. The* Panchatantra*, which means the "Five Chapters" in Sanskrit, is based on earlier oral folklore. The collection was composed some time between 100 B.C. and 500 A.D. in a Sanskrit original now lost and is primarily known through an Arabic version of the eighth century and a twelfth-century Hebrew translation, which is the source of most Western versions of the tales. Other translations spread the fables as far as central Europe, Asia, and Indonesia.*

Like many collections of fables, the Panchatantra *is a frame tale, with an introduction containing verse and aphorisms spoken by an eighty-year-old Brahmin teacher named Vishnusharman, who tells the stories over a period of six months for the edification of three foolish princes named Rich-Power, Fierce-Power, and Endless-Power. The stories are didactic, teaching* niti*, the wise conduct of life, and* artha*, practical wisdom that stresses cleverness and self-reliance above more altruistic virtues.*

The Lion, the King of the Animals **from "The Fables of Bidpai," c.1480 (vellum). Musée Condé, Chantilly, France/The Bridgeman Art Library.**

Once a merchant was leading a caravan of heavily-laden camels through a jungle when one of them, overcome by fatigue, collapsed. The merchant decided to leave the camel in the jungle and go on his way. Later, when the camel recovered his strength, he realized that he was alone in a strange jungle. Fortunately there was plenty of grass, and he survived.

One day the king of the jungle, a lion, arrived along with his three friends—a leopard, a fox, and a crow. The king lion wondered what the camel was doing in the jungle! He came near the camel and asked how he, a creature of the desert, had ended up in the hostile jungle. The camel tearfully explained what happened. The lion took pity on him and said, "You have nothing to fear now. Henceforth, you are under my protection and can stay with us." The camel began to live happily in the jungle.

Then one day the lion was wounded in a fight with an elephant. He retired to his cave and stayed there for several days. His friends came to offer their sympathy. They tried to catch prey for the hungry lion but failed. The camel had no problem as he lived on grass while the others were starving.

The fox came up with a plan. He secretly went to the lion and suggested that the camel be sacrificed for the good of the others. The lion got furious, "I can never kill an animal who is under my protection."

The fox humbly said, "But Lord, you have provided us food all the 5
time. If any one of us voluntarily offered himself to save your life, I hope you won't mind!" The hungry lion did not object to that and agreed to take the offer.

The fox went back to his companions and said, "Friends, our king is dying of starvation. Let us go and beg him to eat one of us. It is the least we can do for such a noble soul."

So they went to the king and the crow offered his life. The fox interrupted, and said, "You are a small creature, the master's hunger will hardly be appeased by eating you. May I humbly offer my life to satisfy my master's hunger."

The leopard stepped forward and said, "You are no bigger than the crow, it is me whom our master should eat."

The foolish camel thought, "Everyone has offered to lay down their lives for the king, but he has not hurt any one. It is now my turn to offer myself." So he stepped forward and said, "Stand aside friend leopard, the king and you have close family ties. It is me whom the master must eat."

An ominous silence greeted the camel's offer. Then the king gladly 10
said, "I accept your offer, O noble camel." And in no time he was killed by the three rogues, the false friends.

Moral: Be careful in choosing your friends.

Parable

Another traditional form of storytelling is the **parable**. Like a fable, a parable is a brief narrative that delivers a moral, but unlike a fable, its plot is plausibly realistic, and the main characters are human rather than anthropomorphized animals or natural forces. The other key difference is that parables usually possess a more mysterious and suggestive tone. A fable customarily ends by explicitly stating its moral, but parables often present their morals implicitly, and their meanings can be open to several interpretations.

In the Western tradition, the literary conventions of the parable are largely based on the brief stories told by Jesus in his preaching. The forty-three parables recounted in the four Gospels reveal how frequently he used the form to teach. Jesus designed his parables to have two levels of meaning—a literal story that could immediately be understood by the crowds he addressed and a deeper meaning fully comprehended only by his disciples, an inner circle who understood the nature of his ministry. (You can see the richness of interpretations suggested by Jesus's parables by reading and analyzing "The Parable of the Prodigal Son" from St. Luke's Gospel, which appears in Chapter 6.) The parable was also widely used by Eastern philosophers. The Taoist sage Chuang Tzu often portrayed the principles of Tao—which he called the "Way of Nature"—in witty parables such as the following one, traditionally titled "Independence."

Chuang Tzu

Independence

Chou Dynasty (4th century B.C.)

Translated by Herbert Giles

Chuang Chou, usually known as Chuang Tzu (approximately 390–365 B.C.), was one of the great philosophers of the Chou period in China. He was born in the Sung feudal state and received an excellent education. Unlike most educated men, however, Chuang Tzu did not seek public office or political power. Influenced by Taoist philosophy, he believed that individuals should transcend their desire for success and wealth, as well as their fear of failure and poverty. True freedom, he maintained, came from escaping the distractions of worldly affairs. Chuang Tzu's writings have been particularly praised for their combination of humor and wisdom. His parables and stories are classics of Chinese literature.

Chuang Tzu was one day fishing, when the Prince of Ch'u sent two high officials to interview him, saying that his Highness would be glad of Chuang Tzu's assistance in the administration of his government. The latter quietly fished on, and without looking round, replied, "I have heard that in the State of Ch'u there is a sacred tortoise, which has been dead three thousand years, and which the prince keeps packed up in a box on the altar in his ancestral shrine. Now do you think that tortoise would rather be dead and have its remains thus honoured, or be alive and wagging its tail in the mud?" The two officials answered that no doubt it would rather be alive and wagging its tail in the mud; whereupon Chuang Tzu cried out "Begone! I too elect to remain wagging my tail in the mud."

Questions

1. What part of this story is the exposition? How many sentences does Chuang Tzu use to set up the dramatic situation?
2. Why does the protagonist change the subject and mention the sacred tortoise? Why doesn't he answer the request directly and immediately? Does it serve any purpose that Chuang Tzu makes the officials answer a question to which he knows the answer?
3. What does this story tell us about the protagonist Chuang Tzu's personality?

Tale

The name *tale* (from the Old English *talu*, "speech") is sometimes applied to any story, whether short or long, true or fictitious. *Tale* being a more evocative name than *story*, writers sometimes call their stories "tales" as if to imply something handed down from the past. But defined in a more limited sense, a **tale** is a story, usually short, that sets forth strange and wonderful events in more or less bare summary, without detailed character-drawing. "Tale" is pretty much synonymous with "yarn," for it implies a story in which the goal is revelation of the marvelous rather than revelation of character.

In the English folktale "Jack and the Beanstalk," we take away a more vivid impression of the miraculous beanstalk and the giant who dwells at its top than of Jack's mind or personality. Because such venerable stories were told aloud before someone set them down in writing, the storytellers had to limit themselves to brief descriptions. Probably spoken around a fire or hearth, such a tale tends to be less complicated and less closely detailed than a story written for the printed page, whose reader can linger over it. Still, such tales *can* be complicated. It is not merely greater length that makes a short story different from a tale or a fable: one mark of a short story is a fully delineated character.

Types of Tales

Even modern tales favor supernatural or fantastic events: for instance, the **tall tale**, a variety of folk story that recounts the deeds of a superhero (such as the giant lumberjack Paul Bunyan) or of the storyteller. If the storyteller is describing his or her own imaginary experience, the bragging yarn is usually told with a straight face to listeners who take pleasure in scoffing at it. Although the **fairy tale**, set in a world of magic and enchantment, is sometimes the work of a modern author (notably Hans Christian Andersen), well-known examples are those German folktales that probably originated in the Middle Ages, collected by the Brothers Grimm. The label *fairy tale* is something of an English misnomer, for in the Grimm stories, though witches and goblins abound, fairies are a minority.

Jakob and Wilhelm Grimm

Godfather Death

1812 (from oral tradition)

Translated by Dana Gioia

Jakob and Wilhelm Grimm

Jakob Grimm (1785–1863) and Wilhelm Grimm (1786–1859), brothers and scholars, were born near Frankfurt am Main, Germany. For most of their lives they worked together—lived together, too, even when in 1825 Wilhelm married. In 1838, as librarians, they began toiling on their Deutsch Wörterbuch, *or German dictionary, a vast project that was to outlive them by a century. (It was completed only in 1960.) In 1840 King Friedrich Wilhelm IV appointed both brothers to the Royal Academy of Sciences, and both taught at the University of Berlin for the rest of their days.*

The name Grimm is best known to us for that splendid collection of ancient German folk stories we call Grimm's Fairy Tales*—in German,* Kinder- und Hausmärchen *("Childhood and Household Tales," 1812–1815). This classic work spread German children's stories around the world. Many tales we hear early in life were collected by the Grimms: "Hansel and Gretel," "Snow White and the Seven Dwarfs," "Rapunzel," "Tom Thumb," "Little Red Riding Hood," "Rumpelstiltskin." Versions of some of these tales had been written down as early as the sixteenth century, but mainly the brothers relied on the memories of Hessian peasants who recited the stories aloud for them.*

A poor man had twelve children and had to work day and night just to give them bread. Now when the thirteenth came into the world, he did not know what to do, so he ran out onto the main highway intending to ask the first one he met to be the child's godfather.

The first person he met was the good Lord God, who knew very well what was weighing on the man's heart. And He said to him, "Poor man, I am sorry for you. I will hold your child at the baptismal font. I will take care of him and fill his days with happiness."

The man asked, "Who are you?"

"I am the good Lord."

"Then I don't want you as godfather. You give to the rich and let the poor starve."

The man spoke thus because he did not know how wisely God portions out wealth and poverty. So he turned away from the Lord and went on.

Then the Devil came up to him and said, "What are you looking for? If you take me as your child's sponsor, I will give him gold heaped high and wide and all the joys of this world."

The man asked, "Who are you?"

"I am the Devil."

"Then I don't want you as godfather," said the man. "You trick men and lead them astray."

He went on, and bone-thin Death strode up to him and said, "Choose me as godfather."

The man asked, "Who are you?"

"I am Death, who makes all men equal."

Then the man said, "You are the right one. You take the rich and the poor without distinction. You will be the godfather."

Death answered, "I will make your child rich and famous. Whoever has me as a friend shall lack for nothing."

The man said, "The baptism is next Sunday. Be there on time."

Death appeared just as he had promised and stood there as a proper godfather.

When the boy had grown up, his godfather walked in one day and said to come along with him. Death led him out into the woods, showed him an herb, and said, "Now you are going to get your christening present. I am making you a famous doctor. When you are called to a patient, I will always appear to you. If I stand next to the sick person's head, you may speak boldly that you will make him healthy again. Give him some of this herb, and he will recover. But if you see me standing by the sick person's feet, then he is mine. You must say that nothing can be done and that no doctor in the world can save him. But beware of using the herb against my will, or it will turn out badly for you."

It was not long before the young man was the most famous doctor in the whole world. "He needs only to look at the sick person," everyone said, "and then he knows how things stand—whether the patient will get well again or whether he must die." People came from far and wide to bring their sick and gave him so much gold that he quickly became quite rich.

Now it soon happened that the king grew ill, and the doctor was summoned to say whether a recovery was possible. But when he came to the bed, Death was standing at the sick man's feet, and now no herb grown could save him.

"If I cheat Death this one time," thought the doctor, "he will be angry, but since I am his godson, he will turn a blind eye, so I will risk it." He took up the sick man and turned him around so that his head was now where Death stood. Then he gave the king some of the herb. The king recovered and grew healthy again.

But Death then came to the doctor with a dark and angry face and threatened him with his finger. "You have hoodwinked me this time," he said. "And I will forgive you once because you are my godson. But if you try such a thing again, it will be your neck, and I will take you away with me."

Not long after, the king's daughter fell into a serious illness. She was his only child, and he wept day and night until his eyes went blind. He let it be known that whoever saved her from death would become her husband and inherit the crown.

When the doctor came to the sick girl's bed, he saw Death standing at her feet. He should have remembered his godfather's warning, but the princess's great beauty and the happy prospect of becoming her husband so infatuated him that he flung all caution to the wind. He didn't notice that Death stared at him angrily or that he raised his hand and shook his bony fist. The doctor picked up the sick girl and turned her around to place her head where her feet had been. He gave her the herb, and right away her cheeks grew rosy and she stirred again with life.

When Death saw that he had been cheated out of his property a 25
second time, he strode with long steps up to the doctor and said, "It is all over for you. Now it's your turn." Death seized him so firmly with his ice-cold hand that the doctor could not resist. He led him into an underground cavern. There the doctor saw thousands and thousands of candles burning in endless rows. Some were tall, others medium-sized, and others quite small. Every moment some went out and others lit up, so that the tiny flames seemed to jump to and fro in perpetual motion.

"Look," said Death, "these are the life lights of mankind. The tall ones belong to children, the middle-size ones to married people in the prime of life, and the short ones to the very old. But sometimes even children and young people have only a short candle."

"Show me my life light," said the doctor, assuming it would be very tall.

Death pointed to a small stub that seemed about to flicker out.

"Oh, dear godfather!" cried the terrified doctor. "Light a new candle for me. If you love me, do it, so that I may enjoy my life, become king, and marry the beautiful princess."

"That I cannot do," Death replied. "One candle must first go out 30
before a new one is lighted."

"Then put my old one on top of a new candle that will keep burning when the old one goes out," begged the doctor.

Death acted as if he were going to grant the wish and picked up a tall new candle. But because he wanted revenge, he deliberately fumbled in placing the new candle, and the stub toppled over and went out. The doctor immediately dropped to the ground and fell into the hands of Death.

PLOT

Like a fable, the Grimm brothers' tale seems stark in its lack of detail and in the swiftness of its telling. Compared with the fully portrayed characters of many modern stories, the characters of father, son, king, princess, and even Death himself seem hardly more than stick figures. It may have been that to draw ample characters would not have contributed to the storytellers' design; that, indeed, to have done so would have been inartistic. Yet "Godfather Death" is a compelling story. By what methods does it arouse and sustain our interest?

Elements of Plot

Plot sometimes refers simply to the events in a story. In this book, though, **plot** will mean the artistic arrangement of those events. From the opening sentence of "Godfather Death," we watch the unfolding of a **dramatic situation**: a person is involved in some **conflict**. First, this character is a poor man with children to feed, in conflict with the world; very soon, we find him in conflict with God and with the Devil besides. Drama in fiction occurs in any clash of wills, desires, or powers—whether it be a conflict of character against character, character against society, character against some natural force, or, as in "Godfather Death," character against some supernatural entity.

Like any shapely tale, "Godfather Death" has a beginning, a middle, and an end. In fact, it is unusual to find a story so clearly displaying the elements of structure that critics have found in many classic works of fiction and drama. The tale begins with an **exposition**: the opening portion that sets the scene (if any), introduces the main characters, tells us what happened before the story opened, and provides any other background information that we need in order to understand and care about the events to follow. In "Godfather Death," the exposition is brief—all in the opening paragraph. The middle section of the story begins with Death's giving the herb to the boy and his warning not to defy him. This moment introduces a new conflict (a **complication**), and by this time it is clear that the son and not the father is to be the central human character of the story.

Protagonist Versus Antagonist

Death's godson is the principal person who strives: the **protagonist** (a better term than **hero**, for it may apply equally well to a central character who is not especially brave or virtuous). The **suspense**, the pleasurable anxiety we feel that heightens our attention to the story, resides in our wondering how it will all turn out. Will the doctor triumph over Death? Even though we suspect, early in the story, that the doctor stands no chance against such a superhuman **antagonist**, we want to see for ourselves the outcome of his defiance.

Crisis and Climax

When the doctor defies his godfather for the first time—when he saves the king—we have a **crisis**, a moment of high tension. The tension is momentarily resolved when Death lets him off. Then an even greater crisis—the turning point in the action—occurs with the doctor's second defiance in restoring the princess to life. In the last section of the story, with the doctor in the underworld, events come to a **climax**, the moment of greatest tension at which the outcome is to be decided, when the terrified doctor begs for a new candle. Will Death grant him one? Will he live, become king, and marry the princess? The outcome or **conclusion**—also called the **resolution** or **dénouement** (French for "the untying of the knot")—quickly follows as Death allows the little candle to go out.

Narrative Techniques

The treatment of plot is one aspect of an author's artistry. Different arrangements of the same material are possible. A writer might decide to tell of the events in chronological order, beginning with the earliest; or he or she might open the story with the last event, then tell what led up to it. Sometimes a writer chooses to skip rapidly over the exposition and begin ***in medias res*** (Latin for "in the midst of things"), first presenting some exciting or significant moment, then filling in what happened earlier. This method is by no means a modern invention: Homer begins the *Odyssey* with his hero mysteriously late in returning from war and his son searching for him; John Milton's *Paradise Lost* opens with Satan already defeated in his revolt against God. A device useful to writers for filling in what happened earlier is the **flashback** (or **retrospect**), a scene relived in a character's memory. Alternatively, a storyteller can try to incite our anticipation by giving us some **foreshadowing** or indication of events to come. In "Godfather Death" the foreshadowings are apparent in Death's warnings ("But if you try such a thing again, it will be your neck").

THE SHORT STORY

The teller of tales relies heavily on the method of **summary**: terse, general narration. In a **short story**, a form more realistic than the tale and of modern origin, the writer usually presents the main events in greater fullness. Fine writers of short stories, although they may use summary at times (often to give some portion of a story less emphasis), are skilled in rendering a **scene**: a vivid or dramatic moment described in enough detail to create the illusion that the reader is practically there. Avoiding long summary, they try to *show* rather than simply to *tell*, as if following Mark Twain's advice to authors: "Don't say, 'The old lady screamed.' Bring her on and let her scream."

A short story is more than just a sequence of happenings. A finely wrought short story has the richness and conciseness of an excellent lyric poem. Spontaneous and natural as the finished story may seem, the writer has crafted it so artfully that there is meaning in even seemingly casual speeches and apparently trivial details. If we skim it hastily, skipping the descriptive passages, we miss significant parts.

Some literary short stories, unlike commercial fiction in which the main interest is in physical action or conflict, tell of an **epiphany**: some moment of insight, discovery, or revelation by which a character's life, or view of life, is greatly altered. The term, which means "showing forth" in Greek, was first used in Christian theology to signify the manifestation of God's presence in the world. This theological idea was adapted by James Joyce to refer to a heightened moment of secular revelation. (For such moments in fiction, see the stories in this book by Joyce, John Steinbeck, and Joyce Carol Oates.) Other short stories tell of a character initiated into experience or maturity: one such **story of initiation** is William Faulkner's "Barn Burning" (Chapter 5), in which a boy finds it necessary to defy his father and suddenly grows into manhood. Less obviously dramatic, perhaps, than "Godfather Death," such a story may be no less powerful.

The fable and the tale are ancient forms; the short story is of more recent origin. In the nineteenth century, writers of fiction were encouraged by a large, literate audience of middle-class readers who wanted to see their lives reflected in faithful mirrors. Skillfully representing ordinary life, many writers perfected the art of the short story: in Russia, Anton Chekhov, and in America, Nathaniel Hawthorne and Edgar Allan Poe (although the Americans seem less fond of everyday life than of dream and fantasy). It would be false to claim that, in passing from the fable and the tale to the short story, fiction has made triumphant progress; or to claim that, because short stories are modern, they are superior to fables and tales. Fable, tale, and short story are distinct forms, each achieving its own effects. Far from being extinct, fable and tale have enjoyed a resurgence in recent years. Jorge Luis Borges, Italo Calvino, and Gabriel García Márquez have all used fable and folktale to create memorable and very modern fiction. All forms of fiction are powerful in the right authorial hands.

Let's begin with a contemporary short story whose protagonist undergoes an initiation into maturity. To notice the difference between a short story and a tale, you may find it helpful to compare John Updike's "A & P" with "Godfather Death." Although Updike's short story is centuries distant from the Grimm tale in its setting and its method of telling, you may be reminded of "Godfather Death" in the main character's dramatic situation. To defend a young woman, a young man has to defy his mentor—here, the boss of a supermarket. In so doing, he places himself in jeopardy. Updike has the protagonist tell his own story, amply and with humor. How does it differ from a tale?

John Updike

A & P

1961

John Updike

John Updike (1932–2009) was born in Reading, Pennsylvania, received his B.A. from Harvard, and then went to Oxford to study drawing and fine art. In the mid-1950s he worked on the staff of the New Yorker, *at times doing errands for the aged James Thurber. Although he left the magazine to become a full-time writer, Updike continued to supply it with memorable stories, witty light verse, and searching reviews. A famously prolific writer, he published more than fifty books. Updike is best known as a hardworking, versatile, highly productive writer of fiction. For his novel* The Centaur *(1963) he received a National*

Book Award, and for Rabbit Is Rich *(1982) a Pulitzer Prize and an American Book Award. The fourth and last Rabbit Angstrom novel,* Rabbit at Rest *(1990), won him a second Pulitzer. Updike is one of the few Americans ever to be awarded both the National Medal of Arts (1989) and the National Humanities Medal (2003)—the nation's highest honors in each respective field. His many other books include* The Witches of Eastwick *(1984), made into a successful film starring Jack Nicholson,* Terrorist *(2006), and his final novel,* The Widows of Eastwick *(2008).*

Almost uniquely among contemporary American writers, Updike moved back and forth successfully among a variety of literary genres: light verse, serious poetry, drama, criticism, children's books, novels, and short stories. But it is perhaps in short fiction that he did his finest work. Many critics agree with the Washington Post *writer Jonathan Yardley, who wrote: "It is in his short stories that we find Updike's most assured work, and no doubt it is upon the best of them that his reputation ultimately will rest."*

In walks three girls in nothing but bathing suits. I'm in the third check-out slot, with my back to the door, so I don't see them until they're over by the bread. The one that caught my eye first was the one in the plaid green two-piece. She was a chunky kid, with a good tan and a sweet broad soft-looking can with those two crescents of white just under it, where the sun never seems to hit, at the top of the backs of her legs. I stood there with my hand on a box of HiHo crackers trying to remember if I rang it up or not. I ring it up again and the customer starts giving me hell. She's one of these cash-register-watchers, a witch about fifty with rouge on her cheekbones and no eyebrows, and I know it made her day to trip me up. She'd been watching cash registers for fifty years and probably never seen a mistake before.

By the time I got her feathers smoothed and her goodies into a bag—she gives me a little snort in passing, if she'd been born at the right time they would have burned her over in Salem—by the time I get her on her way the girls had circled around the bread and were coming back, without a pushcart, back my way along the counters, in the aisle between the check-outs and the Special bins. They didn't even have shoes on. There was this chunky one, with the two-piece—it was bright green and the seams on the bra were still sharp and her belly was still pretty pale so I guessed she just got it (the suit)—there was this one, with one of those chubby berry-faces, the lips all bunched together under her nose, this one, and a tall one, with black hair that hadn't quite frizzed right, and one of these sunburns right across under the eyes, and a chin that was too long—you know, the kind of girl other girls think is very "striking" and "attractive" but never quite makes it, as they very well know, which is why they like her so much—and then the third one, that wasn't quite so tall. She was the queen. She kind of led them, the other two peeking around and making their shoulders round. She didn't look around, not this queen, she just walked straight on slowly, on these long white prima-donna legs. She came down a little hard on her heels, as if she didn't walk in her bare feet that much, putting down her heels and then letting the weight move along to her toes as if she was testing the floor with every step, putting a little deliberate extra action into it. You never know for sure how girls' minds work (do you really think it's a mind in there or just a little buzz like a bee in a glass jar?) but you got the idea she had talked the other two into coming in here with her, and now she was showing them how to do it, walk slow and hold yourself straight.

She had on a kind of dirty-pink—beige maybe, I don't know—bathing suit with a little nubble all over it and, what got me, the straps were down. They were off her shoulders looped loose around the cool tops of her arms, and I guess as a result the suit had slipped a little on her, so all around the top of the cloth there was this shining rim. If it hadn't been there you wouldn't have known there could have been anything whiter than those shoulders. With the straps pushed off, there was nothing between the top of the suit and the top of her head except just *her*, this clean bare plane of the top of her chest down from the shoulder bones like a dented sheet of metal tilted in the light. I mean, it was more than pretty.

She had sort of oaky hair that the sun and salt had bleached, done up in a bun that was unraveling, and a kind of prim face. Walking into the A & P with your straps down, I suppose it's the only kind of face you *can* have. She held her head so high her neck, coming up out of those white shoulders, looked kind of stretched, but I didn't mind. The longer her neck was, the more of her there was.

She must have felt in the corner of her eye me and over my shoulder 5
Stokesie in the second slot watching, but she didn't tip. Not this queen. She kept her eyes moving across the racks, and stopped, and turned so slow it made my stomach rub the inside of my apron, and buzzed to the other two, who kind of huddled against her for relief, and they all three of them went up the cat-and-dog-food-breakfast-cereal-macaroni-rice-raisins-seasonings-spreads-spaghetti-soft-drinks-crackers-and-cookies aisle. From the third slot I look straight up this aisle to the meat counter, and I watched them all the way. The fat one with the tan sort of fumbled with the cookies, but on second thought she put the packages back. The sheep pushing their carts down the aisle—the girls were walking against the usual traffic (not that we have one-way signs or anything)—were pretty hilarious. You could see them, when Queenie's white shoulders dawned on them, kind of jerk, or hop, or hiccup, but their eyes snapped back to their own baskets and on they pushed. I bet you could set off dynamite in an A & P and the people would by and large keep reaching and checking oatmeal off their lists and muttering "Let me see, there was a third thing, began with A, asparagus, no, ah, yes, applesauce!" or whatever it is they do mutter. But there was no doubt, this jiggled them. A few houseslaves in pin curlers even looked around after pushing their carts past to make sure what they had seen was correct.

You know, it's one thing to have a girl in a bathing suit down on the beach, where what with the glare nobody can look at each other much anyway, and another thing in the cool of the A & P, under the fluorescent lights, against all those stacked packages, with her feet padding along naked over our checkerboard green-and-cream rubber-tile floor.

"Oh Daddy," Stokesie said beside me. "I feel so faint."

"Darling," I said. "Hold me tight." Stokesie's married, with two babies chalked up on his fuselage already, but as far as I can tell that's the only difference. He's twenty-two, and I was nineteen this April.

"Is it done?" he asks, the responsible married man finding his voice. I forgot to say he thinks he's going to be manager some sunny day, maybe in 1990 when it's called the Great Alexandrov and Petrooshki Tea Company or something.

What he meant was, our town is five miles from a beach, with a big 10
summer colony out on the Point, but we're right in the middle of town, and the women generally put on a shirt or shorts or something before they get out of the car into the street. And anyway these are usually women with six children and varicose veins mapping their legs and nobody, including them, could care less. As I say, we're right in the middle of town, and if you stand at our front doors you can see two banks and the Congregational church and the newspaper store and three real-estate offices and about twenty-seven old freeloaders tearing up Central Street because the sewer broke again. It's not as if we're on the Cape; we're north of Boston and there's people in this town haven't seen the ocean for twenty years. The girls had reached the meat counter and were asking McMahon something. He pointed, they pointed, and they shuffled out of sight behind a pyramid of Diet Delight peaches. All that was left for us to see was old McMahon patting his mouth and looking after them sizing up their joints. Poor kids, I began to feel sorry for them, they couldn't help it.

Now here comes the sad part of the story, at least my family says it's sad but I don't think it's sad myself. The store's pretty empty, it being Thursday afternoon, so there was nothing much to do except lean on the register and wait for the girls to show up again. The whole store was like a pinball machine and I didn't know which tunnel they'd come out of. After a while they come around out of the far aisle, around the light bulbs, records at discount of the Caribbean Six or Tony Martin Sings or some such gunk you wonder they waste the wax on, six-packs of candy bars, and plastic toys done up in cellophane that fall apart when a kid looks at them anyway. Around they come, Queenie still leading the way, and holding a little gray jar in her hand. Slots Three through Seven are unmanned and I could see her wondering between Stokes and me, but Stokesie with his usual luck draws an old party in baggy gray pants who stumbles up with four giant cans of pineapple juice (what do these bums *do* with all that pineapple juice? I've often asked myself) so the girls come to me. Queenie puts down the jar and I take it into my fingers icy cold. Kingfish Fancy Herring Snacks in Pure Sour Cream: 49¢. Now her hands are empty, not a ring or a bracelet, bare as God made them, and I wonder where the money's coming from. Still with that prim look she lifts a folded dollar bill out of the hollow at the center of her nubbled pink top. The jar went heavy in my hand. Really, I thought that was so cute.

Then everybody's luck begins to run out. Lengel comes in from haggling with a truck full of cabbages on the lot and is about to scuttle into that door marked MANAGER behind which he hides all day when the girls touch his eye. Lengel's pretty dreary, teaches Sunday school and the rest, but he doesn't miss that much. He comes over and says, "Girls, this isn't the beach."

Queenie blushes, though maybe it's just a brush of sunburn I was noticing for the first time, now that she was so close. "My mother asked me to pick up a jar of herring snacks." Her voice kind of startled me, the way voices do when you see the people first, coming out so flat and dumb yet kind of tony, too, the way it ticked over "pick up" and "snacks." All of a sudden I slid right down her voice into her living room. Her father and the other men were standing around in ice-cream coats and bow ties and the women were in sandals picking up herring snacks on toothpicks off a big plate and they were all holding drinks the color of water with olives and sprigs of mint in them. When my parents have somebody over they get lemonade and if it's a real racy affair Schlitz in tall glasses with "They'll Do It Every Time" cartoons stencilled on.

"That's all right," Lengel said. "But this isn't the beach." His repeating this struck me as funny, as if it had just occurred to him, and he had been thinking all these years the A & P was a great big dune and he was the head lifeguard. He didn't like my smiling—as I say he doesn't miss much—but he concentrates on giving the girls that sad Sunday-school-superintendent stare.

Queenie's blush is no sunburn now, and the plump one in plaid, that 15
I liked better from the back—a really sweet can—pipes up, "We weren't doing any shopping. We just came in for the one thing."

"That makes no difference," Lengel tells her, and I could see from the way his eyes went that he hadn't noticed she was wearing a two-piece before. "We want you decently dressed when you come in here."

"We *are* decent," Queenie says suddenly, her lower lip pushing, getting sore now that she remembers her place, a place from which the crowd that runs the A & P must look pretty crummy. Fancy Herring Snacks flashed in her very blue eyes.

"Girls, I don't want to argue with you. After this come in here with your shoulders covered. It's our policy." He turns his back. That's policy for you. Policy is what the kingpins want. What the others want is juvenile delinquency.

All this while, the customers had been showing up with their carts but, you know, sheep, seeing a scene, they had all bunched up on Stokesie, who shook open a paper bag as gently as peeling a peach, not wanting to miss a word. I could feel in the silence everybody getting nervous, most of all Lengel, who asks me, "Sammy, have you rung up this purchase?"

20 I thought and said "No" but it wasn't about that I was thinking. I go through the punches, 4, 9, GROC, TOT—it's more complicated than you think, and after you do it often enough, it begins to make a little song, that you hear words to, in my case "Hello (*bing*) there, you (*gung*) hap-py *pee*-pul (*splat*)!"—the *splat* being the drawer flying out. I uncrease the bill, tenderly as you may imagine, it just having come from between the two smoothest scoops of vanilla I had ever known were there, and pass a half and a penny into her narrow pink palm, and nestle the herrings in a bag and twist its neck and hand it over, all the time thinking.

The girls, and who'd blame them, are in a hurry to get out, so I say "I quit" to Lengel quick enough for them to hear, hoping they'll stop and watch me, their unsuspected hero. They keep right on going, into the electric eye; the door flies open and they flicker across the lot to their car, Queenie and Plaid and Big Tall Goony-Goony (not that as raw material she was so bad), leaving me with Lengel and a kink in his eyebrow.

"Did you say something, Sammy?"

"I said I quit."

"I thought you did."

25 "You didn't have to embarrass them."

"It was they who were embarrassing us."

I started to say something that came out "Fiddle-de-doo." It's a saying of my grandmother's, and I know she would have been pleased.

"I don't think you know what you're saying," Lengel said.

"I know you don't," I said. "But I do." I pull the bow at the back of my apron and start shrugging it off my shoulders. A couple customers that had been heading for my slot begin to knock against each other, like scared pigs in a chute.

30 Lengel sighs and begins to look very patient and old and gray. He's been a friend of my parents for years. "Sammy, you don't want to do this to your Mom and Dad," he tells me. It's true, I don't. But it seems to me that once you begin a gesture it's fatal not to go through with it. I fold the apron, "Sammy" stitched in red on the pocket, and put it on the counter, and drop the bow tie on top of it. The bow tie is theirs, if you've ever wondered. "You'll feel this for the rest of your life," Lengel says, and I know that's true, too, but remembering how he made that pretty girl blush makes me so scrunchy inside I punch the No Sale tab and the machine whirs "pee-pul" and the drawer splats out. One advantage to this scene taking place in summer, I can follow this up with a clean exit, there's no fumbling around getting your coat and galoshes, I just saunter into the electric eye in my white shirt that my mother ironed the night before, and the door heaves itself open, and outside the sunshine is skating around on the asphalt.

I look around for my girls, but they're gone, of course. There wasn't anybody but some young married screaming with her children about some candy they didn't get by the door of a powder-blue Falcon station wagon. Looking back in the big windows, over the bags of peat moss and aluminum lawn furniture stacked on the pavement, I could see Lengel in my place in the slot, checking the sheep through. His face was dark gray and his back stiff, as if he'd just had an injection of iron, and my stomach kind of fell as I felt how hard the world was going to be to me hereafter.

Questions

1. Notice how artfully Updike arranges details to set the story in a perfectly ordinary supermarket. What details stand out for you as particularly true to life? What does this close attention to detail contribute to the story?
2. How fully does Updike draw the character of Sammy? What traits (admirable or otherwise) does Sammy show? Is he any less a hero for wanting the girls to notice his heroism? To what extent is he more thoroughly and fully portrayed than the doctor in "Godfather Death"?
3. What part of the story seems to be the exposition? (See the definition of *exposition* in the discussion of plot earlier in the chapter.) Of what value to the story is the carefully detailed portrait of Queenie, the leader of the three girls?
4. Where in "A & P" does the dramatic conflict become apparent? What moment in the story brings the crisis? What is the climax of the story?
5. Why, exactly, does Sammy quit his job?
6. Does anything lead you to *expect* Sammy to make some gesture of sympathy for the three girls? What incident earlier in the story (before Sammy quits) seems a foreshadowing?
7. What do you understand from the conclusion of the story? What does Sammy mean when he acknowledges "how hard the world was going to be . . . hereafter"?
8. What comment does Updike—through Sammy—make on supermarket society?

WRITING *effectively*

THINKING ABOUT PLOT

A day without conflict is pleasant, but a story without conflict is boring. The plot of every short story, novel, or movie derives its energy from conflict. A character desperately wants something he or she can't have, or is frantic to avoid an unpleasant (or deadly) event. In most stories, conflict is established and tension builds, leading to a crisis and, finally, a resolution of some sort. When analyzing a story, be sure to remember these points:

- **Plotting isn't superficial.** Although plot might seem like the most obvious and superficial part of a story, it is an important expressive device. Plot combines with the other elements of fiction—imagery, style, and symbolism, for example—to create an emotional response in the reader: suspense, humor, sadness, excitement, terror.
- **Small events can have large consequences.** In most short stories, plot depends less on large external events than on small occurrences that set off large internal changes in the main character.
- **Action reveals character.** Good stories are a lot like life: the protagonist's true nature is usually revealed not just by what he or she says but also by what he or she does. Stories often show how the protagonist comes to a personal turning point, or how his or her character is tested or revealed by events.
- **Plot is about cause and effect.** Plot is more than simply a sequence of events ("First A happens, and then B, and then C . . ."). The actions, events, and situations described in most stories are related to each other by more than just accident ("First A happens, which causes B to happen, which makes C all the more surprising, or inevitable, or ironic . . .").

CHECKLIST: Writing About Plot

- ☐ What is the story's central conflict?
- ☐ Who is the protagonist? What does he or she want?
- ☐ What is at stake for the protagonist in the conflict?
- ☐ What stands in the way of the protagonist's easily achieving his or her goal?
- ☐ What are the main events that take place in the story? How does each event relate to the protagonist's struggle?
- ☐ Where do you find the story's climax, or crisis?
- ☐ How is the conflict resolved?
- ☐ Does the protagonist succeed in achieving his or her goals?
- ☐ What is the impact of success, failure, or a surprising outcome on the protagonist?

TOPICS FOR WRITING ON PLOT

1. Choose and read a story from this collection, and write a brief description of its plot and main characters. Then write at length about how the protagonist is changed or tested by the story's events. What do the main character's actions reveal about his or her personality? Some possible story choices are Updike's "A & P," Alice Walker's "Everyday Use" (Chapter 9), and Joyce Carol Oates's "Where Are You Going, Where Have You Been?" (Chapter 3).

2. Briefly list the events described in "A & P." Now write several paragraphs about the ways in which the story adds up to more than the sum of its events. Why should the reader care about Sammy's thoughts and decisions?
3. How do Sammy's actions in "A & P" reveal his character? In what ways are his thoughts and actions at odds with each other?
4. Write a brief fable modeled on either "Death Has an Appointment in Samarra," "The Fox and the Grapes," or "The Camel and His Friends." Begin with a familiar proverb—"A penny saved is a penny earned" or "Too many cooks spoil the broth"—and invent a story to make the moral convincing.
5. With "Godfather Death" in mind, write a fairy tale set in the present, in a town or city much like your own. After you've completed your fairy tale, write a paragraph explaining what aspects of the fairy tale by the Brothers Grimm you hoped to capture in your story.
6. The Brothers Grimm collected and wrote down many of our best-known fairy tales—"Cinderella," "Snow White and the Seven Dwarfs," and "Little Red Riding Hood," for example. If you have strong childhood recollections of one of these stories—perhaps based on picture books or on the animated Disney versions—find and read the Brothers Grimm version. Are you surprised by the differences? Write a brief essay contrasting the original with your remembered version. What does the original offer that the adaptation does not?

▶ TERMS FOR *review*

Types of Short Fiction

Fable ▶ A brief, often humorous narrative told to illustrate a moral. The characters in fables are traditionally animals whose personality traits symbolize human traits.

Parable ▶ A brief, usually allegorical narrative that teaches a moral. In parables, unlike fables (where the moral is explicitly stated within the narrative), the moral themes are implicit and can often be interpreted in several ways.

Tale ▶ A short narrative without a complex plot. Tales are an ancient form of narrative found in folklore, and traditional tales often contain supernatural elements. A tale differs from a short story by its tendency toward lesser-developed characters and linear plotting.

Tall tale ▶ A humorous short narrative that provides a wildly exaggerated version of events. Originally an oral form, the tall tale usually assumes that its audience knows the narrator is distorting the events. The form is often associated with the American frontier.

Fairy tale, folktale ▶ A traditional form of short narrative folklore, originally transmitted orally, which features supernatural characters such as witches, giants, fairies, or animals with human personality traits. Fairy tales often feature a hero or heroine who strives to achieve some desirable fate—such as marrying royalty or finding great wealth.

Short story ▶ A prose narrative too brief to be published in a separate volume—as novellas and novels frequently are. The short story is usually a focused narrative that presents one or two characters involved in a single compelling action.

Initiation story (also called **coming-of-age story**) ▶ A narrative in which the main character, usually a child or adolescent, undergoes an important experience (or "rite of passage") that prepares him or her for adulthood.

Elements of Plot

Protagonist ▶ The main or central character in a narrative. The protagonist usually initiates the main action of the story, often in conflict with the antagonist.

Antagonist ▶ The most significant character or force that opposes the protagonist in a narrative. The antagonist may be another character, society itself, a force of nature, or even—in some modern literature—conflicting impulses within the protagonist.

Exposition ▶ The opening portion of a narrative. In the exposition, the scene is set, the protagonist is introduced, and the author discloses any other background information necessary for the reader to understand the events that follow.

Conflict ▶ The central struggle between two or more forces in a story. Conflict generally occurs when some person or thing prevents the protagonist from achieving his or her goal. Conflict is the basic material out of which most plots are made.

Complication ▶ The introduction of a significant development in the central conflict between characters (or between a character and his or her situation). Complications may be external (an outside problem that the characters cannot avoid) or internal (a complication that originates in some important aspect of a character's values or personality).

Crisis ▶ The point in a narrative when the crucial action, decision, or realization must take place. From the Greek word *krisis*, meaning "decision."

Climax ▶ The moment of greatest intensity in a story, which almost inevitably occurs toward the end of the work. The climax often takes the form of a decisive confrontation between the protagonist and antagonist.

Conclusion ▶ In plotting, the logical end or outcome of a unified plot, shortly following the climax. Also called **resolution** or **dénouement** ("the untying of the knot"), as in resolving—or untying the knots created by—plot complications earlier in the narrative.

Narrative Techniques

Foreshadowing ▶ An indication of events to come in a narrative. The author may introduce specific words, images, or actions in order to suggest significant later events.

Flashback ▶ A scene relived in a character's memory. Flashbacks may be related by the narrator in a summary, or they may be experienced by the characters themselves. Flashbacks allow the author to include significant events that occurred before the opening of the story.

Epiphany ▶ A moment of profound insight or revelation by which a character's life is greatly altered.

In medias res ▶ A Latin phrase meaning "in the midst of things"; refers to the narrative device of beginning a story midway in the events it depicts (usually at an exciting or significant moment) before explaining the context or preceding actions.

2 POINT OF VIEW

What You Will Learn in This Chapter

- To identify the point of view from which a story is told
- To describe different types of narrators
- To explain stream-of-consciousness narration
- To analyze the role of point of view in a story

In the opening lines of *The Adventures of Huckleberry Finn*, Mark Twain takes care to separate himself from the leading character, who is to tell his own story:

> You don't know about me, without you have read a book by the name of *The Adventures of Tom Sawyer*, but that ain't no matter. That book was made by Mr. Mark Twain, and he told the truth, mainly.

Twain wrote the novel, but the **narrator** or speaker is Huck Finn, a fictional character who supposedly tells the story. Of course in *Huckleberry Finn*, the narrator of the story is not the same person as the "real-life" author. In employing Huck as his narrator, Twain selects a special angle of vision: not his own, exactly, but that of a resourceful boy moving through the thick of events, with a mind at times shrewd, at other times innocent. Through Huck's eyes, Twain takes in certain scenes, actions, and characters and—as only Huck's angle of vision could have enabled Twain to do so well—records them memorably.

IDENTIFYING POINT OF VIEW

Narrators come in many forms. Because stories usually are told by someone, almost every story has some kind of narrator. Some theorists reserve the term *narrator* for a character who tells a story in the first person. We use it in a wider sense, to mean a recording consciousness that an author creates, who may or may not be a participant in the events of the story. Real persons can tell stories in a factual way, but when such a story is *written*, the result is usually *nonfiction*: a memoir, a travelogue, an autobiography.

To identify a story's **point of view**, describe the role the narrator plays in the events and any limits placed on his or her knowledge of the events. In a short story, it is usual for the writer to maintain one point of view from beginning to end, but there is nothing to stop him or her from introducing other points of view as well. In his long, panoramic novel *War and Peace*, encompassing the vast drama of Napoleon's invasion of Russia, Leo Tolstoy freely shifts the point of view in and out of the minds of many characters, among them Napoleon himself.

TYPES OF NARRATORS

Theoretically, a great many points of view are possible. One initial way to determine a story's point of view is to identify whether or not the narrator appears as a major or minor character, as a sideline observer, or as an unnamed nonparticipant.

Participant Narrator

When the narrator is cast as a **participant** in the events of the story, he or she is a dramatized character who writes in the first person, who says "I." Such a narrator may be the protagonist (Huck Finn) or may be an **observer**, a minor character standing a little to one side, watching a story unfold that mainly involves other characters. A famous example of a participant narrator occurs in F. Scott Fitzgerald's *The Great Gatsby*. The novel's narrator is not Jay Gatsby, but his neighbor and friend Nick Carraway, who knows only portions of Gatsby's mysterious life.

Nonparticipant Narrator

A narrator who remains a **nonparticipant** does not appear in the story as a character. Viewing the characters, perhaps seeing into the minds of one or more of them, such a narrator refers to them as "he," "she," or "they." In the tale of "Godfather Death," we have a narrator who is not a character in the story at all, someone who is not even named, who stands at a distance from the action while recording what the main characters say and do.

HOW MUCH DOES A NARRATOR KNOW?

The narrator of a story can possess different levels of knowledge about the characters' thoughts, feelings, and actions—from total omniscience to almost total ignorance. Those levels of knowledge can be categorized in the following ways.

All-knowing

The **all-knowing** (or **omniscient**) narrator sees into the minds of any or all of the characters, moving when necessary from one to another. This is the point of view in "Godfather Death," in which the narrator knows the feelings and motives of the father, of the doctor, and even of Death himself. Since he adds an occasional comment or opinion, this narrator may be said also to show **editorial omniscience** (as we can tell from his disapproving remark that the doctor "should have remembered" and his observation that the father did not understand "how wisely God shares out wealth and poverty"). A narrator who shows **impartial omniscience** presents the thoughts and actions of the characters but does not judge them or comment on them.

Limited Omniscience

When a nonparticipating narrator sees events through the eyes of a single character, whether a major character or a minor one, the resulting point of view is sometimes called **limited omniscience** or **selective omniscience**. The author, of course, selects which character's perspective to see from; the omniscience is his and not the narrator's. In William Faulkner's "Barn Burning" (Chapter 5), the narrator is almost entirely confined to knowing the thoughts and perceptions of a boy, the central character.

Objective Point of View

In the **objective point of view**, the narrator does not enter the mind of any character but describes events from the outside. Telling us what people say and how their faces look, he or she leaves us to infer their thoughts and feelings. So inconspicuous is the narrator that this point of view has been called "the fly on the wall." Some critics would say that in the objective point of view, the narrator disappears altogether.

Unreliable Narrator

In a story told by an **unreliable narrator**, the point of view is that of a person who, we perceive, is deceptive, self-deceptive, deluded, or deranged. Although this narrative device has long been employed by great authors of the past, such as Edgar Allan Poe and Eudora Welty, contemporary writers have been particularly fond of unreliable narrators. For a famous example, consider the demented and unstable condition of Poe's narrator in "The Tell-Tale Heart" in this chapter.

Other Narrative Points of View

Besides the common points of view just listed, uncommon points of view are possible. In Jack London's adventure novel *The Call of the Wild*, the story is told from the perspective of its protagonist, a dog.

Also possible, but unusual, is a story written in the second person, "you." This point of view results in a startling directness, as in Jay McInerney's novel *Bright Lights, Big City* (1985), which begins:

> You are not the kind of guy who would be at a place like this at this time of the morning. But here you are, and you cannot say that the terrain is entirely unfamiliar, although the details are fuzzy. You are at a nightclub talking to a girl with a shaved head.

The attitudes and opinions of a narrator aren't necessarily those of the author; in fact, we may notice a lively conflict between what we are told and what, apparently, we are meant to believe. A story may be told by an innocent narrator or a **naive narrator**, a character who fails to understand all the implications of the story. One such innocent narrator (despite his sometimes shrewd perceptions) is Huckleberry Finn. Because Huck accepts without question the morality and lawfulness of slavery, he feels guilty about helping Jim, a runaway slave. But, far from condemning Huck for his defiance of the law—"All right, then, I'll *go* to hell," Huck tells himself, deciding against returning Jim to captivity—the author, and the reader along with him, silently applaud.

STREAM OF CONSCIOUSNESS

One popular modern method of writing is called **stream of consciousness**, from a phrase coined by psychologist William James to describe the procession of thoughts passing through the mind. In fiction, the stream of consciousness is a kind of selective omniscience: the presentation of thoughts and sense impressions in a lifelike fashion—not in a sequence arranged by logic, but mingled randomly. When in his novel *Ulysses* James Joyce takes us into the mind of Leopold Bloom, an ordinary Dublin mind well-stocked with trivia and fragments of odd learning, the reader may have an impression not of a smoothly flowing stream but of an ocean of miscellaneous things, all crowded and jostling.

> As he set foot on O'Connell bridge a puffball of smoke plumed up from the parapet. Brewery barge with export stout. England. Sea air sours it, I heard. Be interesting some day to get a pass through Hancock to see the brewery. Regular world in itself. Vats of porter, wonderful. Rats get in too. Drink themselves bloated as big as a collie floating.

Stream-of-consciousness writing usually occurs in relatively short passages, but in *Ulysses* Joyce employs it extensively. Similar in method, an **interior monologue** is an extended presentation of a character's thoughts, not in the seemingly helter-skelter order of a stream of consciousness, but in an arrangement as if the character were speaking out loud to himself, for us to overhear.

Every point of view has limitations. Even **total omniscience**, a knowledge of the minds of all the characters, has its disadvantages. Such a point of view requires high skill to manage, without the storyteller's losing his or her way in a multitude of perspectives. In fact, there are evident advantages in having a narrator not know everything. We are accustomed to seeing the world through one pair of eyes, to having truths gradually occur to us.

By using a particular point of view, an author may artfully withhold information, if need be, rather than immediately present it to us. If, for instance, the suspense in a story depends on our not knowing until the end that the protagonist is a spy, the author would be ill advised to tell the story from the protagonist's point of view. Clearly, the author makes a fundamental decision in selecting, from many possibilities, a story's point of view.

Here is a short story memorable for many reasons, among them its point of view.

William Faulkner

A Rose for Emily

1931

William Faulkner

William Faulkner (1897–1962) spent most of his days in Oxford, Mississippi, where he attended the University of Mississippi and where he served as postmaster until angry townspeople ejected him because they had failed to receive mail. During World War I he joined the Royal Canadian Air Force and afterward worked as a feature writer for the New Orleans Times-Picayune. *Faulkner's private life was a long struggle to stay solvent: even after fame came to him, he had to write Hollywood scripts and teach at the University of Virginia to support himself. His violent comic novel* Sanctuary *(1931) caused a stir and turned a profit, but critics tend most to admire* The Sound and the Fury *(1929), a tale partially told through the eyes of an idiot;* As I Lay Dying *(1930);* Light in August *(1932);* Absalom, Absalom *(1936); and* The Hamlet *(1940). Beginning with* Sartoris *(1929), Faulkner in his fiction imagines a Mississippi county named Yoknapatawpha and traces the fortunes of several of its families, including the aristocratic Compsons and Sartorises and the white-trash, dollar-grabbing Snopeses, from the Civil War to the mid-twentieth century. His influence on his fellow Southern writers (and others) has been profound. In 1950 he received the Nobel Prize in Literature. Although we think of Faulkner primarily as a novelist, he wrote nearly a hundred short stories. Forty-two of the best are available in his* Collected Stories *(1950; 1995).*

I

When Miss Emily Grierson died, our whole town went to her funeral: the men through a sort of respectful affection for a fallen monument, the women mostly out of curiosity to see the inside of her house, which no one save an old manservant—a combined gardener and cook—had seen in at least ten years.

It was a big, squarish frame house that had once been white, decorated with cupolas and spires and scrolled balconies in the heavily lightsome style of the seventies, set on what had once been our most select street. But garages and cotton gins had encroached and obliterated even the august names of that neighborhood; only Miss Emily's house was left, lifting its stubborn and coquettish decay above the cotton wagons and the gasoline pumps—an eyesore among eyesores. And now Miss Emily had gone to join the representatives of those august names where they lay in the cedar-bemused cemetery among the ranked and anonymous graves of Union and Confederate soldiers who fell at the battle of Jefferson.

Alive, Miss Emily had been a tradition, a duty, and a care; a sort of hereditary obligation upon the town, dating from that day in 1894 when Colonel Sartoris, the mayor—he who fathered the edict that no Negro woman should appear on the streets without an apron—remitted her taxes, the dispensation dating from the death of her father on into perpetuity. Not that Miss Emily would have accepted charity. Colonel Sartoris invented an involved tale to the effect that Miss Emily's father had loaned money to the town, which the town, as a matter of business, preferred this way of repaying. Only a man of Colonel Sartoris' generation and thought could have invented it, and only a woman could have believed it.

When the next generation, with its more modern ideas, became mayors and aldermen, this arrangement created some little dissatisfaction. On the first of the year they mailed her a tax notice. February came, and there was no reply. They wrote her a formal letter, asking her to call at the sheriff's office at her convenience. A week later the mayor wrote her himself, offering to call or to send his car for her, and received in reply a note on paper of an archaic shape, in a thin, flowing calligraphy in faded ink, to the effect that she no longer went out at all. The tax notice was also enclosed, without comment.

They called a special meeting of the Board of Aldermen. A depu- 5
tation waited upon her, knocked at the door through which no visitor had passed since she ceased giving china-painting lessons eight or ten years earlier. They were admitted by the old Negro into a dim hall from which a stairway mounted into still more shadow. It smelled of dust and disuse—a close, dank smell. The Negro led them into the parlor. It was furnished in heavy, leather-covered furniture. When the Negro opened the blinds of one window, they could see that the leather was cracked; and when they sat down, a faint dust rose sluggishly about their thighs, spinning with slow motes in the single sun-ray. On a tarnished gilt easel before the fireplace stood a crayon portrait of Miss Emily's father.

They rose when she entered—a small, fat woman in black, with a thin gold chain descending to her waist and vanishing into her belt, leaning on an ebony cane with a tarnished gold head. Her skeleton was small and spare; perhaps that was why what would have been merely plumpness in another was obesity in her. She looked bloated, like a body long submerged in motionless water, and of that pallid hue. Her eyes, lost in the fatty ridges of her face, looked like two small pieces of coal pressed into a lump of dough as they moved from one face to another while the visitors stated their errand.

She did not ask them to sit. She just stood in the door and listened quietly until the spokesman came to a stumbling halt. Then they could hear the invisible watch ticking at the end of the gold chain.

Her voice was dry and cold. "I have no taxes in Jefferson. Colonel Sartoris explained it to me. Perhaps one of you can gain access to the city records and satisfy yourselves."

"But we have. We are the city authorities, Miss Emily. Didn't you get a notice from the sheriff, signed by him?"

"I received a paper, yes," Miss Emily said. "Perhaps he considers himself the sheriff . . . I have no taxes in Jefferson."

"But there is nothing on the books to show that, you see. We must go by the—"

"See Colonel Sartoris. I have no taxes in Jefferson."

"But, Miss Emily—"

"See Colonel Sartoris." (Colonel Sartoris had been dead almost ten years.) "I have no taxes in Jefferson. Tobe!" The Negro appeared. "Show these gentlemen out."

II

So she vanquished them, horse and foot, just as she had vanquished their fathers thirty years before about the smell. That was two years after her father's death and a short time after her sweetheart—the one we believed would marry her—had deserted her. After her father's death she went out very little; after her sweetheart went away, people hardly saw her at all. A few of the ladies had the temerity to call, but were not received, and the only sign of life about the place was the Negro man—a young man then—going in and out with a market basket.

"Just as if a man—any man—could keep a kitchen properly," the ladies said; so they were not surprised when the smell developed. It was another link between the gross, teeming world and the high and mighty Griersons.

A neighbor, a woman, complained to the mayor, Judge Stevens, eighty years old.

"But what will you have me do about it, madam?" he said.

"Why, send her word to stop it," the woman said. "Isn't there a law?"

"I'm sure that won't be necessary," Judge Stevens said. "It's probably just a snake or a rat that nigger of hers killed in the yard. I'll speak to him about it."

The next day he received two more complaints, one from a man who came in diffident deprecation. "We really must do something about it, Judge. I'd be the last one in the world to bother Miss Emily, but we've got to do something." That night the Board of Aldermen met—three graybeards and one younger man, a member of the rising generation.

"It's simple enough," he said. "Send her word to have her place cleaned up. Give her a certain time to do it in, and if she don't . . ."

"Dammit, sir," Judge Stevens said, "will you accuse a lady to her face of smelling bad?"

So the next night, after midnight, four men crossed Miss Emily's lawn and slunk about the house like burglars, sniffing along the base of the brickwork and at the cellar openings while one of them performed a regular sowing motion with his hand out of a sack slung from his shoulder. They broke open the cellar door and sprinkled lime there, and in all the outbuildings. As they recrossed the lawn, a window that had been dark was lighted and

Miss Emily sat in it, the light behind her, and her upright torso motionless as that of an idol. They crept quietly across the lawn and into the shadow of the locusts that lined the street. After a week or two the smell went away.

That was when people had begun to feel really sorry for her. People 25
in our town, remembering how old lady Wyatt, her great-aunt, had gone completely crazy at last, believed that the Griersons held themselves a little too high for what they really were. None of the young men were quite good enough for Miss Emily and such. We had long thought of them as a tableau, Miss Emily a slender figure in white in the background, her father a spraddled silhouette in the foreground, his back to her and clutching a horsewhip, the two of them framed by the back-flung front door. So when she got to be thirty and was still single, we were not pleased exactly, but vindicated; even with insanity in the family she wouldn't have turned down all of her chances if they had really materialized.

When her father died, it got about that the house was all that was left to her; and in a way, people were glad. At last they could pity Miss Emily. Being left alone, and a pauper, she had become humanized. Now she too would know the old thrill and the old despair of a penny more or less.

The day after his death all the ladies prepared to call at the house and offer condolence and aid, as is our custom. Miss Emily met them at the door, dressed as usual and with no trace of grief on her face. She told them that her father was not dead. She did that for three days, with the ministers calling on her, and the doctors, trying to persuade her to let them dispose of the body. Just as they were about to resort to law and force, she broke down, and they buried her father quickly.

We did not say she was crazy then. We believed she had to do that. We remembered all the young men her father had driven away, and we knew that with nothing left, she would have to cling to that which had robbed her, as people will.

III

She was sick for a long time. When we saw her again, her hair was cut short, making her look like a girl, with a vague resemblance to those angels in colored church windows—sort of tragic and serene.

The town had just let the contracts for paving the sidewalks, and 30
in the summer after her father's death they began the work. The construction company came with niggers and mules and machinery, and a foreman named Homer Barron, a Yankee—a big, dark, ready man, with a big voice and eyes lighter than his face. The little boys would follow in groups to hear him cuss the niggers, and the niggers singing in time to the rise and fall of picks. Pretty soon he knew everybody in town. Whenever you heard a lot of laughing anywhere about the square, Homer Barron would be in the center of the group. Presently we began to see him and Miss Emily on Sunday afternoons driving in the yellow-wheeled buggy and the matched team of bays from the livery stable.

At first we were glad that Miss Emily would have an interest, because the ladies all said, "Of course a Grierson would not think seriously of a Northerner, a day laborer." But there were still others, older people, who said that even grief could not cause a real lady to forget *noblesse oblige*°—without calling it *noblesse oblige*. They just said, "Poor Emily. Her kinsfolk should come to her." She had some kin in Alabama; but years ago her father had fallen out with them over the estate of old lady Wyatt, the crazy woman, and there was no communication between the two families. They had not even been represented at the funeral.

And as soon as the old people said, "Poor Emily," the whispering began. "Do you suppose it's really so?" they said to one another. "Of course it is. What else could . . ." This behind their hands; rustling of craned silk and satin behind jalousies closed upon the sun of Sunday afternoon as the thin, swift clop-clop-clop of the matched team passed: "Poor Emily."

She carried her head high enough—even when we believed that she was fallen. It was as if she demanded more than ever the recognition of her dignity as the last Grierson; as if it had wanted that touch of earthiness to reaffirm her imperviousness. Like when she bought the rat poison, the arsenic. That was over a year after they had begun to say "Poor Emily," and while the two female cousins were visiting her.

"I want some poison," she said to the druggist. She was over thirty then, still a slight woman, though thinner than usual, with cold, haughty black eyes in a face the flesh of which was strained across the temples and about the eye-sockets as you imagine a lighthouse-keeper's face ought to look. "I want some poison," she said.

"Yes, Miss Emily. What kind? For rats and such? I'd recom—" 35

"I want the best you have. I don't care what kind."

The druggist named several. "They'll kill anything up to an elephant. But what you want is—"

"Arsenic," Miss Emily said. "Is that a good one?"

"Is . . . arsenic? Yes, ma'am. But what you want—"

"I want arsenic." 40

The druggist looked down at her. She looked back at him, erect, her face like a strained flag. "Why, of course," the druggist said. "If that's what you want. But the law requires you to tell what you are going to use it for."

Miss Emily just stared at him, her head tilted back in order to look him eye for eye, until he looked away and went and got the arsenic and wrapped it up. The Negro delivery boy brought her the package; the druggist didn't come back. When she opened the package at home there was written on the box, under the skull and bones: "For rats."

noblesse oblige: the obligation of a member of the nobility to behave with honor and dignity.

IV

So the next day we all said, "She will kill herself"; and we said it would be the best thing. When she had first begun to be seen with Homer Barron, we had said, "She will marry him." Then we said, "She will persuade him yet," because Homer himself had remarked—he liked men, and it was known that he drank with the younger men in the Elks' Club—that he was not a marrying man. Later we said, "Poor Emily," behind the jalousies as they passed on Sunday afternoon in the glittering buggy, Miss Emily with her head high and Homer Barron with his hat cocked and a cigar in his teeth, reins and whip in a yellow glove.

Then some of the ladies began to say that it was a disgrace to the town and a bad example to the young people. The men did not want to interfere, but at last the ladies forced the Baptist minister—Miss Emily's people were Episcopal—to call upon her. He would never divulge what happened during that interview, but he refused to go back again. The next Sunday they again drove about the streets, and the following day the minister's wife wrote to Miss Emily's relations in Alabama.

So she had blood-kin under her roof again and we sat back to watch developments. At first nothing happened. Then we were sure that they were to be married. We learned that Miss Emily had been to the jeweler's and ordered a man's toilet set in silver, with the letters H.B. on each piece. Two days later we learned that she had bought a complete outfit of men's clothing, including a nightshirt, and we said, "They are married." We were really glad. We were glad because the two female cousins were even more Grierson than Miss Emily had ever been.

So we were not surprised when Homer Barron—the streets had been finished some time since—was gone. We were a little disappointed that there was not a public blowing-off, but we believed that he had gone on to prepare for Miss Emily's coming, or to give her a chance to get rid of the cousins. (By that time it was a cabal, and we were all Miss Emily's allies to help circumvent the cousins.) Sure enough, after another week they departed. And, as we had expected all along, within three days Homer Barron was back in town. A neighbor saw the Negro man admit him at the kitchen door at dusk one evening.

And that was the last we saw of Homer Barron. And of Miss Emily for some time. The Negro man went in and out with the market basket, but the front door remained closed. Now and then we would see her at a window for a moment, as the men did that night when they sprinkled the lime, but for almost six months she did not appear on the streets. Then we knew that this was to be expected too; as if that quality of her father which had thwarted her woman's life so many times had been too virulent and too furious to die.

When we next saw Miss Emily, she had grown fat and her hair was turning gray. During the next few years it grew grayer and grayer until it attained an even pepper-and-salt iron-gray, when it ceased turning. Up to the day of her death at seventy-four it was still that vigorous iron-gray, like the hair of an active man.

From that time on her front door remained closed, save for a period of six or seven years, when she was about forty, during which she gave lessons in china-painting. She fitted up a studio in one of the downstairs rooms, where the daughters and granddaughters of Colonel Sartoris' contemporaries were sent to her with the same regularity and in the same spirit that they were sent to church on Sundays with a twenty-five-cent piece for the collection plate. Meanwhile her taxes had been remitted.

Then the newer generation became the backbone and the spirit 50
of the town, and the painting pupils grew up and fell away and did not send their children to her with boxes of color and tedious brushes and pictures cut from the ladies' magazines. The front door closed upon the last one and remained closed for good. When the town got free postal delivery, Miss Emily alone refused to let them fasten the metal numbers above her door and attach a mailbox to it. She would not listen to them.

Daily, monthly, yearly we watched the Negro grow grayer and more stooped, going in and out with the market basket. Each December we sent her a tax notice, which would be returned by the post office a week later, unclaimed. Now and then we would see her in one of the downstairs windows—she had evidently shut up the top floor of the house—like the carven torso of an idol in a niche, looking or not looking at us, we could never tell which. Thus she passed from generation to generation—dear, inescapable, impervious, tranquil, and perverse.

And so she died. Fell ill in the house filled with dust and shadows, with only a doddering Negro man to wait on her. We did not even know she was sick; we had long since given up trying to get any information from the Negro. He talked to no one, probably not even to her, for his voice had grown harsh and rusty, as if from disuse.

She died in one of the downstairs rooms, in a heavy walnut bed with a curtain, her gray head propped on a pillow yellow and moldy with age and lack of sunlight.

V

The Negro met the first of the ladies at the front door and let them in, with their hushed, sibilant voices and their quick, curious glances, and then he disappeared. He walked right through the house and out the back and was not seen again.

The two female cousins came at once. They held the funeral on the 55
second day, with the town coming to look at Miss Emily beneath a mass of bought flowers, with the crayon face of her father musing profoundly above the bier and the ladies sibilant and macabre; and the very old

men—some in their brushed Confederate uniforms—on the porch and the lawn, talking of Miss Emily as if she had been a contemporary of theirs, believing that they had danced with her and courted her perhaps, confusing time with its mathematical progression, as the old do, to whom all the past is not a diminishing road but, instead, a huge meadow which no winter ever quite touches, divided from them now by the narrow bottleneck of the most recent decade of years.

Already we knew that there was one room in that region above stairs which no one had seen in forty years, and which would have to be forced. They waited until Miss Emily was decently in the ground before they opened it.

The violence of breaking down the door seemed to fill this room with pervading dust. A thin, acrid pall as of the tomb seemed to lie everywhere upon this room decked and furnished as for a bridal: upon the valance curtains of faded rose color, upon the rose-shaded lights, upon the dressing table, upon the delicate array of crystal and the man's toilet things backed with tarnished silver, silver so tarnished that the monogram was obscured. Among them lay collar and tie, as if they had just been removed, which, lifted, left upon the surface a pale crescent in the dust. Upon a chair hung the suit, carefully folded; beneath it the two mute shoes and the discarded socks.

The man himself lay in the bed.

For a long while we just stood there, looking down at the profound and fleshless grin. The body had apparently once lain in the attitude of an embrace, but now the long sleep that outlasts love, that conquers even the grimace of love, had cuckolded him. What was left of him, rotted beneath what was left of the nightshirt, had become inextricable from the bed in which he lay; and upon him and upon the pillow beside him lay that even coating of the patient and biding dust.

Then we noticed that in the second pillow was the indentation of a head. One of us lifted something from it, and leaning forward, that faint and invisible dust dry and acrid in the nostrils, we saw a long strand of iron-gray hair.

Questions

1. What is meaningful in the final detail that the strand of hair on the second pillow is "iron-gray"?
2. Who is the unnamed narrator? For whom does he (or she?) profess to be speaking?
3. Why does "A Rose for Emily" seem better told from his or her point of view than if it were told (like John Updike's "A & P" in Chapter 1) from the point of view of the main character?
4. What foreshadowings of the discovery of the body of Homer Barron are we given earlier in the story? Share your experience in reading "A Rose for Emily": did the foreshadowings give away the ending for you? Did they heighten your interest?
5. What contrasts does the narrator draw between changing reality and Emily's refusal or inability to recognize change?

6. How do the character and background of Emily Grierson differ from those of Homer Barron? What general observations about the society that Faulkner depicts can be made from his portraits of these two characters and from his account of life in this one Mississippi town?
7. Does the story seem to you totally grim, or do you find any humor in it?
8. What do you infer to be the author's attitude toward Emily Grierson? Is she simply a murderous madwoman? Why do you suppose Faulkner calls his story "A Rose . . ."?

Edgar Allan Poe

The Tell-Tale Heart

(1843) 1850

Edgar Allan Poe

Edgar Poe (1809–1849) was born in Boston, the second son of actors Eliza and David Poe. Edgar inherited his family's legacy of artistic talent, financial instability, and social inferiority (actors were not considered respectable in the nineteenth century), as well as his father's problems with alcohol. David Poe abandoned his family after the birth of Edgar's little sister, Rosalie, and Eliza died of tuberculosis in a Richmond, Virginia, boardinghouse before Edgar turned three. He was taken in by the wealthy John and Frances Allan of Richmond, whose name he added to his own. Allan educated Poe at first-rate schools, where he excelled in all subjects. But he grew into a moody adolescent, and his relationship with his foster father deteriorated.

Poe's first year at the University of Virginia was marked by scholastic success, alcoholic binges, and gambling debts. Disgraced, he fled to Boston and joined the army under the name Edgar Perry. He performed well as an enlisted man and published his first collection of poetry, Tamerlane and Other Poems, *at the age of eighteen. After an abortive stint at West Point led to a final break with the Allans, Poe embarked on a full-time literary career. A respected critic and editor, he sharply improved both the content and circulation of every magazine with which he was associated. But, morbidly sensitive to criticism, paranoid and belligerent when drunk, he left or was fired from every post he held. Poorly paid as both an editor and a writer, he earned almost nothing from the works that made him famous, such as "The Fall of the House of Usher" and "The Raven."*

After the break with his foster family, Poe rediscovered his own. From 1831, he lived with his father's widowed sister, Maria Clemm, and her daughter, Virginia. In 1836 Poe married this thirteen-year-old first cousin. These women provided him with much-needed emotional stability. However, like his mother, Poe's wife died of tuberculosis at age twenty-four, her demise doubtless hastened by poverty. Afterward, Poe's life came apart; his drinking intensified, as did his self-destructive tendencies. In October 1849 he died in mysterious circumstances, a few days after being found sick and incoherent on a Baltimore street.

True!—nervous—very, very dreadfully nervous I had been and am; but why *will* you say that I am mad? The disease had sharpened my senses—not destroyed—not dulled them. Above all was the sense of hearing acute. I heard all things in the heaven and in the earth. I heard many things in hell. How, then, am I mad? Hearken! and observe how healthily—how calmly, I can tell you the whole story.

It is impossible to say how first the idea entered my brain; but once conceived, it haunted me day and night. Object there was none. Passion there was none. I loved the old man. He had never wronged me. He had never given me insult. For his gold I had no desire. I think it was his eye! yes, it was this! One of his eyes resembled that of a vulture—a pale blue eye, with a film over it. Whenever it fell upon me, my blood ran cold; and so by degrees—very gradually—I made up my mind to take the life of the old man, and thus rid myself of the eye forever.

Now this is the point. You fancy me mad. Madmen know nothing. But you should have seen *me*. You should have seen how wisely I proceeded—with what caution—with what foresight—with what dissimulation I went to work! I was never kinder to the old man than during the whole week before I killed him. And every night, about midnight, I turned the latch of his door and opened it—oh, so gently! And then, when I had made an opening sufficient for my head, I put in a dark lantern, all closed, closed, so that no light shone out, and then I thrust in my head. Oh, you would have laughed to see how cunningly I thrust it in! I moved it slowly—very, very slowly, so that I might not disturb the old man's sleep. It took me an hour to place my whole head within the opening so far that I could see him as he lay upon his bed. Ha!—would a madman have been so wise as this? And then, when my head was well in the room, I undid the lantern cautiously—oh, so cautiously—cautiously (for the hinges creaked)—I undid it just so much that a single thin ray fell upon the vulture eye. And this I did for seven long nights—every night just at midnight—but I found the eye always closed; and so it was impossible to do the work; for it was not the old man who vexed me, but his Evil Eye. And every morning, when the day broke, I went boldly into the chamber, and spoke courageously to him, calling him by name in a hearty tone, and inquiring how he had passed the night. So you see he would have been a very profound old man, indeed, to suspect that every night, just at twelve, I looked in upon him while he slept.

Upon the eighth night I was more than usually cautious in opening the door. A watch's minute hand moves more quickly than did mine. Never before that night had I *felt* the extent of my own powers—of my sagacity. I could scarcely contain my feelings of triumph. To think that there I was, opening the door, little by little, and he not even to dream of my secret deeds or thoughts. I fairly chuckled at the idea; and perhaps he heard me; for he moved on the bed suddenly, as if startled. Now you may think that I drew back—but no. His room was as black as pitch with the thick darkness (for the shutters were close fastened, through fear of robbers), and so I knew that he could not see the opening of the door, and I kept pushing it on steadily, steadily.

I had my head in, and was about to open the lantern, when my thumb slipped upon the tin fastening, and the old man sprang up in the bed, crying out—"Who's there?"

I kept quite still and said nothing. For a whole hour I did not move a muscle, and in the meantime I did not hear him lie down. He was still sitting up in the bed, listening;—just as I have done, night after night, hearkening to the death watches° in the wall.

Presently I heard a slight groan, and I knew it was the groan of mortal terror. It was not a groan of pain or of grief—oh, no!—it was the low stifled sound that arises from the bottom of the soul when overcharged with awe. I knew the sound very well. Many a night, just at midnight, when all the world slept, it has welled up from my own bosom, deepening, with its dreadful echo, the terrors that distracted me. I say I knew it well. I knew what the old man felt, and pitied him, although I chuckled at heart. I knew that he had been lying awake ever since the first slight noise, when he had turned in the bed. His fears had been ever since growing upon him. He had been trying to fancy them causeless, but could not. He had been saying to himself—"It is nothing but the wind in the chimney—it is only a mouse crossing the floor," or "it is merely a cricket which has made a single chirp." Yes, he had been trying to comfort himself with these suppositions; but he had found all in vain. *All in vain*; because Death, in approaching him, had stalked with his black shadow before him, and enveloped the victim. And it was the mournful influence of the unperceived shadow that caused him to feel—although he neither saw nor heard—to *feel* the presence of my head within the room.

When I had waited a long time, very patiently, without hearing him lie down, I resolved to open a little—a very, very little crevice in the lantern. So I opened it—you cannot imagine how stealthily, stealthily—until, at length, a single dim ray, like the thread of the spider, shot from out of the crevice and fell upon the vulture eye.

It was open—wide, wide open—and I grew furious as I gazed upon it. I saw it with perfect distinctness—all a dull blue, with a hideous veil over it that chilled the very marrow in my bones; but I could see nothing else of the old man's face or person: for I had directed the ray as if by instinct, precisely upon the damned spot.

And now have I not told you that what you mistake for madness is but over-acuteness of the senses?—now, I say, there came to my ears a low, dull, quick sound, such as a watch makes when enveloped in cotton. I knew *that* sound well, too. It was the beating of the old man's

death watches: beetles that infest timbers. Their clicking sound was thought to be an omen of death.

heart. It increased my fury, as the beating of a drum stimulates the soldier into courage.

But even yet I refrained and kept still. I scarcely breathed. I held the lantern motionless. I tried how steadily I could maintain the ray upon the eye. Meantime the hellish tattoo of the heart increased. It grew quicker and quicker, and louder and louder every instant. The old man's terror *must* have been extreme! It grew louder, I say, louder every moment!—do you mark me well? I have told you that I am nervous: so I am. And now at the dead hour of the night, amid the dreadful silence of that old house, so strange a noise as this excited me to uncontrollable terror. Yet, for some minutes longer I refrained and stood still. But the beating grew louder, louder! I thought the heart must burst. And now a new anxiety seized me—the sound would be heard by a neighbor! The old man's hour had come! With a loud yell, I threw open the lantern and leaped into the room. He shrieked once—once only. In an instant I dragged him to the floor, and pulled the heavy bed over him. I then smiled gaily, to find the deed so far done. But, for many minutes, the heart beat on with a muffled sound. This, however, did not vex me; it would not be heard through the wall. At length it ceased. The old man was dead. I removed the bed and examined the corpse. Yes, he was stone, stone dead. I placed my hand upon the heart and held it there many minutes.

If still you think me mad, you will think so no longer when I describe the wise precautions I took for the concealment of the body. The night waned, and I worked hastily, but in silence. First of all I dismembered the corpse. I cut off the head and the arms and the legs.

I then took up three planks from the flooring of the chamber, and deposited all between the scantlings. I then replaced the boards so cleverly, so cunningly, that no human eye—not even *his*—could have detected anything wrong. There was nothing to wash out—no stain of any kind—no blood-spot whatever. I had been too wary for that. A tub had caught all—ha! ha!

When I had made an end of these labors, it was four o'clock—still dark as midnight. As the bell sounded the hour, there came a knocking at the street door. I went down to open it with a light heart,—for what had I *now* to fear? There entered three men, who introduced themselves, with perfect suavity, as officers of the police. A shriek had been heard by a neighbor during the night; suspicion of foul play had been aroused, information had been lodged at the police office, and they (the officers) had been deputed to search the premises.

I smiled,—for *what* had I to fear? I bade the gentlemen welcome. The shriek, I said, was my own in a dream. The old man, I mentioned, was absent in the country. I took my visitors all over the house. I bade them search—search *well*. I led them, at length, to *his* chamber. I showed them his treasures, secure, undisturbed. In the enthusiasm of my confidence, I brought chairs into the room, and desired them *here* to rest from their fatigues, while

I myself, in the wild audacity of my perfect triumph, placed my own seat upon the very spot beneath which reposed the corpse of the victim.

The officers were satisfied. My *manner* had convinced them. I was singularly at ease. They sat, and while I answered cheerily, they chatted of familiar things. But, ere long, I felt myself getting pale and wished them gone. My head ached, and I fancied a ringing in my ears: but still they sat and still chatted. The ringing became more distinct:—it continued and became more distinct: I talked more freely to get rid of the feeling: but it continued and gained definitiveness—until, at length, I found that the noise was *not* within my ears.

No doubt I now grew *very* pale:—but I talked more fluently, and with a heightened voice. Yet the sound increased—and what could I do? It was a *low, dull, quick sound—much such a sound as a watch makes when enveloped in cotton*. I gasped for breath—and yet the officers heard it not. I talked more quickly—more vehemently; but the noise steadily increased. I arose and argued about trifles, in a high key and with violent gesticulations; but the noise steadily increased. Why *would* they not be gone? I paced the floor to and fro with heavy strides, as if excited to fury by the observations of the men—but the noise steadily increased. Oh God! what *could* I do? I foamed—I raved—I swore! I swung the chair upon which I had been sitting, and grated it upon the boards, but the noise arose over all and continually increased. It grew louder—louder—*louder*! And still the men chatted pleasantly, and smiled. Was it possible they heard not? Almighty God!—no, no! They heard!—they suspected!—they *knew!*—they were making a mockery of my horror!—this I thought, and this I think. But anything was better than this agony! Anything was more tolerable than this derision! I could bear those hypocritical smiles no longer! I felt that I must scream or die!—and now—again!—hark! louder! louder! louder! *louder*!—

"Villains!" I shrieked, "dissemble no more! I admit the deed!—tear up the planks!—here, here!—it is the beating of his hideous heart!"

Questions

1. From what point of view is Poe's story told? Why is this point of view particularly effective for "The Tell-Tale Heart"?
2. Point to details in the story that identify its speaker as an unreliable narrator.
3. What do we know about the old man in the story? What motivates the narrator to kill him?
4. In spite of all his precautions, the narrator does not commit the perfect crime. What trips him up?
5. How do you account for the police officers chatting calmly with the murderer instead of reacting to the sound that stirs the murderer into a frenzy?

Eudora Welty

A Worn Path

1941

Eudora Welty

Eudora Welty (1909–2001) was born in Jackson, Mississippi, the daughter of an insurance company president. Like William Faulkner, another Mississippi writer, she stayed close to her roots for practically all her life, except for short sojourns at the University of Wisconsin, where she took her B.A., and in New York City, where she studied advertising. She lived most of her life in her childhood home in Jackson, within a stone's throw of the state capitol. Although Welty was a novelist distinguished for The Robber Bridegroom *(1942),* Delta Wedding *(1946),* The Ponder Heart *(1954),* Losing Battles *(1970), and* The Optimist's Daughter *(1972), many critics think her finest work was in the short-story form.* The Collected Stories of Eudora Welty *(1980) gathers the work of more than forty years. Welty's other books include a memoir,* One Writer's Beginnings *(1984), and* The Eye of the Story *(1977), a book of sympathetic criticism on the fiction of other writers, including Willa Cather, Virginia Woolf, Katherine Anne Porter, and Isak Dinesen.* One Time, One Place, *a book of photographs of everyday life that Welty took in Mississippi during the Depression, was republished in a revised edition in 1996.*

It was December—a bright frozen day in the early morning. Far out in the country there was an old Negro woman with her head tied in a red rag, coming along a path through the pinewoods. Her name was Phoenix Jackson. She was very old and small and she walked slowly in the dark pine shadows, moving a little from side to side in her steps, with the balanced heaviness and lightness of a pendulum in a grandfather clock. She carried a thin, small cane made from an umbrella, and with this she kept tapping the frozen earth in front of her. This made a grave and persistent noise in the still air, that seemed meditative like the chirping of a solitary little bird.

She wore a dark striped dress reaching down to her shoe tops, and an equally longapron of bleached sugar sacks, with a full pocket: all neat and tidy, but every time she took a step she might have fallen over her shoelaces, which dragged from her unlaced shoes. She looked straight ahead. Her eyes were blue with age. Her skin had a pattern all its own of numberless branching wrinkles and as though a whole little tree stood in the middle of her forehead, but a golden color ran underneath, and the two knobs of her cheeks were illumined by a yellow burning under the dark. Under the red rag her hair came down on her neck in the frailest of ringlets, still black, and with an odor like copper.

Now and then there was a quivering in the thicket. Old Phoenix said, "Out of my way, all you foxes, owls, beetles, jack rabbits, coons and wild animals! . . . Keep out from under these feet, little bob-whites. . . . Keep the big wild hogs out of my path. Don't let none of those come running my direction. I got a long way." Under her small black-freckled hand her cane, limber as a buggy whip, would switch at the brush as if to rouse up any hiding things.

On she went. The woods were deep and still. The sun made the pine needles almost too bright to look at, up where the wind rocked. The cones dropped as light as feathers. Down in the hollow was the mourning dove—it was not too late for him.

The path ran up a hill. "Seem like there is chains about my feet, 5
time I get this far," she said, in the voice of argument old people keep to use with themselves. "Something always take a hold of me on this hill—pleads I should stay."

After she got to the top she turned and gave a full, severe look behind her where she had come. "Up through pines," she said at length. "Now down through oaks."

Her eyes opened their widest, and she started down gently. But before she got to the bottom of the hill a bush caught her dress.

Her fingers were busy and intent, but her skirts were full and long, so that before she could pull them free in one place they were caught in another. It was not possible to allow the dress to tear. "I in the thorny bush," she said. "Thorns, you doing your appointed work. Never want to let folks pass, no sir. Old eyes thought you was a pretty little *green* bush."

Finally, trembling all over, she stood free, and after a moment dared to stoop for her cane.

"Sun so high!" she cried, leaning back and looking, while the thick 10
tears went over her eyes. "The time getting all gone here."

At the foot of this hill was a place where a log was laid across the creek.

"Now comes the trial," said Phoenix.

Putting her right foot out, she mounted the log and shut her eyes. Lifting her skirt, leveling her cane fiercely before her, like a festival figure in some parade, she began to march across. Then she opened her eyes and she was safe on the other side.

"I wasn't as old as I thought," she said.

But she sat down to rest. She spread her skirts on the bank around 15
her and folded her hands over her knees. Up above her was a tree in a pearly cloud of mistletoe. She did not dare to close her eyes, and when a little boy brought her a plate with a slice of marble-cake on it she spoke to him. "That would be acceptable," she said. But when she went to take it there was just her own hand in the air.

So she left that tree, and had to go through a barbed-wire fence. There she had to creep and crawl, spreading her knees and stretching

"There is no telling, mister," she said, "no telling."

Then she gave a little cry and clapped her hands and said, "Git on away from here, dog! Look! Look at that dog!" She laughed as if in admiration. "He ain't scared of nobody. He a big black dog." She whispered, "Sic him!"

"Watch me get rid of that cur," said the man. "Sic him, Pete! Sic him!"

Phoenix heard the dogs fighting, and heard the man running and throwing sticks. She even heard a gunshot. But she was slowly bending forward by that time, further and further forward, the lids stretched down over her eyes, as if she were doing this in her sleep. Her chin was lowered almost to her knees. The yellow palm of her hand came out from the fold of her apron. Her fingers slid down and along the ground under the piece of money with the grace and care they would have in lifting an egg from under a setting hen. Then she slowly straightened up, she stood erect, and the nickel was in her apron pocket. A bird flew by. Her lips moved. "God watching me the whole time. I come to stealing."

The man came back, and his own dog panted about them. "Well, I 55
scared him off that time," he said, and then he laughed and lifted his gun and pointed it at Phoenix.

She stood straight and faced him.

"Doesn't the gun scare you?" he said, still pointing it.

"No, sir, I seen plenty go off closer by, in my day, and for less than what I done," she said, holding utterly still.

He smiled, and shouldered the gun. "Well, Granny," he said, "you must be a hundred years old, and scared of nothing. I'd give you a dime if I had any money with me. But you take my advice and stay home, and nothing will happen to you."

"I bound to go on my way, mister," said Phoenix. She inclined her 60
head in the red rag. Then they went in different directions, but she could hear the gun shooting again and again over the hill.

She walked on. The shadows hung from the oak trees to the road like curtains. Then she smelled wood-smoke, and smelled the river, and she saw a steeple and the cabins on their steep steps. Dozens of little black children whirled around her. There ahead was Natchez shining. Bells were ringing. She walked on.

In the paved city it was Christmas time. There were red and green electric lights strung and crisscrossed everywhere, and all turned on in the daytime. Old Phoenix would have been lost if she had not distrusted her eyesight and depended on her feet to know where to take her.

She paused quietly on the sidewalk where people were passing by. A lady came along in the crowd, carrying an armful of red-, green- and silver-wrapped presents; she gave off perfume like the red roses in hot summer, and Phoenix stopped her.

"Please, missy, will you lace up my shoe?" She held up her foot.

"What do you want, Grandma?" 65

"See my shoe," said Phoenix. "Do all right for out in the country, but wouldn't look right to go in a big building."

"Stand still then, Grandma," said the lady. She put her packages down on the sidewalk beside her and laced and tied both shoes tightly.

"Can't lace 'em with a cane," said Phoenix, "Thank you, missy. I doesn't mind asking a nice lady to tie up my shoe, when I gets out on the street."

Moving slowly and from side to side, she went into the big building, and into a tower of steps, where she walked up and around and around until her feet knew to stop.

She entered a door, and there she saw nailed up on the wall the document that had been stamped with the gold seal and framed in the gold frame, which matched the dream that was hung up in her head.

"Here I be," she said. There was a fixed and ceremonial stiffness over her body.

"A charity case, I suppose," said an attendant who sat at the desk before her.

But Phoenix only looked above her head. There was sweat on her face, the wrinkles in her skin shone like a bright net.

"Speak up, Grandma," the woman said. "What's your name? We must have your history, you know. Have you been here before? What seems to be the trouble with you?"

Old Phoenix only gave a twitch to her face as if a fly were bothering her.

"Are you deaf?" cried the attendant.

But then the nurse came in.

"Oh, that's just old Aunt Phoenix," she said. "She doesn't come for herself—she has a little grandson. She makes these trips just as regular as clockwork. She lives away back off the Old Natchez Trace." She bent down. "Well, Aunt Phoenix, why don't you just take a seat? We won't keep you standing after your long trip." She pointed.

The old woman sat down, bolt upright in the chair.

"Now, how is the boy?" asked the nurse.

Old Phoenix did not speak.

"I said, how is the boy?"

But Phoenix only waited and stared straight ahead, her face very solemn and withdrawn into rigidity.

"Is his throat any better?" asked the nurse. "Aunt Phoenix, don't you hear me? Is your grandson's throat any better since the last time you came for the medicine?"

With her hands on her knees, the old woman waited, silent, erect and motion less, just as if she were in armor.

"You mustn't take up our time this way, Aunt Phoenix," the nurse said. "Tell us quickly about your grandson, and get it over. He isn't dead, is he?"

At last there came a flicker and then a flame of comprehension across her face, and she spoke.

"My grandson. It was my memory had left me. There I sat and forgot why I made my long trip."

"Forgot?" The nurse frowned. "After you came so far?"

Then Phoenix was like an old woman begging a dignified forgiveness 90
for waking up frightened in the night. "I never did go to school, I was too old at the Surrender," she said in a soft voice. "I'm an old woman without an education. It was my memory fail me. My little grandson, he is just the same, and I forgot it in the coming."

"Throat never heals, does it?" said the nurse, speaking in a loud, sure voice to old Phoenix. By now she had a card with something written on it, a little list. "Yes. Swallowed lye. When was it?—January—two-three years ago—"

Phoenix spoke unasked now. "No, missy, he not dead, he just the same. Every little while his throat begin to close up again, and he not able to swallow. He not get his breath. He not able to help himself. So the time come around, and I go on another trip for the soothing medicine."

"All right. The doctor said as long as you came to get it, you could have it," said the nurse. "But it's an obstinate case."

"My little grandson, he sit up there in the house all wrapped up, waiting by himself," Phoenix went on. "We is the only two left in the world. He suffer and it don't seem to put him back at all. He got a sweet look. He going to last. He wear a little patch quilt and peep out holding his mouth open like a little bird. I remembers so plain now. I not going to forget him again, no, the whole enduring time. I could tell him from all the others in creation."

"All right." The nurse was trying to hush her now. She brought her 95
a bottle of medicine. "Charity," she said, making a check mark in a book.

Old Phoenix held the bottle close to her eyes, and then carefully put it into her pocket.

"I thank you," she said.

"It's Christmas time, Grandma," said the attendant. "Could I give you a few pennies out of my purse?"

"Five pennies is a nickel," said Phoenix stiffly.

"Here's a nickel," said the attendant. 100

Phoenix rose carefully and held out her hand. She received the nickel and then fished the other nickel out of her pocket and laid it beside the new one. She stared at her palm closely, with her head on one side.

Then she gave a tap with her cane on the floor.

"This is what come to me to do," she said. "I going to the store and buy my child a little windmill they sells, made out of paper. He going to find it hard to believe there such a thing in the world. I'll march myself back where he waiting, holding it straight up in this hand."

She lifted her free hand, gave a little nod, turned around, and walked out of the doctor's office. Then her slow step began on the stairs, going down.

Questions

1. What point of view is used in this story? Explain your answer.
2. What is the significance of the old woman being named Phoenix?
3. Welty presents Phoenix's dreams and hallucinations as if they were as real as everything else she encounters. What does this technique contribute to the story's effect?
4. How would you characterize the way Phoenix is viewed and treated by the white people she meets? Does their behavior toward her give you any indication of where the story is set and when it takes place?
5. In paragraph 52, Phoenix laughs at the black dog "as if in admiration." What does she admire about him, and what does this attitude tell us about her?
6. "With her hands on her knees, the old woman waited, silent, erect and motionless, just as if she were in armor" (paragraph 85). Is the comparison at the end of this sentence just a striking visual image, or does it have a larger relevance?

Flannery O'Connor

A Good Man Is Hard to Find 1955

Flannery O'Connor

Mary Flannery O'Connor (1925–1964) was born in Savannah, Georgia, but spent most of her life in the small town of Milledgeville. While attending Georgia State College for Women, she won a local reputation for her fledgling stories and satiric cartoons. After graduating in 1945, she went on to study at the University of Iowa, where she earned an M.F.A. in 1947. Diagnosed in 1950 with disseminated lupus, the same incurable illness that had killed her father, O'Connor returned home and spent the last decade of her life living with her mother in Milledgeville. Back on the family dairy farm, she wrote, maintained an extensive literary correspondence, raised peacocks, and underwent medical treatment. When her illness occasionally went into a period of remission, she made trips to lecture and read her stories to college audiences. Her health declined rapidly after surgery early in 1964 for an unrelated complaint. She died at thirty-nine.

O'Connor is unusual among modern American writers in the depth of her Christian vision. A devout Roman Catholic, she attended mass daily while growing up and living in the largely Protestant South. As a latter-day satirist in the manner of Jonathan Swift, O'Connor levels the eye of an uncompromising moralist on the violence and spiritual disorder of the modern world, focusing on what she calls "the action of grace in territory held largely by the devil." She is sometimes called a "Southern Gothic" writer because of her fascination with grotesque incidents and characters. Throughout her career she depicted the South as a troubled region in which the social, racial, and religious status quo that had existed since before the Civil War was coming to a violent end. Despite the inherent seriousness of her religious and social themes, O'Connor's mordant and frequently outrageous humor is everywhere apparent. Her combination of profound vision and dark comedy is the distinguishing characteristic of her literary sensibilities.

O'Connor's published work includes two short novels, Wise Blood *(1952) and* The Violent Bear It Away *(1960), and two collections of short stories,* A Good Man Is Hard to Find *(1955) and* Everything That Rises Must Converge, *published posthumously in 1965. A collection of essays and miscellaneous prose,* Mystery and Manners *(1969), and her selected letters,* The Habit of Being *(1979), reveal an innate cheerfulness and engaging personal warmth that are not always apparent in her fiction.* The Complete Stories of Flannery O'Connor *was posthumously awarded the National Book Award in 1971.*

The grandmother didn't want to go to Florida. She wanted to visit some of her connections in east Tennessee and she was seizing at every chance to change Bailey's mind. Bailey was the son she lived with, her only boy. He was sitting on the edge of his chair at the table, bent over the orange sports section of the *Journal*. "Now look here, Bailey," she said, "see here, read this," and she stood with one hand on her thin hip and the other rattling the newspaper at his bald head. "Here this fellow that calls himself The Misfit is aloose from the Federal Pen and headed toward Florida and you read here what it says he did to these people. Just you read it. I wouldn't take my children in any direction with a criminal like that aloose in it. I couldn't answer to my conscience if I did."

Bailey didn't look up from his reading so she wheeled around then and faced the children's mother, a young woman in slacks, whose face was as broad and innocent as a cabbage and was tied around with a green head-kerchief that had two points on the top like rabbit's ears. She was sitting on the sofa, feeding the baby his apricots out of a jar. "The children have been to Florida before," the old lady said. "You all ought to take them somewhere else for a change so they would see different parts of the world and be broad. They never have been to east Tennessee."

The children's mother didn't seem to hear her but the eight-year-old boy, John Wesley, a stocky child with glasses, said, "If you don't want to go to Florida, why dontcha stay at home?" He and the little girl, June Star, were reading the funny papers on the floor.

"She wouldn't stay at home to be queen for a day," June Star said without raising her yellow head.

"Yes and what would you do if this fellow, The Misfit, caught you?" 5
the grandmother said.

"I'd smack his face," John Wesley said.

"She wouldn't stay at home for a million bucks," June Star said. "Afraid she'd miss something. She has to go everywhere we go."

"All right, Miss," the grandmother said. "Just remember that the next time you want me to curl your hair."

June Star said her hair was naturally curly.

The next morning the grandmother was the first one in the car, 10
ready to go. She had her big black valise that looked like the head of a hippopotamus in one corner, and underneath it she was hiding a basket with Pitty Sing, the cat, in it. She didn't intend for the cat to be left alone in the house for three days because he would miss her too much and she was afraid he might brush against one of the gas burners and accidentally asphyxiate himself. Her son, Bailey, didn't like to arrive at a motel with a cat.

She sat in the middle of the back seat with John Wesley and June Star on either side of her. Bailey and the children's mother and the baby sat in front and they left Atlanta at eight forty-five with the mileage on the car at 55890. The grandmother wrote this down because she thought it would be interesting to say how many miles they had been when they got back. It took them twenty minutes to reach the outskirts of the city.

The old lady settled herself comfortably, removing her white cotton gloves and putting them up with her purse on the shelf in front of the back window. The children's mother still had on slacks and still had her hair tied up in a green kerchief, but the grandmother had on a navy blue straw sailor hat with a bunch of white violets on the brim and a navy blue dress with a small white dot in the print. Her collars and cuffs were white organdy trimmed with lace and at her neckline she had pinned a purple spray of cloth violets containing a sachet. In case of an accident, anyone seeing her dead on the highway would know at once that she was a lady.

She said she thought it was going to be a good day for driving, neither too hot nor too cold, and she cautioned Bailey that the speed limit was fifty-five miles an hour and that the patrolmen hid themselves behind billboards and small clumps of trees and sped out after you before you had a chance to slow down. She pointed out interesting details of the scenery: Stone Mountain; the blue granite that in some places came up to both sides of the highway; the brilliant red clay banks slightly streaked with purple; and the various crops that made rows of green lace-work on the ground. The trees were full of silver-white sunlight and the meanest of them sparkled. The children were reading comic magazines and their mother had gone back to sleep.

"Let's go through Georgia fast so we won't have to look at it much," John Wesley said.

"If I were a little boy," said the grandmother, "I wouldn't talk about 15
my native state that way. Tennessee has the mountains and Georgia has the hills."

"Tennessee is just a hillbilly dumping ground," John Wesley said, "and Georgia is a lousy state too."

"You said it," June Star said.

"In my time," said the grandmother, folding her thin veined fingers, "children were more respectful of their native states and their parents and everything else. People did right then. Oh look at the cute little pickaninny!" she said and pointed to a Negro child standing in the door of a shack. "Wouldn't that make a picture, now?" she asked and they all turned and looked at the little Negro out of the back window. He waved.

"He didn't have any britches on," June Star said.

"He probably didn't have any," the grandmother explained. "Little 20
niggers in the country don't have things like we do. If I could paint, I'd paint that picture," she said.

The children exchanged comic books.

The grandmother offered to hold the baby and the children's mother passed him over the front seat to her. She set him on her knee and bounced him and told him about the things they were passing. She rolled her eyes and screwed up her mouth and stuck her leathery thin face into his smooth bland one. Occasionally he gave her a faraway smile. They passed a large cotton field with five or six graves fenced in the middle of it, like a small island. "Look at the graveyard!" the grandmother said, pointing it out. "That was the old family burying ground. That belonged to the plantation."

"Where's the plantation?" John Wesley asked.

"Gone With the Wind," said the grandmother. "Ha. Ha."

When the children finished all the comic books they had brought, 25
they opened the lunch and ate it. The grandmother ate a peanut butter sandwich and an olive and would not let the children throw the box and the paper napkins out the window. When there was nothing else to do they played a game by choosing a cloud and making the other two guess what shape it suggested. John Wesley took one the shape of a cow and June Star guessed a cow and John Wesley said, no, an automobile, and June Star said he didn't play fair, and they began to slap each other over the grandmother.

The grandmother said she would tell them a story if they would keep quiet. When she told a story, she rolled her eyes and waved her head and was very dramatic. She said once when she was a maiden lady she had been courted by a Mr. Edgar Atkins Teagarden from Jasper, Georgia. She said he was a very good-looking man and a gentleman and that he brought her a watermelon every Saturday afternoon with his initials cut in it, E. A. T. Well, one Saturday, she said, Mr. Teagarden brought the watermelon and there was nobody at home and he left it on the front porch and returned in his buggy to Jasper, but she never got the watermelon, she said, because a nigger boy ate it when he saw the initials, E. A. T.! This story tickled John Wesley's funny bone and he giggled and giggled but June Star didn't think it was any good. She said she wouldn't marry a man that just brought her a watermelon on Saturday. The grandmother said she would have done well to marry Mr. Teagarden because he was a gentleman and had bought Coca-Cola stock when it first came out and that he had died only a few years ago, a very wealthy man.

They stopped at The Tower for barbecued sandwiches. The Tower was a part stucco and part wood filling station and dance hall set in a clearing outside of Timothy. A fat man named Red Sammy Butts ran it and there were signs stuck here and there on the building and for miles up and down the highway saying, TRY RED SAMMY'S FAMOUS BARBECUE. NONE LIKE FAMOUS RED SAMMY'S! RED SAM! THE FAT BOY WITH THE HAPPY LAUGH. A VETERAN! RED SAMMY'S YOUR MAN!

Red Sammy was lying on the bare ground outside The Tower with his head under a truck while a gray monkey about a foot high, chained to a small chinaberry tree, chattered nearby. The monkey sprang back into the tree and got on the highest limb as soon as he saw the children jump out of the car and run toward him.

Inside, The Tower was a long dark room with a counter at one end and tables at the other and dancing space in the middle. They all sat down at a board table next to the nickelodeon and Red Sam's wife, a tall burnt-brown woman with hair and eyes lighter than her skin, came and took their order. The children's mother put a dime in the machine and played "The Tennessee Waltz," and the grandmother said that tune always made her want to dance. She asked Bailey if he would like to dance but he only glared at her. He didn't have a naturally sunny disposition like she did and trips made him nervous. The grandmother's brown eyes were very bright. She swayed her head from side to side and pretended she was dancing in her chair. June Star said play something she could tap to so the children's mother put in another dime and played a fast number and June Star stepped out onto the dance floor and did her tap routine.

"Ain't she cute?" Red Sam's wife said, leaning over the counter. 30
"Would you like to come be my little girl?"

"No I certainly wouldn't," June Star said. "I wouldn't live in a broken-down place like this for a million bucks!" and she ran back to the table.

"Ain't she cute?" the woman repeated, stretching her mouth politely.

"Aren't you ashamed?" hissed the grandmother.

Red Sam came in and told his wife to quit lounging on the counter and hurry up with these people's order. His khaki trousers reached just to his hip bones and his stomach hung over them like a sack of meal swaying under his shirt. He came over and sat down at a table nearby and let out a combination sigh and yodel. "You can't win," he said. "You can't win," and he wiped his sweating red face off with a gray handkerchief. "These days you don't know who to trust," he said. "Ain't that the truth?"

"People are certainly not nice like they used to be," said the 35
grandmother.

"Two fellers come in here last week," Red Sammy said, "driving a Chrysler. It was a old beat-up car but it was a good one and these boys looked all right to me. Said they worked at the mill and you know I let them fellers charge the gas they bought? Now why did I do that?"

"Because you're a good man!" the grandmother said at once.

"Yes'm, I suppose so," Red Sam said as if he were struck with this answer.

His wife brought the orders, carrying the five plates all at once without a tray, two in each hand and one balanced on her arm. "It isn't a soul in this green world of God's that you can trust," she said. "And I don't count nobody out of that, not nobody," she repeated, looking at Red Sammy.

"Did you read about that criminal, The Misfit, that's escaped?" asked 40
the grandmother.

"I wouldn't be a bit surprised if he didn't attact this place right here," said the woman. "If he hears about it being here, I wouldn't be none surprised to see him. If he hears it's two cent in the cash register, I wouldn't be a-tall surprised if he . . ."

"That'll do," Red Sam said. "Go bring these people their Co'-Colas," and the woman went off to get the rest of the order.

"A good man is hard to find," Red Sammy said. "Everything is getting terrible. I remember the day you could go off and leave your screen door unlatched. Not no more."

He and the grandmother discussed better times. The old lady said that in her opinion Europe was entirely to blame for the way things were now. She said the way Europe acted you would think we were made of money and Red Sam said it was no use talking about it, she was exactly right. The children ran outside into the white sunlight and looked at the monkey in the lacy chinaberry tree. He was busy catching fleas on himself and biting each one carefully between his teeth as if it were a delicacy.

They drove off again into the hot afternoon. The grandmother took 45
cat naps and woke up every five minutes with her own snoring. Outside of Toombsboro she woke up and recalled an old plantation that she had visited in this neighborhood once when she was a young lady. She said the house had six white columns across the front and that there was an avenue of oaks leading up to it and two little wooden trellis arbors on either side in front where you sat down with your suitor after a stroll in the garden. She recalled exactly which road to turn off to get to it. She knew that Bailey would not be willing to lose any time looking at an old house, but the more she talked about it, the more she wanted to see it once again

and find out if the little twin arbors were still standing. "There was a secret panel in this house," she said craftily, not telling the truth but wishing that she were, "and the story went that all the family silver was hidden in it when Sherman° came through but it was never found . . ."

"Hey!" John Wesley said. "Let's go see it! We'll find it! We'll poke all the woodwork and find it! Who lives there? Where do you turn off at? Hey, Pop, can't we turn off there?"

"We never have seen a house with a secret panel!" June Star shrieked. "Let's go to the house with the secret panel! Hey Pop, can't we go see the house with the secret panel!"

"It's not far from here, I know," the grandmother said. "It wouldn't take over twenty minutes."

Bailey was looking straight ahead. His jaw was as rigid as a horseshoe. "No," he said.

The children began to yell and scream that they wanted to see the 50
house with the secret panel. John Wesley kicked the back of the front seat and June Star hung over her mother's shoulder and whined desperately into her ear that they never had any fun even on their vacation, that they could never do what THEY wanted to do. The baby began to scream and John Wesley kicked the back of the seat so hard that his father could feel the blows in his kidney.

"All right!" he shouted and drew the car to a stop at the side of the road. "Will you all shut up? Will you all just shut up for one second? If you don't shut up, we won't go anywhere."

"It would be very educational for them," the grandmother murmured.

"All right," Bailey said, "but get this: this is the only time we're going to stop for anything like this. This is the one and only time."

"The dirt road that you have to turn down is about a mile back," the grandmother directed. "I marked it when we passed."

"A dirt road," Bailey groaned. 55

After they had turned around and were headed toward the dirt road, the grandmother recalled other points about the house, the beautiful glass over the front doorway and the candle-lamp in the hall. John Wesley said that the secret panel was probably in the fireplace.

"You can't go inside this house," Bailey said. "You don't know who lives there."

"While you all talk to the people in front, I'll run around behind and get in a window," John Wesley suggested.

"We'll all stay in the car," his mother said.

They turned onto the dirt road and the car raced roughly along in a 60
swirl of pink dust. The grandmother recalled the times when there were no paved roads and thirty miles was a day's journey. The dirt road was

Sherman: General William Tecumseh Sherman, Union commander, whose troops burned Atlanta in 1864 and then made a devastating march to the sea.

hilly and there were sudden washes in it and sharp curves on dangerous embankments. All at once they would be on a hill, looking down over the blue tops of trees for miles around, then the next minute, they would be in a red depression with the dust-coated trees looking down on them.

"This place had better turn up in a minute," Bailey said, "or I'm going to turn around."

The road looked as if no one had traveled on it for months.

"It's not much farther," the grandmother said and just as she said it, a horrible thought came to her. The thought was so embarrassing that she turned red in the face and her eyes dilated and her feet jumped up, upsetting her valise in the corner. The instant the valise moved, the newspaper top she had over the basket under it rose with a snarl and Pitty Sing, the cat, sprang onto Bailey's shoulder.

The children were thrown to the floor and their mother, clutching the baby, was thrown out the door onto the ground; the old lady was thrown into the front seat. The car turned over once and landed right-side-up in a gulch off the side of the road. Bailey remained in the driver's seat with the cat—gray-striped with a broad white face and an orange nose—clinging to his neck like a caterpillar.

As soon as the children saw they could move their arms and legs, 65
they scrambled out of the car, shouting, "We've had an ACCIDENT!" The grandmother was curled up under the dashboard, hoping she was injured so that Bailey's wrath would not come down on her all at once. The horrible thought she had had before the accident was that the house she had remembered so vividly was not in Georgia but in Tennessee.

Bailey removed the cat from his neck with both hands and flung it out the window against the side of a pine tree. Then he got out of the car and started looking for the children's mother. She was sitting against the side of the red gutted ditch, holding the screaming baby, but she only had a cut down her face and a broken shoulder. "We've had an ACCIDENT!" the children screamed in a frenzy of delight.

"But nobody's killed," June Star said with disappointment as the grandmother limped out of the car, her hat still pinned to her head but the broken front brim standing up at a jaunty angle and the violet spray hanging off the side. They all sat down in the ditch, except the children, to recover from the shock. They were all shaking.

"Maybe a car will come along," said the children's mother hoarsely.

"I believe I have injured an organ," said the grandmother, pressing her side, but no one answered her. Bailey's teeth were clattering. He had on a yellow sport shirt with bright blue parrots designed in it and his face was as yellow as the shirt. The grandmother decided that she would not mention that the house was in Tennessee.

The road was about ten feet above and they could see only the tops 70
of the trees on the other side of it. Behind the ditch they were sitting in

there were more woods, tall and dark and deep. In a few minutes they saw a car some distance away on top of a hill, coming slowly as if the occupants were watching them. The grandmother stood up and waved both her arms dramatically to attract their attention. The car continued to come on slowly, disappeared around a bend and appeared again, moving even slower, on top of the hill they had gone over. It was a big black battered hearse-like automobile. There were three men in it.

It came to a stop just over them and for some minutes, the driver looked down with a steady expressionless gaze to where they were sitting, and didn't speak. Then he turned his head and muttered something to the other two and they got out. One was a fat boy in black trousers and a red sweat shirt with a silver stallion embossed on the front of it. He moved around on the right side of them and stood staring, his mouth partly open in a kind of loose grin. The other had on khaki pants and a blue striped coat and a gray hat pulled down very low, hiding most of his face. He came around slowly on the left side. Neither spoke.

The driver got out of the car and stood by the side of it, looking down at them. He was an older man than the other two. His hair was just beginning to gray and he wore silver-rimmed spectacles that gave him a scholarly look. He had a long creased face and didn't have on any shirt or undershirt. He had on blue jeans that were too tight for him and was holding a black hat and a gun. The two boys also had guns.

"We've had an ACCIDENT!" the children screamed.

The grandmother had the peculiar feeling that the bespectacled man was someone she knew. His face was as familiar to her as if she had known him all her life but she could not recall who he was. He moved away from the car and began to come down the embankment, placing his feet carefully so that he wouldn't slip. He had on tan and white shoes and no socks, and his ankles were red and thin. "Good afternoon," he said. "I see you all had you a little spill."

"We turned over twice!" said the grandmother. 75

"Oncet," he corrected. "We seen it happen. Try their car and see will it run, Hiram," he said quietly to the boy with the gray hat.

"What you got that gun for?" John Wesley asked. "Whatcha gonna do with that gun?"

"Lady," the man said to the children's mother, "would you mind calling them children to sit down by you? Children make me nervous. I want all you all to sit down right together there where you're at."

"What are you telling US what to do for?" June Star asked.

Behind them the line of woods gaped like a dark open mouth. "Come 80
here," said their mother.

"Look here now," Bailey began suddenly, "we're in a predicament! We're in . . ."

The grandmother shrieked. She scrambled to her feet and stood staring. "You're The Misfit!" she said. "I recognized you at once!"

"Yes'm," the man said, smiling slightly as if he were pleased in spite of himself to be known, "but it would have been better for all of you, lady, if you hadn't of reckernized me."

Bailey turned his head sharply and said something to his mother that shocked even the children. The old lady began to cry and The Misfit reddened.

"Lady," he said, "don't you get upset. Sometimes a man says things 85
he don't mean. I don't reckon he meant to talk to you thataway."

"You wouldn't shoot a lady, would you?" the grandmother said and removed a clean handkerchief from her cuff and began to slap at her eyes with it.

The Misfit pointed the toe of his shoe into the ground and made a little hole and then covered it up again. "I would hate to have to," he said.

"Listen," the grandmother almost screamed, "I know you're a good man. You don't look a bit like you have common blood. I know you must come from nice people!"

"Yes mam," he said, "finest people in the world." When he smiled he showed a row of strong white teeth. "God never made a finer woman than my mother and my daddy's heart was pure gold," he said. The boy with the red sweat shirt had come around behind them and was standing with his gun at his hip. The Misfit squatted down on the ground. "Watch them children, Bobby Lee," he said. "You know they make me nervous." He looked at the six of them huddled together in front of him and he seemed to be embarrassed as if he couldn't think of anything to say. "Ain't a cloud in the sky," he remarked, looking up at it. "Don't see no sun but don't see no cloud neither."

"Yes, it's a beautiful day," said the grandmother. "Listen," she said, 90
"you shouldn't call yourself The Misfit because I know you're a good man at heart. I can just look at you and tell."

"Hush!" Bailey yelled. "Hush! Everybody shut up and let me handle this!" He was squatting in the position of a runner about to sprint forward but he didn't move.

"I pre-chate that, lady," The Misfit said and drew a little circle in the ground with the butt of his gun.

"It'll take a half a hour to fix this here car," Hiram called, looking over the raised hood of it.

"Well, first you and Bobby Lee get him and that little boy to step over yonder with you," The Misfit said, pointing to Bailey and John Wesley. "The boys want to ast you something," he said to Bailey. "Would you mind stepping back in them woods there with them?"

"Listen," Bailey began, "we're in a terrible predicament! Nobody 95
realizes what this is," and his voice cracked. His eyes were as blue and intense as the parrots in his shirt and he remained perfectly still.

The grandmother reached up to adjust her hat brim as if she were going to the woods with him but it came off in her hand. She stood staring at it and after a second she let it fall on the ground. Hiram pulled Bailey up by the arm as if he were assisting an old man. John Wesley caught hold of his father's hand and Bobby Lee followed. They went off toward the woods and just as they reached the dark edge, Bailey turned and supporting himself against a gray naked pine trunk, he shouted, "I'll be back in a minute, Mamma, wait on me!"

"Come back this instant!" his mother shrilled but they all disappeared into the woods.

"Bailey Boy!" the grandmother called in a tragic voice but she found she was looking at The Misfit squatting on the ground in front of her. "I just know you're a good man," she said desperately. "You're not a bit common!"

"Nome, I ain't a good man," The Misfit said after a second as if he had considered her statement carefully, "but I ain't the worst in the world neither. My daddy said I was a different breed of dog from my brothers and sisters. 'You know,' Daddy said, 'it's some that can live their whole life out without asking about it and it's others has to know why it is, and this boy is one of the latters. He's going to be into everything!'" He put on his black hat and looked up suddenly and then away deep into the woods as if he were embarrassed again. "I'm sorry I don't have on a shirt before you ladies," he said, hunching his shoulders slightly. "We buried our clothes that we had on when we escaped and we're just making do until we can get better. We borrowed these from some folks we met," he explained.

"That's perfectly all right," the grandmother said. "Maybe Bailey has 100
an extra shirt in his suitcase."

"I'll look and see terrectly," The Misfit said.

"Where are they taking him?" the children's mother screamed.

"Daddy was a card himself," The Misfit said. "You couldn't put anything over on him. He never got in trouble with the Authorities though. Just had the knack of handling them."

"You could be honest too if you'd only try," said the grandmother. "Think how wonderful it would be to settle down and live a comfortable life and not have to think about somebody chasing you all the time."

The Misfit kept scratching in the ground with the butt of his gun as 105
if he were thinking about it. "Yes'm, somebody is always after you," he murmured.

The grandmother noticed how thin his shoulder blades were just behind his hat because she was standing up looking down on him. "Do you ever pray?" she asked.

He shook his head. All she saw was the black hat wiggle between his shoulder blades. "Nome," he said.

There was a pistol shot from the woods, followed closely by another. Then silence. The old lady's head jerked around. She could hear the wind move through the tree tops like a long satisfied insuck of breath. "Bailey Boy!" she called.

"I was a gospel singer for a while," The Misfit said. "I been most everything. Been in the arm service, both land and sea, at home and abroad, been twict married, been an undertaker, been with the railroads, plowed Mother Earth, been in a tornado, seen a man burnt alive oncet," and he looked up at the children's mother and the little girl who were sitting close together, their faces white and their eyes glassy; "I even seen a woman flogged," he said.

"Pray, pray," the grandmother began, "pray, pray . . ." 110

"I never was a bad boy that I remember of," The Misfit said in an almost dreamy voice, "but somewheres along the line I done something wrong and got sent to the penitentiary. I was buried alive," and he looked up and held her attention to him by a steady stare.

"That's when you should have started to pray," she said. "What did you do to get sent to the penitentiary that first time?"

"Turn to the right, it was a wall," The Misfit said, looking up again at the cloudless sky. "Turn to the left, it was a wall. Look up it was a ceiling, look down it was a floor. I forget what I done, lady. I set there and set there, trying to remember what it was I done and I ain't recalled it to this day. Oncet in a while, I would think it was coming to me, but it never come."

"Maybe they put you in by mistake," the old lady said vaguely.

"Nome," he said. "It wasn't no mistake. They had the papers on me." 115

"You must have stolen something," she said.

The Misfit sneered slightly. "Nobody had nothing I wanted," he said. "It was a head-doctor at the penitentiary said what I had done was kill my daddy but I known that for a lie. My daddy died in nineteen ought nineteen of the epidemic flu and I never had a thing to do with it. He was buried in the Mount Hopewell Baptist churchyard and you can go there and see for yourself."

"If you would pray," the old lady said, "Jesus would help you."

"That's right," The Misfit said.

"Well then, why don't you pray?" she asked trembling with delight 120
suddenly.

"I don't want no hep," he said. "I'm doing all right by myself."

Bobby Lee and Hiram came ambling back from the woods. Bobby Lee was dragging a yellow shirt with bright blue parrots in it.

"Thow me that shirt, Bobby Lee," The Misfit said. The shirt came flying at him and landed on his shoulder and he put it on. The grandmother couldn't name what the shirt reminded her of. "No, lady," The Misfit said while he was buttoning it up, "I found out the crime don't matter. You can do one thing or you can do another, kill a man or take a tire off his car, because sooner or later you're going to forget what it was you done and just be punished for it."

The children's mother had begun to make heaving noises as if she couldn't get her breath. "Lady," he asked, "would you and that little girl like to step off yonder with Bobby Lee and Hiram and join your husband?"

"Yes, thank you," the mother said faintly. Her left arm dangled help- 125
lessly and she was holding the baby, who had gone to sleep, in the other. "Hep that lady up, Hiram," The Misfit said as she struggled to climb out of the ditch, "and Bobby Lee, you hold onto that little girl's hand."

"I don't want to hold hands with him," June Star said. "He reminds me of a pig."

The fat boy blushed and laughed and caught her by the arm and pulled her off into the woods after Hiram and her mother.

Alone with The Misfit, the grandmother found that she had lost her voice. There was not a cloud in the sky nor any sun. There was nothing around her but woods. She wanted to tell him that he must pray. She opened and closed her mouth several times before anything came out. Finally she found herself saying, "Jesus. Jesus," meaning, Jesus will help you, but the way she was saying it, it sounded as if she might be cursing.

"Yes'm," The Misfit said as if he agreed. "Jesus thown everything off balance. It was the same case with Him as with me except He hadn't committed any crime and they could prove I had committed one because they had the papers on me. Of course," he said, "they never shown me my papers. That's why I sign myself now. I said long ago, you get you a signature and sign everything you do and keep a copy of it. Then you'll know what you done and you can hold up the crime to the punishment and see do they match and in the end you'll have something to prove you ain't been treated right. I call myself The Misfit," he said, "because I can't make what all I done wrong fit what all I gone through in punishment."

There was a piercing scream from the woods, followed closely by a 130
pistol report. "Does it seem right to you, lady, that one is punished a heap and another ain't punished at all?"

"Jesus!" the old lady cried. "You've got good blood! I know you wouldn't shoot a lady! I know you come from nice people! Pray! Jesus, you ought not to shoot a lady. I'll give you all the money I've got!"

"Lady," The Misfit said, looking beyond her far into the woods, "there never was a body that give the undertaker a tip."

There were two more pistol reports and the grandmother raised her head like a parched old turkey hen crying for water and called, "Bailey Boy, Bailey Boy!" as if her heart would break.

"Jesus was the only One that ever raised the dead," The Misfit continued, "and He shouldn't have done it. He thown everything off balance. If He did what He said, then it's nothing for you to do but thow away everything and follow Him, and if He didn't, then it's nothing for you to do but enjoy the few minutes you got left the best way you can—by killing somebody or burning down his house or doing some other meanness to him. No pleasure but meanness," he said and his voice had become almost a snarl.

"Maybe He didn't raise the dead," the old lady mumbled, not know- 135
ing what she was saying and feeling so dizzy that she sank down in the ditch with her legs twisted under her.

"I wasn't there so I can't say He didn't," The Misfit said. "I wisht I had of been there," he said, hitting the ground with his fist. "It ain't right I wasn't there because if I had of been there I would of known. Listen lady," he said in a high voice, "if I had of been there I would of known and I wouldn't be like I am now." His voice seemed about to crack and the grandmother's head cleared for an instant. She saw the man's face twisted close to her own as if he were going to cry and she murmured, "Why you're one of my babies. You're one of my own children!" She reached out and touched him on the shoulder. The Misfit sprang back as if a snake had bitten him and shot her three times through the chest. Then he put his gun down on the ground and took off his glasses and began to clean them.

Hiram and Bobby Lee returned from the woods and stood over the ditch, looking down at the grandmother who half sat and half lay in a puddle of blood with her legs crossed under her like a child's and her face smiling up at the cloudless sky.

Without his glasses, The Misfit's eyes were red-rimmed and pale and defenseless-looking. "Take her off and thow her where you thown the others," he said, picking up the cat that was rubbing itself against his leg.

"She was a talker, wasn't she?" Bobby Lee said, sliding down the ditch with a yodel.

"She would of been a good woman," The Misfit said, "if it had been 140
somebody there to shoot her every minute of her life."

"Some fun!" Bobby Lee said.

"Shut up, Bobby Lee," The Misfit said. "It's no real pleasure in life."

Questions

1. How early in the story does O'Connor foreshadow what will happen in the end? What further hints does she give us along the way? How does the scene at Red Sammy's Barbecue advance the story toward its conclusion?
2. When we first meet the grandmother, what kind of person is she? What do her various remarks reveal about her? Does she remain a static character, or does she change in any way as the story goes on?
3. When the grandmother's head clears for an instant (paragraph 136), what does she suddenly understand? Reread this passage carefully and prepare to discuss what it means.
4. What do we learn from the conversation between The Misfit and the grandmother while the others go out to the woods? How would you describe The Misfit's outlook on the world? Compare it with the author's, from whatever you know about Flannery O'Connor and from the story itself.
5. How would you respond to a reader who complained, "The title of this story is just an obvious platitude"?

WRITING *effectively*

THINKING ABOUT POINT OF VIEW

When we hear an outlandish piece of news, something that doesn't quite add up, we're well advised, as the saying goes, to consider the source. The same is true when we read a short story.

- **Consider who is telling the story.** A story's point of view determines how much confidence a reader should have in the events related. A story told from a third-person omniscient point of view generally provides a sense of authority and stability that makes the narrative seem reliable.
- **Ask why the narrator is telling the story.** The use of a first-person narrator, on the other hand, often suggests a certain bias, especially when the narrator relates events in which he or she has played a part. In such cases the narrator sometimes has an obvious interest in the audience's accepting his or her version of the story as truth.
- **Think about whether anything important is being left out of the story.** Is something of obvious importance to the situation not being reported? Understanding the limits of a narrator's point of view is key to interpreting what a story says.

CHECKLIST: Writing About Point of View

- ☐ How is the story narrated? Is it told in the third or the first person?
- ☐ If the story is told in the third person, is the point of view omniscient or does it confine itself to what is perceived by a particular character?
- ☐ What is gained by this choice?
- ☐ If the story is told by a first-person narrator, what is the speaker's main reason for telling the story? What does the narrator have to gain by making us believe his or her account?
- ☐ Does the first-person narrator fully understand his or her own motivations? Is there some important aspect of the narrator's character or situation that is being overlooked?
- ☐ Is there anything peculiar about the first-person narrator? Does this peculiarity create any suspicions about the narrator's accuracy or reliability?
- ☐ What does the narrator's perspective add? Would the story seem as memorable if related from another narrative angle?

TOPICS FOR WRITING ON POINT OF VIEW

1. Retell the events in "A & P" (Chapter 1) from the point of view of one of the story's minor characters: Lengel, or Stokesie, or one of the girls. How does the story's emphasis change?
2. Here is another writing exercise to help you sense what a difference point of view makes. Write a short statement from the point of view of William Faulkner's Homer Barron on "My Affair with Miss Emily."
3. Imagine a story such as "A & P" or "A Rose for Emily" told by an omniscient third-person narrator. Write several paragraphs about what would be lost (or gained) by such a change.
4. Choose any tale from "Gallery of International Voices" (Chapter 8) or "Stories for Further Reading" (Chapter 9), and, in a paragraph or two, describe how point of view colors the general meaning. If you like, you may argue that the story might be told more effectively from an alternate point of view.
5. Think back to a confrontation in your own life, and describe that event from a point of view contrary to your own. Try to imagine yourself inside your speaker's personality, and present the facts as that person would, as convincingly as you can.
6. Tell the story of a confrontation—biographical or fictional—from the point of view of a minor character peripheral to the central action. You could, for instance, tell the story of a disastrous first date from the point of view of the unlucky waitress who serves the couple dinner.

▶ TERMS FOR *review*

Points of View

Total omniscience ▶ Point of view in which the narrator knows everything about all of the characters and events in a story. A narrator with total omniscience can move freely from one character to another. Generally, a totally omniscient narrative is written in the third person.

Limited or selective omniscience ▶ Point of view in which the narrator sees into the minds of some but not all of the characters. Most typically, limited omniscience sees through the eyes of one major or minor character.

Impartial omniscience ▶ Point of view employed when an omniscient narrator, who presents the thoughts and actions of the characters, does not judge them or comment on them.

Editorial omniscience ▶ Point of view employed when an omniscient narrator goes beyond reporting the thoughts of his characters to make a critical judgment or commentary, revealing the narrator's own thoughts or attitudes.

Objective point of view ▶ Point of view in which the third-person narrator merely reports dialogue and action with little or no interpretation or access to the characters' minds.

Types of Narrators

Omniscient or all-knowing narrator ▶ A narrator who has the ability to move freely through the consciousness of any character. The omniscient narrator also has complete knowledge of all of the external events in a story.

Participant or first-person narrator ▶ A narrator who is a participant in the action. Such a narrator refers to himself or herself as "I" and may be a major or minor character in the story.

Observer ▶ A first-person narrator who is relatively detached from or plays only a minor role in the events described.

Nonparticipant or third-person narrator ▶ A narrator who does not appear in the story as a character but is usually capable of revealing the thoughts and motives of one or more characters.

Innocent or naive narrator ▶ A character who fails to understand all the implications of the story he or she tells. The innocent narrator—often a child or childlike adult—is frequently used by an author to generate irony, sympathy, or pity by creating a gap between what the narrator perceives and what the reader knows.

Unreliable narrator ▶ A narrator who—intentionally or unintentionally—relates events in a subjective or distorted manner. The author usually provides some indication early on in such stories that the narrator is not to be completely trusted.

Narrative Techniques

Interior monologue ▶ An extended presentation of a character's thoughts in a narrative. Usually written in the present tense and printed without quotation marks, an interior monologue reads as if the character were speaking aloud to himself or herself, for the reader to overhear.

Stream of consciousness ▶ A type of modern narration that uses various literary devices, especially interior monologue, in an attempt to duplicate the subjective and associative nature of human consciousness.

3 CHARACTER

What You Will Learn in This Chapter

- To define *character*
- To identify types of characters
- To explain motivation and development
- To analyze the role of a character in a story

From popular fiction and drama, both classic and contemporary, we are acquainted with many stereotyped characters. Called **stock characters**, they are often known by some outstanding trait or traits: the *bragging* soldier of Greek and Roman comedy, the Prince *Charming* of fairy tales, the *mad* scientist of horror movies, the *fearlessly reckless* police detective of urban action films, the *brilliant but alcoholic* brain surgeon of medical thrillers on television. Stock characters are especially convenient for writers of commercial fiction: they require little detailed portraiture, for we already know them well. Most writers of the literary story, however, attempt to create characters who strike us not as stereotypes but as unique individuals. While stock characters tend to have single dominant virtues and vices, characters in the finest contemporary short stories tend to have many facets, like people we meet.

A **character**, then, is presumably an imagined person who inhabits a story. Usually we recognize, in the main characters of a story, human personalities that become familiar to us. If the story seems "true to life," we generally find that its characters act in a reasonably consistent manner and that the author has provided them with motivation: sufficient reason to behave as they do. Should a character behave in a sudden and unexpected way, seeming to deny what we have been told about his or her nature or personality, we trust that there was a reason for this behavior and that sooner or later we will discover it.

In good fiction, characters often change or develop. In *A Christmas Carol*, Charles Dickens tells how Ebenezer Scrooge, a tightfisted miser, reforms overnight, suddenly gives to the poor, and endeavors to assist his clerk's struggling family. But Dickens amply demonstrates why Scrooge had such a change of heart—four ghostly visitors, stirring kind memories the old miser had forgotten and also warning him of the probable consequences of his habits—provide the character (and hence the story) with adequate motivation.

CHARACTERIZATION

To borrow the useful terms of the English novelist E. M. Forster, characters may seem flat or round, depending on whether a writer sketches or sculpts them. A **flat character** has only one outstanding trait or feature, or at most a few distinguishing marks: for example, the familiar stock character of the mad scientist, with his lust for absolute power and his crazily gleaming eyes. Flat characters, however, need not be stock characters: in all of literature there is probably only one Tiny Tim, though his functions in *A Christmas Carol* are mainly to invoke blessings and to remind others of their Christian duties.

Some writers, such as George R. R. Martin, populate their novels with hosts of characters. Often they distinguish the flat ones by giving each a single odd physical feature or mannerism—a nervous twitch, a piercing gaze, an obsessive fondness for oysters. **Round characters**, however, present us with more facets—that is, their authors portray them in greater depth and in more generous detail. Such a round character may appear to us only as he appears to the other characters in the story. If their views of him differ, we will see him from more than one side. In other stories, we enter a character's mind and come to know him through his own thoughts, feelings, and perceptions.

Character Development

Flat characters tend to stay the same throughout a story, but round characters often change—they learn or become enlightened, they grow or deteriorate. In William Faulkner's "Barn Burning" (Chapter 5), the boy Sarty Snopes, driven to defy his proud and violent father, becomes at the story's end more knowing and more mature. (Some critics call a fixed character **static**; a changing one, **dynamic**.) This is not to damn a flat character as an inferior creation. In most fiction—even the greatest—minor characters tend to be flat instead of round. Why? Rounding them would cost time and space; and so enlarged, they might only distract us from the main characters.

What's in a Name?

"A character, first of all, is the noise of his name," according to novelist William Gass. Names, chosen artfully, can indicate natures. A simple illustration is the completely virtuous Squire Allworthy, the foster father in *Tom Jones* by Henry Fielding. Subtler, perhaps, is the custom of giving a character a name that makes an **allusion**: a reference to some famous person, place, or thing. For his central characters in *Moby-Dick*, Herman Melville chose names from the Old Testament, calling his tragic and domineering Ahab after a biblical tyrant who came to a bad end, and his wandering narrator Ishmael after a biblical outcast. Whether or not it includes such a reference, a good name

"Damned unfair," he said, "Tragic, really. If they're not chopping off the wrong leg, or bombing your ancestral village, they're closing their positions."

She stood her ground. "I didn't say it was tragic," she said, "I just think it's a pretty lousy way to treat your customers."

"Unforgivable," Anders said, "Heaven will take note."

She sucked in her cheeks but stared past him and said nothing. Anders saw that the other woman, her friend, was looking in the same direction. And then the tellers stopped what they were doing, and the customers slowly turned, and silence came over the bank. Two man wearing black ski masks and blue business suits were standing to the side of the door. One of them had a pistol pressed against the guard's neck. The guard's eyes were closed, and his lips were moving. The other man had a sawed-off shotgun. "Keep your big mouth shut!" the man with the pistol said, though no one had spoken a word. "One of you tellers hits the alarm, you're all dead meat. Got it?"

The tellers nodded.

"Oh, bravo," Anders said. "*Dead meat*." He turned to the woman in front of him. "Great script, eh? The stern, brass-knuckled poetry of the dangerous classes."

She looked at him with drowning eyes.

The man with the shotgun pushed the guard to his knees. He handed the shotgun to his partner and yanked the guard's wrists up behind his back and locked them together with a pair of handcuffs. He toppled him onto the floor with a kick between the shoulder blades. Then he took his shotgun back and went over to the security gate at the end of the counter. He was short and heavy and moved with peculiar slowness, even torpor. "Buzz him in," his partner said. The man with the shotgun opened the gate and sauntered along the line of tellers, handing each of them a Hefty bag. When he came to the empty position he looked over at the man with the pistol, who said, "Whose slot is that?"

Anders watched the teller. She put her hand to her throat and turned to the man she'd been talking to. He nodded. "Mine," she said.

"Then get your ugly ass in gear and fill that bag."

"There you go," Anders said to the woman in front of him. "Justice is done."

"Hey! Bright boy! Did I tell you to talk?"

"No," Anders said.

"Then shut your trap."

"Did you hear that?" Anders said. "'Bright boy.' Right out of 'The Killers.'"°

"The Killers": a short story by Ernest Hemingway about two gangsters who visit a suburban Chicago diner in search of a prizefighter they have been told to murder. They use the term "bright boy" to condescendingly and aggressively address the other men in the diner.

"Please be quiet," the woman said.

"Hey, you deaf or what?" The man with the pistol walked over to Anders. He poked the weapon into Anders' gut. "You think I'm playing games?"

"No," Anders said, but the barrel tickled like a stiff finger and he had to fight back the titters. He did this by making himself stare into the man's eyes, which were clearly visible behind the holes in the mask: pale blue and rawly red-rimmed. The man's left eyelid kept twitching. He breathed out a piercing, ammoniac smell that shocked Anders more than anything that had happened, and he was beginning to develop a sense of unease when the man prodded him again with the pistol.

"You like me, bright boy!" he said. "You want to suck my dick!"

"No," Anders said.

"Then stop looking at me."

Anders fixed his gaze on the man's shiny wing-tip shoes.

"Not down there. Up there." He stuck the pistol under Anders' chin and pushed it upwards until Anders was looking at the ceiling.

Anders had never paid much attention to that part of the bank, a pompous old building with marble floors and counters and pillars, and gilt scrollwork over the tellers' cages. The domed ceiling had been decorated with mythological figures whose fleshy, toga-draped ugliness Anders had taken in at a glance years earlier and afterward declined to notice. Now he had no choice but to scrutinize the painter's work. It was even worse than he remembered, and all of it executed with the utmost gravity. The artist had a few tricks up his sleeve and used them again and again—a certain rosy blush on the underside of the clouds, a coy backwards glance on the faces of the cupids and fauns. The ceiling was crowded with various dramas, but the one that caught Anders' eye was Zeus and Europa—portrayed, in this rendition, as a bull ogling a cow from behind a haystack. To make the cow sexy, the painter had canted her hips suggestively and given her long, droopy eyelashes through which she gazed back at the bull with sultry welcome. The bull wore a smirk and his eyebrows were arched. If there'd been a bubble coming out of his mouth, it would have said, "Hubba hubba."

"What's so funny, bright boy?"

"Nothing."

"You think I'm comical? You think I'm some kind of clown?"

"No."

"Fuck with me again, you're history. *Capiche?*"

Anders burst out laughing. He covered his mouth with both hands and said, "I'm sorry, I'm sorry," then snorted helplessly through his fingers and said, "*Capiche*—oh, God—*capiche*," and at that the man with the pistol raised the pistol and shot Anders right in the head.

The bullet smashed Anders' skull and ploughed through his brain and exited behind his right ear, scattering shards of bone into the cerebral cortex, the corpus callosum, back toward the basal ganglia, and down into the thalamus. But before all this occurred, the first appearance of the bullet in the cerebrum set off a crackling chain of iron transports and neuro-transmissions. Because of their peculiar origin these traced a peculiar pattern, flukishly calling into life a summer afternoon some forty years past, and long since lost to memory. After striking the cranium the bullet was moving at 900 feet per second, a pathetically sluggish, glacial pace compared to the synaptic lightning that flashed around it. Once in the brain, that is, the bullet came under the mediation of brain time, which gave Anders plenty of leisure to contemplate the scene that, in a phrase he would have abhorred, "passed before his eyes."

It is worth noting what Anders did not remember, given what he did remember. He did not remember his first lover, Sherry, or what he had most madly loved about her, before it came to irritate him—her unembarrassed carnality, and especially the cordial way she had with his unit, which she called Mr. Mole, as in, "Uh-oh, looks like Mr. Mole wants to play," and, "let's hide Mr. Mole!" Anders did not remember his wife, whom he had also loved before she exhausted him with her predictability, or his daughter, now a sullen professor of economics at Dartmouth. He did not remember standing just outside his daughter's door as she lectured her bear about his naughtiness and described the truly appalling punishment Paws would receive unless he changed his ways. He did not remember a single line of the hundreds of poems he committed to memory in his youth so that he could give himself the shivers at will—not "Silent, upon a peak in Darien," or "My God, I heard this day," or "All my pretty ones? Did you say all? O hell-kite! All?" None of these did he remember; not one. Anders did not remember his dying mother saying of his father, "I should have stabbed him in his sleep."

He did not remember Professor Josephs telling his class how Athenian prisoners in Sicily had been released if they could recite Aeschylus, and then reciting Aeschylus himself, right there, in the Greek. Anders did not remember how his eyes had burned at those sounds. He did not remember the surprise of seeing a college classmate's name on the jacket of a novel not long after they graduated, or the respect he had felt after reading the book. He did not remember the pleasure of giving respect.

Nor did Anders remember seeing a woman leap to her death from the building opposite his own just days after his daughter was born. He did not remember shouting, "Lord have mercy!" He did not remember deliberately crashing his father's car into a tree, or having his ribs kicked in by three policemen at an anti-war rally, or waking himself up with laughter. He did not remember when he began to regard the heap of books on his desk with boredom and dread, or when he grew angry at writers for writing them. He did not remember when everything began to remind him of something else.

This is what Anders remembered. Heat. A baseball field. Yellow grass, the whirr of insects, himself leaning against a tree as the boys of the neighborhood gather for a pickup game. He looks on as the others argue the relative genius of Mantle and Mays. They have been worrying this subject all summer, and it has become tedious to Anders; an oppression, like the heat.

Then the last two boys arrive, Coyle and a cousin of his from Mississippi. Anders has never met Coyle's cousin before and will never see him again. He says hi with the rest but takes no further notice of him until they've chosen sides and someone asks the cousin what position he wants to play. "Shortstop," the boy says. "Short's the best position they is." Anders turns and looks at him. He wants to hear Coyle's cousin repeat what he's just said, but he knows better than to ask. The others will think he's being a jerk, ragging the kid for his grammar. But that isn't it, not at all—it's that Anders is strangely roused, elated, by those final two words, their pure unexpectedness and their music. He takes the field in a trance, repeating them to himself.

The bullet is already in the brain; it won't be outrun forever, or charmed to a halt. In the end it will do its work and leave the troubled skull behind, dragging its comet's tail of memory and hope and talent and love into the marble hall of commerce. That can't be helped. But for now Anders can still make time. Time for the shadows to lengthen on the grass, time for the tethered dog to bark at the flying ball, time for the boy in right field to smack his sweat-blackened mitt and softly chant, *They is*, *They is*, *They is*.

Questions

1. Describe the character of the adult Anders. Why do you think Wolff chose to make him a book critic?
2. Does Anders seem to experience the robbery as a real-life event? In what ways is his reaction different than the other customers, and why do you suppose that is?
3. Is there anything symbolic about setting the story in a "marble hall of commerce," especially in contrast to the baseball field conjured up in his memory?
4. Who in the story would you say is a *stock character*?
5. Why did Wolff decide to tell us what Anders did *not* remember?
6. What is the significance of the afternoon that Anders does remember? What do the final words, *They is,* symbolize for him?
7. How has Anders changed during the course of his life?

Joyce Carol Oates

Where Are You Going, Where Have You Been? 1970

Joyce Carol Oates

Joyce Carol Oates was born in 1938 into a blue-collar, Catholic family in Lockport, New York. As an undergraduate at Syracuse University, she won a Mademoiselle *magazine award for fiction. After graduating with top honors, she took a master's degree in English at the University of Wisconsin and went on to teach at several universities: Detroit, Windsor, and Princeton. A remarkably prolific writer, Oates has produced more than twenty-five collections of stories, including* Lovely, Dark, and Deep *(2014), and more than forty novels, including* them *(1969), winner of a National Book Award,* Because It Is Bitter, and Because It Is My Heart *(1990),* Blonde *(2000), and, more recently,* A Man Without Shadow *(2016) and* A Book of American Martyrs *(2017). She also writes poetry, plays, and literary criticism.* On Boxing *(1987) is her nonfiction memoir and study of fighters and fighting. Violence and the macabre may inhabit her best stories, but Oates has insisted that these elements in her work are never gratuitous. The 1985 film* Smooth Talk, *directed by Joyce Chopra, was based on "Where Are You Going, Where Have You Been?"*

For Bob Dylan

Her name was Connie. She was fifteen and she had a quick nervous giggling habit of craning her neck to glance into mirrors, or checking other people's faces to make sure her own was all right. Her mother, who noticed everything and knew everything and who hadn't much reason any longer to look at her own face, always scolded Connie about it. "Stop gawking at yourself, who are you? You think you're so pretty?" she would say. Connie would raise her eyebrows at these familiar complaints and look right through her mother, into a shadowy vision of herself as she was right at that moment: she knew she was pretty and that was everything. Her mother had been pretty once too, if you could believe those old snapshots in the album, but now her looks were gone and that was why she was always after Connie.

"Why don't you keep your room clean like your sister? How've you got your hair fixed—what the hell stinks? Hair spray? You don't see your sister using that junk."

Her sister June was twenty-four and still lived at home. She was a secretary in the high school Connie attended, and if that wasn't bad enough—with her in the same building—she was so plain and chunky and steady that Connie had to hear her praised all the time by her mother and her mother's sisters. June did this, June did that, she saved money and helped clean the house and cooked and Connie couldn't do a thing, her mind was all filled with trashy daydreams. Their father was away at work most of the time and when he came home he wanted supper and he read the newspaper at supper and after supper he went to bed. He didn't bother talking much to them, but around his bent head Connie's mother kept picking at her until Connie wished her mother was dead and she herself was dead and it was all over. "She makes me want to throw up sometimes," she complained to her friends. She had a high, breathless, amused voice which made everything she said sound a little forced, whether it was sincere or not.

There was one good thing: June went places with girl friends of hers, girls who were just as plain and steady as she, and so when Connie wanted to do that her mother had no objections. The father of Connie's best girl friend drove the girls the three miles to town and left them off at a shopping plaza, so that they could walk through the stores or go to a movie, and when he came to pick them up again at eleven he never bothered to ask what they had done.

They must have been familiar sights, walking around that shopping 5
plaza in their shorts and flat ballerina slippers that always scuffed the sidewalk, with charm bracelets jingling on their thin wrists; they would lean together to whisper and laugh secretly if someone passed by who amused or interested them. Connie had long dark blond hair that drew anyone's eye to it, and she wore part of it pulled up on her head and puffed out and the rest of it she let fall down her back. She wore a pull-over jersey blouse that looked one way when she was at home and another way when she was away from home. Everything about her had two sides to it, one for home and one for anywhere that was not home: her walk that could be childlike and bobbing, or languid enough to make anyone think she was hearing music in her head, her mouth which was pale and smirking most of the time, but bright and pink on these evenings out, her laugh which was cynical and drawling at home—"Ha, ha, very funny"—but high-pitched and nervous anywhere else, like the jingling of the charms on her bracelet.

Sometimes they did go shopping or to a movie, but sometimes they went across the highway, ducking fast across the busy road, to a drive-in restaurant where older kids hung out. The restaurant was shaped like a big bottle, though squatter than a real bottle, and on its cap was a revolving figure of a grinning boy who held a hamburger aloft. One night in mid-summer they ran across, breathless with daring, and right away someone leaned out a car window and invited them over, but it was just a boy from high school they didn't like. It made them feel good to be able to ignore him. They went up through the maze of parked and cruising cars to the bright-lit, fly-infested restaurant, their faces pleased and expectant as if they were entering a sacred building that loomed out of the night to give them what haven and what blessing they yearned for.

They sat at the counter and crossed their legs at the ankles, their thin shoulders rigid with excitement, and listened to the music that made everything so good: the music was always in the background like music at a church service, it was something to depend upon.

A boy named Eddie came in to talk with them. He sat backwards on his stool, turning himself jerkily around in semi-circles and then stopping and turning again, and after a while he asked Connie if she would like something to eat. She said she did and so she tapped her friend's arm on her way out—her friend pulled her face up into a brave droll look—and Connie said she would meet her at eleven, across the way. "I just hate to leave her like that," Connie said earnestly, but the boy said that she wouldn't be alone for long. So they went out to his car and on the way Connie couldn't help but let her eyes wander over the windshields and faces all around her, her face gleaming with a joy that had nothing to do with Eddie or even this place; it might have been the music. She drew her shoulders up and sucked in her breath with the pure pleasure of being alive, and just at that moment she happened to glance at a face just a few feet from hers. It was a boy with shaggy black hair, in a convertible jalopy painted gold. He stared at her and then his lips widened into a grin. Connie slit her eyes at him and turned away, but she couldn't help glancing back and there he was still watching her. He wagged a finger and laughed and said, "Gonna get you, baby," and Connie turned away again without Eddie noticing anything.

She spent three hours with him, at the restaurant where they ate hamburgers and drank Cokes in wax cups that were always sweating, and then down an alley a mile or so away, and when he left her off at five to eleven only the movie house was still open at the plaza. Her girl friend was there, talking with a boy. When Connie came up the two girls smiled at each other and Connie said, "How was the movie?" and the girl said, "*You* should know." They rode off with the girl's father, sleepy and pleased, and Connie couldn't help but look at the darkened shopping plaza with its big empty parking lot and its signs that were faded and ghostly now, and over at the drive-in restaurant where cars were still circling tirelessly. She couldn't hear the music at this distance.

Next morning June asked her how the movie was and Connie said, "So-so."

She and that girl and occasionally another girl went out several 10
times a week that way, and the rest of the time Connie spent around the house—it was summer vacation—getting in her mother's way and thinking, dreaming, about the boys she met. But all the boys fell back and dissolved into a single face that was not even a face, but an idea, a feeling, mixed up with the urgent insistent pounding of the music and the humid night air of July. Connie's mother kept dragging her back to the daylight by finding things for her to do or saying, suddenly, "What's this about the Pettinger girl?"

And Connie would say nervously, "Oh, her. That dope." She always drew thick clear lines between herself and such girls, and her mother was simple and kindly enough to believe her. Her mother was so simple, Connie thought, that it was maybe cruel to fool her so much. Her mother went scuffling around the house in old bedroom slippers and complained over the telephone to one sister about the other, then the other called up and the two of them complained about the third one. If June's name was mentioned her mother's tone was approving, and if Connie's name was mentioned it was disapproving. This did not really mean she disliked Connie and actually Connie thought that her mother preferred her to June because she was prettier, but the two of them kept up a pretense of exasperation, a sense that they were tugging and struggling over something of little value to either of them. Sometimes, over coffee, they were almost friends, but something would come up—some vexation that was like a fly buzzing suddenly around their heads—and their faces went hard with contempt.

One Sunday Connie got up at eleven—none of them bothered with church—and washed her hair so that it could dry all day long, in the sun. Her parents and sister were going to a barbecue at an aunt's house and Connie said no, she wasn't interested, rolling her eyes to let her mother know just what she thought of it. "Stay home alone then," her mother said sharply. Connie sat out back in a lawn chair and watched them drive away, her father quiet and bald, hunched around so that he could back the car out, her mother with a look that was still angry and not at all softened through the windshield, and in the back seat poor old June all dressed up as if she didn't know what a barbecue was, with all the running yelling kids and the flies. Connie sat with her eyes closed in the sun, dreaming and dazed with the warmth about her as if this were a kind of love, the caresses of love, and her mind slipped over onto thoughts of the boy she had been with the night before and how nice he had been, how sweet it always was, not the way someone like June would suppose but sweet, gentle, the way it was in movies and promised in songs; and when she opened her eyes she hardly knew where she was, the back yard ran off into weeds and a fence-line of trees and behind it the sky was perfectly blue and still. The asbestos "ranch house" that was now three years old startled her—it looked small. She shook her head as if to get awake.

It was too hot. She went inside the house and turned on the radio to drown out the quiet. She sat on the edge of her bed, barefoot, and listened for an hour and a half to a program called XYZ Sunday Jamboree, record after record of hard, fast, shrieking songs she sang along with, interspersed by exclamations from "Bobby King": "An' look here you girls at Napoleon's—Son and Charley want you to pay real close attention to this song coming up!"

And Connie paid close attention herself, bathed in a glow of slow-pulsed joy that seemed to rise mysteriously out of the music itself and lay languidly about the airless little room, breathed in and breathed out with each gentle rise and fall of her chest.

After a while she heard a car coming up the drive. She sat up at 15
once, startled, because it couldn't be her father so soon. The gravel kept crunching all the way in from the road—the driveway was long—and Connie ran to the window. It was a car she didn't know. It was an open jalopy, painted a bright gold that caught the sunlight opaquely. Her heart began to pound and her fingers snatched at her hair, checking it, and she whispered "Christ, Christ," wondering how bad she looked. The car came to a stop at the side door and the horn sounded four short taps as if this were a signal Connie knew.

She went into the kitchen and approached the door slowly, then hung out the screen door, her bare toes curling down off the step. There were two boys in the car and now she recognized the driver: he had shaggy, shabby black hair that looked crazy as a wig and he was grinning at her.

"I ain't late, am I?" he said.

"Who the hell do you think you are?" Connie said.

"Toldja I'd be out, didn't I?"

"I don't even know who you are." 20

She spoke sullenly, careful to show no interest or pleasure, and he spoke in a fast bright monotone. Connie looked past him to the other boy, taking her time. He had fair brown hair, with a lock that fell onto his forehead. His sideburns gave him a fierce, embarrassed look, but so far he hadn't even bothered to glance at her. Both boys wore sunglasses. The driver's glasses were metallic and mirrored everything in miniature.

"You wanta come for a ride?" he said.

Connie smirked and let her hair fall loose over one shoulder.

"Don'tcha like my car? New paint job," he said. "Hey."

"What?" 25

"You're cute."

She pretended to fidget, chasing flies away from the door.

"Don'tcha believe me, or what?" he said.

"Look, I don't even know who you are," Connie said in disgust.

"Hey, Ellie's got a radio, see. Mine's broke down." He lifted his 30
friend's arm and showed her the little transistor the boy was holding, and now Connie began to hear the music. It was the same program that was playing inside the house.

"Bobby King?" she said.

"I listen to him all the time. I think he's great."

"He's kind of great," Connie said reluctantly.

"Listen, that guy's *great*. He knows where the action is."

Connie blushed a little, because the glasses made it impossible for 35
her to see just what this boy was looking at. She couldn't decide if she liked him or if he was just a jerk, and so she dawdled in the doorway and

wouldn't come down or go back inside. She said, "What's all that stuff painted on your car?"

"Can'tcha read it?" He opened the door very carefully, as if he was afraid it might fall off. He slid out just as carefully, planting his feet firmly on the ground, the tiny metallic world in his glasses slowing down like gelatine hardening and in the midst of it Connie's bright green blouse. "This here is my name, to begin with," he said. ARNOLD FRIEND was written in tarlike black letters on the side, with a drawing of a round grinning face that reminded Connie of a pumpkin, except it wore sunglasses. "I wanta introduce myself, I'm Arnold Friend and that's my real name and I'm gonna be your friend, honey, and inside the car's Ellie Oscar, he's kinda shy." Ellie brought his transistor radio up to his shoulder and balanced it there. "Now these numbers are a secret code, honey," Arnold Friend explained. He read off the numbers 33, 19, 17 and raised his eyebrows at her to see what she thought of that, but she didn't think much of it. The left rear fender had been smashed and around it was written, on the gleaming gold background: DONE BY CRAZY WOMAN DRIVER. Connie had to laugh at that. Arnold Friend was pleased at her laughter and looked up at her. "Around the other side's a lot more—you wanta come and see them?"

"No."

"Why not?"

"Why should I?"

"Don'tcha wanta see what's on the car? Don'tcha wanta go for a 40
ride?"

"I don't know."

"Why not?"

"I got things to do."

"Like what?"

"Things." 45

He laughed as if she had said something funny. He slapped his thighs. He was standing in a strange way, leaning back against the car as if he were balancing himself. He wasn't tall, only an inch or so taller than she would be if she came down to him. Connie liked the way he was dressed, which was the way all of them dressed: tight faded jeans stuffed into black, scuffed boots, a belt that pulled his waist in and showed how lean he was, and a white pull-over shirt that was a little soiled and showed the hard small muscles of his arms and shoulders. He looked as if he probably did hard work, lifting and carrying things. Even his neck looked muscular. And his face was a familiar face, somehow: the jaw and chin and cheeks slightly darkened, because he hadn't shaved for a day or two, and the nose long and hawk-like, sniffing as if she were a treat he was going to gobble up and it was all a joke.

"Connie, you ain't telling the truth. This is your day set aside for a ride with me and you know it," he said, still laughing. The way he straightened and recovered from his fit of laughing showed that it had been all fake.

"How do you know what my name is?" she said suspiciously.

"It's Connie."

"Maybe and maybe not." 50

"I know my Connie," he said, wagging his finger. Now she remembered him even better, back at the restaurant, and her cheeks warmed at the thought of how she sucked in her breath just at the moment she passed him—how she must have looked to him. And he had remembered her. "Ellie and I come out here especially for you," he said. "Ellie can sit in back. How about it?"

"Where?"

"Where what?"

"Where're we going?"

He looked at her. He took off the sunglasses and she saw how pale 55
the skin around his eyes was, like holes that were not in shadow but instead in light. His eyes were chips of broken glass that catch the light in an amiable way. He smiled. It was as if the idea of going for a ride somewhere, to some place, was a new idea to him.

"Just for a ride, Connie sweetheart."

"I never said my name was Connie," she said.

"But I know what it is. I know your name and all about you, lots of things," Arnold Friend said. He had not moved yet but stood still leaning back against the side of his jalopy. "I took a special interest in you, such a pretty girl, and found out all about you like I know your parents and sister are gone somewheres and I know where and how long they're going to be gone, and I know who you were with last night, and your best girl friend's name is Betty. Right?"

He spoke in a simple lilting voice, exactly as if he were reciting the words to a song. His smile assured her that everything was fine. In the car Ellie turned up the volume on his radio and did not bother to look around at them.

"Ellie can sit in the back seat," Arnold Friend said. He indicated 60
his friend with a casual jerk of his chin, as if Ellie did not count and she should not bother with him.

"How'd you find out all that stuff?" Connie said.

"Listen: Betty Schultz and Tony Fitch and Jimmy Pettinger and Nancy Pettinger," he said, in a chant. "Raymond Stanley and Bob Hutter—"

"Do you know all those kids?"

"I know everybody."

"Look, you're kidding. You're not from around here." 65

"Sure."

"But—how come we never saw you before?"

"Sure you saw me before," he said. He looked down at his boots, as if he were a little offended. "You just don't remember."

"I guess I'd remember you," Connie said.

70 "Yeah?" He looked up at this, beaming. He was pleased. He began to mark time with the music from Ellie's radio, tapping his fists lightly together. Connie looked away from his smile to the car, which was painted so bright it almost hurt her eyes to look at it. She looked at that name, ARNOLD FRIEND. And up at the front fender was an expression that was familiar—MAN THE FLYING SAUCERS. It was an expression kids had used the year before, but didn't use this year. She looked at it for a while as if the words meant something to her that she did not yet know.

"What're you thinking about? Huh?" Arnold Friend demanded. "Not worried about your hair blowing around in the car, are you?"

"No."

"Think I maybe can't drive good?"

"How do I know?"

75 "You're a hard girl to handle. How come?" he said. "Don't you know I'm your friend? Didn't you see me put my sign in the air when you walked by?"

"What sign?"

"My sign." And he drew an X in the air, leaning out toward her. They were maybe ten feet apart. After his hand fell back to his side the X was still in the air, almost visible. Connie let the screen door close and stood perfectly still inside it, listening to the music from her radio and the boy's blend together. She stared at Arnold Friend. He stood there so stiffly relaxed, pretending to be relaxed, with one hand idly on the door handle as if he were keeping himself up that way and had no intention of ever moving again. She recognized most things about him, the tight jeans that showed his thighs and buttocks and the greasy leather boots and the tight shirt, and even that slippery friendly smile of his, that sleepy dreamy smile that all the boys used to get across ideas they didn't want to put into words. She recognized all this and also the singsong way he talked, slightly mocking, kidding, but serious and a little melancholy, and she recognized the way he tapped one fist against the other in homage to the perpetual music behind him. But all these things did not come together.

She said suddenly, "Hey, how old are you?"

His smile faded. She could see then that he wasn't a kid, he was much older—thirty, maybe more. At this knowledge her heart began to pound faster.

80 "That's a crazy thing to ask. Can'tcha see I'm your own age?"

"Like hell you are."

"Or maybe a coupla years older, I'm eighteen."

"Eighteen?" she said doubtfully.

He grinned to reassure her and lines appeared at the corners of his mouth. His teeth were big and white. He grinned so broadly his eyes became slits and she saw how thick the lashes were, thick and black as if painted with a black tarlike material. Then he seemed to become embarrassed, abruptly, and looked over his shoulder at Ellie. "*Him,* he's crazy," he said. "Ain't he a riot, he's a nut, a real character." Ellie was still listening to the music. His sunglasses told nothing about what he was thinking. He wore a bright orange shirt unbuttoned halfway to show his chest, which was a pale, bluish chest and not muscular like Arnold Friend's. His shirt collar was turned up all around and the very tips of the collar pointed out past his chin as if they were protecting him. He was pressing the transistor radio up against his ear and sat there in a kind of daze, right in the sun.

"He's kinda strange," Connie said. 85

"Hey, she says you're kinda strange! Kinda strange!" Arnold Friend cried. He pounded on the car to get Ellie's attention. Ellie turned for the first time and Connie saw with shock that he wasn't a kid either—he had a fair, hairless face, cheeks reddened slightly as if the veins grew too close to the surface of his skin, the face of a forty-year-old baby. Connie felt a wave of dizziness rise in her at this sight and she stared at him as if waiting for something to change the shock of the moment, make it all right again. Ellie's lips kept shaping words, mumbling along with the words blasting in his ear.

"Maybe you two better go away," Connie said faintly.

"What? How come?" Arnold Friend cried. "We come out here to take you for a ride. It's Sunday." He had the voice of the man on the radio now. It was the same voice, Connie thought. "Don'tcha know it's Sunday all day and honey, no matter who you were with last night today you're with Arnold Friend and don't you forget it!—Maybe you better step out here," he said, and this last was in a different voice. It was a little flatter, as if the heat was finally getting to him.

"No. I got things to do."

"Hey." 90

"You two better leave."

"We ain't leaving until you come with us."

"Like hell I am—"

"Connie, don't fool around with me. I mean, I mean, don't fool *around,*" he said, shaking his head. He laughed incredulously. He placed his sunglasses on top of his head, carefully, as if he were indeed wearing a wig, and brought the stems down behind his ears. Connie stared at him, another wave of dizziness and fear rising in her so that for a moment he wasn't even in focus but was just a blur, standing there against his gold car, and she had the idea that he had driven up the driveway all right but had come from nowhere before that and belonged nowhere and that everything about him and even about the music that was so familiar to her was only half real.

"If my father comes and sees you—" 95

"He ain't coming. He's at a barbecue."

"How do you know that?"

"Aunt Tillie's. Right now they're—uh—they're drinking. Sitting around," he said vaguely, squinting as if he were staring all the way to town and over to Aunt Tillie's backyard. Then the vision seemed to get clear and he nodded energetically. "Yeah. Sitting around. There's your sister in a blue dress, huh? And high heels, the poor sad bitch—nothing like you, sweetheart! And your mother's helping some fat woman with the corn, they're cleaning the corn—husking the corn—"

"What fat woman?" Connie cried.

"How do I know what fat woman. I don't know every goddam fat 100
woman in the world!" Arnold Friend laughed.

"Oh, that's Mrs. Hornby. . . . Who invited her?" Connie said. She felt a little light-headed. Her breath was coming quickly.

"She's too fat. I don't like them fat. I like them the way you are, honey," he said, smiling sleepily at her. They stared at each other for a while, through the screen door. He said softly, "Now what you're going to do is this: you're going to come out that door. You're going to sit up front with me and Ellie's going to sit in the back, the hell with Ellie, right? This isn't Ellie's date. You're my date. I'm your lover, honey."

"What? You're crazy—"

"Yes, I'm your lover. You don't know what that is but you will," he said. "I know that too. I know all about you. But look: it's real nice and you couldn't ask for nobody better than me, or more polite. I always keep my word. I'll tell you how it is, I'm always nice at first, the first time. I'll hold you so tight you won't think you have to try to get away or pretend anything because you'll know you can't. And I'll come inside you where it's all secret and you'll give in to me and you'll love me—"

"Shut up! You're crazy!" Connie said. She backed away from the 105
door. She put her hands against her ears as if she'd heard something terrible, something not meant for her. "People don't talk like that, you're crazy," she muttered. Her heart was almost too big now for her chest and its pumping made sweat break out all over her. She looked out to see Arnold Friend pause and then take a step toward the porch lurching. He almost fell. But, like a clever drunken man, he managed to catch his balance. He wobbled in his high boots and grabbed hold of one of the porch posts.

"Honey?" he said. "You still listening?"

"Get the hell out of here!"

"Be nice, honey. Listen."

"I'm going to call the police—"

He wobbled again and out of the side of his mouth came a fast spat 110
curse, an aside not meant for her to hear. But even this "Christ!" sounded forced. Then he began to smile again. She watched this smile come, awkward as if he were smiling from inside a mask. His whole face was a mask, she thought wildly, tanned down onto his throat but then running out as if he had plastered makeup on his face but had forgotten about his throat.

"Honey—? Listen, here's how it is. I always tell the truth and I promise you this: I ain't coming in that house after you."

"You better not! I'm going to call the police if you—if you don't—"

"Honey," he said, talking right through her voice, "honey, I'm not coming in there but you are coming out here. You know why?"

She was panting. The kitchen looked like a place she had never seen before, some room she had run inside but which wasn't good enough, wasn't going to help her. The kitchen window had never had a curtain, after three years, and there were dishes in the sink for her to do—probably—and if you ran your hand across the table you'd probably feel something sticky there.

"You listening, honey? Hey?" 115

"—going to call the police—"

"Soon as you touch the phone I don't need to keep my promise and can come inside. You won't want that."

She rushed forward and tried to lock the door. Her fingers were shaking. "But why lock it," Arnold Friend said gently, talking right into her face. "It's just a screen door. It's just nothing." One of his boots was at a strange angle, as if his foot wasn't in it. It pointed out to the left, bent at the ankle. "I mean, anybody can break through a screen door and glass and wood and iron or anything else if he needs to, anybody at all and specially Arnold Friend. If the place got lit up with a fire honey you'd come running out into my arms, right into my arms and safe at home—like you knew I was your lover and'd stopped fooling around. I don't mind a nice shy girl but I don't like no fooling around." Part of those words were spoken with a slight rhythmic lilt, and Connie somehow recognized them—the echo of a song from last year, about a girl rushing into her boyfriend's arms and coming home again—

Connie stood barefoot on the linoleum floor, staring at him. "What do you want?" she whispered.

"I want you," he said. 120

"What?"

"Seen you that night and thought, that's the one, yes sir. I never needed to look any more."

"But my father's coming back. He's coming to get me. I had to wash my hair first—" She spoke in a dry, rapid voice, hardly raising it for him to hear.

"No, your daddy is not coming and yes, you had to wash your hair and you washed it for me. It's nice and shining and all for me, I thank you, sweetheart," he said, with a mock bow, but again he almost lost his balance. He had to bend and adjust his boots. Evidently his feet did not go all the way down; the boots must have been stuffed with something so that he would seem taller. Connie stared out at him and behind him Ellie in the car, who seemed to be looking off toward Connie's right, into nothing. This Ellie said, pulling the words out of the air one after another as if he were just discovering them, "You want me to pull out the phone?"

"Shut your mouth and keep it shut," Arnold Friend said, his face red 125
from bending over or maybe from embarrassment because Connie had seen his boots. "This ain't none of your business."

"What—what are you doing? What do you want?" Connie said. "If I call the police they'll get you, they'll arrest you—"

"Promise was not to come in unless you touch that phone, and I'll keep that promise," he said. He resumed his erect position and tried to force his shoulders back. He sounded like a hero in a movie, declaring something important. He spoke too loudly and it was as if he were speaking to someone behind Connie. "I ain't made plans for coming in that house where I don't belong but just for you to come out to me, the way you should. Don't you know who I am?"

"You're crazy," she whispered. She backed away from the door but did not want to go into another part of the house, as if this would give him permission to come through the door. "What do you . . . You're crazy, you . . ."

"Huh? What're you saying, honey?"

Her eyes darted everywhere in the kitchen. She could not remember 130
what it was, this room.

"This is how it is, honey: you come out and we'll drive away, have a nice ride. But if you don't come out we're gonna wait till your people come home and then they're all going to get it."

"You want that telephone pulled out?" Ellie said. He held the radio away from his ear and grimaced, as if without the radio the air was too much for him.

"I toldja shut up, Ellie," Arnold Friend said, "you're deaf, get a hearing aid, right? Fix yourself up. This little girl's no trouble and's gonna be nice to me, so Ellie keep to yourself, this ain't your date—right? Don't hem in on me. Don't hog. Don't crush. Don't bird dog. Don't trail me," he said in a rapid meaningless voice, as if he were running through all the expressions he'd learned but was no longer sure which one of them was in style, then rushing on to new ones, making them up with his eyes closed, "Don't crawl under my fence, don't squeeze in my chipmunk hole, don't sniff my glue, suck my popsicle, keep your own greasy fingers on yourself!" He shaded his eyes and peered in at Connie, who was backed against the kitchen table. "Don't mind him honey he's just a creep. He's a dope. Right? I'm the boy for you and like I said you come out here nice like a lady and give me your hand, and nobody else gets hurt, I mean, your nice old bald-headed daddy and your mummy and your sister in her high heels. Because listen: why bring them in this?"

"Leave me alone," Connie whispered.

"Hey, you know that old woman down the road, the one with the 135
chickens and stuff—you know her?"

"She's dead!"

"Dead? What? You know her?" Arnold Friend said.

"She's dead—"

"Don't you like her?"

"She's dead—she's—she isn't here any more—" 140

"But don't you like her, I mean, you got something against her? Some grudge or something?" Then his voice dipped as if he were conscious of a rudeness. He touched the sunglasses perched on top of his head as if to make sure they were still there. "Now you be a good girl."

"What are you going to do?"

"Just two things, or maybe three," Arnold Friend said. "But I promise it won't last long and you'll like me that way you get to like people you're close to. You will. It's all over for you here, so come on out. You don't want your people in any trouble, do you?"

She turned and bumped against a chair or something, hurting her leg, but she ran into the back room and picked up the telephone. Something roared in her ear, a tiny roaring, and she was so sick with fear that she could do nothing but listen to it—the telephone was clammy and very heavy and her fingers groped down to the dial but were too weak to touch it. She began to scream into the phone, into the roaring. She cried out, she cried for her mother, she felt her breath start jerking back and forth in her lungs as if it were something Arnold Friend were stabbing her with again and again with no tenderness. A noisy sorrowful wailing rose all about her and she was locked inside it the way she was locked inside the house.

After a while she could hear again. She was sitting on the floor with 145
her wet back against the wall.

Arnold Friend was saying from the door, "That's a good girl. Put the phone back."

She kicked the phone away from her.

"No, honey. Pick it up. Put it back right."

She picked it up and put it back. The dial tone stopped.

"That's a good girl. Now come outside." 150

She was hollow with what had been fear, but what was now just an emptiness. All that screaming had blasted it out of her. She sat, one leg cramped under her, and deep inside her brain was something like a pinpoint of light that kept going and would not let her relax. She thought, I'm not going to see my mother again. She thought, I'm not going to sleep in my bed again. Her bright green blouse was all wet.

Arnold Friend said, in a gentle-loud voice that was like a stage voice, "The place where you came from ain't there any more, and where you had in mind to go is cancelled out. This place you are now—inside your daddy's house—is nothing but a cardboard box I can knock down any time. You know that and always did know it. You hear me?"

She thought, I have got to think. I have to know what to do.

"We'll go out to a nice field, out in the country here where it smells so nice and it's sunny," Arnold Friend said. "I'll have my arms around you so you won't need to try to get away and I'll show you what love is like, what it does. The hell with this house! It looks solid all right," he said. He ran a fingernail down the screen and the noise did not make Connie shiver, as it would have the day before. "Now put your hand on your heart, honey. Feel that? That feels solid too but we know better, be nice to me, be sweet like you can because what else is there for a girl like you but to be sweet and pretty and give in?—and get away before her people come back?"

She felt her pounding heart. Her hand seemed to enclose it. She 155
thought for the first time in her life that it was nothing that was hers, that belonged to her, but just a pounding, living thing inside this body that wasn't really hers either.

"You don't want them to get hurt," Arnold Friend went on. "Now get up, honey. Get up all by yourself."

She stood up.

"Now turn this way. That's right. Come over here to me—Ellie, put that away, didn't I tell you? You dope. You miserable creepy dope," Arnold Friend said. His words were not angry but only part of an incantation. The incantation was kindly. "Now come out through the kitchen to me honey and let's see a smile, try it, you're a brave sweet little girl and now they're eating corn and hotdogs cooked to bursting over an outdoor fire, and they don't know one thing about you and never did and honey you're better than them because not a one of them would have done this for you."

Connie felt the linoleum under her feet; it was cool. She brushed her hair back out of her eyes. Arnold Friend let go of the post tentatively and opened his arms for her, his elbows pointing in toward each other and his wrists limp, to show that this was an embarrassed embrace and a little mocking, he didn't want to make her self-conscious.

She put out her hand against the screen. She watched herself push 160
the door slowly open as if she were safe back somewhere in the other doorway, watching this body and this head of long hair moving out into the sunlight where Arnold Friend waited.

"My sweet little blue-eyed girl," he said, in a half-sung sigh that had nothing to do with her brown eyes but was taken up just the same by the vast sunlit reaches of the land behind him and on all sides of him, so much land that Connie had never seen before and did not recognize except to know that she was going to it.

Questions

1. How is Connie characterized in the first few pages of the story, and how is this characterization important in the events that follow?
2. What hints does Oates give us that Arnold Friend is not what he seems? Do you find him funny—or frightening? Why?

3. How does music work in the story? Does music seem to affect the way that Connie acts and thinks?
4. Oates has described Connie's choice at the end as a selfless, almost heroic, choice. Do you agree with this view? How do you interpret her actions at the end of the story?
5. What do you think happens at the end of the story? What are the possible outcomes of the situation? Which ending do you consider most likely and why?

Toni Morrison

Recitatif

1983

Toni Morrison

Toni Morrison (b. 1931) grew up on the banks of Lake Erie, in the Rust Belt town of Lorain, Ohio. She was the first person in her family to attend college, and decades later, after a remarkable career, she became the first African American woman to win the Nobel Prize in Literature. Other high honors include the Pulitzer Prize and American Book Award for her masterpiece novel Beloved *(1987) and the 2012 Presidential Medal of Freedom, the nation's most prestigious civilian award. Morrison was born Chloe Ardella Wofford, the daughter of a welder and a maid. One of four children, she left working-class Lorain to attend Howard University in Washington, D.C., and later earned a master's degree at Cornell. Morrison worked as a professor and as an editor at Random House, publishing* The Bluest Eye *(1970), her first novel, at age thirty-nine, which she wrote while teaching at Howard and raising two children alone. Other novels include* Sula *(1973),* Song of Solomon *(1977),* Jazz *(1992), and* God Help the Child *(2015).*

In a 1993 interview with the Paris Review, *Morrison spoke about why race is central to her artistic identity. She was asked if she wouldn't rather be thought of as a great writer of literature, rather than specifically as an African American writer: "It's very important to me that my work be African-American; if it assimilates into a different or larger pool, so much the better. But I shouldn't be asked to do that. Joyce is not asked to do that. Tolstoy is not. I mean, they can all be Russian, French, Irish, or Catholic, they write out of where they come from, and I do too. It just so happens that that space for me is African American; it could be Catholic, it could be midwestern. I'm those things too, and they are all important."*

My mother danced all night and Roberta's was sick. That's why we were taken to St. Bonny's. People want to put their arms around you when you tell them you were in a shelter, but it really wasn't bad. No big long room with one hundred beds like Bellevue. There were four to a room, and when Roberta and me came, there was a shortage of state kids, so we were the only ones assigned to 406 and could go from bed to bed if we wanted to. And we wanted to, too. We changed beds every night and for the whole four months we were there we never picked one out as our own permanent bed.

It didn't start out that way. The minute I walked in and the Big Bozo introduced us, I got sick to my stomach. It was one thing to be taken out of your own bed early in the morning—it was something else to be stuck in a strange place with a girl from a whole other race. And Mary, that's my mother, she was right. Every now and then she would stop dancing long enough to tell me something important and one of the things she said was that they never washed their hair and they smelled funny. Roberta sure did. Smell funny, I mean. So when the Big Bozo (nobody ever called her Mrs. Itkin, just like nobody ever said St. Bonaventure)—when she said, "Twyla, this is Roberta. Roberta, this is Twyla. Make each other welcome." I said, "My mother won't like you putting me in here."

"Good," said Bozo. "Maybe then she'll come and take you home."

How's that for mean? If Roberta had laughed I would have killed her, but she didn't. She just walked over to the window and stood with her back to us.

"Turn around," said the Bozo. "Don't be rude. Now Twyla. Roberta. 5
When you hear a loud buzzer, that's the call for dinner. Come down to the first floor. Any fights and no movie." And then, just to make sure we knew what we would be missing, "*The Wizard of Oz.*"

Roberta must have thought I meant that my mother would be mad about my being put in the shelter. Not about rooming with her, because as soon as Bozo left she came over to me and said, "Is your mother sick too?"

"No," I said. "She just likes to dance all night."

"Oh," she nodded her head and I liked the way she understood things so fast. So for the moment it didn't matter that we looked like salt and pepper standing there and that's what the other kids called us sometimes. We were eight years old and got F's all the time. Me because I couldn't remember what I read or what the teacher said. And Roberta because she couldn't read at all and didn't even listen to the teacher. She wasn't good at anything except jacks, at which she was a killer: pow scoop pow scoop pow scoop.

We didn't like each other all that much at first, but nobody else wanted to play with us because we weren't real orphans with beautiful dead parents in the sky. We were dumped. Even the New York City Puerto Ricans and the upstate Indians ignored us. All kinds of kids were in there, black ones, white ones, even two Koreans. The food was good, though. At least I thought so. Roberta hated it and left whole pieces of things on her plate: Spam, Salisbury steak—even jello with fruit cocktail in it, and she didn't care if I ate what she wouldn't. Mary's idea of supper was popcorn and a can of Yoo-Hoo. Hot mashed potatoes and two weenies was like Thanksgiving for me.

It really wasn't bad, St. Bonny's. The big girls on the second floor 10
pushed us around now and then. But that was all. They wore lipstick and eyebrow pencil and wobbled their knees while they watched TV. Fifteen, sixteen, even, some of them were. They were put-out girls, scared runaways most of them. Poor little girls who fought their uncles off but looked tough to us, and mean. God did they look mean. The staff tried to keep them separate from the younger children, but sometimes they caught us watching them in the orchard where they played radios and danced with each other. They'd light out after us and pull our hair or twist our arms. We were scared of them, Roberta and me, but neither of us wanted the other one to know it. So we got a good list of dirty names we could shout back when we ran from them through the orchard. I used to dream a lot and almost always the orchard was there. Two acres, four maybe, of these little apple trees. Hundreds of them. Empty and crooked like beggar women when I first came to St. Bonny's but fat with flowers when I left. I don't know why I dreamt about that orchard so much. Nothing really happened there. Nothing all that important, I mean. Just the big girls dancing and playing the radio. Roberta and me watching. Maggie fell down there once. The kitchen woman with legs like parentheses. And the big girls laughed at her. We should have helped her up, I know, but we were scared of those girls with lipstick and eyebrow pencil. Maggie couldn't talk. The kids said she had her tongue cut out, but I think she was just born that way: mute. She was old and sandy-colored and she worked in the kitchen. I don't know if she was nice or not. I just remember her legs like parentheses and how she rocked when she walked. She worked from early in the morning till two o'clock, and if she was late, if she had too much cleaning and didn't get out till two-fifteen or so, she'd cut through the orchard so she wouldn't miss her bus and have to wait another hour. She wore this really stupid little hat—a kid's hat with ear flaps—and she wasn't much taller than we were. A really awful little hat. Even for a mute, it was dumb—dressing like a kid and never saying anything at all.

"But what about if somebody tries to kill her?" I used to wonder about that. "Or what if she wants to cry? Can she cry?"

"Sure," Roberta said. "But just tears. No sounds come out."

"She can't scream?"

"Nope. Nothing."

"Can she hear?" 15

"I guess."

"Let's call her," I said. And we did.

"Dummy! Dummy!" She never turned her head.

"Bow legs! Bow legs!" Nothing. She just rocked on, the chin straps of her baby-boy hat swaying from side to side. I think we were wrong. I think she could hear and didn't let on. And it shames me even now to think there was somebody in there after all who heard us call her those names and couldn't tell on us.

We got along all right, Roberta and me. Changed beds every night, 20
got F's in civics and communication skills and gym. The Bozo was disappointed in us, she said. Out of 130 of us state cases, 90 were under twelve. Almost all were real orphans with beautiful dead parents in the sky. We were the only ones dumped and the only ones with F's in three classes including gym. So we got along—what with her leaving whole pieces of things on her plate and being nice about not asking questions.

I think it was the day before Maggie fell down that we found out our mothers were coming to visit us on the same Sunday. We had been at the shelter twenty-eight days (Roberta twenty-eight and a half) and this was their first visit with us. Our mothers would come at ten o'clock in time for chapel, then lunch with us in the teachers' lounge. I thought if my dancing mother met her sick mother it might be good for her. And Roberta thought her sick mother would get a big bang out of a dancing one. We got excited about it and curled each other's hair. After breakfast we sat on the bed watching the road from the window. Roberta's socks were still wet. She washed them the night before and put them on the radiator to dry. They hadn't, but she put them on anyway because their tops were so pretty—scalloped in pink. Each of us had a purple construction-paper basket that we had made in craft class. Mine had a yellow crayon rabbit on it. Roberta's had eggs with wiggly lines of color. Inside were cellophane grass and just the jelly beans because I'd eaten the two marshmallow eggs they gave us. The Big Bozo came herself to get us. Smiling she told us we looked very nice and to come downstairs. We were so surprised by the smile we'd never seen before, neither of us moved.

"Don't you want to see your mommies?"

I stood up first and spilled the jelly beans all over the floor. Bozo's smile disappeared while we scrambled to get the candy up off the floor and put it back in the grass.

She escorted us downstairs to the first floor, where the other girls were lining up to file into the chapel. A bunch of grown-ups stood to one side. Viewers mostly. The old biddies who wanted servants and the fags who wanted company looking for children they might want to adopt. Once in a while a grandmother. Almost never anybody young or anybody whose face wouldn't scare you in the night. Because if any of the real orphans had young relatives they wouldn't be real orphans. I saw Mary right away. She had on those green slacks I hated and hated even more now because didn't she know we were going to chapel? And that fur jacket with the pocket linings so ripped she had to pull to get her hands out of them. But her face was pretty—like always, and she smiled and waved like she was the little girl looking for her mother—not me.

I walked slowly, trying not to drop the jelly beans and hoping the 25
paper handle would hold. I had to use my last Chiclet because by the

time I finished cutting everything out, all the Elmer's was gone. I am left-handed and the scissors never worked for me. It didn't matter, though; I might just as well have chewed the gum. Mary dropped to her knees and grabbed me, mashing the basket, the jelly beans, and the grass into her ratty fur jacket.

"Twyla, baby. Twyla, baby!"

I could have killed her. Already I heard the big girls in the orchard the next time saying, "Twyyyyyla, baby!" But I couldn't stay mad at Mary while she was smiling and hugging me and smelling of Lady Esther dusting powder. I wanted to stay buried in her fur all day.

To tell the truth I forgot about Roberta. Mary and I got in line for the traipse into chapel and I was feeling proud because she looked so beautiful even in those ugly green slacks that made her behind stick out. A pretty mother on earth is better than a beautiful dead one in the sky even if she did leave you all alone to go dancing.

I felt a tap on my shoulder, turned, and saw Roberta smiling. I smiled back, but not too much lest somebody think this visit was the biggest thing that ever happened in my life. Then Roberta said, "Mother, I want you to meet my roommate, Twyla. And that's Twyla's mother."

I looked up it seemed for miles. She was big. Bigger than any man 30
and on her chest was the biggest cross I'd ever seen. I swear it was six inches long each way. And in the crook of her arm was the biggest Bible ever made.

Mary, simple-minded as ever, grinned and tried to yank her hand out of the pocket with the raggedy lining—to shake hands, I guess. Roberta's mother looked down at me and then looked down at Mary too. She didn't say anything, just grabbed Roberta with her Bible-free hand and stepped out of line, walking quickly to the rear of it. Mary was still grinning because she's not too swift when it comes to what's really going on. Then this light bulb goes off in her head and she says "That bitch!" really loud and us almost in the chapel now. Organ music whining; the Bonny Angels singing sweetly. Everybody in the world turned around to look. And Mary would have kept it up—kept calling names if I hadn't squeezed her hand as hard as I could. That helped a little, but she still twitched and crossed and uncrossed her legs all through service. Even groaned a couple of times. Why did I think she would come there and act right? Slacks. No hat like the grandmothers and viewers, and groaning all the while. When we stood for hymns she kept her mouth shut. Wouldn't even look at the words on the page. She actually reached in her purse for a mirror to check her lipstick. All I could think of was that she really needed to be killed. The sermon lasted a year, and I knew the real orphans were looking smug again.

We were supposed to have lunch in the teachers' lounge, but Mary didn't bring anything, so we picked fur and cellophane grass off the mashed jelly beans and ate them. I could have killed her. I sneaked a look at Roberta. Her mother had brought chicken legs and ham sandwiches and oranges and a whole box of chocolate-covered grahams. Roberta drank milk from a thermos while her mother read the Bible to her.

Things are not right. The wrong food is always with the wrong people. Maybe that's why I got into waitress work later—to match up the right people with the right food. Roberta just let those chicken legs sit there, but she did bring a stack of grahams up to me later when the visit was over. I think she was sorry that her mother would not shake my mother's hand. And I liked that and I liked the fact that she didn't say a word about Mary groaning all the way through the service and not bringing any lunch.

Roberta left in May when the apple trees were heavy and white. On her last day we went to the orchard to watch the big girls smoke and dance by the radio. It didn't matter that they said, "Twyyyyyla, baby." We sat on the ground and breathed. Lady Esther. Apple blossoms. I still go soft when I smell one or the other. Roberta was going home. The big cross and the big Bible was coming to get her and she seemed sort of glad and sort of not. I thought I would die in that room of four beds without her and I knew Bozo had plans to move some other dumped kid in there with me. Roberta promised to write every day, which was really sweet of her because she couldn't read a lick so how could she write anybody. I would have drawn pictures and sent them to her but she never gave me her address. Little by little she faded. Her wet socks with the pink scalloped tops and her big serious-looking eyes—that's all I could catch when I tried to bring her to mind.

I was working behind the counter at the Howard Johnson's on the 35
Thruway just before the Kingston exit. Not a bad job. Kind of a long ride from Newburgh,° but okay once I got there. Mine was the second night shift—eleven to seven. Very light until a Greyhound checked in for breakfast around six-thirty. At that hour the sun was all the way clear of the hills behind the restaurant. The place looked better at night—more like shelter—but I loved it when the sun broke in, even if it did show all the cracks in the vinyl and the speckled floor looked dirty no matter what the mop boy did.

It was August and a bus crowd was just unloading. They would stand around a long while: going to the john, and looking at gifts and junk-for-sale machines, reluctant to sit down so soon. Even to eat. I was trying to fill the coffee pots and get them all situated on the electric burners when I saw her. She was sitting in a booth smoking a cigarette with two guys smothered in head and facial hair. Her own hair was so big and wild I could hardly see her face. But the eyes. I would know them anywhere. She had on a powder-blue halter and shorts outfit and earrings the size of bracelets. Talk about lipstick and eyebrow pencil. She made the big girls look like

Newburgh: A city of roughly 30,000 people located sixty miles north of Manhattan along the Hudson River. Newburgh was the site of race riots in the 1960s.

nuns. I couldn't get off the counter until seven o'clock, but I kept watching the booth in case they got up to leave before that. My replacement was on time for a change, so I counted and stacked my receipts as fast as I could and signed off. I walked over to the booth, smiling and wondering if she would remember me. Or even if she wanted to remember me. Maybe she didn't want to be reminded of St. Bonny's or to have anybody know she was ever there. I know I never talked about it to anybody.

I put my hands in my apron pockets and leaned against the back of the booth facing them.

"Roberta? Roberta Fisk?"

She looked up. "Yeah?"

"Twyla."

She squinted for a second and then said, "Wow."

"Remember me?"

"Sure. Hey. Wow."

"It's been a while," I said, and gave a smile to the two hairy guys.

"Yeah. Wow. You work here?"

"Yeah," I said. "I live in Newburgh."

"Newburgh? No kidding?" She laughed then a private laugh that included the guys but only the guys, and they laughed with her. What could I do but laugh too and wonder why I was standing there with my knees showing out from under that uniform. Without looking I could see the blue and white triangle on my head, my hair shapeless in a net, my ankles thick in white oxfords. Nothing could have been less sheer than my stockings. There was this silence that came down right after I laughed. A silence it was her turn to fill up. With introductions, maybe, to her boyfriends or an invitation to sit down and have a Coke. Instead she lit a cigarette off the one she'd just finished and said, "We're on our way to the Coast. He's got an appointment with Hendrix."

She gestured casually toward the boy next to her.

"Hendrix? Fantastic," I said. "Really fantastic. What's she doing now?"

Roberta coughed on her cigarette and the two guys rolled their eyes up at the ceiling.

"Hendrix. Jimi Hendrix, asshole. He's only the biggest—Oh, wow. Forget it."

I was dismissed without anyone saying goodbye, so I thought I would do it for her.

"How's your mother?" I asked.

Her grin cracked her whole face. She swallowed. "Fine," she said. "How's yours?"

"Pretty as a picture," I said and turned away. The backs of my knees were damp. Howard Johnson's really was a dump in the sunlight.

James is as comfortable as a house slipper. He liked my cooking and I liked his big loud family. They have lived in Newburgh all of their lives and talk about it the way people do who have always known a home. His grandmother is a porch swing older than his father and when they talk about streets and avenues and buildings they call them names they no longer have. They still call the A & P° Rico's because it stands on property once a mom and pop store owned by Mr. Rico. And they call the new community college Town Hall because it once was. My mother-in-law puts up jelly and cucumbers and buys butter wrapped in cloth from a dairy. James and his father talk about fishing and baseball and I can see them all together on the Hudson in a raggedy skiff. Half the population of Newburgh is on welfare now, but to my husband's family it was still some upstate paradise of a time long past. A time of ice houses and vegetable wagons, coal furnaces and children weeding gardens. When our son was born my mother-in-law gave me the crib blanket that had been hers.

But the town they remembered had changed. Something quick was in the air. Magnificent old houses, so ruined they had become shelter for squatters and rent risks, were bought and renovated. Smart IBM° people moved out of their suburbs back into the city and put shutters up and herb gardens in their backyards. A brochure came in the mail announcing the opening of a Food Emporium. Gourmet food it said—and listed items the rich IBM crowd would want. It was located in a new mall at the edge of town and I drove out to shop there one day—just to see. It was late in June. After the tulips were gone and the Queen Elizabeth roses were open everywhere. I trailed my cart along the aisle tossing in smoked oysters and Robert's sauce and things I knew would sit in my cupboard for years. Only when I found some Klondike ice cream bars did I feel less guilty about spending James's fireman's salary so foolishly. My father-in-law ate them with the same gusto little Joseph did.

Waiting in the check-out line I heard a voice say, "Twyla!"

The classical music piped over the aisles had affected me and the woman leaning toward me was dressed to kill. Diamonds on her hand, a smart white summer dress. "I'm Mrs. Benson," I said.

"Ho. Ho. The Big Bozo," she sang.

For a split second I didn't know what she was talking about. She had a bunch of asparagus and two cartons of fancy water.

"Roberta!"

"Right."

"For heaven's sake. Roberta."

"You look great," she said.

"So do you. Where are you? Here? In Newburgh?"

"Yes. Over in Annandale." °

A & P: Iconic grocery store chain that ceased operations in 2015 after a century and a half in business *IBM:* One of the first computer and technology companies and still among the most successful. *Annandale:* A more affluent town than Newburgh, forty miles north, Annandale-on-Hudson is home to Bard College.

I was opening my mouth to say more when the cashier called my attention to her empty counter.

"Meet you outside." Roberta pointed her finger and went into the express line.

I placed the groceries and kept myself from glancing around to check Roberta's progress. I remembered Howard Johnson's and looking for a chance to speak only to be greeted with a stingy "wow." But she was waiting for me and her huge hair was sleek now, smooth around a small, nicely shaped head. Shoes, dress, everything lovely and summery and rich. I was dying to know what happened to her, how she got from Jimi Hendrix to Annandale, a neighborhood full of doctors and IBM executives. Easy, I thought. Everything is so easy for them. They think they own the world.

"How long," I asked her. "How long have you been here?"

"A year. I got married to a man who lives here. And you, you're married too, right? Benson, you said."

"Yeah. James Benson."

"And is he nice?"

"Oh, is he nice?"

"Well, is he?" Roberta's eyes were steady as though she really meant the question and wanted an answer.

"He's wonderful, Roberta. Wonderful."

"So you're happy."

"Very."

"That's good," she said and nodded her head. "I always hoped you'd be happy. Any kids? I know you have kids."

"One. A boy. How about you?"

"Four."

"Four?"

She laughed. "Step kids. He's a widower."

"Oh."

"Got a minute? Let's have a coffee."

I thought about the Klondikes melting and the inconvenience of going all the way to my car and putting the bags in the trunk. Served me right for buying all that stuff I didn't need. Roberta was ahead of me.

"Put them in my car. It's right here."

And then I saw the dark blue limousine.

"You married a Chinaman?"

"No," she laughed. "He's the driver."

"Oh, my. If the Big Bozo could see you now."

We both giggled. Really giggled. Suddenly, in just a pulse beat, twenty years disappeared and all of it came rushing back. The big girls (whom we called gar girls—Roberta's misheard word for the evil stone faces described in a civics class) there dancing in the orchard, the ploppy mashed potatoes, the double weenies, the Spam with pineapple. We went into the coffee shop holding onto one another and I tried to think why we were glad to see each other this time and not before. Once, twelve years ago, we passed like strangers. A black girl and a white girl meeting in a Howard Johnson's on the road and having nothing to say. One in a blue and white triangle waitress hat—the other on her way to see Hendrix. Now we were behaving like sisters separated for much too long. Those four short months were nothing in time. Maybe it was the thing itself. Just being there, together. Two little girls who knew what nobody else in the world knew—how not to ask questions. How to believe what had to be believed. There was politeness in that reluctance and generosity as well. Is your mother sick too? No, she dances all night. Oh—and an understanding nod.

We sat in a booth by the window and fell into recollection like veterans.

"Did you ever learn to read?"

"Watch." She picked up the menu. "Special of the day. Cream of corn soup. Entrées. Two dots and a wriggly line. Quiche. Chef salad, scallops. . ."

I was laughing and applauding when the waitress came up.

"Remember the Easter baskets?"

"And how we tried to *introduce* them?"

"Your mother with that cross like two telephone poles."

"And yours with those tight slacks."

We laughed so loudly heads turned and made the laughter harder to suppress.

"What happened to the Jimi Hendrix date?"

Roberta made a blow-out sound with her lips.

"When he died I thought about you."

"Oh, you heard about him finally?"

"Finally. Come on, I was a small-town country waitress."

"And I was a small-town country dropout. God, were we wild. I still don't know how I got out of there alive."

"But you did."

"I did. I really did. Now I'm Mrs. Kenneth Norton."

"Sounds like a mouthful."

"It is."

"Servants and all?"

Roberta held up two fingers.

"Ow! What does he do?"

"Computers and stuff. What do I know?"

"I don't remember a hell of a lot from those days, but Lord, St. Bonny's is as clear as daylight. Remember Maggie? The day she fell down and those gar girls laughed at her?"

Roberta looked up from her salad and stared at me. "Maggie didn't fall," she said.

"Yes, she did. You remember."

"No, Twyla. They knocked her down. Those girls pushed her down and tore her clothes. In the orchard."

"I don't—that's not what happened."

"Sure it is. In the orchard. Remember how scared we were?"

"Wait a minute. I don't remember any of that."

"And Bozo was fired."

"You're crazy. She was there when I left. You left before me."

"I went back. You weren't there when they fired Bozo."

"What?"

"Twice. Once for a year when I was about ten, another for two months when I was fourteen. That's when I ran away."

"You ran away from St. Bonny's?"

"I had to. What do you want? Me dancing in that orchard?"

"Are you sure about Maggie?"

"Of course I'm sure. You've blocked it, Twyla. It happened. Those girls had behavior problems, you know."

"Didn't they, though. But why can't I remember the Maggie thing?"

"Believe me. It happened. And we were there."

"Who did you room with when you went back?" I asked her as if I would know her. The Maggie thing was troubling me.

"Creeps. They tickled themselves in the night."

My ears were itching and I wanted to go home suddenly. This was all very well but she couldn't just comb her hair, wash her face and pretend everything was hunky-dory. After the Howard Johnson's snub. And no apology. Nothing.

"Were you on dope or what that time at Howard Johnson's?" I tried to make my voice sound friendlier than I felt.

"Maybe, a little. I never did drugs much. Why?"

"I don't know; you acted sort of like you didn't want to know me then."

"Oh, Twyla, you know how it was in those days: black—white. You know how everything was."

But I didn't know. I thought it was just the opposite. Busloads of blacks and whites came into Howard Johnson's together. They roamed together then: students, musicians, lovers, protesters. You got to see everything at Howard Johnson's and blacks were very friendly with whites in those days. But sitting there with nothing on my plate but two hard tomato wedges wondering about the melting Klondikes it seemed childish remembering the slight. We went to her car, and with the help of the driver, got my stuff into my station wagon.

"We'll keep in touch this time," she said.

"Sure," I said. "Sure. Give me a call."

"I will," she said, and then just as I was sliding behind the wheel, she leaned into the window. "By the way. Your mother. Did she ever stop dancing?"

I shook my head. "No. Never."

Roberta nodded.

"And yours? Did she ever get well?"

She smiled a tiny sad smile. "No. She never did. Look, call me, okay?"

"Okay," I said, but I knew I wouldn't. Roberta had messed up my past somehow with that business about Maggie. I wouldn't forget a thing like that. Would I? 150

Strife came to us that fall. At least that's what the paper called it. Strife. Racial strife. The word made me think of a bird—a big shrieking bird out of 1,000,000,000 B.C. Flapping its wings and cawing. Its eye with no lid always bearing down on you. All day it screeched and at night it slept on the rooftops. It woke you in the morning and from the *Today* show to the eleven o'clock news it kept you an awful company. I couldn't figure it out from one day to the next. I knew I was supposed to feel something strong, but I didn't know what, and James wasn't any help. Joseph was on the list of kids to be transferred from the junior high school to another one at some far-out-of-the-way place and I thought it was a good thing until I heard it was a bad thing. I mean I didn't know. All the schools seemed dumps to me, and the fact that one was nicer looking didn't hold much weight. But the papers were full of it and then the kids began to get jumpy. In August, mind you. Schools weren't even open yet. I thought Joseph might be frightened to go over there, but he didn't seem scared so I forgot about it, until I found myself driving along Hudson Street out there by the school they were trying to integrate and saw a line of women marching. And who do you suppose was in line, big as life, holding a sign in front of her bigger than her mother's cross? MOTHERS HAVE RIGHTS TOO! it said.

I drove on, and then changed my mind. I circled the block, slowed down, and honked my horn.

Roberta looked over and when she saw me she waved. I didn't wave back, but I didn't move either. She handed her sign to another woman and came over to where I was parked.

"Hi."

"What are you doing?" 155

"Picketing. What's it look like?"

"What for?"

"What do you mean, 'What for?' They want to take my kids and send them out of the neighborhood. They don't want to go."

"So what if they go to another school? My boy's being bussed too, and I don't mind. Why should you?"

"It's not about us, Twyla. Me and you. It's about our kids." 160

"What's more *us* than that?"

"Well, it is a free country."

"Not yet, but it will be."

"What the hell does that mean? I'm not doing anything to you."

"You really think that?" 165

"I know it."

"I wonder what made me think you were different."

"I wonder what made me think you were different."

"Look at them," I said. "Just look. Who do they think they are? Swarming all over the place like they own it. And now they think they can decide where my child goes to school. Look at them, Roberta. They're Bozos."

170 Roberta turned around and looked at the women. Almost all of them were standing still now, waiting. Some were even edging toward us. Roberta looked at me out of some refrigerator behind her eyes. "No, they're not. They're just mothers."

"And what am I? Swiss cheese?"

"I used to curl your hair."

"I hated your hands in my hair."

The women were moving. Our faces looked mean to them of course and they looked as though they could not wait to throw themselves in front of a police car, or better yet, into my car and drag me away by my ankles. Now they surrounded my car and gently, gently began to rock it. I swayed back and forth like a sideways yo-yo. Automatically I reached for Roberta, like the old days in the orchard when they saw us watching them and we had to get out of there, and if one of us fell the other pulled her up and if one of us was caught the other stayed to kick and scratch, and neither would leave the other behind. My arm shot out of the car window but no receiving hand was there. Roberta was looking at me sway from side to side in the car and her face was still. My purse slid from the car seat down under the dashboard. The four policemen who had been drinking Tab in their car finally got the message and strolled over, forcing their way through the women. Quietly, firmly they spoke. "Okay, ladies. Back in line or off the streets."

175 Some of them went away willingly; others had to be urged away from the car doors and the hood. Roberta didn't move. She was looking steadily at me. I was fumbling to turn on the ignition, which wouldn't catch because the gearshift was still in drive. The seats of the car were a mess because the swaying had thrown my grocery coupons all over it and my purse was sprawled on the floor.

"Maybe I am different now, Twyla. But you're not. You're the same little state kid who kicked a poor old black lady when she was down on the ground. You kicked a black lady and you have the nerve to call me a bigot."

The coupons were everywhere and the guts of my purse were bunched under the dashboard. What was she saying? Black? Maggie wasn't black.

"She wasn't black," I said.

"Like hell she wasn't, and you kicked her. We both did. You kicked a black lady who couldn't even scream."

180 "Liar!"

"You're the liar! Why don't you just go on home and leave us alone, huh?"

She turned away and I skidded away from the curb.

The next morning I went into the garage and cut the side out of the carton our portable TV had come in. It wasn't nearly big enough, but after a while I had a decent sign: red spray-painted letters on a white background—AND SO DO CHILDREN ****. I meant just to go down to the school and tack it up somewhere so those cows on the picket line across the street could see it, but when I got there, some ten or so others had already assembled—protesting the cows across the street. Police permits and everything. I got in line and we strutted in time on our side while Roberta's group strutted on theirs. That first day we were all dignified, pretending the other side didn't exist. The second day there was name calling and finger gestures. But that was about all. People changed signs from time to time, but Roberta never did and neither did I. Actually my sign didn't make sense without Roberta's. "And so do children what?" one of the women on my side asked me. Have rights, I said, as though it was obvious.

Roberta didn't acknowledge my presence in any way and I got to thinking maybe she didn't know I was there. I began to pace myself in the line, jostling people one minute and lagging behind the next, so Roberta and I could reach the end of our respective lines at the same time and there would be a moment in our tum when we would face each other. Still, I couldn't tell whether she saw me and knew my sign was for her. The next day I went early before we were scheduled to assemble. I waited until she got there before I exposed my new creation. As soon as she hoisted her MOTHERS HAVE RIGHTS TOO I began to wave my new one, which said, HOW WOULD YOU KNOW? I know she saw that one, but I had gotten addicted now. My signs got crazier each day, and the women on my side decided that I was a kook. They couldn't make heads or tails out of my brilliant screaming posters.

I brought a painted sign in queenly red with huge black letters that said, IS YOUR MOTHER WELL? Roberta took her lunch break and didn't come back for the rest of the day or any day after. Two days later I stopped going too and couldn't have been missed because nobody understood my signs anyway.

It was a nasty six weeks. Classes were suspended and Joseph didn't go to anybody's school until October. The children—everybody's children—soon got bored with that extended vacation they thought was going to be so great. They looked at TV until their eyes flattened. I spent a couple of mornings tutoring my son, as the other mothers said we should. Twice I opened a text from last year that he had never turned in. Twice he yawned in my face. Other mothers organized living room sessions so the kids would keep up. None of the kids could concentrate so they drifted back to *The Price Is Right* and *The Brady Bunch*. When the school finally opened there were fights once or twice and some sirens roared through the streets every once in a while. There were a lot of photographers from Albany. And just when ABC was about to send up a news crew, the kids settled down like nothing in the world had happened. Joseph hung my HOW WOULD YOU KNOW? sign in his bedroom. I don't know what became of AND SO DO CHILDREN ****. I think my father-in-law cleaned some fish

could, if she wanted, wear green eye-shadow around one eye, a straight pin in her nostril, yellow slacks, and purple shoes, no matter. And then to slip off into death, the blind man's hand on her hand, his blind eyes streaming tears—I'm imagining now—her last thought maybe this: that he never even knew what she looked like, and she on an express to the grave. Robert was left with a small insurance policy and a half of a twenty-peso Mexican coin. The other half of the coin went into the box with her. Pathetic.

So when the time rolled around, my wife went to the depot to pick him up. With nothing to do but wait—sure, I blamed him for that—I was having a drink and watching the TV when I heard the car pull into the drive. I got up from the sofa with my drink and went to the window to have a look.

I saw my wife laughing as she parked the car. I saw her get out of the car and shut the door. She was still wearing a smile. Just amazing. She went around to the other side of the car to where the blind man was already starting to get out. This blind man, feature this, he was wearing a full beard! A beard on a blind man! Too much, I say. The blind man reached into the backseat and dragged out a suitcase. My wife took his arm, shut the car door, and, talking all the way, moved him down the drive and then up the steps to the front porch. I turned off the TV. I finished my drink, rinsed the glass, dried my hands. Then I went to the door.

My wife said, "I want you to meet Robert. Robert, this is my husband. I've told you all about him." She was beaming. She had this blind man by his coat sleeve.

The blind man let go of his suitcase and up came his hand.

I took it. He squeezed hard, held my hand, and then he let it go.

"I feel like we've already met," he boomed.

"Likewise," I said. I didn't know what else to say. Then I said, "Welcome. I've heard a lot about you." We began to move then, a little group, from the porch into the living room, my wife guiding him by the arm. The blind man was carrying his suitcase in his other hand. My wife said things like, "To your left here, Robert. That's right. Now watch it, there's a chair. That's it. Sit down right here. This is the sofa. We just bought this sofa two weeks ago."

I started to say something about the old sofa. I'd liked that old sofa. But I didn't say anything. Then I wanted to say something else, small-talk, about the scenic ride along the Hudson. How going *to* New York, you should sit on the right-hand side of the train, and coming *from* New York, the left-hand side.

"Did you have a good train ride?" I said. "Which side of the train did you sit on, by the way?"

"What a question, which side!" my wife said. "What's it matter which side?" she said.

"I just asked," I said.

"Right side," the blind man said. "I hadn't been on a train in nearly forty years. Not since I was a kid. With my folks. That's been a long time. I'd nearly forgotten the sensation. I have winter in my beard now," he said. "So I've been told, anyway. Do I look distinguished, my dear?" the blind man said to my wife.

"You look distinguished, Robert," she said. "Robert," she said. "Robert, it's just so good to see you."

My wife finally took her eyes off the blind man and looked at me. I had the feeling she didn't like what she saw. I shrugged.

I've never met, or personally known, anyone who was blind. This blind man was late forties, a heavy-set, balding man with stooped shoulders, as if he carried a great weight there. He wore brown slacks, brown shoes, a light-brown shirt, a tie, a sports coat. Spiffy. He also had this full beard. But he didn't use a cane and he didn't wear dark glasses. I'd always thought dark glasses were a must for the blind. Fact was, I wished he had a pair. At first glance, his eyes looked like anyone else's eyes. But if you looked close, there was something different about them. Too much white in the iris, for one thing, and the pupils seemed to move around in the sockets without his knowing it or being able to stop it. Creepy. As I stared at his face, I saw the left pupil turn in toward his nose while the other made an effort to keep in one place. But it was only an effort, for that eye was on the roam without his knowing it or wanting it to be.

I said, "Let me get you a drink. What's your pleasure? We have a little of everything. It's one of our pastimes."

"Bub, I'm a Scotch man myself," he said fast enough in this big voice.

"Right," I said. Bub! "Sure you are. I knew it."

He let his fingers touch his suitcase, which was sitting alongside the sofa. He was taking his bearings. I didn't blame him for that.

"I'll move that up to your room," my wife said.

"No, that's fine," the blind man said loudly. "It can go up when I go up."

"A little water with the Scotch?" I said.

"Very little," he said.

"I knew it," I said.

He said, "Just a tad. The Irish actor, Barry Fitzgerald? I'm like that fellow. When I drink water, Fitzgerald said, I drink water. When I drink whiskey, I drink whiskey." My wife laughed. The blind man brought his hand up under his beard. He lifted his beard slowly and let it drop.

I did the drinks, three big glasses of Scotch with a splash of water in each. Then we made ourselves comfortable and talked about Robert's travels. First the long flight from the West Coast to Connecticut, we covered that. Then from Connecticut up here by train. We had another drink concerning that leg of the trip.

I remembered having read somewhere that the blind didn't smoke because, as speculation had it, they couldn't see the smoke they exhaled.

I thought I knew that much and that much only about blind people. But this blind man smoked his cigarette down to the nubbin and then lit another one. This blind man filled his ashtray and my wife emptied it.

When we sat down at the table for dinner, we had another drink. My wife heaped Robert's plate with cube steak, scalloped potatoes, green beans. I buttered him up two slices of bread. I said, "Here's bread and butter for you." I swallowed some of my drink. "Now let us pray," I said, and the blind man lowered his head. My wife looked at me, her mouth agape. "Pray the phone won't ring and the food doesn't get cold," I said.

We dug in. We ate everything there was to eat on the table. We 45
ate like there was no tomorrow. We didn't talk. We ate. We scarfed. We grazed that table. We were into serious eating. The blind man had right away located his foods, he knew just where everything was on his plate. I watched with admiration as he used his knife and fork on the meat. He'd cut two pieces of meat, fork the meat into his mouth, and then go all out for the scalloped potatoes, the beans next, and then he'd tear off a hunk of buttered bread and eat that. He'd follow this up with a big drink of milk. It didn't seem to bother him to use his fingers once in a while, either.

We finished everything, including half a strawberry pie. For a few moments, we sat as if stunned. Sweat beaded on our faces. Finally, we got up from the table and left the dirty plates. We didn't look back. We took ourselves into the living room and sank into our places again. Robert and my wife sat on the sofa. I took the big chair. We had us two or three more drinks while they talked about the major things that had come to pass for them in the past ten years. For the most part, I just listened. Now and then I joined in. I didn't want him to think I'd left the room, and I didn't want her to think I was feeling left out. They talked of things that had happened to them—to them!—these past ten years. I waited in vain to hear my name on my wife's sweet lips: "And then my dear husband came into my life"—something like that. But I heard nothing of the sort. More talk of Robert. Robert had done a little of everything, it seemed, a regular blind jack-of-all-trades. But most recently he and his wife had had an Amway distributorship, from which, I gathered, they'd earned their living, such as it was. The blind man was also a ham radio operator. He talked in his loud voice about conversations he'd had with fellow operators in Guam, in the Philippines, in Alaska, and even in Tahiti. He said he'd have a lot of friends there if he ever wanted to go visit those places. From time to time, he'd turn his blind face toward me, put his hand under his beard, ask me something. How long had I been in my present position? (Three years.) Did I like my work? (I didn't.) Was I going to stay with it? (What were the options?) Finally, when I thought he was beginning to run down, I got up and turned on the TV.

My wife looked at me with irritation. She was heading toward a boil. Then she looked at the blind man and said, "Robert, do you have a TV?"

The blind man said, "My dear, I have two TVs. I have a color set and a black-and-white thing, an old relic. It's funny, but if I turn the TV on, and I'm always turning it on, I turn on the color set. It's funny, don't you think?"

I didn't know what to say to that. I had absolutely nothing to say to that. No opinion. So I watched the news program and tried to listen to what the announcer was saying.

"This is a color TV," the blind man said. "Don't ask me how, but I 50
can tell."

"We traded up a while ago," I said.

The blind man had another taste of his drink. He lifted his beard, sniffed it, and let it fall. He leaned forward on the sofa. He positioned his ashtray on the coffee table, then put the lighter to his cigarette. He leaned back on the sofa and crossed his legs at the ankles.

My wife covered her mouth, and then she yawned. She stretched. She said, "I think I'll go upstairs and put on my robe. I think I'll change into something else. Robert, you make yourself comfortable," she said.

"I'm comfortable," the blind man said.

"I want you to feel comfortable in this house," she said. 55

"I am comfortable," the blind man said.

After she'd left the room, he and I listened to the weather report and then to the sports roundup. By that time, she'd been gone so long I didn't know if she was going to come back. I thought she might have gone to bed. I wished she'd come back downstairs. I didn't want to be left alone with a blind man. I asked him if he wanted another drink, and he said sure. Then I asked if he wanted to smoke some dope with me. I said I'd just rolled a number. I hadn't, but I planned to do so in about two shakes.

"I'll try some with you," he said.

"Damm right," I said. "That's the stuff."

I got our drinks and sat down on the sofa with him. Then I rolled 60
us two fat numbers. I lit one and passed it. I brought it to his fingers. He took it and inhaled.

"Hold it as long as you can," I said. I could tell he didn't know the first thing.

My wife came back downstairs wearing her pink robe and her pink slippers.

"What do I smell?" she said.

"We thought we'd have us some cannabis," I said.

My wife gave me a savage look. Then she looked at the blind man 65
and said, "Robert, I didn't know you smoked."

He said, "I do now, my dear. There's a first time for everything. But I don't feel anything yet."

"This stuff is pretty mellow," I said. "This stuff is mild. It's dope you can reason with," I said. "It doesn't mess you up."

"Not much it doesn't, bub," he said, and laughed.

My wife sat on the sofa between the blind man and me. I passed her the number. She took it and toked and then passed it back to me. "Which way is this going?" she said. Then she said, "I shouldn't be smoking this. I can hardly keep my eyes open as it is. That dinner did me in. I shouldn't have eaten so much."

"It was the strawberry pie," the blind man said. "That's what did it," he said, and he laughed his big laugh. Then he shook his head.

"There's more strawberry pie," I said.

"Do you want some more, Robert?" my wife said.

"Maybe in a little while," he said.

We gave our attention to the TV. My wife yawned again. She said, "Your bed is made up when you feel like going to bed, Robert. I know you must have had a long day. When you're ready to go to bed, say so." She pulled his arm. "Robert?"

He came to and said, "I've had a real nice time. This beats tapes, doesn't it?"

I said, "Coming at you," and I put the number between his fingers. He inhaled, held the smoke, and then let it go. It was like he'd been doing it since he was nine years old.

"Thanks, bub," he said. "But I think this is all for me. I think I'm beginning to feel it," he said. He held the burning roach out for my wife.

"Same here," she said. "Ditto. Me, too." She took the roach and passed it to me. "I may just sit here for a while between you two guys with my eyes closed. But don't let me bother you, okay? Either one of you. If it bothers you, say so. Otherwise, I may just sit here with my eyes closed until you're ready to go to bed," she said. "Your bed's made up, Robert, when you're ready. It's right next to our room at the top of the stairs. We'll show you up when you're ready. You wake me up now, you guys, if I fall asleep." She said that and then she closed her eyes and went to sleep.

The news program ended. I got up and changed the channel. I sat back down on the sofa. I wished my wife hadn't pooped out. Her head lay across the back of the sofa, her mouth open. She'd turned so that her robe slipped away from her legs, exposing a juicy thigh. I reached to draw her robe back over her, and it was then that I glanced at the blind man. What the hell! I flipped the robe open again.

"You say when you want some strawberry pie," I said.

"I will," he said.

I said, "Are you tired? Do you want me to take you up to your bed? Are you ready to hit the hay?"

"Not yet," he said. "No, I'll stay up with you, bub. If that's all right. I'll stay up until you're ready to turn in. We haven't had a chance to talk. Know what I mean? I feel like me and her monopolized the evening." He lifted his beard and he let it fall. He picked up his cigarettes and his lighter.

"That's all right," I said. Then I said, "I'm glad for the company."

And I guess I was. Every night I smoked dope and stayed up as long 85
as I could before I fell asleep. My wife and I hardly ever went to bed at the same time. When I did go to sleep, I had these dreams. Sometimes I'd wake up from one of them, my heart going crazy.

Something about the church and the Middle Ages was on the TV. Not your run-of-the-mill TV fare. I wanted to watch something else. I turned to the other channels. But there was nothing on them, either. So I turned back to the first channel and apologized.

"Bub, it's all right," the blind man said. "It's fine with me. Whatever you want to watch is okay. I'm always learning something. Learning never ends. It won't hurt me to learn something tonight. I got ears," he said.

We didn't say anything for a time. He was leaning forward with his head turned at me, his right ear aimed in the direction of the set. Very disconcerting. Now and then his eyelids drooped and then they snapped open again. Now and then he put his fingers into his beard and tugged, like he was thinking about something he was hearing on the television.

On the screen, a group of men wearing cowls was being set upon and tormented by men dressed in skeleton costumes and men dressed as devils. The men dressed as devils wore devil masks, horns, and long tails. This pageant was part of a procession. The Englishman who was narrating the thing said it took place in Spain once a year. I tried to explain to the blind man what was happening.

"Skeletons," he said. "I know about skeletons," he said, and he nodded. 90

The TV showed this one cathedral. Then there was a long, slow look at another one. Finally, the picture switched to the famous one in Paris, with its flying buttresses and its spires reaching up to the clouds. The camera pulled away to show the whole of the cathedral rising above the skyline.

There were times when the Englishman who was telling the thing would shut up, would simply let the camera move around the cathedrals. Or else the camera would tour the countryside, men in fields walking behind oxen. I waited as long as I could. Then I felt I had to say something. I said, "They're showing the outside of this cathedral now. Gargoyles. Little statues carved to look like monsters. Now I guess they're in Italy. Yeah, they're in Italy. There's paintings on the walls of this one church."

"Are those fresco paintings, bub?" he asked, and he sipped from his drink.

I reached for my glass. But it was empty. I tried to remember what I could remember. "You're asking me are those frescoes?" I said. "That's a good question. I don't know."

The camera moved to a cathedral outside Lisbon. The differences 95
in the Portuguese cathedral compared with the French and Italian were not that great. But they were there. Mostly the interior stuff. Then something occurred to me, and I said, "Something has occurred to me. Do you

have any idea what a cathedral is? What they look like, that is? Do you follow me? If somebody says cathedral to you, do you have any notion what they're talking about? Do you know the difference between that and a Baptist church, say?"

He let the smoke dribble from his mouth. "I know they took hundreds of workers fifty or a hundred years to build," he said. "I just heard the man say that, of course. I know generations of the same families worked on a cathedral. I heard him say that, too. The men who began their life's work on them, they never lived to see the completion of their work. In that wise, bub, they're no different from the rest of us, right?" He laughed. Then his eyelids drooped again. His head nodded. He seemed to be snoozing. Maybe he was imagining himself in Portugal. The TV was showing another cathedral now. This one was in Germany. The Englishman's voice droned on. "Cathedrals," the blind man said. He sat up and rolled his head back and forth. "If you want the truth, bub, that's about all I know. What I just said. What I heard him say. But maybe you could describe one to me? I wish you'd do it. I'd like that. If you want to know, I really don't have a good idea."

I stared hard at the shot of the cathedral on the TV. How could I even begin to describe it? But say my life depended on it. Say my life was being threatened by an insane guy who said I had to do it or else.

I stared some more at the cathedral before the picture flipped off into the countryside. There was no use. I turned to the blind man and said, "To begin with, they're very tall." I was looking around the room for clues. "They reach way up. Up and up. Toward the sky. They're so big, some of them, they have to have these supports. To help hold them up, so to speak. These supports are called buttresses. They remind me of viaducts, for some reason. But maybe you don't know viaducts, either? Sometimes the cathedrals have devils and such carved into the front. Sometimes lords and ladies. Don't ask me why this is," I said.

He was nodding. The whole upper part of his body seemed to be moving back and forth.

"I'm not doing so good, am I?" I said.

He stopped nodding and leaned forward on the edge of the sofa. As he listened to me, he was running his fingers through his beard. I wasn't getting through to him, I could see that. But he waited for me to go on just the same. He nodded, like he was trying to encourage me. I tried to think what else to say. "They're really big," I said. "They're massive. They're built of stone. Marble, too, sometimes. In those olden days, when they built cathedrals, men wanted to be close to God. In those olden days, God was an important part of everyone's life. You could tell this from their cathedral-building. I'm sorry," I said, "but it looks like that's the best I can do for you. I'm just no good at it."

"That's all right, bub," the blind man said. "Hey, listen. I hope you don't mind my asking you. Can I ask you something? Let me ask you a simple question, yes or no. I'm just curious and there's no offense. You're my host. But let me ask if you are in any way religious? You don't mind my asking?"

I shook my head. He couldn't see that, though. A wink is the same as a nod to a blind man. "I guess I don't believe in it. In anything. Sometimes it's hard. You know what I'm saying?"

"Sure, I do," he said.

"Right," I said. 105

The Englishman was still holding forth. My wife sighed in her sleep. She drew a long breath and went on with her sleeping.

"You'll have to forgive me," I said. "But I can't tell you what a cathedral looks like. It just isn't in me to do it. I can't do any more than I've done."

The blind man sat very still, his head down, as he listened to me.

I said, "The truth is, cathedrals don't mean anything special to me. Nothing. Cathedrals. They're something to look at on late-night TV. That's all they are."

It was then that the blind man cleared his throat. He brought some- 110
thing up. He took a handkerchief from his back pocket. Then he said, "I get it, bub. It's okay. It happens. Don't worry about it," he said. "Hey, listen to me. Will you do me a favor? I got an idea. Why don't you find us some heavy paper? And a pen. We'll do something. We'll draw one together. Get us a pen and some heavy paper. Go on, bub, get the stuff," he said.

So I went upstairs. My legs felt like they didn't have any strength in them. They felt like they did after I'd done some running. In my wife's room I looked around. I found some ballpoints in a little basket on her table. And then I tried to think where to look for the kind of paper he was talking about.

Downstairs, in the kitchen, I found a shopping bag with onion skins in the bottom of the bag. I emptied the bag and shook it. I brought it into the living room and sat down with it near his legs. I moved some things, smoothed the wrinkles from the bag, spread it out on the coffee table.

The blind man got down from the sofa and sat next to me on the carpet.

He ran his fingers over the paper. He went up and down the sides of the paper. The edges, even the edges. He fingered the corners.

"All right," he said. "All right, let's do her." 115

He found my hand, the hand with the pen. He closed his hand over my hand. "Go ahead, bub, draw," he said. "Draw. You'll see. I'll follow along with you. It'll be okay. Just begin now like I'm telling you. You'll see. Draw," the blind man said.

So I began. First I drew a box that looked like a house. It could have been the house I lived in. Then I put a roof on it. At either end of the roof, I drew spires. Crazy.

"Swell," he said. "Terrific. You're doing fine," he said. "Never thought anything like this could happen in your lifetime, did you, bub? Well, it's a strange life, we all know that. Go on now. Keep it up."

I put in windows with arches. I drew flying buttresses. I hung great doors. I couldn't stop. The TV station went off the air. I put down the pen and closed and opened my fingers. The blind man felt around over the paper. He moved the tips of his fingers over the paper, all over what I had drawn, and he nodded.

"Doing fine," the blind man said. 120

I took up the pen again, and he found my hand. I kept at it. I'm no artist. But I kept drawing just the same.

My wife opened up her eyes and gazed at us. She sat up on the sofa, her robe hanging open. She said, "What are you doing? Tell me, I want to know."

I didn't answer her.

The blind man said, "We're drawing a cathedral. Me and him are working on it. Press hard," he said to me. "That's right. That's good," he said. "Sure. You got it, bub, I can tell. You didn't think you could. But you can, can't you? You're cooking with gas now. You know what I'm saying? We're going to really have us something here in a minute. How's the old arm?" he said. "Put some people in there now. What's a cathedral without people?"

My wife said, "What's going on? Robert, what are you doing? What's 125
going on?"

"It's all right," he said to her. "Close your eyes now," the blind man said to me.

I did it. I closed them just like he said.

"Are they closed?" he said. "Don't fudge."

"They're closed," I said.

"Keep them that way," he said. He said, "Don't stop now. Draw." 130

So we kept on with it. His fingers rode my fingers as my hand went over the paper. It was like nothing else in my life up to now.

Then he said, "I think that's it. I think you got it," he said. "Take a look. What do you think?"

But I had my eyes closed. I thought I'd keep them that way for a little longer. I thought it was something I ought to do.

"Well?" he said. "Are you looking?"

My eyes were still closed. I was in my house. I knew that. But I didn't 135
feel like I was inside anything.

"It's really something," I said.

Questions

1. What details in "Cathedral" make clear the narrator's initial attitude toward blind people? What hints does the author give about the reasons for this attitude? At what point in the story do the narrator's preconceptions about blind people start to change?

2. For what reason does the wife keep asking Robert if he'd like to go to bed (paragraphs 74–78)? What motivates the narrator to make the same suggestion in paragraph 82? What effect does Robert's reply have on the narrator?
3. What makes the narrator start explaining what he's seeing on television?
4. How does the point of view contribute to the effectiveness of the story?
5. At the end, the narrator has an epiphany. How would you describe it?
6. Would you describe the narrator as an antihero? Use specific details from the story to back up your response.
7. Is the wife a flat or a round character? What about Robert? Support your conclusion about each of them.
8. In a good story, a character doesn't suddenly become a completely different sort of person. Find details early in the story that show the narrator's more sensitive side and thus help to make his development credible and persuasive.

WRITING *effectively*

THINKING ABOUT CHARACTER

Although readers usually consider plot the central element of fiction, writers usually remark that stories begin with characters.

- **Identify the most important character.** The central character is the one who must deal with the plot complications and the central crisis of the story. The choices made by this character communicate his or her attitudes as well as the story's themes.
- **Consider the ways the characters' personalities and values are communicated.** Note that the way characters speak can immediately reveal important things about their personalities, beliefs, and behavior. A single line of dialogue can tell the audience a great deal.
- **Consider how the story's action grows out of its central character.** A story's action usually grows out of the personality of its protagonist and the situation he or she faces. As novelist Phyllis Bottome observed, "If a writer is true to his characters, they will give him his plot."

CHECKLIST: Writing About Character

- ☐ Who is the main character or protagonist of the story?
- ☐ Make a quick list of the character's physical, mental, moral, or behavioral traits. Which seem especially significant to the action of the story?

- ☐ Does the main character have an antagonist in the story? How do they differ?
- ☐ Does the way the protagonist speaks reveal anything about his or her personality?
- ☐ If the story is told in the first person, what is revealed about how the protagonist views his or her surroundings?
- ☐ What is the character's primary motivation? Does this motivation seem reasonable to you?
- ☐ Does the protagonist fully understand his or her motivations?
- ☐ In what ways is the protagonist changed or tested by the events of the story?

TOPICS FOR WRITING ON CHARACTER

1. Choose a story with a dynamic protagonist. (See the beginning of this chapter for a discussion of dynamic characters.) Write an essay exploring how that character evolves over the course of the story, providing evidence from the story to back up your argument. Some good story choices might be Faulkner's "Barn Burning" (Chapter 5), Carver's "Cathedral," Morrison's "Recitatif," and Wolff's "Bullet in the Brain."
2. Using a story from this book, write a short essay that explains why a protagonist takes a crucial life-changing action. What motivates this character to do something that seems bold or surprising? You might consider:
   - What motivates the narrator to overcome his instinctive antipathy to the blind man in "Cathedral"?
   - Why does Anders provoke the bank robber in "Bullet in the Brain"?
3. Choose a minor character from any of the stories in this book, and write briefly on what the story reveals about that person, reading closely for even the smallest of details. Is he or she a stock character? Why or why not?
4. Choose a story in which the main character has an obvious antagonist, such as "Cathedral" or "A & P" (Chapter 1). What role does this second character play in bringing the protagonist to a new awareness of life?
5. Choose a favorite character from a television show you watch regularly. What details are provided (either in the show's dialogue or in its visuals) to communicate the personality of this character? Would you say this person is a stock character or a rounded one? Write a brief essay making a case for your position.
6. Browse through magazines and newspapers to find a picture of a person you can't identify. Cut out the picture. Create a character based on the picture. As many writers do, make a list of characteristics, from the major (her life's ambition) to the minor (his favorite breakfast cereal). As you build your list, make sure your details add up to a rounded character.

▸ TERMS FOR *review*

Characterization ▸ The techniques a writer uses to create, reveal, or develop the characters in a narrative.

Character description ▸ An aspect of characterization through which the author overtly relates either physical or mental traits of a character. This description is almost invariably a sign of what lurks beneath the surface of the character.

Character development ▸ The process by which a character is introduced, advanced, and possibly transformed in a story.

Motivation ▸ What a character in a narrative wants; the reasons an author provides for a character's actions. Motivation can be either explicit (the reasons are specifically stated in a story) or implicit (the reasons are only hinted at or partially revealed).

Flat (or **static**) **character** ▸ A term coined by English novelist E. M. Forster to describe a character with only one outstanding trait. Flat characters are rarely the central characters in a narrative and stay the same throughout a story.

Round (or **dynamic**) **character** ▸ A term also coined by Forster to describe a complex character who is presented in depth in a narrative. Round characters are those who change significantly during the course of a narrative or whose full personalities are revealed gradually throughout the story.

Stock character ▸ A common or stereotypical character. Examples of stock characters are the mad scientist, the battle-scarred veteran, and the strong but silent cowboy.

Hero ▸ The central character in a narrative. The term *hero* often implies positive moral attributes.

Antihero ▸ A protagonist who is lacking in one or more of the conventional qualities attributed to a hero. Instead of being dignified, brave, idealistic, or purposeful, for instance, the antihero may be buffoonish, cowardly, self-interested, or weak.

4 SETTING

What You Will Learn in This Chapter

- To understand and define *setting*
- To identify the elements of setting—including place, time, weather, and atmosphere
- To describe literary modes such as *historical fiction*, *regionalism*, and *naturalism*
- To analyze the role of setting in a story

ELEMENTS OF SETTING

By the **setting** of a story, we mean its time and place. Yet often, in an effective short story, setting may figure as more than mere background or underpinning. It can make things happen. It can prompt characters to act, bring them to realizations, or cause them to reveal their inmost natures.

Place

Of course, the idea of setting includes the physical environment of a story: a house, a street, a city, a landscape, a region. *Where* a story takes place is often called its **locale**. Physical places mattered so greatly to French novelist Honoré de Balzac that sometimes, before writing a story set in a particular town, he would visit that town, select a few houses, and describe them in detail, down to their very smells.

Time

In addition to place, setting may crucially involve the *time* of the story—the hour, year, or century. It might matter greatly that a story takes place at dawn, or on the day of the first moon landing. When we begin to read a historical novel, we are soon made aware that we aren't reading about modern-day life. In *The Scarlet Letter*, nineteenth-century author Nathaniel Hawthorne, by a long introduction and a vivid opening scene at a prison door, prepares us to witness events in the Puritan community of Boston in the seventeenth century. This setting, together with scenes of Puritan times we recall from high school history, helps us understand what happens in the novel. We can appreciate the shocked agitation in town when a woman is accused of adultery: she has given illegitimate birth. Such an event might seem common today, but in the stern, God-fearing New England Puritan community, it was a flagrant defiance of church and state, which were all-powerful (and were all one).

That reader will make no sense of *The Scarlet Letter* who ignores its setting—if it is even possible to ignore the historical setting. The fact that Hawthorne's novel takes place in a time remote from our own leads us to expect different customs and different attitudes. Some critics and teachers regard the setting of a story as its whole society, including the beliefs and assumptions of its characters.

Weather

Besides time and place, setting may also include the weather, which in some stories is a crucial element. Climate seems as substantial as any character in William Faulkner's story "Dry September." After sixty-two rainless days, a long unbroken spell of late-summer heat has frayed every nerve in a small town and caused the main character, a hotheaded white supremacist, to feel more and more irritated. The weather, someone remarks, is "enough to make a man do anything." When a false report circulates that a white woman has been raped by a black man, the rumor, like a match flung into a dry field, ignites rage and provokes a lynching. To fully understand the story we have to recognize its locale, a small town in Mississippi in the 1930s during an infernal heat wave.

Atmosphere

Atmosphere is the dominant mood or feeling that pervades all parts of a literary work. Atmosphere refers to the total effect conveyed by the author's use of language, images, and physical setting. But as the term *atmosphere* suggests, aspects of the physical setting (place, time, and weather) are usually essential elements in achieving the author's intention. In some stories, a writer will seem to draw a setting mainly to evoke atmosphere. In such a story, setting starts us feeling whatever the storyteller would have us feel. In "The Tell-Tale Heart," Poe's having set the action in an old, dark, lantern-lit house greatly contributes to our sense of unease—and so helps the story's effectiveness.

HISTORICAL FICTION

One example of how time can become a major element of setting is in **historical fiction**, where the author tries to recreate a faithful picture of daily life in another time and place. The historical period might be long ago, such as ancient Rome in Robert Graves's novel *I, Claudius* (1934), or it may be more recent, as in the setting of early twentieth-century Britain in Ian McEwan's *Atonement* (2001). Historical fiction sometimes introduces well-known figures from the past. Thornton Wilder's *Ides of March* (1948) includes Julius Caesar and Cleopatra among its many characters. Ron Hansen's *Exiles* (2008) depicts the life of English poet Gerard Manley Hopkins. More often, historical fiction presents imaginary characters in a carefully reconstructed version of a particular period of the past. Part of the pleasure of reading this sort of fiction comes from experiencing the many details of another time, just as films carefully set in a particular historical moment, such as Ridley Scott's *Gladiator* (2000) and James Cameron's *Titanic* (1997), let us see meticulously recreated settings of another time and place.

REGIONALISM

Physical place is especially vital to a **regional writer**, who usually sets stories in one geographic area. Such a writer, often a native of the place, tries to bring it alive for readers who live elsewhere. William Faulkner, a distinguished regional writer, almost always set his novels and stories in his native Mississippi. Kate Chopin became known as a regional writer because she wrote about Louisiana in many of her short stories and in her novel *The Awakening*. Willa Cather, for her novels of frontier Nebraska, is often regarded as another outstanding regionalist (though she also set fiction in Quebec, the Southwest, and, in "Paul's Case" (Chapter 14), Pittsburgh and New York).

There is often something arbitrary, however, about calling an author a regional writer. The label sometimes has a political tinge; it means that the author describes an area outside the political and economic centers of a society. In a sense, we might think of James Joyce as a regional writer, in that all his fiction takes place in the city of Dublin, but instead we usually call him an Irish author.

As such writers show, a place can profoundly affect the character of someone who grew up in it. Willa Cather is fond of portraying strong-minded, independent women, such as the heroine of her novel *My Antonía*, strengthened in part by years of coping with the hardships of life on the wind-lashed prairie.

NATURALISM

Some writers consider the social and economic setting the most important element in the story. They present social environment as the determining factor in human behavior. Their approach is called **naturalism**—fiction of grim realism, in which the writer observes human characters like a scientist observing ants, seeing them as the products and victims of environment and heredity. Naturalism was first consciously developed in fiction in the late nineteenth century by French novelist Émile Zola. Important American naturalists include Jack London, Stephen Crane, and Theodore Dreiser. Dreiser's novel *The Financier* (1912) begins in a city setting. A young boy (who will grow up to be a ruthless industrialist) is watching a battle to the death between a lobster and a squid in a fish-market tank. Dented for the rest of his life by this grim scene, he decides that's exactly the way human society functions.

HOW SETTING CAN HARMONIZE WITH OTHER ELEMENTS OF A STORY

Setting usually operates subtly, and often, setting and character will reveal each other. Recall how Faulkner, at the start of "A Rose for Emily" (Chapter 2), depicts Emily Grierson's house, once handsome but now "an eyesore among eyesores" surrounded by gas stations. Still standing, refusing to yield its old-time horse-and-buggy splendor to the age of the automobile, the house in "its stubborn and coquettish decay" embodies the character of its owner. In John Steinbeck's "The Chrysanthemums" (Chapter 7), the story begins with a fog that has sealed off a valley from the rest of the world—a fog like the lid on a pot. That physical setting helps convey the isolation and loneliness of the protagonist's situation.

But be warned: you'll meet stories in which setting appears hardly to matter. In the Sufi fable "Death Has an Appointment in Samarra" (Chapter 1), all we need to be told about the setting is that it is an inn in Baghdad. In that brief fable, the inevitability of death is the point, not an exotic setting. In this chapter, though, you will meet four fine stories in which setting, for one reason or another, counts greatly. Without it, none of these stories could take place.

Kate Chopin

The Storm (1898)

Kate Chopin

Kate Chopin (1851–1904) was born Katherine O'Flaherty in St. Louis, the daughter of an Irish immigrant grown wealthy in retailing. On his death, young Kate was raised by her mother's family: aristocratic Creoles, descendants of the French and Spaniards who had colonized Louisiana. She received a convent schooling and at nineteen married Oscar Chopin, a Creole cotton broker from New Orleans. Later, the Chopins lived on a plantation near Cloutierville, Louisiana, a region whose varied people—Creoles, Cajuns, blacks—Kate Chopin was later to write about with loving care in Bayou Folk *(1894) and* A Night in Arcadie *(1897). The shock of her husband's sudden death in 1883, which left her with the raising of six children, seems to have plunged Kate Chopin into writing. She read and admired fine woman writers of her day, such as the Maine realist Sarah Orne Jewett. She also read Maupassant, Zola, and other new (and scandalous) French naturalist writers. She began to bring into American fiction some of their hard-eyed observation and their passion for telling unpleasant truths. Determined, in defiance of her times, frankly to show the sexual feelings of her characters, Chopin suffered from neglect and censorship. When her major novel,* The Awakening, *appeared in 1899, critics were outraged by her candid portrait of a woman who seeks sexual and professional independence. After causing such a literary scandal, Chopin was unable to get her later work published, and wrote little more before she died.* The Awakening *and many of her stories had to wait seven decades for a sympathetic audience.*

I

The leaves were so still that even Bibi thought it was going to rain. Bobinôt, who was accustomed to converse on terms of perfect equality with his little son, called the child's attention to certain somber clouds that were rolling with sinister intention from the west, accompanied by a sullen, threatening roar. They were at Friedheimer's store and decided to remain there till the storm had passed. They sat within the door on two empty kegs. Bibi was four years old and looked very wise.

"Mama'll be 'fraid, yes," he suggested with blinking eyes.

"She'll shut the house. Maybe she got Sylvie helpin' her this evenin'," Bobinôt responded reassuringly.

"No; she ent got Sylvie. Sylvie was helpin' her yistiday," piped Bibi.

Bobinôt arose and going across to the counter purchased a can of 5
shrimps, of which Calixta was very fond. Then he returned to his perch on the keg and sat stolidly holding the can of shrimps while the storm burst. It shook the wooden store and seemed to be ripping great furrows in the distant field. Bibi laid his little hand on his father's knee and was not afraid.

II

Calixta, at home, felt no uneasiness for their safety. She sat at a side window sewing furiously on a sewing machine. She was greatly occupied and did not notice the approaching storm. But she felt very warm and often stopped to mop her face on which the perspiration gathered in beads. She unfastened her white sacque at the throat. It began to grow dark, and suddenly realizing the situation she got up hurriedly and went about closing windows and doors.

Out on the small front gallery she had hung Bobinôt's Sunday clothes to air and she hastened out to gather them before the rain fell. As she stepped outside, Alcée Laballière rode in at the gate. She had not seen him very often since her marriage, and never alone. She stood there with Bobinôt's coat in her hands, and the big rain drops began to fall. Alcée rode his horse under the shelter of a side projection where the chickens had huddled and there were plows and a harrow piled up in the corner.

"May I come and wait on your gallery till the storm is over, Calixta?" he asked.

"Come 'long in, M'sieur Alcée."

His voice and her own startled her as if from a trance, and she seized 10
Bobinôt's vest. Alcée, mounting to the porch, grabbed the trousers and snatched Bibi's braided jacket that was about to be carried away by a sudden gust of wind. He expressed an intention to remain outside, but it was soon apparent that he might as well have been out in the open: the water beat in upon the boards in driving sheets, and he went inside, closing the door after him. It was even necessary to put something beneath the door to keep the water out.

"My! what a rain! It's good two years sence it rain' like that," exclaimed Calixta as she rolled up a piece of bagging and Alcée helped her to thrust it beneath the crack.

She was a little fuller of figure than five years before when she married; but she had lost nothing of her vivacity. Her blue eyes still retained their melting quality; and her yellow hair, dishevelled by the wind and rain, kinked more stubbornly than ever about her ears and temples.

The rain beat upon the low, shingled roof with a force and clatter that threatened to break an entrance and deluge them there. They were in the dining room—the sitting room—the general utility room. Adjoining was her bed room, with Bibi's couch along side her own. The door stood open, and the room with its white, monumental bed, its closed shutters, looked dim and mysterious.

Alcée flung himself into a rocker and Calixta nervously began to gather up from the floor the lengths of a cotton sheet which she had been sewing.

"If this keeps up, *Dieu sait*° if the levees goin' to stan' it!" she exclaimed. 15

"What have you got to do with the levees?"

"I got enough to do! An' there's Bobinôt with Bibi out in that storm—if he only didn' left Friedheimer's!"

"Let us hope, Calixta, that Bobinôt's got sense enough to come in out of a cyclone."

She went and stood at the window with a greatly disturbed look on her face. She wiped the frame that was clouded with moisture. It was stiflingly hot. Alcée got up and joined her at the window, looking over her shoulder. The rain was coming down in sheets obscuring the view of faroff cabins and enveloping the distant wood in a gray mist. The playing of the lightning was incessant. A bolt struck a tall chinaberry tree at the edge of the field. It filled all visible space with a blinding glare and the crash seemed to invade the very boards they stood upon.

Calixta put her hands to her eyes, and with a cry, staggered backward. Alcée's arm encircled her, and for an instant he drew her close and spasmodically to him. 20

"*Bonté!*"° she cried, releasing herself from his encircling arm and retreating from the window, "the house'll go next! If I only knew w'ere Bibi was!" She would not compose herself; she would not be seated. Alcée clasped her shoulders and looked into her face. The contact of her warm, palpitating body when he had unthinkingly drawn her into his arms, had aroused all the old-time infatuation and desire for her flesh.

"Calixta," he said, "don't be frightened. Nothing can happen. The house is too low to be struck, with so many tall trees standing about. There! aren't you going to be quiet? say, aren't you?" He pushed her hair back from her face that was warm and steaming. Her lips were as red and moist as pomegranate seed. Her white neck and a glimpse of her full, firm bosom disturbed him powerfully. As she glanced up at him the fear in her liquid blue eyes had given place to a drowsy gleam that unconsciously betrayed a sensuous desire. He looked down into her eyes and there was nothing for him to do but gather her lips in a kiss. It reminded him of Assumption.°

Dieu sait: French for "God only knows." *Bonté!*: Heavens! *Assumption:* a parish west of New Orleans.

"Do you remember—in Assumption, Calixta?" he asked in a low voice broken by passion. Oh! she remembered; for in Assumption he had kissed her and kissed and kissed her; until his senses would well nigh fail, and to save her he would resort to a desperate flight. If she was not an immaculate dove in those days, she was still inviolate; a passionate creature whose very defenselessness had made her defense, against which his honor forbade him to prevail. Now—well, now—her lips seemed in a manner free to be tasted, as well as her round, white throat and her whiter breasts.

They did not heed the crashing torrents, and the roar of the elements made her laugh as she lay in his arms. She was a revelation in that dim, mysterious chamber; as white as the couch she lay upon. Her firm, elastic flesh that was knowing for the first time its birthright, was like a creamy lily that the sun invites to contribute its breath and perfume to the undying life of the world.

The generous abundance of her passion, without guile or trickery, 25
was like a white flame which penetrated and found response in depths of his own sensuous nature that had never yet been reached.

When he touched her breasts they gave themselves up in quivering ecstasy, inviting his lips. Her mouth was a fountain of delight. And when he possessed her, they seemed to swoon together at the very borderland of life's mystery.

He stayed cushioned upon her, breathless, dazed, enervated, with his heart beating like a hammer upon her. With one hand she clasped his head, her lips lightly touching his forehead. The other hand stroked with a soothing rhythm his muscular shoulders.

The growl of the thunder was distant and passing away. The rain beat softly upon the shingles, inviting them to drowsiness and sleep. But they dared not yield.

The rain was over; and the sun was turning the glistening green world into a palace of gems. Calixta, on the gallery, watched Alcée ride away. He turned and smiled at her with a beaming face; and she lifted her pretty chin in the air and laughed aloud.

III

Bobinôt and Bibi, trudging home, stopped without at the cistern to 30
make themselves presentable.

"My! Bibi, w'at will yo' mama say! You ought to be ashame'. You oughtn' put on those good pants. Look at 'em! An' that mud on yo' collar! How you got that mud on yo' collar, Bibi? I never saw such a boy!" Bibi was the picture of pathetic resignation. Bobinôt was the embodiment of serious solicitude as he strove to remove from his own person and his son's the signs of their tramp over heavy roads and through wet fields. He scraped the mud off Bibi's bare legs and feet with a stick and carefully removed all traces from his heavy brogans. Then, prepared for the worst—the meeting with an overscrupulous housewife, they entered cautiously at the back door.

Calixta was preparing supper. She had set the table and was dripping coffee at the hearth. She sprang up as they came in.

"Oh, Bobinôt! You back! My! but I was uneasy. W'ere you been during the rain? An' Bibi? he ain't wet? he ain't hurt?" She had clasped Bibi and was kissing him effusively. Bobinôt's explanations and apologies which he had been composing all along the way, died on his lips as Calixta felt him to see if he were dry, and seemed to express nothing but satisfaction at their safe return.

"I brought you some shrimps, Calixta," offered Bobinôt, hauling the can from his ample side pocket and laying it on the table.

"Shrimps! Oh, Bobinôt! you too good fo' anything!" and she gave him a smacking kiss on the cheek that resounded. "*J'vous réponds,*° we'll have a feas' to night! umph-umph!"

Bobinôt and Bibi began to relax and enjoy themselves, and when the three seated themselves at table they laughed much and so loud that anyone might have heard them as far away as Laballière's.

IV

Alcée Laballière wrote to his wife, Clarisse, that night. It was a loving letter, full of tender solicitude. He told her not to hurry back, but if she and the babies liked it at Biloxi, to stay a month longer. He was getting on nicely; and though he missed them, he was willing to bear the separation a while longer—realizing that their health and pleasure were the first things to be considered.

V

As for Clarisse, she was charmed upon receiving her husband's letter. She and the babies were doing well. The society was agreeable; many of her old friends and acquaintances were at the bay. And the first free breath since her marriage seemed to restore the pleasant liberty of her maiden days. Devoted as she was to her husband, their intimate conjugal life was something which she was more than willing to forego for a while.

So the storm passed and everyone was happy.

Questions

1. Exactly where does Chopin's story take place? How can you tell?
2. What circumstances introduced in Part I turn out to have a profound effect on events in the story?
3. What details in "The Storm" emphasize the fact that Bobinôt loves his wife? What details reveal how imperfectly he comprehends her nature?
4. What general attitudes toward sex, love, and marriage does Chopin imply? Cite evidence to support your answer.
5. What meanings do you find in the title "The Storm"?
6. In the story as a whole, how do setting and plot reinforce each other?

J'vous réponds: Let me tell you.

Jack London

To Build a Fire

1910

Jack London (1876–1916), born in San Francisco, won a large popular audience for his novels of the sea and the Yukon: The Call of the Wild *(1903),* The Sea-Wolf *(1904), and* White Fang *(1906). Like Ernest Hemingway, he was a writer who lived a strenuous and eventful life. In 1893, he marched cross-country in Coxey's Army, an organized protest of the unemployed; in 1897, he took part in the Klondike Gold Rush; and later, as a reporter, he covered the Russo-Japanese War and the Mexican Revolution. Son of an unmarried mother and a father who denied his paternity, London grew up in poverty. At fourteen, he began holding hard jobs: working in a canning factory and a jute mill, serving as a deck hand, pirating oysters in San Francisco Bay. These experiences persuaded him to join the Socialist Labor Party and crusade for workers' rights. In his political novel* The Iron Heel *(1908), London envisions a grim totalitarian America. Like himself, the hero of his novel* Martin Eden *(1909) is a man of brief schooling who gains fame as a writer, works for a cause, loses faith in it, and finds life without meaning. Though endowed with immense physical energy—he wrote fifty volumes—London drank hard, spent fast, and played out early. While his reputation as a novelist may have declined since his own day, some of his short stories have lasted triumphantly.*

Jack London

Day had broken cold and gray, exceedingly cold and gray, when the man turned aside from the main Yukon trail and climbed the high earth-bank, where a dim and little-travelled trail led eastward through the fat spruce timberland. It was a steep bank, and he paused for breath at the top, excusing the act to himself by looking at his watch. It was nine o'clock. There was no sun nor hint of sun, though there was not a cloud in the sky. It was a clear day, and yet there seemed an intangible pall over the face of things, a subtle gloom that made the day dark, and that was due to the absence of sun. This fact did not worry the man. He was used to the lack of sun. It had been days since he had seen the sun, and he knew that a few more days must pass before that cheerful orb, due south, would just peep above the sky line and dip immediately from view.

The man flung a look back along the way he had come. The Yukon lay a mile wide and hidden under three feet of ice. On top of this ice were as many feet of snow. It was all pure white, rolling in gentle undulations where the ice jams of the freeze-up had formed. North and south, as far as the eye could see, it was unbroken white, save for a dark hairline that curved and twisted from around the spruce-covered island to the south, and that curved and twisted away into the north, where it disappeared behind another spruce-covered island. This dark hairline was the trail—the main trail—that led south five hundred miles to the Chilcoot Pass, Dyea, and salt water; and that led north seventy miles to Dawson, and still on to the north a thousand miles to Nulato, and finally to St. Michael, on Bering Sea, a thousand miles and half a thousand more.

But all this—the mysterious, far-reaching hairline trail, the absence of sun from the sky, the tremendous cold, and the strangeness and weirdness of it all—made no impression on the man. It was not because he was long used to it. He was a newcomer in the land, a *chechaquo*, and this was his first winter. The trouble with him was that he was without imagination. He was quick and alert in the things of life, but only in the things, and not in the significances. Fifty degrees below zero meant eighty-odd degrees of frost. Such fact impressed him as being cold and uncomfortable, and that was all. It did not lead him to meditate upon his frailty as a creature of temperature, and upon man's frailty in general, able only to live within certain narrow limits of heat and cold; and from there on it did not lead him to the conjectural field of immortality and man's place in the universe. Fifty degrees below zero stood for a bite of frost that hurt and that must be guarded against by the use of mittens, ear flaps, warm moccasins, and thick socks. Fifty degrees below zero was to him just precisely fifty degrees below zero. That there should be anything more to it than that was a thought that never entered his head.

As he turned to go on, he spat speculatively. There was a sharp, explosive crackle that startled him. He spat again. And again, in the air, before it could fall to the snow, the spittle crackled. He knew that at fifty below spittle crackled on the snow, but this spittle had crackled in the air. Undoubtedly it was colder than fifty below—how much colder he did not know. But the temperature did not matter. He was bound for the old claim on the left fork of Henderson Creek, where the boys were already. They had come over across the divide from the Indian Creek country, while he had come the roundabout way to take a look at the possibilities of getting out logs in the spring from the islands in the Yukon. He would be in to camp by six o'clock; a bit after dark, it was true, but the boys would be there, a fire would be going, and a hot supper would be ready. As for lunch, he pressed his hand against the protruding bundle under his jacket. It was also under his shirt, wrapped up in a handkerchief and lying against the naked skin. It was the only way to keep the biscuits from freezing. He smiled agreeably to himself as he thought of those biscuits, each cut open and sopped in bacon grease, and each enclosing a generous slice of fried bacon.

He plunged in among the big spruce trees. The trail was faint. A foot of snow had fallen since the last sled had passed over, and he was glad he was without a sled, travelling light. In fact, he carried nothing but the lunch wrapped in the handkerchief. He was surprised, however, at the cold. It certainly was cold, he concluded, as he rubbed his numb nose and cheekbones with his mittened hand. He was a warm-whiskered man, but the hair on his face did not protect the high cheekbones and the eager nose that thrust itself aggressively into the frosty air.

At the man's heels trotted a dog, a big native husky, the proper wolf dog, gray-coated and without any visible or temperamental difference from its brother, the wild wolf. The animal was depressed by the tremendous cold. It knew that it was no time for travelling. Its instinct told it a truer tale than was told to the man by the man's judgment. In reality, it was not merely colder than fifty below zero; it was colder than sixty below, than seventy below. It was seventy-five below zero. Since the freezing point is thirty-two above zero, it meant that one hundred and seven degrees of frost obtained. The dog did not know anything about thermometers. Possibly in its brain there was no sharp consciousness of a condition of very cold such as was in the man's brain. But the brute had its instinct. It experienced a vague but menacing apprehension that subdued it and made it slink along at the man's heels, and that made it question eagerly every unwonted movement of the man as if expecting him to go into camp or to seek shelter somewhere and build a fire. The dog had learned fire, and it wanted fire, or else to burrow under the snow and cuddle its warmth away from the air.

The frozen moisture of its breathing had settled on its fur in a fine powder of frost, and especially were its jowls, muzzle, and eyelashes whitened by its crystalled breath. The man's red beard and mustache were likewise frosted, but more solidly, the deposit taking the form of ice and increasing with every warm, moist breath he exhaled. Also, the man was chewing tobacco, and the muzzle of ice held his lips so rigidly that he was unable to clear his chin when he expelled the juice. The result was that a crystal beard of the color and solidity of amber was increasing its length on his chin. If he fell down it would shatter itself, like glass, into brittle fragments. But he did not mind the appendage. It was the penalty all tobacco chewers paid in that country, and he had been out before in two cold snaps. They had not been so cold as this, he knew, but by the spirit thermometer at Sixty Mile he knew they had been registered at fifty below and at fifty-five.

He held on through the level stretch of woods for several miles, crossed a wide flat, and dropped down a bank to the frozen bed of a small stream. This was Henderson Creek, and he knew he was ten miles from the forks. He looked at his watch. It was ten o'clock. He was making four miles an hour, and he calculated that he would arrive at the forks at half-past twelve. He decided to celebrate that event by eating his lunch there.

The dog dropped in again at his heels, with a tail drooping discouragement, as the man swung along the creek bed. The furrow of the old sled trail was plainly visible, but a dozen inches of snow covered the marks of the last runners. In a month no man had come up or down that silent creek. The man held steadily on. He was not much given to thinking, and just then particularly he had nothing to think about save that he would eat lunch at the forks and that at six o'clock he would be in camp with the boys. There was nobody to talk to; and, had there been, speech would have been impossible because of the ice muzzle on his mouth. So he continued monotonously to chew tobacco and to increase the length of his amber beard.

Once in a while the thought reiterated itself that it was very cold and that he had never experienced such cold. As he walked along he rubbed his cheekbones and nose with the back of his mittened hand. He did this automatically, now and again changing hands. But, rub as he would, the instant he stopped his cheekbones were numb, and the following instant the end of his nose went numb. He was sure to frost his cheeks; he knew that, and experienced a pang of regret that he had not devised a nose strap of the sort Bud wore in cold snaps. Such a strap passed across the cheeks, as well, and saved them. But it didn't matter much, after all. What were frosted cheeks? A bit painful, that was all; they were never serious.

Empty as the man's mind was of thoughts, he was keenly observant, and he noticed the changes in the creek, the curves and bends and timber jams, and always he sharply noted where he placed his feet. Once, coming around a bend, he shied abruptly, like a startled horse, curved away from the place where he had been walking, and retreated several paces back along the trail. The creek he knew was frozen clear to the bottom—no creek could contain water in that arctic winter—but he knew also that there were springs that bubbled out from the hillsides and ran along under the snow and on top the ice of the creek. He knew that the coldest snaps never froze these springs, and he knew likewise their danger. They were traps. They hid pools of water under the snow that might be three inches deep, or three feet. Sometimes a skin of ice half an inch thick covered them, and in turn was covered by the snow. Sometimes there were alternate layers of water and ice skin, so that when one broke through he kept on breaking through for a while, sometimes wetting himself to the waist.

That was why he had shied in such panic. He had felt the give under his feet and heard the crackle of a snow-hidden ice skin. And to get his feet wet in such a temperature meant trouble and danger. At the very least it meant delay, for he would be forced to stop and build a fire, and under its protection to bare his feet while he dried his socks and moccasins. He stood and studied the creek bed and its banks, and decided that the flow of water came from the right. He reflected awhile, rubbing his nose and cheeks, then skirted to the left, stepping gingerly and testing the footing for each step. Once clear of the danger, he took a fresh chew of tobacco and swung along at his four-mile gait.

In the course of the next two hours he came upon several similar traps. Usually the snow above the hidden pools had a sunken, candied appearance that advertised the danger. Once again, however, he had a close call; and once, suspecting danger, he compelled the dog to go on in front. The dog did not want to go. It hung back until the man shoved it forward, and then it went quickly across the white, unbroken surface. Suddenly it broke through, floundered to one side, and got away to firmer footing. It had wet its forefeet and legs, and almost immediately the water that clung to it turned to ice. It made quick efforts to lick the ice off its legs, then dropped down in the snow and began to bite out the ice that had formed between the toes. This was a matter of instinct. To permit the ice to remain would mean sore feet. It did not know this. It merely obeyed the mysterious prompting that arose from the deep crypts of its being. But the man knew, having achieved a judgment on the subject, and he removed the mitten from his right hand and helped tear out the ice particles. He did not expose his fingers more than a minute, and was astonished at the swift numbness that smote them. It certainly was cold. He pulled on the mitten hastily, and beat the hand savagely across his chest.

At twelve o'clock the day was at its brightest. Yet the sun was too far south on its winter journey to clear the horizon. The bulge of the earth intervened between it and Henderson Creek, where the man walked under a clear sky at noon and cast no shadow. At half-past twelve, to the minute, he arrived at the forks of the creek. He was pleased at the speed he had made. If he kept it up, he would certainly be with the boys by six. He unbuttoned his jacket and shirt and drew forth his lunch. The action consumed no more than a quarter of a minute, yet in that brief moment the numbness laid hold of the exposed fingers. He did not put the mitten on, but, instead, struck the fingers a dozen sharp smashes against his leg. Then he sat down on a snow-covered log to eat. The sting that followed upon the striking of his fingers against his leg ceased so quickly that he was startled. He had had no chance to take a bite of biscuit. He struck the fingers repeatedly and returned them to the mitten, baring the other hand for the purpose of eating. He tried to take a mouthful, but the ice muzzle prevented. He had forgotten to build a fire and thaw out. He chuckled at his foolishness, and as he chuckled he noted the numbness creeping into the exposed fingers. Also, he noted that the stinging which had first come to his toes when he sat down was already passing away. He wondered whether the toes were warm or numb. He moved them inside the moccasins and decided that they were numb.

He pulled the mitten on hurriedly and stood up. He was a bit fright- 15
ened. He stamped up and down until the stinging returned into the feet. It certainly was cold, was his thought. That man from Sulphur Creek had spoken the truth when telling how cold it sometimes got in the country. And he had laughed at him at the time! That showed one must not be too sure of things. There was no mistake about it, it *was* cold. He strode up and down, stamping his feet and threshing his arms, until reassured by

the returning warmth. Then he got out matches and proceeded to make a fire. From the undergrowth, where high water of the previous spring had lodged a supply of seasoned twigs, he got his firewood. Working carefully from a small beginning, he soon had a roaring fire, over which he thawed the ice from his face and in the protection of which he ate his biscuits. For the moment the cold of space was outwitted. The dog took satisfaction in the fire, stretching out close enough for warmth and far enough away to escape being singed.

When the man had finished, he filled his pipe and took his comfortable time over a smoke. Then he pulled on his mittens, settled the ear flaps of his cap firmly about his ears, and took the creek trail up the left fork. The dog was disappointed and yearned back toward the fire. This man did not know cold. Possibly all the generations of his ancestry had been ignorant of cold, of real cold, of cold one hundred and seven degrees below freezing point. But the dog knew; all its ancestry knew, and it had inherited the knowledge. And it knew that it was not good to walk abroad in such fearful cold. It was the time to lie snug in a hole in the snow and wait for a curtain of cloud to be drawn across the face of outer space whence this cold came. On the other hand, there was no keen intimacy between the dog and the man. The one was the toil slave of the other, and the only caresses it had ever received were the caresses of the whip lash and of harsh and menacing throat sounds that threatened the whip lash. So the dog made no effort to communicate its apprehension to the man. It was not concerned in the welfare of the man; it was for its own sake that it yearned back toward the fire. But the man whistled, and spoke to it with the sound of whip lashes, and the dog swung in at the man's heels and followed after.

The man took a chew of tobacco and proceeded to start a new amber beard. Also, his moist breath quickly powdered with white his mustache, eyebrows, and lashes. There did not seem to be so many springs on the left fork of the Henderson, and for half an hour the man saw no signs of any. And then it happened. At a place where there were no signs, where the soft, unbroken snow seemed to advertise solidity beneath, the man broke through. It was not deep. He wet himself halfway to the knees before he floundered out to the firm crust.

He was angry, and cursed his luck aloud. He had hoped to get into camp with the boys at six o'clock, and this would delay him an hour, for he would have to build a fire and dry out his footgear. This was imperative at that low temperature—he knew that much; and he turned aside to the bank, which he climbed. On top, tangled in the underbrush about the trunks of several small spruce trees, was a high-water deposit of dry firewood—sticks and twigs, principally, but also larger portions of seasoned branches and fine, dry, last year's grasses. He threw down several large pieces on top of the snow. This served for a foundation and prevented the young flame from drowning itself in the snow it otherwise would melt. The flame he got by touching a match to a small shred of birch bark that he took from his pocket. This burned even more readily than paper. Placing it on the foundation, he fed the young flame with wisps of dry grass and with the tiniest dry twigs.

He worked slowly and carefully, keenly aware of his danger. Gradually, as the flame grew stronger, he increased the size of the twigs with which he fed it. He squatted in the snow, pulling the twigs out from their entanglement in the brush and feeding directly to the flame. He knew there must be no failure. When it is seventy-five below zero, a man must not fail in his first attempt to build a fire—that is, if his feet are wet. If his feet are dry, and he fails, he can run along the trail for half a mile and restore his circulation. But the circulation of wet and freezing feet cannot be restored by running when it is seventy-five below. No matter how fast he runs, the wet feet will freeze the harder.

All this the man knew. The old-timer on Sulphur Creek had told 20
him about it the previous fall, and now he was appreciating the advice. Already all sensation had gone out of his feet. To build the fire he had been forced to remove his mittens, and the fingers had quickly gone numb. His pace of four miles an hour had kept his heart pumping blood to the surface of his body and to all the extremities. But the instant he stopped, the action of the pump eased down. The cold of space smote the unprotected tip of the planet, and he, being on that unprotected tip, received the full force of the blow. The blood of his body recoiled before it. The blood was alive, like the dog, and like the dog it wanted to hide away and cover itself up from the fearful cold. So long as he walked four miles an hour, he pumped that blood, willy-nilly, to the surface; but now it ebbed away and sank down into the recesses of his body. The extremities were the first to feel its absence. His wet feet froze the faster, and his exposed fingers numbed the faster, though they had not yet begun to freeze. Nose and cheeks were already freezing, while the skin of all his body chilled as it lost its blood.

But he was safe. Toes and nose and cheeks would be only touched by the frost, for the fire was beginning to burn with strength. He was feeding it with twigs the size of his finger. In another minute he would be able to feed it with branches the size of his wrist, and then he could remove his wet footgear, and, while it dried, he could keep his naked feet warm by the fire, rubbing them at first, of course, with snow. The fire was a success. He was safe. He remembered the advice of the old-timer on Sulphur Creek, and smiled. The old-timer had been very serious in laying down the law that no man must travel alone in the Klondike after fifty below. Well, here he was; he had had the accident; he was alone; and he had saved himself. Those old-timers were rather womanish, some of them, he thought. All a man had to do was to keep his head, and he was all right. Any man who was a man could travel alone. But it was surprising, the rapidity with which his cheeks and nose were freezing. And he had not thought his fingers could go lifeless in so short a time. Lifeless they were, for he could scarcely make them move together to grip a twig, and they seemed remote from his body and from him. When he touched a twig, he had to look and see whether or not he had hold of it. The wires were pretty well down between him and his finger ends.

All of which counted for little. There was the fire, snapping and crackling and promising life with every dancing flame. He started to untie his moccasins. They were coated with ice; the thick German socks were like sheaths of iron halfway to the knees; and the moccasin strings were like rods of steel all twisted and knotted as by some conflagration. For a moment he tugged with his numb fingers, then, realizing the folly of it, he drew his sheath knife.

But before he could cut the strings, it happened. It was his own fault or, rather, his mistake. He should not have built the fire under the spruce tree. He should have built it in the open. But it had been easier to pull the twigs from the brush and drop them directly on the fire. Now the tree under which he had done this carried a weight of snow on its boughs. No wind had blown for weeks, and each bough was fully freighted. Each time he had pulled a twig he had communicated a slight agitation to the tree—an imperceptible agitation, so far as he was concerned, but an agitation sufficient to bring about the disaster. High up in the tree one bough capsized its load of snow. This fell on the boughs beneath, capsizing them. This process continued, spreading out and involving the whole tree. It grew like an avalanche, and it descended without warning upon the man and the fire, and the fire was blotted out! Where it had burned was a mantle of fresh and disordered snow.

The man was shocked. It was as though he had just heard his own sentence of death. For a moment he sat and stared at the spot where the fire had been. Then he grew very calm. Perhaps the old-timer on Sulphur Creek was right. If he had only had a trail mate he would have been in no danger now. The trail mate could have built the fire. Well, it was up to him to build the fire over again, and this second time there must be no failure. Even if he succeeded, he would most likely lose some toes. His feet must be badly frozen by now, and there would be some time before the second fire was ready.

Such were his thoughts, but he did not sit and think them. He was 25
busy all the time they were passing through his mind. He made a new foundation for a fire, this time in the open, where no treacherous tree could blot it out. Next he gathered dry grasses and tiny twigs from the high-water flotsam. He could not bring his fingers together to pull them out, but he was able to gather them by the handful. In this way he got many rotten twigs and bits of green moss that were undesirable, but it was the best he could do. He worked methodically, even collecting an armful of the larger branches to be used later when the fire gathered strength. And all the while the dog sat and watched him, a certain yearning

wistfulness in its eye, for it looked upon him as the fire provider, and the fire was slow in coming.

When all was ready, the man reached in his pocket for a second piece of birch bark. He knew the bark was there, and, though he could not feel it with his fingers, he could hear its crisp rustling as he fumbled for it. Try as he would, he could not clutch hold of it. And all the time, in his consciousness, was the knowledge that each instant his feet were freezing. This thought tended to put him in a panic, but he fought against it and kept calm. He pulled on his mittens with his teeth, and threshed his arms back and forth, beating his hands with all his might against his sides. He did this sitting down, and he stood up to do it; and all the while the dog sat in the snow, its wolf brush of a tail curled around warmly over its forefeet, its sharp wolf ears pricked forward intently as it watched the man. And the man, as he beat and threshed with his arms and hands, felt a great surge of envy as he regarded the creature that was warm and secure in its natural covering.

After a time he was aware of the first faraway signals of sensation in his beaten fingers. The faint tingling grew stronger till it evolved into a stinging ache that was excruciating, but which the man hailed with satisfaction. He stripped the mitten from his right hand and fetched forth the birch bark. The exposed fingers were quickly going numb again. Next he brought out his bunch of sulphur matches. But the tremendous cold had already driven the life out of his fingers. In his effort to separate one match from the others, the whole bunch fell in the snow. He tried to pick it out of the snow, but failed. The dead fingers could neither touch nor clutch. He was very careful. He drove the thought of his freezing feet, and nose, and cheeks, out of his mind, devoting his whole soul to the matches. He watched, using the sense of vision in place of that of touch, and when he saw his fingers on each side the bunch, he closed them—that is, he willed to close them, for the wires were down, and the fingers did not obey. He pulled the mitten on the right hand, and beat it fiercely against his knee. Then, with both mittened hands, he scooped the bunch of matches, along with much snow, into his lap. Yet he was no better off.

After some manipulation he managed to get the bunch between the heels of his mittened hands. In this fashion he carried it to his mouth. The ice crackled and snapped when by a violent effort he opened his mouth. He drew the lower jaw in, curled the upper lip out of the way, and scraped the bunch with his upper teeth in order to separate a match. He succeeded in getting one, which he dropped on his lap. He was no better off. He could not pick it up. Then he devised a way. He picked it up in his teeth and scratched it on his leg. Twenty times he scratched before he succeeded in lighting it. As it flamed he held it with his teeth to the birch bark. But the burning brimstone went up his nostrils and into his lungs, causing him to cough spasmodically. The match fell into the snow and went out.

The old-timer on Sulphur Creek was right, he thought in the moment of controlled despair that ensued: after fifty below, a man should travel with a partner. He beat his hands, but failed in exciting any sensation. Suddenly he bared both hands, removing the mittens with his teeth. He caught the whole bunch between the heels of his hands. His arm muscles not being frozen enabled him to press the hand heels tightly against the matches. Then he scratched the bunch along his leg. It flared into flame, seventy sulphur matches at once! There was no wind to blow them out. He kept his head to one side to escape the strangling fumes, and held the blazing bunch to the birch bark. As he so held it, he became aware of sensation in his hand. His flesh was burning. He could smell it. Deep down below the surface he could feel it. The sensation developed into pain that grew acute. And still he endured it, holding the flame of the matches clumsily to the bark that would not light readily because his own burning hands were in the way, absorbing most of the flame.

At last, when he could endure no more, he jerked his hands apart. The blazing matches fell sizzling into the snow, but the birch bark was alight. He began laying dry grasses and the tiniest twigs on the flame. He could not pick and choose, for he had to lift the fuel between the heels of his hands. Small pieces of rotten wood and green moss clung to the twigs, and he bit them off as well as he could with his teeth. He cherished the flame carefully and awkwardly. It meant life, and it must not perish. The withdrawal of blood from the surface of his body now made him begin to shiver, and he grew more awkward. A large piece of green moss fell squarely on the little fire. He tried to poke it out with his fingers, but his shivering frame made him poke too far, and he disrupted the nucleus of the little fire, the burning grasses and tiny twigs separating and scattering. He tried to poke them together again, but in spite of the tenseness of the effort, his shivering got away from him, and the twigs were hopelessly scattered. Each twig gushed a puff of smoke and went out. The fire provider had failed. As he looked apathetically about him, his eyes chanced on the dog, sitting across the ruins of the fire from him, in the snow, making restless, hunching movements, slightly lifting one forefoot and then the other, shifting its weight back and forth on them with wistful eagerness.

The sight of the dog put a wild idea into his head. He remembered the tale of the man, caught in the blizzard, who killed a steer and crawled inside the carcass, and so was saved. He would kill the dog and bury his hands in the warm body until the numbness went out of them. Then he could build another fire. He spoke to the dog, calling it to him; but in his voice was a strange note of fear that frightened the animal, who had never known the man to speak in such a way before. Something was the matter, and its suspicious nature sensed danger—it knew not what danger, but somewhere, somehow, in its brain arose an apprehension of the man. It flattened its ears down at the sound of the man's voice, and its restless, hunching movements and the liftings and shiftings of its forefeet became more pronounced; but it would not come to the man. He got on his hands and knees and crawled toward the dog. This unusual posture again excited suspicion, and the animal sidled mincingly away.

The man sat up in the snow for a moment and struggled for calmness. Then he pulled on his mittens, by means of his teeth, and got upon his feet. He glanced down at first in order to assure himself that he was really standing up, for the absence of sensation in his feet left him unrelated to the earth. His erect position in itself started to drive the webs of suspicion from the dog's mind; and when he spoke peremptorily, with the sound of whip lashes in his voice, the dog rendered its customary allegiance and came to him. As it came within reaching distance, the man lost his control. His arms flashed out to the dog, and he experienced genuine surprise when he discovered that his hands could not clutch, that there was neither bend nor feeling in the fingers. He had forgotten for the moment that they were frozen and that they were freezing more and more. All this happened quickly, and before the animal could get away, he encircled its body with his arms. He sat down in the snow, and in this fashion held the dog, while it snarled and whined and struggled.

But it was all he could do, hold its body encircled in his arms and sit there. He realized that he could not kill the dog. There was no way to do it. With his helpless hands he could neither draw nor hold his sheath knife nor throttle the animal. He released it, and it plunged wildly away, with tail between its legs, and still snarling. It halted forty feet away and surveyed him curiously, with ears sharply pricked forward.

The man looked down at his hands in order to locate them, and found them hanging on the ends of his arms. It struck him as curious that one should have to use his eyes in order to find out where his hands were. He began threshing his arms back and forth, beating the mittened hands against his sides. He did this for five minutes, violently, and his heart pumped enough blood up to the surface to put a stop to his shivering. But no sensation was aroused in the hands. He had an impression that they hung like weights on the ends of his arms, but when he tried to run the impression down, he could not find it.

A certain fear of death, dull and oppressive, came to him. This fear 35
quickly became poignant as he realized that it was no longer a mere matter of freezing his fingers and toes, or of losing his hands and feet, but that it was a matter of life and death with the chances against him. This threw him into a panic, and he turned and ran up the creek bed along the old, dim trail. The dog joined in behind and kept up with him. He ran blindly, without intention, in fear such as he had never known in his life. Slowly, as he plowed and floundered through the snow, he began to see things again—the banks of the creek, the old timber jams, the leafless

aspens, and the sky. The running made him feel better. He did not shiver. Maybe, if he ran on, his feet would thaw out; and anyway, if he ran far enough, he would reach camp and the boys. Without doubt he would lose some fingers and toes and some of his face; but the boys would take care of him, and save the rest of him when he got there. And at the same time there was another thought in his mind that said he would never get to the camp and the boys; that it was too many miles away, that the freezing had too great a start on him, and that he would soon be stiff and dead. This thought he kept in the background and refused to consider. Sometimes it pushed itself forward and demanded to be heard, but he thrust it back and strove to think of other things.

It struck him as curious that he could run at all on feet so frozen that he could not feel them when they struck the earth and took the weight of his body. He seemed to himself to skim along above the surface, and to have no connection with the earth. Somewhere he had once seen a winged Mercury, and he wondered if Mercury felt as he felt when skimming over the earth.

His theory of running until he reached the camp and the boys had one flaw in it: he lacked the endurance. Several times he stumbled, and finally he tottered, crumpled up, and fell. When he tried to rise, he failed. He must sit and rest, he decided, and next time he would merely walk and keep on going. As he sat and regained his breath, he noted that he was feeling quite warm and comfortable. He was not shivering, and it even seemed that a warm glow had come to his chest and trunk. And yet, when he touched his nose and cheeks, there was no sensation. Running would not thaw them out. Nor would it thaw out his hands and feet. Then the thought came to him that the frozen portions of his body must be extending. He tried to keep this thought down, to forget it, to think of something else; he was aware of the panicky feeling that it caused, and he was afraid of the panic. But the thought asserted itself, and persisted, until it produced a vision of his body totally frozen. This was too much, and he made another wild run along the trail. Once he slowed down to a walk, but the thought of the freezing extending itself made him run again.

And all the time the dog ran with him, at his heels. When he fell down a second time, it curled its tail over its forefeet and sat in front of him, facing him, curiously eager and intent. The warmth and security of the animal angered him, and he cursed it till it flattened down its ears appeasingly. This time the shivering came more quickly upon the man. He was losing in his battle with the frost. It was creeping into his body from all sides. The thought of it drove him on, but he ran no more than a hundred feet, when he staggered and pitched headlong. It was his last panic. When he had recovered his breath and control, he sat up and entertained in his mind the conception of meeting death with dignity. However, the conception did not come to him in such terms. His idea of it was that he had been making a fool of himself, running around like a chicken with its head cut off—such was the simile that occurred to him. Well, he was bound to freeze anyway, and he might as well take it decently. With this new-found peace of mind came the first glimmerings of drowsiness. A good idea, he thought, to sleep off to death. It was like taking an anesthetic. Freezing was not so bad as people thought. There were lots worse ways to die.

He pictured the boys finding his body next day. Suddenly he found himself with them, coming along the trail and looking for himself. And, still with them, he came around a turn in the trail and found himself lying in the snow. He did not belong with himself any more, for even then he was out of himself, standing with the boys and looking at himself in the snow. It certainly was cold, was his thought. When he got back to the States he could tell the folks what real cold was. He drifted on from this to a vision of the old-timer on Sulphur Creek. He could see him quite clearly, warm and comfortable, and smoking a pipe.

"You were right, old hoss; you were right," the man mumbled to the 40
old-timer of Sulphur Creek.

Then the man drowsed off into what seemed to him the most comfortable and satisfying sleep he had ever known. The dog sat facing him and waiting. The brief day drew to a close in a long, slow twilight. There were no signs of a fire to be made, and, besides, never in the dog's experience had it known a man to sit like that in the snow and make no fire. As the twilight drew on, its eager yearning for the fire mastered it, and with a great lifting and shifting of forefeet, it whined softly, then flattened its ears down in anticipation of being chidden by the man. But the man remained silent. Later the dog whined loudly. And still later it crept close to the man and caught the scent of death. This made the animal bristle and back away. A little longer it delayed, howling under the stars that leaped and danced and shone brightly in the cold sky. Then it turned and trotted up the trail in the direction of the camp it knew, where were the other food providers and fire providers.

Questions

1. Roughly how much of London's story is devoted to describing the setting? What particular details make it memorable?
2. To what extent does setting determine what happens in this story?
3. From what point of view is London's story told?
4. In "To Build a Fire" the man is never given a name. What is the effect of his being called simply "the man" throughout the story?
5. From the evidence London gives us, what stages are involved in the process of freezing to death? What does the story gain from London's detailed account of the man's experience with each successive stage?
6. What are the most serious mistakes the man makes? To what factors do you attribute these errors?

Jorge Luis Borges

The Gospel According to Mark 1970

Translated by Andrew Hurley

Jorge Luis Borges

Jorge Luis Borges (1899–1986), an outstanding modern writer of Latin America, was born in Buenos Aires into a family prominent in Argentine history. His father, with whom he had a very close relationship, was a lawyer and teacher. Borges grew up bilingual, learning English from his English grandmother and receiving his early education from an English tutor. In later years, he would translate work by Poe, Melville, Whitman, Faulkner, and others into Spanish. Caught in Europe by the outbreak of World War I, Borges lived in Switzerland—where he learned French and taught himself German—and later Spain, where he joined the Ultraists, a group of experimental poets who renounced realism. On returning to Argentina, he edited a poetry magazine printed in the form of a poster and affixed to city walls. In his early writings, Borges favored the style of Criollismo (regionalism), but by the mid-1930s he had begun to take a more cosmopolitan and internationalist approach; in this same period, his principal literary mode began to shift from poetry to fiction. In 1946, for his opposition to the regime of Colonel Juan Perón, Borges was forced to resign his post as a librarian and was mockingly offered a job as a chicken inspector. In 1955, after Perón was deposed, Borges became director of the National Library and professor of English literature at the University of Buenos Aires. A sufferer since childhood from poor eyesight, Borges eventually went blind. His eye problems may have encouraged him to work mainly in short, highly crafted forms: stories, essays, fables, and lyric poems full of elaborate music. His short stories, in Ficciones *(1944),* El hacedor *(1960; translated as* Dreamtigers*, 1964), and* Labyrinths *(1962), have been admired worldwide.*

The incident took place on the Los Alamos ranch, south of the small town of Junín, in late March of 1928. Its protagonist was a medical student named Baltasar Espinosa. We might define him for the moment as a Buenos Aires youth much like many others, with no traits worthier of note than the gift for public speaking that had won him more than one prize at the English school° in Ramos Mejía and an almost unlimited goodness. He didn't like to argue; he preferred that his interlocutor rather than he himself be right. And though he found the chance twists and turns of gambling interesting, he was a poor gambler, because he didn't like to win. He was intelligent and open to learning, but he was lazy; at thirty-three he had not yet completed the last requirements for his

English school: a prep school that emphasized English. (Well-to-do Argentines of this era wanted their children to learn English.)

degree. (The work he still owed, incidentally, was for his favorite class.) His father, like all the gentlemen of his day a freethinker,° had instructed Espinosa in the doctrines of Herbert Spencer,° but once, before he set off on a trip to Montevideo, his mother had asked him to say the Lord's Prayer every night and make the sign of the cross, and never in all the years that followed did he break that promise. He did not lack courage; one morning, with more indifference than wrath, he had traded two or three blows with some of his classmates that were trying to force him to join a strike at the university. He abounded in debatable habits and opinions, out of a spirit of acquiescence: his country mattered less to him than the danger that people in other countries might think the Argentines still wore feathers; he venerated France but had contempt for the French; he had little respect for Americans but took pride in the fact that there were skyscrapers in Buenos Aires; he thought that the gauchos° of the plains were better horsemen than the gauchos of the mountains. When his cousin Daniel invited him to spend the summer at Los Alamos, he immediately accepted—not because he liked the country but out of a natural desire to please, and because he could find no good reason for saying no.

The main house at the ranch was large and a bit run-down; the quarters for the foreman, a man named Gutre, stood nearby. There were three members of the Gutre family: the father, the son (who was singularly rough and unpolished), and a girl of uncertain paternity. They were tall, strong, and bony, with reddish hair and Indian features. They rarely spoke. The foreman's wife had died years before.

In the country, Espinosa came to learn things he hadn't known, had never even suspected; for example, that when you're approaching a house there's no reason to gallop and that nobody goes out on a horse unless there's a job to be done. As the summer wore on, he learned to distinguish birds by their call.

Within a few days, Daniel had to go to Buenos Aires to close a deal on some livestock. At the most, he said, the trip would take a week. Espinosa, who was already a little tired of his cousin's *bonnes fortunes* and his indefatigable interest in the vagaries of men's tailoring, stayed behind on the ranch with his textbooks. The heat was oppressive, and not even nightfall brought relief. Then one morning toward dawn, he was awakened by thunder. Wind lashed the casuarina trees. Espinosa heard the first drops of rain and gave thanks to God. Suddenly the wind blew cold. That afternoon, the Salado overflowed.

The next morning, as he stood on the porch looking out over the 5
flooded plains, Baltasar Espinosa realized that the metaphor equating the pampas with the sea was not, at least that morning, an altogether false

freethinker: person who rejects traditional beliefs, especially religious dogma, in favor of rational inquiry. *Herbert Spencer:* a British philosopher (1820–1903) who championed the theory of evolution. *gauchos:* South American cowboys.

one, though Hudson° had noted that the sea seems the grander of the two because we view it not from horseback or our own height, but from the deck of a ship. The rain did not let up; the Gutres, helped (or hindered) by the city dweller, saved a good part of the livestock, though many animals were drowned. There were four roads leading to the ranch; all were under water. On the third day, when a leaking roof threatened the foreman's house, Espinosa gave the Gutres a room at the back of the main house, alongside the toolshed. The move brought Espinosa and the Gutres closer, and they began to eat together in the large dining room. Conversation was not easy; the Gutres, who knew so much about things in the country, did not know how to explain them. One night Espinosa asked them if people still remembered anything about the Indian raids, back when the military command for the frontier had been in Junín. They told him they did, but they would have given the same answer if he had asked them about the day Charles I° had been beheaded. Espinosa recalled that his father used to say that all the cases of longevity that occur in the country are the result of either poor memory or a vague notion of dates—gauchos quite often know neither the year they were born in nor the name of the man that fathered them.

In the entire house, the only reading material to be found were several copies of a farming magazine, a manual of veterinary medicine, a deluxe edition of the romantic verse drama *Tabaré*, a copy of *The History of the Shorthorn in Argentina*, several erotic and detective stories, and a recent novel that Espinosa had not read—*Don Segundo Sombra*, by Ricardo Güiraldes. In order to put some life into the inevitable afterdinner attempt at conversation, Espinosa read a couple of chapters of the novel to the Gutres, who did not know how to read or write. Unfortunately, the foreman had been a cattle drover himself, and he could not be interested in the adventures of another such a one. It was easy work, he said; they always carried along a pack mule with everything they might need. If he had not been a cattle drover, he announced, he'd never have seen Lake Gómez, or the Bragado River, or even the Núñez ranch, in Chacabuco. . . .

In the kitchen there was a guitar; before the incident I am narrating, the laborers would sit in a circle and someone would pick up the guitar and strum it, though never managing actually to play it. That was called "giving it a strum."

Espinosa, who was letting his beard grow out, would stop before the mirror to look at his changed face; he smiled to think that he'd soon be boring the fellows in Buenos Aires with his stories about the Salado overrunning its banks. Curiously, he missed places in the city he never went, and would never go: a street corner on Cabrera where a mailbox stood; two cement lions on a porch on Calle Jujuy a few blocks from the

Hudson: W. H. Hudson was an English naturalist and author (1841–1922) who wrote extensively about South America. *Charles I:* King of England, beheaded in 1649.

Plaza del Once; a tile-floored corner grocery-store-and-bar (whose location he couldn't quite remember). As for his father and his brothers, by now Daniel would have told them that he had been isolated—the word was etymologically precise—by the floodwaters.

Exploring the house still cut off by the high water, he came upon a Bible printed in English. On its last pages the Guthries (for that was their real name) had kept their family history. They had come originally from Inverness° and had arrived in the New World—doubtlessly as peasant laborers—in the early nineteenth century; they had intermarried with Indians. The chronicle came to an end in the eighteen-seventies; they no longer knew how to write. Within a few generations they had forgotten their English; by the time Espinosa met them, even Spanish gave them some difficulty. They had no faith, though in their veins, alongside the superstitions of the pampas, there still ran a dim current of the Calvinist's harsh fanaticism. Espinosa mentioned his find to them, but they hardly seemed to hear him.

He leafed through the book, and his fingers opened it to the first verses of the Gospel According to St. Mark. To try his hand at translating, and perhaps to see if they might understand a little of it, he decided that that would be the text he read the Gutres after dinner. He was surprised that they listened first attentively and then with mute fascination. The presence of gold letters on the binding may have given it increased authority. "It's in their blood," he thought. It also occurred to him that throughout history, humankind has told two stories: the story of a lost ship sailing the Mediterranean seas in quest of a beloved isle, and the story of a god who allows himself to be crucified on Golgotha. He recalled his elocution classes in Ramos Mejía, and he rose to his feet to preach the parables.

In the following days, the Gutres would wolf down the spitted beef and canned sardines in order to arrive sooner at the Gospel.

The girl had a little lamb; it was her pet, and she prettied it with a sky blue ribbon. One day it cut itself on a piece of barbed wire; to stanch the blood, the Gutres were about to put spiderwebs on the wound, but Espinosa treated it with pills. The gratitude awakened by that cure amazed him. At first, he had not trusted the Gutres and had hidden away in one of his books the two hundred forty pesos he'd brought; now, with Daniel gone, he had taken the master's place and begun to give timid orders, which were immediately followed. The Gutres would trail him through the rooms and along the hallway, as though they were lost. As he read, he noticed that they would sweep away the crumbs he had left on the table. One afternoon, he surprised them as they were discussing him in brief, respectful words. When he came to the end of the Gospel According to St. Mark, he started to read another of the three remaining gospels, but the father asked him to reread the one he'd just finished,

Inverness: a county in Scotland.

so they could understand it better. Espinosa felt they were like children, who prefer repetition to variety or novelty. One night he dreamed of the Flood (which is not surprising) and was awakened by the hammering of the building of the Ark, but he told himself it was thunder. And in fact the rain, which had let up for a while, had begun again; it was very cold. The Gutres told him the rain had broken through the roof of the toolshed; when they got the beams repaired, they said, they'd show him where. He was no longer a stranger, a foreigner, and they all treated him with respect; he was almost spoiled. None of them liked coffee, but there was always a little cup for him, with spoonfuls of sugar stirred in.

That second storm took place on a Tuesday. Thursday night there was a soft knock on his door; because of his doubts about the Gutres he always locked it. He got up and opened the door; it was the girl. In the darkness he couldn't see her, but he could tell by her footsteps that she was barefoot, and afterward, in the bed, that she was naked—that in fact she had come from the back of the house that way. She did not embrace him, or speak a word; she lay down beside him and she was shivering. It was the first time she had lain with a man. When she left, she did not kiss him; Espinosa realized that he didn't even know her name. Impelled by some sentiment he did not attempt to understand, he swore that when he returned to Buenos Aires, he'd tell no one of the incident.

The next day began like all the others, except that the father spoke to Espinosa to ask whether Christ had allowed himself to be killed in order to save all mankind. Espinosa, who was a freethinker like his father but felt obliged to defend what he had read them, paused.

"Yes," he finally replied. "To save all mankind from hell."

"What *is* hell?" Gutre then asked him.

"A place underground where souls will burn in fire forever."

"And those that drove the nails will also be saved?"

"Yes," replied Espinosa, whose theology was a bit shaky. (He had worried that the foreman wanted to have a word with him about what had happened last night with his daughter.)

After lunch they asked him to read the last chapters again.

Espinosa had a long siesta that afternoon, although it was a light sleep, interrupted by persistent hammering and vague premonitions. Toward evening he got up and went out into the hall.

"The water's going down," he said, as though thinking out loud. "It won't be long now."

"Not long now," repeated Gutre, like an echo.

The three of them had followed him. Kneeling on the floor, they asked his blessing. Then they cursed him, spat on him, and drove him to the back of the house. The girl was weeping. Espinosa realized what awaited him on the other side of the door. When they opened it, he saw the sky. A bird screamed; *it's a goldfinch*, Espinosa thought. There was no roof on the shed; they had torn down the roof beams to build the Cross.

Questions

1. What is about to happen to Baltasar Espinosa at the end of this story?
2. How old is Espinosa? What is ironic about his age?
3. Why is the isolated rural setting crucial to the story? Could the events have occurred in a large city like Buenos Aires?
4. What lessons does Espinosa learn in the country? What important lessons does he not notice as the weeks of his stay drag on?
5. How does weather affect the outcome of the story?
6. What is the background of the Gutre family? How did they come to own an English Bible? Why is it ironic that they own this book?
7. When Espinosa begins reading the Gospel of Saint Mark to the Gutres, what changes in their behavior does he notice?
8. What other action does Espinosa perform that earns the Gutres's gratitude?
9. Why do the Gutres kill Espinosa? What do they hope to gain?

Amy Tan

A Pair of Tickets 1989

Amy Tan

Amy Tan was born in Oakland, California, in 1952. Both of her parents were recent Chinese immigrants. Her father was an electrical engineer (as well as a Baptist minister); her mother was a vocational nurse. When her father and older brother both died of brain tumors, the fifteen-year-old Tan moved with her mother and younger brother to Switzerland, where she attended high school. On their return to the United States, Tan attended Linfield College, a Baptist school in Oregon, but she eventually transferred to San Jose State University. At this time Tan and her mother argued about her future. The mother insisted her daughter pursue premedical studies in preparation for becoming a neurosurgeon, but Tan wanted to do something else. For six months the two did not speak to each other. Tan worked for IBM writing computer manuals and also wrote freelance business articles under a pseudonym. In 1987 she and her mother visited China together. This experience, which is reflected in "A Pair of Tickets," deepened Tan's sense of her Chinese American identity. "As soon as my feet touched China," she wrote, "I became Chinese." Soon after, she began writing her first novel, The Joy Luck Club *(1989), which consists of sixteen interrelated stories about a group of Chinese American mothers and their daughters. (The club of the title is a woman's social group.)* The Joy Luck Club *became both a critical success and a best seller, and was made into a movie in 1993. In 1991 Tan published her second novel,* The Kitchen God's Wife. *Her later novels include* The Bonesetter's Daughter *(2001),* Saving Fish from Drowning *(2005), and* The Valley of Amazement *(2013). She lives north of San Francisco with her husband.*

The minute our train leaves the Hong Kong border and enters Shenzhen, China, I feel different. I can feel the skin on my forehead tingling, my blood rushing through a new course, my bones aching with a familiar old pain. And I think, My mother was right. I am becoming Chinese.

"Cannot be helped," my mother said when I was fifteen and had vigorously denied that I had any Chinese whatsoever below my skin. I was a sophomore at Galileo High in San Francisco, and all my Caucasian friends agreed: I was about as Chinese as they were. But my mother had studied at a famous nursing school in Shanghai, and she said she knew all about genetics. So there was no doubt in her mind, whether I agreed or not: Once you are born Chinese, you cannot help but feel and think Chinese.

"Someday you will see," said my mother. "It is in your blood, waiting to be let go."

And when she said this, I saw myself transforming like a werewolf, a mutant tag of DNA suddenly triggered, replicating itself insidiously into a *syndrome,*° a cluster of telltale Chinese behaviors, all those things my mother did to embarrass me—haggling with store owners, pecking her mouth with a toothpick in public, being color-blind to the fact that lemon yellow and pale pink are not good combinations for winter clothes.

But today I realize I've never really known what it means to be Chi- 5
nese. I am thirty-six years old. My mother is dead and I am on a train, carrying with me her dreams of coming home. I am going to China.

We are first going to Guangzhou, my seventy-two-year-old father, Canning Woo, and I, where we will visit his aunt, whom he has not seen since he was ten years old. And I don't know whether it's the prospect of seeing his aunt or if it's because he's back in China, but now he looks like he's a young boy, so innocent and happy I want to button his sweater and pat his head. We are sitting across from each other, separated by a little table with two cold cups of tea. For the first time I can ever remember, my father has tears in his eyes, and all he is seeing out the train window is a sectioned field of yellow, green, and brown, a narrow canal flanking the tracks, low rising hills, and three people in blue jackets riding an ox-driven cart on this early October morning. And I can't help myself. I also have misty eyes, as if I had seen this a long, long time ago, and had almost forgotten.

In less than three hours, we will be in Guangzhou, which my guidebook tells me is how one properly refers to Canton these days. It seems all the cities I have heard of, except Shanghai, have changed their spellings. I think they are saying China has changed in other ways as well. Chungking is Chongqing. And Kweilin is Guilin. I have looked these names up,

syndrome: a group of symptoms that occur together as the sign of a particular disease or abnormality.

because after we see my father's aunt in Guangzhou, we will catch a plane to Shanghai, where I will meet my two half-sisters for the first time.

They are my mother's twin daughters from her first marriage, little babies she was forced to abandon on a road as she was fleeing Kweilin for Chungking in 1944. That was all my mother had told me about these daughters, so they had remained babies in my mind, all these years, sitting on the side of a road, listening to bombs whistling in the distance while sucking their patient red thumbs.

And it was only this year that someone found them and wrote with this joyful news. A letter came from Shanghai, addressed to my mother. When I first heard about this, that they were alive, I imagined my identical sisters transforming from little babies into six-year-old girls. In my mind, they were seated next to each other at a table, taking turns with the fountain pen. One would write a neat row of characters: *Dearest Mama. We are alive.* She would brush back her wispy bangs and hand the other sister the pen, and she would write: *Come get us. Please hurry.*

Of course they could not know that my mother had died three 10
months before, suddenly, when a blood vessel in her brain burst. One minute she was talking to my father, complaining about the tenants upstairs, scheming how to evict them under the pretense that relatives from China were moving in. The next minute she was holding her head, her eyes squeezed shut, groping for the sofa, and then crumpling softly to the floor with fluttering hands.

So my father had been the first one to open the letter, a long letter it turned out. And they did call her Mama. They said they always revered her as their true mother. They kept a framed picture of her. They told her about their life, from the time my mother last saw them on the road leaving Kweilin to when they were finally found.

And the letter had broken my father's heart so much—these daughters calling my mother from another life he never knew—that he gave the letter to my mother's old friend Auntie Lindo and asked her to write back and tell my sisters, in the gentlest way possible, that my mother was dead.

But instead Auntie Lindo took the letter to the Joy Luck Club and discussed with Auntie Ying and Auntie An-mei what should be done, because they had known for many years about my mother's search for her twin daughters, her endless hope. Auntie Lindo and the others cried over this double tragedy, of losing my mother three months before, and now again. And so they couldn't help but think of some miracle, some possible way of reviving her from the dead, so my mother could fulfill her dream.

So this is what they wrote to my sisters in Shanghai: "Dearest Daughters, I too have never forgotten you in my memory or in my heart. I never gave up hope that we would see each other again in a joyous reunion. I am only sorry it has been too long. I want to tell you everything about my life since I last saw you. I want to tell you this when our family comes to see you in China. . . ." They signed it with my mother's name.

It wasn't until all this had been done that they first told me about my 15
sisters, the letter they received, the one they wrote back.

"They'll think she's coming, then," I murmured. And I had imagined my sisters now being ten or eleven, jumping up and down, holding hands, their pigtails bouncing, excited that their mother—*their* mother—was coming, whereas my mother was dead.

"How can you say she is not coming in a letter?" said Auntie Lindo. "She is their mother. She is your mother. You must be the one to tell them. All these years, they have been dreaming of her." And I thought she was right.

But then I started dreaming, too, of my mother and my sisters and how it would be if I arrived in Shanghai. All these years, while they waited to be found, I had lived with my mother and then had lost her. I imagined seeing my sisters at the airport. They would be standing on their tip-toes, looking anxiously, scanning from one dark head to another as we got off the plane. And I would recognize them instantly, their faces with the identical worried look.

"*Jyejye, Jyejye*. Sister, Sister. We are here," I saw myself saying in my poor version of Chinese.

"Where is Mama?" they would say, and look around, still smiling, 20
two flushed and eager faces. "Is she hiding?" And this would have been like my mother, to stand behind just a bit, to tease a little and make people's patience pull a little on their hearts. I would shake my head and tell my sisters she was not hiding.

"Oh, that must be Mama, no?" one of my sisters would whisper excitedly, pointing to another small woman completely engulfed in a tower of presents. And that, too, would have been like my mother, to bring mountains of gifts, food, and toys for children—all bought on sale—shunning thanks, saying the gifts were nothing, and later turning the labels over to show my sisters, "Calvin Klein, 100% wool."

I imagined myself starting to say, "Sisters, I am sorry, I have come alone . . ." and before I could tell them—they could see it in my face—they were wailing, pulling their hair, their lips twisted in pain, as they ran away from me. And then I saw myself getting back on the plane and coming home.

After I had dreamed this scene many times—watching their despair turn from horror into anger—I begged Auntie Lindo to write another letter. And at first she refused.

"How can I say she is dead? I cannot write this," said Auntie Lindo with a stubborn look.

"But it's cruel to have them believe she's coming on the plane," I 25
said. "When they see it's just me, they'll hate me."

"Hate you? Cannot be." She was scowling. "You are their own sister, their only family."

"You don't understand," I protested.

"What I don't understand?" she said.

And I whispered, "They'll think I'm responsible, that she died because I didn't appreciate her."

And Auntie Lindo looked satisfied and sad at the same time, as if 30
this were true and I had finally realized it. She sat down for an hour, and when she stood up she handed me a two-page letter. She had tears in her eyes. I realized that the very thing I had feared, she had done. So even if she had written the news of my mother's death in English, I wouldn't have had the heart to read it.

"Thank you," I whispered.

The landscape has become gray, filled with low flat cement buildings, old factories, and then tracks and more tracks filled with trains like ours passing by in the opposite direction. I see platforms crowded with people wearing drab Western clothes, with spots of bright colors: little children wearing pink and yellow, red and peach. And there are soldiers in olive green and red, and old ladies in gray tops and pants that stop mid-calf. We are in Guangzhou.

Before the train even comes to a stop, people are bringing down their belongings from above their seats. For a moment there is a dangerous shower of heavy suitcases laden with gifts to relatives, half-broken boxes wrapped in miles of string to keep the contents from spilling out, plastic bags filled with yarn and vegetables and packages of dried mushrooms, and camera cases. And then we are caught in a stream of people rushing, shoving, pushing us along, until we find ourselves in one of a dozen lines waiting to go through customs. I feel as if I were getting on the number 30 Stockton bus in San Francisco. I am in China, I remind myself. And somehow the crowds don't bother me. It feels right. I start pushing too.

I take out the declaration forms and my passport. "Woo," it says at the top, and below that, "June May," who was born in "California, U.S.A.," in 1951. I wonder if the customs people will question whether I'm the same person in the passport photo. In this picture, my chin-length hair is swept back and artfully styled. I am wearing false eyelashes, eye shadow, and lip liner. My cheeks are hollowed out by bronze blusher. But I had not expected the heat in October. And now my hair hangs limp with the humidity. I wear no makeup; in Hong Kong my mascara had melted into dark circles and everything else had felt like layers of grease. So today my face is plain, unadorned except for a thin mist of shiny sweat on my forehead and nose.

Even without makeup, I could never pass for true Chinese. I stand 35
five-foot-six, and my head pokes above the crowd so that I am eye level only with other tourists. My mother once told me my height came from my grandfather, who was a northerner, and may have even had some Mongol blood. "This is what your grandmother once told me," explained

my mother. "But now it is too late to ask her. They are all dead, your grandparents, your uncles, and their wives and children, all killed in the war, when a bomb fell on our house. So many generations in one instant."

She had said this so matter-of-factly that I thought she had long since gotten over any grief she had. And then I wondered how she knew they were all dead.

"Maybe they left the house before the bomb fell," I suggested.

"No," said my mother. "Our whole family is gone. It is just you and I."

"But how do you know? Some of them could have escaped."

"Cannot be," said my mother, this time almost angrily. And then her 40
frown was washed over by a puzzled blank look, and she began to talk as if she were trying to remember where she had misplaced something. "I went back to that house. I kept looking up to where the house used to be. And it wasn't a house, just the sky. And below, underneath my feet, were four stories of burnt bricks and wood, all the life of our house. Then off to the side I saw things blown into the yard, nothing valuable. There was a bed someone used to sleep in, really just a metal frame twisted up at one corner. And a book, I don't know what kind, because every page had turned black. And I saw a teacup which was unbroken but filled with ashes. And then I found my doll, with her hands and legs broken, her hair burned off. . . . When I was a little girl, I had cried for that doll, seeing it all alone in the store window, and my mother had bought it for me. It was an American doll with yellow hair. It could turn its legs and arms. The eyes moved up and down. And when I married and left my family home, I gave the doll to my youngest niece, because she was like me. She cried if that doll was not with her always. Do you see? If she was in the house with that doll, her parents were there, and so everybody was there, waiting together, because that's how our family was."

The woman in the customs booth stares at my documents, then glances at me briefly, and with two quick movements stamps everything and sternly nods me along. And soon my father and I find ourselves in a large area filled with thousands of people and suitcases. I feel lost and my father looks helpless.

"Excuse me," I say to a man who looks like an American. "Can you tell me where I can get a taxi?" He mumbles something that sounds Swedish or Dutch.

"Syau Yen! Syau Yen!" I hear a piercing voice shout from behind me. An old woman in a yellow knit beret is holding up a pink plastic bag filled with wrapped trinkets. I guess she is trying to sell us something. But my father is staring down at this tiny sparrow of a woman, squinting into her eyes. And then his eyes widen, his face opens up and he smiles like a pleased little boy.

"*Aiyi! Aiyi!*"—Auntie Auntie!—he says softly.

"Syau Yen!" coos my great-aunt. I think it's funny she has just called 45
my father "Little Wild Goose." It must be his baby milk name, the name used to discourage ghosts from stealing children.

They clasp each other's hands—they do not hug—and hold on like this, taking turns saying, "Look at you! You are so old. Look how old you've become!" They are both crying openly, laughing at the same time, and I bite my lip, trying not to cry. I'm afraid to feel their joy. Because I am thinking how different our arrival in Shanghai will be tomorrow, how awkward it will feel.

Now Aiyi beams and points to a Polaroid picture of my father. My father had wisely sent pictures when he wrote and said we were coming. See how smart she was, she seems to intone as she compares the picture to my father. In the letter, my father had said we would call her from the hotel once we arrived, so this is a surprise, that they've come to meet us. I wonder if my sisters will be at the airport.

It is only then that I remember the camera. I had meant to take a picture of my father and his aunt the moment they met. It's not too late.

"Here, stand together over here," I say, holding up the Polaroid. The camera flashes and I hand them the snapshot. Aiyi and my father still stand close together, each of them holding a corner of the picture, watching as their images begin to form. They are almost reverentially quiet. Aiyi is only five years older than my father, which makes her around seventy-seven. But she looks ancient, shrunken, a mummified relic. Her thin hair is pure white, her teeth are brown with decay. So much for stories of Chinese women looking young forever, I think to myself.

Now Aiyi is crooning to me: "*Jandale*." So big already. She looks up 50
at me, at my full height, and then peers into her pink plastic bag—her gifts to us, I have figured out—as if she is wondering what she will give to me, now that I am so old and big. And then she grabs my elbow with her sharp pincerlike grasp and turns me around. A man and woman in their fifties are shaking hands with my father, everybody smiling and saying, "Ah! Ah!" They are Aiyi's oldest son and his wife, and standing next to them are four other people, around my age, and a little girl who's around ten. The introductions go by so fast, all I know is that one of them is Aiyi's grandson, with his wife, and the other is her granddaughter, with her husband. And the little girl is Lili, Aiyi's great-granddaughter.

Aiyi and my father speak the Mandarin dialect from their childhood, but the rest of the family speaks only the Cantonese of their village. I understand only Mandarin but can't speak it that well. So Aiyi and my father gossip unrestrained in Mandarin, exchanging news about people from their old village. And they stop only occasionally to talk to the rest of us, sometimes in Cantonese, sometimes in English.

"Oh, it is as I suspected," says my father, turning to me. "He died last summer." And I already understood this. I just don't know who this person, Li Gong, is. I feel as if I were in the United Nations and the translators had run amok.

"Hello," I say to the little girl. "My name is Jing-mei." But the little girl squirms to look away, causing her parents to laugh with embarrassment.

I try to think of Cantonese words I can say to her, stuff I learned from friends in Chinatown, but all I can think of are swear words, terms for bodily functions, and short phrases like "tastes good," "tastes like garbage," and "she's really ugly." And then I have another plan: I hold up the Polaroid camera, beckoning Lili with my finger. She immediately jumps forward, places one hand on her hip in the manner of a fashion model, juts out her chest, and flashes me a toothy smile. As soon as I take the picture she is standing next to me, jumping and giggling every few seconds as she watches herself appear on the greenish film.

By the time we hail taxis for the ride to the hotel, Lili is holding tight onto my hand, pulling me along.

In the taxi, Aiyi talks nonstop, so I have no chance to ask her about 55
the different sights we are passing by.

"You wrote and said you would come only for one day," says Aiyi to my father in an agitated tone. "One day! How can you see your family in one day! Toishan is many hours' drive from Guangzhou. And this idea to call us when you arrive. This is nonsense. We have no telephone."

My heart races a little. I wonder if Auntie Lindo told my sisters we would call from the hotel in Shanghai?

Aiyi continues to scold my father. "I was so beside myself, ask my son, almost turned heaven and earth upside down trying to think of a way! So we decided the best was for us to take the bus from Toishan and come into Guangzhou—meet you right from the start."

And now I am holding my breath as the taxi driver dodges between trucks and buses, honking his horn constantly. We seem to be on some sort of long freeway overpass, like a bridge above the city. I can see row after row of apartments, each floor cluttered with laundry hanging out to dry on the balcony. We pass a public bus, with people jammed in so tight their faces are nearly wedged against the window. Then I see the skyline of what must be downtown Guangzhou. From a distance, it looks like a major American city, with high rises and construction going on everywhere. As we slow down in the more congested part of the city, I see scores of little shops, dark inside, lined with counters and shelves. And then there is a building, its front laced with scaffolding made of bamboo poles held together with plastic strips. Men and women are standing on narrow platforms, scraping the sides, working without safety straps or helmets. Oh, would OSHA° have a field day here, I think.

Aiyi's shrill voice rises up again: "So it is a shame you can't see our 60
village, our house. My sons have been quite successful, selling our vegetables in the free market. We had enough these last few years to build a big house, three stories, all of new brick, big enough for our whole family and then some. And every year, the money is even better. You Americans aren't the only ones who know how to get rich!"

OSHA: Occupational Safety and Health Administration, a U.S. federal agency that regulates and monitors workplace safety conditions.

The taxi stops and I assume we've arrived, but then I peer out at what looks like a grander version of the Hyatt Regency. "This is communist China?" I wonder out loud. And then I shake my head toward my father. "This must be the wrong hotel." I quickly pull out our itinerary, travel tickets, and reservations. I had explicitly instructed my travel agent to choose something inexpensive, in the thirty-to-forty-dollar range. I'm sure of this. And there it says on our itinerary: Garden Hotel, Huanshi Dong Lu. Well, our travel agent had better be prepared to eat the extra, that's all I have to say.

The hotel is magnificent. A bellboy complete with uniform and sharp-creased cap jumps forward and begins to carry our bags into the lobby. Inside, the hotel looks like an orgy of shopping arcades and restaurants all encased in granite and glass. And rather than be impressed, I am worried about the expense, as well as the appearance it must give Aiyi, that we rich Americans cannot be without our luxuries even for one night.

But when I step up to the reservation desk, ready to haggle over this booking mistake, it is confirmed. Our rooms are prepaid, thirty-four dollars each. I feel sheepish, and Aiyi and the others seem delighted by our temporary surroundings. Lili is looking wide-eyed at an arcade filled with video games.

Our whole family crowds into one elevator, and the bellboy waves, saying he will meet us on the eighteenth floor. As soon as the elevator door shuts, everybody becomes very quiet, and when the door finally opens again, everybody talks at once in what sounds like relieved voices. I have the feeling Aiyi and the others have never been on such a long elevator ride.

Our rooms are next to each other and are identical. The rugs, drapes, bedspreads are all in shades of taupe. There's a color television with remote-control panels built into the lamp table between the two twin beds. The bathroom has marble walls and floors. I find a built-in wet bar with a small refrigerator stocked with Heineken beer, Coke Classic, and Seven-Up, mini-bottles of Johnnie Walker Red, Bacardi rum, and Smirnoff vodka, and packets of M & M's, honey-roasted cashews, and Cadbury chocolate bars. And again I say out loud, "This is communist China?"

My father comes into my room. "They decided we should just stay here and visit," he says, shrugging his shoulders. "They say, Less trouble that way. More time to talk."

"What about dinner?" I ask. I have been envisioning my first real Chinese feast for many days already, a big banquet with one of those soups steaming out of a carved winter melon, chicken wrapped in clay, Peking duck, the works.

My father walks over and picks up a room service book next to a *Travel & Leisure* magazine. He flips through the pages quickly and then points to the menu. "This is what they want," says my father.

So it's decided. We are going to dine tonight in our rooms, with our family, sharing hamburgers, french fries, and apple pie à la mode.

Aiyi and her family are browsing the shops while we clean up. After 70
a hot ride on the train, I'm eager for a shower and cooler clothes.

The hotel has provided little packets of shampoo which, upon opening, I discover is the consistency and color of hoisin sauce. This is more like it, I think. This is China. And I rub some in my damp hair.

Standing in the shower, I realize this is the first time I've been by myself in what seems like days. But instead of feeling relieved, I feel forlorn. I think about what my mother said, about activating my genes and becoming Chinese. And I wonder what she meant.

Right after my mother died, I asked myself a lot of things, things that couldn't be answered, to force myself to grieve more. It seemed as if I wanted to sustain my grief, to assure myself that I had cared deeply enough.

But now I ask the questions mostly because I want to know the answers. What was that pork stuff she used to make that had the texture of sawdust? What were the names of the uncles who died in Shanghai? What had she dreamt all these years about her other daughters? All the times when she got mad at me, was she really thinking about them? Did she wish I were they? Did she regret that I wasn't?

At one o'clock in the morning, I awake to tapping sounds on the 75
window. I must have dozed off and now I feel my body uncramping itself. I'm sitting on the floor, leaning against one of the twin beds. Lili is lying next to me. The others are asleep, too, sprawled out on the beds and floor. Aiyi is seated at a little table, looking very sleepy. And my father is staring out the window, tapping his fingers on the glass. The last time I listened my father was telling Aiyi about his life since he last saw her. How he had gone to Yenching University, later got a post with a newspaper in Chungking, met my mother there, a young widow. How they later fled together to Shanghai to try to find my mother's family house, but there was nothing there. And then they traveled eventually to Canton and then to Hong Kong, then Haiphong and finally to San Francisco. . . .

"Suyuan didn't tell me she was trying all these years to find her daughters," he is now saying in a quiet voice. "Naturally, I did not discuss her daughters with her. I thought she was ashamed she had left them behind."

"Where did she leave them?" asks Aiyi. "How were they found?"

I am wide awake now. Although I have heard parts of this story from my mother's friends.

"It happened when the Japanese took over Kweilin," says my father.

"Japanese in Kweilin?" says Aiyi. "That was never the case. Couldn't 80
be. The Japanese never came to Kweilin."

"Yes, that is what the newspapers reported. I know this because I was working for the news bureau at the time. The Kuomintang often told us what we could say and could not say. But we knew the Japanese had come into Kwangsi Province. We had sources who told us how they had captured the Wuchang-Canton railway. How they were coming overland, making very fast progress, marching toward the provincial capital."

Aiyi looks astonished. "If people did not know this, how could Suyuan know the Japanese were coming?"

"An officer of the Kuomintang secretly warned her," explains my father. "Suyuan's husband also was an officer and everybody knew that officers and their families would be the first to be killed. So she gathered a few possessions and, in the middle of the night, she picked up her daughters and fled on foot. The babies were not even one year old."

"How could she give up those babies!" sighs Aiyi. "Twin girls. We have never had such luck in our family." And then she yawns again.

"What were they named?" she asks. I listen carefully. I had been planning on using just the familiar "Sister" to address them both. But now I want to know how to pronounce their names.

"They have their father's surname, Wang," says my father. "And their given names are Chwun Yu and Chwun Hwa."

"What do the names mean?" I ask.

"Ah." My father draws imaginary characters on the window. "One means 'Spring Rain,' the other 'Spring Flower,'" he explains in English, "because they born in the spring, and of course rain come before flower, same order these girls are born. Your mother like a poet, don't you think?"

I nod my head. I see Aiyi nod her head forward, too. But it falls forward and stays there. She is breathing deeply, noisily. She is asleep.

"And what does Ma's name mean?" I whisper.

"'Suyuan,'" he says, writing more invisible characters on the glass. "The way she write it in Chinese, it mean 'Long-Cherished Wish.' Quite a fancy name, not so ordinary like flower name. See this first character, it mean something like 'Forever Never Forgotten.' But there is another way to write 'Suyuan.' Sound exactly the same, but the meaning is opposite." His finger creates the brushstrokes of another character. "The first part look the same: 'Never Forgotten.' But the last part add to first part make the whole word mean 'Long-Held Grudge.' Your mother get angry with me, I tell her her name should be Grudge."

My father is looking at me, moist-eyed. "See, I pretty clever, too, hah?"

I nod, wishing I could find some way to comfort him. "And what about my name," I ask, "what does 'Jing-mei' mean?"

"Your name also special," he says. I wonder if any name in Chinese is not something special. "'Jing' like excellent *jing*. Not just good, it's something pure, essential, the best quality. *Jing* is good leftover stuff when you take impurities out of something like gold, or rice, or salt. So what is left—just pure essence. And 'Mei,' this is common *mei*, as in *meimei*, 'younger sister.'"

I think about this. My mother's long-cherished wish. Me, the younger sister who was supposed to be the essence of the others. I feed myself with the old grief, wondering how disappointed my mother must have been. Tiny Aiyi stirs suddenly, her head rolls and then falls back, her mouth opens as if to answer my question. She grunts in her sleep, tucking her body more closely into the chair.

"So why did she abandon those babies on the road?" I need to know, because now I feel abandoned too.

"Long time I wondered this myself," says my father. "But then I read that letter from her daughters in Shanghai now, and I talk to Auntie Lindo, all the others. And then I knew. No shame in what she done. None."

"What happened?"

"Your mother running away—" begins my father.

"No, tell me in Chinese," I interrupt. "Really, I can understand."

He begins to talk, still standing at the window, looking into the night.

After fleeing Kweilin, your mother walked for several days trying to find a main road. Her thought was to catch a ride on a truck or wagon, to catch enough rides until she reached Chungking, where her husband was stationed.

She had sewn money and jewelry into the lining of her dress, enough, she thought, to barter rides all the way. If I am lucky, she thought, I will not have to trade the heavy gold bracelet and jade ring. These were things from her mother, your grandmother.

By the third day, she had traded nothing. The roads were filled with people, everybody running and begging for rides from passing trucks. The trucks rushed by, afraid to stop. So your mother found no rides, only the start of dysentery pains in her stomach.

Her shoulders ached from the two babies swinging from scarf slings. Blisters grew on her palms from holding two leather suitcases. And then the blisters burst and began to bleed. After a while, she left the suitcases behind, keeping only the food and a few clothes. And later she also dropped the bags of wheat flour and rice and kept walking like this for many miles, singing songs to her little girls, until she was delirious with pain and fever.

Finally, there was not one more step left in her body. She didn't have the strength to carry those babies any farther. She slumped to the ground. She knew she would die of her sickness, or perhaps from thirst, from starvation, or from the Japanese, who she was sure were marching right behind her.

She took the babies out of the slings and sat them on the side of the road, then lay down next to them. You babies are so good, she said, so quiet. They smiled back, reaching their chubby hands for her, wanting to be picked up again. And then she knew she could not bear to watch her babies die with her.

She saw a family with three young children in a cart going by. "Take my babies, I beg you," she cried to them. But they stared back with empty eyes and never stopped.

She saw another person pass and called out again. This time a man turned around, and he had such a terrible expression—your mother said it looked like death itself—she shivered and looked away.

When the road grew quiet, she tore open the lining of her dress, and 110
stuffed jewelry under the shirt of one baby and money under the other. She reached into her pocket and drew out the photos of her family, the picture of her father and mother, the picture of herself and her husband on their wedding day. And she wrote on the back of each the names of the babies and this same message: "Please care for these babies with the money and valuables provided. When it is safe to come, if you bring them to Shanghai, 9 Weichang Lu, the Li family will be glad to give you a generous reward. Li Suyuan and Wang Fuchi."

And then she touched each baby's cheek and told her not to cry. She would go down the road to find them some food and would be back. And without looking back, she walked down the road, stumbling and crying, thinking only of this one last hope, that her daughters would be found by a kindhearted person who would care for them. She would not allow herself to imagine anything else.

She did not remember how far she walked, which direction she went, when she fainted, or how she was found. When she awoke, she was in the back of a bouncing truck with several other sick people, all moaning. And she began to scream, thinking she was now on a journey to Buddhist hell. But the face of an American missionary lady bent over her and smiled, talking to her in a soothing language she did not understand. And yet she could somehow understand. She had been saved for no good reason, and it was now too late to go back and save her babies.

When she arrived in Chungking, she learned her husband had died two weeks before. She told me later she laughed when the officers told her this news, she was so delirious with madness and disease. To come so far, to lose so much and to find nothing.

I met her in a hospital. She was lying on a cot, hardly able to move, her dysentery had drained her so thin. I had come in for my foot, my missing toe, which was cut off by a piece of falling rubble. She was talking to herself, mumbling.

"Look at these clothes," she said, and I saw she had on a rather 115
unusual dress for wartime. It was silk satin, quite dirty, but there was no doubt it was a beautiful dress.

"Look at this face," she said, and I saw her dusty face and hollow cheeks, her eyes shining back. "Do you see my foolish hope?"

"I thought I had lost everything, except these two things," she murmured. "And I wondered which I would lose next. Clothes or hope? Hope or clothes?"

"But now, see here, look what is happening," she said, laughing, as if all her prayers had been answered. And she was pulling hair out of her head as easily as one lifts new wheat from wet soil.

It was an old peasant woman who found them. "How could I resist?" the peasant woman later told your sisters when they were older. They were still sitting obediently near where your mother had left them, looking like little fairy queens waiting for their sedan to arrive.

120 The woman, Mei Ching, and her husband, Mei Han, lived in a stone cave. There were thousands of hidden caves like that in and around Kweilin so secret that the people remained hidden even after the war ended. The Meis would come out of their cave every few days and forage for food supplies left on the road, and sometimes they would see something that they both agreed was a tragedy to leave behind. So one day they took back to their cave a delicately painted set of rice bowls, another day a little footstool with a velvet cushion and two new wedding blankets. And once, it was your sisters.

They were pious people, Muslims, who believed the twin babies were a sign of double luck, and they were sure of this when, later in the evening, they discovered how valuable the babies were. She and her husband had never seen rings and bracelets like those. And while they admired the pictures, knowing the babies came from a good family, neither of them could read or write. It was not until many months later that Mei Ching found someone who could read the writing on the back. By then, she loved these baby girls like her own.

In 1952 Mei Han, the husband, died. The twins were already eight years old, and Mei Ching now decided it was time to find your sisters' true family.

She showed the girls the picture of their mother and told them they had been born into a great family and she would take them back to see their true mother and grandparents. Mei Ching told them about the reward, but she swore she would refuse it. She loved these girls so much, she only wanted them to have what they were entitled to—a better life, a fine house, educated ways. Maybe the family would let her stay on as the girls' amah. Yes, she was certain they would insist.

Of course, when she found the place at 9 Weichang Lu, in the old French Concession, it was something completely different. It was the site of a factory building, recently constructed, and none of the workers knew what had become of the family whose house had burned down on that spot.

125 Mei Ching could not have known, of course, that your mother and I, her new husband, had already returned to that same place in 1945 in hopes of finding both her family and her daughters.

Your mother and I stayed in China until 1947. We went to many different cities—back to Kweilin, to Changsha, as far south as Kunming. She was always looking out of one corner of her eye for twin babies, then little girls. Later we went to Hong Kong, and when we finally left in 1949 for the United States, I think she was even looking for them on the boat. But when we arrived, she no longer talked about them. I thought, At last, they have died in her heart.

When letters could be openly exchanged between China and the United States, she wrote immediately to old friends in Shanghai and Kweilin. I did not know she did this. Auntie Lindo told me. But of course, by then, all the street names had changed. Some people had died, others had moved away. So it took many years to find a contact. And when she did find an old schoolmate's address and wrote asking her to look for her daughters, her friend wrote back and said this was impossible, like looking for a needle on the bottom of the ocean. How did she know her daughters were in Shanghai and not somewhere else in China? The friend, of course, did not ask, How do you know your daughters are still alive?

So her schoolmate did not look. Finding babies lost during the war was a matter of foolish imagination, and she had no time for that.

But every year, your mother wrote to different people. And this last year, I think she got a big idea in her head, to go to China and find them herself. I remember she told me, "Canning, we should go, before it is too late, before we are too old." And I told her we were already too old, it was already too late.

I just thought she wanted to be a tourist! I didn't know she wanted to go and look for her daughters. So when I said it was too late, that must have put a terrible thought in her head that her daughters might be dead. And I think this possibility grew bigger and bigger in her head, until it killed her.

Maybe it was your mother's dead spirit who guided her Shanghai schoolmate to find her daughters. Because after your mother died, the schoolmate saw your sisters, by chance, while shopping for shoes at the Number One Department Store on Nanjing Dong Road. She said it was like a dream, seeing these two women who looked so much alike, moving down the stairs together. There was something about their facial expressions that reminded the schoolmate of your mother.

She quickly walked over to them and called their names, which of course, they did not recognize at first, because Mei Ching had changed their names. But your mother's friend was so sure, she persisted. "Are you not Wang Chwun Yu and Wang Chwun Hwa?" she asked them. And then these double-image women became very excited, because they remembered the names written on the back of an old photo, a photo of a young man and woman they still honored, as their much-loved first parents, who had died and become spirit ghosts still roaming the earth looking for them.

At the airport, I am exhausted. I could not sleep last night. Aiyi had followed me into my room at three in the morning, and she instantly fell asleep on one of the twin beds, snoring with the might of a lumberjack. I lay awake thinking about my mother's story, realizing how much I have never known about her, grieving that my sisters and I had both lost her.

And now at the airport, after shaking hands with everybody, waving good-bye, I think about all the different ways we leave people in this world. Cheerily waving good-bye to some at airports, knowing we'll never see each other again. Leaving others on the side of the road, hoping that we will. Finding my mother in my father's story and saying good-bye before I have a chance to know her better.

Aiyi smiles at me as we wait for our gate to be called. She is so old. I put 135
one arm around her and one around Lili. They are the same size, it seems. And then it's time. As we wave good-bye one more time and enter the waiting area, I get the sense I am going from one funeral to another. In my hand I'm clutching a pair of tickets to Shanghai. In two hours we'll be there.

The plane takes off. I close my eyes. How can I describe to them in my broken Chinese about our mother's life? Where should I begin?

"Wake up, we're here," says my father. And I awake with my heart pounding in my throat. I look out the window and we're already on the runway. It's gray outside.

And now I'm walking down the steps of the plane, onto the tarmac and toward the building. If only, I think, if only my mother had lived long enough to be the one walking toward them. I am so nervous I cannot even feel my feet. I am just moving somehow.

Somebody shouts, "She's arrived!" And then I see her. Her short hair. Her small body. And that same look on her face. She has the back of her hand pressed hard against her mouth. She is crying as though she had gone through a terrible ordeal and were happy it is over.

And I know it's not my mother, yet it is the same look she had 140
when I was five and had disappeared all afternoon, for such a long time, that she was convinced I was dead. And when I miraculously appeared, sleepy-eyed, crawling from underneath my bed, she wept and laughed, biting the back of her hand to make sure it was true.

And now I see her again, two of her, waving, and in one hand there is a photo, the Polaroid I sent them. As soon as I get beyond the gate, we run toward each other, all three of us embracing, all hesitations and expectations forgotten.

"Mama, Mama," we all murmur, as if she is among us.

My sisters look at me, proudly. "*Meimei jandale*," says one sister proudly to the other. "Little Sister has grown up." I look at their faces again and I see no trace of my mother in them. Yet they still look familiar. And now I also see what part of me is Chinese. It is so obvious. It is my family. It is in our blood. After all these years, it can finally be let go.

My sisters and I stand, arms around each other, laughing and wiping the tears from each other's eyes. The flash of the Polaroid goes off and my father hands me the snapshot. My sisters and I watch quietly together, eager to see what develops.

The gray-green surface changes to the bright colors of our three images, sharpening and deepening all at once. And although we don't speak, I know we all see it: Together we look like our mother. Her same eyes, her same mouth, open in surprise to see, at last, her long-cherished wish.

Questions

1. How is the external setting of "A Pair of Tickets" essential to what happens internally to the narrator in the course of this story?
2. How does the narrator's view of her father change by seeing him in a different setting?
3. In what ways does the narrator feel at home in China? In what ways does she feel foreign?
4. What do the narrator and her half-sisters have in common? How does this element relate to the theme of the story?
5. In what ways does the story explore specifically Chinese American experiences? In what other ways is the story grounded in universal family issues?

WRITING *effectively*

THINKING ABOUT SETTING

The time and place in which a story is set serve as more than mere backdrop. When preparing to write about a story, be sure to consider where and when it is set, and what role the setting plays.

- **Ask whether setting helps motivate the plot.** The external pressure of the setting is often the key factor that compels or invites the protagonist into action. Setting can play as large a role as plot and characters do by prompting a protagonist into an action he or she might not otherwise take.
- **Consider whether the external setting suggests the character's inner reality.** A particular setting can create a mood or provide clues to a protagonist's nature. To write about a story's setting, therefore, invites you to study not only the time and place but also their relation to the protagonist. Does the external reality provide a clue to the protagonist's inner reality?

- **Notice whether the setting changes as the plot progresses.** The settings in a story are not static. Characters can move from place to place, and their actions may bring them into significantly different external and internal places.

CHECKLIST: Writing About Setting

- ☐ Where does the story take place?
- ☐ What does the setting suggest about the characters' lives?
- ☐ Are there significant differences in the settings for different characters? What does this suggest about each person?
- ☐ When does the story take place? Is the time of year or time of day significant?
- ☐ Does the weather play a meaningful role in the story's action?
- ☐ What is the protagonist's relationship to the setting?
- ☐ Does the setting of the story in some way compel the protagonist into action?
- ☐ Does the story's time or place suggest something about the character of the protagonist?
- ☐ Does a change in setting during the story suggest some internal change in the protagonist?

TOPICS FOR WRITING ON SETTING

1. Choose a story from this chapter, and explore how character and setting are interrelated. How does the setting of the climax of the story contribute to a change in the character's personal perspective?
2. Write about how setting functions as a kind of character in "To Build a Fire." Do the landscape and weather act as the antagonist in the story's plot?
3. How is the plot of Jorge Luis Borges's "The Gospel According to Mark" dependent on the story's setting? Illustrate and analyze how the setting motivates and influences the story's main characters.
4. Take any story in this chapter and analyze how the author presents the key setting. Don't pay special attention to the protagonist or other human characters, but focus on the setting that surrounds him or her and how it emerges as a force in the story.
5. Think of a place to which you often return. If possible, go there. Make a list of every physical detail you can think of to describe that place. Then look the list over and write a paragraph on what sort of mood is suggested by it. If you were to describe your emotional connection to the place, which three details would you choose? Why?
6. Choose any story in this book, and pay careful attention to setting as you read it. Write several paragraphs reflecting on the following questions: What details in the story suggest the time and place in which it is set? Is setting central to the story? If the action were transplanted to some other place and time, how would the story change?

▶ TERMS FOR *review*

Setting ▶ The time and place of a story. The setting may also include the climate and even the social, psychological, or spiritual state of the characters.

Locale ▶ The location where a story takes place.

Atmosphere ▶ The dominant mood or feeling that pervades all or part of a literary work. Atmosphere is the total effect conveyed by the author's use of language, images, and physical setting.

Historical fiction ▶ A type of fiction in which the narrative is set in an earlier time or place, sometimes including well-known figures from the past.

Regionalism ▶ The literary representation of a specific locale that consciously uses the particulars of geography, custom, history, folklore, or speech. In regional narratives, the locale plays a crucial role in the presentation and progression of the story.

Naturalism ▶ A type of fiction in which the characters are presented as products or victims of environment and heredity. Naturalism is considered an extreme form of **realism** (the attempt to reproduce faithfully the surface appearance of life, especially that of ordinary people in everyday situations).

5 TONE AND STYLE

What You Will Learn in This Chapter

- To identify the *tone* of a story
- To describe the elements of an author's style
- To define *irony* and identify its many forms
- To analyze the tone and style of a story

When the narrator of Joseph Conrad's *Heart of Darkness* comes upon an African outpost littered with abandoned machines and notices "a boiler wallowing in the grass," the exact word *wallowing* conveys an attitude: that there is something swinish about this scene of careless waste. If Conrad had selected a different word than *wallowing*—say, *resting*—his description would have carried less meaning. His example reminds us that not only an author's choice of details may lead us to infer his or her attitude, but also the choice of words, as well as characters, events, and situations.

TONE

Whatever helps us understand the author's attitude is commonly called **tone**. Like a tone of voice, the tone of a story may communicate amusement, anger, affection, sorrow, contempt. It implies the feelings of the author, so far as we can sense them. Those feelings may be similar to feelings expressed by the narrator of the story (or by any character), but sometimes they may be dissimilar, even sharply opposed. The characters in a story may regard an event as sad, but we sense that the author regards it as funny. To understand the tone of a story, then, is to understand some attitude more fundamental to the story than whatever attitudes the characters explicitly declare.

The tone of a story, like a tone of voice, may convey not simply one attitude, but a medley. Reading "A & P" (Chapter 1), we have mingled feelings about Sammy: delight in his wicked comments about other people and his skewering of hypocrisy; irritation at his smugness and condescension; admiration for his readiness to take a stand; sympathy for the pain of his disillusionment. Often the tone of a literary story will be too rich and complicated to sum up in one or two words. But to try to describe the tone of such a story may be a useful way to penetrate to its center and to grasp the whole of it.

STYLE

One of the clearest indications of the tone of a story is the **style** in which it is written. In general, style refers to the individual traits or characteristics of a piece of writing: to a writer's particular ways of managing words that we come to recognize as habitual or customary. It includes all the ways in which a writer uses words, imagery, tone, syntax, and figurative language.

A distinctive style marks the work of a fine writer: we can tell his or her work from that of anyone else. From one story to another, however, the writer may fittingly change style; and in some stories, style may be altered meaningfully as the story goes along. In his novel *As I Lay Dying*, William Faulkner changes narrators with every chapter, and he distinguishes the narrators from one another by giving each an individual style or manner of speaking. Though each narrator has his or her own style, the book as a whole demonstrates Faulkner's style as well. For instance, one chapter is written from the point of view of a small boy, Vardaman Bundren, member of a family of poor Mississippi tenant farmers, whose view of a horse in a barn reads like this:

> It is as though the dark were resolving him out of his integrity, into an unrelated scattering of components—snuffings and stampings; smells of cooling flesh and ammoniac hair; an illusion of a co-ordinated whole of splotched hide and strong bones within which, detached and secret and familiar, an *is* different from my *is*.

How can a small boy unaccustomed to libraries use words like *integrity*, *components*, *ammoniac*, *illusion*, and *co-ordinated*? Elsewhere in the story, Vardaman says aloud, with no trace of literacy, "Hit was a-laying right there on the ground." Apparently, in the passage it is not the voice of the boy that we are hearing, but something resembling the voice of William Faulkner, elevated and passionate, expressing the boy's thoughts in a style that admits Faulknerian words.

DICTION

Usually, *style* indicates a mode of expression: the language a writer uses. In this sense, the notion of style includes such traits as the length and complexity of sentences, and **diction**, or choice of words: abstract or concrete, bookish ("unrelated scattering of components") or close to speech ("Hit was a-laying right there on the ground"). Involved in the idea of style, too, is any habitual use of imagery, patterns of sound, figures of speech, or other devices.

Several writers of realistic fiction known as **minimalists**—Ann Beattie, Raymond Carver, Bobbie Ann Mason—have written with a flat, laid-back, unemotional tone, in an appropriately bare, unadorned style. Minimalists seem to give nothing but facts drawn from ordinary life, sometimes in picayune detail. Here is a sample passage from Raymond Carver's story "A Small, Good Thing":

> She pulled into the driveway and cut the engine. She closed her eyes and leaned her head against the wheel for a minute. She listened to the ticking sounds the engine made as it began to cool. Then she got out of the car. She could hear the dog barking inside the house. She went to the front door, which was unlocked. She went inside and turned on lights and put on a kettle of water for tea. She opened some dog food and fed Slug on the back porch. The dog ate in hungry little smacks. It kept running into the kitchen to see that she was going to stay.

Explicit feeling and showy language are kept at a minimum here. Notice how Carver's diction relies on everyday words—mostly words of only one or two syllables. Taken out of context, this description may strike you as banal, as if the writer himself were bored; but it works effectively as a part of Carver's entire story. As in all good writing, the style here seems a faithful mirror of what is said in it. At its best, such writing achieves "a hard-won reduction, a painful stripping away of richness, a baring of bone."[1]

Two Examples of Style: Hemingway Versus Faulkner

To see what style means, compare the stories in this chapter by William Faulkner ("Barn Burning") and by Ernest Hemingway ("A Clean, Well-Lighted Place"). Faulkner frequently falls into a style in which a statement, as soon as it is uttered, is followed by another statement expressing the idea in a more emphatic way. Sentences are interrupted with parenthetical elements (asides, like this) thrust into them unexpectedly. At times, Faulkner writes of seemingly ordinary matters as if giving a speech in a towering passion. Here, from "Barn Burning," is a description of how a boy's father delivers a rug:

> "Don't you want me to help?" he whispered. His father did not answer and now he heard again that stiff foot striking the hollow portico with that wooden and clocklike deliberation, that outrageous overstatement of the weight it carried. The rug, hunched, not flung (the boy could tell that even in the darkness) from his father's shoulder struck the angle of wall and floor with a sound unbelievably loud, thunderous, then the foot again, unhurried and enormous; a light came on in the house and the boy sat, tense, breathing steadily and quietly and just a little fast, though the foot itself did not increase its beat at all, descending the steps now; now the boy could see him.

Faulkner is not merely indulging in language for its own sake. As you will find when you read the whole story, this rug delivery is vital to the story, and so too is the father's profound defiance—indicated by his walk. By devices of style—by *metaphor* and *simile* ("wooden and clocklike"), by exact qualification

[1] Letter in the *New York Times Book Review*, 5 June 1988.

("not flung"), by emphatic adjectives ("loud, thunderous")—Faulkner is carefully placing his emphases.

By the words he selects to describe the father's stride, Faulkner directs how we feel toward the man and perhaps also indicates his own wondering but skeptical attitude toward a character whose very footfall is "outrageous" and "enormous." (Fond of long sentences like the last one in the quoted passage, Faulkner remarked that there are sentences that need to be written in the way a circus acrobat pedals a bicycle on a high wire: rapidly, so as not to fall off.)

Hemingway's famous style includes both short sentences and long. His long compound sentences tend to be relatively simple in construction (clause plus clause plus clause), sometimes joined with the use of *and*. He interrupts such a sentence with a dependent clause or a parenthetical element much less frequently than Faulkner does. The effect is like listening to speech:

> In the day time the street was dusty, but at night the dew settled the dust and the old man liked to sit late because he was deaf and now at night it was quiet and he felt the difference.

Hemingway is a master of swift, terse dialogue and often casts whole scenes in the form of conversation. As if he were a closemouthed speaker unwilling to let his feelings loose, the narrator of a Hemingway story often addresses us in understatement, implying greater depths of feeling than he puts into words. Read the following story and you will see that its style and tone cannot be separated.

Ernest Hemingway

A Clean, Well-Lighted Place 1933

Ernest Hemingway

Ernest Hemingway (1899–1961), born in Oak Park, Illinois, skipped college to become a cub reporter. In World War I, as an eighteen-year-old volunteer ambulance driver in Italy, he was wounded in action. In 1922 he settled in Paris, then aswarm with writers; he later recalled that time in the autobiographical essays in A Moveable Feast *(1964). Hemingway won swift acclaim for his early stories,* In Our Time *(1925), and for his first, perhaps finest, novel,* The Sun Also Rises *(1926), portraying a "lost generation" of postwar American drifters in France and Spain.* For Whom the Bell Tolls *(1940) depicts life during the Spanish Civil War. Hemingway became a celebrity, often photographed as a marlin fisherman or a lion hunter. A fan of bullfighting, he wrote two nonfiction books on the subject:* Death in the Afternoon *(1932) and* The Dangerous Summer *(posthumously published in 1985). After World War II, with his fourth wife, journalist Mary Welsh, he made his home in Cuba, where he wrote* The Old Man and the Sea *(1952). The Nobel Prize in Literature came his way in 1954. In 1961, mentally distressed and physically ailing, he shot himself. Hemingway brought a hard-bitten realism to American fiction. His heroes live dangerously, by personal codes of honor, courage, and endurance. Hemingway's distinctively crisp, unadorned style left American literature permanently changed.*

It was late and every one had left the café except an old man who sat in the shadow the leaves of the tree made against the electric light. In the day time the street was dusty, but at night the dew settled the dust and the old man liked to sit late because he was deaf and now at night it was quiet and he felt the difference. The two waiters inside the café knew that the old man was a little drunk, and while he was a good client they knew that if he became too drunk he would leave without paying, so they kept watch on him.

"Last week he tried to commit suicide," one waiter said.

"Why?"

"He was in despair."

"What about?" 5

"Nothing."

"How do you know it was nothing?"

"He has plenty of money."

They sat together at a table that was close against the wall near the door of the café and looked at the terrace where the tables were all empty except where the old man sat in the shadow of the leaves of the tree that moved slightly in the wind. A girl and a soldier went by in the street. The street light shone on the brass number on his collar. The girl wore no head covering and hurried beside him.

"The guard will pick him up," one waiter said. 10

"What does it matter if he gets what he's after?"

"He had better get off the street now. The guard will get him. They went by five minutes ago."

The old man sitting in the shadow rapped on his saucer with his glass. The younger waiter went over to him.

"What do you want?"

The old man looked at him. "Another brandy," he said. 15

"You'll be drunk," the waiter said. The old man looked at him. The waiter went away.

"He'll stay all night," he said to his colleague. "I'm sleepy now. I never get into bed before three o'clock. He should have killed himself last week."

The waiter took the brandy bottle and another saucer from the counter inside the café and marched out to the old man's table. He put down the saucer and poured the glass full of brandy.

"You should have killed yourself last week," he said to the deaf man. The old man motioned with his finger. "A little more," he said. The waiter poured on into the glass so that the brandy slopped over and ran down the stem into the top saucer of the pile. "Thank you," the old man said. The waiter took the bottle back inside the café. He sat down at the table with his colleague again.

"He's drunk now," he said.

"He's drunk every night."°

"What did he want to kill himself for?"

"How should I know?"

"How did he do it?"

"He hung himself with a rope."

"Who cut him down?"

"His niece."

"Why did they do it?"

"Fear for his soul."

"How much money has he got?"

"He's got plenty."

"He must be eighty years old."

"Anyway I should say he was eighty."°

"I wish he would go home. I never get to bed before three o'clock. What kind of hour is that to go to bed?"

"He stays up because he likes it."

"He's lonely. I'm not lonely. I have a wife waiting in bed for me."

"He had a wife once too."

"A wife would be no good to him now."

"You can't tell. He might be better with a wife."

"His niece looks after him."

"I know. You said she cut him down."

"I wouldn't want to be that old. An old man is a nasty thing."

"Not always. This old man is clean. He drinks without spilling. Even now, drunk. Look at him."

"I don't want to look at him. I wish he would go home. He has no regard for those who must work."

The old man looked from his glass across the square, then over at the waiters.

"Another brandy," he said, pointing to his glass. The waiter who was in a hurry came over.

"Finished," he said, speaking with that omission of syntax stupid people employ when talking to drunken people or foreigners. "No more tonight. Close now."

"Another," said the old man.

"He's drunk now," he said. "He's drunk every night": The younger waiter perhaps says both these lines. A device of Hemingway's style is sometimes to have a character pause, then speak again—as often happens in actual speech. *"He must be eighty years old." "Anyway I should say he was eighty"*: Is this another instance of the same character's speaking twice? Clearly, it is the younger waiter who says the next line, "I wish he would go home."

"No. Finished." The waiter wiped the edge of the table with a towel and shook his head.

The old man stood up, slowly counted the saucers, took a leather coin purse from his pocket and paid for the drinks, leaving half a peseta tip.

The waiter watched him go down the street, a very old man walking unsteadily but with dignity.

"Why didn't you let him stay and drink?" the unhurried waiter asked. They were putting up the shutters. "It is not half-past two."

"I want to go home to bed."

"What is an hour?"

"More to me than to him."

"An hour is the same."

"You talk like an old man yourself. He can buy a bottle and drink at home."

"It's not the same."

"No, it is not," agreed the waiter with a wife. He did not wish to be unjust. He was only in a hurry.

"And you? You have no fear of going home before the usual hour?"

"Are you trying to insult me?"

"No, hombre, only to make a joke."

"No," the waiter who was in a hurry said, rising from pulling down the metal shutters. "I have confidence. I am all confidence."

"You have youth, confidence, and a job," the older waiter said. "You have everything."

"And what do you lack?"

"Everything but work."

"You have everything I have."

"No. I have never had confidence and I am not young."

"Come on. Stop talking nonsense and lock up."

"I am of those who like to stay late at the café," the older waiter said. "With all those who do not want to go to bed. With all those who need a light for the night."

"I want to go home and into bed."

"We are of two different kinds," the older waiter said. He was not dressed to go home. "It is not only a question of youth and confidence although those things are very beautiful. Each night I am reluctant to close up because there may be some one who needs the café."

"Hombre, there are bodegas° open all night long."

"You do not understand. This is a clean and pleasant café. It is well lighted. The light is very good and also, now, there are shadows of the leaves."

"Good night," said the younger waiter.

"Good night," the other said. Turning off the electric light he continued the conversation with himself. It is the light of course but it is

bodegas: wineshops.

necessary that the place be clean and pleasant. You do not want music. Certainly you do not want music. Nor can you stand before a bar with dignity although that is all that is provided for these hours. What did he fear? It was not fear or dread. It was a nothing that he knew too well. It was all a nothing and a man was nothing too. It was only that and light was all it needed and a certain cleanness and order. Some lived in it and never felt it but he knew it all was nada y pues nada y nada y pues nada.° Our nada who art in nada, nada be thy name thy kingdom nada thy will be nada in nada as it is in nada. Give us this nada our daily nada and nada us our nada as we nada our nadas and nada us not into nada but deliver us from nada; pues nada. Hail nothing full of nothing, nothing is with thee. He smiled and stood before a bar with a shining steam pressure coffee machine.

"What's yours?" asked the barman.

"Nada."

"Otro loco más,"° said the barman and turned away.

"A little cup," said the waiter.

The barman poured it for him.

"The light is very bright and pleasant but the bar is unpolished," the waiter said.

The barman looked at him but did not answer. It was too late at night for conversation.

"You want another copita?"° the barman asked.

"No, thank you," said the waiter and went out. He disliked bars and bodegas. A clean, well-lighted café was a very different thing. Now, without thinking further, he would go home to his room. He would lie in the bed and finally, with daylight, he would go to sleep. After all, he said to himself, it is probably only insomnia. Many must have it.

Questions

1. What besides insomnia makes the older waiter reluctant to go to bed? Comment especially on his meditation with its *nada* refrain. Why does he understand so well the old man's need for a café? What does the café represent for the two of them?
2. Compare the younger waiter and the older waiter in their attitudes toward the old man. Whose attitude do you take to be closer to that of the author? Even though Hemingway does not editorially state his own feelings, how does he make them clear to us?
3. Point to sentences that establish the style of the story. What is distinctive in them? What repetitions of words or phrases seem particularly effective? Does Hemingway seem to favor a simple or an erudite vocabulary?
4. What is the story's point of view? Discuss its appropriateness.

nada y pues . . . nada: nothing and then nothing and nothing and then nothing. *Otro loco más:* another lunatic. *copita:* little cup.

William Faulkner

Barn Burning 1939

William Faulkner (1897–1962) receives a capsule biography in Chapter 2, page 32, along with his story "A Rose for Emily." "Barn Burning" is among his many contributions to the history of Yoknapatawpha, an imaginary Mississippi county in which the Sartorises and the de Spains are landed aristocrats living by a code of honor, and the Snopeses—most of them—are shiftless ne'er-do-wells.

The store in which the Justice of the Peace's court was sitting smelled of cheese. The boy, crouched on his nail keg at the back of the crowded room, knew he smelled cheese, and more: from where he sat he could see the ranked shelves close-packed with the solid, squat, dynamic shapes of tin cans whose labels his stomach read, not from the lettering which meant nothing to his mind but from the scarlet devils and the silver curve of fish—this, the cheese which he knew he smelled and the hermetic meat which his intestines believed he smelled coming in intermittent gusts momentary and brief between the other constant one, the smell and sense just a little of fear because mostly of despair and grief, the old fierce pull of blood. He could not see the table where the Justice sat and before which his father and his father's enemy (*our enemy* he thought in that despair: *ourn! mine and hisn both! He's my father!*) stood, but he could hear them, the two of them that is, because his father had said no word yet:

"But what proof have you, Mr. Harris?"

"I told you. The hog got into my corn. I caught it up and sent it back to him. He had no fence that would hold it. I told him so, warned him. The next time I put the hog in my pen. When he came to get it I gave him enough wire to patch up his pen. The next time I put the hog up and kept it. I rode down to his house and saw the wire I gave him still rolled on to the spool in his yard. I told him he could have the hog when he paid me a dollar pound fee. That evening a nigger came with the dollar and got the hog. He was a strange nigger. He said, 'He say to tell you wood and hay kin burn.' I said, 'What?' 'That whut he say to tell you,' the nigger said. 'Wood and hay kin burn.' That night my barn burned. I got the stock out but I lost the barn."

"Where's the nigger? Have you got him?"

"He was a strange nigger, I tell you. I don't know what became of 5
him."

"But that's not proof. Don't you see that's not proof?"

"Get that boy up here. He knows." For a moment the boy thought too that the man meant his older brother until Harris said, "Not him. The little one. The boy," and, crouching, small for his age, small and wiry like his father, in patched and faded jeans even too small for him, with straight, uncombed, brown hair and eyes gray and wild as storm scud, he saw the men between himself and the table part and become a lane of grim faces, at the end of which he saw the Justice, a shabby, collarless, graying man in spectacles, beckoning him. He felt no floor under his bare feet; he seemed to walk beneath the palpable weight of the grim turning faces. His father, still in his black Sunday coat donned not for the trial but for the moving, did not even look at him. *He aims for me to lie*, he thought, again with that frantic grief and despair. *And I will have to do hit.*

"What's your name, boy?" the Justice said.

"Colonel Sartoris Snopes," the boy whispered.

"Hey?" the Justice said. "Talk louder. Colonel Sartoris? I reckon any- 10
body named for Colonel Sartoris in this country can't help but tell the truth, can they?" The boy said nothing. *Enemy! Enemy!* he thought; for a moment he could not even see, could not see that the Justice's face was kindly nor discern that his voice was troubled when he spoke to the man named Harris: "Do you want me to question this boy?" But he could hear, and during those subsequent long seconds while there was absolutely no sound in the crowded little room save that of quiet and intent breathing it was as if he had swung outward at the end of a grape vine, over a ravine, and at the top of the swing had been caught in a prolonged instant of mesmerized gravity, weightless in time.

"No!" Harris said violently, explosively. "Damnation! Send him out of here!" Now time, the fluid world, rushed beneath him again, the voices coming to him again through the smell of cheese and sealed meat, the fear and despair and the old grief of blood:

"This case is closed. I can't find against you, Snopes, but I can give you advice. Leave this country and don't come back to it."

His father spoke for the first time, his voice cold and harsh, level, without emphasis: "I aim to. I don't figure to stay in a country among people who . . ." he said something unprintable and vile, addressed to no one.

"That'll do," the Justice said. "Take your wagon and get out of this country before dark. Case dismissed."

His father turned, and he followed the stiff black coat, the wiry fig- 15
ure walking a little stiffly from where a Confederate provost's man's musket ball had taken him in the heel on a stolen horse thirty years ago, followed the two backs now, since his older brother had appeared from somewhere in the crowd, no taller than the father but thicker, chewing tobacco steadily, between the two lines of grim-faced men and out of the store and across the worn gallery and down the sagging steps and among the dogs and half-grown boys in the mild May dust, where as he passed a voice hissed:

"Barn burner!"

Again he could not see, whirling; there was a face in a red haze, moonlike, bigger than the full moon, the owner of it half again his size, he leaping in the red haze toward the face, feeling no blow, feeling no shock when his head struck the earth, scrabbling up and leaping again, feeling no blow this time either and tasting no blood, scrabbling up to see the other boy in full flight and himself already leaping into pursuit as his father's hand jerked him back, the harsh, cold voice speaking above him: "Go get in the wagon."

It stood in a grove of locusts and mulberries across the road. His two hulking sisters in their Sunday dresses and his mother and her sister in calico and sunbonnets were already in it, sitting on and among the sorry residue of the dozen and more movings which even the boy could remember—the battered stove, the broken beds and chairs, the clock inlaid with mother-of-pearl, which would not run, stopped at some fourteen minutes past two o'clock of a dead and forgotten day and time, which had been his mother's dowry. She was crying, though when she saw him she drew her sleeve across her face and began to descend from the wagon. "Get back," the father said.

"He's hurt. I got to get some water and wash his . . ."

20 "Get back in the wagon," his father said. He got in too, over the tailgate. His father mounted to the seat where the older brother already sat and struck the gaunt mules two savage blows with the peeled willow, but without heat. It was not even sadistic; it was exactly that same quality which in later years would cause his descendants to over-run the engine before putting a motor car into motion, striking and reining back in the same movement. The wagon went on, the store with its quiet crowd of grimly watching men dropped behind; a curve in the road hid it. *Forever* he thought. *Maybe he's done satisfied now, now that he has* . . . stopping himself, not to say it aloud even to himself. His mother's hand touched his shoulder.

"Does hit hurt?" she said.

"Naw," he said. "Hit don't hurt. Lemme be."

"Can't you wipe some of the blood off before hit dries?"

"I'll wash to-night," he said. "Lemme be, I tell you."

25 The wagon went on. He did not know where they were going. None of them ever did or ever asked, because it was always somewhere, always a house of sorts waiting for them a day or two days or even three days away. Likely his father had already arranged to make a crop on another farm before he . . . Again he had to stop himself. He (the father) always did. There was something about his wolflike independence and even courage when the advantage was at least neutral which impressed strangers, as if they got from his latent ravening ferocity not so much a sense of dependability as a feeling that his ferocious conviction in the rightness of his own actions would be of advantage to all whose interest lay with his.

That night they camped, in a grove of oaks and beeches where a spring ran. The nights were still cool and they had a fire against it, of a rail lifted from a nearby fence and cut into lengths—a small fire, neat, niggard almost, a shrewd fire; such fires were his father's habit and custom always, even in freezing weather. Older, the boy might have remarked this and wondered why not a big one; why should not a man who had not only seen the waste and extravagance of war, but who had in his blood an inherent voracious prodigality with material not his own, have burned everything in sight? Then he might have gone a step farther and thought that that was the reason: that niggard blaze was the living fruit of nights passed during those four years in the woods hiding from all men, blue and gray, with his strings of horses (captured horses, he called them). And older still, he might have divined the true reason: that the element of fire spoke to some deep mainspring of his father's being, as the element of steel or of powder spoke to other men, as the one weapon for the preservation of integrity, else breath were not worth the breathing, and hence to be regarded with respect and used with discretion.

But he did not think this now and he had seen those same niggard blazes all his life. He merely ate his supper beside it and was already half asleep over his iron plate when his father called him, and once more he followed the stiff back, the stiff and ruthless limp, up the slope and on to the starlit road where, turning, he could see his father against the stars but without face or depth—a shape black, flat, and bloodless as though cut from tin in the iron folds of the frockcoat which had not been made for him, the voice harsh like tin and without heat like tin:

"You were fixing to tell them. You would have told him." He didn't answer. His father struck him with the flat of his hand on the side of the head, hard but without heat, exactly as he had struck the two mules at the store, exactly as he would strike either of them with any stick in order to kill a horse fly, his voice without heat or anger: "You're getting to be a man. You got to learn. You got to learn to stick to your own blood or you ain't going to have any blood to stick to you. Do you think either of them, any man there this morning, would? Don't you know all they wanted was a chance to get at me because they knew I had them beat? Eh?" Later, twenty years later, he was to tell himself, "If I had said they wanted only truth, justice, he would have hit me again." But now he said nothing. He was not crying. He just stood there. "Answer me," his father said.

"Yes," he whispered. His father turned.

"Get on to bed. We'll be there tomorrow." 30

Tomorrow they were there. In the early afternoon the wagon stopped before a paintless two-room house identical almost with the dozen others it had stopped before even in the boy's ten years, and again, as on the other dozen occasions, his mother and aunt got down and began to unload the wagon, although his two sisters and his father and brother had not moved.

"Likely hit ain't fitten for hawgs," one of the sisters said.

"Nevertheless, fit it will and you'll hog it and like it," his father said. "Get out of them chairs and help your Ma unload."

The two sisters got down, big, bovine, in a flutter of cheap ribbons; one of them drew from the jumbled wagon bed a battered lantern, the other a worn broom. His father handed the reins to the older son and began to climb stiffly over the wheel. "When they get unloaded, take the team to the barn and feed them." Then he said, and at first the boy thought he was still speaking to his brother: "Come with me."

"Me?" he said. 35

"Yes," his father said. "You."

"Abner," his mother said. His father paused and looked back—the harsh level stare beneath the shaggy, graying, irascible brows.

"I reckon I'll have a word with the man that aims to begin to-morrow owning me body and soul for the next eight months."

They went back up the road. A week ago—or before last night, that is—he would have asked where they were going, but not now. His father had struck him before last night but never before had he paused afterward to explain why; it was as if the blow and the following calm, outrageous voice still rang, repercussed, divulging nothing to him save the terrible handicap of being young, the light weight of his few years, just heavy enough to prevent his soaring free of the world as it seemed to be ordered but not heavy enough to keep him footed solid in it, to resist it and try to change the course of its events.

Presently he could see the grove of oaks and cedars and the other 40
flowering trees and shrubs where the house would be, though not the house yet. They walked beside a fence massed with honeysuckle and Cherokee roses and came to a gate swinging open between two brick pillars, and now, beyond a sweep of drive, he saw the house for the first time and at that instant he forgot his father and the terror and despair both, and even when he remembered his father again (who had not stopped) the terror and despair did not return. Because, for all the twelve movings, they had sojourned until now in a poor country, a land of small farms and fields and houses, and he had never seen a house like this before. *Hit's big as a courthouse* he thought quietly, with a surge of peace and joy whose reason he could not have thought into words, being too young for that: *They are safe from him. People whose lives are a part of this peace and dignity are beyond his touch, he no more to them than a buzzing wasp: capable of stinging for a little moment but that's all; the spell of this peace and dignity rendering even the barns and stable and cribs which belong to it impervious to the puny flames he might contrive* . . . this, the peace and joy, ebbing for an instant as he looked again at the stiff black back, the stiff and implacable limp of the figure which was not dwarfed by the house, for the reason that it had never looked big anywhere and which now, against the serene columned backdrop, had more than ever that impervious quality of something cut ruthlessly from tin, depthless, as though, sidewise to the sun, it would cast no shadow. Watching him, the boy remarked the absolutely undeviating course which his father held and saw the stiff foot come squarely down in a pile of fresh droppings where a horse had stood in the drive and which his father could have avoided by a simple change of stride.

But it ebbed only a moment, though he could not have thought this into words either, walking on in the spell of the house, which he could even want but without envy, without sorrow, certainly never with that ravening and jealous rage which unknown to him walked in the ironlike black coat before him: *Maybe he will feel it too. Maybe it will even change him now from what maybe he couldn't help but be.*

They crossed the portico. Now he could hear his father's stiff foot as it came down on the boards with clocklike finality, a sound out of all proportion to the displacement of the body it bore and which was not dwarfed either by the white door before it, as though it had attained to a sort of vicious and ravening minimum not to be dwarfed by anything—the flat, wide, black hat, the formal coat of broadcloth which had once been black but which had now that friction-glazed greenish cast of the bodies of old house flies, the lifted sleeve which was too large, the lifted hand like a curled claw. The door opened so promptly that the boy knew the Negro must have been watching them all the time, an old man with neat grizzled hair, in a linen jacket, who stood barring the door with his body, saying, "Wipe yo foots, white man, fo you come in here. Major ain't home nohow."

"Get out of my way, nigger," his father said, without heat too, flinging the door back and the Negro also and entering, his hat still on his head. And now the boy saw the prints of the stiff foot on the doorjamb and saw them appear on the pale rug behind the machinelike deliberation of the foot which seemed to bear (or transmit) twice the weight which the body compassed. The Negro was shouting "Miss Lula! Miss Lula!" somewhere behind them, then the boy, deluged as though by a warm wave by a suave turn of the carpeted stair and a pendant glitter of chandeliers and a mute gleam of gold frames, heard the swift feet and saw her too, a lady—perhaps he had never seen her like before either—in a gray, smooth gown with lace at the throat and an apron tied at the waist and the sleeves turned back, wiping cake or biscuit dough from her hands with a towel as she came up the hall, looking not at his father at all but at the tracks on the blond rug with an expression of incredulous amazement.

"I tried," the Negro cried. "I tole him to . . ."

"Will you please go away?" she said in a shaking voice. "Major de Spain is not at home. Will you please go away?"

His father had not spoken again. He did not speak again. He did not 45
even look at her. He just stood stiff in the center of the rug, in his hat, the shaggy iron-gray brows twitching slightly above the pebble-colored eyes as he appeared to examine the house with brief deliberation. Then with the same deliberation he turned; the boy watched him pivot on the good leg and saw the stiff foot drag around the arc of the turning, leaving a final long and fading smear. His father never looked at it, he never once looked down at the rug. The Negro held the door. It closed behind them,

upon the hysteric and indistinguishable woman-wail. His father stopped at the top of the steps and scraped his boot clean on the edge of it. At the gate he stopped again. He stood for a moment, planted stiffly on the stiff foot, looking back at the house. "Pretty and white, ain't it?" he said. "That's sweat. Nigger sweat. Maybe it ain't white enough yet to suit him. Maybe he wants to mix some white sweat with it."

Two hours later the boy was chopping wood behind the house within which his mother and aunt and the two sisters (the mother and aunt, not the two girls, he knew that; even at this distance and muffled by walls the flat loud voices of the two girls emanated an incorrigible idle inertia) were setting up the stove to prepare a meal, when he heard the hooves and saw the linen-clad man on a fine sorrel mare, whom he recognized even before he saw the rolled rug in front of the Negro youth following on a fat bay carriage horse—a suffused, angry face vanishing, still at full gallop, beyond the corner of the house where his father and brother were sitting in the two tilted chairs; and a moment later, almost before he could have put the axe down, he heard the hooves again and watched the sorrel mare go back out of the yard, already galloping again. Then his father began to shout one of the sisters' names, who presently emerged backward from the kitchen door dragging the rolled rug along the ground by one end while the other sister walked behind it.

"If you ain't going to tote, go on and set up the wash pot," the first said.

"You, Sarty!" the second shouted. "Set up the wash pot!" His father appeared at the door, framed against that shabbiness, as he had been against that other bland perfection, impervious to either, the mother's anxious face at his shoulder.

"Go on," the father said. "Pick it up." The two sisters stooped, broad, lethargic; stooping, they presented an incredible expanse of pale cloth and a flutter of tawdry ribbons.

"If I thought enough of a rug to have to git hit all the way from 50
France I wouldn't keep hit where folks coming in would have to tromp on hit," the first said. They raised the rug.

"Abner," the mother said. "Let me do it."

"You go back and git dinner," his father said. "I'll tend to this."

From the woodpile through the rest of the afternoon the boy watched them, the rug spread flat in the dust beside the bubbling wash pot, the two sisters stooping over it with that profound and lethargic reluctance, while the father stood over them in turn, implacable and grim, driving them though never raising his voice again. He could smell the harsh homemade lye they were using; he saw his mother come to the door once and look toward them with an expression not anxious now but very like despair; he saw his father turn, and he fell to with the axe and saw from the corner of his eye his father raise from the ground a flattish fragment of field stone and examine it and return to the pot, and this time his mother actually spoke: "Abner. Abner. Please don't. Please, Abner."

Then he was done too. It was dusk; the whippoorwills had already begun. He could smell coffee from the room where they would presently eat the cold food remaining from the mid-afternoon meal, though when he entered the house he realized they were having coffee again probably because there was a fire on the hearth, before which the rug now lay spread over the backs of the two chairs. The tracks of his father's foot were gone. Where they had been were now long, water-cloudy scoriations resembling the sporadic course of a lilliputian mowing machine.

55 It still hung there while they ate the cold food and then went to bed, scattered without order or claim up and down the two rooms, his mother in one bed, where his father would later lie, the older brother in the other, himself, the aunt, and the two sisters on pallets on the floor. But his father was not in bed yet. The last thing the boy remembered was the depthless, harsh silhouette of the hat and coat bending over the rug and it seemed to him that he had not even closed his eyes when the silhouette was standing over him, the fire almost dead behind it, the stiff foot prodding him awake. "Catch up the mule," his father said.

When he returned with the mule his father was standing in the back door, the rolled rug over his shoulder. "Ain't you going to ride?" he said.

"No. Give me your foot."

He bent his knee into his father's hand, the wiry, surprising power flowed smoothly, rising, he rising with it, on to the mule's bare back (they had owned a saddle once; the boy could remember it though not when or where) and with the same effortlessness his father swung the rug up in front of him. Now in the starlight they retraced the afternoon's path, up the dusty road rife with honeysuckle, through the gate and up the black tunnel of the drive to the lightless house, where he sat on the mule and felt the rough warp of the rug drag across his thighs and vanish.

"Don't you want me to help?" he whispered. His father did not answer and now he heard again that stiff foot striking the hollow portico with that wooden and clocklike deliberation, that outrageous overstatement of the weight it carried. The rug, hunched, not flung (the boy could tell that even in the darkness) from his father's shoulder struck the angle of wall and floor with a sound unbelievably loud, thunderous, then the foot again, unhurried and enormous; a light came on in the house and the boy sat, tense, breathing steadily and quietly and just a little fast, though the foot itself did not increase its beat at all, descending the steps now; now the boy could see him.

60 "Don't you want to ride now?" he whispered. "We kin both ride now," the light within the house altering now, flaring up and sinking. *He's coming down the stairs now*, he thought. He had already ridden the mule up beside the horse block; presently his father was up behind him and he doubled the reins over and slashed the mule across the neck, but before the animal could begin to trot the hard, thin arm came around him, the hard, knotted hand jerking the mule back to a walk.

In the first red rays of the sun they were in the lot, putting plow gear on the mules. This time the sorrel mare was in the lot before he heard it at all, the rider collarless and even bareheaded, trembling, speaking in a shaking voice as the woman in the house had done, his father merely looking up once before stooping again to the hame° he was buckling, so that the man on the mare spoke to his stooping back:

"You must realize you have ruined that rug. Wasn't there anybody here, any of your women . . ." he ceased, shaking, the boy watching him, the older brother leaning now in the stable door, chewing, blinking slowly and steadily at nothing apparently. "It cost a hundred dollars. But you never had a hundred dollars. You never will. So I'm going to charge you twenty bushels of corn against your crop. I'll add it in your contract and when you come to the commissary you can sign it. That won't keep Mrs. de Spain quiet but maybe it will teach you to wipe your feet off before you enter her house again."

Then he was gone. The boy looked at his father, who still had not spoken or even looked up again, who was now adjusting the logger-head in the hame.

"Pap," he said. His father looked at him—the inscrutable face, the shaggy brows beneath where the gray eyes glinted coldly. Suddenly the boy went toward him, fast, stopping as suddenly. "You done the best you could!" he cried. "If he wanted hit done different why didn't he wait and tell you how? He won't git no twenty bushels! He won't git none! We'll gather hit and hide hit! I kin watch . . ."

"Did you put the cutter back in that straight stock like I told you?" 65

"No, sir," he said.

"Then go do it."

That was Wednesday. During the rest of that week he worked steadily, at what was within his scope and some which was beyond it, with an industry that did not need to be driven nor even commanded twice; he had this from his mother, with the difference that some at least of what he did he liked to do, such as splitting wood with the half-size axe which his mother and aunt had earned, or saved money somehow, to present him with at Christmas. In company with the two older women (and on one afternoon, even one of the sisters), he built pens for the shoat and the cow which were a part of his father's contract with the landlord, and one afternoon, his father being absent, gone somewhere on one of the mules, he went to the field.

They were running a middle buster now, his brother holding the plow straight while he handled the reins, and walking beside the straining mule, the rich black soil shearing cool and damp against his bare ankles, he thought *Maybe this is the end of it. Maybe even that twenty bushels that seems hard to have to pay for just a rug will be a cheap price for him to*

hame: a curved section of the harness of a draft animal.

stop forever and always from being what he used to be; thinking, dreaming now, so that his brother had to speak sharply to him to mind the mule: *Maybe he even won't collect the twenty bushels. Maybe it will all add up and balance and vanish—corn, rug, fire; the terror and grief; the being pulled two ways like between two teams of horses—gone, done with for ever and ever.*

Then it was Saturday; he looked up from beneath the mule he was harnessing and saw his father in the black coat and hat. "Not that," his father said. "The wagon gear." And then, two hours later, sitting in the wagon bed behind his father and brother on the seat, the wagon accomplished a final curve, and he saw the weathered paintless store with its tattered tobacco- and patent-medicine posters and the tethered wagons and saddle animals below the gallery. He mounted the gnawed steps behind his father and brother, and there again was the lane of quiet, watching faces for the three of them to walk through. He saw the man in spectacles sitting at the plank table and he did not need to be told this was a Justice of the Peace; he sent one glare of fierce, exultant, partisan defiance at the man in collar and cravat now, whom he had seen but twice before in his life, and that on a galloping horse, who now wore on his face an expression not of rage but of amazed unbelief which the boy could not have known was at the incredible circumstance of being sued by one of his own tenants, and came and stood against his father and cried at the Justice: "He ain't done it! He ain't burnt . . ."

"Go back to the wagon," his father said.

"Burnt?" the Justice said. "Do I understand this rug was burned too?"

"Does anybody here claim it was?" his father said. "Go back to the wagon." But he did not, he merely retreated to the rear of the room, crowded as that other had been, but not to sit down this time, instead, to stand pressing among the motionless bodies, listening to the voices:

"And you claim twenty bushels of corn is too high for the damage you did to the rug?"

"He brought the rug to me and said he wanted the tracks washed out of it. I washed the tracks out and took the rug back to him."

"But you didn't carry the rug back to him in the same condition it was in before you made the tracks on it."

His father did not answer, and now for perhaps half a minute there was no sound at all save that of breathing, the faint, steady suspiration of complete and intent listening.

"You decline to answer that, Mr. Snopes?" Again his father did not answer. "I'm going to find against you, Mr. Snopes. I'm going to find that you were responsible for the injury to Major de Spain's rug and hold you liable for it. But twenty bushels of corn seems a little high for a man in your circumstances to have to pay. Major de Spain claims it cost a hundred dollars. October corn will be worth about fifty cents. I figure that if Major de Spain can stand a ninety-five dollar loss on something he paid cash for, you can stand a five-dollar loss you haven't earned yet. I hold you in damages to Major de Spain to the amount of ten bushels of corn over and above your contract with him, to be paid to him out of your crop at gathering time. Court adjourned."

It had taken no time hardly, the morning was but half begun. He thought they would return home and perhaps back to the field, since they were late, far behind all other farmers. But instead his father passed on behind the wagon, merely indicating with his hand for the older brother to follow with it, and crossed the road toward the blacksmith shop opposite, pressing on after his father, overtaking him, speaking, whispering up at the harsh, calm face beneath the weathered hat: "He won't git no ten bushels either. He won't git one. We'll . . ." until his father glanced for an instant down at him, the face absolutely calm, the grizzled eyebrows tangled above the cold eyes, the voice almost pleasant, almost gentle:

"You think so? Well, we'll wait till October anyway." 80

The matter of the wagon—the setting of a spoke or two and the tightening of the tires—did not take long either, the business of the tires accomplished by driving the wagon into the spring branch behind the shop and letting it stand there, the mules nuzzling into the water from time to time, and the boy on the seat with the idle reins, looking up the slope and through the sooty tunnel of the shed where the slow hammer rang and where his father sat on an upended cypress bolt, easily, either talking or listening, still sitting there when the boy brought the dripping wagon up out of the branch and halted it before the door.

"Take them on to the shade and hitch," his father said. He did so and returned. His father and the smith and a third man squatting on his heels inside the door were talking, about crops and animals; the boy, squatting too in the ammoniac dust and hoof-parings and scales of rust, heard his father tell a long and unhurried story out of the time before the birth of the older brother even when he had been a professional horsetrader. And then his father came up beside him where he stood before a tattered last year's circus poster on the other side of the store, gazing rapt and quiet at the scarlet horses, the incredible poisings and convulsions of tulle and tights and the painted leers of comedians, and said, "It's time to eat."

But not at home. Squatting beside his brother against the front wall, he watched his father emerge from the store and produce from a paper sack a segment of cheese and divide it carefully and deliberately into three with his pocket knife and produce crackers from the same sack. They all three squatted on the gallery and ate, slowly, without talking; then in the store again, they drank from a tin dipper tepid water smelling of the cedar bucket and of living beech trees. And still they did not go home. It was a horse lot this time, a tall rail fence upon and along which men stood and sat and out of which one by one horses were led, to be walked and trotted and then cantered back and forth along the road while the slow swapping and buying went on and the sun began to slant westward, they—the three of them—watching and listening, the older brother with his muddy eyes and his steady, inevitable tobacco, the father commenting now and then on certain of the animals, to no one in particular.

It was after sundown when they reached home. They ate supper by lamplight, then, sitting on the doorstep, the boy watched the night fully accomplish, listening to the whippoorwills and the frogs, when he heard his mother's voice: "Abner! No! No! Oh, God. Oh, God. Abner!" and he rose, whirled, and saw the altered light through the door where a candle stub now burned in a bottle neck on the table and his father, still in the hat and coat, at once formal and burlesque as though dressed carefully for some shabby and ceremonial violence, emptying the reservoir of the lamp back into the five-gallon kerosene can from which it had been filled, while the mother tugged at his arm until he shifted the lamp to the other hand and flung her back, not savagely or viciously, just hard, into the wall, her hands flung out against the wall for balance, her mouth open and in her face the same quality of hopeless despair as had been in her voice. Then his father saw him standing in the door.

"Go to the barn and get that can of oil we were oiling the wagon with," he said. The boy did not move. Then he could speak.

"What . . ." he cried. "What are you . . ."

"Go get that oil," his father said. "Go."

Then he was moving, running, outside the house, toward the stable: this the old habit, the old blood which he had not been permitted to choose for himself, which had been bequeathed him willy nilly and which had run for so long (and who knew where, battening on what of outrage and savagery and lust) before it came to him. *I could keep on*, he thought. *I could run on and on and never look back, never need to see his face again. Only I can't. I can't*, the rusted can in his hand now, the liquid sploshing in it as he ran back to the house and into it, into the sound of his mother's weeping in the next room, and handed the can to his father.

"Ain't you going to even send a nigger?" he cried. "At least you sent a nigger before!"

This time his father didn't strike him. The hand came even faster than the blow had, the same hand which had set the can on the table with almost excruciating care flashing from the can toward him too quick for him to follow it, gripping him by the back of his shirt and on to tiptoe before he had seen it quit the can, the face stooping at him in breathless and frozen ferocity, the cold, dead voice speaking over him to the older brother who leaned against the table, chewing with that steady, curious, sidewise motion of cows:

"Empty the can into the big one and go on. I'll catch up with you."

"Better tie him up to the bedpost," the brother said.

"Do like I told you," the father said. Then the boy was moving, his bunched shirt and the hard, bony hand between his shoulder-blades, his toes just touching the floor, across the room and into the other one, past the sisters sitting with spread heavy thighs in the two chairs over the cold hearth, and to where his mother and aunt sat side by side on the bed, the aunt's arm about his mother's shoulders.

"Hold him," the father said. The aunt made a startled movement. "Not you," the father said. "Lennie. Take hold of him. I want to see you do it." His mother took him by the wrist. "You'll hold him better than that. If he gets loose don't you know what he is going to do? He will go up yonder." He jerked his head toward the road. "Maybe I'd better tie him."

95 "I'll hold him," his mother whispered.

"See you do then." Then his father was gone, the stiff foot heavy and measured upon the boards, ceasing at last.

Then he began to struggle. His mother caught him in both arms, he jerking and wrenching at them. He would be stronger in the end, he knew that. But he had no time to wait for it. "Lemme go!" he cried. "I don't want to have to hit you!"

"Let him go!" the aunt said. "If he don't go, before God, I am going up there myself!"

"Don't you see I can't?" his mother cried. "Sarty! Sarty! No! No! Help me, Lizzie!"

100 Then he was free. His aunt grasped at him but it was too late. He whirled, running, his mother stumbled forward on to her knees behind him, crying to the nearer sister: "Catch him, Net! Catch him!" But that was too late too, the sister (the sisters were twins, born at the same time, yet either of them now gave the impression of being, encompassing as much living meat and volume and weight as any other two of the family) not yet having begun to rise from the chair, her head, face, alone merely turned, presenting to him in the flying instant an astonishing expanse of young female features untroubled by any surprise even, wearing only an expression of bovine interest. Then he was out of the room, out of the house, in the mild dust of the starlit road and the heavy rifeness of honeysuckle, the pale ribbon unspooling with terrific slowness under his running feet, reaching the gate at last and turning in, running, his heart and lungs drumming, on up the drive toward the lighted house, the lighted door. He did not knock, he burst in, sobbing for breath, incapable for the moment of speech; he saw the astonished face of the Negro in the linen jacket without knowing when the Negro had appeared.

"De Spain!" he cried, panted. "Where's . . ." then he saw the white man too emerging from a white door down the hall. "Barn!" he cried. "Barn!"

"What?" the white man said. "Barn?"

"Yes!" the boy cried. "Barn!"

"Catch him!" the white man shouted.

105 But it was too late this time too. The Negro grasped his shirt, but the entire sleeve, rotten with washing, carried away, and he was out that door too and in the drive again, and had actually never ceased to run even while he was screaming into the white man's face.

Behind him the white man was shouting, "My horse! Fetch my horse!" and he thought for an instant of cutting across the park and climbing the fence into the road, but he did not know the park nor how high the vine-massed fence might be and he dared not risk it. So he ran on down the drive, blood and breath roaring; presently he was in the road again though he could not see it. He could not hear either: the galloping mare was almost upon him before he heard her, and even then he held his course, as if the very urgency of his wild grief and need must in a moment more find him wings, waiting until the ultimate instant to hurl himself aside and into the weed-choked roadside ditch as the horse thundered past and on, for an instant in furious silhouette against the stars, the tranquil early summer night sky which, even before the shape of the horse and rider vanished, stained abruptly and violently upward: a long, swirling roar incredible and soundless, blotting the stars, and he springing up and into the road again, running again, knowing it was too late yet still running even after he heard the shot and, an instant later, two shots, pausing now without knowing he had ceased to run, crying, "Pap! Pap!," running again before he knew he had begun to run, stumbling, tripping over something and scrabbling up again without ceasing to run, looking backward over his shoulder at the glare as he got up, running on among the invisible trees, panting, sobbing, "Father! Father!"

At midnight he was sitting on the crest of a hill. He did not know it was midnight and he did not know how far he had come. But there was no glare behind him now and he sat now, his back toward what he had called home for four days anyhow, his face toward the dark woods which he would enter when breath was strong again, small, shaking steadily in the chill darkness, hugging himself into the remainder of his thin, rotten shirt, the grief and despair now no longer terror and fear but just grief and despair. *Father. My father*, he thought. "He was brave!" he cried suddenly, aloud but not loud, no more than a whisper. "He was! He was in the war! He was in Colonel Sartoris' cav'ry!" not knowing that his father had gone to that war a private in the fine old European sense, wearing no uniform, admitting the authority of and giving fidelity to no man or army or flag, going to war as Malbrouck° himself did: for booty—it meant nothing and less than nothing to him if it were enemy booty or his own.

The slow constellations wheeled on. It would be dawn and then sun-up after a while and he would be hungry. But that would be to-morrow and now he was only cold, and walking would cure that. His breathing was easier now and he decided to get up and go on, and then he found that he had been asleep because he knew it was almost dawn, the night

Malbrouck: John Churchill, Duke of Marlborough (1650–1722), English general victorious in the Battle of Blenheim (1704), a triumph that drove the French army out of Germany. The French called him Malbrouck, a name they found easier to pronounce.

almost over. He could tell that from the whippoorwills. They were everywhere now among the dark trees below him, constant and inflectioned and ceaseless, so that, as the instant for giving over to the day birds drew nearer and nearer, there was no interval at all between them. He got up. He was a little stiff, but walking would cure that too as it would the cold, and soon there would be the sun. He went on down the hill, toward the dark woods within which the liquid silver voices of the birds called unceasing—the rapid and urgent beating of the urgent and quiring heart of the late spring night. He did not look back.

Questions

1. After delivering his warning to Major de Spain, the boy Snopes does not actually witness what happens to his father and brother, or what happens to the Major's barn. But what do you assume happens? What evidence is given in the story?
2. What do you understand to be Faulkner's opinion of Abner Snopes? Make a guess, indicating details in the story that convey attitudes.
3. Which adjectives best describe the general tone of the story: *calm, amused, disinterested, scornful, marveling, excited, impassioned*? Point out passages that may be so described. What do you notice about the style in which these passages are written?
4. In tone and style, how does "Barn Burning" compare with Faulkner's story "A Rose for Emily" (Chapter 2)? To what do you attribute any differences?
5. Suppose that, instead of "Barn Burning," Faulkner had written a story told by Abner Snopes in the first person. Why would such a story need a style different from that of "Barn Burning"? (Suggestion: Notice Faulkner's descriptions of Abner Snopes's voice.)
6. Although "Barn Burning" takes place some thirty years after the Civil War, how does the war figure in it?

IRONY

If a friend declares, "Oh, sure, I just *love* to have four papers due on the same day," you detect that the statement contains **irony**. This is **verbal irony**, the most familiar kind, in which we understand the speaker's meaning to be far from the usual meaning of the words—in this case, quite the opposite. (When the irony is found, as here, in a somewhat sour statement tinged with mockery, it is called **sarcasm**.)

Irony, of course, occurs in writing as well as in conversation. When in a comic moment in Isaac Bashevis Singer's "Gimpel the Fool" the sexton announces, "The wealthy Reb Gimpel invites the congregation to a feast in honor of the birth of a son," the people at the synagogue burst into laughter. They know that Gimpel, in contrast to the sexton's words, is not a wealthy man but a humble baker; that the son is not his own but his wife's lover's; and that the birth brings no honor to anybody. Verbal irony, then, implies a contrast or discrepancy between what is *said* and what is *meant*.

Dramatic Irony

There are also times when the speaker, unlike the reader, does not realize the ironic dimension of his or her words; such instances are known as **dramatic irony**. The most famous example occurs in Sophocles's tragic drama *Oedipus the King*, when Oedipus vows to find and punish the murderer of King Laius, unaware that he himself is the man he seeks, and adds: "If by any chance / he proves to be an intimate of our house, / here at my hearth, with my full knowledge, / may the curse I just called down on him strike me!" Stories often contain other kinds of irony. A situation, for example, can be ironic if it contains some wry contrast or incongruity. In Jack London's "To Build a Fire" (Chapter 4), it is ironic that a freezing man, desperately trying to strike a match to light a fire and save himself, accidentally ignites all his remaining matches.

Irony as Point of View

An entire story may be told from an **ironic point of view**. Whenever we sense a sharp distinction between the narrator of a story and the author, irony is likely to occur—especially when the narrator is telling us something that we are clearly expected to doubt or to interpret very differently. In "A & P," Sammy (who tells his own story) makes many smug and cruel observations about the people around him; but the author makes clear to us that much of his superiority is based on immaturity and lack of self-knowledge. (This irony, by the way, does not negate the fact that Sammy makes some very telling comments about society's superficial values and rigid and judgmental attitudes, comments that Updike seems to endorse and wants us to endorse as well.) And when we read Hemingway's "A Clean, Well-Lighted Place," surely we feel that most of the time the older waiter speaks for the author. Though the waiter gives us a respectful, compassionate view of a lonely old man, and we don't doubt that the view is Hemingway's, still, in the closing lines of the story we are reminded that author and waiter are not identical. Musing on the sleepless night ahead of him, the waiter tries to shrug off his problem—"After all, it is probably only insomnia"—but the reader, who recalls the waiter's bleak view of *nada*, nothingness, knows that it certainly isn't mere insomnia that keeps him awake but a dread of solitude and death. At that crucial moment, Hemingway and the older waiter part company, and we perceive an ironic point of view, and also a verbal irony, "After all, it is probably only insomnia."

Cosmic Irony

Storytellers are sometimes fond of ironic twists of fate—developments that reveal a terrible distance between what people deserve and what they get, between what is and what ought to be. In the novels of Thomas Hardy, some hostile fate keeps playing tricks to thwart the main characters. In *Tess of the D'Urbervilles*, an all-important letter, thrust under a door, by chance slides beneath a carpet and is not received. Such an irony is sometimes called an **irony of fate** or a **cosmic irony**, for it suggests that some malicious fate (or other spirit in the universe) is deliberately frustrating human efforts. Evidently, there is an irony of fate in the student's futile attempt to escape Death in the fable "Death Has an Appointment in Samarra," and perhaps in the flaring up of the all-precious matches in "To Build a Fire," as well. To notice an irony gives pleasure. It may move us to laughter, make us feel wonder, or arouse our sympathy. By so involving us, irony—whether in a statement, a situation, an unexpected event, or a point of view—can render a story more likely to strike us, to affect us, and to be remembered.

O. Henry (William Sydney Porter)

The Gift of the Magi

1906

O. Henry

William Sydney Porter (1862–1910), known to the world as O. Henry, was born in Greensboro, North Carolina. He began writing in his mid-twenties, contributing humorous sketches to various periodicals. In 1896 he was indicted for embezzlement from the First National Bank of Austin, Texas; he fled to Honduras before his trial but returned when he found that his wife was terminally ill. He was convicted and served three years of a five-year sentence; his guilt or innocence has never been definitively established. Released in 1901, he moved to New York the following year. Already a well-known writer, for the next three years he produced a story every week for the New York World *while also contributing tales and sketches to magazines. Beginning with* Cabbages and Kings *in 1904, his stories were published in nine highly successful collections in the few remaining years of his life, as well as in three posthumously issued volumes. Financial extravagance and alcoholism darkened his last days, culminating in his death from tuberculosis at the age of forty-seven. Ranked during his lifetime with Hawthorne and Poe, O. Henry is more likely now to be invoked in negative terms, for his sentimentality and especially for his reliance on frequently forced trick endings, but the most prestigious annual volume of the best American short fiction is still called* The O. Henry Prize Stories, *and the best of his own work is loved by millions of readers.*

One dollar and eighty-seven cents. That was all. And sixty cents of it was in pennies. Pennies saved one and two at a time by bulldozing the grocer and the vegetable man and the butcher until one's cheeks burned with the silent imputation of parsimony that such close dealing implied. Three times Della counted it. One dollar and eighty-seven cents. And the next day would be Christmas.

There was clearly nothing to do but flop down on the shabby little couch and howl. So Della did it. Which instigates the moral reflection that life is made up of sobs, sniffles, and smiles, with sniffles predominating.

While the mistress of the home is gradually subsiding from the first stage to the second, take a look at the home. A furnished flat at $8 per week. It did not exactly beggar description, but it certainly had that word on the lookout for the mendicancy squad.

In the vestibule below was a letter-box into which no letter would go, and an electric button from which no mortal finger could coax a ring. Also appertaining thereunto was a card bearing the name "Mr. James Dillingham Young."

The "Dillingham" had been flung to the breeze during a former 5
period of prosperity when its possessor was being paid $30 per week. Now, when the income was shrunk to $20, the letters of "Dillingham" looked blurred, as though they were thinking seriously of contracting to a modest and unassuming D. But whenever Mr. James Dillingham Young came home and reached his flat above he was called "Jim" and greatly hugged by Mrs. James Dillingham Young, already introduced to you as Della. Which is all very good.

Della finished her cry and attended to her cheeks with the powder rag. She stood by the window and looked out dully at a grey cat walking a grey fence in a grey backyard. Tomorrow would be Christmas Day, and she had only $1.87 with which to buy Jim a present. She had been saving every penny she could for months, with this result. Twenty dollars a week doesn't go far. Expenses had been greater than she had calculated. They always are. Only $1.87 to buy a present for Jim. Her Jim. Many a happy hour she had spent planning for something nice for him. Something fine and rare and sterling—something just a little bit near to being worthy of the honor of being owned by Jim.

There was a pier-glass between the windows of the room. Perhaps you have seen a pier-glass in an $8 flat. A very thin and very agile person may, by observing his reflection in a rapid sequence of longitudinal strips, obtain a fairly accurate conception of his looks. Della, being slender, had mastered the art.

Suddenly she whirled from the window and stood before the glass. Her eyes were shining brilliantly, but her face had lost its color within twenty seconds. Rapidly she pulled down her hair and let it fall to its full length.

Now, there were two possessions of the James Dillingham Youngs in which they both took a mighty pride. One was Jim's gold watch that had been his father's and his grandfather's. The other was Della's hair. Had the Queen of Sheba lived in the flat across the airshaft, Della would have let her hair hang out the window some day to dry just to depreciate Her Majesty's jewels and gifts. Had King Solomon been the janitor, with all his treasures piled up in the basement, Jim would have pulled out his watch every time he passed, just to see him pluck at his beard from envy.

So now Della's beautiful hair fell about her, rippling and shining like 10
a cascade of brown waters. It reached below her knee and made itself almost a garment for her. And then she did it up again nervously and quickly. Once she faltered for a minute and stood still while a tear or two splashed on the worn red carpet.

On went her old brown jacket; on went her old brown hat. With a whirl of skirts and with the brilliant sparkle still in her eyes, she fluttered out the door and down the stairs to the street.

Where she stopped the sign read: "Mme. Sofronie. Hair Goods of All Kinds." One flight up Della ran, and collected herself, panting. Madame, large, too white, chilly, hardly looked the "Sofronie."

"Will you buy my hair?" asked Della.

"I buy hair," said Madame. "Take yer hat off and let's have a sight at the looks of it."

Down rippled the brown cascade. 15

"Twenty dollars," said Madame, lifting the mass with a practiced hand.

"Give it to me quick," said Della.

Oh, and the next two hours tripped by on rosy wings. Forget the hashed metaphor. She was ransacking the stores for Jim's present.

She found it at last. It surely had been made for Jim and no one else. There was no other like it in any of the stores, and she had turned all of them inside out. It was a platinum fob chain simple and chaste in design, properly proclaiming its value by substance alone and not by meretricious ornamentation—as all good things should do. It was even worthy of The Watch. As soon as she saw it she knew that it must be Jim's. It was like him. Quietness and value—the description applied to both. Twenty-one dollars they took from her for it, and she hurried home with the 87 cents. With that chain on his watch Jim might be properly anxious about the time in any company. Grand as the watch was, he sometimes looked at it on the sly on account of the old leather strap that he used in place of a chain.

When Della reached home her intoxication gave way a little to pru- 20
dence and reason. She got out her curling irons and lighted the gas and went to work repairing the ravages made by generosity added to love. Which is always a tremendous task, dear friends—a mammoth task.

Within forty minutes her head was covered with tiny, close-lying curls that made her look wonderfully like a truant schoolboy. She looked at her reflection in the mirror long, carefully, and critically.

"If Jim doesn't kill me," she said to herself, "before he takes a second look at me, he'll say I look like a Coney Island chorus girl. But what could I do—oh! What could I do with a dollar and eighty-seven cents?"

At 7 o'clock the coffee was made and the frying-pan was on the back of the stove hot and ready to cook the chops.

Jim was never late. Della doubled the fob chain in her hand and sat on the corner of the table near the door that he always entered. Then she heard his step on the stair away down on the first flight, and she turned white for just a moment. She had a habit of saying little silent prayers about the simplest everyday things, and now she whispered: "Please God, make him think I am still pretty."

The door opened and Jim stepped in and closed it. He looked thin and very serious. Poor fellow, he was only twenty-two—and to be burdened with a family! He needed a new overcoat and he was without gloves.

Jim stopped inside the door, as immovable as a setter at the scent of quail. His eyes were fixed upon Della, and there was an expression in them that she could not read, and it terrified her. It was not anger, nor surprise, nor disapproval, nor horror, nor any of the sentiments that she had been prepared for. He simply stared at her fixedly with that peculiar expression on his face.

Della wriggled off the table and went for him.

"Jim, darling," she cried, "don't look at me that way. I had my hair cut off and sold because I couldn't have lived through Christmas without giving you a present. It'll grow out again—you won't mind, will you? I just had to do it. My hair grows awfully fast. Say 'Merry Christmas!' Jim, and let's be happy. You don't know what a nice—what a beautiful, nice gift I've got for you."

"You've cut off your hair?" asked Jim, laboriously, as if he had not arrived at that patent fact yet even after the hardest mental labor.

"Cut it off and sold it," said Della. "Don't you like me just as well, anyhow? I'm me without my hair, ain't I?"

Jim looked about the room curiously.

"You say your hair is gone?" he said, with an air almost of idiocy.

"You needn't look for it," said Della. "It's sold, I tell you—sold and gone, too. It's Christmas Eve, boy. Be good to me, for it went for you. Maybe the hairs of my head were numbered," she went on with a sudden serious sweetness, "but nobody could ever count my love for you. Shall I put the chops on, Jim?"

Out of his trance Jim seemed quickly to wake. He enfolded his Della. For ten seconds let us regard with discreet scrutiny some inconsequential object in the other direction. Eight dollars a week or a million a year—what is the difference? A mathematician or a wit would give you the wrong answer. The magi brought valuable gifts, but that was not among them. This dark assertion will be illuminated later on.

Jim drew a package from his overcoat pocket and threw it upon the table.

"Don't make any mistake, Dell," he said, "about me. I don't think there's anything in the way of a haircut or a shave or a shampoo that could make me like my girl any less. But if you'll unwrap that package you may see why you had me going a while at first."

White fingers and nimble tore at the string and paper. And then an ecstatic scream of joy; and then, alas! a quick feminine change to hysterical tears and wails, necessitating the immediate employment of all the comforting powers of the lord of the flat.

For there lay The Combs—the set of combs, side and back, that Della had worshipped for long in a Broadway window. Beautiful combs, pure tortoise shell, with jewelled rims—just the shade to wear in the beautiful vanished hair. They were expensive combs, she knew, and her heart had simply craved and yearned over them without the least hope of possession. And now, they were hers, but the tresses that should have adorned the coveted adornments were gone.

But she hugged them to her bosom, and at length she was able to look up with dim eyes and a smile and say: "My hair grows so fast, Jim!"

And then Della leaped up like a little singed cat and cried, "Oh, oh!" 40

Jim had not yet seen his beautiful present. She held it out to him eagerly upon her open palm. The dull precious metal seemed to flash with a reflection of her bright and ardent spirit.

"Isn't it a dandy, Jim? I hunted all over town to find it. You'll have to look at the time a hundred times a day now. Give me your watch. I want to see how it looks on it."

Instead of obeying, Jim tumbled down on the couch and put his hands under the back of his head and smiled.

"Dell," said he, "let's put our Christmas presents away and keep 'em a while. They're too nice to use just at present. I sold the watch to get the money to buy your combs. And now suppose you put the chops on."

The magi, as you know, were wise men—wonderfully wise men— 45
who brought gifts to the Babe in the manger. They invented the art of giving Christmas presents. Being wise, their gifts were no doubt wise ones, possibly bearing the privilege of exchange in case of duplication. And here I have lamely related to you the uneventful chronicle of two foolish children in a flat who most unwisely sacrificed for each other the greatest treasures of their house. But in a last word to the wise of these days let it be said that of all who give gifts these two were the wisest. Of all who give and receive gifts, such as they are wisest. Everywhere they are wisest. They are the magi.

Questions

1. How would you describe the style of this story? Does the author's tone tell you anything about his attitude toward the characters and events of the narrative?
2. What do the details in paragraph 7 tell you about Della and Jim's financial situation?
3. O. Henry tells us that Jim "needed a new overcoat and he was without gloves" (paragraph 25). Why do you think Della didn't buy him these things for Christmas and instead got him a watch chain?

4. "Eight dollars a week or a million a year—what is the difference? A mathematician or a wit would give you the wrong answer" (paragraph 34). What, in your view, is "the wrong answer," and why is it wrong? What might the right answer be?
5. What is ironic about the story's ending? Is this plot twist the most important element of the conclusion? If not, what is?

Margaret Atwood

Happy Endings

1983

Margaret Atwood

Born in Ottawa, Ontario, in 1939, Margaret Eleanor Atwood was the daughter of an entomologist and spent her childhood summers in the forests of northern Quebec, where her father carried out research. Atwood began writing at the age of five and had already seriously entertained thoughts of becoming a professional writer before she finished high school. She graduated from the University of Toronto in 1961 and then got a master's degree from Radcliffe. Atwood initially gained prominence as a poet. Her first full-length collection of poems, The Circle Game *(1966), was awarded a Governor General's Award, Canada's most prestigious literary honor, and she has since published nearly twenty volumes of verse. Atwood also began to write fiction seriously in graduate school. Her short stories were first collected in* Dancing Girls *(1977), followed by numerous additional collections, most recently* Stone Mattress *(2014).*

A dedicated feminist, Atwood's works of fiction explore the complex relations between the sexes, most incisively in The Handmaid's Tale *(1985), a futuristic novel about a world in which gender roles are ruthlessly enforced by a society based on religious fundamentalism. (*The Handmaid's Tale *was adapted as a 2017 award-winning TV series.) In 1986 Atwood was named Woman of the Year by* Ms. *magazine. Subsequent novels include* Cat's Eye *(1988),* The Robber Bride *(1993),* The Blind Assassin *(2000),* MaddAddam *(2013), and* The Hag-Seed *(2016), a modern version of Shakespeare's* The Tempest.

John and Mary meet.
What happens next?
If you want a happy ending, try A.

A

John and Mary fall in love and get married. They both have worthwhile and remunerative jobs which they find stimulating and challenging. They buy a charming house. Real estate values go up. Eventually, when they can afford live-in help, they have two children, to whom they are devoted. The children turn out well. John and Mary have a stimulating and challenging sex life and worthwhile friends. They go on fun vacations together. They retire. They both have hobbies which they find stimulating and challenging. Eventually they die. This is the end of the story.

B

Mary falls in love with John but John doesn't fall in love with Mary. 5
He merely uses her body for selfish pleasure and ego gratification of a tepid kind. He comes to her apartment twice a week and she cooks him dinner, you'll notice that he doesn't even consider her worth the price of a dinner out, and after he's eaten the dinner he fucks her and after that he falls asleep, while she does the dishes so he won't think she's untidy, having all those dirty dishes lying around, and puts on fresh lipstick so she'll look good when he wakes up, but when he wakes up he doesn't even notice, he puts on his socks and his shorts and his pants and his shirt and his tie and his shoes, the reverse order from the one in which he took them off. He doesn't take off Mary's clothes, she takes them off herself, she acts as if she's dying for it every time, not because she likes sex exactly, she doesn't, but she wants John to think she does because if they do it often enough surely he'll get used to her, he'll come to depend on her and they will get married, but John goes out the door with hardly so much as a goodnight and three days later he turns up at six o'clock and they do the whole thing over again.

Mary gets run down. Crying is bad for your face, everyone knows that and so does Mary but she can't stop. People at work notice. Her friends tell her John is a rat, a pig, a dog, he isn't good enough for her, but she can't believe it. Inside John, she thinks, is another John, who is much nicer. This other John will emerge like a butterfly from a cocoon, a Jack from a box, a pit from a prune, if the first John is only squeezed enough.

One evening John complains about the food. He has never complained about the food before. Mary is hurt.

Her friends tell her they've seen him in a restaurant with another woman, whose name is Madge. It's not even Madge that finally gets to Mary; it's the restaurant. John has never taken Mary to a restaurant. Mary collects all the sleeping pills and aspirins she can find, and takes them and a half a bottle of sherry. You can see what kind of a woman she is by the fact that it's not even whiskey. She leaves a note for John. She hopes he'll discover her and get her to the hospital in time and repent and then they can get married, but this fails to happen and she dies.

John marries Madge and everything continues as in A.

C

John, who is an older man, falls in love with Mary, and Mary, who is 10
only twenty-two, feels sorry for him because he's worried about his hair falling out. She sleeps with him even though she's not in love with him.

She met him at work. She's in love with someone called James, who is twenty-two also and not yet ready to settle down.

John on the contrary settled down long ago: this is what is bothering him. John has a steady, respectable job and is getting ahead in his field, but Mary isn't impressed by him, she's impressed by James, who has a motorcycle and a fabulous record collection. But James is often away on his motorcycle, being free. Freedom isn't the same for girls, so in the meantime Mary spends Thursday evenings with John. Thursdays are the only days John can get away.

John is married to a woman called Madge and they have two children, a charming house which they bought just before the real estate values went up, and hobbies which they find stimulating and challenging, when they have the time. John tells Mary how important she is to him, but of course, he can't leave his wife because a commitment is a commitment. He goes on about this more than is necessary and Mary finds it boring, but older men can keep it up longer so on the whole she has a fairly good time.

One day James breezes in on his motorcycle with some top-grade California hybrid and James and Mary get higher than you'd believe possible and they climb into bed. Everything becomes very underwater, but along comes John, who has a key to Mary's apartment. He finds them stoned and entwined. He's hardly in any position to be jealous, considering Madge, but nevertheless he's overcome with despair. Finally he's middle-aged, in two years he'll be bald as an egg and he can't stand it. He purchases a handgun, saying he needs it for target practice—this is the thin part of the plot, but it can be dealt with later—and shoots the two of them and himself.

Madge, after a suitable period of mourning, marries an understanding man called Fred and everything continues as in A, but under different names.

D

Fred and Madge have no problems. They get along exceptionally 15
well and are good at working out any little difficulties that may arise. But their charming house is by the seashore and one day a giant tidal wave approaches. Real estate values go down. The rest of the story is about what caused the tidal wave and how they escape from it. They do, though thousands drown, but Fred and Madge are virtuous and lucky. Finally on high ground they clasp each other, wet and dripping and grateful, and continue as in A.

E

Yes, but Fred has a bad heart. The rest of the story is about how kind and understanding they both are until Fred dies. Then Madge devotes herself to charity work until the end of A. If you like, it can be "Madge," "cancer," "guilty and confused," and "bird watching."

F

If you think this is all too bourgeois, make John a revolutionary and Mary a counterespionage agent and see how far that gets you. Remember, this is Canada. You'll still end up with A, though in between you may get a lustful brawling saga of passionate involvement, a chronicle of our times, sort of.

You'll have to face it, the endings are the same however you slice it. Don't be deluded by any other endings, they're all fake, either deliberately fake, with malicious intent to deceive, or just motivated by excessive optimism if not by downright sentimentality.

The only authentic ending is the one provided here:

John and Mary die. John and Mary die. John and Mary die.

So much for endings. Beginnings are always more fun. True connoisseurs, however, are known to favor the stretch in between, since it's the hardest to do anything with.

That's about all that can be said for plots, which anyway are just one thing after another, a what and a what and a what.

Now try How and Why.

Questions

1. Why does Atwood present the story (or stories) in this manner? What point is she trying to make about the conventions of narrative storytelling?
2. What effect does her method of storytelling have on your understanding of the characters?
3. How would you describe the various possible scenarios for John, Mary, Fred, and Madge?
4. What does "Happy Endings" suggest about love and romance?
5. Despite the dark content, how would you describe Atwood's tone?
6. Is there really a "happy ending" in this story?

WRITING *effectively*

THINKING ABOUT TONE AND STYLE

If you look around a crowded classroom, you will notice—consciously or not—the styles of your fellow students. The way they dress, talk, and even sit conveys information about their attitudes. A haircut, T-shirt, tattoo, or piece of jewelry all silently say something. Similarly, a writer's style—his or her own distinct voice—can give the reader crucial extra information. To analyze a writer's style, think about:

- **Diction: Consider the flavor of words chosen by the author for a particular story.** In "A Clean, Well-Lighted Place," for example, Hemingway favors simple, unemotional, and descriptive language, whereas in "The Storm" (Chapter 4), Chopin uses extravagant and emotionally charged diction. Each choice reveals something important about the story.
- **Sentence structure: Look for patterns in a story's sentence structure.** Hemingway is famous for his short, clipped sentences, which often repeat certain key words. Faulkner, however, favors complex, elaborate syntax that immerses the reader in the emotion of the narrative.
- **Tone: Try to determine the writer's attitude toward the story he or she is telling.** In "The Gospel According to Mark" (Chapter 4), Borges uses dispassionate restraint to present a central irony, a tragic misunderstanding that will doom his protagonist. Tan's "A Pair of Tickets" (Chapter 4), by contrast, creates a tone of hushed excitement and direct emotional involvement.
- **Organization: Examine the order in which information is presented.** Borges tells his story in a straightforward, chronological manner, which eventually makes it possible for us to appreciate the tale's complex undercurrents. Other stories (for example, Atwood's "Happy Endings") present the narrative's events in more complicated and surprising ways.

CHECKLIST: Writing About Tone and Style

- ☐ Does the writer use word choice in a distinctive way?
- ☐ Is the diction unusual in any way?
- ☐ Does the author tend toward long or short—even fragmented—sentences?
- ☐ How would you characterize the writer's voice? Is it formal or casual? Distant or intimate? Impassioned or restrained?
- ☐ Can the narrator's words be taken at face value? Is there anything ironic about the narrator's voice?
- ☐ How does the writer arrange the material? Is information delivered chronologically, or is the organization more complex?
- ☐ What is the writer's attitude toward the material?

TOPICS FOR WRITING ON TONE AND STYLE

1. Examine a short story with a style you admire. Write an essay in which you analyze the author's approach toward diction, sentence structure, tone, and organization.

How do these elements work together to create a certain mood? How does that mood contribute to the story's meaning? If your chosen story has a first-person narrator, how do stylistic choices help to create a sense of that particular character?

2. Write a brief analysis of irony in "The Gift of the Magi" or "Happy Endings." What sorts of irony does your story employ?
3. Consider a short story in which the narrator is the central character, perhaps "A & P" (Chapter 1), "Araby" (Chapter 9), or "Cathedral" (Chapter 3). In a brief essay, show how the character of the narrator determines the style of the story. Examine language in particular—words or phrases, slang expressions, figures of speech, local or regional usage.
4. Write a page in which you describe eating a meal in the company of others. Using sensory details, convey a sense of the setting, the quality of the food, and the presence of your dining companions. Now rewrite your paragraph as Ernest Hemingway. Finally, rewrite it as William Faulkner.
5. In a paragraph, describe a city street as seen through the eyes of a college graduate who has just moved to the city to start a new career. Now describe that same street in the voice of an old woman walking home from the hospital where her husband has just died. Finally, describe the street in the voice of a teenage runaway. In each paragraph, refrain from identifying your character or saying anything about his or her circumstances. Simply present the street as each character would perceive it.

▶ TERMS FOR *review*

Tone ▶ The attitude toward a subject conveyed in a literary work. No single stylistic device creates tone; it is the net result of the various elements an author brings to creating the work's feeling and manner.

Style ▶ All the distinctive ways in which an author uses language to create a literary work. An author's style depends on his or her characteristic use of diction, imagery, tone, syntax, and figurative language.

Diction ▶ Word choice or vocabulary. Diction refers to the class of words that an author decides is appropriate to use in a particular work.

Irony ▶ A literary device in which a discrepancy of meaning is masked beneath the surface of the language. Irony is present when a writer says one thing but means something quite the opposite.

Verbal irony ▶ A statement in which the speaker or writer says the opposite of what is really meant. For example, a friend might say, "How graceful!" after you trip clumsily on a stair.

Sarcasm ▶ A conspicuously bitter form of irony in which the ironic statement is designed to hurt or mock its target.

Dramatic irony ▶ Where the reader understands the implication and meaning of a situation and may foresee the oncoming disaster or triumph while the character does not.

Cosmic irony (or **irony of fate**) ▶ A type of situational irony that emphasizes the discrepancy between what characters deserve and what they get, between a character's aspirations and the treatment he or she receives at the hands of fate.

6 THEME

What You Will Learn in This Chapter

- To define *theme*
- To explain the difference between theme and plot summary
- To summarize a story's theme in a single sentence
- To analyze the role of a theme in a story

The **theme** of a story is whatever general idea or insight the entire story reveals. In some stories the theme is unmistakable. At the end of Aesop's fable about the council of the mice that can't decide who will take on the dangerous task of hanging a warning bell around the neck of the cat, the theme is stated in the moral: *It is easier to propose a thing than to carry it out.*

In a work of commercial fiction, too, the theme (if any) is usually obvious. Consider a typical detective thriller in which, say, a rookie police officer trained in scientific methods of crime detection sets out to solve a mystery sooner than his or her rival, a veteran sleuth whose only laboratory is carried under his hat. Perhaps the veteran solves the case, leading to the conclusion (and the theme), "The old ways are the best ways after all." Or the story might dramatize the same rivalry but reverse the outcome, having the rookie win, thereby reversing the theme: "The times are changing! Let's shake loose from old-fashioned ways."

PLOT VERSUS THEME

In literary fiction, a theme is seldom so obvious. That is, a theme need not be a moral or a message; it may be what the events add up to, what the story is about. When we come to the end of a finely wrought short story such as Ernest Hemingway's "A Clean, Well-Lighted Place" (Chapter 5), it may be easy to sum up the plot—to say what happens—but it is more difficult to sum up the story's main idea. Hemingway relates the events—how a younger waiter gets rid of an old man and how an older waiter then goes to a coffee bar—but in themselves these events seem relatively slight, though the story as a whole seems large (for its size) and full of meaning. A **summary**, a brief condensation of the main idea or plot of a literary work, may be helpful, but it tends to focus on the surface events of a story. A theme aims for a deeper and more comprehensive statement of its larger meaning.

For the meaning, we must look to other elements in the story besides simply what happens in it. It is clear that Hemingway is most deeply interested in the thoughts and feelings of the older waiter, the character who has more and more to say as the story progresses, until at the end the story is entirely confined to his thoughts and perceptions. What is meaningful in these thoughts and perceptions? The older waiter understands the old man and sympathizes with his need for a clean, well-lighted place. If we say that, we are still talking about what happens in the story, though we have gone beyond merely recording its external events. But a theme is usually stated in *general* words. Another try: "Solitary people who cannot sleep need a cheerful, orderly place where they can drink with dignity." That's a little better. We have indicated, at least, that Hemingway's story is about more than just an old man and a couple of waiters. But what about the older waiter's meditation on *nada*, nothingness? Coming near the end of the story, it is given great emphasis, and probably no good statement of Hemingway's theme can leave it out. Still another try at a thematic statement: "Solitary people need a place of refuge from their terrible awareness that their lives (or, perhaps, human lives) are essentially meaningless." Neither this nor any other statement of the story's theme is unarguably right, but at least the sentence helps the reader to bring into focus one primary idea that Hemingway seems to be driving at.

Moral inferences may be drawn from the story, no doubt, for Hemingway is indirectly giving us advice about properly regarding and sympathizing with the lonely, the uncertain, and the old. But the story doesn't set forth a lesson that we are supposed to put into practice. One could argue that "A Clean, Well-Lighted Place" contains *several* themes, and other statements could be made to include Hemingway's views of love, of communication between people, of dignity. Great short stories, like great symphonies, frequently have more than one theme.

SUMMARIZING THE THEME

In many a fine short story, theme is the center, the moving force, the principle of unity. Clearly, such a theme is something other than the characters or plot of a story. To say that James Joyce's "Araby" (Chapter 9) is a short story about a boy who goes to a bazaar to buy a gift for a young woman, only to arrive too late, is to summarize the plot, not the theme. (The theme *might* be put, "The romantic illusions of a young man are vulnerable to the lessons of reality," or it might be put in any of a hundred other ways.) Although the title of Shirley Jackson's "The Lottery" (Chapter 7), with its hint of the lure of easy riches, may arouse pleasant expectations, which the neutral tone of the narrative does nothing initially to dispel, the theme—the larger realization that the story leaves us with—has to do with the ways in which cruel and insensitive social practices can come to seem like normal and natural ones.

Sometimes you will hear it said that the theme of a story (say, Faulkner's "Barn Burning" in Chapter 5) is "loss of innocence" or that the theme of some other story (Hurston's "Sweat," in Chapter 9 for instance) is "the revolt of the downtrodden." Although such general descriptions of theme in a short phrase can be useful, we suggest that you work to be more specific. Try to sum up the theme in a short sentence that gives a fuller and more vivid sense of whatever truth or insight you think the story reveals. Crafting that sentence, you will find yourself looking closely at the story as you attempt to define its principal meaning.

FINDING THE THEME

You may find it helpful, in making a one-sentence statement of theme, to consider these questions:

1. Look back at the title of the story. From what you have read, what does it indicate?
2. Does the main character change in any way over the course of the story? Does this character arrive at any eventual realization or understanding? Are you left with any realization or understanding you did not have before?
3. Does the author make any general observations about life or human nature? Do the characters make any? (Caution: Characters now and again will utter opinions with which the reader is not necessarily supposed to agree.)
4. Does the story contain any especially curious objects, mysterious flat characters, significant animals, repeated names, song titles, or whatever, that hint at meanings larger than such things ordinarily have? In literary stories, such symbols may point to central themes.
5. When you have worded your statement of theme, have you cast it in general language, not just given a plot summary?
6. Does your statement hold true for the story as a whole, not for just part of it?

In distilling a statement of theme from a rich and complicated story, we have, of course, no more encompassed the whole story than a paleontologist taking a plaster mold of a petrified footprint has captured a living stegosaurus. A writer (other than a fabulist) does not usually set out with theme in hand, determined to make every detail in the story work to demonstrate it. Well then, the skeptical reader may ask, if only *some* stories have themes, if those themes may be hard to sum up, and if readers will probably disagree in their summations, why bother to state themes? Isn't it too much trouble? Surely it is, unless the effort to state a theme ends in pleasure and profit. Trying to sum up the point of a story in our own words is merely one way to make ourselves better aware of whatever we may have understood vaguely and tentatively. Attempted with loving care, such statements may bring into focus our scattered impressions of a rewarding story, may help to clarify and hold fast whatever wisdom the storyteller has offered us.

Tim O'Brien

The Things They Carried 1990

Tim O'Brien

Tim O'Brien was born in 1946 in Austin, Minnesota. Immediately after graduating summa cum laude from Macalester College in 1968, he was drafted into the US Army. Serving as an infantryman in Vietnam, O'Brien attained the rank of sergeant and was awarded a Purple Heart after being wounded by shrapnel. Upon his discharge in 1970, he began graduate work at Harvard. In 1973 he published If I Die in a Combat Zone, Box Me Up and Ship Me Home, *a mixture of memoir and fiction about his wartime experiences. His 1978 novel* Going After Cacciato *won the National Book Award, and is considered by some critics to be the best book of American fiction about the Vietnam War. "The Things They Carried" was first published in* Esquire *in 1986, and later became the title piece in a book of interlocking short stories published in 1990. His other novels include* The Nuclear Age *(1985),* In the Lake of the Woods *(1994),* Tomcat in Love *(1998), and* July, July *(2002). O'Brien currently teaches at Texas State University–San Marcos.*

First Lieutenant Jimmy Cross carried letters from a girl named Martha, a junior at Mount Sebastian College in New Jersey. They were not love letters, but Lieutenant Cross was hoping, so he kept them folded in plastic at the bottom of his rucksack. In the late afternoon, after a day's march, he would dig his foxhole, wash his hands under a canteen, unwrap the letters, hold them with the tips of his fingers, and spend the last hour of light pretending. He would imagine romantic camping trips into the White Mountains in New Hampshire. He would sometimes taste the envelope flaps, knowing her tongue had been there. More than anything, he wanted Martha to love him as he loved her, but the letters were mostly chatty, elusive on the matter of love. She was a virgin, he was almost sure. She was an English major at Mount Sebastian, and she wrote beautifully about her professors and roommates and midterm exams, about her respect for Chaucer and her great affection for Virginia Woolf. She often quoted lines of poetry; she never mentioned the war, except to say, Jimmy, take care of yourself. The letters weighed 10 ounces. They were signed Love, Martha, but Lieutenant Cross understood that Love was only a way of signing and did not mean what he sometimes pretended it meant. At dusk, he would carefully return the letters to his rucksack. Slowly, a bit distracted, he would get up and move among his men, checking the perimeter; then at full dark he would return to his hole and watch the night and wonder if Martha was a virgin.

The things they carried were largely determined by necessity. Among the necessities or near-necessities were P-38 can openers, pocket knives, heat tabs, wristwatches, dog tags, mosquito repellent, chewing gum, candy, cigarettes, salt tablets, packets of Kool-Aid, lighters, matches, sewing kits, Military Payment Certificates, C rations, and two or three canteens of water. Together, these items weighed between 15 and 20 pounds, depending upon a man's habits or rate of metabolism. Henry Dobbins, who was a big man, carried extra rations; he was especially fond of canned peaches in heavy syrup over pound cake. Dave Jensen, who practiced field hygiene, carried a toothbrush, dental floss, and several hotel-sized bars of soap he'd stolen on R&R° in Sydney, Australia. Ted Lavender, who was scared, carried tranquilizers until he was shot in the head outside the village of Than Khe in mid-April. By necessity, and because it was SOP,° they all carried steel helmets that weighed 5 pounds including the liner and camouflage cover. They carried the standard fatigue jackets and trousers. Very few carried underwear. On their feet they carried jungle boots—2.1 pounds—and Dave Jensen carried three pairs of socks and a can of Dr. Scholl's foot powder as a precaution against trench foot. Until he was shot, Ted Lavender carried six or seven ounces of premium dope, which for him was a necessity. Mitchell Sanders, the RTO,° carried condoms. Norman Bowker carried a diary. Rat Kiley carried comic books. Kiowa, a devout Baptist, carried an illustrated New Testament that had been presented to him by his father, who taught Sunday school in Oklahoma City, Oklahoma. As a hedge against bad times, however, Kiowa also carried his grandmother's distrust of the white man, his grandfather's old hunting hatchet. Necessity dictated. Because the land was mined and booby-trapped, it was SOP for each man to carry a steel-centered, nylon-covered flak jacket, which weighed 6.7 pounds, but which on hot days seemed much heavier. Because you could die so quickly, each man carried at least one large compress bandage, usually in the helmet band for easy access. Because the nights were cold, and because the monsoons were wet, each carried a green plastic poncho that could be used as a raincoat or groundsheet or makeshift tent. With its quilted liner, the poncho weighed almost two pounds, but it was worth every ounce. In April, for instance, when Ted Lavender was shot, they used his poncho to wrap him up, then to carry him across the paddy, then to lift him into the chopper that took him away.

They were called legs or grunts.

To carry something was to hump it, as when Lieutenant Jimmy Cross humped his love for Martha up the hills and through the swamps. In its intransitive form, to hump meant to walk, or to march, but it implied burdens far beyond the intransitive.

Almost everyone humped photographs. In his wallet, Lieutenant 5
Cross carried two photographs of Martha. The first was a Kodacolor

R&R: the military abbreviation for "rest and relaxation," a brief vacation from active service. *SOP*: standard operating procedure. *RTO*: radio and telephone operator.

snapshot signed Love, though he knew better. She stood against a brick wall. Her eyes were gray and neutral, her lips slightly open as she stared straight-on at the camera. At night, sometimes, Lieutenant Cross wondered who had taken the picture, because he knew she had boyfriends, because he loved her so much, and because he could see the shadow of the picture-taker spreading out against the brick wall. The second photograph had been clipped from the 1968 Mount Sebastian yearbook. It was an action shot—women's volleyball—and Martha was bent horizontal to the floor, reaching, the palms of her hands in sharp focus, the tongue taut, the expression frank and competitive. There was no visible sweat. She wore white gym shorts. Her legs, he thought, were almost certainly the legs of a virgin, dry and without hair, the left knee cocked and carrying her entire weight, which was just over one hundred pounds. Lieutenant Cross remembered touching that left knee. A dark theater, he remembered, and the movie was *Bonnie and Clyde*, and Martha wore a tweed skirt, and during the final scene, when he touched her knee, she turned and looked at him in a sad, sober way that made him pull his hand back, but he would always remember the feel of the tweed skirt and the knee beneath it and the sound of the gunfire that killed Bonnie and Clyde, how embarrassing it was, how slow and oppressive. He remembered kissing her good night at the dorm door. Right then, he thought, he should've done something brave. He should've carried her up the stairs to her room and tied her to the bed and touched that left knee all night long. He should've risked it. Whenever he looked at the photographs, he thought of new things he should've done.

What they carried was partly a function of rank, partly of field specialty.

As a first lieutenant and platoon leader, Jimmy Cross carried a compass, maps, code books, binoculars, and a .45-caliber pistol that weighed 2.9 pounds fully loaded. He carried a strobe light and the responsibility for the lives of his men.

As an RTO, Mitchell Sanders carried the PRC-25 radio, a killer, 26 pounds with its battery.

As a medic, Rat Kiley carried a canvas satchel filled with morphine and plasma and malaria tablets and surgical tape and comic books and all the things a medic must carry, including M&M's for especially bad wounds, for a total weight of nearly 20 pounds.

As a big man, therefore a machine gunner, Henry Dobbins carried 10
the M-60, which weighed 23 pounds unloaded, but which was almost always loaded. In addition, Dobbins carried between 10 and 15 pounds of ammunition draped in belts across his chest and shoulders.

As PFCs or Spec 4s, most of them were common grunts and carried the standard M-16 gas-operated assault rifle. The weapon weighed 7.5 pounds unloaded, 8.2 pounds with its full 20-round magazine. Depending on numerous factors, such as topography and psychology, the riflemen carried anywhere from 12 to 20 magazines, usually in cloth bandoliers, adding on another 8.4 pounds at minimum, 14 pounds at maximum. When it was available, they also carried M-16 maintenance gear—rods and steel brushes and swabs and tubes of LSA oil—all of which weighed about a pound. Among the grunts, some carried the M-79 grenade launcher, 5.9 pounds unloaded, a reasonably light weapon except for the ammunition, which was heavy. A single round weighed 10 ounces. The typical load was 25 rounds. But Ted Lavender, who was scared, carried 34 rounds when he was shot and killed outside Than Khe, and he went down under an exceptional burden, more than 20 pounds of ammunition, plus the flak jacket and helmet and rations and water and toilet paper and tranquilizers and all the rest, plus the unweighed fear. He was dead weight. There was no twitching or flopping. Kiowa, who saw it happen, said it was like watching a rock fall, or a big sandbag or something—just boom, then down—not like the movies where the dead guy rolls around and does fancy spins and goes ass over teakettle—not like that, Kiowa said, the poor bastard just flat-fuck fell. Boom. Down. Nothing else. It was a bright morning in mid-April. Lieutenant Cross felt the pain. He blamed himself. They stripped off Lavender's canteens and ammo, all the heavy things, and Rat Kiley said the obvious, the guy's dead, and Mitchell Sanders used his radio to report one U.S. KIA° and to request a chopper. Then they wrapped Lavender in his poncho. They carried him out to a dry paddy, established security, and sat smoking the dead man's dope until the chopper came. Lieutenant Cross kept to himself. He pictured Martha's smooth young face, thinking he loved her more than anything, more than his men, and now Ted Lavender was dead because he loved her so much and could not stop thinking about her. When the dustoff arrived, they carried Lavender aboard. Afterward they burned Than Khe. They marched until dusk, then dug their holes, and that night Kiowa kept explaining how you had to be there, how fast it was, how the poor guy just dropped like so much concrete. Boom-down, he said. Like cement.

In addition to the three standard weapons—the M-60, M-16, and M-79—they carried whatever presented itself, or whatever seemed appropriate as a means of killing or staying alive. They carried catch-as-catch-can. At various times, in various situations, they carried M-14s and CAR-15s and Swedish Ks and grease guns and captured AK-47s and Chi-Coms and RPGs and Simonov carbines and black market Uzis and .38-caliber Smith & Wesson handguns and 66 mm LAWs and shotguns and silencers and blackjacks and bayonets and C-4 plastic explosives. Lee Strunk carried a slingshot; a weapon of last resort, he called it. Mitchell Sanders carried brass knuckles. Kiowa carried his grandfather's feathered

KIA: killed in action.

hatchet. Every third or fourth man carried a Claymore antipersonnel mine—3.5 pounds with its firing device. They all carried fragmentation grenades—14 ounces each. They all carried at least one M-18 colored smoke grenade—24 ounces. Some carried CS or tear gas grenades. Some carried white phosphorus grenades. They carried all they could bear, and then some, including a silent awe for the terrible power of the things they carried.

In the first week of April, before Lavender died, Lieutenant Jimmy Cross received a good-luck charm from Martha. It was a simple pebble, an ounce at most. Smooth to the touch, it was a milky white color with flecks of orange and violet, oval-shaped, like a miniature egg. In the accompanying letter, Martha wrote that she had found the pebble on the Jersey shoreline, precisely where the land touched water at high tide, where things came together but also separated. It was this separate-but-together quality, she wrote, that had inspired her to pick up the pebble and to carry it in her breast pocket for several days, where it seemed weightless, and then to send it through the mail, by air, as a token of her truest feelings for him. Lieutenant Cross found this romantic. But he wondered what her truest feelings were, exactly, and what she meant by separate-but-together. He wondered how the tides and waves had come into play on that afternoon along the Jersey shoreline when Martha saw the pebble and bent down to rescue it from geology. He imagined bare feet. Martha was a poet, with the poet's sensibilities, and her feet would be brown and bare, the toenails unpainted, the eyes chilly and somber like the ocean in March, and though it was painful, he wondered who had been with her that afternoon. He imagined a pair of shadows moving along the strip of sand where things came together but also separated. It was phantom jealousy, he knew, but he couldn't help himself. He loved her so much. On the march, through the hot days of early April, he carried the pebble in his mouth, turning it with his tongue, tasting sea salt and moisture. His mind wandered. He had difficulty keeping his attention on the war. On occasion he would yell at his men to spread out the column, to keep their eyes open, but then he would slip away into daydreams, just pretending, walking barefoot along the Jersey shore, with Martha, carrying nothing. He would feel himself rising. Sun and waves and gentle winds, all love and lightness.

What they carried varied by mission.

When a mission took them to the mountains, they carried mosquito 15
netting, machetes, canvas tarps, and extra bug juice.

If a mission seemed especially hazardous, or if it involved a place they knew to be bad, they carried everything they could. In certain heavily mined AOs,° where the land was dense with Toe Poppers and

AOs: areas of operation.

Bouncing Betties, they took turns humping a 28-pound mine detector. With its headphones and big sensing plate, the equipment was a stress on the lower back and shoulders, awkward to handle, often useless because of the shrapnel in the earth, but they carried it anyway, partly for safety, partly for the illusion of safety.

On ambush, or other night missions, they carried peculiar little odds and ends. Kiowa always took along his New Testament and a pair of moccasins for silence. Dave Jensen carried night-sight vitamins high in carotene. Lee Strunk carried his slingshot; ammo, he claimed, would never be a problem. Rat Kiley carried brandy and M&M's candy. Until he was shot, Ted Lavender carried the starlight scope, which weighed 6.3 pounds with its aluminum carrying case. Henry Dobbins carried his girlfriend's pantyhose wrapped around his neck as a comforter. They all carried ghosts. When dark came, they would move out single file across the meadows and paddies to their ambush coordinates, where they would quietly set up the Claymores and lie down and spend the night waiting.

Other missions were more complicated and required special equipment. In mid-April, it was their mission to search out and destroy the elaborate tunnel complexes in the Than Khe area south of Chu Lai. To blow the tunnels, they carried one-pound blocks of pentrite high explosives, four blocks to a man, 68 pounds in all. They carried wiring, detonators, and battery-powered clackers. Dave Jensen carried earplugs. Most often, before blowing the tunnels, they were ordered by higher command to search them, which was considered bad news, but by and large they just shrugged and carried out orders. Because he was a big man, Henry Dobbins was excused from tunnel duty. The others would draw numbers. Before Lavender died there were 17 men in the platoon, and whoever drew the number 17 would strip off his gear and crawl in headfirst with a flashlight and Lieutenant Cross's .45-caliber pistol. The rest of them would fan out as security. They would sit down or kneel, not facing the hole, listening to the ground beneath them, imagining cobwebs and ghosts, whatever was down there—the tunnel walls squeezing in—how the flashlight seemed impossibly heavy in the hand and how it was tunnel vision in the very strictest sense, compression in all ways, even time, and how you had to wiggle in—ass and elbows—a swallowed-up feeling—and how you found yourself worrying about odd things: Will your flashlight go dead? Do rats carry rabies? If you screamed, how far would the sound carry? Would your buddies hear it? Would they have the courage to drag you out? In some respects, though not many, the waiting was worse than the tunnel itself. Imagination was a killer.

On April 16, when Lee Strunk drew the number 17, he laughed and muttered something and went down quickly. The morning was hot and very still. Not good, Kiowa said. He looked at the tunnel opening, then out across a dry paddy toward the village of Than Khe. Nothing moved. No clouds or birds or people. As they waited, the men smoked and drank

Kool-Aid, not talking much, feeling sympathy for Lee Strunk but also feeling the luck of the draw. You win some, you lose some, said Mitchell Sanders, and sometimes you settle for a rain check. It was a tired line and no one laughed.

Henry Dobbins ate a tropical chocolate bar. Ted Lavender popped a 20
tranquilizer and went off to pee.

After five minutes, Lieutenant Jimmy Cross moved to the tunnel, leaned down, and examined the darkness. Trouble, he thought—a cave-in maybe. And then suddenly, without willing it, he was thinking about Martha. The stresses and fractures, the quick collapse, the two of them buried alive under all that weight. Dense, crushing love. Kneeling, watching the hole, he tried to concentrate on Lee Strunk and the war, all the dangers, but his love was too much for him, he felt paralyzed, he wanted to sleep inside her lungs and breathe her blood and be smothered. He wanted her to be a virgin and not a virgin, all at once. He wanted to know her. Intimate secrets: Why poetry? Why so sad? Why that grayness in her eyes? Why so alone? Not lonely, just alone—riding her bike across campus or sitting off by herself in the cafeteria—even dancing, she danced alone—and it was the aloneness that filled him with love. He remembered telling her that one evening. How she nodded and looked away. And how, later, when he kissed her, she received the kiss without returning it, her eyes wide open, not afraid, not a virgin's eyes, just flat and uninvolved.

Lieutenant Cross gazed at the tunnel. But he was not there. He was buried with Martha under the white sand at the Jersey shore. They were pressed together, and the pebble in his mouth was her tongue. He was smiling. Vaguely, he was aware of how quiet the day was, the sullen paddies, yet he could not bring himself to worry about matters of security. He was beyond that. He was just a kid at war, in love. He was twenty-four years old. He couldn't help it.

A few moments later Lee Strunk crawled out of the tunnel. He came up grinning, filthy but alive. Lieutenant Cross nodded and closed his eyes while the others clapped Strunk on the back and made jokes about rising from the dead.

Worms, Rat Kiley said. Right out of the grave. Fuckin' zombie.

The men laughed. They all felt great relief. 25

Spook city, said Mitchell Sanders.

Lee Strunk made a funny ghost sound, a kind of moaning, yet very happy, and right then, when Strunk made that high happy moaning sound, when he went *Ahhooooo*, right then Ted Lavender was shot in the head on his way back from peeing. He lay with his mouth open. The teeth were broken. There was a swollen black bruise under his left eye. The cheekbone was gone. Oh shit, Rat Kiley said, the guy's dead. The guy's dead, he kept saying, which seemed profound—the guy's dead. I mean really.

The things they carried were determined to some extent by superstition. Lieutenant Cross carried his good-luck pebble. Dave Jensen carried a rabbit's foot. Norman Bowker, otherwise a very gentle person, carried a thumb that had been presented to him as a gift by Mitchell Sanders. The thumb was dark brown, rubbery to the touch, and weighed four ounces at most. It had been cut from a VC corpse, a boy of fifteen or sixteen. They'd found him at the bottom of an irrigation ditch, badly burned, flies in his mouth and eyes. The boy wore black shorts and sandals. At the time of his death he had been carrying a pouch of rice, a rifle, and three magazines of ammunition.

You want my opinion, Mitchell Sanders said, there's a definite moral here.

He put his hand on the dead boy's wrist. He was quiet for a time, as if counting a pulse, then he patted the stomach, almost affectionately, and used Kiowa's hunting hatchet to remove the thumb.

Henry Dobbins asked what the moral was.

Moral?

You know. *Moral*.

Sanders wrapped the thumb in toilet paper and handed it across to Norman Bowker. There was no blood. Smiling, he kicked the boy's head, watched the flies scatter, and said, It's like with that old TV show—Paladin. Have gun, will travel.

Henry Dobbins thought about it.

Yeah, well, he finally said. I don't see no moral.

There it *is*, man.

Fuck off.

They carried USO stationery and pencils and pens. They carried Sterno, safety pins, trip flares, signal flares, spools of wire, razor blades, chewing tobacco, liberated joss sticks and statuettes of the smiling Buddha, candles, grease pencils, *The Stars and Stripes*, fingernail clippers, Psy Ops leaflets, bush hats, bolos, and much more. Twice a week, when the resupply choppers came in, they carried hot chow in green mermite cans and large canvas bags filled with iced beer and soda pop. They carried plastic water containers, each with a two-gallon capacity. Mitchell Sanders carried a set of starched tiger fatigues for special occasions. Henry Dobbins carried Black Flag insecticide. Dave Jensen carried empty sandbags that could be filled at night for added protection. Lee Strunk carried tanning lotion. Some things they carried in common. Taking turns, they carried the big PRC-77 scrambler radio, which weighed 30 pounds with its battery. They shared the weight of memory. They took up what others could no longer bear. Often, they carried each other, the wounded or weak. They carried infections. They carried chess sets, basketballs, Vietnamese-English dictionaries, insignia of rank, Bronze Stars and Purple Hearts, plastic cards imprinted with the Code of Conduct. They carried diseases, among them malaria and dysentery. They carried lice and ringworm and leeches and paddy algae and various rots and molds. They carried the land itself—Vietnam, the place, the soil—a powdery orange-red dust that covered their boots and fatigues and faces. They carried the sky. The whole atmosphere, they carried it, the humidity, the monsoons, the stink of fungus and decay, all of it, they carried gravity. They moved like mules. By daylight they took sniper fire, at night they were mortared, but it was not battle, it was just the endless march, village to village, without purpose, nothing won or lost. They marched for the sake of the march. They plodded along slowly, dumbly, leaning forward against the heat, unthinking, all blood and bone, simple grunts, soldiering with their legs, toiling up the hills and down into the paddies and across the rivers and up again and down, just humping, one step and then the next and then another, but no volition, no will, because it was automatic, it was anatomy, and the war was entirely a matter of posture and carriage, the hump was everything, a kind of inertia, a kind of emptiness, a dullness of desire and intellect and conscience and hope and human sensibility. Their principles were in their feet. Their calculations were biological. They had no sense of strategy or mission. They searched the villages without knowing what to look for, not caring, kicking over jars of rice, frisking children and old men, blowing tunnels, sometimes setting fires and sometimes not, then forming up and moving on to the next village, then other villages, where it would always be the same. They carried their own lives. The pressures were enormous. In the heat of early afternoon, they would remove their helmets and flak jackets, walking bare, which was dangerous but which helped ease the strain. They would often discard things along the route of march. Purely for comfort, they would throw away rations, blow their Claymores and grenades, no matter, because by nightfall the resupply choppers would arrive with more of the same, then a day or two later still more, fresh watermelons and crates of ammunition and sunglasses and woolen sweaters—the resources were stunning—sparklers for the Fourth of July, colored eggs for Easter—it was the great American war chest—the fruits of science, the smokestacks, the canneries, the arsenals at Hartford, the Minnesota forests, the machine shops, the vast fields of corn and wheat—they carried like freight trains; they carried it on their backs and shoulders—and for all the ambiguities of Vietnam, all the mysteries and unknowns, there was at least the single abiding certainty that they would never be at a loss for things to carry.

After the chopper took Lavender away, Lieutenant Jimmy Cross led 40
his men into the village of Than Khe. They burned everything. They shot chickens and dogs, they trashed the village well, they called in artillery and watched the wreckage, then they marched for several hours through the hot afternoon, and then at dusk, while Kiowa explained how Lavender died, Lieutenant Cross found himself trembling.

He tried not to cry. With his entrenching tool, which weighed five pounds, he began digging a hole in the earth.

He felt shame. He hated himself. He had loved Martha more than his men, and as a consequence Lavender was now dead, and this was something he would have to carry like a stone in his stomach for the rest of the war.

All he could do was dig. He used his entrenching tool like an ax, slashing, feeling both love and hate, and then later, when it was full dark, he sat at the bottom of his foxhole and wept. It went on for a long while. In part, he was grieving for Ted Lavender, but mostly it was for Martha, and for himself, because she belonged to another world, which was not quite real, and because she was a junior at Mount Sebastian College in New Jersey, a poet and a virgin and uninvolved, and because he realized she did not love him and never would.

Like cement, Kiowa whispered in the dark. I swear to God—boom, down. Not a word.

I've heard this, said Norman Bowker.

A pisser, you know? Still zipping himself up. Zapped while zipping.

All right, fine. That's enough.

Yeah, but you had to see it, the guy just—

I *heard*, man. Cement. So why not shut the fuck *up*?

Kiowa shook his head sadly and glanced over at the hole where Lieutenant Jimmy Cross sat watching the night. The air was thick and wet. A warm dense fog had settled over the paddies and there was the stillness that precedes rain.

After a time Kiowa sighed.

One thing for sure, he said. The lieutenant's in some deep hurt. I mean that crying jag—the way he was carrying on—it wasn't fake or anything, it was real heavy-duty hurt. The man cares.

Sure, Norman Bowker said.

Say what you want, the man does care.

We all got problems.

Not Lavender.

No, I guess not, Bowker said. Do me a favor, though.

Shut up?

That's a smart Indian. Shut up.

Shrugging, Kiowa pulled off his boots. He wanted to say more, just to lighten up his sleep, but instead he opened his New Testament and arranged it beneath his head as a pillow. The fog made things seem hollow and unattached. He tried not to think about Ted Lavender, but then he was thinking how fast it was, no drama, down and dead, and how it was hard to feel anything except surprise. It seemed unchristian. He wished he could find some great sadness, or even anger, but the emotion wasn't there and he couldn't make it happen. Mostly he felt pleased to be alive. He liked the smell of the New Testament under his cheek, the leather and ink and paper and glue, whatever the chemicals were. He liked hearing the sounds of night. Even his fatigue, it felt fine, the stiff muscles and the prickly awareness of his own body, a floating feeling. He enjoyed not being dead. Lying there, Kiowa admired Lieutenant Jimmy Cross's capacity for grief. He wanted to share the man's pain, he wanted to care as Jimmy Cross cared. And yet when he closed his eyes, all he could think was Boom-down, and all he could feel was the pleasure of having his boots off and the fog curling in around him and the damp soil and the Bible smells and the plush comfort of night.

After a moment Norman Bowker sat up in the dark.

What the hell, he said. You want to talk, *talk*. Tell it to me.

Forget it.

No, man, go on. One thing I hate, it's a silent Indian.

For the most part they carried themselves with poise, a kind of 65
dignity. Now and then, however, there were times of panic, when they squealed or wanted to squeal but couldn't, when they twitched and made moaning sounds and covered their heads and said Dear Jesus and flopped around on the earth and fired their weapons blindly and cringed and sobbed and begged for the noise to stop and went wild and made stupid promises to themselves and to God and to their mothers and fathers, hoping not to die. In different ways, it happened to all of them. Afterward, when the firing ended, they would blink and peek up. They would touch their bodies, feeling shame, then quickly hiding it. They would force themselves to stand. As if in slow motion, frame by frame, the world would take on the old logic—absolute silence, then the wind, then sunlight, then voices. It was the burden of being alive. Awkwardly, the men would reassemble themselves, first in private, then in groups, becoming soldiers again. They would repair the leaks in their eyes. They would check for casualties, call in dustoffs, light cigarettes, try to smile, clear their throats and spit and begin cleaning their weapons. After a time someone would shake his head and say, No lie, I almost shit my pants, and someone else would laugh, which meant it was bad, yes, but the guy had obviously not shit his pants, it wasn't that bad, and in any case nobody would ever do such a thing and then go ahead and talk about it. They would squint into the dense, oppressive sunlight. For a few moments, perhaps, they would fall silent, lighting a joint and tracking its passage from man to man, inhaling, holding in the humiliation. Scary stuff, one of them might say. But then someone else would grin or flick his eyebrows and say, Roger-dodger, almost cut me a new asshole, *almost*.

There were numerous such poses. Some carried themselves with a sort of wistful resignation, others with pride or stiff soldierly discipline or good humor or macho zeal. They were afraid of dying but they were even more afraid to show it.

They found jokes to tell.

They used a hard vocabulary to contain the terrible softness. *Greased*, they'd say. *Offed, lit up, zapped while zipping*. It wasn't cruelty, just stage presence. They were actors. When someone died, it wasn't quite dying, because in a curious way it seemed scripted, and because they had their lines mostly memorized, irony mixed with tragedy, and because they called it by other names, as if to encyst and destroy the reality of death itself. They kicked corpses. They cut off thumbs. They talked grunt lingo. They told stories about Ted Lavender's supply of tranquilizers, how the poor guy didn't feel a thing, how incredibly tranquil he was.

There's a moral here, said Mitchell Sanders.

They were waiting for Lavender's chopper, smoking the dead man's dope.

The moral's pretty obvious, Sanders said, and winked. Stay away from drugs. No joke, they'll ruin your day every time.

Cute, said Henry Dobbins.

Mind blower, get it? Talk about wiggy. Nothing left, just blood and brains.

They made themselves laugh.

There it is, they'd say. Over and over—there it is, my friend, there it is—as if the repetition itself were an act of poise, a balance between crazy and almost crazy, knowing without going, there it is, which meant be cool, let it ride, because Oh yeah, man, you can't change what can't be changed, there it is, there it absolutely and positively and fucking well *is*.

They were tough.

They carried all the emotional baggage of men who might die. Grief, terror, love, longing—these were intangibles, but the intangibles had their own mass and specific gravity, they had tangible weight. They carried shameful memories. They carried the common secret of cowardice barely restrained, the instinct to run or freeze or hide, and in many respects this was the heaviest burden of all, for it could never be put down, it required perfect balance and perfect posture. They carried their reputations. They carried the soldier's greatest fear, which was the fear of blushing. Men killed, and died, because they were embarrassed not to. It was what had brought them to the war in the first place, nothing positive, no dreams of glory or honor, just to avoid the blush of dishonor. They died so as not to die of embarrassment. They crawled into tunnels and walked point and advanced under fire. Each morning, despite the unknowns, they made their legs move. They endured. They kept humping. They did not submit to the obvious alternative, which was simply to close the eyes and fall. So easy, really. Go limp and tumble to the ground and let the muscles unwind and not speak and not budge until your buddies picked you up and lifted you into the chopper that would roar and dip its nose and carry you off to the world. A mere matter of falling, yet no one ever fell. It was not courage, exactly; the object was not valor. Rather, they were too frightened to be cowards.

By and large they carried these things inside, maintaining the masks of composure. They sneered at sick call. They spoke bitterly about guys who had found release by shooting off their own toes or fingers. Pussies, they'd say. Candy-asses. It was fierce, mocking talk, with only a trace of envy or awe, but even so the image played itself out behind their eyes.

They imagined the muzzle against flesh. So easy: squeeze the trigger and blow away a toe. They imagined it. They imagined the quick, sweet pain, then the evacuation to Japan, then a hospital with warm beds and cute geisha nurses.

And they dreamed of freedom birds. 80

At night, on guard, staring into the dark, they were carried away by jumbo jets. They felt the rush of takeoff. *Gone!* they yelled. And then velocity—wings and engines—a smiling stewardess—but it was more than a plane, it was a real bird, a big sleek silver bird with feathers and talons and high screeching. They were flying. The weights fell off; there was nothing to bear. They laughed and held on tight, feeling the cold slap of wind and altitude, soaring, thinking *It's over, I'm gone!*—they were naked, they were light and free—it was all lightness, bright and fast and buoyant, light as light, a helium buzz in the brain, a giddy bubbling in the lungs as they were taken up over the clouds and the war, beyond duty, beyond gravity and mortification and global entanglements—*Sin loi!*° they yelled. *I'm sorry, mother-fuckers, but I'm out of it, I'm goofed, I'm on a space cruise, I'm gone!*—and it was a restful, unencumbered sensation, just riding the light waves, sailing that big silver freedom bird over the mountains and oceans, over America, over the farms and great sleeping cities and cemeteries and highways and the golden arches of McDonald's, it was flight, a kind of fleeing, a kind of falling, falling higher and higher, spinning off the edge of the earth and beyond the sun and through the vast, silent vacuum where there were no burdens and where everything weighed exactly nothing—*Gone!* they screamed. *I'm sorry but I'm gone!*—and so at night, not quite dreaming, they gave themselves over to lightness, they were carried, they were purely borne.

On the morning after Ted Lavender died, First Lieutenant Jimmy Cross crouched at the bottom of his foxhole and burned Martha's letters. Then he burned the two photographs. There was a steady rain falling, which made it difficult, but he used heat tabs and Sterno to build a small fire, screening it with his body, holding the photographs over the tight blue flame with the tips of his fingers.

He realized it was only a gesture. Stupid, he thought. Sentimental, too, but mostly just stupid.

Lavender was dead. You couldn't burn the blame.

Besides, the letters were in his head. And even now, without pho- 85
tographs, Lieutenant Cross could see Martha playing volleyball in her white gym shorts and yellow T-shirt. He could see her moving in the rain.

Sin loi: Vietnamese for "sorry."

When the fire died out, Lieutenant Cross pulled his poncho over his shoulders and ate breakfast from a can.

There was no great mystery, he decided.

In those burned letters Martha had never mentioned the war, except to say, Jimmy, take care of yourself. She wasn't involved. She signed the letters Love, but it wasn't love, and all the fine lines and technicalities did not matter. Virginity was no longer an issue. He hated her. Yes, he did. He hated her. Love, too, but it was a hard, hating kind of love.

The morning came up wet and blurry. Everything seemed part of everything else, the fog and Martha and the deepening rain.

He was a soldier, after all. 90

Half smiling, Lieutenant Jimmy Cross took out his maps. He shook his head hard, as if to clear it, then bent forward and began planning the day's march. In ten minutes, or maybe twenty, he would rouse the men and they would pack up and head west, where the maps showed the country to be green and inviting. They would do what they had always done. The rain might add some weight, but otherwise it would be one more day layered upon all the other days.

He was realistic about it. There was that new hardness in his stomach. He loved her but he hated her.

No more fantasies, he told himself.

Henceforth, when he thought about Martha, it would be only to think that she belonged elsewhere. He would shut down the daydreams. This was not Mount Sebastian, it was another world, where there were no pretty poems or midterm exams, a place where men died because of carelessness and gross stupidity. Kiowa was right. Boom-down, and you were dead, never partly dead.

Briefly, in the rain, Lieutenant Cross saw Martha's gray eyes gazing 95
back at him.

He understood.

It was very sad, he thought. The things men carried inside. The things men did or felt they had to do.

He almost nodded at her, but didn't.

Instead he went back to his maps. He was now determined to perform his duties firmly and without negligence. It wouldn't help Lavender, he knew that, but from this point on he would comport himself as an officer. He would dispose of his good-luck pebble. Swallow it, maybe, or use Lee Strunk's slingshot, or just drop it along the trail. On the march he would impose strict field discipline. He would be careful to send out flank security, to prevent straggling or bunching up, to keep his troops moving at the proper pace and at the proper interval. He would insist on clean weapons. He would confiscate the remainder of Lavender's dope. Later in the day, perhaps, he would call the men together and speak to them plainly. He would accept the blame for what had happened to Ted Lavender. He would be a man about it. He would look them in the eyes, keeping his chin level, and he would issue the new SOPs in a calm, impersonal tone of voice, a lieutenant's voice, leaving no room for argument or discussion. Commencing immediately, he'd tell them, they would no longer abandon equipment along the route of march. They would police up their acts. They would get their shit together, and keep it together, and maintain it neatly and in good working order.

He would not tolerate laxity. He would show strength, distancing 100
himself.

Among the men there would be grumbling, of course, and maybe worse, because their days would seem longer and their loads heavier, but Lieutenant Jimmy Cross reminded himself that his obligation was not to be loved but to lead. He would dispense with love; it was not now a factor. And if anyone quarreled or complained, he would simply tighten his lips and arrange his shoulders in the correct command posture. He might give a curt little nod. Or he might not. He might just shrug and say, Carry on, then they would saddle up and form into a column and move out toward the villages west of Than Khe.

Questions

1. How many soldiers are there in the platoon? Name them all.
2. Throughout the story the narrator uses the phrase "the things they carried" or some variation of it. What effect does it have to characterize people by the physical objects they bear?
3. Take any character in the story and list several of the things he carries. What do they tell us about his personality and values?
4. What non-physical things do the men carry?
5. Why does the lieutenant Jimmy Cross burn Martha's photographs and letters the morning after Lavender's death?
6. What does this story suggest about what troops carry home when they return from war?
7. What theme seems most important to you? Is it stated anywhere in the story?

Sandra Cisneros

Barbie-Q

1991

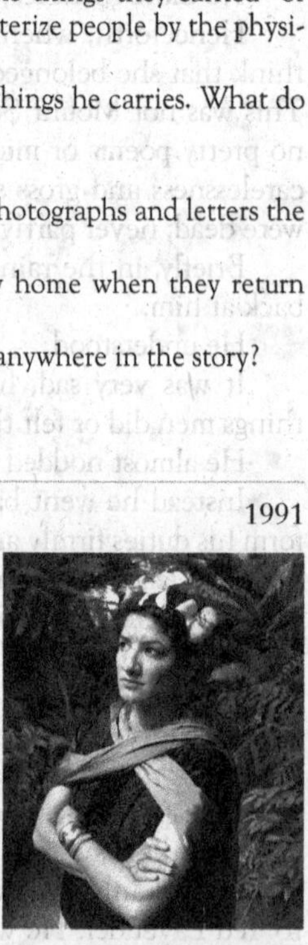
Sandra Cisneros

Sandra Cisneros was born in Chicago in 1954. The child of a Mexican father and a Mexican American mother, she was the only daughter in a family of seven children. She attended Loyola University Chicago and then received a master's degree from the University of Iowa Writers' Workshop. She has instructed high-school dropouts and more recently taught as a visiting writer at numerous universities, including the Universities of California at Irvine and Berkeley and the University of Michigan. Her honors include fellowships from the National Endowment for the Arts and the MacArthur Foundation, an American Book Award, and a 2015 National Medal of Arts. Cisneros's first published work was poetry: Bad Boys *(1980), followed by* My Wicked Wicked Ways *(1987) and* Loose Woman *(1994). Her fiction collections,* The House on Mango Street *(1984) and* Woman Hollering Creek *(1991), earned her a broader audience. She has also published a bilingual children's book,* Hairs/Pelitos *(1994), a novel,* Caramelo *(2002), an illustrated fable for adults,* Have You Seen Marie? (2012), *and a collection of autobiographical essays,* A House of My Own *(2015). Cisneros lives in San Antonio, Texas.*

For Licha

Yours is the one with mean eyes and a ponytail. Striped swimsuit, stilettos, sunglasses, and gold hoop earrings. Mine is the one with bubble hair. Red swimsuit, stilettos, pearl earrings, and a wire stand. But that's all we can afford, besides one extra outfit apiece. Yours, "Red Flair," sophisticated A-line coatdress with a Jackie Kennedy pillbox hat, white gloves, handbag, and heels included. Mine, "Solo in the Spotlight," evening elegance in black glitter strapless gown with a puffy skirt at the bottom like a mermaid tail, formal-length gloves, pink chiffon scarf, and mike included. From so much dressing and undressing, the black glitter wears off where her titties stick out. This and a dress invented from an old sock when we cut holes here and here and here, the cuff rolled over for the glamorous, fancy-free, off-the-shoulder look.

Every time the same story. Your Barbie is roommates with my Barbie, and my Barbie's boyfriend comes over and your Barbie steals him, okay? Kiss kiss kiss. Then the two Barbies fight. You dumbbell! He's mine. Oh no he's not, you stinky! Only Ken's invisible, right? Because we don't have money for a stupid-looking boy doll when we'd both rather ask for a new Barbie outfit next Christmas. We have to make do with your mean-eyed Barbie and my bubblehead Barbie and our one outfit apiece not including the sock dress.

Until next Sunday when we are walking through the flea market on Maxwell Street° and *there!* Lying on the street next to some tool bits, and platform shoes with the heels all squashed, and a fluorescent green wicker wastebasket, and aluminum foil, and hubcaps, and a pink shag rug, and windshield wiper blades, and dusty mason jars, and a coffee can full of rusty nails. *There!* Where? Two Mattel boxes. One with the "Career Gal" ensemble, snappy black-and-white business suit, three-quarter-length sleeve jacket with kick-pleated skirt, red sleeveless shell, gloves, pumps, and matching hat included. The other, "Sweet Dreams," dreamy pink-and-white plaid nightgown and matching robe, lace-trimmed slippers,

Maxwell Street: In a historically immigrant Chicago neighborhood, Maxwell Street was the site of a century-old flea market that closed in 1994.

hair-brush and hand mirror included. How much? Please, please, please, please, please, please, please, until they say okay.

On the outside you and me skipping and humming but inside we are doing loopity-loops and pirouetting. Until at the next vendor's stand, next to boxed pies, and bright orange toilet brushes, and rubber gloves, and wrench sets, and bouquets of feather flowers, and glass towel racks, and steel wool, and Alvin and the Chipmunks records, *there!* And *there!* And *there!* And *there!* and *there!* and *there!* and *there!* Bendable Legs Barbie with her new page-boy hairdo. Midge, Barbie's best friend. Ken, Barbie's boyfriend. Skipper, Barbie's little sister. Tutti and Todd, Barbie and Skipper's tiny twin sister and brother. Skipper's friends, Scooter and Ricky. Alan, Ken's buddy. And Francie, Barbie' MOD'ern cousin.

Everybody today selling toys, all of them damaged with water and 5
smelling of smoke. Because a big toy warehouse on Halsted Street burned down yesterday—see there?—the smoke still rising and drifting across the Dan Ryan expressway.° And now there is a big fire sale at Maxwell Street, today only.

So what if we didn't get our new Bendable Legs Barbie and Midge and Ken and Skipper and Tutti and Todd and Scooter and Ricky and Alan and Francie in nice clean boxes and had to buy them on Maxwell Street, all water-soaked and sooty. So what if our Barbies smell like smoke when you hold them up to your nose even after you wash and wash and wash them. And if the prettiest doll, Barbie's MOD'ern cousin Francie with real eyelashes, eyelash brush included, has a left foot that's melted a little—so? If you dress her in her new "Prom Pinks" outfit, satin splendor with matching coat, gold belt, clutch, and hair bow included, so long as you don't lift her dress, right?—who's to know.

Questions

1. What would you guess to be the age of the narrator? What elements of the narration offer clues?
2. Identify places where the narrator seems to have gotten her descriptions from marketing and advertising. Also find language that starkly contrasts the dreamy names and phrases, suggesting a clash of two different worlds.
3. What do we know about the narrator's social class? Why is that important to our understanding of the story?
4. The classic Barbie doll is blond and Caucasian, and she has an unrealistic "idealized" female body. What is significant about the narrator's acceptance of the damaged and deformed dolls? Does the story seem to make a statement about class and privilege in our society?
5. Try to formulate a one-sentence thematic statement of "Barbie-Q," using the guidelines provided earlier in the chapter to assist you.

Dan Ryan expressway: freeway that connects downtown Chicago to the city's South Side neighborhood.

Luke

The Parable of the Prodigal Son

(King James Version, 1611)

Luke (first century) is traditionally considered the author of the Gospel bearing his name and the Acts of the Apostles in the New Testament. A physician who lived in the Greek city of Antioch (now in Syria), Luke accompanied the Apostle Paul on some of his missionary journeys. Luke's elegantly written Gospel includes some of the Bible's most beloved parables, including that of the Good Samaritan and the Prodigal Son.

And he said, A certain man had two sons: And the younger of them said to his father, Father, give me the portion of goods that falleth to me. And he divided unto them his living. And not many days after the younger son gathered all together, and took his journey into a far country, and there wasted his substance with riotous living. And when he had spent all, there arose a mighty famine in that land; and he began to be in want. And he went and joined himself to a citizen of that country; and he sent him into his fields to feed swine. And he would fain have filled his belly with the husks that the swine did eat: and no man gave unto him. And when he came to himself, he said, How many hired servants of

***The Prodigal Son*, woodcut by Gustave Doré, 1865.**

my father's have bread enough and to spare, and I perish with hunger! I will arise and go to my father, and will say unto him, Father I have sinned against heaven, and before thee, and am no more worthy to be called thy son; make me as one of thy hired servants. And he arose, and came to his father. But when he was yet a great way off, his father saw him, and had compassion, and ran, and fell on his neck, and kissed him. And the son said unto him, Father I have sinned against heaven, and in thy sight, and am no more worthy to be called thy son. But the father said to his servants, Bring forth the best robe, and put it on him; and put a ring on his hand, and shoes on his feet: And bring hither the fatted calf, and kill it; and let us eat, and be merry: For this my son was dead, and is alive again; he was lost, and is found. And they began to be merry. Now his elder son was in the field: and he came and drew nigh to the house, he heard music and dancing. And he called one of the servants, and asked what these things meant. And he said unto him, Thy brother is come; and thy father hath killed the fatted calf, because he hath received him safe and sound. And he was angry, and would not go in: therefore came his father out, and entreated him. And he answering said to his father, Lo, these many years do I serve thee, neither transgressed I at any time thy commandment; and yet thou never gavest me a kid, that I might make merry with my friends: But as soon as this thy son was come, which hath devoured thy living with harlots, thou hast killed for him the fatted calf. And he said unto him, Son thou art ever with me, and all that I have is thine. It was meet that we should make merry, and be glad: for this thy brother was dead, and is alive again; and was lost, and is found.

—Luke 15:11-32

Questions

1. This story has traditionally been called "The Parable of the Prodigal Son." What does *prodigal* mean (make a guess, and then look it up)? Which of the two brothers is prodigal?
2. What position does the younger son expect when he returns to his father's house? What does the father give him?
3. When the older brother sees the celebration for his younger brother's return, he grows angry. He makes a very reasonable set of complaints to his father. He has indeed been a loyal and moral son, but what virtue does the older brother lack?
4. Is the father fair to the elder son? Explain your answer.
5. Theologians have discussed this parable's religious significance for two thousand years. What, in your own words, is the human theme of the story?

Kurt Vonnegut Jr.

Harrison Bergeron

1961

Kurt Vonnegut Jr.

Kurt Vonnegut Jr. (1922–2007) was born in Indianapolis. During the Depression his father, a well-to-do architect, had virtually no work, and the family lived in reduced circumstances. Vonnegut attended Cornell University, where he majored in chemistry and was also managing editor of the daily student newspaper. In 1943 he enlisted in the US Army. During the Battle of the Bulge he was captured by German troops and interned as a prisoner of war in Dresden, where he survived the massive Allied firebombing, which killed tens of thousands of people, mostly civilians. (The firebombing of Dresden became the central incident in Vonnegut's best-selling 1969 novel, Slaughterhouse-Five.*) After the war, Vonnegut worked as a reporter and later as a public relations man for General Electric in Schenectady, New York. He quit his job in 1951 to write full-time after publishing several science fiction stories in national magazines. His first novel,* Player Piano, *appeared in 1952, followed by* Sirens of Titan *(1959) and his first best seller,* Cat's Cradle *(1963)—all now considered classics of literary science fiction. Among his many other books are* Mother Night *(1961),* Jailbird *(1979), and a book of biographical essays,* A Man Without a Country *(2005). His short fiction was collected in* Welcome to the Monkey House *(1968) and* Bagombo Snuff Box *(1999). Vonnegut was a singular figure in modern American fiction. An ingenious comic writer, he fused the popular genre of science fiction with the literary tradition of dark satire—a combination splendidly realized in "Harrison Bergeron."*

The year was 2081, and everybody was finally equal. They weren't only equal before God and the law. They were equal every which way. Nobody was smarter than anybody else. Nobody was better looking than anybody else. Nobody was stronger or quicker than anybody else. All this equality was due to the 211th, 212th, and 213th Amendments to the Constitution, and to the unceasing vigilance of agents of the United States Handicapper General.

Some things about living still weren't quite right, though. April, for instance, still drove people crazy by not being springtime. And it was in that clammy month that the H-G men took George and Hazel Bergeron's fourteen-year-old son, Harrison, away.

It was tragic, all right, but George and Hazel couldn't think about it very hard. Hazel had a perfectly average intelligence, which meant she couldn't think about anything except in short bursts. And George, while his intelligence was way above normal, had a little mental handicap radio in his ear. He was required by law to wear it at all times. It was tuned to a government transmitter. Every twenty seconds or so, the transmitter would send out some sharp noise to keep people like George from taking unfair advantage of their brains.

George and Hazel were watching television. There were tears on Hazel's cheeks, but she'd forgotten for the moment what they were about.

On the television screen were ballerinas.

A buzzer sounded in George's head. His thoughts fled in panic, like bandits from a burglar alarm.

"That was a real pretty dance, that dance they just did," said Hazel.

"Huh?" said George.

"That dance—it was nice," said Hazel.

"Yup," said George. He tried to think a little about the ballerinas. They weren't really very good—no better than anybody else would have been, anyway. They were burdened with sashweights and bags of birdshot, and their faces were masked, so that no one, seeing a free and graceful gesture or a pretty face, would feel like something the cat drug in. George was toying with the vague notion that maybe dancers shouldn't be handicapped. But he didn't get very far with it before another noise in his ear radio scattered his thoughts.

George winced. So did two out of the eight ballerinas.

Hazel saw him wince. Having no mental handicap herself, she had to ask George what the latest sound had been.

"Sounded like somebody hitting a milk bottle with a ball peen hammer," said George.

"I'd think it would be real interesting, hearing all the different sounds," said Hazel, a little envious. "All the things they think up."

"Um," said George.

"Only, if I was Handicapper General, you know what I would do?" said Hazel. Hazel, as a matter of fact, bore a strong resemblance to the Handicapper General, a woman named Diana Moon Glampers. "If I was Diana Moon Glampers," said Hazel, "I'd have chimes on Sunday—just chimes. Kind of in honor of religion."

"I could think, if it was just chimes," said George.

"Well—maybe make 'em real loud," said Hazel. "I think I'd make a good Handicapper General."

"Good as anybody else," said George.

"Who knows better'n I do what normal is?" said Hazel.

"Right," said George. He began to think glimmeringly about his abnormal son who was now in jail, about Harrison, but a twenty-one-gun salute in his head stopped that.

"Boy!" said Hazel, "that was a doozy, wasn't it?"

It was such a doozy that George was white and trembling, and tears stood on the rims of his red eyes. Two of the eight ballerinas had collapsed to the studio floor, were holding their temples.

"All of a sudden you look so tired," said Hazel. "Why don't you stretch out on the sofa, so's you can rest your handicap bag on the pillows, honeybunch." She was referring to the forty-seven pounds of birdshot in a canvas bag, which was padlocked around George's neck. "Go on and rest the bag for a little while," she said. "I don't care if you're not equal to me for a while."

George weighed the bag with his hands. "I don't mind it," he said. "I don't notice it any more. It's just a part of me."

"You been so tired lately—kind of wore out," said Hazel. "If there was just some way we could make a little hole in the bottom of the bag, and just take out a few of them lead balls. Just a few."

"Two years in prison and two thousand dollars fine for every ball I took out," said George. "I don't call that a bargain."

"If you could just take a few out when you came home from work," said Hazel. "I mean—you don't compete with anybody around here. You just set around."

"If I tried to get away with it," said George, "then other people'd get away with it—and pretty soon we'd be right back to the dark ages again, with everybody competing against everybody else. You wouldn't like that, would you?"

"I'd hate it," said Hazel.

"There you are," said George. "The minute people start cheating on laws, what do you think happens to society?"

If Hazel hadn't been able to come up with an answer to this question, George couldn't have supplied one. A siren was going off in his head.

"Reckon it'd fall all apart," said Hazel.

"What would?" said George blankly.

"Society," said Hazel uncertainly. "Wasn't that what you just said?"

"Who knows?" said George.

The television program was suddenly interrupted for a news bulletin. It wasn't clear at first as to what the bulletin was about, since the announcer, like all announcers, had a serious speech impediment. For about half a minute, and in a state of high excitement, the announcer tried to say, "Ladies and gentlemen—"

He finally gave up, handed the bulletin to a ballerina to read.

"That's all right—" Hazel said of the announcer, "he tried. That's the big thing. He tried to do the best he could with what God gave him. He should get a nice raise for trying so hard."

"Ladies and gentlemen—" said the ballerina, reading the bulletin. She must have been extraordinarily beautiful, because the mask she wore was hideous. And it was easy to see that she was the strongest and most graceful of all the dancers, for her handicap bags were as big as those worn by two-hundred-pound men.

And she had to apologize at once for her voice, which was a very unfair voice for a woman to use. Her voice was a warm, luminous, timeless melody. "Excuse me—" she said, and she began again, making her voice absolutely uncompetitive.

"Harrison Bergeron, age fourteen," she said in a grackle squawk, "has just escaped from jail, where he was held on suspicion of plotting to overthrow the government. He is a genius and an athlete, is under-handicapped, and should be regarded as extremely dangerous."

A police photograph of Harrison Bergeron was flashed on the screen upside down, then sideways, upside down again, then right side up. The picture showed the full length of Harrison against a background calibrated in feet and inches. He was exactly seven feet tall.

The rest of Harrison's appearance was Halloween and hardware. Nobody had ever borne heavier handicaps. He had outgrown hindrances faster than the H-G men could think them up. Instead of a little ear radio for a mental handicap, he wore a tremendous pair of earphones, and spectacles with thick wavy lenses. The spectacles were intended to make him not only half blind, but to give him whanging headaches besides.

Scrap metal was hung all over him. Ordinarily, there was a certain 45
symmetry, a military neatness to the handicaps issued to strong people, but Harrison looked like a walking junkyard. In the race of life, Harrison carried three hundred pounds.

And to offset his good looks, the H-G men required that he wear at all times a red rubber ball for a nose, keep his eyebrows shaved off, and cover his even white teeth with black caps at snaggle-tooth random.

"If you see this boy," said the ballerina, "do not—I repeat, do not—try to reason with him."

There was the shriek of a door being torn from its hinges.

Screams and barking cries of consternation came from the television set. The photograph of Harrison Bergeron on the screen jumped again and again, as though dancing to the tune of an earthquake.

George Bergeron correctly identified the earthquake, and well he 50
might have—for many was the time his own home had danced to the same crashing tune. "My God—" said George, "that must be Harrison!"

The realization was blasted from his mind instantly by the sound of an automobile collision in his head.

When George could open his eyes again, the photograph of Harrison was gone. A living, breathing Harrison filled the screen.

Clanking, clownish, and huge, Harrison stood in the center of the studio. The knob of the uprooted studio door was still in his hand. Ballerinas, technicians, musicians, and announcers cowered on their knees before him, expecting to die.

"I am the Emperor!" cried Harrison. "Do you hear? I am the Emperor! Everybody must do what I say at once!" He stamped his foot and the studio shook.

"Even as I stand here—" he bellowed, "crippled, hobbled, sickened—I 55
am a greater ruler than any man who ever lived! Now watch me become what I *can* become!"

Harrison tore the straps of his handicap harness like wet tissue paper, tore straps guaranteed to support five thousand pounds.

Harrison's scrap-iron handicaps crashed to the floor.

Harrison thrust his thumbs under the bar of the padlock that secured his head harness. The bar snapped like celery. Harrison smashed his headphones and spectacles against the wall.

He flung away his rubber-ball nose, revealed a man that would have awed Thor, the god of thunder.

"I shall now select my Empress!" he said, looking down on the cowering people. "Let the first woman who dares rise to her feet claim her mate and her throne!"

A moment passed, and then a ballerina arose, swaying like a willow.

Harrison plucked the mental handicap from her ear, snapped off her physical handicaps with marvelous delicacy. Last of all, he removed her mask.

She was blindingly beautiful.

"Now—" said Harrison, taking her hand, "shall we show the people the meaning of the word dance? Music!" he commanded.

The musicians scrambled back into their chairs, and Harrison stripped them of their handicaps, too. "Play your best," he told them, "and I'll make you barons and dukes and earls."

The music began. It was normal at first—cheap, silly, false. But Harrison snatched two musicians from their chairs, waved them like batons as he sang the music as he wanted it played. He slammed them back into their chairs.

The music began again and was much improved.

Harrison and his Empress merely listened to the music for a while—listened gravely, as though synchronizing their heartbeats with it.

They shifted their weights to their toes.

Harrison placed his big hands on the girl's tiny waist, letting her sense the weightlessness that would soon be hers.

And then, in an explosion of joy and grace, into the air they sprang!

Not only were the laws of the land abandoned, but the law of gravity and the laws of motion as well.

They reeled, whirled, swiveled, flounced, capered, gamboled, and spun.

They leaped like deer on the moon.

The studio ceiling was thirty feet high, but each leap brought the dancers nearer to it.

It became their obvious intention to kiss the ceiling.

They kissed it.

And then, neutralizing gravity with love and pure will, they remained suspended in air inches below the ceiling, and they kissed each other for a long, long time.

It was then that Diana Moon Glampers, the Handicapper General, came into the studio with a double-barreled ten-gauge shotgun. She fired twice, and the Emperor and the Empress were dead before they hit the floor.

Diana Moon Glampers loaded the gun again. She aimed it at the musicians and told them they had ten seconds to get their handicaps back on. 80

It was then that the Bergerons' television tube burned out.

Hazel turned to comment about the blackout to George. But George had gone out into the kitchen for a can of beer.

George came back in with the beer, paused while a handicap signal shook him up. And then he sat down again. "You been crying?" he said to Hazel.

"Yup," she said.

"What about?" he said. 85

"I forget," she said. "Something real sad on television."

"What was it?" he said.

"It's all kind of mixed up in my mind," said Hazel.

"Forget sad things," said George.

"I always do," said Hazel. 90

"That's my girl," said George. He winced. There was the sound of a rivetting gun in his head.

"Gee—I could tell that one was a doozy," said Hazel.

"You can say that again," said George.

"Gee—" said Hazel, "I could tell that one was a doozy."

Questions

1. What tendencies in present-day American society is Vonnegut satirizing? Does the story argue *for* anything? How would you sum up its theme?
2. Is Diana Moon Glampers a "flat" or a "round" character? (If you need to review these terms, see the discussion of character in Chapter 3.) Would you call Vonnegut's characterization of her "realistic"? If not, why doesn't it need to be?
3. From what point of view is the story told? Why is it more effective than if Harrison Bergeron had told his own story in the first person?
4. Two sympathetic critics of Vonnegut's work, Karen and Charles Wood, have said of his stories: "Vonnegut proves repeatedly . . . that men and women remain fundamentally the same, no matter what technology surrounds them." Try applying this comment to "Harrison Bergeron." Do you agree?
5. Stanislaw Lem, Polish author of *Solaris* and other novels, once made this thoughtful criticism of many of his contemporaries among science fiction writers:

   > The revolt against the machine and against civilization, the praise of the "aesthetic" nature of catastrophe, the dead-end course of human civilization—these are their foremost problems, the intellectual content of their works. Such SF is as it were *a priori* vitiated by pessimism, in the sense that anything that may happen will be for the worse. ("The Time-Travel Story and Related Matters of SF Structuring," *Science Fiction Studies* 1 [1974], 143–54.)

   How might Lem's objection be raised against "Harrison Bergeron"? In your opinion, does it negate the value of Vonnegut's story?

WRITING *effectively*

THINKING ABOUT THEME

A clear, precise statement about a story's theme can serve as a promising thesis for a writing assignment. After you read a short story, you will probably have some vague sense of its theme—the central unifying idea, or the point of the story. How do you hone that vague sense of theme into a sharp and intriguing thesis?

- **Start by making a list of phrases or ideas that suggest the story's possible theme.** If you are discussing Chinua Achebe's "Dead Men's Path" (Chapter 8), your initial list might look like this:

  new ideas versus tradition
  danger of inflexibility
  importance of compromise
  necessity of inclusiveness
  stubbornness of youth
  changing cultures
  wisdom of elders

- **Choose the most important points and then combine them into a single sentence.** For Achebe, you might have circled "new ideas versus tradition," "importance of compromise," and "necessity of inclusiveness," and your summary might be this:

  The central theme of "Dead Men's Path" is that lasting progress is best made in a spirit of compromise and inclusivity, not by insensitivity to the feelings of those who follow the old ways.

- **Refine your sentence to capture the story's essence as clearly and specifically as possible.** Remember, your goal is to transcend a mere one-sentence plot summary. How can you clearly express the central theme in a few words? Your refinement might read as follows:

  The theme of "Dead Men's Path" is that progress requires compromise and inclusiveness, which recognizes the feelings of those who follow the old ways.

CHECKLIST: Writing About Theme

- ☐ List as many possible themes as you can.
- ☐ Circle the two or three most important points and try to combine them into a sentence.

- ☐ Relate particular details of the story to the theme you have spelled out. Consider plot details, dialogue, setting, point of view, title—any elements that seem especially pertinent.
- ☐ Check whether all the elements of the story fit your thesis.
- ☐ Have you missed an important aspect of the story? Or, have you chosen to focus on a secondary idea, overlooking the central one?
- ☐ If necessary, rework your thesis until it applies to every element in the story.

TOPICS FOR WRITING ON THEME

1. Choose a story that catches your attention, and go through the steps outlined above to develop a strong thesis sentence about the story's theme. Then flesh out your argument into an essay, supporting your thesis with evidence from the text, including quotations. Some good story choices might be "A Clean, Well-Lighted Place" (Chapter 5), "The Chrysanthemums" (Chapter 7), "A Good Man Is Hard to Find," (Chapter 2) and "The Lottery" (Chapter 7).
2. Define the central theme of "Harrison Bergeron." Is Vonnegut's early-1960s vision of the future still relevant today? Why or why not?
3. Write a short parable in the style of Aesop's "The Fox and the Grapes" (Chapter 1), and explicitly state your theme at the end of the story.
4. A recent *Time* magazine article describes a young California woman who distanced herself from her Chinese heritage until reading *The Joy Luck Club* "turned her into a 'born-again Asian.' It gave her new insights into why her mom was so hard on her and why the ways she showed love—say, through food—were different from those of the families [she] saw on TV, who seemed to say 'I love you' all day long." Have you ever had a similar experience, in which something you read gave you a better understanding of a loved one, or even yourself?

▶ TERMS FOR *review*

Summary ▶ A brief condensation of the main idea or plot of a literary work. A summary is similar to a paraphrase, but less detailed.

Theme ▶ The main idea or larger meaning of a work of literature. A theme may be a message or a moral, but it is more likely to be a central, unifying insight or viewpoint.

7 SYMBOL

What You Will Learn in This Chapter

- To recognize and define a *literary symbol*
- To explain *allegory* and describe its characteristics
- To identify and describe symbolic characters and symbolic acts
- To analyze a symbol's role in a story

In F. Scott Fitzgerald's novel *The Great Gatsby*, a huge pair of bespectacled eyes stares across a wilderness of ash heaps, from a billboard advertising the services of an oculist. Repeatedly entering into the story, the advertisement comes to mean more than simply the availability of eye examinations. Fitzgerald has a character liken it to the eyes of God; he hints that some sad, compassionate spirit is brooding as it watches the passing procession of humanity. Such an object is a **symbol**: in literature, a person, place, or thing that suggests more than its literal meaning.

Symbols generally do not "stand for" any single meaning, nor for anything absolutely definite; they point, they hint, or, as Henry James put it, they cast long shadows. To take a large example: in Herman Melville's *Moby-Dick*, the great white whale of the book's title apparently means more than the literal dictionary-definition meaning of an aquatic mammal. He also suggests more than the devil, to whom some of the characters liken him. The great whale, as the story unfolds, comes to imply an amplitude of meanings, among them the forces of nature and the whole created universe.

ALLEGORY

This indefinite multiplicity of meanings is characteristic of a symbolic story and distinguishes it from an **allegory**, a story in which persons, places, and things form a system of clearly labeled equivalents. In a simple allegory, characters and other elements often stand for abstractions. You will meet such a character in another story in this book, Nathaniel Hawthorne's "Young Goodman Brown" (Chapter 9). This tale's main female character, Faith, represents the religious virtue suggested by her name. Supreme allegories are found in some biblical parables ("The Kingdom of Heaven is like a man who sowed good seed in his field . . . ," Matthew 13:24–30).

A classic allegory is the medieval play *Everyman*, whose hero represents us all, and who, deserted by false friends called Kindred and Goods, faces the judgment of God accompanied only by a faithful friend called Good Deeds. In John Bunyan's seventeenth-century allegory *Pilgrim's Progress*, the protagonist, Christian, struggles along the difficult road toward salvation, meeting along the way persons such as Mr. Worldly Wiseman, who directs him into a more comfortable path (a wrong turn), and the residents of a town called Fair Speech, among them a hypocrite named Mr. Facing-both-ways. Not all allegories are simple: Dante's *Divine Comedy*, written during the Middle Ages, continues to reveal new meanings to careful readers. Allegory was much beloved in the Middle Ages, but in contemporary fiction it is rare. One modern instance is George Orwell's long fable *Animal Farm*, in which (among its double meanings) barnyard animals stand for human victims and totalitarian oppressors.

SYMBOLS

Symbols in fiction are not generally abstract terms such as *love* or *truth*, but are likely to be perceptible objects. In William Faulkner's "A Rose for Emily" (Chapter 2), Miss Emily's invisible watch ticking at the end of a golden chain not only indicates the passage of time, but also suggests that time passes without even being noticed by the watch's owner, and the golden chain carries suggestions of wealth and authority. Objects (and creatures) that seem insignificant in themselves can take on a symbolic importance in the larger context.

Often the symbols we meet in fiction are inanimate objects, but other things also may function symbolically. In James Joyce's "Araby" (Chapter 9), the very name of the bazaar, Araby—the poetic name for Arabia—suggests magic, romance, and *The Arabian Nights*; its syllables (the narrator tells us) "cast an Eastern enchantment over me." Even a locale, or a feature of physical topography, can provide rich suggestions. Recall Ernest Hemingway's "A Clean, Well-Lighted Place" (Chapter 5), in which the café is not merely a café, but an island of refuge from night, chaos, loneliness, old age, and impending death.

Symbolic Characters

In some novels and stories, symbolic characters make brief cameo appearances. Such characters often are not well-rounded and fully known, but are seen fleetingly and remain slightly mysterious. Usually such a symbolic character is more a portrait than a person—or somewhat portraitlike, as Faulkner's Miss Emily, who twice appears at a window of her house "like the carven torso of an idol in a niche." Though Faulkner invests Miss Emily with life and vigor, he also clothes her in symbolic hints: she seems almost to personify the vanishing aristocracy of the antebellum South, still maintaining a black servant and being ruthlessly betrayed by a moneymaking Yankee. Sometimes a part of a character's body or an attribute may convey symbolic meaning: a baleful eye, as in Edgar Allan Poe's "The Tell-Tale Heart" (Chapter 2).

Symbolic Acts

Much as a symbolic whale holds more meaning than an ordinary whale, a **symbolic act** is a gesture with larger significance than usual. For the boy's father in Faulkner's "Barn Burning" (Chapter 5), the act of destroying a barn is no mere act of spite, but an expression of his profound hatred for anything not belonging to him. Faulkner adds that burning a barn reflects the father's memories of the "waste and extravagance of war," and further adds that "the element of fire spoke to some deep mainspring" in his being. A symbolic act, however, doesn't have to be a gesture as large as starting a conflagration. Before setting out in pursuit of the great white whale, Melville's Captain Ahab in *Moby-Dick* deliberately snaps his tobacco pipe and throws it away, as if to suggest (among other things) that he will let no pleasure or pastime distract him from his vengeance.

Why Use Symbols?

Why do writers have to symbolize—why don't they tell us outright? One advantage of a symbol is that it is so compact, and yet so fully laden. Both starkly concrete and slightly mysterious, like Miss Emily's invisible ticking watch, it may impress us with all the force of something beheld in a dream or in a nightmare. The watch suggests, among other things, the slow and invisible passage of time. What this symbol says, it says more fully and more memorably than could be said, perhaps, in a long essay on the subject.

To some extent (it may be claimed), all stories are symbolic. Merely by holding up for our inspection these characters and their actions, the writer lends them *some* special significance. But this is to think of *symbol* in an extremely broad and inclusive way. For the usual purposes of reading a story and understanding it, there is probably little point in looking for symbolism in every word, in every stick or stone, in every striking of a match, in every minor character. Still, to be on the alert for symbols when reading fiction is perhaps wiser than to ignore them. Not to admit that symbolic meanings may be present, or to refuse to think about them, would be another way to misread a story—or to read no further than its outer edges.

RECOGNIZING SYMBOLS

How, then, do you recognize a symbol in fiction when you meet it? Fortunately, the storyteller often gives the symbol particular emphasis. It may be mentioned repeatedly throughout the story; it may even supply the story with a title ("Barn Burning," "A Clean, Well-Lighted Place," "Araby"). At times, a crucial symbol will open a story or end it. Unless an object, act, or character is given some such special emphasis and importance, we may generally feel safe in taking it at face value. Probably it isn't a symbol if it points clearly and unmistakably toward some one meaning, like a whistle in a factory, whose blast at noon means lunch. But an object, an act, or a character is surely symbolic (and almost as surely displays high literary art) if, when we finish the story, we realize that it was that item—that gigantic eye; that clean, well-lighted café; that burning of a barn—which led us to the author's theme, the essential meaning.

John Steinbeck

The Chrysanthemums 1938

John Steinbeck

John Steinbeck (1902–1968) was born in Salinas, California, in the fertile valley he remembers in "The Chrysanthemums." Off and on, he attended Stanford University, and then he sojourned in New York as a reporter and a bricklayer. After years of struggle to earn his living by fiction, Steinbeck reached a large audience with Tortilla Flat *(1935), a loosely woven novel portraying Mexican Americans in Monterey with fondness and sympathy. Great acclaim greeted* The Grapes of Wrath *(1939), the story of a family of Oklahoma farmers who, ruined by dust storms in the 1930s, join a mass migration to California. In 1962 he became the seventh American to win the Nobel Prize in Literature, but many critics resisted placing Steinbeck on the same high shelf as Faulkner and Hemingway. He wrote much, not all good, and yet his best work adds up to an impressive total. Besides* The Grapes of Wrath, *it includes* In Dubious Battle *(1936), a novel of an apple-pickers' strike;* Of Mice and Men *(1937), a powerful short novel of comradeship between a hobo and a man; the short stories in* The Long Valley *(1938); and the masterful* East of Eden *(1952), the sweeping history of a pair of families in the author's native Salinas Valley. Throughout the fiction he wrote in his prime, Steinbeck maintains an appealing sympathy for the poor and downtrodden, the lonely and dispossessed.*

The high grey-flannel fog of winter closed off the Salinas Valley° from the sky and from all the rest of the world. On every side it sat like a lid on the mountains and made of the great valley a closed pot. On the broad, level land floor the gang plows bit deep and left the black earth shining like metal where the shares had cut. On the foothill ranches across the Salinas River, the yellow stubble fields seemed to be bathed in pale cold sunshine, but there was no sunshine in the valley now in December. The thick willow scrub along the river flamed with sharp and positive yellow leaves.

It was a time of quiet and of waiting. The air was cold and tender. A light wind blew up from the southwest so that the farmers were mildly hopeful of a good rain before long; but fog and rain do not go together.

Salinas Valley: south of San Francisco in Monterey County, a fertile agricultural region just inland from California's central coast.

Across the river, on Henry Allen's foothill ranch there was little work to be done, for the hay was cut and stored and the orchards were plowed up to receive the rain deeply when it should come. The cattle on the higher slopes were becoming shaggy and rough-coated.

Elisa Allen, working in her flower garden, looked down across the yard and saw Henry, her husband, talking to two men in business suits. The three of them stood by the tractor shed, each man with one foot on the side of the little Fordson. They smoked cigarettes and studied the machine as they talked.

Elisa watched them for a moment and then went back to her work. 5
She was thirty-five. Her face was lean and strong and her eyes were as clear as water. Her figure looked blocked and heavy in her gardening costume, a man's black hat pulled low down over her eyes, clodhopper shoes, a figured print dress almost completely covered by a big corduroy apron with four big pockets to hold the snips, the trowel and scratcher, the seeds and the knife she worked with. She wore heavy leather gloves to protect her hands while she worked.

She was cutting down the old year's chrysanthemum stalks with a pair of short and powerful scissors. She looked down toward the men by the tractor shed now and then. Her face was eager and mature and handsome; even her work with the scissors was over-eager, over-powerful. The chrysanthemum stems seemed too small and easy for her energy.

She brushed a cloud of hair out of her eyes with the back of her glove, and left a smudge of earth on her cheek in doing it. Behind her stood the neat white farm house with red geraniums close-banked around it as high as the windows. It was a hard-swept looking little house with hard-polished windows, and a clean mud-mat on the front steps.

Elisa cast another glance toward the tractor shed. The strangers were getting into their Ford coupe. She took off a glove and put her strong fingers down into the forest of new green chrysanthemum sprouts that were growing around the old roots. She spread the leaves and looked down among the close-growing stems. No aphids were there, no sowbugs or snails or cutworms. Her terrier fingers destroyed such pests before they could get started.

Elisa started at the sound of her husband's voice. He had come near quietly, and he leaned over the wire fence that protected her flower garden from cattle and dogs and chickens.

"At it again," he said. "You've got a strong new crop coming." 10

Elisa straightened her back and pulled on the gardening glove again. "Yes. They'll be strong this coming year." In her tone and on her face there was a little smugness.

"You've got a gift with things," Henry observed. "Some of those yellow chrysanthemums you had this year were ten inches across. I wish you'd work out in the orchard and raise some apples that big."

Her eyes sharpened. "Maybe I could do it, too. I've a gift with things, all right. My mother had it. She could stick anything in the ground and make it grow. She said it was having planters' hands that knew how to do it."

"Well, it sure works with flowers," he said.

"Henry, who were those men you were talking to?"

"Why, sure, that's what I came to tell you. They were from the Western Meat Company. I sold those thirty head of three-year-old steers. Got nearly my own price, too."

"Good," she said. "Good for you."

"And I thought," he continued, "I thought how it's Saturday afternoon, and we might go into Salinas for dinner at a restaurant, and then to a picture show—to celebrate, you see."

"Good," she repeated. "Oh, yes. That will be good."

Henry put on his joking tone. "There's fights tonight. How'd you like to go to the fights?"

"Oh, no," she said breathlessly. "No, I wouldn't like fights."

"Just fooling, Elisa. We'll go to a movie. Let's see. It's two now. I'm going to take Scotty and bring down those steers from the hill. It'll take us maybe two hours. We'll go in town about five and have dinner at the Cominos Hotel. Like that?"

"Of course I'll like it. It's good to eat away from home."

"All right, then. I'll go get up a couple of horses."

She said, "I'll have plenty of time to transplant some of these sets, I guess."

She heard her husband calling Scotty down by the barn. And a little later she saw the two men ride up the pale yellow hillside in search of the steers.

There was a little square sandy bed kept for rooting the chrysanthemums. With her trowel she turned the soil over and over, and smoothed it and patted it firm. Then she dug ten parallel trenches to receive the sets. Back at the chrysanthemum bed she pulled out the little crisp shoots, trimmed off the leaves of each one with her scissors and laid it on a small orderly pile.

A squeak of wheels and plod of hoofs came from the road. Elisa looked up. The country road ran along the dense bank of willows and cottonwoods that bordered the river, and up this road came a curious vehicle, curiously drawn. It was an old spring-wagon, with a round canvas top on it like the cover of a prairie schooner. It was drawn by an old bay horse and a little grey-and-white burro. A big stubble-bearded man sat between the cover flaps and drove the crawling team. Underneath the wagon, between the hind wheels, a lean and rangy mongrel dog walked sedately. Words were painted on the canvas, in clumsy, crooked letters. "Pots, pans, knives, sisors, lawn mores, Fixed." Two rows of articles, and the triumphantly definitive "Fixed" below. The black paint had run down in little sharp points beneath each letter.

Elisa, squatting on the ground, watched to see the crazy, loose-jointed wagon pass by. But it didn't pass. It turned into the farm road in front of her house, crooked old wheels skirling and squeaking. The rangy dog darted from between the wheels and ran ahead. Instantly the two ranch shepherds flew out at him. Then all three stopped, and with stiff and quivering tails, with taut straight legs, with ambassadorial dignity, they slowly circled, sniffing daintily. The caravan pulled up to Elisa's wire fence and stopped. Now the newcomer dog, feeling out-numbered, lowered his tail and retired under the wagon with raised hackles and bared teeth.

The man on the wagon seat called out, "That's a bad dog in a fight when he gets started."

Elisa laughed. "I see he is. How soon does he generally get started?"

The man caught up her laughter and echoed it heartily. "Sometimes not for weeks and weeks," he said. He climbed stiffly down, over the wheel. The horse and the donkey drooped like unwatered flowers.

Elisa saw that he was a very big man. Although his hair and beard were greying, he did not look old. His worn black suit was wrinkled and spotted with grease. The laughter had disappeared from his face and eyes the moment his laughing voice ceased. His eyes were dark, and they were full of the brooding that gets in the eyes of teamsters and of sailors. The calloused hands he rested on the wire fence were cracked, and every crack was a black line. He took off his battered hat.

"I'm off my general road, ma'am," he said. "Does this dirt road cut over across the river to the Los Angeles highway?"

Elisa stood up and shoved the thick scissors in her apron pocket. "Well, yes, it does, but it winds around and then fords the river. I don't think your team could pull through the sand."

He replied with some asperity, "It might surprise you what them beasts can pull through."

"When they get started?" she asked.

He smiled for a second. "Yes. When they get started."

"Well," said Elisa, "I think you'll save time if you go back to the Salinas road and pick up the highway there."

He drew a big finger down the chicken wire and made it sing. "I ain't in any hurry, ma'am. I go from Seattle to San Diego and back every year. Takes all my time. About six months each way. I aim to follow nice weather."

Elisa took off her gloves and stuffed them in the apron pocket with the scissors. She touched the under edge of her man's hat, searching for fugitive hairs. "That sounds like a nice kind of a way to live," she said.

He leaned confidentially over the fence. "Maybe you noticed the writing on my wagon. I mend pots and sharpen knives and scissors. You got any of them things to do?"

"Oh, no," she said quickly. "Nothing like that." Her eyes hardened with resistance.

"Scissors is the worst thing," he explained. "Most people just ruin scissors trying to sharpen 'em, but I know how. I got a special tool. It's a little bobbit kind of thing, and patented. But it sure does the trick."

"No. My scissors are all sharp."

"All right, then. Take a pot," he continued earnestly, "a bent pot, or a pot with a hole. I can make it like new so you don't have to buy no new ones. That's a saving for you."

"No," she said shortly. "I tell you I have nothing like that for you to do."

His face fell to an exaggerated sadness. His voice took on a whining undertone. "I ain't had a thing to do today. Maybe I won't have no supper tonight. You see I'm off my regular road. I know folks on the highway clear from Seattle to San Diego. They save their things for me to sharpen up because they know I do it so good and save them money."

"I'm sorry," Elisa said irritably. "I haven't anything for you to do."

His eyes left her face and fell to searching the ground. They roamed about until they came to the chrysanthemum bed where she had been working. "What's them plants, ma'am?"

The irritation and resistance melted from Elisa's face. "Oh, those are chrysanthemums, giant whites and yellows. I raise them every year, bigger than anybody around here."

"Kind of a long-stemmed flower? Looks like a quick puff of colored smoke?" he asked.

"That's it. What a nice way to describe them."

"They smell kind of nasty till you get used to them," he said.

"It's a good bitter smell," she retorted, "not nasty at all."

He changed his tone quickly. "I like the smell myself."

"I had ten-inch blooms this year," she said.

The man leaned farther over the fence. "Look. I know a lady down the road a piece, has got the nicest garden you ever seen. Got nearly every kind of flower but no chrysanthemums. Last time I was mending a copper-bottom washtub for her (that's a hard job but I do it good), she said to me, 'If you ever run acrost some nice chrysanthemums I wish you'd try to get me a few seeds.' That's what she told me."

Elisa's eyes grew alert and eager. "She couldn't have known much about chrysanthemums. You *can* raise them from seed, but it's much easier to root the little sprouts you see there."

"Oh," he said. "I s'pose I can't take none to her, then."

"Why yes you can," Elisa cried. "I can put some in damp sand, and you can carry them right along with you. They'll take root in the pot if you keep them damp. And then she can transplant them."

"She'd sure like to have some, ma'am. You say they're nice ones?"

"Beautiful," she said. "Oh, beautiful." Her eyes shone. She tore off the battered hat and shook out her dark pretty hair. "I'll put them in a flower pot, and you can take them right with you. Come into the yard."

While the man came through the picket gate Elisa ran excitedly along the geranium-bordered path to the back of the house. And she returned carrying a big red flower pot. The gloves were forgotten now. She kneeled on the ground by the starting bed and dug up the sandy soil with her fingers and scooped it into the bright new flower pot. Then she picked up the little pile of shoots she had prepared. With her strong fingers she pressed them in the sand and tamped around them with her knuckles. The man stood over her. "I'll tell you what to do," she said. "You remember so you can tell the lady."

"Yes, I'll try to remember."

"Well, look. These will take root in about a month. Then she must set them out, about a foot apart in good rich earth like this, see?" She lifted a handful of dark soil for him to look at. "They'll grow fast and tall. Now remember this: In July tell her to cut them down, about eight inches from the ground."

"Before they bloom?" he asked.

"Yes, before they bloom." Her face was tight with eagerness. "They'll grow right up again. About the last of September the buds will start."

She stopped and seemed perplexed. "It's the budding that takes the most care," she said hesitantly. "I don't know how to tell you." She looked deep into his eyes, searchingly. Her mouth opened a little, and she seemed to be listening. "I'll try to tell you," she said. "Did you ever hear of planting hands?"

"Can't say I have, ma'am."

"Well, I can only tell you what it feels like. It's when you're picking off the buds you don't want. Everything goes right down into your fingertips. You watch your fingers work. They do it themselves. You can feel how it is. They pick and pick the buds. They never make a mistake. They're with the plant. Do you see? Your fingers and the plant. You can feel that, right up your arm. They know. They never make a mistake. You can feel it. When you're like that you can't do anything wrong. Do you see that? Can you understand that?"

She was kneeling on the ground looking up at him. Her breast swelled passionately.

The man's eyes narrowed. He looked away self-consciously. "Maybe I know," he said. "Sometimes in the night in the wagon there—"

Elisa's voice grew husky. She broke in on him, "I've never lived as you do, but I know what you mean. When the night is dark—why, the stars are sharp-pointed, and there's quiet. Why, you rise up and up! Every pointed star gets driven into your body. It's like that. Hot and sharp and—lovely."

Kneeling there, her hand went out toward his legs in the greasy black trousers. Her hesitant fingers almost touched the cloth. Then her hand dropped to the ground. She crouched low like a fawning dog.

He said, "It's nice, just like you say. Only when you don't have no dinner, it ain't."

She stood up then, very straight, and her face was ashamed. She held the flower pot out to him and placed it gently in his arms. "Here. Put it in your wagon, on the seat, where you can watch it. Maybe I can find something for you to do."

At the back of the house she dug in the can pile and found two old and battered aluminum saucepans. She carried them back and gave them to him. "Here, maybe you can fix these."

His manner changed. He became professional. "Good as new I can fix them." At the back of his wagon he set a little anvil, and out of an oily tool box dug a small machine hammer. Elisa came through the gate to watch him while he pounded out the dents in the kettles. His mouth grew sure and knowing. At a difficult part of the work he sucked his under-lip.

"You sleep right in the wagon?" Elisa asked. 80

"Right in the wagon, ma'am. Rain or shine I'm dry as a cow in there."

"It must be nice," she said. "It must be very nice. I wish women could do such things."

"It ain't the right kind of a life for a woman."

Her upper lip raised a little, showing her teeth. "How do you know? How can you tell?" she said.

"I don't know, ma'am," he protested. "Of course I don't know. Now 85
here's your kettles, done. You don't have to buy no new ones."

"How much?"

"Oh, fifty cents'll do. I keep my prices down and my work good. That's why I have all them satisfied customers up and down the highway."

Elisa brought him a fifty-cent piece from the house and dropped it in his hand. "You might be surprised to have a rival some time. I can sharpen scissors, too. And I can beat the dents out of little pots. I could show you what a woman might do."

He put his hammer back in the oily box and shoved the little anvil out of sight. "It would be a lonely life for a woman, ma'am, and a scarey life, too, with animals creeping under the wagon all night." He climbed over the singletree, steadying himself with a hand on the burro's white rump. He settled himself in the seat, picked up the lines. "Thank you kindly, ma'am," he said. "I'll do like you told me; I'll go back and catch the Salinas road."

"Mind," she called, "if you're long in getting there, keep the sand 90
damp."

"Sand, ma'am? . . . Sand? Oh, sure. You mean around the chrysanthemums. Sure I will." He clucked his tongue. The beasts leaned luxuriously into their collars. The mongrel dog took his place between the back wheels. The wagon turned and crawled out the entrance road and back the way it had come, along the river.

Elisa stood in front of her wire fence watching the slow progress of the caravan. Her shoulders were straight, her head thrown back, her eyes half-closed, so that the scene came vaguely into them. Her lips moved silently, forming the words "Good-bye—good-bye." Then she whispered, "That's a bright direction. There's a glowing there." The sound of her whisper startled her. She shook herself free and looked about to see whether anyone had been listening. Only the dogs had heard. They lifted their heads toward her from their sleeping in the dust, and then stretched out their chins and settled asleep again. Elisa turned and ran hurriedly into the house.

In the kitchen she reached behind the stove and felt the water tank. It was full of hot water from the noonday cooking. In the bathroom she tore off her soiled clothes and flung them into the corner. And then she scrubbed herself with a little block of pumice, legs and thighs, loins and chest and arms, until her skin was scratched and red. When she had dried herself she stood in front of a mirror in her bedroom and looked at her body. She tightened her stomach and threw out her chest. She turned and looked over her shoulder at her back.

After a while she began to dress, slowly. She put on her newest underclothing and her nicest stockings and the dress which was the symbol of her prettiness. She worked carefully on her hair, penciled her eyebrows and rouged her lips.

Before she was finished she heard the little thunder of hoofs and the 95
shouts of Henry and his helper as they drove the red steers into the corral. She heard the gate bang shut and set herself for Henry's arrival.

His step sounded on the porch. He entered the house calling, "Elisa, where are you?"

"In my room, dressing. I'm not ready. There's hot water for your bath. Hurry up. It's getting late."

When she heard him splashing in the tub, Elisa laid his dark suit on the bed, and shirt and socks and tie beside it. She stood his polished shoes on the floor beside the bed. Then she went to the porch and sat primly and stiffly down. She looked toward the river road where the willow-line was still yellow with frosted leaves so that under the high grey fog they seemed a thin band of sunshine. This was the only color in the grey afternoon. She sat unmoving for a long time. Her eyes blinked rarely.

Henry came banging out of the door, shoving his tie inside his vest as he came. Elisa stiffened and her face grew tight. Henry stopped short and looked at her. "Why—why, Elisa. You look so nice!"

"Nice? You think I look nice? What do you mean by 'nice'?" 100

Henry blundered on. "I don't know. I mean you look different, strong and happy."

"I am strong? Yes, strong. What do you mean 'strong'?"

He looked bewildered. "You're playing some kind of a game," he said helplessly. "It's a kind of a play. You look strong enough to break a calf over your knee, happy enough to eat it like a watermelon."

For a second she lost her rigidity. "Henry! Don't talk like that. You didn't know what you said." She grew complete again. "I'm strong," she boasted. "I never knew before how strong."

Henry looked down toward the tractor shed, and when he brought 105
his eyes back to her, they were his own again. "I'll get out the car. You can put on your coat while I'm starting."

Elisa went into the house. She heard him drive to the gate and idle down his motor, and then she took a long time to put on her hat. She pulled it here and pressed it there. When Henry turned the motor off she slipped into her coat and went out.

The little roadster bounced along on the dirt road by the river, raising the birds and driving the rabbits into the brush. Two cranes flapped heavily over the willow-line and dropped into the river-bed.

Far ahead on the road Elisa saw a dark speck. She knew.

She tried not to look as they passed it, but her eyes would not obey. She whispered to herself sadly, "He might have thrown them off the road. That wouldn't have been much trouble, not very much. But he kept the pot," she explained. "He had to keep the pot. That's why he couldn't get them off the road."

The roadster turned a bend and she saw the caravan ahead. She 110
swung full around toward her husband so she could not see the little covered wagon and the mismatched team as the car passed them.

In a moment it was over. The thing was done. She did not look back.

She said loudly, to be heard above the motor, "It will be good, tonight, a good dinner."

"Now you're changed again," Henry complained. He took one hand from the wheel and patted her knee. "I ought to take you in to dinner oftener. It would be good for both of us. We get so heavy out on the ranch."

"Henry," she asked, "could we have wine at dinner?"

"Sure we could. Say! That will be fine." 115

She was silent for a while; then she said, "Henry, at those prize fights, do the men hurt each other very much?"

"Sometimes a little, not often. Why?"

"Well, I've read how they break noses, and blood runs down their chests. I've read how the fighting gloves get heavy and soggy with blood."

He looked around at her. "What's the matter, Elisa? I didn't know you read things like that." He brought the car to a stop, then turned to the right over the Salinas River bridge.

"Do any women ever go to the fights?" she asked. 120

"Oh, sure, some. What's the matter, Elisa? Do you want to go? I don't think you'd like it, but I'll take you if you really want to go."

She relaxed limply in the seat. "Oh, no. No. I don't want to go. I'm sure I don't." Her face was turned away from him. "It will be enough if we can have wine. It will be plenty." She turned up her coat collar so he could not see that she was crying weakly—like an old woman.

Questions

1. When we first meet Elisa Allen in her garden, with what details does Steinbeck delineate her character for us?
2. Elisa works inside a "wire fence that protected her flower garden from cattle and dogs and chickens" (paragraph 9). What does this wire fence suggest?
3. How would you describe Henry and Elisa's marriage? Cite details from the story.
4. With what motive does the traveling salesman take an interest in Elisa's chrysanthemums? What immediate effect does his interest have on Elisa?
5. For what possible purpose does Steinbeck give us such a detailed account of Elisa's preparations for her evening out? Notice her tearing off her soiled clothes and her scrubbing her body with pumice (paragraphs 93–94).
6. Of what significance to Elisa is the sight of the contents of the flower pot discarded in the road? Notice that, as her husband's car overtakes the covered wagon, Elisa turns away; and then Steinbeck adds, "In a moment it was over. The thing was done. She did not look back" (paragraph 111). Explain this passage.
7. How do you interpret Elisa's asking for wine with dinner? How do you account for her new interest in prizefights?
8. In a sentence, try to state this short story's theme.
9. Why are Elisa Allen's chrysanthemums so important to this story? Sum up what you understand them to mean.

Charlotte Perkins Gilman

The Yellow Wallpaper 1892

Charlotte Perkins Gilman

Charlotte Perkins Gilman (1860–1935) was born in Hartford, Connecticut. Her father was the writer Frederick Beecher Perkins (a nephew of reformer-novelist Harriet Beecher Stowe, author of Uncle Tom's Cabin, *and abolitionist minister Henry Ward Beecher), but he abandoned the family shortly after his daughter's birth. Raised in meager surroundings, the young Gilman adopted her intellectual Beecher aunts as role models. Because she and her mother moved from one relation to another, Gilman's early education was neglected—at fifteen, she had had only four years of schooling. In 1878 she studied commercial art at the Rhode Island School of Design. In 1884 she married Walter Stetson, an artist. After the birth of her one daughter, she experienced a severe depression. The rest cure her doctor prescribed became the basis of her most famous story, "The Yellow Wallpaper." This tale combines standard elements of Gothic fiction (the isolated country mansion, the brooding atmosphere of the room, the aloof but dominating husband) with the fresh clarity of Gilman's feminist perspective. Gilman's first marriage ended in an amicable divorce. A celebrated essayist and public speaker, she became an important early figure in American feminism. Her study* Women and Economics *(1898) stressed the importance of both sexes having a place in the working world. Her feminist-Utopian novel* Herland *(1915) describes a thriving nation of women without men. In 1900 Gilman married a second time—this time, more happily—to her cousin George Houghton Gilman. Following his sudden death in 1934, Gilman discovered she had inoperable breast cancer. After finishing her autobiography, she killed herself with chloroform in Pasadena, California.*

It is very seldom that mere ordinary people like John and myself secure ancestral halls for the summer.

A colonial mansion, a hereditary estate, I would say a haunted house and reach the height of romantic felicity—but that would be asking too much of fate!

Still I will proudly declare that there is something queer about it.

Else, why should it be let so cheaply? And why have stood so long untenanted?

John laughs at me, of course, but one expects that in marriage. 5

John is practical in the extreme. He has no patience with faith, an intense horror of superstition, and he scoffs openly at any talk of things not to be felt and seen and put down in figures.

John is a physician, and *perhaps*—(I would not say it to a living soul, of course, but this is dead paper and a great relief to my mind)—*perhaps* that is one reason I do not get well faster.

You see he does not believe I am sick!

And what can one do?

If a physician of high standing, and one's own husband, assures 10 friends and relatives that there is really nothing the matter with one but temporary nervous depression—a slight hysterical tendency—what is one to do?

My brother is also a physician, and also of high standing, and he says the same thing.

So I take phosphates or phosphites—whichever it is—and tonics, and journeys, and air, and exercise, and am absolutely forbidden to "work" until I am well again.

Personally, I disagree with their ideas.

Personally, I believe that congenial work, with excitement and change, would do me good.

But what is one to do? 15

I did write for a while in spite of them; but it *does* exhaust me a good deal—having to be so sly about it, or else meet with heavy opposition.

I sometimes fancy that in my condition if I had less opposition and more society and stimulus—but John says the very worst thing I can do is to think about my condition, and I confess it always makes me feel bad.

So I will let it alone and talk about the house.

The most beautiful place! It is quite alone, standing well back from the road, quite three miles from the village. It makes me think of English places that you read about, for there are hedges and walls and gates that lock, and lots of separate little houses for the gardeners and people.

There is a *delicious* garden! I never saw such a garden—large and shady, full of box-bordered paths, and lined with long grape-covered arbors with seats under them.

There were greenhouses, too, but they are all broken now.

There was some legal trouble, I believe, something about the heirs and co-heirs; anyhow, the place has been empty for years.

That spoils my ghostliness, I am afraid, but I don't care—there is something strange about the house—I can feel it.

I even said so to John one moonlight evening, but he said what I felt was a *draught*, and shut the window.

I get unreasonably angry with John sometimes. I'm sure I never used to be so sensitive. I think it is due to this nervous condition.

But John says if I feel so, I shall neglect proper self-control; so I take pains to control myself—before him, at least, and that makes me very tired.

I don't like our room a bit. I wanted one downstairs that opened on the piazza and had roses all over the window, and such pretty old-fashioned chintz hangings! But John would not hear of it.

He said there was only one window and not room for two beds, and no near room for him if he took another.

He is very careful and loving, and hardly lets me stir without special direction.

I have a schedule prescription for each hour in the day; he takes all care from me, and so I feel basely ungrateful not to value it more.

He said we came here solely on my account, that I was to have perfect rest and all the air I could get. "Your exercise depends on your strength, my dear," said he, "and your food somewhat on your appetite; but air you can absorb all the time." So we took the nursery at the top of the house.

It is a big, airy room, the whole floor nearly, with windows that look all ways, and air and sunshine galore. It was a nursery first and then playroom and gymnasium, I should judge; for the windows are barred for little children, and there are rings and things in the walls.

The paint and paper look as if a boys' school had used it. It is stripped off—the paper—in great patches all around the head of my bed, about as far as I can reach, and in a great place on the other side of the room low down. I never saw a worse paper in my life.

One of those sprawling flamboyant patterns committing every artistic sin.

It is dull enough to confuse the eye in following, pronounced enough to constantly irritate and provoke study, and when you follow the lame uncertain curves for a little distance they suddenly commit suicide—plunge off at outrageous angles, destroy themselves in unheard of contradictions.

The color is repellent, almost revolting; a smouldering unclean yellow, strangely faded by the slow-turning sunlight.

It is a dull yet lurid orange in some places, a sickly sulphur tint in others.

No wonder the children hated it! I should hate it myself if I had to live in this room long.

There comes John, and I must put this away—he hates to have me write a word.

We have been here two weeks, and I haven't felt like writing before, since that first day.

I am sitting by the window now, up in this atrocious nursery, and there is nothing to hinder my writing as much as I please, save lack of strength.

John is away all day, and even some nights when his cases are serious.

I am glad my case is not serious!

But these nervous troubles are dreadfully depressing.

John does not know how much I really suffer. He knows there is no *reason* to suffer, and that satisfies him.

Of course it is only nervousness. It does weigh on me so not to do my duty in any way!

I meant to be such a help to John, such a real rest and comfort, and here I am a comparative burden already!

Nobody would believe what an effort it is to do what little I am able—to dress and entertain, and order things.

It is fortunate Mary is so good with the baby. Such a dear baby!

And yet I *cannot* be with him, it makes me so nervous.

I suppose John never was nervous in his life. He laughs at me so about this wallpaper!

At first he meant to repaper the room, but afterward he said that I was letting it get the better of me, and that nothing was worse for a nervous patient than to give way to such fancies.

He said that after the wallpaper was changed it would be the heavy bedstead, and then the barred windows, and then that gate at the head of the stairs, and so on.

"You know the place is doing you good," he said, "and really, dear, I don't care to renovate the house just for a three months' rental."

"Then do let us go downstairs," I said, "there are such pretty rooms there."

Then he took me in his arms and called me a blessed little goose, and said he would go down cellar, if I wished, and have it whitewashed into the bargain.

But he is right enough about the beds and windows and things.

It is as airy and comfortable a room as any one need wish, and, of course, I would not be so silly as to make him uncomfortable just for a whim.

I'm really getting quite fond of the big room, all but that horrid paper.

Out of one window I can see the garden, those mysterious deep-shaded arbors, the riotous old-fashioned flowers, and bushes and gnarly trees.

Out of another I get a lovely view of the bay and a little private wharf belonging to the estate. There is a beautiful shaded lane that runs down there from the house. I always fancy I see people walking in these numerous paths and arbors, but John has cautioned me not to give way to fancy in the least. He says that with my imaginative power and habit of story-making, a nervous weakness like mine is sure to lead to all manner of excited fancies, and that I ought to use my will and good sense to check the tendency. So I try.

I think sometimes that if I were only well enough to write a little it would relieve the press of ideas and rest me.

But I find I get pretty tired when I try.

It is so discouraging not to have any advice and companionship about my work. When I get really well, John says we will ask Cousin Henry and Julia down for a long visit; but he says he would as soon put fireworks in my pillow-case as to let me have those stimulating people about now.

I wish I could get well faster.

But I must not think about that. This paper looks to me as if it *knew* what a vicious influence it had!

There is a recurrent spot where the pattern lolls like a broken neck and two bulbous eyes stare at you upside down.

I get positively angry with the impertinence of it and the everlastingness. Up and down and sideways they crawl, and those absurd unblinking eyes are everywhere. There is one place where two breadths didn't match, and the eyes go all up and down the line, one a little higher than the other.

I never saw so much expression in an inanimate thing before, and we all know how much expression they have! I used to lie awake as a child and get more entertainment and terror out of blank walls and plain furniture than most children could find in a toy-store.

I remember what a kindly wink the knobs of our big, old bureau used to have, and there was one chair that always seemed like a strong friend.

I used to feel that if any of the other things looked too fierce I could always hop into that chair and be safe.

The furniture in this room is no worse than inharmonious, however, for we had to bring it all from downstairs. I suppose when this was used as a playroom they had to take the nursery things out, and no wonder! I never saw such ravages as the children have made here.

The wallpaper, as I said before, is torn off in spots, and it sticketh closer than a brother°—they must have had perseverance as well as hatred.

it sticketh . . . brother: From Proverbs 18:24: "There is a friend that sticketh closer than a brother."

Then the floor is scratched and gouged and splintered, the plaster itself is dug out here and there, and this great heavy bed, which is all we found in the room, looks as if it had been through the wars.

But I don't mind it a bit—only the paper. 75

There comes John's sister. Such a dear girl as she is, and so careful of me! I must not let her find me writing.

She is a perfect and enthusiastic housekeeper, and hopes for no better profession. I verily believe she thinks it is the writing which made me sick!

But I can write when she is out, and see her a long way off from these windows.

There is one that commands the road, a lovely shaded winding road, and one that just looks off over the country. A lovely country, too, full of great elms and velvet meadows.

This wallpaper has a kind of sub-pattern in a different shade, a par- 80
ticularly irritating one, for you can only see it in certain lights, and not clearly then.

But in the places where it isn't faded and where the sun is just so—I can see a strange, provoking, formless sort of figure, that seems to skulk about behind that silly and conspicuous front design.

There's sister on the stairs!

Well, the Fourth of July is over! The people are all gone and I am tired out. John thought it might do me good to see a little company, so we just had Mother and Nellie and the children down for a week.

Of course I didn't do a thing. Jennie sees to everything now.

But it tired me all the same. 85

John says if I don't pick up faster he shall send me to Weir Mitchell° in the fall.

But I don't want to go there at all. I had a friend who was in his hands once, and she says he is just like John and my brother, only more so!

Besides, it is such an undertaking to go so far.

I don't feel as if it was worthwhile to turn my hand over for anything, and I'm getting dreadfully fretful and querulous.

I cry at nothing, and cry most of the time. 90

Of course I don't when John is here, or anybody else, but when I am alone.

And I am alone a good deal just now. John is kept in town very often by serious cases, and Jennie is good and lets me alone when I want her to.

So I walk a little in the garden or down that lovely lane, sit on the porch under the roses, and lie down up here a good deal.

Weir Mitchell: (1829–1914): famed nerve specialist who actually treated the author, Charlotte Perkins Gilman, for nervous prostration with his well-known "rest cure." (The cure was not successful.) Also the author of *Diseases of the Nervous System, Especially of Women* (1881).

I'm getting really fond of the room in spite of the wallpaper. Perhaps *because* of the wallpaper.

It dwells in my mind so! 95

I lie here on this great immovable bed—it is nailed down, I believe—and follow that pattern about by the hour. It is as good as gymnastics, I assure you. I start, we'll say, at the bottom, down in the corner over there where it has not been touched, and I determine for the thousandth time that I *will* follow that pointless pattern to some sort of a conclusion.

I know a little of the principle of design, and I know this thing was not arranged on any laws of radiation,° or alternation, or repetition, or symmetry, or anything else that I ever heard of.

It is repeated, of course, by the breadths, but not otherwise.

Looked at in one way, each breadth stands alone, the bloated curves and flourishes—a kind of "debased Romanesque" with *delirium tremens*—go waddling up and down in isolated columns of fatuity.

But, on the other hand, they connect diagonally, and the sprawling out- 100
lines run off in great slanting waves of optic horror, like a lot of wallowing sea-weeds in full chase.

The whole thing goes horizontally, too, at least it seems so, and I exhaust myself trying to distinguish the order of its going in that direction.

They have used a horizontal breadth for a frieze, and that adds wonderfully to the confusion.

There is one end of the room where it is almost intact, and there, when the crosslights fade and the low sun shines directly upon it, I can almost fancy radiation after all—the interminable grotesques seem to form around a common centre and rush off in headlong plunges of equal distraction.

It makes me tired to follow it. I will take a nap I guess.

I don't know why I should write this. 105

I don't want to.

I don't feel able.

And I know John would think it absurd. But I *must* say what I feel and think in some way—it is such a relief!

But the effort is getting to be greater than the relief.

Half the time now I am awfully lazy, and lie down ever so much. 110

John says I mustn't lose my strength, and has me take cod liver oil and lots of tonics and things, to say nothing of ale and wine and rare meat.

Dear John! He loves me very dearly, and hates to have me sick. I tried to have a real earnest reasonable talk with him the other day, and tell him how I wish he would let me go and make a visit to Cousin Henry and Julia.

laws of radiation: a principle of design in which all elements are arranged in some circular pattern around a center.

But he said I wasn't able to go, nor able to stand it after I got there; and I did not make out a very good case for myself, for I was crying before I had finished.

It is getting to be a great effort for me to think straight. Just this nervous weakness I suppose.

And dear John gathered me up in his arms, and just carried me upstairs and laid me on the bed, and sat by me and read to me till it tired my head.

He said I was his darling and his comfort and all he had, and that I must take care of myself for his sake, and keep well.

He says no one but myself can help me out of it, that I must use my will and self-control and not let any silly fancies run away with me.

There's one comfort, the baby is well and happy, and does not have to occupy this nursery with the horrid wallpaper.

If we had not used it, that blessed child would have! What a fortunate escape! Why, I wouldn't have a child of mine, an impressionable little thing, live in such a room for worlds.

I never thought of it before, but it is lucky that John kept me here after all, I can stand it so much easier than a baby, you see.

Of course I never mention it to them any more—I am too wise—but I keep watch of it all the same.

There are things in that paper that nobody knows but me, or ever will.

Behind that outside pattern the dim shapes get clearer every day.

It is always the same shape, only very numerous.

And it is like a woman stooping down and creeping about behind that pattern. I don't like it a bit. I wonder—I begin to think—I wish John would take me away from here!

It is so hard to talk with John about my case, because he is so wise, and because he loves me so.

But I tried it last night.

It was moonlight. The moon shines in all around just as the sun does.

I hate to see it sometimes, it creeps so slowly, and always comes in by one window or another.

John was asleep and I hated to waken him, so I kept still and watched the moonlight on that undulating wallpaper till I felt creepy.

The faint figure behind seemed to shake the pattern, just as if she wanted to get out.

I got up softly and went to feel and see if the paper *did* move, and when I came back John was awake.

"What is it, little girl?" he said. "Don't go walking about like that—you'll get cold."

I thought it was a good time to talk, so I told him that I really was not gaining here, and that I wished he would take me away.

"Why, darling!" said he, "our lease will be up in three weeks, and I can't see how to leave before.

"The repairs are not done at home, and I cannot possibly leave town just now. Of course if you were in any danger, I could and would, but you really are better, dear, whether you can see it or not. I am a doctor, dear, and I know. You are gaining flesh and color, your appetite is better, I feel really much easier about you."

"I don't weigh a bit more," said I, "nor as much; and my appetite may be better in the evening when you are here, but it is worse in the morning when you are away!"

"Bless her little heart!" said he with a big hug, "she shall be as sick as she pleases! But now let's improve the shining hours by going to sleep, and talk about it in the morning!"

"And you won't go away?" I asked gloomily.

"Why, how can I, dear? It is only three weeks more and then we will take a nice little trip of a few days while Jennie is getting the house ready. Really, dear, you are better!"

"Better in body perhaps—" I began, and stopped short, for he sat up straight and looked at me with such a stern, reproachful look that I could not say another word.

"My darling," said he, "I beg of you, for my sake and for our child's sake, as well as for your own, that you will never for one instant let that idea enter your mind! There is nothing so dangerous, so fascinating, to a temperament like yours. It is a false and foolish fancy. Can you not trust me as a physician when I tell you so?"

So of course I said no more on that score, and we went to sleep before long. He thought I was asleep first, but I wasn't, and lay there for hours trying to decide whether that front pattern and the back pattern really did move together or separately.

On a pattern like this, by daylight, there is a lack of sequence, a defiance of law, that is a constant irritant to a normal mind.

The color is hideous enough, and unreliable enough, and infuriating enough, but the pattern is torturing.

You think you have mastered it, but just as you get well underway in following, it turns a back-somersault and there you are. It slaps you in the face, knocks you down, and tramples upon you. It is like a bad dream.

The outside pattern is a florid arabesque,° reminding one of a fungus. If you can imagine a toadstool in joints, an interminable string of toadstools, budding and sprouting in endless convolutions—why, that is something like it.

That is, sometimes!

arabesque: a type of ornamental style (Arabic in origin) that uses flowers, foliage, fruit, or other figures to create an intricate pattern of interlocking shapes and lines.

There is one marked peculiarity about this paper, a thing nobody seems to notice but myself, and that is that it changes as the light changes.

When the sun shoots in through the east window—I always watch 150
for that first long, straight ray—it changes so quickly that I never can quite believe it.

That is why I watch it always.

By moonlight—the moon shines in all night when there is a moon—I wouldn't know it was the same paper.

At night in any kind of light, in twilight, candlelight, lamplight, and worst of all by moonlight, it becomes bars! The outside pattern, I mean, and the woman behind it is as plain as can be.

I didn't realize for a long time what the thing was that showed behind, that dim sub-pattern, but now I am quite sure it is a woman.

By daylight she is subdued, quiet. I fancy it is the pattern that keeps 155
her so still. It is so puzzling. It keeps me quiet by the hour.

I lie down ever so much now. John says it is good for me, and to sleep all I can.

Indeed he started the habit by making me lie down for an hour after each meal.

It is a very bad habit, I am convinced, for you see I don't sleep.

And that cultivates deceit, for I don't tell them I'm awake—O, no!

The fact is I am getting a little afraid of John. 160

He seems very queer sometimes, and even Jennie has an inexplicable look.

It strikes me occasionally, just as a scientific hypothesis, that perhaps it is the paper!

I have watched John when he did not know I was looking, and come into the room suddenly on the most innocent excuses, and I've caught him several times *looking at the paper*! And Jennie too. I caught Jennie with her hand on it once.

She didn't know I was in the room, and when I asked her in a quiet, a very quiet voice, with the most restrained manner possible, what she was doing with the paper—she turned around as if she had been caught stealing, and looked quite angry—asked me why I should frighten her so!

Then she said that the paper stained everything it touched, that she 165
had found yellow smooches° on all my clothes and John's, and she wished we would be more careful!

Did not that sound innocent? But I know she was studying that pattern, and I am determined that nobody shall find it out but myself!

Life is very much more exciting now than it used to be. You see I have something more to expect, to look forward to, to watch. I really do eat better, and am more quiet than I was.

smooches: smudges or smears.

John is so pleased to see me improve! He laughed a little the other day, and said I seemed to be flourishing in spite of my wallpaper.

I turned it off with a laugh. I had no intention of telling him it was *because* of the wallpaper—he would make fun of me. He might even want to take me away.

I don't want to leave now until I have found it out. There is a week 170
more, and I think that will be enough.

I'm feeling ever so much better! I don't sleep much at night, for it is so interesting to watch developments; but I sleep a good deal in the daytime.

In the daytime it is tiresome and perplexing.

There are always new shoots on the fungus, and new shades of yellow all over it. I cannot keep count of them, though I have tried conscientiously.

It is the strangest yellow, that wallpaper! It makes me think of all the yellow things I ever saw—not beautiful ones like buttercups, but old foul, bad yellow things.

But there is something else about that paper—the smell! I noticed 175
it the moment we came into the room, but with so much air and sun it was not bad. Now we have had a week of fog and rain, and whether the windows are open or not, the smell is here.

It creeps all over the house.

I find it hovering in the dining-room, skulking in the parlor, hiding in the hall, lying in wait for me on the stairs.

It gets into my hair.

Even when I go to ride, if I turn my head suddenly and surprise it—there is that smell!

Such a peculiar odor, too! I have spent hours in trying to analyze it, 180
to find what it smelled like.

It is not bad—at first—and very gentle, but quite the subtlest, most enduring odor I ever met.

In this damp weather it is awful. I wake up in the night and find it hanging over me.

It used to disturb me at first. I thought seriously of burning the house—to reach the smell.

But now I am used to it. The only thing I can think of that it is like is the *color* of the paper! A yellow smell.

There is a very funny mark on this wall, low down, near the mop- 185
board. A streak that runs round the room. It goes behind every piece of furniture, except the bed, a long, straight, even *smooch*, as if it had been rubbed over and over.

I wonder how it was done and who did it, and what they did it for. Round and round and round—round and round and round—it makes me dizzy!

***

I really have discovered something at last.

Through watching so much at night, when it changes so, I have finally found out.

The front pattern *does* move—and no wonder! The woman behind shakes it!

Sometimes I think there are a great many women behind, and sometimes only one, and she crawls around fast, and her crawling shakes it all over.

Then in the very bright spots she keeps still, and in the very shady spots she just takes hold of the bars and shakes them hard.

And she is all the time trying to climb through. But nobody could climb through that pattern—it strangles so; I think that is why it has so many heads.

They get through, and then the pattern strangles them off and turns them upside down, and makes their eyes white!

If those heads were covered or taken off it would not be half so bad.

I think that woman gets out in the daytime!

And I'll tell you why—privately—I've seen her!

I can see her out of every one of my windows!

It is the same woman, I know, for she is always creeping, and most women do not creep by daylight.

I see her in that long shaded lane, creeping up and down. I see her in those dark grape arbors, creeping all round the garden.

I see her on that long road under the trees, creeping along, and when a carriage comes she hides under the blackberry vines.

I don't blame her a bit. It must be very humiliating to be caught creeping by daylight!

I always lock the door when I creep by daylight. I can't do it at night, for I know John would suspect something at once.

And John is so queer now, that I don't want to irritate him. I wish he would take another room! Besides, I don't want anybody to get that woman out at night but myself.

I often wonder if I could see her out of all the windows at once.

But, turn as fast as I can, I can only see out of one at one time.

And though I always see her, she *may* be able to creep faster than I can turn!

I have watched her sometimes away off in the open country, creeping as fast as a cloud shadow in a high wind.

If only that top pattern could be gotten off from the under one! I mean to try it, little by little.

I have found out another funny thing, but I shan't tell it this time! It does not do to trust people too much.

There are only two more days to get this paper off, and I believe John is beginning to notice. I don't like the look in his eyes.

And I heard him ask Jennie a lot of professional questions about me. She had a very good report to give.

She said I slept a good deal in the daytime.

John knows I don't sleep very well at night, for all I'm so quiet!

He asked me all sorts of questions, too, and pretended to be very loving and kind.

As if I couldn't see through him!

Still, I don't wonder he acts so, sleeping under this paper for three months.

It only interests me, but I feel sure John and Jennie are affected by it.

Hurrah! This is the last day, but it is enough. John had to stay in town over night, and won't be out until this evening.

Jennie wanted to sleep with me—the sly thing—but I told her I should undoubtedly rest better for a night all alone.

That was clever, for really I wasn't alone a bit! As soon as it was moonlight and that poor thing began to crawl and shake the pattern, I got up and ran to help her.

I pulled and she shook, I shook and she pulled, and before morning we had peeled off yards of that paper.

A strip about as high as my head and half around the room.

And then when the sun came and that awful pattern began to laugh at me, I declared I would finish it to-day!

We go away to-morrow, and they are moving all my furniture down again to leave things as they were before.

Jennie looked at the wall in amazement, but I told her merrily that I did it out of pure spite at the vicious thing.

She laughed and said she wouldn't mind doing it herself, but I must not get tired.

How she betrayed herself that time!

But I am here, and no person touches this paper but me—not *alive*!

She tried to get me out of the room—it was too patent! But I said it was so quiet and empty and clean now that I believed I would lie down again and sleep all I could; and not to wake me even for dinner—I would call when I woke.

So now she is gone, and the servants are gone, and the things are gone, and there is nothing left but that great bedstead nailed down, with the canvas mattress we found on it.

We shall sleep downstairs to-night, and take the boat home to-morrow.

I quite enjoy the room, now it is bare again.

How those children did tear about here!

This bedstead is fairly gnawed!

But I must get to work.

I have locked the door and thrown the key down into the front path.

I don't want to go out, and I don't want to have anybody come in, till John comes.

I want to astonish him.

I've got a rope up here that even Jennie did not find. If that woman does get out, and tries to get away, I can tie her!

But I forgot I could not reach far without anything to stand on!

This bed will *not* move!

I tried to lift and push it until I was lame, and then I got so angry I bit off a little piece at one corner—but it hurt my teeth.

Then I peeled off all the paper I could reach standing on the floor. It sticks horribly and the pattern just enjoys it! All those strangled heads and bulbous eyes and waddling fungus growths just shriek with derision!

I am getting angry enough to do something desperate. To jump out of the window would be admirable exercise, but the bars are too strong even to try.

Besides, I wouldn't do it. Of course not. I know well enough that a step like that is improper and might be misconstrued.

I don't like to *look* out of the windows even—there are so many of those creeping women, and they creep so fast.

I wonder if they all come out of that wallpaper as I did!

But I am securely fastened now by my well-hidden rope—you don't get *me* out in the road there!

I suppose I shall have to get back behind the pattern when it comes night, and that is hard!

It is so pleasant to be out in this great room and creep around as I please!

I don't want to go outside. I won't, even if Jennie asks me to.

For outside you have to creep on the ground, and everything is green instead of yellow.

But here I can creep smoothly on the floor, and my shoulder just fits in that long smooch around the wall, so I cannot lose my way.

Why, there's John at the door!

It is no use, young man, you can't open it!

How he does call and pound!

Now he's crying for an axe.

It would be a shame to break down that beautiful door!

"John, dear!" said I in the gentlest voice, "the key is down by the front steps, under a plantain leaf!"

That silenced him for a few moments.

Then he said—very quietly indeed—"Open the door, my darling!"

"I can't," said I. "The key is down by the front door under a plantain leaf!"

And then I said it again, several times, very gently and slowly, and said it so often that he had to go and see, and he got it of course, and came in. He stopped short by the door.

"What is the matter?" he cried. "For God's sake, what are you doing!"

I kept on creeping just the same, but I looked at him over my shoulder. 265

"I've got out at last," said I, "in spite of you and Jane! And I've pulled off most of the paper, so you can't put me back!"

Now why should that man have fainted? But he did, and right across my path by the wall, so that I had to creep over him every time!

Questions

1. Several times at the beginning of the story, the narrator says such things as "What is one to do?" and "What can one do?" What do these comments refer to? What, if anything, do they suggest about women's roles at the time the story was written?
2. The narrator says, "I get unreasonably angry with John sometimes" (paragraph 25). How unreasonable is her anger at him? What does the fact that she feels it is unreasonable say about her?
3. What do her changing feelings about the wallpaper tell us about her condition?
4. As the story progresses, the wallpaper begins to acquire powerful associations. What does it come to symbolize at the story's end?
5. "It is so hard to talk with John about my case, because he is so wise, and because he loves me so" (paragraph 126). His wisdom is, to say the least, open to question, but what about his love? Do you think he suffers merely from a failure of perception, or is there a failure of affection as well? Explain your response.
6. Where precisely in the story do you think it becomes clear that she has begun to hallucinate?
7. What does the woman behind the wallpaper represent? Why does the narrator come to identify with her?
8. How ill does the narrator seem at the beginning of the story? How ill does she seem at the end? How do you account for the change in her condition?

Ursula K. Le Guin

The Ones Who Walk Away from Omelas 1975

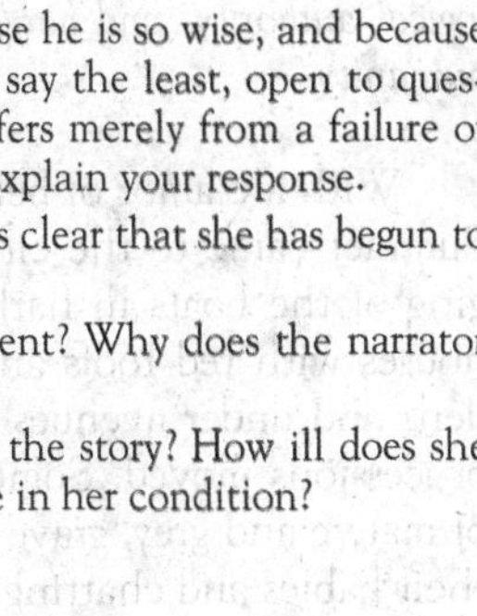

Ursula K. Le Guin

Ursula Kroeber Le Guin (1929–2018) was born on St. Ursula's Day (October 21) in Berkeley, California, the only daughter and youngest child of Theodora Kroeber, a folklorist, and Alfred Kroeber, a renowned anthropologist. Le Guin attended Radcliffe College, and then entered Columbia University to do graduate work in French and Italian literature. While completing her master's, she wrote her first stories. In the early sixties Le Guin began publishing in both science fiction pulp magazines and academic journals. In 1966 her first novel, Rocannon's World, *was published as an Ace science fiction paperback original—hardly a respectable format for the debut of one of America's premier writers. In 1968 Le Guin published* A Wizard of Earthsea, *the first novel in her Earthsea series, now*

considered a classic of young adult literature. The next two volumes, The Tombs of Atuan *(1971), which won a Newbery citation, and* The Farthest Shore *(1972), which won a National Book Award, brought Le Guin mainstream acclaim.*

Le Guin's novels The Left Hand of Darkness (1969) *and* The Dispossessed (1974) *won both the Hugo and the Nebula awards, science fiction's two most prized honors. She also twice won the Hugo for best short story, including the 1974 award for "The Ones Who Walk Away from Omelas." Le Guin published more than thirty novels and many volumes of short stories, poetry, and essays. Le Guin died in 2018 at her long-time home in Portland, Oregon.*

One of the few science fiction writers whose work has earned general critical acclaim, Le Guin belongs most naturally in the company of major novelists of ideas such as Aldous Huxley, George Orwell, and Anthony Burgess, who have used the genre of science fiction to explore the possible consequences of ideological rather than technological change. Le Guin was especially concerned with issues of social justice and equality. In her short stories—including "The Ones Who Walk Away from Omelas"—she created complex imaginary civilizations, envisioned with anthropological authority, and her aim was less to imagine alien cultures than to explore humanity.

With a clamor of bells that set the swallows soaring, the Festival of Summer came to the city Omelas, bright-towered by the sea. The rigging of the boats in harbor sparkled with flags. In the streets between houses with red roofs and painted walls, between old moss-grown gardens and under avenues of trees, past great parks and public buildings, processions moved. Some were decorous: old people in long stiff robes of mauve and grey, grave master workmen, quiet, merry women carrying their babies and chatting as they walked. In other streets the music beat faster, a shimmering of gong and tambourine, and the people went dancing, the procession was a dance. Children dodged in and out, their high calls rising like the swallows' crossing flights over the music and the singing. All the processions wound towards the north side of the city, where on the great water-meadow called the Green Fields boys and girls, naked in the bright air, with mud-stained feet and ankles and long, lithe arms, exercised their restive horses before the race. The horses wore no gear at all but a halter without bit. Their manes were braided with streamers of silver, gold, and green. They flared their nostrils and pranced and boasted to one another; they were vastly excited, the horse being the only animal who has adopted our ceremonies as his own. Far off to the north and west the mountains stood up half encircling Omelas on her bay. The air of morning was so clear that the snow still crowning the Eighteen Peaks burned with white-gold fire across the miles of sunlit air, under the dark blue of the sky. There was just enough wind to make the banners that marked the racecourse snap and flutter now and then. In the silence of the broad green meadows one could hear the music winding through the city streets, farther and nearer and ever approaching, a cheerful faint sweetness of the air that from time to time trembled and gathered together and broke out into the great joyous clanging of the bells.

Joyous! How is one to tell about joy? How describe the citizens of Omelas?

They were not simple folk, you see, though they were happy. But we do not say the words of cheer much any more. All smiles have become archaic. Given a description such as this one tends to make certain assumptions. Given a description such as this one tends to look next for the King, mounted on a splendid stallion and surrounded by his noble knights, or perhaps in a golden litter borne by great-muscled slaves. But there was no king. They did not use swords, or keep slaves. They were not barbarians. I do not know the rules and laws of their society, but I suspect that they were singularly few. As they did without monarchy and slavery, so they also got on without the stock exchange, the advertisement, the secret police, and the bomb. Yet I repeat that these were not simple folk, not dulcet shepherds, noble savages, bland utopians. They were not less complex than us. The trouble is that we have a bad habit, encouraged by pedants and sophisticates, of considering happiness as something rather stupid. Only pain is intellectual, only evil interesting. This is the treason of the artist: a refusal to admit the banality of evil and the terrible boredom of pain. If you can't lick 'em, join 'em. If it hurts, repeat it. But to praise despair is to condemn delight, to embrace violence is to lose hold of everything else. We have almost lost hold; we can no longer describe a happy man, nor make any celebration of joy. How can I tell you about the people of Omelas? They were not naïve and happy children—though their children were, in fact, happy. They were mature, intelligent, passionate adults whose lives were not wretched. O miracle! but I wish I could describe it better. I wish I could convince you. Omelas sounds in my words like a city in a fairy tale, long ago and far away, once upon a time. Perhaps it would be best if you imagined it as your own fancy bids, assuming it will rise to the occasion, for certainly I cannot suit you all. For instance, how about technology? I think that there would be no cars or helicopters in and above the streets; this follows from the fact that the people of Omelas are happy people. Happiness is based on a just discrimination of what is necessary, what is neither necessary nor destructive, and what is destructive. In the middle category, however—that of the unnecessary but undestructive, that of comfort, luxury, exuberance, etc.—they could perfectly well have central heating, subway trains, washing machines, and all kinds of marvelous devices not yet invented here, floating light-sources, fuelless power, a cure for the common cold. Or they could have none of that: it doesn't matter. As you like it. I incline to think that people from towns up and down the coast have been coming in to Omelas during the last days before the Festival on very fast little trains and double-decked trams, and that the train station of Omelas is actually the handsomest building in town, though plainer than the magnificent Farmers' Market. But even granted trains, I fear that Omelas so far strikes some of you as goody-goody. Smiles, bells, parades, horses, bleh. If so, please add an orgy. If an orgy would help, don't hesitate. Let us not, however, have temples from which issue beautiful nude priests and priestesses already half in ecstasy and ready to copulate with any man or woman, lover or stranger, who desires union with the deep godhead of the blood, although that was my first idea. But really it would be better not to have any temples in Omelas—at least, not manned temples. Religion yes, clergy no. Surely the beautiful nudes can just wander about, offering themselves like divine soufflés to the hunger of the needy and the rapture of the flesh. Let them join the processions. Let tambourines be struck above the copulations, and the glory of desire be proclaimed upon the gongs, and (a not unimportant point) let the offspring of these delightful rituals be beloved and looked after by all. One thing I know there is none of in Omelas is guilt. But what else should there be? I thought at first there were no drugs, but that is puritanical. For those who like it, the faint insistent sweetness of *drooz* may perfume the ways of the city, *drooz* which first brings a great lightness and brilliance to the mind and limbs, and then after some hours a dreamy languor, and wonderful visions at last of the very arcana and inmost secrets of the Universe, as well as exciting the pleasure of sex beyond all belief; and it is not habit-forming. For more modest tastes I think there ought to be beer. What else, what else belongs in the joyous city? The sense of victory, surely, the celebration of courage. But as we did without clergy, let us do without soldiers. The joy built upon successful slaughter is not the right kind of joy; it will not do; it is fearful and it is trivial. A boundless and generous contentment, a magnanimous triumph felt not against some outer enemy but in communion with the finest and fairest in the souls of all men everywhere and the splendor of the world's summer: this is what swells the hearts of the people of Omelas, and the victory they celebrate is that of life. I really don't think many of them need to take *drooz*.

Most of the processions have reached the Green Fields by now. A marvelous smell of cooking goes forth from the red and blue tents of the provisioners. The faces of small children are amiably sticky; in the benign grey beard of a man a couple of crumbs of rich pastry are entangled. The youths and girls have mounted their horses and are beginning to group around the starting line of the course. An old woman, small, fat, and laughing, is passing out flowers from a basket, and tall young men wear her flowers in their shining hair. A child of nine or ten sits at the edge of the crowd, alone, playing on a wooden flute. People pause to listen, and they smile, but they do not speak to him, for he never ceases playing and never sees them, his dark eyes wholly rapt in the sweet, thin magic of the tune.

He finishes, and slowly lowers his hands holding the wooden flute. 5

As if that little private silence were the signal, all at once a trumpet sounds from the pavilion near the starting line: imperious, melancholy, piercing. The horses rear on their slender legs, and some of them neigh in answer. Sober-faced, the young riders stroke the horses' necks and soothe them, whispering, "Quiet, quiet, there my beauty, my hope. . . ." They begin to form in rank along the starting line. The crowds along the racecourse are like a field of grass and flowers in the wind. The Festival of Summer has begun.

Do you believe? Do you accept the festival, the city, the joy? No? Then let me describe one more thing.

In a basement under one of the beautiful public buildings of Omelas, or perhaps in the cellar of one of its spacious private homes, there is a room. It has one locked door, and no window. A little light seeps in dustily between cracks in the boards, secondhand from a cobwebbed window somewhere across the cellar. In one corner of the little room a couple of mops, with stiff, clotted, foul-smelling heads, stand near a rusty bucket. The floor is dirt, a little damp to the touch, as cellar dirt usually is. The room is about three paces long and two wide: a mere broom closet or disused tool room. In the room a child is sitting. It could be a boy or a girl. It looks about six, but actually is nearly ten. It is feeble-minded. Perhaps it was born defective, or perhaps it has become imbecile through fear, malnutrition, and neglect. It picks its nose and occasionally fumbles vaguely with its toes or genitals, as it sits hunched in the corner farthest from the bucket and the two mops. It is afraid of the mops. It finds them horrible. It shuts its eyes, but it knows the mops are still standing there; and the door is locked; and nobody will come. The door is always locked; and nobody ever comes, except that sometimes—the child has no understanding of time or interval—sometimes the door rattles terribly and opens, and a person, or several people, are there. One of them may come in and kick the child to make it stand up. The others never come close, but peer in at it with frightened, disgusted eyes. The food bowl and the water jug are hastily filled, the door is locked, the eyes disappear. The people at the door never say anything, but the child, who has not always lived in the tool room, and can remember sunlight and its mother's voice, sometimes speaks. "I will be good," it says. "Please let me out. I will be good!" They never answer. The child used to scream for help at night, and cry a good deal, but now it only makes a kind of whining, "eh-haa, eh-haa," and it speaks less and less often. It is so thin there are no calves to its legs; its belly protrudes; it lives on a half-bowl of corn meal and grease a day. It is naked. Its buttocks and thighs are a mass of festered sores, as it sits in its own excrement continually.

They all know it is there, all the people of Omelas. Some of them have come to see it, others are content merely to know it is there. They all know that it has to be there. Some of them understand why, and some do not, but they all understand that their happiness, the beauty of their city, the tenderness of their friendships, the health of their children, the wisdom of their scholars, the skill of their makers, even the abundance of their harvest and the kindly weathers of their skies, depend wholly on this child's abominable misery.

This is usually explained to children when they are between eight and twelve, whenever they seem capable of understanding; and most of those who come to see the child are young people, though often enough an adult comes, or comes back, to see the child. No matter how well the matter has been explained to them, these young spectators are always shocked and sickened at the sight. They feel disgust, which they had thought themselves superior to. They feel anger, outrage, impotence, despite all the explanations. They would like to do something for the child. But there is nothing they can do. If the child were brought up into the sunlight out of that vile place, if it were cleaned and fed and comforted, that would be a good thing, indeed; but if it were done, in that day and hour all the prosperity and beauty and delight of Omelas would wither and be destroyed. Those are the terms. To exchange all the goodness and grace of every life in Omelas for that single, small improvement: to throw away the happiness of thousands for the chance of the happiness of one: that would be to let guilt within the walls indeed.

The terms are strict and absolute; there may not even be a kind word spoken to the child.

Often the young people go home in tears, or in a tearless rage, when they have seen the child and faced this terrible paradox. They may brood over it for weeks or years. But as time goes on they begin to realize that even if the child could be released, it would not get much good of its freedom: a little vague pleasure of warmth and food, no doubt, but little more. It is too degraded and imbecile to know any real joy. It has been afraid too long ever to be free of fear. Its habits are too uncouth for it to respond to humane treatment. Indeed, after so long it would probably be wretched without walls about it to protect it, and darkness for its eyes, and its own excrement to sit in. Their tears at the bitter injustice dry when they begin to perceive the terrible justice of reality, and to accept it. Yet it is their tears and anger, the trying of their generosity and the acceptance of their helplessness, which are perhaps the true source of the splendor of their lives. Theirs is no vapid, irresponsible happiness. They know that they, like the child, are not free. They know compassion. It is the existence of the child, and their knowledge of its existence, that makes possible the nobility of their architecture, the poignancy of their music, the profundity of their science. It is because of the child that they are so gentle with children. They know that if the wretched one were not there snivelling in the dark, the other one, the flute-player, could make no joyful music as the young riders line up in their beauty for the race in the sunlight of the first morning of summer.

Now do you believe in them? Are they not more credible? But there is one more thing to tell, and this is quite incredible.

At times one of the adolescent girls or boys who go to see the child does not go home to weep or rage, does not, in fact, go home at all. Sometimes also a man or woman much older falls silent for a day or two, and then leaves home. These people go out into the street, and walk down the street alone. They keep walking, and walk straight out of the city of Omelas, through the beautiful gates. They keep walking across the farmlands of Omelas. Each one goes alone, youth or girl, man or woman. Night falls; the traveler must pass down village streets, between the houses with yellow-lit windows, and on out into the darkness of the fields. Each alone, they go west or north, toward the mountains. They go on. They leave Omelas, they walk ahead into the darkness, and they do not come back. The place they go towards is a place even less imaginable to most of us than the city of happiness. I cannot describe it at all. It is possible that it does not exist. But they seem to know where they are going, the ones who walk away from Omelas.

Questions

1. Does the narrator live in Omelas? What do we know about the narrator's society?
2. What is the narrator's opinion of Omelas? Does the author seem to share that opinion?
3. What is the narrator's attitude toward "the ones who walk away from Omelas"? Would the narrator have been one of those who walked away?
4. How do you account for the narrator's willingness to let readers add anything they like to the story?—"If an orgy would help, don't hesitate" (paragraph 3). Didn't Ursula K. Le Guin care what her story includes?
5. What is suggested by the locked, dark cellar in which the child sits? What other details in the story are suggestive enough to be called symbolic?
6. Do you find in the story any implied criticism of our own society?

Shirley Jackson

The Lottery

1948

Shirley Jackson

*Shirley Jackson (1919–1965), a native of San Francisco, moved in her teens to Rochester, New York. She started college at the University of Rochester, but had to drop out, stricken by severe depression, a problem that was to recur at intervals throughout her life. Later she graduated from Syracuse University. With her husband, Stanley Edgar Hyman, a literary critic, she settled in Bennington, Vermont, in a sprawling house built in the nineteenth century. There Jackson conscientiously set herself to produce a fixed number of words each day. She wrote novels—*The Road Through the Wall *(1948)—and three psychological thrillers—*Hangsaman *(1951),* The Haunting of Hill House *(1959), and* We Have Always Lived in the Castle *(1962). She wrote light, witty articles for*

Good Housekeeping *and other popular magazines about the horrors of housekeeping and rearing four children, collected in* Life Among the Savages *(1953) and* Raising Demons *(1957); but she claimed to have written them only for money. When "The Lottery" appeared in the* New Yorker *in 1948, that issue of the magazine quickly sold out. Her purpose in writing the story, Jackson declared, had been "to shock the story's readers with a graphic demonstration of the pointless violence and general inhumanity in their own lives."*

The morning of June 27th was clear and sunny, with the fresh warmth of a full-summer day; the flowers were blossoming profusely and the grass was richly green. The people of the village began to gather in the square, between the post office and the bank, around ten o'clock; in some towns there were so many people that the lottery took two days and had to be started on June 26th, but in this village, where there were only about three hundred people, the whole lottery took less than two hours, so it could begin at ten o'clock in the morning and still be through in time to allow the villagers to get home for noon dinner.

The children assembled first, of course. School was recently over for the summer, and the feeling of liberty sat uneasily on most of them; they tended to gather together quietly for a while before they broke into boisterous play, and their talk was still of the classroom and the teacher, of books and reprimands. Bobby Martin had already stuffed his pockets full of stones, and the other boys soon followed his example, selecting the smoothest and roundest stones; Bobby and Harry Jones and Dickie Delacroix—the villagers pronounced this name "Dellacroy"—eventually made a great pile of stones in one corner of the square and guarded it against the raids of the other boys. The girls stood aside, talking among themselves, looking over their shoulders at the boys, and the very small children rolled in the dust or clung to the hands of their older brothers or sisters.

Soon the men began to gather, surveying their own children, speaking of planting and rain, tractors and taxes. They stood together, away from the pile of stones in the corner, and their jokes were quiet and they smiled rather than laughed. The women, wearing faded house dresses and sweaters, came shortly after their menfolk. They greeted one another and exchanged bits of gossip as they went to join their husbands. Soon the women, standing by their husbands, began to call to their children, and the children came reluctantly, having to be called four or five times. Bobby Martin ducked under his mother's grasping hand and ran, laughing, back to the pile of stones. His father spoke up sharply, and Bobby came quickly and took his place between his father and his oldest brother.

The lottery was conducted—as were the square dances, the teenage club, the Halloween program—by Mr. Summers, who had time and energy to devote to civic activities. He was a roundfaced, jovial man and he ran the coal business, and people were sorry for him, because he had no children and his wife was a scold. When he arrived in the square, carrying the black wooden box, there was a murmur of conversation among the villagers and he waved and called, "Little late today, folks." The postmaster, Mr. Graves, followed him, carrying a three-legged stool, and the stool was put in the center of the square and Mr. Summers set the black box down on it. The villagers kept their distance, leaving a space between themselves and the stool, and when Mr. Summers said, "Some of you fellows want to give me a hand?" there was a hesitation before two men, Mr. Martin and his oldest son, Baxter, came forward to hold the box steady on the stool while Mr. Summers stirred up the papers inside it.

The original paraphernalia for the lottery had been lost long ago, 5
and the black box now resting on the stool had been put into use even before Old Man Warner, the oldest man in town, was born. Mr. Summers spoke frequently to the villagers about making a new box, but no one liked to upset even as much tradition as was represented by the black box. There was a story that the present box had been made with some pieces of the box that had preceded it, the one that had been constructed when the first people settled down to make a village here. Every year, after the lottery, Mr. Summers began talking again about a new box, but every year the subject was allowed to fade off without anything's being done. The black box grew shabbier each year; by now it was no longer completely black but splintered badly along one side to show the original wood color, and in some places faded or stained.

Mr. Martin and his oldest son, Baxter, held the black box securely on the stool until Mr. Summers had stirred the papers thoroughly with his hand. Because so much of the ritual had been forgotten or discarded, Mr. Summers had been successful in having slips of paper substituted for the chips of wood that had been used for generations. Chips of wood, Mr. Summers had argued, had been all very well when the village was tiny, but now that the population was more than three hundred and likely to keep on growing, it was necessary to use something that would fit more easily into the black box. The night before the lottery, Mr. Summers and Mr. Graves made up the slips of paper and put them in the box, and it was then taken to the safe of Mr. Summers's coal company and locked up until Mr. Summers was ready to take it to the square next morning. The rest of the year, the box was put away, sometimes one place, sometimes another; it had spent one year in Mr. Graves's barn and another year underfoot in the post office, and sometimes it was set on a shelf in the Martin grocery and left there.

There was a great deal of fussing to be done before Mr. Summers declared the lottery open. There were lists to make up—of heads of families, heads of households in each family, members of each household in each family. There was the proper swearing-in of Mr. Summers by the postmaster, as the official of the lottery; at one time, some people remembered, there had been a recital of some sort, performed by the official of the lottery, a perfunctory, tuneless chant that had been rattled off duly each year; some people believed that the official of the lottery used to stand just so when he said or sang it, others believed that he was supposed to walk among the people, but years and years ago this part of the ritual had been allowed to lapse. There had been, also, a ritual salute, which the official of the lottery had had to use in addressing each person who came up to draw from the box, but this also had changed with time, until now it was felt necessary only for the official to speak to each person approaching. Mr. Summers was very good at all this; in his clean white shirt and blue jeans, with one hand resting carelessly on the black box, he seemed very proper and important as he talked interminably to Mr. Graves and the Martins.

Just as Mr. Summers finally left off talking and turned to the assembled villagers, Mrs. Hutchinson came hurriedly along the path to the square, her sweater thrown over her shoulders, and slid into place in the back of the crowd. "Clean forgot what day it was," she said to Mrs. Delacroix, who stood next to her, and they both laughed softly. "Thought my old man was out back stacking wood," Mrs. Hutchinson went on, "and then I looked out the window and the kids were gone, and then I remembered it was the twenty-seventh and came a-running." She dried her hands on her apron, and Mrs. Delacroix said, "You're in time, though. They're still talking away up there."

Mrs. Hutchinson craned her neck to see through the crowd and found her husband and children standing near the front. She tapped Mrs. Delacroix on the arm as a farewell and began to make her way through the crowd. The people separated good-humoredly to let her through; two or three people said, in voices just loud enough to be heard across the crowd, "Here comes your Missus, Hutchinson," and "Bill, she made it after all." Mrs. Hutchinson reached her husband, and Mr. Summers, who had been waiting, said cheerfully, "Thought we were going to have to get on without you, Tessie." Mrs. Hutchinson said, grinning, "Wouldn't have me leave m'dishes in the sink, now would you, Joe?" and soft laughter ran through the crowd as the people stirred back into position after Mrs. Hutchinson's arrival.

"Well, now," Mr. Summers said soberly, "guess we better get started, 10
get this over with, so's we can go back to work. Anybody ain't here?"

"Dunbar," several people said. "Dunbar, Dunbar."

Mr. Summers consulted his list. "Clyde Dunbar," he said. "That's right. He's broke his leg, hasn't he? Who's drawing for him?"

"Me, I guess," a woman said, and Mr. Summers turned to look at her. "Wife draws for her husband," Mr. Summers said. "Don't you have a grown boy to do it for you, Janey?" Although Mr. Summers and everyone else in the village knew the answer perfectly well, it was the business of the official of the lottery to ask such questions formally. Mr. Summers waited with an expression of polite interest while Mrs. Dunbar answered.

"Horace's not but sixteen yet," Mrs. Dunbar said regretfully. "Guess I gotta fill in for the old man this year."

"Right," Mr. Summers said. He made a note on the list he was holding. 15 Then he asked, "Watson boy drawing this year?"

A tall boy in the crowd raised his hand. "Here," he said. "I'm drawing for m'mother and me." He blinked his eyes nervously and ducked his head as several voices in the crowd said things like "Good fellow, Jack," and "Glad to see your mother's got a man to do it."

"Well," Mr. Summers said, "guess that's everyone. Old Man Warner make it?"

"Here," a voice said, and Mr. Summers nodded.

A sudden hush fell on the crowd as Mr. Summers cleared his throat and looked at the list. "All ready?" he called. "Now, I'll read the names—heads of families first—and the men come up and take a paper out of the box. Keep the paper folded in your hand without looking at it until everyone has had a turn. Everything clear?"

The people had done it so many times that they only half listened to 20 the directions; most of them were quiet, wetting their lips, not looking around. Then Mr. Summers raised one hand high and said, "Adams." A man disengaged himself from the crowd and came forward. "Hi, Steve," Mr. Summers said, and Mr. Adams said, "Hi, Joe." They grinned at one another humorlessly and nervously. Then Mr. Adams reached into the black box and took out a folded paper. He held it firmly by one corner as he turned and went hastily back to his place in the crowd, where he stood a little apart from his family, not looking down at his hand.

"Allen," Mr. Summers said. "Anderson. . . . Bentham."

"Seems like there's no time at all between lotteries any more," Mrs. Delacroix said to Mrs. Graves in the back row. "Seems like we got through with the last one only last week."

"Time sure goes fast," Mrs. Graves said.

"Clark. . . . Delacroix."

"There goes my old man," Mrs. Delacroix said. She held her breath 25 while her husband went forward.

"Dunbar," Mr. Summers said, and Mrs. Dunbar went steadily to the box while one of the women said, "Go on, Janey," and another said, "There she goes."

"We're next," Mrs. Graves said. She watched while Mr. Graves came around from the side of the box, greeted Mr. Summers gravely, and selected a slip of paper from the box. By now, all through the crowd there were men holding the small folded papers in their large hands, turning them over and over nervously. Mrs. Dunbar and her two sons stood together, Mrs. Dunbar holding the slip of paper.

"Harburt. . . . Hutchinson."

"Get up there, Bill," Mrs. Hutchinson said, and the people near her laughed.

"Jones." 30

"They do say," Mr. Adams said to Old Man Warner, who stood next to him, "that over in the north village they're talking of giving up the lottery."

Old Man Warner snorted. "Pack of crazy fools," he said. "Listening to the young folks, nothing's good enough for *them*. Next thing you know, they'll be wanting to go back to living in caves, nobody work any more, live *that* way for a while. Used to be a saying about 'Lottery in June, corn be heavy soon.' First thing you know, we'd all be eating stewed chickweed and acorns. There's *always* been a lottery," he added petulantly. "Bad enough to see young Joe Summers up there joking with everybody."

"Some places have already quit lotteries," Mrs. Adams said.

"Nothing but trouble in *that*," Old Man Warner said stoutly. "Pack of young fools."

35 "Martin." And Bobby Martin watched his father go forward. "Overdyke. . . . Percy."

"I wish they'd hurry," Mrs. Dunbar said to her older son. "I wish they'd hurry."

"They're almost through," her son said.

"You get ready to run tell Dad," Mrs. Dunbar said.

Mr. Summers called his own name and then stepped forward precisely and selected a slip from the box. Then he called, "Warner."

40 "Seventy-seventh year I been in the lottery," Old Man Warner said as he went through the crowd. "Seventy-seventh time."

"Watson." The tall boy came awkwardly through the crowd. Someone said, "Don't be nervous, Jack," and Mr. Summers said, "Take your time, son."

"Zanini."

After that, there was a long pause, a breathless pause, until Mr. Summers, holding his slip of paper in the air, said, "All right, fellows." For a minute, no one moved, and then all the slips of paper were opened. Suddenly, all the women began to speak at once, saying, "Who is it?" "Who's got it?" "Is it the Dunbars?" "Is it the Watsons?" Then the voices began to say, "It's Hutchinson. It's Bill." "Bill Hutchinson's got it."

"Go tell your father," Mrs. Dunbar said to her older son.

45 People began to look around to see the Hutchinsons. Bill Hutchinson was standing quiet, staring down at the paper in his hand. Suddenly, Tessie Hutchinson shouted to Mr. Summers, "You didn't give him time enough to take any paper he wanted. I saw you. It wasn't fair!"

"Be a good sport, Tessie," Mrs. Delacroix called, and Mrs. Graves said, "All of us took the same chance."

"Shut up, Tessie," Bill Hutchinson said.

"Well, everyone," Mr. Summers said, "that was done pretty fast, and now we've got to be hurrying a little more to get done in time." He consulted his next list. "Bill," he said, "you draw for the Hutchinson family. You got any other households in the Hutchinsons?"

"There's Don and Eva," Mrs. Hutchinson yelled. "Make them take their chance!"

"Daughters draw with their husbands' families, Tessie," Mr. Summers said gently. "You know that as well as anyone else."

"It wasn't fair," Tessie said.

"I guess not, Joe," Bill Hutchinson said regretfully. "My daughter draws with her husband's family, that's only fair. And I've got no other family except the kids."

"Then, as far as drawing for families is concerned, it's you," Mr. Summers said in explanation, "and as far as drawing for households is concerned, that's you, too. Right?"

"Right," Bill Hutchinson said.

"How many kids, Bill?" Mr. Summers asked formally.

"Three," Bill Hutchinson said. "There's Bill, Jr., and Nancy, and little Dave. And Tessie and me."

"All right, then," Mr. Summers said. "Harry, you got their tickets back?"

Mr. Graves nodded and held up the slips of paper. "Put them in the box, then," Mr. Summers directed. "Take Bill's and put it in."

"I think we ought to start over," Mrs. Hutchinson said, as quietly as she could. "I tell you it wasn't *fair*. You didn't give him time enough to choose. *Every*body saw that."

Mr. Graves had selected the five slips and put them in the box, and he dropped all the papers but those onto the ground, where the breeze caught them and lifted them off.

"Listen, everybody," Mrs. Hutchinson was saying to the people around her.

"Ready, Bill?" Mr. Summers asked, and Bill Hutchinson, with one quick glance around at his wife and children, nodded.

"Remember," Mr. Summers said, "take the slips and keep them folded until each person has taken one. Harry, you help little Dave." Mr. Graves took the hand of the little boy, who came willingly with him up to the box. "Take a paper out of the box, Davy," Mr. Summers said. Davy put his hand into the box and laughed. "Take just *one* paper," Mr. Summers said. "Harry, you hold it for him." Mr. Graves took the child's hand and removed the folded paper from the tight fist and held it while little Dave stood next to him and looked up at him wonderingly.

"Nancy next," Mr. Summers said. Nancy was twelve, and her school friends breathed heavily as she went forward, switching her skirt, and took a slip daintily from the box. "Bill, Jr.," Mr. Summers said, and Billy, his face red and his feet over-large, nearly knocked the box over as he got a paper out. "Tessie," Mr. Summers said. She hesitated for a minute, looking around defiantly, and then set her lips and went up to the box. She snatched a paper out and held it behind her.

"Bill," Mr. Summers said, and Bill Hutchinson reached into the box and felt around, bringing his hand out at last with the slip of paper in it.

The crowd was quiet. A girl whispered, "I hope it's not Nancy," and the sound of the whisper reached the edges of the crowd.

"It's not the way it used to be," Old Man Warner said clearly. "People ain't the way they used to be."

"All right," Mr. Summers said. "Open the papers. Harry, you open little Dave's."

Mr. Graves opened the slip of paper and there was a general sigh through the crowd as he held it up and everyone could see that it was blank. Nancy and Bill, Jr., opened theirs at the same time, and both beamed and laughed, turning around to the crowd and holding their slips of paper above their heads.

"Tessie," Mr. Summers said. There was a pause, and then Mr. Sum- 70
mers looked at Bill Hutchinson, and Bill unfolded his paper and showed it. It was blank.

"It's Tessie," Mr. Summers said, and his voice was hushed. "Show us her paper, Bill."

Bill Hutchinson went over to his wife and forced the slip of paper out of her hand. It had a black spot on it, the black spot Mr. Summers had made the night before with the heavy pencil in the coal-company office. Bill Hutchinson held it up, and there was a stir in the crowd.

"All right, folks," Mr. Summers said, "Let's finish quickly."

Although the villagers had forgotten the ritual and lost the original black box, they still remembered to use stones. The pile of stones the boys had made earlier was ready; there were stones on the ground with the blowing scraps of paper that had come out of the box. Mrs. Delacroix selected a stone so large she had to pick it up with both hands and turned to Mrs. Dunbar. "Come on," she said. "Hurry up."

Mrs. Dunbar had small stones in both hands, and she said, gasping 75
for breath, "I can't run at all. You'll have to go ahead and I'll catch up with you."

The children had stones already, and someone gave little Davy Hutchinson a few pebbles.

Tessie Hutchinson was in the center of a cleared space by now, and she held her hands out desperately as the villagers moved in on her. "It isn't fair," she said. A stone hit her on the side of the head.

Old Man Warner was saying, "Come on, come on, everyone." Steve Adams was in the front of the crowd of villagers, with Mrs. Graves beside him.

"It isn't fair, it isn't right," Mrs. Hutchinson screamed, and then they were upon her.

Questions

1. Where do you think "The Lottery" takes place? What purpose do you suppose the writer has in making this setting appear so familiar and ordinary?
2. What details in paragraphs 2 and 3 foreshadow the ending of the story?

3. Take a close look at Jackson's description of the black wooden box (paragraph 5) and of the black spot on the fatal slip of paper (paragraph 72). What do these objects suggest to you? Are there any other symbols in the story?
4. What do you understand to be the writer's own attitude toward the lottery and the stoning? Exactly what in the story makes her attitude clear to us?
5. What do you make of Old Man Warner's saying, "Lottery in June, corn be heavy soon" (paragraph 32)?
6. What do you think Shirley Jackson is driving at? Consider each of the following interpretations and, looking at the story, see if you can find any evidence for it:

   Jackson takes a primitive fertility rite and playfully transfers it to a small town in North America.

   Jackson, writing her story soon after World War II, indirectly expresses her horror at the Holocaust. She assumes that the massacre of the Jews was carried out by unwitting, obedient people, like these villagers.

   Jackson is satirizing our own society, in which men are selected for the army by lottery.

   Jackson is just writing a memorable story that signifies nothing at all.

WRITING *effectively*

THINKING ABOUT SYMBOLS

One danger in analyzing a story's symbolism is the temptation to read symbolic meaning into *everything*. An image acquires symbolic resonance because it is organically important to the actions and emotions of the story.

- **Consider a symbolic object's relevance to the plot.** What events, characters, and ideas are associated with it? It also helps to remember that some symbols arrive with cultural baggage. Any great white whale that swims into a work of contemporary fiction will inevitably summon up the symbolic associations of Melville's Moby Dick.
- **Ask yourself what the symbol means to the protagonist of your story.** Writers don't simply assign arbitrary meanings to items in their stories; generally, a horse is a horse, and a hammer is just a hammer. Sometimes, though, an object means something more to a character. Think of the flowers in "The Chrysanthemums."
- **Remember: in literature, few symbols are hidden.** Don't go on a symbol hunt. As you read or reread a story, any real symbol will usually

find you. If an object appears time and again, or is tied inextricably to the story's events, it is likely to suggest something beyond itself. When an object, an action, or a place has emotional or intellectual power beyond its literal importance, then it is a genuine symbol.

CHECKLIST: Writing About Symbols

- ☐ Which objects, actions, or places seem unusually significant?
- ☐ List the specific objects, people, and ideas with which a particular symbol is associated.
- ☐ Locate the exact place in the story where the symbol links itself to the other thing.
- ☐ Ask whether each symbol comes with ready-made cultural associations.
- ☐ Avoid far-fetched interpretations. Focus first on the literal things, places, and actions in the story.
- ☐ Don't make a symbol mean too much or too little. Don't limit it to one narrow association or claim it summons up many different things.
- ☐ Be specific. Identify the exact place in the story where a symbol takes on a deeper meaning.

TOPICS FOR WRITING ON SYMBOLS

1. From the stories in this book, choose one with a strong central symbol. Explain how the symbol helps to communicate the story's meaning, citing specific moments in the text.
2. Choose a story from this chapter. Describe your experience of reading that story, and of encountering its symbols. At what point did the main symbol's meaning become clear? What in the story indicated the larger importance of that symbol?
3. From any story in this book, select an object, or place, or action that seems clearly symbolic. How do you know? Now select an object, place, or action from the same story that clearly seems to signify no more than itself. How can you tell?
4. Analyze the symbolism in either "Dead Men's Path" (Chapter 8) or "The Story of an Hour" (Chapter 9). Consider a symbol that recurs over the course of the story, and look closely at each appearance it makes. How does the story's use of the symbol evolve?
5. In an essay of 600 to 800 words, compare and contrast the symbolic use of the scapegoat in "The Lottery" and "The Ones Who Walk Away from Omelas."

▶ TERMS FOR *review*

Symbol ▶ A person, place, or thing in a narrative that suggests meanings beyond its literal sense. Symbol is related to allegory, but it works more complexly. A symbol often contains multiple meanings and associations.

Conventional symbol ▶ A literary symbol that has a conventional or customary meaning for most readers—for example, a black cat crossing a path or a young bride in a white dress.

Symbolic act ▶ An action whose significance goes well beyond its literal meaning. In literature, symbolic acts often involve some conscious or unconscious ritual element such as rebirth, purification, forgiveness, vengeance, or initiation.

Allegory ▶ A narrative in which the literal events (persons, places, and things) consistently point to a parallel sequence of symbolic equivalents. This narrative strategy is often used to dramatize abstract ideas, historical events, religious systems, or political issues. An allegory has two levels of meaning: a literal level that tells a surface story and a symbolic level in which the abstract ideas unfold.

8 GALLERY OF INTERNATIONAL VOICES

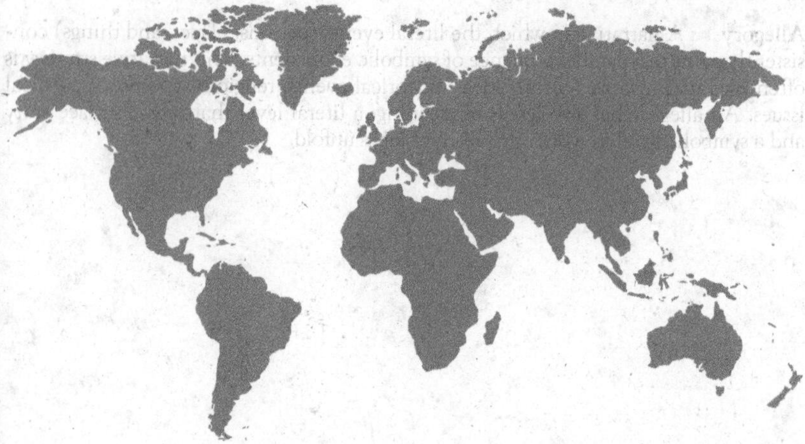

Stories from Around the World

Chinua Achebe—*Nigeria*
Inés Arredondo—*Mexico*
Gabriel García Márquez—*Colombia*
Ha Jin—*China*
Jamaica Kincaid—*Antigua*
Naguib Mahfouz—*Egypt*
Bharati Mukherjee—*India*

NIGERIA

Chinua Achebe

Dead Men's Path

(1953) 1972

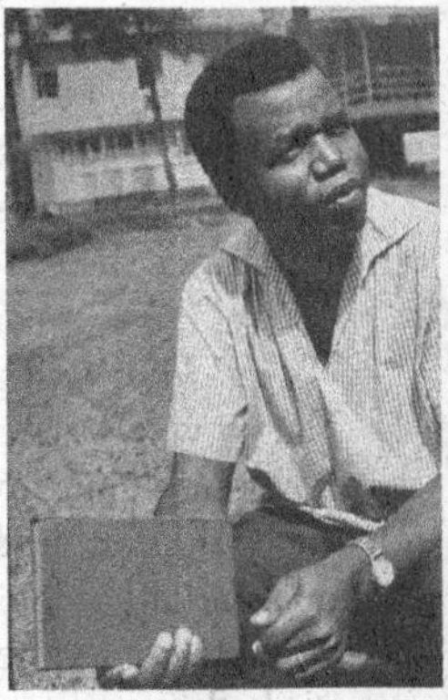

Chinua Achebe

Chinua Achebe (1930–2013) was born in Ogidi, a village in eastern Nigeria. His father was a missionary schoolteacher, and Achebe had a devout Christian upbringing. A member of the Ibo tribe, the future writer grew up speaking Igbo, but at the age of eight, he began learning English. He went abroad to study at London University but returned to Africa to complete his BA at the University College of Ibadan in 1953. Achebe worked for years in Nigerian radio. Shortly after Nigeria's independence from Great Britain in 1963, civil war broke out, and the nation split in two. Achebe left his job to join the Ministry of Information for Biafra, the new country created from eastern Nigeria. It was not until 1970 that the bloody civil war ended. Approximately one million Ibos lay dead from war, disease, and starvation as the defeated Biafrans reunited with Nigeria. Achebe was often considered Africa's premier novelist. His novels included Things Fall Apart *(1958),* No Longer at Ease *(1962),* A Man of the People *(1966), and* Anthills of the Savannah *(1987). His short stories were collected in* Girls at War *(1972). He also published poetry, children's stories, and several volumes of essays, the last of which is* Home and Exile *(2000). In 1990 Achebe suffered massive injuries in a car accident outside Lagos that left him paralyzed from the waist down. Following the accident, he taught at Bard College in upstate New York for almost nineteen years. In 1999 he visited Nigeria again after a deliberate nine-year absence to protest government dictatorship, and his homecoming became a national event. In 2007 he was awarded the second Man Booker International Prize for his lifetime contribution to world literature. He died at age 82.*

Michael Obi's hopes were fulfilled much earlier than he had expected. He was appointed headmaster of Ndume Central School in January 1949. It had always been an unprogressive school, so the Mission authorities decided to send a young and energetic man to run it. Obi accepted this responsibility with enthusiasm. He had many wonderful ideas and this was an opportunity to put them into practice. He had had sound secondary school education which designated him a "pivotal teacher" in the official records and set him apart from the other headmasters in the mission field. He was outspoken in his condemnation of the narrow views of these older and often less-educated ones.

"We shall make a good job of it, shan't we?" he asked his young wife when they first heard the joyful news of his promotion.

"We shall do our best," she replied. "We shall have such beautiful gardens and everything will be just *modern* and delightful . . ." In their two years of married life she had become completely infected by his passion for "modern methods" and his denigration of "these old and superannuated people in the teaching field who would be better employed as traders in the Onitsha market." She began to see herself already as the admired wife of the young headmaster, the queen of the school.

The wives of the other teachers would envy her position. She would set the fashion in everything . . . Then, suddenly, it occurred to her that there might not be other wives. Wavering between hope and fear, she asked her husband, looking anxiously at him.

"All our colleagues are young and unmarried," he said with enthusiasm 5
which for once she did not share. "Which is a good thing," he continued.

"Why?"

"Why? They will give all their time and energy to the school."

Nancy was downcast. For a few minutes she became skeptical about the new school; but it was only for a few minutes. Her little personal misfortune could not blind her to her husband's happy prospects. She looked at him as he sat folded up in a chair. He was stoop-shouldered and looked frail. But he sometimes surprised people with sudden bursts of physical energy. In his present posture, however, all his bodily strength seemed to have retired behind his deep-set eyes, giving them an extraordinary power of penetration. He was only twenty-six, but looked thirty or more. On the whole, he was not unhandsome.

"A penny for your thoughts, Mike," said Nancy after a while, imitating the woman's magazine she read.

"I was thinking what a grand opportunity we've got at last to show 10
these people how a school should be run."

Ndume School was backward in every sense of the word. Mr. Obi put his whole life into the work, and his wife hers too. He had two aims. A high standard of teaching was insisted upon, and the school compound was to be turned into a place of beauty. Nancy's dream-gardens came to life with the coming of the rains, and blossomed. Beautiful hibiscus and allamanda hedges in brilliant red and yellow marked out the carefully tended school compound from the rank neighborhood bushes.

One evening as Obi was admiring his work he was scandalized to see an old woman from the village hobble right across the compound, through a marigold flower-bed and the hedges. On going up there he found faint signs of an almost disused path from the village across the school compound to the bush on the other side.

"It amazes me," said Obi to one of his teachers who had been three years in the school, "that you people allowed the villagers to make use of this footpath. It is simply incredible." He shook his head.

"The path," said the teacher apologetically, "appears to be very important to them. Although it is hardly used, it connects the village shrine with their place of burial."

"And what has that got to do with the school?" asked the headmaster. 15

"Well, I don't know," replied the other with a shrug of the shoulders. "But I remember there was a big row some time ago when we attempted to close it."

"That was some time ago. But it will not be used now," said Obi as he walked away. "What will the Government Education Officer think of this when he comes to inspect the school next week? The villagers might, for all I know, decide to use the schoolroom for a pagan ritual during the inspection."

Heavy sticks were planted closely across the path at the two places where it entered and left the school premises. These were further strengthened with barbed wire.

Three days later the village priest of *Ani* called on the headmaster. He was an old man and walked with a slight stoop. He carried a stout walking-stick which he usually tapped on the floor, by way of emphasis, each time he made a new point in his argument.

"I have heard," he said after the usual exchange of cordialities, "that 20
our ancestral footpath has recently been closed . . ."

"Yes," replied Mr. Obi. "We cannot allow people to make a highway of our school compound."

"Look here, my son," said the priest bringing down his walking-stick, "this path was here before you were born and before your father was born. The whole life of this village depends on it. Our dead relatives depart by it and our ancestors visit us by it. But most important, it is the path of children coming in to be born . . ."

Mr. Obi listened with a satisfied smile on his face.

"The whole purpose of our school," he said finally, "is to eradicate just such beliefs as that. Dead men do not require footpaths. The whole idea is just fantastic. Our duty is to teach your children to laugh at such ideas."

"What you say may be true," replied the priest, "but we follow the 25
practices of our fathers. If you reopen the path we shall have nothing to quarrel about. What I always say is: let the hawk perch and let the eagle perch." He rose to go.

"I am sorry," said the young headmaster. "But the school compound cannot be a thoroughfare. It is against our regulations. I would suggest your constructing another path, skirting our premises. We can even get our boys to help in building it. I don't suppose the ancestors will find the little detour too burdensome."

"I have no more words to say," said the old priest, already outside.

Two days later a young woman in the village died in childbed. A diviner was immediately consulted and he prescribed heavy sacrifices to propitiate ancestors insulted by the fence.

Obi woke up next morning among the ruins of his work. The beautiful hedges were torn up not just near the path but right round the school, the flowers trampled to death and one of the school buildings pulled down . . . That day, the white Supervisor came to inspect the school and wrote a nasty report on the state of the premises but more seriously about the "tribal-war situation developing between the school and the village, arising in part from the misguided zeal of the new headmaster."

MEXICO

Inés Arredondo

The Shunammite 1965

Translated by Alberto Manguel

Inés Arredondo

Inés Arredondo (1928–1989) was born in Culiacán, the capital and largest city of the state of Sinaloa, Mexico, the daughter of a doctor. In 1947 she enrolled in the National Autonomous University of Mexico, but in the following year experienced a spiritual and emotional crisis that brought her close to suicide. In 1953 she married the writer Tomas Segovia; the union, which produced three children, was troubled, leading to separation in 1962 and divorce three years later. In 1972 she married Carlos Ruiz Sanchez, a physician. Throughout her adult life, financial necessity caused Arredondo to work at a variety of jobs—librarian, editor, translator, and professor. Because of spinal problems she was forced to undergo five operations and was ultimately confined to a wheelchair. Beginning in 1965, she published several small volumes of short fiction, which brought her several awards and established her reputation as a major writer. "The Shunammite" was filmed, with a screenplay by Arredondo, as a segment in a 1965 Mexican movie called Amor Amor Amor *and was the basis for a 1991 opera by Marcela Rodríguez.* Underground River and Other Stories *(1996) presents twelve of her stories in English translation.*

> *So they sought for a fair damsel throughout all the coasts of Israel, and found Abishag, a Shunammite,° and brought her to the king.*
> *And the damsel was very fair, and cherished the king, and ministered to him; but the king knew her not.*
>
> —1 KINGS 1:3–4

Abishag, a Shunammite: Among the tasks Abishag was called upon to perform for the dying King David was to lie with him and warm him with her body, yet there was no sexual contact between them. A Shunammite was someone from the town of Shunem in ancient Palestine.

The summer had been a fiery furnace. The last summer of my youth.

Tense, concentrated in the arrogance that precedes combustion, the city shone in a dry and dazzling light. I stood in the very midst of the light, dressed in mourning, proud, feeding the flames with my blonde hair, alone. Men's sly glances slid over my body without soiling it, and my haughty modesty forced them to barely nod at me, full of respect. I was certain of having the power to dominate passions, to purify anything in the scorching air that surrounded but did not singe me.

Nothing changed when I received the telegram; the sadness it brought me did not affect in the least my feelings towards the world. My uncle Apolonio was dying at the age of seventy-odd years and wanted to see me. I had lived as a daughter in his house for many years and I sincerely felt pain at the thought of his inevitable death. All this was perfectly normal, and not a single omen, not a single shiver made me suspect anything. Quickly I made arrangements for the journey, in the very same untouchable midst of the motionless summer.

I arrived at the village during the hour of siesta.

Walking down the empty streets with my small suitcase, I fell to 5
daydreaming, in that dusky zone between reality and time, born of the excessive heat. I was not remembering; I was almost reliving things as they had been. "Look, Licha, the *amapas*° are blooming again." The clear voice, almost childish. "I want you to get yourself a dress like that of Margarita Ibarra to wear on the sixteenth." I could hear her, feel her walking by my side, her shoulders bent a little forwards, light in spite of her plumpness, happy and old. I carried on walking in the company of my aunt Panchita, my mother's sister. "Well, my dear, if you *really* don't like Pepe . . . but he's such a *nice* boy." Yes, she had used those exact words, here, in front of Tichi Valenzuela's window, with her gay smile, innocent and impish. I walked a little further, where the paving stones seemed to fade away in the haze, and when the bells rang, heavy and real, ending the siesta and announcing the Rosary, I opened my eyes and gave the village a good, long look: it was not the same. The *amapas* had not bloomed and I was crying, in my mourning dress, at the door of my uncle's house.

The front gate was open, as always, and at the end of the courtyard rose the bougainvillea. As always: but not the same. I dried my tears, and felt that I was not arriving: I was leaving. Everything looked motionless, pinioned in my memory, and the heat and the silence seemed to wither it all. My footsteps echoed with a new sound, and María came out to greet me.

"Why didn't you let us know? We'd have sent . . ."

We went straight into the sick man's room. As I entered, I felt cold. Silence and gloom preceded death.

amapa: a small tree that is covered, when in bloom, by masses of yellow, pink, or purple tubular flowers.

"Luisa, is that you?"

The dear voice was dying out and would soon be silent for ever.

"I'm here, uncle."

"God be praised! I won't die alone."

"Don't say that; you'll soon be much better."

He smiled sadly; he knew I was lying but he did not want to make me cry.

"Yes, my daughter. Yes. Now have a rest, make yourself at home and then come and keep me company. I'll try to sleep a little."

Shriveled, wizened, toothless, lost in the immense bed and floating senselessly in whatever was left of his life, he was painful to be with, like something superfluous, out of place, like so many others at the point of death. Stepping out of the overheated passageway, one would take a deep breath, instinctively, hungry for light and air.

I began to nurse him and I felt happy doing it. This house was *my* house, and in the morning, while tidying up, I would sing long-forgotten songs. The peace that surrounded me came perhaps from the fact that my uncle no longer awaited death as something imminent and terrible, but instead let himself be carried by the passing days towards a more or less distant or nearby future, with the unconscious tenderness of a child. He would go over his past life with great pleasure and enjoy imagining that he was bequeathing me his images, as grandparents do with their children.

"Bring me that small chest, there, in the large wardrobe. Yes, that one. The key is underneath the mat, next to Saint Anthony. Bring the key as well."

And his sunken eyes would shine once again at the sight of all his treasures.

"Look: this necklace—I gave it to your aunt for our tenth wedding anniversary. I bought it in Mazatlán from a Polish jeweler who told me God-knows-what story about an Austrian princess, and asked an impossible price for it. I brought it back hidden in my pistol-holder and didn't sleep a wink in the stagecoach—I was so afraid someone would steal it!"

The light of dusk made the young, living stones glitter in his calloused hands.

"This ring, so old, belonged to my mother; look carefully at the miniature in the other room and you'll see her wearing it. Cousin Begoña would mutter behind her back that a sweetheart of hers . . ."

The ladies in the portraits would move their lips and speak, once again, would breathe again—all these ladies he had seen, he had touched. I would picture them in my mind and understand the meaning of these jewels.

"Have I told you about the time we traveled to Europe, in 1908, before the Revolution?° You had to take a ship to Colima. And in Venice

the Revolution: The Mexican Revolution, which toppled the dictator Porfirio Díaz and led to a decade of political unrest and civil war, began in 1910.

your aunt Panchita fell in love with a certain pair of earrings. They were much too expensive, and I told her so. 'They are fit for a queen.' Next day I bought them for her. You just can't imagine what it was like because all this took place long, long before you were born, in 1908, in Venice, when your aunt was so young, so . . . "

"Uncle, you're getting tired, you should rest."

"You're right, I'm tired. Leave me a while and take the small chest to your room. It's yours."

"But, uncle . . . "

"It's all yours, that's all! I trust I can give away whatever I want!"

His voice broke into a sob: the illusion was vanishing and he found himself again on the point of dying, of saying goodbye to the things he had loved. He turned to the wall and I left with the box in my hands, not knowing what to do.

On other occasions he would tell me about "the year of the famine," or "the year of the yellow corn," or "the year of the plague," and very old tales of murderers and ghosts. Once he even tried to sing a *corrido*° from his youth, but it shattered in his jagged voice. He was leaving me his life, and he was happy.

The doctor said that yes, he could see some recovery, but that we were not to raise our hopes, there was no cure, it was merely a matter of a few days more or less.

One afternoon of menacing dark clouds, when I was bringing in the clothes hanging out to dry in the courtyard, I heard María cry out. I stood still, listening to her cry as if it were a peal of thunder, the first of the storm to come. Then silence, and I was left alone in the courtyard, motionless. A bee buzzed by and the rain did not fall. No one knows as well as I do how awful a foreboding can be, a premonition hanging above a head turned towards the sky.

"Lichita, he's dying! He's gasping for air!"

"Go get the doctor . . . No! I'll go. But call doña Clara to stay with you till I'm back."

"And the priest, fetch the priest."

I ran, I ran away from that unbearable moment, blunt and asphyxiating. I ran, hurried back, entered the house, made coffee; I greeted the relatives who began to arrive dressed in half-mourning; I ordered candles; I asked for a few holy relics; I kept on feverishly trying to fulfill my only obligation at the time, to be with my uncle. I asked the doctor: he had given him an injection, so as not to leave anything untried, but he knew it was useless. I saw the priest arrive with the Eucharist, even then I lacked the courage to enter. I knew I would regret it afterwards. "Thank

corrido: a kind of narrative ballad; *corridos* were originally about romantic love, but at the time of the Revolution they were frequently political in nature.

God, now I won't die alone"—but I couldn't. I covered my face with my hands and prayed.

The priest came and touched my shoulder. I thought that all was over and I shivered.

"He's calling you. Come in."

I don't know how I reached the door. Night had fallen and the room, lit by a bedside lamp, seemed enormous. The furniture, larger than life, looked black, and a strange clogging atmosphere hung about the bed. Trembling, I felt I was inhaling death.

"Stand next to him," said the priest.

I obeyed, moving towards the foot of the bed, unable to look even at the sheets.

"Your uncle's wish, unless you say otherwise, is to marry you *in articulo mortis*,° so that you may inherit his possessions. Do you accept?"

I stifled a cry of horror. I opened my eyes wide enough to let in the whole terrible room. "Why does he want to drag me into his grave?" I felt death touching my skin.

"Luisa . . ."

It was uncle Apolonio. Now I had to look at him. He could barely mouth the words, his jaw seemed slack and he spoke moving his face like that of a ventriloquist's doll.

"Please."

And he fell silent with exhaustion.

I could take no more. I left the room. That was not my uncle, it did not even look like him. Leave everything to me, yes, but not only his possessions, his stories, his life. I didn't want it, his life, his death. I didn't want it. When I opened my eyes I was standing once again in the courtyard and the sky was still overcast. I breathed in deeply, painfully.

"Already?" the relatives drew near to ask, seeing me so distraught.

I shook my head. Behind me, the priest explained.

"Don Apolonio wants to marry her with his last breath, so that she may inherit him."

"And you won't?" the old servant asked anxiously. "Don't be silly, no one deserves it more than you. You were a daughter to them, and you have worked very hard looking after him. If you don't marry him, the cousins in Mexico City will leave you without a cent. Don't be silly!"

"It's a fine gesture on his part."

"And afterwards you'll be left a rich widow, as untouched as you are now." A young cousin laughed nervously.

"It's a considerable fortune, and I, as your uncle several times removed, would advise you to . . ."

in articulo mortis: "at the point of death." Such marriages were allowed to take place without the usual formalities and were considered binding even if, as here, the dying party subsequently recovered.

"If you think about it, not accepting shows a lack of both charity and humility."

"That's true, that's absolutely true."

I did not want to give an old man his last pleasure, a pleasure I should, after all, be thankful for, because my youthful body, of which I felt so proud, had not dwelt in any of the regions of death. I was overcome by nausea. That was my last clear thought that night. I woke from a kind of hypnotic slumber as they forced me to hold his hand covered in cold sweat. I felt nauseous again, but said "yes."

I remember vaguely that they hovered over me all the time, talking all at once, taking me over there, bringing me over here, making me sign, making me answer. The taste of that night—a taste that has stayed with me for the rest of my life—was that of an evil ring-around-the-rosies turning vertiginously around me, while everyone laughed and sang grotesquely

This is the way the widow is wed,
The widow is wed, the widow is wed

while I stood, a slave, in the middle. Something inside me hurt, and I could not lift my eyes.

When I came to my senses, all was over, and on my hand shone the braided ring which I had seen so many times on my aunt Panchita's finger: there had been no time for anything else.

The guests began to leave.

"If you need me, don't hesitate to call. In the meantime give him these drops every six hours."

"May God bless you and give you strength."

"Happy honeymoon," whispered the young cousin in my ear, with a nasty laugh.

I returned to the sickbed. "Nothing has changed, nothing has changed." My fear certainly had not changed. I convinced María to stay and help me look after uncle Apolonio. I only calmed down once I saw dawn was breaking. It had started to rain, but without thunder or lightning, very still.

It kept on drizzling that day and the next, and the day after. Four days of anguish. Nobody came to visit, nobody other than the doctor and the priest. On days like these no one goes out, everyone stays indoors and waits for life to start again. These are the days of the spirit, sacred days.

If at least the sick man had needed plenty of attention my hours would have seemed shorter, but there was little that could be done for him.

On the fourth night María went to bed in a room close by, and I stayed alone with the dying man. I was listening to the monotonous rain and praying unconsciously, half asleep and unafraid, waiting. My fingers stopped turning the rosary, and as I held the beads I could feel through my fingertips a peculiar warmth, a warmth both alien and intimate, the warmth we leave in things and which is returned to us transformed, a comrade, a brother foreshadowing the warmth of others, a warmth both unknown and recollected, never quite grasped and yet inhabiting the core of my bones. Softly, deliciously, my nerves relaxed, my fingers felt light, I fell asleep.

I must have slept many hours: it was dawn when I woke up. I knew because the lights had been switched off and the electric plant stops working at two in the morning. The room, barely lit by an oil lamp at the feet of the Holy Virgin on the chest of drawers, made me think of the wedding night, my wedding night. It was so long ago, an empty eternity.

From the depth of the gloomy darkness don Apolonio's broken and tired breathing reached me. There he still was, not the man himself, simply the persistent and incomprehensible shred that hangs on, with no goal, with no apparent motive. Death is frightening, but life mingled with death, soaked in death, is horrible in a way that owes little to either life or death. Silence, corruption of the flesh, the stench, the monstrous transformation, the final vanishing act, all this is painful, but it reaches a climax and then gives way, dissolves into the earth, into memory, into history. But not this: this arrangement worked out between life and death—echoed in the useless exhaling and inhaling—could carry on forever. I would hear him trying to clear his anaesthetized throat and it occurred to me that air was not entering that body, or rather, that it was not a human body breathing the air: it was a machine, puffing and panting, stopping in a curious game, a game to kill time without end. That thing was no human being: it was somebody playing with huffs and snores. And the horror of it all won me over: I began to breathe to the rhythm of his panting; to inhale, stop suddenly, choke, breathe, choke again, unable to control myself, until I realized I had been deceived by what I thought was the sense of the game. What I really felt was the pain and shortness of breath of an animal in pain. But I kept on, on, until there was one single breathing, one single inhuman breath, one single agony. I felt calmer, terrified but calmer: I had lifted the barrier, I could let myself go and simply wait for the common end. It seemed to me that by abandoning myself, by giving myself up unconditionally, the end would happen quickly, would not be allowed to continue. It would have fulfilled its purpose and its persistent search in the world.

Not a hint of farewell, not a glimmer of pity towards me. I carried on the mortal game for a long, long while, from someplace where time had ceased to matter.

The shared breathing became less agitated, more peaceful, but also weaker. I seemed to be drifting back. I felt so tired I could barely move, exhaustion nestling in forever inside my body. I opened my eyes. Nothing had changed.

No: far away, in the shadows, is a rose. Alone, unique, alive. There it is, cut out against the darkness, clear as day, with its fleshy, luminous petals, shining. I look at it and my hand moves and I remember its touch and the simple act of putting it in a vase. I looked at it then, but I only understand it now. I stir, I blink, and the rose is still there, in full bloom, identical to itself.

I breathe freely, with my own breath. I pray, I remember, I doze off, and the untouched rose mounts guard over the dawning light and my secret. Death and hope suffer change.

And now day begins to break and in the clean sky I see that at last 75
the days of rain are over. I stay at the window a long time, watching everything change in the sun. A strong ray enters and the suffering seems a lie. Unjustified bliss fills my lungs and unwittingly I smile. I turn to the rose as if to an accomplice but I can't find it: the sun has withered it.

Clear days came again, and maddening heat. The people went to work, and sang, but don Apolonio would not die; in fact he seemed to get better. I kept on looking after him, but no longer in a cheerful mood—my eyes downcast, I turned the guilt I felt into hard work. My wish, now clearly, was that it all end, that he die. The fear, the horror I felt looking at him, at his touch, his voice, were unjustified because the link between us was not real, could never be real, and yet he felt like a dead weight upon me. Through politeness and shame I wanted to get rid of it.

Yes, don Apolonio was visibly improving. Even the doctor was surprised and offered no explanation.

On the very first morning I sat him up among the pillows, I noticed that certain look in my uncle's eyes. The heat was stifling and I had to lift him all by myself. Once I had propped him up I noticed: the old man was staring as if dazed at my heaving chest, his face distorted and his trembling hands unconsciously moving towards me. I drew back instinctively and turned my head away.

"Please close the blinds, it's too hot."

His almost dead body was growing warm. 80

"Come here, Luisa, sit by my side. Come."

"Yes, uncle." I sat, my knees drawn up, at the foot of the bed, without looking at him.

"Polo, you must call me Polo, after all we are closer relatives now." There was mockery in the tone of his voice.

"Yes, uncle."

"Polo, Polo." His voice was again sweet and soft. "You'll have a lot to 85
forgive me. I'm old and sick, and a man in my condition is like a child."

"Yes."

"Let's see. Try saying, 'Yes, Polo.'"

"Yes, Polo."

The name on my lips seemed to me an aberration, made me nauseated.

Polo got better, but became fussy and irritable. I realized he was 90
fighting to be the man he once had been, and yet the resurrected self was not the same, but another.

"Luisa, bring me . . . Luisa, give me . . . Luisa, plump up my pillows . . . pour me some water . . . prop up my leg . . ."

He wanted me to be there all day long, always by his side, seeing to his needs, touching him. And the fixed look and distorted face kept coming back, more and more frequently, growing over his features like a mask.

"Pick up my book. It fell underneath the bed, on this side."

I kneeled and stuck my head and almost half my body underneath the bed, and had to stretch my arm as far as it would go, to reach it. At first I thought it had been my own movements, or maybe the bedclothes, but once I had the book in my hand and was shuffling to get out, I froze, stunned by what I had long foreseen, even expected: the outburst, the scream, the thunder. A rage never before felt raced through me when the realization of what was happening reached my consciousness, when his shaking hand, taking advantage of my amazement, became surer and heavier, and enjoyed itself, adventuring with no restraints, feeling and exploring my thighs—a fleshless hand glued to my skin, fingering my body with delight, a dead hand searching impatiently between my legs, a bodyless hand.

I rose as quickly as I could, my face burning with shame and determination, but when I saw him I forgot myself and entered like an automaton into the nightmare. Polo was laughing softly through his toothless mouth. And then, suddenly serious, with a coolness that terrified me, he said:

"What? Aren't you my wife before God and men? Come here, I'm cold, heat my bed. But first take off your dress, you don't want to get it creased."

What followed, I know, is my story, my life, but I can barely remember it; like a disgusting dream I can't even tell whether it was long or short. Only one thought kept me sane during the early days: "This can't go on, it can't go on." I imagined that God would not allow it, would prevent it in some way or another. He, personally, God, would interfere. Death, once dreaded, seemed my only hope. Not Apolonio's—he was a demon of death—but mine, the just and necessary death for my corrupted flesh. But nothing happened. Everything stayed on, suspended in time, without future. Then, one morning, taking nothing with me, I left.

It was useless. Three days later they let me know that my husband was dying, and they called me back. I went to see the father confessor and told him my story.

"What keeps him alive is lust, the most horrible of all sins. This isn't life, Father, it's death. Let him die!"

"He would die in despair. I can't allow it."

"And I?"

"I understand, but if you don't go to him, it would be like murder. Try not to arouse him, pray to the Blessed Virgin, and keep your mind on your duties."

I went back. And lust drew him out of the grave once more.

Fighting, endlessly fighting, I managed, after several years, to overcome my hatred, and finally, at the very end, I even conquered the beast: Apolonio died in peace, sweetly, his old self again.

But I was not able to go back to who I was. Now wickedness, malice, shine in the eyes of the men who look at me, and I feel I have become an occasion of sin for all, I, the vilest of harlots. Alone, a sinner, totally engulfed by the never-ending flames of this cruel summer which surrounds us all, like an army of ants.

COLOMBIA

Gabriel García Márquez

The Handsomest Drowned Man in the World 1968

Translated by Gregory Rabassa

Gabriel García Márquez

Gabriel García Márquez (1928–2014), among the most eminent Latin American writers, was born in Aracataca, a Caribbean port in Colombia, one of sixteen children of an impoverished telegraph operator. For a time he studied law in Bogotá; later he then became a newspaper reporter. Although he never joined the Communist Party, García Márquez outspokenly advocated many left-wing proposals for reform. In 1954, despairing of any prospect for political change, he left Colombia to live in Mexico City. Though at nineteen he had already completed a book of short stories, La hojarasca (Leaf Storm)*, he waited until 1955 to publish it. Soon he began to build a towering reputation among readers of Spanish. His celebrated novel* Cien años de soledad *(1967), published in English as* One Hundred Years of Solitude *(1969), traces the history of a Colombian family through six generations. Called by Chilean poet Pablo Neruda "the greatest revelation in the Spanish language since* Don Quixote,*" the book has sold more than thirty million copies in thirty-five languages. In 1982 García Márquez was awarded the Nobel Prize in Literature. His fiction, rich in myth and invention, has reminded American readers of the work of William Faulkner, another explorer of his native ground; indeed, García Márquez called Faulkner "my master." His later novels include* Love in the Time of Cholera *(1988),* The General in His Labyrinth *(1990),* Of Love and Other Demons

(1995), and Memories of My Melancholy Whores *(2005). His* Collected Stories *was published in 1994.* Living to Tell the Tale *(2003), the first volume of an autobiographical trilogy, traces the author's life up to the beginning of his journalistic career, and offers many insights into the sources and techniques of his works of fiction. García Márquez died in Mexico City in 2014. In a note of mourning after the author's death, the president of his native country called him "the greatest Colombian of all time."*

A Tale for Children

The first children who saw the dark and slinky bulge approaching through the sea let themselves think it was an empty ship. Then they saw it had no flags or masts and they thought it was a whale. But when it washed up on the beach, they removed the clumps of seaweed, the jellyfish tentacles, and the remains of fish and flotsam, and only then did they see that it was a drowned man.

They had been playing with him all afternoon, burying him in the sand and digging him up again, when someone chanced to see them and spread the alarm in the village. The men who carried him to the nearest house noticed that he weighed more than any dead man they had ever known, almost as much as a horse, and they said to each other that maybe he'd been floating too long and the water had got into his bones. When they laid him on the floor they said he'd been taller than all the other men because there was barely enough room for him in the house, but they thought that maybe the ability to keep on growing after death was part of the nature of certain drowned men. He had the smell of the sea about him and only his shape gave one to suppose that it was the corpse of a human being, because the skin was covered with a crust of mud and scales.

They did not even have to clean off his face to know that the dead man was a stranger. The village was made up of only twenty-odd wooden houses that had stone courtyards with no flowers and which were spread about on the end of a desertlike cape. There was so little land that mothers always went about with the fear that the wind would carry off their children and the few dead that the years had caused among them had to be thrown off the cliffs. But the sea was calm and bountiful and all the men fit into seven boats. So when they found the drowned man they simply had to look at one another to see that they were all there. That night they did not go out to work at sea. While the men went to find out if anyone was missing in neighboring villages, the women stayed behind to care for the drowned man. They took the mud off with grass swabs, they removed the underwater stones entangled in his hair, and they scraped the crust off with tools used for scaling fish. As they were doing that they noticed that the vegetation on him came from faraway oceans and deep water and that his clothes were in tatters, as if he had sailed through labyrinths of coral. They noticed too that he bore his death with pride, for he did not have the lonely look of other drowned men who came out of the sea or that haggard, needy look of men who drowned in rivers. But only when they finished cleaning him off did they become aware of the kind of man he was and it left them breathless. Not only was he the tallest, strongest, most virile, and best built man they had ever seen, but even though they were looking at him there was no room for him in their imagination.

They could not find a bed in the village large enough to lay him on nor was there a table solid enough to use for his wake. The tallest men's holiday pants would not fit him, nor the fattest ones' Sunday shirts, nor the shoes of the one with the biggest feet. Fascinated by his huge size and his beauty, the women then decided to make him some pants from a large piece of sail and a shirt from some bridal brabant linen so that he could continue through his death with dignity. As they sewed, sitting in a circle and gazing at the corpse between stitches, it seemed to them that the wind had never been so steady nor the sea so restless as on that night and they supposed that the change had something to do with the dead man. They thought that if that magnificent man had lived in the village, his house would have had the widest doors, the highest ceiling, and the strongest floor, his bedstead would have been made from a midship frame held together by iron bolts, and his wife would have been the happiest woman. They thought that he would have had so much authority that he could have drawn fish out of the sea simply by calling their names and that he would have put so much work into his land that springs would have burst forth from among the rocks so that he would have been able to plant flowers on the cliffs. They secretly compared him to their own men, thinking that for all their lives theirs were incapable of doing what he could do in one night, and they ended up dismissing them deep in their hearts as the weakest, meanest, and most useless creatures on earth. They were wandering through the maze of fantasy when the oldest woman, who as the oldest had looked upon the drowned man with more compassion than passion, sighed:

"He has the face of someone called Esteban." 5

It was true. Most of them had only to take another look at him to see that he could not have any other name. The more stubborn among them, who were the youngest, still lived for a few hours with the illusion that when they put his clothes on and he lay among the flowers in patent leather shoes his name might be Lautaro. But it was a vain illusion. There had not been enough canvas, the poorly cut and worse sewn pants were too tight, and the hidden strength of his heart popped the buttons on his shirt. After midnight the whistling of the wind died down and the sea fell into its Wednesday drowsiness. The silence put an end to any last doubts: he was Esteban. The women who had dressed him, who had combed his hair, had cut his nails and shaved him were unable to hold back a shudder of pity when they had to resign themselves to his being dragged along the ground. It was then that they understood how unhappy he must have been with that huge body since it bothered him even after death. They could see him in life, condemned to going through doors sideways, cracking his head on crossbeams, remaining on his feet during visits, not knowing what to do with his soft, pink, sea lion hands while the lady of the house looked for her most resistant chair and begged him, frightened to death, sit here, Esteban, please, and he, leaning against the wall, smiling, don't bother, ma'am, I'm fine where I am, his heels raw and his back roasted from having done the same thing so many times whenever he paid a visit, don't bother, ma'am, I'm fine where I am, just to avoid the embarrassment of breaking up the chair, and never knowing perhaps that the ones who said don't go, Esteban, at least wait till the coffee's ready, were the ones who later on would whisper the big boob finally left, how nice, the handsome fool has gone. That was what the women were thinking beside the body a little before dawn. Later, when they covered his face with a handkerchief so that the light would not bother him, he looked so forever dead, so defenseless, so much like their men that the first furrows of tears opened in their hearts. It was one of the younger ones who began the weeping. The others, coming to, went from sighs to wails, and the more they sobbed the more they felt like weeping, because the drowned man was becoming all the more Esteban for them, and so they wept so much, for he was the most destitute, most peaceful, and most obliging man on earth, poor Esteban. So when the men returned with the news that the drowned man was not from the neighboring villages either, the women felt an opening of jubilation in the midst of their tears.

"Praise the Lord," they sighed, "he's ours!"

The men thought the fuss was only womanish frivolity. Fatigued because of the difficult nighttime inquiries, all they wanted was to get rid of the bother of the newcomer once and for all before the sun grew strong on that arid, windless day. They improvised a litter with the remains of foremasts and gaffs, tying it together with rigging so that it would bear the weight of the body until they reached the cliffs. They wanted to tie the anchor from a cargo ship to him so that he would sink easily into the deepest waves, where fish are blind and divers die of nostalgia, and bad currents would not bring him back to shore, as had happened with other bodies. But the more they hurried, the more the women thought of ways to waste time. They walked about like startled hens, pecking with the sea charms on their breasts, some interfering on one side to put a scapular of the good wind on the drowned man, some on the other side to put a wrist compass on him, and after a great deal of *get away from there, woman, stay out of the way, look, you almost made me fall on top of the dead man*, the men began to feel mistrust in their livers and started grumbling about why so many main-altar decorations for a stranger, because no matter how many nails and holy-water jars he had on him, the sharks would chew him all the same, but the women kept piling on their junk relics, running back and forth, stumbling, while they released in sighs what they did not in tears, so that the men finally exploded with *since when has there ever been such a fuss over a drifting corpse, a drowned nobody, a piece of cold Wednesday meat.* One of the women, mortified by so much lack of care, then removed the handkerchief from the dead man's face and the men were left breathless too.

He was Esteban. It was not necessary to repeat it for them to recognize him. If they had been told Sir Walter Raleigh,° even they might have been impressed with his gringo accent, the macaw on his shoulder, his cannibal-killing blunderbuss, but there could be only one Esteban in the world and there he was, stretched out like a sperm whale, shoeless, wearing the pants of an undersized child, and with those stony nails that had to be cut with a knife. They only had to take the handkerchief off his face to see that he was ashamed, that it was not his fault that he was so big or so heavy or so handsome, and if he had known that this was going to happen, he would have looked for a more discreet place to drown in, seriously, I even would have tied the anchor off a galleon around my neck and staggered off a cliff like someone who doesn't like things in order not to be upsetting people now with this Wednesday dead body, as you people say, in order not to be bothering anyone with this filthy piece of cold meat that doesn't have anything to do with me. There was so much truth in his manner that even the most mistrustful men, the ones who felt the bitterness of endless nights at sea fearing that their women would tire of dreaming about them and begin to dream of drowned men, even they and others who were harder still shuddered in the marrow of their bones at Esteban's sincerity.

That was how they came to hold the most splendid funeral they could 10
conceive of for an abandoned drowned man. Some women who had gone to get flowers in the neighboring villages returned with other women who could not believe what they had been told, and those women went back for more flowers when they saw the dead man, and they brought more and more until there were so many flowers and so many people that it was hard to walk about. At the final moment it pained them to return him to the waters as an orphan and they chose a father and mother from among the best people, and aunts and uncles and cousins, so that through him all the inhabitants of the village became kinsmen. Some sailors who heard weeping from a distance went off course and people heard of one who had himself tied to the mainmast, remembering ancient fables about sirens. While they fought for the privilege of carrying him on their shoulders along the steep escarpment by the cliffs, men and women became aware for the first time of the desolation of their streets, the dryness of their courtyards, the narrowness of their dreams as they faced the splendor and beauty of their drowned man. They let him go without an anchor so that he could come back if he wished and whenever he wished, and they all held their breath for the fraction of centuries the body took to fall into the abyss. They did not need to look at one another to realize that they were no longer all present, that they would never be. But they

Sir Walter Raleigh: Elizabethan explorer and statesman (1552–1618)

also knew that everything would be different from then on, that their houses would have wider doors, higher ceilings, and stronger floors so that Esteban's memory could go everywhere without bumping into beams and so that no one in the future would dare whisper the big boob finally died, too bad, the handsome fool has finally died, because they were going to paint their house fronts gay colors to make Esteban's memory eternal and they were going to break their backs digging for springs among the stones and planting flowers on the cliffs so that in future years at dawn the passengers on great liners would awaken, suffocated by the smell of gardens on the high seas, and the captain would have to come down from the bridge in his dress uniform, with his astrolabe, his pole star, and his row of war medals and, pointing to the promontory of roses on the horizon, he would say in fourteen languages, look there, where the wind is so peaceful now that it's gone to sleep beneath the beds, over there, where the sun's so bright that the sunflowers don't know which way to turn, yes, that's Esteban's village.

CHINA

Ha Jin

Saboteur

2000

Ha Jin

Ha Jin is the pen name of Xuefei Jin, who was born in Liaoning, China, in 1956. The son of military doctors, Jin grew up during the turbulent Cultural Revolution, a ten-year upheaval initiated by the Communist Party in 1966 to transform China into a Marxist workers' society by destroying all remnants of the nation's ancient past. During this period many schools and universities were closed and intellectuals were required to work in proletarian jobs. Jin taught himself English by listening to the radio. At fourteen, he joined the People's Liberation Army, where he remained for nearly six years, and he later worked as a telegraph operator for a railroad company. He then attended Heilongjiang University, where in 1981 he received a BA in English. After earning an MA in American literature from Shangdong University in 1984, Jin traveled to the United States to work on a PhD at Brandeis University. He intended to return to China, but the Communist Party's violent suppression of the student movement in 1989 made him decide to stay in the United States and write only in English. "It's such a brutal government," he commented. "I was very angry, and I decided not to return to China." "Writing in English became my means of survival," he remarked, "of spending or wasting my life, of retrieving losses, mine, and those of others." Jin has published both poetry and fiction, including the novels Waiting *(1999, National Book Award),* War Trash *(2004, PEN/Faulkner Award),* A Free Life *(2007),* Nanjing Requiem *(2011), and* The Boat Rocker *(2016). His first volume of short fiction,* Ocean of Words *(1996), was drawn from his experience in the People's Liberation Army and won the PEN/Hemingway Award. He teaches creative writing at Boston University.*

Mr. Chiu and his bride were having lunch in the square before Muji Train Station. On the table between them were two bottles of soda spewing out brown foam and two paper boxes of rice and sautéed cucumber and pork. "Let's eat," he said to her, and broke the connected ends of the chopsticks. He picked up a slice of streaky pork and put it into his mouth. As he was chewing, a few crinkles appeared on his thin jaw.

To his right, at another table, two railroad policemen were drinking tea and laughing; it seemed that the stout, middle-aged man was telling a joke to his young comrade, who was tall and of athletic build. Now and again they would steal a glance at Mr. Chiu's table.

The air smelled of rotten melon. A few flies kept buzzing above the couple's lunch. Hundreds of people were rushing around to get on the platform or to catch buses to downtown. Food and fruit vendors were crying for customers in lazy voices. About a dozen young women, representing the local hotels, held up placards which displayed the daily prices and words as large as a palm, like FREE MEALS, AIR-CONDITIONING, and ON THE RIVER. In the center of the square stood a concrete statue of Chairman Mao, at whose feet peasants were napping, their backs on the warm granite and their faces toward the sunny sky. A flock of pigeons perched on the Chairman's raised hand and forearm.

The rice and cucumber tasted good, and Mr. Chiu was eating unhurriedly. His sallow face showed exhaustion. He was glad that the honeymoon was finally over and that he and his bride were heading back for Harbin. During the two weeks' vacation, he had been worried about his liver, because three months ago he had suffered from acute hepatitis; he was afraid he might have a relapse. But he had had no severe symptoms, despite his liver being still big and tender. On the whole he was pleased with his health, which could endure even the strain of a honeymoon; indeed, he was on the course of recovery. He looked at his bride, who took off her wire glasses, kneading the root of her nose with her fingertips. Beads of sweat coated her pale cheeks.

"Are you all right, sweetheart?" he asked. 5

"I have a headache. I didn't sleep well last night."

"Take an aspirin, will you?"

"It's not that serious. Tomorrow is Sunday and I can sleep in. Don't worry."

As they were talking, the stout policeman at the next table stood up and threw a bowl of tea in their direction. Both Mr. Chiu's and his bride's sandals were wet instantly.

"Hooligan!" she said in a low voice.

Mr. Chiu got to his feet and said out loud, "Comrade Policeman, why did you do this?" He stretched out his right foot to show the wet sandal.

"Do what?" the stout man asked huskily, glaring at Mr. Chiu while the young fellow was whistling.

"See, you dumped tea on our feet."

"You're lying. You wet your shoes yourself."

"Comrade Policemen, your duty is to keep order, but you purposely tortured us common citizens. Why violate the law you are supposed to enforce?" As Mr. Chiu was speaking, dozens of people began gathering around.

With a wave of his hand, the man said to the young fellow, "Let's get hold of him!"

They grabbed Mr. Chiu and clamped handcuffs around his wrists. He cried, "You can't do this to me. This is utterly unreasonable."

"Shut up!" The man pulled out his pistol. "You can use your tongue at our headquarters."

The young fellow added, "You're a saboteur, you know that? You're disrupting public order."

The bride was too petrified to say anything coherent. She was a recent college graduate, had majored in fine arts, and had never seen the police make an arrest. All she could say was, "Oh, please, please!"

The policemen were pulling Mr. Chiu, but he refused to go with them, holding the corner of the table and shouting, "We have a train to catch. We already bought the tickets."

The stout man punched him in the chest. "Shut up. Let your ticket expire." With the pistol butt he chopped Mr. Chiu's hands, which at once released the table. Together the two men were dragging him away to the police station.

Realizing he had to go with them, Mr. Chiu turned his head and shouted to his bride, "Don't wait for me here. Take the train. If I'm not back by tomorrow morning, send someone over to get me out."

She nodded, covering her sobbing mouth with her palm.

After removing his belt, they locked Mr. Chiu into a cell in the back of the Railroad Police Station. The single window in the room was blocked by six steel bars; it faced a spacious yard, in which stood a few pines. Beyond the trees, two swings hung from an iron frame, swaying gently in the breeze. Somewhere in the building a cleaver was chopping rhythmically. There must be a kitchen upstairs, Mr. Chiu thought.

He was too exhausted to worry about what they would do to him, so he lay down on the narrow bed and shut his eyes. He wasn't afraid. The Cultural Revolution was over already, and recently the Party had been propagating the idea that all citizens were equal before the law. The police ought to be a law-abiding model for common people. As long as he remained coolheaded and reasoned with them, they probably wouldn't harm him.

Late in the afternoon he was taken to the Interrogation Bureau on the second floor. On his way there, in the stairwell, he ran into the middle-aged policeman who had manhandled him. The man grinned, rolling his bulgy eyes and pointing his fingers at him as if firing a pistol. Egg of a tortoise! Mr. Chiu cursed mentally.

The moment he sat down in the office, he burped, his palm shielding his mouth. In front of him, across a long desk, sat the chief of the bureau and a donkey-faced man. On the glass desktop was a folder containing information on his case. He felt it bizarre that in just a matter of hours they had accumulated a small pile of writing about him. On second thought he began to wonder whether they had kept a file on him all the time. How could this have happened? He lived and worked in Harbin, more than three hundred miles away, and this was his first time in Muji City.

The chief of the bureau was a thin, bald man who looked serene and intelligent. His slim hands handled the written pages in the folder in the manner of a lecturing scholar. To Mr. Chiu's left sat a young scribe, with a clipboard on his knee and a black fountain pen in his hand.

"Your name?" the chief asked, apparently reading out the question from a form.

"Chiu Maguang."

"Age?"

"Thirty-four."

"Profession?"

"Lecturer."

"Work unit?"

"Harbin University."

"Political status?"

"Communist Party member."

The chief put down the paper and began to speak. "Your crime is sabotage, although it hasn't induced serious consequences yet. Because you are a Party member, you should be punished more. You have failed to be a model for the masses and you—"

"Excuse me, sir," Mr. Chiu cut him off.

"What?"

"I didn't do anything. Your men are the saboteurs of our social order. They threw hot tea on my feet and on my wife's feet. Logically speaking, you should criticize them, if not punish them."

"That statement is groundless. You have no witness. Why should I believe you?" the chief said matter-of-factly.

"This is my evidence." He raised his right hand. "Your man hit my fingers with a pistol."

"That doesn't prove how your feet got wet. Besides, you could have hurt your fingers yourself."

"But I am telling the truth!" Anger flared up in Mr. Chiu. "Your police station owes me an apology. My train ticket has expired, my new leather sandals are ruined, and I am late for a conference in the provincial capital. You must compensate me for the damage and losses. Don't mistake me for a common citizen who would tremble when you sneeze. I'm a scholar, a philosopher, and an expert in dialectical materialism. If necessary, we will argue about this in *The Northeastern Daily*, or we will go to the highest People's Court in Beijing. Tell me, what's your name?" He got carried away with his harangue, which was by no means trivial and had worked to his advantage on numerous occasions.

"Stop bluffing us," the donkey-faced man broke in. "We have seen a lot of your kind. We can easily prove you are guilty. Here are some of the statements given by eyewitnesses." He pushed a few sheets of paper toward Mr. Chiu.

Mr. Chiu was dazed to see the different handwritings, which all stated that he had shouted in the square to attract attention and refused to obey the police. One of the witnesses had identified herself as a purchasing agent from a shipyard in Shanghai. Something stirred in Mr. Chiu's stomach, a pain rising to his rib. He gave out a faint moan.

"Now you have to admit you are guilty," the chief said. "Although it's 50
a serious crime, we won't punish you severely, provided you write out a self-criticism and promise that you won't disrupt the public order again. In other words, your release will depend on your attitude toward this crime."

"You're daydreaming," Mr. Chiu cried. "I won't write a word, because I'm innocent. I demand that you provide me with a letter of apology so I can explain to my university why I'm late."

Both the interrogators smiled contemptuously. "Well, we've never done that," said the chief, taking a puff of his cigarette.

"Then make this a precedent."

"That's unnecessary. We are pretty certain that you will comply with our wishes." The chief blew a column of smoke toward Mr. Chiu's face.

At the tilt of the chief's head, two guards stepped forward and 55
grabbed the criminal by the arms. Mr. Chiu meanwhile went on saying, "I shall report you to the Provincial Administration. You'll have to pay for this! You are worse than the Japanese military police."

They dragged him out of the room.

After dinner, which consisted of a bowl of millet porridge, a corn bun, and a piece of pickled turnip, Mr. Chiu began to have a fever, shaking with a chill and sweating profusely. He knew that the fire of anger had gotten into his liver and that he was probably having a relapse. No medicine was available, because his briefcase had been left with his bride. At home it would have been time for him to sit in front of their color TV, drinking jasmine tea and watching the evening news. It was so lonesome in here. The orange bulb above the single bed was the only source of light, which enabled the guards to keep him under surveillance at night. A moment ago he had asked them for a newspaper or a magazine to read, but they turned him down.

Through the small opening on the door noises came in. It seemed that the police on duty were playing cards or chess in a nearby office; shouts and laughter could be heard now and then. Meanwhile, an accordion kept coughing from a remote corner in the building. Looking at the ballpoint and the letter paper left for him by the guards when they took him back from the Interrogation Bureau, Mr. Chiu remembered the old saying, "When a scholar runs into soldiers, the more he argues, the muddier his point becomes." How ridiculous this whole thing was. He ruffled his thick hair with his fingers.

He felt miserable, massaging his stomach continually. To tell the truth, he was more upset than frightened, because he would have to catch up with his work once he was back home—a paper that was due at the printers next week, and two dozen books he ought to read for the courses he was going to teach in the fall.

A human shadow flitted across the opening. Mr. Chiu rushed to the 60
door and shouted through the hole, "Comrade Guard, Comrade Guard!"

"What do you want?" a voice rasped.

"I want you to inform your leaders that I'm very sick. I have heart disease and hepatitis. I may die here if you keep me like this without medication."

"No leader is on duty on the weekend. You have to wait till Monday."

"What? You mean I'll stay in here tomorrow?"

"Yes." 65

"Your station will be held responsible if anything happens to me."

"We know that. Take it easy, you won't die."

It seemed illogical that Mr. Chiu slept quite well that night, though the light above his head had been on all the time and the straw mattress was hard and infested with fleas. He was afraid of ticks, mosquitoes, cockroaches—any kind of insect but fleas and bedbugs. Once, in the countryside, where his school's faculty and staff had helped the peasants harvest crops for a week, his colleagues had joked about his flesh, which they said must have tasted nonhuman to fleas. Except for him, they were all afflicted with hundreds of bites.

More amazing now, he didn't miss his bride a lot. He even enjoyed sleeping alone, perhaps because the honeymoon had tired him out and he needed more rest.

The backyard was quiet on Sunday morning. Pale sunlight streamed 70
through the pine branches. A few sparrows were jumping on the ground, catching caterpillars and ladybugs. Holding the steel bars, Mr. Chiu inhaled the morning air, which smelled meaty. There must have been an eatery or a cooked-meat stand nearby. He reminded himself that he should take this detention with ease. A sentence that Chairman Mao

had written to a hospitalized friend rose in his mind: "Since you are already in here, you may as well stay and make the best of it."

His desire for peace of mind originated in his fear that his hepatitis might get worse. He tried to remain unperturbed. However, he was sure that his liver was swelling up, since the fever still persisted. For a whole day he lay in bed, thinking about his paper on the nature of contradictions. Time and again he was overwhelmed by anger, cursing aloud, "A bunch of thugs!" He swore that once he was out, he would write an article about this experience. He had better find out some of the policemen's names.

It turned out to be a restful day for the most part; he was certain that his university would send somebody to his rescue. All he should do now was remain calm and wait patiently. Sooner or later the police would have to release him, although they had no idea that he might refuse to leave unless they wrote him an apology. Damn those hoodlums, they had ordered more than they could eat!

When he woke up on Monday morning, it was already light. Somewhere a man was moaning; the sound came from the backyard. After a long yawn, and kicking off the tattered blanket, Mr. Chiu climbed out of bed and went to the window. In the middle of the yard, a young man was fastened to a pine, his wrists handcuffed around the trunk from behind. He was wriggling and swearing loudly, but there was no sight of anyone else in the yard. He looked familiar to Mr. Chiu.

Mr. Chiu squinted his eyes to see who it was. To his astonishment, he recognized the man, who was Fenjin, a recent graduate from the Law Department at Harbin University. Two years ago Mr. Chiu had taught a course in Marxist materialism, in which Fenjin had enrolled. Now, how on earth had this young devil landed here?

Then it dawned on him that Fenjin must have been sent over by his bride. What a stupid woman! A bookworm, who only knew how to read foreign novels! He had expected that she would contact the school's Security Section, which would for sure send a cadre here. Fenjin held no official position; he merely worked in a private law firm that had just two lawyers; in fact, they had little business except for some detective work for men and women who suspected their spouses of having extramarital affairs. Mr. Chiu was overcome with a wave of nausea.

Should he call out to let his student know he was nearby? He decided not to, because he didn't know what had happened. Fenjin must have quarreled with the police to incur such a punishment. Yet this could never have occurred if Fenjin hadn't come to his rescue. So no matter what, Mr. Chiu had to do something. But what could he do?

It was going to be a scorcher. He could see purple steam shimmering and rising from the ground among the pines. Poor devil, he thought, as he raised a bowl of corn glue to his mouth, sipped, and took a bite of a piece of salted celery.

When a guard came to collect the bowl and the chopsticks, Mr. Chiu asked him what had happened to the man in the backyard. "He called our boss 'bandit,'" the guard said. "He claimed he was a lawyer or something. An arrogant son of a rabbit."

Now it was obvious to Mr. Chiu that he had to do something to help his rescuer. Before he could figure out a way, a scream broke out in the backyard. He rushed to the window and saw a tall policeman standing before Fenjin, an iron bucket on the ground. It was the same young fellow who had arrested Mr. Chiu in the square two days before. The man pinched Fenjin's nose, then raised his hand, which stayed in the air for a few seconds, then slapped the lawyer across the face. As Fenjin was groaning, the man lifted up the bucket and poured water on his head.

"This will keep you from getting sunstroke, boy. I'll give you some 80
more every hour," the man said loudly.

Fenjin kept his eyes shut, yet his wry face showed that he was struggling to hold back from cursing the policeman, or, more likely, that he was sobbing in silence. He sneezed, then raised his face and shouted, "Let me go take a piss."

"Oh, yeah?" the man bawled. "Pee in your pants."

Still Mr. Chiu didn't make any noise, gripping the steel bars with both hands, his fingers white. The policeman turned and glanced at the cell's window; his pistol, partly holstered, glittered in the sun. With a snort he spat his cigarette butt to the ground and stamped it into the dust.

Then the door opened and the guards motioned Mr. Chiu to come out. Again they took him upstairs to the Interrogation Bureau.

The same men were in the office, though this time the scribe was 85
sitting there empty-handed. At the sight of Mr. Chiu the chief said, "Ah, here you are. Please be seated."

After Mr. Chiu sat down, the chief waved a white silk fan and said to him, "You may have seen your lawyer. He's a young man without manners, so our director had him taught a crash course in the backyard."

"It's illegal to do that. Aren't you afraid to appear in a newspaper?"

"No, we are not, not even on TV. What else can you do? We are not afraid of any story you make up. We call it fiction. What we do care about is that you cooperate with us. That is to say, you must admit your crime."

"What if I refuse to cooperate?"

"Then your lawyer will continue his education in the sunshine." 90

A swoon swayed Mr. Chiu, and he held the arms of the chair to steady himself. A numb pain stung him in the upper stomach and nauseated him, and his head was throbbing. He was sure that the hepatitis was finally attacking him. Anger was flaming up in his chest; his throat was tight and clogged.

The chief resumed, "As a matter of fact, you don't even have to write out your self-criticism. We have your crime described clearly here. All we need is your signature."

Holding back his rage, Mr. Chiu said, "Let me look at that."

With a smirk the donkey-faced man handed him a sheet which carried these words:

> I hereby admit that on July 13 I disrupted public order at Muji Train Station, and that I refused to listen to reason when the railroad police issued their warning. Thus I myself am responsible for my arrest. After two days' detention, I have realized the reactionary nature of my crime. From now on, I shall continue to educate myself with all my effort and shall never commit this kind of crime again.

A voice started screaming in Mr. Chiu's ears, "Lie, lie!" But he shook 95
his head and forced the voice away. He asked the chief, "If I sign this, will you release both my lawyer and me?"

"Of course, we'll do that." The chief was drumming his fingers on the blue folder—their file on him.

Mr. Chiu signed his name and put his thumbprint under his signature.

"Now you are free to go," the chief said with a smile, and handed him a piece of paper to wipe his thumb with.

Mr. Chiu was so sick that he couldn't stand up from the chair at first try. Then he doubled his effort and rose to his feet. He staggered out of the building to meet his lawyer in the backyard, having forgotten to ask for his belt back. In his chest he felt as though there were a bomb. If he were able to, he would have razed the entire police station and eliminated all their families. Though he knew he could do nothing like that, he made up his mind to do something.

"I'm sorry about this torture, Fenjin," Mr. Chiu said when they met. 100

"It doesn't matter. They are savages." The lawyer brushed a patch of dirt off his jacket with trembling fingers. Water was still dribbling from the bottoms of his trouser legs.

"Let's go now," the teacher said.

The moment they came out of the police station, Mr. Chiu caught sight of a tea stand. He grabbed Fenjin's arm and walked over to the old woman at the table. "Two bowls of black tea," he said and handed her a one-yuan note.

After the first bowl, they each had another one. Then they set out for the train station. But before they walked fifty yards, Mr. Chiu insisted on eating a bowl of tree-ear soup at a food stand. Fenjin agreed. He told his teacher, "You mustn't treat me like a guest."

"No, I want to eat something myself." 105

As if dying of hunger, Mr. Chiu dragged his lawyer from restaurant to restaurant near the police station, but at each place he ordered no more than two bowls of food. Fenjin wondered why his teacher wouldn't stay at one place and eat his fill.

Mr. Chiu bought noodles, wonton, eight-grain porridge, and chicken soup, respectively, at four restaurants. While eating, he kept saying through his teeth, "If only I could kill all the bastards!" At the last place he merely took a few sips of the soup without tasting the chicken cubes and mushrooms.

Fenjin was baffled by his teacher, who looked ferocious and muttered to himself mysteriously, and whose jaundiced face was covered with dark puckers. For the first time Fenjin thought of Mr. Chiu as an ugly man.

Within a month over eight hundred people contracted acute hepatitis in Muji. Six died of the disease, including two children. Nobody knew how the epidemic had started.

ANTIGUA

Jamaica Kincaid

Girl 1983

Jamaica Kincaid

Jamaica Kincaid was born Elaine Potter Richardson in 1949 in St. John's, capital of the West Indian island nation of Antigua and Barbuda (she adopted the name Jamaica Kincaid in 1973 because of her family's disapproval of her writing). In 1965 she was sent to Westchester County, New York, to work as an au pair (or "servant," as she prefers to describe it). She attended Franconia College in New Hampshire, but did not complete a degree. Kincaid worked as a staff writer for the New Yorker for nearly twenty years; Talk Stories *(2001) is a collection of seventy-seven short pieces that she wrote for the magazine. She won wide attention for* At the Bottom of the River *(1983), the volume of her stories that includes "Girl." In 1985 she published* Annie John, *an interlocking cycle of short stories about growing up in Antigua.* Lucy *(1990) was her first novel; it was followed by* The Autobiography of My Mother *(1996) and* Mr. Potter *(2002), novels inspired by the lives of her parents. Kincaid is also the author of* A Small Place *(1988), a memoir of her homeland and meditation on the destructiveness of colonialism, and* My Brother *(1997), a reminiscence of her brother Devon, who died of AIDS at thirty-three. Her recent works include a travel book titled* Among Flowers: A Walk in the Himalaya *(2005) and a novel,* See Now Then *(2013). A naturalized US citizen, Kincaid has said of her adopted country: "It's given me a place to be myself—but myself as I was formed somewhere else."*

Wash the white clothes on Monday and put them on the stone heap; wash the color clothes on Tuesday and put them on the clothesline to dry; don't walk barehead in the hot sun; cook pumpkin fritters in very hot sweet oil; soak your little cloths right after you take them off; when buying cotton to make yourself a nice blouse, be sure that it doesn't have gum on it, because that way it won't hold up well after a wash; soak salt fish overnight before you cook it; is it true that you sing benna° in Sunday school?; always eat your food in such a way that it won't turn someone else's stomach; on Sundays try to walk like a lady and not like the slut you are so bent on becoming; don't sing benna in Sunday school; you mustn't speak to wharf-rat boys, not even to give directions; don't eat fruits on the street—flies will follow you; *but I don't sing benna on Sundays at all and never in Sunday school*; this is how to sew on a button; this is how to make a buttonhole for the button you have just sewed on; this is how to hem a dress when you see the hem coming down and so to prevent yourself from looking like the slut I know you are so bent on becoming; this is how you iron your father's khaki shirt so that it doesn't have a crease; this is how you iron your father's khaki pants so that they don't have a crease; this is how you grow okra—far from the house, because okra tree harbors red ants; when you are growing dasheen, make sure it gets plenty of water or else it makes your throat itch when you are eating it; this is how you sweep a corner; this is how you sweep a whole house; this is how you sweep a yard; this is how you smile to someone you don't like too much; this is how you smile to someone you don't like at all; this is how you smile to someone you like completely; this is how you set a table for tea; this is how you set a table for dinner; this is how you set a table for dinner with an important guest; this is how you set a table for lunch; this is how you set a table for breakfast; this is how to behave in the presence of men who don't know you very well, and this way they won't recognize immediately the slut I have warned you against becoming; be sure to wash every day, even if it is with your own spit; don't squat down to play marbles—you are not a boy, you know; don't pick people's flowers—you might catch something; don't throw stones at blackbirds, because it might not be a blackbird at all; this is how to make a bread pudding; this is how to make doukona°; this is how to make pepper pot; this is how to make a good medicine for a cold; this is how to make a good medicine to throw away a child before it even becomes a child; this is how to catch a fish; this is how to throw back a fish you don't like, and that way something bad won't fall on you; this is how to bully a man; this is how a man bullies you; this is how to love a man, and if this doesn't work there are other ways, and if they don't work don't feel too bad about giving up; this is how to spit up in the air if you feel like it, and this is how to move quick so that it doesn't fall on you; this is how to make ends meet; always squeeze bread to make sure it's fresh; *but what if the baker won't let me feel the bread?*; you mean to say that after all you are really going to be the kind of woman who the baker won't let near the bread?

benna: Kincaid defined this word, for two editors who inquired, as meaning "songs of the sort your parents didn't want you to sing, at first calypso and later rock and roll" (quoted by Sylvan Barnet and Marcia Stubbs, *The Little Brown Reader*, 2nd ed. [Boston: Little, 1980] 74). *doukona:* a pudding made from sweet potato, coconut, and spices.

EGYPT

Naguib Mahfouz

The Lawsuit 1989

Translated by Denys Johnson-Davies

Naguib Mahfouz

Naguib Mahfouz (1911–2006) was born in Cairo, Egypt, where he spent his entire life and which served as the setting for his thirty-four novels and fourteen collections of short stories. His father was a civil servant, a path that Mahfouz himself would follow, spending most of his career in the Ministry of Culture. Mahfouz graduated from Cairo University in 1934 with a degree in philosophy but abandoned his post-graduate studies to pursue writing, concentrating so intently on this goal that he even deferred marriage until 1943. Prose fiction was a relatively new genre in Arabic literature, and Mahfouz—who had read and admired many Western novelists, including Melville, Dostoevsky, Balzac, and Camus—was enormously influential in modernizing its language, techniques, and subject matter. He planned a sequence of novels telling the entire history of Egypt, but after writing three novels set in the time of the Pharaohs he abandoned this project in favor of contemporary settings. Among his most important works are The Cairo Trilogy *(which includes* Palace Walk, Palace of Desire, Sugar Street, *1956–1957), depicting three generations of a middle-class Cairo family, and* Children of Gebelawi *(1959), an allegorical treatment of the development of Judaism, Christianity, and Islam. Considered blasphemous, this novel has not been published in the Arabic world, except in Lebanon. Mahfouz further alienated Islamic fundamentalists through his condemnation of the fatwa against Salman Rushdie for* The Satanic Verses *in 1989. Although Mahfouz regarded Rushdie's novel as offensive, he supported the author's freedom of expression. As a result of defending Rushdie, Mahfouz was stabbed in the neck by an Islamic fundamentalist. He recovered, but was left with permanent nerve damage that impaired his ability to write. In 1988 Mahfouz became the first Arabic writer to win the Nobel Prize in Literature. Though the award had little effect on his modest lifestyle, it had an immense impact on his literary fortunes: previously almost unknown outside the Arab world, he became a widely translated author with an international reputation.*

I found myself suddenly the subject of a lawsuit. My father's widow was demanding maintenance. Awakened from the depths of time, the past with its memories had invaded me. After reading the petition I exclaimed, "When did she go broke? Has she in her turn been robbed?"

"This woman robbed us and deprived us of our legal rights," I said to my lawyer.

I felt a strong desire to see her, not through any temptation to gloat over her but in order to see what effects time had had upon her. Today, like me, she was in her forties. Had her beauty withstood the passage of time? Was it holding out against poverty? If the lawsuit was not genuine, would she have stretched out a demanding hand to one of her enemies? On the other hand, if it was specious, why had she not stretched out her hand before? What a ravishing beauty she had been!

"My father married her," I told the lawyer, "when he was in his middle fifties and she a girl of twenty." A semiliterate, old-fashioned contractor, he did not deal with banks but stored his profits away in a large cupboard in his bedroom. We were happy about this so long as we were a single family. The announcement of the new marriage was like a bomb exploding among us—my mother, my elder brother, and myself, as well as my sisters in their various homes. The top floor was given over to my father, the bride, and the cupboard. We were struck dumb by her youth and beauty. My mother said in a quavering voice choked with weeping, "What a catastrophe! We'll end up without a bean."

5 My elder brother was illiterate and mentally retarded. He was without work, but considered himself a landowner. He flared up in a rage, declaring, "I'll defend myself to the very death."

Some of our relatives advised us to consult a lawyer, but my father threatened my mother with divorce if we were to entertain any such move. "I'm not gullible or an idiot, and no one's rights will be lost."

I was the one least affected by the disaster, partly because of my youth and partly because I was the only one in the family who wanted to study, hoping to enter the engineering college. Yet even so, I did not miss the significance of the facts—my father's age and that of his beautiful bride, and the fortune under threat. By way of smoothing things over, I would say, "I have confidence in my father."

"If we say nothing," my brother would say, "we'll find the cupboard empty."

I shared his fears but affected outwardly what I did not feel inwardly. All the time I felt that our oasis, which had appeared so tranquil, was being subjected to a wild wind and that on the horizon black clouds were gathering. My mother took refuge in silent anxiety, with each new day giving her warning of a bad outcome. As for my elder brother, he would brave the lion in his lair, pleading with his father. "I am the firstborn, uneducated as you can see, and without means of support, so give me my share."

10 "Do you want to inherit from me while I'm still alive? It's a disgrace for you to doubt me—no one's rights will be lost." But my brother would not calm down and would pester my father whenever they met. He would hurl threats at him from behind his back, and my mother would say that she was more worried about my brother than she was about the fortune.

For my part, I wondered whether my father, that capable master of his trade, the man who was such a meticulous accountant despite his illiteracy, would meet defeat at the hands of a pretty girl. Yet, without doubt, he was changing, slipping down little by little each day. He would take himself off to the Turkish baths twice a month, would clip his beard and trim his mustache every week, and would strut about in new clothes. Finally he took to dyeing his hair. Precious gifts embellished the bride's neck, bosom, and arms. Now there was a Chevrolet and a chauffeur waiting in front of our house.

My brother became more and more angry. "Where did he get her from?" he would say to me. Was it so impossible that she might get hold of the key and find her way to opening the cupboard? Would she not take from him something to secure her future? Did she not have the power to make him happy or to turn his life into one of misery and turmoil as she wished?

Arguments would develop between my brother and my father that would go beyond the bounds of propriety. My father would grow angry and spit in my brother's face. In an explosive outburst, my brother seized hold of a table lamp and hurled it at his father, drawing blood. Seeing the blood, my brother was scared, but even so persevered in his attempts to do Father in, with the cook and the chauffeur intervening. My father insisted on informing the police, and my brother was taken off to court and from there to prison, where he died after a year.

"How did she find the courage to bring her case?" I asked the lawyer.

"Necessity has its own rules."

In the midst of our alarm and our mourning for my brother, my mother and I heard the noise of something striking the floor above us. We hurried upstairs and found ourselves standing aghast over my father's body. As is usual in such circumstances, we asked ourselves again and again what could have happened, but no amount of questioning can bring back the dead. It seems that he had had a paralyzing stroke a whole day before his death without our knowing.

We waited till he had been buried and the rites of mourning were over, and then the family gathered together. My sisters, their husbands, and their husbands' parents were there, and the lawyer was present as well. We asked about the key to the cupboard, and the young widow answered quite simply that she knew nothing about it. Sometimes the mind boggles at the sheer brazenness of lying. But what could be done? We then came across the key, and the cupboard finally divulged its secrets, exhibiting to us with profound mockery a bundle of notes that did not exceed five thousand pounds. "Then where is the man's fortune?" everyone called out.

All eyes were fixed on the beautiful widow, who answered defiantly. We had recourse to the police, and there were investigations and searches. As my mother had predicted, we came out of it all "without a bean." The beautiful widow went off to her parents' house, and the curtain was brought down upon her and the inheritance. My mother died. I got a job, married, and achieved a notable success. I became oblivious of the past until the lawsuit brought me back to it.

"It's really the height of irony," I said to the lawyer, "that I should be required to pay maintenance to that woman."

His voice came to me from between the files on his desk. "The old story does on the face of it appear worthy of being put forward, but what's the point of unearthing it when we have no evidence against her?"

"Even if the old story may not be open for discussion, it's a good starting point, whose effect should not be underrated."

"On the contrary, we would be providing the woman's lawyer with the chance to take the offensive and to attract sympathy for her."

"Sympathy?"

"Steady now. Let's think about it a bit objectively. An old man hoards his wealth in a cupboard in his bedroom. He then buys himself a beautiful girl of twenty when he's a man of fifty-five. Such and such happens to his family and such and such to his beautiful wife. Fine, who was to blame?" He was silent for a while, scowling, then continued. "Let's look at it from your side. You're a man who's earning and has a family, and the cost of living is unbearably high, and so on and so forth. . . . Let's content ourselves by settling on a reasonable sum for maintenance."

"Too bad!" I muttered. "She robbed us; then there was the death of my brother and my mother's distress."

"I'm sorry about that, but she's as much a victim as you are. Even the fortune she made off with brought her to disaster. And now here she is begging."

Prompted by casual curiosity, I said, "It's as though you know something about her."

He shook his head with diplomatic vagueness. "A woman who couldn't have children, she was married and divorced several times when she was in her prime. In middle age she fell in love with a student, who, in his turn, robbed her and went off."

He did not divulge the sources of his information, but I surmised the logical progression of events. I experienced a feeling of gratification, which a sense of decency prevented me from showing.

On the day of the court session, I was again seized by a mysterious desire to set eyes on her. I recognized her as she waited in front of the lawyers' room. I knew her by conjecture before actually recognizing her, for the beauty that had made away with our fortune and ruined us had completely vanished. She was fat, excessively and unacceptably so, and the charming freshness had leaked away from her face. What little beauty was left seemed insipid. A veneer of perpetual dejection acted like a screen between her and other people. Without giving the matter any thought, I went up to her, inclined my head in greeting, and said, "I remember you . . . perhaps you remember me?"

At first she gazed at me in surprise, then in confusion. She returned the greeting with a gesture of her covered head. "I'm sorry to cause you trouble," she said, as though apologizing, "but I am forced to do so."

I forgot what I wanted to say. In fact words failed me, and I felt an inner peace. "Don't worry—let the Lord do as He wills." I quietly moved away as I said to myself, "Why not? Even a farce must continue right to the final act."

INDIA

Bharati Mukherjee

Saints 1985

Bharati Mukherjee

Bharati Mukherjee (1940–2017) spent her earliest years in Calcutta, raised in a large family compound of nearly fifty relatives, which was financially supported by her father, the proprietor of a thriving pharmaceutical company. When Mukherjee was eight, the family traveled abroad, and she received her education for three years in England and Switzerland. Upon return to Calcutta, Mukherjee was placed in a Roman Catholic school run by Irish nuns. She later studied English at the University of Calcutta and earned a master's degree from the University of Baroda. In the early 1960s, she came to the United States to study in the prestigious writing program at the University of Iowa. Mukherjee wrote eight novels, including The Tiger's Daughter *(1971),* Jasmine *(1989),* Desirable Daughters *(2002), and* Miss New India *(2011), as well as a memoir and three books of nonfiction. A short story collection,* The Middleman and Other Stories *(1988), won the National Book Critics Circle Award. Mukherjee taught at several universities in Canada and the United States, most notably the University of California at Berkeley, where she joined the English department in 1989. Although India was Mukherjee's home country into adulthood, she had intimate, firsthand knowledge of the immigrant experience—moving from India to Europe to America to Canada and back to America. The challenge of immigrant life—which she called "the epic narrative of this millennium"—was the primary subject of her strongest fiction. In a* Boston Globe *interview upon the publication of* The Holder of the World *(1993; a retelling of Hawthorne's* The Scarlet Letter*), Mukherjee said: "While I have changed in my 30 years in this country, it has also had to change because of the hundreds of thousands of people like me, forcing the culture, moment by moment, into something new. I am looking for that new, constantly evolving thing."*

"And one more thing," Mom says. "Your father can't take you this August."

I can tell from the way she fusses with the placemats that she is interested in my reaction. The placemats are made of pinkish linen and I can see a couple of ironing marks, like shiny little arches. Wayne is coming for dinner. Wayne Latta is her new friend. It's the first time she's having him over with others, but that's not why she's nervous.

"That's okay," I tell her. "Tran and I have plans for the summer."

Mom rolls up the spray-starched napkins and knots them until they look like nesting birds on each dinner plate. "It isn't that he's really busy," she says. She gives me one of her I-know-you-are-hurting, son, looks. "I don't see why he can't take you. He says he has a conference to go to in Hong Kong at the end of July, so he might as well do China in August."

"It's okay. Really," I say. It's true, I am okay. At fifteen I'm too old to 5
be a pawn between them, and too young to get caught in problems of my own. I'm in a state of grace. I want to get to my room in this state of grace before it disintegrates, and start a new game of "Geopolitique 1990" on the Apple II-Plus Dad gave me last Christmas.

"Can you get the flower holders, Shawn?" Mom asks.

I take a wide, flat cardboard box out of the buffet.

She lifts eight tiny glass holders out of the box, and lines them up in the center of the table. She hasn't used them since things started going bad between Dad and her. When things blew up, they sold the big house in New Jersey and Mom and I moved to this college town in upstate New York. Mom works in the Admissions Office. Wayne calls it a college for rich bitches who were too dumb to get into Bennington or Barnard.

"Get me a pitcher of water and the flowers," Mom says.

In a dented aluminum pot in the kitchen sink, eight yellow rosebuds 10
are soaking up water. Granules of sugar are whitish and still sludgy in the bottom of the pot. Mom's a believer; she's read somewhere that sugar in lukewarm water keeps cut flowers fresh. I move the pot to one side and fill a quart-sized measuring cup with lukewarm water. I know her routines.

It's going to be an anxious evening for Mom. She's set out extra goblets for spritzers on a tray lined with paper towels. Index cards typed up with recipes for dips and sauces are stacked on the windowsill. She shouldn't do sauces, nothing that requires last-minute frying and stirring. She's the flustery type, and she's only setting herself up for failure.

"What happened to the water, Shawn?"

It's a Pizza Hut night for me, definitely. I know what she's going through with Wayne. He's not at all like Dad, the good Dr. Manny Patel, who soothes crazies at Creedmore all day. Nights he's a playboy and slum landlord, Mom says.

Mom says, "Your father will call you tomorrow, he said. He wants to talk to you himself. He wants to know what you want this Christmas."

This is only the first Thursday in November. Dad's planning ahead is a joke with us. Foresight is what got him out of Delhi to New York. "Could I have become a psychiatrist and a near-millionaire if I hadn't planned well ahead?" Dad used to tell Mom in the medium-bad days.

Mom thinks making a million is a vicious, selfish aim. But Dad's really very generous. He sends money to relatives and to Indian orphanages. He's generous but practical. He says he doesn't want to send me stuff—cashmere sweaters and Ultrasuede jackets, the stuff he likes—that'll end up in basement cedar closets.

"I'll be late tomorrow," I remind Mom. "Fridays I have my chess club."

Actually, Tran and I and a bunch of other guys from the chess club play four afternoons a week. Thursdays we don't play because Tran has Debate Workshop.

"You know what I want, Mom. You can tell him."

I ask for computer games, video cassettes, nothing major. So twice a year Dad sends big checks. Dad's real generous with me. It makes him feel the big benefactor, Mom says, whenever a check comes in the mail. But that's only because things went really bad two years ago. They sent me away to boarding school, but they still couldn't work things out between them.

At five, Wayne comes into our driveway in his blue Toyota pickup. The wheels squeal and rock in the deep, snowy ruts. Wayne has a cord of firewood in the back of the truck. Mom paid him for the firewood yesterday and for the time he put in picking up the cord from some French guy in Ballston Spa. Wayne's a writer; meantime he works as a janitor in the college. A "mopologist" is what he calls himself. It's so corny, but every time Wayne uses that word, Mom gives him a tinkly, supportive laugh. Janitors are more caring than shrinks, the laugh seems to say.

We hear Wayne on the back porch, cursing as he drops an armload of logs. For all his muscles, he's a clumsy man. But then Mom could never have gotten Dad to carry the logs himself. Dad would have had them delivered or done without them.

Mom takes five-dollar bills out of the buffet drawer and counts out thirty dollars. "For the wine, would you give it to him? I couldn't do a production all by myself on a weeknight."

"Why do a production at all?"

She stiffens. "I'm not ashamed of Wayne," she says. "Wayne is who he is.

Wayne finally comes into the dining room. I slip him the money: it's more than he expected. "I got some beer too, Mila." Mom's name is Camille but he calls her Mila. That's a hard thing to get used to. He drops my rucksack on the floor, turns the chair around and straddles it. There are five other chairs around the table and two folding chairs brought up from the basement for tonight. Under Wayne's muscular thighs, the dining room chair looks rickety, absurdly elegant. Red longjohns show through the knee rips of his blue jeans. He keeps his red knit cap on. But he's not as tough as he looks. He keeps the cap on because he's sensitive about his bald, baby-pink head.

"Hey, Shawn," he says to me. "Still baking the competition?"

It's Wayne's usual joke about my playing competitive chess. Our school team has T-shirts that we paid for by working the concession stands on basketball nights last winter. Tran plays varsity first board, I play third. Now we need chess cheerleaders, Wayne kids me. *"Hey, hey, push that pawn! Dee-fense, dee-fense. King's Indian dee-fense!"* Wayne isn't a bad sort, not for around here. Last year we went for trout out on the Battenkill. The day with Wayne wasn't bad, given our complicated situation. I went back to the creek with Tran a week later, but it was different. Tran's idea of fishing is throwing a net across the river, tossing in a stick of dynamite, then pulling it up.

"You'll like Milos and Verna," Mom tells Wayne. "They're both painters in the Art Department. From Yugoslavia, but I think they're hoping to stay in the States."

From the soft, nervous look she's giving Wayne, I know it isn't the Yugoslavs she's thinking of right at the moment. Wayne grabs her throat in his thick hairy hands. She lifts her face. Then she glances at me in a quick guilty way as if she's already given away too much.

I know about feelings. I've got a secret life, too.

"D'you have enough for a pizza?" Mom asks me. She's moved away from Wayne.

Yeah, I have enough.

From the Pizza Hut, Tran and I go back to Tran's place. Tran's sixteen and he owns a noisy used Plymouth. It's two-tone, white and aquamarine. I like the colors. Tran's a genuine boatperson. When he was younger, the English teacher made him tell the class about having to hide from pirates and having to chew on raw fish just to stay alive. Women on his boat hid any valuable stuff they had in their vaginas. "That's enough, Tran, thank you," the teacher said. Now he never mentions his cruise to America.

We skid to a stop inside the Indian Lookout Point Trailer Park where he lives with his mother in a flash of aqua. The lights are on in Tran's mobile home. Tran's mother's muddy Chevy and his stepfather's Dodge Ram are angle-parked. Tran's real father got left behind in Saigon.

"I don't know," Tran says. He doesn't cut the engine. We sit in the warm, dark car. "Maybe we ought to go on to your place. He never gets home this early."

It's minus ten outside, maybe worse with the wind-chill factor. I open the car door softly. The car light on Tran's face makes his face look ochre-dingy, mottled with pimples.

"Mom's entertaining tonight," I warn him. The snow is slippery cold under my Adidas. I pick my way through icy patches to the trailer, and look in a little front window.

Tran's mom is at the kitchen sink, washing a glass. She's still wearing her wool coat and plaid scarf. Her face has an odd puffy quiver. There are no signs of physical violence, but someone's sure been hurt. Tran's stepfather (he didn't, and can't, adopt Tran until some agency can locate Tran's real father, and get his consent) is sitting hunched forward in a rocker, and drinking Miller Lite.

Like Tran, I've learned to discount homey scenes.

"That's okay," Tran says. He's calling out from the car. His sad face is in the opened window. "Your place is bigger."

It makes sense, but I can't move away from his little window.

"I can show you a move that'll bake Sato," he says. "I mean really bake his ass."

We both hate Sato but Sato isn't smart enough to wince under our hate or even smart enough to know when his ass has really been baked.

"Okay." There's that new killer chess move, and a new Peter Gabriel for us to listen to. Tran's chess rating is just under 1900. Farelli's is higher, but Farelli is more than arrogant. He's so arrogant he dropped off the team. He goes down to Manhattan instead and hustles games in Times Square or in the chess clubs. Tran's a little guilty about playing first board; he knows he owes it to Farelli's vanity. The difference between Farelli and Tran is about the same as between Tran and me. Farelli wants to charge the club four-fifty an hour for tutoring. He's the only real American in the club. The rest of us have names like Sato, Chin, Duoc, Cho and Prasad. My name's Patel, Shawn Patel. Mom took back her maiden name, Belliveau, when we moved out of Upper Montclair. We're supposed to be out of Dad's reach here, except for checks.

A week after Mom's dinner party, Tran and I are coming out of an arcade on Upper Broadway Street when we see Wayne walking our way. Upper Broadway's short and squat. The storefronts have shallow doorways you can't hide in. Wayne is with the Yugoslav woman, the painter who doesn't intend to go back to her country. They aren't holding hands or anything, they aren't even touching shoulders, but I can tell they want to do things. The Yugoslav has both her hands in the pockets of her duffle coat. A toggle at her throat is missing and the loop has nothing to weigh it down. The Yugoslav has red cheeks. With her red cheeks, her button nose and her long, loose hair, she looks very young. Maybe it's a trick of afternoon light or of European make-up, but she looks too young to be a friend of Mom's.

Wayne wants to hug her. I can tell from the way he arches his upper body inside his coat. He wants to sneak his hand into her pocket, pull out her fist, swing hands on Upper Broadway and be stared at by everyone.

I pull Tran back inside the arcade.

"I got to get to Houston," Tran says. We're playing "Joust," his favorite game, but his slight body is twisted in misery.

"It'll work out," I tell him. Wanting to go to Houston has to do with his mother and stepfather. Things always go bad between parents. "You can't leave in the middle of the semester. It doesn't make sense."

"What does?"

Tran has an older brother in Houston, in engineering school. Tran thinks his mother will come up with the bus fare south. She works at Grand Union, and weekends she waitresses. "My luck's got to change," he says.

Luck has nothing to do with anything, I want to say. You're out of the clutch of pirates now. No safe hiding places.

Wayne and his painter make us spend too many tokens on this Joust machine.

Mom's in the eating nook of the kitchen, reading a book on English gardens when I come in the back door. She's wearing a long skirt made of quilted fabric and a matching jacket. The quilting makes her look fat, and ridiculous.

She catches my grin. "It's warm, don't knock it," she says of her skirt. These upstate houses are drafty. Then she pulls her feet up under her and wriggles her raised knees gracelessly under the long skirt. "And I love the color on me."

I bleed. Mom should have had a daughter. Two women could have consoled each other. I can only think of Wayne, how even now he's slipping the loops over Serbian toggles. It's a complicated feeling. I bleed because I'm disloyal.

"Your father's sent a present by UPS," she says. She doesn't look up from the illustration of a formal garden of a lord. A garden with a stiff, bristly hedged maze to excite desire and contain it. "I put the package on your desk upstairs. It looks like a book."

She means to say, Dad's presents are always impersonal.

Actually it's two books that Dad has sent me this time. The thick, heavy one is an art book, reproductions of Moghul paintings that Dad loves. Even India was once an empire-building nation. The other is a thin book with bad binding put out by a religious printing house in Madras. The little book is about a Hindu saint who had visions. Dad has sent me a book about visions.

May this book bring you as much happiness as it did me when I was your age, Dad's inscription reads. Then a p.s. *The saint died of throat cancer and was briefly treated by your great-uncle, the cancer specialist in Calcutta.*

Forty pages into the book, the saint describes a vision. "I see the Divine Mother in all things." He sees Her in ants, dogs, flowers, the latrine bowls in the temple. He keeps falling into trances as he goes for walks or as he says his prayers. In this perfect state, sometimes the saint kicks his disciples. He eats garbage thrown out by temple cooks for cows and pariah dogs.

"Did I kick you?" the saint asks when he comes out of his trance. "Kick, kick," beg the disciples as they push each other to get near enough for a saintly touch.

My father, healer of derangements, slum landlord with income properties on two continents, believer of visions, pleasure-taker where none seems present, is a mystery.

Downstairs Mom is dialing Wayne's number. In the whir of the tele- 65
phone dial, I read the new rhythms of her agony. Wayne will not answer his phone tonight. Wayne is in bed with his naked Yugoslav.

It's my turn to call. I slip my bony finger into the dial's fingerholes. "Want to ball?" I whisper into the mouthpiece. My throat is raspy from the fullness of desire.

"What?" It's a girlish voice at the other end. "What did you say?"

The girl giggles. "You dumb pervert." She leaves it to me to hang up first.

The next night, a Friday night, Tran and I come down from my room to get Mountain Dew out of the fridge. Mom and Wayne are making out in the kitchen. He has her jammed up against the eating nook's wall. There are Indian paintings on that wall. She kept the paintings and gave Dad the statues and framed batiks. Wayne holds Mom's head against dusty glass, behind which an emperor in Moghul battledress is leading his army out of the capital. Wayne's got his knee high up Mom's quilted skirt. The knee presses in, hard. I see love's monstrous force bloat her face. Wayne has her head in his grasp. Her orange hair tufts out between his knuckles, and its orange mist covers the bygone emperor and his soldiers.

Tran's used to living in small, usurped spaces. He drops a shy, civil 70
little cough, and right away Wayne lets go of Mom's hair. But his knee is still raised, still pressing into her skirt.

"Get outta here, guys," he says. He looks pleased, he sounds good-natured. "You got better things to do. Go push your pawns."

"Tell her about the painter," I say. My voice is even, not emotional.

"What're you talking about? What's the matter with you?"

Tran says, "Let's get the soda, Shawn." He picks up the six-pack and two glasses and pushes me toward the stairwell.

Upstairs, Tran and I take turns dialing the town's other insomniacs. 75
"Do you have soft breasts?" I ask. I really want to know. "Yes," one of them confesses. "Very soft and very white and I'm so lonely tonight. Do you want to touch?"

Tran reads aloud an episode from the life of the Hindu saint. Reaching the state of perfection while strolling along the Ganges one day, the saint fell and broke his arm. The saint had been thinking of his love for the young boy followers who lived in the temple. He had been thinking of his love for them—love as for a sweetheart, he says—when he slipped into a trance and stumbled. Love and pain: in the saint's mind there is no separation.

Trans makes the last of our calls for the night. "You bitch," he says as he shakes his thin body in a parody of undulation. To me he says, "Mother won't come through with the bus fare to Houston."

Tonight Tran wants to sleep over in my room. Tomorrow we'll find a way to raise the bus fare.

I want to tell him things, to console him. Bad luck and good luck even out over a lifetime. Cancer can ravage an ecstatic saint. Things pass. I don't remember Dad in any intimate way except that he embarrassed me when he came to pick me up from my old boarding school. The overstated black Mercedes, the hugging and kissing in such a foreign way.

A little before midnight, Tran's moan startles me awake. He must be dreaming of fathers, pirates, saints and Houston. For me the worst isn't dreams. It's having to get out of the house at night and walk around. At midnight I float like a ghost through other people's gardens. I peer into other boys' bedrooms, I become somebody else's son.

Tonight I'm more restless than other nights. I look for an Indian name in the phone book. The directory in our upstate town is thin; it caves against my eager arms. The first name I spot is Batliwalla. Meaning perhaps bottle-walla, a dealer in bottles in the ancestral long-ago. Batliwalla, Jamshed S., M.D.

I dress in the dark for a night of cold roaming. It'll be a night of walking in a state of perfect grace. For disguise, I choose Mom's red cloth coat from the hall cupboard and her large red wool beret into which she has stuck a pheasant feather. She keeps five more feathers, like a bouquet, in a candy jar. The feathers are from Wayne the hunter. Wayne's promised to put a pheasant on our table for Thanksgiving dinner. I can taste its hard, stringy birdflesh and pellets of buckshot.

Like the Hindu saint, I walk my world in boots and a trance. But in this upstate town the only body of water is an icy creek, not the Ganges.

The Batliwallas have no curtains on their back windows. I look into a back bedroom that glows from a bedside lamp. A kid in pajamas is sitting up in bed, a book in his hands. He's a little kid, a junior high kid, or maybe a studious dwarf. The dwarfkid rocks back and forth under his bedclothes. He seems to be learning something, maybe a poem, by heart. He's the conqueror of alien syllables. His fleshy, brown lips purse and pout ferociously. His tiny head in its helmet of glossy black hair bumps, bumps, bumps the bed's white vinyl headboard. The dwarfkid's eyes are screwed tightly shut, and his long eyelashes look like tiny troughs for ghosts to drink out of. Wanting good grades, the dwarfkid studies into the night. He rocks, he shouts, he bumps his head. I can't hear the words, but I want to reach out to a fellow saint.

When I get home, the back porch is dark but the kitchen light is on. I sit on the stack of firewood and look in. I'm not cold, or sleepy. Wayne and Mom are fighting in the kitchen, literally slugging each other. I had Wayne figured wrong. He isn't the sly operator after all. He's opened up my Mom's upper lip. It's blood Mom is washing off.

"Get out," Mom screams at him. This time I can make out all the words. I feel like a god, overseeing lives.

The faucet is running as it had done the day there were yellow rosebuds in a kitchen pot. Steam from the hot, running water frizzes Mom's hair. She looks old. "Get out of my house."

"I'm getting out." Wayne says. But he doesn't leave. First he lights a cigarette, something Mom doesn't permit. Then he flops down on one of the two kitchen stools, props his work boots on the other and starts to adjust the laces. "I wouldn't stay if you begged me."

"Get out, out!" Mom's still screaming as I turn my house key in the lock. She might as well know it all. "Do me a favor, get out. Lace your goddamn boots in your goddamn truck. Please get out."

I move through the bright kitchen into the dark dining room, and wait for the lovers to finish.

In a while Wayne leaves. He doesn't slam the door. He doesn't toss the key on the floor. The pickup's low beams dance on frozen bushes.

"My god, Shawn! "Mom has switched on a wall light in the dining room. She's staring at me, she's really looking at me. Finally. "My god, what have you done to your face, poor baby."

Her fingers scrape at the muck on my face, the cheek-blush, lipstick, eyeshadow. Her bruised mouth is on my hair. I can feel her warm, wet sobs, but I don't hurt. I am in a trance in the middle of a November night. I can't hurt for me, for Dad, I can't hurt for anyone in the world. I feel so strong, so much a potentate in battledress.

How wondrous to be a visionary. If I were to touch someone now, I'd be touching god.

9 STORIES FOR FURTHER READING

Sherman Alexie

This Is What It Means to Say Phoenix, Arizona 1993

Sherman Alexie

Sherman Alexie was born in 1966 on the Spokane Indian Reservation in Wellpinit, Washington. Hydrocephalic at birth, he underwent surgery at the age of six months. At first he was expected not to survive; when that prognosis proved wrong, it was predicted, again wrongly, that he would be severely mentally disabled. Alexie attended Gonzaga University in Spokane and graduated from Washington State University with a degree in American studies. His first book, a collection of poems called The Business of Fancydancing, *appeared in 1991, and he has published prolifically since then, averaging a book a year. He is the author of several volumes of poetry as well as four collections of stories—*The Lone Ranger and Tonto Fistfight in Heaven *(1993),* The Toughest Indian in the World *(2000),* Ten Little Indians *(2003), and* War Dances *(2009), which won the PEN/Faulkner Award, and* Blasphemy *(2012)—and three novels—*Reservation Blues *(1995),* Indian Killer *(1996), and* Flight *(2007), and the semi-autobiographical novel depicting his adolescent years,* The Absolutely True Diary of a Part-Time Indian *(2007), which won a National Book Award. A memoir of his childhood,* You Don't Have to Say You Love Me, *appeared in 2017. In addition to his writing, Alexie won the World Heavyweight Poetry Bout competition an unprecedented four consecutive times (1998–2001); he has appeared on television discussion programs hosted by Bill Maher, Bill Moyers, and Jim Lehrer (a 1998 "Dialogue on Race" whose participants also included President Bill Clinton); he has performed frequently as a stand-up comedian; and he co-produced and wrote the 1998 feature film* Smoke Signals, *based on "This Is What It Means to Say Phoenix, Arizona." Alexie lives with his wife and two sons in Seattle, Washington.*

Just after Victor lost his job at the BIA,° he also found out that his father had died of a heart attack in Phoenix, Arizona. Victor hadn't seen his father in a few years, only talked to him on the telephone once or twice, but there still was a genetic pain, which was soon to be pain as real and immediate as a broken bone.

BIA: Bureau of Indian Affairs, a federal agency responsible for management of Indian lands and concerns.

Victor didn't have any money. Who does have money on a reservation, except the cigarette and fireworks salespeople? His father had a savings account waiting to be claimed, but Victor needed to find a way to get to Phoenix. Victor's mother was just as poor as he was, and the rest of his family didn't have any use at all for him. So Victor called the Tribal Council.

"Listen," Victor said. "My father just died. I need some money to get to Phoenix to make arrangements."

"Now, Victor," the council said. "You know we're having a difficult time financially."

"But I thought the council had special funds set aside for stuff like this."

"Now, Victor, we do have some money available for the proper return of tribal members' bodies. But I don't think we have enough to bring your father all the way back from Phoenix."

"Well," Victor said. "It ain't going to cost all that much. He had to be cremated. Things were kind of ugly. He died of a heart attack in his trailer and nobody found him for a week. It was really hot, too. You get the picture."

"Now, Victor, we're sorry for your loss and the circumstances. But we can really only afford to give you one hundred dollars."

"That's not even enough for a plane ticket."

"Well, you might consider driving down to Phoenix."

"I don't have a car. Besides, I was going to drive my father's pickup back up here."

"Now, Victor," the council said. "We're sure there is somebody who could drive you to Phoenix. Or is there somebody who could lend you the rest of the money?"

"You know there ain't nobody around with that kind of money."

"Well, we're sorry, Victor, but that's the best we can do."

Victor accepted the Tribal Council's offer. What else could he do? So he signed the proper papers, picked up his check, and walked over to the Trading Post to cash it.

While Victor stood in line, he watched Thomas Builds-the-Fire standing near the magazine rack, talking to himself. Like he always did. Thomas was a storyteller that nobody wanted to listen to. That's like being a dentist in a town where everybody has false teeth.

Victor and Thomas Builds-the-Fire were the same age, had grown up and played in the dirt together. Ever since Victor could remember, it was Thomas who always had something to say.

Once, when they were seven years old, when Victor's father still lived with the family, Thomas closed his eyes and told Victor this story: "Your father's heart is weak. He is afraid of his own family. He is afraid of you. Late at night he sits in the dark. Watches the television until there's nothing but that white noise. Sometimes he feels like he wants to buy a motorcycle and ride away. He wants to run and hide. He doesn't want to be found."

Thomas Builds-the-Fire had known that Victor's father was going to leave, knew it before anyone. Now Victor stood in the Trading Post with a one-hundred-dollar check in his hand, wondering if Thomas knew that Victor's father was dead, if he knew what was going to happen next.

Just then Thomas looked at Victor, smiled, and walked over to him. 20

"Victor, I'm sorry about your father," Thomas said.

"How did you know about it?" Victor asked.

"I heard it on the wind. I heard it from the birds. I felt it in the sunlight. Also, your mother was just in here crying."

"Oh," Victor said and looked around the Trading Post. All the other Indians stared, surprised that Victor was even talking to Thomas. Nobody talked to Thomas anymore because he told the same damn stories over and over again. Victor was embarrassed, but he thought that Thomas might be able to help him. Victor felt a sudden need for tradition.

"I can lend you the money you need," Thomas said suddenly. "But 25 you have to take me with you."

"I can't take your money," Victor said. "I mean, I haven't hardly talked to you in years. We're not really friends anymore."

"I didn't say we were friends. I said you had to take me with you."

"Let me think about it."

Victor went home with his one hundred dollars and sat at the kitchen table. He held his head in his hands and thought about Thomas Builds-the-Fire, remembered little details, tears and scars, the bicycle they shared for a summer, so many stories.

Thomas Builds-the-Fire sat on the bicycle, waited in Victor's yard. 30 He was ten years old and skinny. His hair was dirty because it was the Fourth of July.

"Victor," Thomas yelled. "Hurry up. We're going to miss the fireworks."

After a few minutes, Victor ran out of his house, jumped the porch railing, and landed gracefully on the sidewalk.

"And the judges award him a 9.95, the highest score of the summer," Thomas said, clapped, laughed.

"That was perfect, cousin," Victor said. "And it's my turn to ride the bike."

Thomas gave up the bike and they headed for the fairgrounds. It was 35 nearly dark and the fireworks were about to start.

"You know," Thomas said. "It's strange how us Indians celebrate the Fourth of July. It ain't like it was our independence everybody was fighting for."

"You think about things too much," Victor said. "It's just supposed to be fun. Maybe Junior will be there."

"Which Junior? Everybody on this reservation is named Junior."

And they both laughed.

The fireworks were small, hardly more than a few bottle rockets and a fountain. But it was enough for two Indian boys. Years later, they would need much more.

Afterwards, sitting in the dark, fighting off mosquitoes, Victor turned to Thomas Builds-the-Fire.

"Hey," Victor said. "Tell me a story."

Thomas closed his eyes and told this story: "There were these two Indian boys who wanted to be warriors. But it was too late to be warriors in the old way. All the horses were gone. So the two Indian boys stole a car and drove to the city. They parked the stolen car in front of the police station and then hitchhiked back home to the reservation. When they got back, all their friends cheered and their parents' eyes shone with pride. *You were very brave*, everybody said to the two Indian boys. *Very brave*."

"Ya-hey," Victor said. "That's a good one. I wish I could be a warrior."

"Me, too," Thomas said.

They went home together in the dark, Thomas on the bike now, Victor on foot. They walked through shadows and light from streetlamps.

"We've come a long ways," Thomas said. "We have outdoor lighting."

"All I need is the stars," Victor said. "And besides, you still think about things too much."

They separated then, each headed for home, both laughing all the way.

Victor sat at his kitchen table. He counted his one hundred dollars again and again. He knew he needed more to make it to Phoenix and back. He knew he needed Thomas Builds-the-Fire. So he put his money in his wallet and opened the front door to find Thomas on the porch.

"Ya-hey, Victor," Thomas said. "I knew you'd call me."

Thomas walked into the living room and sat down on Victor's favorite chair.

"I've got some money saved up," Thomas said. "It's enough to get us down there, but you have to get us back."

"I've got this hundred dollars," Victor said. "And my dad had a savings account I'm going to claim."

"How much in your dad's account?"

"Enough. A few hundred."

"Sounds good. When we leaving?"

When they were fifteen and had long since stopped being friends, Victor and Thomas got into a fistfight. That is, Victor was really drunk and beat Thomas up for no reason at all. All the other Indian boys stood around and watched it happen. Junior was there and so were Lester, Seymour, and a lot of others. The beating might have gone on until Thomas was dead if Norma Many Horses hadn't come along and stopped it.

"Hey, you boys," Norma yelled and jumped out of her car. "Leave him alone."

If it had been someone else, even another man, the Indian boys 60
would've just ignored the warnings. But Norma was a warrior. She was powerful. She could have picked up any two of the boys and smashed their skulls together. But worse than that, she would have dragged them all over to some tipi and made them listen to some elder tell a dusty old story.

The Indian boys scattered, and Norma walked over to Thomas and picked him up.

"Hey, little man, are you okay?" she asked.

Thomas gave her a thumbs up.

"Why they always picking on you?"

Thomas shook his head, closed his eyes, but no stories came to him, 65
no words or music. He just wanted to go home, to lie in his bed and let his dreams tell his stories for him.

Thomas Builds-the-Fire and Victor sat next to each other in the airplane, coach section. A tiny white woman had the window seat. She was busy twisting her body into pretzels. She was flexible.

"I have to ask," Thomas said, and Victor closed his eyes in embarrassment.

"Don't," Victor said.

"Excuse me, miss," Thomas asked. "Are you a gymnast or something?"

"There's no something about it," she said. "I was first alternate on 70
the 1980 Olympic team."

"Really?" Thomas asked.

"Really."

"I mean, you used to be a world-class athlete?" Thomas asked.

"My husband still thinks I am."

Thomas Builds-the-Fire smiled. She was a mental gymnast, too. She 75
pulled her leg straight up against her body so that she could've kissed her kneecap.

"I wish I could do that," Thomas said.

Victor was ready to jump out of the plane. Thomas, that crazy Indian storyteller with ratty old braids and broken teeth, was flirting with a beautiful Olympic gymnast. Nobody back home on the reservation would ever believe it.

"Well," the gymnast said. "It's easy. Try it."

Thomas grabbed at his leg and tried to pull it up into the same position as the gymnast. He couldn't even come close, which made Victor and the gymnast laugh.

"Hey," she asked. "You two are Indian, right?" 80

"Full-blood," Victor said.

"Not me," Thomas said. "I'm half magician on my mother's side and half clown on my father's."

They all laughed.

"What are your names?" she asked.

"Victor and Thomas."

"Mine is Cathy. Pleased to meet you all."

The three of them talked for the duration of the flight. Cathy the gymnast complained about the government, how they screwed the 1980 Olympic team by boycotting.°

"Sounds like you all got a lot in common with Indians," Thomas said.

Nobody laughed.

After the plane landed in Phoenix and they had all found their way to the terminal, Cathy the gymnast smiled and waved good-bye.

"She was really nice," Thomas said.

"Yeah, but everybody talks to everybody on airplanes," Victor said. "It's too bad we can't always be that way."

"You always used to tell me I think too much," Thomas said. "Now it sounds like you do."

"Maybe I caught it from you."

"Yeah."

Thomas and Victor rode in a taxi to the trailer where Victor's father died.

"Listen," Victor said as they stopped in front of the trailer. "I never told you I was sorry for beating you up that time."

"Oh, it was nothing. We were just kids and you were drunk."

"Yeah, but I'm still sorry."

"That's all right."

Victor paid for the taxi and the two of them stood in the hot Phoenix summer. They could smell the trailer.

"This ain't going to be nice," Victor said. "You don't have to go in."

"You're going to need help."

Victor walked to the front door and opened it. The stink rolled out and made them both gag. Victor's father had lain in that trailer for a week in hundred-degree temperatures before anyone found him. And the only reason anyone found him was because of the smell. They needed dental records to identify him. That's exactly what the coroner said. They needed dental records.

"Oh, man," Victor said. "I don't know if I can do this."

"Well, then don't."

"But there might be something valuable in there."

they screwed the 1980 Olympic team by boycotting: in an international movement led by the United States at the direction of President Jimmy Carter, some sixty nations boycotted the 1980 Summer Olympic Games in Moscow as a protest against the Soviet invasion of Afghanistan in December 1979.

"I thought his money was in the bank."

"It is. I was talking about pictures and letters and stuff like that."

"Oh," Thomas said as he held his breath and followed Victor into the trailer.

When Victor was twelve, he stepped into an underground wasp nest. His foot was caught in the hole, and no matter how hard he struggled, Victor couldn't pull free. He might have died there, stung a thousand times, if Thomas Builds-the-Fire had not come by.

"Run," Thomas yelled and pulled Victor's foot from the hole. They ran then, hard as they ever had, faster than Billy Mills, faster than Jim Thorpe,° faster than the wasps could fly.

Victor and Thomas ran until they couldn't breathe, ran until it was cold and dark outside, ran until they were lost and it took hours to find their way home. All the way back, Victor counted his stings.

"Seven," Victor said. "My lucky number."

Victor didn't find much to keep in the trailer. Only a photo album and a stereo. Everything else had that smell stuck in it or was useless anyway.

"I guess this is all," Victor said. "It ain't much."

"Better than nothing," Thomas said.

"Yeah, and I do have the pickup."

"Yeah," Thomas said. "It's in good shape."

"Dad was good about that stuff."

"Yeah, I remember your dad."

"Really?" Victor asked. "What do you remember?"

Thomas Builds-the-Fire closed his eyes and told this story: "I remember when I had this dream that told me to go to Spokane, to stand by the Falls in the middle of the city and wait for a sign. I knew I had to go there but I didn't have a car. Didn't have a license. I was only thirteen. So I walked all the way, took me all day, and I finally made it to the Falls. I stood there for an hour waiting. Then your dad came walking up. *What the hell are you doing here?* he asked me. I said, *Waiting for a vision*. Then your father said, *All you're going to get here is mugged*. So he drove me over to Denny's, bought me dinner, and then drove me home to the reservation. For a long time I was mad because I thought my dreams had lied to me. But they didn't. Your dad was my vision. *Take care of each other* is what my dreams were saying. *Take care of each other*."

Billy Mills . . . Jim Thorpe: William Mervin "Billy" Mills (born 1938), a member of the Sioux tribe, won a gold medal in the 10,000-meter run at the 1964 Summer Olympic Games in Tokyo, Japan. Jacobus Franciscus "Jim" Thorpe (1888–1953), of the Sac and Fox tribe, is widely regarded as one of the greatest American athletes of the twentieth century; he won gold medals in the pentathlon and decathlon at the 1912 Summer Olympic Games in Stockholm, Sweden. He also played professional football, baseball, and basketball.

Victor was quiet for a long time. He searched his mind for memories of his father, found the good ones, found a few bad ones, added it all up, and smiled.

"My father never told me about finding you in Spokane," Victor said.

"He said he wouldn't tell anybody. Didn't want me to get in trouble. But he said I had to watch out for you as part of the deal."

"Really?"

"Really. Your father said you would need the help. He was right."

"That's why you came down here with me, isn't it?" Victor asked.

"I came because of your father."

Victor and Thomas climbed into the pickup, drove over to the bank, and claimed the three hundred dollars in the savings account.

Thomas Builds-the-Fire could fly.

Once, he jumped off the roof of the tribal school and flapped his arms like a crazy eagle. And he flew. For a second, he hovered, suspended above all the other Indian boys who were too smart or too scared to jump.

"He's flying," Junior yelled, and Seymour was busy looking for the trick wires or mirrors. But it was real. As real as the dirt when Thomas lost altitude and crashed to the ground.

He broke his arm in two places.

"He broke his wing," Victor chanted, and the other Indian boys joined in, made it a tribal song.

"He broke his wing, he broke his wing, he broke his wing," all the Indian boys chanted as they ran off, flapping their wings, wishing they could fly, too. They hated Thomas for his courage, his brief moment as a bird. Everybody has dreams about flying. Thomas flew.

One of his dreams came true for just a second, just enough to make it real.

Victor's father, his ashes, fit in one wooden box with enough left over to fill a cardboard box.

"He always was a big man," Thomas said.

Victor carried part of his father and Thomas carried the rest out to the pickup. They set him down carefully behind the seats, put a cowboy hat on the wooden box and a Dodgers cap on the cardboard box. That's the way it was supposed to be.

"Ready to head back home," Victor asked.

"It's going to be a long drive."

"Yeah, take a couple days, maybe."

"We can take turns," Thomas said.

"Okay," Victor said, but they didn't take turns. Victor drove for sixteen hours straight north, made it halfway up Nevada toward home before he finally pulled over.

"Hey, Thomas," Victor said. "You got to drive for a while."

"Okay."

Thomas Builds-the-Fire slid behind the wheel and started off down the road. All through Nevada, Thomas and Victor had been amazed at the lack of animal life, at the absence of water, of movement.

"Where is everything?" Victor had asked more than once. 150

Now when Thomas was finally driving they saw the first animal, maybe the only animal in Nevada. It was a long-eared jackrabbit.

"Look," Victor yelled. "It's alive."

Thomas and Victor were busy congratulating themselves on their discovery when the jackrabbit darted out into the road and under the wheels of the pickup.

"Stop the goddamn car," Victor yelled, and Thomas did stop, backed the pickup to the dead jackrabbit.

"Oh, man, he's dead," Victor said as he looked at the squashed animal. 155

"Really dead."

"The only thing alive in this whole state and we just killed it."

"I don't know," Thomas said. "I think it was suicide."

Victor looked around the desert, sniffed the air, felt the emptiness and loneliness, and nodded his head.

"Yeah," Victor said. "It had to be suicide." 160

"I can't believe this," Thomas said. "You drive for a thousand miles and there ain't even any bugs smashed on the windshield. I drive for ten seconds and kill the only living thing in Nevada."

"Yeah," Victor said. "Maybe I should drive."

"Maybe you should."

Thomas Builds-the-Fire walked through the corridors of the tribal school by himself. Nobody wanted to be anywhere near him because of all those stories. Story after story.

Thomas closed his eyes and this story came to him: "We are all given 165 one thing by which our lives are measured, one determination. Mine are the stories which can change or not change the world. It doesn't matter which as long as I continue to tell the stories. My father, he died on Okinawa in World War II, died fighting for this country, which had tried to kill him for years. My mother, she died giving birth to me, died while I was still inside her. She pushed me out into the world with her last breath. I have no brothers or sisters. I have only my stories which came to me before I even had the words to speak. I learned a thousand stories before I took my first thousand steps. They are all I have. It's all I can do."

Thomas Builds-the-Fire told his stories to all those who would stop and listen. He kept telling them long after people had stopped listening.

Victor and Thomas made it back to the reservation just as the sun was rising. It was the beginning of a new day on earth, but the same old shit on the reservation.

"Good morning," Thomas said.

"Good morning."

The tribe was waking up, ready for work, eating breakfast, reading the newspaper, just like everybody else does. Willene LeBret was out in her garden wearing a bathrobe. She waved when Thomas and Victor drove by.

"Crazy Indians made it," she said to herself and went back to her roses.

Victor stopped the pickup in front of Thomas Builds-the-Fire's HUD house.° They both yawned, stretched a little, shook dust from their bodies.

"I'm tired," Victor said.

"Of everything," Thomas added.

They both searched for words to end the journey. Victor needed to thank Thomas for his help, for the money, and make the promise to pay it all back.

"Don't worry about the money," Thomas said. "It don't make any difference anyhow."

"Probably not, enit?"

"Nope."

Victor knew that Thomas would remain the crazy storyteller who talked to dogs and cars, who listened to the wind and pine trees. Victor knew that he couldn't really be friends with Thomas, even after all that had happened. It was cruel but it was real. As real as the ashes, as Victor's father, sitting behind the seats.

"I know how it is," Thomas said. "I know you ain't going to treat me any better than you did before. I know your friends would give you too much shit about it."

Victor was ashamed of himself. Whatever happened to the tribal ties, the sense of community? The only real thing he shared with anybody was a bottle and broken dreams. He owed Thomas something, anything.

"Listen," Victor said and handed Thomas the cardboard box which contained half of his father. "I want you to have this."

Thomas took the ashes and smiled, closed his eyes, and told this story: "I'm going to travel to Spokane Falls one last time and toss these ashes into the water. And your father will rise like a salmon, leap over the bridge, over me, and find his way home. It will be beautiful. His teeth will shine like silver, like a rainbow. He will rise, Victor, he will rise."

Victor smiled.

"I was planning on doing the same thing with my half," Victor said. "But I didn't imagine my father looking anything like a salmon. I thought it'd be like cleaning the attic or something. Like letting things go after they've stopped having any use."

HUD house: housing subsidized by the U.S. Department of Housing and Urban Development.

"Nothing stops, cousin," Thomas said. "Nothing stops."

Thomas Builds-the-Fire got out of the pickup and walked up his driveway. Victor started the pickup and began the drive home.

"Wait," Thomas yelled suddenly from his porch. "I just got to ask one favor."

Victor stopped the pickup, leaned out the window, and shouted back. "What do you want?"

"Just one time when I'm telling a story somewhere, why don't you stop and listen?" Thomas asked.

"Just once?"

"Just once."

Victor waved his arms to let Thomas know that the deal was good. It was a fair trade, and that was all Victor had ever wanted from his whole life. So Victor drove his father's pickup toward home while Thomas went into his house, closed the door behind him, and heard a new story come to him in the silence afterwards.

T. Coraghessan Boyle

Greasy Lake

1985

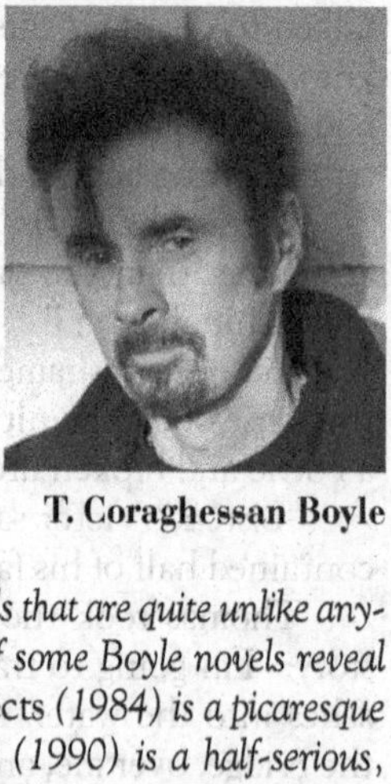

T. Coraghessan Boyle

T. Coraghessan Boyle (the T. stands for Tom) was born in 1948 in Peekskill, New York, the son of Irish immigrants. He grew up, he recalls, "as a sort of pampered punk" who did not read a book until he was eighteen. After a brief period as a high school teacher, he studied in the University of Iowa Writers' Workshop, submitting a collection of stories for his Phd. His stories in Esquire, Paris Review, *the* Atlantic, *and other magazines quickly won him notice for their outrageous macabre humor and bizarre inventiveness. Boyle has published many volumes of short stories, including* Greasy Lake *(1985),* T. C. Boyle Stories *(1998), and* Tooth and Claw *(2005). He has also published more than a dozen novels that are quite unlike anything else in contemporary American fiction. The subjects of some Boyle novels reveal his wide-ranging and idiosyncratic interests.* Budding Prospects *(1984) is a picaresque romp among adventurous marijuana growers.* East Is East *(1990) is a half-serious, half-comic story of a Japanese fugitive in an American writers' colony.* The Road to Wellville *(1993) takes place in 1907 in a sanitarium run by Dr. John Harvey Kellogg of corn flakes fame, with cameo appearances by Henry Ford, Thomas Edison, and Harvey Firestone. A recent novel—his sixteenth—is* The Terranauts *(2016). Boyle is Distinguished Professor of English at University of Southern California.*

It's about a mile down on the dark side of Route 88.
—BRUCE SPRINGSTEEN

There was a time when courtesy and winning ways went out of style, when it was good to be bad, when you cultivated decadence like a taste. We were all dangerous characters then. We wore torn-up leather jackets, slouched around with toothpicks in our mouths, sniffed glue and ether and what somebody claimed was cocaine. When we wheeled our parents' whining station wagons out onto the street we left a patch of rubber half a block long. We drank gin and grape juice, Tango, Thunderbird, and Bali Hai. We were nineteen. We were bad. We read André Gide° and struck elaborate poses to show that we didn't give a shit about anything. At night, we went up to Greasy Lake.

Through the center of town, up the strip, past the housing developments and shopping malls, street lights giving way to the thin streaming illumination of the headlights, trees crowding the asphalt in a black unbroken wall: that was the way out to Greasy Lake. The Indians had called it Wakan, a reference to the clarity of its waters. Now it was fetid and murky, the mud banks glittering with broken glass and strewn with beer cans and the charred remains of bonfires. There was a single ravaged island a hundred yards from shore, so stripped of vegetation it looked as if the air force had strafed it. We went up to the lake because everyone went there, because we wanted to snuff the rich scent of possibility on the breeze, watch a girl take off her clothes and plunge into the festering murk, drink beer, smoke pot, howl at the stars, savor the incongruous full-throated roar of rock and roll against the primeval susurrus of frogs and crickets. This was nature.

I was there one night, late, in the company of two dangerous characters. Digby wore a gold star in his right ear and allowed his father to pay his tuition at Cornell; Jeff was thinking of quitting school to become a painter/musician/head-shop proprietor. They were both expert in the social graces, quick with a sneer, able to manage a Ford with lousy shocks over a rutted and gutted blacktop road at eighty-five while rolling a joint as compact as a Tootsie Roll Pop stick. They could lounge against a bank of booming speakers and trade "man"s with the best of them or roll out across the dance floor as if their joints worked on bearings. They were slick and quick and they wore their mirror shades at breakfast and dinner, in the shower, in closets and caves. In short, they were bad.

I drove. Digby pounded the dashboard and shouted along with Toots & the Maytals while Jeff hung his head out the window and streaked the side of my mother's Bel Air with vomit. It was early June, the air soft as a hand on your cheek, the third night of summer vacation. The first two nights we'd been out till dawn, looking for something we never found. On this,

André Gide: controversial French writer (1869–1951) whose novels, including *The Counterfeiters* and *Lafcadio's Adventures,* often show individuals in conflict with accepted morality.

the third night, we'd cruised the strip sixty-seven times, been in and out of every bar and club we could think of in a twenty-mile radius, stopped twice for bucket chicken and forty-cent hamburgers, debated going to a party at the house of a girl Jeff's sister knew, and chucked two dozen raw eggs at mailboxes and hitchhikers. It was 2:00 A.M.; the bars were closing. There was nothing to do but take a bottle of lemon-flavored gin up to Greasy Lake.

The taillights of a single car winked at us as we swung into the dirt 5
lot with its tufts of weed and washboard corrugations; '57 Chevy, mint, metallic blue. On the far side of the lot, like the exoskeleton of some gaunt chrome insect, a chopper leaned against its kickstand. And that was it for excitement: some junkie halfwit biker and a car freak pumping his girlfriend. Whatever it was we were looking for, we weren't about to find it at Greasy Lake. Not that night.

But then all of a sudden Digby was fighting for the wheel. "Hey, that's Tony Lovett's car! Hey!" he shouted, while I stabbed at the brake pedal and the Bel Air nosed up to the gleaming bumper of the parked Chevy. Digby leaned on the horn, laughing, and instructed me to put my brights on. I flicked on the brights. This was hilarious. A joke. Tony would experience premature withdrawal and expect to be confronted by grim-looking state troopers with flashlights. We hit the horn, strobed the lights, and then jumped out of the car to press our witty faces to Tony's windows; for all we knew we might even catch a glimpse of some little fox's tit, and then we could slap backs with red-faced Tony, roughhouse a little, and go on to new heights of adventure and daring.

The first mistake, the one that opened the whole floodgate, was losing my grip on the keys. In the excitement, leaping from the car with the gin in one hand and a roach clip in the other, I spilled them in the grass—in the dark, rank, mysterious nighttime grass of Greasy Lake. This was a tactical error, as damaging and irreversible in its way as Westmoreland's decision to dig in at Khe Sanh.° I felt it like a jab of intuition, and I stopped there by the open door, peering vaguely into the night that puddled up round my feet.

The second mistake—and this was inextricably bound up with the first—was identifying the car as Tony Lovett's. Even before the very bad character in greasy jeans and engineer boots ripped out of the driver's door, I began to realize that this chrome blue was much lighter than the robin's-egg of Tony's car, and that Tony's car didn't have rear-mounted speakers. Judging from their expressions, Digby and Jeff were privately groping toward the same inevitable and unsettling conclusion as I was.

Westmoreland's decision . . . Khe Sanh: General William C. Westmoreland commanded U.S. troops in Vietnam (1964–1968). In late 1967 the North Vietnamese and Viet Cong forces attacked Khe Sanh (or Khesanh) with a show of strength, causing Westmoreland to expend great effort to defend a plateau of relatively little tactical importance.

In any case, there was no reasoning with this bad greasy character—clearly he was a man of action. The first lusty Rockette° kick of his steel-toed boot caught me under the chin, chipped my favorite tooth, and left me sprawled in the dirt. Like a fool, I'd gone down on one knee to comb the stiff hacked grass for the keys, my mind making connections in the most dragged-out, testudineous way, knowing that things had gone wrong, that I was in a lot of trouble, and that the lost ignition key was my grail and my salvation. The three or four succeeding blows were mainly absorbed by my right buttock and the tough piece of bone at the base of my spine.

Meanwhile, Digby vaulted the kissing bumpers and delivered a sav- 10
age kung-fu blow to the greasy character's collarbone. Digby had just finished a course in martial arts for phys-ed credit and had spent the better part of the past two nights telling us apocryphal tales of Bruce Lee types and of the raw power invested in lightning blows shot from coiled wrists, ankles, and elbows. The greasy character was unimpressed. He merely backed off a step, his face like a Toltec mask, and laid Digby out with a single whistling roundhouse blow . . . but by now Jeff had got into the act, and I was beginning to extricate myself from the dirt, a tinny compound of shock, rage, and impotence wadded in my throat.

Jeff was on the guy's back, biting at his ear. Digby was on the ground, cursing. I went for the tire iron I kept under the driver's seat. I kept it there because bad characters always keep tire irons under the driver's seat, for just such an occasion as this. Never mind that I hadn't been involved in a fight since sixth grade, when a kid with a sleepy eye and two streams of mucus depending from his nostrils hit me in the knee with a Louisville slugger,° never mind that I'd touched the tire iron exactly twice before, to change tires: it was there. And I went for it.

I was terrified. Blood was beating in my ears, my hands were shaking, my heart turning over like a dirtbike in the wrong gear. My antagonist was shirtless, and a single cord of muscle flashed across his chest as he bent forward to peel Jeff from his back like a wet overcoat. "Motherfucker," he spat, over and over, and I was aware in that instant that all four of us—Digby, Jeff, and myself included—were chanting "motherfucker, motherfucker," as if it were a battle cry. (What happened next? the detective asks the murderer from beneath the turned-down brim of his porkpie hat. I don't know, the murderer says, something came over me. Exactly.)

Digby poked the flat of his hand in the bad character's face and I came at him like a kamikaze, mindless, raging, stung with humiliation—the whole thing, from the initial boot in the chin to this murderous primal instant involving no more than sixty hyperventilating, gland-flooding seconds—I came at him and brought the tire iron down across his ear. The effect was instantaneous, astonishing. He was a stunt man and this was Hollywood, he was a big grimacing toothy balloon and I was a man with a straight pin. He collapsed. Wet his pants. Went loose in his boots.

Rockette: member of a dance troupe in the stage show at Radio City Music Hall, New York; the dancers are famous for their ability to kick fast and high with wonderful coordination. *Louisville slugger:* a brand of baseball bat.

A single second, big as a zeppelin, floated by. We were standing over him in a circle, gritting our teeth, jerking our necks, our limbs and hands and feet twitching with glandular discharges. No one said anything. We just stared down at the guy, the car freak, the lover, the bad greasy character laid low. Digby looked at me; so did Jeff. I was still holding the tire iron, a tuft of hair clinging to the crook like dandelion fluff, like down. Rattled, I dropped it in the dirt, already envisioning the headlines, the pitted faces of the police inquisitors, the gleam of handcuffs, clank of bars, the big black shadows rising from the back of the cell . . . when suddenly a raw torn shriek cut through me like all the juice in all the electric chairs in the country.

It was the fox. She was short, barefoot, dressed in panties and a man's 15
shirt. "Animals!" she screamed, running at us with her fists clenched and wisps of blow-dried hair in her face. There was a silver chain round her ankle, and her toenails flashed in the glare of the headlights. I think it was the toenails that did it. Sure, the gin and the cannabis and even the Kentucky Fried may have had a hand in it, but it was the sight of those flaming toes that set us off—the toad emerging from the loaf in *Virgin Spring*,° lipstick smeared on a child; she was already tainted. We were on her like Bergman's deranged brothers—see no evil, hear none, speak none—panting, wheezing, tearing at her clothes, grabbing for flesh. We were bad characters, and we were scared and hot and three steps over the line—anything could have happened.

It didn't.

Before we could pin her to the hood of the car, our eyes masked with lust and greed and the purest primal badness, a pair of headlights swung into the lot. There we were, dirty, bloody, guilty, dissociated from humanity and civilization, the first of the Ur-crimes behind us, the second in progress, shreds of nylon panty and spandex brassiere dangling from our fingers, our flies open, lips licked—there we were, caught in the spotlight. Nailed.

We bolted. First for the car, and then, realizing we had no way of starting it, for the woods. I thought nothing. I thought escape. The headlights came at me like accusing fingers. I was gone.

Ram-bam-bam, across the parking lot, past the chopper and into the feculent undergrowth at the lake's edge, insects flying up in my face, weeds whipping, frogs and snakes and red-eyed turtles splashing off into the night: I was already ankle-deep in muck and tepid water and still going strong. Behind me, the girl's screams rose in intensity, disconsolate, incriminating, the screams of the Sabine women,° the Christian martyrs,

Virgin Spring: film about a rape by Swedish director Ingmar Bergman (1960). *Sabine women*: members of an ancient tribe in Italy, according to legend, forcibly carried off by the early Romans under Romulus to be their wives. The incident is depicted in a famous painting, *The Rape of the Sabine Women*, by seventeenth-century French artist Nicolas Poussin.

Anne Frank° dragged from the garret. I kept going, pursued by those cries, imagining cops and bloodhounds. The water was up to my knees when I realized what I was doing: I was going to swim for it. Swim the breadth of Greasy Lake and hide myself in the thick clot of woods on the far side. They'd never find me there.

I was breathing in sobs, in gasps. The water lapped at my waist as I 20
looked out over the moon-burnished ripples, the mats of algae that clung to the surface like scabs. Digby and Jeff had vanished. I paused. Listened. The girl was quieter now, screams tapering to sobs, but there were male voices, angry, excited, and the high-pitched ticking of the second car's engine. I waded deeper, stealthy, hunted, the ooze sucking at my sneakers. As I was about to take the plunge—at the very instant I dropped my shoulder for the first slashing stroke—I blundered into something. Something unspeakable, obscene, something soft, wet, moss-grown. A patch of weed? A log? When I reached out to touch it, it gave like a rubber duck, it gave like flesh.

In one of those nasty little epiphanies for which we are prepared by films and TV and childhood visits to the funeral home to ponder the shrunken painted forms of dead grandparents, I understood what it was that bobbed there so inadmissibly in the dark. Understood, and stumbled back in horror and revulsion, my mind yanked in six different directions (I was nineteen, a mere child, an infant, and here in the space of five minutes I'd struck down one greasy character and blundered into the waterlogged carcass of a second), thinking, The keys, the keys, why did I have to go and lose the keys? I stumbled back, but the muck took hold of my feet—a sneaker snagged, balance lost—and suddenly I was pitching face forward into the buoyant black mass, throwing out my hands in desperation while simultaneously conjuring the image of reeking frogs and muskrats revolving in slicks of their own deliquescing juices. AAAAArrrgh! I shot from the water like a torpedo, the dead man rotating to expose a mossy beard and eyes cold as the moon. I must have shouted out, thrashing around in the weeds, because the voices behind me suddenly became animated.

"What was that?"

"It's them, it's them: they tried to, tried to . . . rape me!" Sobs.

A man's voice, flat Midwestern accent. "You sons a bitches, we'll kill you!"

Frogs, crickets. 25

Then another voice, harsh, *r*-less, Lower East Side: "Motherfucker!" I recognized the verbal virtuosity of the bad greasy character in the engineer boots. Tooth chipped, sneakers gone, coated in mud and slime and worse, crouching breathless in the weeds waiting to have my ass

Anne Frank: German Jewish girl (1929–1945) whose diary written during the Nazi occupation of the Netherlands later became world-famous. She hid with her family in a secret attic in Amsterdam, but was caught by the Gestapo and sent to the concentration camp at Belsen, where she died.

thoroughly and definitively kicked and fresh from the hideous stinking embrace of a three-days-dead-corpse, I suddenly felt a rush of joy and vindication: the son of a bitch was alive! Just as quickly, my bowels turned to ice. "Come on out of there, you pansy mothers!" the bad greasy character was screaming. He shouted curses till he was out of breath.

The crickets started up again, then the frogs. I held my breath. All at once there was a sound in the reeds, a swishing, a splash: thunk-a-thunk. They were throwing rocks. The frogs fell silent. I cradled my head. Swish, swish, thunk-a-thunk. A wedge of feldspar the size of a cue ball glanced off my knee. I bit my finger.

It was then that they turned to the car. I heard a door slam, a curse, and then the sound of the headlights shattering—almost a good-natured sound, celebratory, like corks popping from the necks of bottles. This was succeeded by the dull booming of the fenders, metal on metal, and then the icy crash of the windshield. I inched forward, elbows and knees, my belly pressed to the muck, thinking of guerrillas and commandos and *The Naked and the Dead*.° I parted the weeds and squinted the length of the parking lot.

The second car—it was a Trans-Am—was still running, its high beams washing the scene in a lurid stagy light. Tire iron flailing, the greasy bad character was laying into the side of my mother's Bel Air like an avenging demon, his shadow riding up the trunks of the trees. Whomp. Whomp. Whomp-whomp. The other two guys—blond types, in fraternity jackets—were helping out with tree branches and skull-sized boulders. One of them was gathering up bottles, rocks, muck, candy wrappers, used condoms, poptops, and other refuse and pitching it through the window on the driver's side. I could see the fox, a white bulb behind the windshield of the '57 Chevy. "Bobbie," she whined over the thumping, "come on." The greasy character paused a moment, took one good swipe at the left taillight, and then heaved the tire iron halfway across the lake. Then he fired up the '57 and was gone.

Blond head nodded at blond head. One said something to the other, 30
too low for me to catch. They were no doubt thinking that in helping to annihilate my mother's car they'd committed a fairly rash act, and thinking too that there were three bad characters connected with that very car watching them from the woods. Perhaps other possibilities occurred to them as well—police, jail cells, justices of the peace, reparations, lawyers, irate parents, fraternal censure. Whatever they were thinking, they suddenly dropped branches, bottles, and rocks and sprang for their car in unison, as if they'd choreographed it. Five seconds. That's all it took. The engine shrieked, the tires squealed, a cloud of dust rose from the rutted lot and then settled back on darkness.

The Naked and the Dead: 1948 novel by Norman Mailer, about US Army life in World War II.

I don't know how long I lay there, the bad breath of decay all around me, my jacket heavy as a bear, the primordial ooze subtly reconstituting itself to accommodate my upper thighs and testicles. My jaws ached, my knee throbbed, my coccyx was on fire. I contemplated suicide, wondered if I'd need bridgework, scraped the recesses of my brain for some sort of excuse to give my parents—a tree had fallen on the car, I was blinded by a bread truck, hit and run, vandals had got to it while we were playing chess at Digby's. Then I thought of the dead man. He was probably the only person on the planet worse off than I was. I thought about him, fog on the lake, insects chirring eerily, and felt the tug of fear, felt the darkness opening up inside me like a set of jaws. Who was he, I wondered, this victim of time and circumstance bobbing sorrowfully in the lake at my back. The owner of the chopper, no doubt, a bad older character come to this. Shot during a murky drug deal, drowned while drunkenly frolicking in the lake. Another headline. My car was wrecked; he was dead.

When the eastern half of the sky went from black to cobalt and the trees began to separate themselves from the shadows, I pushed myself up from the mud and stepped out into the open. By now the birds had begun to take over for the crickets, and dew lay slick on the leaves. There was a smell in the air, raw and sweet at the same time, the smell of the sun firing buds and opening blossoms. I contemplated the car. It lay there like a wreck along the highway, like a steel sculpture left over from a vanished civilization. Everything was still. This was nature.

I was circling the car, as dazed and bedraggled as the sole survivor of an air blitz, when Digby and Jeff emerged from the trees behind me. Digby's face was crosshatched with smears of dirt; Jeff's jacket was gone and his shirt was torn across the shoulder. They slouched across the lot, looking sheepish, and silently came up beside me to gape at the ravaged automobile. No one said a word. After a while Jeff swung open the driver's door and began to scoop the broken glass and garbage off the seat. I looked at Digby. He shrugged. "At least they didn't slash the tires," he said.

It was true: the tires were intact. There was no windshield, the headlights were staved in, and the body looked as if it had been sledgehammered for a quarter a shot at the county fair, but the tires were inflated to regulation pressure. The car was drivable. In silence, all three of us bent to scrape the mud and shattered glass from the interior. I said nothing about the biker. When we were finished, I reached in my pocket for the keys, experienced a nasty stab of recollection, cursed myself, and turned to search the grass. I spotted them almost immediately, no more than five feet from the open door, glinting like jewels in the first tapering shaft of sunlight. There was no reason to get philosophical about it: I eased into the seat and turned the engine over.

It was at that precise moment that the silver Mustang with the flame 35
decals rumbled into the lot. All three of us froze; then Digby and Jeff slid into the car and slammed the door. We watched as the Mustang rocked

and bobbed across the ruts and finally jerked to a halt beside the forlorn chopper at the far end of the lot. "Let's go," Digby said. I hesitated, the Bel Air wheezing beneath me.

Two girls emerged from the Mustang. Tight jeans, stiletto heels, hair like frozen fur. They bent over the motorcycle, paced back and forth aimlessly, glanced once or twice at us, and then ambled over to where the reeds sprang up in a green fence round the perimeter of the lake. One of them cupped her hands to her mouth. "Al," she called. "Hey, Al!"

"Come on," Digby hissed. "Let's get out of here."

But it was too late. The second girl was picking her way across the lot, unsteady on her heels, looking up at us and then away. She was older—twenty-five or -six—and as she came closer we could see there was something wrong with her: she was stoned or drunk, lurching now and waving her arms for balance. I gripped the steering wheel as if it were the ejection lever of a flaming jet, and Digby spat out my name, twice, terse and impatient.

"Hi," the girl said.

We looked at her like zombies, like war veterans, like deaf-and-dumb 40
pencil peddlers.

She smiled, her lips cracked and dry. "Listen," she said, bending from the waist to look in the window, "you guys seen Al?" Her pupils were pinpoints, her eyes glass. She jerked her neck. "That's his bike over there—Al's. You seen him?"

Al. I didn't know what to say. I wanted to get out of the car and retch, I wanted to go home to my parents' house and crawl into bed. Digby poked me in the ribs. "We haven't seen anybody," I said.

The girl seemed to consider this, reaching out a slim veiny arm to brace herself against the car. "No matter," she said, slurring the *t*'s, "he'll turn up." And then, as if she'd just taken stock of the whole scene—the ravaged car and our battered faces, the desolation of the place—she said: "Hey, you guys look like some pretty bad characters—been fightin', huh?" We stared straight ahead, rigid as catatonics. She was fumbling in her pocket and muttering something. Finally she held out a handful of tablets in glassine wrappers: "Hey, you want to party, you want to do some of these with me and Sarah?"

I just looked at her. I thought I was going to cry. Digby broke the silence. "No, thanks," he said, leaning over me. "Some other time."

I put the car in gear and it inched forward with a groan, shaking off 45
pellets of glass like an old dog shedding water after a bath, heaving over the ruts on its worn springs, creeping toward the highway. There was a sheen of sun on the lake. I looked back. The girl was still standing there, watching us, her shoulders slumped, hand outstretched.

Ray Bradbury

A Sound of Thunder

1953

Ray Bradbury

Raymond Douglas Bradbury (1920–2012) was born in Waukegan, Illinois, a small Midwestern town he has frequently evoked in his fiction. His mother was a Swedish immigrant and his father an electrical lineman. In 1934, Bradbury's unemployed father moved the family from the Depression-ravaged Midwest to Los Angeles, where Ray entered high school. The teenaged Bradbury soon discovered science fiction and began publishing stories in his high school magazine. Unable to afford college, he took odd jobs while making his way as a writer. By 1941 he was publishing fiction in commercial magazines and very quickly developed a personal style that was strikingly unlike the conventional science fiction of the era. His stories were quietly poetic, evocatively detailed, overtly symbolic, and often suffused with nostalgia. Bradbury's first collection, Dark Carnival *(1947), made a modest impression, but his 1950 cycle of stories about mankind's doomed colonization of Mars,* The Martian Chronicles, *was immediately recognized as a classic of science fiction. The success of* The Martian Chronicles *made Bradbury the first American science-fiction writer to cross over into the mainstream literary market. His novels became both critical and popular successes, especially* Fahrenheit 451 *(1953),* Dandelion Wine *(1957), and* Something Wicked This Way Comes *(1962), but he was best known for his short stories, which were collected in volumes such as* The Illustrated Man *(1951),* The Golden Apples of the Sun *(1953),* A Medicine for Melancholy *(1959), and* I Sing the Body Electric! *(1969). Bradbury's literary vision has also been disseminated through film, television, and theater. Although at his best an elegant stylist, Bradbury was perhaps primarily a mythmaker. His science fiction and fantasy narratives have given contemporary readers the stories, situations, images, and symbols necessary to a complex, and rapidly changing, technology-driven society. Bradbury received many honors, including the National Medal of Arts in 2004 and a lifetime Pulitzer Prize in 2007. He died in Los Angeles, where he had lived for his entire adult life, at age ninety-one.*

The sign on the wall seemed to quaver under a film of sliding warm water. Eckels felt his eyelids blink over his stare, and the sign burned in this momentary darkness:

TIME SAFARI, INC.

SAFARIS TO ANY YEAR IN THE

PAST.

YOU NAME THE ANIMAL.

WE TAKE YOU THERE.

YOU SHOOT IT.

A warm phlegm gathered in Eckels' throat; he swallowed and pushed it down. The muscles around his mouth formed a smile as he put his hand slowly out upon the air, and in that hand waved a check for ten thousand dollars to the man behind the desk.

"Does this safari guarantee I come back alive?"

"We guarantee nothing," said the official, "except the dinosaurs." He turned. "This is Mr. Travis, your Safari Guide in the Past. He'll tell you what and where to shoot. If he says no shooting, no shooting. If you disobey instructions, there's a stiff penalty of another ten thousand dollars, plus possible government action, on your return."

Eckels glanced across the vast office at a mass and tangle, a snaking 5
and humming of wires and steel boxes, at an aurora that flickered now orange, now silver, now blue. There was a sound like a gigantic bonfire burning all of Time, all the years and all the parchment calendars, all the hours piled high and set aflame.

A touch of the hand and this burning would, on the instant, beautifully reverse itself. Eckels remembered the wording in the advertisements to the letter. Out of chars and ashes, out of dust and coals, like golden salamanders, the old years, the green years, might leap; roses sweeten the air, white hair turn Irish-black, wrinkles vanish; all, everything fly back to seed, flee death, rush down to their beginnings, suns rise in western skies and set in glorious easts, moons eat themselves opposite to the custom, all and everything cupping one in another like Chinese boxes, rabbits into hats, all and everything returning to the fresh death, the seed death, the green death, to the time before the beginning. A touch of a hand might do it, the merest touch of a hand.

"Unbelievable." Eckels breathed, the light of the Machine on his thin face. "A real Time Machine." He shook his head. "Makes you think, If the election had gone badly yesterday, I might be here now running away from the results. Thank God Keith won. He'll make a fine President of the United States."

"Yes," said the man behind the desk. "We're lucky. If Deutscher had gotten in, we'd have the worst kind of dictatorship. There's an anti everything man for you, a militarist, anti-Christ, anti-human, anti-intellectual. People called us up, you know, joking but not joking. Said if Deutscher became President they wanted to go live in 1492. Of course it's not our business to conduct Escapes, but to form Safaris. Anyway, Keith's President now. All you got to worry about is—"

"Shooting my dinosaur," Eckels finished it for him.

"A *Tyrannosaurus rex*. The Tyrant Lizard, the most incredible mon- 10
ster in history. Sign this release. Anything happens to you, we're not responsible. Those dinosaurs are hungry."

Eckels flushed angrily. "Trying to scare me!"

"Frankly, yes. We don't want anyone going who'll panic at the first shot. Six Safari leaders were killed last year, and a dozen hunters. We're here to give you the severest thrill a *real* hunter ever asked for. Traveling you back sixty million years to bag the biggest game in all of Time. Your personal check's still there. Tear it up."

Mr. Eckels looked at the check. His fingers twitched.

"Good luck," said the man behind the desk. "Mr. Travis, he's all yours."

They moved silently across the room, taking their guns with them, toward the Machine, toward the silver metal and the roaring light.

First a day and then a night and then a day and then a night, then it was day-night-day-night-day. A week, a month, a year, a decade! A.D. 2055. A.D. 2019. 1999! 1957! Gone! The Machine roared.

They put on their oxygen helmets and tested the intercoms.

Eckels swayed on the padded seat, his face pale, his jaw stiff. He felt the trembling in his arms and he looked down and found his hands tight on the new rifle. There were four other men in the Machine. Travis, the Safari Leader, his assistant, Lesperance, and two other hunters, Billings and Kramer. They sat looking at each other, and the years blazed around them.

"Can these guns get a dinosaur cold?" Eckels felt his mouth saying.

"If you hit them right," said Travis on the helmet radio. "Some dinosaurs have two brains, one in the head, another far down the spinal column. We stay away from those. That's stretching luck. Put your first two shots into the eyes, if you can, blind them, and go back into the brain."

The Machine howled. Time was a film run backward. Suns fled and ten million moons fled after them. "Think," said Eckels. "Every hunter that ever lived would envy us today. This makes Africa seem like Illinois."

The Machine slowed; its scream fell to a murmur. The Machine stopped.

The sun stopped in the sky.

The fog that had enveloped the Machine blew away and they were in an old time, a very old time indeed, three hunters and two Safari Heads with their blue metal guns across their knees.

"Christ isn't born yet," said Travis. "Moses has not gone to the mountain to talk with God. The Pyramids are still in the earth, waiting to be cut out and put up. *Remember* that. Alexander, Caesar, Napoleon, Hitler—none of them exists."

The man nodded.

"That"—Mr. Travis pointed—"is the jungle of sixty million two thousand and fifty-five years before President Keith."

He indicated a metal path that struck off into green wilderness, over streaming swamp, among giant ferns and palms.

"And that," he said, "is the Path, laid by Time Safari for your use. It floats six inches above the earth. Doesn't touch so much as one grass blade, flower, or tree. It's an anti-gravity metal. Its purpose is to keep you from touching this world of the past in any way. Stay on the Path. Don't go off it. I repeat. *Don't go off.* For *any* reason! If you fall off, there's a penalty. And don't shoot any animal we don't okay."

"Why?" asked Eckels. 30

They sat in the ancient wilderness. Far birds' cries blew on a wind, and the smell of tar and an old salt sea, moist grasses, and flowers the color of blood.

"We don't want to change the Future. We don't belong here in the Past. The government doesn't *like* us here. We have to pay big graft to keep our franchise. A Time Machine is finicky business. Not knowing it, we might kill an important animal, a small bird, a roach, a flower even, thus destroying an important link in a growing species."

"That's not clear," said Eckels.

"All right," Travis continued, "say we accidentally kill one mouse here. That means all the future families of this one particular mouse are destroyed, right?"

"Right." 35

"And all the families of the families of the families of that one mouse! With a stamp of your foot, you annihilate first one, then a dozen, then a thousand, a million, a billion possible mice!"

"So they're dead," said Eckels. "So what?"

"So what?" Travis snorted quietly. "Well, what about the foxes that'll need those mice to survive? For want of ten mice, a fox dies. For want of ten foxes a lion starves. For want of a lion, all manner of insects, vultures, infinite billions of life forms are thrown into chaos and destruction. Eventually it all boils down to this: fifty-nine million years later, a caveman, one of a dozen on the *entire world*, goes hunting wild boar or saber-toothed tiger for food. But you, friend, have stepped on all the tigers in that region. By stepping on *one* single mouse. So the caveman starves. And the caveman, please note, is not just *any* expendable man, no! He is an *entire future nation.* From his loins would have sprung ten sons. From their loins one hundred sons, and thus onward to a civilization. Destroy this one man, and you destroy a race, a people, an entire history of life. It is comparable to slaying some of Adam's grandchildren. The stomp of your foot, on one mouse, could start an earthquake, the effects of which could shake our earth and destinies down through Time, to their very foundations. With the death of that one caveman, a billion others yet unborn are throttled in the womb. Perhaps Rome never rises on its seven hills. Perhaps Europe is forever a dark forest, and only Asia waxes healthy and teeming. Step on a mouse and you crush the Pyramids. Step on a mouse and you leave your print, like a Grand Canyon, across Eternity. Queen Elizabeth might never be born, Washington might not cross the Delaware, there might never be a United States at all. So be careful. Stay on the Path. *Never* step off!"

"I see," said Eckels. "Then it wouldn't pay for us even to touch the *grass?*"

"Correct. Crushing certain plants could add up infinitesimally. A little 40
error here would multiply in sixty million years, all out of proportion.

Of course maybe our theory is wrong. Maybe Time *can't* be changed by us. Or maybe it can be changed only in little subtle ways. A dead mouse here makes an insect imbalance there, a population disproportion later, a bad harvest further on, a depression, mass starvation, and finally, a change in *social* temperament in far-flung countries. Something much more subtle, like that. Perhaps only a soft breath, a whisper, a hair, pollen on the air, such a slight, slight change that unless you looked close you wouldn't see it. Who knows? Who really can say he knows? We don't know. We're guessing. But until we do know for certain whether our messing around in Time *can* make a big roar or a little rustle in history, we're being careful. This Machine, this Path, your clothing and bodies, were sterilized, as you know, before the journey. We wear these oxygen helmets so we can't introduce our bacteria into an ancient atmosphere."

"How do we know which animals to shoot?"

"They're marked with red paint," said Travis. "Today, before our journey, we sent Lesperance here back with the Machine. He came to this particular era and followed certain animals."

"Studying them?"

"Right," said Lesperance. "I track them through their entire existence, noting which of them lives longest. Very few. How many times they mate. Not often. Life's short. When I find one that's going to die when a tree falls on him, or one that drowns in a tar pit, I note the exact hour, minute, and second. I shoot a paint bomb. It leaves a red patch on his side. We can't miss it. Then I correlate our arrival in the Past so that we meet the Monster not more than two minutes before he would have died anyway. This way, we kill only animals with no future, that are never going to mate again. You see how *careful* we are?"

"But if you came back this morning in Time," said Eckels eagerly, you 45
must've bumped into *us*, our Safari! How did it turn out? Was it successful? Did all of us get through—alive?"

Travis and Lesperance gave each other a look.

"That'd be a paradox," said the latter. "Time doesn't permit that sort of mess—a man meeting himself. When such occasions threaten, Time steps aside. Like an airplane hitting an air pocket. You felt the Machine jump just before we stopped? That was us passing ourselves on the way back to the Future. We saw nothing. There's no way of telling *if* this expedition was a success, *if* we got our monster, or whether all of us—meaning *you*, Mr. Eckels—got out alive."

Eckels smiled palely.

"Cut that," said Travis sharply. "Everyone on his feet!"

They were ready to leave the Machine. 50

The jungle was high and the jungle was broad and the jungle was the entire world forever and forever. Sounds like music and sounds like flying tents filled the sky, and those were pterodactyls soaring with cavernous gray wings, gigantic bats of delirium and night fever.

Eckels, balanced on the narrow Path, aimed his rifle playfully.

"Stop that!" said Travis. "Don't even aim for fun, blast you! If your guns should go off—"

Eckels flushed. "Where's our *Tyrannosaurus?*"

Lesperance checked his wristwatch. "Up ahead. We'll bisect his trail in sixty seconds. Look for the red paint! Don't shoot till we give the word. Stay on the Path. *Stay on the Path!*"

They moved forward in the wind of morning.

"Strange," murmured Eckels. "Up ahead, sixty million years, Election Day over. Keith made President. Everyone celebrating. And here we are, a million years lost, and they don't exist. The things we worried about for months, a lifetime, not even born or thought of yet."

"Safety catches off, everyone!" ordered Travis. "You, first shot, Eckels. Second, Billings, Third, Kramer."

"I've hunted tiger, wild boar, buffalo, elephant, but now, this is *it*," said Eckels. "I'm shaking like a kid."

"Ah," said Travis.

Everyone stopped.

Travis raised his hand. "Ahead," he whispered. "In the mist. There he is. There's His Royal Majesty now."

The jungle was wide and full of twitterings, rustlings, murmurs, and sighs.

Suddenly it all ceased, as if someone had shut a door.

Silence.

A sound of thunder.

Out of the mist, one hundred yards away, came *Tyrannosaurus rex.*

"It," whispered Eckels. "It . . ."

"Sh!"

It came on great oiled, resilient, striding legs. It towered thirty feet above half of the trees, a great evil god, folding its delicate watchmaker's claws close to its oily reptilian chest. Each lower leg was a piston, a thousand pounds of white bone, sunk in thick ropes of muscle, sheathed over in a gleam of pebbled skin like the mail of a terrible warrior. Each thigh was a ton of meat, ivory, and steel mesh. And from the great breathing cage of the upper body those two delicate arms dangled out front, arms with hands which might pick up and examine men like toys, while the snake neck coiled. And the head itself, a ton of sculptured stone, lifted easily upon the sky. Its mouth gaped, exposing a fence of teeth like daggers. Its eyes rolled, ostrich eggs, empty of all expression save hunger. It closed its mouth in a death grin. It ran, its pelvic bones crushing aside trees and bushes, its taloned feet clawing damp earth, leaving prints six inches deep wherever it settled its weight.

It ran with a gliding ballet step, far too poised and balanced for its ten tons. It moved into a sunlit area warily, its beautifully reptilian hands feeling the air.

"Why, why," Eckels twitched his mouth. "It could reach up and grab the moon."

"Sh!" Travis jerked angrily. "He hasn't seen us yet."

"It can't be killed," Eckels pronounced this verdict quietly, as if there could be no argument. He had weighed the evidence and this was his considered opinion. The rifle in his hands seemed a cap gun. "We were fools to come. This is impossible."

"Shut up!" hissed Travis.

"Nightmare."

"Turn around," commanded Travis. "Walk quietly to the Machine. We'll remit half your fee."

"I didn't realize it would be this *big*," said Eckels. "I miscalculated, that's all. And now I want out."

"It *sees* us!"

"There's the red paint on its chest!"

The Tyrant Lizard raised itself. Its armored flesh glittered like a thousand green coins. The coins, crusted with slime, steamed. In the slime, tiny insects wriggled, so that the entire body seemed to twitch and undulate, even while the monster itself did not move. It exhaled. The stink of raw flesh blew down the wilderness.

"Get me out of here," said Eckels. "It was never like this before. I was always sure I'd come through alive. I had good guides, good safaris, and safety. This time, I figured wrong. I've met my match and admit it. This is too much for me to get hold of."

"Don't run," said Lesperance. "Turn around. Hide in the Machine."

"Yes." Eckels seemed to be numb. He looked at his feet as if trying to make them move. He gave a grunt of helplessness.

"Eckels!"

He took a few steps, blinking, shuffling.

"Not *that* way!"

The Monster, at the first motion, lunged forward with a terrible scream. It covered one hundred yards in six seconds. The rifles jerked up and blazed fire. A windstorm from the beast's mouth engulfed them in the stench of slime and old blood. The Monster roared, teeth glittering with sun.

Eckels, not looking back, walked blindly to the edge of the Path, his gun limp in his arms, stepped off the Path, and walked, not knowing it, in the jungle. His feet sank into green moss. His legs moved him, and he felt alone and remote from the events behind.

The rifles cracked again. Their sound was lost in shriek and lizard thunder. The great level of the reptile's tail swung up, lashed sideways. Trees exploded in clouds of leaf and branch. The Monster twitched its jeweler's hands down to fondle at the men, to twist them in half, to crush them like berries, to cram them into its teeth and its screaming throat. Its boulderstone eyes leveled with the men. They saw themselves mirrored. They fired at the metallic eyelids and the blazing black iris.

Like a stone idol, like a mountain avalanche, *Tyrannosaurus* fell. Thundering, it clutched trees, pulled them with it. It wrenched and tore the metal Path. The men flung themselves back and away. The body hit, ten tons of cold flesh and stone. The guns fired. The Monster lashed its armored tail, twitched its snake jaws, and lay still. A fount of blood spurted from its throat. Somewhere inside, a sac of fluids burst. Sickening gushes drenched the hunters. They stood, red and glistening.

The thunder faded.

The jungle was silent. After the avalanche, a green peace. After the nightmare, morning.

Billings and Kramer sat on the pathway and threw up. Travis and Lesperance stood with smoking rifles, cursing steadily.

95 In the Time Machine, on his face, Eckels lay shivering. He had found his way back to the Path, climbed into the Machine.

Travis came walking, glanced at Eckels, took cotton gauze from a metal box, and returned to the others, who were sitting on the Path.

"Clean up."

They wiped the blood from their helmets. They began to curse too. The Monster lay, a hill of solid flesh. Within, you could hear the sighs and murmurs as the furthest chambers of it died, the organs malfunctioning, liquids running a final instant from pocket to sac to spleen, everything shutting off, closing up forever. It was like standing by a wrecked locomotive or a steam shovel at quitting time, all valves being released or levered tight. Bones cracked; the tonnage of its own flesh, off balance, dead weight, snapped the delicate forearms, caught underneath. The meat settled, quivering.

Another cracking sound. Overhead, a gigantic tree branch broke from its heavy mooring, fell. It crashed upon the dead beast with finality.

100 "There." Lesperance checked his watch. "Right on time. That's the giant tree that was scheduled to fall and kill this animal originally." He glanced at the two hunters. "You want the trophy picture?"

"What?"

"We can't take a trophy back to the Future. The body has to stay right here where it would have died originally, so the insects, birds, and bacteria can get at it, as they were intended to. Everything in balance. The body stays. But we *can* take a picture of you standing near it."

The two men tried to think, but gave up, shaking their heads.

They let themselves be led along the metal Path. They sank wearily into the Machine cushions. They gazed back at the ruined Monster, the stagnating mound, where already strange reptilian birds and golden insects were busy at the steaming armor. A sound on the floor of the Time Machine stiffened them. Eckels sat there, shivering.

105 "I'm sorry," he said at last.

"Get up!" cried Travis.

Eckels got up.

"Go out on that Path alone," said Travis. He had his rifle pointed, "You're not coming back in the Machine. We're leaving you here!"

Lesperance seized Travis's arm. "Wait—"

"Stay out of this!" Travis shook his hand away. "This fool nearly 110
killed us. But it isn't *that* so much, no. It's his *shoes*! Look at them! He ran off the Path. That *ruins* us! We'll forfeit! Thousands of dollars of insurance! We guarantee no one leaves the Path. He left it. Oh, the fool! I'll have to report to the government. They might revoke our license to travel. Who knows *what* he's done to Time, to History!"

"Take it easy, all he did was kick up some dirt."

"How do we *know?*" cried Travis. "We don't know anything! It's all a mystery! Get out of here, Eckels!"

Eckels fumbled his shirt. "I'll pay anything. A hundred thousand dollars!"

Travis glared at Eckels' checkbook and spat. "Go out there. The Monster's next to the Path. Stick your arms up to your elbows in his mouth. Then you can come back with us."

"That's unreasonable!" 115

"The Monster's dead, you idiot. The bullets! The bullets can't be left behind. They don't belong in the Past; they might change anything. Here's my knife. Dig them out!"

The jungle was alive again, full of the old tremorings and bird cries. Eckels turned slowly to regard the primeval garbage dump, that hill of nightmares and terror. After a long time, like a sleepwalker he shuffled out along the Path.

He returned, shuddering, five minutes later, his arms soaked and red to the elbows. He held out his hands. Each held a number of steel bullets. Then he fell. He lay where he fell, not moving.

"You didn't have to make him do that," said Lesperance.

"Didn't I? It's too early to tell." Travis nudged the still body. "He'll 120
live. Next time he won't go hunting game like this. Okay." He jerked his thumb wearily at Lesperance. "Switch on. Let's go home."

1492. 1776. 1812.

They cleaned their hands and faces. They changed their caking shirts and pants. Eckels was up and around again, not speaking. Travis glared at him for a full ten minutes.

"Don't look at me," cried Eckels. "I haven't done anything."

"Who can tell?"

"Just ran off the Path, that's all, a little mud on my shoes—what do 125
you want me to do—get down and pray?"

"We might need it. I'm warning you, Eckels, I might kill you yet. I've got my gun ready."

"I'm innocent. I've done nothing!"

1999. 2000. 2055.

The Machine stopped.

"Get out," said Travis. 130

The room was there as they had left it. But not the same as they had left it. The same man sat behind the same desk. But the same man did not quite sit behind the same desk. Travis looked around swiftly. "Everything okay here?" he snapped.

"Fine. Welcome home!"

Travis did not relax. He seemed to be looking through the one high window.

"Okay, Eckels, get out. Don't ever come back." Eckels could not move.

"You heard me," said Travis. "What're you *staring* at?" 135

Eckels stood smelling of the air, and there was a thing to the air, a chemical taint so subtle, so slight, that only a faint cry of his subliminal senses warned him it was there. The colors, white, gray, blue, orange, in the wall, in the furniture, in the sky beyond the window, were . . . were. . . . And there was a *feel*. His flesh twitched. His hands twitched. He stood drinking the oddness with the pores of his body. Somewhere, someone must have been screaming one of those whistles that only a dog can hear. His body screamed silence in return. Beyond this room, beyond this wall, beyond this man who was not quite the same man seated at this desk that was not quite the same desk . . . lay an entire world of streets and people. What sort of world it was now, there was no telling. He could feel them moving there, beyond the walls, almost, like so many chess pieces blown in a dry wind. . . .

But the immediate thing was the sign painted on the office wall, the same sign he had read earlier today on first entering. Somehow, the sign had changed:

TYME SEFARI INC.
SEFARIS TU ANY YEER EN THE
PAST.
YU NAIM THE ANIMALL.
WEE TAEKYUTHAIR.
YU SHOOT ITT.

Eckels felt himself fall into a chair. He fumbled crazily at the thick slime on his boots. He held up a clod of dirt, trembling, "No, it *can't* be. Not a *little* thing like that. No!"

Embedded in the mud, glistening green and gold and black, was a butterfly, very beautiful and very dead.

"Not a little thing like *that*! Not a butterfly!" cried Eckels. 140

It fell to the floor, an exquisite thing, a small thing that could upset balances and knock down a line of small dominoes and then big dominoes and then gigantic dominoes, all down the years across Time. Eckels' mind whirled. It *couldn't* change things. Killing one butterfly couldn't be *that* important! Could it?

His face was cold. His mouth trembled, asking: "Who—who won the presidential election yesterday?"

The man behind the desk laughed. "You joking? You know very well. Deutscher, of course! Who else? Not that fool weakling Keith. We got an iron man now, a man with guts!" The official stopped. "What's wrong?"

Eckels moaned. He dropped to his knees. He scrabbled at the golden butterfly with shaking fingers. "Can't we," he pleaded to the world, to himself, to the officials, to the Machine, "can't we take it back, can't we make it alive again? Can't we start over? Can't we—"

He did not move. Eyes shut, he waited, shivering. He heard Travis breathe loud in the room; he heard Travis shift his rifle, click the safety catch, and raise the weapon.

There was a sound of thunder.

Kate Chopin

The Story of an Hour

1894

Kate Chopin

Kate Chopin (1851–1904) was born Katherine O'Flaherty in St. Louis, the daughter of an Irish immigrant grown wealthy in retailing. On his death, young Kate was raised by her mother's family: aristocratic Creoles, descendants of the French and Spaniards who had colonized Louisiana. She received a convent schooling and at nineteen married Oscar Chopin, a Creole cotton broker from New Orleans. Later, the Chopins lived on a plantation near Cloutierville, Louisiana, a region whose varied people—Creoles, Cajuns, blacks—Kate Chopin was later to write about with loving care in Bayou Folk *(1894) and* A Night in Arcadie *(1897). The shock of her husband's sudden death in 1883, which left her with the raising of six children, seems to have plunged Kate Chopin into writing. She read and admired fine woman writers of her day, such as the Maine realist Sarah Orne Jewett. She also read Maupassant, Zola, and other new (and scandalous) French naturalist writers. She began to bring into American fiction some of their hard-eyed observation and their passion for telling unpleasant truths. Determined, in defiance of her times, frankly to show the sexual feelings of her characters, Chopin suffered from neglect and censorship. When her major novel,* The Awakening, *appeared in 1899, critics were outraged by her candid portrait of a woman who seeks sexual and professional independence. After causing such a literary scandal, Chopin was unable to get her later work published and wrote little more before she died.* The Awakening *and many of her stories had to wait seven decades for a sympathetic audience.*

Knowing that Mrs. Mallard was afflicted with a heart trouble, great care was taken to break to her as gently as possible the news of her husband's death.

It was her sister Josephine who told her, in broken sentences; veiled hints that revealed in half concealing. Her husband's friend Richards was there, too, near her. It was he who had been in the newspaper office when intelligence of the railroad disaster was received, with Brently Mallard's name leading the list of "killed." He had only taken the time to assure himself of its truth by a second telegram, and had hastened to forestall any less careful, less tender friend in bearing the sad message.

She did not hear the story as many women have heard the same, with a paralyzed inability to accept its significance. She wept at once, with sudden, wild abandonment, in her sister's arms. When the storm of grief had spent itself she went away to her room alone. She would have no one follow her.

There stood, facing the open window, a comfortable, roomy armchair. Into this she sank, pressed down by a physical exhaustion that haunted her body and seemed to reach into her soul.

She could see in the open square before her house the tops of trees 5
that were all aquiver with the new spring life. The delicious breath of rain was in the air. In the street below a peddler was crying his wares. The notes of a distant song which some one was singing reached her faintly, and countless sparrows were twittering in the eaves.

There were patches of blue sky showing here and there through the clouds that had met and piled one above the other in the west facing her window.

She sat with her head thrown back upon the cushion of the chair, quite motionless, except when a sob came up into her throat and shook her, as a child who has cried itself to sleep continues to sob in its dreams.

She was young, with a fair, calm face, whose lines bespoke repression and even a certain strength. But now there was a dull stare in her eyes, whose gaze was fixed away off yonder on one of those patches of blue sky. It was not a glance of reflection, but rather indicated a suspension of intelligent thought.

There was something coming to her and she was waiting for it, fearfully. What was it? She did not know; it was too subtle and elusive to name. But she felt it, creeping out of the sky, reaching toward her through the sounds, the scents, the color that filled the air.

Now her bosom rose and fell tumultuously. She was beginning to 10
recognize this thing that was approaching to possess her, and she was striving to beat it back with her will—as powerless as her two white slender hands would have been.

When she abandoned herself a little whispered word escaped her slightly parted lips. She said it over and over under her breath: "free, free, free!" The vacant stare and the look of terror that had followed it went from her eyes. They stayed keen and bright. Her pulses beat fast, and the coursing blood warmed and relaxed every inch of her body.

She did not stop to ask if it were or were not a monstrous joy that held her. A clear and exalted perception enabled her to dismiss the suggestion as trivial.

She knew that she would weep again when she saw the kind, tender hands folded in death; the face that had never looked save with love upon her, fixed and gray and dead. But she saw beyond that bitter moment a long procession of years to come that would belong to her absolutely. And she opened and spread her arms out to them in welcome.

There would be no one to live for her during those coming years; she would live for herself. There would be no powerful will bending hers in that blind persistence with which men and women believe they have a right to impose a private will upon a fellow-creature. A kind intention or a cruel intention made the act seem no less a crime as she looked upon it in that brief moment of illumination.

And yet she had loved him—sometimes. Often she had not. What did it matter! What could love, the unsolved mystery, count for in face of this possession of self-assertion which she suddenly recognized as the strongest impulse of her being!

"Free! Body and soul free!" she kept whispering.

Josephine was kneeling before the closed door with her lips to the keyhole, imploring for admission. "Louise, open the door! I beg; open the door—you will make yourself ill. What are you doing, Louise? For heaven's sake open the door."

"Go away. I am not making myself ill." No; she was drinking in a very elixir of life through that open window.

Her fancy was running riot along those days ahead of her. Spring days, and summer days, and all sorts of days that would be her own. She breathed a quick prayer that life might be long. It was only yesterday she had thought with a shudder that life might be long.

She arose at length and opened the door to her sister's importunities. There was a feverish triumph in her eyes, and she carried herself unwittingly like a goddess of Victory. She clasped her sister's waist, and together they descended the stairs. Richards stood waiting for them at the bottom.

Some one was opening the front door with a latchkey. It was Brently Mallard who entered, a little travel-stained, composedly carrying his grip-sack and umbrella. He had been far from the scene of the accident, and did not even know there had been one. He stood amazed at Josephine's piercing cry; at Richards' quick motion to screen him from the view of his wife.

But Richards was too late.

When the doctors came they said she had died of heart disease—of joy that kills.

Neil Gaiman

How to Talk to Girls at Parties

2006

Neil Gaiman

Neil Gaiman was born in Hampshire, England, in 1960 to a father who worked for a chain of grocery stores and a mother who was a pharmacist. When still a young boy, his parents quit their jobs, moved the family, and joined the Church of Scientology, for which his father became a public relations official. Gaiman has stated that he practices neither Scientology nor Judaism, his family's other religion, although that odd combination of fantasy and tradition pervades his writing. He did not attend university, but instead began a prolific career in literature—initially as a writer of graphic novels. Early on, Gaiman worked as a journalist and book reviewer on his way to becoming one of the most successful living writers of several imaginative genres, including literary fiction, fantasy, and comic books. He has also written horror, children's literature, and screenplays for television and film. Gaiman's first novel, Good Omens *(1990), was penned in collaboration with the fantasy writer Terry Pratchett. He launched to fame with the publication of* The Sandman *(1989–1996), a series that became one of DC Comic's bestselling titles in their storied history, even surpassing the sales of such classics as* Superman *and* Batman.

Gaiman started reading at age four and was soon immersed in the works of C. S. Lewis, J. R. R. Tolkien, Ursula K. Le Guin, Edgar Allan Poe, Lewis Carroll, and others. His writing is full of allusion; the depth and diversity of his literary accomplishments were influenced by spending countless hours in the library throughout his childhood. "I wouldn't be who I am without libraries," he has said. "I was the sort of kid who devoured books, and my happiest times as a boy were when I persuaded my parents to drop me off in the local library on their way to work, and I spent the day there." Gaiman has three children from his first marriage. He lives near Minneapolis and is married to the musician Amanda Palmer.

"Come on," said Vic. "It'll be great."

"No, it won't," I said, although I'd lost this fight hours ago, and I knew it.

"It'll be brilliant," said Vic, for the hundredth time. "Girls! Girls! Girls!" He grinned with white teeth.

We both attended an all-boys' school in south London. While it would be a lie to say that we had no experience with girls—Vic seemed to have had many girlfriends, while I had kissed three of my sister's friends—it would, I think, be perfectly true to say that we both chiefly spoke to, interacted with, and only truly understood, other boys. Well, I did, anyway. It's hard to speak for someone else, and I've not seen Vic for thirty years. I'm not sure that I would know what to say to him now if I did.

We were walking the backstreets that used to twine in a grimy maze 5
behind East Croydon station—a friend had told Vic about a party, and

Vic was determined to go whether I liked it or not, and I didn't. But my parents were away that week at a conference, and I was Vic's guest at his house, so I was trailing along beside him.

"It'll be the same as it always is," I said. "After an hour you'll be off somewhere snogging the prettiest girl at the party, and I'll be in the kitchen listening to somebody's mum going on about politics or poetry or something."

"You just have to talk to them," he said. "I think it's probably that road at the end here." He gestured cheerfully, swinging the bag with the bottle in it.

"Don't you know?"

"Alison gave me directions and I wrote them on a bit of paper, but I left it on the hall table. S'okay. I can find it."

"How?" Hope welled slowly up inside me. 10

"We walk down the road," he said, as if speaking to an idiot child. "And we look for the party. Easy."

I looked, but saw no party: just narrow houses with rusting cars or bikes in their concreted front gardens; and the dusty glass fronts of newsagents, which smelled of alien spices and sold everything from birthday cards and secondhand comics to the kind of magazines that were so pornographic that they were sold already sealed in plastic bags. I had been there when Vic had slipped one of those magazines beneath his sweater, but the owner caught him on the pavement outside and made him give it back.

We reached the end of the road and turned into a narrow street of terraced houses. Everything looked very still and empty in the Summer's evening. "It's all right for you," I said. "They fancy you. You don't actually have to talk to them." It was true: one urchin grin from Vic and he could have his pick of the room.

"Nah. S'not like that. You've just got to talk."

The times I had kissed my sister's friends I had not spoken to them. 15
They had been around while my sister was off doing something elsewhere, and they had drifted into my orbit, and so I had kissed them. I do not remember any talking. I did not know what to say to girls, and I told him so.

"They're just girls," said Vic. "They don't come from another planet."

As we followed the curve of the road around, my hopes that the party would prove unfindable began to fade: a low pulsing noise, music muffled by walls and doors, could be heard from a house up ahead. It was eight in the evening, not that early if you aren't yet sixteen, and we weren't. Not quite.

I had parents who liked to know where I was, but I don't think Vic's parents cared that much. He was the youngest of five boys. That in itself seemed magical to me: I merely had two sisters, both younger than I was, and I felt both unique and lonely. I had wanted a brother as far back as

I could remember. When I turned thirteen, I stopped wishing on falling stars or first stars, but back when I did, a brother was what I had wished for.

We went up the garden path, crazy paving leading us past a hedge and a solitary rosebush to a pebble-dashed facade. We rang the doorbell, and the door was opened by a girl. I could not have told you how old she was, which was one of the things about girls I had begun to hate: when you start out as kids you're just boys and girls, going through time at the same speed, and you're all five, or seven, or eleven, together. And then one day there's a lurch and the girls just sort of sprint off into the future ahead of you, and they know all about everything, and they have periods and breasts and makeup and God-only-knew-what-else—for I certainly didn't. The diagrams in biology textbooks were no substitute for being, in a very real sense, young adults. And the girls of our age were.

Vic and I weren't young adults, and I was beginning to suspect that 20
even when I started needing to shave every day, instead of once every couple of weeks, I would still be way behind.

The girl said, "Hello?"

Vic said, "We're friends of Alison's." We had met Alison, all freckles and orange hair and a wicked smile, in Hamburg, on a German exchange. The exchange organizers had sent some girls with us, from a local girls' school, to balance the sexes. The girls, our age, more or less, were raucous and funny, and had more or less adult boyfriends with cars and jobs and motorbikes and—in the case of one girl with crooked teeth and a raccoon coat, who spoke to me about it sadly at the end of a party in Hamburg, in, of course, the kitchen—a wife and kids.

"She isn't here," said the girl at the door. "No Alison."

"Not to worry," said Vic, with an easy grin. "I'm Vic. This is Enn." A beat, and then the girl smiled back at him. Vic had a bottle of white wine in a plastic bag, removed from his parents' kitchen cabinet. "Where should I put this, then?"

She stood out of the way, letting us enter. "There's a kitchen in the 25
back," she said. "Put it on the table there, with the other bottles." She had golden, wavy hair, and she was very beautiful. The hall was dim in the twilight, but I could see that she was beautiful.

"What's your name, then?" said Vic.

She told him it was Stella, and he grinned his crooked white grin and told her that that had to be the prettiest name he had ever heard. Smooth bastard. And what was worse was that he said it like he meant it.

Vic headed back to drop off the wine in the kitchen, and I looked into the front room, where the music was coming from. There were people dancing in there. Stella walked in, and she started to dance, swaying to the music all alone, and I watched her.

This was during the early days of punk. On our own record players we would play the Adverts and the Jam, the Stranglers and the Clash and the Sex Pistols. At other people's parties you'd hear ELO or 10cc or even Roxy Music. Maybe some Bowie, if you were lucky. During the German exchange, the only LP that we had all been able to agree on was Neil Young's *Harvest*, and his song "Heart of Gold" had threaded through the trip like a refrain: *I crossed the ocean for a heart of gold*. . . .

The music playing in that front room wasn't anything I recognized. 30

It sounded a bit like a German electronic pop group called Kraftwerk, and a bit like an LP I'd been given for my last birthday, of strange sounds made by the BBC Radiophonic Workshop. The music had a beat, though, and the half-dozen girls in that room were moving gently to it, although I only looked at Stella. She shone.

Vic pushed past me, into the room. He was holding a can of lager. "There's booze back in the kitchen," he told me. He wandered over to Stella and he began to talk to her. I couldn't hear what they were saying over the music, but I knew that there was no room for me in that conversation.

I didn't like beer, not back then. I went off to see if there was something I wanted to drink. On the kitchen table stood a large bottle of Coca-Cola, and I poured myself a plastic tumblerful, and I didn't dare say anything to the pair of girls who were talking in the underlit kitchen. They were animated and utterly lovely. Each of them had very black skin and glossy hair and movie star clothes, and their accents were foreign, and each of them was out of my league.

I wandered, Coke in hand.

The house was deeper than it looked, larger and more complex than 35
the two-up two-down model I had imagined. The rooms were underlit—I doubt there was a bulb of more than 40 watts in the building—and each room I went into was inhabited: in my memory, inhabited only by girls. I did not go upstairs.

A girl was the only occupant of the conservatory. Her hair was so fair it was white, and long, and straight, and she sat at the glass-topped table, her hands clasped together, staring at the garden outside, and the gathering dusk. She seemed wistful.

"Do you mind if I sit here?" I asked, gesturing with my cup. She shook her head, and then followed it up with a shrug, to indicate that it was all the same to her. I sat down.

Vic walked past the conservatory door. He was talking to Stella, but he looked in at me, sitting at the table, wrapped in shyness and awkwardness, and he opened and closed his hand in a parody of a speaking mouth. Talk. Right.

"Are you from around here?" I asked the girl.

She shook her head. She wore a low-cut silvery top, and I tried not 40
to stare at the swell of her breasts.

I said, "What's your name? I'm Enn."

"Wain's Wain," she said, or something that sounded like it. "I'm a second."

“That’s uh. That’s a different name.”

She fixed me with huge, liquid eyes. “It indicates that my progenitor was also Wain, and that I am obliged to report back to her. I may not breed.”

45 “Ah. Well. Bit early for that anyway, isn’t it?”

She unclasped her hands, raised them above the table, spread her fingers. “You see?” The little finger on her left hand was crooked, and it bifurcated at the top, splitting into two smaller fingertips. A minor deformity. “When I was finished a decision was needed. Would I be retained, or eliminated? I was fortunate that the decision was with me. Now, I travel, while my more perfect sisters remain at home in stasis. They were firsts. I am a second.

“Soon I must return to Wain, and tell her all I have seen. All my impressions of this place of yours.”

“I don’t actually live in Croydon,” I said. “I don’t come from here.” I wondered if she was American. I had no idea what she was talking about.

“As you say,” she agreed, “neither of us comes from here.” She folded her six- fingered left hand beneath her right, as if tucking it out of sight. “I had expected it to be bigger, and cleaner, and more colorful. But still, it is a jewel.”

50 She yawned, covered her mouth with her right hand, only for a moment, before it was back on the table again. “I grow weary of the journeying, and I wish sometimes that it would end. On a street in Rio at Carnival, I saw them on a bridge, golden and tall and insect-eyed and winged, and elated I almost ran to greet them, before I saw that they were only people in costumes. I said to Hola Colt, ‘Why do they try so hard to look like us?’ and Hola Colt replied, ‘Because they hate themselves, all shades of pink and brown, and so small.’ It is what I experience, even me, and I am not grown. It is like a world of children, or of elves.” Then she smiled, and said, “It was a good thing they could not any of them see Hola Colt.”

“Um,” I said, “do you want to dance?”

She shook her head immediately. “It is not permitted,” she said. “I can do nothing that might cause damage to property. I am Wain’s.”

“Would you like something to drink, then?”

“Water,” she said.

55 I went back to the kitchen and poured myself another Coke, and filled a cup with water from the tap. From the kitchen back to the hall, and from there into the conservatory, but now it was quite empty.

I wondered if the girl had gone to the toilet, and if she might change her mind about dancing later. I walked back to the front room and stared in. The place was filling up. There were more girls dancing, and several lads I didn’t know, who looked a few years older than me and Vic. The lads and the girls all kept their distance, but Vic was holding Stella’s hand as they danced, and when the song ended he put an arm around her, casually, almost proprietorially, to make sure that nobody else cut in.

I wondered if the girl I had been talking to in the conservatory was now upstairs, as she did not appear to be on the ground floor.

I walked into the living room, which was across the hall from the room where the people were dancing, and I sat down on the sofa. There was a girl sitting there already. She had dark hair, cut short and spiky, and a nervous manner.

Talk, I thought. "Um, this mug of water's going spare," I told her, "if you want it?"

She nodded, and reached out her hand and took the mug, extremely 60
carefully, as if she were unused to taking things, as if she could trust neither her vision nor her hands.

"I love being a tourist," she said, and smiled hesitantly. She had a gap between her two front teeth, and she sipped the tap water as if she were an adult sipping a fine wine. "The last tour, we went to sun, and we swam in sunfire pools with the whales. We heard their histories and we shivered in the chill of the outer places, then we swam deepward where the heat churned and comforted us.

"I wanted to go back. This time, I wanted it. There was so much I had not seen. Instead we came to world. Do you like it?"

"Like what?"

She gestured vaguely to the room—the sofa, the armchairs, the curtains, the unused gas fire.

"It's all right, I suppose." 65

"I told them I did not wish to visit world," she said. "My parent-teacher was unimpressed. 'You will have much to learn,' it told me. I said, 'I could learn more in sun, again. Or in the deeps. Jessa spun webs between galaxies. I want to do that.'

"But there was no reasoning with it, and I came to world. Parent-teacher engulfed me, and I was here, embodied in a decaying lump of meat hanging on a frame of calcium. As I incarnated I felt things deep inside me, fluttering and pumping and squishing. It was my first experience with pushing air through the mouth, vibrating the vocal cords on the way, and I used it to tell parent-teacher that I wished that I would die, which it acknowledged was the inevitable exit strategy from world."

There were black worry beads wrapped around her wrist, and she fiddled with them as she spoke. "But knowledge is there, in the meat," she said, "and I am resolved to learn from it."

We were sitting close at the center of the sofa now. I decided I should put an arm around her, but casually. I would extend my arm along the back of the sofa and eventually sort of creep it down, almost imperceptibly, until it was touching her. She said, "The thing with the liquid in the eyes, when the world blurs. Nobody told me, and I still do not understand. I have touched the folds of the Whisper and pulsed and flown with the tachyon swans, and I still do not understand."

She wasn't the prettiest girl there, but she seemed nice enough, and 70
she was a girl, anyway. I let my arm slide down a little, tentatively, so that it made contact with her back, and she did not tell me to take it away.

Vic called to me then, from the doorway. He was standing with his arm around Stella, protectively, waving at me. I tried to let him know, by shaking my head, that I was onto something, but he called my name and, reluctantly, I got up from the sofa and walked over to the door. "What?"

"Er. Look. The party," said Vic, apologetically. "It's not the one I thought it was. I've been talking to Stella and I figured it out. Well, she sort of explained it to me. We're at a different party."

"Christ. Are we in trouble? Do we have to go?"

Stella shook her head. He leaned down and kissed her, gently, on the lips. "You're just happy to have me here, aren't you darlin'?"

"You know I am," she told him.

He looked from her back to me, and he smiled his white smile: roguish, lovable, a little bit Artful Dodger, a little bit wide-boy Prince Charming. "Don't worry. They're all tourists here anyway. It's a foreign exchange thing, innit? Like when we all went to Germany."

"It is?"

"Enn. You got to talk to them. And that means you got to listen to them, too. You understand?"

"I did. I already talked to a couple of them."

"You getting anywhere?"

"I was till you called me over."

"Sorry about that. Look, I just wanted to fill you in. Right?"

And he patted my arm and he walked away with Stella. Then, together, the two of them went up the stairs.

Understand me, all the girls at that party, in the twilight, were lovely; they all had perfect faces but, more important than that, they had whatever strangeness of proportion, of oddness or humanity it is that makes a beauty something more than a shop window dummy.

Stella was the most lovely of any of them, but she, of course, was Vic's, and they were going upstairs together, and that was just how things would always be.

There were several people now sitting on the sofa, talking to the gap-toothed girl. Someone told a joke, and they all laughed. I would have had to push my way in there to sit next to her again, and it didn't look like she was expecting me back, or cared that I had gone, so I wandered out into the hall. I glanced in at the dancers, and found myself wondering where the music was coming from. I couldn't see a record player or speakers.

From the hall I walked back to the kitchen.

Kitchens are good at parties. You never need an excuse to be there, and, on the good side, at this party I couldn't see any signs of someone's mum. I inspected the various bottles and cans on the kitchen table, then I poured a half an inch of Pernod into the bottom of my plastic cup, which I filled to the top with Coke. I dropped in a couple of ice cubes and took a sip, relishing the sweet-shop tang of the drink.

"What's that you're drinking?" A girl's voice.

"It's Pernod," I told her. "It tastes like aniseed balls, only it's alcoholic." I didn't say that I only tried it because I'd heard someone in the crowd ask for a Pernod on a live Velvet Underground LP.

"Can I have one?" I poured another Pernod, topped it off with Coke, passed it to her. Her hair was a coppery auburn, and it tumbled around her head in ringlets. It's not a hair style you see much now, but you saw it a lot back then.

"What's your name?" I asked.

"Triolet," she said.

"Pretty name," I told her, although I wasn't sure that it was. She was pretty, though.

"It's a verse form," she said, proudly. "Like me."

"You're a poem?"

She smiled, and looked down and away, perhaps bashfully. Her profile was almost flat—a perfect Grecian nose that came down from her forehead in a straight line. We did Antigone in the school theater the previous year. I was the messenger who brings Creon the news of Antigone's death. We wore half-masks that made us look like that. I thought of that play, looking at her face, in the kitchen, and I thought of Barry Smith's drawings of women in the Conan comics: five years later I would have thought of the Pre-Raphaelites, of Jane Morris and Lizzie Siddall. But I was only fifteen then.

"You're a poem?" I repeated.

She chewed her lower lip. "If you want. I am a poem, or I am a pattern, or a race of people whose world was swallowed by the sea."

"Isn't it hard to be three things at the same time?"

"What's your name?"

"Enn."

"So you are Enn," she said. "And you are a male. And you are a biped. Is it hard to be three things at the same time?"

"But they aren't different things. I mean, they aren't contradictory." It was a word I had read many times but never said aloud before that night, and I put the stresses in the wrong places. *Contradictory.*

She wore a thin dress made of a white, silky fabric. Her eyes were a pale green, a color that would now make me think of tinted contact lenses; but this was thirty years ago; things were different then. I remember wondering about Vic and Stella, upstairs. By now, I was sure that they were in one of the bedrooms, and I envied Vic so much it almost hurt.

Still, I was talking to this girl, even if we were talking nonsense, even if her name wasn't really Triolet (my generation had not been given hippie names: all the Rainbows and the Sunshines and the Moons, they were only six, seven, eight years old back then). She said, "We knew that it would soon be over, and so we put it all into a poem, to tell the universe who we were, and why we were here, and what we said and did and thought and dreamed and yearned for. We wrapped our dreams in words and patterned the words so that they would live forever, unforgettable. Then we sent the poem as a pattern of flux, to wait in the heart of a star, beaming out its message in pulses and bursts and fuzzes across the electromagnetic spectrum, until the time when, on worlds a thousand sun systems distant, the pattern would be decoded and read, and it would become a poem once again."

"And then what happened?"

She looked at me with her green eyes, and it was as if she stared out at me from her own Antigone half-mask; but as if her pale green eyes were just a different, deeper, part of the mask. "You cannot hear a poem without it changing you," she told me. "They heard it, and it colonized them. It inherited them and it inhabited them, its rhythms becoming part of the way that they thought; its images permanently transmuting their metaphors; its verses, its outlook, its aspirations becoming their lives. Within a generation their children would be born already knowing the poem, and, sooner rather than later, as these things go, there were no more children born. There was no need for them, not any longer. There was only a poem, which took flesh and walked and spread itself across the vastness of the known."

I edged closer to her, so I could feel my leg pressing against hers.

She seemed to welcome it: she put her hand on my arm, affection- 110
ately, and I felt a smile spreading across my face.

"There are places that we are welcomed," said Triolet, "and places where we are regarded as a noxious weed, or as a disease, something immediately to be quarantined and eliminated. But where does contagion end and art begin?"

"I don't know," I said, still smiling. I could hear the unfamiliar music as it pulsed and scattered and boomed in the front room.

She leaned into me then and—I suppose it was a kiss. . . . I suppose. She pressed her lips to my lips, anyway, and then, satisfied, she pulled back, as if she had now marked me as her own.

"Would you like to hear it?" she asked, and I nodded, unsure what she was offering me, but certain that I needed anything she was willing to give me.

She began to whisper something in my ear. It's the strangest thing 115
about poetry—you can tell it's poetry, even if you don't speak the language. You can hear Homer's Greek without understanding a word, and you still know it's poetry. I've heard Polish poetry, and Inuit poetry, and I knew what it was without knowing. Her whisper was like that. I didn't know the language, but her words washed through me, perfect, and in my mind's eye I saw towers of glass and diamond; and people with eyes of the palest green; and, unstoppable, beneath every syllable, I could feel the relentless advance of the ocean.

Perhaps I kissed her properly. I don't remember. I know I wanted to.

And then Vic was shaking me violently. "Come on!" he was shouting. "Quickly. Come on!"

In my head I began to come back from a thousand miles away.

"Idiot. Come on. Just get a move on," he said, and he swore at me. There was fury in his voice.

For the first time that evening I recognized one of the songs being 120
played in the front room. A sad saxophone wail followed by a cascade of liquid chords, a man's voice singing cut-up lyrics about the sons of the silent age.° I wanted to stay and hear the song.

She said, "I am not finished. There is yet more of me."

"Sorry love," said Vic, but he wasn't smiling any longer. "There'll be another time," and he grabbed me by the elbow and he twisted and pulled, forcing me from the room. I did not resist. I knew from experience that Vic could beat the stuffing out me if he got it into his head to do so. He wouldn't do it unless he was upset or angry, but he was angry now.

Out into the front hall. As Vic pulled open the door, I looked back one last time, over my shoulder, hoping to see Triolet in the doorway to the kitchen, but she was not there. I saw Stella, though, at the top of the stairs. She was staring down at Vic, and I saw her face.

This all happened thirty years ago. I have forgotten much, and I will forget more, and in the end I will forget everything; yet, if I have any certainty of life beyond death, it is all wrapped up not in psalms or hymns, but in this one thing alone: I cannot believe that I will ever forget that moment, or forget the expression on Stella's face as she watched Vic hurrying away from her. Even in death I shall remember that.

Her clothes were in disarray, and there was makeup smudged across 125
her face, and her eyes—

You wouldn't want to make a universe angry. I bet an angry universe would look at you with eyes like that.

We ran then, me and Vic, away from the party and the tourists and the twilight, ran as if a lightning storm was on our heels, a mad helter-skelter dash down the confusion of streets, threading through the maze, and we did not look back, and we did not stop until we could not breathe; and then we stopped and panted, unable to run any longer. We were in pain. I held on to a wall, and Vic threw up, hard and long, into the gutter.

He wiped his mouth.

"She wasn't a—" He stopped.

He shook his head. 130

Then he said, "You know . . . I think there's a thing. When you've gone as far as you dare. And if you go any further, you wouldn't be you anymore? You'd be the person who'd done that? The places you just can't go. . . . I think that happened to me tonight."

sons of the silent age: "Sons of the Silent Age" is a song by David Bowie from his 1977 album *Heroes*, the second of three dark, minimalist records that were known as the "Berlin Trilogy."

I thought I knew what he was saying. "Screw her, you mean?" I said.

He rammed a knuckle hard against my temple, and twisted it violently. I wondered if I was going to have to fight him—and lose—but after a moment he lowered his hand and moved away from me, making a low, gulping noise.

I looked at him curiously, and I realized that he was crying: his face was scarlet; snot and tears ran down his cheeks. Vic was sobbing in the street, as unselfconsciously and heartbreakingly as a little boy.

He walked away from me then, shoulders heaving, and he hurried down the road so he was in front of me and I could no longer see his face. I wondered what had occurred in that upstairs room to make him behave like that, to scare him so, and I could not even begin to guess.

The streetlights came on, one by one; Vic stumbled on ahead, while I trudged down the street behind him in the dusk, my feet treading out the measure of a poem that, try as I might, I could not properly remember and would never be able to repeat.

Nathaniel Hawthorne

Young Goodman Brown

(1835) 1846

Nathaniel Hawthorne

Nathaniel Hawthorne (1804–1864) was born in the clipper-ship seaport of Salem, Massachusetts, son of a merchant captain (who died when the future novelist was only four years old) and great-great-grandson of a magistrate involved in the notorious Salem witchcraft trials. Hawthorne takes a keen interest in New England's sin-and-brimstone Puritan past in many of his stories, especially "Young Goodman Brown," and in the classic novel The Scarlet Letter *(1850), his deepest exploration of his major themes of conscience, sin, and guilt. In 1825 Hawthorne graduated from Bowdoin College; one of his classmates—and his lifelong best friend—was Franklin Pierce, who in 1852 would be elected president of the United States. After college, Hawthorne lived at home and trained to be a writer. His first novel,* Fanshawe *(1828), begun while he was still an undergraduate, was published anonymously and at his own expense. During this period, Hawthorne also experienced great difficulty in trying to publish his short fiction, both in magazines and in book form, until the appearance of* Twice-Told Tales *(1837). In 1841, he was appointed to a position in the Boston Custom House; in the following year he married Sophia Peabody. The newlyweds settled in the Old Manse in Concord, Massachusetts. Three more novels followed:* The House of the Seven Gables *(1851, the story of a family curse, tinged with nightmarish humor),* The Blithedale Romance *(1852, drawn from his short, irritating stay at a Utopian commune, Brook Farm), and* The Marble Faun *(1860, inspired by a stay in Italy). When Franklin Pierce ran for president, Hawthorne wrote his campaign biography. After taking office, Pierce appointed his old friend American consul at Liverpool, England. Depressed by ill health and the terrible toll of the Civil War, Hawthorne died suddenly while on a tour with Pierce of New Hampshire's White Mountains. With his contemporary Edgar Allan Poe, Hawthorne transformed the American short story from popular magazine filler into a major literary form.*

Young Goodman° Brown came forth, at sunset, into the street of Salem village,° but put his head back, after crossing the threshold, to exchange a parting kiss with his young wife. And Faith, as the wife was aptly named, thrust her own pretty head into the street, letting the wind play with the pink ribbons of her cap, while she called to Goodman Brown.

"Dearest heart," whispered she, softly and rather sadly, when her lips were close to his ear, "pray thee, put off your journey until sunrise, and sleep in your own bed to-night. A lone woman is troubled with such dreams and such thoughts, that she's afraid of herself, sometimes. Pray, tarry with me this night, dear husband, of all nights in the year!"

"My love and my Faith," replied young Goodman Brown, "of all nights in the year, this one night must I tarry away from thee. My journey, as thou callest it, forth and back again, must needs be done 'twixt now and sunrise. What, my sweet, pretty wife, dost thou doubt me already, and we but three months married!"

"Then, God bless you!" said Faith, with the pink ribbons, "and may you find all well, when you come back."

"Amen!" cried Goodman Brown. "Say thy prayers, dear Faith, and 5
go to bed at dusk, and no harm will come to thee."

So they parted; and the young man pursued his way, until, being about to turn the corner by the meeting-house, he looked back, and saw the head of Faith still peeping after him, with a melancholy air, in spite of her pink ribbons.

"Poor little Faith!" thought he, for his heart smote him. "What a wretch am I, to leave her on such an errand! She talks of dreams, too. Methought, as she spoke, there was trouble in her face, as if a dream had warned her what work is to be done tonight. But, no, no! 'twould kill her to think it. Well; she's a blessed angel on earth; and after this one night, I'll cling to her skirts and follow her to Heaven."

With this excellent resolve for the future, Goodman Brown felt himself justified in making more haste on his present evil purpose. He had taken a dreary road, darkened by all the gloomiest trees of the forest, which barely stood aside to let the narrow path creep through, and closed immediately behind. It was all as lonely as could be; and there is this peculiarity in such a solitude, that the traveller knows not who may

Goodman: title given by Puritans to a male head of a household; a farmer or other ordinary citizen. *Salem village:* in England's Massachusetts Bay Colony.

be concealed by the innumerable trunks and the thick boughs overhead; so that, with lonely footsteps, he may yet be passing through an unseen multitude.

"There may be a devilish Indian behind every tree," said Goodman Brown, to himself; and he glanced fearfully behind him, as he added, "What if the devil himself should be at my very elbow!"

His head being turned back, he passed a crook of the road, and looking forward again, beheld the figure of a man, in grave and decent attire, seated at the foot of an old tree. He arose, at Goodman Brown's approach, and walked onward, side by side with him.

"You are late, Goodman Brown," said he. "The clock of the Old South was striking as I came through Boston; and that is full fifteen minutes agone."°

"Faith kept me back awhile," replied the young man, with a tremor in his voice, caused by the sudden appearance of his companion, though not wholly unexpected.

It was now deep dusk in the forest, and deepest in that part of it where these two were journeying. As nearly as could be discerned, the second traveller was about fifty years old, apparently in the same rank of life as Goodman Brown, and bearing a considerable resemblance to him, though perhaps more in expression than features. Still, they might have been taken for father and son. And yet, though the elder person was as simply clad as the younger, and as simple in manner too, he had an indescribable air of one who knew the world, and would not have felt abashed at the governor's dinner-table, or in King William's court,° were it possible that his affairs should call him thither. But the only thing about him, that could be fixed upon as remarkable, was his staff, which bore the likeness of a great black snake, so curiously wrought, that it might almost be seen to twist and wriggle itself, like a living serpent. This, of course, must have been an ocular deception, assisted by the uncertain light.

"Come, Goodman Brown!" cried his fellow-traveller, "this is dull pace for the beginning of a journey. Take my staff, if you are so soon weary."

"Friend," said the other, exchanging his slow pace for a full stop, "having kept covenant by meeting thee here, it is my purpose now to return whence I came. I have scruples, touching the matter thou wot'st° of."

"Sayest thou so?" replied he of the serpent, smiling apart. "Let us walk on, nevertheless, reasoning as we go, and if I convince thee not, thou shalt turn back. We are but a little way in the forest, yet."

full fifteen minutes agone: Apparently this mystery man has traveled in a flash from Boston's Old South Church all the way to the woods beyond Salem—as the crow flies, a good sixteen miles. *King William's court:* back in England, where William III reigned from 1689 to 1702. *wot'st:* know.

"Too far, too far!" exclaimed the goodman, unconsciously resuming his walk. "My father never went into the woods on such an errand, nor his father before him. We have been a race of honest men and good Christians, since the days of the martyrs.° And shall I be the first of the name of Brown, that ever took this path, and kept—"

"Such company, thou wouldst say," observed the elder person, interpreting his pause. "Well said, Goodman Brown! I have been as well acquainted with your family as with ever a one among the Puritans; and that's no trifle to say. I helped your grandfather, the constable, when he lashed the Quaker woman so smartly through the streets of Salem. And it was I that brought your father a pitch-pine knot, kindled at my own hearth, to set fire to an Indian village, in King Philip's war.° They were my good friends, both; and many a pleasant walk have we had along this path, and returned merrily after midnight. I would fain be friends with you, for their sake."

"If it be as thou sayest," replied Goodman Brown, "I marvel they never spoke of these matters. Or, verily, I marvel not, seeing that the least rumor of the sort would have driven them from New England. We are a people of prayer, and good works, to boot, and abide no such wickedness."

"Wickedness or not," said the traveller with the twisted staff, "I have 20
a very general acquaintance here in New England. The deacons of many a church have drunk the communion wine with me; the selectmen, of divers towns, make me their chairman; and a majority of the Great and General Court are firm supporters of my interest. The governor and I, too—but these are state-secrets."

"Can this be so!" cried Goodman Brown, with a stare of amazement at his undisturbed companion. "Howbeit, I have nothing to do with the governor and council; they have their own ways, and are no rule for a simple husbandman, like me. But, were I to go on with thee, how should I meet the eye of that good old man, our minister, at Salem village? Oh, his voice would make me tremble, both Sabbath-day and lecture-day!"°

Thus far, the elder traveller had listened with due gravity, but now burst into a fit of irrepressible mirth, shaking himself so violently, that his snake-like staff actually seemed to wriggle in sympathy.

"Ha! ha! ha!" shouted he, again and again; then composing himself, "Well, go on, Goodman Brown, go on; but pray thee, don't kill me with laughing!"

days of the martyrs: a time when many forebears of the New England Puritans had given their lives for religious convictions—when Mary I (Mary Tudor, nicknamed "Bloody Mary"), queen of England from 1553 to 1558, briefly reestablished the Roman Catholic Church in England and launched a campaign of persecution against Protestants. *King Philip's war:* Metacomet, or King Philip (as the English called him), chief of the Wampanoag Indians, had led a bitter, widespread uprising of several New England tribes (1675–1678). Metacomet died in the war, as did one out of every ten white male colonists. *lecture-day:* a weekday when everyone had to go to church to hear a sermon or Bible-reading.

"Well, then, to end the matter at once," said Goodman Brown, considerably nettled, "there is my wife, Faith. It would break her dear little heart; and I'd rather break my own!"

"Nay, if that be the case," answered the other, "e'en go thy ways, 25
Goodman Brown. I would not, for twenty old women like the one hobbling before us, that Faith should come to any harm."

As he spoke, he pointed his staff at a female figure on the path, in whom Goodman Brown recognized a very pious and exemplary dame, who had taught him his catechism, in youth, and was still his moral and spiritual adviser, jointly with the minister and Deacon Gookin.

"A marvel, truly, that Goody° Hoyse should be so far in the wilderness, at nightfall!" said he. "But, with your leave, friend, I shall take a cut through the woods, until we have left this Christian woman behind. Being a stranger to you, she might ask whom I was consorting with, and whither I was going."

"Be it so," said his fellow-traveller. "Betake you to the woods, and let me keep the path."

Accordingly, the young man turned aside, but took care to watch his companion, who advanced softly along the road, until he had come within a staff's length of the old dame. She, meanwhile, was making the best of her way, with singular speed for so aged a woman, and mumbling some indistinct words, a prayer, doubtless, as she went. The traveller put forth his staff, and touched her withered neck with what seemed the serpent's tail.

"The devil!" screamed the pious old lady. 30

"Then Goody Cloyse knows her old friend?" observed the traveller, confronting her, and leaning on his writhing stick.

"Ah, forsooth, and is it your worship, indeed?" cried the good dame. "Yea, truly is it, and in the very image of my old gossip,° Goodman Brown, the grandfather of the silly fellow that now is. But—would your worship believe it?—my broomstick hath strangely disappeared, stolen, as I suspect, by that unhanged witch, Goody Cory, and that, too, when I was all anointed with the juice of smallage and cinquefoil and wolfs bane—"°

"Mingled with fine wheat and the fat of a new-born babe," said the shape of old Goodman Brown.

"Ah, your worship knows the receipt,"° cried the old lady, cackling aloud. "So, as I was saying, being all ready for the meeting, and no horse to ride on, I made up my mind to foot it; for they tell me, there is a nice

Goody: short for Goodwife, title for a married woman of ordinary station. In his story, Hawthorne borrows from history the names of two "Goodys"—Goody Cloyse and Goody Cory—and one unmarried woman, Martha Carrier. In 1692 Hawthorne's great-great-grandfather John Hathorne, a judge in the Salem witchcraft trials, had condemned all three to be hanged. *gossip:* friend or kinsman. *smallage and cinquefoil and wolf's bane:* wild plants—here, ingredients for a witch's brew. *receipt:* recipe.

young man to be taken into communion to-night. But now your good worship will lend me your arm, and we shall be there in a twinkling."

"That can hardly be," answered her friend. "I may not spare you my arm, Goody Cloyse, but here is my staff, if you will."

So saying, he threw it down at her feet, where, perhaps, it assumed life, being one of the rods which its owner had formerly lent to the Egyptian Magi.° Of this fact, however, Goodman Brown could not take cognizance. He had cast up his eyes in astonishment, and looking down again, beheld neither Goody Cloyse nor the serpentine staff, but his fellow-traveller alone, who waited for him as calmly as if nothing had happened.

"That old woman taught me my catechism!" said the young man; and there was a world of meaning in this simple comment.

They continued to walk onward, while the elder traveller exhorted his companion to make good speed and persevere in the path, discoursing so aptly, that his arguments seemed rather to spring up in the bosom of his auditor, than to be suggested by himself. As they went, he plucked a branch of maple, to serve for a walking-stick, and began to strip it of the twigs and little boughs, which were wet with evening dew. The moment his fingers touched them, they became strangely withered and dried up, as with a week's sunshine. Thus the pair proceeded, at a good free pace, until suddenly, in a gloomy hollow of the road, Goodman Brown sat himself down on the stump of a tree, and refused to go any farther.

"Friend," said he, stubbornly, "my mind is made up. Not another step will I budge on this errand. What if a wretched old woman do choose to go to the devil, when I thought she was going to Heaven! Is that any reason why I should quit my dear Faith, and go after her?"

"You will think better of this, by-and-by," said his acquaintance, composedly. "Sit here and rest yourself awhile; and when you feel like moving again, there is my staff to help you along."

Without more words, he threw his companion the maple stick, and was as speedily out of sight, as if he had vanished into the deepening gloom. The young man sat a few moments, by the road-side, applauding himself greatly, and thinking with how clear a conscience he should meet the minister, in his morning-walk, nor shrink from the eye of good old Deacon Gookin. And what calm sleep would be his, that very night, which was to have been spent so wickedly, but purely and sweetly now, in the arms of Faith! Amidst these pleasant and praiseworthy meditations, Goodman Brown heard the tramp of horses along the road, and deemed it advisable to conceal himself within the verge of the forest, conscious of the guilty purpose that had brought him thither, though now so happily turned from it.

Egyptian Magi: In the Bible, Pharaoh's wise men and sorcerers who by their magical powers changed their rods into live serpents. (This incident, part of the story of Moses and Aaron, is related in Exodus 7:8–12.)

On came the hoof-tramps and the voices of the riders, two grave old voices, conversing soberly as they drew near. These mingled sounds appeared to pass along the road, within a few yards of the young man's hiding-place; but owing, doubtless, to the depth of the gloom, at that particular spot, neither the travellers nor their steeds were visible. Though their figures brushed the small boughs by the way-side, it could not be seen that they intercepted, even for a moment, the faint gleam from the strip of bright sky, athwart which they must have passed. Goodman Brown alternately crouched and stood on tip-toe, pulling aside the branches, and thrusting forth his head as far as he durst, without discerning so much as a shadow. It vexed him the more, because he could have sworn, were such a thing possible, that he recognized the voices of the minister and Deacon Gookin, jogging along quietly, as they were wont to do, when bound to some ordination or ecclesiastical council. While yet within hearing, one of the riders stopped to pluck a switch.

"Of the two, reverend Sir," said the voice like the deacon's, "I had rather miss an ordination-dinner than to-night's meeting. They tell me that some of our community are to be here from Falmouth and beyond, and others from Connecticut and Rhode Island; besides several of the Indian powows,° who, after their fashion, know almost as much deviltry as the best of us. Moreover, there is a goodly young woman to be taken into communion."

"Mighty well, Deacon Gookin!" replied the solemn old tones of the minister. "Spur up, or we shall be late. Nothing can be done, you know, until I get on the ground."

45 The hoofs clattered again, and the voices, talking so strangely in the empty air, passed on through the forest, where no church had ever been gathered, nor solitary Christian prayed. Whither, then, could these holy men be journeying, so deep into the heathen wilderness? Young Goodman Brown caught hold of a tree, for support, being ready to sink down on the ground, faint and overburdened with the heavy sickness of his heart. He looked up to the sky, doubting whether there really was a Heaven above him. Yet, there was the blue arch, and the stars brightening in it.

"With Heaven above, and Faith below, I will yet stand firm against the devil!" cried Goodman Brown.

While he still gazed upward, into the deep arch of the firmament, and had lifted his hands to pray, a cloud, though no wind was stirring, hurried across the zenith, and hid the brightening stars. The blue sky was still visible, except directly overhead, where this black mass of cloud was sweeping swiftly northward. Aloft in the air, as if from the depths of the cloud, came a confused and doubtful sound of voices. Once, the listener fancied that he could distinguish the accents of town's-people of his own,

powows: Indian priests or medicine men.

men and women, both pious and ungodly, many of whom he had met at the communion-table, and had seen others rioting at the tavern. The next moment, so indistinct were the sounds, he doubted whether he had heard aught but the murmur of the old forest, whispering without a wind. Then came a stronger swell of those familiar tones, heard daily in the sunshine, at Salem village, but never, until now, from a cloud of night. There was one voice, of a young woman, uttering lamentations, yet with an uncertain sorrow, and entreating for some favor, which, perhaps, it would grieve her to obtain. And all the unseen multitude, both saints and sinners, seemed to encourage her onward.

"Faith!" shouted Goodman Brown, in a voice of agony and desperation; and the echoes of the forest mocked him, crying—"Faith! Faith!" as if bewildered wretches were seeking her, all through the wilderness.

The cry of grief, rage, and terror, was yet piercing the night, when the unhappy husband held his breath for a response. There was a scream, drowned immediately in a louder murmur of voices, fading into far-off laughter, as the dark cloud swept away, leaving the clear and silent sky above Goodman Brown. But something fluttered lightly down through the air, and caught on the branch of a tree. The young man seized it, and beheld a pink ribbon.

"My Faith is gone!" cried he, after one stupefied moment. "There is no good on earth; and sin is but a name. Come, devil! for to thee is this world given."

And maddened with despair, so that he laughed loud and long, did Goodman Brown grasp his staff and set forth again, at such a rate, that he seemed to fly along the forest-path, rather than to walk or run. The road grew wilder and drearier, and more faintly traced, and vanished at length, leaving him in the heart of the dark wilderness, still rushing onward, with the instinct that guides mortal man to evil. The whole forest was peopled with frightful sounds; the creaking of the trees, the howling of wild beasts, and the yell of Indians; while, sometimes, the wind tolled like a distant church-bell, and sometimes gave a broad roar around the traveller, as if all Nature were laughing him to scorn. But he was himself the chief horror of the scene, and shrank not from its other horrors.

"Ha! ha! ha!" roared Goodman Brown, when the wind laughed at him. "Let us hear which will laugh loudest! Think not to frighten me with your deviltry! Come witch, come wizard, come Indian powow, come devil himself! and here comes Goodman Brown. You may as well fear him as he fear you!"

In truth, all through the haunted forest, there could be nothing more frightful than the figure of Goodman Brown. On he flew, among the black pines, brandishing his staff with frenzied gestures, now giving vent to an inspiration of horrid blasphemy, and now shouting forth such laughter, as set all the echoes of the forest laughing like demons around him. The fiend in his own shape is less hideous, than when he rages in the breast of man. Thus sped the demoniac on his course, until, quivering among the trees, he saw a red light before him, as when the felled trunks and branches of a clearing have been set on fire, and throw up their lurid blaze against the sky, at the hour of midnight. He paused, in a lull of the tempest that had driven him onward, and heard the swell of what seemed a hymn, rolling solemnly from a distance, with the weight of many voices. He knew the tune; it was a familiar one in the choir of the village meeting-house. The verse died heavily away, and was lengthened by a chorus, not of human voices, but of all the sounds of the benighted wilderness, pealing in awful harmony together. Goodman Brown cried out; and his cry was lost to his own ear, by its unison with the cry of the desert.

In the interval of silence, he stole forward, until the light glared full upon his eyes. At one extremity of an open space, hemmed in by the dark wall of the forest, arose a rock, bearing some rude, natural resemblance either to an altar or a pulpit, and surrounded by four blazing pines, their tops aflame, their stems untouched, like candles at an evening meeting. The mass of foliage, that had overgrown the summit of the rock, was all on fire, blazing high into the night, and fitfully illuminating the whole field. Each pendent twig and leafy festoon was in a blaze. As the red light arose and fell, a numerous congregation alternately shone forth, then disappeared in shadow, and again grew, as it were, out of the darkness, peopling the heart of the solitary woods at once.

"A grave and dark-clad company!" quoth Goodman Brown. 55

In truth, they were such. Among them, quivering to-and-fro, between gloom and splendor, appeared faces that would be seen, next day, at the council-board of the province, and others which, Sabbath after Sabbath, looked devoutly heavenward, and benignantly over the crowded pews, from the holiest pulpits in the land. Some affirm that the lady of the governor was there. At least, there were high dames well known to her, and wives of honored husbands, and widows, a great multitude, and ancient maidens, all of excellent repute, and fair young girls, who trembled, lest their mothers should espy them. Either the sudden gleams of light, flashing over the obscure field, bedazzled Goodman Brown, or he recognized a score of the church-members of Salem village, famous for their especial sanctity. Good old Deacon Gookin had arrived, and waited at the skirts of that venerable saint, his revered pastor. But, irreverently consorting with these grave, reputable, and pious people, these elders of the church, these chaste dames and dewy virgins, there were men of dissolute lives and women of spotted fame, wretches given over to all mean and filthy vice, and suspected even of horrid crimes. It was strange to see, that the good shrank not from the wicked, nor were the sinners abashed by the saints. Scattered, also, among their pale-faced enemies, were the Indian priests, or powows, who had often scared their native forest with more hideous incantations than any known to English witchcraft.

"But, where is Faith?" thought Goodman Brown; and, as hope came into his heart, he trembled.

Another verse of the hymn arose, a slow and mournful strain, such as the pious love, but joined to words which expressed all that our nature can conceive of sin, and darkly hinted at far more. Unfathomable to mere mortals is the lore of fiends. Verse after verse was sung, and still the chorus of the desert swelled between, like the deepest tone of a mighty organ. And, with the final peal of that dreadful anthem, there came a sound, as if the roaring wind, the rushing streams, the howling beasts, and every other voice of the unconverted wilderness, were mingling and according with the voice of guilty man, in homage to the prince of all. The four blazing pines threw up a loftier flame, and obscurely discovered shapes and visages of horror on the smoke-wreaths, above the impious assembly. At the same moment, the fire on the rock shot redly forth, and formed a glowing arch above its base, where now appeared a figure. With reverence be it spoken, the figure bore no slight similitude, both in garb and manner, to some grave divine of the New England churches.

"Bring forth the converts!" cried a voice, that echoed through the field and rolled into the forest.

At the word, Goodman Brown stepped forth from the shadow of the 60
trees, and approached the congregation, with whom he felt a loathful brotherhood, by the sympathy of all that was wicked in his heart. He could have well nigh sworn, that the shape of his own dead father beckoned him to advance, looking downward from a smoke-wreath, while a woman, with dim features of despair, threw out her hand to warn him back. Was it his mother? But he had no power to retreat one step, nor to resist, even in thought, when the minister and good old Deacon Gookin seized his arms, and led him to the blazing rock. Thither came also the slender form of a veiled female, led between Goody Cloyse, that pious teacher of the catechism, and Martha Carrier, who had received the devil's promise to be queen of hell. A rampant hag was she! And there stood the proselytes,° beneath the canopy of fire.

"Welcome, my children," said the dark figure, "to the communion of your race! Ye have found, thus young, your nature and your destiny. My children, look behind you!"

They turned; and flashing forth, as it were, in a sheet of flame, the fiend-worshippers were seen; the smile of welcome gleamed darkly on every visage.

"There," resumed the sable form, "are all whom ye have reverenced from youth. Ye deemed them holier than yourselves, and shrank from your own sin, contrasting it with their lives of righteousness, and prayerful aspirations heavenward. Yet, here are they all, in my worshipping

proselytes: new converts.

assembly! This night it shall be granted you to know their secret deeds; how hoary-bearded elders of the church have whispered wanton words to the young maids of their households; how many a woman, eager for widow's weeds, has given her husband a drink at bedtime, and let him sleep his last sleep in her bosom; how beardless youths have made haste to inherit their fathers' wealth; and how fair damsels—blush not, sweet ones!—have dug little graves in the garden, and bidden me, the sole guest, to an infant's funeral. By the sympathy of your human hearts for sin, ye shall scent out all the places—whether in church, bed-chamber, street, field, or forest—where crime has been committed, and shall exult to behold the whole earth one stain of guilt, one mighty bloodspot. Far more than this! It shall be yours to penetrate, in every bosom, the deep mystery of sin, the fountain of all wicked arts, and which inexhaustibly supplies more evil impulses than human power—than my power, at its utmost!—can make manifest in deeds. And now, my children, look upon each other."

They did so; and, by the blaze of the hell-kindled torches, the wretched man beheld his Faith, and the wife her husband, trembling before that unhallowed altar.

"Lo! there ye stand, my children," said the figure, in a deep and sol- 65
emn tone, almost sad, with its despairing awfulness, as if his once angelic nature could yet mourn for our miserable race. "Depending upon one another's hearts, ye had still hoped, that virtue were not all a dream. Now are ye undeceived! Evil is the nature of mankind. Evil must be your only happiness. Welcome, again, my children, to the communion of your race!"

"Welcome!" repeated the fiend-worshippers, in one cry of despair and triumph.

And there they stood, the only pair, as it seemed, who were yet hesitating on the verge of wickedness, in this dark world. A basin was hollowed, naturally, in the rock. Did it contain water, reddened by the lurid light? or was it blood? or, perchance, a liquid flame? Herein did the Shape of Evil dip his hand, and prepare to lay the mark of baptism upon their foreheads, that they might be partakers of the mystery of sin, more conscious of the secret guilt of others, both in deed and thought, than they could now be of their own. The husband cast one look at his pale wife, and Faith at him. What polluted wretches would the next glance show them to each other, shuddering alike at what they disclosed and what they saw!

"Faith! Faith!" cried the husband. "Look up to Heaven, and resist the Wicked one!"

Whether Faith obeyed, he knew not. Hardly had he spoken, when he found himself amid calm night and solitude, listening to a roar of the wind, which died heavily away through the forest. He staggered against the rock and felt it chill and damp, while a hanging twig, that had been all on fire, besprinkled his cheek with the coldest dew.

The next morning, young Goodman Brown came slowly into the 70
street of Salem village, staring around him like a bewildered man. The good old minister was taking a walk along the grave-yard, to get an appetite for breakfast and meditate his sermon, and bestowed a blessing, as he passed, on Goodman Brown. He shrank from the venerable saint, as if to avoid an anathema.° Old Deacon Goodkin was at domestic worship, and the holy words of his prayer were heard through the open window. "What God doth the wizard pray to?" quoth Goodman Brown. Goody Cloyse, that excellent old Christian, stood in the early sunshine, at her own lattice, catechizing a little girl, who had brought her a pint of morning's milk. Goodman Brown snatched away the child, as from the grasp of the fiend himself. Turning the corner by the meeting-house, he spied the head of Faith, with the pink ribbons, gazing anxiously forth, and bursting into such joy at sight of him, that she skipt along the street, and almost kissed her husband before the whole village. But, Goodman Brown looked sternly and sadly into her face, and passed on without a greeting.

Had Goodman Brown fallen asleep in the forest, and only dreamed a wild dream of a witch-meeting?

Be it so, if you will. But, alas! it was a dream of evil omen for young Goodman Brown. A stern, a sad, a darkly meditative, a distrustful, if not a desperate man, did he become, from the night of that fearful dream. On the Sabbath-day, when the congregation were singing a holy psalm, he could not listen, because an anthem of sin rushed loudly upon his ear, and drowned all the blessed strain. When the minister spoke from the pulpit, with power and fervid eloquence, and, with his hand on the open Bible, of the sacred truths of our religion, and of saint-like lives and triumphant deaths, and of future bliss or misery unutterable, then did Goodman Brown turn pale, dreading, lest the roof should thunder down upon the gray blasphemer and his hearers. Often, awakening suddenly at midnight, he shrank from the bosom of Faith, and at morning or eventide, when the family knelt down at prayer, he scowled, and muttered to himself, and gazed sternly at his wife, and turned away. And when he had lived long, and was borne to his grave, a hoary corpse, followed by Faith, an aged woman, and children and grandchildren, a goodly procession, besides neighbors, not a few, they carved no hopeful verse upon his tombstone; for his dying hour was gloom.

anathema: an official curse, a decree that casts communicants out of a church and bans them from receiving the sacraments.

Zora Neale Hurston

Sweat

1926

Zora Neale Hurston

Zora Neale Hurston (1901?–1960) was born in Eatonville, Florida, but no record of her actual date of birth exists (best guesses range from 1891 to 1901). Hurston was one of eight children. Her father, a carpenter and Baptist preacher, was also the three-term mayor of Eatonville, the first all-black town incorporated in the United States. When Hurston's mother died in 1912, the father moved the children from one relative to another. Consequently, Hurston never finished grammar school, although in 1918 she began taking classes at Howard University, paying her way through school by working as a manicurist and maid. While at Howard, she published her first story. In early 1925 she moved to New York, arriving with "$1.50, no job, no friends, and a lot of hope." She soon became an important member of the Harlem Renaissance, a group of young black artists (including Langston Hughes, Countee Cullen, Jean Toomer, and Claude McKay) who sought "spiritual emancipation" for African Americans by exploring black heritage and identity in the arts. Hurston eventually became, according to critic Laura Zaidman, "the most prolific black American woman writer of her time." In 1925 she became the first African American student at Barnard College, where she completed a B.A. in anthropology. Hurston's most famous story, "Sweat," appeared in the only issue of Fire!!*, a 1926 avant-garde Harlem Renaissance magazine edited by Hurston, Hughes, and Wallace Thurman. This powerful story of an unhappy marriage turned murderous was particularly noteworthy for having the characters speak in the black country dialect of Hurston's native Florida. Hurston achieved only modest success during her lifetime, despite the publication of her memorable novel* Their Eyes Were Watching God *(1937) and her many contributions to the study of African American folklore. She died, poor and neglected, in a Florida welfare home and was buried in an unmarked grave. In 1973 novelist Alice Walker erected a gravestone for her carved with the words:*

Zora Neale Hurston
"A Genius of the South"
1901–1960
Novelist, Folklorist
Anthropologist

I

It was eleven o'clock of a Spring night in Florida. It was Sunday. Any other night, Delia Jones would have been in bed for two hours by this time. But she was a washwoman, and Monday morning meant a great deal to her. So she collected the soiled clothes on Saturday when she returned the clean things. Sunday night after church, she sorted and put the white things to soak. It saved her almost a half-day's start. A great hamper in the bedroom held the clothes that she brought home. It was so much neater than a number of bundles lying around.

She squatted on the kitchen floor beside the great pile of clothes, sorting them into small heaps according to color, and humming a song in a mournful key, but wondering through it all where Sykes, her husband, had gone with her horse and buckboard.°

Just then something long, round, limp, and black fell upon her shoulders and slithered to the floor beside her. A great terror took hold of her. It softened her knees and dried her mouth so that it was a full minute before she could cry out or move. Then she saw that it was the big bull whip her husband liked to carry when he drove.

She lifted her eyes to the door and saw him standing there bent over with laughter at her fright. She screamed at him.

"Sykes, what you throw dat whip on me like dat? You know it would 5
skeer me—looks just like a snake, an' you knows how skeered Ah is of snakes."

"Course Ah knowed it! That's how come Ah done it." He slapped his leg with his hand and almost rolled on the ground in his mirth. "If you such a big fool dat you got to have a fit over a earth worm or a string, Ah don't keer how bad Ah skeer you."

"You ain't got no business doing it. Gawd knows it's a sin. Some day Ah'm gointuh drop dead from some of yo' foolishness. 'Nother thing, where you been wid mah rig? Ah feeds dat pony. He ain't fuh you to be drivin' wid no bull whip."

"You sho' is one aggravatin' nigger woman!" he declared and stepped into the room. She resumed her work and did not answer him at once. "Ah done tole you time and again to keep them white folks' clothes outa dis house."

He picked up the whip and glared at her. Delia went on with her work. She went out into the yard and returned with a galvanized tub and set it on the wash-bench. She saw that Sykes had kicked all of the clothes together again, and now stood in her way truculently, his whole manner hoping, *praying*, for an argument. But she walked calmly around him and commenced to re-sort the things.

"Next time, Ah'm gointer kick 'em outdoors," he threatened as he 10
struck a match along the leg of his corduroy breeches.

Delia never looked up from her work, and her thin, stooped shoulders sagged further.

"Ah ain't for no fuss t'night Sykes. Ah just come from taking sacrament at the church house."

buckboard: a four-wheeled open carriage with the seat resting on a spring platform.

He snorted scornfully. "Yeah, you just come from de church house on a Sunday night, but heah you is gone to work on them clothes. You ain't nothing but a hypocrite. One of them amen-corner Christians—sing, whoop, and shout, then come home and wash white folks' clothes on the Sabbath."

He stepped roughly upon the whitest pile of things, kicking them helter-skelter as he crossed the room. His wife gave a little scream of dismay, and quickly gathered them together again.

"Sykes, you quit grindin' dirt into these clothes! How can Ah git 15
through by Sat'day if Ah don't start on Sunday?"

"Ah don't keer if you never git through. Anyhow, Ah done promised Gawd and a couple of other men, Ah ain't gointer have it in mah house. Don't gimme no lip neither, else Ah'll throw 'em out and put mah fist up side yo' head to boot."

Delia's habitual meekness seemed to slip from her shoulders like a blown scarf. She was on her feet; her poor little body, her bare knuckly hands bravely defying the strapping hulk before her.

"Looka heah, Sykes, you done gone too fur. Ah been married to you fur fifteen years, and Ah been takin' in washin' fur fifteen years. Sweat, sweat, sweat! Work and sweat, cry and sweat, pray and sweat!"

"What's that got to do with me?" he asked brutally.

"What's it got to do with you, Sykes? Mah tub of suds is filled yo' 20
belly with vittles more times than yo' hands is filled it. Mah sweat is done paid for this house and Ah reckon Ah kin keep on sweatin' in it."

She seized the iron skillet from the stove and struck a defensive pose, which act surprised him greatly, coming from her. It cowed him and he did not strike her as he usually did.

"Naw you won't," she panted, "that ole snaggle-toothed black woman you runnin' with ain't comin' heah to pile up on *mah* sweat and blood. You ain't paid for nothin' on this place, and Ah'm gointer stay right heah till Ah'm toted out foot foremost."

"Well, you better quit gittin' me riled up, else they'll be totin' you out sooner than you expect. Ah'm so tired of you Ah don't know whut to do. Gawd! How Ah hates skinny wimmen!"

A little awed by this new Delia, he sidled out of the door and slammed the back gate after him. He did not say where he had gone, but she knew too well. She knew very well that he would not return until nearly daybreak also. Her work over, she went on to bed but not to sleep at once. Things had come to a pretty pass!

She lay awake, gazing upon the debris that cluttered their matrimonial 25
trail. Not an image left standing along the way. Anything like flowers had long ago been drowned in the salty stream that had been pressed from her heart. Her tears, her sweat, her blood. She had brought love to the union and he had brought a longing after the flesh. Two months after the wedding, he had given her the first brutal beating. She had the memory of his numerous trips to Orlando with all of his wages when he had returned to

her penniless, even before the first year had passed. She was young and soft then, but now she thought of her knotty, muscled limbs, her harsh knuckly hands, and drew herself up into an unhappy little ball in the middle of the big feather bed. Too late now to hope for love, even if it were not Bertha it would be someone else. This case differed from the others only in that she was bolder than the others. Too late for everything except her little home. She had built it for her old days, and planted one by one the trees and flowers there. It was lovely to her, lovely.

Somehow, before sleep came, she found herself saying aloud: "Oh well, whatever goes over the Devil's back, is got to come under his belly. Sometime or ruther, Sykes, like everybody else, is gointer reap his sowing." After that she was able to build a spiritual earthworks° against her husband. His shells could no longer reach her. AMEN. She went to sleep and slept until he announced his presence in bed by kicking her feet and rudely snatching the covers away.

"Gimme some kivah heah, an' git yo' damn foots over on yo' own side! Ah oughter mash you in yo' mouf fuh drawing dat skillet on me."

Delia went clear to the rail without answering him. A triumphant indifference to all that he was or did.

II

The week was full of work for Delia as all other weeks, and Saturday found her behind her little pony, collecting and delivering clothes.

It was a hot, hot day near the end of July. The village men on Joe Clarke's porch even chewed cane listlessly. They did not hurl the cane-knots as usual. They let them dribble over the edge of the porch. Even conversation had collapsed under the heat.

"Heah come Delia Jones," Jim Merchant said, as the shaggy pony came 'round the bend of the road toward them. The rusty buckboard was heaped with baskets of crisp, clean laundry.

"Yep," Joe Lindsay agreed. "Hot or col', rain or shine, jes'ez reg'lar ez de weeks roll roun' Delia carries 'em an' fetches 'em on Sat'day."

"She better if she wanter eat," said Moss. "Syke Jones ain't wuth de shot an' powder hit would tek tuh kill 'im. Not to *huh* he ain't."

"He sho' ain't," Walter Thomas chimed in. "It's too bad, too, cause she wuz a right pretty li'l trick when he got huh. Ah'd uh mah'ied huh mahself if he hadnter beat me to it."

Delia nodded briefly at the men as she drove past.

"Too much knockin' will ruin *any* 'oman. He done beat huh 'nough tuh kill three women, let 'lone change they looks," said Elijah Moseley. "How Syke kin stommuck dat big black greasy Mogul he's layin' roun'

spiritual earthworks: earthworks are military fortifications made of earth; here Hurston uses it metaphorically to mean Delia's emotional defenses.

wid, gits me. Ah swear dat eight-rock couldn't kiss a sardine can Ah done thowed out de back do' 'way las' yeah."

"Aw, she's fat, thass how come. He's allus been crazy 'bout fat women," put in Merchant. "He'd a' been tied up wid one long time ago if he could a' found one tuh have him. Did Ah tell yuh 'bout him come sidlin' roun' *mah* wife—bringin' her a basket uh peecans outa his yard fuh a present? Yessir, mah wife! She tol' him tuh take 'em right straight back home, 'cause Delia works so hard ovah dat washtub she reckon everything on de place taste lak sweat an' soapsuds. Ah jus' wisht Ah'd a' caught 'im 'roun' dere! Ah'd a' made his hips ketch on fiah down dat shell road."

"Ah know he done it, too. Ah sees 'im grinnin' at every 'oman dat passes," Walter Thomas said. "But even so, he useter eat some mighty big hunks uh humble pie tuh git dat li'l 'oman he got. She wuz ez pritty ez a speckled pup! Dat wuz fifteen years ago. He useter be so skeered uh losin' huh, she could make him do some parts of a husband's duty. Dey never wuz de same in de mind."

"There oughter be a law about him," said Lindsay. "He ain't fit tuh carry guts tuh a bear."

Clarke spoke for the first time. "Tain't no law on earth dat kin make 40
a man be decent if it ain't in 'im. There's plenty men dat takes a wife lak dey do a joint uh sugar-cane. It's round, juicy, an' sweet when dey gits it. But dey squeeze an' grind, squeeze an' grind an' wring tell dey wring every drop uh pleasure dat's in 'em out. When dey's satisfied dat dey is wrung dry, dey treats 'em jes' lak dey do a cane-chew. Dey thows 'em away. Dey knows whut dey is doin' while dey is at it, an' hates theirselves fuh it but they keeps on hangin' after huh tell she's empty. Den dey hates huh fuh bein' a cane-chew an' in de way."

"We oughter take Syke an' dat stray 'oman uh his'n down in Lake Howell swamp an' lay on de rawhide till they cain't say Lawd a' mussy. He allus wuz uh ovahbearin niggah, but since dat white 'oman from up north done teached 'im how to run a automobile, he done got too biggety to live—an' we oughter kill 'im," Old Man Anderson advised.

A grunt of approval went around the porch. But the heat was melting their civic virtue and Elijah Moseley began to bait Joe Clarke.

"Come on, Joe, git a melon outa dere an' slice it up for yo' customers. We'se all sufferin' wid de heat. De bear's done got *me!*"

"Thass right, Joe, a watermelon is jes' whut Ah needs tuh cure de eppizudicks," Walter Thomas joined forces with Moseley. "Come on dere, Joe. We all is steady customers an' you ain't set us up in a long time. Ah chooses dat long, bowlegged Floridy favorite."

"A god, an' be dough. You all gimme twenty cents and slice away," 45
Clarke retorted. "Ah needs a col' slice m'self. Heah, everybody chip in. Ah'll lend y'all mah meat knife."

The money was all quickly subscribed and the huge melon brought forth. At that moment, Sykes and Bertha arrived. A determined silence fell on the porch and the melon was put away again.

Merchant snapped down the blade of his jackknife and moved toward the store door.

"Come on in, Joe, an' gimme a slab uh sow belly an' uh pound uh coffee—almost fuhgot 'twas Sat'day. Got to git on home." Most of the men left also.

Just then Delia drove past on her way home, as Sykes was ordering magnificently for Bertha. It pleased him for Delia to see.

"Git whutsoever yo' heart desires, Honey. Wait a minute, Joe. Give huh two bottles uh strawberry soda-water, uh quart parched ground-peas, an' a block uh chewin' gum."

With all this they left the store, with Sykes reminding Bertha that this was his town and she could have it if she wanted it.

The men returned soon after they left, and held their watermelon feast.

"Where did Syke Jones git da 'oman from nohow?" Lindsay asked.

"Ovah Apopka. Guess dey musta been cleanin' out de town when she lef'. She don't look lak a thing but a hunk uh liver wid hair on it."

"Well, she sho' kin squall," Dave Carter contributed. "When she gits ready tuh laff, she jes' opens huh mouf an' latches it back tuh de las' notch. No ole granpa alligator down in Lake Bell ain't got nothin' on huh."

III

Bertha had been in town three months now. Sykes was still paying her room-rent at Della Lewis'—the only house in town that would have taken her in. Sykes took her frequently to Winter Park to "stomps." He still assured her that he was the swellest man in the state.

"Sho' you kin have dat li'l ole house soon's Ah git dat 'oman outa-dere. Everything b'longs tuh me an' you sho' kin have it. Ah sho' 'bomi-nates uh skinny 'oman. Lawdy, you sho' is got one portly shape on you! You kin git *anything* you wants. Dis is *mah* town an' you sho' kin have it."

Delia's work-worn knees crawled over the earth in Gethsemane° and up the rocks of Calvary° many, many times during these months. She avoided the villagers and meeting places in her efforts to be blind and deaf. But Bertha nullified this to a degree, by coming to Delia's house to call Sykes out to her at the gate.

Delia and Sykes fought all the time now with no peaceful interludes. They slept and ate in silence. Two or three times Delia had attempted a timid friendliness, but she was repulsed each time. It was plain that the breaches must remain agape.

The sun had burned July to August. The heat streamed down like a million hot arrows, smiting all things living upon the earth. Grass with-ered, leaves browned, snakes went blind in shedding, and men and dogs went mad. Dog days!

Gethsemane: the garden outside Jerusalem that was the scene of Jesus's agony and arrest (see Matthew 26:36–57); hence, a scene of great suffering. *Calvary*: the hill outside Jerusalem where Jesus was crucified.

Delia came home one day and found Sykes there before her. She wondered, but started to go on into the house without speaking, even though he was standing in the kitchen door and she must either stoop under his arm or ask him to move. He made no room for her. She noticed a soap box beside the steps, but paid no particular attention to it, knowing that he must have brought it there. As she was stooping to pass under his outstretched arm, he suddenly pushed her backward, laughingly.

"Look in de box dere, Delia, Ah done brung yuh somethin'!"

She nearly fell upon the box in her stumbling, and when she saw what it held, she all but fainted outright.

"Syke! Syke, mah Gawd! You take dat rattlesnake 'way from heah! You *gottuh*. Oh, Jesus, have mussy!"

"Ah ain't got tuh do nuthin' uh de kin'—fact is Ah ain't got tuh do nothin' but die. Tain't no use uh you puttin' on airs makin' out lak you skeered uh dat snake—he's gointer stay right heah tell he die. He wouldn't bite me cause Ah knows how tuh handle 'im. Nohow he wouldn't risk breakin' out his fangs 'gin *yo* skinny laigs."

"Naw, now Syke, don't keep dat thing 'round tryin' tuh skeer me tuh death. You knows Ah'm even feared uh earth worms. Thass de biggest snake Ah evah did see. Kill 'im, Syke, please."

"Doan ast me tuh do nothin' fuh yuh. Goin' 'round tryin' tuh be so damn asterperious.° Naw, Ah ain't gonna kill it. Ah think uh damn sight mo' uh him dan you! Dat's a nice snake an' anybody doan lak 'im kin jes' hit de grit."

The village soon heard that Sykes had the snake, and came to see and ask questions.

"How de hen-fire did you ketch dat six-foot rattler, Syke?" Thomas asked.

"He's full uh frogs so he cain't hardly move, thass how Ah eased up on 'im. But Ah'm a snake charmer an' knows how tuh handle 'em. Shux, dat ain't nothin'. Ah could ketch one eve'y day if Ah so wanted tuh."

"Whut he needs is a heavy hick'ry club leaned real heavy on his head. Dat's de bes' way tuh charm a rattlesnake."

"Naw, Walt, y'all jes' don't understand dese diamon' backs lak Ah do," said Sykes in a superior tone of voice.

The village agreed with Walter, but the snake stayed on. His box remained by the kitchen door with its screen wire covering. Two or three days later it had digested its meal of frogs and literally came to life. It rattled at every movement in the kitchen or the yard. One day as Delia came down the kitchen steps she saw his chalky-white fangs curved like scimitars hung in the wire meshes. This time she did not run away with

asterperious: haughty.

averted eyes as usual. She stood for a long time in the doorway in a red fury that grew bloodier for every second that she regarded the creature that was her torment.

That night she broached the subject as soon as Sykes sat down to the table.

"Syke, Ah wants you tuh take dat snake 'way fum heah. You done starved me an' Ah put up widcher, you done beat me an Ah took dat, but you done kilt all mah insides bringin' dat varmint heah."

Sykes poured out a saucer full of coffee and drank it deliberately before he answered her.

"A whole lot Ah keer 'bout how you feels inside uh out. Dat snake ain't goin' no damn wheah till Ah gits ready fuh 'im tuh go. So fur as beatin' is concerned, yuh ain't took near all dat you gointer take ef yuh stay 'round *me*."

Delia pushed back her plate and got up from the table. "Ah hates you, Sykes," she said calmly. "Ah hates you tuh de same degree dat Ah useter love yuh. Ah done took an' took till mah belly is full up tuh mah neck. Dat's de reason Ah got mah letter fum de church an' moved mah membership tuh Woodbridge—so Ah don't haftuh take no sacrament wid yuh. Ah don't wantuh see yuh 'round me atall. Lay 'round wid dat 'oman all yuh wants tuh, but gwan 'way fum me an' mah house. Ah hates yuh lak uh suck-egg dog."

Sykes almost let the huge wad of corn bread and collard greens he was chewing fall out of his mouth in amazement. He had a hard time whipping himself up to the proper fury to try to answer Delia.

"Well, Ah'm glad you does hate me. Ah'm sho' tiahed uh you hangin' ontuh me. Ah don't want yuh. Look at yuh stringey ole neck! Yo' raw-bony laigs an' arms is enough tuh cut uh man tuh death. You looks jes' lak de devvul's doll-baby tuh *me*. You cain't hate me no worse dan Ah hates you. Ah been hatin' *you* fuh years."

"Yo' ole black hide don't look lak nothin' tuh me, but uh passle uh wrinkled up rubber, wid yo' big ole yeahs flappin' on each side lak uh paih uh buzzard wings. Don't think Ah'm gointuh be run 'way fum mah house neither. Ah'm goin' tuh de white folks 'bout *you*, mah young man, de very nex' time you lay yo' han's on me. Mah cup is done run ovah." Delia said this with no signs of fear and Sykes departed from the house, threatening her, but made not the slightest move to carry out any of them.

That night he did not return at all, and the next day being Sunday, Delia was glad she did not have to quarrel before she hitched up her pony and drove the four miles to Woodbridge.

She stayed to the night service—"love feast"—which was very warm and full of spirit. In the emotional winds her domestic trials were borne far and wide so that she sang as she drove homeward,

Jurden water,° black an' col
Chills de body, not de soul
An' Ah wantah cross Jurden in uh calm time.

She came from the barn to the kitchen door and stopped.

"Whut's de mattah, ol' Satan, you ain't kickin' up yo' racket?" She 85
addressed the snake's box. Complete silence. She went on into the house with a new hope in its birth struggles. Perhaps her threat to go to the white folks had frightened Sykes! Perhaps he was sorry! Fifteen years of misery and suppression had brought Delia to the place where she would hope *anything* that looked towards a way over or through her wall of inhibitions.

She felt in the match-safe behind the stove at once for a match. There was only one there.

"Dat niggah wouldn't fetch nothin' heah tuh save his rotten neck, but he kin run thew whut Ah brings quick enough. Now he done toted off nigh on tuh haff uh box uh matches. He done had dat 'oman heah in mah house, too."

Nobody but a woman could tell how she knew this even before she struck the match. But she did and it put her into a new fury.

Presently she brought in the tubs to put the white things to soak. This time she decided she need not bring the hamper out of the bedroom; she would go in there and do the sorting. She picked up the pot-bellied lamp and went in. The room was small and the hamper stood hard by the foot of the white iron bed. She could sit and reach through the bedposts—resting as she worked.

"*Ah wantah cross Jurden in uh calm time.*" She was singing again. The 90
mood of the "love feast" had returned. She threw back the lid of the basket almost gaily. Then, moved by both horror and terror, she sprang back toward the door. *There lay the snake in the basket!* He moved sluggishly at first, but even as she turned round and round, jumped up and down in an insanity of fear, he began to stir vigorously. She saw him pouring his awful beauty from the basket upon the bed, then she seized the lamp and ran as fast as she could to the kitchen. The wind from the open door blew out the light and the darkness added to her terror. She sped to the darkness of the yard, slamming the door after her before she thought to set down the lamp. She did not feel safe even on the ground, so she climbed up in the hay barn.

There for an hour or more she lay sprawled upon the hay a gibbering wreck.

Finally she grew quiet, and after that came coherent thought. With this stalked through her a cold, bloody rage. Hours of this. A period of introspection, a space of retrospection, then a mixture of both. Out of this an awful calm.

Jurden water: black Southern dialect for the River Jordan, which represents the last boundary before entering heaven. It comes from the Old Testament, when the Jews had to cross the River Jordan to reach the Promised Land.

"Well, Ah done de bes' Ah could. If things ain't right, Gawd knows tain't mah fault."

She went to sleep—a twitch sleep—and woke up to a faint gray sky. There was a loud hollow sound below. She peered out. Sykes was at the wood-pile, demolishing a wire-covered box.

He hurried to the kitchen door, but hung outside there some minutes before he entered, and stood some minutes more inside before he closed it after him.

The gray in the sky was spreading. Delia descended without fear now, and crouched beneath the low bedroom window. The drawn shade shut out the dawn, shut in the night. But the thin walls held back no sound.

"Dat ol' scratch° is woke up now!" She mused at the tremendous whirr inside, which every woodsman knows, is one of the sound illusions. The rattler is a ventriloquist. His whirr sounds to the right, to the left, straight ahead, behind, close under foot—everywhere but where it is. Woe to him who guesses wrong unless he is prepared to hold up his end of the argument! Sometimes he strikes without rattling at all.

Inside, Sykes heard nothing until he knocked a pot lid off the stove while trying to reach the match-safe in the dark. He had emptied his pockets at Bertha's.

The snake seemed to wake up under the stove and Sykes made a quick leap into the bedroom. In spite of the gin he had had, his head was clearing now.

"Mah Gawd!" he chattered, "ef Ah could on'y strack uh light!"

The rattling ceased for a moment as he stood paralyzed. He waited. It seemed that the snake waited also.

"Oh, fuh de light! Ah thought he'd be too sick"—Sykes was muttering to himself when the whirr began again, closer, right underfoot this time. Long before this, Sykes' ability to think had been flattened down to primitive instinct and he leaped—onto the bed.

Outside Delia heard a cry that might have come from a maddened chimpanzee, a stricken gorilla. All the terror, all the horror, all the rage that man possibly could express, without a recognizable human sound.

A tremendous stir inside there, another series of animal screams, the intermittent whirr of the reptile. The shade torn violently down from the window, letting in the red dawn, a huge brown hand seizing the window stick, great dull blows upon the wooden floor punctuating the gibberish of sound long after the rattle of the snake had abruptly subsided. All this Delia could see and hear from her place beneath the window, and it made her ill. She crept over to the four-o'clocks and stretched herself on the cool earth to recover.

She lay there. "Delia, Delia!" She could hear Sykes calling in a most despairing tone as one who expected no answer. The sun crept on up,

scratch: a folk expression for the devil.

and he called. Delia could not move—her legs had gone flabby. She never moved, he called, and the sun kept rising.

"Mah Gawd!" She heard him moan, "Mah Gawd fum Heben!" She heard him stumbling about and got up from her flower-bed. The sun was growing warm. As she approached the door she heard him call out hopefully, "Delia, is dat you Ah heah?"

She saw him on his hands and knees as soon as she reached the door. He crept an inch or two toward her—all that he was able, and she saw his horribly swollen neck and his one open eye shining with hope. A surge of pity too strong to support bore her away from that eye that must, could not, fail to see the tubs. He would see the lamp. Orlando with its doctors was too far. She could scarcely reach the chinaberry tree, where she waited in the growing heat while inside she knew the cold river was creeping up and up to extinguish that eye which must know by now that she knew.

James Joyce

Araby 1914

James Joyce

James Joyce (1882–1941) quit Ireland at twenty to spend his mature life in voluntary exile on the continent, writing of nothing but Dublin, where he was born. In Trieste, Zurich, and Paris, he supported his family with difficulty, sometimes teaching in Berlitz language schools, until his writing won him fame and wealthy patrons. At first Joyce met difficulty in getting his work printed and circulated. Publication of Dubliners *(1914), the collection of stories that includes "Araby," was delayed seven years because its prospective Irish publisher feared libel suits. (The book depicts local citizens, some of them recognizable, and views Dubliners mostly as a thwarted, self-deceived lot.)* A Portrait of the Artist as a Young Man *(1916), a novel of thinly veiled autobiography, recounts a young intellectual's breaking away from country, church, and home. Joyce's immense comic novel* Ulysses *(1922), a parody of the* Odyssey, *spans eighteen hours in the life of a wandering Jew, a Dublin seller of advertising. Frank about sex but untitillating, the book was banned at one time by the U.S. Post Office. Joyce's later work stepped up its demands on readers. The challenging* Finnegans Wake *(1939), if read aloud, sounds as though a learned comic poet were sleep-talking, jumbling several languages. Joyce was an innovator whose bold experiments showed many other writers possibilities in fiction that had not earlier been imagined.*

North Richmond Street, being blind,° was a quiet street except at the hour when the Christian Brothers' School set the boys free. An

being blind: being a dead-end street.

uninhabited house of two stories stood at the blind end, detached from its neighbors in a square ground. The other houses of the street, conscious of decent lives within them, gazed at one another with brown imperturbable faces.

The former tenant of our house, a priest, had died in the back drawing-room. Air, musty from having been long enclosed, hung in all the rooms, and the waste room behind the kitchen was littered with old useless papers. Among these I found a few paper-covered books, the pages of which were curled and damp: *The Abbot*, by Walter Scott, *The Devout Communicant* and *The Memoirs of Vidocq.*° I liked the last best because its leaves were yellow. The wild garden behind the house contained a central apple-tree and a few straggling bushes under one of which I found the late tenant's rusty bicycle-pump. He had been a very charitable priest: in his will he had left all his money to institutions and the furniture of his house to his sister.

When the short days of winter came dusk fell before we had well eaten our dinners. When we met in the street the houses had grown somber. The space of sky above us was the color of ever-changing violet and towards it the lamps of the street lifted their feeble lanterns. The cold air stung us and we played till our bodies glowed. Our shouts echoed in the silent street. The career of our play brought us through the dark muddy lanes behind the houses where we ran the gauntlet of the rough tribes from the cottages, to the back doors of the dark dripping gardens where odors arose from the ashpits, to the dark odorous stables where a coachman smoothed and combed the horse or shook music from the buckled harness. When we returned to the street light from the kitchen windows had filled the areas. If my uncle was seen turning the corner we hid in the shadow until we had seen him safely housed. Or if Mangan's sister° came out on the doorstep to call her brother in to his tea we watched her from our shadow peer up and down the street. We waited to see whether she would remain or go in and, if she remained, we left our shadow and walked up to Mangan's steps resignedly. She was waiting for us, her figure defined by the light from the half-opened door. Her brother always teased her before he obeyed and I stood by the railings looking at her. Her dress swung as she moved her body and the soft rope of her hair tossed from side to side.

Every morning I lay on the floor in the front parlor watching her door. The blind was pulled down within an inch of the sash so that I could not be seen. When she came out on the doorstep my heart leaped. I ran to the hall, seized my books and followed her. I kept her brown figure always in my eye and, when we came near the point at which

The Abbot . . . Vidocq: a popular historical romance (1820); a book of pious meditations by an eighteenth-century English Franciscan, Pacificus Baker; and the autobiography of François-Jules Vidocq (1775–1857), a criminal who later turned detective. *Mangan's sister:* an actual young woman in this story, but the phrase recalls Irish poet James Clarence Mangan (1803–1849) and his best-known poem, "Dark Rosaleen," which personifies Ireland as a beautiful woman for whom the poet yearns.

our ways diverged, I quickened my pace and passed her. This happened morning after morning. I had never spoken to her, except for a few casual words, and yet her name was like a summons to all my foolish blood.

Her image accompanied me even in places the most hostile to 5
romance. On Saturday evenings when my aunt went marketing I had to go to carry some of the parcels. We walked through the flaring streets, jostled by drunken men and bargaining women, amid the curses of laborers, the shrill litanies of shopboys who stood on guard by the barrels of pigs' cheeks, the nasal chanting of street-singers, who sang a *come-all-you* about O'Donovan Rossa,° or a ballad about the troubles in our native land. These noises converged in a single sensation of life for me: I imagined that I bore my chalice safely through a throng of foes. Her name sprang to my lips at moments in strange prayers and praises which I myself did not understand. My eyes were often full of tears (I could not tell why) and at times a flood from my heart seemed to pour itself out into my bosom. I thought little of the future. I did not know whether I would ever speak to her or not or, if I spoke to her, how I could tell her of my confused adoration. But my body was like a harp and her words and gestures were like fingers running upon the wires.

One evening I went into the back drawing-room in which the priest had died. It was a dark rainy evening and there was no sound in the house. Through one of the broken panes I heard the rain impinge upon the earth, the fine incessant needles of water playing in the sodden beds. Some distant lamp or lighted window gleamed below me. I was thankful that I could see so little. All my senses seemed to desire to veil themselves and, feeling that I was about to slip from them, I pressed the palms of my hands together until they trembled, murmuring: *O love! O love!* many times.

At last she spoke to me. When she addressed the first words to me I was so confused that I did not know what to answer. She asked me was I going to *Araby*. I forget whether I answered yes or no. It would be a splendid bazaar, she said; she would love to go.

—And why can't you? I asked.

While she spoke she turned a silver bracelet round and round her wrist. She could not go, she said, because there would be a retreat that week in her convent.° Her brother and two other boys were fighting for their caps and I was alone at the railings. She held one of the spikes, bowing her head towards me. The light from the lamp opposite our door caught the white curve of her neck, lit up her hair that rested there and, falling, lit

come-all-you about O'Donovan Rossa: the street singers earned their living by singing timely songs that usually began, "Come all you gallant Irishmen / And listen to my song." Their subject, also called Dynamite Rossa, was a popular hero jailed by the British for advocating violent rebellion. *a retreat . . . in her convent:* a week devoted to religious observances more intense than usual, at the convent school Miss Mangan attends; probably she will have to listen to a number of hellfire sermons.

up the hand upon the railing. It fell over one side of her dress and caught the white border of a petticoat, just visible as she stood at ease.

—It's well for you, she said.

—If I go, I said, I will bring you something.

What innumerable follies laid waste my waking and sleeping thoughts after that evening! I wished to annihilate the tedious intervening days. I chafed against the work of school. At night in my bedroom and by day in the classroom her image came between me and the page I strove to read. The syllables of the word *Araby* were called to me through the silence in which my soul luxuriated and cast an Eastern enchantment over me. I asked for leave to go to the bazaar on Saturday night. My aunt was surprised and hoped it was not some Freemason° affair. I answered few questions in class. I watched my master's face pass from amiability to sternness; he hoped I was not beginning to idle. I could not call my wandering thoughts together. I had hardly any patience with the serious work of life which, now that it stood between me and my desire, seemed to me child's play, ugly monotonous child's play.

On Saturday morning I reminded my uncle that I wished to go to the bazaar in the evening. He was fussing at the hallstand, looking for the hatbrush, and answered me curtly:

—Yes, boy, I know.

As he was in the hall I could not go into the front parlor and lie at the window. I left the house in bad humor and walked slowly towards the school. The air was pitilessly raw and already my heart misgave me.

When I came home to dinner my uncle had not yet been home. Still it was early. I sat staring at the clock for some time and, when its ticking began to irritate me, I left the room. I mounted the staircase and gained the upper part of the house. The high cold empty gloomy rooms liberated me and I went from room to room singing. From the front window I saw my companions playing below in the street. Their cries reached me weakened and indistinct and, leaning my forehead against the cool glass, I looked over at the dark house where she lived. I may have stood there for an hour, seeing nothing but the brown-clad figure cast by my imagination, touched discreetly by the lamplight at the curved neck, at the hand upon the railings and at the border below the dress.

When I came downstairs again I found Mrs. Mercer sitting at the fire. She was an old garrulous woman, a pawnbroker's widow, who collected used stamps for some pious purpose. I had to endure the gossip of the tea-table. The meal was prolonged beyond an hour and still my uncle did not come. Mrs. Mercer stood up to go: she was sorry she couldn't wait any longer, but it was after eight o'clock and she did not like to be out

Freemason: Catholics in Ireland viewed the Masonic order as a Protestant conspiracy against them.

late, as the night air was bad for her. When she had gone I began to walk up and down the room, clenching my fists. My aunt said:

—I'm afraid you may put off your bazaar for this night of Our Lord.

At nine o'clock I heard my uncle's latchkey in the halldoor. I heard him talking to himself and heard the hallstand rocking when it had received the weight of his overcoat. I could interpret these signs. When he was midway through his dinner I asked him to give me the money to go to the bazaar. He had forgotten.

—The people are in bed and after their first sleep now, he said. 20

I did not smile. My aunt said to him energetically:

—Can't you give him the money and let him go? You've kept him late enough as it is.

My uncle said he was very sorry he had forgotten. He said he believed in the old saying: *All work and no play makes Jack a dull boy*. He asked me where I was going and, when I had told him a second time he asked me did I know *The Arab's Farewell to His Steed.*° When I left the kitchen he was about to recite the opening lines of the piece to my aunt.

I held a florin tightly in my hands as I strode down Buckingham Street towards the station. The sight of the streets thronged with buyers and glaring with gas recalled to me the purpose of my journey. I took my seat in a third-class carriage of a deserted train. After an intolerable delay the train moved out of the station slowly. It crept onward among ruinous houses and over the twinkling river. At Westland Row Station a crowd of people pressed to the carriage doors; but the porters moved them back, saying that it was a special train for the bazaar. I remained alone in the bare carriage. In a few minutes the train drew up beside an improvised wooden platform. I passed out on to the road and saw by the lighted dial of a clock that it was ten minutes to ten. In front of me was a large building which displayed the magical name.

I could not find any sixpenny entrance and, fearing that the bazaar 25
would be closed, I passed in quickly through a turnstile, handing a shilling to a weary-looking man. I found myself in a big hall girdled at half its height by a gallery. Nearly all the stalls were closed and the greater part of the hall was in darkness. I recognized a silence like that which pervades a church after a service. I walked into the center of the bazaar timidly. A few people were gathered about the stalls which were still open. Before a curtain, over which the words *Café Chantant*° were written in colored lamps, two men were counting money on a salver.° I listened to the fall of the coins.

The Arab's Farewell to His Steed: This sentimental ballad by a popular poet, Caroline Norton (1808–1877), tells the story of a nomad of the desert who, in a fit of greed, sells his beloved horse, then regrets the loss, flings away the gold he had received, and takes back his horse. Notice the echo of "Araby" in the song title. *Café Chantant:* name for a Paris nightspot featuring topical songs. *salver*: a tray like that used in serving Holy Communion.

Remembering with difficulty why I had come I went over to one of the stalls and examined porcelain vases and flowered tea-sets. At the door of the stall a young lady was talking and laughing with two young gentlemen. I remarked their English accents and listened vaguely to their conversation.

—O, I never said such a thing!

—O, but you did!

—O, but I didn't!

—Didn't she say that?

—Yes. I heard her.

—O, there's a . . . fib!

Observing me the young lady came over and asked me did I wish to buy anything. The tone of her voice was not encouraging; she seemed to have spoken to me out of a sense of duty. I looked humbly at the great jars that stood like eastern guards at either side of the dark entrance to the stall and murmured:

—No, thank you.

The young lady changed the position of one of the vases and went back to the two young men. They began to talk of the same subject. Once or twice the young lady glanced at me over her shoulder.

I lingered before her stall, though I knew my stay was useless, to make my interest in her wares seem the more real. Then I turned away slowly and walked down the middle of the bazaar. I allowed the two pennies to fall against the sixpence in my pocket. I heard a voice call from one end of the gallery that the light was out. The upper part of the hall was now completely dark.

Gazing up into the darkness I saw myself as a creature driven and derided by vanity; and my eyes burned with anguish and anger.

Franz Kafka

Before the Law 1919

Translated by John Siscoe

Franz Kafka

Franz Kafka (1883–1924) was born into a German-speaking Jewish family in Prague, Czechoslovakia (then part of the Austro-Hungarian empire). He was the only surviving son of a domineering, successful father. After earning a law degree, Kafka worked as a claims investigator for the state accident insurance company. He worked on his stories at night, especially during his frequent bouts of insomnia. He never married, and lived mostly with his parents. Kafka was such a careful and self-conscious writer that he found it difficult to finish his work and send it out for publication. During his lifetime he published only a few thin volumes of short fiction, most notably The Metamorphosis *(1915) and* In the Penal Colony *(1919). He never finished to his own satisfaction any of his three novels (all published posthumously):* The Trial *(1925),* The Castle *(1926), and* Amerika *(1927). As Kafka was dying of tuberculosis, he begged his friend and literary executor Max Brod to burn his uncompleted manuscripts. Brod pondered this request but luckily didn't obey. Kafka's two major novels,* The Trial *and* The Castle, *both depict huge, remote, bumbling, irresponsible bureaucracies in whose power the individual feels helpless and blind. Kafka's works appear startlingly prophetic to readers looking back on them in the later light of Stalinism, World War II, and the Holocaust. His haunting vision of an alienated modern world led the poet W. H. Auden to remark at midcentury, "Had one to name the author who comes nearest to bearing the same kind of relation to our age as Dante, Shakespeare, and Goethe bore to theirs, Kafka is the first one would think of." The ironic and devastating parable "Before the Law" contains the distilled essence of what we mean by the term "Kafkaesque."*

Before the Law stands a doorkeeper. To this doorkeeper comes a man from the country who asks to be admitted to the Law. But the doorkeeper says that he can't let the man in just now. The man thinks this over and then asks if he will be allowed to enter later. "It's possible," answers the doorkeeper, "but not just now." Since the door to the Law stands open as usual and the doorkeeper steps aside, the man bends down to look through the doorway into the interior. Seeing this, the doorkeeper laughs and says: "If you find it so compelling, then try to enter despite my prohibition. But bear in mind that I am powerful. And I am only the lowest doorkeeper. In hall after hall, keepers stand at every door. The mere sight of the third one is more than even I can bear." These are difficulties which the man from the country has not expected; the Law, he thinks, should be always available to everyone. But when he looks more closely at the doorkeeper in his furred robe, with his large pointed nose and his long, thin, black Tartar beard, he decides that it would be better to wait until he receives permission to enter. The doorkeeper gives him a stool and allows him to sit down beside the door. There he sits for days and years. He makes many attempts to be let in, and wearies the doorkeeper with his pleas. The doorkeeper often questions him casually about his home and many other matters, but the questions are asked with indifference, the way important men might ask them, and always conclude with the statement the man can't be admitted at this time. The man, who has equipped himself with many things for his journey, spends all that he has, regardless of value, in order to bribe the doorkeeper. The doorkeeper accepts it all, though saying each time as he does so, "I'm taking this only so that you won't feel that you haven't tried everything." During these long years the man watches the doorkeeper almost continuously. He forgets about the other doorkeepers, and imagines that this first one is the sole obstacle barring his way to the Law. In the early years he loudly bewails his misfortune; later, as he grows old, he merely grumbles to himself. He becomes childish, and since during his long study of the doorkeeper he has gotten to know even the fleas in the fur collar, he begs these fleas to help him change the doorkeeper's mind. At last his eyesight grows dim and he cannot tell whether it is really growing darker or whether his eyes are simply deceiving him. Yet in the darkness he can now perceive that radiance that streams inextinguishably from the door of the Law. Now his life is nearing its end. Before he dies, all his experiences during this long time coalesce in his mind into a single question, one which he has never yet asked the doorkeeper. He beckons to the doorkeeper, for he can no longer raise his stiffening body. The doorkeeper has to bend low to hear him, since the difference in size between them has increased very much to the man's disadvantage. "What do you want to know now?" asks the doorkeeper, "you are insatiable." "Surely everyone strives to reach the Law," says the man, "why then is it that in all these years no one has come seeking admittance but me?" The doorkeeper realizes that the man has reached his end and that his hearing is failing so he yells in his ear: "No one but you could have been admitted here, since this entrance was meant for you alone. Now I am going to shut it."

Katherine Mansfield

Miss Brill 1922

Katherine Mansfield

Katherine Mansfield Beauchamp (1888–1923), was born into a sedate Victorian family in New Zealand, the daughter of a successful businessman. At fifteen, she emigrated to England to attend school and did not ever permanently return Down Under. In 1918, after a time of wild-oat sowing in bohemian London, she married the journalist and critic John Middleton Murry. All at once, Mansfield found herself struggling to define her sexual identity, to earn a living by her pen, to endure World War I (in which her brother was killed in action), and to survive the ravages of tuberculosis. She died at thirty-four, in France, at a spiritualist commune where she had sought to regain her health. Mansfield wrote no novels, but during her brief career concentrated on the short story, in which she has few peers. Bliss *(1920) and* The Garden-Party and Other Stories *(1922) were greeted with an acclaim that has continued; her collected short stories were published in 1937. Some of her stories celebrate life, others wryly poke fun at it. Many reveal, in ordinary lives, small incidents that open like doorways into significances.*

Although it was so brilliantly fine—the blue sky powdered with gold and great spots of light like white wine splashed over the Jardins Publiques—Miss Brill was glad that she had decided on her fur. The air was motionless, but when you opened your mouth there was just a faint chill, like a chill from a glass of iced water before you sip, and now and again a leaf came drifting—from nowhere, from the sky. Miss Brill put up her hand and touched her fur. Dear little thing! It was nice to feel it again. She had taken it out of its box that afternoon, shaken out the moth-powder, given it a good brush, and rubbed the life back into the dim little eyes. "What has been happening to me?" said the sad little eyes. Oh, how sweet it was to see them snap at her again from the red eiderdown! . . . But the nose, which was of some black composition, wasn't at all firm. It must have had a knock, somehow. Never mind—a little dab of black sealing-wax when the time came—when it was absolutely necessary. . . . Little rogue! Yes, she really felt like that about it. Little rogue biting its tail just by her left ear. She could have taken it off and laid it on her lap and stroked it. She felt a tingling in her hands and arms, but that came from walking, she supposed. And when she breathed, something light and sad—no, not sad, exactly—something gentle seemed to move in her bosom.

There were a number of people out this afternoon, far more than last Sunday. And the band sounded louder and gayer. That was because the Season had begun. For although the band played all year round on Sundays, out of season it was never the same. It was like some one playing with only the family to listen; it didn't care how it played if there weren't any strangers present. Wasn't the conductor wearing a new coat, too? She was sure it was new. He scraped with his foot and flapped his arms like a rooster about to crow, and the bandsmen sitting in the green rotunda blew out their cheeks and glared at the music. Now there came a little "flutey" bit—very pretty!—a little chain of bright drops. She was sure it would be repeated. It was; she lifted her head and smiled.

Only two people shared her "special" seat: a fine old man in a velvet coat, his hands clasped over a huge carved walking-stick, and a big old woman, sitting upright, with a roll of knitting on her embroidered apron. They did not speak. This was disappointing, for Miss Brill always looked forward to the conversation. She had become really quite expert, she thought, at listening as though she didn't listen, at sitting in other people's lives just for a minute while they talked round her.

She glanced, sideways, at the old couple. Perhaps they would go soon. Last Sunday, too, hadn't been as interesting as usual. An Englishman and his wife, he wearing a dreadful Panama hat and she button boots. And she'd gone on the whole time about how she ought to wear spectacles; she knew she needed them; but that it was no good getting any; they'd be sure to break and they'd never keep on. And he'd been so patient. He'd suggested everything—gold rims, the kind that curved round your ears, little pads inside the bridge. No, nothing would please her. "They'll always be sliding down my nose!" Miss Brill wanted to shake her.

The old people sat on the bench, still as statues. Never mind, there 5
was always the crowd to watch. To and fro, in front of the flower-beds and the band rotunda, the couples and groups paraded, stopped to talk,

to greet, to buy a handful of flowers from the old beggar who had his tray fixed to the railings. Little children ran among them, swooping and laughing; little boys with big white silk bows under their chins, little girls, little French dolls, dressed up in velvet and lace. And sometimes a tiny staggerer came suddenly rocking into the open from under the trees, stopped, stared, as suddenly sat down "flop," until its small high-stepping mother, like a young hen, rushed scolding to its rescue. Other people sat on the benches and green chairs, but they were nearly always the same, Sunday after Sunday, and—Miss Brill had often noticed—there was something funny about nearly all of them. They were odd, silent, nearly all old, and from the way they stared they looked as though they'd just come from dark little rooms or even—even cupboards!

Behind the rotunda the slender trees with yellow leaves down drooping, and through them just a line of sea, and beyond the blue sky with gold-veined clouds.

Tum-tum-tum tiddle-um! tiddle-um! tum tiddley-um tum ta! blew the band.

Two young girls in red came by and two young soldiers in blue met them, and they laughed and paired and went off arm-in-arm. Two peasant women with funny straw hats passed, gravely, leading beautiful smoke-colored donkeys. A cold, pale nun hurried by. A beautiful woman came along and dropped her bunch of violets, and a little boy ran after to hand them to her, and she took them and threw them away as if they'd been poisoned. Dear me! Miss Brill didn't know whether to admire that or not! And now an ermine toque and a gentleman in grey met just in front of her. He was tall, stiff, dignified, and she was wearing the ermine toque she'd bought when her hair was yellow. Now everything, her hair, her face, even her eyes, was the same color as the shabby ermine, and her hand, in its cleaned glove, lifted to dab her lips, was a tiny yellowish paw. Oh, she was so pleased to see him—delighted! She rather thought they were going to meet that afternoon. She described where she'd been—everywhere, here, there, along by the sea. The day was so charming—didn't he agree? And wouldn't he, perhaps? . . . But he shook his head, lighted a cigarette, slowly breathed a great deep puff into her face, and, even while she was still talking and laughing, flicked the match away and walked on. The ermine toque was alone; she smiled more brightly than ever. But even the band seemed to know what she was feeling and played more softly, played tenderly, and the drum beat, "The Brute! The Brute!" over and over. What would she do? What was going to happen now? But as Miss Brill wondered, the ermine toque turned, raised her hand as though she'd seen some one else, much nicer, just over there, and pattered away. And the band changed again and played more quickly, more gaily than ever, and the old couple on Miss Brill's seat got up and marched away, and such a funny old man with long whiskers hobbled along in time to the music and was nearly knocked over by four girls walking abreast.

Oh, how fascinating it was! How she enjoyed it! How she loved sitting here, watching it all! It was like a play. It was exactly like a play. Who could believe the sky at the back wasn't painted? But it wasn't till a little brown dog trotted on solemn and then slowly trotted off, like a little "theatre" dog, a little dog that had been drugged, that Miss Brill discovered what it was that made it so exciting. They were all on the stage. They weren't only the audience, not only looking on; they were acting. Even she had a part and came every Sunday. No doubt somebody would have noticed if she hadn't been there; she was part of the performance after all. How strange she'd never thought of it like that before! And yet it explained why she made such a point of starting from home at just the same time each week—so as not to be late for the performance—and it also explained why she had quite a queer, shy feeling at telling her English pupils how she spent her Sunday afternoons. No wonder! Miss Brill nearly laughed out loud. She was on the stage. She thought of the old invalid gentleman to whom she read the newspaper four afternoons a week while he slept in the garden. She had got quite used to the frail head on the cotton pillow, the hollowed eyes, the open mouth and the high pinched nose. If he'd been dead she mightn't have noticed for weeks; she wouldn't have minded. But suddenly he knew he was having the paper read to him by an actress! "An actress!" The old head lifted; two points of light quivered in the old eyes. "An actress—are ye?" And Miss Brill smoothed the newspaper as though it were the manuscript of her part and said gently: "Yes, I have been an actress for a long time."

The band had been having a rest. Now they started again. And 10
what they played was warm, sunny, yet there was just a faint chill—a something, what was it?—not sadness—no, not sadness—a something that made you want to sing. The tune lifted, lifted, the light shone; and it seemed to Miss Brill that in another moment all of them, all the whole company, would begin singing. The young ones, the laughing ones who were moving together, they would begin, and the men's voices, very resolute and brave, would join them. And then she too, she too, and the others on the benches—they would come in with a kind of accompaniment—something low, that scarcely rose or fell, something so beautiful—moving . . . And Miss Brill's eyes filled with tears and she looked smiling at all the other members of the company. Yes, we understand, we understand, she thought—though what they understood she didn't know.

Just at that moment a boy and a girl came and sat down where the old couple had been. They were beautifully dressed; they were in love. The hero and heroine, of course, just arrived from his father's yacht. And still soundlessly singing, still with that trembling smile, Miss Brill prepared to listen.

"No, not now," said the girl. "Not here, I can't."

"But why? Because of that stupid old thing at the end there?" asked the boy. "Why does she come here at all—who wants her? Why doesn't she keep her silly old mug at home?"

"It's her fu-fur which is so funny," giggled the girl. "It's exactly like a fried whiting."

"Ah, be off with you!" said the boy in an angry whisper. Then: "Tell me, my petite cherie—"

"No, not here," said the girl. "Not *yet*."

On her way home she usually bought a slice of honeycake at the baker's. It was her Sunday treat. Sometimes there was an almond in her slice, sometimes not. It made a great difference. If there was an almond it was like carrying home a tiny present—a surprise—something that might very well not have been there. She hurried on the almond Sundays and struck the match for the kettle in quite a dashing way.

But today she passed the baker's boy, climbed the stairs, went into the little dark room—her room like a cupboard—and sat down on the red eiderdown. She sat there for a long time. The box that the fur came out of was on the bed. She unclasped the necklet quickly; quickly, without looking, laid it inside. But when she put the lid on she thought she heard something crying.

Alice Walker

Everyday Use 1973

Alice Walker, a leading black writer and social activist, was born in 1944 in Eatonton, Georgia, the youngest of eight children. Her father, a sharecropper and dairy farmer, earned about $300 a year; her mother helped by working as a maid. Both entertained their children by telling stories. When Alice Walker was eight, she was accidentally struck by a pellet from a brother's BB gun. She lost the sight of her right eye because the Walkers had no car to rush her to the hospital. Later she attended Spelman College in Atlanta and finished college at Sarah Lawrence College on a scholarship. While working for the civil rights movement in Mississippi, she met a young lawyer, Melvyn Leventhal. In 1967 they settled in Jackson, Mississippi, the first legally married interracial couple in town. After much racial harassment, they returned to New York in 1974, later divorcing.

Alice Walker

First known as a poet, Walker has published nine books of verse. She has edited a collection of the work of the then-neglected writer Zora Neale Hurston, written a study of Langston Hughes, and published many volumes of nonfiction, including the essay collection In Search of Our Mothers' Gardens: Womanist Prose *(1983).*

(By womanist *she means "black feminist.") But the largest part of Walker's reading audience knows her fiction: four story collections, including* In Love and Trouble *(1973), from which "Everyday Use" is taken, and her many novels. Her best-known novel,* The Color Purple *(1982), won both a Pulitzer Prize and National Book Award and was made into a film by Steven Spielberg in 1985. Recent novels include* By the Light of My Father's Smile *(1998) and* Now Is the Time to Open Your Heart *(2004). Walker lives in Northern California.*

for your grandmama

I will wait for her in the yard that Maggie and I made so clean and wavy yesterday afternoon. A yard like this is more comfortable than most people know. It is not just a yard. It is like an extended living room. When the hard clay is swept clean as a floor and the fine sand around the edges lined with tiny, irregular grooves, anyone can come and sit and look up into the elm tree and wait for the breezes that never come inside the house.

Maggie will be nervous until after her sister goes: she will stand hopelessly in corners, homely and ashamed of the burn scars down her arms and legs, eyeing her sister with a mixture of envy and awe. She thinks her sister has held life always in the palm of one hand, that "no" is a word the world never learned to say to her.

You've no doubt seen those TV shows where the child who has "made it" is confronted, as a surprise, by her own mother and father, tottering in weakly from backstage. (A pleasant surprise, of course: What would they do if parent and child came on the show only to curse out and insult each other?) On TV mother and child embrace and smile into each other's faces. Sometimes the mother and father weep, the child wraps them in her arms and leans across the table to tell how she would not have made it without their help. I have seen these programs.°

Sometimes I dream a dream in which Dee and I are suddenly brought together on a TV program of this sort. Out of a dark and soft-seated limousine I am ushered into a bright room filled with many people. There I meet a smiling, gray, sporty man like Johnny Carson who shakes my hand and tells me what a fine girl I have. Then we are on the stage and Dee is embracing me with tears in her eyes. She pins on my dress a large orchid, even though she has told me once that she thinks orchids are tacky flowers.

In real life I am a large, big-boned woman with rough, man-working 5
hands. In the winter I wear flannel nightgowns to bed and overalls during the day. I can kill and clean a hog as mercilessly as a man. My fat keeps

these programs: On the NBC television show *This Is Your Life*, people were publicly and often tearfully reunited with friends, relatives, and teachers they had not seen in years.

me hot in zero weather. I can work outside all day, breaking ice to get water for washing. I can eat pork liver cooked over the open fire minutes after it comes steaming from the hog. One winter I knocked a bull calf straight in the brain between the eyes with a sledge hammer and had the meat hung up to chill before nightfall. But of course all this does not show on television. I am the way my daughter would want me to be: a hundred pounds lighter, my skin like an uncooked barley pancake. My hair glistens in the hot bright lights. Johnny Carson has much to do to keep up with my quick and witty tongue.

But that is a mistake. I know even before I wake up. Who ever knew a Johnson with a quick tongue? Who can even imagine me looking a strange white man in the eye? It seems to me I have talked to them always with one foot raised in flight, with my head turned in whichever way is farthest from them. Dee, though. She would always look anyone in the eye. Hesitation was no part of her nature.

"How do I look, Mama?" Maggie says, showing just enough of her thin body enveloped in pink skirt and red blouse for me to know she's there, almost hidden by the door.

"Come out into the yard," I say.

Have you ever seen a lame animal, perhaps a dog run over by some careless person rich enough to own a car, sidle up to someone who is ignorant enough to be kind to him? That is the way my Maggie walks. She has been like this, chin on chest, eyes on ground, feet in shuffle, ever since the fire that burned the other house to the ground.

Dee is lighter than Maggie, with nicer hair and a fuller figure. She's a 10
woman now, though sometimes I forget. How long ago was it that the other house burned? Ten, twelve years? Sometimes I can still hear the flames and feel Maggie's arms sticking to me, her hair smoking and her dress falling off her in little black papery flakes. Her eyes seemed stretched open, blazed open by the flames reflected in them. And Dee. I see her standing off under the sweet gum tree she used to dig gum out of; a look of concentration on her face as she watched the last dingy gray board of the house fall in toward the red-hot brick chimney. Why don't you do a dance around the ashes? I'd wanted to ask her. She had hated the house that much.

I used to think she hated Maggie, too. But that was before we raised the money, the church and me, to send her to Augusta to school. She used to read to us without pity; forcing words, lies, other folks' habits, whole lives upon us two, sitting trapped and ignorant underneath her voice. She washed us in a river of make-believe, burned us with a lot of knowledge we didn't necessarily need to know. Pressed us to her with the serious way she read, to shove us away at just the moment, like dimwits, we seemed about to understand.

Dee wanted nice things. A yellow organdy dress to wear to her graduation from high school; black pumps to match a green suit she'd made from an old suit somebody gave me. She was determined to stare down any disaster in her efforts. Her eyelids would not flicker for minutes at a time. Often I fought off the temptation to shake her. At sixteen she had a style of her own: and knew what style was.

I never had an education myself. After second grade the school was closed down. Don't ask me why: in 1927 colored asked fewer questions than they do now. Sometimes Maggie reads to me. She stumbles along good-naturedly but can't see well. She knows she is not bright. Like good looks and money, quickness passed her by. She will marry John Thomas (who has mossy teeth in an earnest face) and then I'll be free to sit here and I guess just sing church songs to myself. Although I never was a good singer. Never could carry a tune. I was always better at a man's job. I used to love to milk till I was hoofed in the side in '49. Cows are soothing and slow and don't bother you, unless you try to milk them the wrong way.

I have deliberately turned my back on the house. It is three rooms, just like the one that burned, except the roof is tin; they don't make shingle roofs any more. There are no real windows, just some holes cut in the sides, like the portholes in a ship, but not round and not square, with rawhide holding the shutters up on the outside. This house is in a pasture, too, like the other one. No doubt when Dee sees it she will want to tear it down. She wrote me once that no matter where we "choose" to live, she will manage to come see us. But she will never bring her friends. Maggie and I thought about this and Maggie asked me, "Mama, when did Dee ever *have* any friends?"

She had a few. Furtive boys in pink shirts hanging about on washday 15
after school. Nervous girls who never laughed. Impressed with her they worshiped the well-turned phrase, the cute shape, the scalding humor that erupted like bubbles in lye. She read to them.

When she was courting Jimmy T she didn't have much time to pay to us, but turned all her faultfinding power on him. He *flew* to marry a cheap city girl from a family of ignorant flashy people. She hardly had time to recompose herself.

When she comes I will meet—but there they are!

Maggie attempts to make a dash for the house, in her shuffling way, but I stay her with my hand. "Come back here," I say. And she stops and tries to dig a well in the sand with her toe.

It is hard to see them clearly through the strong sun. But even the first glimpse of leg out of the car tells me it is Dee. Her feet were always neat-looking, as if God himself had shaped them with a certain style. From the other side of the car comes a short, stocky man. Hair is all over his head a foot long and hanging from his chin like a kinky mule tail. I hear Maggie suck in her breath. "Uhnnnh," is what it sounds like. Like when you see the wriggling end of a snake just in front of your foot on the road. "Uhnnnh."

Dee next. A dress down to the ground, in this hot weather. A dress 20
so loud it hurts my eyes. There are yellows and oranges enough to throw back the light of the sun. I feel my whole face warming from the heat waves it throws out. Earrings, too, gold and hanging down to her shoulders. Bracelets dangling and making noises when she moves her arm up to shake the folds of the dress out of her armpits. The dress is loose and flows, and as she walks closer, I like it. I hear Maggie go "Uhnnnh" again. It is her sister's hair. It stands straight up like the wool on a sheep. It is black as night and around the edges are two long pigtails that rope about like small lizards disappearing behind her ears.

"Wa-su-zo-Tean-o!"° she says, coming on in that gliding way the dress makes her move. The short stocky fellow with the hair to his navel is all grinning and he follows up with "Asalamalakim,° my mother and sister!" He moves to hug Maggie but she falls back, right up against the back of my chair. I feel her trembling there and when I look up I see the perspiration falling off her chin.

"Don't get up," says Dee. Since I am stout it takes something of a push. You can see me trying to move a second or two before I make it. She turns, showing white heels through her sandals, and goes back to the car. Out she peeks next with a Polaroid. She stoops down quickly and lines up picture after picture of me sitting there in front of the house with Maggie cowering behind me. She never takes a shot without making sure the house is included. When a cow comes nibbling around the edge of the yard she snaps it and me and Maggie *and* the house. Then she puts the Polaroid in the back seat of the car, and comes up and kisses me on the forehead.

Meanwhile Asalamalakim is going through the motions with Maggie's hand. Maggie's hand is as limp as a fish, and probably as cold, despite the sweat, and she keeps trying to pull it back. It looks like Asalamalakim wants to shake hands but wants to do it fancy. Or maybe he don't know how people shake hands. Anyhow, he soon gives up on Maggie.

"Well," I say. "Dee."

"No, Mama," she says. "Not 'Dee,' Wangero Leewanika Kemanjo!" 25

"What happened to 'Dee'?" I wanted to know.

"She's dead," Wangero said. "I couldn't bear it any longer, being named after the people who oppress me."

"You know as well as me you was named after your aunt Dicie," I said. Dicie is my sister. She named Dee. We called her "Big Dee" after Dee was born.

Wa-su-zo-Tean-o!: salutation in Swahili, an African language. Notice that Dee has to sound it out, syllable by syllable. *Asalamalakim*: salutation in Arabic: "Peace be upon you."

"But who was *she* named after?" asked Wangero.

"I guess after Grandma Dee," I said.

"And who was she named after?" asked Wangero.

"Her mother," I said, and saw Wangero was getting tired. "That's about as far back as I can trace it," I said. Though, in fact, I probably could have carried it back beyond the Civil War through the branches.

"Well," said Asalamalakim, "there you are."

"Uhnnnh," I heard Maggie say.

"There I was not," I said, "before 'Dicie' cropped up in our family, so why should I try to trace it that far back?"

He just stood there grinning, looking down on me like somebody inspecting a Model A car.° Every once in a while he and Wangero sent eye signals over my head.

"How do you pronounce this name?" I asked.

"You don't have to call me by it if you don't want to," said Wangero.

"Why shouldn't I?" I asked. "If that's what you want us to call you, we'll call you."

"I know it might sound awkward at first," said Wangero.

"I'll get used to it," I said. "Ream it out again."

Well, soon we got the name out of the way. Asalamalakim had a name twice as long and three times as hard. After I tripped over it two or three times he told me to just call him Hakim-a-barber. I wanted to ask him was he a barber, but I didn't really think he was, so I didn't ask.

"You must belong to those beef-cattle peoples down the road," I said. They said "Asalamalakim" when they met you, too, but they didn't shake hands. Always too busy: feeding the cattle, fixing the fences, putting up salt-lick shelters, throwing down hay. When the white folks poisoned some of the herd the men stayed up all night with rifles in their hands. I walked a mile and a half just to see the sight.

Hakim-a-barber said, "I accept some of their doctrines, but farming and raising cattle is not my style." (They didn't tell me, and I didn't ask, whether Wangero (Dee) had really gone and married him.)

We sat down to eat and right away he said he didn't eat collards and pork was unclean. Wangero, though, went on through the chitlins and corn bread, the greens and everything else. She talked a blue streak over the sweet potatoes. Everything delighted her. Even the fact that we still used the benches her daddy made for the table when we couldn't afford to buy chairs.

"Oh, Mama!" she cried. Then turned to Hakim-a-barber. "I never knew how lovely these benches are. You can feel the rump prints," she said, running her hands underneath her and along the bench. Then she gave a sigh and her hand closed over Grandma Dee's butter dish.

Model A car: popular low-priced automobile introduced by the Ford Motor Company in 1927.

"That's it!" she said. "I knew there was something I wanted to ask you if I could have." She jumped up from the table and went over in the corner where the churn stood, the milk in it clabber° by now. She looked at the churn and looked at it.

"This churn top is what I need," she said. "Didn't Uncle Buddy whittle it out of a tree you all used to have?"

"Yes," I said.

"Uh huh," she said happily. "And I want the dasher, too."

"Uncle Buddy whittle that, too?" asked the barber. 50

Dee (Wangero) looked up at me.

"Aunt Dee's first husband whittled the dash," said Maggie so low you almost couldn't hear her. "His name was Henry, but they called him Stash."

"Maggie's brain is like an elephant's," Wangero said, laughing. "I can use the churn top as a centerpiece for the alcove table," she said, sliding a plate over the churn, "and I'll think of something artistic to do with the dasher."

When she finished wrapping the dasher the handle stuck out. I took it for a moment in my hands. You didn't even have to look close to see where hands pushing the dasher up and down to make butter had left a kind of sink in the wood. In fact, there were a lot of small sinks; you could see where thumbs and fingers had sunk into the wood. It was beautiful light yellow wood, from a tree that grew in the yard where Big Dee and Stash had lived.

After dinner Dee (Wangero) went to the trunk at the foot of my 55
bed and started rifling through it. Maggie hung back in the kitchen over the dishpan. Out came Wangero with two quilts. They had been pieced by Grandma Dee and then Big Dee and me had hung them on the quilt frames on the front porch and quilted them. One was in the Lone Star pattern. The other was Walk Around the Mountain. In both of them were scraps of dresses Grandma Dee had worn fifty and more years ago. Bits and pieces of Grandpa Jarrell's paisley shirts. And one teeny faded blue piece, about the size of a penny matchbox, that was from Great Grandpa Ezra's uniform that he wore in the Civil War.

"Mama," Wangero said sweet as a bird. "Can I have these old quilts?"

I heard something fall in the kitchen, and a minute later the kitchen door slammed.

"Why don't you take one or two of the others?" I asked. "These old things was just done by me and Big Dee from some tops your grandma pieced before she died."

"No," said Wangero. "I don't want those. They are stitched around the borders by machine."

"That'll make them last better," I said. 60

clabber: sour milk or buttermilk.

"That's not the point," said Wangero. "These are all pieces of dresses Grandma used to wear. She did all this stitching by hand. Imagine!" She held the quilts securely in her arms, stroking them.

"Some of the pieces, like those lavender ones, come from old clothes her mother handed down to her," I said, moving up to touch the quilts. Dee (Wangero) moved back just enough so that I couldn't reach the quilts. They already belonged to her.

"Imagine!" she breathed again, clutching them closely to her bosom.

"The truth is," I said, "I promised to give them quilts to Maggie, for when she marries John Thomas."

She gasped like a bee had stung her. 65

"Maggie can't appreciate these quilts!" she said. "She'd probably be backward enough to put them to everyday use."

"I reckon she would," I said. "God knows I been saving 'em for long enough with nobody using 'em. I hope she will!" I didn't want to bring up how I had offered Dee (Wangero) a quilt when she went away to college. Then she had told me they were old-fashioned, out of style.

"But they're *priceless*!" she was saying now, furiously; for she has a temper. "Maggie would put them on the bed and in five years they'd be in rags. Less than that!"

"She can always make some more," I said. "Maggie knows how to quilt."

Dee (Wangero) looked at me with hatred. "You just will not under- 70
stand. The point is these quilts, *these* quilts!"

"Well," I said, stumped. "What would *you* do with them?"

"Hang them," she said. As if that was the only thing you *could* do with quilts.

Maggie by now was standing in the door. I could almost hear the sound her feet made as they scraped over each other.

"She can have them, Mama," she said, like somebody used to never winning anything, or having anything reserved for her. "I can 'member Grandma Dee without the quilts."

I looked at her hard. She had filled her bottom lip with checkerberry 75
snuff and it gave her face a kind of dopey, hangdog look. It was Grandma Dee and Big Dee who taught her how to quilt herself. She stood there with her scarred hands hidden in the folds of her skirt. She looked at her sister with something like fear but she wasn't mad at her. This was Maggie's portion. This was the way she knew God to work.

When I looked at her like that something hit me in the top of my head and ran down to the soles of my feet. Just like when I'm in church and the spirit of God touches me and I get happy and shout. I did something I never had done before: hugged Maggie to me, then dragged her on into the room, snatched the quilts out of Miss Wangero's hands and dumped them into Maggie's lap. Maggie just sat there on my bed with her mouth open.

"Take one or two of the others," I said to Dee.

But she turned without a word and went out to Hakim-a-barber.

"You just don't understand," she said, as Maggie and I came out to the car.

"What don't I understand?" I wanted to know.

"Your heritage," she said. And then she turned to Maggie, kissed her, and said, "You ought to try to make something of yourself, too, Maggie. It's really a new day for us. But from the way you and Mama still live you'd never know it."

She put on some sunglasses that hid everything above the tip of her nose and her chin.

Maggie smiled; maybe at the sunglasses. But a real smile, not scared. After we watched the car dust settle I asked Maggie to bring me a dip of snuff. And then the two of us sat there just enjoying, until it was time to go in the house and go to bed.

Virginia Woolf

A Haunted House 1921

Virginia Woolf

Adeline Virginia Stephen Woolf (1882–1941) was born in London, the daughter of Sir Leslie Stephen, an influential critic and editor of the voluminous Dictionary of National Biography. *Virginia and her sister Vanessa (later Vanessa Bell) were largely self-educated in their father's extensive library while—in a distinction not lost on them—their brothers were sent to college. After their father's death in 1904, Virginia and Vanessa moved to Bloomsbury, a bohemian London neighborhood, and became the center of the "Bloomsbury Group" of progressive artists and intellectuals. Always in frail health, Virginia experienced episodes of mental disturbance. In 1912 she married Leonard Woolf, a journalist and novelist. In 1917 as therapy, they set up a hand-press in their home and started the Hogarth Press, which became one of the most celebrated small presses of the century. In addition to Woolf's books, it issued works by T. S. Eliot, Katherine Mansfield, Robinson Jeffers, Edwin Arlington Robinson, and Sigmund Freud. Woolf's first novel was* The Voyage Out *(1915); though realistic in technique, it foreshadowed the psychological depth and poetic force of her late work. In innovative novels such as* Mrs. Dalloway *(1925) and* To the Lighthouse *(1927), Woolf became one of the central Modernist writers in English and a pioneer of stream-of-consciousness narration, which portrays the random flow of thoughts and feelings through a character's mind. Her critical essays are collected in* The Common Reader *(1925, second series 1932); her long essay* A Room of One's Own *(1929) is a feminist classic. After several nervous breakdowns, Woolf, fearing for her sanity, drowned herself in 1941.*

Whatever hour you woke there was a door shutting. From room to room they went, hand in hand, lifting here, opening there, making sure—a ghostly couple.

"Here we left it," she said. And he added, "Oh, but here too!" "It's upstairs," she murmured. "And in the garden," he whispered. "Quietly," they said, "or we shall wake them."

But it wasn't that you woke us. Oh, no. "They're looking for it; they're drawing the curtain," one might say, and so read on a page or two. "Now they've found it," one would be certain, stopping the pencil on the margin. And then, tired of reading, one might rise and see for oneself, the house all empty, the doors standing open, only the wood pigeons bubbling with content and the hum of the threshing machine sounding from the farm. "What did I come in here for? What did I want to find?" My hands were empty. "Perhaps it's upstairs then?" The apples were in the loft. And so down again, the garden still as ever, only the book had slipped into the grass.

But they had found it in the drawing room. Not that one could ever see them. The window panes reflected apples, reflected roses; all the leaves were green in the glass. If they moved in the drawing room, the apple only turned its yellow side. Yet, the moment after, if the door was opened, spread about the floor, hung upon the walls, pendant from the ceiling—what? My hands were empty. The shadow of a thrush crossed the carpet; from the deepest wells of silence the wood pigeon drew its bubble of sound. "Safe, safe, safe," the pulse of the house beat softly. "The treasure buried; the room . . ." the pulse stopped short. Oh, was that the buried treasure?

A moment later the light had faded. Out in the garden then? But the 5
trees spun darkness for a wandering beam of sun. So fine, so rare, coolly sunk beneath the surface the beam I sought always burnt behind the glass. Death was the glass; death was between us; coming to the woman first, hundreds of years ago, leaving the house, sealing all the windows; the rooms were darkened. He left it, left her, went North, went East, saw the stars turned in the Southern sky; sought the house, found it dropped beneath the Downs. "Safe, safe, safe," the pulse of the house beat gladly. "The Treasure yours."

The wind roars up the avenue. Trees stoop and bend this way and that. Moonbeams splash and spill wildly in the rain. But the beam of the lamp falls straight from the window. The candle burns stiff and still. Wandering through the house, opening the windows, whispering not to wake us, the ghostly couple seek their joy.

"Here we slept" she says. And he adds, "Kisses without number." "Waking in the morning—" "Silver between the trees—" "Upstairs—" "In the garden—" "When summer came—" "In winter snowtime—" The doors go shutting far in the distance, gently knocking like the pulse of a heart.

Nearer they come; cease at the doorway. The wind falls, the rain slides silver down the glass. Our eyes darken; we hear no steps beside us; we see no lady spread her ghostly cloak. His hands shield the lantern. "Look," he breathes. "Sound asleep. Love upon their lips."

Stooping, holding their silver lamp above us, long they look and deeply. Long they pause. The wind drives straightly; the flame stoops slightly. Wild beams of moonlight cross both floor and wall, and, meeting, stain the faces bent; the faces pondering; the faces that search the sleepers and seek their hidden joy.

"Safe, safe, safe," the heart of the house beats proudly. "Long years—" he sighs. "Again you found me." "Here," she murmurs, "sleeping; in the garden reading; laughing, rolling apples in the loft. Here we left our treasure—" Stooping, their light lifts the lids upon my eyes. "Safe! safe! safe!" the pulse of the house beats wildly. Waking, I cry "Oh, is this *your* buried treasure? The light in the heart."

Kay Ryan, US Poet Laureate, 2008–2010

POETRY

TALKING WITH *Kay Ryan*

"Language That Lasts"

Dana Gioia Interviews Former US Poet Laureate Kay Ryan

Q: When did you start writing poetry?

KAY RYAN: In a way I'd say I started writing poetry when I started collecting language, which was as soon as I could. I loved hearing a new word or phrase, and I had a private game of trying to say things differently than I'd said them before. I remember when I was quite advanced in this language study, in ninth grade, I went on a summer trip with my friend and her parents down to Texas. I was sitting there quietly in the small hot living room of my friend's aunt, listening to the adult conversation. Someone said something irritated along the lines of, "Tracy totaled Teddy's Toronado, and Tyler tattled it to Tina!" and I just burst out laughing: that accidental string of T's nobody else seemed to notice. Language brought me constant, secret pleasure, and it was free; I could have as much as I wanted, which is nice if you're poor.

As to writing-writing, I fooled around with writing poetry during high school and college and even after I'd become a community college teacher, trying to keep it at arm's length because I didn't want to be exposed the way poetry makes you exposed. I wanted to stay superficial. But by the time I was thirty I could see that poetry was eating away at my mind anyhow. Why not accept it and try to get really good at it? So, either I started writing poetry at three or thirty.

Q: Did poetry play much of a part in your childhood?

KAY RYAN: I guess the short answer would be no. But my mother had one lovely poem about a dead kitten that she liked to say. I always enjoyed feeling tender and sad when she did; it was a kind of intimacy with a mother who wasn't very intimate. And my mother's mother liked to recite poems when she came to visit. They made me feel very serious, and that is a lovely feeling for a child: "Life is real! Life is earnest! / And the grave is not its goal; / Dust thou art, to dust returnest / Was not spoken of the soul!" My grandmother grew up in a time when people really memorized poetry for pleasure, and I loved hearing it.

My only other contact with poetry—but it was an important one—was in sixth grade. My enlightened teacher, Mrs. Kimball, at Roosevelt Elementary School in Bakersfield, California, had us do "choral reading," meaning the whole class memorized poems and stood up on the stage like a chorus at assemblies and recited them with great gusto. So I got a chance, like my grandmother, to memorize poetry for pleasure and have the pleasure of saying it aloud.

Q: Whom do you write for?

KAY RYAN: This is a devilish question. I'll have to answer it in parts.

First, when I write a poem I'm completely occupied with trying to net some elusive fish; I'm desperate to get the net (made of words) knotted in such a way that it will catch this desired fish (a half-formed idea, a wisp of a feeling). I'm not thinking of anything but that; I'm not thinking of me, I'm not thinking of you.

But then later, after I've finished writing the poem and have let it sit for days or months and look back to see if there's a fish in the net after all (many times, I'm sorry to say, there is no fish), I begin thinking of you. Have I put the necessary connections in the poem, or are some of them still in my head? Have I shaped the lines so they will present the reader with the most pleasure in discovering the secret rhymes? Have I removed self-indulgences? Because a poem, by its nature, must please others. If it doesn't, it can't last; and if it doesn't last it wasn't a poem, because poems are language that lasts.

Q: What gives you pleasure in writing?

KAY RYAN: People have dreams where they begin noticing that their house is lots bigger than they knew; they realize there is a maze of rooms behind the ones they've been occupying. The dreamer (I've had this dream) doesn't know why she hasn't noticed this before, because it's fascinating.

Writing a poem is like this; I go back behind my usual mind and find places I didn't know about, places that only the activity of writing a poem can let me into.

Q: Who are your favorite poets?

KAY RYAN: My favorite American poets are Emily Dickinson and Robert Frost. British favorites include John Donne, Gerard Manley Hopkins, Philip Larkin, and Stevie Smith. Favorites in other languages are Fernando Pessoa and Constantine Cavafy.

Q: Did a poem ever change your life?

KAY RYAN: A dream poem might have. When I was around ten, I dreamed that a piece of white paper was blowing around and I was chasing it. I knew it had the most beautiful poem in the world written on it. I couldn't catch it.

I never forgot that dream, although at the time I wasn't even thinking of trying to write poetry. Still, maybe some deep part of me was busy at it even then. I'm still trying to catch that piece of paper.

Kay Ryan with Dana Gioia

Q: What is the purpose of poetry? Why do people need poetry?

KAY RYAN: The secret, long-term purpose of poetry is to create more space between everything. Poetry is the main engine of the expanding universe. You yourself will have noticed how reading a poem that really strikes you (that will be one in 25, if you're lucky; a poem can be great and still not strike YOU) makes you feel freer and less burdened, even if it's about death. You feel fresher, more awake. This proves my point; your atoms have been subtly distanced from each other, like a breeze is blowing through your DNA. That's poetry loosening you.

To the Muse

Give me leave, Muse, in plain view to array
Your shift and bodice by the light of day.
I would have brought an epic. Be not vexed
Instead to grace a niggling schoolroom text;
Let down your sanction, help me to oblige
Those who would lead fresh devots to your liege,
And at your altar, grant that in a flash
Readers and I know incense from dead ash.

—X. J. K.

10 READING A POEM

What You Will Learn in This Chapter

- To paraphrase a poem
- To recognize and define *lyric poetry*
- To define the other major kinds of poetry—*narrative, dramatic, didactic*
- To define and differentiate *subject* and *theme*

How do you read a poem? The literal-minded might say, "Just let your eye light on it"; but there is more to poetry than meets the eye. What Shakespeare called "the mind's eye" also plays a part. Many readers who have no trouble understanding and enjoying prose find poetry difficult. This is to be expected. At first glance, a poem usually will make some sense and give some pleasure, but it may not yield everything at once. Poetry is not to be galloped over like the daily news: a poem differs from most prose in that it is to be read slowly, carefully, and attentively. Not all poems are difficult, of course, and some can be understood and enjoyed on first encounter. But good poems yield more if read twice; and the best poems—after ten, twenty, or a hundred readings—still go on yielding.

POETRY OR VERSE

Approaching a thing written in lines and surrounded with white space, we need not expect it to be a poem just because it is verse. (Any composition in lines of more or less regular rhythm, often ending in rimes, is **verse**.) Here, for instance, is a specimen of verse that few will call poetry:

Thirty days hath September,
April, June, and November;
All the rest have thirty-one
Excepting February alone,
To which we twenty-eight assign
Till leap year makes it twenty-nine.

To a higher degree than that classic memory-tickler, poetry appeals to the mind and arouses feelings. Poetry may state facts, but, more important, it makes imaginative statements that we may value even if its facts are incorrect. Coleridge's error in placing a star within the horns of the crescent moon in "The Rime of the Ancient Mariner" does not stop the passage from being good poetry, though it is faulty astronomy. According to poet Gerard Manley Hopkins, poetry is "to be heard for its own sake and interest even over and above its interest of meaning." There are other elements in a poem besides plain prose sense: sounds, images, rhythms, figures of speech. These may strike us and please us even before we ask, "But what does it all mean?"

This is a truth not readily grasped by anyone who regards a poem as a kind of puzzle written in secret code with a message slyly concealed. The effect of a poem (our whole mental and emotional response to it) consists of much more than simply a message. By its musical qualities, by its suggestions, it can work on the reader's unconscious. T. S. Eliot put it well when he said in *The Use of Poetry and the Use of Criticism* that the prose sense of a poem is chiefly useful in keeping the reader's mind "diverted and quiet, while the poem does its work upon him." Eliot went on to liken the meaning of a poem to the bit of meat a burglar brings along to throw to the family dog. What is the work of a poem? To touch us, to stir us, to make us glad, and possibly even to tell us something.

HOW TO READ A POEM

How to set about reading a poem? Here are a few suggestions. To begin with, read the poem once straight through, with no particular expectations; read open-mindedly. Let yourself experience whatever you find, without worrying just yet about the large general and important ideas the poem contains (if indeed it contains any). Don't dwell on a troublesome word or difficult passage—just push on. Some of the difficulties may seem smaller when you read the poem for a second time; at least, they will have become parts of a whole for you.

On the second reading, read for the exact sense of all the words; if there are words you don't understand, look them up in a dictionary. Dwell on any difficult parts as long as you need to.

If you read the poem silently, sound its words in your mind. Better still, read the poem aloud, or listen to someone else reading it. You may discover meanings you didn't perceive in it before. To decide how to speak a poem can be an excellent method of getting to understand it.

PARAPHRASE

Try to **paraphrase** the poem as a whole, or perhaps just the more difficult lines. In paraphrasing, we put into our own words what we understand the poem to say, restating ideas that seem essential, coming out and stating what the poem may only suggest. This may sound like a heartless thing to do to a poem, but good poems can stand it. In fact, to compare a poem to its paraphrase is a good way to see the distance between poetry and prose.

calls for. The reader who can't stand "The Lake Isle of Innisfree" because she is afraid of bees isn't reading a poem by Yeats, but one of her own invention.

Now and again we meet a poem—perhaps startling and memorable—into which the method of paraphrase won't take us far. Some portion of any deep poem resists explanation, but certain poems resist it almost entirely. Many poems by religious mystics seem closer to dream than waking. So do poems that purport to record drug experiences, such as Coleridge's "Kubla Khan" (Chapter 23). So do nonsense poems, translations of primitive folk songs, and surreal poems. Such poetry may move us and give pleasure (although not, perhaps, the pleasure of intellectual understanding). We do it no harm by trying to paraphrase it, though we may fail. Whether logically clear or strangely opaque, good poems appeal to the intelligence and do not shrink from it.

So far, we have taken for granted that poetry differs from prose; yet all our strategies for reading poetry—plowing straight on through and then going back, isolating difficulties, trying to paraphrase, reading aloud, using a dictionary—are no different from those we might employ in unraveling a complicated piece of prose. Poetry, after all, is similar to prose in most respects. At the very least, it is written in the same language. Like prose, poetry shares knowledge with us. It tells us, for instance, of a beautiful island in Lake Gill, County Sligo, Ireland, and of how one man feels about it.

LYRIC POETRY

Originally, as its Greek name suggests, a *lyric* was a poem sung to the music of a lyre. This earlier meaning—a poem made for singing—is still current today, when we use *lyrics* to mean the words of a popular song. But the kind of printed poem we now call a *lyric* is usually something else, as over the past five hundred years the nature of lyric poetry has changed greatly. Ever since the invention of the printing press in the fifteenth century, poets have written less often for singers, more often for readers. In general, this tendency has made lyric poems contain less word-music and (since they can be pondered on a page) more thought—and perhaps more complicated feelings.

What Is a Lyric Poem?

Here is a rough definition of a **lyric poem** as it is written today: a short poem expressing the thoughts and feelings of a single speaker. Often a poet will write a lyric in the first person ("I will arise and go now, and go to Innisfree"), but not always. A lyric can also be in the first person plural, as in Paul Laurence Dunbar's "We Wear the Mask" (Chapter 18). Or, a lyric might describe an object or recall an experience without the speaker's ever bringing himself or herself into it. (For an example of such a lyric, one in which the poet refrains from saying "I," see Theodore Roethke's "Root Cellar" or Gerard Manley Hopkins's "Pied Beauty," both found in Chapter 14.)

Perhaps because, rightly or wrongly, some people still think of lyrics as lyre-strummings, they expect a lyric to be an outburst of feeling, somewhat resembling a song, at least containing musical elements such as rime, rhythm, or sound effects. Such expectations are fulfilled in "The Lake Isle of Innisfree," that impassioned lyric full of language rich in sound. Many contemporary poets, however, write short poems in which they voice opinions or complicated feelings—poems that no reader would dream of trying to sing.

But in the sense in which we use it, *lyric* will usually apply to a kind of poem you can easily recognize. Here, for instance, are two lyrics. They differ sharply in subject and theme, but they have traits in common: both are short, and (as you will find) both set forth one speaker's definite, unmistakable feelings.

Robert Hayden (1913–1980)

Those Winter Sundays 1962

Sundays too my father got up early
and put his clothes on in the blueblack cold,
then with cracked hands that ached
from labor in the weekday weather made
banked fires blaze. No one ever thanked him.

I'd wake and hear the cold splintering, breaking.
When the rooms were warm, he'd call,
and slowly I would rise and dress,
fearing the chronic angers of that house,

Speaking indifferently to him,
who had driven out the cold
and polished my good shoes as well.
What did I know, what did I know
of love's austere and lonely offices?

Questions

1. Jot down a brief paraphrase of this poem. In your paraphrase, clearly show what the speaker finds himself remembering.
2. What are the speaker's various feelings? What do you understand from the words "chronic angers" and "austere"?
3. With what specific details does the poem make the past seem real?
4. What is the subject of Hayden's poem? How would you state its theme?

Adrienne Rich (1929–2012)

Aunt Jennifer's Tigers 1951

Aunt Jennifer's tigers prance across a screen,
Bright topaz denizens of a world of green.
They do not fear the men beneath the tree;
They pace in sleek chivalric certainty.

Aunt Jennifer's fingers fluttering through her wool
Find even the ivory needle hard to pull.
The massive weight of Uncle's wedding band
Sits heavily upon Aunt Jennifer's hand.

When Aunt is dead, her terrified hands will lie
Still ringed with ordeals she was mastered by.
The tigers in the panel that she made
Will go on prancing, proud and unafraid.

NARRATIVE POETRY

Although a lyric sometimes relates an incident, or like "Those Winter Sundays" draws a scene, it does not usually relate a series of events. That happens in a **narrative poem**, one whose main purpose is to tell a story.

Narrative poetry dates back to the Babylonian *Epic of Gilgamesh* (composed before 2000 B.C.) and Homer's epics the *Iliad* and the *Odyssey* (composed before 700 B.C.). The **epic**, which is a long narrative form often tracing the adventures of a legendary or mythic hero, may well have originated much earlier. In England and Scotland, storytelling poems, such as *Beowulf*, have long been popular; in the late Middle Ages, **ballads**—or storytelling songs—circulated widely. Some, such as "Sir Patrick Spence" and "Bonny Barbara Allan," survive in our day, and folksingers sometimes perform them.

The art of narrative poetry invites the skills of a writer of fiction: the ability to draw characters and settings, to engage attention, to shape a plot. Needless to say, it calls for all the skills of a poet as well. In the English language today, lyrics seem more plentiful than other kinds of poetry. Although there has recently been a revival of interest in writing narrative poems, they have a far smaller audience than the readership enjoyed by long verse narratives in the nineteenth century, such as Henry Wadsworth Longfellow's *Evangeline* and Alfred, Lord Tennyson's *Idylls of the King*.

Here are two narrative poems: one medieval, one modern. How would you paraphrase the stories they tell? How do they hold your attention on their stories?

Anonymous (traditional Scottish ballad)

Sir Patrick Spence

The king sits in Dumferling toune,
  Drinking the blude-reid wine:
"O whar will I get guid sailor
  To sail this schip of mine?"

Up and spak an eldern knicht,° *knight*
  Sat at the kings richt kne:
"Sir Patrick Spence is the best sailor
  That sails upon the se."

The king has written a braid letter,
  And signed it wi' his hand,
And sent it to Sir Patrick Spence,
  Was walking on the sand.

The first line that Sir Patrick red,
  A loud lauch lauchèd he;
The next line that Sir Patrick red,
  The teir blinded his ee.

"O wha° is this has don this deid, *who*
  This ill deid don to me,
To send me out this time o' the yeir,
  To sail upon the se!

"Mak haste, mak haste, my mirry men all,
  Our guid schip sails the morne."
"O say na sae,° my master deir, *so*
  For I feir a deadlie storme.

"Late late yestreen I saw the new moone,
  Wi' the auld moone in hir arme,
And I feir, I feir, my deir master,
  That we will cum to harme."

O our Scots nobles wer richt laith° *loath*
  To weet° their cork-heild schoone,° *wet; shoes*
Bot lang owre° a' the play wer playd, *long before*
  Their hats they swam aboone.° *above (their heads)*

O lang, lang may their ladies sit,
  Wi' their fans into their hand,
Or ere° they se Sir Patrick Spence *before*
  Cum sailing to the land.

O lang, lang may the ladies stand,
  Wi' their gold kems° in their hair, *combs*
Waiting for their ain° deir lords, *own*
  For they'll se thame na mair.

Haf owre,° haf owre to Aberdour, *halfway over*
  It's fiftie fadom deip,
And thair lies guid Sir Patrick Spence,
  Wi' the Scots lords at his feit.

Sir Patrick Spence. 9 *braid:* Broad, but broad in what sense? The poet could have meant *plain-spoken, official,* or *on wide paper.*

Questions

1. That the king drinks "blude-reid wine" (line 2)—what meaning do you find in that detail? What does it hint at or foreshadow? (If the phrase "blude-reid" is confusing, trying saying it aloud, and your ear may pick up its meaning.)
2. What do you make of this king and his motives for sending Spence and the Scots lords into an impending storm? Is he a fool, is he cruel and inconsiderate, is he deliberately trying to drown Sir Patrick and his crew, or is it impossible for us to know? Let your answer rely on the poem alone, not on anything you read into it.
3. Comment on this ballad's methods of storytelling. Is the story told too briefly for us to care what happens to Spence and his men, or are there any means by which the poet makes us feel compassion for them? Do you resent the lack of a detailed account of the shipwreck?
4. Lines 25–28—the new moon with the old moon in her arm—have been much admired as poetry. In what way does this stanza also contribute to the story of the poem?

Robert Frost (1874–1963)

"Out, Out—" 1916

The buzz-saw snarled and rattled in the yard
And made dust and dropped stove-length sticks of wood,
Sweet-scented stuff when the breeze drew across it.
And from there those that lifted eyes could count
Five mountain ranges one behind the other
Under the sunset far into Vermont.
And the saw snarled and rattled, snarled and rattled,
As it ran light, or had to bear a load.
And nothing happened: day was all but done.
Call it a day, I wish they might have said
To please the boy by giving him the half hour
That a boy counts so much when saved from work.
His sister stood beside them in her apron
To tell them "Supper." At the word, the saw,
As if to prove saws knew what supper meant,
Leaped out at the boy's hand, or seemed to leap—
He must have given the hand. However it was,
Neither refused the meeting. But the hand!
The boy's first outcry was a rueful laugh,
As he swung toward them holding up the hand
Half in appeal, but half as if to keep
The life from spilling. Then the boy saw all—
Since he was old enough to know, big boy
Doing a man's work, though a child at heart—

He saw all spoiled. "Don't let him cut my hand off—
The doctor, when he comes. Don't let him, sister!"
So. But the hand was gone already.
The doctor put him in the dark of ether.
He lay and puffed his lips out with his breath.
And then—the watcher at his pulse took fright.
No one believed. They listened at his heart.
Little—less—nothing!—and that ended it.
No more to build on there. And they, since they
Were not the one dead, turned to their affairs.

"Out, Out—." The title of this poem echoes the words of Shakespeare's Macbeth on receiving news that his queen is dead: "Out, out, brief candle! / Life's but a walking shadow, a poor player / That struts and frets his hour upon the stage / And then is heard no more. It is a tale / Told by an idiot, full of sound and fury, / Signifying nothing" (*Macbeth* 5.5.23–28).

Questions

1. How does Frost make the buzz-saw appear sinister? How does he make it seem, in another way, like a friend?
2. What do you make of the people who surround the boy—the "they" of the poem? Who might they be? Do they seem to you concerned and compassionate, cruel, indifferent, or what?
3. What does Frost's reference to *Macbeth* contribute to your understanding of "'Out, Out—'"? How would you state the theme of Frost's poem?
4. Set this poem beside "Sir Patrick Spence." How does "'Out, Out—'" resemble or differ from that medieval folk ballad in subject? How is Frost's poem similar or different in its way of telling a story?

DRAMATIC POETRY

A third kind of poetry is **dramatic poetry**, which presents the voice of an imaginary character (or characters) speaking directly, without any additional narration by the author.

A dramatic poem, according to T. S. Eliot, does not consist of "what the poet would say in his own person, but only what he can say within the limits of one imaginary character addressing another imaginary character." Strictly speaking, the term *dramatic poetry* describes any verse written for the stage (and until a few centuries ago most playwrights, like Shakespeare and Molière, wrote their plays mainly in verse).

Dramatic Monologue

The term *dramatic poetry* most often refers to the **dramatic monologue**, a poem written as a speech made by a character (other than the author) at some decisive moment. A dramatic monologue is usually addressed by the speaker to some other character who remains silent. If the listener replies, the poem becomes a dialogue (such as Thomas Hardy's "The Ruined Maid" in Chapter 12) in which the story unfolds in the conversation between two speakers.

The dramatic monologue has been a popular form among American poets, including Edwin Arlington Robinson, Robert Frost, Ezra Pound, Randall Jarrell, Sylvia Plath, and David Mason. The Victorian poet Robert Browning, who developed the form of the dramatic monologue, liked to put words in the mouths of characters who were conspicuously nasty, weak, reckless, or crazy: The most famous dramatic monologue ever written is probably Browning's "My Last Duchess," in which the poet conjures up a Renaissance Italian duke whose words reveal much more about himself than the aristocratic speaker intends.

Robert Browning (1812–1889)

My Last Duchess 1842

Ferrara

That's my last Duchess painted on the wall,
Looking as if she were alive. I call
That piece a wonder, now: Frà Pandolf's hands
Worked busily a day, and there she stands.
Will't please you sit and look at her? I said
"Frà Pandolf" by design, for never read
Strangers like you that pictured countenance,
The depth and passion of its earnest glance,
But to myself they turned (since none puts by
The curtain I have drawn for you, but I)
And seemed as they would ask me, if they durst,
How such a glance came there; so, not the first
Are you to turn and ask thus. Sir, 'twas not
Her husband's presence only, called that spot
Of joy into the Duchess' cheek: perhaps
Frà Pandolf chanced to say, "Her mantle laps
Over my lady's wrist too much," or "Paint
Must never hope to reproduce the faint
Half-flush that dies along her throat": such stuff
Was courtesy, she thought, and cause enough
For calling up that spot of joy. She had
A heart—how shall I say?—too soon made glad,
Too easily impressed; she liked whate'er
She looked on, and her looks went everywhere.
Sir, 'twas all one! My favor at her breast,
The dropping of the daylight in the West,
The bough of cherries some officious fool
Broke in the orchard for her, the white mule
She rode with round the terrace—all and each

Would draw from her alike the approving speech,
Or blush, at least. She thanked men,—good! but thanked
Somehow—I know not how—as if she ranked
My gift of a nine-hundred-years-old name
With anybody's gift. Who'd stoop to blame
This sort of trifling? Even had you skill
In speech—(which I have not)—to make your will
Quite clear to such an one, and say, "Just this
Or that in you disgusts me; here you miss,
Or there exceed the mark"—and if she let
Herself be lessoned so, nor plainly set
Her wits to yours, forsooth, and made excuse,
—E'en then would be some stooping; and I choose
Never to stoop. Oh sir, she smiled, no doubt,
Whene'er I passed her; but who passed without
Much the same smile? This grew; I gave commands;
Then all smiles stopped together. There she stands
As if alive. Will't please you rise? We'll meet
The company below, then. I repeat,
The Count your master's known munificence
Is ample warrant that no just pretense
Of mine for dowry will be disallowed;
Though his fair daughter's self, as I avowed
At starting, is my object. Nay, we'll go
Together down, sir. Notice Neptune, though,
Taming a sea-horse, thought a rarity,
Which Claus of Innsbruck cast in bronze for me!

My Last Duchess. Ferrara, a city in northern Italy, is the scene. Browning may have modeled his speaker after Alonzo, Duke of Ferrara (1533–1598). 3 *Frà Pandolf* and 56 *Claus of Innsbruck:* names of fictitious artists.

Questions

1. Whom is the Duke addressing? What is this person's business in Ferrara?
2. What is the Duke's opinion of his last Duchess's personality? Do we see her character differently?
3. If the Duke was unhappy with the Duchess's behavior, why didn't he make his displeasure known? Cite a specific passage to explain his reticence.
4. How much do we know about the fate of the last Duchess? Would it help our understanding of the poem to know more?
5. Does Browning imply any connection between the Duke's art collection and his attitude toward his wife?

DIDACTIC POETRY

More fashionable in former times was a fourth variety of poetry, **didactic poetry**: poetry or verse written to state a message or teach a body of knowledge. In a lyric, a speaker may express sadness; in a **didactic poem**, he or she may explain that sadness is inherent in life. Poems that impart a body of knowledge, such as Ovid's *Art of Love* and Lucretius's *On the Nature of Things*, are didactic. Such instructive poetry was favored especially by classical Latin poets and by English poets of the eighteenth century. In *The Fleece* (1757), John Dyer celebrated the British woolen industry and included practical advice on raising sheep:

> In cold stiff soils the bleaters oft complain
> Of gouty ails, by shepherds termed the halt:
> Those let the neighboring fold or ready crook
> Detain, and pour into their cloven feet
> Corrosive drugs, deep-searching arsenic,
> Dry alum, verdigris, or vitriol keen.

One might agree with Dr. Johnson's comment on Dyer's effort: "The subject, Sir, cannot be made poetical." But it may be argued that the subject of didactic poetry does not make it any less poetical. Good poems, it seems, can be written about anything under the sun. Like Dyer, John Milton described sick sheep in "Lycidas," a poem few readers have thought unpoetic:

> The hungry sheep look up, and are not fed,
> But, swoll'n with wind and the rank mist they draw,
> Rot inwardly, and foul contagion spread . . .

What makes Milton's lines better poetry than Dyer's is, among other things, a difference in attitude. Sick sheep to Dyer mean the loss of a few shillings and pence; to Milton, whose sheep stand for English Christendom, they mean a moral catastrophe.

WRITING *effectively*

THINKING ABOUT PARAPHRASING

A poet takes pains to choose each word of a poem for both its sound and its exact shade of meaning. Since a poem's full effect is so completely wedded to its precise wording, some would say that no poem can be truly paraphrased. But even though it represents an imperfect approximation of the real thing, a paraphrase can be useful to write and read. It can clearly map out a poem's key images, actions, and ideas. A map is no substitute for a landscape, but a good map often helps us find our way through the landscape without getting lost.

William Stafford (1914–1993)

Ask Me 1975

Some time when the river is ice ask me
mistakes I have made. Ask me whether
what I have done is my life. Others
have come in their slow way into
my thought, and some have tried to help
or to hurt—ask me what difference
their strongest love or hate has made.

I will listen to what you say.
You and I can turn and look
at the silent river and wait. We know
the current is there, hidden; and there
are comings and goings from miles away
that hold the stillness exactly before us.
What the river says, that is what I say.

William Stafford (1914–1993)

A Paraphrase of "Ask Me" 1977

I think my poem can be paraphrased—and that any poem can be paraphrased. But every pass through the material, using other words, would have to be achieved at certain costs, either in momentum, or nuance, or dangerously explicit (and therefore misleading in tone) adjustments. I'll try one such pass through the poem:

> When it's quiet and cold and we have some chance to interchange without hurry, confront me if you like with a challenge about whether I think I have made mistakes in my life—and ask me, if you want to, whether to me my life is actually the sequence of events or exploits others would see. Well, those others tag along in my living, and some of them in fact have played significant roles in the narrative run of my world; they have intended either helping or hurting (but by implication in the way I am saying this you will know that neither effort is conclusive). So—ask me how important their good or bad intentions have been (both intentions get a drastic *leveling* judgment from this cool stating of it all). You, too, will be entering that realm of maybe-help-maybe-hurt, by entering that far into my life by asking this serious question—so: I will stay still and consider. Out there will be the world confronting us both; we will both know we are surrounded by mystery, tremendous things that do not reveal themselves to us. That river, that world—and our lives—all share the depth and stillness of much

> more significance than our talk, or intentions. There is a steadiness and somehow a solace in knowing that what is around us so greatly surpasses our human concerns.
>
> From "Ask Me"

CHECKLIST: Writing a Paraphrase

- ☐ **Read the poem closely.** It is important to read it more than once to understand it well.
- ☐ **Go through it line by line.** Don't skip lines or stanzas or any key details. In your own words, what does each line say?
- ☐ **Write your paraphrase as prose.**
- ☐ **State the poem's literal meaning.** Don't worry about deeper meanings.
- ☐ **Reread your statement to see if you have missed anything important.** Check to see if you have captured the overall significance of the poem along with the details.

TOPICS FOR WRITING ON PARAPHRASING

1. Paraphrase any short poem from Chapter 23, "Poems for Further Reading." Be sure to do a careful line-by-line reading. Include the most vital points and details, and state the poem's main thought or theme without quoting any original passage.
2. In a paragraph, contrast William Stafford's poem with his paraphrase. What does the poem offer that the paraphrase does not? What, then, is the value of the paraphrase?
3. Write a two-page paraphrase of the events described in "'Out, Out—.'" Then take your paraphrase further: summarize the poem's message in a single sentence.

▶ TERMS FOR *review*

Analytic Terms

Verse ▶ This term has two major meanings. It refers to any single line of poetry or to any composition written in separate lines of more or less regular rhythm, in contrast to prose.

Paraphrase ▶ The restatement in one's own words of what one understands a poem to say or suggest. A paraphrase is similar to a summary, although not as brief or simple.

Summary ▶ A brief condensation of the main idea or plot of a work. A summary is similar to a paraphrase, but less detailed.

Subject ▶ The main topic of a work, whatever the work is "about."

Theme ▶ A generally recurring subject or idea noticeably evident in a literary work. Not all subjects in a work can be considered themes, only the central one(s).

Types of Poetry

Lyric poem ▶ A short poem expressing the thoughts and feelings of a single speaker. Often written in the first person, it traditionally has a songlike immediacy and emotional force.

Narrative poem ▶ A poem that tells a story. **Epics** and **ballads** are two common forms of narrative poetry.

Dramatic monologue ▶ A poem written as a speech made by a character at some decisive moment. The speaker is usually addressing a silent listener.

Didactic poem ▶ A poem intended to teach a moral lesson or impart a body of knowledge.

11 LISTENING TO A VOICE

What You Will Learn in This Chapter

- To identify the speaker in a poem
- To understand and characterize the tone of a poem
- To define *irony* in its major forms
- To analyze the role of a speaker in a poem

TONE

In old Western movies, when one hombre taunts another, it is customary for the second to drawl, "Smile when you say that, pardner" or "Mister, I don't like your tone of voice." Sometimes in reading a poem, although we can neither see a face nor hear a voice, we can infer the poet's attitude from other evidence.

Like tone of voice, **tone** in literature often conveys an attitude toward the person addressed. Like the manner of a person, the manner of a poem may be friendly or belligerent toward its reader, condescending or respectful. Again like tone of voice, the tone of a poem may tell us how the speaker feels about himself or herself: cocksure or humble, sad or glad. But usually when we ask "What is the tone of a poem?" we mean "What attitude does the poet take toward a theme or a subject?" Is the poet being affectionate, hostile, earnest, playful, sarcastic, or what? We may never be able to know, of course, the poet's personal feelings. All we need know is how to feel when we read the poem.

Strictly speaking, tone isn't an attitude; it is whatever in the poem makes an attitude clear to us: the choice of certain words instead of others, the picking out of certain details. In A. E. Housman's "Loveliest of trees" (Chapter 23), for example, the poet communicates his admiration for a cherry tree's beauty by singling out its white blossoms for attention; had he wanted to show his dislike for the tree, he might have concentrated on its broken branches, birdlime, or snails. To perceive the tone of a poem rightly, we need to read the poem carefully, paying attention to whatever suggestions we find in it.

Theodore Roethke (1908–1963)

My Papa's Waltz 1948

The whiskey on your breath
Could make a small boy dizzy;
But I hung on like death:
Such waltzing was not easy.

We romped until the pans
Slid from the kitchen shelf;
My mother's countenance
Could not unfrown itself.

The hand that held my wrist
Was battered on one knuckle;
At every step you missed
My right ear scraped a buckle.

You beat time on my head
With a palm caked hard by dirt,
Then waltzed me off to bed
Still clinging to your shirt.

What is the tone of this poem? Most readers find the speaker's attitude toward his father critical, but nonetheless affectionate. They take this recollection of childhood to be an odd but happy one. Other readers, however, concentrate on other details, such as the father's rough manners and drunkenness. One reader has written that "Roethke expresses his resentment for his father, a drunken brute with dirty hands and whiskey breath who carelessly hurt the child's ear and manhandled him." Although this reader accurately noticed some of the events in the poem and perceived that there was something desperate in the son's hanging onto the father "like death," he simplifies the tone of the poem and so misses its humorous side.

While "My Papa's Waltz" contains the dark elements of manhandling and drunkenness, the tone remains grotesquely comic. The rollicking rhythms of the poem underscore Roethke's complex humor—half loving and half censuring of the unwashed, intoxicated father. The humor is further reinforced by playful rimes such as *dizzy* and *easy*, *knuckle* and *buckle*, as well as the joyful suggestions of the words *waltz*, *waltzing*, and *romped*. The scene itself is comic, with kitchen pans falling because of the father's roughhousing while the mother looks on unamused. However much the speaker satirizes the overly rambunctious father, he does not have the boy identify with the soberly disapproving mother. Not all comedy is comfortable and reassuring. Certainly, this small boy's family life has its frightening side, but the last line suggests the boy is *still clinging* to his father with persistent if also complicated love.

Satiric Poetry

"My Papa's Waltz," though it includes lifelike details that aren't pretty, has a tone relatively easy to recognize. So does **satiric poetry**, a kind of comic poetry that generally conveys a message. Usually its tone is one of detached amusement, withering contempt, and implied superiority. In a satiric poem, the poet ridicules some person or persons (or perhaps some type of human behavior), examining the victim by the light of certain principles and implying that the reader, too, ought to feel contempt for the victim.

Stephen Crane (1871–1900)

The Wayfarer 1899

The wayfarer,
Perceiving the pathway to truth,
Was struck with astonishment.
It was thickly grown with weeds.
"Ha," he said,
"I see that none has passed here
In a long time."
Later he saw that each weed
Was a singular knife.
"Well," he mumbled at last,
"Doubtless there are other roads."

Questions

1. What is Crane's message?
2. How would you characterize the tone of this poem? Disillusioned? Amused?

A Spectrum of Tones

In some poems the poet's attitude may be plain enough, while in other poems attitudes may be so mingled that it is hard to describe them tersely without doing injustice to the poem. Does Andrew Marvell in "To His Coy Mistress" (Chapter 23) take a serious or playful attitude toward the fact that he and his lady are destined to be food for worms? No one-word answer will suffice. And what of T. S. Eliot's "The Love Song of J. Alfred Prufrock" (Chapter 23)? In his attitude toward his redemption-seeking hero who wades with trousers rolled, Eliot is seriously funny. The following poem by Rhina Espaillat mingles not only tones but also languages.

Rhina Espaillat (b. 1932)

Bilingual/*Bilingüe* 1998

My father liked them separate, one there,
one here (*allá y aquí*), as if aware

that words might cut in two his daughter's heart
(*el corazón*) and lock the alien part

to what he was—his memory, his name
(*su nombre*)—with a key he could not claim.

"English outside this door, Spanish inside,"
he said, "*y basta.*" But who can divide

the world, the word (*mundo y palabra*) from
any child? I knew how to be dumb

and stubborn (*testaruda*); late, in bed,
I hoarded secret syllables I read

until my tongue (*mi lengua*) learned to run
where his stumbled. And still the heart was one.

I like to think he knew that, even when,
proud (*orgulloso*) of his daughter's pen,

he stood outside *mis versos*, half in fear
of words he loved but wanted not to hear.

Questions

1. Espaillat's poem is full of Spanish words and phrases. (Even the title is given in both languages.) What does the Spanish add to the poem? Could we remove the phrases without changing the poem?
2. How does the father want to divide his daughter's world, at least in terms of language? Does his request suggest any other divisions he hopes to enforce in her life?
3. How does the daughter respond to her father's request to leave English outside their home?
4. "And still the heart was one," states the speaker of the poem. Should we take her statement at face value or do we sense a cost to her bilingual existence? Agree or disagree with the daughter's statement, but state the reasons for your opinion.

Franz Wright (1953-2015)

Alcohol 1989

You do look a little ill.

But we can do something about that, now.

Can't we.

The fact is you're a shocking wreck.

Do you hear me.

You aren't all alone.

And you could use some help today, packing in the dark, boarding
buses north, putting the seat back and grinning with terror flowing over your legs through your fingers and hair . . .

I was always waiting, always here.

Know anyone else who can say that?

My advice to you is think of her for what she is: one more name cut
in the scar of your tongue.

What was it you said, "To rather be harmed than harm is not abject."

Please.

Can we be leaving now.

We like bus trips, remember. Together
we could watch these winter fields slip past, and never care again,

think of it.

I don't have to be anywhere.

Questions

1. Who or what is the speaker in the poem? Who is being addressed?
2. Does the poem provide clues toward a backstory, a conflict, or a situation?
3. What is the effect of the unusual spacing and the often ungrammatical punctuation?

Weldon Kees (1914–1955)

For My Daughter 1940

Looking into my daughter's eyes I read
Beneath the innocence of morning flesh
Concealed, hintings of death she does not heed.
Coldest of winds have blown this hair, and mesh
Of seaweed snarled these miniatures of hands;
The night's slow poison, tolerant and bland,
Has moved her blood. Parched years that I have seen
That may be hers appear: foul, lingering
Death in certain war, the slim legs green.
Or, fed on hate, she relishes the sting
Of others' agony; perhaps the cruel
Bride of a syphilitic or a fool.
These speculations sour in the sun.
I have no daughter. I desire none.

Questions

1. How does the last line of this sonnet affect the meaning of the poem?
2. "For My Daughter" was first published in 1940. What considerations might a potential American parent have felt at that time? Are these historical concerns mirrored in the poem?
3. Donald Justice has said that "Kees is one of the bitterest poets in history." Is bitterness the only attitude the speaker reveals in this poem?

THE SPEAKER IN THE POEM

The tone of a poem, we said, is like tone of voice in that both communicate feelings. Still, this comparison raises a question: when we read a poem, whose "voice" speaks to us?

"The poet's" is one possible answer; and in the case of many a poem that answer may be right. In order to read a poem, we seldom need to read a poet's biography; but in truth there are certain poems whose full effect depends upon our knowing at least a fact or two of the poet's life. Here is one such poem.

Natasha Trethewey (b. 1966)

White Lies 2000

The lies I could tell,
when I was growing up
light-bright, near-white,
high-yellow, red-boned
in a black place,
were just white lies.

I could easily tell the white folks
that we lived uptown,
not in that pink and green
shanty-fied shotgun section
along the tracks. I could act
like my homemade dresses
came straight out the window
of Maison Blanche. I could even
keep quiet, quiet as kept,
like the time a white girl said
(squeezing my hand), *Now
we have three of us in this class*.

But I paid for it every time
Mama found out.
She laid her hands on me,
then washed out my mouth
with Ivory soap. *This*

is to purify, she said,
and cleanse your lying tongue.
Believing her, I swallowed suds
thinking they'd work
from the inside out.

Through its pattern of vivid color imagery, Trethewey's poem tells of a black child light enough to "pass for white" in a society that was still extremely race-sensitive. But knowing the author's family background gives us a deeper insight into the levels of meaning in the poem. Trethewey was born in Mississippi in 1966, at a time when her parents' interracial marriage was a criminal act in that state. On her birth certificate, her mother's race was given as "colored"; in the box intended to record the race of her father—who was white and had been born in Nova Scotia—appeared the word "Canadian" (although her parents divorced before she began grade school, she remained extremely close to both of them). Trethewey has said of her birth certificate: "Something is left out of the official record that way. The irony isn't lost on me. Even in documenting myself as a person there is a little fiction." "White Lies" succeeds admirably on its own, but these biographical details allow us to read it as an even more complex meditation on issues of racial definition and personal identity in America.

Persona

Most of us can tell the difference between a person we meet in life and a person we meet in a work of art. And yet, in reading poems, we are liable to temptation. When the poet says "I," we may want to assume that he or she is making a personal statement. But reflect: do all poems have to be personal? Here is a brief poem inscribed on the tombstone of an infant in Burial Hill Cemetery, Plymouth, Massachusetts:

Since I have been so quickly done for,
I wonder what I was begun for.

We do not know who wrote those lines, but it is clear that the poet was not a short-lived infant writing from personal experience. In some poems, the speaker is obviously a **persona**, or fictitious character: not the poet, but the poet's creation. As a grown man, William Blake, a skilled professional engraver, wrote a poem in the voice of a boy, an illiterate chimney sweeper. (The poem appears later in this chapter.)

Let's consider a poem spoken not by a poet, but by a persona—in this case a mysterious one. Edwin Arlington Robinson's "Luke Havergal" is a dramatic monologue, but the identity of the speaker is never clearly stated. In 1905, upon first reading the poem in Robinson's *The Children of the Night* (1897), President Theodore Roosevelt was so moved that he wrote an essay about the book that made the author famous. Roosevelt, however, admitted that he found the musically seductive poem difficult. "I am not sure I understand 'Luke Havergal,'" he wrote, "but I am entirely sure I like it." Possibly what most puzzled our twenty-sixth president was who was speaking in the poem. How much does Robinson let us know about the voice and the person it addresses?

Edwin Arlington Robinson (1869–1935)

Luke Havergal

1897

Go to the western gate, Luke Havergal,
There where the vines cling crimson on the wall,
And in the twilight wait for what will come.
The leaves will whisper there of her, and some,
Like flying words, will strike you as they fall;
But go, and if you listen she will call.
Go to the western gate, Luke Havergal—
Luke Havergal.

No, there is not a dawn in eastern skies
To rift the fiery night that's in your eyes;
But there, where western glooms are gathering,
The dark will end the dark, if anything:
God slays Himself with every leaf that flies,
And hell is more than half of paradise.
No, there is not a dawn in eastern skies—
In eastern skies.

Out of a grave I come to tell you this,
Out of a grave I come to quench the kiss
That flames upon your forehead with a glow
That blinds you to the way that you must go.
Yes, there is yet one way to where she is,
Bitter, but one that faith may never miss.
Out of a grave I come to tell you this—
To tell you this.

There is the western gate, Luke Havergal,
There are the crimson leaves upon the wall.
Go, for the winds are tearing them away,—
Nor think to riddle the dead words they say,
Nor any more to feel them as they fall;
But go, and if you trust her she will call.
There is the western gate, Luke Havergal—
Luke Havergal.

Questions

1. Who is the speaker of the poem? What specific details does the author reveal about the speaker?

2. What does the speaker ask Luke Havergal to do?
3. What do you understand "the western gate" to be?
4. Would you advise Luke Havergal to follow the speaker's advice? Why or why not?

No literary law decrees that the speaker in a poem even has to be human. Good poems have been uttered by clouds, pebbles, clocks, and animals. Here is a comic poem spoken by man's best friend, a dog.

Anonymous

Dog Haiku

2001

Today I sniffed
Many dog behinds—I celebrate
By kissing your face.

*

I sound the alarm!
Garbage man—come to kill us all—
Look! Look! Look! Look! Look!

*

How do I love thee?
The ways are numberless as
My hairs on the rug.

*

I sound the alarm!
Paper boy—come to kill us all—
Look! Look! Look! Look! Look!

*

I am your best friend,
Now, always, and especially
When you are eating.

Questions

1. Who is the "I" in the poem? Who is the "you"?
2. Do you recognize the allusion in lines 7–9?
3. What elements create the humorous effect of the poem?

The Art of Imagination

We need not deny that a poet's experience can contribute to a poem or that the emotion in the poem can indeed be the poet's. Still, to write a good poem one has to do more than live and feel. Writing poetry takes skill and imagination—qualities that extensive travel and wide experience do not necessarily give. Emily Dickinson seldom strayed from her family's house and grounds in Amherst, Massachusetts, yet her rimed life studies of a snake, a bee, and a hummingbird contain more poetry than we find in any firsthand description (so far) of the surface of the moon.

Langston Hughes (1902–1967)

Theme for English B

1951

The instructor said,
Go home and write
a page tonight.
And let that page come out of you—
Then, it will be true.

I wonder if it's that simple?
I am twenty-two, colored, born in Winston-Salem.
I went to school there, then Durham, then here
to this college on the hill above Harlem.
I am the only colored student in my class.
The steps from the hill lead down into Harlem,
through a park, then I cross St. Nicholas,
Eighth Avenue, Seventh, and I come to the Y,
the Harlem Branch Y, where I take the elevator
up to my room, sit down, and write this page:

It's not easy to know what is true for you or me
at twenty-two, my age. But I guess I'm what
I feel and see and hear, Harlem, I hear you:
hear you, hear me—we two—you, me, talk on this page.
(I hear New York, too.) Me—who?
Well, I like to eat, sleep, drink, and be in love.
I like to work, read, learn, and understand life.
I like a pipe for a Christmas present,
or records—Bessie, bop, or Bach.
I guess being colored doesn't make me *not* like
the same things other folks like who are other races.
So will my page be colored that I write?
Being me, it will not be white.
But it will be
a part of you, instructor.
You are white—
yet a part of me, as I am a part of you.
That's American.
Sometimes perhaps you don't want to be a part of me.
Nor do I often want to be a part of you.
But we are, that's true!
As I learn from you,
I guess you learn from me—
although you're older—and white—

and somewhat more free.
This is my page for English B.

THEME FOR ENGLISH B. 9 *college on the hill above Harlem:* Columbia University, where Hughes was briefly a student. (Note, however, that this poem is not autobiographical. The young speaker is a character invented by the middle-aged author.) 24 *Bessie:* Bessie Smith (1898?–1937) was a popular blues singer often called the "Empress of the Blues."

Karen An-hwei Lee (b. 1973)

Rainfall 2002

I wonder what is seen when it is raining. In the streets, the birds flying up—I hear them; and the children running; the leaves shivering, turning up lighter sides; rain skirting the curbs, rushing through open gutters, washed under, to the open sea; the long legs of a bird flying up, the tumult of rain closing, the sky's heart roving, and great cool light ensuing.

Questions

1. From the details she chooses, what do you suppose are the poet's feelings about rain?
2. How would you describe the tone of the poem?
3. What is the effect of the poem being set as one long line, rather than being split into short lines and stanzas? Does it alter the cadence with which you read it?

William Carlos Williams (1883–1963)

The Red Wheelbarrow 1923

so much depends
upon

a red wheel
barrow

glazed with rain
water

beside the white
chickens

Experiment: Reading With and Without Biography

1. Write a paragraph summing up your initial reactions to "The Red Wheelbarrow."
2. Now write a second paragraph with the benefit of this snippet of biographical information: Inspiration for this poem apparently came to Dr. Williams as he was gazing from the window of a house where one of his patients, a small girl, lay suspended between life and death.[1] How does this information affect your reading of the poem?

[1]This account, from the director of the public library in Williams's native Rutherford, New Jersey, is given by Geri M. Rhodes in "The Paterson Metaphor in William Carlos Williams's *Paterson*," master's thesis, Tufts University, 1965.

IRONY

To see a distinction between the poet and the words of a fictitious character—between Robert Browning and "My Last Duchess"—is to be aware of **irony**: a manner of speaking that implies a discrepancy. If the mask says one thing and we sense that the writer is in fact saying something else, the writer has adopted an **ironic point of view**. No finer illustration exists in English than Jonathan Swift's "A Modest Proposal," an essay in which Swift speaks as an earnest, humorless citizen who sets forth his reasonable plan to aid the Irish poor. The plan is so monstrous no sane reader can assent to it: the poor are to sell their children as meat for the tables of their landlords. From behind his false face, Swift is actually recommending not cannibalism but love and Christian charity.

A poem is often made complicated and more interesting by another kind of irony. **Verbal irony** occurs whenever words say one thing but mean something else, usually the opposite. The word *love* means *hate* here: "I just *love* to stay home and scroll through Instagram on a Saturday night!"

Sarcasm

When verbal irony is conspicuously bitter, heavy-handed, and mocking, it is defined as **sarcasm**: "Oh, he's the biggest spender in the world, all right!" (The sarcasm, if that statement were spoken, would be underscored by the speaker's tone of voice.) A famous instance of sarcasm occurs in Shakespeare's *Julius Caesar* in Mark Antony's oration over the body of the slain Caesar: "Brutus is an honorable man." Antony repeats this line until the enraged populace begins shouting exactly what he means to call Brutus and the other conspirators: traitors, villains, murderers. We had best be alert for irony on the printed page, for if we miss it, our interpretations of a poem may go wild.

Robert Creeley (1926–2005)

Oh No

1959

If you wander far enough
you will come to it
and when you get there
they will give you a place to sit
for yourself only, in a nice chair,
and all your friends will be there
with smiles on their faces
and they will likewise all have places.

This poem is rich in verbal irony. The title helps point out that between the speaker's words and attitude lie deep differences. In line 2, what is *it*? Old age?

The wandering suggests a conventional metaphor: the journey of life. Is *it* literally a rest home for "senior citizens," or perhaps some naïve popular concept of heaven (such as we meet in comic strips: harps, angels with hoops for halos) in which the saved all sit around in a ring, smugly congratulating one another? We can't be sure, but the speaker's attitude toward this final sitting-place is definite. It is a place for the selfish, as we infer from the phrase *for yourself only*. And *smiles on their faces* may hint that the smiles are unchanging and forced. There is a difference between saying "They had smiles on their faces" and "They smiled": the latter suggests that the smiles came from within. The word *nice* is to be regarded with distrust. If we see through this speaker, as Creeley implies we can, we realize that, while pretending to be sweet-talking us into a seat, actually he is revealing the horror of a little hell. And the title is the poet's reaction to it (or the speaker's unironic, straightforward one): "Oh no! Not *that*!"

Dramatic Irony

Dramatic irony, like verbal irony, contains an element of contrast, but it usually refers to a situation in a play wherein a character whose knowledge is limited says, does, or encounters something of greater significance than he or she knows. We, the spectators, realize the meaning of this speech or action, for the playwright has afforded us superior knowledge. In Sophocles's *Oedipus the King* (Chapter 26), when Oedipus vows to punish whoever has brought down a plague upon the city of Thebes, we know—as he does not—that the man he would punish is himself. The situation of Oedipus also contains **cosmic irony**, or **irony of fate**: some Fate with a grim sense of humor seems cruelly to trick a human being. Cosmic irony clearly exists in poems in which fate or the Fates are personified and seen as hostile.

To sum up: the effect of irony depends on the reader's noticing some incongruity or discrepancy between two things. In *verbal irony*, there is a contrast between the speaker's words and meaning; in an *ironic point of view*, between the writer's attitude and what is spoken by a fictitious character; in *dramatic irony*, between the limited knowledge of a character and the fuller knowledge of the reader or spectator; in *cosmic irony*, between a character's position or aspiration and the treatment he or she receives at the hands of Fate. Although, in the work of an inept poet, irony can be crude and obvious sarcasm, it is invaluable to a poet of more complicated mind, who imagines more than one perspective.

W. H. Auden (1907–1973)

The Unknown Citizen 1940

(To JS/07/M/378
This Marble Monument Is Erected by the State)

He was found by the Bureau of Statistics to be
One against whom there was no official complaint,

And all the reports on his conduct agree
That, in the modern sense of an old-fashioned word, he was a saint,
For in everything he did he served the Greater Community.
Except for the War till the day he retired
He worked in a factory and never got fired,
But satisfied his employers, Fudge Motors Inc.
Yet he wasn't a scab or odd in his views,
For his Union reports that he paid his dues,
(Our report on his Union shows it was sound)
And our Social Psychology workers found
That he was popular with his mates and liked a drink.
The Press are convinced that he bought a paper every day
And that his reactions to advertisements were normal in every way.
Policies taken out in his name prove that he was fully insured,
And his Health-card shows he was once in hospital but left it cured.
Both Producers Research and High-Grade Living declare
He was fully sensible to the advantages of the Installment Plan
And had everything necessary to the Modern Man,
A phonograph, a radio, a car and a frigidaire.
Our researchers into Public Opinion are content
That he held the proper opinions for the time of year;
When there was peace, he was for peace; when there was war, he went.
He was married and added five children to the population,
Which our Eugenist says was the right number for a parent of his generation,
And our teachers report that he never interfered with their education.
Was he free? Was he happy? The question is absurd:
Had anything been wrong, we should certainly have heard.

Questions

1. Read the two-line epitaph at the beginning of the poem as carefully as you read what follows. How does the epitaph help establish the voice by which the rest of the poem is spoken?
2. Who is speaking?
3. What ironic discrepancies do you find between the speaker's attitude toward the subject and that of the poet himself? By what is the poet's attitude made clear?
4. In the phrase "The Unknown Soldier" (of which "The Unknown Citizen" reminds us), what does the word *unknown* mean? What does it mean in the title of Auden's poem?
5. What tendencies in our civilization does Auden satirize?
6. How would you expect the speaker to define a Modern Man, if an iPod, a radio, a car, and a refrigerator are "everything" a Modern Man needs?

Sharon Olds (b. 1942)

Rite of Passage 1983

As the guests arrive at my son's party
they gather in the living room—
short men, men in first grade
with smooth jaws and chins.
Hands in pockets, they stand around
jostling, jockeying for place, small fights
breaking out and calming. One says to another
How old are you? Six. I'm seven. So?
They eye each other, seeing themselves
tiny in the other's pupils. They clear their
throats a lot, a room of small bankers,
they fold their arms and frown. *I could beat you*
up, a seven says to a six,
the dark cake, round and heavy as a
turret, behind them on the table. My son,
freckles like specks of nutmeg on his cheeks,
chest narrow as the balsa keel of a
model boat, long hands
cool and thin as the day they guided him
out of me, speaks up as a host
for the sake of the group.
We could easily kill a two-year-old,
he says in his clear voice. The other
men agree, they clear their throats
like Generals, they relax and get down to
playing war, celebrating my son's life.

Questions

1. What is ironic about the way the speaker describes the first-grade boys at her son's birthday party?
2. What other irony does the author underscore in the last two lines?
3. Does this mother sentimentalize her own son by seeing him as better than the other boys?

Edna St. Vincent Millay (1892–1950)

Second Fig 1920

Safe upon the solid rock the ugly houses stand:
Come and see my shining palace built upon the sand!

Question

Do you think the author is making fun of the speaker's attitude or agreeing with it?

Exercise: Detecting Irony

Point out the kinds of irony that occur in "The Workbox."

Thomas Hardy (1840–1928)

The Workbox

1914

"See, here's the workbox, little wife,
  That I made of polished oak."
He was a joiner,° of village life;
  She came of borough folk.

He holds the present up to her
  As with a smile she nears
And answers to the profferer,
  "'Twill last all my sewing years!"

"I warrant it will. And longer too.
  'Tis a scantling that I got
Off poor John Wayward's coffin, who
  Died of they knew not what.

"The shingled pattern that seems to cease
  Against your box's rim
Continues right on in the piece
  That's underground with him.

"And while I worked it made me think
  Of timber's varied doom:
One inch where people eat and drink,
  The next inch in a tomb.

"But why do you look so white, my dear,
  And turn aside your face?
You knew not that good lad, I fear,
  Though he came from your native place?"

"How could I know that good young man,
  Though he came from my native town,
When he must have left far earlier than
  I was a woman grown?"

"Ah, no. I should have understood!
  It shocked you that I gave
To you one end of a piece of wood
  Whose other is in a grave?"

° joiner: *carpenter*

"Don't, dear, despise my intellect,
  Mere accidental things
Of that sort never have effect
  On my imaginings."

Yet still her lips were limp and wan,
  Her face still held aside,
As if she had known not only John,
  But known of what he died.

FOR REVIEW AND FURTHER STUDY

William Blake (1757–1827)

The Chimney Sweeper 1789

When my mother died I was very young,
And my father sold me while yet my tongue
Could scarcely cry "'weep! 'weep! 'weep! 'weep!"
So your chimneys I sweep, and in soot I sleep.

There's little Tom Dacre, who cried when his head,
That curled like a lamb's back, was shaved: so I said
"Hush, Tom! never mind it, for when your head's bare
You know that the soot cannot spoil your white hair."

And so he was quiet, and that very night,
As Tom was a-sleeping, he had such a sight!
That thousands of sweepers, Dick, Joe, Ned, and Jack,
Were all of them locked up in coffins of black.

And by came an Angel who had a bright key,
And he opened the coffins and set them all free;
Then down a green plain leaping, laughing, they run,
And wash in a river, and shine in the sun.

Then naked and white, all their bags left behind,
They rise upon clouds and sport in the wind;
And the Angel told Tom, if he'd be a good boy,
He'd have God for his father, and never want° joy. *lack*

And so Tom awoke; and we rose in the dark,
And got with our bags and our brushes to work.
Though the morning was cold, Tom was happy and warm;
So if all do their duty they need not fear harm.

Questions

1. What does Blake's poem reveal about conditions of life in the London of his day?
2. What does this poem have in common with "The Golf Links"?
3. Sum up your impressions of the speaker's character. What does he say and do that displays it to us?
4. What pun do you find in line 3? Is its effect comic or serious?
5. In Tom Dacre's dream (lines 11–20), what wishes come true? Do you understand them to be the wishes of the chimney sweepers, of the poet, or of both?
6. In the last line, what is ironic in the speaker's assurance that the dutiful "need not fear harm"? What irony is there in his urging all to "do their duty"? (Who have failed in their duty to him?)
7. What is the tone of Blake's poem? Angry? Hopeful? Sorrowful? Compassionate? (Don't feel obliged to sum it up in a single word.)

Exercise: Telling Tone

Here are two radically different poems on a similar subject. Try stating the theme of each poem in your own words. How is the tone (the speaker's attitude) different in the two poems?

Richard Lovelace (1618–1658)

To Lucasta

1649

On Going to the Wars

Tell me not, Sweet, I am unkind
  That from the nunnery
Of thy chaste breast and quiet mind,
  To war and arms I fly.

True, a new mistress now I chase,
  The first foe in the field;
And with a stronger faith embrace
  A sword, a horse, a shield.

Yet this inconstancy is such
  As you too shall adore;
I could not love thee, Dear, so much,
  Loved I not Honor more.

Wilfred Owen (1893–1918)

Dulce et Decorum Est

1920

Bent double, like old beggars under sacks,
Knock-kneed, coughing like hags, we cursed through sludge,
Till on the haunting flares we turned our backs

And towards our distant rest began to trudge.
Men marched asleep. Many had lost their boots
But limped on, blood-shod. All went lame; all blind;
Drunk with fatigue; deaf even to the hoots
Of tired, outstripped Five-Nines that dropped behind.

Gas! GAS! Quick, boys!—An ecstasy of fumbling,
Fitting the clumsy helmets just in time;
But someone still was yelling out and stumbling,
And flound'ring like a man in fire or lime . . .
Dim, through the misty panes and thick green light,
As under a green sea, I saw him drowning.

In all my dreams, before my helpless sight,
He plunges at me, guttering, choking, drowning.
If in some smothering dreams you too could pace
Behind the wagon that we flung him in,
And watch the white eyes writhing in his face,
His hanging face, like a devil's sick of sin;
If you could hear, at every jolt, the blood
Come gargling from the froth-corrupted lungs,
Obscene as cancer, bitter as the cud
Of vile, incurable sores on innocent tongues,—
My friend, you would not tell with such high zest
To children ardent for some desperate glory,
The old Lie: Dulce et decorum est
Pro patria mori.

DULCE ET DECORUM EST. Owen's title is the beginning of the famous Latin quotation from the Roman poet Horace with which he ends this poem: "*Dulce et decorum est pro patria mori.*" It is translated as "It is sweet and proper to die for your country." 8 *Five-Nines:* German howitzers often used to shoot poison gas shells. 17 *you too:* Some manuscript versions of this poem carry the dedication "To Jessie Pope" (a writer of patriotic verse) or "To a certain Poetess."

WRITING *effectively*

THINKING ABOUT TONE

To understand the tone of a poem, we need to listen to the words, as we might listen to an actual conversation. The key is to hear not only *what* is being said but also *how* it is being said. Does the speaker sound noticeably surprised, angry, nostalgic, or tender? Begin with an obvious but often overlooked question: who is speaking? Don't assume that every poem is spoken by its author.

- **Look for the ways—large and small—in which the speaker reveals aspects of his or her character.** Attitudes may be revealed directly or indirectly. Often, emotions must be intuited. The details a poet chooses to convey can reveal much about a speaker's stance toward his or her subject matter.
- **Consider also how the speaker addresses the listener.** Again, listen to the sound of the poem as you would listen to the sound of someone's voice—is it shrill, or soothing, or sarcastic?
- **Look for an obvious difference between the speaker's attitude and your own honest reaction toward what is happening in the poem.** If the gap between the two responses is wide, the poem may be taken as ironic.
- **Remember that many poets strive toward understatement, writing matter-of-factly about occasions of intense sorrow, horror, or joy.** In poems, as in conversation, understatement can be a powerful tool, more convincing—and often more moving—than hyperbole.

CHECKLIST: Writing About Tone

- ☐ Who is speaking the poem?
- ☐ Is the narrator's voice close to the poet's, or is it the voice of a fictional or historical person?
- ☐ How does the speaker address the listener?
- ☐ Does the poem directly reveal an emotion or attitude?
- ☐ Does it indirectly reveal any attitudes or emotions?
- ☐ Does your reaction to what is happening in the poem differ widely from that of the speaker? If so, what does that difference suggest? Is the poem in some way ironic?
- ☐ What adjectives would best describe the poem's tone?

TOPICS FOR WRITING ON TONE

1. Describe the tone of W. H. Auden's "The Unknown Citizen," quoting as necessary to back up your argument. How does the poem's tone contribute to its meaning?
2. Write an analysis of Thomas Hardy's "The Workbox," focusing on what the poem leaves unsaid.
3. In an essay of 250 to 500 words, compare and contrast the tone of two poems on a similar subject. You might examine how Walt Whitman and Emily Dickinson treat the subject of locomotives, or how Richard Lovelace and Wilfred Owen write about war. (For advice on writing about poetry by the method of comparison and contrast, see the chapter "Writing About Literature.")

4. Look closely at any poem in this chapter. Going through it line by line, make a list of the sensory details the poem provides. Now write briefly about how those details combine to create a particular tone. Two choices are Theodore Roethke's "My Papa's Waltz" and Sharon Olds's "Rite of Passage."

▶ TERMS FOR *review*

Tone ▶ The mood or manner of expression of a literary work, which conveys an attitude toward the work's subject, which may be playful, sarcastic, ironic, sad, solemn, or any other possible attitude. Tone helps to establish the reader's relationship to the characters or ideas presented in the work.

Satiric poetry ▶ Poetry that blends criticism with humor to convey a message, usually through the use of irony and a tone of detached amusement, withering contempt, and implied superiority.

Persona ▶ Latin for "mask." A fictitious character created by an author to be the speaker of a literary work.

Types of Irony

Irony ▶ In language, a discrepancy between what is said and what is meant. In life, a discrepancy between what is expected and what occurs.

Verbal irony ▶ A mode of expression in which the speaker or writer says the opposite of what is really meant, such as saying "Great story!" in response to a boring, pointless anecdote.

Sarcasm ▶ A style of bitter irony intended to hurt or mock its target.

Dramatic irony ▶ A situation in which the larger implications of a character's words, actions, or situation are unrealized by that character but seen by the author and the reader or audience.

Cosmic irony ▶ The contrast between a character's position or aspiration and the treatment he or she receives at the hands of a seemingly hostile fate; also called **irony of fate**.

12 WORDS

What You Will Learn in This Chapter

- To define *diction*
- To recognize and define the standard *levels of diction*
- To recognize and explain allusions in a poem
- To analyze the role of diction in a poem

LITERAL MEANING: WHAT A POEM SAYS FIRST

Although successful as a painter, Edgar Degas found poetry discouragingly hard to write. To his friend, the poet Stéphane Mallarmé, he complained, "What a business! My whole day gone on a blasted sonnet, without getting an inch further . . . and it isn't ideas I'm short of . . . I'm full of them, I've got too many. . . ."

"But Degas," said Mallarmé, "you can't make a poem with ideas—you make it with *words*!"

Like the celebrated painter, some people assume that all it takes to make a poem is a bright idea. Poems state ideas, to be sure, and sometimes the ideas are invaluable; and yet the most impressive idea in the world will not make a poem, unless its words are selected and arranged with loving art. Some poets take great pains to find the right word. Unable to fill a two-syllable gap in an unfinished line that went, "The seal's wide _____ gaze toward Paradise," Hart Crane paged through an unabridged dictionary. When he reached S, he found the object of his quest in *spindrift*: "spray skimmed from the sea by a strong wind." The word is exact and memorable.

In reading a poem, some people assume that its words can be skipped over rapidly, and they try to leap at once to the poem's general theme. It is as if they fear being thought clods unless they can find huge ideas in the poem (whether or not there are any). Such readers often ignore the literal meanings of words: the ordinary, matter-of-fact sense to be found in a dictionary. (As you will see in the next chapter, "Saying and Suggesting," words possess not only dictionary meanings—denotations—but also many associations and suggestions—connotations.) Consider the following poem and see what you make of it.

William Carlos Williams (1883–1963)

This Is Just to Say 1934

I have eaten
the plums
that were in
the icebox

and which
you were probably
saving
for breakfast

Forgive me
they were delicious
so sweet
and so cold

Some readers distrust a poem so simple and candid. They think, "What's wrong with me? There has to be more to it than this!" But poems seldom are puzzles in need of solutions. We can begin by accepting the poet's statements, without suspecting the poet of trying to hoodwink us. On later reflection, of course, we might possibly decide that the poet is playfully teasing or being ironic; but Williams gives us no reason to think that. There seems no need to look beyond the literal sense of his words, no profit in speculating that the plums symbolize worldly joys and that the icebox stands for the universe. Clearly, a reader who held such a grand theory would have overlooked (in eagerness to find a significant idea) the plain truth that the poet makes clear to us: that ice-cold plums are a joy to taste.

To be sure, Williams's small poem is simpler than most poems are; and yet in reading any poem, no matter how complicated, you will do well to reach slowly and reluctantly for a theory to explain it by. To find the general theme of a poem, you first need to pay attention to its words. Recall Yeats's "The Lake Isle of Innisfree" (Chapter 10), a poem that makes a statement—crudely summed up, "I yearn to leave the city and retreat to a place of ideal peace and happiness." And yet before we can realize this theme, we have to notice details: nine bean rows, a glade loud with bees, "lake water lapping with low sounds by the shore," the gray of a pavement. These details and not some abstract remark make clear what the poem is saying: that the city is drab, while the island hideaway is sublimely beautiful.

DICTION

If a poem says *daffodils* instead of *plant life* or *diaper years* instead of *infancy*, we call its **diction**, or choice of words, **concrete** rather than **abstract**. Concrete words refer to what we can immediately perceive with our senses: *dog*, *actor*, *chemical*, or particular individuals who belong to those general classes: *Bonzo the fox terrier*, *Ryan Gosling*, *hydrogen sulfate*. Abstract words express ideas or concepts: *love*, *time*, *truth*. In abstracting, we leave out some characteristics found in each individual, and instead observe a quality common to many. The word *beauty*, for instance, denotes what may be observed in numerous persons, places, and things.

Ezra Pound gave a famous piece of advice to his fellow poets: "Go in fear of abstractions." This is not to say that a poet cannot employ abstract words, nor that all poems have to be about physical things. Much of T. S. Eliot's *Four Quartets* is concerned with time, eternity, history, language, reality, and other things that cannot be physically handled. But Eliot, however high he may soar for a larger view, keeps returning to earth. He makes us aware of *things*.

Here is a famous poem that groups together some very specific things: certain ships and their cargoes.

John Masefield (1878–1967)

Cargoes 1902

Quinquireme of Nineveh from distant Ophir,
Rowing home to haven in sunny Palestine,
With a cargo of ivory,
And apes and peacocks,
Sandalwood, cedarwood, and sweet white wine.

Stately Spanish galleon coming from the Isthmus,
Dipping through the Tropics by the palm-green shores,
With a cargo of diamonds,
Emeralds, amethysts,
Topazes, and cinnamon, and gold moidores.

Dirty British coaster with a salt-caked smoke stack,
Butting through the Channel in the mad March days,
With a cargo of Tyne coal,
Road-rails, pig-lead,
Firewood, iron-ware, and cheap tin trays.

CARGOES. 1 *Quinquireme:* ancient Assyrian vessel propelled by sails and oars. *Ninevah:* capital of ancient Assyrian empire. *Ophir:* a vanished place, possibly in Arabia; according to the Bible, King Solomon sent expeditions there for its celebrated pure gold, and also for ivory, apes, peacocks, and other luxury items. (See I Kings 9–10.) 10 *Moidores:* Portuguese coins. 13 *Tyne:* a river in Scotland.

Questions

1. Does this poem use elevated language or everyday words?
2. Pick out some examples of unusual words in this poem.

John Donne (1572–1631)

Batter my heart, three-personed God, for You (about 1610)

Batter my heart, three-personed God, for You
As yet but knock, breathe, shine, and seek to mend.
That I may rise and stand, o'erthrow me, and bend
Your force to break, blow, burn, and make me new.
I, like an usurped town to another due,
Labor to admit You, but Oh! to no end.
Reason, Your viceroy in me, me should defend,
But is captived, and proves weak or untrue.
Yet dearly I love You, and would be lovèd fain,
But am betrothed unto Your enemy;
Divorce me, untie or break that knot again;
Take me to You, imprison me, for I,
Except You enthrall me, never shall be free,
Nor ever chaste, except You ravish me.

Questions

1. In the last line of this sonnet, to what does Donne compare the onslaught of God's love? Do you think the poem is weakened by the poet's comparing a spiritual experience to something so grossly carnal? Discuss.
2. Explain the seeming contradiction in the last line: in what sense can a ravished person be "chaste"? Explain the seeming contradictions in lines 3–4 and 12–13: how can a person thrown down and destroyed be enabled to "rise and stand"; an imprisoned person be "free"?
3. In lines 5–6 the speaker compares himself to a "usurped town" trying to throw off its conqueror by admitting an army of liberation. Who is the "usurper" in this comparison?
4. Explain the comparison of "Reason" to a "viceroy" (lines 7–8).
5. Sum up in your own words the message of Donne's poem. In stating its theme, did you have to read the poem for literal meanings, figurative comparisons, or both?

THE VALUE OF A DICTIONARY

Use the dictionary. It's better than the critics.

—ELIZABETH BISHOP TO HER STUDENTS

If a poet troubles to seek out the best words available, the least we can do is to find out what the words mean. The dictionary is a firm ally in reading poems; if the poems are more than a century old, it is indispensable. Meanings change. When the Elizabethan poet George Gascoigne wrote, "O Abraham's brats, O brood of blessed seed," the word *brats* implied neither irritation nor contempt. When in the seventeenth century Andrew Marvell imagined two lovers' "vegetable love," he referred to a vegetative or growing love, not one resembling a lettuce. And when Queen Anne, in a famous anecdote, called the just-completed Saint Paul's

Cathedral "awful, artificial, and amusing," its architect, Sir Christopher Wren, was overwhelmed with joy and gratitude, for what she had told him was that it was awe-inspiring, artful, and stimulating to contemplate (or *muse* upon).

In reading poetry, there is nothing to be done about the inevitable tendency of language to change except to watch out for it. If you suspect that a word has shifted in meaning over the years, most standard desk dictionaries will be helpful, an unabridged dictionary more helpful still, and most helpful of all the *Oxford English Dictionary (OED)*, which gives, for each definition, successive examples of the word's written use through the past thousand years. You need not feel a grim obligation to keep interrupting a poem in order to rummage in the dictionary; but if the poem is worth reading very closely, you may wish for any aid you can find.

"Every word which is used to express a moral or intellectual fact," said Emerson in his study *Nature*, "if traced to its root, is found to be borrowed from some material appearance. *Right* means straight; *wrong* means twisted. *Spirit* primarily means wind; *transgression*, the crossing of a line; *supercilious*, the raising of an eyebrow." Browse in a dictionary and you will discover such original concretenesses. These are revealed in your dictionary's etymologies, or brief notes on the derivation of words, given in most dictionaries near the beginning of an entry on a word; in some dictionaries, at the end of the entry. Look up *squirrel*, for instance, and you will find it comes from two Greek words meaning "shadow-tail." For another example of a common word that originally contained a poetic metaphor, look up the origin of *daisy*.

Experiment: Use the Dictionary to Read Longfellow's "Aftermath"

The following short poem seems very simple and straightforward, but much of its total effect depends on the reader knowing the literal meanings of several words. The most crucial word is in the title—"aftermath." Most readers today will assume that they know what that word means, but in this poem Longfellow uses it in both its current sense and its original, more literal meaning. Read the poem twice—first without a dictionary, then a second time after looking up the meanings of "aftermath," "fledged," "rowen," and "mead." How does knowing the exact meanings of these words add to both your literal and critical reading of the poem?

Henry Wadsworth Longfellow (1807–1882)

Aftermath

1873

When the summer fields are mown,
When the birds are fledged and flown,
  And the dry leaves strew the path;
With the falling of the snow,
With the cawing of the crow,
Once again the fields we mow
  And gather in the aftermath.

Not the sweet, new grass with flowers
In this harvesting of ours;
  Not the upland clover bloom;
But the rowen mixed with weeds,
Tangled tufts from marsh and meads,
Where the poppy drops its seeds
  In the silence and the gloom.

Questions

1. How do the etymology and meaning of "aftermath" help explain this poem? (Look the word up in your dictionary.)
2. What is the meaning of "fledged" (line 2) and "rowen" (line 11)?
3. Once you understand the literal meaning of the poem, do you think that Longfellow intended any further significance to it?

Allusion

An **allusion** is an indirect reference to any person, place, or thing—fictitious, historical, or actual. Sometimes, to understand an allusion in a poem, we have to find out something we didn't know before. But usually the poet asks of us only common knowledge. When, in his poem "To Helen," Edgar Allan Poe refers to "the glory that was Greece / And the grandeur that was Rome," he assumes that we have heard of those places. He also expects that we will understand his allusion to the cultural achievements of those ancient nations and perhaps even catch the subtle contrast between those two similar words *glory* and *grandeur*, with its suggestion that, for all its merits, Roman civilization was also more pompous than Greek.

Allusions not only enrich the meaning of a poem, they also save space. In "The Love Song of J. Alfred Prufrock" (Chapter 23), T. S. Eliot, by giving a brief introductory quotation from the speech of a damned soul in Dante's *Inferno*, is able to suggest that his poem will be the confession of a soul in torment, who sees no chance of escape and who feels the need to confide in someone, yet trusts that his secrets will be kept safe.

Often in reading a poem, you will meet a name you don't recognize, on which the meaning of a line (or perhaps a whole poem) seems to depend. In this book, most such unfamiliar references and allusions are glossed or footnoted, but when you venture out on your own in reading poems, you may find yourself needlessly perplexed unless you look up such names, the way you look up any other words. Unless the name is one that the poet made up, you will probably find it in one of the larger desk dictionaries, such as *Merriam-Webster's Collegiate Dictionary* or the *American Heritage Dictionary*. If you don't solve your problem there, try an online search of the word or phrase, as some allusions are quotations from other poems.

Exercise: Catching Allusions

From your knowledge, supplemented by a dictionary or other reference work if need be, explain the allusions in the following poems.

J. V. Cunningham (1911–1985)

Friend, on this scaffold Thomas More lies dead — 1960

Friend, on this scaffold Thomas More lies dead
Who would not cut the Body from the Head.

Samuel Menashe (1925–2011)

Bread — 1985

Thy will be done
By crust and crumb
And loaves left over
The sea is swollen
With the bread I throw
Upon the water

Questions

1. Can you identify the two allusions Menashe uses in this poem? (Hint: The first allusion occurs in line 1; the second in lines 5–6).
2. Paraphrase the content of the poem in a few sentences.
3. How do you think these references add meaning to this very short poem?

Carl Sandburg (1878–1967)

Grass — 1918

Pile the bodies high at Austerlitz and Waterloo.
Shovel them under and let me work—
  I am the grass; I cover all.

And pile them high at Gettysburg
And pile them high at Ypres and Verdun.
Shovel them under and let me work.
Two years, ten years, and passengers ask the conductor:
  What place is this?
  Where are we now?

  I am the grass.
  Let me work.

Questions

1. What do the five proper nouns in Sandburg's poem have in common?
2. How much does the reader need to understand about the allusions in "Grass" to appreciate their importance to the literal meaning of the poem?

WORD CHOICE AND WORD ORDER

Even if Samuel Johnson's famous *Dictionary* of 1755 had been as thick as Webster's unabridged, an eighteenth-century poet searching through it for words would have had a narrower choice. For in English literature of the neoclassical period, many poets subscribed to a belief in **poetic diction**: "A system of words," said Dr. Johnson, "refined from the grossness of domestic use." The system admitted into a serious poem only certain words and subjects, excluding others as violations of **decorum** (propriety). Accordingly, such common words as *rat*, *cheese*, *big*, *sneeze*, and *elbow*, although admissible to satire, were thought inconsistent with the loftiness of tragedy, epic, ode, and elegy. Dr. Johnson's biographer, James Boswell, tells how a poet writing an epic reconsidered the word "rats" and instead wrote "the whiskered vermin race." Johnson himself objected to Lady Macbeth's allusion to her "keen knife," saying that "we do not immediately conceive that any crime of importance is to be committed with a knife; or who does not, at last, from the long habit of connecting a knife with sordid offices, feel aversion rather than terror?"

Anglo-Saxon Versus Latinate Diction

When Wordsworth, in his Preface to *Lyrical Ballads*, asserted that "the language really spoken by men," especially by humble rustics, is plainer and more emphatic, and conveys "elementary feelings . . . in a state of greater simplicity," he was, in effect, advocating a new poetic diction. Wordsworth's ideas invited freshness into English poetry and, by admitting words that neoclassical poets would have called "low" ("His poor old *ankles* swell"), helped rid poets of the fear of being thought foolish for mentioning a commonplace.

This theory of the superiority of rural diction was, as Coleridge pointed out, hard to adhere to, and, in practice, Wordsworth was occasionally to write a language as Latinate and citified as these lines on yew trees:

> Huge trunks!—and each particular trunk a growth
> Of intertwisted fibers serpentine
> Up-coiling, and inveterately convolved . . .

Language so Latinate sounds pedantic to us, especially the phrase *inveterately convolved*. In fact, some poets, notably Gerard Manley Hopkins, have subscribed to the view that English words derived from Anglo-Saxon (Old English) have more force and flavor than their Latin equivalents. *Kingly*, one may feel, has more power than *regal*. One argument for this view is that so many words of Old English origin—*man*, *wife*, *child*, *house*, *eat*, *drink*, *sleep*—are basic to our living speech. Yet Latinate diction is not necessarily elevated. We use Latinate words every day, such as *station*, *office*, *order*, and *human*. None of these terms seem "inveterately convolved." Word choice is a subtle and flexible art.

Levels of Diction

When E. E. Cummings begins a poem, "mr youse needn't be so spry/concernin questions arty," we recognize another kind of diction available to poetry: **low diction** (or **vulgate**, speech not much affected by schooling). Handbooks of grammar sometimes distinguish various **levels of diction**. A sort of ladder is imagined, on whose rungs words, phrases, and sentences may be ranked in an ascending order of formality, from the curses of an illiterate thug to the commencement-day address of a doctor of divinity. These levels range from vulgate through **colloquial** (the casual conversation or informal writing of literate people) and **middle diction** (or **general English**, most literate speech and writing, more studied than colloquial but not pretentious), up to **high diction** (or **formal English**, the impersonal language of educated persons, usually only written, possibly spoken on dignified occasions). Recently, however, lexicographers have been shunning such labels. The designation *colloquial* was expelled from *Webster's Third New International Dictionary* on the grounds that "it is impossible to know whether a word out of context is colloquial or not" and that the diction of Americans nowadays is more fluid than the labels suggest. Aware that we are being unscientific, you may find the labels useful. They may help roughly to describe what happens when, as in the following poem, a poet shifts from one level of usage to another.

Robert Herrick (1591–1674)

Upon Julia's Clothes 1648

Whenas in silks my Julia goes,
Then, then, methinks, how sweetly flows
That liquefaction of her clothes.

Next, when I cast mine eyes and see
That brave vibration each way free,
O how that glittering taketh me!

UPON JULIA'S CLOTHES. 3 *liquefaction:* becoming fluid, turning to liquid. 5 *brave:* Herrick uses *brave* in its original sense, meaning excellent or fine.

Even in so short a poem as "Upon Julia's Clothes," we see how a sudden shift in the level of diction can produce a surprising and memorable effect. One word in each stanza—*liquefaction* in the first, *vibration* in the second—stands out from the standard, but not extravagant, language that surrounds it. Try to imagine the entire poem being written in such formal English, in mostly unfamiliar words of several syllables each: the result, in all likelihood, would be merely an oddity, and a turgid one at that. But by using such terms sparingly, Herrick allows them to take on a greater strength and significance through their contrast with the words that surround them. It is *liquefaction* in particular that strikes the reader: like a great catch by an outfielder, it impresses both for its appropriateness in the situation and for its sheer beauty as a demonstration of superior skill. Once we have read the poem, we realize that the effect would be severely compromised, if not ruined, by the substitution of any other word in its place.

Dialect

At present, most poetry in English avoids elaborate literary expressions such as "fleecy care" in favor of more colloquial language. In many English-speaking areas, such as Scotland, there has even been a movement to write poems in regional dialects. (A **dialect** is a particular variety of language spoken by an identifiable regional group or social class of persons.) Dialect poets frequently try to capture the freshness and authenticity of the language spoken in their immediate locale.

Kay Ryan (b. 1945)

Blandeur 2000

If it please God,
let less happen.
Even out Earth's
rondure, flatten
Eiger, blanden
the Grand Canyon.
Make valleys
slightly higher,
widen fissures
to arable land,
remand your
terrible glaciers
and silence
their calving,
halving or doubling
all geographical features
toward the mean.
Unlean against our hearts.
Withdraw your grandeur
from these parts.

BLANDEUR. 4 *rondure:* an elegant curvature. 5 *Eiger:* a mountain in the Alps. 11 *remand:* send back; often a legal term meaning to send back to a lower court. 14 *calving:* when a small glacier splits from a larger one; often an agricultural term for when a cow births a calf.

Questions

1. The title of Ryan's poem is a word that she invented. What do you think it means? Explain the reasoning behind your theory.
2. Where else does Ryan use a different form of this new word?
3. What other unusual but real words does the author use?

Thomas Hardy (1840–1928)

The Ruined Maid

1901

"O 'Melia, my dear, this does everything crown!
Who could have supposed I should meet you in Town?
And whence such fair garments, such prosperi-ty?"—
"O didn't you know I'd been ruined?" said she.

—"You left us in tatters, without shoes or socks,
Tired of digging potatoes, and spudding up docks;° *spading up dockweed*
And now you've gay bracelets and bright feathers three!"
"Yes: that's how we dress when we're ruined," said she.

—"At home in the barton° you said 'thee' and 'thou,' *farmyard*
And 'thik oon,' and 'theäs oon,' and 't'other'; but now
Your talking quite fits 'ee for high compa-ny!"—
"Some polish is gained with one's ruin," said she.

—"Your hands were like paws then, your face blue and bleak
But now I'm bewitched by your delicate cheek,
And your little gloves fit as on any la-dy!"—
"We never do work when we're ruined," said she.

—"You used to call home-life a hag-ridden dream,
And you'd sigh, and you'd sock;° but at present you seem *groan*
To know not of megrims° or melancho-ly!"— *blues*
"True. One's pretty lively when ruined," said she.

—"I wish I had feathers, a fine sweeping gown,
And a delicate face, and could strut about Town!"—
"My dear—a raw country girl, such as you be,
Cannot quite expect that. You ain't ruined," said she.

Questions

1. Where does this dialogue take place? Who are the two speakers?
2. Comment on Hardy's use of the word *ruined*. What is the conventional meaning of the word when applied to a woman? As 'Melia applies it to herself, what is its meaning?
3. Sum up the attitude of each speaker toward the other. What details of the new 'Melia does the first speaker most dwell on? Would you expect Hardy to be so impressed by all these details, or is there, between his view of the characters and their view of themselves, any hint of an ironic discrepancy?

4. In losing her country dialect ("thik oon" and "theäs oon" for "this one" and "that one"), 'Melia is presumed to have gained in sophistication. What does Hardy suggest by her "ain't" in the last line?

Julie Larios (b. 1949)

What Bee Did 2006

Bee not only buzzed.
When swatted at, Bee deviled,
Bee smirched. And when fuddled,
like many of us, Bee labored, Bee reaved.
He behaved as well as any Bee can have.

Bee never lied. Bee never lated.
And despite the fact Bee took, Bee also stowed.
In love, Bee seiged. Bee seeched.
Bee moaned, Bee sighed himself,
Bee gat with his Beloved.

And because Bee tokened summer
(the one season we all, like Bee, must lieve)
Bee also dazzled.

Questions

1. Can you identify the play on words or running joke in this poem? It may help to read the poem aloud.
2. Even when some of the words aren't used in their common or correct forms, does the poem instill them with new meaning and surprising humor? Point out some examples.

FOR REVIEW AND FURTHER STUDY

E. E. Cummings (1894–1962)

anyone lived in a pretty how town 1940

anyone lived in a pretty how town
(with up so floating many bells down)
spring summer autumn winter
he sang his didn't he danced his did.

Women and men(both little and small)
cared for anyone not at all
they sowed their isn't they reaped their same
sun moon stars rain

children guessed(but only a few
and down they forgot as up they grew

autumn winter spring summer)
that noone loved him more by more

when by now and tree by leaf
she laughed his joy she cried his grief
bird by snow and stir by still
anyone's any was all to her

someones married their everyones
laughed their cryings and did their dance
(sleep wake hope and then)they
said their nevers they slept their dream

stars rain sun moon
(and only the snow can begin to explain
how children are apt to forget to remember
with up so floating many bells down)

one day anyone died i guess
(and noone stooped to kiss his face)
busy folk buried them side by side
little by little and was by was

all by all and deep by deep
and more by more they dream their sleep
noone and anyone earth by april
wish by spirit and if by yes.

Women and men(both dong and ding)
summer autumn winter spring
reaped their sowing and went their came
sun moon stars rain

Questions

1. Summarize the story told in this poem. Who are the characters?
2. Rearrange the words in the two opening lines into the order you would expect them usually to follow. What effect does Cummings obtain by his unconventional word order?
3. Another of Cummings's strategies is to use one part of speech as if it were another; for instance, in line 4, *didn't* and *did* ordinarily are verbs, but here they are used as nouns. What other words in the poem perform functions other than their expected ones?

Sarah Cortez (b. 1950)

Adam 2016

What song is being sung
by your bones? The pink
ache of sunrise? The small

Adam Ayala by Dan Streck.

birds' hollow worries? Sighs
that cannot affix themselves
to your wealth of ruffled flowers?

Both my feet prickle
with the humming
from your tibia and pelvis,
collarbone, and metatarsals
strung like dominoes
who love a careful distance
but find their meaning
only in collapse
and closeness, followed
by stacking in a lidded box.

ADAM. This is an example of an **ekphrastic poem**—a poem created in response to a visual image such as a painting or photograph.

Questions

1. "Adam" was included in an anthology of poems inspired by roadside crosses in Texas. Does that change your understanding of the poem?
2. Why does the poem meditate on bones?
3. What is the "lidded box" in the final line?
4. What elements in Dan Streck's photograph do you see reflected in the poem?

Exercise: Different Kinds of English

Read the following poems and see what kinds of diction and word order you find in them. Which poems are least formal in their language and which most formal? Is there any use of low diction? Any dialect? What does each poem achieve that its own kind of English makes possible?

Anonymous (American oral verse)

Carnation Milk (about 1900?)

Carnation Milk is the best in the land;
Here I sit with a can in my hand—
No tits to pull, no hay to pitch,
You just punch a hole in the son of a bitch.

CARNATION MILK. "This quatrain is imagined as the caption under a picture of a rugged-looking cowboy seated upon a bale of hay," notes William Harmon in his *Oxford Book of American Light Verse* (New York: Oxford UP, 1979). Possibly the first to print this work was David Ogilvy (1911–1999), who quotes it in his *Confessions of an Advertising Man* (New York: Atheneum, 1963).

Gina Valdés (b. 1943)

English con Salsa 1993

Welcome to ESL 100, English Surely Latinized,
inglés con chile y cilantro, English as American
as Benito Juárez. Welcome, muchachos from Xochicalco,
learn the language of dólares and dolores, of kings
and queens, of Donald Duck and Batman. Holy Toluca!
In four months you'll be speaking like George Washington,
in four weeks you can ask, More coffee? In two months
you can say, May I take your order? In one year you
can ask for a raise, cool as the Tuxpan River.

Welcome, muchachas from Teocaltiche, in this class
we speak English refrito, English con sal y limón,
English thick as mango juice, English poured from
a clay jug, English tuned like a requinto from Uruapan,
English lighted by Oaxacan dawns, English spiked
with mezcal from Mitla, English with a red cactus
flower blooming in its heart.

Welcome, welcome, amigos del sur, bring your Zapotec
tongues, your Nahuatl tones, your patience of pyramids,
your red suns and golden moons, your guardian angels,
your duendes, your patron saints, Santa Tristeza,
Santa Alegría, Santo Todolopuede. We will sprinkle
holy water on pronouns, make the sign of the cross
on past participles, jump like fish from Lake Pátzcuaro

say shoes and shit, grab a cool verb and a pollo loco
and dance on the walls like chapulines.

When a teacher from La Jolla or a cowboy from Santee
asks you, Do you speak English? You'll answer, Sí,
yes, simón, of course, I love English!
And you'll hum
A Mixtec chant that touches la tierra and the heavens.

ENGLISH CON SALSA. 3 *Benito Juárez:* Mexican statesman (1806–1872), president of Mexico in the 1860s and 1870s.

William Wordsworth (1770–1850)

My heart leaps up when I behold

1807

My heart leaps up when I behold
A rainbow in the sky:
So was it when my life began;
So is it now I am a man;
So be it when I shall grow old,
Or let me die!
The Child is father of the Man;
And I could wish my days to be
Bound each to each by natural piety.

William Wordsworth (1770–1850)

Mutability

1822

From low to high doth dissolution climb,
And sink from high to low, along a scale
Of awful notes, whose concord shall not fail;
A musical but melancholy chime,
Which they can hear who meddle not with crime,
Nor avarice, nor over-anxious care.
Truth fails not; but her outward forms that bear
The longest date do melt like frosty rime,° *frozen dew*
That in the morning whitened hill and plain
And is no more; drop like the tower sublime
Of yesterday, which royally did wear
His crown of weeds, but could not even sustain
Some casual shout that broke the silent air,
Or the unimaginable touch of Time.

Lewis Carroll
[*Charles Lutwidge Dodgson*] (1832–1898)

Jabberwocky 1871

The Jabberwock, as illustrated by John Tenniel, 1872.

’Twas brillig, and the slithy toves
Did gyre and gimble in the wabe:
All mimsy were the borogoves,
And the mome raths outgrabe.

“Beware the Jabberwock, my son!
The jaws that bite, the claws that catch!
Beware the Jubjub bird, and shun
The frumious Bandersnatch!”

He took his vorpal sword in hand:
Long time the manxome foe he sought—
So rested he by the Tumtum tree
And stood awhile in thought.

And, as in uffish thought he stood,
The Jabberwock, with eyes of flame,
Came whiffling through the tulgey wood,
And burbled as it came!

One, two! One, two! And through and through
The vorpal blade went snicker-snack!
He left it dead, and with its head
He went galumphing back.

“And hast thou slain the Jabberwock?
Come to my arms, my beamish boy!
O frabjous day! Callooh! Callay!”
He chortled in his joy.

’Twas brillig, and the slithy toves
Did gyre and gimble in the wabe:
All mimsy were the borogoves,
And the mome raths outgrabe.

JABBERWOCKY. Fussy about pronunciation, Carroll in his preface to *The Hunting of the Snark* declares: “The first ‘o’ in ‘borogoves’ is pronounced like the ‘o’ in ‘borrow.’ I have heard people try to give it the sound of the ‘o’ in ‘worry.’ Such is Human Perversity.” *Toves*, he adds, rimes with *groves*.

Questions

1. Look up *chortled* (line 24) in your dictionary and find out its definition and origin.
2. In *Through the Looking Glass*, Alice seeks the aid of Humpty Dumpty to decipher the meaning of this nonsense poem. “*Brillig*,” he explains, “means four o’clock in

the afternoon—the time when you begin *broiling* things for dinner." Does "brillig" sound like any other familiar word?

3. "*Slithy*," the explanation goes on, "means 'lithe and slimy.' 'Lithe' is the same as 'active.' You see it's like a portmanteau—there are two meanings packed up into one word." "Mimsy" is supposed to pack together both "flimsy" and "miserable." In the rest of the poem, what other portmanteau—or packed suitcase—words can you find?

WRITING *effectively*

THINKING ABOUT DICTION

Although a poem may contain images and ideas, it is made up of words. Language is the medium of poetry, and a poem's diction—its exact wording—is the chief source of its power. Writers labor to shape each word and phrase to create particular effects. Poets choose words for their meanings, their associations, and even their sounds. Changing a single word may ruin a poem's effect, just as changing one letter or number in an online password makes all the other characters useless.

- **As you prepare to write about a poem, ask yourself if some particular word or combination of words gives you particular pleasure or especially intrigues you.** Don't worry yet about why the word or words impress you. Don't even worry about the meaning. Just underline the words in your book.
- **Try to determine what about the word or phrase commanded your attention.** Maybe a word strikes you as being unexpected but just right. A phrase might seem especially musical or it might call forth a vivid picture in your imagination.
- **Consider your underlined words and phrases in the context of the poem.** How does each relate to the words around it? What does it add to the poem?
- **Think about the poem as a whole.** What sort of language does it rely on? Many poems favor the plain, straightforward language people use in everyday conversation, but others reach for more elegant diction. Choices such as these contribute to the poem's distinctive flavor, as well as to its ultimate meaning.

CHECKLIST: Writing About Diction

- ☐ As you read, underline words or phrases that appeal to you or seem especially significant.
- ☐ What is it about each underlined word or phrase that appeals to you?
- ☐ How does the word or phrase relate to the other lines? What does it contribute to the poem's effect?
- ☐ How does the sound of a word you've chosen add to the poem's mood?
- ☐ What would be lost if synonyms were substituted for your favorite words?
- ☐ What sort of diction does the poem use? Conversational? Lofty? Monosyllabic? Polysyllabic? Concrete? Abstract?
- ☐ How does diction contribute to the poem's flavor and meaning?

TOPICS FOR WRITING ON WORD CHOICE

1. Find two poems in this book that use very different sorts of diction to address similar subjects. You might choose one with formal and elegant language and another with very down-to-earth or slangy word choices. A good choice might be John Milton's "When I consider how my light is spent" and Seamus Heaney's "Digging" (both in Chapter 23). In a short essay (750 to 1,000 words), discuss how the difference in diction affects the tones of the two poems.
2. Browse through Chapter 23, "Poems for Further Reading," for a poem that catches your interest. Within that poem, find a word or phrase that particularly intrigues you. Write a paragraph on what the word or phrase adds to the poem, including how it shades the meaning and contributes to the overall effect.
3. Choose a brief poem from this chapter. Type the poem out, substituting synonyms for each of its nouns and verbs, using a thesaurus if necessary. Next, write a one-page analysis of the difference in feel and meaning between the original and your creation.
4. Choose a poem that strikes you as particularly inventive or unusual in its language, such as E. E. Cummings's "anyone lived in a pretty how town," Gerard Manley Hopkins's "The Windhover" (Chapter 23), or Kay Ryan's "Blandeur," and write a brief analysis of it. Concentrate on the diction of the poem and word order. For what possible purposes does the poet depart from standard English or incorporate unusual vocabulary?
5. Writers are notorious word junkies who often jot down interesting words they stumble across in daily life. Over the course of a day, keep a list of any intriguing words you encounter in your reading, music listening, or television viewing. Even street signs and advertisements can supply surprising words. After twenty-four hours of list-keeping, choose your five favorites. Write a five-line poem, incorporating your five words, letting them take you where they will. Then write a page-long description of the process. What appealed to you in the words you chose? What did you learn about the process of composing a poem?

▶ TERMS FOR *review*

Diction and Allusion

Diction ▶ Word choice or vocabulary. Diction refers to the class of words that an author chooses as appropriate for a particular work.

Concrete diction ▶ Words that specifically name or describe things or persons. *Concrete diction* refers to what we can immediately perceive with our senses.

Abstract diction ▶ Words that express general ideas or concepts.

Poetic diction ▶ Strictly speaking, *poetic diction* means any language deemed suitable for verse, but the term generally refers to elevated language intended for poetry rather than common use.

Allusion ▶ A brief, sometimes indirect, reference in a text to a person, place, or thing. Allusions imply a common body of knowledge between reader and writer and act as a literary shorthand to enrich the meaning of a text.

Levels of Diction

Low diction (or **vulgate**) ▶ The language of the common people. Not necessarily containing foul or inappropriate language, it refers simply to unschooled, everyday speech. The term *vulgate* comes from the Latin word *vulgus*, meaning "mob" or "common people."

Colloquial English ▶ The casual or informal but correct language of ordinary native speakers. Conversational in tone, it may include contractions, slang, and shifts in grammar, vocabulary, and diction.

Middle diction (or **general English**) ▶ The ordinary speech of educated native speakers. Most literate speech and writing is in middle diction, which is more educated than **colloquial English**, yet not as elevated as **high diction**.

High diction (or **formal English**) ▶ The heightened, impersonal language of educated persons, usually only written, although possibly spoken on dignified occasions.

Dialect ▶ A particular variety of language spoken by an identifiable regional group or social class.

13 SAYING AND SUGGESTING

What You Will Learn in This Chapter

- To understand and define *denotation*
- To understand and define *connotation*
- To explain the difference between what words say and suggest in a poem
- To analyze the role of suggestion in a poem

The goal of scientists—according to Bishop Thomas Sprat, who lived in the seventeenth century—was to write so clearly that they might bring "all things as near the mathematical plainness" as possible. Such an effort would seem bound to fail, because words, unlike numbers, are ambiguous indicators. Although it may have troubled Bishop Sprat, the tendency of a word to have multiplicity of meaning rather than mathematical plainness opens broad avenues to poetry.

DENOTATION AND CONNOTATION

Every word has at least one **denotation**: a dictionary definition, also known as a **literal meaning**. But the English language has many a common word with so many denotations that a reader may need to think twice to see what it means in a specific context. The noun *field*, for instance, can denote an expanse of land, a sports arena, the scene of a battle, part of a flag, a profession, and a number system in mathematics. Further, the word can be used as a verb ("he fielded a grounder") or an adjective ("field trip," "field glasses").

A word also has **connotations**: overtones or suggestions of additional meaning that it gains from all the contexts in which we have met it in the past. **Suggestion** is the power of a word to imply unspoken associations, in addition to its literal meaning. Suggestion is one of the greatest powers of poetry. The word *skeleton*, according to a dictionary, denotes "the bony framework of a human being or other vertebrate animal, which supports the flesh and protects the organs." But by its associations, the word can rouse thoughts of war, of disease and death, of Halloween, or of one's plans to go to medical school. Think, too, of the difference between "Old Doc Jones" and "Theodore E. Jones, M.D." In the mind's eye, the former appears in his shirt-sleeves; the latter has a gold nameplate on his door.

That some words denote the same thing but have sharply different connotations is pointed out in this anonymous Victorian jingle:

Here's a little ditty that you really ought to know:
Horses "sweat" and men "perspire," but ladies only "glow."

Poets aren't the only people who care about the connotations of language. Advertisers know that connotations make money. Nowadays many automobile dealers advertise their secondhand cars not as "used" but as "pre-owned," as if fearing that "used car" would connote an old heap with soiled upholstery and mysterious engine troubles. "Pre-owned," however, suggests that the previous owner has kindly taken the trouble of breaking in the car for you.

In imaginative writing, connotations are as crucial as they are in advertising. Consider this sentence: "A new brand of journalism is being born, or spawned" (Dwight Macdonald writing in the *New York Review of Books*). The last word, by its associations with fish and crustaceans, suggests that this new journalism is scarcely the product of human beings.

William Blake was a master at choosing words loaded with connotation, as in this classic poem.

William Blake (1757–1827)

London 1794

I wander through each chartered street,
Near where the chartered Thames does flow,
And mark in every face I meet
Marks of weakness, marks of woe.

In every cry of every man,
In every infant's cry of fear,
In every voice, in every ban,
The mind-forged manacles I hear.

How the chimney-sweeper's cry
Every black'ning church appalls
And the hapless soldier's sigh
Runs in blood down palace walls.

But most through midnight streets I hear
How the youthful harlot's curse
Blasts the new-born infant's tear
And blights with plagues the marriage hearse.

Here are only a few of the possible meanings of four of Blake's words:

- ***chartered*** (lines 1, 2)

Denotations: Established by a charter (a written grant or a certificate of incorporation); leased or hired.

Connotations: Defined, limited, restricted, channeled, mapped, bound by law; bought and sold (like a slave or an inanimate object); Magna Carta; charters given to crown colonies by the King.

Other words in the poem with similar connotations: Ban, which can denote (1) a legal prohibition; (2) a churchman's curse or malediction; (3) in medieval times, an order summoning a king's vassals to fight for him. *Manacles*, or shackles, restrain movement. *Chimney-sweeper*, *soldier*, and *harlot* are all hirelings.

Interpretation of the lines: The street has had mapped out for it the direction in which it must go; the Thames has had laid down to it the course it must follow. Street and river are channeled, imprisoned, enslaved (like every inhabitant of London).

- ***black'ning*** (line 10)

Denotation: Becoming black.

Connotations: The darkening of something once light, the defilement of something once clean, the deepening of guilt, the gathering of darkness at the approach of night.

Other words in the poem with similar connotations: Objects becoming marked or smudged (*marks of weakness*, *marks of woe* in the faces of passersby; bloodied walls of a palace; marriage blighted with plagues); the word *appalls* (denoting not only "to overcome with horror" but "to make pale" and also "to cast a pall or shroud over"); *midnight streets*.

Interpretation of the line: Literally, every London church grows black from soot and hires a chimney-sweeper (a small boy) to help clean it. But Blake suggests too that by profiting from the suffering of the child laborer, the church is soiling its original purity.

- ***Blasts, blights*** (lines 15, 16)

Denotations: Both *blast* and *blight* mean "to cause to wither" or "to ruin and destroy." Both are terms from horticulture. Frost *blasts* a bud and kills it; disease *blights* a growing plant.

Connotations: Sickness and death; gardens shriveled and dying; gusts of wind and the ravages of insects; things blown to pieces or rotted and warped.

Other words in the poem with similar connotations: Faces marked with weakness and woe; the child becomes a chimney-sweep; the soldier killed by war; blackening church and bloodied palace; young girl turned harlot; wedding carriage transformed into a hearse.

Interpretation of the lines: Literally, the harlot spreads the plague of syphilis, which, carried into marriage, can cause a baby to be born blind. In a larger and more meaningful sense, Blake sees the prostitution of even one young girl corrupting the entire institution of matrimony and endangering every child.

Some of these connotations are more to the point than others; the reader of a poem nearly always has the problem of distinguishing relevant associations from irrelevant ones. We need to read a poem in its entirety and, when a word leaves us in doubt, look for other things in the poem to corroborate or refute what we think it means. Relatively simple and direct in its statement, Blake's account of his stroll through the city at night becomes an indictment of a whole social and religious order. The indictment could hardly be this effective if it were "mathematically plain," its every word restricted to one denotation clearly spelled out.

Wallace Stevens (1879–1955)

Disillusionment of Ten O'Clock

1923

The houses are haunted
By white night-gowns.
None are green,
Or purple with green rings,
Or green with yellow rings,
Or yellow with blue rings.
None of them are strange,
With socks of lace
And beaded ceintures.
People are not going
To dream of baboons and periwinkles.
Only, here and there, an old sailor,
Drunk and asleep in his boots,
Catches tigers
In red weather.

Questions

1. What are "beaded ceintures"? What does the phrase suggest?
2. What contrast does Stevens draw between the people who live in these houses and the old sailor? What do the connotations of "white night-gowns" and "sailor" add to this contrast?
3. What is lacking in these people who wear white night-gowns? Why should the poet's view of them be a "disillusionment"?

Robert Frost (1874–1963)

Fire and Ice

1923

Some say the world will end in fire,
Some say in ice.
From what I've tasted of desire
I hold with those who favor fire.
But if it had to perish twice,
I think I know enough of hate
To say that for destruction ice
Is also great
And would suffice.

Questions

1. To whom does Frost refer in line 1? In line 2?
2. What connotations of *fire* and *ice* contribute to the richness of Frost's comparison?

Timothy Steele (b. 1948)

Epitaph

1979

Here lies Sir Tact, a diplomatic fellow
Whose silence was not golden, but just yellow.

Questions

1. To what famous saying does the poet allude?
2. What are the connotations of "golden"? Of "yellow"?

Hieu Minh Nguyen (b. 1991)

Arranged

2014

my grandmother tells me you are very pretty
your smile not of a girl but of a package
teeth straight and perfectly arranged
like each petal in a bride's bouquet

your smile not of a girl but of a package
you are presented to me as a trophy
like each petal in a bride's bouquet
a haunting hiding underneath a veil

you are presented to me as a trophy
in my sheets there's a continent between us
a haunting hiding underneath a veil
we will sleep in separate beds

in my sheets there's a continent between us
wedding photos hang in the walk-in closet
we will sleep in separate beds
make a habit out of undressing in the bathroom

wedding photos hang in the walk-in closet
teeth straight and perfectly arranged
make a habit out of undressing in the bathroom
my grandmother tells me you are very pretty

Questions

1. What is the dictionary definition of "arranged," as used in first and last stanzas of the poem? Does the word take on another meaning when you look more closely at the poem?
2. The form of "Arranged" is a **pantoum**, a Malayan poetic form that was adopted by the French and then made its way into English. Study the line repetitions in the poem. Can you determine the pattern? How does the use of this form enhance the meaning of the poem?

H.D. [Hilda Doolittle] (1886–1961)

Sea Rose 1916

Rose, harsh rose,
marred and with stint of petals,
meagre flower, thin,
sparse of leaf,

more precious
than a wet rose
single on a stem—
you are caught in the drift.

Stunted, with small leaf,
you are flung on the sand,
you are lifted
in the crisp sand
that drives in the wind.

Can the spice-rose
drip such acrid fragrance
hardened in a leaf?

Alfred, Lord Tennyson (1809–1892)

Tears, Idle Tears

1847

Tears, idle tears, I know not what they mean,
Tears from the depth of some divine despair
Rise in the heart, and gather to the eyes,
In looking on the happy Autumn-fields,
And thinking of the days that are no more.

Fresh as the first beam glittering on a sail,
That brings our friends up from the underworld,
Sad as the last which reddens over one
That sinks with all we love below the verge;
So sad, so fresh, the days that are no more.

Ah, sad and strange as in dark summer dawns
The earliest pipe of half-awakened birds
To dying ears, when unto dying eyes
The casement slowly grows a glimmering square;
So sad, so strange, the days that are no more.

Dear as remembered kisses after death,
And sweet as those by hopeless fancy feigned
On lips that are for others; deep as love,
Deep as first love, and wild with all regret;
O Death in Life, the days that are no more.

Question

Why is the speaker crying?

Richard Wilbur (1921–2017)

Love Calls Us to the Things of This World

1956

The eyes open to a cry of pulleys,
And spirited from sleep, the astounded soul
Hangs for a moment bodiless and simple
As false dawn.
Outside the open window
The morning air is all awash with angels.

Some are in bed-sheets, some are in blouses,
Some are in smocks: but truly there they are.
Now they are rising together in calm swells
Of halcyon feeling, filling whatever they wear
With the deep joy of their impersonal breathing;

Now they are flying in place, conveying
The terrible speed of their omnipresence, moving
And staying like white water; and now of a sudden
They swoon down into so rapt a quiet
That nobody seems to be there.
The soul shrinks

From all that it is about to remember,
From the punctual rape of every blessèd day,
And cries,
"Oh, let there be nothing on earth but laundry,
Nothing but rosy hands in the rising steam
And clear dances done in the sight of heaven."

Yet, as the sun acknowledges
With a warm look the world's hunks and colors,
The soul descends once more in bitter love
To accept the waking body, saying now
In a changed voice as the man yawns and rises,

"Bring them down from their ruddy gallows;
Let there be clean linen for the backs of thieves;
Let lovers go fresh and sweet to be undone,
And the heaviest nuns walk in a pure floating
Of dark habits,
keeping their difficult balance."

Love Calls Us to the Things of This World. Wilbur once said that his title was taken from St. Augustine, but in a later interview he admitted that neither he nor any critic has ever been able to locate the quotation. Whatever its source, however, the title establishes the poem's central idea that love allows us to return from the divine world of the spirit to the imperfect world of our everyday lives.

Questions

1. What are the "angels" in line 5? Why does this metaphor seem appropriate to the situation?
2. What is "the punctual rape of every blessèd day"? Who is being raped? Who or what commits the rape? Why would Wilbur choose this particular word with all its violent associations?
3. Whom or what does the soul love in line 23, and why is that love bitter?
4. Is it merely obesity that make the nuns' balance "difficult" in the two final lines of the poem? What other "balance" does Wilbur's poem suggest?
5. The soul has two speeches in the poem. How do they differ in tone and imagery?
6. The spiritual world is traditionally considered invisible. What concrete images does Wilbur use to express its special character?

WRITING *effectively*

THINKING ABOUT DENOTATION AND CONNOTATION

People often convey their feelings indirectly, through body language, facial expression, tone of voice, and other ways. Similarly, the imagery, tone, and diction of a poem can suggest a message so clearly that it doesn't need to be stated outright.

- **Pay careful attention to what a poem suggests.** Jot down a few key observations both about what the poem says directly and what you might want to know but aren't told. What important details are you left to infer for yourself?
- **Establish what the poem actually says.** When journalists write a news story, they usually try to cover the "five W's" in the opening paragraph—who, what, when, where, and why. These questions are worthwhile ones to ask about a poem:

  Who? Who is the speaker or central figure of the poem? (In William Blake's "London," for instance, the speaker is also the protagonist who witnesses the hellish horror of the city.) If the poem seems to be addressed not simply to the reader but to a more specific listener, identify that listener as well.

  What? What objects or events are being seen or presented? Does the poem ever suddenly change its subject? (In Wallace Stevens's "Disillusionment of Ten O'Clock," for example, there are essentially two scenes—one dull and proper, the other wild and disreputable. What does that obvious shift suggest about Stevens's meaning?)

  When? When does the poem take place? If a poet explicitly states a time of day or a season of the year, it is likely that the *when* of the poem is important. (The fact that Stevens's poem takes place at 10 P.M. and not 2 A.M. tells us a great deal about the people it describes.)

  Where? Where is the poem set? Often the setting suggests something important, or plays a role in setting the mood.

  Why? If the poem describes a dramatic action but does not provide an overt reason for the occurrence, perhaps the reader is meant to draw his or her own conclusions on the subject. (Tennyson's "Tears, Idle Tears" becomes more evocative by not being explicit about why the speaker weeps.)

- **Remember, it is almost as important to know what a poem does not tell us as to know what it does.**

CHECKLIST: Writing About What a Poem Says and Suggests

- ☐ Who speaks the words of the poem? Is it a voice close to the poet's own? A fictional character? A real person?
- ☐ Who is the poem's central figure?
- ☐ To whom—if anyone—is the poem addressed?
- ☐ What objects or events are depicted?
- ☐ When does the poem take place? Is that timing significant in any way?
- ☐ Where does the action of the poem take place?
- ☐ Why does the action of the poem take place? Is there some significant motivation?
- ☐ Does the poem leave any of the above information out? If so, what does that lack of information reveal about the poem's intentions?

TOPICS FOR WRITING ON DENOTATION AND CONNOTATION

1. Search a poem of your own choosing for the answers to the "five W's"—*Who? What? When? Where? Why?* Indicate, with details, which of the questions are explicitly answered by the poem and which are left unaddressed.
2. Look closely at the central image of Richard Wilbur's "Love Calls Us to the Things of This World." Why does such an ordinary sight cause such intense feelings in the poem's speaker? Give evidence from the poem to back up your theory.
3. What do the various images in Tennyson's "Tears, Idle Tears" suggest about the speaker's reasons for weeping? Address each image, and explain what the images add up to.
4. Browse through a newspaper or magazine for an advertisement that tries to surround a product with an aura. A new car, for instance, might be described in terms of some powerful jungle cat ("purring power, ready to spring"). Clip or photocopy the ad and circle words in it that seem especially suggestive. Then, in an accompanying essay, unfold the suggestions in these words and try to explain the ad's appeal. What differences can you see between how poetry and advertising copy use connotative language?

▶ TERMS FOR *review*

Denotation ▶ The literal, dictionary meaning of a word.

Connotation ▶ An association or additional meaning that a word, image, or phrase may carry, apart from its literal denotation or dictionary definition. A word may pick up connotations from the uses to which it has been put in the past.

Suggestion ▶ The power of a word to imply unspoken associations, in addition to its literal meaning.

14 IMAGERY

What You Will Learn in This Chapter

- To define *imagery*
- To differentiate and explain the major types of imagery
- To recognize and describe haiku as a literary form
- To analyze the role of imagery in a poem

Ezra Pound (1885–1972)

In a Station of the Metro 1916

The apparition of these faces in the crowd;
Petals on a wet, black bough.

Pound said he wrote this poem to convey an experience: emerging one day from a train in the Paris subway (*Métro*), he beheld "suddenly a beautiful face, and then another and another." Originally he had described his impression in a poem thirty lines long. In this final version, each line contains an image, which, like a picture, may take the place of a thousand words.

Though the term **image** suggests a thing seen, when speaking of images in poetry, we generally mean *a word or sequence of words that refers to any sensory experience*. Often this experience is a sight (**visual imagery**, as in Pound's poem), but it may be a sound (**auditory imagery**) or a touch (**tactile imagery**, such as a perception of roughness or smoothness). It may be an odor or a taste or perhaps a bodily sensation such as pain, the prickling of gooseflesh, the quenching of thirst, or—as in the following brief poem—the perception of something cold.

Taniguchi Buson (1716–1783)

The piercing chill I feel (about 1760)

The piercing chill I feel:
  my dead wife's comb, in our bedroom,
    under my heel . . .

—*Translated by Harold G. Henderson*

As in this haiku (in Japanese, a poem typically of three lines and seventeen syllables), an image can convey a flash of understanding. Had he wished, the poet might have spoken of the dead woman, of the contrast between her death and his memory of her, of his feelings toward death in general. But such a discussion would be quite different from the poem he actually wrote. Striking his bare foot against the comb, now cold and motionless but associated with the living wife (perhaps worn in her hair), the widower feels a shock as if he had touched the woman's corpse. A literal, physical sense of death is conveyed; the abstraction "death" is understood through the senses. To render the abstract in concrete terms is what poets often try to do; in this attempt, an image can be valuable.

IMAGERY

An image may occur in a single word, a phrase, a sentence, or, as in this case, an entire short poem. To speak of the **imagery** of a poem—all its images taken together—is often more useful than to speak of separate images. To divide Buson's haiku into five images—*chill*, *wife*, *comb*, *bedroom*, *heel*—is possible, for any noun that refers to a visible object or a sensation is an image, but this is to draw distinctions that in themselves mean little and to disassemble a single experience.

Some literary critics look for much of the meaning of a poem in its imagery, wherein they expect to see the mind of the poet more truly revealed than in whatever the poet explicitly claims to believe. Though Shakespeare's Theseus (in *A Midsummer Night's Dream*) accuses poets of being concerned with "airy nothings," poets are usually very much concerned with what is in front of them. This concern is of use to us. Involved in our personal hopes and apprehensions, anticipating the future so hard that much of the time we see the present through a film of thought across our eyes, perhaps we need a poet occasionally to remind us that even the coffee we absentmindedly sip comes (as Yeats put it) in a "heavy spillable cup."

T. S. Eliot (1888–1965)

The winter evening settles down 1917

The winter evening settles down
With smell of steaks in passageways.
Six o'clock.
The burnt-out ends of smoky days.
And now a gusty shower wraps
The grimy scraps
Of withered leaves about your feet
And newspapers from vacant lots;

The showers beat
On broken blinds and chimney-pots,
And at the corner of the street
A lonely cab-horse steams and stamps.

And then the lighting of the lamps.

Questions

1. What mood is evoked by the images in Eliot's poem?
2. What kind of city neighborhood has the poet chosen to describe? How can you tell?

Theodore Roethke (1908–1963)

Root Cellar

1948

Nothing would sleep in that cellar, dank as a ditch,
Bulbs broke out of boxes hunting for chinks in the dark,
Shoots dangled and drooped,
Lolling obscenely from mildewed crates,
Hung down long yellow evil necks, like tropical snakes.
And what a congress of stinks!—
Roots ripe as old bait,
Pulpy stems, rank, silo-rich,
Leaf-mold, manure, lime, piled against slippery planks.
Nothing would give up life:
Even the dirt kept breathing a small breath.

Questions

1. As a boy growing up in Saginaw, Michigan, Theodore Roethke spent much of his time in a large commercial greenhouse run by his family. What details in his poem show more than a passing acquaintance with growing things?
2. What varieties of image does "Root Cellar" contain? Point out examples.
3. What do you understand to be Roethke's attitude toward the root cellar? Does he view it as a disgusting chamber of horrors? Pay special attention to the last two lines.

Elizabeth Bishop (1911–1979)

The Fish

1946

I caught a tremendous fish
and held him beside the boat
half out of water, with my hook
fast in a corner of his mouth.
He didn't fight.
He hadn't fought at all.
He hung a grunting weight,

battered and venerable
and homely. Here and there
his brown skin hung in strips
like ancient wallpaper,
and its pattern of darker brown
was like wallpaper:
shapes like full-blown roses
stained and lost through age.
He was speckled with barnacles,
fine rosettes of lime,
and infested
with tiny white sea-lice,
and underneath two or three
rags of green weed hung down.
While his gills were breathing in
the terrible oxygen
—the frightening gills,
fresh and crisp with blood,
that can cut so badly—
I thought of the coarse white flesh
packed in like feathers,
the big bones and the little bones,
the dramatic reds and blacks
of his shiny entrails,
and the pink swim-bladder
like a big peony.
I looked into his eyes
which were far larger than mine
but shallower, and yellowed,
the irises backed and packed
with tarnished tinfoil
seen through the lenses
of old scratched isinglass.
They shifted a little, but not
to return my stare.
—It was more like the tipping
of an object toward the light.
I admired his sullen face,
the mechanism of his jaw,
and then I saw
that from his lower lip
—if you could call it a lip—
grim, wet, and weaponlike,
hung five old pieces of fish-line,
or four and a wire leader

with the swivel still attached,
with all their five big hooks
grown firmly in his mouth.
A green line, frayed at the end
where he broke it, two heavier lines,
and a fine black thread
still crimped from the strain and snap
when it broke and he got away.
Like medals with their ribbons
frayed and wavering,
a five-haired beard of wisdom
trailing from his aching jaw.
I stared and stared
and victory filled up
the little rented boat,
from the pool of bilge
where oil had spread a rainbow
around the rusted engine
to the bailer rusted orange,
the sun-cracked thwarts,
the oarlocks on their strings,
the gunnels—until everything
was rainbow, rainbow, rainbow!
And I let the fish go.

Questions

1. How many abstract words does this poem contain? What proportion of the poem is imagery?
2. What is the speaker's attitude toward the fish? Comment in particular on lines 61–64.
3. What attitude do the images of the rainbow of oil (line 69), the orange bailer (bailing bucket, line 71), and the "sun-cracked thwarts" (line 72) convey? Does the poet expect us to feel mournful because the boat is in such sorry condition?
4. What is meant by "rainbow, rainbow, rainbow"?
5. How do these images prepare us for the conclusion? Why does the speaker let the fish go?

Emily Dickinson (1830–1886)

A Route of Evanescence

(about 1879)

A Route of Evanescence
With a revolving Wheel –
A Resonance of Emerald –
A Rush of Cochineal° –

° *red dye*

And every Blossom on the Bush
Adjusts its tumbled Head –
The mail from Tunis, probably,
An easy Morning's Ride –

A ROUTE OF EVANESCENCE. Dickinson titled this poem "A Humming-bird" in an 1880 letter to a friend. 1 *Evanescence:* ornithologist's term for the luminous sheen of certain birds' feathers. 7 *Tunis:* capital city of Tunisia, North Africa.

Question

What is the subject of this poem? How can you tell?

Jean Toomer (1894–1967)

Reapers

1923

Black reapers with the sound of steel on stones
Are sharpening scythes. I see them place the hones
In their hip-pockets as a thing that's done,
And start their silent swinging, one by one.
Black horses drive a mower through the weeds,
And there, a field rat, startled, squealing bleeds,
His belly close to ground. I see the blade,
Blood-stained, continue cutting weeds and shade.

Questions

1. Imagine the scene Toomer describes. What details most vividly strike the mind's eye?
2. What kind of image is "silent swinging"?
3. Read the poem aloud. Notice especially the effect of the words "sound of steel on stones" and "field rat, startled, squealing bleeds." What interesting sounds are present in the very words that contain these images?
4. What feelings do you get from this poem as a whole? Besides appealing to our auditory and visual imagination, what do the images contribute?

Gerard Manley Hopkins (1844–1889)

Pied Beauty

(1877)

Glory be to God for dappled things—
  For skies of couple-color as a brinded° cow; *streaked*
    For rose-moles all in stipple° upon trout that swim; *speckled or dotted*
Fresh-firecoal chestnut-falls; finches' wings;
  Landscape plotted and pieced—fold, fallow, and plow;
    And áll trádes, their gear and tackle and trim.° *equipment*

All things counter, original, spare, strange;
  Whatever is fickle, freckled (who knows how?)

With swift, slow; sweet, sour; adazzle, dim;
He fathers-forth whose beauty is past change:
Praise him.

Questions

1. What does the word "pied" mean? (Hint: what does a Pied Piper look like?)
2. According to Hopkins, what do "skies," "cow," "trout," "ripe chestnuts," "finches' wings," and "landscapes" all have in common? What landscapes can the poet have in mind? (Have you ever seen any "dappled" landscape while looking down from an airplane, or from a mountain or high hill?)
3. What do you make of line 6? What can carpenters' saws and ditch-diggers' spades possibly have in common with the dappled things in lines 2–4?
4. Does Hopkins refer only to visual contrasts? What other kinds of variation interest him?
5. Try to state in your own words the theme of this poem. How essential to our understanding of this theme are Hopkins's images?

ABOUT HAIKU

Arakida Moritake (1473–1549)

The falling flower

The falling flower
I saw drift back to the branch
Was a butterfly.

—*Translated by Babette Deutsch*

Haiku means "beginning-verse" in Japanese—perhaps because the form may have originated in a game. Players, given a haiku, were supposed to extend its three lines into a longer poem. Haiku (the word can also be plural) consist mainly of imagery, but, as we saw in Buson's lines about the cold comb, their imagery is not always only pictorial; it can involve any of the five senses. Haiku are so short that they depend on imagery to trigger associations and responses in the reader. A haiku in Japanese is rimeless; its seventeen syllables are traditionally arranged in three lines, usually following a pattern of five, seven, and five syllables. English haiku frequently ignore such a pattern, being rimed or unrimed as the poet prefers. What English haiku do try to preserve is the powerful way Japanese haiku capture the intensity of a particular moment, usually by linking two concrete images. There is little room for abstract thoughts or general observations. The following attempt, though containing seventeen syllables, is far from haiku in spirit:

Now that our love is gone
I feel within my soul
a nagging distress.

Unlike the author of those lines, haiku poets look out upon a literal world, seldom looking inward to *discuss* their feelings. Japanese haiku tend to be seasonal in subject, but because they are so highly compressed, they usually only *imply* a season: a blossom indicates spring; a crow on a branch, autumn; snow, winter. Not just pretty little sketches of nature (as some Westerners think), haiku assume a view of the universe in which observer and nature are not separated.

Haiku emerged in sixteenth-century Japan and soon developed into a deeply esteemed form. Even today, Japanese soldiers, stockbrokers, scientists, schoolchildren, and the emperor himself (who abdicated in 2017, possibly to dedicate more time to poetry) still find occasion to pen haiku. Soon after the form first captured the attention of Western poets at the end of the nineteenth century, it became immensely influential for modern poets, such as Ezra Pound, William Carlos Williams, and H.D., as a model for the kind of verse they wanted to write—concise, direct, and imagistic.

The Japanese consider the poems of the "Three Masters"—Basho, Buson, and Issa—to be the pinnacle of the classical haiku. Each poet had his own personality: Basho, the ascetic seeker of Zen enlightenment; Buson, the worldly artist; Issa, the sensitive master of wit and pathos. Here are liberal translations of poems from each of the "Three Masters."

Matsuo Basho (1644–1694)

Heat-lightning streak

Heat-lightning streak—
through darkness pierces
the heron's shriek.

—*Translated by X. J. Kennedy*

In the old stone pool

In the old stone pool
a frogjump:
splishhhhh.

—*Translated by X. J. Kennedy*

Taniguchi Buson (1716–1783)

On the one-ton temple bell

On the one-ton temple bell
a moonmoth, folded into sleep,
sits still.

—*Translated by X. J. Kennedy*

Moonrise on mudflats

Moonrise on mudflats,
the line of water and sky
blurred by a bullfrog

—*Translated by Michael Stillman*

Kobayashi Issa (1763–1827)

only one guy

only one guy and
only one fly trying to
make the guest room do.

—*Translated by Cid Corman*

Cricket

Cricket, be
careful! I'm rolling
over!

—*Translated by Robert Bly*

HAIKU FROM JAPANESE INTERNMENT CAMPS

Japanese immigrants brought the tradition of haiku-writing to the United States, often forming local clubs to pursue their shared literary interests. During World War II, when Japanese Americans were unjustly considered "enemy aliens" and confined to federal internment camps, these poets continued to write in their bleak new surroundings. Today these haiku provide a vivid picture of the deprivations suffered by the poets, their families, and their fellow internees.

Suiko Matsushita

Cosmos in bloom

Cosmos in bloom
as if no war
were taking place

—*Translated by Violet Kazue de Cristoforo*

Hakuro Wada

Even the croaking of frogs

Even the croaking of frogs
comes from outside the barbed wire fence
this is our life

—*Translated by Violet Kazue de Cristoforo*

CONTEMPORARY HAIKU

Here are four more recent haiku written in English. (Don't expect them all to observe a strict arrangement of seventeen syllables, however.) Haiku, in any language, is an art of few words but many suggestions. A haiku starts us thinking and telling.

Nick Virgilio (1928–1989)

The Old Neighborhood

the old neighborhood
falling to the wrecking ball:
names in the sidewalk

Adelle Foley (1940–2016)

Learning to Shave (Father Teaching Son)

A nick on the jaw
The razor's edge of manhood
Along the bloodline.

FOR REVIEW AND FURTHER STUDY

John Keats (1795–1821)

Bright star, would I were steadfast as thou art (1819)

Bright star, would I were steadfast as thou art—
Not in lone splendor hung aloft the night,
And watching, with eternal lids apart,
Like Nature's patient, sleepless Eremite,° *hermit*
The moving waters at their priestlike task
Of pure ablution round earth's human shores,
Or gazing on the new soft-fallen mask
Of snow upon the mountains and the moors—
No—yet still steadfast, still unchangeable,
Pillowed upon my fair love's ripening breast,
To feel for ever its soft swell and fall,
Awake for ever in a sweet unrest,
Still, still to hear her tender-taken breath,
And so live ever—or else swoon to death.

Questions

1. Stars are conventional symbols for love and a loved one. (Love, Shakespeare tells us in a sonnet, "is the star to every wandering bark.") In this sonnet, why is it not possible for the star to have this meaning? How does Keats use it?
2. What seems concrete and particular in the speaker's observations?
3. Suppose Keats had said "slow and easy" instead of "tender-taken" in line 13. What would have been lost?

Experiment: Writing with Images

Taking the following poems as examples from which to start rather than as models to be slavishly copied, try to compose a brief poem that consists largely of imagery.

William Carlos Williams (1883–1963)

El Hombre 1917

It's a strange courage
you give me ancient star:

Shine alone in the sunrise
toward which you lend no part!

Gary Snyder (b. 1930)

Mid-August at Sourdough Mountain Lookout 1959

Down valley a smoke haze
Three days heat, after five days rain
Pitch glows on the fir-cones
Across rocks and meadows
Swarms of new flies.

I cannot remember things I once read
A few friends, but they are in cities.
Drinking cold snow-water from a tin cup
Looking down for miles
Through high still air.

MID-AUGUST AT SOURDOUGH MOUNTAIN LOOKOUT. *Sourdough Mountain:* in the state of Washington, where the poet's job at the time was to watch for forest fires.

Angela Alaimo O'Donnell (b. 1960)

Tattoo 2007

Queequeg himself in his own proper person was a riddle to unfold, a wondrous work in one volume.

—*Moby Dick*

Aureola of vaccination, small sun.
Stippled freckles burnt deep by Spain.

The bite of escalator steps, right knee.
The scalpel's ounce of flesh, right breast.

Lines of longitude etched along the belly
By swell and swell and swell of child.

Wrinkled forehead, crinkled brow of poor sight.
Neat print of crow's feet at each eye.

The moles doled out at birth.
The stiff lip of strong-limbed women.

These marks, too, hieroglyphic,
A language of eternity and once.

Story inscribed on warm parchment
That breathes and beats beneath life's needle.

Stevie Smith (1902–1971)

Not Waving but Drowning 1957

Nobody heard him, the dead man,
But still he lay moaning:
I was much further out than you thought
And not waving but drowning.

Poor chap, he always loved larking
And now he's dead
It must have been too cold for him his heart gave way,
They said.

Oh, no no no, it was too cold always
(Still the dead one lay moaning)
I was much too far out all my life
And not waving but drowning.

Robert Bly (b. 1926)

Driving to Town Late to Mail a Letter 1962

It is a cold and snowy night. The main street is deserted.
The only things moving are swirls of snow.
As I lift the mailbox door, I feel its cold iron.
There is a privacy I love in this snowy night.
Driving around, I will waste more time.

WRITING *effectively*

THINKING ABOUT IMAGERY

Images are powerful things—thus the old saw, "A picture is worth a thousand words." A poem, however, must build its pictures from words. By taking note of its imagery, and watching how the nature of those images evolves from start to finish, you can go a long way toward a better understanding of the poem. The following steps can help:

- **Make a short list of the poem's key images.** Be sure to write them down in the order they appear, because the sequence can be as important as the images themselves.

- **Take the poem's title into account.** A title often points the way to important insights.
- **Remember: not all images are visual.** Images can draw on any or all of the five senses.
- **Jot down key adjectives or other qualifying words.**
- **Go back through your list and take notes about what moods or attitudes are suggested by each image.** What do you notice about the movement from the first image to the last?

Example: Robert Bly's "Driving to Town Late to Mail a Letter"

Let's try this method on a short poem. An initial list of images in Bly's "Driving to Town Late to Mail a Letter" might look like this:

cold and snowy night
deserted main street
mailbox door—cold iron
snowy night (speaker loves its privacy)
speaker drives around (to waste time)

Bly's title also contains several crucial images. Let's add them to the top of the list:

driving (to town)
late night
a letter (to be mailed)

Looking over our list, we see how the images provide an outline of the poem's story. We also see how Bly begins the poem without providing an initial sense of how his speaker feels about the situation. Is driving to town late on a snowy evening a positive, negative, or neutral experience? By noting where (in line 4) the speaker reveals a subjective response to an image ("There is a privacy I love in this snowy night"), we begin to grasp the poem's overall emotional structure. We might also note on our list how the poem begins and ends with the same image (driving), but uses it for different effects. At the beginning, the speaker is driving for the practical purpose of mailing a letter, but at the end, he drives purely for pleasure.

Simply by noting the images from start to finish, we have already worked out a rough essay outline—all on a single sheet of paper or a few inches of computer screen.

CHECKLIST: Writing About Imagery

☐ List a poem's key images, in the order in which they appear.
☐ What does the poem's title suggest?
☐ Remember, images can draw on all five senses—not just the visual.
☐ List key adjectives or other qualifying words.

- ☐ What emotions or attitudes are suggested by each image?
- ☐ Does the mood of the imagery change from start to finish?
- ☐ What is suggested by the movement from one image to the next? Remember that the order or sequence of images is almost as important as the images themselves.

TOPICS FOR WRITING ON IMAGERY

1. Apply the steps listed in "Checklist: Writing About Imagery" to one of the poems in this chapter. Stevie Smith's "Not Waving but Drowning," John Keats's "Bright star, would I were steadfast as thou art," and Jean Toomer's "Reapers" would each make a good subject. Make a brief list of images, and jot down notes on what the images suggest. Now write a two-page description of this process—what it revealed about the poem itself, and about reading poetry in general.
2. Choose a small, easily overlooked object in your home that has special significance to you. Write a paragraph-long, excruciatingly detailed description of the item, putting at least four senses into play. Without making any direct statements about the item's importance to you, try to let the imagery convey the mood you associate with it. Bring your paragraph to class, exchange it with a partner, and see if he or she can identify the mood you were trying to convey.
3. Reread the section on haiku in this chapter. Write three or four haiku of your own and a brief prose account of your experience in writing them. Did anything about the process surprise you?
4. Examining any poem in this chapter, demonstrate how its imagery helps communicate its general theme. Be specific in noting how each key image contributes to the poem's total effect. Feel free to consult criticism on the poem but make sure to credit any observation you borrow from a critical source.

▶ TERMS FOR *review*

Image ▶ A word or series of words that refers to any sensory experience (usually sight, although also sound, smell, touch, or taste). An image is a direct or literal recreation of physical experience and adds immediacy to literary language.

Imagery ▶ The collective set of images in a poem or other literary work.

Visual imagery ▶ Imagery that refers to the sense of sight or presents something one may see.

Auditory imagery ▶ Imagery that refers to the sense of hearing.

Tactile imagery ▶ Imagery that refers to the sense of touch.

Haiku ▶ A Japanese verse form that typically has three unrhymed lines of five, seven, and five syllables. Traditional haiku is often serious and spiritual in tone, relying mostly on imagery, and usually set (often by implication instead of direct statement) in one of the four seasons. Modern haiku in English sometimes ignore strict syllable count and may have a more playful, worldly tone.

15 FIGURES OF SPEECH

What You Will Learn in This Chapter

- To define *simile*
- To define *metaphor*
- To recognize the major figures of speech
- To analyze the role of figurative speech in a poem

WHY SPEAK FIGURATIVELY?

"I will speak daggers to her, but use none," says Hamlet, preparing to confront his mother. His statement makes sense only because we realize that *daggers* is to be taken two ways: literally (denoting sharp, pointed weapons) and nonliterally (referring to something that can be used *like* weapons—namely, words). Reading poetry, we often meet comparisons between two things whose similarity we have never noticed before. When Marianne Moore observes that a fir tree has "an emerald turkey-foot at the top," the result is a pleasure that poetry richly affords: the sudden recognition of likenesses.

A treetop like a turkey-foot, words like daggers—such comparisons are called **figures of speech**. A figure of speech occurs whenever a speaker or writer, for the sake of freshness or emphasis, departs from the usual denotations, or literal definitions, of words. Certainly, when Hamlet says he will speak daggers, no one expects him to release pointed weapons from his lips, for *daggers* is not to be read solely for its denotation. Its connotations, or suggested meanings—sharp, stabbing, piercing, wounding—also come to mind, and we see ways in which words and daggers might work alike.

Figures of speech are not devices to state what is demonstrably untrue. Indeed they often state truths that more literal language cannot communicate; they call attention to such truths; they lend them emphasis.

Alfred, Lord Tennyson (1809–1892)

The Eagle 1851

He clasps the crag with crooked hands;
Close to the sun in lonely lands,

Ringed with the azure world, he stands.
The wrinkled sea beneath him crawls;
He watches from his mountain walls,
And like a thunderbolt he falls.

This brief poem is rich in figurative language. In the first line, the phrase *crooked hands* may surprise us. An eagle does not have hands, we might protest; but the objection would be a quibble, for evidently Tennyson is indicating exactly how an eagle clasps a crag, in the way that human fingers clasp a thing. By implication, too, the eagle is a person. *Close to the sun*, if taken literally, is an absurd exaggeration, the sun being a mean distance of 93 million miles from the earth. For the eagle to be closer to it by the altitude of a mountain is so minor as to be insignificant. But figuratively, Tennyson conveys that the eagle stands above the clouds, perhaps silhouetted against the sun, and for the moment belongs to the heavens rather than to the land and sea. The word *ringed* makes a circle of the whole world's horizons and suggests that we see the world from the eagle's height; the *wrinkled sea* becomes an aged, sluggish animal; *mountain walls*, possibly literal, also suggests a fort or castle; and finally the eagle itself is likened to a thunderbolt in speed and in power, perhaps also in that its beak is—like our abstract conception of a lightning bolt—pointed. How much of the poem can be taken literally? Only *he clasps the crag, he stands, he watches, he falls*. The rest is made of figures of speech. The result is that, reading Tennyson's poem, we gain a bird's-eye view of sun, sea, and land—and even of bird. Like imagery, figurative language refers us to the physical world.

William Shakespeare (1564–1616)

Shall I compare thee to a summer's day? (Sonnet 18) 1609

Shall I compare thee to a summer's day?
Thou art more lovely and more temperate.
Rough winds do shake the darling buds of May,
And summer's lease hath all too short a date.
Sometime too hot the eye of heaven shines,
And often is his gold complexion dimmed;
And every fair° from fair sometimes declines, *fair one*
By chance, or nature's changing course, untrimmed:
But thy eternal summer shall not fade,
Nor lose possession of that fair thou ow'st,° *ownest, have*
Nor shall death brag thou wand'rest in his shade,
When in eternal lines to time thou grow'st.
So long as men can breathe or eyes can see,
So long lives this, and this gives life to thee.

Howard Moss (1922–1987)

Shall I Compare Thee to a Summer's Day? 1976

Who says you're like one of the dog days?
You're nicer. And better.
Even in May, the weather can be gray,
And a summer sub-let doesn't last forever.
Sometimes the sun's too hot;
Sometimes it is not.
Who can stay young forever?
People break their necks or just drop dead!
But you? Never!
If there's just one condensed reader left
Who can figure out the abridged alphabet,
After you're dead and gone,
In this poem you'll live on!

SHALL I COMPARE THEE TO A SUMMER'S DAY? (Moss). 1 *dog days*: the hottest days of summer. The ancient Romans believed that the Dog-star, Sirius, added heat to summer months.

Questions

1. In Howard Moss's streamlined version of Shakespeare, from a series called "Modified Sonnets (Dedicated to adapters, abridgers, digesters, and condensers everywhere)," to what extent does the poet use figurative language? In Shakespeare's original sonnet, how high a proportion of Shakespeare's language is figurative?
2. Compare some of Moss's lines to the corresponding lines in Shakespeare's sonnet. Why is "Even in May, the weather can be gray" less interesting than the original? In the lines on the sun (5–6 in both versions), what has Moss's modification deliberately left out? Why is Shakespeare's seeing death as a braggart memorable? Why aren't you greatly impressed by Moss's last two lines?
3. Can you explain Shakespeare's play on the word "untrimmed" (line 8)? Evidently the word can mean "divested of trimmings," but what other suggestions do you find in it?
4. How would you answer someone who argued, "Maybe Moss's language isn't as good as Shakespeare's, but the meaning is still there. What's wrong with putting Shakespeare into up-to-date words that can be understood by everybody?"

METAPHOR AND SIMILE

Life, like a dome of many-colored glass,
Stains the white radiance of Eternity.

The first of these lines (from Shelley's "Adonais") is a **simile**: a comparison of two things, indicated by some connective, usually *like*, *as*, *than*, or a verb such as *resembles*. A simile expresses a similarity. Still, for a simile to exist, the things compared have to be dissimilar in kind. It is no simile to say "Your fingers are like mine"; it is a literal observation. But to say "Your fingers are like sausages" is to use a simile. Omit the connective—say "Your fingers are sausages"—and the result is a **metaphor**, a statement that one thing *is* something else, which, in a literal sense, it is not. In the second of Shelley's lines, it is *assumed* that Eternity is light or radiance, and we have an **implied metaphor**, one that uses neither a connective nor the verb *to be*. Here are examples:

Oh, my love is like a red, red rose.	*Simile*
Oh, my love resembles a red, red rose.	*Simile*
Oh, my love is redder than a rose.	*Simile*
Oh, my love is a red, red rose.	*Metaphor*
Oh, my love has red petals and sharp thorns.	*Implied metaphor*

Often you can tell a metaphor from a simile by much more than just the presence or absence of a connective. In general, a simile refers to only one characteristic that two things have in common, while a metaphor is not plainly limited in the number of resemblances it may indicate. To use the simile "He eats like a pig" is to compare man and animal in one respect: eating habits. But to say "He's a pig" is to use a metaphor that might also involve comparisons of appearance and morality.

The Usefulness of Metaphors

For scientists as well as poets, the making of metaphors is customary. As astrophysicist and novelist Alan Lightman has noted, we can't help envisioning scientific discoveries in terms of things we know from daily life—spinning balls, waves in water, pendulums, weights on springs. "We have no other choice," Lightman reasons. "We cannot avoid forming mental pictures when we try to grasp the meaning of our equations, and how can we picture what we have not seen?"[1] In science as well as in poetry, it would seem, metaphors are necessary instruments of understanding.

Mixed Metaphors

In everyday speech, simile and metaphor occur frequently. We use metaphors ("She's a doll") and similes ("The tickets are selling like hotcakes") without being fully conscious of them. If, however, we are aware that words possess literal meanings as well as figurative ones, we should avoid using what are called **mixed metaphors** and not follow the example of the writer who advised, "Water the spark of knowledge and it will bear fruit," or the speaker who urged, "To get ahead, keep your nose to the grindstone, your shoulder

[1]"Physicists' Use of Metaphor," *The American Scholar* (Winter 1989): 99.

to the wheel, your ear to the ground, and your eye on the ball." Perhaps the unintended humor of these statements comes from our seeing that the writer, busy stringing together stale metaphors, was not aware that they had any physical reference.

Poetry and Metaphor

A poem may make a series of comparisons, or the whole poem may be one extended comparison:

Emily Dickinson (1830–1886)

My Life had stood – a Loaded Gun (about 1863)

My Life had stood – a Loaded Gun –
In Corners – till a Day
The Owner passed – identified –
And carried Me away –

And now We roam in Sovereign Woods –
And now We hunt the Doe –
And every time I speak for Him –
The Mountains straight reply –

And do I smile, such cordial light
Upon the Valley glow –
It is as a Vesuvian face
Had let its pleasure through –

And when at Night – Our good Day done –
I guard My Master's Head –
'Tis better than the Eider-Duck's
Deep Pillow – to have shared –

To foe of His – I'm deadly foe –
None stir the second time –
On whom I lay a Yellow Eye –
Or an emphatic Thumb –

Though I than He – may longer live
He longer must – than I –
For I have but the power to kill,
Without – the power to die –

How much life metaphors can bring to poetry may be seen by comparing two poems by Tennyson and Blake.

Alfred, Lord Tennyson (1809–1892)

Flower in the Crannied Wall 1869

Flower in the crannied wall,
I pluck you out of the crannies,
I hold you here, root and all, in my hand,
Little flower—but *if* I could understand
What you are, root and all, and all in all,
I should know what God and man is.

How many metaphors does this poem contain? None. Compare it with a briefer poem on a similar theme: the quatrain that begins Blake's "Auguries of Innocence." (We follow here the opinion of W. B. Yeats, who, in editing Blake's poems, thought the lines, each with its own metaphor, deserved to be printed separately.)

William Blake (1757–1827)

To see a world in a grain of sand (about 1803)

To see a world in a grain of sand
And a heaven in a wild flower,
Hold infinity in the palm of your hand
And eternity in an hour.

Set beside Blake's poem, Tennyson's—short though it is—seems lengthy. What contributes to the richness of "To see a world in a grain of sand" is Blake's use of a metaphor in every line. And every metaphor is loaded with suggestion. Our world does indeed resemble a grain of sand: in being round, in being stony, in being one of a myriad (the suggestions go on and on). Like Blake's grain of sand, a metaphor holds much within a small circumference.

Sylvia Plath (1932–1963)

Metaphors 1960

I'm a riddle in nine syllables,
An elephant, a ponderous house,
A melon strolling on two tendrils.
O red fruit, ivory, fine timbers!
This loaf's big with its yeasty rising.
Money's new-minted in this fat purse.
I'm a means, a stage, a cow in calf.
I've eaten a bag of green apples,
Boarded the train there's no getting off.

Questions

1. To what central fact do all the metaphors in this poem refer?
2. In the first line, what has the speaker in common with a riddle? Why does she say she has *nine* syllables? What patterns using the number nine do you find in the poem?

N. Scott Momaday (b. 1934)

Simile
1974

What did we say to each other
that now we are as the deer
who walk in single file
with heads high
with ears forward
with eyes watchful
with hooves always placed on firm ground
in whose limbs there is latent flight

Questions

1. Momaday never tells us what was said. Does this omission keep us from understanding the comparison?
2. The comparison is extended with each detail adding some new twist. Explain the implications of the last line.

Experiment: Likening

Write a poem that follows the method of N. Scott Momaday's "Simile," consisting of one long comparison between two objects. Possible subjects might include talking to a loved one long-distance; how you feel going to a weekend job; being on a diet; not being noticed by someone you love; winning a lottery.

Jill Alexander Essbaum (b. 1971)

The Heart
2007

Four simple chambers.
A thousand complicated doors.

One of them is yours.

Questions

1. Which line contains a figure of speech?
2. Is that figure a metaphor or a simile? Explain.

Cody Walker (b. 1967)

I'm Like 2016

I'm like a twenty-inch Fatbike: extra-tired.
I'm like milk from the Third Reich: expired.
I'm like a word deleted from *Leaves of Grass*.
I'm like a bird homing in on a sheet of glass.
I'm like a gnome transported to the dreary present.
I'm like a Roman laborer or a wounded pheasant.
I'm like the neighbor you watch till he lowers his light.
I'm like a kid with a light saber and a Diet Sprite.
I'm like the guy at Kroger who left his wallet in the car.
I'm like a Geiger counter. I'm like the devil's cigar.

Question

Describe what each simile adds to the poem. What is the accumulative effect?

Exercise: What Is Similar?

Each of these quotations contains a simile or a metaphor. In each of these figures of speech, what two things are being compared? Try to state exactly what you understand the two things to have in common: the most striking similarity or similarities that the poet sees.

1. All the world's a stage,
And all the men and women merely players:
They have their exits and their entrances,
And one man in his time plays many parts,
His acts being seven ages.
—William Shakespeare, *As You Like It*

2. "Hope" is the thing with feathers –
That perches in the soul –
And sings the tune without the words –
And never stops – at all –
—Emily Dickinson, an untitled poem

3. Why should I let the toad *work*
Squat on my life?
Can't I use my wit as a pitchfork
And drive the brute off?
—Philip Larkin, "Toads"

4. I wear my patience like a light-green dress
and wear it thin.
—Emily Grosholz, "Remembering the Ardèche"

OTHER FIGURES OF SPEECH

When Shakespeare asks, in a sonnet,

> O! how shall summer's honey breath hold out
> Against the wrackful siege of batt'ring days,

it might seem at first that he mixes metaphors. How can a *breath* confront the battering ram of an invading army? But it is summer's breath and, by giving it to summer, Shakespeare makes the season seem human. It is as if the fragrance of summer were the breath within a person's body, and winter were the onslaught of old age.

Personification

Such is Shakespeare's instance of **personification**: a figure of speech in which a thing, an animal, or an abstract term (*truth*, *nature*) is made human. A personification extends throughout the following short poem, in which the wind is a wild man, and evidently it is not just any autumn breeze but a hurricane or at least a stiff gale.

James Stephens (1882–1950)

The Wind 1915

The wind stood up, and gave a shout;
He whistled on his fingers, and

Kicked the withered leaves about,
And thumped the branches with his hand,

And said he'd kill, and kill, and kill;
And so he will! And so he will!

Apostrophe

Hand in hand with personification often goes **apostrophe**: a way of addressing someone or something invisible or not ordinarily spoken to. In an apostrophe, a poet (in these examples Wordsworth) may address an inanimate object ("Spade! with which Wilkinson hath tilled his lands"), some dead or absent person ("Milton! thou shouldst be living at this hour"), an abstract thing ("Return, Delights!"), or a spirit ("Thou Soul that art the eternity of thought"). More often than not, the poet uses apostrophe to announce a lofty and serious tone. An "O" may even be put in front of it ("O moon!") since, according to W. D. Snodgrass, every poet has a right to do so at least once in a lifetime. But apostrophe doesn't have to be highfalutin. It is a means of giving life to the inanimate. It is a way of giving body to the intangible, a way of speaking to it person to person, as in the words of a moving American spiritual: "Death, ain't you got no shame?"

Robinson Jeffers (1887–1962)

Hands

1929

Inside a cave in a narrow canyon near Tassajara
The vault of rock is painted with hands,
A multitude of hands in the twilight, a cloud of men's palms,
 no more,
No other picture. There's no one to say
Whether the brown shy quiet people who are dead intended
Religion or magic, or made their tracings
In the idleness of art; but over the division of years these careful
Signs-manual are now like a sealed message
Saying: "Look: we also were human; we had hands, not paws.
 All hail
You people with the cleverer hands, our supplanters
In the beautiful country; enjoy her a season, her beauty, and
 come down
And be supplanted; for you also are human."

Question

Can you identify examples of personification and apostrophe in "Hands"?

Overstatement and Understatement

Most of us, from time to time, emphasize a point with a statement containing exaggeration: "Faster than greased lightning"; "I've told him a thousand times." We speak, then, not literal truth but use a figure of speech called **overstatement** (or **hyperbole**). Poets too, being fond of emphasis, often exaggerate for effect. Instances are Marvell's profession of a love that should grow "Vaster than empires, and more slow" and John Burgon's description of Petra: "A rose-red city, half as old as Time." Overstatement can be used also for humorous purposes, as in a fat woman's boast (from a blues song): "Every time I shake, some skinny gal loses her home."[2] The opposite is **understatement,** implying more than is said. Mark Twain in *Life on the Mississippi* recalls how, as an apprentice steamboat-pilot asleep when supposed to be on watch, he was roused by the pilot and sent clambering to the pilot house: "Mr. Bixby was close behind, commenting." Another example is Robert Frost's line "One could do worse than be a swinger of birches"—the conclusion of a poem that has suggested that to swing on a birch tree is one of the most deeply satisfying activities in the world.

Pun

Asked to tell the difference between men and women, Samuel Johnson replied, "I can't conceive, madam, can you?" The great dictionary-maker was

[2]Quoted by Amiri Baraka [LeRoi Jones] in *Blues People* (New York: Morrow, 1963), 92.

using a figure of speech known to classical rhetoricians as *paronomasia*, better known to us as a **pun** or play on words. How does a pun operate? Usually with humorous intent, it reminds us of another word (or other words) of similar or identical sound but of very different denotation. Although puns at their worst can be mere piddling quibbles, at best they can sharply point to surprising but genuine resemblances. The name of a dentist's country estate, Tooth Acres, is accurate: aching teeth paid for the property. In his novel *Moby-Dick*, Herman Melville takes up questions about whales that had puzzled scientists: for instance, are the whale's spoutings water or gaseous vapor? When Melville speaks pointedly of the great whale "sprinkling and mistifying the gardens of the deep," we catch his pun and conclude that the creature both mistifies and mystifies at once.

In poetry, a pun may be facetious, as in Thomas Hood's ballad of "Faithless Nelly Gray":

> Ben Battle was a soldier bold,
>   And used to war's alarms;
> But a cannon-ball took off his legs,
>   So he laid down his arms!

Or it may be serious, as in these lines on war by E. E. Cummings:

> the bigness of cannon
> is skilful,

(*is skilful* becoming *is kill-ful* when read aloud), or perhaps, as in Shakespeare's song in *Cymbeline*, "Fear no more the heat o' th' sun," both facetious and serious at once:

> Golden lads and girls all must,
> As chimney-sweepers, come to dust.

Poets often make puns on images, thereby combining the sensory force of imagery with the verbal pleasure of wordplay.

To sum up: even though figures of speech are not to be taken *only* literally, they refer us to a tangible world. By *personifying* an eagle, Tennyson reminds us that the bird and humankind have certain characteristics in common. Through *hyperbole* and *understatement*, a poet can make us see the physical actuality in back of words. *Pun* causes us to realize this actuality, too, and probably surprise us enjoyably at the same time. Through *apostrophe*, the poet animates the inanimate and asks it to listen—speaks directly to an immediate god or to the revivified dead. Put to such uses, figures of speech have power. They are more than just ways of playing with words.

Dana Gioia (b. 1950)

Money 1991

Money is a kind of poetry.
—Wallace Stevens

Money, the long green,
cash, stash, rhino, jack
or just plain dough.

Chock it up, fork it over,
shell it out. Watch it
burn holes through pockets.

To be made of it! To have it
to burn! Greenbacks, double eagles,
megabucks and Ginnie Maes.

It greases the palm, feathers a nest,
holds heads above water,
makes both ends meet.

Money breeds money.
Gathering interest, compounding daily.
Always in circulation.

Money. You don't know where it's been,
but you put it where your mouth is.
And it talks.

Question

What figures of speech can you identify in this poem?

Carl Sandburg (1878–1967)

Fog 1916

The fog comes
on little cat feet.

It sits looking
over harbor and city
on silent haunches
and then moves on.

Questions

1. What figure of speech does this poem use?
2. Which specific feline qualities does the speaker impute to the fog?

FOR REVIEW AND FURTHER STUDY

Exercise: Figures of Speech

Identify the central figure of speech in each of the following short poems.

Robert Frost (1874–1963)

A Patch of Old Snow 1916

There's a patch of old snow in a corner
 That I should have guessed
Was a blow-away paper the rain
 Had brought to rest.

It is speckled with grime as if
 Small print overspread it,
The news of a day I've forgotten—
 If I ever read it.

Kay Ryan (b. 1945)

Turtle 1994

Who would be a turtle who could help it?
A barely mobile hard roll, a four-oared helmet,
she can ill afford the chances she must take
in rowing toward the grasses that she eats.
Her track is graceless, like dragging
a packing case places, and almost any slope
defeats her modest hopes. Even being practical,
she's often stuck up to the axle on her way
to something edible. With everything optimal,
she skirts the ditch which would convert
her shell into a serving dish. She lives
below luck-level, never imagining some lottery
will change her load of pottery to wings.
Her only levity is patience,
the sport of truly chastened things.

Emily Brontë (1818–1848)

Love and Friendship (1839)

Love is like the wild rose-briar;
Friendship like the holly-tree—

The holly is dark when the rose-briar blooms
But which will bloom most constantly?

The wild rose-briar is sweet in spring,
Its summer blossoms scent the air;
Yet wait till winter comes again
And who will call the wild-briar fair?

Then scorn the silly rose-wreath now
And deck thee with the holly's sheen,
That when December blights thy brow
He still may leave thy garland green.

John Keats (1795–1821)

Ode on a Grecian Urn

1820

Thou still unravished bride of quietness,
  Thou foster-child of silence and slow time,
Sylvan historian, who canst thus express
  A flowery tale more sweetly than our rhyme:
What leaf-fringed legend haunts about thy shape
  Of deities or mortals, or of both,
    In Tempe or the dales of Arcady?
  What men or gods are these? What maidens loth?
What mad pursuit? What struggle to escape?
    What pipes and timbrels? What wild ecstasy?

Heard melodies are sweet, but those unheard
  Are sweeter; therefore, ye soft pipes, play on;
Not to the sensual° ear, but, more endeared, *physical*
  Pipe to the spirit ditties of no tone:
Fair youth, beneath the trees, thou canst not leave
  Thy song, nor ever can those trees be bare;
    Bold Lover, never, never canst thou kiss,
Though winning near the goal—yet, do not grieve;
    She cannot fade, though thou hast not thy bliss,
  For ever wilt thou love, and she be fair!

Ah, happy, happy boughs! that cannot shed
  Your leaves, nor ever bid the Spring adieu;
And, happy melodist, unwearièd,
  For ever piping songs for ever new;
More happy love! more happy, happy love!
  For ever warm and still to be enjoyed,
    For ever panting, and for ever young;

All breathing human passion far above,
That leaves a heart high-sorrowful and cloyed,
A burning forehead, and a parching tongue.

Who are these coming to the sacrifice?
To what green altar, O mysterious priest,
Lead'st thou that heifer lowing at the skies,
And all her silken flanks with garlands drest?
What little town by river or sea shore,
Or mountain-built with peaceful citadel,
Is emptied of this folk, this pious morn?
And, little town, thy streets for evermore
Will silent be; and not a soul to tell
Why thou art desolate, can e'er return.

O Attic shape! Fair attitude! with brede° *design*
Of marble men and maidens overwrought,
With forest branches and the trodden weed;
Thou, silent form, dost tease us out of thought
As doth eternity: Cold Pastoral!
When old age shall this generation waste,
Thou shalt remain, in midst of other woe
Than ours, a friend to man, to whom thou say'st,
Beauty is truth, truth beauty,—that is all
Ye know on earth, and all ye need to know.

ODE ON A GRECIAN URN. 7 *Tempe, dales of Arcady:* valleys in Greece. 41 *Attic:* Athenian, possessing a classical simplicity and grace. 49–50: if Keats had put the urn's words in quotation marks, critics might have been spared much ink. Does the urn say just "beauty is truth, truth beauty," or does its statement take in the whole of the last two lines?

WRITING *effectively*

THINKING ABOUT METAPHORS

Metaphors are more than mere decoration. Sometimes, for example, they help us envision an unfamiliar thing more clearly by comparing it with another, more familiar item. A metaphor can reveal interesting aspects of both items. Usually we can see the main point of a good metaphor immediately, but in interpreting a poem, the practical issue sometimes arises of how far to extend a comparison.

- **To write effectively about a metaphorical poem, start by considering the general scope of its key metaphor.** In what ways, for instance, do the characters resemble deer in N. Scott Momaday's "Simile"?
- **Before you begin to write, clarify which aspects of the comparison are true and which are false.** While the characters in Momaday's poem may resemble alert, anxious deer in their emotional response to their conflict, they probably don't actually have hooves and forward-pointing ears.
- **Make a list of metaphors and key images in the poem.** Then draw lines to connect the ones that seem to be related.
- **Notice whether there are obvious connections among all the metaphors or similes in a poem.** Perhaps all of them are threatening, or inviting, or nocturnal, or exaggerated. Such similarities, if they occur, will almost certainly be significant.

CHECKLIST: Writing About Metaphors

- ☐ Underline a poem's key comparisons. Look for both similes and metaphors.
- ☐ How are the two things being compared alike?
- ☐ In what ways are the two things unlike each other?
- ☐ Do the metaphors or similes in the poem have anything in common?
- ☐ If so, what does that commonality suggest?

TOPICS FOR WRITING ON FIGURES OF SPEECH

1. In a brief essay of approximately 500 words, analyze the figures of speech to be found in any poem in this chapter. To what effect does the poem employ metaphors, similes, hyperbole, overstatement, paradox, or any other figure of speech?
2. Whip up some similes of your own. Choose someone likely to be unfamiliar to your classmates—your brother or your best friend from home, for example. Write a paragraph in which you use multiple metaphors and similes to communicate a sense of what that person looks, sounds, and acts like. Come up with at least one figure of speech in each sentence.
3. Write a paragraph on any topic, tossing in as many hyperbolic statements as possible. Then write another version, changing all your exaggeration to understatement. In one last paragraph, sum up what this experience taught you about figurative language.
4. Rewrite a short poem rich in figurative language: for example, William Shakespeare's "Shall I compare thee to a summer's day?" or Sylvia Plath's "Metaphors." Taking for your model Howard Moss's deliberately bepiddling version of Shakespeare's poem, use language as flat and unsuggestive as possible. Eliminate every figure of speech. (Ignore any rime or rhythm in the original.) Then, in a paragraph, indicate lines in your revised version that seem glaringly worsened. In conclusion, sum up what your barbaric rewrite tells you about the nature of poetry.

▶ TERMS FOR *review*

Simile and Metaphor

Simile ▶ A comparison of two things, indicated by some connective, usually *like*, *as*, or *than*, or a verb such as *resembles*. A simile usually compares two things that initially seem unlike but are shown to have a significant resemblance. "Cool as a cucumber" and "My love is like a red, red rose" are examples of similes.

Metaphor ▶ A statement that one thing *is* something else, which, in a literal sense, it is not. A metaphor creates a close association between the two entities and underscores some important similarity between them. An example of metaphor is "Richard is a pig."

Implied metaphor ▶ A metaphor that uses neither connectives nor the verb *to be*. If we say "John crowed over his victory," we imply metaphorically that John is a rooster but do not say so specifically.

Mixed metaphor ▶ The (usually unintentional) combining of two or more incompatible metaphors, resulting in ridiculousness or nonsense. For example, "Mary was such a tower of strength that she breezed her way through all the work." ("Towers" do not "breeze.")

Other Figures of Speech

Personification ▶ The endowing of a thing, an animal, or an abstract term with human characteristics. Personification dramatizes the nonhuman world in tangibly human terms.

Apostrophe ▶ A direct address to someone or something. In an apostrophe, a speaker may address an inanimate object, a dead or absent person, an abstract thing, or a spirit.

Overstatement ▶ Also called **hyperbole**. Exaggeration used to emphasize a point.

Understatement ▶ An ironic figure of speech that deliberately describes something in a way that is less than the case.

Pun ▶ A play on words, usually for humorous effect, in which one word is substituted for another of similar or identical sound but of very different meaning.

16 SOUND

What You Will Learn in This Chapter

- To recognize and define *alliteration* and *assonance*
- To differentiate and define *euphony*, *cacophony*, and *onomatopoeia*
- To recognize and define the major types of *rime*
- To analyze the role of sound in a poem

SOUND AS MEANING

Isak Dinesen, in a memoir of her life on a plantation in East Africa, tells how some Kikuyu tribesmen reacted to their first hearing of rimed verse:

> The Natives, who have a strong sense of rhythm, know nothing of verse, or at least did not know anything before the times of the schools, where they were taught hymns. One evening out in the maize-field, where we had been harvesting maize, breaking off the cobs and throwing them on to the ox-carts, to amuse myself, I spoke to the field laborers, who were mostly quite young, in Swahili verse. There was no sense in the verse, it was made for the sake of the rime—"Ngumbe na-penda chumbe, Malaya-mbaya. Wakamba nakula mamba." The oxen like salt—whores are bad,—The Wakamba do eat snakes. It caught the interest of the boys, they formed a ring round me. They were quick to understand that the meaning in poetry is of no consequence, and they did not question the thesis of the verse, but waited eagerly for the rime, and laughed at it when it came. I tried to make them themselves find the rime and finish the poem when I had begun it, but they could not, or would not, do that, and turned away their heads. As they had become used to the idea of poetry, they begged: "Speak again. Speak like rain." Why they should feel verse to be like rain I do not know. It must have been, however, an expression of applause, since in Africa rain is always longed for and welcomed.[1]

What the tribesmen had discovered is that poetry, like music, appeals to the ear. However limited it may be in comparison with the sound of an orchestra—or a tribal drummer—the sound of words in itself gives pleasure.

[1]Isak Dinesen, *Out of Africa* (New York: Random, 1972).

However, we might doubt Isak Dinesen's assumption that "meaning in poetry is of no consequence." "Hey nonny-nonny" and such nonsense has a place in song lyrics and other poems, and we might take pleasure in hearing rimes in Swahili; but most good poetry has meaningful sound as well as musical sound. Certainly the words of a song have an effect different from that of wordless music: they go along with their music and, by making statements, add more meaning. In the response of the Kikuyu tribesmen, there may have been not only the pleasure of hearing sounds but also the agreeable surprise of finding that things not usually associated had been brought together.

Euphony and Cacophony

More powerful when in the company of meaning, not apart from it, the sounds of consonants and vowels can contribute greatly to a poem's effect. The sound of s, which can suggest the swishing of water, has rarely been used more accurately than in Surrey's line "Calm is the sea, the waves work less and less." When, in a poem, the sound of words working together with meaning pleases mind and ear, the effect is **euphony**, as in the following lines from Tennyson's "Come down, O maid":

> Myriads of rivulets hurrying through the lawn,
> The moan of doves in immemorial elms,
> And murmuring of innumerable bees.

Its opposite is **cacophony**: a harsh, discordant effect. It too is chosen for the sake of meaning. We hear it in Milton's scornful reference in "Lycidas" to corrupt clergymen whose songs "Grate on their scrannel pipes of wretched straw." (Read that line and one of Tennyson's aloud and see which requires lips, teeth, and tongue to do more work.) But note that although Milton's line is harsh in sound, the line (when we meet it in his poem) is pleasing because it is artful.

Is sound identical with meaning in lines such as these? Not quite. In the passage from Tennyson, for instance, the cooing of doves is not *exactly* a moan. As John Crowe Ransom pointed out, the sound would be almost the same but the meaning entirely different in "The murdering of innumerable beeves." While it is true that the consonant sound *sl-* will often begin a word that conveys ideas of wetness and smoothness—*slick*, *slimy*, *slippery*, *slush*—we are so used to hearing it in words that convey nothing of the kind—*slave*, *slow*, *sledgehammer*—that it is doubtful whether, all by itself, the sound communicates anything definite. The most beautiful phrase in the English language, according to Dorothy Parker, is *cellar door*. Another wit once nominated, as our most euphonious word, not *sunrise* or *silvery* but *syphilis*.

Onomatopoeia

Relating sound more closely to meaning, the device called **onomatopoeia** is an attempt to represent a thing or action by a word that imitates the sound associated with it: *zoom*, *whiz*, *crash*, *bang*, *ding-dong*, *pitter-patter*, *yakety-yak*.

Onomatopoeia is often effective in poetry, as in Emily Dickinson's line about the fly with its "uncertain stumbling Buzz," in which the nasal sounds *n*, *m*, *ng* and the sibilants *c*, *s* help make a droning buzz.

Like the Kikuyu tribesmen, others who care for poetry have discovered in the sound of words something of the refreshment of cool rain. Dylan Thomas, describing how he began to write poetry, said that from early childhood words were to him "as the notes of bells, the sounds of musical instruments, the noises of wind, sea, and rain, the rattle of milk carts, the clopping of hooves on cobbles, the fingering of branches on the window pane, might be to someone, deaf from birth, who has miraculously found his hearing."[2] For readers, too, the sound of words can have a magical spell, most powerful when it points to meaning.

William Butler Yeats (1865–1939)

Who Goes with Fergus? 1892

Who will go drive with Fergus now,
And pierce the deep wood's woven shade,
And dance upon the level shore?
Young man, lift up your russet brow,
And lift your tender eyelids, maid,

And brood on hopes and fear no more.
And no more turn aside and brood
Upon love's bitter mystery;
For Fergus rules the brazen cars,° *chariots*
And rules the shadows of the wood,
And the white breast of the dim sea
And all dishevelled wandering stars.

WHO GOES WITH FERGUS? *Fergus:* Irish king who gave up his throne to be a wandering poet.

Questions

1. In what lines do you find euphony?
2. In what line do you find cacophony?
3. How do the sounds of these lines stress what is said in them?

Exercise: Listening to Meaning

Read aloud the following brief poems. In the sounds of which particular words are meanings well captured? In which of the two poems do you find onomatopoeia?

[2] "Notes on the Art of Poetry," *Modern Poetics*, ed. James Scully (New York: McGraw-Hill, 1965).

Edgar Allan Poe (1809–1849)

from Ulalume 1847

The skies they were ashen and sober;
  The leaves they were crispéd and sere—
  The leaves they were withering and sere;
It was night, in the lonesome October
  Of my most immemorial year;
It was hard by the dim lake of Auber,
  In the misty mid region of Weir—
It was down by the dank tarn of Auber,
  In the ghoul-haunted woodland of Weir.

William Wordsworth (1770–1850)

A Slumber Did My Spirit Seal 1800

A slumber did my spirit seal;
  I had no human fears—
She seemed a thing that could not feel
  The touch of earthly years.

No motion has she now, no force;
  She neither hears nor sees;
Rolled round in earth's diurnal course,
  With rocks, and stones, and trees.

ALLITERATION AND ASSONANCE

Listening to a symphony in which themes are repeated throughout each movement, we enjoy both their recurrence and their variation. We take similar pleasure in the repetition of a phrase or a single chord. Something like this pleasure is afforded us frequently in poetry.

Analogies between poetry and wordless music, it is true, tend to break down when carried far, since poetry—to mention a single difference—has words with literal meanings. But like musical compositions, poems have patterns of sounds. Among such patterns long popular in English poetry is **alliteration**, which has been defined as a succession of similar sounds. Alliteration occurs in the repetition of the same consonant sound at the beginning of successive words—"round and round the rugged rocks the ragged rascal ran." Or it may occur inside the words, as in Milton's description of the gates of Hell:

> On a sudden open fly
> With impetuous recoil and ja*rr*ing sound
> The infernal doo*r*s, and on thei*r* hinges g*r*ate
> Ha*r*sh thunde*r*, that the lowest bottom shook
> Of E*r*ebus.

The former kind is called **initial alliteration**, the latter **internal alliteration** or **hidden alliteration**. We recognize alliteration by sound, not by spelling: *know* and *nail* alliterate, *know* and *key* do not. In a line by E. E. Cummings, "colossal hoax of clocks and calendars," the sound of *x* within *hoax* alliterates with the *cks* in clo*cks*.

As we have seen, to repeat the sound of a consonant is to produce alliteration, but to repeat the sound of a *vowel* is to produce **assonance**. Like alliteration, assonance may occur either initially—"*a*ll the *aw*ful *au*guries"—or internally—Edmund Spenser's "Her goodly *eyes* l*i*ke sapph*i*res sh*i*ning br*i*ght, / Her forehead *i*vory wh*i*te . . ."—and it can help make common phrases unforgettable: "eager beaver," "holy smoke." Like alliteration, it slows the reader down and focuses attention.

Frances Cornford (1886–1960)

The Watch 1910

I wakened on my hot, hard bed,
Upon the pillow lay my head;
Beneath the pillow I could hear
My little watch was ticking clear.
I thought the throbbing of it went
Like my continual discontent;
I thought it said in every tick:
I am so sick, so sick, so sick;
O Death, come quick, come quick, come quick,
Come quick, come quick, come quick, come quick.

Questions

1. Read the poem aloud, and identify examples of internal alliteration.
2. What do the hard *ck* sounds at the end of the poem resemble, and how does that fit with the poem's theme and subject?

Experiment: Reading for Assonance

Try reading aloud as rapidly as possible the following poem by Tennyson. From the difficulties you encounter, you may be able to sense the slowing effect of assonance. Then read the poem aloud a second time, with consideration.

Alfred, Lord Tennyson (1809–1892)

The splendor falls on castle walls 1847

The splendor falls on castle walls
    And snowy summits old in story:
The long light shakes across the lakes,
    And the wild cataract leaps in glory.

Blow, bugle, blow, set the wild echoes flying,
Blow, bugle; answer, echoes, dying, dying, dying.

O hark, O hear! how thin and clear,
And thinner, clearer, farther going!
O sweet and far from cliff and scar° *jutting rock*
The horns of Elfland faintly blowing!
Blow, let us hear the purple glens replying:
Blow, bugle; answer, echoes, dying, dying, dying.

O love, they die in yon rich sky,
They faint on hill or field or river:
Our echoes roll from soul to soul,
And grow for ever and for ever.
Blow, bugle, blow, set the wild echoes flying,
And answer, echoes, answer, dying, dying, dying.

RIME

Isak Dinesen's tribesmen, to whom rime was a new phenomenon, recognized at once that rimed language is special language. So do we, for, although much English poetry is unrimed, rime is one means of setting poetry apart from ordinary conversation and bringing it closer to music. A **rime** (or rhyme), defined most narrowly, occurs when two or more words or phrases contain an identical or similar vowel sound, usually accented, and the consonant sounds (if any) that follow the vowel sound are identical: *hay* and *sleigh*, *prairie schooner* and *piano tuner*. These examples demonstrate that rime depends not on spelling but on sound.

Excellent rimes surprise. It is all very well that a reader may anticipate which vowel sound is coming next, for patterns of rime give pleasure by satisfying expectations; but riming becomes dull clunking if, at the end of each line, the reader can predict the word that will end the next. Hearing many a jukebox song for the first time, a listener can do so: *charms* lead to *arms*, *skies above* to *love*. As Alexander Pope observes of the habits of dull rimesters,

Where'er you find "the cooling western breeze,"
In the next line it "whispers through the trees";
If crystal streams "with pleasing murmurs creep,"
The reader's threatened (not in vain) with "sleep" . . .

Robert Herrick made good use of rime to indicate a startling contrast:

Then while time serves, and we are but decaying,
Come, my Corinna, come, let's go a-Maying.

Though good rimes seem fresh, not all will startle us, and probably few will call to mind things so unlike as *May* and *decay*. Some masters of rime often link words that, taken out of context, might seem common and unevocative. Here are the opening lines of Rachel Hadas's poem "Three Silences," which describe an infant feeding at a mother's breast:

Of all the times when not to speak is best,
mother's and infant's is the easiest,
the milky mouth still warm against her breast.

Hadas's rimes are not memorable in themselves, and yet these lines are—at least in part because they rime so well. The quiet echo of sound at the end of each line reinforces the intimate tone of the mother's moment with her child. Poetic invention may be driven home without rime, but sometimes it is rime that rings the doorbell.

Some rimes wear thin from too much use. Rimes such as *moon, June, croon* seem leaden and would need an extremely powerful context to ring true. *Death, breath* is a rime that poets have used with wearisome frequency; another is *birth, earth, mirth*. And yet we cannot exclude these from the diction of poetry, for they might be the very words a poet would need in order to say something new and original.

Types of Rime

To have an **exact rime**, sounds following the vowel sound have to be the same: *red* and *bread*, *wealthily* and *stealthily*, *walk to her* and *talk to her*. If final consonant sounds are the same but the vowel sounds are different, the result is **slant rime**, also called **near rime**, **off rime**, or **imperfect rime**: *sun* riming with *bone*, *moon*, *rain*, *green*, *gone*, *thin*. By not satisfying the reader's expectation of an exact chime, but instead giving a clunk, a slant rime can help a poet say some things in a particular way. It works especially well for disappointed letdowns, negations, and denials, as in Blake's couplet:

He who the ox to wrath has moved
Shall never be by woman loved.

Consonance, a kind of slant rime, occurs when the rimed words or phrases have the same beginning and ending consonant sounds but a different vowel, as in *chitter* and *chatter*. Consonance is used in a traditional nonsense poem, "The Cutty Wren": "'O where are you going?' says *Milder* to *Malder*." (W. H. Auden wrote a variation on it that begins, "'O where are you going?' said *reader* to *rider*," thus keeping the consonance.)

End rime, as its name indicates, comes at the ends of lines; **internal rime** within them. Most rime tends to be end rime. Few recent poets have used internal rime so heavily as Wallace Stevens in the beginning of "Bantams in Pine-Woods": "Chieftain Iffucan of Azcan in caftan / Of tan with henna hackles, halt!" (lines also heavy on alliteration). A poet may employ both end rime and internal rime in the same poem, as in Robert Burns's satiric ballad "The Kirk's Alarm":

Orthodox, Orthodox, wha believe in John Knox,
  Let me sound an alarm to your conscience:
A heretic blast has been blawn i' the wast,° *west*
  That "what is not sense must be nonsense."

Masculine rime is a rime of one-syllable words (*jail, bail*) or (in words of more than one syllable) stressed final syllables: *di-VORCE, re-MORSE*, or *horse, re-MORSE*.

Feminine rime is a rime of two or more syllables, with stress on a syllable other than the last: *TUR-tle, FER-tile*, or (to take an example from Byron) *in-tel-LECT-u-al, hen-PECKED you all.* Often it lends itself to comic verse, but it can occasionally be valuable to serious poems, as in Wordsworth's "Resolution and Independence":

We poets in our youth begin in gladness,
But thereof come in the end despondency and madness.

Artfully used, feminine rime can give a poem a heightened musical effect for the simple reason that it offers the listener twice as many riming syllables in each line. In the wrong hands, however, that sonic abundance can make a bad poem twice as painful to endure. Serious poems containing feminine rimes of three syllables have been attempted, notably by Thomas Hood in "The Bridge of Sighs":

Take her up tenderly,
Lift her with care;
Fashioned so slenderly,
Young, and so fair!

But the pattern is hard to sustain without lapsing into unintended comedy, as in the same poem:

Still, for all slips of hers,
One of Eve's family—
Wipe those poor lips of hers,
Oozing so clammily.

It works better when the comedy is intentional.

Hilaire Belloc (1870–1953)

The Hippopotamus 1896

I shoot the Hippopotamus
  with bullets made of platinum,
Because if I use leaden ones
  his hide is sure to flatten 'em.

Bob Kaufman (1925–1986)

No More Jazz at Alcatraz (1967)

No More Jazz
at Alcatraz
No more piano
for Lucky Luciano
No more trombone
for Al Capone
No More Jazz
at Alcatraz
No more cello
for Frank Costello
No more screeching of the
Seagulls
As they line up for
Chow
No More Jazz
at Alcatraz

NO MORE JAZZ AT ALCATRAZ. *Alcatraz*: maximum security federal prison on an island in the San Francisco Bay, closed down in 1963; now a popular tourist attraction. The prison once had an all-inmate jazz band. 4, 6, 10 *Lucky Luciano, Al Capone, Frank Costello*: famous Mafia gangsters.

Questions

1. What is unusual about Kaufman's rimes?
2. The poem describes one of the harshest prisons in American history. What is surprising about the poem's mood? How does the poet achieve that effect?

David Barber (b. 1960)

Aria 2013

What if it were possible to vanquish
All this shame with a wash of varnish
Instead of wishing the stain would vanish?

What if you gave it a glossy finish?
What if there were a way to burnish
All this foolishness, all the anguish?

What if you gave yourself leave to ravish
All these ravages with famished relish?
What if this were your way to flourish?

What if the self you love to punish—
Knavish, peevish, wolfish, sheepish—
Were all slicked up in something lavish?

Why so squeamish? Why make a fetish
Out of everything you must relinquish?
Why not embellish what you can't abolish?

What would be left if you couldn't brandish
All the slavishness you've failed to banish?
What would you be without this gibberish?

What if the true worth of the varnish
Were to replenish your resolve to vanquish
Every vain wish before you vanish?

Gerard Manley Hopkins (1844–1889)

God's Grandeur (1877)

The world is charged with the grandeur of God.
  It will flame out, like shining from shook foil;
  It gathers to a greatness, like the ooze of oil
Crushed. Why do men then now not reck his rod?
Generations have trod, have trod, have trod;
  And all is seared with trade; bleared, smeared with toil;
  And wears man's smudge and shares man's smell: the soil
Is bare now, nor can foot feel, being shod.

And for all this, nature is never spent;
  There lives the dearest freshness deep down things;
And though the last lights off the black West went
  Oh, morning, at the brown brink eastward, springs—
Because the Holy Ghost over the bent
  World broods with warm breast and with ah! bright wings.

God's Grandeur. 1 *charged:* as though with electricity. 3–4 *It gathers . . . Crushed:* The grandeur of God will rise and be manifest, as oil rises and collects from crushed olives or grain. 4 *reck his rod:* heed His law. 10 *deep down things:* Tightly packing the poem, Hopkins omits the preposition *in* or *within* before *things*. 11 *last lights . . . went:* When in 1534 Henry VIII broke ties with the Roman Catholic Church and created the Church of England.

Questions

1. In a letter Hopkins explained "shook foil" (line 2): "I mean foil in its sense of leaf or tinsel. . . . Shaken goldfoil gives off broad glares like sheet lightning and also, and this is true of nothing else, owing to its zigzag dints and creasings and network of small many cornered facets, a sort of fork lightning too." What do you think he meant by the phrase "ooze of oil" (line 3)? Would you call this phrase an example of alliteration?

2. What instances of internal rime does the poem contain? How would you describe their effects?
3. Point out some of the poet's uses of alliteration and assonance. Do you believe that Hopkins perhaps goes too far in his heavy use of devices of sound, or would you defend his practice?
4. Why do you suppose Hopkins, in the last two lines, says "over the bent / World" instead of (as we might expect) *bent over the world*? How can the world be bent? Can you make any sense out of this wording, or is Hopkins just trying to get his rime scheme to work out?

HOW TO READ A POEM ALOUD

There is no better way to understand a poem than to read it aloud. Developing skill at reading poems aloud will not only deepen your understanding of literature, but it will also improve your ability to speak in public.

Before trying to read a poem aloud to other people, understand its meaning as thoroughly as possible. If you know what the poet is saying and the poet's attitude toward it, you will be able to find an appropriate tone of voice and to give each part of the poem a proper emphasis.

Except in the most informal situations and in some class exercises, read a poem to yourself before trying it on an audience. No actor goes before the footlights without first having studied the script, and the language of poems usually demands even more consideration than the language of most contemporary plays. Prepare your reading in advance. Check pronunciations you are not sure of. Underline words that should be emphasized.

Read more slowly than you normally would. Keep in mind that you are saying something to somebody. Don't race through the poem as if you are eager to get it over with.

Don't lapse into singsong. A poem may have a definite swing, but swing should never be exaggerated at the cost of sense. If you understand what the poem is saying and speak the poem as if you do, the temptation to fall into such a mechanical intonation should not occur. Observe the punctuation, making slight pauses for commas and longer pauses for full stops (periods, question marks, exclamation points).

If the poem is rimed, don't raise your voice and make the rimes stand out unnaturally. They should receive no more volume than other words in the poem, though a faint pause at the end of each line will call the listener's attention to them.

If, in first listening to a poem, you don't take in all its meaning, don't be discouraged. With more practice in listening, your attention span and your ability to understand poems read aloud will increase. Incidentally, following the text of poems in a book while hearing them read aloud may increase your comprehension, but it may not necessarily help you to *listen*. At least some of the time, close your book and let your ears make the poems welcome. That way, their sounds may better work for you.

Gerard Manley Hopkins (1844–1889)

Spring and Fall (1880)

To a young child

Márgarét, áre you gríeving
Over Goldengrove unleaving?° *shedding its leaves*
Leáves, líke the things of man, you
With your fresh thoughts care for, can you?
Áh! ás the heart grows older
It will come to such sights colder
By and by, nor spare a sigh
Though worlds of wanwood leafmeal lie;
And yet you wíll weep and know why.
Now no matter, child, the name:
Sórrow's spríngs áre the same.
Nor mouth had, no nor mind, expressed
What heart heard of, ghost° guessed: *spirit*
It ís the blight man was born for,
It is Margaret you mourn for.

Exercise: Reading for Sound and Meaning

Read this brief poem aloud. What devices of sound do you find? Try to explain what sound contributes to the total effect of the poem and how it reinforces what the poet is saying.

Michael Stillman (b. 1940)

In Memoriam John Coltrane 1972

Listen to the coal
rolling, rolling through the cold
steady rain, wheel on

wheel, listen to the
turning of the wheels this night
black as coal dust, steel

on steel, listen to
these cars carry coal, listen
to the coal train roll.

IN MEMORIAM JOHN COLTRANE. John Coltrane (1926–1967) was a saxophonist whose originality, passion, and technical wizardry have had a deep influence on the history of modern jazz.

WRITING *effectively*

THINKING ABOUT A POEM'S SOUND

A poem's music—the distinct way it sounds—is an important element of its effect and a large part of what separates it from prose. Describing a poem's sound can be tricky, though. Critics often disagree about the sonic effects of particular poems. Cataloguing every auditory element of a poem would be a huge, unwieldy job. The easiest way to write about sound is to focus your discussion. Concentrate on a single, clearly defined sonic element that strikes you as especially noteworthy. Simply try to understand how that element helps communicate the poem's main theme.

- **You might examine, for example, how certain features (such as rime, rhythm, meter, or alliteration) add force to the literal meaning of each line.** Or, for an ironic poem, you might look at how those same elements undercut and change the surface meaning of the poem.
- **Keep in mind that for a detailed analysis of this sort, it often helps to choose a short poem.** If you want to write about a longer poem, focus on a short passage that strikes you as especially rich in sonic effects.
- **Let your data build up before you force any conclusions about the poem's auditory effects.** As your list grows, a pattern should emerge, and ideas will probably occur to you that were not apparent earlier.

CHECKLIST: Writing About a Poem's Sound

- ☐ List the main auditory elements you find in the poem.
- ☐ Look for rime, meter, alliteration, assonance, euphony, cacophony, repetition, onomatopoeia.
- ☐ Is there a pattern in your list? Is the poem particularly heavy in alliteration or repetition, for example?
- ☐ Limit your discussion to one or two clearly defined sonic effects.
- ☐ How do your chosen effects help communicate the poem's main theme?
- ☐ How does the sound of the words add to the poem's mood?

TOPICS FOR WRITING ON SOUND

1. Choose a brief poem from this chapter or Chapter 23 and examine how one or two elements of sound work throughout the poem to strengthen its meaning. Before you write, review the elements of sound described in this chapter. Back up your argument with specific quotations from the poem.
2. Silently read Dylan Thomas's "Fern Hill" (Chapter 23). Then read the poem aloud, to yourself or to a friend. Now write briefly. What did you perceive about the poem from reading it aloud that you hadn't noticed before?
3. Consider the verbal music of Michael Stillman's "In Memoriam John Coltrane" (or a selection from Chapter 23). Read the poem both silently and aloud, listening for sonic effects. Describe how the poem's sound underscores its meaning.

▶ TERMS FOR *review*

Sound Effects

Alliteration ▶ The repetition of a consonant sound in a line of verse or prose. Alliteration can be used at the beginning of words (**initial alliteration** as in "cool cats") or internally on stressed syllables (**internal alliteration** as in "I met a traveler from an antique land.").

Assonance ▶ The repetition of two or more vowel sounds in successive words, which creates a kind of rime. Like alliteration, the assonance may occur initially ("*a*ll the *aw*ful *au*guries") or internally ("wh*i*te l*i*lacs").

Cacophony ▶ A harsh, discordant sound often mirroring the meaning of the context in which it is used. The opposite of cacophony is **euphony.**

Euphony ▶ The harmonious effect when the sounds of the words connect with the meaning in a way pleasing to the ear and mind. The opposite of euphony is **cacophony.**

Onomatopoeia ▶ An attempt to represent a thing or action by a word that imitates the sound associated with it.

Rime

Rime ▶ Two or more words that contain an identical or similar vowel sound, usually accented, with following consonant sounds (if any) identical as well (*woo* and *stew*). An **exact rime** is a full rime in which the sounds following the initial letters of the words are identical in sound (*follow* and *hollow*).

Consonance ▶ Also called **slant rime.** A kind of rime in which the linked words share similar consonant sounds but have different vowel sounds, as in *reason* and *raisin*, *mink* and *monk*. Sometimes only the final consonant sound is identical, as in *fame* and *room*.

End rime ▶ Rime that occurs at the ends of lines, rather than within them. End rime is the most common kind of rime in English-language poetry.

Internal rime ▶ Rime that occurs within a line of poetry, as opposed to **end rime.**

Masculine rime ▶ Either a rime of one-syllable words (*fox* and *socks*) or—in polysyllabic words—a rime on the stressed final syllables (con-*trive* and sur-*vive*).

Feminine rime ▶ A rime of two or more syllables with stress on a syllable other than the last (*tur*-tle and *fer*-tile).

17 RHYTHM

What You Will Learn in This Chapter

- To define *rhythm* and *stress*
- To define *prosody* and *scansion*
- To recognize and define the four major English meters
- To analyze the role of rhythm in a poem

STRESSES AND PAUSES

Rhythms affect us powerfully. We are lulled by a hammock's sway, awakened by an alarm clock's repeated yammer. Long after we come home from a beach, the rising and falling of waves and tides continue in memory. How powerfully the rhythms of poetry also move us may be felt in folk songs of railroad workers and chain gangs whose words were chanted in time to the lifting and dropping of a sledgehammer, and in verse that marching soldiers shout, putting a stress on every word that coincides with a footfall:

> Your LEFT! TWO! THREE! FOUR!
> Your LEFT! TWO! THREE! FOUR!
> You LEFT your WIFE and TWEN-ty-one KIDS
> And you LEFT! TWO! THREE! FOUR!
> You'll NEV-er get HOME to-NIGHT!

A rhythm is produced by a series of recurrences: the returns and departures of the seasons, the repetitions of an engine's stroke, the beats of the heart. A rhythm may be produced by the recurrence of a sound (the throb of a drum, a telephone's busy signal), but rhythm and sound are not identical. A totally deaf person at a parade can sense rhythm from the motions of the marchers' arms and feet, from the shaking of the pavement as they tramp. Rhythms inhere in the motions of the moon and stars, even though when they move, we hear no sound.

Rhythm

In poetry, several kinds of recurrent *sound* are possible, including (as we saw in the previous chapter) rime, alliteration, and assonance. But most often when we speak of the **rhythm** of a poem, we mean the recurrence of stresses and pauses in it. When we hear a poem read aloud, stresses and pauses are, of course, part of its sound. It is possible to be aware of rhythms in poems read silently, too.

Stresses

A **stress** (or **accent**) is a greater amount of force given to one syllable in speaking than is given to another. We favor a stressed syllable with a little more breath and emphasis, with the result that it comes out slightly louder, higher in pitch, or longer in duration than other syllables. In this manner we place a stress on the first syllable of words such as *eagle*, *impact*, *open*, and *statue*, and on the second syllable in *cigar*, *mystique*, *precise*, and *until*.

Each word in English carries at least one stress, except (usually) for the articles *a*, *an*, and *the*, the conjunction *and*, and one-syllable prepositions: *at*, *by*, *for*, *from*, *of*, *to*, *with*. One word by itself is seldom long enough for us to notice a rhythm in it. Usually a sequence of at least a few words is needed for stresses to establish their pattern: a line, a passage, a whole poem.

Strong rhythms may be seen in most Mother Goose rimes, to which children have been responding for hundreds of years. This rime is for an adult to chant while bouncing a child up and down on a knee:

  Here goes my lord
A trot, a trot, a trot, a trot!
  Here goes my lady
A canter, a canter, a canter, a canter!
  Here goes my young master
Jockey-hitch, jockey-hitch, jockey-hitch, jockey-hitch!
  Here goes my young miss
An amble, an amble, an amble, an amble!
  The footman lags behind to tipple ale and wine
And goes gallop, a gallop, a gallop, to make up his time.

More than one rhythm occurs in these lines, as the make-believe horse changes pace. How do these rhythms differ? From one line to the next, the interval between stresses lengthens or grows shorter. In "a TROT a TROT a TROT a TROT," the stress falls on every other syllable. But in the middle of the line "A CAN-ter a CAN-ter a CAN-ter a CAN-ter," the stress falls on every third syllable. When stresses recur at fixed intervals as in these lines, the result is called a **meter**.

STRESS AND MEANING

Stresses embody meanings. Whenever two or more fall side by side, words gain in emphasis. Consider these hard-hitting lines from John Donne, in which accent marks have been placed, dictionary-fashion, to indicate the stressed syllables:

Bát·ter my héart, thrée-pér·soned Gód, for Yóu
As yét but knóck, bréathe, shíne, and séek to ménd.
That Í may ríse and stánd, o'er·thrów me, and bénd
Your fórce to bréak, blów, búrn, and máke me néw.

When unstressed (or **slack) syllables** recur in pairs, the result is a rhythm that trips and bounces, as in Robert Service's rollicking line:

A bunch of the boys were whoop·ing it up in the Ma·la·mute sa·loon . . .

or in Edgar Allan Poe's lines—also light but meant to be serious:

For the moon nev·er beams, with·out bring·ing me dreams
Of the beau·ti·ful An·na·bel Lee.

Apart from the words that convey it, the rhythm of a poem has no meaning. There are no essentially sad rhythms, nor any essentially happy ones. But some rhythms enforce certain meanings better than others do. The bouncing rhythm of Service's line seems fitting for an account of a merry night in a Klondike saloon; but it may be distracting when encountered in Poe's wistful elegy.

The special power of poetry comes from allowing us to hear simultaneously every level of meaning in language—denotation and connotation, image and idea, abstract content and physical sound. Since sound stress is one of the ways that the English language most clearly communicates meaning, any regular rhythmic pattern will influence the poem's effect. As film directors know, any movie scene's effect can change dramatically if different background music accompanies the images. Master of the suspense film Alfred Hitchcock, for instance, could fill an ordinary scene with tension or terror just by playing nervous, grating music underneath it.

Exercise: Get with the Beat

Describe how the strong rhythm in these passages helps establish the tone and meaning of the poem.

1. I couldn't be cooler, I come from Missoula,
And I rope and I chew and I ride.
But I'm a heroin dealer, and I drive a four-wheeler
With stereo speakers inside.
My ol' lady Phoebe's out rippin' off C.B.'s
From the rigs at the Wagon Wheel Bar,
Near a Montana truck stop and a shit-outta-luck stop
For a trucker who's driven too far.
— Greg Keeler, from "There Ain't No Such
Thing as a Montana Cowboy" (a song lyric)

2. Oh newsprint moonprint Marilyn!
Rub ink from a finger
to make your beauty mark.
—Rachel Eisler, from "Marilyn's Nocturne"
(a poem about a newspaper photograph of
Marilyn Monroe)

Pauses

Rhythms in poetry are due not only to stresses but also to pauses. "Every nice ear," observed Alexander Pope, "must, I believe, have observed that in any smooth English verse of ten syllables, there is naturally a pause either at the fourth, fifth, or sixth syllable." Such a light but definite pause within a line is called a **cesura** (or **caesura**), Latin for "a cutting." More liberally than Pope, we apply the name to a pause in a line of any length, after any word in the line. In studying a poem, we indicate a cesura by double vertical lines (||). A cesura often occurs at a punctuation mark, but there can be a cesura even if no punctuation is present. Sometimes you will find it at the end of a phrase or clause or, as in these lines by William Blake, after an internal rime:

> And priests in black gowns || were walking their rounds
> And binding with briars || my joys and desires.

Lines of ten or twelve syllables (as Pope knew) tend to have just one cesura, though sometimes there are more, as in John Webster's line from *The Duchess of Malfi*:

> Cover her face: || mine eyes dazzle: || she died young.

LINE ENDINGS

Pauses also tend to recur at more prominent places—namely, after each line. At the end of a verse (from *versus*, Latin for "a turning"), the reader's eye, before turning to go on to the next line, makes a pause, however brief. If a line ends in a full pause—usually indicated by some mark of punctuation—we call it **end-stopped**. All the lines in this passage from Christopher Marlowe's *Doctor Faustus* (in which Faustus addresses the apparition of Helen of Troy) are end-stopped:

> Was this the face that launch'd a thousand ships,
> And burnt the topless towers of Ilium?
> Sweet Helen, make me immortal with a kiss.
> Her lips suck forth my soul: see, where it flies!
> Come, Helen, come, give me my soul again.
> Here will I dwell, for heaven is in these lips,
> And all is dross that is not Helena.

A line that does not end in punctuation and that therefore is read with only a slight pause after it is called a **run-on line**. Because a run-on line gives us only part of a phrase, clause, or sentence, we have to read on to the line or lines following, in order to complete a thought. All these lines from Robert Browning's "My Last Duchess" (Chapter 9) are run-on lines:

Sir, 'twas not
Her husband's presence only, called that spot
Of joy into the Duchess' cheek: perhaps
Frà Pandolf chanced to say "Her mantle laps
Over my lady's wrist too much," or "Paint
Must never hope to reproduce the faint
Half-flush that dies along her throat": such stuff
Was courtesy, she thought . . .

A passage in run-on lines has a rhythm different from that of a passage like Marlowe's in end-stopped lines. When emphatic pauses occur in the quotation from Browning, they fall within a line rather than at the end of one. Marlowe's and Browning's passages are in lines of the same meter (iambic) and the same length (ten syllables). What makes the big difference in their rhythms is the running on, or lack of it.

To sum up: rhythm is recurrence. In poems, it is made of stresses and pauses. The poet can produce it by doing any of several things: making the intervals between stresses fixed or varied, long or short; indicating pauses (cesuras) within lines; end-stopping lines or running them over; writing in short or long lines. Rhythm in itself cannot convey meaning. And yet if a poet's words have meaning, their rhythm must be one with it.

Gwendolyn Brooks (1917–2000)

We Real Cool — 1960

The Pool Players.
Seven at the Golden Shovel.

We real cool. We
Left school. We

Lurk late. We
Strike straight. We

Sing sin. We
Thin gin. We

Jazz June. We
Die soon.

Question

Describe the rhythms of this poem. By what techniques are they produced?

Alfred, Lord Tennyson (1809–1892)

Break, Break, Break (1834)

Break, break, break,
  On thy cold gray stones, O Sea!
And I would that my tongue could utter
  The thoughts that arise in me.

O well for the fisherman's boy,
  That he shouts with his sister at play!
O well for the sailor lad,
  That he sings in his boat on the bay!

And the stately ships go on
  To their haven under the hill;
But O for the touch of a vanish'd hand,
  And the sound of a voice that is still!

Break, break, break,
  At the foot of thy crags, O Sea!
But the tender grace of a day that is dead
  Will never come back to me.

Questions

1. Read the first line aloud. What effect does it create at the beginning of the poem?
2. Is there a regular rhythmic pattern in this poem? If so, how would you describe it?
3. The speaker claims that his or her thoughts are impossible to utter. Using evidence from the poem, can you describe the speaker's thoughts and feelings?

Dorothy Parker (1893–1967)

Résumé 1926

Razors pain you;
Rivers are damp;
Acids stain you;
And drugs cause cramp.
Guns aren't lawful;
Nooses give;
Gas smells awful;
You might as well live.

Questions

1. Which of the following words might be used to describe the rhythm of this poem, and which might not—*flowing, jaunty, mournful, tender, abrupt*?
2. Is this light verse or a serious poem? Can it be both?

METER

Meter is the rhythmic pattern of stresses in verse. To enjoy the rhythms of a poem, no special knowledge of meter is necessary. All you need do is pay attention to stresses and where they fall, and you will perceive the basic pattern, if there is any. There is nothing occult about the study of meter. Most people find they can master its essentials in no more time than it takes to learn a new video game. If you take the time, you will then have the pleasure of knowing what is happening in the rhythms of many a fine poem, and pleasurable knowledge may even deepen your insight into poetry. The study of metrical structures in poetry is called **prosody**.

Scansion

To make ourselves aware of a meter, we need only listen to a poem, or sound its words to ourselves. If we care to work out exactly what a poet is doing, we *scan* a line or a poem by indicating the stresses in it. **Scansion**, the art of so doing, is not just a matter of pointing to syllables; it is also a matter of listening to a poem and making sense of it. To scan a poem is one way to indicate how to read it aloud; in order to see where stresses fall, you have to see the places where the poet wishes to put emphasis. That is why, when scanning a poem, you may find yourself suddenly understanding it.

The idea in scanning a poem is not to reproduce the sound of a human voice. To scan a poem, rather, is to make a diagram of the stresses (and absences of stress) to show its rhythmical shape, its musical beat. Various marks are used in scansion; in this book we use ′ for a stressed syllable and ˘ for an unstressed syllable.

Types of Meter

There are four common accentual-syllabic meters in English: iambic, anapestic, trochaic, and dactylic. Each is named for its basic **foot** (usually a unit of two or three syllables that contains one strong stress) or building block.

1. **Iambic**—the most common meter in English poetry. An iambic line is made up primarily of **iambs**, an unstressed syllable followed by a stressed syllable, ˘ ′. Many writers, such as Robert Frost, feel iambs most easily capture the natural rhythms of our speech.

   ˘ ′ ˘ ′ ˘ ′ ˘ ′ ˘ ′
   But soft, | what light | through yon | der win | dow breaks?
   —*William Shakespeare*

   ˘ ′ ˘ ′ ˘ ′ ˘ ′ ˘ ′
   When I | have fears | that I | may cease | to be
   —*John Keats*

2. **Anapestic**—a galloping meter. The anapestic line is made up primarily of **anapests**, two unstressed syllables followed by a stressed

syllable, ˘˘ ′. Anapestic meter resembles iambic but contains an extra unstressed syllable. Totally anapestic lines often roll with such speed that poets sometimes slow them down by substituting an iambic foot (as Poe does in "Annabel Lee").

> Now this | is the Law | of the Jun | gle—as old | and as true
> | as the sky;
> And the Wolf | that shall keep | it may pros | per, | but the Wolf
> | that shall break | it must die.
>
> —*Rudyard Kipling*

> It was ma | ny and ma | ny a year | a go,
> In a king | dom by | the sea,
> That a maid | en there lived | whom you | may know
> By the name | of An | na·bel Lee.
>
> —*Edgar Allan Poe*

3. **Trochaic**—often associated with songs, chants, and magic spells in English. The trochaic line is made up primarily of **trochees**, a stressed syllable followed by an unstressed syllable, ′ ˘. Trochees make a strong, emphatic meter that is often very mnemonic—that is, "helping, or meant to help, the memory." Shakespeare used trochaic meter to exploit its magical associations.

> Dou·ble, | dou·ble, | toil and | trou·ble,
> Fi·re | burn and | caul·dron | bub·ble.
>
> —*William Shakespeare*

4. **Dactylic**—a less common meter for English poetry, with a gently rolling meter. The dactylic line is made up primarily of **dactyls**, one stressed syllable followed by two unstressed syllables, ′ ˘˘. The dactylic meter is more often found in classical languages such as Greek or Latin. Used carefully, dactylic meter can sound stately, as in Longfellow's *Evangeline*.

> This is the | for·est pri | me·val. The | mur·mur·ing | pines and the
> | hem·lock
>
> —*Henry Wadsworth Longfellow*

But it also easily becomes a prancing, propulsive measure and is often used in comic verse.

> Puss·y·cat, | puss·y·cat, | where have you | been?
>
> —*Mother Goose*

In the twentieth century, the bouncing meters—anapestic and dactylic—were used more often for comic verse than for serious poetry. Called feet, though they contain no unaccented syllables, are the **monosyllabic foot** (′) and the **spondee** (″). Meters are not ordinarily made up of them; if one were, it would be like the steady impact of nails being hammered into a board—no pleasure to hear or to dance to. But inserted now and then, they can lend emphasis and variety to a meter, as Yeats well knew when he broke up the predominantly iambic rhythm of "Who Goes with Fergus?" (Chapter 16) with a line in which two spondees occur.

> And the white breast of the dim sea.

The Poetic Line

Meters are classified also by line lengths: *trochaic monometer*, for instance, is a line one trochee long, as in this anonymous brief comment on microbes:

> Adam
> Had 'em.

A frequently used meter is **iambic pentameter**: a line of five iambs, a meter especially familiar because it occurs in heroic couplets, sonnets, and blank verse (such as Shakespeare's plays and Milton's *Paradise Lost*).

Line Lengths

Here are the commonly used names for line lengths:

monometer	one foot
dimeter	two feet
trimeter	three feet
tetrameter	four feet
pentameter	five feet
hexameter	six feet
heptameter	seven feet
octameter	eight feet

Lines of more than eight feet are possible but are rare. They tend to break up into shorter lengths in the listening ear.

Like a basic dance step, a meter is not to be slavishly adhered to. The fun in reading a metrical poem often comes from watching the poet continually departing from perfect regularity, giving a few heel-kicks to display a bit of joy or ingenuity, then easing back into the basic step again. Because meter is orderly and the rhythms of living speech are unruly, poets can play one against the other, in a sort of counterpoint. Robert Frost, a master at pitting a line of iambs against a very natural-sounding and irregular sentence, declared, "I am never more pleased than when I can get these into strained relation. I like to drag and break the intonation across the meter as waves first comb and then break stumbling on the shingle."[1]

Accentual Meter

Besides iambic, anapestic, trochaic, and dactylic, English poets have another valuable meter, which is commonly found in spoken forms of poetry, such as the ballad and rap music. It is **accentual meter**, in which the poet does not write in feet but instead counts stresses, typically having the same number of stresses in each line. The poet may place them anywhere in the line and may include practically any number of unstressed syllables. In "Christabel," for instance, Coleridge keeps four stresses to a line, though the first line has only eight syllables and the last line has eleven:

> There is nót wínd e·nóugh to twírl
> The óne réd léaf, the lást of its clán,
> That dán·ces as óf·ten as dánce it cán,
> Háng·ing so líght, and háng·ing so hígh,
> On the tóp-most twíg that lóoks úp at the ský.

Meter has seen a great return to popularity in the past many years. Most contemporary poets now explore the rhythmic possibilities of regular meter in their work, following the examples of major poets from Shakespeare through Yeats, who fashioned their work by it. To enjoy metrical poetry—even to write it—you do not have to slice lines into feet; yet you *do* need to recognize when a meter is present in a line, and when the line departs from it. Meter can remind us of body rhythms such as breathing, walking, the beating of the heart. In an effective metrical poem, these rhythms cannot be separated from what the poet is saying—or, in the words of an old jazz song of Duke Ellington's, "It don't mean a thing if it ain't got that swing."

Exercise: Recognizing Rhythms

Which of the following poems contain predominant meters? Which poems are not wholly metrical, but are metrical in certain lines? Point out any such lines. What reasons do you see, in such places, for the poet's seeking a metrical effect?

[1]Letter to John Cournos in 1914, in *Selected Letters of Robert Frost*, ed. Lawrance Thompson (New York: Holt, 1964) 128.

Edith Sitwell (1887–1964)

Mariner Man

1918

"What are you staring at, mariner man,
Wrinkled as sea-sand and old as the sea?"
"Those trains will run over their tails, if they can,
Snorting and sporting like porpoises! Flee
The burly, the whirligig wheels of the train,
As round as the world and as large again,
Running half the way over to Babylon, down
Through fields of clover to gay Troy town—
A-puffing their smoke as grey as the curl
On my forehead as wrinkled as sands of the sea!—
But what can that matter to you, my girl?
(And what can that matter to me?)"

A. E. Housman (1859–1936)

When I was one-and-twenty

1896

When I was one-and-twenty
  I heard a wise man say,
"Give crowns and pounds and guineas
  But not your heart away;
Give pearls away and rubies
  But keep your fancy free."
But I was one-and-twenty,
  No use to talk to me.

When I was one-and-twenty
  I heard him say again,
"The heart out of the bosom
  Was never given in vain;
'Tis paid with sighs a plenty
  And sold for endless rue."
And I am two-and-twenty,
  And oh, 'tis true, 'tis true.

Edgar Allan Poe (1809–1849)

Annabel Lee

1849

It was many and many a year ago,
  In a kingdom by the sea,
That a maiden there lived whom you may know
  By the name of Annabel Lee;

And this maiden she lived with no other thought
  Than to love and be loved by me.

I was a child and *she* was a child,
  In this kingdom by the sea,
But we loved with a love that was more than love—
  I and my Annabel Lee—
With a love that the wingéd seraphs of Heaven
  Coveted her and me.

And this was the reason that, long ago,
  In this kingdom by the sea,
A wind blew out of a cloud, chilling
  My beautiful Annabel Lee;
So that her highborn kinsmen came
  And bore her away from me,
To shut her up in a sepulchre
  In this kingdom by the sea.

The angels, not half so happy in Heaven,
  Went envying her and me:—
Yes!—that was the reason (as all men know,
  In this kingdom by the sea)
That the wind came out of the cloud by night,
  Chilling and killing my Annabel Lee.

But our love it was stronger by far than the love
  Of those who were older than we—
  Of many far wiser than we—
And neither the angels in Heaven above,
  Nor the demons down under the sea,
Can ever dissever my soul from the soul
  Of the beautiful Annabel Lee:—

For the moon never beams, without bringing me dreams
  Of the beautiful Annabel Lee;
And the stars never rise, but I feel the bright eyes
  Of the beautiful Annabel Lee:
And so, all the night-tide, I lie down by the side
Of my darling—my darling—my life and my bride,
  In the sepulchre there by the sea—
  In her tomb by the sounding sea.

Walt Whitman (1819–1892)

Beat! Beat! Drums! (1861)

Beat! beat! drums!—blow! bugles! blow!
Through the windows—through doors—burst like a ruthless force,
Into the solemn church, and scatter the congregation,
Into the school where the scholar is studying;
Leave not the bridegroom quiet—no happiness must he have now with
his bride,
Nor the peaceful farmer any peace, ploughing his field or gathering his
grain,
So fierce you whirr and pound you drums—so shrill you bugles blow.

Beat! beat! drums!—blow! bugles! blow!
Over the traffic of cities—over the rumble of wheels in the streets;
Are beds prepared for sleepers at night in the houses? no sleepers must
sleep in those beds,
No bargainers' bargains by day—no brokers or speculators—would
they continue?
Would the talkers be talking? would the singer attempt to sing?
Would the lawyer rise in the court to state his case before the judge?
Then rattle quicker, heavier drums—you bugles wilder blow.

Beat! beat! drums!—blow! bugles! blow!
Make no parley—stop for no expostulation,
Mind not the timid—mind not the weeper or prayer,
Mind not the old man beseeching the young man,
Let not the child's voice be heard, nor the mother's entreaties,
Make even the trestles to shake the dead where they lie awaiting
the hearses,
So strong you thump O terrible drums—so loud you bugles blow.

WRITING *effectively*

THINKING ABOUT RHYTHM

When we read casually, we don't need to think very hard about a poem's rhythm. We *feel* it as we read, even if we aren't consciously paying attention to matters such as iambs or anapests. When analyzing a poem, though, it helps to have a clear sense of how the rhythm works, and the best way to reach that understanding is through scansion. A scansion gives us a picture of the poem's most important sound patterns. Scanning a poem can seem a bit intimidating at first, but it really isn't all that difficult.

- **Read the poem aloud, marking the stressed syllables as you go.**
- **If you're having a hard time hearing the stresses, read the line a few different ways.** Try to detect which way seems most like natural speech.

***Example*: Tennyson's "Break, Break, Break"**

A simple scansion of the opening of Tennyson's poem might look like this:

Break, break, break	(3 syllables)
On thy cold gray stones, O Sea!	(7 syllables, rime)
And I would that my tongue could utter	(9 syllables)
The thoughts that arise in me.	(7 syllables, rime)

By now some basic organizing principles of the poem have become clear. The lines are rimed *a b c b*, but they contain an irregular number of syllables. The number of strong stresses, however, seems to be constant, at least in the opening stanza.

Now that you have a visual diagram of the poem's sound, the rhythm will be much easier to write about. This diagram will also lead you to a richer understanding of how the poet's artistry reinforces the poem's meaning. The three sharp syllables of the first line give the reader an immediate sense of the depth and intensity of the speaker's feelings. The sudden burst of syllables in the third line underscores the rush of passion that wells up in his breast and outstrips his ability to give voice to it. And the rhythm of the last two lines—the rising intensity of the third line followed by the ebb of the fourth—subtly suggests the effect of the surging and receding of the waves.

CHECKLIST: Scanning a Poem

- ☐ Read the poem aloud.
- ☐ Mark the main speech stresses. When in doubt, read the line aloud several different ways. Which way seems most natural?
- ☐ Are there rimes? Indicate where they occur.
- ☐ How many syllables are there in each line?
- ☐ Do any other recurring sound patterns strike you?
- ☐ Does the poem set up a reliable pattern and then diverge from it? If so, how does that irregularity underscore the line's meaning?

TOPICS FOR WRITING ON RHYTHM

1. Scan the rhythm of a passage from any poem in this chapter, following the guidelines listed above. Discuss how the poem uses rhythm to create certain key effects. Be sure that your scansion shows all the elements you've chosen to discuss.
2. With a classmate, take turns reading a poem from this chapter out loud to each other. Now write briefly on what you learned about the poem's rhythm by speaking and hearing it.
3. How do rhythm and other kinds of sonic effects (alliteration and consonance, for example) combine to make meaning in Edna St. Vincent Millay's "Counting-out Rhyme"?
4. Scan a stanza of Walt Whitman's "Beat! Beat! Drums!" What do you notice about the poem's rhythms? How do the rhythms underscore the poem's meaning?
5. Scan two poems, one in free verse, and the other in regular meter. For a free verse poem you might pick Allen Ginsberg's "A Supermarket in California" (Chapter 22) or Stephen Crane's "The Wayfarer" (Chapter 10); for a poem in regular meter you could go with one of the poems in this chapter, for example, A. E. Housman's "When I was one-and-twenty." Now write about the experience. Do you detect any particular strengths offered by regular meter? How about by free verse?

▶ TERMS FOR *review*

Pattern and Structure

Rhythm ▶ The recurring pattern of stresses and pauses in a poem. A fixed rhythm in a poem is called **meter**.

Stress ▶ An emphasis, or **accent**, placed on a syllable in speech. An unstressed syllable in a line of verse is called a **slack syllable**.

Cesura or caesura ▶ A light but definite pause within a line of verse. Cesuras often appear near the middle of a line, but their placement may be varied for rhythmic effect.

Run-on line ▶ A line of verse that does not end in punctuation but carries on grammatically to the next line. The use of run-on lines is called *enjambment*.

End-stopped line ▶ A line of verse that ends in a full pause, often indicated by a mark of punctuation.

Meter

Prosody ▶ The study of metrical structures in poetry.

Scansion ▶ A practice used to describe rhythmic patterns in a poem by separating the metrical feet, counting the syllables, marking the accents, and indicating the cesuras.

Foot ▶ The basic unit of measurement in metrical poetry. Each separate meter is identified by the pattern and order of stressed and unstressed syllables in its foot.

Iamb ▶ A metrical foot in verse in which an unaccented syllable is followed by an accented one (◡ ′). The iambic measure is the most common one used in English poetry.

Iambic pentameter ▶ The most common meter in English verse, five iambic feet per line. Many fixed forms, such as the sonnet and heroic couplets, employ iambic pentameter.

Anapest ▶ A metrical foot in verse in which two unstressed syllables are followed by a stressed syllable (◡◡ ′).

Trochee ▶ A metrical foot in which a stressed syllable is followed by an unstressed one (′ ◡).

Dactyl ▶ A metrical foot in which one stressed syllable is followed by two unstressed ones (′ ◡◡). Dactylic meter is less common in English than in classical Greek and Latin.

Spondee ▶ A metrical foot of verse consisting of two stressed syllables (′ ′).

Accentual meter ▶ Verse meter based on the number of stresses per line, not the number of syllables.

18 CLOSED FORM

What You Will Learn in This Chapter

- To define *form* as a literary concept
- To describe and differentiate *closed* and *open forms*
- To recognize and describe the two major *sonnet* forms, Italian and English
- To analyze the role of form in a poem

Form, as a general idea, is the design of a thing as a whole, the configuration of all its parts. No poem can escape having some kind of form, whether its lines are as various in length as a tree's branches or all in hexameter. To put this point in another way: if you were to listen to a poem read aloud in a language unknown to you, or if you saw the poem printed in that foreign language, whatever in the poem you could see or hear would be the form of it.

Writing in **closed form**, a poet follows (or finds) some sort of pattern, such as that of a sonnet with its rime scheme and its fourteen lines of iambic pentameter. On a page, poems in closed form tend to look regular and symmetrical, often falling into stanzas that indicate groups of rimes. Along with William Butler Yeats, who held that a successful poem will "come shut with a click, like a closing box," the poet who writes in closed form apparently strives for a kind of perfection—seeking, perhaps, to lodge words so securely in place that no word can be budged without a worsening. For the sake of meaning, though, a competent poet often will depart from a symmetrical pattern. As Robert Frost observed, there is satisfaction to be found in things not mechanically regular: "We enjoy the straight crookedness of a good walking stick."

The poet who writes in **open form** usually seeks no final click. Often, such a poet views the writing of a poem as a process, rather than a quest for an absolute. Free to use white space for emphasis, able to shorten or lengthen lines as the sense seems to require, the poet lets the poem discover its shape as it goes along, moving as water flows downhill, adjusting to its terrain, engulfing obstacles. (Open form provides the focus of Chapter 19.)

Most poetry of the past is in closed form, exhibiting at least a pattern of rime or meter, but since the early 1960s the majority of American poets have preferred forms that stay open. Lately, the situation has been changing yet again, with closed form reappearing in much recent poetry. Whatever the fashion of the moment, the reader who seeks a wide understanding of poetry of both the present and the past will need to know both the closed and open varieties.

THE VALUE OF FORM

Closed form gives some poems a valuable advantage: it makes them more easily memorable. The **epic** poems of nations—long narratives tracing the adventures of popular heroes: the Greek *Iliad* and *Odyssey*, the French *Song of Roland*, the Spanish *Cid*—tend to occur in patterns of fairly consistent line length or number of stresses because these works were sometimes transmitted orally. Sung to the music of a lyre or chanted to a drumbeat, they may have been easier to memorize because of their patterns. If a singer forgot something, the song would have a noticeable hole in it, so rime or fixed meter probably helped prevent an epic from deteriorating when passed along from one singer to another. It is no coincidence that so many English playwrights of Shakespeare's day favored iambic pentameter. Companies of actors, often called on to perform a different play each day, could count on a fixed line length to aid their burdened memories.

Some poets complain that closed form is a straitjacket, a limit to free expression. Other poets, however, feel that, like fires held fast in a narrow space, thoughts stated in a tightly binding form may take on a heightened intensity. "Limitation makes for power," according to one contemporary practitioner of closed form, Richard Wilbur; "the strength of the genie comes of his being confined in a bottle." Compelled by some strict pattern to arrange and rearrange words, delete, and exchange them, poets must focus on them the keenest attention. Often they stand a chance of discovering words more meaningful than the ones they started out with. And at times, in obedience to a rime scheme, the poet may be surprised by saying something quite unexpected.

FORMAL PATTERNS

The best-known line-by-line pattern for a poem in English is **blank verse**: unrimed iambic pentameter. Most portions of Shakespeare's plays are in blank verse, and so are Milton's *Paradise Lost*, Tennyson's "Ulysses," certain dramatic monologues of Browning and Frost, and thousands of other poems. Here are some lines of blank verse that begin Robert Frost's "Mending Wall":

Something there is that doesn't love a wall,
That sends the frozen-ground-swell under it,
And spills the upper boulders in the sun;
And makes gaps even two can pass abreast.

The Couplet

The **couplet** is a two-line stanza, usually rimed. Its lines often tend to be equal in length, whether short or long. Here are two examples:

Blow,
Snow!

As I in hoary winter's night stood shivering in the snow,
Surprised I was with sudden heat which made my heart to glow.

Actually, any pair of rimed lines that contains a complete thought is called a couplet, even if it is not a stanza, such as the couplet that ends a sonnet by Shakespeare. Unlike other stanzas, couplets are often printed solid; one couplet is not separated from the next by white space. This practice is usual in writing the **heroic couplet**—or **closed couplet**—two rimed lines of iambic pentameter, with the first ending in a light pause and the second more heavily end-stopped. George Crabbe, in *The Parish Register*, described a shotgun wedding:

Next at our altar stood a luckless pair,
Brought by strong passions and a warrant there:
By long rent cloak, hung loosely, strove the bride,
From every eye, what all perceived, to hide;
While the boy bridegroom, shuffling in his pace,
Now hid awhile and then exposed his face.
As shame alternately with anger strove
The brain confused with muddy ale to move,
In haste and stammering he performed his part,
And looked the rage that rankled in his heart.

Though employed by Chaucer, the heroic couplet was named from its later use by John Dryden and others in poems, translations of classical epics, and verse plays of epic heroes. It continued in favor through most of the eighteenth century. Much of our pleasure in reading good heroic couplets comes from the seemingly easy precision with which a skilled poet unites statements and strict pattern.

The Tercet

A **tercet** is a group of three lines. If rimed, they usually keep to one rime sound, as in this anonymous English children's jingle:

Julius Caesar,
The Roman geezer,
Squashed his wife with a lemon-squeezer.

(That, by the way, is a great demonstration of surprising and unpredictable rimes.) ***Terza rima***, the form Dante employs in *The Divine Comedy*, is made of tercets linked together by the rime scheme *a b a*, *b c b*, *c d c*, *d e d*, *e f e*, and so on. Harder to do in English than in Italian—with its greater resources of riming words—the form nevertheless was managed by Shelley in "Ode to the West Wind" (with the aid of some slant rimes):

Make me thy lyre, even as the forest is:
What if my leaves are falling like its own!
The tumult of thy mighty harmonies

Will take from both a deep, autumnal tone,
Sweet though in sadness. Be thou, Spirit fierce,
My spirit! Be thou me, impetuous one!

The Quatrain

The workhorse of English poetry is the **quatrain**, a stanza consisting of four lines. Quatrains are used in rimed poems more often than any other form.

Ernest Dowson (1867–1900)

Days of wine and roses 1896

Vitae summa brevis spem nos vetat incohare longam

They are not long, the weeping and the laughter,
Love and desire and hate:
I think they have no portion in us after
We pass the gate.

They are not long, the days of wine and roses:
Out of a misty dream
Our path emerges for a while, then closes
Within a dream.

DAYS OF WINE AND ROSES. The epigraph, from Horace's *Odes* Book 1, 4, translates as "the brief sum of life forbids us the hope of enduring long."

Question

What elements of sound and rhythm are consistent between the two stanzas?

Quatrains come in many line lengths, and sometimes contain lines of varying length. Most often, poets rime the second and fourth lines of quatrains, as in the ballad, but the rimes can occur in any combination the poet chooses.

Longer and more complicated stanzas are, of course, possible, but couplet, tercet, and quatrain have been called the building blocks of our poetry because most longer stanzas are made up of them. What short stanzas does John Donne mortar together to make the longer stanza of his "Song"?

John Donne (1572–1631)

Song 1633

Go and catch a falling star,
Get with child a mandrake root,
Tell me where all past years are,
Or who cleft the Devil's foot,

Teach me to hear mermaids singing,
Or to keep off envy's stinging,
And find
What wind
Serves to advance an honest mind.

If thou be'st borne to strange sights,
Things invisible to see,
Ride ten thousand days and nights,
Till age snow white hairs on thee,
Thou, when thou return'st, wilt tell me
All strange wonders that befell thee,
And swear
Nowhere
Lives a woman true, and fair.

If thou findst one, let me know,
Such a pilgrimage were sweet—
Yet do not, I would not go,
Though at next door we might meet;
Though she were true, when you met her,
And last, till you write your letter,
Yet she
Will be
False, ere I come, to two, or three.

BALLADS

Any narrative song might be called a **ballad**. In English, some of the most famous ballads are **folk ballads**, loosely defined as anonymous story-songs transmitted orally before they were ever written down. Sir Walter Scott, a pioneer collector of Scottish folk ballads, drew the ire of an old woman whose songs he had transcribed: "They were made for singing and no' for reading, but ye ha'e broken the charm now and they'll never be sung mair." The old singer had a point. Print freezes songs and tends to hold them fast to a single version. If Scott and others had not written them down, however, many would have been lost.

Anonymous (traditional Scottish ballad)

Bonny Barbara Allan

It was in and about the Martinmas time,
When the green leaves were afalling,
That Sir John Graeme, in the West Country,
Fell in love with Barbara Allan.

He sent his men down through the town,
To the place where she was dwelling;
"O haste and come to my master dear,
Gin° ye be Barbara Allan." *if*

O hooly,° hooly rose she up, *slowly*
To the place where he was lying,
And when she drew the curtain by:
"Young man, I think you're dying."

"O it's I'm sick, and very, very sick,
And 'tis a' for Barbara Allan."—
"O the better for me ye's never be,
Tho your heart's blood were aspilling.

"O dinna ye mind,° young man," said she, *don't you remember*
"When ye was in the tavern adrinking,
That ye made the health° gae round and round, *toasts*
And slighted Barbara Allan?"

He turned his face unto the wall,
And death was with him dealing:
"Adieu, adieu, my dear friends all,
And be kind to Barbara Allan."

And slowly, slowly raise she up,
And slowly, slowly left him,
And sighing said she could not stay,
Since death of life had reft him.

She had not gane a mile but twa,
When she heard the dead-bell ringing,
And every jow° that the dead-bell geid,° *stroke, gave*
It cried, "Woe to Barbara Allan!"

"O mother, mother, make my bed!
O make it saft and narrow!
Since my love died for me today,
I'll die for him tomorrow."

BONNY BARBARA ALLAN. 1 *Martinmas:* Saint Martin's Day, November 11.

Questions

1. Without ever coming out and explicitly calling Barbara hard-hearted, this ballad reveals that she is. In which stanza and by what means is her cruelty demonstrated?
2. At what point does Barbara evidently have a change of heart? Again, how does the poem dramatize this change without explicitly talking about it?
3. Paraphrase lines 9, 15–16, 22, and 25–28. By putting these lines into prose, what has been lost?

As you can see from "Bonny Barbara Allan," in a traditional English or Scottish folk ballad the storyteller speaks of the lives and feelings of others. Even if the pronoun "I" occurs, it rarely has much personality. Characters often exchange dialogue, but no one character speaks all the way through. Events move rapidly, perhaps because some of the dull transitional stanzas have been forgotten.

Ballad Stanza

One favorite pattern of ballad-makers is the so-called **ballad stanza**, four lines rimed *a b c b*, tending to fall into 8, 6, 8, and 6 syllables:

Clerk Saunders and Maid Margaret
  Walked owre yon garden green,
And deep and heavy was the love
  That fell thir twa between.° *between those two*

Though not the only possible stanza for a ballad, this easily singable quatrain has continued to attract poets since the Middle Ages. Close kin to the ballad stanza is **common meter**, a stanza found in hymns such as "Amazing Grace," by the eighteenth-century English hymnist John Newton:

Amazing grace! how sweet the sound
  That saved a wretch like me!
I once was lost, but now am found,
  Was blind, but now I see.

Notice that its pattern is that of the ballad stanza except for its *two* pairs of rimes. That all its lines rime is probably a sign of more literate artistry than we usually hear in folk ballads. Another sign of schoolteachers' influence is that Newton's rimes are exact. (Rimes in folk ballads are often rough-and-ready, as if made by ear, rather than polished and exact, as if the riming words had been matched for their similar spellings. In "Barbara Allan," for instance, the hard-hearted lover's name rimes with *afalling*, *dwelling*, *aspilling*, *dealing*, and even with *ringing* and *adrinking*.) That so many hymns were written in common meter may have been due to convenience. If a congregation didn't know the tune to a hymn in common meter, they readily could sing its words to the tune of another such hymn they knew.

Literary Ballads

Literary ballads, not meant for singing, are written by sophisticated poets for book-educated readers who enjoy being reminded of folk ballads. Literary ballads imitate certain features of folk ballads: they may tell of dramatic conflicts or of mortals who encounter the supernatural; they may use conventional figures of speech or ballad stanzas. Well-known poems of this kind include Keats's "La Belle Dame sans Merci," Coleridge's "Rime of the Ancient Mariner," and (more recently) Dudley Randall's "Ballad of Birmingham."

Dudley Randall (1914–2000)

Ballad of Birmingham 1966

(On the Bombing of a Church in Birmingham, Alabama, 1963)

"Mother dear, may I go downtown
Instead of out to play,
And march the streets of Birmingham
In a Freedom March today?"

"No, baby, no, you may not go,
For the dogs are fierce and wild,
And clubs and hoses, guns and jails
Aren't good for a little child."

"But, mother, I won't be alone.
Other children will go with me,
And march the streets of Birmingham
To make our country free."

"No, baby, no, you may not go,
For I fear those guns will fire.
But you may go to church instead
And sing in the children's choir."

She has combed and brushed her night-dark hair,
And bathed rose petal sweet,
And drawn white gloves on her small brown hands,
And white shoes on her feet.

The mother smiled to know her child
Was in the sacred place,
But that smile was the last smile
To come upon her face.

For when she heard the explosion,
Her eyes grew wet and wild.
She raced through the streets of Birmingham
Calling for her child.

She clawed through bits of glass and brick,
Then lifted out a shoe.
"O here's the shoe my baby wore,
But, baby, where are you?"

Questions

1. This poem, about a dynamite blast set off in an African American church by a racial terrorist (later convicted), delivers a message without preaching. How would you sum up this message, its implied theme?
2. What is ironic in the mother's denying her child permission to take part in a protest march?
3. How does this modern poem resemble a traditional ballad?

THE SONNET

When we speak of "traditional verse forms," we usually mean **fixed forms**. If written in a fixed form, a poem inherits from other poems certain familiar elements of structure: an unvarying number of lines, say, or a stanza pattern. In addition, it may display certain **conventions**: expected features such as themes, subjects, attitudes, or figures of speech. In medieval folk ballads a "milk-white steed" is a conventional figure of speech; and if its rider be a cruel and beautiful witch who kidnaps mortals, she is a conventional character.

In the poetry of western Europe and America, the **sonnet** is the fixed form that has attracted for the longest time the largest number of noteworthy practitioners. Originally an Italian form (*sonetto*: "little song"), the sonnet owes much of its prestige to Petrarch (1304–1374), who wrote in it of his love for the unattainable Laura. So great was the vogue for sonnets in England at the end of the sixteenth century that a gentleman might have been thought a boor if he couldn't turn out a decent one. Not content to adopt merely the sonnet's fourteen-line pattern, English poets also tried on its conventional mask of the tormented lover. They borrowed some of Petrarch's similes (a lover's heart, for instance, is like a storm-tossed boat) and invented others.

Soon after English poets imported the sonnet in the sixteenth century, they worked out their own rime scheme—one easier for them to follow than Petrarch's, which calls for a greater number of riming words than English can readily provide. (It's a popular though exaggerated belief that in Italian, practically everything rimes.) In the following **English sonnet**, sometimes called a **Shakespearean sonnet**, the rimes cohere in four clusters: *a b a b*, *c d c d*, *e f e f*, *g g*. Because a rime scheme tends to shape the poet's statements to it, the English sonnet has three places where the procession of thought is likely to turn in another direction. Within its form, a poet may pursue one idea throughout the three quatrains and then in the couplet end with a surprise.

William Shakespeare (1564–1616)

Let me not to the marriage of true minds (Sonnet 116) 1609

Let me not to the marriage of true minds
Admit impediments; love is not love
Which alters when it alteration finds,

Or bends with the remover to remove.
O, no, it is an ever-fixèd mark
That looks on tempests and is never shaken;
It is the star to every wand'ring bark,
Whose worth's unknown, although his height be taken.
Love's not Time's fool, though rosy lips and cheeks
Within his bending sickle's compass° come; *range*
Love alters not with his° brief hours and weeks, *Time's*
But bears° it out even to the edge of doom. *endures*
    If this be error and upon me proved,
    I never writ, nor no man ever loved.

LET ME NOT TO THE MARRIAGE OF TRUE MINDS. 5 *ever-fixèd mark:* a sea-mark like a beacon or a lighthouse that provides mariners with safe bearings. 7 *the star:* presumably the North Star, which gave sailors the most dependable bearing at sea. 12 *edge of doom:* either the brink of death or—taken more generally—Judgment Day.

Less frequently met in English poetry, the **Italian sonnet**, or **Petrarchan sonnet**, follows the rime scheme *a b b a a b b a* in its first eight lines, called the **octave**, and then adds new rime sounds in the last six lines, called the **sestet**. The sestet may rime *c d c d c d*, *c d e c d e*, *c d c c d c*, or in almost any other variation that doesn't end in a couplet. This organization into two parts sometimes helps arrange the poet's thoughts. In the octave, the poet may state a problem, and then, in the sestet, may offer a resolution. A lover, for example, may lament all octave long that a loved one is neglectful, then in line 9 begin to foresee some outcome: the speaker will die, or accept unhappiness, or trust that the beloved will have a change of heart.

Edna St. Vincent Millay (1892–1950)

What lips my lips have kissed, and where, and why 1923

What lips my lips have kissed, and where, and why,
I have forgotten, and what arms have lain
Under my head till morning; but the rain
Is full of ghosts tonight, that tap and sigh
Upon the glass and listen for reply,
And in my heart there stirs a quiet pain
For unremembered lads that not again
Will turn to me at midnight with a cry.
Thus in the winter stands the lonely tree,
Nor knows what birds have vanished one by one,
Yet knows its boughs more silent than before:
I cannot say what loves have come and gone,
I only know that summer sang in me
A little while, that in me sings no more.

In this Italian sonnet, the turn of thought comes at the traditional point—the beginning of the ninth line. Many English-speaking poets, however, feel free to vary its placement. In John Milton's commanding sonnet on his blindness ("When I consider how my light is spent" in Chapter 23), the turn comes midway through line 8, and no one has ever thought the worse of it for bending the rules.

When we hear the terms *closed form* or *fixed form*, we imagine traditional poetic forms as a series of immutable rules. But, in the hands of the best poets, metrical forms are fluid concepts that change to suit the occasion. Here, for example, is a haunting poem by Robert Frost that simultaneously fulfills the rules of two traditional forms. Is it an innovative sonnet or a poem in *terza rima?* Frost combined the features of both forms to create a compressed and powerfully lyric poem.

Robert Frost (1874–1963)

Acquainted with the Night 1928

I have been one acquainted with the night.
I have walked out in rain—and back in rain.
I have outwalked the furthest city light.

I have looked down the saddest city lane.
I have passed by the watchman on his beat
And dropped my eyes, unwilling to explain.

I have stood still and stopped the sound of feet
When far away an interrupted cry
Came over houses from another street,

But not to call me back or say good-by;
And further still at an unearthly height,
One luminary clock against the sky

Proclaimed the time was neither wrong nor right.
I have been one acquainted with the night.

"The sonnet," quipped poet-critic Robert Bly, "is where old professors go to die." And certainly in the hands of an unskilled practitioner, the form can seem moribund. Considering the impressive number of powerful sonnets by modern poets such as Yeats, Frost, Auden, Millay, Cummings, Kees, and Heaney, however, the form hardly appears to be exhausted. No law compels sonnets to adopt an exalted tone or confines them to an Elizabethan vocabulary, as demonstrated in these two contemporary examples.

Kim Addonizio (b. 1954)

First Poem for You 1994

I like to touch your tattoos in complete
darkness, when I can't see them. I'm sure of
where they are, know by heart the neat
lines of lightning pulsing just above
your nipple, can find, as if by instinct, the blue
swirls of water on your shoulder where a serpent
twists, facing a dragon. When I pull you
to me, taking you until we're spent
and quiet on the sheets, I love to kiss
the pictures in your skin. They'll last until
you're seared to ashes; whatever persists
or turns to pain between us, they will still
be there. Such permanence is terrifying.
So I touch them in the dark; but touch them, trying.

Questions

1. What is the speaker of this poem "sure of "? What, by implication, is she not sure of?
2. Why do you think the speaker feels that "Such permanence is terrifying"?
3. What, in your view, is she "trying" to do in the poem's last line?

R. S. Gwynn (b. 1948)

Shakespearean Sonnet 2002

With a first line taken from the TV listings

A man is haunted by his father's ghost.
Boy meets girl while feuding families fight.
A Scottish king is murdered by his host.
Two couples get lost on a summer night.
A hunchback slaughters all who block his way.
A ruler's rivals plot against his life.
A fat man and a prince make rebels pay.
A noble Moor has doubts about his wife.
An English king decides to conquer France.
A duke finds out his best friend is a she.
A forest sets the scene for this romance.
An old man and his daughters disagree.
A Roman leader makes a big mistake.
A sexy queen is bitten by a snake.

Questions

1. Explain the play on words in the title.
2. How many of the texts described in this sonnet can you identify?
3. Does this poem intend merely to amuse, or does it have a larger point?

Sherman Alexie (b. 1966)

The Facebook Sonnet

2011

Welcome to the endless high-school
Reunion. Welcome to past friends
And lovers, however kind or cruel.
Let's undervalue and unmend

The present. Why can't we pretend
Every stage of life is the same?
Let's exhume, resume, and extend
Childhood. Let's play all the games

That occupy the young. Let fame
And shame intertwine. Let one's search
For God become public domain.
Let church.com become our church.

Let's sign up, sign in, and confess
Here at the altar of loneliness.

Questions

1. How would you paraphrase this poem? What are the speaker's objections to social media?
2. Read the poem aloud, pausing slightly at the line endings. What is the rhythmic effect of the run-on lines?

THE EPIGRAM

Oscar Wilde said that a cynic is "a man who knows the price of everything and the value of nothing." Such a terse, pointed statement is called an epigram. In poetry, however, an **epigram** is a form: "A short poem ending in a witty or ingenious turn of thought, to which the rest of the composition is intended to lead up" (according to the *Oxford English Dictionary*). Often it is a malicious gibe with an unexpected stinger in the final line—perhaps in the very last word.

Sir John Harrington (1561?–1612)

Of Treason 1618

Treason doth never prosper; what's the reason?
For if it prosper, none dare call it treason.

Anonymous

Epitaph on a dentist

Stranger, approach this spot with gravity;
John Brown is filling his last cavity.

Wendy Videlock (b. 1961)

If Not for the Dark 2013

If not for the dark,
no
spark.

OTHER FORMS

There are many other verse forms used in English. Some forms, like the villanelle and sestina, come from other European literatures. But English has borrowed fixed forms from an astonishing variety of sources. The haiku and tanka, for instance, originated in Japan. Other borrowed forms include the ghazal (Arabic), rubaiyat (Persian), pantoum (Malay), and sapphics (Greek). Even blank verse, which seems as English as the royal family, began as an attempt by Elizabethan poets to copy an Italian eleven-syllable line. To conclude this chapter, here are poems in three widely used closed forms—the villanelle, rondeau, and sestina. Their patterns, which are sometimes called "French forms," have been particularly fascinating to English-language poets because they do not merely require the repetition of rime sounds; instead, they demand more elaborate echoing, involving the repetition of either full words or whole lines of verse. Sometimes difficult to master, these forms can create a powerful musical effect unlike ordinary riming.

Dylan Thomas (1914–1953)

Do not go gentle into that good night 1952

Do not go gentle into that good night,
Old age should burn and rave at close of day;
Rage, rage against the dying of the light.

Though wise men at their end know dark is right,
Because their words had forked no lightning they
Do not go gentle into that good night.

Good men, the last wave by, crying how bright
Their frail deeds might have danced in a green bay,
Rage, rage against the dying of the light.

Wild men who caught and sang the sun in flight,
And learn, too late, they grieved it on its way,
Do not go gentle into that good night.

Grave men, near death, who see with blinding sight
Blind eyes could blaze like meteors and be gay,
Rage, rage against the dying of the light.

And you, my father, there on the sad height,
Curse, bless, me now with your fierce tears, I pray,
Do not go gentle into that good night.
Rage, rage against the dying of the light.

Questions

1. "Do not go gentle into that good night" is a **villanelle**: a fixed form originated by French courtly poets of the Middle Ages. What are its rules?
2. Whom does the poem address? What is the speaker saying?
3. Villanelles are sometimes criticized as elaborate exercises in trivial wordplay. How would you defend Thomas's poem against this charge?

Paul Laurence Dunbar (1872–1906)

We Wear the Mask

1895

We wear the mask that grins and lies,
It hides our cheeks and shades our eyes,—
This debt we pay to human guile;
With torn and bleeding hearts we smile,
And mouth with myriad subtleties.

Why should the world be over-wise,
In counting all our tears and sighs?
Nay, let them only see us, while
  We wear the mask.

We smile, but, O great Christ, our cries
To thee from tortured souls arise.
We sing, but oh the clay is vile

Beneath our feet, and long the mile;
But let the world dream otherwise,
  We wear the mask!

Question

"We Wear the Mask" uses another French form, the **rondeau.** Where do you find patterns of repetition, and how is that repetition effective at expressing the poem's theme?

Elizabeth Bishop (1911–1979)

Sestina

1965

September rain falls on the house.
In the failing light, the old grandmother
sits in the kitchen with the child
beside the Little Marvel Stove,
reading the jokes from the almanac,
laughing and talking to hide her tears.

She thinks that her equinoctial tears
and the rain that beats on the roof of the house
were both foretold by the almanac,
but only known to a grandmother.
The iron kettle sings on the stove.
She cuts some bread and says to the child,

It's time for tea now; but the child
is watching the teakettle's small hard tears
dance like mad on the hot black stove,
the way the rain must dance on the house.
Tidying up, the old grandmother
hangs up the clever almanac

on its string. Birdlike, the almanac
hovers half open above the child,
hovers above the old grandmother
and her teacup full of dark brown tears.
She shivers and says she thinks the house
feels chilly, and puts more wood in the stove.

It was to be, says the Marvel Stove.
I know what I know, says the almanac.
With crayons the child draws a rigid house
and a winding pathway. Then the child
puts in a man with buttons like tears
and shows it proudly to the grandmother.

But secretly, while the grandmother
busies herself about the stove,
the little moons fall down like tears
from between the pages of the almanac
into the flower bed the child
has carefully placed in the front of the house.

Time to plant tears, says the almanac.
The grandmother sings to the marvellous stove
and the child draws another inscrutable house.

SESTINA. As its title indicates, this poem is written in the trickiest of medieval fixed forms, that of the **sestina** (or "song of sixes"), said to have been invented in Provence in the thirteenth century by the troubadour poet Arnaut Daniel. In six six-line stanzas, the poet repeats six end-words (in a prescribed order) and then reintroduces the six repeated words (in any order) in a closing **envoy** of three lines. Elizabeth Bishop strictly follows the troubadour rules for the order in which the end-words recur. (If you'd like, you can figure out the formula: in the first stanza, the six words are arranged A B C D E F; in the second, F A E B D C; and so on.)

Questions

1. A perceptive comment from a student: "Something seems to be going on here that the child doesn't understand. Maybe some terrible loss has happened." Test this guess by reading the poem closely.
2. In the "little moons" that fall from the almanac (line 33), does the poem introduce dream or fantasy, or do you take these to be small round pieces of paper?
3. What is the tone of this poem—the speaker's apparent attitude toward the scene described?

WRITING *effectively*

THINKING ABOUT A SONNET

A poem's form is closely tied to its meaning. This is especially true of the sonnet, a form whose rules dictate not only the sound of a poem but also, to a certain extent, its sense. A sonnet traditionally looks at a single theme, but reverses its stance on the subject somewhere along the way. One possible definition of the sonnet might be a fourteen-line poem divided into two unequal parts. Traditionally, Italian sonnets divide their parts into an octave (the first eight lines) and a sestet (the last six), while English sonnets are more lopsided, with a final couplet balanced against three preceding quatrains. The moment when a sonnet changes its direction is commonly called "the turn."

- **Identifying the moment when the poem "turns" helps in understanding both its theme and its structure.** In a Shakespearean sonnet, the turn usually—but not always—comes in the final couplet. In modern sonnets, the turn is often less overt.
- **To find that moment, study the poem's opening.** Latch on to the mood and manner of the opening lines. Is the feeling joyful or sad, loving or angry?
- **Read the poem from this opening perspective until you feel it tug strongly in another direction.** Sometimes the second part of a sonnet will directly contradict the opening. More often it explains, augments, or qualifies the opening.

CHECKLIST: Writing About a Sonnet

- ☐ Read the poem carefully.
- ☐ What is the mood of its opening lines?
- ☐ At what line do you feel a shift in the mood?
- ☐ What is the tone after the sonnet's turn away from its opening direction?
- ☐ What do the two alternative points of view add up to?
- ☐ How does the poem reconcile its contrasting sections?

TOPICS FOR WRITING ON CLOSED FORM

1. Examine a sonnet from anywhere in this book. Explain how its two parts combine to create a total effect neither part could achieve alone. Be sure to identify the turning point. Paraphrase what each of the poem's two sections says and describe how the poem as a whole reconciles the two contrasting parts. (In addition to the sonnets in this chapter, you might consider any of the following from Chapter 23: Elizabeth Barrett Browning's "How Do I Love Thee?"; Gerard Manley Hopkins's "The Windhover"; John Milton's "When I consider how my light is spent"; William Shakespeare's "When in disgrace with Fortune and men's eyes"; or William Wordsworth's "Composed upon Westminster Bridge.")
2. Select a poem from Chapter 23 that incorporates rime. Write a paragraph describing how the rime scheme helps to advance the poem's meaning.
3. Write ten lines of blank verse on a topic of your own choice. Then write about the experience. What aspects of writing in regular meter did you find most challenging? What did you learn about reading blank verse from trying your hand at writing it?
4. William Carlos Williams, in an interview, delivered this blast:

   > Forcing twentieth-century America into a sonnet—gosh, how I hate sonnets—is like putting a crab into a square box. You've got to cut his legs off to make him fit. When you get through, you don't have a crab any more.

   In a two-page essay, defend the modern American sonnet against Williams's charge. Or instead, open fire on it, using Williams's view for ammunition. Some sonnets to consider: Sherman Alexie's "The Facebook Sonnet"; Kim Addonizio's "First Poem for You"; and R. S. Gwynn's "Shakespearean Sonnet."

5. Write a sestina and see what you find out by doing so. (Even if you fail in the attempt, you just might learn something interesting.) To start, pick six words you think are worth repeating six times. This elaborate pattern gives you much help: as John Ashbery has pointed out, writing a sestina is "like riding downhill on a bicycle and having the pedals push your feet." Here is some encouragement from a poet and critic, John Heath-Stubbs: "I have never read a sestina that seemed to me a total failure."

▶ TERMS FOR *review*

Form

Form ▶ In a general sense, form is the means by which a literary work expresses its content. In poetry, form is usually used to describe the design of a poem.

Fixed form ▶ A traditional verse form requiring certain predetermined elements of structure—for example, a stanza pattern, set meter, or predetermined line length.

Closed form ▶ A generic term that describes poetry written in a pattern of meter, rime, lines, or stanzas. A closed form adheres to a set structure.

Open form ▶ Verse that has no set scheme—no regular meter, rime, or stanzaic pattern. Open form has also been called **free verse**.

Blank verse ▶ Verse that contains five iambic feet per line (iambic pentameter) and is not rimed. ("Blank" means unrimed.)

Couplet ▶ A two-line stanza in poetry, usually rimed and with lines of roughly equal length.

Closed couplet ▶ Two rimed lines of iambic pentameter that usually contain an independent and complete thought or statement. Also called **heroic couplet**.

Quatrain ▶ A stanza consisting of four lines, it is the most common stanza form used in English-language poetry.

Epic ▶ A long narrative poem tracing the adventures of a popular hero. Epic poems are usually written in a consistent form and meter throughout.

Epigram ▶ A very short comic poem, often turning at the end with some sharp wit or unexpected stinger.

Ballads

Ballad ▶ Traditionally, a song that tells a story. Ballads are characteristically compressed, dramatic, and objective in their narrative style.

Folk ballads ▶ Anonymous narrative songs, usually in ballad meter. They were originally created for oral performance, often resulting in many versions of a single ballad.

Ballad stanza ▶ The most common pattern for a ballad, consisting of four lines rimed *a b c b*, in which the first and third lines have four metrical feet (usually eight syllables) and the second and fourth lines have three feet (usually six syllables). **Common meter,** often used in hymns, is a variation rimed *a b a b.*

Literary ballad ▶ A ballad not meant for singing, written by a sophisticated poet for educated readers, rather than arising from the anonymous oral tradition.

The Sonnet

Sonnet ▶ A fixed form of fourteen lines, traditionally written in iambic pentameter and rimed throughout.

Italian sonnet ▶ Also called **Petrarchan sonnet**, it rimes the **octave** (eight lines) *a b b a a b b a*; the **sestet** (last six lines) may follow any rime pattern, as long as it does not end in a couplet. The poem traditionally turns, or shifts in mood or tone, after the octave.

English sonnet ▶ Also called **Shakespearean sonnet**, it has the following rime scheme organized into three quatrains and a concluding couplet: *a b a b c d c d e f e f g g.* The poem may turn—that is, shift in mood or tone—between any of the rime clusters.

19 OPEN FORM

What You Will Learn in This Chapter

- To recognize and describe *free verse* and *open form*
- To explain how line breaks contribute to the meaning of a free verse poem
- To analyze the role of free verse in shaping the meaning of a poem

Writing in **open form**, a poet seeks to discover a fresh and individual arrangement for words in every poem. Such a poem, generally speaking, has neither a rime scheme nor a basic meter informing the whole of it. Doing without those powerful (some would say hypnotic) elements, the poet who writes in open form relies on other means to engage and sustain the reader's attention. Novice poets often think that open form looks easy, not nearly so hard as riming everything; but in truth, formally open poems are easy to write only if written carelessly. To compose lines with keen awareness of open form's demands, and of its infinite possibilities, calls for skill: at least as much as that needed to write in meter and rime, if not more. Should the poet succeed, then the discovered arrangement will seem exactly right for what the poem is saying.

Denise Levertov (1923–1997)

Ancient Stairway 1999

Footsteps like water hollow
the broad curves of stone
ascending, descending
century by century.
Who can say if the last
to climb these stairs
will be journeying
downward or upward?

Open form, in this brief poem, affords Denise Levertov certain advantages. Able to break off a line at whatever point she likes (a privilege not available to the poet writing, say, a conventional sonnet, who has to break off each line after its tenth syllable), she selects her pauses artfully. Line breaks lend emphasis: a word or phrase at the end of a line takes a little more stress (and receives a little more attention), because the ending of the line compels the reader to make a slight pause, if only for the brief moment it takes to sling back one's eyes and fix them on the line following. Slight pauses, then, follow the words and phrases *hollow/stone/descending/century/last/stairs/journeying/upward*—all these being elements that apparently the poet wishes to call our attention to. (The pause after a line break also casts a little more weight on the *first* word or phrase of each succeeding line.)

Levertov makes the most of white space—another means of calling attention to things, as any good picture-framer knows. She has greater control over the shape of the poem, its look on the page, than would be allowed by the demands of meter; she uses that control to stack on top of one another lines that appear much like the steps of a staircase. The opening line with its quick stresses might suggest to us the feet passing over the steps. From there, Levertov slows the rhythm to the heavy beats of lines 3–4, which could communicate a sense of repeated trudging up and down the stairs (in a particularly effective touch, all four of the stressed syllables in these two lines make the same sound), a sense that is reinforced by the poem's last line, which echoes the rhythm of line 3. In all likelihood, we perceive these effects instinctively, not consciously (which may also be the way the author created them), but no matter how we apprehend them, they serve to deepen our understanding of and pleasure in the text.

FREE VERSE

Poetry in open form can also be called **free verse** (from the French ***vers libre***), suggesting a kind of verse liberated from the shackles of rime and meter. "Writing free verse," said Robert Frost, who wasn't interested in it, "is like playing tennis with the net down." And yet, as Denise Levertov and many other poets demonstrate, high scores can be made in such an unconventional game, provided it doesn't straggle all over the court. For a successful poem in open form, the term *free verse* seems inaccurate. "Being an art form," said William Carlos Williams, "verse cannot be 'free' in the sense of having *no* limitations or guiding principles."[1] Various substitute names have been suggested: organic poetry, composition by field, raw (as opposed to cooked) poetry, open form poetry. "But what does it matter what you call it?" remark the editors of a 1969 anthology called *Naked Poetry*. "The best poems of the last thirty years don't rhyme (usually) and don't move on feet of more or less equal duration (usually). That nondescription moves toward the only technical principle they all have in common."[2]

[1]"Free Verse," *Princeton Encyclopedia of Poetry and Poetics*, 2nd ed., 1975.
[2]Stephen Berg and Robert Mezey, eds., foreword, *Naked Poetry: Recent American Poetry in Open Forms* (Indianapolis: Bobbs, 1969).

Free Verse Lines

To the poet working in open form, no less than to the poet writing a sonnet, line length can be valuable. Walt Whitman, who loved to expand vast sentences for line after line, knew well that an impressive rhythm can accumulate if the poet will keep long lines approximately the same length, causing a pause to recur at about the same interval after every line. Sometimes, too, Whitman repeats the same words at each line's opening. An instance is the masterly sixth section of "When Lilacs Last in the Dooryard Bloom'd," an elegy for Abraham Lincoln:

> Coffin that passes through lanes and streets,
> Through day and night with the great cloud darkening the land,
> With the pomp of the inloop'd flags with the cities draped in black,
> With the show of the States themselves as of crape-veil'd women
>   standing,
> With processions long and winding and the flambeaus of the night,
> With the countless torches lit, with the silent sea of faces and the
>   unbared heads,
> With the waiting depot, the arriving coffin, and the somber faces,
> With dirges through the night, with the thousand voices rising strong
>   and solemn,
> With all the mournful voices of the dirges pour'd around the coffin,
> The dim-lit churches and the shuddering organs—where amid these you
>   journey,
> With the tolling tolling bells' perpetual clang,
> Here, coffin that slowly passes,
> I give you my sprig of lilac.

There is music in such solemn, operatic arias. Whitman's lines echo another model: the Hebrew **psalms**, or sacred songs, as translated in the King James Version of the Bible. In Psalm 150, repetition also occurs inside of lines:

> Praise ye the Lord. Praise God in his sanctuary: praise him in the firmament
>   of his power.
> Praise him for his mighty acts: praise him according to his excellent
>   greatness.
> Praise him with the sound of the trumpet: praise him with the psaltery
>   and harp.
> Praise him with the timbrel and dance: praise him with stringed instruments
>   and organs.
> Praise him upon the loud cymbals: praise him upon the high sounding
>   cymbals.
> Let every thing that hath breath praise the Lord. Praise ye the Lord.

Sound and Rhythm in Free Verse

In many classics of open form poetry, sound and rhythm are positive forces. When speaking a poem in open form, you often may find that it makes a difference for the better if you pause at the end of each line. Why do the pauses matter? Open form poetry usually has no meter to lend it rhythm. *Some* lines in an open form poem, as we have seen in Whitman's "dimes on the eyes" passage, do fall into metrical feet; sometimes the whole poem does. Usually lacking meter's aid, however, open form, in order to have more and more noticeable rhythms, has need of all the recurring pauses it can get.

Some poems, to be sure, seem more widely open in form than others. A poet may wish to avoid the rigidity and predictability of fixed line lengths and stanzaic forms but still wish to hold a poem together through a strong rhythmic impulse and even a discernible metrical emphasis. A poet may employ rime, but have the rimes recur at various intervals, or perhaps rime lines of varying lengths. In a 1917 essay called "Reflections on *Vers Libre*" (French for "free verse"), T. S. Eliot famously observed, "No *vers* is *libre* for the man who wants to do a good job."

E. E. Cummings (1894–1962)

Buffalo Bill 's

1923

Buffalo Bill 's
defunct
        who used to
        ride a watersmooth-silver
                                        stallion
and break onetwothreefourfive pigeonsjustlikethat
                                                            Jesus
he was a handsome man
                              and what i want to know is
how do you like your blueeyed boy
Mister Death

Question

If set as conventional prose, Cumming's poem would look like this:

> Buffalo Bill's defunct, who used to ride a water-smooth silver stallion and break one, two, three, four, five pigeons just like that. Jesus, he was a handsome man. And what I want to know is: "How do you like your blue-eyed boy, Mister Death?"

By what characteristics would this still be recognizable as poetry? What would be lost?

***The Kermess* or *Peasant Dance* by Pieter Brueghel the Elder (1520?–1569).**

William Carlos Williams (1883–1963)

The Dance

1944

In Brueghel's great picture, The Kermess,
the dancers go round, they go round and
around, the squeal and the blare and the
tweedle of bagpipes, a bugle and fiddles
tipping their bellies (round as the thick-
sided glasses whose wash they impound)
their hips and their bellies off balance
to turn them. Kicking and rolling about
the Fair Grounds, swinging their butts, those
shanks must be sound to bear up under such
rollicking measures, prance as they dance
in Brueghel's great picture, The Kermess.

THE DANCE. 1 *Brueghel:* Flemish painter known for his scenes of peasant activities. *The Kermess:* painting of a celebration on the feast day of a local patron saint.

Questions

1. Scan this poem and try to describe the effect of its rhythms.
2. Williams, widely admired for his free verse, insisted for many years that what he sought was a form not in the least bit free. What effect does he achieve by ending lines on such weak words as the articles "and" and "the"? By splitting "thick- / sided"? By splitting a prepositional phrase with the break at the end of line 8? By using

line breaks to split "those" and "such" from what they modify? What do you think he is trying to convey?

3. Is there any point in his making line 12 a repetition of the opening line?
4. Look at the reproduction of Brueghel's painting *The Kermess* (also called *Peasant Dance*). Aware that the rhythms of dancers, the rhythms of a painting, and the rhythms of a poem are not all the same, can you put in your own words what Brueghel's dancing figures have in common with Williams's descriptions of them?
5. Compare "The Dance" with another poem that refers to a Brueghel painting: W. H. Auden's "Musée des Beaux Arts" (Chapter 23). What seems to be each poet's main concern: to convey in words a sense of the painting, or to visualize the painting in order to state some theme?

Stephen Crane (1871–1900)

The Heart

1895

In the desert
I saw a creature, naked, bestial,
Who, squatting upon the ground,
Held his heart in his hands,
And ate of it.
I said, "Is it good, friend?"
"It is bitter—bitter," he answered;
"But I like it
Because it is bitter,
And because it is my heart."

Walt Whitman (1819–1892)

I Hear America Singing

1860

I hear America singing, the varied carols I hear,
Those of mechanics, each one singing his as it should be blithe and strong,
The carpenter singing his as he measures his plank or beam,
The mason singing his as he makes ready for work, or leaves off work,
The boatman singing what belongs to him in his boat, the deckhand singing on the steamboat deck,
The shoemaker singing as he sits on his bench, the hatter singing as he stands,
The wood-cutter's song, the ploughboy's on his way in the morning, or at noon intermission or at sundown,
The delicious singing of the mother, or of the young wife at work, or of the girl sewing or washing,
Each singing what belongs to him or her and to none else,
The day what belongs to the day—at night the party of young fellows, robust, friendly,
Singing with open mouths their strong melodious songs.

Questions: Crane Versus Whitman

The following nit-picking questions are intended to help you see exactly what makes these two open form poems by Crane and Whitman so different in their music.

1. After reading Whitman's poem aloud, how would you describe its rhythm? In what way, and to what effect, does he use repetition?
2. How would you describe the rhythm of Crane's poem, and how is that rhythm determined by the shorter lines and more frequent punctuation?
3. Point out words in Whitman's poem that seem musical. Is "melodious," the word found in Whitman's final line, an apt description of "I Hear America Singing"?
4. Do you find many melodious words in "The Heart"? Is Crane's poem necessarily an inferior poem for having less music?

Analyzing Line Breaks

Wallace Stevens's lineation in "Thirteen Ways of Looking at a Blackbird" allows us not only to see but also to savor the connections between the poem's ideas and images. Consider section II of the poem:

> I was of three minds,
> Like a tree
> In which there are three blackbirds.

On a purely semantic level, these lines may mean the same as the prose statement, "I was of three minds, like a tree in which there are three blackbirds," but Stevens's choice of line breaks adds special emphasis at several points. Each of these three lines isolates and presents a separate image (the speaker, the tree, and the blackbirds). The placement of *three* in the opening and closing lines helps us feel the similar nature of the two statements. The short middle line allows us to see the image of the tree before we fully understand why it is parallel to the divided mind—thus adding a touch of suspense that the prose version of this statement just can't supply. Ending each line with a key noun and image also gives the poem a concrete feel not altogether evident in the prose.

Wallace Stevens (1879–1955)

Thirteen Ways of Looking at a Blackbird

1923

I

Among twenty snowy mountains,
The only moving thing
Was the eye of the blackbird.

II

I was of three minds,
Like a tree
In which there are three blackbirds.

III

The blackbird whirled in the autumn winds.
It was a small part of the pantomime.

IV

A man and a woman
Are one.
A man and a woman and a blackbird
Are one.

V

I do not know which to prefer,
The beauty of inflections
Or the beauty of innuendoes,
The blackbird whistling
Or just after.

VI

Icicles filled the long window
With barbaric glass.
The shadow of the blackbird
Crossed it, to and fro.
The mood
Traced in the shadow
An indecipherable cause.

VII

O thin men of Haddam,
Why do you imagine golden birds?
Do you not see how the blackbird
Walks around the feet
Of the women about you?

VIII

I know noble accents
And lucid, inescapable rhythms;
But I know, too,
That the blackbird is involved
In what I know.

IX

When the blackbird flew out of sight,
It marked the edge
Of one of many circles.

X

At the sight of blackbirds
Flying in a green light,
Even the bawds of euphony
Would cry out sharply.

XI

He rode over Connecticut
In a glass coach.
Once, a fear pierced him,
In that he mistook
The shadow of his equipage
For blackbirds.

XII

The river is moving.
The blackbird must be flying.

XIII

It was evening all afternoon.
It was snowing
And it was going to snow.
The blackbird sat
In the cedar-limbs.

THIRTEEN WAYS OF LOOKING AT A BLACKBIRD. 25 *Haddam:* This biblical-sounding name is that of a town in Connecticut.

Questions

1. What is the speaker's attitude toward the men of Haddam? What attitude toward this world does he suggest they lack? What is implied by calling them "thin" (line 25)?
2. What do the landscapes of winter contribute to the poem's effectiveness? If Stevens had chosen images of summer lawns, what would have been lost?
3. In which sections of the poem does Stevens suggest that a unity exists between human being and blackbird, between blackbird and the entire natural world? Can we say that Stevens "philosophizes"? What role does imagery play in Stevens's statement of his ideas?
4. What sense can you make of Part X? Make an enlightened guess.
5. Consider any one of the thirteen parts. What patterns of sound and rhythm do you find in it? What kind of structure does it have?
6. If the thirteen parts were arranged in some different order, would the poem be just as good? Or can you find a justification for its beginning with Part I and ending with Part XIII?
7. Does the poem seem an arbitrary combination of thirteen separate poems? Or is there any reason to call it a whole?

FOR REVIEW AND FURTHER STUDY

***Exercise:* Seeing the Logic of Open Form Verse**

Read the following poems in open form silently to yourself, noticing what each poet does with white space, repetitions, line breaks, and indentations. Then read the poems aloud, trying to indicate by slight pauses where lines end and also pausing slightly at any space inside a line. Can you see any reasons for the poet's placing his or her words in this arrangement rather than in a prose paragraph? Do any of these poets seem to care also about visual effect?

E. E. Cummings (1894–1962)

in Just- 1923

in Just-
spring   when the world is mud-
luscious the little
lame balloonman

whistles   far   and wee

and eddieandbill come
running from marbles and
piracies and it's
spring

when the world is puddle-wonderful

the queer
old balloonman whistles
far   and   wee
and bettyandisbel come dancing

from hop-scotch and jump-rope and

it's
spring
and
   the

      goat-footed

balloonMan   whistles
far
and
wee

Langston Hughes (1901–1967)

I, Too 1926

I, too, sing America.

I am the darker brother.
They send me to eat in the kitchen
When company comes,
But I laugh,
And eat well,
And grow strong.

Tomorrow,
I'll be at the table
When company comes.
Nobody'll dare
Say to me,
"Eat in the kitchen,"
Then.

Besides,
They'll see how beautiful I am
And be ashamed—

I, too, am America.

Questions

1. Who do you imagine to be the speaker of this poem?
2. What is suggested by the final line?

Francisco X. Alarcón (b. 1954)

Frontera	**Border** 2003
ninguna	no
frontera	border
podrá	can ever
separanos	separate us

Question

How would the meaning of this short poem change if you dropped one of the languages?

Carole Satyamurti (b. 1939)

I Shall Paint My Nails Red

1990

Because a bit of color is a public service.
Because I am proud of my hands.
Because it will remind me I'm a woman.
Because I will look like a survivor.
Because I can admire them in traffic jams.
Because my daughter will say ugh.
Because my lover will be surprised.
Because it is quicker than dyeing my hair.
Because it is a ten-minute moratorium.
Because it is reversible.

Question

"I Shall Paint My Nails Red" is written in free verse, but the poem has several organizing principles. How many can you discover?

WRITING *effectively*

THINKING ABOUT FREE VERSE

"That's not poetry! It's just chopped-up prose." So runs one old-fashioned complaint about free verse. Such criticism may be true of inept poems, but in the best free verse the line endings transform language in ways beyond the possibilities of prose. A line break implies a slight pause so that the last word of each line receives special emphasis. The last word in a line is meant to linger, however briefly, in the listener's ear. With practice and attention, you can easily develop a better sense of how a poem's line breaks operate.

- **Note whether the breaks tend to come at the end of sentences or phrases, or in the middle of an idea.** An abundance of breaks in mid-thought can create a tumbling, headlong effect, forcing your eye to speed down the page. Conversely, lines that tend to break at the end of a full idea can give a more stately rhythm to a poem.
- **Determine whether the lines tend to be all brief, all long, or a mix.** A very short line forces us to pay special attention to its every word, no matter how small.

- **Ask yourself how the poet's choices about line breaks help to reinforce the poem's meaning.** Can you identify any example of a line break affecting the meaning of a phrase or sentence?

CHECKLIST: Writing About Line Breaks

- ☐ Reread a poem, paying attention to where its lines end.
- ☐ Do the breaks tend to come at the end of the sentences or phrases?
- ☐ Do they tend to come in the middle of an idea?
- ☐ Do the lines tend to be long? Short? A mix of both?
- ☐ Is the poem broken into stanzas? Are they long? Short? A mix of both?
- ☐ What mood is created by the breaks?
- ☐ How do line breaks and stanza breaks reinforce the poem's meaning as a whole?

TOPICS FOR WRITING ON OPEN FORM

1. Retype a free verse poem as prose, adding conventional punctuation and capitalization if necessary. Then compare and contrast the prose version with the poem itself. How do the two texts differ in tone, rhythm, emphasis, and effect? How do they remain similar? Use any poem from this chapter or any of the following from Chapter 23: W. H. Auden's "Musée des Beaux Arts"; Ezra Pound's "The River-Merchant's Wife: A Letter"; or William Carlos Williams's "Queen-Anne's-Lace."
2. Write a 500-word essay on how the line breaks and white space (or lack thereof) in E. E. Cummings's "Buffalo Bill 's" contribute to the poem's effect.
3. Read aloud William Carlos Williams's "The Dance." Examine how the poem's line breaks and sonic effects underscore the poem's meaning.
4. Compare any poem in this chapter with a poem in rime and meter. Discuss several key features that they have in common despite their apparent differences in style. Features it might be useful to compare include imagery, tone, figures of speech, and word choice.
5. Write an imitation of Wallace Stevens's "Thirteen Ways of Looking at a Blackbird." Come up with thirteen ways of looking at your car, a can opener, a housecat—or any object that intrigues you. Choose your line breaks carefully, to recreate some of the mood of the original. You might also have a look at Aaron Abeyta's parody "thirteen ways of looking at a tortilla" in Chapter 23.

▶ TERMS FOR *review*

Open form ▶ Poems that have neither a rime scheme nor a basic meter are in open form. Open form has also been called **free verse.**

Free verse ▶ From the French ***vers libre.*** Free verse is poetry whose lines follow no consistent meter. It may be rimed, but usually is not. In the last hundred years, free verse has become a common practice.

20 SYMBOL

What You Will Learn in This Chapter

- To recognize and define a *poetic symbol*
- To identify and define *symbolic actions*
- To describe *allegory* and its characteristics
- To analyze the role of a symbol in a poem

The national flag is supposed to stir our patriotic feelings. When a black cat crosses his path, a superstitious man shivers, foreseeing bad luck. To each of these, by custom, our society expects a standard response. A flag, a black cat crossing one's path—each is a **symbol**: a visible object or action that suggests some further meaning in addition to itself. In literature, a symbol might be the word *flag* or the words *a black cat crossed his path* or every description of flag or cat in an entire novel, story, play, or poem.

A flag and the crossing of a black cat may be called **conventional symbols**, since they can have a conventional or customary effect on us. Conventional symbols are also part of the language of poetry, as we know when we meet the red rose, emblem of love, in a lyric, or the Christian cross in the devotional poems of George Herbert. More often, however, symbols in literature have no conventional, long-established meaning, but particular meanings of their own. In Melville's novel *Moby-Dick*, to take a rich example, whatever we associate with the great white whale is *not* attached unmistakably to white whales by custom. Though Melville tells us that men have long regarded whales with awe and relates Moby Dick to the celebrated fish that swallowed Jonah, the reader's response is to one particular whale, the creature of Herman Melville. Only the experience of reading the novel in its entirety can give Moby Dick his particular meaning.

THE MEANINGS OF A SYMBOL

As Eudora Welty has observed, it is a good thing Melville made Moby Dick a whale, a creature large enough to contain all that critics have found in him. A symbol in literature, if not conventional, has more than just one meaning. In "The Raven," by Edgar Allan Poe, the appearance of a strange black bird in the narrator's study is sinister; and indeed, if we take the poem seriously, we may even respond with a sympathetic shiver of dread. Does the bird mean death, fate, melancholy, the loss of a loved one, knowledge in the service of evil? All of these, perhaps. Like any well-chosen symbol, Poe's raven sets off within the reader an unending train of feelings and associations.

We miss the value of a symbol, however, if we think it can mean absolutely anything we wish. If a poet has any control over our reactions, the poem will guide our responses in a certain direction.

T. S. Eliot (1888–1965)

The *Boston Evening Transcript* 1917

The readers of the *Boston Evening Transcript*
Sway in the wind like a field of ripe corn.

When evening quickens faintly in the street,
Wakening the appetites of life in some
And to others bringing the *Boston Evening Transcript*,
I mount the steps and ring the bell, turning
Wearily, as one would turn to nod good-bye to La Rochefoucauld,
If the street were time and he at the end of the street,
And I say, "Cousin Harriet, here is the *Boston Evening Transcript*."

The newspaper, whose name Eliot purposely repeats so monotonously, indicates what this poem is about. Now defunct, the *Transcript* covered in detail the slightest activity of Boston's leading families and was noted for the great length of its obituaries. Eliot, then, uses the newspaper as a symbol for an existence of boredom, fatigue ("Wearily"), petty and unvarying routine (since an evening newspaper, like night, arrives on schedule). The *Transcript* evokes a way of life without zest or passion, for, opposed to people who read it, Eliot sets people who do not: those whose desires revive, not expire, when the working day is through. Suggestions abound in the ironic comparison of the *Transcript*'s readers to a cornfield late in summer. To mention only a few: the readers sway because they are sleepy; they vegetate; they are drying up; each makes a rattling sound when turning a page. It is not necessary that we know the remote and similarly disillusioned friend to whom the speaker might nod: La Rochefoucauld, for example, whose cynical *Maxims* entertained Parisian society under Louis XIV. We understand that the nod is symbolic of an immense weariness of spirit. We know nothing about Cousin Harriet, whom the speaker addresses, but imagine from the greeting she inspires that she is probably a bore.

If Eliot wishes to say that certain Bostonians lead lives of sterile boredom, why does he couch his meaning in symbols? Why doesn't he tell us directly what he means? These questions imply two assumptions not necessarily true: first, that Eliot has a message to impart; second, that he is concealing it. We have reason to think that Eliot did not usually have a message in mind when beginning a poem, for as he once told a critic: "The conscious problems with which one is concerned in the actual writing are more those of a quasi-musical nature . . . than of a conscious exposition of ideas." Poets sometimes discover what they have to say while in the act of saying it. And it may be that in his *Transcript* poem, Eliot is saying exactly what he means. By communicating his meaning through symbols instead of statements, he may be choosing the only kind of language appropriate to an idea of great subtlety and complexity. (The paraphrase "Certain Bostonians are bored" hardly begins to describe the poem in all its possible meanings.) And by his use of symbolism, Eliot affords us the pleasure of finding our own entrances to his poem.

This power of suggestion that a symbol contains is, perhaps, its greatest advantage. Sometimes, as in the following poem by Emily Dickinson, a symbol will lead us from a visible object to something too vast to be perceived.

Emily Dickinson (1830–1886)

The Lightning is a yellow Fork (about 1870)

The Lightning is a yellow Fork
From Tables in the sky
By inadvertent fingers dropt
The awful Cutlery

Of mansions never quite disclosed
And never quite concealed
The Apparatus of the Dark
To ignorance revealed.

If the lightning is a fork, then whose are the fingers that drop it, the table from which it slips, the household to which it belongs? The poem implies this question without giving an answer. An obvious answer is "God," but can we be sure? We wonder, too, about these partially lighted mansions: if our vision were clearer, what would we behold?

IDENTIFYING SYMBOLS

You might wonder, "But how am I supposed to know a symbol when I see one?" The best approach is to read poems closely, taking comfort in the likelihood that it is better not to notice symbols at all than to find significance in every literal stone and huge meanings in every thing. In looking for the symbols in a poem, pick out all the references to concrete objects—newspapers, black cats, twisted pins. Consider these with special care. Notice any that the poet emphasizes by detailed description, by repetition, or by placing them at the very beginning or end of the poem. Ask: What is the poem about; what does it add up to? If, when the poem is paraphrased, the paraphrase depends primarily on the meaning of certain concrete objects, these richly suggestive objects may be the symbols.

There are some things a literary symbol usually is *not*. A symbol is not an abstraction. Such terms as *truth*, *death*, *love*, and *justice* cannot work as symbols (unless personified, as in the traditional figure of Justice holding a scale). Most often, a symbol is something we can see in the mind's eye: a newspaper, a lightning bolt, a gesture of nodding good-bye.

In narratives, a well-developed character who speaks much dialogue and is not the least bit mysterious is usually not a symbol. But watch out for an executioner in a black hood; a character, named for a biblical prophet, who does little but utter a prophecy; a trio of old women who resemble the Three Fates. (It has been argued, with good reason, that Milton's fully rounded character of Satan in *Paradise Lost* is a symbol embodying evil and human pride, but a narrower definition of symbol is more frequently useful.) A symbol *may* be a part of a person's body (the baleful eye of the murder victim in Poe's story "The Tell-Tale Heart") or a look, a voice, or a mannerism.

A symbol usually is not the second term of a metaphor. In the line "The Lightning is a yellow Fork," the symbol is the lightning, not the fork.

Sometimes a symbol addresses a sense other than sight: in William Faulkner's tale "A Rose for Emily" (Chapter 2), the odor of decay that surrounds the house of the last survivor of a town's leading family suggests not only physical dissolution but also the decay of a social order. A symbol is a special kind of image, for it exceeds the usual image in the richness of its connotations. The dead wife's cold comb in the haiku of Buson (Chapter 14) works symbolically, suggesting among other things the chill of the grave, the contrast between the living and the dead.

Symbolic Action

Holding a narrower definition than that used in this book, some readers of poetry prefer to say that a symbol is always a concrete object, never an act. They would deny the label "symbol" to Ahab's breaking his tobacco pipe before setting out to pursue Moby Dick (suggesting, perhaps, his determination to allow no pleasure to distract him from the chase) or to any large motion (such as Ahab's whole quest). This distinction, while confining, does have the merit of sparing one from seeing all motion to be possibly symbolic. Some would call Ahab's gesture not a symbol but a **symbolic act**.

To sum up: a symbol radiates hints or casts long shadows (to use Henry James's metaphor). We are unable to say it "stands for" or "represents" a meaning. It evokes, it suggests, it manifests. It demands no single necessary interpretation, such as the interpretation a driver gives to a red traffic light. Rather, like Emily Dickinson's lightning bolt, it points toward an indefinite meaning, which may lie in part beyond the reach of words.

Thomas Hardy (1840–1928)

Neutral Tones

1898

We stood by a pond that winter day,
And the sun was white, as though chidden of° God, *rebuked by*
And a few leaves lay on the starving sod;
—They had fallen from an ash, and were gray.

Your eyes on me were as eyes that rove
Over tedious riddles of years ago;
And some words played between us to and fro
On which lost the more by our love.

The smile on your mouth was the deadest thing
Alive enough to have strength to die;
And a grin of bitterness swept thereby
Like an ominous bird a-wing. . . .

Since then, keen lessons that love deceives,
And wrings with wrong, have shaped to me
Your face, and the God-curst sun, and a tree,
And a pond edged with grayish leaves.

Questions

1. Sum up the story told in this poem. In lines 1–12, what is the dramatic situation? What has happened in the interval between the experience related in these lines and the reflection in the last stanza?
2. What meanings do you find in the title?
3. Explain in your own words the metaphor in line 2.
4. What connotations appropriate to this poem does the "ash" (line 4) have that *oak* or *maple* would lack?
5. What visible objects in the poem function symbolically? What actions or gestures?

Yusef Komunyakaa (b. 1947)

Facing It

1988

My black face fades,
hiding inside the black granite.
I said I wouldn't,
dammit: No tears.
I'm stone. I'm flesh.
My clouded reflection eyes me
like a bird of prey, the profile of night
slanted against morning. I turn
this way—the stone lets me go.
I turn that way—I'm inside
the Vietnam Veterans Memorial

again, depending on the light
to make a difference.
I go down the 58,022 names,
half-expecting to find
my own in letters like smoke.
I touch the name Andrew Johnson;
I see the booby trap's white flash.
Names shimmer on a woman's blouse
but when she walks away
the names stay on the wall.
Brushstrokes flash, a red bird's
wings cutting across my stare.
The sky. A plane in the sky.
A white vet's image floats
closer to me, then his pale eyes
look through mine. I'm a window.
He's lost his right arm
inside the stone. In the black mirror
a woman's trying to erase names:
No, she's brushing a boy's hair.

Questions

1. How does the title of "Facing It" relate to the poem? Does it have more than one meaning?
2. The narrator describes the people around him by their reflections on the polished granite rather than by looking at them directly. What does this indirect way of scrutinizing contribute to the poem?

William Butler Yeats (1865–1939)

He wishes for the Cloths of Heaven 1899

Had I the heavens' embroidered cloths,
Enwrought with golden and silver light,
The blue and the dim and the dark cloths
Of night and light and the half light,
I would spread the cloths under your feet:
But I, being poor, have only my dreams;
I have spread my dreams under your feet;
Tread softly because you tread on my dreams.

ALLEGORY

If we read of a ship, its captain, its sailors, and the rough seas, and we realize we are reading about a commonwealth and how its rulers and workers keep it going even in difficult times, then we are reading an **allegory**. Closely akin to symbolism, allegory is a description—usually narrative—in which persons, places, and things are employed in a continuous and consistent system of equivalents. In an allegory an object has a single additional significance, one largely determined by convention. When an allegory appears in a work, it usually has a one-to-one relationship to an abstract entity, recognizable to readers and audiences familiar with the cultural context of the work.

Although more strictly limited in its suggestions than symbolism, allegory need not be thought inferior. Few poems continue to interest readers more than Dante's allegorical *Divine Comedy*. Sublime evidence of the appeal of allegory may be found in Jesus's use of the **parable**: a brief narrative—usually allegorical but sometimes not—that teaches a moral.

Matthew

The Parable of the Good Seed

(King James Version, 1611)

The kingdom of heaven is likened unto a man which sowed good seed in his field:
But while men slept, his enemy came and sowed tares among the wheat, and went his way.
But when the blade was sprung up, and brought forth fruit, then appeared the tares also.
So the servants of the householder came and said unto him, Sir, didst not thou sow good seed in thy field? From whence then hath it tares?
He said unto them, An enemy hath done this. The servants said unto him, Wilt thou then that we go and gather them up?
But he said, Nay; lest while ye gather up the tares, ye root up also the wheat with them.
Let both grow together until the harvest: and in the time of harvest I will say to the reapers, Gather ye together first the tares, and bind them in bundles to burn them: but gather the wheat into my barn.

—Matthew 13:24–30

THE PARABLE OF THE GOOD SEED. 2 *tares*: harmful weeds.

Jesus explains this parable to his disciples, saying that the sower is the Son of man, the field is the world, the good seed are the children of the Kingdom, the tares are the children of the wicked one, the enemy is the devil, the harvest is the end of the world, the reapers are angels. "As therefore the tares are gathered and burned in the fire; so shall it be in the end of this world" (Matthew 13:36–42).

Usually the meanings of an allegory are plainly labeled or thinly disguised. An allegory, when carefully built, is systematic. It makes one principal comparison, the working out of whose details may lead to further comparisons.

George Herbert (1593–1633)

Redemption 1633

Having been tenant long to a rich Lord,
  Not thriving, I resolved to be bold,
  And make a suit unto him, to afford
A new small-rented lease, and cancel th' old.

In Heaven at his manor I him sought:
  They told me there, that he was lately gone
  About some land, which he had dearly bought
Long since on earth, to take possession.

I straight returned, and knowing his great birth,
  Sought him accordingly in great resorts;
  In cities, theaters, ga rdens, parks, and courts:
At length I heard a ragged noise and mirth

  Of thieves and murderers: there I him espied,
  Who straight, *Your suit is granted*, said, and died.

Questions

1. In this allegory, what equivalents does Herbert give each of these terms: "tenant," "Lord," "not thriving," "suit," "new lease," "old lease," "manor," "land," "dearly bought," "take possession," "his great birth"?
2. What scene is depicted in the last three lines?

An object in an allegory is like a bird whose cage is clearly lettered with its identity—"RAVEN, *Corvus corax*; habitat of specimen, Maine." A symbol, by contrast, is a bird with piercing eyes that mysteriously appears one evening in your library. It is there; you can touch it. But what does it mean?

Edwin Markham (1852–1940)

Outwitted 1914

He drew a circle that shut me out—
Heretic, rebel, a thing to flout.
But Love and I had the wit to win:
We drew a circle that took him in!

Question

What does a circle symbolize here? The same thing both times it is mentioned?

Suji Kwock Kim (b. 1968)

Occupation

2003

The soldiers
are hard at work
building a house.
They hammer
bodies into the earth
like nails,
they paint the walls
with blood.
Inside the doors
stay shut, locked
as eyes of stone.
Inside the stairs
feel slippery,
all flights go down.
There is no floor:
only a roof,
where ash is falling—
dark snow,
human snow,
thickly, mutely
falling.
Come, they say.
This house will
last forever.
You must occupy it.
And you, and you—
Come, they say.
There is room
for everyone.

Questions

1. What materials do the soldiers use to build the house?
2. What is unusual about the interior of the house?
3. How is the ash unusual?
4. The title contains a pun. Find and explain it.
5. What does the soldiers' house seem to symbolize?

Whether an object in literature is a symbol, part of an allegory, or no such thing at all, it has at least one sure meaning. Moby Dick is first a whale, and the *Boston Evening Transcript* is a newspaper. Besides deriving a multitude of intangible suggestions from the title symbol in Eliot's long poem *The Waste Land*, its readers cannot fail to carry away a sense of the land's physical appearance: a river choked with sandwich papers and cigarette ends, London Bridge "under the brown fog of a winter dawn." The most vital element of a literary work may pass us by, unless, before seeking further depths in a thing, we look to the thing itself.

Antonio Machado (1875–1939)

Proverbios y Cantares (XXIX) 1912

Caminante, son tus huellas
el camino, y nada más;
caminante, no hay camino,
se hace camino al andar.
Al andar se hace camino,
y al volver la vista atrás
se ve la senda que nunca
se ha de volver a pisar.
Caminante, no hay camino
sino estelas en la mar.

Traveler 2011

Traveler, your footsteps are
the road, there's nothing more;
traveler, there is no road,
the road is made by walking.
Walking makes the road,
and if you turn around,
you only see the path
you cannot walk again.
Traveler, there is no road,
only a track of foam
upon the sea.

—*Translated by Michael Ortiz*

Questions

Compare Machado's poem with Robert Frost's famous "The Road Not Taken." In what ways does Machado's use of the road as a symbol resemble Frost's use? In what ways does it differ?

Robert Frost (1874–1963)

The Road Not Taken 1916

Two roads diverged in a yellow wood,
And sorry I could not travel both
And be one traveler, long I stood
And looked down one as far as I could
To where it bent in the undergrowth;

Then took the other, as just as fair,
And having perhaps the better claim,
Because it was grassy and wanted wear;
Though as for that the passing there
Had worn them really about the same,

And both that morning equally lay
In leaves no step had trodden black.
Oh, I kept the first for another day!
Yet knowing how way leads on to way,
I doubted if I should ever come back.

I shall be telling this with a sigh
Somewhere ages and ages hence:
Two roads diverged in a wood, and I—
I took the one less traveled by,
And that has made all the difference.

Question

What symbolism do you find in this poem, if any? Back up your claim with evidence.

Christina Rossetti (1830–1894)

Up-Hill 1862

Does the road wind up-hill all the way?
  Yes, to the very end.
Will the day's journey take the whole long day?
  From morn to night, my friend.

But is there for the night a resting-place?
  A roof for when the slow dark hours begin.
May not the darkness hide it from my face?
  You cannot miss that inn.

Shall I meet other wayfarers at night?
  Those who have gone before.
Then must I knock, or call when just in sight?
  They will not keep you standing at that door.

Shall I find comfort, travel-sore and weak?
  Of labor you shall find the sum.
Will there be beds for me and all who seek?
  Yea, beds for all who come.

Questions

1. In reading this poem, at what line did you realize that the poet is building an allegory?
2. For what does each thing stand?
3. What does the title of the poem suggest to you?
4. Recast the meaning of line 14, a knotty line, in your own words.

5. Discuss the possible identities of the two speakers—the apprehensive traveler and the character with all the answers. Are they specific individuals? Allegorical figures?
6. Compare "Up-Hill" with Robert Creeley's "Oh No" (Chapter 11). What striking similarities do you find in these two dissimilar poems?

FOR REVIEW AND FURTHER STUDY

Mary Oliver (b. 1935)

Wild Geese

1986

You do not have to be good.
You do not have to walk on your knees
for a hundred miles through the desert, repenting.
You only have to let the soft animal of your body
  love what it loves.
Tell me about despair, yours, and I will tell you mine.
Meanwhile the world goes on.
Meanwhile the sun and the clear pebbles of the rain
are moving across the landscapes,
over the prairies and the deep trees,
the mountains and the rivers.
Meanwhile the wild geese, high in the clean blue air,
are heading home again.
Whoever you are, no matter how lonely,
the world offers itself to your imagination,
calls to you like the wild geese, harsh and exciting—
over and over announcing your place
in the family of things.

Questions

1. Is this poem addressed to a specific person?
2. What is meant by "good" in the first line?
3. What do the wild geese symbolize? What is the significance of the use of the term "wild"?
4. What other adjectives are used to describe the phenomena of nature? What thematic purpose is served by this characterization of the natural world?

Emma Lazarus (1849–1887)

The New Colossus

(1883) 1888

Not like the brazen giant of Greek fame,
With conquering limbs astride from land to land;
Here at our sea-washed, sunset gates shall stand

A mighty woman with a torch, whose flame
Is the imprisoned lightning, and her name
Mother of Exiles. From her beacon-hand
Glows world-wide welcome; her mild eyes command
The air-bridged harbor that twin cities frame.
"Keep, ancient lands, your storied pomp!" cries she
With silent lips. "Give me your tired, your poor,
Your huddled masses yearning to breathe free,
The wretched refuse of your teeming shore.
Send these, the homeless, tempest-tost to me,
I lift my lamp beside the golden door!"

THE NEW COLOSSUS. In 1883, a committee was formed to raise funds to build a pedestal for what would be the largest statue in the world, "Liberty Enlightening the World" by Fréderic-Auguste Bartholdi, which was a gift from the French people to celebrate America's centennial. American authors were asked to donate manuscripts for a fund-raising auction. The young poet Emma Lazarus sent in this sonnet composed for the occasion. When President Grover Cleveland unveiled the Statue of Liberty in October 1886, Lazarus's sonnet was read at the ceremony. In 1903, the poem was carved on the statue's pedestal. The reference in the opening line to "the brazen giant of Greek fame" is to the famous Colossus of Rhodes, a huge bronze statue that once stood in the harbor on the Aegean island of Rhodes. Built to commemorate a military victory, it was one of the so-called Seven Wonders of the World.

Karen Holden (b. 1955)

Bats in a Box

2010

Strange and beautiful, the bats
cling to the corrugated corner, dead to day

This tiny tribe of sleepers and I, somnambulist
travel from house to woods in quiet camaraderie

I carry them the way I would anything precious
hands held out in astonishment and cupped as if

cradling water or the world, as if this moment
is the gift I was waiting for all along.

Lorine Niedecker (1903–1970)

Popcorn-can cover

(about 1959)

Popcorn-can cover
screwed to the wall
over a hole
          so the cold
can't mouse in

Tami Haaland (b. 1960)

Lipstick 2001

I wonder how they do it, those women
who can slip lipstick over lips without
looking, after they've finished a meal
or when they ride in cars. Satin Claret
or Plum or Twig or Pecan. I can't stay
inside the lines, late comer to lipstick
that I am, and sometimes get messy
even in front of a mirror. But these
women know where lips end and plain
skin begins, probably know how to put
their hair in a knot with a single pin.

Questions

1. How does the speaker use lipstick differently from the way "those women" do?
2. Why do the other women know how to apply lipstick more accurately? What does this knowledge suggest about the difference between them and the speaker?
3. What does lipstick seem to suggest in the poem? Support your ideas with specific examples from the poem.

Wallace Stevens (1879–1955)

Anecdote of the Jar 1923

I placed a jar in Tennessee,
And round it was, upon a hill.
It made the slovenly wilderness
Surround that hill.

The wilderness rose up to it,
And sprawled around, no longer wild.
The jar was round upon the ground
And tall and of a port in air.

It took dominion everywhere.
The jar was gray and bare.
It did not give of bird or bush,
Like nothing else in Tennessee.

WRITING *effectively*

THINKING ABOUT SYMBOLS

A symbol, to use poet John Drury's concise definition, is "an image that radiates meanings." While images in a poem can and should be read as what they literally are, images often do double duty, suggesting deeper meanings. Exactly what those meanings are, however, often differs from poem to poem.

Some symbols have been used so often and effectively over time that a traditional reading of them has developed. At times a poet clearly adopts an image's traditional symbolic meaning. Some poems, however, deliberately play against a symbol's conventional associations.

- **To determine the meaning (or meanings) of a symbol, start by asking if it has traditional associations.** If so, consider whether the symbol is being used in the expected way or if the poet is playing with those associations.
- **Consider the symbol's relationship to the rest of the poem.** Let context be your guide. The image might have a unique meaning to the poem's speaker.
- **Consider the emotions that the image evokes.** If the image recurs in the poem, pay attention to how it changes from one appearance to the next.
- **Keep in mind that not everything is a symbol.** If an image doesn't appear to radiate meanings above and beyond its literal sense, don't feel you have failed as a critic. As Sigmund Freud once said about symbol-hunting, "Sometimes a cigar is just a cigar."

CHECKLIST: Writing About Symbols

- ☐ Is the symbol a traditional one?
- ☐ If so, is it being used in the expected way? Or is the poet playing with its associations?
- ☐ What does the image seem to mean to the poem's speaker?
- ☐ What emotions are evoked by the image?
- ☐ If an image recurs in a poem, how does it change from one appearance to the next?
- ☐ Does the image radiate meaning beyond its literal sense? If not, it might not be intended as a symbol.

TOPICS FOR WRITING ON SYMBOLISM

1. Do an in-depth analysis of the symbolism in a poem of your choice from Chapter 23, "Poems for Further Reading." Two likely choices would be Gerard Manley Hopkins's "The Windhover" and Wallace Stevens's "The Snow Man."
2. Compare and contrast the use of roads as symbols in Christina Rossetti's "Up-Hill" and Robert Frost's "The Road Not Taken." What does the use of this image suggest in each poem?
3. Discuss "Anecdote of the Jar" in terms of Wallace Stevens's use of symbolism to portray the relationship between humanity and nature.
4. Write an explication of any poem from this chapter, paying careful attention to its symbols. Some good choices are Mary Oliver's "Wild Geese," Thomas Hardy's "Neutral Tones," and Christina Rossetti's "Up-Hill." For a further description of poetic explication, see the chapter, "Writing About Literature."
5. Take a relatively simple, straightforward poem, such as William Carlos Williams's "This Is Just to Say" (Chapter 12), and write a burlesque critical interpretation of it. Claim to discover symbols that the poem doesn't contain. While running wild with your "reading into" the poem, don't invent anything that you can't somehow support from the text of the poem itself. At the end of your burlesque, sum up in a paragraph what this exercise taught you about how to read poems, or how not to.

▶ TERMS FOR *review*

Symbol ▶ A person, place, or thing in a narrative that suggests meanings beyond its literal sense. Symbol is related to *allegory*, but it works more complexly. A symbol bears multiple suggestions and associations. It is unique to the work, not common to a culture.

Allegory ▶ A description—often a narrative—in which the literal events (persons, places, and things) consistently point to a parallel sequence of ideas, values, or other recognizable abstractions. An allegory has two levels of meaning: a literal level that tells a surface story and a symbolic level in which the abstractions unfold.

Symbolic act ▶ An action whose significance goes well beyond its literal meaning. In literature, symbolic acts often involve a primal or unconscious ritual element such as rebirth, purification, forgiveness, vengeance, or initiation.

Conventional symbols ▶ Symbols that, because of their frequent use, have acquired a standard significance. They may range from complex metaphysical images such as those of Christian saints in Gothic art to social customs such as a young bride in a white dress. They are conventional symbols because they carry recognizable meanings and suggestions.

21 MYTH

What You Will Learn in This Chapter

- To define *myth* and *mythology*
- To recognize and describe an *archetype*
- To describe personal myth
- To analyze the role of myth and archetype in a poem

Poets have long been fond of retelling **myths**, narrowly defined as traditional stories about the exploits of immortal beings. Such stories taken collectively may also be called myth or **mythology**.

Our use of the term *myth* in discussing poetry, then, differs from its use in expressions such as "the myth of communism" and "the myth of democracy." In these examples, *myth* is used broadly to represent any idea people believe in, whether true or false. In the following discussion, *myth* will mean a kind of story—either from ancient or modern sources—whose actions implicitly symbolize some profound truth about human or natural existence.

THE SUBJECTS AND USES OF MYTH

Traditional myths tell us stories of gods or heroes—their battles, their lives, their loves, and often their suffering—all on a scale of magnificence larger than our life. These exciting stories usually reveal part of a culture's worldview. Myths often try to explain universal natural phenomena, like the phases of the moon or the turning of the seasons.

Modern psychologists, such as Sigmund Freud and Carl Jung, have been fascinated by myth and legend, since they believe these stories symbolically enact deep truths about human nature. Our myths, psychologists insist, express our wishes, dreams, and nightmares. Whether or not we believe myths, we recognize their psychological power. Even in the first century B.C., the Roman poet Ovid did not believe in the literal truth of the legends he so suavely retold; he confessed, "I prate of ancient poets' monstrous lies."

Poets have many coherent mythologies on which to draw; perhaps those most frequently consulted by British and American poets are the classical, the Christian, the Norse, the Native American, and the folktales of the American frontier (embodying the deeds of superhuman characters such as Paul Bunyan). Some poets have taken inspiration from other myths as well:

T. S. Eliot's *The Waste Land*, for example, is enriched by allusions to Buddhism and to pagan vegetation cults.

A tour through any good art museum will demonstrate how thoroughly myth pervades the painting and sculpture of nearly every civilization. In literature, one evidence of its continuing value to recent poets and storytellers is how frequently ancient myths are retold. Even in modern society, writers often turn to myth when they try to tell stories of deep significance. Mythic structures still touch a powerful and primal part of the human imagination. William Faulkner's story "The Bear" recalls tales of Indian totem animals; James Joyce's *Ulysses* transposes the *Odyssey* to modern Dublin (and the Coen brothers' film *O Brother, Where Art Thou?* reimagines Homer's epic in Depression-era Mississippi); Rita Dove's play *The Darker Face of the Earth* recasts the story of Oedipus in the slave-era South; Bernard Shaw retells the story of Pygmalion in his popular Edwardian social comedy *Pygmalion*, later the basis of the hit musical *My Fair Lady*. Popular interest in such works may testify to the profound appeal myths continue to hold for us. Like other varieties of poetry, myth is a kind of knowledge, not at odds with scientific knowledge but existing in addition to it.

Robert Frost (1874–1963)

Nothing Gold Can Stay 1923

Nature's first green is gold,
Her hardest hue to hold.
Her early leaf's a flower;
But only so an hour.
Then leaf subsides to leaf.
So Eden sank to grief,
So dawn goes down to day.
Nothing gold can stay.

Questions

1. To what myth does this poem allude? Does Frost sound as though he believes in the myth or as though he rejects it?
2. When Frost says, "Nature's first green is gold," he is describing how many leaves first appear as tiny yellow buds and blossoms. But what else does this line imply?
3. What would happen to the poem's meaning if line 6 were omitted?

William Wordsworth (1770–1850)

The world is too much with us 1807

The world is too much with us; late and soon,
Getting and spending, we lay waste our powers:
Little we see in Nature that is ours;

We have given our hearts away, a sordid boon!
This Sea that bares her bosom to the moon;
The winds that will be howling at all hours,
And are up-gathered now like sleeping flowers;
For this, for everything, we are out of tune;
It moves us not.—Great God! I'd rather be
A Pagan suckled in a creed outworn;
So might I, standing on this pleasant lea,
Have glimpses that would make me less forlorn;
Have sight of Proteus rising from the sea;
Or hear old Triton blow his wreathèd horn.

Questions

1. What condition does the speaker complain of in this sonnet? To what does he attribute this condition?
2. How does this situation affect him personally?

H.D. [Hilda Doolittle] (1886–1961)

Helen

1924

All Greece hates
the still eyes in the white face,
the lustre as of olives
where she stands,
and the white hands.

All Greece reviles
the wan face when she smiles,
hating it deeper still
when it grows wan and white,
remembering past enchantments
and past ills.

Greece sees, unmoved,
God's daughter, born of love,
the beauty of cool feet
and slenderest knees,
could love indeed the maid,
only if she were laid,
white ash amid funereal cypresses.

HELEN. In Greek mythology, Helen, most beautiful of all women, was the daughter of a mortal, Leda, by the god Zeus. Her abduction set off the long and devastating Trojan War. While married to Menelaus, king of the Greek city-state of Sparta, Helen was carried off by Paris, prince of Troy. Menelaus and his brother, Agamemnon, raised an army, besieged Troy for ten years, and eventually recaptured her. One episode of the Trojan War is related in the *Iliad*, Homer's epic poem, composed before 700 B.C.

Questions

1. At what point in the Troy narrative does this poem appear to be set?
2. What connotations does the color white usually possess? Does it have those same associations here?

ARCHETYPE

An important concept in understanding myth is the **archetype**, a basic image, character, situation, or symbol that appears so often in literature and legend that it evokes a deep universal response. (The Greek root of *archetype* means "original pattern.") The term was borrowed by literary critics from the writings of the Swiss psychologist Carl Jung, a serious scholar of myth and religion, who formulated a theory of the "collective unconscious," a set of primal memories common to the entire human race. Archetypal patterns emerged, he speculated, in prerational thought and often reflect key primordial experiences such as birth, growth, sexual awakening, family, generational struggle, and death, as well as primal elements such as fire, sun, moon, blood, and water. Jung also believed that these situations, images, and figures had actually been genetically coded into the human brain and are passed down to successive generations, but no one has ever been able to prove a biological base for the undeniable phenomenon of similar characters, stories, and symbols appearing across widely separated and diverse cultures.

Whatever their origin, archetypal images do seem verbally coded in most myths, legends, and traditional tales. One sees enough recurring patterns and figures from Greek myth to *Star Wars*, from Hindu epic to Marvel superhero comics, to strongly suggest that there is some common psychic force at work. Typical archetypal figures include the trickster, the cruel stepmother, the rebellious young man, the beautiful but destructive woman, and the stupid youngest son who succeeds through simple goodness. Any one of these figures can be traced from culture to culture. The trickster, for instance, appears in American Indian coyote tales, Norse myths about the fire god Loki, Marx Brothers films, and *Batman* comic books and movies featuring the Joker.

Archetypal myths are the basic conventions of human storytelling, which we learn without necessarily being aware of the process. The patterns we absorb in our first nursery rhymes and fairy tales, as mythological critic Northrop Frye has demonstrated, underlie—though often very subtly—the most sophisticated poems and novels. One powerful archetype seen across many cultures is the demon-goddess who immobilizes men by locking them into a deathly trance or—in the most primitive forms of the myth—turning them to stone. Here is a modern version of this ancient myth in the following poem.

Louise Bogan (1897–1970)

Medusa 1923

I had come to the house, in a cave of trees,
Facing a sheer sky.
Everything moved,—a bell hung ready to strike,
Sun and reflection wheeled by.

When the bare eyes were before me
And the hissing hair,
Held up at a window, seen through a door.
The stiff bald eyes, the serpents on the forehead
Formed in the air.

This is a dead scene forever now.
Nothing will ever stir.
The end will never brighten it more than this,
Nor the rain blur.

The water will always fall, and will not fall,
And the tipped bell make no sound.
The grass will always be growing for hay
Deep on the ground.

And I shall stand here like a shadow
Under the great balanced day,
My eyes on the yellow dust, that was lifting in the wind,
And does not drift away.

MEDUSA. One of the Gorgons of Greek mythology. Hideously ugly with snakes for hair, Medusa turned those who looked upon her face into stone.

Questions

1. Who is the speaker of the poem?
2. Why are the first two stanzas spoken in the past tense while the final three are mainly in the future tense?
3. What is the speaker's attitude toward Medusa? Is there anything surprising about his or her reaction to being transformed into stone?
4. Does Bogan merely dramatize an incident from classical mythology, or does the poem suggest other interpretations as well?

John Keats (1795–1821)

La Belle Dame sans Merci 1819

I

O what can ail thee, knight at arms,
  Alone and palely loitering?

The sedge has wither'd from the lake,
And no birds sing.

II

O what can ail thee, knight at arms,
So haggard and so woe-begone?
The squirrel's granary is full,
And the harvest's done.

III

I see a lily on thy brow
With anguish moist and fever dew,
And on thy cheeks a fading rose
Fast withereth too.

IV

I met a lady in the meads,
Full beautiful, a fairy's child;
Her hair was long, her foot was light,
And her eyes were wild.

V

I made a garland for her head,
And bracelets too, and fragrant zone;
She look'd at me as she did love,
And made sweet moan.

VI

I set her on my pacing steed,
And nothing else saw all day long,
For sidelong would she bend, and sing
A fairy's song.

VII

She found me roots of relish sweet,
And honey wild, and manna dew,
And sure in language strange she said—
I love thee true.

VIII

She took me to her elfin grot,
And there she wept, and sigh'd full sore,
And there I shut her wild wild eyes
With kisses four.

IX

And there she lulled me asleep,
And there I dream'd—Ah! woe betide!

The latest dream I ever dream'd
  On the cold hill's side.

X

I saw pale kings, and princes too,
  Pale warriors, death pale were they all;
They cried—"La belle dame sans merci
  Hath thee in thrall!"

XI

I saw their starv'd lips in the gloam
  With horrid warning gaped wide,
And I awoke and found me here
  On the cold hill's side.

XII

And this is why I sojourn here,
  Alone and palely loitering,
Though the sedge is wither'd from the lake,
  And no birds sing.

La Belle Dame sans Merci. The title is French for "the beautiful woman without mercy." Keats borrowed the title from a fifteenth-century French poem.

Questions

1. What time of year is suggested by the details of the first two stanzas? What is the significance of the season in the larger context of the poem?
2. How many speakers are there? Where does the change of speaker occur?
3. What details throughout the text tell us that *la belle dame* is no ordinary woman?
4. Why do you think the poet chose to imitate the form of the folk ballad in this poem?

A. E. Stallings (b. 1968)

First Love: A Quiz

2006

He came up to me:
  a. in his souped-up Camaro
  b. to talk to my skinny best friend
  c. and bumped my glass of wine so I wore the ferrous stain on
    my sleeve
  d. from the ground, in a lead chariot drawn by a team of stal-
    lions black as crude oil and breathing sulfur; at his heart, he
    sported a tiny golden arrow

He offered me:
  a. a ride
  b. dinner and a movie, with a wink at the cliché

c. an excuse not to go back alone to the apartment with its sink
of dirty knives
d. a narcissus with a hundred dazzling petals that breathed a
sweetness as cloying as decay

I went with him because:
a. even his friends told me to beware
b. I had nothing to lose except my virginity
c. he placed his hand in the small of my back and I felt the
tread of honeybees
d. he was my uncle, the one who lived in the half-finished basement, and he took me by the hair

The place he took me to:
a. was dark as my shut eyes
b. and where I ate bitter seed and became ripe
c. and from which my mother would never take me wholly
back, though she wept and walked the earth and made the
bearded ears of barley wither on their stalks and the blasted
flowers drop from their sepals
d. is called by some men hell and others love
e. all of the above

First Love: A Quiz. Stallings's poem alludes to the classical myth of Persephone. A beautiful young goddess, the daughter of Zeus and Demeter, she was abducted by Hades, the ruler of the Underworld (and the brother of Zeus). Her mother Demeter, the goddess of agriculture, became so grief-stricken that plants stopped growing. Eventually, Persephone was permitted to spend six months on the earth each year, which allows spring and summer to return, before descending again to Hades, which brings back winter.

Questions

1. How does Stallings adapt a classical myth of abduction and rape into a contemporary story? Give specific examples.
2. In each option, does the speaker see the man as dangerous? If so, why does she go with him?
3. What is your interpretation of the last line?

PERSONAL MYTH

Sometimes poets have been inspired to make up myths of their own, to embody their own visions of life. "I must create a system or be enslaved by another man's," said William Blake, who in his "prophetic books" peopled the cosmos with supernatural beings having names such as Los, Urizen, and Vala (side by side with recognizable figures from the Old and New Testaments). This kind of system-making probably has advantages and drawbacks. T. S. Eliot, in his essay on Blake, wishes that the author of *The Four Zoas* had accepted traditional myths, and he compares Blake's thinking to a piece of homemade furniture whose construction diverted valuable energy from the writing of poems. Others have found Blake's untraditional cosmos an achievement—notably William Butler Yeats, himself the creator of an elaborate personal mythology. Although we need not know all of Yeats's mythology to enjoy his poems, to know of its existence can make a few great poems deeper for us and less difficult.

William Butler Yeats (1865–1939)

The Second Coming 1921

Turning and turning in the widening gyre° *spiral*
The falcon cannot hear the falconer;
Things fall apart; the center cannot hold;
Mere anarchy is loosed upon the world,
The blood-dimmed tide is loosed, and everywhere
The ceremony of innocence is drowned;
The best lack all conviction, while the worst
Are full of passionate intensity.

Surely some revelation is at hand;
Surely the Second Coming is at hand.
The Second Coming! Hardly are those words out
When a vast image out of *Spiritus Mundi*
Troubles my sight: somewhere in sands of the desert
A shape with lion body and the head of a man,
A gaze blank and pitiless as the sun,
Is moving its slow thighs, while all about it
Reel shadows of the indignant desert birds.
The darkness drops again; but now I know
That twenty centuries of stony sleep
Were vexed to nightmare by a rocking cradle,
And what rough beast, its hour come round at last,
Slouches towards Bethlehem to be born?

What kind of Second Coming does Yeats expect? Evidently it is not to be a Christian one. Yeats saw human history as governed by the turning of a Great Wheel, whose phases influence events and determine human personalities—rather like the signs of the Zodiac in astrology. Every two thousand years comes a horrendous moment: the Wheel completes a turn; one civilization ends and another begins. In 1919 when Yeats wrote "The Second Coming," his Ireland was in the midst of turmoil and bloodshed; the Western Hemisphere had been severely shaken by World War I and the Russian Revolution. A new millennium seemed imminent. What sphinxlike, savage deity would next appear on earth, with birds proclaiming it angrily? Yeats imagines it emerging from *Spiritus Mundi*, Soul of the World, a collective unconscious from which a human being (since the individual soul touches it) receives dreams, nightmares, and memories.

Diane Thiel (b. 1967)

Memento Mori in Middle School

2000

When I was twelve, I chose Dante's *Inferno*
in gifted class—an oral presentation
with visual aids. My brother, *il miglior fabbro*,

said he would draw the tortures. We used ten
red posterboards. That day, for school, I dressed
in pilgrim black, left earlier to hang them

around the class. The students were impressed.
The teacher, too. She acted quite amused
and peered too long at all the punishments.

We knew by reputation she was cruel.
The class could see a hint of twisted forms
and asked to be allowed to round the room

as I went through my final presentation.
We passed the first one, full of poets cut
out of a special issue of *Horizon*.

The class thought these were such a boring set,
they probably deserved their tedious fates.
They liked the next, though—bodies blown about,

the lovers kept outside the tinfoil gates.
We had a new boy in our class named Paolo
and when I noted Paolo's wind-blown state

and pointed out Francesca, people howled.
I knew that more than one of us not-so-
covertly liked him. It seemed like hours

before we moved on to the gluttons, though,
where they could hold the cool fistfuls of slime
I brought from home. An extra touch. It sold

in canisters at toy stores at the time.
The students recognized the River Styx,
the logo of a favorite band of mine.

We moved downriver to the town of Dis,
which someone loudly re-named Dis and Dat.
And for the looming harpies and the furies,

who shrieked and tore things up, I had clipped out
the shrillest, most deserving teacher's heads
from our school paper, then thought better of it.

At the wood of suicides, we quieted.
Though no one in the room would say a word,
I know we couldn't help but think of Fred.

His name was in the news, though we had heard
he might have just been playing with the gun.
We moved on quickly by that huge, dark bird

and rode the flying monster, Geryon,
to reach the counselors, each wicked face,
again, I had resisted pasting in.

To represent the ice in that last place,
where Satan chewed the traitors' frozen heads,
my mother had insisted that I take

an ice-chest full of popsicles—to end
my gruesome project on a lighter note.
"It *is* a comedy, isn't it," she said.

She hadn't read the poem, or seen our art,
but asked me what had happened to the sweet,
angelic poems I once read and wrote.

The class, though, was delighted by the treat,
and at the last round, they all pushed to choose
their colors quickly, so they wouldn't melt.

The bell rang. Everyone ran out of school,
as always, yelling at the top of their lungs,
The *Inferno* fast forgotten, but their howls

showed off their darkened red and purple tongues.

Memento Mori in Middle School. *Memento Mori:* Latin for "Remember you must die," the phrase now means any reminder of human mortality and the need to lead a virtuous life. 1 *Dante's* Inferno: The late medieval epic poem by the Italian poet Dante Alighieri describes a Christian soul's journey through hell. (*Inferno* means "hell" in Italian.) 3 *il miglior fabbro:* the better craftsman—Dante's term for fellow poet Arnaut Daniel, which T. S. Eliot later famously quoted to praise Ezra Pound. 15 Horizon: a magazine of art and culture. 20–23: *Paolo . . . Francesca:* two lovers in Dante's *Inferno* who have been damned for their adultery. 29 *River Styx:* the river that flows around hell to mark its boundary. 31 *Dis:* the main city of hell named after its ruler, Dis (Pluto). 43 *Geryon:* a mythical monster Dante places in his *Inferno.*

Sylvia Plath (1932–1963)

Lady Lazarus

(1962) 1965

I have done it again.
One year in every ten
I manage it—

A sort of walking miracle, my skin
Bright as a Nazi lampshade,
My right foot

A paperweight,
My face a featureless, fine
Jew linen.

Peel off the napkin
O my enemy.
Do I terrify?—

The nose, the eye pits, the full set of teeth?
The sour breath
Will vanish in a day.

Soon, soon the flesh
The grave cave ate will be
At home on me

And I a smiling woman.
I am only thirty.
And like the cat I have nine times to die.

This is Number Three.
What a trash
To annihilate each decade.

What a million filaments.
The peanut-crunching crowd
Shoves in to see

Them unwrap me hand and foot—
The big strip tease.
Gentleman, ladies

These are my hands
My knees.
I may be skin and bone,

Nevertheless, I am the same, identical woman.
The first time it happened I was ten.
It was an accident.

The second time I meant
To last it out and not come back at all.
I rocked shut

As a seashell.
They had to call and call
And pick the worms off me like sticky pearls.

Dying
Is an art, like everything else.
I do it exceptionally well.

I do it so it feels like hell.
I do it so it feels real.
I guess you could say I've a call.

It's easy enough to do it in a cell.
It's easy enough to do it and stay put.
It's the theatrical

Comeback in broad day
To the same place, the same face, the same brute
Amused shout:

"A miracle!"
That knocks me out.
There is a charge

For the eyeing of my scars, there is a charge
For the hearing of my heart—
It really goes.

And there is a charge, a very large charge,
For the word or a touch
Or a bit of blood

Or a piece of my hair or my clothes.
So, so, Herr Doktor.
So, Herr Enemy.

I am your opus,° *work, work of art*
I am your valuable,
The pure gold baby

That melts to a shriek.
I turn and burn.
Do not think I underestimate your great concern.

Ash, ash—
You poke and stir.
Flesh, bone, there is nothing there—

A cake of soap,
A wedding ring,
A gold filling,

Herr God, Herr Lucifer
Beware
Beware.

Out of the ash
I rise with my red hair
And I eat men like air.

Questions

1. What or whom does the title, "Lady Lazarus," allude to?
2. Although the poem is openly autobiographical, Plath uses certain symbols to represent herself (Lady Lazarus, a Jew murdered in a concentration camp, a cat with nine lives, and so on). What do these symbols tell us about Plath's attitude toward herself and the world around her?
3. In her biography of Plath, *Bitter Fame*, the poet Anne Stevenson says that this poem penetrates "the furthest reaches of disdain and rage . . . bereft of all 'normal' human feelings." What do you think Stevenson means? Does anything in the poem strike you as particularly chilling?
4. The speaker in "Lady Lazarus" says, "Dying / Is an art, like everything else" (lines 43–44). What sense do you make of this metaphor?
5. Does the ending of "Lady Lazarus" imply that the speaker assumes that she will outlive her suicide attempts? Set forth your final understanding of the poem.

MYTH AND POPULAR CULTURE

If one can find myths in an art museum, one can also find them abundantly in popular culture. Movies and comic books, for example, are full of myths in modern guise. What is Superman, if not a mythic hero who has adapted himself to modern urban life? Marvel Comics even made the Norse thunder god, Thor, into a superhero, although they initially obliged him, like Clark Kent, to get a job. We also see myths retold on the technicolor screen. Sometimes Hollywood presents the traditional story directly, as in Walt Disney's *Cinderella*; more often the ancient tales acquire contemporary settings, as in another celluloid Cinderella story, *Pretty Woman*. George Lucas's *Star Wars* series borrowed the structure of medieval quest legends. In quest stories, young knights pursued their destiny, often by seeking the Holy Grail, the cup Christ used at the Last Supper; in *Star Wars*, Luke Skywalker searched for his own parentage and identity, but his interstellar quest brought him to a surprisingly similar cast of knights, monsters, princesses, and wizards. Medieval Grail romances, which influenced Eliot's *The Waste Land* and J. R. R. Tolkien's *The Lord of the Rings* trilogy, also shaped films such as *The Matrix*. Science fiction commonly uses myth to original effect. Extraterrestrial visitors usually appear as either munificent mythic gods or nightmarish demons. Steven Spielberg's *E.T.*, for example, revealed a gentle, Christ-like alien recognized by innocent children, but persecuted by adults. E.T. even healed the sick, fell into a deathlike coma, and was resurrected.

Why do poets retell myths? Why don't they just make up their own stories? First, using myth allows poets to be concise. By alluding to stories that their audiences know, they can draw on powerful associations with just a few words. If someone describes an acquaintance, "He thinks he's James Bond," that one allusion speaks volumes. Likewise, when Robert Frost inserts the single line "So Eden sank to grief" in "Nothing Gold Can Stay," those five words summon up a wealth of associations. They tie the perishable quality of spring's beauty to the equally transient nature of human youth. They also suggest that everything in the human world is subject to time's ravages, that perfection is impossible for us to maintain, just as it was for Adam and Eve.

Second, poets know that many stories fall into familiar mythic patterns, and that the most powerful stories of human existence tend to be the same, generation after generation. Sometimes using an old story allows a writer to describe a new situation in a fresh and surprising way.

Aimee Nezhukumatathil (b. 1974)

What I Learned from the Incredible Hulk 2003

When it comes to clothes, make
an allowance for the unexpected.
Be sure the spare in the trunk
of your station wagon with wood paneling

isn't in need of repair. A simple jean jacket
says *Hey, if you aren't trying to smuggle*
rare Incan coins through this peaceful
little town and kidnap the local orphan,

I can be one heck of a mellow kinda guy.
But no matter how angry a man gets, a smile
and a soft stroke on his bicep can work
wonders. I learned that male chests

also have nipples, warm and established—
green doesn't always mean envy.
It's the meadows full of clover
and chicory the Hulk seeks for rest, a return

to normal. And sometimes, a woman
gets to go with him, her tiny hands
correcting his rumpled hair, the cuts
in his hand. Green is the space between

water and sun, cover for a quiet man,
each rib shuttling drops of liquid light.

Questions

1. What is the joke of lines 1 and 2?
2. How is the color green used in the poem?
3. In what way does the poem cast the Incredible Hulk as a mythic hero of popular culture? Does the poet assume that her audience has a shared knowledge of the character and history of the Hulk?

4. How might this poem be different if a man had written it?
5. Describe the tone of the first nine lines. How does that tone shift in line ten, and how would you describe the second half of the poem?

FOR REVIEW AND FURTHER STUDY

Alfred, Lord Tennyson (1809–1892)

Ulysses (1833)

It little profits that an idle king,
By this still hearth, among these barren crags,
Matched with an agèd wife, I mete and dole° *measure and dispense*
Unequal laws unto a savage race
That hoard, and sleep, and feed, and know not me.

I cannot rest from travel; I will drink
Life to the lees.° All times I have enjoyed *to the bottom, the dregs*
Greatly, have suffered greatly, both with those
That loved me, and alone; on shore, and when
Through scudding drifts the rainy Hyades
Vexed the dim sea. I am become a name;
For always roaming with a hungry heart
Much have I seen and known—cities of men
And manners, climates, councils, governments,
Myself not least, but honored of them all—
And drunk delight of battle with my peers,
Far on the ringing plains of windy Troy.
I am a part of all that I have met;
Yet all experience is an arch wherethrough
Gleams that untraveled world whose margin fades
Forever and forever when I move.
How dull it is to pause, to make an end,
To rust unburnished, not to shine in use!
As though to breathe were life! Life piled on life
Were all too little, and of one to me
Little remains; but every hour is saved
From that eternal silence, something more,
A bringer of new things; and vile it were
For some three suns to store and hoard myself,
And this grey spirit yearning in desire
To follow knowledge like a sinking star,
Beyond the utmost bound of human thought.

This is my son, mine own Telemachus,
To whom I leave the scepter and the isle—
Well-loved of me, discerning to fulfill

This labor, by slow prudence to make mild
A rugged people, and through soft degrees
Subdue them to the useful and the good.
Most blameless is he, centered in the sphere
Of common duties, decent not to fail
In offices of tenderness, and pay
Meet adoration to my household gods,
When I am gone. He works his work, I mine.

There lies the port; the vessel puffs her sail;
There gloom the dark, broad seas. My mariners,
Souls that have toiled, and wrought, and thought with me—
That ever with a frolic welcome took
The thunder and the sunshine, and opposed
Free hearts, free foreheads—you and I are old;
Old age hath yet his honor and his toil.
Death closes all; but something ere the end,
Some work of noble note, may yet be done,
Not unbecoming men that strove with Gods.
The lights begin to twinkle from the rocks;
The long day wanes; the slow moon climbs; the deep
Moans round with many voices. Come, my friends,
'Tis not too late to seek a newer world.
Push off, and sitting well in order smite
The sounding furrows; for my purpose holds
To sail beyond the sunset, and the baths
Of all the western stars, until I die.
It may be that the gulfs will wash us down;
It may be we shall touch the Happy Isles,
And see the great Achilles, whom we knew.
Though much is taken, much abides; and though
We are not now that strength which in old days
Moved earth and heaven, that which we are, we are—
One equal temper of heroic hearts,
Made weak by time and fate, but strong in will
To strive, to seek, to find, and not to yield.

ULYSSES. Known as Odysseus in Greek, Ulysses was the king of Ithaca and a hero of the Trojan War. His ten-year journey home was portrayed in Homer's epic poem the *Odyssey*. 10 *Hyades:* daughters of Atlas, who were transformed into a group of stars. Their rising with the sun was thought to be a sign of rain. 33 *Telemachus:* son of Ulysses and Prince of Ithaca. 63 *Happy Isles:* Elysium, a paradise believed to be attainable by sailing west. 64 *Achilles:* also a hero of the Trojan War, a great warrior whose only vulnerability was found on a single spot on his heel.

Questions

1. Who is the speaker of this poem? What details tell us so?
2. What does the speaker mean by "'Tis not too late to seek a newer world" (line 57)?
3. What do you know, or what can you find out, about Ulysses's life that may shed light on what is said here?

WRITING *effectively*

THINKING ABOUT MYTH

Of the many myths conjured by the poets in these pages, you may know some by heart, some only vaguely, and others not at all. When reading a poem inspired by myth, there's no way around it: your understanding will be more precise if you know the mythic story the poem refers to. With the vast resources available on the Web, it's never hard to find a description of a myth, whether traditional or contemporary. While different versions of most myths exist, what usually remains fixed is the tale's basic pattern. A familiarity with that narrative is a key to the meaning—both intellectual and emotional—of any poem that makes reference to mythology.

- **Start with the underlying pattern of the narrative in question.** Does the basic shape of the poem's story seem familiar? Does it have some recognizable source in myth or legend? Even if the poem has no obvious narrative line, does it call to mind other stories?
- **Notice what new details the poem has added, and what it inevitably leaves out.** The difference between the poem and the source material will reveal something about the author's attitude toward the original, and may give you a sense of his or her intentions in reworking the original myth.

CHECKLIST: Writing About Myth

- ☐ Does the poem have a recognizable source in myth or legend?
- ☐ What new details has the poet added to the original myth?
- ☐ What do these details reveal about the poet's attitude toward the source material?
- ☐ Have important elements of the original been discarded? What does their absence suggest about the author's primary focus?
- ☐ Does the poem rely heavily on its mythic imagery? Or is myth tangential to the poem's theme?
- ☐ How do mythic echoes underscore the poem's meaning?

TOPICS FOR WRITING ON MYTH

1. Anne Sexton's "Cinderella" freely mixes period detail and slang from twentieth-century American life with elements from the original fairy tale. (You can read the original in Charles Perrault's *Mother Goose Tales*.) Write an analysis of the effect of all this anachronistic mixing and matching. Be sure to look up any period details you don't recognize.

2. Provide an explication of Louise Bogan's "Medusa." For tips on poetic explication, refer to the chapter "Writing About Literature."
3. Write an essay of approximately 750 words discussing A. E. Stallings's "First Love: A Quiz." How does the poet combine modern circumstances and mythological allusions to suggest personal meaning for the reader?
4. You're probably familiar with an urban legend or two—near-fantastical stories passed on from one person to another, with the suggestion that they really happened to a friend of a friend of the person who told you the tale. Retell an urban myth in free-verse form. If you don't know any urban myths, an Internet search engine can lead you to scores of them.
5. Retell a famous myth or fairy tale to reflect your personal worldview.

▶ TERMS FOR *review*

Myth ▶ A traditional narrative of anonymous authorship that arises out of a culture's oral tradition. The characters in traditional myths are often gods or heroic figures engaged in significant actions and decisions. Myth is usually differentiated from *legend*, which has a specific historical base.

Mythology ▶ The body of myths belonging to a particular culture.

Archetype ▶ A recurring symbol, character, landscape, or event found in myth and literature across different cultures and eras, one that appears so often that it evokes a universal response.

22 WHAT IS POETRY?

What You Will Learn in This Chapter

- To appreciate the diverse ways in which poetry has been defined

By now, perhaps, you have formed your own idea of what poetry is, whether or not you can easily define it. Robert Frost made a try at a definition: "A poem is an idea caught in the act of dawning." Just in case further efforts at definition may be useful, here are a few memorable ones. Poetry is:

> things that are true expressed in words that are beautiful.
> —*Dante*

> the best words in the best order.
> —*Samuel Taylor Coleridge*

> the spontaneous overflow of powerful feelings.
> —*William Wordsworth*

> emotion put into measure.
> —*Thomas Hardy*

> a way of remembering what it would impoverish us to forget.
> —*Robert Frost*

> a revelation in words by means of the words.
> —*Wallace Stevens*

> Poetry is prose bewitched.
> —*Mina Loy*

> the clear expression of mixed feelings.
> —*W. H. Auden*

> an angel with a gun in its hand . . .
> —*José Garcia Villa*

> the language in which man explores his own amazement.
> —*Christopher Fry*

> hundreds of things coming together at the right moment.
> —*Elizabeth Bishop*

Poetry is a sound art.
—*Joy Harjo*

Reduced to its simplest and most essential form, the poem is a song.
Song is neither discourse nor explanation.
—*Octavio Paz*

Poems come out of wonder, not out of knowing.
—*Lucille Clifton*

Poetry is always the cat concert under the window of the room
in which the official version of reality is being written.
—*Charles Simic*

A poem differs from most prose in several ways. For one, both writer and reader tend to regard it differently. The poet's attitude is something like this: I offer this piece of writing to be read not as prose but as a poem—that is, more perceptively, thoughtfully, and creatively, with more attention to sounds and connotations. This is a great deal to expect, but in return, the reader, too, has a right to certain expectations.

Approaching the poem in the anticipation of out-of-the-ordinary knowledge and pleasure, the reader assumes that the poem may use certain enjoyable devices not available to prose: rime, alliteration, meter, and rhythms—definite, various, or emphatic. (The poet may not *always* decide to use these things.) The reader expects the poet to make greater use, perhaps, of resources of meaning such as figurative language, allusion, symbol, and imagery. As readers of prose, we might seek no more than meaning: no more than what could be paraphrased without serious loss. Meeting any figurative language or graceful turns of word order, we think them pleasant extras. But in poetry all these "extras" matter as much as the paraphrasable content, if not more. For, when we finish reading a good poem, we cannot explain precisely to ourselves what we have experienced—without repeating, word for word, the language of the poem itself. Archibald MacLeish makes this point memorably in "Ars Poetica":

A poem should not mean
But be.

Throughout this book, we have been working on the assumption that the patient and conscious explication of poems will sharpen unconscious perceptions. We can only hope that it will; the final test lies in whether you care to go on by yourself, reading other poems, finding in them pleasure and enlightenment. Pedagogy must have a stop; so too must the viewing of poems as if their elements fell into chapters. For the total experience of reading a poem surpasses the mind's categories. The wind in the grass, says a proverb, cannot be taken into the house.

23 POEMS FOR FURTHER READING

Aaron Abeyta

Aaron Abeyta (b. 1971)

thirteen ways of looking at a tortilla 2001

i.

among twenty different tortillas
the only thing moving
was the mouth of the niño

ii.

i was of three cultures
like a tortilla
for which there are three bolios

iii.

the tortilla grew on the wooden table
it was a small part of the earth

iv.

a house and a tortilla
are one
a man a woman and a tortilla
are one

v.

i do not know which to prefer
the beauty of the red wall
or the beauty of the green wall
the tortilla fresh
or just after

vi.

tortillas filled the small kitchen
with ancient shadows

the shadow of Maclovia
cooking long ago
the tortilla
rolled from the shadow
the innate roundness

vii.

o thin viejos of chimayo
why do you imagine biscuits
do you not see how the tortilla
lives with the hands
of the women about you

viii.

i know soft corn
and beautiful inescapable sopapillas
but i know too
that the tortilla
has taught me what I know

ix.

when the tortilla is gone
it marks the end
of one of many tortillas

x.

at the sight of tortillas
browning on a black comal°
even the pachucos of española
would cry out sharply

comal: flat griddle pan

xi.

he rode over new mexico
in a pearl low rider
once he got a flat
in that he mistook
the shadow of his spare
for a tortilla

xii.

the abuelitas are moving
the tortilla must be baking

xiii.

it was cinco de mayo all year
it was warm
and it was going to get warmer
the tortilla sat
on the frijolito plate

Francisco X. Alarcón (1954–2016)

The X in My Name

1993

the poor
signature
of my illiterate
and peasant
self
giving away
all rights
in a deceiving
contract for life

Anonymous (Navajo mountain chant)

Last Words of the Prophet

Farewell, younger brother!
From the holy places the gods come for me.
You will never see me again; but when the showers pass and the thunder peals,
"There," you will say, "is the voice of my elder brother."
And when the harvest comes, of the beautiful birds and grasshoppers you will say,
"There is the ordering of my elder brother!"

—*Translated by Washington Matthews*

Matthew Arnold (1822–1888)

Dover Beach

1867

The sea is calm to-night.
The tide is full, the moon lies fair
Upon the straits; on the French coast the light
Gleams and is gone; the cliffs of England stand,
Glimmering and vast, out in the tranquil bay.
Come to the window, sweet is the night-air!
Only, from the long line of spray

Where the sea meets the moon-blanched land,
Listen! you hear the grating roar
Of pebbles which the waves draw back, and fling,
At their return, up the high strand,
Begin, and cease, and then again begin,
With tremulous cadence slow, and bring
The eternal note of sadness in.

Sophocles long ago
Heard it on the Aegean, and it brought
Into his mind the turbid ebb and flow
Of human misery; we
Find also in the sound a thought,
Hearing it by this distant northern sea.

The Sea of Faith
Was once, too, at the full, and round earth's shore
Lay like the folds of a bright girdle furled.
But now I only hear
Its melancholy, long, withdrawing roar,
Retreating, to the breath
Of the night-wind, down the vast edges drear
And naked shingles° of the world. *gravel beaches*

Ah, love, let us be true
To one another! for the world, which seems
To lie before us like a land of dreams,
So various, so beautiful, so new,
Hath really neither joy, nor love, nor light,
Nor certitude, nor peace, nor help for pain;
And we are here as on a darkling° plain *darkened or darkening*
Swept with confused alarms of struggle and flight,
Where ignorant armies clash by night.

The Fall of Icarus **by Pieter Brueghel the Elder (1520?–1569).**

W. H. Auden (1907–1973)

Musée des Beaux Arts

1940

About suffering they were never wrong,
The Old Masters: how well they understood
Its human position; how it takes place
While someone else is eating or opening a window or just walking
    dully along;
How, when the aged are reverently, passionately waiting
For the miraculous birth, there always must be
Children who did not specially want it to happen, skating
On a pond at the edge of the wood:
They never forgot
That even the dreadful martyrdom must run its course
Anyhow in a corner, some untidy spot
Where the dogs go on with their doggy life and the torturer's horse
Scratches its innocent behind on a tree.

In Brueghel's *Icarus*, for instance: how everything turns away
Quite leisurely from the disaster; the ploughman may
Have heard the splash, the forsaken cry,
But for him it was not an important failure; the sun shone
As it had to on the white legs disappearing into the green
Water; and the expensive delicate ship that must have seen
Something amazing, a boy falling out of the sky,
Had somewhere to get to and sailed calmly on.

Elizabeth Bishop

Elizabeth Bishop (1911–1979)

One Art

1976

The art of losing isn't hard to master;
so many things seem filled with the intent
to be lost that their loss is no disaster.

Lose something every day. Accept the fluster
of lost door keys, the hour badly spent.
The art of losing isn't hard to master.

Then practice losing farther, losing faster:
places, and names, and where it was you meant
to travel. None of these will bring disaster.

I lost my mother's watch. And look! my last, or
next-to-last, of three loved houses went.
The art of losing isn't hard to master.

I lost two cities, lovely ones. And, vaster,
some realms I owned, two rivers, a continent.
I miss them, but it wasn't a disaster.

—Even losing you (the joking voice, a gesture
I love) I shan't have lied. It's evident
the art of losing's not too hard to master
though it may look like (*Write* it!) like disaster.

Illuminated manuscript of William Blake's "The Tyger."

William Blake (1757–1827)

The Tyger 1794

Tyger! Tyger! burning bright
In the forests of the night,
What immortal hand or eye
Could frame thy fearful symmetry?

In what distant deeps or skies
Burnt the fire of thine eyes?
On what wings dare he aspire?
What the hand dare seize the fire?

And what shoulder, and what art,
Could twist the sinews of thy heart?
And when thy heart began to beat,
What dread hand? and what dread feet?

What the hammer? what the chain?
In what furnace was thy brain?
What the anvil? what dread grasp
Dare its deadly terrors clasp?

When the stars threw down their spears,
And watered heaven with their tears,
Did he smile his work to see?
Did he who made the Lamb make thee?

Tyger! Tyger! burning bright
In the forests of the night,
What immortal hand or eye
Dare frame thy fearful symmetry?

Gwendolyn Brooks

Gwendolyn Brooks (1917–2000)

the mother

1945

Abortions will not let you forget.
You remember the children you got that you did not get,
The damp small pulps with a little or with no hair,
The singers and workers that never handled the air.
You will never neglect or beat
Them, or silence or buy with a sweet.
You will never wind up the sucking-thumb
Or scuttle off ghosts that come.
You will never leave them, controlling your luscious sigh,
Return for a snack of them, with gobbling mother-eye.

I have heard in the voices of the wind the voices of my dim killed
children.
I have contracted. I have eased
My dim dears at the breasts they could never suck.
I have said, Sweets, if I sinned, if I seized
Your luck
And your lives from your unfinished reach,
If I stole your births and your names,
Your straight baby tears and your games,
Your stilted or lovely loves, your tumults, your marriages, aches, and
your deaths,
If I poisoned the beginnings of your breaths,
Believe that even in my deliberateness I was not deliberate.
Though why should I whine,
Whine that the crime was other than mine?—
Since anyhow you are dead.
Or rather, or instead,
You were never made.
But that too, I am afraid,
Is faulty: oh, what shall I say, how is the truth to be said?
You were born, you had body, you died.
It is just that you never giggled or planned or cried.

Believe me, I loved you all.
Believe me, I knew you, though faintly, and I loved, I loved you
All.

Elizabeth Barrett Browning (1806–1861)

How Do I Love Thee? Let Me Count the Ways — 1850

How do I love thee? Let me count the ways.
I love thee to the depth and breadth and height
My soul can reach, when feeling out of sight
For the ends of Being and ideal Grace.
I love thee to the level of every day's
Most quiet need, by sun and candle-light.
I love thee freely, as men strive for Right;
I love thee purely, as they turn from Praise.
I love thee with the passion put to use
In my old griefs, and with my childhood's faith.
I love thee with a love I seemed to lose
With my lost saints,—I love thee with the breath,
Smiles, tears, of all my life!—and, if God choose,
I shall but love thee better after death.

Charles Bukowski

Charles Bukowski (1920–1994)

Dostoevsky — 1997

against the wall, the firing squad ready.
then he got a reprieve.
suppose they had shot Dostoevsky?
before he wrote all that?
I suppose it wouldn't have
mattered
not directly.
there are billions of people who have

never read him and never
will.
but as a young man I know that he
got me through the factories,
past the whores,
lifted me high through the night
and put me down
in a better
place.
even while in the bar
drinking with the other
derelicts,
I was glad they gave Dostoevsky a
reprieve,
it gave me one,
allowed me to look directly at those
rancid faces
in my world,
death pointing its finger,
I held fast,
an immaculate drunk
sharing the stinking dark with
my
brothers.

DOSTOEVSKY. The Russian novelist Fyodor Dostoevsky (1821–1880), author of *Crime and Punishment* and *The Brothers Karamazov*, was arrested in 1849 in a czarist crackdown on liberal organizations and sentenced to death. It was not until the members of the firing squad had aimed their rifles and were awaiting the order to fire that he was informed that his sentence had been commuted to four years of hard labor in Siberia.

Judith Ortiz Cofer (b. 1952)

Quinceañera 1987

My dolls have been put away like dead
children in a chest I will carry
with me when I marry.
I reach under my skirt to feel
a satin slip bought for this day. It is soft
as the inside of my thighs. My hair
has been nailed back with my mother's
black hairpins to my skull. Her hands
stretched my eyes open as she twisted
braids into a tight circle at the nape
of my neck. I am to wash my own clothes
and sheets from this day on, as if

the fluids of my body were poison, as if
the little trickle of blood I believe
travels from my heart to the world were
shameful. Is not the blood of saints and
men in battle beautiful? Do Christ's hands
not bleed into your eyes from His cross?
At night I hear myself growing and wake
to find my hands drifting of their own will
to soothe skin stretched tight
over my bones.
I am wound like the guts of a clock,
waiting for each hour to release me.

QUINCEAÑERA. The title refers to a fifteen-year-old girl's coming-out party in Latin cultures.

Samuel Taylor Coleridge (1772–1834)

Kubla Khan (1797–1798)

Or, a Vision in a Dream. A Fragment.

In Xanadu did Kubla Khan
A stately pleasure-dome decree:
Where Alph, the sacred river, ran
Through caverns measureless to man
  Down to a sunless sea.
So twice five miles of fertile ground
With walls and towers were girdled round:
And here were gardens bright with sinuous rills,
Where blossomed many an incense-bearing tree;
And here were forests ancient as the hills,
Enfolding sunny spots of greenery.

But oh! that deep romantic chasm which slanted
Down the green hill athwart a cedarn cover!
A savage place! as holy and enchanted
As e'er beneath a waning moon was haunted
By woman wailing for her demon-lover!
And from this chasm, with ceaseless turmoil seething,
As if this earth in fast thick pants were breathing,
A mighty fountain momently was forced:
Amid whose swift half-intermitted burst
Huge fragments vaulted like rebounding hail,
Or chaffy grain beneath the thresher's flail:
And 'mid these dancing rocks at once and ever
It flung up momently the sacred river.
Five miles meandering with a mazy motion

Through wood and dale the sacred river ran,
Then reached the caverns measureless to man,
And sank in tumult to a lifeless ocean:
And 'mid this tumult Kubla heard from far
Ancestral voices prophesying war!

The shadow of the dome of pleasure
Floated midway on the waves;
Where was heard the mingled measure
From the fountain and the caves.
It was a miracle of rare device,
A sunny pleasure-dome with caves of ice!

A damsel with a dulcimer
In a vision once I saw:
It was an Abyssinian maid,
And on her dulcimer she played,
Singing of Mount Abora.
Could I revive within me
Her symphony and song,
To such a deep delight 'twould win me,
That with music loud and long,
I would build that dome in air,
That sunny dome! those caves of ice!
And all who heard should see them there,
And all should cry, Beware! Beware!
His flashing eyes, his floating hair!
Weave a circle round him thrice,
And close your eyes with holy dread,
For he on honey-dew hath fed,
And drunk the milk of Paradise.

Kubla Khan. There was an actual Kublai Khan, a thirteenth-century Mongol emperor, and a Chinese city of Xanadu; but Coleridge's dream vision also borrows from travelers' descriptions of such other exotic places as Abyssinia and America. 51 *circle:* a magic circle drawn to keep away evil spirits.

Billy Collins

Billy Collins (b. 1941)

Introduction to Poetry

1988

I ask them to take a poem
and hold it up to the light
like a color slide

or press an ear against its hive.

I say drop a mouse into a poem
and watch him probe his way out,

or walk inside the poem's room
and feel the walls for a light switch.

I want them to waterski
across the surface of a poem
waving at the author's name on the shore.

But all they want to do
is tie the poem to a chair with rope
and torture a confession out of it.

They begin beating it with a hose
to find out what it really means.

E. E. Cummings

E. E. Cummings (1894–1962)

somewhere i have never travelled,gladly beyond 1931

somewhere i have never travelled,gladly beyond
any experience,your eyes have their silence:
in your most frail gesture are things which enclose me,
or which i cannot touch because they are too near

your slightest look easily will unclose me
though i have closed myself as fingers,
you open always petal by petal myself as Spring opens
(touching skilfully,mysteriously)her first rose

or if your wish be to close me,i and
my life will shut very beautifully,suddenly,
as when the heart of this flower imagines
the snow carefully everywhere descending;

nothing which we are to perceive in this world equals
the power of your intense fragility:whose texture
compels me with the colour of its countries,
rendering death and forever with each breathing

(i do not know what it is about you that closes
and opens;only something in me understands
the voice of your eyes is deeper than all roses)
nobody,not even the rain,has such small hands

Emily Dickinson (1830–1886)

Wild Nights – Wild Nights! (about 1861)

Wild Nights – Wild Nights!
Were I with thee
Wild Nights should be
Our luxury!

Futile – the Winds –
To a Heart in port –
Done with the Compass –
Done with the Chart!

Rowing in Eden –
Ah, the Sea!
Might I but moor – Tonight –
In Thee!

Emily Dickinson (1830–1886)

I felt a Funeral, in my Brain (about 1861)

I felt a Funeral, in my Brain,
And Mourners to and fro
Kept treading – treading – till it seemed
That Sense was breaking through –

And when they all were seated,
A Service, like a Drum –
Kept beating – beating – till I thought
My Mind was going numb –

And then I heard them lift a Box
And creak across my Soul
With those same Boots of Lead, again,
Then Space – began to toll,

As all the Heavens were a Bell,
And Being, but an Ear,
And I, and Silence, some strange Race
Wrecked, solitary, here –

And Then a Plank in Reason, broke,
And I dropped down, and down –
And hit a World, at every plunge,
And Finished knowing – then –

Emily Dickinson

Emily Dickinson (1830–1886)

Because I could not stop for Death (about 1863)

Because I could not stop for Death –
He kindly stopped for me –
The Carriage held but just Ourselves –
And Immortality.

We slowly drove – He knew no haste
And I had put away
My labor and my leisure too,
For His Civility –

We passed the School, where Children strove
At Recess – in the Ring –
We passed the Fields of Gazing Grain –
We passed the Setting Sun –

Or rather – He passed Us –
The Dews drew quivering and chill –
For only Gossamer, my Gown –
My Tippet° – only Tulle –

° *cape*

We paused before a House that seemed
A Swelling of the Ground –
The Roof was scarcely visible –
The Cornice – in the Ground –

Since then – 'tis Centuries – and yet
Feels shorter than the Day
I first surmised the Horses' Heads
Were toward Eternity –

John Donne (1572–1631)

Death be not proud (about 1610)

Death be not proud, though some have callèd thee
Mighty and dreadful, for thou art not so;
For those whom thou think'st thou dost overthrow
Die not, poor death, nor yet canst thou kill me.
From rest and sleep, which but thy pictures be,
Much pleasure, then from thee much more must flow,
And soonest our best men with thee do go,
Rest of their bones, and soul's delivery.
Thou art slave to fate, chance, kings, and desperate men,
And dost with poison, war, and sickness dwell,
And poppy, or charms can make us sleep as well,
And better than thy stroke; why swell'st thou then?
One short sleep past, we wake eternally,
And death shall be no more; death, thou shalt die.

John Donne (1572–1631)

The Flea 1633

Mark but this flea, and mark in this
How little that which thou deny'st me is;
It sucked me first, and now sucks thee,
And in this flea our two bloods mingled be;
Thou know'st that this cannot be said
A sin, nor shame, nor loss of maidenhead,
  Yet this enjoys before it woo,
  And pampered swells with one blood made of two,
  And this, alas, is more than we would do.

Oh stay, three lives in one flea spare,
Where we almost, yea more than married are.
This flea is you and I, and this
Our marriage bed, and marriage temple is;
Though parents grudge, and you, we're met
And cloistered in these living walls of jet.
  Though use° make you apt to kill me, *custom*
  Let not to that, self-murder added be,
  And sacrilege, three sins in killing three.

Cruel and sudden, hast thou since
Purpled thy nail in blood of innocence?
Wherein could this flea guilty be,
Except in that drop which it sucked from thee?

Yet thou triumph'st, and say'st that thou
Find'st not thyself, nor me, the weaker now;
'Tis true; then learn how false, fears be;
Just so much honor, when thou yield'st to me,
Will waste, as this flea's death took life from thee.

T. S. Eliot

T. S. Eliot (1888–1965)

The Love Song of J. Alfred Prufrock 1917

S'io credessi che mia risposta fosse
a persona che mai tornasse al mondo,
questa fiamma staria senza più scosse.
Ma per ciò che giammai di questo fondo
non tornò vivo alcun, s'i'odo il vero,
senza tema d'infamia ti rispondo.

Let us go then, you and I,
When the evening is spread out against the sky
Like a patient etherized upon a table;
Let us go, through certain half-deserted streets,
The muttering retreats
Of restless nights in one-night cheap hotels
And sawdust restaurants with oyster-shells:
Streets that follow like a tedious argument
Of insidious intent
To lead you to an overwhelming question . . .
Oh, do not ask, "What is it?"
Let us go and make our visit.

In the room the women come and go
Talking of Michelangelo.

The yellow fog that rubs its back upon the window-panes,
The yellow smoke that rubs its muzzle on the window-panes,
Licked its tongue into the corners of the evening,
Lingered upon the pools that stand in drains,

Let fall upon its back the soot that falls from chimneys,
Slipped by the terrace, made a sudden leap,
And seeing that it was a soft October night,
Curled once about the house, and fell asleep.

And indeed there will be time
For the yellow smoke that slides along the street
Rubbing its back upon the window-panes;
There will be time, there will be time
To prepare a face to meet the faces that you meet;
There will be time to murder and create,
And time for all the works and days of hands
That lift and drop a question on your plate;
Time for you and time for me,
And time yet for a hundred indecisions,
And for a hundred visions and revisions,
Before the taking of a toast and tea.

In the room the women come and go
Talking of Michelangelo.
And indeed there will be time
To wonder, "Do I dare?" and, "Do I dare?"
Time to turn back and descend the stair,
With a bald spot in the middle of my hair—
(They will say: "How his hair is growing thin!")
My morning coat, my collar mounting firmly to the chin,
My necktie rich and modest, but asserted by a simple pin—
(They will say: "But how his arms and legs are thin!")
Do I dare
Disturb the universe?
In a minute there is time
For decisions and revisions which a minute will reverse.
For I have known them all already, known them all—
Have known the evenings, mornings, afternoons,
I have measured out my life with coffee spoons;
I know the voices dying with a dying fall
Beneath the music from a farther room.
So how should I presume?

And I have known the eyes already, known them all—
The eyes that fix you in a formulated phrase,
And when I am formulated, sprawling on a pin,
When I am pinned and wriggling on the wall,
Then how should I begin
To spit out all the butt-ends of my days and ways?
And how should I presume?

And I have known the arms already, known them all—
Arms that are braceleted and white and bare
(But in the lamplight, downed with light brown hair!)
Is it perfume from a dress
That makes me so digress?
Arms that lie along a table, or wrap about a shawl.
    And should I then presume?
    And how should I begin?

. . . . .

Shall I say, I have gone at dusk through narrow streets
And watched the smoke that rises from the pipes
Of lonely men in shirt-sleeves, leaning out of windows? . . .

I should have been a pair of ragged claws
Scuttling across the floors of silent seas.

. . . . .

And the afternoon, the evening, sleeps so peacefully!
Smoothed by long fingers,
Asleep ... tired ... or it malingers,
Stretched on the floor, here beside you and me.
Should I, after tea and cakes and ices,
Have the strength to force the moment to its crisis?
But though I have wept and fasted, wept and prayed,
Though I have seen my head (grown slightly bald) brought in upon
    a platter,
I am no prophet—and here's no great matter;
I have seen the moment of my greatness flicker,
And I have seen the eternal Footman hold my coat, and snicker,
And in short, I was afraid.
And would it have been worth it, after all,
After the cups, the marmalade, the tea,
Among the porcelain, among some talk of you and me,
Would it have been worth while,
To have bitten off the matter with a smile,
To have squeezed the universe into a ball
To roll it toward some overwhelming question,
To say: "I am Lazarus, come from the dead,
Come back to tell you all, I shall tell you all"—
If one, settling a pillow by her head,
    Should say: "That is not what I meant at all.
    That is not it, at all."

And would it have been worth it, after all,
Would it have been worth while,
After the sunsets and the dooryards and the sprinkled streets,

After the novels, after the teacups, after the skirts that trail along
the floor—
And this, and so much more?—
It is impossible to say just what I mean!
But as if a magic lantern threw the nerves in patterns on a screen:
Would it have been worth while
If one, settling a pillow or throwing off a shawl,
And turning toward the window, should say:
"That is not it at all,
That is not what I meant, at all."

. . . . .

No! I am not Prince Hamlet, nor was meant to be;
Am an attendant lord, one that will do
To swell a progress, start a scene or two,
Advise the prince; no doubt, an easy tool,
Deferential, glad to be of use,
Politic, cautious, and meticulous;
Full of high sentence, but a bit obtuse;
At times, indeed, almost ridiculous—
Almost, at times, the Fool.

I grow old ... I grow old ...
I shall wear the bottoms of my trousers rolled.

Shall I part my hair behind? Do I dare to eat a peach?
I shall wear white flannel trousers, and walk upon the beach.
I have heard the mermaids singing, each to each.

I do not think that they will sing to me.
I have seen them riding seaward on the waves
Combing the white hair of the waves blown back
When the wind blows the water white and black.

We have lingered in the chambers of the sea
By sea-girls wreathed with seaweed red and brown
Till human voices wake us, and we drown.

THE LOVE SONG OF J. ALFRED PRUFROCK. The epigraph, from Dante's *Inferno*, is the speech of one dead and damned, who thinks that his hearer also is going to remain in Hell. Count Guido da Montefeltro, whose sin has been to give false counsel after a corrupt prelate had offered him prior absolution and whose punishment is to be wrapped in a constantly burning flame, offers to tell Dante his story:

If I thought my answer were to someone who
might see the world again, then there would be
no more stirrings of this flame. Since it is true
that no one leaves these depths of misery
alive, from all that I have heard reported,
I answer you without fear of infamy.

(Translation by Michael Palma from: Dante Alighieri, *Inferno: A New Verse Translation* [New York: Norton, 2002].) 29 *works and days:* title of a poem by Hesiod (eighth century B.C.), depicting his life as a hardworking Greek farmer and exhorting his brother to be like him. 82 *head . . . platter:* like that of John the Baptist, prophet and praiser of chastity, whom King Herod beheaded at the demand of Herodias, his unlawfully wedded wife (see Mark 6:17–28). 92–93 *squeezed . . . To roll it:* an echo from Marvell's "To His Coy Mistress," lines 41–42. 94 *Lazarus:* probably the Lazarus whom Jesus called forth from the tomb (John 11:1–44), but possibly the beggar seen in Heaven by the rich man in Hell (Luke 16:19–25). 105 *magic lantern:* an early type of projector used to display still pictures from transparent slides.

Robert Frost

Robert Frost (1874–1963)

Mending Wall

1914

Something there is that doesn't love a wall,
That sends the frozen-ground-swell under it,
And spills the upper boulders in the sun;
And makes gaps even two can pass abreast.
The work of hunters is another thing:
I have come after them and made repair
Where they have left not one stone on a stone,
But they would have the rabbit out of hiding,
To please the yelping dogs. The gaps I mean,
No one has seen them made or heard them made,
But at spring mending-time we find them there.
I let my neighbor know beyond the hill;
And on a day we meet to walk the line
And set the wall between us once again.
We keep the wall between us as we go.
To each the boulders that have fallen to each.
And some are loaves and some so nearly balls
We have to use a spell to make them balance:
"Stay where you are until our backs are turned!"
We wear our fingers rough with handling them.
Oh, just another kind of outdoor game,
One on a side. It comes to little more:

There where it is we do not need the wall:
He is all pine and I am apple orchard.
My apple trees will never get across
And eat the cones under his pines, I tell him.
He only says, "Good fences make good neighbors."
Spring is the mischief in me, and I wonder
If I could put a notion in his head:
"*Why* do they make good neighbors? Isn't it
Where there are cows? But here there are no cows.
Before I built a wall I'd ask to know
What I was walling in or walling out,
And to whom I was like to give offence.
Something there is that doesn't love a wall,
That wants it down." I could say "Elves" to him,
But it's not elves exactly, and I'd rather
He said it for himself. I see him there
Bringing a stone grasped firmly by the top
In each hand, like an old-stone savage armed.
He moves in darkness as it seems to me,
Not of woods only and the shade of trees.
He will not go behind his father's saying,
And he likes having thought of it so well
He says again, "Good fences make good neighbors."

Robert Frost (1874–1963)

Stopping by Woods on a Snowy Evening 1923

Whose woods these are I think I know.
His house is in the village though;
He will not see me stopping here
To watch his woods fill up with snow.

My little horse must think it queer
To stop without a farmhouse near
Between the woods and frozen lake
The darkest evening of the year.

He gives his harness bells a shake
To ask if there is some mistake.
The only other sound's the sweep
Of easy wind and downy flake.

The woods are lovely, dark and deep,
But I have promises to keep,
And miles to go before I sleep,
And miles to go before I sleep.

Allen Ginsberg

Allen Ginsberg (1926–1997)

A Supermarket in California 1956

What thoughts I have of you tonight, Walt Whitman, for I walked down the sidestreets under the trees with a headache self-conscious looking at the full moon.

In my hungry fatigue, and shopping for images, I went into the neon fruit supermarket, dreaming of your enumerations!

What peaches and what penumbras! Whole families shopping at night! Aisles full of husbands! Wives in the avocados, babies in the tomatoes!—and you, García Lorca, what were you doing down by the watermelons?

I saw you, Walt Whitman, childless, lonely old grubber, poking among the meats in the refrigerator and eyeing the grocery boys.

I heard you asking questions of each: Who killed the pork chops? What price bananas? Are you my Angel?

I wandered in and out of the brilliant stacks of cans following you, and followed in my imagination by the store detective.

We strode down the open corridors together in our solitary fancy tasting artichokes, possessing every frozen delicacy, and never passing the cashier.

Where are we going, Walt Whitman? The doors close in an hour. Which way does your beard point tonight?

(I touch your book and dream of our odyssey in the supermarket and feel absurd.)

Will we walk all night through solitary streets? The trees add shade to shade, lights out in the houses, we'll both be lonely.

Will we stroll dreaming of the lost America of love past blue automobiles in driveways, home to our silent cottage?

Ah, dear father, graybeard, lonely old courage-teacher, what America did you have when Charon quit poling his ferry and you got out on a smoking bank and stood watching the boat disappear on the black waters of Lethe?

A SUPERMARKET IN CALIFORNIA. 2 *enumerations:* many of Whitman's poems contain lists of observed details. 3 *García Lorca:* modern Spanish poet who wrote an "Ode to Walt Whitman" in his book-length sequence *Poet in New York.* 12 *Charon … Lethe:* Is the poet confusing two underworld rivers? Charon, in Greek and Roman mythology, is the boatman who ferries the souls of the dead across the river Styx. The river Lethe also flows through Hades, and a drink of its waters makes the dead lose their painful memories of loved ones they have left behind.

Thomas Hardy (1840–1928)

The Convergence of the Twain 1912

Lines on the Loss of the "Titanic"

I

In a solitude of the sea
Deep from human vanity,
And the Pride of Life that planned her, stilly couches she.

II

Steel chambers, late the pyres
Of her salamandrine fires,
Cold currents thrid,° and turn to rhythmic tidal lyres. *thread*

III

Over the mirrors meant
To glass the opulent
The sea-worm crawls—grotesque, slimed, dumb, indifferent.

IV

Jewels in joy designed
To ravish the sensuous mind
Lie lightless, all their sparkles bleared and black and blind.

V

Dim moon-eyed fishes near
Gaze at the gilded gear
And query: "What does this vaingloriousness down here?" . . .

VI

Well: while was fashioning
This creature of cleaving wing,
The Immanent Will that stirs and urges everything

VII

Prepared a sinister mate
For her—so gaily great—
A Shape of Ice, for the time far and dissociate.

VIII

And as the smart ship grew
In stature, grace, and hue,
In shadowy silent distance grew the Iceberg too.

IX

Alien they seemed to be:
No mortal eye could see
The intimate welding of their later history,

X

Or sign that they were bent
By paths coincident
On being anon twin halves of one august event,

XI

Till the Spinner of the Years
Said "Now!" And each one hears,
And consummation comes, and jars two hemispheres.

THE CONVERGENCE OF THE TWAIN. The luxury liner *Titanic*, supposedly unsinkable, went down in 1912 after striking an iceberg on its first Atlantic voyage. 5 *salamandrine:* like the salamander, a lizard that supposedly thrives in fires, or like a spirit of the same name that inhabits fire (according to alchemists).

Seamus Heaney (1939–2013)

Digging

1966

Between my finger and my thumb
The squat pen rests; snug as a gun.

Under my window, a clean rasping sound
When the spade sinks into gravelly ground:
My father, digging. I look down

Till his straining rump among the flowerbeds
Bends low, comes up twenty years away
Stooping in rhythm through potato drills
Where he was digging.

The coarse boot nestled on the lug, the shaft
Against the inside knee was levered firmly.
He rooted out tall tops, buried the bright edge deep
To scatter new potatoes that we picked
Loving their cool hardness in our hands.

By God, the old man could handle a spade.
Just like his old man.

My grandfather cut more turf in a day
Than any other man on Toner's bog.
Once I carried him milk in a bottle
Corked sloppily with paper. He straightened up
To drink it, then fell to right away
Nicking and slicing neatly, heaving sods
Over his shoulder, going down and down
For the good turf. Digging.

The cold smell of potato mould, the squelch and slap
Of soggy peat, the curt cuts of an edge
Through living roots awaken in my head.
But I've no spade to follow men like them.

Between my finger and my thumb
The squat pen rests.
I'll dig with it.

William Ernest Henley (1849–1903)

Invictus 1875

Out of the night that covers me,
  Black as the pit from pole to pole,
I thank whatever gods may be
  For my unconquerable soul.

In the fell clutch of circumstance
  I have not winced nor cried aloud.
Under the bludgeonings of chance
  My head is bloody, but unbowed.

Beyond this place of wrath and tears
  Looms but the Horror of the shade,
And yet the menace of the years
  Finds and shall find me unafraid.

It matters not how strait the gate,
  How charged with punishments the scroll,
I am the master of my fate,
  I am the captain of my soul.

George Herbert (1593–1633)

Easter Wings

1633

Lord, who createdst man in wealth and store,
Though foolishly he lost the same,
Decaying more and more
Till he became
Most poor;
With thee
Oh, let me rise
As larks, harmoniously,
And sing this day thy victories;
Then shall the fall further the flight in me.
My tender age in sorrow did begin;
And still with sicknesses and shame
Thou didst so punish sin,
That I became
Most thin.
With thee
Let me combine,
And feel this day thy victory;
For if I imp my wing on thine,
Affliction shall advance the flight in me.

Juan Felipe Herrera (b. 1948)

El Ángel de la Guarda

1999

I should have visited more often.
I should have taken the sour pudding they offered.
I should have danced that lousy beggar shuffle.
I should have painted their rooms in a brighter color.
I should have put a window in there, for the daughters.
I should have provided a decent mountain for a view.
I should have nudged them a little closer to the sky.
I should have guessed they would never come out to wave.
I should have cleaned up that mole, the abyss, in the back.
I should have touched them, thass it, it comes to me now.
I should have touched them.

Linocut by Artemio Rodríguez

Robert Herrick (1591–1674)

To the Virgins, to Make Much of Time 1648

Gather ye rose-buds while ye may,
  Old Time is still a-flying;
And this same flower that smiles today,
  Tomorrow will be dying.

The glorious lamp of heaven, the sun,
  The higher he's a-getting,
The sooner will his race be run,
  And nearer he's to setting.

That age is best which is the first,
  When youth and blood are warmer;
But being spent, the worse, and worst
  Times still succeed the former.

Then be not coy, but use your time,
  And while ye may, go marry;
For having lost but once your prime,
  You may for ever tarry.

Gerard Manley Hopkins

Gerard Manley Hopkins (1844–1889)

The Windhover (1877)

To Christ Our Lord

I caught this morning morning's minion, king-
  dom of daylight's dauphin, dapple-dawn-drawn Falcon, in his riding
  Of the rolling level underneath him steady air, and striding
High there, how he rung upon the rein of a wimpling wing
In his ecstasy! then off, off forth on swing,
  As a skate's heel sweeps smooth on a bow-bend: the hurl and gliding
  Rebuffed the big wind. My heart in hiding
Stirred for a bird, —the achieve of, the mastery of the thing!

Brute beauty and valor and act, oh, air, pride, plume, here
  Buckle! AND the fire that breaks from thee then, a billion
Times told lovelier, more dangerous, O my chevalier!

  No wonder of it: shéer plód makes plough down sillion° *furrow*
Shine, and blue-bleak embers, ah my dear,
  Fall, gall themselves, and gash gold-vermilion.

THE WINDHOVER. A windhover is a kestrel, or small falcon, so called because it can hover upon the wind. 4 *rung . . . wing:* A horse is "rung upon the rein" when its trainer holds the end of a long rein and has the horse circle him. The possible meanings of *wimpling* include: (1) curving; (2) pleated, arranged in many little folds one on top of another; (3) rippling or undulating like the surface of a flowing stream.

A. E. Housman (1859–1936)

Loveliest of trees, the cherry now 1896

Loveliest of trees, the cherry now
Is hung with bloom along the bough,
And stands about the woodland ride° *path*
Wearing white for Eastertide.

Now, of my threescore years and ten,
Twenty will not come again,
And take from seventy springs a score,
It only leaves me fifty more.

And since to look at things in bloom
Fifty springs are little room,
About the woodlands I will go
To see the cherry hung with snow.

Langston Hughes

Langston Hughes (1901–1967)

The Negro Speaks of Rivers (1921) 1926

I've known rivers:
I've known rivers ancient as the world and older than the flow of
human blood in human veins.

My soul has grown deep like the rivers.

I bathed in the Euphrates when dawns were young.
I built my hut near the Congo and it lulled me to sleep.
I looked upon the Nile and raised the pyramids above it.
I heard the singing of the Mississippi when Abe Lincoln went down to New
Orleans, and I've seen its muddy bosom turn all golden in the sunset.

I've known rivers:
Ancient, dusky rivers.

My soul has grown deep like the rivers.

Langston Hughes (1901–1967)

Harlem [Dream Deferred]

1951

What happens to a dream deferred?

Does it dry up
like a raisin in the sun?
Or fester like a sore—
And then run?
Does it stink like rotten meat?
Or crust and sugar over—
like a syrupy sweet?

Maybe it just sags
like a heavy load.

Or does it explode?

Robinson Jeffers

Robinson Jeffers (1887–1962)

Fire on the Hills

1932

The deer were bounding like blown leaves
Under the smoke in front the roaring wave of the brushfire;
I thought of the smaller lives that were caught.
Beauty is not always lovely; the fire was beautiful, the terror
Of the deer was beautiful; and when I returned
Down the back slopes after the fire had gone by, an eagle
Was perched on the jag of a burnt pine,
Insolent and gorged, cloaked in the folded storms of his shoulders.
He had come from far off for the good hunting
With fire for his beater to drive the game; the sky was merciless
Blue, and the hills merciless black,
The sombre-feathered great bird sleepily merciless between them.
I thought, painfully, but the whole mind,
The destruction that brings an eagle from heaven is better than mercy.

Ben Jonson (1573?–1637)

On My First Son (1603)

Farewell, thou child of my right hand, and joy.
My sin was too much hope of thee, loved boy;
Seven years thou wert lent to me, and I thee pay,
Exacted by thy fate, on the just day.
Oh, could I lose all father° now. For why *fatherhood*
Will man lament the state he should envý—
To have so soon 'scaped world's and flesh's rage,
And, if no other misery, yet age?
Rest in soft peace, and asked, say, "Here doth lie
Ben Jonson his best piece of poetry,"
For whose sake henceforth all his vows be such
As what he loves may never like° too much. *thrive*

On My First Son. 1 *child of my right hand:* Jonson's son was named Benjamin; this phrase translates the Hebrew name. 4 *the just day:* the very day. The boy had died on his seventh birthday. 10 *poetry:* Jonson uses the word *poetry* here reflecting its Greek root *poiesis*, which means *creation*.

Donald Justice (1925–2004)

On the Death of Friends in Childhood 1960

We shall not ever meet them bearded in heaven,
Nor sunning themselves among the bald of hell;
If anywhere, in the deserted schoolyard at twilight,
Forming a ring, perhaps, or joining hands
In games whose very names we have forgotten.
Come, memory, let us seek them there in the shadows.

John Keats

John Keats (1795–1821)

When I have fears that I may cease to be (1818)

When I have fears that I may cease to be
  Before my pen has gleaned my teeming brain,
Before high-pilèd books, in charact'ry,° *written language*
  Hold like rich garners° the full-ripened grain; *storehouses*
When I behold, upon the night's starred face,
  Huge cloudy symbols of a high romance,
And think that I may never live to trace
  Their shadows with the magic hand of chance;
And when I feel, fair creature of an hour,
  That I shall never look upon thee more,
Never have relish in the fairy° power *supernatural*
  Of unreflecting love;—then on the shore
Of the wide world I stand alone, and think
Till love and fame to nothingness do sink.

WHEN I HAVE FEARS THAT I MAY CEASE TO BE. 12 *unreflecting:* thoughtless and spontaneous, rather than deliberate.

Philip Larkin (1922–1985)

Poetry of Departures 1955

Sometimes you hear, fifth-hand,
As epitaph:
He chucked up everything
And just cleared off,
And always the voice will sound
Certain you approve
This audacious, purifying,
Elemental move.

And they are right, I think.
We all hate home
And having to be there:
I detest my room,
Its specially-chosen junk,
The good books, the good bed,
And my life, in perfect order:
So to hear it said

He walked out on the whole crowd
Leaves me flushed and stirred,
Like *Then she undid her dress*
Or *Take that you bastard*;
Surely I can, if he did?
And that helps me stay
Sober and industrious.
But I'd go today,

Yes, swagger the nut-strewn roads,
Crouch in the fo'c'sle
Stubbly with goodness, if
It weren't so artificial,
Such a deliberate step backwards
To create an object:
Books; china; a life
Reprehensibly perfect.

POETRY OF DEPARTURES. 26 *fo'c'sle:* nautical term, short for *forecastle*, the front upper deck of a sailing ship.

D. H. Lawrence (1885–1930)

Piano 1918

Softly, in the dusk, a woman is singing to me;
Taking me back down the vista of years, till I see
A child sitting under the piano, in the boom of the tingling strings
And pressing the small, poised feet of a mother who smiles as she sings.

In spite of myself, the insidious mastery of song
Betrays me back, till the heart of me weeps to belong
To the old Sunday evenings at home, with winter outside
And hymns in the cozy parlor, the tinkling piano our guide.

So now it is vain for the singer to burst into clamor
With the great black piano appassionato. The glamour
Of childish days is upon me, my manhood is cast
Down in the flood of remembrance, I weep like a child for the past.

Li-Young Lee

Li-Young Lee (b. 1957)

Night Mirror

2001

Li-Young, don't feel lonely
when you look up
into great night and find
yourself the far face peering
hugely out from between
a star and a star. All that space
the nighthawk plunges through,
homing, all that distance beyond embrace,
what is it but your own infinity.

And don't be afraid
when, eyes closed, you look inside you
and find night is both
the silence tolling after stars
and the final word
that founds all beginning, find night,

abyss and shuttle,
a finished cloth
frayed by the years, then gathered
in the songs and games
mothers teach their children.

Look again
and find yourself changed
and changing, now the bewildered honey
fallen into your own hands,
now the immaculate fruit born of hunger.
Now the unequaled perfume of your dying.
And time? Time is the salty wake
of your stunned entrance upon
no name.

Denise Levertov (1923–1997)

O Taste and See

1964

The world is
not with us enough.
O taste and see

the subway Bible poster said,
meaning **The Lord**, meaning
if anything all that lives
to the imagination's tongue,

grief, mercy, language,
tangerine, weather, to
breathe them, bite,
savor, chew, swallow, transform

into our flesh our
deaths, crossing the street, plum, quince,
living in the orchard and being

hungry, and plucking
the fruit.

Li Po (701–762)

Drinking Alone by Moonlight

(about 750) 1919

A cup of wine, under the flowering trees;
I drink alone, for no friend is near.
Raising my cup I beckon the bright moon,
For he, with my shadow, will make three men.
The moon, alas, is no drinker of wine;
Listless, my shadow creeps about at my side.
Yet with the moon as friend and the shadow as slave
I must make merry before the Spring is spent.
To the songs I sing the moon flickers her beams;
In the dance I weave my shadow tangles and breaks.
While we were sober, three shared the fun;
Now we are drunk, each goes his way.
May we long share our odd, inanimate feast,
And meet at last on the Cloudy River of the sky.

—*Translated by Arthur Waley*

DRINKING ALONE BY MOONLIGHT. 14 *the Cloudy River of the sky*: the Milky Way.

Shirley Geok-lin Lim

Shirley Geok-lin Lim (b. 1944)

Learning to love America

1998

because it has no pure products

because the Pacific Ocean sweeps along the coastline
because the water of the ocean is cold
and because land is better than ocean

because I say we rather than they

because I live in California
I have eaten fresh artichokes
and jacarandas bloom in April and May

because my senses have caught up with my body
my breath with the air it swallows
my hunger with my mouth

because I walk barefoot in my house

because I have nursed my son at my breast
because he is a strong American boy
because I have seen his eyes redden when he is asked who he is
because he answers I don't know

because to have a son is to have a country
because my son will bury me here
because countries are in our blood and we bleed them

because it is late and too late to change my mind
because it is time.

LEARNING TO LOVE AMERICA. 1 *pure products:* an allusion to poem XVIII of *Spring and All* (1923) by William Carlos Williams, which begins: "The pure products of America / go crazy—."

Andrew Marvell (1621–1678)

To His Coy Mistress

1681

Had we but world enough, and time,
This coyness,° Lady, were no crime. *modesty, reluctance*
We would sit down, and think which way
To walk, and pass our long love's day.
Thou by the Indian Ganges' side
Should'st rubies find; I by the tide
Of Humber would complain.° I would *sing sad songs*
Love you ten years before the Flood,
And you should, if you please, refuse
Till the Conversion of the Jews.
My vegetable° love should grow *vegetative, flourishing*
Vaster than empires, and more slow.
An hundred years should go to praise
Thine eyes, and on thy forehead gaze,
Two hundred to adore each breast,
But thirty thousand to the rest.
An age at least to every part,
And the last age should show your heart.
For, Lady, you deserve this state,° *pomp, ceremony*
Nor would I love at lower rate.
  But at my back I always hear
Time's wingèd chariot hurrying near,
And yonder all before us lie
Deserts of vast eternity.
Thy beauty shall no more be found,
Nor, in thy marble vault, shall sound
My echoing song; then worms shall try
That long preserved virginity,
And your quaint honor turn to dust,
And into ashes all my lust.
The grave's a fine and private place,
But none, I think, do there embrace.
  Now therefore, while the youthful hue
Sits on thy skin like morning glew° *glow*
And while thy willing soul transpires
At every pore with instant° fires, *eager*
Now let us sport us while we may;
And now, like amorous birds of prey,
Rather at once our time devour,
Than languish in his slow-chapped° power. *slow-jawed*
Let us roll all our strength, and all

Our sweetness, up into one ball
And tear our pleasures with rough strife,
Thorough° the iron gates of life. *through*
Thus, though we cannot make our sun
Stand still, yet we will make him run.

TO HIS COY MISTRESS. 7 *Humber:* a river that flows by Marvell's town of Hull (on the side of the world opposite from the Ganges). 10 *conversion of the Jews:* an event that, according to St. John the Divine, is to take place just before the end of the world. 35 *transpires:* exudes, as a membrane lets fluid or vapor pass through it.

Claude McKay

Claude McKay (1889–1948)

If We Must Die

1922

If we must die, let it not be like hogs
Hunted and penned in an inglorious spot,
While round us bark the mad and hungry dogs,
Making their mock at our accursèd lot.
If we must die, O let us nobly die,
So that our precious blood may not be shed
In vain; then even the monsters we defy
Shall be constrained to honor us though dead!
O kinsmen! we must meet the common foe!
Though far outnumbered let us show us brave,
And for their thousand blows deal one death-blow!
What though before us lies the open grave?
Like men we'll face the murderous, cowardly pack,
Pressed to the wall, dying, but fighting back!

Edna St. Vincent Millay

Edna St. Vincent Millay (1892–1950)

Recuerdo 1920

We were very tired, we were very merry—
We had gone back and forth all night on the ferry.
It was bare and bright, and smelled like a stable—
But we looked into a fire, we leaned across a table,
We lay on a hill-top underneath the moon;
And the whistles kept blowing, and the dawn came soon.

We were very tired, we were very merry—
We had gone back and forth all night on the ferry;
And you ate an apple, and I ate a pear,
From a dozen of each we had bought somewhere;
And the sky went wan, and the wind came cold,
And the sun rose dripping, a bucketful of gold.

We were very tired, we were very merry,
We had gone back and forth all night on the ferry.
We hailed, "Good morrow, mother!" to a shawl-covered head,
And bought a morning paper, which neither of us read;
And she wept, "God bless you!" for the apples and pears,
And we gave her all our money but our subway fares.

RECUERDO. The Spanish title means "a recollection" or "a memory."

John Milton (1608–1674)

When I consider how my light is spent (1655?)

When I consider how my light is spent,
 Ere half my days in this dark world and wide,
 And that one talent which is death to hide
 Lodged with me useless, though my soul more bent
To serve therewith my Maker, and present
 My true account, lest He returning chide;
 "Doth God exact day-labor, light denied?"
 I fondly° ask. But Patience, to prevent *foolishly*

That murmur, soon replies, "God doth not need
Either man's work or his own gifts. Who best
Bear his mild yoke, they serve him best. His state
Is kingly: thousands at his bidding speed,
And post o'er land and ocean without rest;
They also serve who only stand and wait."

WHEN I CONSIDER HOW MY LIGHT IS SPENT. 1 *my light is spent:* Milton had become blind. 3 *that one talent:* For Jesus's parable of the talents (measures of money), see Matthew 25:14–30.

Marilyn Nelson

Marilyn Nelson (b. 1946)

A Strange Beautiful Woman 1985

A strange beautiful woman
met me in the mirror
the other night.
Hey,
I said,
What you doing here?
She asked me
the same thing.

Pablo Neruda (1904–1973)

We Are Many 1967

Of the many men who I am, who we are,
I can't find a single one;
they disappear among my clothes,
they've left for another city.

When everything seems to be set
to show me off as intelligent,
the fool I always keep hidden
takes over all that I say.

At other times, I'm asleep
among distinguished people,

and when I look for my brave self,
a coward unknown to me
rushes to cover my skeleton
with a thousand fine excuses.

When a decent house catches fire,
instead of the fireman I summon,
an arsonist bursts on the scene,
and that's me. What can I do?

What can I do to distinguish myself?
How can I pull myself together?

All the books I read
are full of dazzling heroes,
always sure of themselves.
I die with envy of them;
and in films full of wind and bullets,
I goggle at the cowboys,
I even admire the horses.

But when I call for a hero,
out comes my lazy old self;
so I never know who I am,
nor how many I am or will be.
I'd love to be able to touch a bell
and summon the real me,
because if I really need myself,
I mustn't disappear.

While I am writing, I'm far away;
and when I come back, I've gone.
I would like to know if others
go through the same things that I do,
have as many selves as I have,
and see themselves similarly;
and when I've exhausted this problem,
I'm going to study so hard
that when I explain myself,
I'll be talking geography.

—Translated by Alastair Reid

Ezra Pound (1885–1972)

The River-Merchant's Wife: A Letter 1915

While my hair was still cut straight across my forehead
I played about the front gate, pulling flowers.
You came by on bamboo stilts, playing horse,
You walked about my seat, playing with blue plums.
And we went on living in the village of Chokan:
Two small people, without dislike or suspicion.

At fourteen I married My Lord you.
I never laughed, being bashful.
Lowering my head, I looked at the wall.
Called to, a thousand times, I never looked back.

At fifteen I stopped scowling,
I desired my dust to be mingled with yours
Forever and forever and forever.
Why should I climb the look out?

At sixteen you departed,
You went into far Ku-to-yen, by the river of swirling eddies,
And you have been gone five months.
The monkeys make sorrowful noise overhead.

You dragged your feet when you went out.
By the gate now, the moss is grown, the different mosses,
Too deep to clear them away!
The leaves fall early this autumn, in wind.
The paired butterflies are already yellow with August
Over the grass in the West garden;
They hurt me. I grow older.

If you are coming down through the narrows of the river Kiang,
Please let me know beforehand,
And I will come out to meet you
As far as Cho-fu-sa.

THE RIVER-MERCHANT'S WIFE: A LETTER. A free translation from the Chinese poet Li Po (eighth century).

Henry Reed (1914–1986)

Naming of Parts 1946

Today we have naming of parts. Yesterday,
We had daily cleaning. And tomorrow morning,
We shall have what to do after firing. But today,
Today we have naming of parts. Japonica

Glistens like coral in all of the neighboring gardens,
And today we have naming of parts.

This is the lower sling swivel. And this
Is the upper sling swivel, whose use you will see,
When you are given your slings. And this is the piling swivel,
Which in your case you have not got. The branches
Hold in the gardens their silent, eloquent gestures,
Which in our case we have not got.

This is the safety-catch, which is always released
With an easy flick of the thumb. And please do not let me
See anyone using his finger. You can do it quite easy
If you have any strength in your thumb. The blossoms
Are fragile and motionless, never letting anyone see
Any of them using their finger.

And this you can see is the bolt. The purpose of this
Is to open the breech, as you see. We can slide it
Rapidly backwards and forwards: we call this
Easing the spring. And rapidly backwards and forwards
The early bees are assaulting and fumbling the flowers:
They call it easing the Spring.

They call it easing the Spring: it is perfectly easy
If you have any strength in your thumb: like the bolt,
And the breech, and the cocking-piece, and the point of balance,
Which in our case we have not got; and the almond-blossom
Silent in all of the gardens and the bees going backwards and forwards,
For today we have naming of parts.

Edwin Arlington Robinson (1869–1935)

Miniver Cheevy 1910

Miniver Cheevy, child of scorn,
Grew lean while he assailed the seasons;
He wept that he was ever born,
And he had reasons.

Miniver loved the days of old
When swords were bright and steeds were prancing;
The vision of a warrior bold
Would set him dancing.

Miniver sighed for what was not,
And dreamed, and rested from his labors;
He dreamed of Thebes and Camelot,
And Priam's neighbors.

Miniver mourned the ripe renown
  That made so many a name so fragrant;
He mourned Romance, now on the town,
  And Art, a vagrant.

Miniver loved the Medici,
  Albeit he had never seen one;
He would have sinned incessantly
  Could he have been one.

Miniver cursed the commonplace
  And eyed a khaki suit with loathing;
He missed the medieval grace
  Of iron clothing.

Miniver scorned the gold he sought,
  But sore annoyed was he without it;
Miniver thought, and thought, and thought,
  And thought about it.

Miniver Cheevy, born too late,
  Scratched his head and kept on thinking;
Miniver coughed, and called it fate,
  And kept on drinking.

MINIVER CHEEVY. 11 *Thebes:* a city in ancient Greece and the setting of many famous Greek myths; *Camelot:* the legendary site of King Arthur's Court. 12 *Priam:* the last king of Troy; his "neighbors" would have included Helen of Troy, Aeneas, and other famous figures. 17 *the Medici:* the ruling family of Florence during the high Renaissance, the Medici were renowned patrons of the arts.

Christina Rossetti (1830–1894)

Song (1848) 1862

When I am dead, my dearest,
  Sing no sad songs for me;
Plant thou no roses at my head,
  Nor shady cypress tree:
Be the green grass above me
  With showers and dewdrops wet;
And if thou wilt, remember,
  And if thou wilt, forget.

I shall not see the shadows,
  I shall not feel the rain;
I shall not hear the nightingale
  Sing on, as if in pain:
And dreaming through the twilight

That doth not rise nor set,
Haply I may remember,
And haply may forget.

William Shakespeare

William Shakespeare (1564–1616)

When, in disgrace with Fortune and men's eyes (Sonnet 29) 1609

When, in disgrace with Fortune and men's eyes,
I all alone beweep my outcast state,
And trouble deaf heaven with my bootless° cries, *futile*
And look upon myself and curse my fate,
Wishing me like to one more rich in hope,
Featured like him, like him with friends possessed,
Desiring this man's art, and that man's scope,
With what I most enjoy contented least,
Yet in these thoughts myself almost despising,
Haply° I think on thee, and then my state, *luckily*
Like to the lark at break of day arising
From sullen earth, sings hymns at heaven's gate;
For thy sweet love rememb'red such wealth brings
That then I scorn to change my state with kings.

William Shakespeare (1564–1616)

My mistress' eyes are nothing like the sun (Sonnet 130) 1609

My mistress' eyes are nothing like the sun;
Coral is far more red than her lips' red;
If snow be white, why then her breasts are dun;
If hairs be wires, black wires grow on her head.
I have seen roses damasked, red and white,
But no such roses see I in her cheeks;
And in some perfumes is there more delight

Than in the breath that from my mistress reeks.
I love to hear her speak, yet well I know
That music hath a far more pleasing sound;
I grant I never saw a goddess go:
My mistress, when she walks, treads on the ground.
    And yet, by heaven, I think my love as rare
    As any she° belied with false compare.

woman

Percy Bysshe Shelley (1792–1822)

Ozymandias

1819

I met a traveler from an antique land
Who said: Two vast and trunkless legs of stone
Stand in the desert. ... Near them, on the sand,
Half sunk, a shattered visage lies, whose frown,
And wrinkled lip, and sneer of cold command,
Tell that its sculptor well those passions read
Which yet survive, stamped on these lifeless things,
The hand that mocked° them, and the heart that fed:
And on the pedestal these words appear:
"My name is Ozymandias, king of kings:
Look on my works, ye Mighty, and despair!"
Nothing beside remains. Round the decay
Of that colossal wreck, boundless and bare
The lone and level sands stretch far away.

imitated

Wallace Stevens (1879–1955)

The Snow Man

1923

One must have a mind of winter
To regard the frost and the boughs
Of the pine-trees crusted with snow;

And have been cold a long time
To behold the junipers shagged with ice,
The spruces rough in the distant glitter

Of the January sun; and not to think
Of any misery in the sound of the wind,
In the sound of a few leaves,

Which is the sound of the land
Full of the same wind
That is blowing in the same bare place

For the listener, who listens in the snow,
And, nothing himself, beholds
Nothing that is not there and the nothing that is.

Dylan Thomas (1914–1953)

Fern Hill

1946

Now as I was young and easy under the apple boughs
About the lilting house and happy as the grass was green,
The night above the dingle° starry,
Time let me hail and climb
Golden in the heydays of his eyes,
And honored among wagons I was prince of the apple towns
And once below a time I lordly had the trees and leaves
Trail with daisies and barley
Down the rivers of the windfall light.

° *wooded valley*

And as I was green and carefree, famous among the barns
About the happy yard and singing as the farm was home,
In the sun that is young once only,
Time let me play and be
Golden in the mercy of his means,
And green and golden I was huntsman and herdsman, the calves
Sang to my horn, the foxes on the hills barked clear and cold,
And the sabbath rang slowly
In the pebbles of the holy streams.

All the sun long it was running, it was lovely, the hay
Fields high as the house, the tunes from the chimneys, it was air
And playing, lovely and watery
And fire green as grass.
And nightly under the simple stars
As I rode to sleep the owls were bearing the farm away,
All the moon long I heard, blessed among stables, the nightjars
Flying with the ricks, and the horses
Flashing into the dark.

And then to awake, and the farm, like a wanderer white
With the dew, come back, the cock on his shoulder: it was all

Shining, it was Adam and maiden,
The sky gathered again
And the sun grew round that very day.
So it must have been after the birth of the simple light
In the first, spinning place, the spellbound horses walking warm
Out of the whinnying green stable
On to the fields of praise.

And honored among foxes and pheasants by the gay house
Under the new made clouds and happy as the heart was long,
In the sun born over and over,
I ran my heedless ways,
My wishes raced through the house high hay
And nothing I cared, at my sky blue trades, that time allows
In all his tuneful turning so few and such morning songs
Before the children green and golden
Follow him out of grace,

Nothing I cared, in the lamb white days, that time would take me
Up to the swallow thronged loft by the shadow of my hand,
In the moon that is always rising,
Nor that riding to sleep
I should hear him fly with the high fields
And wake to the farm forever fled from the childless land.
Oh as I was young and easy in the mercy of his means,
Time held me green and dying
Though I sang in my chains like the sea.

Walt Whitman (1819–1892)

When I Heard the Learn'd Astronomer 1865

When I heard the learn'd astronomer,
When the proofs, the figures, were ranged in columns before me,
When I was shown the charts and diagrams, to add, divide, and measure them,
When I sitting heard the astronomer where he lectured with much applause in the lecture-room,
How soon unaccountable I became tired and sick,
Till rising and gliding out I wander'd off by myself,
In the mystical moist night-air, and from time to time,
Look'd up in perfect silence at the stars.

Walt Whitman

Walt Whitman (1819–1892)

O Captain! My Captain!

1865

O Captain! my Captain! our fearful trip is done,
The ship has weather'd every rack, the prize we sought is won,
The port is near, the bells I hear, the people all exulting,
While follow eyes the steady keel, the vessel grim and daring;
  But O heart! heart! heart!
    O the bleeding drops of red,
      Where on the deck my Captain lies,
        Fallen cold and dead.

O Captain! my Captain! rise up and hear the bells;
Rise up—for you the flag is flung—for you the bugle trills,
For you bouquets and ribbon'd wreaths—for you the shores
    a-crowding,
For you they call, the swaying mass, their eager faces turning;
  Here Captain! dear father!
    This arm beneath your head!
      It is some dream that on the deck,
        You've fallen cold and dead.

My Captain does not answer, his lips are pale and still,
My father does not feel my arm, he has no pulse nor will,
The ship is anchor'd safe and sound, its voyage closed and done,
From fearful trip the victor ship comes in with object won;
  Exult O shores, and ring O bells!
    But I with mournful tread,
      Walk the deck my Captain lies,
        Fallen cold and dead.

O CAPTAIN! MY CAPTAIN! Written soon after the death of Abraham Lincoln, this was, in Whitman's lifetime, by far the most popular of his poems.

William Carlos Williams

William Carlos Williams (1883–1963)

The Widow's Lament in Springtime 1921

Sorrow is my own yard
where the new grass
flames as it has flamed
often before but not
with the cold fire
that closes round me this year.

Thirtyfive years
I lived with my husband.
The plumtree is white today
with masses of flowers.

Masses of flowers
load the cherry branches
and color some bushes
yellow and some red
but the grief in my heart

is stronger than they
for though they were my joy
formerly, today I notice them
and turn away forgetting.
Today my son told me

that in the meadows,
at the edge of the heavy woods
in the distance, he saw
trees of white flowers.
I feel that I would like

to go there
and fall into those flowers
and sink into the marsh near them.

William Carlos Williams (1883–1963)

Queen-Anne's-Lace 1921

Her body is not so white as
anemone petals nor so smooth—nor
so remote a thing. It is a field
of the wild carrot taking
the field by force; the grass
does not raise above it.
Here is no question of whiteness,
white as can be, with a purple mole
at the center of each flower.
Each flower is a hand's span
of her whiteness. Wherever
his hand has lain there is
a tiny purple blemish. Each part
is a blossom under his touch
to which the fibers of her being
stem one by one, each to its end,
until the whole field is a
white desire, empty, a single stem,
a cluster, flower by flower,
a pious wish to whiteness gone over—
or nothing.

William Wordsworth (1770–1850)

Composed upon Westminster Bridge 1807

Earth has not anything to show more fair:
Dull would he be of soul who could pass by
A sight so touching in its majesty:
This City now doth, like a garment, wear
The beauty of the morning; silent, bare,
Ships, towers, domes, theaters, and temples lie
Open unto the fields, and to the sky;
All bright and glittering in the smokeless air.
Never did sun more beautifully steep
In his first splendor, valley, rock, or hill;
Ne'er saw I, never felt, a calm so deep!
The river glideth at his own sweet will:
Dear God! the very houses seem asleep;
And all that mighty heart is lying still!

William Butler Yeats (1865–1939)

Sailing to Byzantium

1927

I

That is no country for old men. The young
In one another's arms, birds in the trees
—Those dying generations—at their song,
The salmon-falls, the mackerel-crowded seas,
Fish, flesh, or fowl, commend all summer long
Whatever is begotten, born, and dies.
Caught in that sensual music all neglect
Monuments of unaging intellect.

II

An aged man is but a paltry thing,
A tattered coat upon a stick, unless
Soul clap its hands and sing, and louder sing
For every tatter in its mortal dress,
Nor is there singing school but studying
Monuments of its own magnificence;
And therefore I have sailed the seas and come
To the holy city of Byzantium.

III

O sages standing in God's holy fire
As in the gold mosaic of a wall,
Come from the holy fire, perne in a gyre,° *spin down a spiral*
And be the singing-masters of my soul.
Consume my heart away; sick with desire
And fastened to a dying animal
It knows not what it is; and gather me
Into the artifice of eternity.

IV

Once out of nature I shall never take
My bodily form from any natural thing,
But such a form as Grecian goldsmiths make
Of hammered gold and gold enameling
To keep a drowsy Emperor awake;
Or set upon a golden bough to sing
To lords and ladies of Byzantium
Of what is past, or passing, or to come.

SAILING TO BYZANTIUM. Byzantium was the capital of the Byzantine Empire, the city now called Istanbul. Yeats means, though, not merely the physical city. Byzantium is also a name for his conception of paradise. 1 *no country for old men:* a line that provided the title for Cormac McCarthy's masterful 2005 novel and for the Coen brothers' 2007 Academy Award-winning film adaptation.

William Butler Yeats

William Butler Yeats (1865–1939)

When You Are Old

1893

When you are old and grey and full of sleep,
And nodding by the fire, take down this book,
And slowly read, and dream of the soft look
Your eyes had once, and of their shadows deep;

How many loved your moments of glad grace,
And loved your beauty with love false or true,
But one man loved the pilgrim soul in you,
And loved the sorrows of your changing face;

And bending down beside the glowing bars,
Murmur, a little sadly, how Love fled
And paced upon the mountains overhead
And hid his face amid a crowd of stars.

Playwright David Ives.

DRAMA

TALKING WITH *David Ives*

"Comedy is just tragedy without the sentimentality."

Dana Gioia Interviews David Ives

Q: When did you first become interested in theater?

DAVID IVES: I played The Wolf opposite drop-dead-sexy Amy Skeehan in our third-grade production of "Little Red Riding Hood" at St. Mary Magdalene School in South Chicago. Basically it was all over after that. The show was so successful Amy and I took it on tour to the fourth and fifth grades. By then I had learned the Great Lesson of Theater, which is: *theater is a great way to hang out with girls*. It may be why Shakespeare became both an actor and a playwright: *more girls*.

Q: When did you discover that you could make people laugh?

DAVID IVES: There's some debate about this. An aunt of mine, a few years ago, said to me, "You're just like you were as a boy. Such a happy, funny child." I reported this to my mother, who said without a pause: "I wouldn't say that." She didn't seem to want to explain. One of my old high-school classmates recently mentioned that I was funny in high school. I only remember reading Russian novels about suicide in high school. Maybe I was funny between novels, but they were pretty thick.

Q: Tell us about your first play.

DAVID IVES: I wrote my first play when I was nine. It was about gangsters and had lots of gunfire and a girl I based on Amy Skeehan. I wrote my second play in high school. It was about Russian-like people talking about suicide a lot. My third play was at college and was The Worst Play Ever Written. From there, I had nowhere to go but up. My next play got produced, and suddenly I was a real live playwright. I've been faking it ever since.

Q: When you see one of your plays onstage, how different is it from what you imagined while writing it?

DAVID IVES: It's always better than I imagined it, unless it's worse.

Q: You are the master of the short comic play. What drew you to this unconventional form?

DAVID IVES: Probably a shorter and shorter attention span, like everybody else. Also, my wife Martha is on the short side and I am very drawn to her, so it is only a short (so to speak) way to short plays. I'm fond in general of the concise, the compact, the jeweled, the specific, and perfect as opposed to the verbose, the bloated, the baggy, and general. A good rock-and-roll song can be three or four minutes long and when it's over, if it's been made right and played right, you feel like you've gotten into a barfight, had a love affair, and ridden a convertible down Pacific Coast One on the

most beautiful day of the year, all in three minutes. Imagine what you can do with a ten- or fifteen-minute play. You can make an audience feel like they've done all those things, plus they've gotten married, had kids, died, and went to heaven. There they are, breathless just inside the pearly gates with their heads still spinning, and only ten minutes have passed. As far as I'm concerned, all plays, short or long, should aspire to the conditions of rock-and-roll, whose purpose is to make us aware of our mortality and the fact that we had better get with it before the song ends. Not a bad rule of thumb for art as a whole.

Q: Who are your favorite comic writers and comedians?

DAVID IVES: Nothing depresses me like comedians. Maybe it's because people who try to make me laugh instantly put me in a really bad mood. I once shot a man in Tucson and spent 38 years in the penitentiary because he tried to tell me a joke that started "A priest, a minister, and a rabbi walk into a bar. . . ." As for funny playwrights, Joe Orton and Noel Coward and Chris Durang do it for me because they're not just trying to be funny. They have a vision of life that happens to be comic. They've also got *style*, which is the outward and visible sign of having a vision of life.

Q: Why do people need comedy?

DAVID IVES: Comedy is important for three reasons. First, it's funny. Second, it makes us laugh. Third, it's easier to get a girl to go see a comedy than, let's say, *Hamlet*. Fourth, it shows us what frigging idiots we can be under the right circumstances. As Wendell Berry once said, "It is not from ourselves that we will learn to be better." Watching idiots cavort around onstage is one possible way to do that. First, of course, you have to be interested in being better.

Q: Comedy seems to get less critical respect than tragedy. Does that seem fair to you?

DAVID IVES: Nothing seems fair to me. That's why I write comedy. If you've ever met a critic you'll understand why they give more respect to sadder plays: because critics are the saddest dogs you'll ever meet. The fact is, comedy is much harder to do—to write, to act—than drama, the same way it's harder to look at life and say, *Okay*, than it is to mope around thinking about Russian roulette all the time. But let's get one thing clear: Comedy is not jokes. It certainly isn't sitcoms, which to me are about as funny as a sack of dead kittens. I'm talking about real comedy—human comedy, which is to say comedy that thinks and feels. I'm talking about *Twelfth Night*, or *The Marriage of Bette and Boo*, or *The Importance of Being Earnest*, where there's truth and sadness mixed in with the joy, just as there is in life. Theater *is* life, and it fails when it settles for merely being funny, the same way life is not enough when it settles for just being funny. In the end, comedy is just tragedy without the sentimentality. Dostoyevsky, anyone?

Drama is life with the dull bits left out.

—ALFRED HITCHCOCK

Unlike a short story or a novel, a **play** is a work of storytelling in which actors represent the characters. A play also differs from a work of fiction in another essential way: it is addressed not to readers but to spectators.

To be part of an audience in a theater is an experience far different from reading a story in solitude. As the house lights dim and the curtain rises, we become members of a community. The responses of people around us affect our own responses. We, too, contribute to the community's response whenever we laugh, sigh, applaud, murmur in surprise, or catch our breath in excitement. In contrast, when we watch a movie by ourselves in our living room—say, a slapstick comedy—we probably laugh less often than if we were watching the same film in a theater, surrounded by a roaring crowd. On the other hand, no one is spilling popcorn down the backs of our necks. Each kind of theatrical experience, to be sure, has its advantages.

A theater of live actors has another advantage: a sensitive give-and-take between actors and audience. (Such rapport, of course, depends on the skill of the actors and the perceptiveness of the audience.) Although professional actors may try to give a first-rate performance on all occasions, it is natural for them to feel more keenly inspired by a lively, appreciative audience than by a lethargic one. As veteran playgoers well know, something unique and wonderful can happen when good actors and a good audience respond to each other.

In another sense, a play is more than actors and audience. Like a short story or a poem, a play is a work of art made of words. Watching a play, of course, we don't notice the playwright standing between us and the characters. If the play is absorbing, it flows before our eyes. In a silent reading, the usual play consists mainly of **dialogue**, exchanges of speech, punctuated by stage directions. In performance, though, stage directions vanish. And although the thoughtful efforts of perhaps a hundred people—actors, director, producer, stage designer, costumer, makeup artist, technicians—may have gone into a production, a successful play makes us forget its artifice. We may even forget that the play is literature, for its gestures, facial expressions, bodily stances, lighting, and special effects are as much a part of it as the playwright's written words. Even though words are not all there is to a living play, they are its bones. And the whole play, the finished production, is the total of whatever takes place on stage.

24 READING A PLAY

What You Will Learn in This Chapter

- To define the play as a literary form
- To identify and describe theatrical conventions
- To recognize and describe the elements of a play
- To analyze a play

Most plays are written not to be read in books but to be performed. Finding plays in a literature anthology, the student may well ask: Isn't there something wrong with the idea of reading plays on the printed page? Isn't that a perversion of their nature?

True, plays are meant to be seen on stage, but equally true, reading a play may afford advantages. One is that it is better to know some masterpieces by reading them than never to know them at all. Even if you live in a large city with many theaters, even if you attend a college with many theatrical productions, to succeed in your lifetime in witnessing, say, all the plays of Shakespeare might well be impossible. In print, they are as near to hand as a book on a shelf, ready to be enacted (if you like) on the stage of the mind.

INTERPRETING PLAYS

After all, a play is literature before it comes alive in a theater, and it might be argued that when we read an unfamiliar play, we meet it in the same form in which it first appears to its actors and its director. If a play is rich and complex or if it dates from the remote past and contains difficulties of language and allusion, to read it on the page enables us to study it at our leisure and return to the parts that demand greater scrutiny.

But even if a play may be seen in a theater, sometimes to read it in print may be our way of knowing it as the author wrote it in its entirety. Far from regarding Shakespeare's words as holy writ, producers of *Hamlet*, *King Lear*, *Othello*, and other masterpieces often shorten or even leave out whole speeches and scenes. Besides, the nature of the play, as far as you can tell from a stage production, may depend on decisions of the director. In one production Othello may dress as a Renaissance Moor, in another as a modern general. Every actor who plays Iago in *Othello* makes his own interpretation of this knotty character. Some see Iago as a figure of pure evil; others, as a madman; still others, as a suffering human being consumed by hatred, jealousy, and pride. What do you think Shakespeare meant? You can always read the play and decide for yourself.

If every stage production of a play is a fresh interpretation, so, too, is every reader's reading of it. Some readers, when silently reading a play to themselves, try to visualize a stage, imagining the characters in costume and under lights. If such a reader is an actor or a director and is reading the play with an eye toward staging it, then he or she may try to imagine every detail of a possible production, even shades of makeup and the loudness of sound effects. But the nonprofessional reader, who regards the play as literature, need not attempt such exhaustive imagining. Although some readers find it enjoyable to imagine the play taking place on a stage, others prefer to imagine the people and events that the play brings vividly to mind. Sympathetically following the tangled life of Nora in *A Doll's House* by Henrik Ibsen, we forget that we are reading printed stage directions and instead feel ourselves in the presence of human conflict. Thus regarded, a play becomes a form of storytelling, and the playwright's instructions to the actors and the director become a conventional mode of narrative that we accept much as we accept the methods of a novel or short story.

THEATRICAL CONVENTIONS

Most plays, whether seen in a theater or in print, employ some **conventions**: customary methods of presenting an action, usual and recognizable devices that an audience is willing to accept. In reading a great play from the past, such as *Oedipus the King* or *Othello*, it will help if we know some of the conventions of the classical Greek theater or the Elizabethan theater. When in *Oedipus the King* we encounter a character called the Chorus, it may be useful to be aware that this is a group of citizens who stand to one side of the action, conversing with the principal character and commenting. In *Othello*, when the sinister Iago, left on stage alone, begins to speak (at the end of Act I, Scene iii), we recognize the conventional device of a **soliloquy**, a monologue in which we seem to overhear the character's inmost thoughts uttered aloud. Another such device is the **aside**, in which a character addresses the audience directly, unheard by the other characters on stage, as when the villain in a melodrama chortles, "Heh! Heh! Now she's in my power!" Like conventions in poetry, such familiar methods of staging a narrative afford us a happy shock of recognition. Often, as in these examples, they are ways of making clear to us exactly what the playwright would have us know.

ELEMENTS OF A PLAY

When we read a play on the printed page and find ourselves swept forward by the motion of its story, we need not wonder how—and from what ingredients—the playwright put it together. Still, to analyze the structure of a play is one way to understand and appreciate a playwright's art. Analysis is complicated, however, because in an excellent play the elements (including plot, theme, and characters) do not stand in isolation. Often, deeds clearly follow from the kinds of people the characters are, and from those deeds it is left to the reader to infer the **theme** of the play—the general point or truth about human beings that may be drawn from it. Perhaps the most meaningful way to study the elements of a play (and certainly the most enjoyable) is to consider a play in its entirety.

Here is a short, famous one-act play worth reading for the boldness of its elements—and for its own sake. *Trifles* tells the story of a murder. As you will discover, the "trifles" mentioned in its title are not of trifling stature. In reading the play, you will probably find yourself imagining what you might see on stage if you were in a theater. You may also want to imagine what took place in the lives of the characters before the curtain rose. All this imagining may sound like a tall order, but don't worry. Just read the play for enjoyment the first time through, and then we will consider what makes it effective.

Susan Glaspell

Trifles

1916

Susan Glaspell (1876–1948) grew up in her native Davenport, Iowa, daughter of a grain dealer. After four years at Drake University and a job as a reporter in Des Moines, she settled in New York's Greenwich Village. In 1915, with her husband, George Cram Cook, a theatrical director, she founded the Provincetown Players, the first influential noncommercial theater troupe in America. During the summers of 1915 and 1916, in a makeshift playhouse on a Cape Cod pier, the Players staged the earliest plays of Eugene O'Neill and works by John Reed, Edna St. Vincent Millay, and Glaspell herself. Transplanting the company to New York in the fall of 1916, Glaspell and Cook renamed it the Playwrights' Theater. Glaspell wrote several still-remembered plays, among them a pioneering work of feminist drama, The Verge *(1921), and the Pulitzer Prize-winning* Alison's House *(1930), about the family of a reclusive poet reminiscent of Emily Dickinson who, after her death, squabble over the right to publish her poems. First widely known for her fiction set in Iowa, Glaspell wrote ten novels, including* Fidelity *(1915) and* The Morning Is Near Us *(1939). Shortly after writing the play Trifles, she rewrote it as a short story, "A Jury of Her Peers."*

Susan Glaspell

CHARACTERS

George Henderson, county attorney
Henry Peters, sheriff
Lewis Hale, a neighboring farmer
Mrs. Peters
Mrs. Hale

SCENE. *The kitchen in the now abandoned farmhouse of John Wright, a gloomy kitchen, and left without having been put in order—unwashed pans under the sink, a loaf of bread outside the breadbox, a dish towel on the table—other signs of incompleted work. At the rear the outer door opens and the Sheriff comes in followed by the County Attorney and Hale. The Sheriff and Hale are men in middle life, the County Attorney is a young man; all are much bundled up and go at once to the stove. They are followed by two women—the Sheriff's wife first; she is a slight wiry woman, a thin nervous face. Mrs. Hale is larger and would ordinarily be called more comfortable looking, but she is disturbed now and looks fearfully about as she enters. The women have come in slowly, and stand close together near the door.*

County Attorney (rubbing his hands): This feels good. Come up to the fire, ladies.

Mrs. Peters (after taking a step forward): I'm not—cold.

Sheriff (unbuttoning his overcoat and stepping away from the stove as if to mark the beginning of official business): Now, Mr. Hale, before we move things about, you explain to Mr. Henderson just what you saw when you came here yesterday morning.

County Attorney: By the way, has anything been moved? Are things just as you left them yesterday?

Sheriff (looking about): It's just the same. When it dropped below zero last night I thought I'd better send Frank out this morning to make a fire for us—no use getting pneumonia with a big case on, but I told him not to touch anything except the stove—and you know Frank.

County Attorney: Somebody should have been left here yesterday.

Sheriff: Oh—yesterday. When I had to send Frank to Morris Center for that man who went crazy—I want you to know I had my hands full yesterday, I knew you could get back from Omaha by today and as long as I went over everything here myself—

County Attorney: Well, Mr. Hale, tell just what happened when you came here yesterday morning.

Hale: Harry and I had started to town with a load of potatoes. We came along the road from my place and as I got here I said, "I'm going to see if I can't get John Wright to go in with me on a party telephone." I spoke to Wright about it once before and he put me off, saying folks talked too much anyway, and all he asked was peace and quiet—I guess you know about how much he talked himself; but I thought maybe if I went to the house and talked about it before his wife, though I said to Harry that I didn't know as what his wife wanted made much difference to John—

County Attorney: Let's talk about that later, Mr. Hale. I do want to talk about that, but tell now just what happened when you got to the house.

Hale: I didn't hear or see anything; I knocked at the door, and still it was all quiet inside. I knew they must be up, it was past eight o'clock. So I knocked again, and I thought I heard somebody say, "Come in." I wasn't sure, I'm not sure yet, but I opened the door—this door *(indicating the door by which the two women are still standing)* and there in that rocker—*(pointing to it)* sat Mrs. Wright.

(They all look at the rocker.)

County Attorney: What—was she doing?

Hale: She was rockin' back and forth. She had her apron in her hand and was kind of—pleating it.

County Attorney: And how did she—look?

Hale: Well, she looked queer.

County Attorney: How do you mean—queer?

Hale: Well, as if she didn't know what she was going to do next. And kind of done up.

County Attorney: How did she seem to feel about your coming?

Hale: Why, I don't think she minded—one way or other. She didn't pay much attention. I said, "How do, Mrs. Wright, it's cold, ain't it?" And she said, "Is it?"—and went on kind of pleating at her apron. Well, I was surprised; she didn't ask me to come up to the stove, or to set down, but just sat there, not even looking at me, so I said, "I want to see John." And then she—laughed. I guess you would call it a laugh. I thought of Harry and the team outside, so I said a little sharp: "Can't I see John?" "No," she says, kind o' dull like. "Ain't he home?" says I. "Yes," says she, "he's home." "Then why can't I see him?" I asked her, out of patience. "'Cause he's dead," says she. "*Dead?*" says I. She just nodded her head, not getting a bit excited, but rockin' back and forth. "Why—where is he?" says I, not knowing what to say. She just pointed upstairs—like that. *(Himself pointing to the room above.)* I got up, with the idea of going up there. I walked from there to here—then I says, "Why, what did he die of?" "He died of a rope round his neck," says she, and just went on pleatin' at her apron. Well, I went out and called Harry. I thought I might—need help. We went upstairs and there he was lyin'—

County Attorney: I think I'd rather have you go into that upstairs, where you can point it all out. Just go on now with the rest of the story.

Hale: Well, my first thought was to get that rope off. It looked ... *(stops, his face twitches)* ... but Harry, he went up to him, and he said, "No, he's dead all right, and we'd better not touch anything." So we went back down stairs. She was still sitting that same way. "Has anybody been notified?" I asked. "No," says she, unconcerned. "Who did this, Mrs. Wright?" said Harry. He said it businesslike—and she stopped pleatin' of her apron. "I don't know," she says. "You don't *know?*" says Harry. "No," says she. "Weren't you sleepin' in the bed with him?" says Harry. "Yes," says she, "but I was on the inside." "Somebody slipped a rope round his neck and strangled him and you didn't wake up?" says Harry. "I didn't wake up," she said after him. We must 'a looked as if we didn't see how that could be, for after a minute she said, "I sleep sound." Harry was going to ask her more questions but I said maybe we ought to let her tell her story first to the coroner, or the sheriff, so Harry went fast as he could to Rivers' place, where there's a telephone.

County Attorney: And what did Mrs. Wright do when she knew that you had gone for the coroner?

Hale: She moved from that chair to this one over here *(pointing to a small chair in the corner)* and just sat there with her hands held together and looking down. I got a feeling that I ought to make some conversation, so I said I had come in to see if John wanted to put in a telephone, and at that she started to laugh, and then she stopped and looked at me—scared. *(The County Attorney, who has had his notebook out, makes a note.)* I dunno, maybe it wasn't scared. I wouldn't like to say it was. Soon Harry got back, and then Dr. Lloyd came, and you, Mr. Peters, and so I guess that's all I know that you don't.

County Attorney (looking around): I guess we'll go upstairs first—and then out to the barn and around there. *(To the Sheriff)* You're convinced that there was nothing important here—nothing that would point to any motive.

Sheriff: Nothing here but kitchen things.

(The County Attorney, after again looking around the kitchen, opens the door of a cupboard closet. He gets up on a chair and looks on a shelf. Pulls his hand away, sticky.)

County Attorney: Here's a nice mess.

(The women draw nearer.)

Mrs. Peters (to the other woman): Oh, her fruit; it did freeze. *(To the County Attorney)* She worried about that when it turned so cold. She said the fire'd go out and her jars would break.

Sheriff: Well, can you beat the women! Held for murder and worryin' about her preserves.

County Attorney: I guess before we're through she may have something more serious than preserves to worry about.

Hale: Well, women are used to worrying over trifles.

(The two women move a little closer together.)

County Attorney (with the gallantry of a young politician): And yet, for all their worries, what would we do without the ladies? *(The women do not unbend. He goes to the sink, takes a dipperful of water from the pail and pouring it into a basin, washes his hands. Starts to wipe them on the roller towel, turns it for a cleaner place.)* Dirty towels! *(Kicks his foot against the pans under the sink.)* Not much of a housekeeper, would you say, ladies?

Mrs. Hale (stiffly): There's a great deal of work to be done on a farm.

County Attorney: To be sure. And yet *(with a little bow to her)* I know there are some Dickson County farmhouses which do not have such roller towels.

(He gives it a pull to expose its full length again.)

Mrs. Hale: Those towels get dirty awful quick. Men's hands aren't always as clean as they might be.

County Attorney: Ah, loyal to your sex, I see. But you and Mrs. Wright were neighbors. I suppose you were friends, too.

Mrs. Hale (shaking her head): I've not seen much of her of late years. I've not been in this house—it's more than a year.

County Attorney: And why was that? You didn't like her?

Mrs. Hale: I liked her all well enough. Farmers' wives have their hands full, Mr. Henderson. And then—

County Attorney: Yes—?

Mrs. Hale (looking about): It never seemed a very cheerful place.

County Attorney: No—it's not cheerful. I shouldn't say she had the home-making instinct.

Mrs. Hale: Well, I don't know as Wright had, either.

County Attorney: You mean that they didn't get on very well?

Mrs. Hale: No, I don't mean anything. But I don't think a place'd be any cheerfuller for John Wright's being in it.

County Attorney: I'd like to talk more of that a little later. I want to get the lay of things upstairs now.

(He goes to the left, where three steps lead to a stair door.)

Sheriff: I suppose anything Mrs. Peters does'll be all right. She was to take in some clothes for her, you know, and a few little things. We left in such a hurry yesterday.

County Attorney: Yes, but I would like to see what you take, Mrs. Peters, and keep an eye out for anything that might be of use to us.

Mrs. Peters: Yes, Mr. Henderson.

(The women listen to the men's steps on the stairs, then look about the kitchen.)

Mrs. Hale: I'd hate to have men coming into my kitchen, snooping around and criticizing.

(She arranges the pans under sink which the County Attorney had shoved out of place.)

Mrs. Peters: Of course it's no more than their duty.

Mrs. Hale: Duty's all right, but I guess that deputy sheriff that came out to make the fire might have got a little of this on. *(Gives the roller towel a pull.)* Wish I'd thought of that sooner. Seems mean to talk about her for not having things slicked up when she had to come away in such a hurry.

Mrs. Peters *(who has gone to a small table in the left rear corner of the room, and lifted one end of a towel that covers a pan)*: She had bread set.

(Stands still.)

Mrs. Hale *(eyes fixed on a loaf of bread beside the breadbox, which is on a low shelf at the other side of the room; moves slowly toward it)*: She was going to put this in there. *(Picks up loaf, then abruptly drops it. In a manner of returning to familiar things.)* It's a shame about her fruit. I wonder if it's all gone. *(Gets up on the chair and looks.)* I think there's some here that's all right, Mrs. Peters. Yes—here; *(holding it toward the window)* this is cherries, too. *(Looking again.)* I declare I believe that's the only one. *(Gets down, bottle in her hand. Goes to the sink and wipes it off on the outside.)* She'll feel awful bad after all her hard work in the hot weather. I remember the afternoon I put up my cherries last summer.

(She puts the bottle on the big kitchen table, center of the room. With a sigh, is about to sit down in the rocking-chair. Before she is seated realizes what chair it is; with a slow look at it, steps back. The chair which she has touched rocks back and forth.)

Mrs. Peters: Well, I must get those things from the front room closet. *(She goes to the door at the right, but after looking into the other room, steps back.)* You coming with me, Mrs. Hale? You could help me carry them.

(They go in the other room; reappear, Mrs. Peters carrying a dress and skirt, Mrs. Hale following with a pair of shoes.)

Mrs. Peters: My, it's cold in there.

(She puts the clothes on the big table, and hurries to the stove.)

Mrs. Hale *(examining her skirt)*: Wright was close. I think maybe that's why she kept so much to herself. She didn't even belong to the Ladies Aid. I suppose she felt she couldn't do her part, and then you don't enjoy things when you feel shabby. She used to wear pretty clothes and be lively, when she was Minnie Foster, one of the town girls singing in the choir. But that—oh, that was thirty years ago. This all you was to take in?

Mrs. *Peters:* She said she wanted an apron. Funny thing to want, for there isn't much to get you dirty in jail, goodness knows. But I suppose just to make her feel more natural. She said they was in the top drawer in this cupboard. Yes, here. And then her little shawl that always hung behind the door. *(Opens stair door and looks.)* Yes, here it is.

(Quickly shuts door leading upstairs.)

Mrs. *Hale (abruptly moving toward her):* Mrs. Peters?

Mrs. *Peters:* Yes, Mrs. Hale?

Mrs. *Hale:* Do you think she did it?

Mrs. *Peters (in a frightened voice):* Oh, I don't know.

Mrs. *Hale:* Well, I don't think she did. Asking for an apron and her little shawl. Worrying about her fruit.

Mrs. *Peters (starts to speak, glances up, where footsteps are heard in the room above; in a low voice):* Mr. Peters says it looks bad for her. Mr. Henderson is awful sarcastic in a speech and he'll make fun of her sayin' she didn't wake up.

Mrs. *Hale:* Well, I guess John Wright didn't wake when they was slipping that rope under his neck.

Mrs. *Peters:* No, it's strange. It must have been done awful crafty and still. They say it was such a—funny way to kill a man, rigging it all up like that.

Mrs. *Hale:* That's just what Mr. Hale said. There was a gun in the house. He says that's what he can't understand.

Mrs. *Peters:* Mr. Henderson said coming out that what was needed for the case was a motive; something to show anger, or—sudden feeling.

Mrs. *Hale (who is standing by the table):* Well, I don't see any signs of anger around here. *(She puts her hand on the dish towel which lies on the table, stands looking down at table, one half of which is clean, the other half messy.)* It's wiped to here. *(Makes a move as if to finish work, then turns and looks at loaf of bread outside the breadbox. Drops towel. In that voice of coming back to familiar things.)* Wonder how they are finding things upstairs. I hope she had it a little more red-up° there. You know, it seems kind of *sneaking*. Locking her up in town and then coming out here and trying to get her own house to turn against her!

Mrs. *Peters:* But Mrs. Hale, the law is the law.

Mrs. *Hale:* I s'pose 'tis. *(Unbuttoning her coat.)* Better loosen up your things, Mrs. Peters. You won't feel them when you go out.

(Mrs. Peters takes off her fur tippet, goes to hang it on hook at back of room, stands looking at the under part of the small corner table.)

Mrs. *Peters:* She was piecing a quilt.

(She brings the large sewing basket and they look at the bright pieces.)

red-up: (slang) readied up, ready to be seen.

Mrs. Hale: It's a log cabin pattern. Pretty, isn't it? I wonder if she was goin' to quilt it or just knot it?

(Footsteps have been heard coming down the stairs. The Sheriff enters followed by Hale and the County Attorney.)

Sheriff: They wonder if she was going to quilt it or just knot it!

(The men laugh; the women look abashed.)

County Attorney (rubbing his hands over the stove): Frank's fire didn't do much up there, did it? Well, let's go out to the barn and get that cleared up.

(The men go outside.)

Mrs. Hale (resentfully): I don't know as there's anything so strange, our takin' up our time with little things while we're waiting for them to get the evidence. *(She sits down at the big table smoothing out a block with decision.)* I don't see as it's anything to laugh about.

Mrs. Peters (apologetically): Of course they've got awful important things on their minds.

(Pulls up a chair and joins Mrs. Hale at the table.)

Mrs. Hale (examining another block): Mrs. Peters, look at this one. Here, this is the one she was working on, and look at the sewing! All the rest of it has been so nice and even. And look at this! It's all over the place! Why, it looks as if she didn't know what she was about!

(After she has said this they look at each, then start to glance back at the door. After an instant Mrs. Hale has pulled at a knot and ripped the sewing.)

Mrs. Peters: Oh, what are you doing, Mrs. Hale?

Mrs. Hale (mildly): Just pulling out a stitch or two that's not sewed very good. *(Threading a needle.)* Bad sewing always made me fidgety.

Mrs. Peters (nervously): I don't think we ought to touch things.

Mrs. Hale: I'll just finish up this end. *(Suddenly stopping and leaning forward.)* Mrs. Peters?

Mrs. Peters: Yes, Mrs. Hale?

Mrs. Hale: What do you suppose she was so nervous about?

Mrs. Peters: Oh—I don't know. I don't know as she was nervous. I sometimes sew awful queer when I'm just tired. *(Mrs. Hale starts to say something, looks at Mrs. Peters, then goes on sewing.)* Well, I must get these things wrapped up. They may be through sooner than we think. *(Putting apron and other things together.)* I wonder where I can find a piece of paper, and string.

Mrs. Hale: In that cupboard, maybe.

Mrs. Peters (looking in cupboard): Why, here's a birdcage. *(Holds it up.)* Did she have a bird, Mrs. Hale?

Mrs. *Hale:* Why, I don't know whether she did or not—I've not been here for so long. There was a man around last year selling canaries cheap, but I don't know as she took one; maybe she did. She used to sing real pretty herself.

Mrs. *Peters (glancing around):* Seems funny to think of a bird here. But she must have had one, or why would she have a cage? I wonder what happened to it.

Mrs. *Hale:* I s'pose maybe the cat got it.

Mrs. *Peters:* No, she didn't have a cat. She's got that feeling some people have about cats—being afraid of them. My cat got in her room and she was real upset and asked me to take it out.

Mrs. *Hale:* My sister Bessie was like that. Queer, ain't it?

Mrs. *Peters (examining the cage):* Why, look at this door. It's broke. One hinge is pulled apart.

Mrs. *Hale (looking too):* Looks as if someone must have been rough with it.

Mrs. *Peters:* Why, yes.

(She brings the cage forward and puts it on the table.)

Mrs. *Hale:* I wish if they're going to find any evidence they'd be about it. I don't like this place.

Mrs. *Peters:* But I'm awful glad you came with me, Mrs. Hale. It would be lonesome for me sitting here alone.

Mrs. *Hale:* It would, wouldn't it? *(Dropping her sewing.)* But I tell you what I do wish, Mrs. Peters. I wish I had come over sometimes when *she* was here. I—*(looking around the room)*—wish I had.

Mrs. *Peters:* But of course you were awful busy, Mrs. Hale—your house and your children.

Mrs. *Hale:* I could've come. I stayed away because it weren't cheerful—and that's why I ought to have come. I—I've never liked this place. Maybe because it's down in a hollow and you don't see the road. I dunno what it is but it's a lonesome place and always was. I wish I had come over to see Minnie Foster sometimes. I can see now—

(Shakes her head.)

Mrs. *Peters:* Well, you mustn't reproach yourself, Mrs. Hale. Somehow we just don't see how it is with other folks until—something comes up.

Mrs. *Hale:* Not having children makes less work—but it makes a quiet house, and Wright out to work all day, and no company when he did come in. Did you know John Wright, Mrs. Peters?

Mrs. *Peters:* Not to know him; I've seen him in town. They say he was a good man.

Mrs. *Hale:* Yes—good; he didn't drink, and kept his word as well as most, I guess, and paid his debts. But he was a hard man, Mrs. Peters. Just to pass the time of day with him—*(shivers)*. Like a raw wind that gets to the bone. *(Pauses, her eye falling on the cage.)* I should think she would'a wanted a bird. But what do you suppose went with it?

Mrs. *Peters:* I don't know, unless it got sick and died.

(She reaches over and swings the broken door, swings it again. Both women watch it.)

Mrs. *Hale:* You weren't raised round here, were you? *(Mrs. Peters shakes her head.)* You didn't know—her?

Mrs. *Peters:* Not till they brought her yesterday.

Mrs. *Hale:* She—come to think of it, she was kind of like a bird herself—real sweet and pretty, but kind of timid and—fluttery. How—she—did—change. *(Silence; then as if struck by a happy thought and relieved to get back to everyday things.)* Tell you what, Mrs. Peters, why don't you take the quilt in with you? It might take up her mind.

Mrs. *Peters:* Why, I think that's a real nice idea, Mrs. Hale. There couldn't possibly be any objection to it, could there? Now, just what would I take? I wonder if her patches are in here—and her things.

(They look in the sewing basket.)

Mrs. *Hale:* Here's some red. I expect this has got sewing things in it. *(Brings out a fancy box.)* What a pretty box. Looks like something somebody would give you. Maybe her scissors are in here. *(Opens box. Suddenly puts her hand to her nose.)* Why—*(Mrs. Peters bends nearer, then turns her face away.)* There's something wrapped up in this piece of silk.

Mrs. *Peters:* Why, this isn't her scissors.

Mrs. *Hale (lifting the silk):* Oh, Mrs. Peters—it's—

(Mrs. Peters bends closer.)

Mrs. *Peters:* It's the bird.

Mrs. *Hale (jumping up):* But, Mrs. Peters—look at it! Its neck! Look at its neck! It's all—other side *to.*

Mrs. *Peters:* Somebody—wrung—its—neck.

(Their eyes meet. A look of growing comprehension, of horror. Steps are heard outside. Mrs. Hale slips box under quilt pieces, and sinks into her chair. Enter Sheriff and County Attorney. Mrs. Peters rises.)

County Attorney (as one turning from serious things to little pleasantries): Well, ladies, have you decided whether she was going to quilt it or knot it?

Mrs. *Peters:* We think she was going to—knot it.

County Attorney: Well, that's interesting, I'm sure. *(Seeing the birdcage.)* Has the bird flown?

Mrs. *Hale (putting more quilt pieces over the box):* We think the—cat got it.

Original 1916 production of *Trifles* at the Wharf Theater in Provincetown, Massachusetts.

County Attorney *(preoccupied)*: Is there a cat?

(Mrs. Hale glances in a quick covert way at Mrs. Peters.)

Mrs. *Peters:* Well, not *now*. They're superstitious, you know. They leave.

County Attorney *(to Sheriff Peters, continuing an interrupted conversation)*: No sign at all of anyone having come from the outside. Their own rope. Now let's go up again and go over it piece by piece. *(They start upstairs.)* It would have to have been someone who knew just the—

(Mrs. Peters sits down. The two women sit there not looking at one another, but as if peering into something and at the same time holding back. When they talk now it is in the manner of feeling their way over strange ground, as if afraid of what they are saying, but as if they cannot help saying it.)

Mrs. *Hale:* She liked the bird. She was going to bury it in that pretty box.

Mrs. *Peters (in a whisper)*: When I was a girl—my kitten—there was a boy took a hatchet, and before my eyes—and before I could get there—*(covers her face an instant)*. If they hadn't held me back I would have—*(catches herself, looks upstairs where steps are heard, falters weakly)*—hurt him.

Mrs. *Hale (with a slow look around her)*: I wonder how it would seem never to have had any children around. *(Pause.)* No, Wright wouldn't like the bird—a thing that sang. She used to sing. He killed that, too.

Mrs. *Peters (moving uneasily)*: We don't know who killed the bird.

Mrs. *Hale:* I knew John Wright.

Mrs. *Peters:* It was an awful thing was done in this house that night, Mrs. Hale. Killing a man while he slept, slipping a rope around his neck that choked the life out of him.

Mrs. Hale: His neck. Choked the life out of him.

(Her hand goes out and rests on the birdcage.)

Mrs. Peters (with rising voice): We don't know who killed him. We don't *know.*

Mrs. Hale (her own feeling not interrupted): If there'd been years and years of nothing, then a bird to sing to you, it would be awful—still, after the bird was still.

Mrs. Peters (something within her speaking): I know what stillness is. When we homesteaded in Dakota, and my first baby died—after he was two years old, and me with no other then—

Mrs. Hale (moving): How soon do you suppose they'll be through looking for the evidence?

Mrs. Peters: I know what stillness is. *(Pulling herself back.)* The law has got to punish crime, Mrs. Hale.

Mrs. Hale (not as if answering that): I wish you'd seen Minnie Foster when she wore a white dress with blue ribbons and stood up there in the choir and sang. *(A look around the room.)* Oh, I *wish* I'd come over here once in a while! That was a crime! That was a crime! Who's going to punish that?

Mrs. Peters (looking upstairs): We mustn't—take on.

Mrs. Hale: I might have known she needed help! I know how things can be—for women. I tell you, it's queer, Mrs. Peters. We live close together and we live far apart. We all go through the same things—it's all just a different kind of the same thing. *(Brushes her eyes; noticing the bottle of fruit, reaches out for it.)* If I was you I wouldn't tell her her fruit was gone. Tell her it *ain't.* Tell her it's all right. Take this in to prove it to her. She—she may never know whether it was broke or not.

Mrs. Peters (takes the bottle, looks about for something to wrap it in; takes petticoat from the clothes brought from the other room, very nervously begins winding this around the bottle; in a false voice): My, it's a good thing the men couldn't hear us. Wouldn't they just laugh! Getting all stirred up over a little thing like a—dead canary. As if that could have anything to do with—with—wouldn't they *laugh*!

(The men are heard coming down stairs.)

Mrs. Hale (under her breath): Maybe they would—maybe they wouldn't.

County Attorney: No, Peters, it's all perfectly clear except a reason for doing it. But you know juries when it comes to women. If there was some definite thing. Something to show—something to make a story about—a thing that would connect up with this strange way of doing it—

(The women's eyes meet for an instant. Enter Hale from outer door.)

Hale: Well, I've got the team around. Pretty cold out there.

County Attorney: I'm going to stay here a while by myself. *(To the Sheriff)* You can send Frank out for me, can't you? I want to go over everything. I'm not satisfied that we can't do better.

Sheriff: Do you want to see what Mrs. Peters is going to take in?

(The County Attorney goes to the table, picks up the apron, laughs.)

County Attorney: Oh, I guess they're not very dangerous things the ladies have picked out. *(Moves a few things about, disturbing the quilt pieces which cover the box. Steps back.)* No, Mrs. Peters doesn't need supervising. For that matter, a sheriff's wife is married to the law. Ever think of it that way, Mrs. Peters?

Mrs. Peters: Not—just that way.

Sheriff (chuckling): Married to the law. *(Moves toward the other room.)* I just want you to come in here a minute, George. We ought to take a look at these windows.

County Attorney (scoffingly): Oh, windows!

Sheriff: We'll be right out, Mr. Hale.

(Hale goes outside. The Sheriff follows the County Attorney into the other room. Then Mrs. Hale rises, hands tight together, looking intensely at Mrs. Peters, whose eyes make a slow turn, finally meeting Mrs. Hale's. A moment Mrs. Hale holds her, then her own eyes point the way to where the box is concealed. Suddenly Mrs. Peters throws back quilt pieces and tries to put the box in the bag she is wearing. It is too big. She opens box, starts to take bird out, cannot touch it, goes to pieces, stands there helpless. Sound of a knob turning in the other room. Mrs. Hale snatches the box and puts it in the pocket of her big coat. Enter County Attorney and Sheriff.)

County Attorney (facetiously): Well, Henry, at least we found out that she was not going to quilt it. She was going to—what is it you call it, ladies?

Mrs. Hale (her hand against her pocket): We call it—knot it, Mr. Henderson.

CURTAIN

Questions

1. What attitudes toward women do the Sheriff and the County Attorney express? How do Mrs. Hale and Mrs. Peters react to these sentiments?
2. Why does the County Attorney care so much about discovering a motive for the killing?
3. What does Glaspell show us about the position of women in this early twentieth-century community?
4. What do we learn about the married life of the Wrights? By what means is this knowledge revealed to us?
5. What is the setting of this play, and how does it help us to understand Mrs. Wright's deed?

6. What do you infer from the wildly stitched block in Minnie's quilt? Why does Mrs. Hale rip out the crazy stitches?
7. What is so suggestive in the ruined birdcage and the dead canary wrapped in silk? What do these objects have to do with Minnie Foster Wright? What similarity do you notice between the way the canary died and John Wright's own death?
8. What thoughts and memories confirm Mrs. Peters and Mrs. Hale in their decision to help Minnie beat the murder rap?
9. In what places does Mrs. Peters show that she is trying to be a loyal, law-abiding sheriff's wife? How do she and Mrs. Hale differ in background and temperament?
10. What ironies does the play contain? Comment on Mrs. Hale's closing speech: "We call it—knot it, Mr. Henderson." Why is that little hesitation before "knot it" such a meaningful pause?
11. Point out some moments in the play when the playwright conveys much to the audience without needing dialogue.
12. How would you sum up the play's major theme?
13. How does this play, first produced in 1916, show its age? In what ways does it seem still remarkably new?
14. "*Trifles* is a lousy mystery. All the action took place before the curtain went up. Almost in the beginning, on the third page, we find out 'who done it.' So there isn't really much reason for us to sit through the rest of the play." Discuss this view.

ANALYZING *TRIFLES*

Some plays endure, perhaps because (among other reasons) actors take pleasure in performing them. *Trifles* is such a play, a showcase for the skills of its two principals. While the men importantly bumble about, trying to discover a motive, Mrs. Peters and Mrs. Hale solve the case right under their dull noses. The two players in these leading roles face a challenging task: to show both characters growing onstage before us. Discovering a secret that binds them, the two women must realize painful truths in their own lives, become aware of all they have in common with Minnie Wright, and gradually resolve to side with the accused against the men. That *Trifles* has enjoyed a revival of attention may reflect its evident feminist views, its convincing portrait of two women forced reluctantly to arrive at a moral judgment and to make a defiant move.

Conflict

Some critics say that the essence of drama is **conflict**, the central struggle between two or more forces in a play. Evidently, Glaspell's play is rich in this essential, even though its most violent conflict—the war between John and Minnie Wright—takes place before the play begins. Right away, when the menfolk barge through the door into the warm room, letting the women trail in after them; right away, when the sheriff makes fun of Minnie for worrying about "trifles" and the county attorney (that slick politician) starts crudely trying to flatter the "ladies," we sense a conflict between officious, self-important men and the women they expect to wait on them. What is the play's *theme*? Surely the title points to it: women, who men say worry over trifles, can find large meanings in those little things.

Plot

Like a carefully constructed traditional short story, *Trifles* has a **plot**, a term sometimes taken to mean whatever happens in a story, but more exactly referring to the unique arrangement of events that the author has made. (For more about plot in a story, see Chapter 1.) If Glaspell had elected to tell the story of John and Minnie Wright in chronological order, the sequence in which events took place in time, she might have written a much longer play, opening perhaps with a scene of Minnie's buying her canary and John's cold complaint, "That damned bird keeps twittering all day long!" She might have included scenes showing John strangling the canary and swearing when it beaks him; the Wrights in their loveless bed while Minnie knots her noose; and farmer Hale's entrance after the murder, with Minnie rocking. Only at the end would she have shown us what happened after the crime. That arrangement of events would have made for a quite different play than the short, tight one Glaspell wrote. By telling of events in retrospect, by having the women detectives piece together what happened, Glaspell leads us to focus not only on the murder but, more importantly, on the developing bond between the two women and their growing compassion for the accused.

Subplot

Tightly packed, the one-act *Trifles* contains a single plot: the story of how two women discover evidence that might hang another woman and then hide it. Some plays, usually longer ones, may be more complicated. They may contain a **double plot** (or **subplot**), a secondary arrangement of incidents, involving not the protagonist but someone less important. In Henrik Ibsen's *A Doll's House*, the main plot involves a woman and her husband; they are joined by a second couple, whose fortunes we also follow with interest and whose futures pose different questions.

Protagonist

If *Trifles* may be said to have a **protagonist**, a leading character—a word we usually save for the primary figure of a larger and more eventful play such as *Othello*—then you would call the two women dual protagonists. They act in unison to make the plot unfold. Or you could argue that Mrs. Hale—because she destroys the wild stitching in the quilt, because she finds the dead canary, because she invents a cat to catch the bird (thus deceiving the county attorney), and because in the end when Mrs. Peters helplessly "goes to pieces" it is she who takes the initiative and seizes the evidence—deserves to be called the protagonist. More than anyone else in the play, you could claim, the more decisive Mrs. Hale makes things happen.

Exposition

A vital part of most plays is an **exposition**, the part in which we first meet the characters, learn what happened before the curtain rose, and find out what is happening now. For a one-act play, *Trifles* has a fairly long exposition, extending from the opening of the kitchen door through the end of farmer Hale's story. Clearly, this substantial exposition is necessary to set the situation and to fill in the facts of the crime. By comparison, Shakespeare's far longer *Tragedy of Richard III* begins almost abruptly, with its protagonist, a duke who yearns to be king, summing up history in an opening speech and revealing his evil character: "And therefore, since I cannot prove a lover . . . I am determined to prove a villain." But Glaspell, too, knows her craft. In the exposition, we are given a **foreshadowing**—a hint of what is to come—in Hale's dry remark, "I didn't know as what his wife wanted made much difference to John." The remark announces the play's theme that men often ignore women's feelings, and it hints at Minnie Wright's motive, later to be revealed. The county attorney, failing to pick up a valuable clue, tables the discussion. (Still another foreshadowing occurs in Mrs. Hale's ripping out the wild, panicky stitches in Minnie's quilt. In the end, Mrs. Hale will make a similar final move to conceal the evidence.)

Dramatic Question

With the county attorney's speech to the sheriff, "You're convinced that there was nothing important here—nothing that would point to any motive," we begin to understand what he seeks. As he will make even clearer later, the attorney needs a motive in order to convict the accused wife of murder in the first degree. Will Minnie's motive in killing her husband be discovered? Through the first two-thirds of *Trifles*, this is the play's **dramatic question**. Whether or not we state such a question in our minds (and it is doubtful that we do), our interest quickens as we sense that here is a problem to be solved, an uncertainty to be cleared up. When Mrs. Hale and Mrs. Peters find the dead canary with the twisted neck, the question is answered. We know that Minnie killed John to repay him for his act of gross cruelty. The playwright, however, now raises a *new* dramatic question. Having discovered Minnie's motive, will the women reveal it to the lawmen? Alternatively (if you care to phrase the new question differently), what will they do with the incriminating evidence? We keep reading, or stay clamped to our theater seats, because we want that question answered. We share the women's secret now, and we want to see what they will do with it.

Climax

Step by step, *Trifles* builds to a **climax**: a moment, usually coming late in a play, when tension reaches its greatest height. At such a moment, we sense that the play's dramatic question (or its final dramatic question, if the writer has posed more than one) is about to be answered. In *Trifles* this climax occurs when Mrs. Peters finds herself torn between her desire to save Minnie and her duty to the law. "It was an awful thing was done in this house that night," she reminds herself in one speech, suggesting that Minnie deserves to be punished; then in the next speech she insists, "We don't know who killed him. We don't *know*." Shortly after that, in one speech she voices two warring attitudes. Remembering the loss of her first child, she sympathizes with Minnie: "I know what stillness is." But in her next breath she recalls once more her duty to be a loyal sheriff's wife: "The law has got to punish crime, Mrs. Hale." For a moment, she is placed in conflict with Mrs. Hale, who knew Minnie personally. The two now stand on the edge of a fateful brink. Which way will they decide?

You will sometimes hear climax used in a different sense to mean any **crisis**—that is, a moment of tension when one or another outcome is possible. What crisis means will be easy to remember if you think of a crisis in medicine: the turning point in an illness when it becomes clear that a patient will either die or recover. In talking about plays, you will probably find both crisis and climax useful. You can say that a play has more than one crisis, perhaps several. In such a play, the last and most decisive crisis is the climax. A play has only one climax.

Resolution and Dénouement

From this moment of climax, the play, like its protagonist (or if you like, protagonists), will make a final move. Mrs. Peters takes her stand. Mrs. Hale, too, decides. She owes Minnie something to make up for her own "crime"—her failure to visit the desperate woman. The plot now charges ahead to its outcome or **resolution**, also called the **conclusion** or **dénouement** (French for "untying of a knot"). The two women act: they scoop up the damaging evidence. Seconds before the very end, Glaspell heightens the **suspense**, our enjoyable anxiety, by making Mrs. Peters fumble with the incriminating box as the sheriff and the county attorney draw near. Mrs. Hale's swift grab for the evidence saves the day and presumably saves Minnie's life. The sound of the doorknob turning in the next room, as the lawmen return, is a small but effective bit of **stage business**—any nonverbal action that engages the attention of an audience. Earlier, when Mrs. Hale almost sits down in Minnie's place, the empty chair that ominously starts rocking is another brilliant piece of stage business. Not only does it give us something interesting to watch, but it also gives us something to think about.

Rising and Falling Action

The German critic Gustav Freytag maintained that events in a plot can be arranged in the outline of a pyramid. In his influential view, a play begins with a **rising action**, that part of the narrative (including the exposition) in which events start moving toward a climax. After the climax, the story tapers off in a **falling action**—that is, the subsequent events, including a resolution.

In a tragedy, this falling action usually is recognizable: the protagonist's fortunes proceed downhill to an inevitable end.

Some plays indeed have demonstrable pyramids. In *Trifles*, we might claim that in the first two-thirds of the play a rising action builds in intensity. It proceeds through each main incident: the finding of the crazily stitched quilt, Mrs. Hale's ripping out the evidence, the discovery of the birdcage, then of the bird itself, and Mrs. Hale's concealing it. At the climax, the peak of the pyramid, the two women seem about to clash as Mrs. Peters wavers uncertainly. The action then falls to a swift resolution. If you outlined that pyramid on paper, however, it would look lopsided—a long rise and a short, steep fall. The pyramid metaphor seems more meaningfully to fit longer plays, among them some classic tragedies, such as *Oedipus the King*. Nevertheless, in most other plays, it is hard to find a symmetrical pyramid.

Unity of Time, Place, and Action

Because its action occurs all at one time and in one place, *Trifles* happens to observe the **unities**, certain principles of good drama laid down by Italian literary critics in the sixteenth century. Interpreting the theories of Aristotle as binding laws, these critics set down three basic principles: a good play, they maintained, should display unity of *action*, unity of *time*, and unity of *place*. In practical terms, this theory maintained that a play must represent a single series of interrelated actions that take place within twenty-four hours in a single location. Furthermore, they insisted, to have true unity of action, a play had to be entirely serious or entirely funny. Mixing tragic and comic elements was not allowed. That Glaspell consciously strove to obey those critics is doubtful, and certainly many great plays, such as Shakespeare's *Othello*, defy such arbitrary rules. Still, it is at least arguable that some of the power of *Trifles* (or Sophocles's *Oedipus the King*) comes from the intensity of the playwright's concentration on what happens in one place, in one short expanse of time.

Symbols in Drama

Brief though it is, *Trifles* has main elements you will find in much longer, more complicated plays. It even has **symbols**, things that hint at large meanings—for example, the broken birdcage and the dead canary, both suggesting the music and the joy that John Wright stifled in Minnie and the terrible stillness that followed his killing the one thing she loved. Perhaps the lone remaining jar of cherries, too, radiates suggestions: it is the one bright, cheerful thing poor Minnie has to show for a whole summer of toil. Plays can also contain symbolic characters (generally flat ones such as a prophet who croaks, "Beware the ides of March"), symbolic settings, and symbolic gestures. Symbols in drama may be as big as a house—the home in Ibsen's *A Doll's House*, for instance—or they may appear to be trifles. In Glaspell's rich art, such trifles aren't trifling at all.

WRITING *effectively*

THINKING ABOUT A PLAY

A good play almost always presents a conflict. Conflict creates suspense and keeps an audience from meandering out to the lobby refreshment stand. Without it, a play would be static and, most likely, dull. When a character intensely desires something but some obstacle—perhaps another character—stands in the way, the result is dramatic tension. To understand a play, it is essential to understand the basic conflicts motivating the plot.

- **Identify the play's protagonist.** Who is the central character of the play? What motivates this character? What does this character want most to achieve or avoid? Is this goal reasonable or does it reflect some delusion on the part of the protagonist?
- **Identify the antagonist.** Who prevents the main character from achieving his or her goal? Is the opposition conscious or accidental? What motivates this character to oppose the protagonist?
- **Identify the central dramatic conflict.** What does the struggle between the protagonist and antagonist focus on? Is it another person, a possession, an action, some sort of recognition, or honor?
- **How does the conflict influence the action of the play?** The central conflict usually fuels the plot, causing characters to do and say all sorts of things they might not otherwise undertake. What series of later events does the central conflict set in motion?

CHECKLIST: Writing About a Play

- ☐ List the play's three or four main characters. Jot down what each character wants most at the play's beginning.
- ☐ Which of these characters is the protagonist?
- ☐ What stands in the way of the protagonist achieving his or her goal?
- ☐ How do the other characters' motivations fit into the central conflict? Identify any double plots or subplots.
- ☐ What are the play's main events? How does each relate to the protagonist's struggle?
- ☐ Where do you find the play's climax?
- ☐ How is the conflict resolved? What qualities in the protagonist's character bring about the play's outcome?
- ☐ Does the protagonist achieve his or her goal? How does success or failure affect the protagonist?

TOPICS FOR WRITING ON *TRIFLES*

1. Write a brief essay on the role gender differences play in Susan Glaspell's *Trifles*.
2. Write an analysis of the exposition—how the scene is set, characters introduced, and background information communicated—in *Trifles*.
3. Describe the significance of setting in *Trifles*.
4. Imagine you are a lawyer hired to defend Minnie Wright. Present your closing argument to the jury.
5. Watch any hour-long television drama. Write about the main conflict that drives the story. What motivates the protagonist? What stands in his or her way? How do each of the drama's main events relate to the protagonist's struggle? How is the conflict resolved? Is the show's outcome connected to the protagonist's character, or do events just happen to him or her? Do you believe the script is well written? Why or why not?
6. Select any short play, and write a brief essay identifying the protagonist, central conflict, and dramatic question.

▶ TERMS FOR *review*

To review definitions of the elements of plot (**protagonist, antagonist, exposition, conflict, complication, crisis, climax,** and **conclusion**), see Chapter 1 "Terms for Review" on pages 26 and 27.

Double plot ▶ Also called **subplot.** A second story or plotline that is complete and interesting in its own right, often doubling or inverting the main plot.

Unities ▶ Unity of time, place, and action, the three formal qualities recommended by Renaissance critics to give a theatrical plot cohesion and integrity. According to this theory, a play should depict the causes and effects of a single action unfolding in one day in one place.

Soliloquy ▶ In drama, a speech by a character alone onstage in which he or she utters his or her thoughts aloud.

Aside ▶ A speech that a character addresses directly to the audience, unheard by the other characters on stage, as when the villain in a melodrama chortles: "Heh! Heh! Now she's in my power!"

Stage business ▶ Nonverbal action that engages the attention of an audience.

25 TRAGEDY AND COMEDY

What You Will Learn in This Chapter

- To define *tragedy* as a dramatic mode
- To define *comedy* as a dramatic mode
- To explain the difference between tragedy and comedy
- To understand and describe the various levels and kinds of comedy

In 1770, Horace Walpole wrote, "the world is a comedy to those that think, a tragedy to those that feel." All of us, of course, both think and feel, and all of us have moments when we stand back and laugh, whether ruefully or with glee, at life's absurdities, just as we all have times when our hearts are broken by its pains and losses. Thus, the modes of tragedy and comedy, diametrically opposed to one another though they are, do not demand that we choose between them: both of them speak to something deep and real within us, and each of them has its own truth to tell about the infinitely complex experience of living in this world.

TRAGEDY

By **tragedy** we mean a play that portrays a serious conflict between human beings and some superior, overwhelming force. It ends sorrowfully and disastrously, and this outcome seems inevitable. Few spectators of *Oedipus the King* wonder how the play will turn out or wish for a happy ending. "In a tragedy," French playwright Jean Anouilh has remarked, "nothing is in doubt and everyone's destiny is known. . . . Tragedy is restful, and the reason is that hope, that foul, deceitful thing, has no part in it. There isn't any hope. You're trapped. The whole sky has fallen on you, and all you can do about it is shout."[1]

Many of our ideas of tragedy (from the Greek *tragoidia*, "goat song," referring to the goatskin dress of the performers) go back to ancient Athens; the plays of the Greek dramatists Sophocles, Aeschylus, and Euripides exemplify the art of tragedy. In the fourth century B.C., the philosopher Aristotle described Sophocles's *Oedipus the King* and other tragedies he had seen, analyzing their elements and trying to account for their power over our emotions.

[1]Anouilh, Jean, "Preface," *Antigone*, trans. Lewis Galantière (New York: Random, 1946) 24.

Aristotle's observations will make more sense after you read *Oedipus the King*, so we will save our principal discussion of them for Chapter 26. But for now, to understand something of the nature of tragedy, let us take a brief overview of the subject.

One of the oldest and most durable of literary genres, tragedy is also one of the simplest—the protagonist undergoes a reversal of fortune, from good to bad, ending in catastrophe. However simple, though, tragedy can be one of the most complex genres to explain satisfactorily, with almost every principal point of its definition open to differing and often hotly debated interpretations. It is a fluid and adaptive genre, and for every one of its defining points, we can cite a tragic masterpiece that fails to observe that particular convention. Its fluidity and adaptability can also be shown by the way in which the classical tragic pattern is played out in pure form in such unlikely places as Orson Welles's film *Citizen Kane* (1941) and Chinua Achebe's great novel *Things Fall Apart* (1958): in each of these works, a man of high position and character—one a multimillionaire newspaper publisher, the other a late nineteenth-century African warrior—moves inexorably to destruction, impelled by his rigidity and self-righteousness. Even a movie such as *King Kong*—despite its oversized and hirsute protagonist—exemplifies some of the principles of tragedy.

To gain a clearer understanding of what tragedy is, let us first take a moment to talk about what it is not. Consider the kinds of events that customarily bring the term "tragedy" to mind: the death of a child, a fire that destroys a family's home and possessions, the killing of a bystander caught in the crossfire of a shootout between criminals, and so on. What all of these unfortunate instances have in common, obviously, is that they involve the infliction of great and irreversible suffering. But what they also share is the sense that the sufferers are innocent, that they have done nothing to cause or to deserve their fate. This is what we usually describe as a tragedy in real life, but tragedy in a literary or dramatic context has a different meaning: most theorists take their lead from Aristotle (see Chapter 26 for a fuller discussion of several of the points raised here) in maintaining that the protagonist's reversal of fortune is brought about through some error or weakness on his part, generally referred to as his **tragic flaw**.

Despite this weakness, the hero is traditionally a person of nobility, of both social rank and personality. Just as the suffering of totally innocent people stirs us to sympathetic sorrow rather than a tragic response, so too the destruction of a purely evil figure, a tyrant or a murderer with no redeeming qualities, would inspire only feelings of relief and satisfaction—hardly the emotions that tragedy seeks to stimulate. In most tragedies, the catastrophe entails not only the loss of outward fortune—things such as reputation, power, and life itself, which even the basest villain may possess and then be deprived of—but also the erosion of the protagonist's moral character and greatness of spirit.

Tragic Style

In keeping with this emphasis on nobility of spirit, tragedies are customarily written in an elevated style, one characterized by dignity and seriousness. In the Middle Ages, just as *tragedy* meant a work written in a high style in which the central character went from good fortune to bad, *comedy* indicated just the opposite, a work written in a low or common style, in which the protagonist moved from adverse circumstances to happy ones—hence Dante's great triptych of hell, purgatory, and heaven, written in everyday Italian rather than scholarly Latin, is known as *The Divine Comedy*, despite the relative absence of humor, let alone hilarity, in its pages. The tragic view of life, clearly, presupposes that in the end we will prove unequal to the challenges we must face, while the comic outlook asserts a view of human possibility in which our common sense and resilience—or pure dumb luck—will enable us to win out.

Tragedy's complexity can be seen also in the response that, according to Aristotle, it seeks to arouse in the viewer: pity and fear. By its very nature, pity distances the one who pities from the object of that pity, since we can feel sorry only for those whom we perceive to be worse off than ourselves. When we watch or read a tragedy, moved as we may be, we observe the downfall of the protagonist with a certain detachment; "better him than me" may be a rather crude way of putting it, but perhaps not an entirely incorrect one. Fear, on the other hand, usually involves an immediate anxiety about our own well-being. Even as we regard the hero's destruction from the safety of a better place, we are made to feel our own vulnerability in the face of life's dangers and instability, because we see that neither position nor virtue can protect even the great from ruin.

The following is a scene from Christopher Marlowe's classic Elizabethan tragedy *Doctor Faustus*. Based on an anonymous pamphlet published in Germany in 1587 and translated into English shortly thereafter, this celebrated play tells the story of an elderly professor who feels that he has wasted his life in fruitless inquiry. Chafing at the limits of human understanding, he makes a pact with the devil to gain forbidden knowledge and power. The scene presented here is the decisive turning point of the play, in which Faustus seals the satanic bargain that will damn him. Stimulated by his thirst for knowledge and experience, spurred on by his pride to assume that the divinely ordained limits of human experience no longer apply to him, he rushes to embrace his own undoing. Marlowe dramatizes Faustus's situation by bringing a good angel and a fallen angel (i.e., a demon) to whisper conflicting advice in this pivotal scene. (This good angel versus bad angel device has proved popular for centuries. We still see it today in everything from TV commercials to cartoons such as *The Simpsons*.) Notice the dignified and often gorgeous language Marlowe employs to create the serious mood necessary for tragedy.

Christopher Marlowe

Scene from **Doctor Faustus**[2] (about 1588)

Edited by Sylvan Barnet

*Christopher Marlowe was born in Canterbury, England, in February 1564, about ten weeks before William Shakespeare. Marlowe, the son of a prosperous shoemaker, received a BA from Cambridge University in 1584 and an MA in 1587, after which he settled in London. The rest of his short life was marked by rumor, secrecy, and violence, including suspicions that he was a secret agent for Queen Elizabeth's government and allegations against him of blasphemy and atheism—no small matter in light of the political instability and religious controversies of the times. Peripherally implicated in several violent deaths, he met his own end in May 1593 when he was stabbed above the right eye during a tavern brawl, under circumstances that have never been fully explained. Brief and crowded as his life was, he wrote a number of intense, powerful, and highly influential tragedies—*Tamburlaine the Great, Parts 1 and 2 *(1587),* Doctor Faustus *(1588),* The Jew of Malta *(1589),* Edward the Second *(c. 1592),* The Massacre at Paris *(1593), and* Dido, Queen of Carthage *(c. 1593, with Thomas Nashe). He is also the author of the lyric poem "The Passionate Shepherd to His Love," with its universally known first line: "Come live with me and be my love."*

Doctor Faustus with the Bad Angel and the Good Angel, from the Utah Shakespearean Festival's 2005 production.

[2]This scene is from the 1616 text, or "B-Text," published as *The Tragicall History of the Life and Death of Doctor Faustus*. Modernizations have been made in spelling and punctuation.

DRAMATIS PERSONAE

Doctor Faustus
Good Angel
Bad Angel
Mephistophilis, a devil

ACT II

SCENE I

(*Enter Faustus in his study.*)

Faustus: Now, Faustus, must thou needs be damned;
Canst thou not be saved!
What boots° it then to think on God or heaven?
Away with such vain fancies, and despair—
Despair in God and trust in Belzebub!
Now go not backward Faustus; be resolute!
Why waver'st thou? O something soundeth in mine ear,
"Abjure this magic, turn to God again."
Ay, and Faustus will turn to God again.
To God? He loves thee not.
The god thou serv'st is thine own appetite
Wherein is fixed the love of Belzebub!
To him I'll build an altar and a church,
And offer lukewarm blood of newborn babes!

(*Enter the two Angels.*)

Bad Angel: Go forward, Faustus, in that famous art.
Good Angel: Sweet Faustus, leave that execrable art.
Faustus: Contrition, prayer, repentance? What of these?
Good Angel: O, they are means to bring thee unto heaven.
Bad Angel: Rather illusions, fruits of lunacy,
That make men foolish that do use them most.
Good Angel: Sweet Faustus, think of heaven and heavenly things.
Bad Angel: No, Faustus, think of honor and of wealth.
(*Exeunt Angels.*)

Faustus: Wealth!
Why, the signory of Emden° shall be mine!
When Mephistophilis shall stand by me
What power can hurt me? Faustus, thou art safe.
Cast no more doubts! Mephistophilis, come,

3 *boots*: avails. 24 *signory of Emden*: lordship of the rich German port at the mouth of the Ems.

And bring glad tidings from great Lucifer.
Is't not midnight? Come Mephistophilis,
Veni, veni, Mephostophile!°

(Enter Mephistophilis.)

Now tell me, what saith Lucifer thy lord?
Mephistophilis: That I shall wait on Faustus whilst he lives,
So he will buy my service with his soul.
Faustus: Already Faustus hath hazarded that for thee.
Mephistophilis: But now thou must bequeath it solemnly
And write a deed of gift with thine own blood,
For that security craves Lucifer.
If thou deny it I must back to hell.
Faustus: Stay Mephistophilis and tell me,
What good will my soul do thy lord?
Mephistophilis: Enlarge his kingdom.
Faustus: Is that the reason why he tempts us thus?
Mephistophilis: Solamen miseris socios habuisse doloris.°
Faustus: Why, have you any pain that torture other?°
Mephistophilis: As great as have the human souls of men.
But tell me, Faustus, shall I have thy soul—
And I will be thy slave and wait on thee
And give thee more than thou hast wit to ask?
Faustus: Ay Mephistophilis, I'll give it him.°
Mephistophilis: Then, Faustus, stab thy arm courageously,
And bind thy soul, that at some certain day
Great Lucifer may claim it as his own.
And then be thou as great as Lucifer!
Faustus: Lo, Mephistophilis: for love of thee
Faustus hath cut his arm, and with his proper° blood
Assures° his soul to be great Lucifer's,
Chief Lord and Regent of perpetual night.
View here this blood that trickles from mine arm,
And let it be propitious for my wish.
Mephistophilis: But, Faustus,
Write it in manner of a deed of gift.
Faustus: Ay, so I do—But Mephistophilis,
My blood congeals and I can write no more.
Mephistophilis: I'll fetch thee fire to dissolve it straight.

(Exit.)

Faustus: What might the staying of my blood portend?

30 *Veni, veni, Mephostophile!*: Come, come, Mephistophilis (Latin). 43 *Solamen ... doloris*: Misery loves company (Latin). 44 *other*: others. 49 *him*: i.e., to Lucifer. 55 *proper*: own. 56 *Assures*: conveys by contract.

Is it unwilling I should write this bill?°
Why streams it not that I may write afresh:
"Faustus gives to thee his soul"? O there it stayed.
Why should'st thou not? Is not thy soul thine own?
Then write again: "Faustus gives to thee his soul."

(Enter Mephistophilis, with the chafer° of fire.)

Mephistophilis: See, Faustus, here is fire. Set it° on.
Faustus: So, now the blood begins to clear again.
Now will I make an end immediately.
Mephistophilis (aside): What will not I do to obtain his soul!
Faustus: Consummatum est!° This bill is ended:
And Faustus hath bequeathed his soul to Lucifer.
—But what is this inscription on mine arm?
Homo fuge!° Whither should I fly?
If unto God, He'll throw me down to hell.
My senses are deceived; here's nothing writ.
O yes, I see it plain! Even here is writ
Homo fuge! Yet shall not Faustus fly!
Mephistophilis (aside): I'll fetch him somewhat° to delight his mind.
(Exit Mephistophilis.)

(Enter Devils, giving crowns and rich apparel to Faustus. They dance and then depart.)

(Enter Mephistophilis.)

Faustus: What means this show? Speak, Mephistophilis.
Mephistophilis: Nothing, Faustus, but to delight thy mind,
And let thee see what magic can perform.
Faustus: But may I raise such spirits when I please?
Mephistophilis: Ay, Faustus, and do greater things than these.
Faustus: Then, Mephistophilis, receive this scroll,
A deed of gift of body and of soul:
But yet conditionally that thou perform
All covenants and articles between us both.
Mephistophilis: Faustus, I swear by hell and Lucifer
To effect all promises between us both.
Faustus: Then hear me read it, Mephistophilis:
"On these conditions following:

66 *bill:* contract. 70 *s.d. chafer:* portable grate. 71 *it:* i.e., the receptacle containing the congealed blood. 75 *Consummatum est:* It is finished. (Latin: a blasphemous repetition of Christ's words on the Cross; see John 19:30.) 78 *Homo fuge:* fly, man (Latin). 83 *somewhat:* something.

First, that Faustus may be a spirit° in form and substance.

Secondly, that Mephistophilis shall be his servant, and be by him commanded.

Thirdly, that Mephistophilis shall do for him and bring him whatsoever.

Fourthly, that he shall be in his chamber or house invisible.

Lastly, that he shall appear to the said John Faustus, at all times, in what shape and form soever he please.

I, John Faustus of Wittenberg, Doctor, by these presents, do give both body and soul to Lucifer, Prince of the East, and his minister Mephistophilis, and furthermore grant unto them that, four and twenty years being expired, and these articles written being inviolate,° full power to fetch or carry the said John Faustus, body and soul, flesh, blood, into their habitation wheresoever.

By me John Faustus."

Mephistophilis: Speak, Faustus, do you deliver this as your deed?
Faustus: Ay, take it, and the devil give thee good of it!
Mephistophilis: So, now Faustus, ask me what thou wilt.
Faustus: First, I will question with thee about hell.
Tell me, where is the place that men call hell?
Mephistophilis: Under the heavens.
Faustus: Ay, so are all things else, but whereabouts?
Mephistophilis: Within the bowels of these elements,
Where we are tortured, and remain forever.
Hell hath no limits, nor is circumscribed,
In one self place, but where we are is hell,
And where hell is there must we ever be.
And to be short, when all the world dissolves,
And every creature shall be purified,
All places shall be hell that is not heaven!
Faustus: I think hell's a fable.
Mephistophilis: Ay, think so still—till experience change thy mind.
Faustus: Why, dost thou think that Faustus shall be damned?
Mephistophilis: Ay, of necessity, for here's the scroll
In which thou hast given thy soul to Lucifer.
Faustus: Ay, and body too; but what of that?
Think'st thou that Faustus is so fond° to imagine,

97 *spirit:* evil spirit, devil. (But to see Faustus as transformed now into a devil deprived of freedom to repent is to deprive the remainder of the play of much of its meaning.) 108 *inviolate:* unviolated. 133 *fond:* foolish.

That after this life there is any pain?
No, these are trifles, and mere old wives' tales.
Mephistophilis: But I am an instance to prove the contrary,
For I tell thee I am damned, and now in hell!
Faustus: Nay, and this be hell, I'll willingly be damned—
What, sleeping, eating, walking, and disputing?
But leaving this, let me have a wife,
The fairest maid in Germany,
For I am wanton and lascivious,
And cannot live without a wife.
Mephistophilis: Well, Faustus, thou shalt have a wife.

(He fetches in a woman devil.)

Faustus: What sight is this?
Mephistophilis: Now, Faustus, wilt thou have a wife?
Faustus: Here's a hot whore indeed! No, I'll no wife.
Mephistophilis: Marriage is but a ceremonial toy,°
(Exit she-devil.)
And if thou lov'st me, think no more of it.
I'll cull thee out° the fairest courtesans
And bring them every morning to thy bed.
She whom thine eye shall like, thy heart shall have,
Were she as chaste as was Penelope,°
As wise as Saba,° or as beautiful
As was bright Lucifer before his fall.
Here, take this book and peruse it well.
The iterating° of these lines brings gold;
The framing° of this circle on the ground
Brings thunder, whirlwinds, storm, and lightning;
Pronounce this thrice devoutly to thyself,
And men in harness° shall appear to thee,
Ready to execute what thou command'st.
Faustus: Thanks, Mephistophilis, for this sweet book.
This will I keep as chary as my life.
(Exeunt.)

Questions

1. What specifically motivates Faustus to make his satanic compact? Cite the text to back up your response.
2. How does his behavior constitute a compromise of his nobility?
3. "Is not thy soul thine own?" Faustus asks rhetorically (line 69). Discuss the implications of this statement in terms of the larger thematic concerns of the work.
4. Does Faustus inspire your pity and fear in this scene? Why or why not?

148 *toy*: trifle. 150 *cull thee out*: select for you. 153 *Penelope*: wife of Ulysses, famed for her fidelity. 154 *Saba*: the Queen of Sheba. 157 *iterating*: repetition. 158 *framing*: drawing. 161 *harness*: armor.

Traditional masks of comedy and tragedy.

COMEDY

The best-known traditional emblem of drama—a pair of masks, one sorrowful (representing tragedy) and one smiling (representing comedy)—suggests that tragedy and comedy, although opposites, are close relatives. Often, comedy shows people getting into trouble through error or weakness; in this respect it is akin to tragedy. An important difference between comedy and tragedy lies in the attitude toward human failing that is expected of us. When a main character in a comedy suffers from overweening pride, as does Oedipus, or if he fails to recognize that his bride-to-be is actually his mother, we laugh—something we would never do in watching a competent performance of *Oedipus the King*.

Comedy, from the Greek *komos*, "a revel," is thought to have originated in festivities to celebrate spring, ritual performances in praise of Dionysus, god of fertility and wine. In drama, comedy may be broadly defined as whatever makes us laugh. A comedy may be a name for one entire play, or we may say that there is comedy in only part of a play—as in a comic character or a comic situation.

Theories of Comedy

Many theories have been propounded to explain why we laugh; most of these notions fall into a few familiar types. One school, exemplified by French philosopher Henri Bergson, sees laughter as a form of ridicule, implying a feeling of disinterested superiority; all jokes are *on* somebody. Bergson suggests that laughter springs from situations in which we sense a conflict between some mechanical or rigid pattern of behavior and our sense of a more natural or "organic" kind of behavior that is possible. An example occurs in Buster Keaton's comic film *The Boat*. Having launched a little boat that springs a leak, Keaton rigidly goes down with it, with frozen face. (The more natural and organic thing to do would be to swim for shore.)

Other thinkers view laughter as our response to expectations fulfilled or to expectations set up but then suddenly frustrated. Some hold it to be the expression of our delight in seeing our suppressed urges acted out (as when a comedian hurls an egg at a pompous stuffed shirt); some, to be our defensive reaction to a painful and disturbing truth.

Satiric Comedy

Derisive humor is basic to **satiric comedy,** in which human weakness or folly is ridiculed from a vantage point of supposedly enlightened superiority. Satiric comedy may be coolly malicious and gently biting, but it tends to be critical of people, their manners, and their morals. It is at least as old as the comedies of Aristophanes, who thrived in the fifth century B.C. In *Lysistrata,* the satirist shows how the women of two warring cities speedily halt a war by agreeing to deny themselves to their husbands. (The satirist's target is men so proud that they go to war rather than make the slightest concession.)

High Comedy

Comedy is often divided into two varieties—"high" and "low." **High comedy** relies more on wit and wordplay than on physical action for its humor. It tries to address the audience's intelligence by pointing out the pretension and hypocrisy of human behavior. High comedy also generally avoids derisive humor. Jokes about physical appearance would, for example, be avoided. One technique it employs to appeal to a sophisticated, verbal audience is use of the **epigram,** a brief and witty statement that memorably expresses some truth, large or small. Oscar Wilde's plays such as *The Importance of Being Earnest* (1895) and *Lady Windermere's Fan* (1892) sparkle with such brilliant epigrams as: "I can resist everything except temptation"; "Experience is the name everyone gives to their mistakes"; "There is only one thing in the world worse than being talked about, and that is not being talked about."

Low Comedy

Low comedy explores the opposite extreme of humor. It places greater emphasis on physical action and visual gags, and its verbal jokes do not require much intellect to appreciate (as in Groucho Marx's pithy put-down to his brother Chico, "You have the brain of a five-year-old, and I bet he was glad to get rid of it!"). Low comedy does not avoid derisive humor; rather, it revels in making fun of whatever will get a good laugh. Drunkenness, stupidity, lust, senility, trickery, insult, and clumsiness are inexhaustible staples of this style of comedy. Although it is all too easy for critics to dismiss low comedy, like high comedy it serves a valuable purpose in satirizing human failings. Shakespeare indulged in coarse humor in some of his noblest plays. Low comedy is usually the preferred style of popular culture, and it has inspired many incisive satires on modern life—from the classic films of W. C. Fields and the Marx Brothers to the weekly TV antics of Matt Groening's *The Simpsons* or Zooey Deschanel's *New Girl*.

Low comedy includes several distinct types. One is the **burlesque**, a broadly humorous parody or travesty of another play or kind of play. (In the United States, *burlesque* is something else: a once-popular form of variety show featuring stripteases interspersed with bits of ribald low comedy.) Another valuable type of low comedy is the **farce**, a broadly humorous play whose action is usually fast-moving and improbable. **Slapstick comedy** (such as that of the Three Stooges) is a kind of farce. Featuring pratfalls, pie-throwing, fisticuffs, and other violent action, it takes its name from a circus clown's prop—a bat with two boards that loudly clap together when one clown swats another.

Romantic Comedy

Romantic comedy, another traditional sort of comedy, is subtler. Its main characters are generally lovers, and its plot unfolds their ultimately successful strivings to be united. Unlike satiric comedy, romantic comedy portrays its characters not with withering contempt but with kindly indulgence. It may take place in the everyday world, or perhaps in some never-never land, such as the forest of Arden in Shakespeare's *As You Like It*. Romantic comedy is also a popular staple of Hollywood, which depicts two people undergoing humorous mishaps on their way to falling in love. The characters often suffer humiliation and discomfort along the way, but these moments are funny rather than sad, and the characters are rewarded in the end by true love.

Here is an example of high comedy—a scene from the first act of Oscar Wilde's classic play, *The Importance of Being Earnest*. Following that is *Sure Thing*, a short contemporary comedy by David Ives, one of America's most ingenious playwrights.

Oscar Wilde

Scene from The Importance of Being Earnest: *Lady Bracknell Interviews Her Daughter's Suitor* 1895

Oscar Fingal O'Flahertie Wills Wilde (1854–1900) was born in Ireland to a mother who wrote revolutionary poetry and a philandering father who was an eye and ear surgeon. Wilde was a top student at Trinity College in Dublin and then Magdalen College in Oxford. After settling in London, Wilde married Constance Lloyd and promptly had two sons. Soon after, he entered his years of great productivity. He published two volumes of fairy tales and his sole novel, The Picture of Dorian Gray *(1891), which critics derided for its homosexual undertones. However, it was Wilde's plays that marked him as one of the great writers of England's late-Victorian era. He wrote a string of successes that started with* Lady Windermere's Fan *(1892) and culminated with his masterpiece,* The Importance of Being Earnest *(1895). His comedies focused on high society, the stratum in which Wilde was famously popular. It was said that he was London's "most sought-after dinner guest" and was known for his boundless wit and his many epigrams, such as "Work is the curse of the drinking classes." In 1895 Wilde endured a very public and humiliating*

A 2008 production of *The Importance of Being Earnest*, by the Vaudeville Theatre of London.

legal battle over accusations of "gross indecency" with men, and he was sentenced to two years of hard labor, which devastated him as an artist. Upon his release, Wilde wandered Europe under the name Sebastian Melmoth. Three years later he died of meningitis in Paris, with barely a penny to his name.

CHARACTERS

Lady Bracknell, mother of Gwendolen Fairfax
Jack, the suitor

SCENE. *Morning-room in Algernon's flat in Half-Moon Street. The room is luxuriously and artistically furnished. The sound of a piano is heard in the adjoining room.*

The following is an excerpt from Act I, Scene 1 of the play.

Lady Bracknell (sitting down): You can take a seat, Mr. Worthing.

(Looks in her pocket for note-book and pencil.)

Jack: Thank you, Lady Bracknell, I prefer standing.
Lady Bracknell (pencil and note-book in hand): I feel bound to tell you that you are not down on my list of eligible young men, although I have the same list as the dear Duchess of Bolton has. We work together, in fact. However, I am quite ready to enter your name, should your answers be what a really affectionate mother requires. Do you smoke?

Jack: Well, yes, I must admit I smoke.

Lady Bracknell: I am glad to hear it. A man should always have an occupation of some kind. There are far too many idle men in London as it is. How old are you?

Jack: Twenty-nine.

Lady Bracknell: A very good age to be married at. I have always been of opinion that a man who desires to get married should know either everything or nothing. Which do you know?

Jack (after some hesitation): I know nothing, Lady Bracknell.

Lady Bracknell: I am pleased to hear it. I do not approve of anything that tampers with natural ignorance. Ignorance is like a delicate exotic fruit; touch it and the bloom is gone. The whole theory of modern education is radically unsound. Fortunately in England, at any rate, education produces no effect whatsoever. If it did, it would prove a serious danger to the upper classes, and probably lead to acts of violence in Grosvenor Square. What is your income?

Jack: Between seven and eight thousand a year.

Lady Bracknell (makes a note in her book): In land, or in investments?

Jack: In investments, chiefly.

Lady Bracknell: That is satisfactory. What between the duties expected of one during one's lifetime, and the duties exacted from one after one's death, land has ceased to be either a profit or a pleasure. It gives one position, and prevents one from keeping it up. That's all that can be said about land.

Jack: I have a country house with some land, of course, attached to it, about fifteen hundred acres, I believe; but I don't depend on that for my real income. In fact, as far as I can make out, the poachers are the only people who make anything out of it.

Lady Bracknell: A country house! How many bedrooms? Well, that point can be cleared up afterwards. You have a town house, I hope? A girl with a simple, unspoiled nature, like Gwendolen, could hardly be expected to reside in the country.

Jack: Well, I own a house in Belgrave Square, but it is let by the year to Lady Bloxham. Of course, I can get it back whenever I like, at six months' notice.

Lady Bracknell: Lady Bloxham? I don't know her.

Jack: Oh, she goes about very little. She is a lady considerably advanced in years.

Lady Bracknell: Ah, nowadays that is no guarantee of respectability of character. What number in Belgrave Square?

Jack: 149.

Lady Bracknell (shaking her head): The unfashionable side. I thought there was something. However, that could easily be altered.

Jack: Do you mean the fashion, or the side?

Lady Bracknell (sternly): Both, if necessary, I presume. What are your politics?

Jack: Well, I am afraid I really have none. I am a Liberal Unionist.

Lady Bracknell: Oh, they count as Tories. They dine with us. Or come in the evening, at any rate. Now to minor matters. Are your parents living?

Jack: I have lost both my parents.

Lady Bracknell: To lose one parent, Mr. Worthing, may be regarded as a misfortune; to lose both looks like carelessness. Who was your father? He was evidently a man of some wealth. Was he born in what the Radical papers call the purple of commerce, or did he rise from the ranks of the aristocracy?

Jack: I am afraid I really don't know. The fact is, Lady Bracknell, I said I had lost my parents. It would be nearer the truth to say that my parents seem to have lost me . . . I don't actually know who I am by birth. I was . . . well, I was found.

Lady Bracknell: Found!

Jack: The late Mr. Thomas Cardew, an old gentleman of a very charitable and kindly disposition, found me, and gave me the name of Worthing, because he happened to have a first-class ticket for Worthing in his pocket at the time. Worthing is a place in Sussex. It is a seaside resort.

Lady Bracknell: Where did the charitable gentleman who had a first-class ticket for this seaside resort find you?

Jack (gravely): In a hand-bag.

Lady Bracknell: A hand-bag?

Jack (very seriously): Yes, Lady Bracknell. I was in a hand-bag—a somewhat large, black leather hand-bag, with handles to it—an ordinary hand-bag in fact.

Lady Bracknell: In what locality did this Mr. James, or Thomas, Cardew come across this ordinary hand-bag?

Jack: In the cloak-room at Victoria Station. It was given to him in mistake for his own.

Lady Bracknell: The cloak-room at Victoria Station?

Jack: Yes. The Brighton line.

Lady Bracknell: The line is immaterial. Mr. Worthing, I confess I feel somewhat bewildered by what you have just told me. To be born, or at any rate bred, in a hand-bag, whether it had handles or not, seems to me to display a contempt for the ordinary decencies of family life that reminds one of the worst excesses of the French Revolution. And I presume you know what that unfortunate movement led to? As for the particular locality in which the hand-bag was found, a cloak-room at a railway station might serve to conceal a social indiscretion—has probably, indeed, been used for that purpose before now—but it could hardly be regarded as an assured basis for a recognised position in good society.

Jack: May I ask you then what you would advise me to do? I need hardly say I would do anything in the world to ensure Gwendolen's happiness.

Lady Bracknell: I would strongly advise you, Mr. Worthing, to try and acquire some relations as soon as possible, and to make a definite effort to produce at any rate one parent, of either sex, before the season is quite over.

Jack: Well, I don't see how I could possibly manage to do that. I can produce the hand-bag at any moment. It is in my dressing-room at home. I really think that should satisfy you, Lady Bracknell.

Lady Bracknell: Me, sir! What has it to do with me? You can hardly imagine that I and Lord Bracknell would dream of allowing our only daughter—a girl brought up with the utmost care—to marry into a cloak-room, and form an alliance with a parcel? Good morning, Mr. Worthing!

(*Lady Bracknell sweeps out in majestic indignation.*)

Questions

1. How would you characterize Lady Bracknell? What are her chief concerns in interviewing her daughter's suitor? Find examples from the text to support your argument.
2. Describe Jack's tone. Does he seem amused with Lady Bracknell, nervous about the interview, or genuinely eager to please her?
3. Would you call this passage high comedy or low? Explain the reasons for your choice.

David Ives

Sure Thing

1988

David Ives

David Ives (b. 1950) grew up on the South Side of Chicago. He attended Catholic schools before entering Northwestern University. Later Ives studied at the Yale Drama School—"a blissful time for me," he recalls, "in spite of the fact that there is slush on the ground in New Haven 238 days a year." Ives received his first professional production in Los Angeles at the age of twenty-one "at America's smallest, and possibly worst theater, in a storefront that had a pillar dead center in the middle of the stage." He continued writing for the theater while working as an editor at Foreign Affairs, *and gradually achieved a reputation in theatrical circles for his wildly original and brilliantly written short comic plays. His public breakthrough came in 1993 with the New York staging of* All in the Timing, *which presented six short comedies. This production earned ecstatic reviews and a busy box office, and in the 1995–1996 season,* All in the Timing *was the most widely performed play in America (except for the works of Shakespeare). His second group of one-act comedies,* Mere Mortals *(1997), was produced with great success in New York*

City, followed by Lives of the Saints, *a third group of one-act plays. Ives's full-length plays* Don Juan in Chicago *(1995)*, Ancient History *(1996)*, The Red Address *(1997), and* Polish Joke *(2000) are collected in the volume* Polish Joke and Other Plays *(2004). A talented adapter, Ives was chosen to rework a newly discovered play by Mark Twain,* Is He Dead?, *which had a successful run on Broadway in 2007. His most recent plays are* Venus in Fur *(2010), which was the most-produced play in the country in 2013–2014, and a number of translations and adaptations of French theater, including Pierre Corneille's comedy* The Liar *(2010) and Molière's* The Misanthrope, *which Ives titled* The School For Lies *(2011). He also writes short stories and screenplays for both motion pictures and television. Ives lives in New York City.*

CHARACTERS

Betty
Bill

SCENE. *A café. Betty, a woman in her late twenties, is reading at a café table. An empty chair is opposite her. Bill, same age, enters.*

Bill: Excuse me. Is this chair taken?
Betty: Excuse me?
Bill: Is this taken?
Betty: Yes it is.
Bill: Oh. Sorry.
Betty: Sure thing.

(A bell rings softly.)

Bill: Excuse me. Is this chair taken?
Betty: Excuse me?
Bill: Is this taken?
Betty: No, but I'm expecting somebody in a minute.
Bill: Oh. Thanks anyway.
Betty: Sure thing.

(A bell rings softly.)

Bill: Excuse me. Is this chair taken?
Betty: No, but I'm expecting somebody very shortly.
Bill: Would you mind if I sit here till he or she or it comes?
Betty (glances at her watch): They do seem to be pretty late. . . .
Bill: You never know who you might be turning down.
Betty: Sorry. Nice try, though.
Bill: Sure thing.

(Bell.)

2003 Off-Broadway production of *Sure Thing* by Primary Stages.

Is this seat taken?
Betty: No it's not.
Bill: Would you mind if I sit here?
Betty: Yes I would.
Bill: Oh.

(Bell.)

Is this chair taken?
Betty: No it's not.
Bill: Would you mind if I sit here?
Betty: No. Go ahead.
Bill: Thanks. *(He sits. She continues reading.)* Everyplace else seems to be taken.
Betty: Mm-hm.
Bill: Great place.
Betty: Mm-hm.
Bill: What's the book?
Betty: I just wanted to read in quiet, if you don't mind.
Bill: No. Sure thing.

(Bell.)

Everyplace else seems to be taken.

Betty: Mm-hm.

Bill: Great place for reading.

Betty: Yes, I like it.

Bill: What's the book?

Betty: The Sound and the Fury.

Bill: Oh. Hemingway.

(Bell.)

What's the book?

Betty: The Sound and the Fury.

Bill: Oh. Faulkner.

Betty: Have you read it?

Bill: Not . . . actually. I've sure read *about* it, though. It's supposed to be great.

Betty: It is great.

Bill: I hear it's great. *(Small pause.)* Waiter?

(Bell.)

What's the book?

Betty: The Sound and the Fury.

Bill: Oh. Faulkner.

Betty: Have you read it?

Bill: I'm a Mets fan, myself.

(Bell.)

Betty: Have you read it?

Bill: Yeah, I read it in college.

Betty: Where was college?

Bill: I went to Oral Roberts University.

(Bell.)

Betty: Where was college?

Bill: I was lying. I never really went to college. I just like to party.

(Bell.)

Betty: Where was college?

Bill: Harvard.

Betty: Do you like Faulkner?

Bill: I love Faulkner. I spent a whole winter reading him once.

Betty: I've just started.

Bill: I was so excited after ten pages that I went out and bought everything else he wrote. One of the greatest reading experiences of my life. I mean, all that incredible psychological understanding. Page after page of gorgeous prose. His profound grasp of the mystery of

time and human existence. The smells of the earth . . . What do you think?
Betty: I think it's pretty boring.

(Bell.)

Bill: What's the book?
Betty: *The Sound and the Fury.*
Bill: Oh! Faulkner!
Betty: Do you like Faulkner?
Bill: I love Faulkner.
Betty: He's incredible.
Bill: I spent a whole winter reading him once.
Betty: I was so excited after ten pages that I went out and bought everything else he wrote.
Bill: All that incredible psychological understanding.
Betty: And the prose is so gorgeous.
Bill: And the way he's grasped the mystery of time—
Betty: —and human existence. I can't believe I've waited this long to read him.
Bill: You never know. You might not have liked him before.
Betty: That's true.
Bill: You might not have been ready for him. You have to hit these things at the right moment or it's no good.
Betty: That's happened to me.
Bill: It's all in the timing. *(Small pause.)* My name's Bill, by the way.
Betty: I'm Betty.
Bill: Hi.
Betty: Hi. *(Small pause.)*
Bill: Yes I thought reading Faulkner was . . . a great experience.
Betty: Yes. *(Small pause.)*
Bill: *The Sound and the Fury. . . . (Another small pause.)*
Betty: Well. Onwards and upwards. *(She goes back to her book.)*
Bill: Waiter—?

(Bell.)

You have to hit these things at the right moment or it's no good.
Betty: That's happened to me.
Bill: It's all in the timing. My name's Bill, by the way.
Betty: I'm Betty.
Bill: Hi.
Betty: Hi.
Bill: Do you come in here a lot?
Betty: Actually I'm just in town for two days from Pakistan.
Bill: Oh. Pakistan.

(Bell.)

My name's Bill, by the way.

Betty: I'm Betty.

Bill: Hi.

Betty: Hi.

Bill: Do you come in here a lot?

Betty: Every once in a while. Do you?

Bill: Not so much anymore. Not as much as I used to. Before my nervous breakdown.

(Bell.)

Do you come in here a lot?

Betty: Why are you asking?

Bill: Just interested.

Betty: Are you really interested, or do you just want to pick me up?

Bill: No, I'm really interested.

Betty: Why would you be interested in whether I come in here a lot?

Bill: I'm just . . . getting acquainted.

Betty: Maybe you're only interested for the sake of making small talk long enough to ask me back to your place to listen to some music, or because you've just rented this great tape for your VCR, or because you've got some terrific unknown Django Reinhardt record, only all you really want to do is fuck—which you won't do very well—after which you'll go into the bathroom and pee very loudly, then pad into the kitchen and get yourself a beer from the refrigerator without asking me whether I'd like anything, and then you'll proceed to lie back down beside me and confess that you've got a girlfriend named Stephanie who's away at medical school in Belgium for a year, and that you've been involved with her—*off and on*—in what you'll call a very "intricate" relationship, for the past *seven YEARS*. None of which *interests* me, mister!

Bill: Okay.

(Bell.)

Do you come in here a lot?

Betty: Every other day, I think.

Bill: I come in here quite a lot and I don't remember seeing you.

Betty: I guess we must be on different schedules.

Bill: Missed connections.

Betty: Yes. Different time zones.

Bill: Amazing how you can live right next door to somebody in this town and never even know it.

Betty: I know.

Bill: City life.

Betty: It's crazy.
Bill: We probably pass each other in the street every day. Right in front of this place, probably.
Betty: Yep.
Bill (looks around): Well the waiters here sure seem to be in some different time zone. I can't seem to locate one anywhere. . . . Waiter! *(He looks back.)* So what do you—*(He sees that she's gone back to her book.)*
Betty: I beg pardon?
Bill: Nothing. Sorry.

(Bell.)

Betty: I guess we must be on different schedules.
Bill: Missed connections.
Betty: Yes. Different time zones.
Bill: Amazing how you can live right next door to somebody in this town and never even know it.
Betty: I know.
Bill: City life.
Betty: It's crazy.
Bill: You weren't waiting for somebody when I came in, were you?
Betty: Actually I was.
Bill: Oh. Boyfriend?
Betty: Sort of.
Bill: What's a sort-of boyfriend?
Betty: My husband.
Bill: Ah-ha.

(Bell.)

You weren't waiting for somebody when I came in, were you?
Betty: Actually I was.
Bill: Oh. Boyfriend?
Betty: Sort of.
Bill: What's a sort-of boyfriend?
Betty: We were meeting here to break up.
Bill: Mm-hm . . .

(Bell.)

What's a sort-of boyfriend?
Betty: My lover. Here she comes right now!

(Bell.)

Bill: You weren't waiting for somebody when I came in, were you?
Betty: No, just reading.

Bill: Sort of a sad occupation for a Friday night, isn't it? Reading here, all by yourself?
Betty: Do you think so?
Bill: Well sure. I mean, what's a good-looking woman like you doing out alone on a Friday night?
Betty: Trying to keep away from lines like that.
Bill: No, listen—

(Bell.)

You weren't waiting for somebody when I came in, were you?
Betty: No, just reading.
Bill: Sort of a sad occupation for a Friday night, isn't it? Reading here all by yourself?
Betty: I guess it is, in a way.
Bill: What's a good-looking woman like you doing out alone on a Friday night anyway? No offense, but . . .
Betty: I'm out alone on a Friday night for the first time in a very long time.
Bill: Oh.
Betty: You see, I just recently ended a relationship.
Bill: Oh.
Betty: Of rather long standing.
Bill: I'm sorry. *(Small pause.)* Well listen, since reading by yourself is such a sad occupation for a Friday night, would you like to go elsewhere?
Betty: No . . .
Bill: Do something else?
Betty: No thanks.
Bill: I was headed out to the movies in a while anyway.
Betty: I don't think so.
Bill: Big chance to let Faulkner catch his breath. All those long sentences get him pretty tired.
Betty: Thanks anyway.
Bill: Okay.
Betty: I appreciate the invitation.
Bill: Sure thing.

(Bell.)

You weren't waiting for somebody when I came in, were you?
Betty: No, just reading.
Bill: Sort of a sad occupation for a Friday night, isn't it? Reading here all by yourself?
Betty: I guess I was trying to think of it as existentially romantic. You know—cappuccino, great literature, rainy night . . .
Bill: That only works in Paris. We *could* hop the late plane to Paris. Get on a Concorde. Find a café . . .

Betty: I'm a little short on plane fare tonight.
Bill: Darn it, so am I.
Betty: To tell you the truth, I was headed to the movies after I finished this section. Would you like to come along? Since you can't locate a waiter?
Bill: That's a very nice offer, but . . .
Betty: Uh-huh. Girlfriend?
Bill: Two, actually. One of them's pregnant, and Stephanie—

(Bell.)

Betty: Girlfriend?
Bill: No, I don't have a girlfriend. Not if you mean the castrating bitch I dumped last night.

(Bell.)

Betty: Girlfriend?
Bill: Sort of. Sort of.
Betty: What's a sort-of girlfriend?
Bill: My mother.

(Bell.)

I just ended a relationship, actually.
Betty: Oh.
Bill: Of rather long standing.
Betty: I'm sorry to hear it.
Bill: This is my first night out alone in a long time. I feel a little bit at sea, to tell you the truth.
Betty: So you didn't stop to talk because you're a Moonie, or you have some weird political affiliation—?
Bill: Nope. Straight-down-the-ticket Republican.

(Bell.)

Straight-down-the-ticket Democrat.

(Bell.)

Can I tell you something about politics?

(Bell.)

I like to think of myself as a citizen of the universe.

(Bell.)

I'm unaffiliated.
Betty: That's a relief. So am I.
Bill: I vote my beliefs.

Betty: Labels are not important.
Bill: Labels are not important, exactly. Take me, for example. I mean, what does it matter if I had a two-point at—

(Bell.)

three-point at—

(Bell.)

four-point at college? Or if I did come from Pittsburgh—

(Bell.)

Cleveland—

(Bell.)

Westchester County?
Betty: Sure.
Bill: I believe that a man is what he is.

(Bell.)

A person is what he is.

(Bell.)

A person is . . . what they are.
Betty: I think so too.
Bill: So what if I admire Trotsky?

(Bell.)

So what if I once had a total-body liposuction?

(Bell.)

So what if I don't have a penis?

(Bell.)

So what if I spent a year in the Peace Corps? I was acting on my convictions.
Betty: Sure.
Bill: You just can't hang a sign on a person.
Betty: Absolutely. I'll bet you're a Scorpio.

(Many bells ring.)

Listen, I was headed to the movies after I finished this section. Would you like to come along?
Bill: That sounds like fun. What's playing?
Betty: A couple of the really early Woody Allen movies.

Bill: Oh.
Betty: You don't like Woody Allen?
Bill: Sure. I like Woody Allen.
Betty: But you're not crazy about Woody Allen.
Bill: Those early ones kind of get on my nerves.
Betty: Uh-huh.

(Bell.)

Bill: Y'know I was headed to the—
Betty (simultaneously): I was thinking about—
Bill: I'm sorry.
Betty: No, go ahead.
Bill: I was going to say that I was headed to the movies in a little while, and . . .
Betty: So was I.
Bill: The Woody Allen festival?
Betty: Just up the street.
Bill: Do you like the early ones?
Betty: I think anybody who doesn't ought to be run off the planet.
Bill: How many times have you seen Bananas?
Betty: Eight times.
Bill: Twelve. So are you still interested? *(Long pause.)*
Betty: Do you like Entenmann's crumb cake . . . ?
Bill: Last night I went out at two in the morning to get one. Did you have an Etch-a-Sketch as a child?
Betty: Yes! And do you like Brussels sprouts? *(Pause.)*
Bill: No, I think they're disgusting.
Betty: They *are* disgusting!
Bill: Do you still believe in marriage in spite of current sentiments against it?
Betty: Yes.
Bill: And children?
Betty: Three of them.
Bill: Two girls and a boy.
Betty: Harvard, Vassar, and Brown.
Bill: And will you love me?
Betty: Yes.
Bill: And cherish me forever?
Betty: Yes.
Bill: Do you still want to go to the movies?
Betty: Sure thing.
Bill and Betty (together): Waiter!

BLACKOUT

Questions

1. Ives originally planned to set *Sure Thing* at a bus stop. What does its current setting in a café suggest about the characters?
2. What happens on stage when the bell rings?
3. Who is the protagonist? What does the protagonist want?
4. Does the play have a dramatic question?
5. When does the climax of the play occur?
6. Is *Sure Thing* a romantic comedy or a farce? (See earlier in this chapter for a discussion of these types of comedy.)
7. "*Sure Thing* was not a funny play because it isn't realistic. Conversations just don't happen this way." Discuss that opinion. Do you agree or disagree?

WRITING *effectively*

THINKING ABOUT COMEDY

If you have ever tried to explain a punch line to an uncomprehending friend, you know how hard it can be to convey the essence of humor. Too much explanation makes any joke fizzle out fast. We don't often stop to analyze why a joke strikes us as funny. It simply makes us laugh. For this reason, writing about comedy can be challenging.

- **What makes the play amusing?** Is there a central gag or situation (such as mistaken identity) that creates comic potential in every scene? Note that the central gag is often visual (such as a disguise), something that the audience constantly sees but is not equally apparent in the written text.
- **What is the flavor of the humor?** Is the comedy high or low? Is it verbal or visual, or both? Is there mostly slapstick action or clever wordplay? Is it a romantic comedy in which love plays a central role? A play often mixes types of comedy, but usually one style predominates. A farce may have a few moments of intellectual wit, but it will mostly keep silly jokes and pratfalls coming fast and furiously.
- **How do the personalities of the main characters intensify the humor?** Even when comedy arises out of a situation, character is likely to play an important role. In *A Midsummer Night's Dream*, for example, the fairy queen Titania is bewitched into falling in love with the weaver Bottom, whose head has been transformed into that of an ass. The

situation is funny in its own right, but the humor is intensified by the personalities involved, the proud fairy queen pursuing the lowly and foolish tradesman. Humor often may be found in the unexpected, a twist on the normal and the logical.

CHECKLIST: Writing About Comedy

- ☐ What kind of comedy is the play? Romantic? Slapstick? Satire? How can you tell?
- ☐ Which style of comedy prevails? Is there more emphasis on high comedy or low? More emphasis on verbal humor or physical comedy?
- ☐ Focus on a key comic moment. Does the comedy grow out of situation? Character? A mix of both?
- ☐ How does the play end? In a wedding or romance? A reconciliation? Mutual understanding?

TOPICS FOR WRITING ABOUT TRAGEDY

1. According to Oscar Wilde, "In this world there are only two tragedies: one is not getting what one wants, and the other is getting it." Write an essay in which you discuss this statement in its application to the scene from *Doctor Faustus*.
2. Imagine that Faustus, after his death, has sought forgiveness and salvation with the claim, "The Devil tricked me. I didn't know what I was doing." Write a "judicial opinion" setting forth the grounds for the denial of his plea.

TOPICS FOR WRITING ABOUT COMEDY

1. What or who is being satirized in *Sure Thing*? How true or incisive do you find this satire? Why?
2. "*Sure Thing* isn't good drama because it doesn't have a plot or conflict." Write a two-page response to that complaint.
3. Write about a recent romantic comedy film. How does its plot fulfill the notion of comedy? Or if it was meant to be funny but fell short, what was lacking?
4. Write your own version of Oscar Wilde's scene, set in the present day, in which a young man is interviewed by his girlfriend's mother. Use Wilde's scene for your model, drawing forth the personalities of each character through their words and reactions.
5. Reread either the scene from *The Importance of Being Earnest* or *Sure Thing*, and write a brief analysis of what makes the selection amusing or humorous. Provide details to back up your argument. Consult the "Comedy" section of this chapter for more information on specific types of humor.

▶ TERMS FOR *review*

Dramatic Genres

Tragedy ▶ A play that portrays a serious conflict between human beings and some superior, overwhelming force. It ends sorrowfully and disastrously, an outcome that seems inevitable.

Comedy ▶ A literary work aimed at amusing an audience. In traditional comedy, the protagonist often faces obstacles and complications that threaten disaster but are overturned at the last moment to produce a happy ending.

Kinds of Comedy

High comedy ▶ A comic genre evoking thoughtful laughter from an audience in response to the play's depiction of the folly, pretense, and hypocrisy of human behavior.

Satiric comedy ▶ A genre using derisive humor to ridicule human weakness and folly or attack political injustices and incompetence. Satiric comedy often focuses on ridiculing overly serious characters who resist the festive mood of comedy.

Romantic comedy ▶ A form of comic drama in which the plot focuses on one or more pairs of young lovers who overcome difficulties to achieve a happy ending (usually marriage).

Low comedy ▶ A comic style arousing laughter through jokes, slapstick antics, sight gags, boisterous clowning, and vulgar humor.

Burlesque ▶ A broadly humorous parody or travesty of another play or kind of play.

Farce ▶ A broadly humorous play whose action is usually fast-moving and improbable.

Slapstick comedy ▶ A kind of farce featuring pratfalls, pie-throwing, fisticuffs, and other violent action. It takes its name from a circus clown's prop—a bat with two boards that loudly clap together when one clown swats another.

26 THE THEATER OF SOPHOCLES

What You Will Learn in This Chapter

- To understand Sophocles's play *Oedipus the King* in its biographical, critical, and cultural contexts

THEATER IN ANCIENT GREECE

For the citizens of Athens in the fifth century B.C., theater was both a religious and a civic occasion. Plays were presented only twice a year at religious festivals, both associated with Dionysus, the god of wine and crops. In January there was the Lenaea, the festival of the winepress, when plays, especially comedies, were performed. But the major theatrical event of the year came in March at the Great Dionysia, a citywide celebration that included sacrifices, prize ceremonies, and spectacular processions as well as three days of drama.

Each day at dawn a different author presented a trilogy of tragic plays—three interrelated dramas that portrayed an important mythic or legendary event. Each intense tragic trilogy was followed by a **satyr play**, an obscene parody of a mythic story, performed with the chorus dressed as satyrs, unruly mythic attendants of Dionysus who were half goat or horse and half human.

The Greeks loved competition and believed it fostered excellence. Even theater was a competitive event—not unlike the Olympic games. A panel of five judges voted each year at the Great Dionysia for the best dramatic presentation, and a substantial cash prize was given to the winning poet-playwright (all plays were written in verse). Any aspiring writer who has ever lost a literary contest may be comforted to learn that Sophocles, who triumphed in the competition twenty-four times, seems not to have won the annual prize for *Oedipus the King*. Although this play ultimately proved to be the most celebrated Greek tragedy ever written, it lost the award to a revival of a popular trilogy by Aeschylus, who had recently died.

Staging

Seated in the open air in a hillside amphitheater, as many as 17,000 spectators could watch a performance that must have somewhat resembled an opera or musical. The audience was arranged in rows, with the Athenian governing council and young military cadets seated in the middle sections. Priests, priestesses, and foreign dignitaries were given special places of honor in the front rows. The performance space they watched was divided into two parts—the

orchestra, a level circular "dancing space" (at the base of the amphitheater), and a slightly raised stage built in front of the ***skene*** or stage house, originally a canvas or wooden hut for costume changes.

The actors spoke and performed primarily on the stage, and the chorus sang and danced in the orchestra. The *skene* served as a general set or backdrop—the exterior of a palace, a temple, a cave, or a military tent, depending on the action of the play. The *skene* had a large door at its center that served as the major entrance for principal characters. When opened wide, the door could be used to frame a striking tableau, as when the body of Eurydice is displayed at the end of Sophocles's play *Antigone*. The *skene* supported a hook and pulley by which actors who played gods could be lowered or lifted—hence the Latin phrase ***deus ex machina*** ("god out of the machine") for any means of bringing a play quickly to a resolution.

What did the actors look like? They wore **masks** (*personae*, the source of our word *person*, "a thing through which sound comes"): some of these masks had exaggerated mouthpieces, possibly designed to project speech across the open air. Certainly, the masks, each of which covered an actor's entire head, helped spectators far away recognize the chief characters. The masks often represented certain conventional types of characters: the old king, the young soldier, the shepherd, the beautiful girl (women's parts were played by male actors). Perhaps in order to gain in both increased dignity and visibility, actors in the Greek theater eventually came to wear **cothurni**, high, thick-soled elevator shoes that made them appear taller than ordinary men. All this equipment must have given the actors a slightly inhuman yet very imposing appearance, but we may infer that the spectators accepted such conventions as easily as opera lovers accept an opera's special artifice or today's football fans hardly notice the elaborate helmets, shoulderpads, gloves, and often brightly colored uniforms worn by their favorite teams.

Dramatic Structure

By Sophocles's time, the tragedy had a conventional structure understood by most of the citizens sitting in the audience. No more than three actors were allowed on stage at any one time, along with a chorus of fifteen (the number was fixed by Sophocles himself). The actors' spoken monologue and dialogue alternated with the chorus's singing and dancing. Each tragedy began with a **prologue**, a preparatory scene. In *Oedipus the King*, for example, the play begins with Oedipus asking the suppliants why they have come and the priest telling him about the plague ravaging Thebes. Next came the ***párodos***, the song for the entrance of the chorus. Then the action was enacted in **episodes**, like the acts or scenes in modern plays; the episodes were separated by danced choral songs or **odes**. Finally, there was a closing ***éxodos***, the last scene, in which the characters and chorus concluded the action and departed.

A modern reconstruction of a classical Athenian theater. Note that the chorus performs in the circular orchestra while the actors stand on the raised stage behind.

THE CIVIC ROLE OF GREEK DRAMA

Athenian drama was supported and financed by the state. Administration of the Great Dionysia fell to the head civil magistrate. He annually appointed three wealthy citizens to serve as *choregoi*, or producers, for the competing plays. Each producer had to equip the chorus and rent the rehearsal space in which the poet-playwright would prepare the new work for the festival. The state covered the expenses of the theater, actors, and prizes (which went to author, actors, and *choregos* alike). Theater tickets were distributed free to citizens, which meant that every registered Athenian, even the poorest, could participate. The playwrights therefore addressed themselves to every element of the Athenian democracy. Only the size of the amphitheater limited the attendance. Holding between 14,000 and 17,000 spectators, it could accommodate slightly less than half of Athens's 40,000 citizens.

Greek theater was directed at the moral and political education of the community. The poet's role was the improvement of the *polis* or city-state (made up of a town and its surrounding countryside). Greek city-states traditionally sponsored public contests between *rhapsodes* (professional poetry performers) reciting stories from Homer's epics, the *Iliad* and *Odyssey*. As Greek society developed and urbanized, however, the competitive and individualized heroism of the Homeric epics had to be tempered with the values of cooperation and compromise necessary to a democracy. Civic theater provided the ideal medium to address these cultural needs.

Tragedy and Empathy

As a public art form, tragedy was not simply a stage for political propaganda to promote the status quo. Nor was it exclusively a celebration of idealized heroes nobly enduring the blows of harsh circumstance and misfortune. Tragedy often enabled its audience to reflect on personal values that might be in conflict with civic ideals, on the claims of minorities that it neglected or excluded from public life, or on its own irrational prejudices toward the foreign or the unknown.

ARISTOTLE'S CONCEPT OF TRAGEDY

> *Tragedy is an imitation of an action of high importance, complete and of some amplitude; in language enhanced by distinct and varying beauties; acted not narrated; by means of pity and fear effecting its purgation of these emotions.*
>
> —ARISTOTLE, *POETICS*, CHAPTER VI

Aristotle's famous definition of tragedy, constructed in the fourth century B.C., is the testimony of one who probably saw many classical tragedies performed. In making his observations, Aristotle does not seem to be laying down laws for what a tragedy ought to be. More likely, he is drawing—from tragedies he has seen or read—a general description of them.

Tragic Hero

Aristotle observes that the protagonist, the hero or chief character of a tragedy, is a person of "high estate," apparently a king or queen or other member of a royal family. In thus being as keenly interested as are contemporary dramatists in the private lives of the powerful, Greek dramatists need not be accused of snobbery. It is the nature of tragedy that the protagonist must fall from power and from happiness; his high estate gives him a place of dignity to fall from and perhaps makes his fall seem all the more a calamity in that it involves an entire nation or people. Nor is the protagonist extraordinary merely by his position in society. Oedipus is not only a king but also a noble soul who suffers profoundly and who employs splendid eloquence to express his suffering.

The tragic hero, however, is not a superman; he is fallible. The hero's downfall is the result, as Aristotle said, of his ***hamartia***: his error or transgression or (as some translators would have it) his flaw or weakness of character. The notion that a tragic hero has such a **tragic flaw** has often been attributed to Aristotle, but it is by no means clear that Aristotle meant just that. According to this interpretation, every tragic hero has some fatal weakness, some moral Achilles's heel, that brings him to a bad end. In some classical tragedies, his transgression is a weakness the Greeks called **hubris**—extreme pride, leading to overconfidence.

Whatever Aristotle had in mind, however, many later critics find value in the idea of the tragic flaw. In this view, the downfall of a hero follows from his very nature. Whatever view we take—whether we find the hero's sufferings due to a flaw of character or to an error of judgment—we will probably find that his downfall results from acts for which he himself is responsible. In a Greek tragedy, the hero is a character amply capable of making choices—capable, too, of accepting the consequences.

Katharsis

It may be useful to take another look at Aristotle's definition of *tragedy*, with which we began. By **purgation** (or ***katharsis***), did the ancient theorist mean that after witnessing a tragedy we feel relief, having released our pent-up emotions? Or did he mean that our feelings are purified, refined into something more ennobling? Scholars continue to argue. Whatever his exact meaning, clearly Aristotle implies that after witnessing a tragedy we feel better, not worse—not depressed, but somehow elated. We take a kind of pleasure in the spectacle of a noble man being brought down, but surely this pleasure is a legitimate one. Part of that catharsis may also be based in our feeling of the "rightness" or accuracy of what we have just witnessed. The terrible but undeniable truth of the tragic vision of life is that blind overreaching and the destruction of hopes and dreams are very much a part of what really happens in the world.

Recognition and Reversal

Aristotle, in describing the workings of this inexorable force in *Oedipus the King*, uses terms that later critics have found valuable. One is **recognition**, or discovery (*anagnorisis*): the revelation of some fact not known before or some person's true identity. Oedipus makes such a discovery: he recognizes that he himself was the child whom his mother had given over to be destroyed. Such a recognition also occurs in Shakespeare's *Macbeth* when Macduff reveals himself to have been "from his mother's womb / Untimely ripped," thus disclosing a double meaning in the witches' prophecy that Macbeth could be harmed by "none of woman born," and sweeping aside Macbeth's last shred of belief that he is infallible. Modern critics have taken the term to mean also the terrible enlightenment that accompanies such a recognition with the protagonist's consequent awareness of his role in his own undoing. "To see things plain—that is *anagnorisis*," Clifford Leech observes, "It is what tragedy ultimately is about: the realization of the unthinkable."

Having made his discovery, Oedipus suffers a reversal in his fortunes; he goes off into exile, blinded and dethroned. Such a fall from happiness seems intrinsic to tragedy, but we should know that Aristotle has a more particular meaning for his term **reversal** (*peripeteia*, anglicized as **peripety**). He means an action that turns out to have the opposite effect from the one its doer had intended. One of his illustrations of such an ironic reversal is from *Oedipus the*

King. The first messenger intends to cheer Oedipus with the partially good news that, contrary to the prophecy that Oedipus would kill his father, his father has died of old age. The reversal is in the fact that, when the messenger further reveals that old Polybus was Oedipus's father only by adoption, the king, instead of having his fears allayed, is stirred to new dread.

We are not altogether sorry, perhaps, to see an arrogant man such as Oedipus humbled, and yet it is difficult not to feel that the punishment of Oedipus is greater than he deserves. Possibly this feeling is what Aristotle meant in his observation that a tragedy arouses our pity and our fear—our compassion for Oedipus and our terror as we sense the remorselessness of a universe in which a man is doomed. Notice, however, that at the end of the play Oedipus does not curse God and die. Although such a complex play is open to many interpretations, it is probably safe to say that the play is not a bitter complaint against the universe. At last, Oedipus accepts the divine will, prays for blessings upon his children, and prepares to endure his exile—fallen from high estate but uplifted, through his newfound humility and piety, in moral dignity.

SOPHOCLES

Sophocles

*Sophocles (496?–406 B.C.) tragic dramatist, priest, for a time one of ten Athenian generals, was one of the three great ancient Greek writers of tragedy whose work has survived. (The other two were his contemporaries: Aeschylus, his senior, and Euripides, his junior.) Sophocles won his first victory in the Athenian spring drama competition in 468 B.C., when a tragedy he had written defeated one by Aeschylus. He went on to win many prizes, writing more than 120 plays, of which only seven have survived in their entirety—*Ajax, Antigone, Oedipus the King, Electra, Philoctetes, The Trachinian Women, *and* Oedipus at Colonus. *(Of the lost plays, about a thousand fragments remain.) In his long life, Sophocles saw Greece rise to supremacy over the Persian Empire. He enjoyed the favor of the statesman Pericles, who, making peace with enemy Sparta, ruled Athens during a Golden Age (461–429 B.C.), during which the Parthenon was built and music, art, drama, and philosophy flourished. The playwright lived on to see his native city-state in decline, its strength drained by the disastrous Peloponnesian War. His last play,* Oedipus at Colonus, *set twenty years after the events of* Oedipus the King, *shows the former king in old age, ragged and blind, cast into exile by his sons, but still accompanied by his faithful daughter Antigone. It was written when Sophocles was nearly ninety.* Oedipus the King *is believed to have been first produced in 425 B.C., five years after the plague had broken out in Athens.*

THE ORIGINS OF *OEDIPUS THE KING*

On a Great Dionysia feast day after Athens had survived a devastating plague, the audience turned out to watch a tragedy by Sophocles, set in the city of Thebes at the moment of another terrible plague. This timely play was *Oedipus*, later given the name (in Greek) *Oedipus Tyrannos* to distinguish it from Sophocles's last Oedipus play, *Oedipus at Colonus*.

A folktale figure, Oedipus gets his name through a complex pun. *Oida* means "to know" (from the root *vid-*, "see"), pointing to the tale's contrasting themes of sight and blindness, wisdom and ignorance. *Oedipus* also means "swollen foot" or "clubfoot," pointing to the injury sustained in the title character's infancy, when his ankles were pinioned together like a goat's. Oedipus is the man who comes to knowledge of his true parentage through the evidence of his feet and his old injury. The term *tyrannos*, in the context of the play, simply means a man who comes to rule through his own intelligence and merit, though not related to the ruling family. The traditional Greek title might be translated, therefore, as *Clubfoot the Ruler*. (*Oedipus Rex*, which means "Oedipus the King," is the conventional Latin title for the play.)

Presumably the audience already knew the story portrayed in the play. They would have known that because a prophecy had foretold that Oedipus would grow up to slay his father, he had been taken out as a newborn to

Laurence Olivier in *Oedipus Rex*.

perish in the wilderness of Mount Cithaeron outside Thebes. (Exposure was the common fate of unwanted children in ancient Greece, though only in the most extraordinary circumstances would a royal heir be exposed.) The audience would also have known that before the baby was left to die, his feet had been pinned together. And they would have known that later, adopted by King Polybus and Queen Merope of Corinth and grown to maturity, Oedipus won both the throne and the recently widowed queen of Thebes as a reward for ridding the city of the Sphinx, a winged, woman-headed lion. All who approached the Sphinx were asked a riddle, and failure to solve it meant death. Her lethal riddle was: "What goes on four legs in the morning, two at noon, and three at evening?" Oedipus correctly answered, "Man." (As a baby he crawls on all fours, as a man he walks erect, and then as an old man he uses a cane.) Chagrined and outwitted, the Sphinx leaped from her rocky perch and dashed herself to death. Familiarity with all these events is necessary to understand *Oedipus the King*, which begins years later, after the title character has long been established as ruler of Thebes.

Oedipus the King

425 B.C.?

Translated by David Grene

CHARACTERS

Oedipus, king of Thebes
Jocasta, his wife
Creon, his brother-in-law
Teiresias, an old blind prophet
A *Priest*
First Messenger
Second Messenger
A Herdsman
A Chorus of old men of Thebes

SCENE. *In front of the palace of Oedipus at Thebes. To the right of the stage near the altar stands the Priest with a crowd of children. Oedipus emerges from the central door.*

Oedipus: Children, young sons and daughters of old Cadmus,°
why do you sit here with your suppliant crowns?°
The town is heavy with a mingled burden
of sounds and smells, of groans and hymns and incense;
I did not think it fit that I should hear
of this from messengers but came myself,—
I Oedipus whom all men call the Great.

(He turns to the Priest.)

1 *Cadmus:* hero who, according to legend, had founded the city of Thebes, where the play takes place. 2 *suppliant crowns:* Suppliants, persons coming to beg a favor of the king, traditionally wore headbands of flowers.

You're old and they are young; come, speak for them.
What do you fear or want, that you sit here
suppliant? Indeed I'm willing to give all
that you may need; I would be very hard
should I not pity suppliants like these.

Priest: O ruler of my country, Oedipus,
you see our company around the altar;
you see our ages; some of us, like these,
who cannot yet fly far, and some of us
heavy with age; these children are the chosen
among the young, and I the priest of Zeus.
Within the market place sit others crowned
with suppliant garlands, at the double shrine
of Pallas and the temple where Ismenus°
gives oracles by fire.° King, you yourself
have seen our city reeling like a wreck
already; it can scarcely lift its prow
out of the depths, out of the bloody surf.
A blight is on the fruitful plants of the earth,
a blight is on the cattle in the fields,
a blight is on our women that no children
are born to them; a God that carries fire,
a deadly pestilence, is on our town,
strikes us and spares not, and the house of Cadmus
is emptied of its people while black Death
grows rich in groaning and in lamentation.
We have not come as suppliants to this altar
because we thought of you as of a God,
but rather judging you the first of men
in all the chances of this life and when
we mortals have to do with more than man.
You came and by your coming saved our city,
freed us from tribute which we paid of old
to the Sphinx, cruel singer. This you did
in virtue of no knowledge we could give you,
in virtue of no teaching; it was God
that aided you, men say, and you are held
with God's assistance to have saved our lives.
Now Oedipus, Greatest in all men's eyes,
here falling at your feet we all entreat you,

20–21 *shrine of Pallas . . . Ismenus:* temples to Athena, goddess of wisdom, and Apollo, god of music, poetry, medicine, and prophecy. 22 *oracles by fire:* The ashes of fires at Ismenus were used to foretell the future. An oracle is a message from a god; it is also the name of a priestess who, while in a trance, would speak the message.

find us some strength for rescue.
Perhaps you'll hear a wise word from some God,
perhaps you will learn something from a man
(for I have seen that for the skilled of practice
the outcome of their counsels live the most).
Noblest of men, go, and raise up our city,
go,—and give heed. For now this land of ours
calls you its savior since you saved it once.
So, let us never speak about your reign
as of a time when first our feet were set
secure on high, but later fell to ruin.
Raise up our city, save it and raise it up.
Once you have brought us luck with happy omen;
be no less now in fortune.
If you will rule this land, as now you rule it,
better to rule it full of men than empty.
For neither tower nor ship is anything
when empty, and none live in it together.
Oedipus: I pity you, children. You have come full of longing,
but I have known the story before you told it
only too well. I know you are all sick,
yet there is not one of you, sick though you are,
that is as sick as I myself.
Your several sorrows each have single scope
and touch but one of you. My spirit groans
for city and myself and you at once.
You have not roused me like a man from sleep;
know that I have given many tears to this,
gone many ways wandering in thought,
but as I thought I found only one remedy
and that I took. I sent Menoeceus' son
Creon, Jocasta's brother, to Apollo,
to his Pythian temple,°
that he might learn there by what act or word
I could save this city. As I count the days,
it vexes me what ails him; he is gone
far longer than he needed for the journey.
But when he comes, then, may I prove a villain,
if I shall not do all the God commands.
Priest: Thanks for your gracious words. Your servants here
signal that Creon is this moment coming.

80 *Pythian temple:* Oedipus has sent his brother-in-law Creon to the oracle at Delphi (or Pytho) to seek divine advice.

Oedipus: His face is bright. O holy Lord Apollo,
grant that his news too may be bright for us
and bring us safety.
Priest: It is happy news,
I think, for else his head would not be crowned
with sprigs of fruitful laurel.
Oedipus: We will know soon,
he's within hail. Lord Creon, my good brother,
what is the word you bring us from the God?

(Creon enters.)

Creon: A good word,—for things hard to bear themselves
if in the final issue all is well
I count complete good fortune.
Oedipus: What do you mean?
What you have said so far
leaves me uncertain whether to trust or fear.
Creon: If you will hear my news before these others
I am ready to speak, or else to go within.
Oedipus: Speak it to all;
the grief I bear, I bear it more for these
than for my own heart.
Creon: I will tell you, then,
what I heard from the God.
King Phoebus° in plain words commanded us
to drive out a pollution from our land,
pollution grown ingrained within the land;
drive it out, said the God, not cherish it,
till it's past cure.
Oedipus: What is the rite
of purification? How shall it be done?
Creon: By banishing a man, or expiation
of blood by blood, since it is murder guilt
which holds our city in this destroying storm.
Oedipus: Who is this man whose fate the God pronounces?
Creon: My Lord, before you piloted the state
we had a king called Laius.
Oedipus: I know of him by hearsay. I have not seen him.
Creon: The God commanded clearly: let some one
punish with force this dead man's murderers.
Oedipus: Where are they in the world? Where would a trace
of this old crime be found? It would be hard
to guess where.

108 *King Phoebus:* the sun god, Phoebus Apollo. In the fifth century B.C., when Sophocles writes, the sun god and Apollo were coming to be regarded as one.

Creon: The clue is in this land;
that which is sought is found;
the unheeded thing escapes:
so said the God.
Oedipus: Was it at home,
or in the country that death came upon him,
or in another country travelling?
Creon: He went, he said himself, upon an embassy,
but never returned when he set out from home.
Oedipus: Was there no messenger, no fellow traveller
who knew what happened? Such a one might tell
something of use.
Creon: They were all killed save one. He fled in terror
and he could tell us nothing in clear terms
of what he knew, nothing, but one thing only.
Oedipus: What was it?
If we could even find a slim beginning
in which to hope, we might discover much.
Creon: This man said that the robbers they encountered
were many and the hands that did the murder
were many; it was no man's single power.
Oedipus: How could a robber dare a deed like this
were he not helped with money from the city,
money and treachery?
Creon: That indeed was thought.
But Laius was dead and in our trouble
there was none to help.
Oedipus: What trouble was so great to hinder you
inquiring out the murder of your king?
Creon: The riddling Sphinx induced us to neglect
mysterious crimes and rather seek solution
of troubles at our feet.
Oedipus: I will bring this to light again. King Phoebus
fittingly took this care about the dead,
and you too fittingly.
And justly you will see in me an ally,
a champion of my country and the God.
For when I drive pollution from the land
I will not serve a distant friend's advantage,
but act in my own interest. Whoever
he was that killed the king may readily
wish to dispatch me with his murderous hand;
so helping the dead king I help myself.

Come, children, take your suppliant boughs and go;
up from the altars now. Call the assembly
and let it meet upon the understanding
that I'll do everything. God will decide
whether we prosper or remain in sorrow.

Priest: Rise, children—it was this we came to seek,
which of himself the king now offers us.
May Phoebus who gave us the oracle
come to our rescue and stay the plague.

(Exeunt all but the Chorus.)

Strophe°

Chorus: What is the sweet spoken word of God from the shrine of Pytho rich in gold
that has come to glorious Thebes?
I am stretched on the rack of doubt, and terror and trembling hold
my heart, O Delian Healer,° and I worship full of fears
for what doom you will bring to pass, new or renewed in the revolving years.
Speak to me, immortal voice,
child of golden Hope.

Antistrophe°

First I call on you, Athene, deathless daughter of Zeus,
and Artemis,° Earth Upholder,
who sits in the midst of the market place in the throne which men call Fame,
and Phoebus, the Far Shooter, three averters of Fate,
come to us now, if ever before, when ruin rushed upon the state,
you drove destruction's flame away
out of our land.

Strophe

Our sorrows defy number;
all the ship's timbers are rotten;
taking of thought is no spear for the driving away of the plague.
There are no growing children in this famous land;
there are no women bearing the pangs of childbirth.
You may see them one with another, like birds swift on the wing,
quicker than fire unmastered,
speeding away to the coast of the Western God.°

Strophe: according to theory, a passage sung while the chorus danced from stage right to stage left. 178 *Delian healer:* Apollo, in his capacity as god of medicine. *Antistrophe:* a passage sung while the chorus danced from stage left to stage right. 183 *Artemis:* twin sister of Apollo, goddess of the moon and of the hunt. 196 *Western God:* Hades, god of the underworld.

Antistrophe

In the unnumbered deaths
of its people the city dies;
those children that are born lie dead on the naked earth
unpitied, spreading contagion of death; and grey haired mothers and wives
everywhere stand at the altar's edge, suppliant, moaning;
the hymn to the healing God rings out but with it the wailing voices are blended.
From these our sufferings grant us, O golden Daughter of Zeus,
glad-faced deliverance.

Strophe

There is no clash of brazen shields but our fight is with the War God,
a War God ringed with the cries of men, a savage God who burns us;
grant that he turn in racing course backwards out of our country's bounds
to the great palace of Amphitrite or where the waves of the Thracian sea
deny the stranger safe anchorage.
Whatsoever escapes the night
at last the light of day revisits;
so smite the War God, Father Zeus,
beneath your thunderbolt,
for you are the Lord of the lightning, the lightning that carries fire.

Antistrophe

And your unconquered arrow shafts, winged by the golden corded bow,
Lycean King, I beg to be at our side for help;
and the gleaming torches of Artemis with which she scours the Lycean hills,
and I call on the God with the turban of gold, who gave his name to this country of ours,
the Bacchic God with the wind flushed face,
Evian One, who travel
with the Maenad company,°
combat the God that burns us
with your torch of pine;
for the God that is our enemy is a God unhonored among the Gods.

(Oedipus returns.)

218–221 *God with the turban of gold . . . Maenad company:* Bacchus, or Dionysus, god of wine, was said to travel with a company of Maenads, female revelers.

Oedipus: For what you ask me—if you will hear my words,
and hearing welcome them and fight the plague,
you will find strength and lightening of your load.

Hark to me; what I say to you, I say
as one that is a stranger to the story
as stranger to the deed. For I would not
be far upon the track if I alone
were tracing it without a clue. But now,
since after all was finished, I became
a citizen among you, citizens—
now I proclaim to all the men of Thebes:
who so among you knows the murderer
by whose hand Laius, son of Labdacus,
died—I command him to tell everything
to me,—yes, though he fears himself to take the blame
on his own head; for bitter punishment
he shall have none, but leave this land unharmed.
Or if he knows the murderer, another,
a foreigner, still let him speak the truth.
For I will pay him and be grateful, too.
But if you shall keep silence, if perhaps
some one of you, to shield a guilty friend,
or for his own sake shall reject my words—
hear what I shall do then:
I forbid that man, whoever he be, my land,
my land where I hold sovereignty and throne;
and I forbid any to welcome him
or cry him greeting or make him a sharer
in sacrifice or offering to the Gods,
or give him water for his hands to wash.
I command all to drive him from their homes,
since he is our pollution, as the oracle
of Pytho's God proclaimed him now to me.
So I stand forth a champion of the God
and of the man who died.
Upon the murderer I invoke this curse—
whether he is one man and all unknown,
or one of many—may he wear out his life
in misery to miserable doom!
If with my knowledge he lives at my hearth
I pray that I myself may feel my curse.
On you I lay my charge to fulfill all this
for me, for the God, and for this land of ours
destroyed and blighted, by the God forsaken.

Even were this no matter of God's ordinance
it would not fit you so to leave it lie,
unpurified, since a good man is dead
and one that was a king. Search it out.
Since I am now the holder of his office,
and have his bed and wife that once was his,
and had his line not been unfortunate
we would have common children—(fortune leaped
upon his head)—because of all these things,
I fight in his defense as for my father,
and I shall try all means to take the murderer
of Laius the son of Labdacus
the son of Polydorus and before him
of Cadmus and before him of Agenor.
Those who do not obey me, may the Gods
grant no crops springing from the ground they plough
nor children to their women! May a fate
like this, or one still worse than this consume them!
For you whom these words please, the other Thebans,
may Justice as your ally and all the Gods
live with you, blessing you now and for ever!

Chorus: As you have held me to my oath, I speak:
I neither killed the king nor can declare
the killer; but since Phoebus set the quest
it is his part to tell who the man is.

Oedipus: Right; but to put compulsion on the Gods
against their will—no man can do that.

Chorus: May I then say what I think second best?

Oedipus: If there's a third best, too, spare not to tell it.

Chorus: I know that what the Lord Teiresias
sees, is most often what the Lord Apollo
sees. If you should inquire of this from him
you might find out most clearly.

Oedipus: Even in this my actions have not been sluggard.
On Creon's word I have sent two messengers
and why the prophet is not here already
I have been wondering.

Chorus: His skill apart
there is besides only an old faint story.

Oedipus: What is it?
I look at every story.

Chorus: It was said
that he was killed by certain wayfarers.

Oedipus: I heard that, too, but no one saw the killer.

Chorus: Yet if he has a share of fear at all,
his courage will not stand firm, hearing your curse.
Oedipus: The man who in the doing did not shrink
will fear no word.
Chorus: Here comes his prosecutor:
led by your men the godly prophet comes
in whom alone of mankind truth is native.

(Enter Teiresias, led by a little boy.)

Oedipus: Teiresias, you are versed in everything,
things teachable and things not to be spoken,
things of the heaven and earth-creeping things.
You have no eyes but in your mind you know
with what a plague our city is afflicted.
My lord, in you alone we find a champion,
in you alone one that can rescue us.
Perhaps you have not heard the messengers,
but Phoebus sent in answer to our sending
an oracle declaring that our freedom
from this disease would only come when we
should learn the names of those who killed King Laius,
and kill them or expel them from our country.
Do not begrudge us oracles from birds,
or any other way of prophecy
within your skill; save yourself and the city,
save me; redeem the debt of our pollution
that lies on us because of this dead man.
We are in your hands; pains are most nobly taken
to help another when you have means and power.
Teiresias: Alas, how terrible is wisdom when
it brings no profit to the man that's wise!
This I knew well, but had forgotten it,
else I would not have come here.
Oedipus: What is this?
How sad you are now you have come!
Teiresias: Let me
go home. It will be easiest for us both
to bear our several destinies to the end
if you will follow my advice.
Oedipus: You'd rob us
of this your gift of prophecy? You talk
as one who had no care for law nor love
for Thebes who reared you.
Teiresias: Yes, but I see that even your own words
miss the mark; therefore I must fear for mine.

Oedipus: For God's sake if you know of anything,
do not turn from us; all of us kneel to you,
all of us here, your suppliants.
Teiresias: All of you here know nothing. I will not
bring to the light of day my troubles, mine—
rather than call them yours.
Oedipus: What do you mean?
You know of something but refuse to speak.
Would you betray us and destroy the city?
Teiresias: I will not bring this pain upon us both,
neither on you nor on myself. Why is it
you question me and waste your labor? I
will tell you nothing.
Oedipus: You would provoke a stone! Tell us, you villain,
tell us, and do not stand there quietly
unmoved and balking at the issue.
Teiresias: You blame my temper but you do not see
your own that lives within you; it is me
you chide.
Oedipus: Who would not feel his temper rise
at words like these with which you shame our city?
Teiresias: Of themselves things will come, although I hide them
and breathe no word of them.
Oedipus: Since they will come
tell them to me.
Teiresias: I will say nothing further.
Against this answer let your temper rage
as wildly as you will.
Oedipus: Indeed I am
so angry I shall not hold back a jot
of what I think. For I would have you know
I think you were complotter of the deed
and doer of the deed save in so far
as for the actual killing. Had you had eyes
I would have said alone you murdered him.
Teiresias: Yes? Then I warn you faithfully to keep
the letter of your proclamation and
from this day forth to speak no word of greeting
to these nor me; you are the land's pollution.
Oedipus: How shamelessly you started up this taunt!
How do you think you will escape?
Teiresias: I have.
I have escaped; the truth is what I cherish
and that's my strength.

Oedipus: And who has taught you truth?
Not your profession surely!
Teiresias: You have taught me,
for you have made me speak against my will.
Oedipus: Speak what? Tell me again that I may learn it better.
Teiresias: Did you not understand before or would you
provoke me into speaking?
Oedipus: I did not grasp it,
not so to call it known. Say it again.
Teiresias: I say you are the murderer of the king
whose murderer you seek.
Oedipus: Not twice you shall
say calumnies like this and stay unpunished.
Teiresias: Shall I say more to tempt your anger more?
Oedipus: As much as you desire; it will be said
in vain.
Teiresias: I say that with those you love best
you live in foulest shame unconsciously
and do not see where you are in calamity.
Oedipus: Do you imagine you can always talk
like this, and live to laugh at it hereafter?
Teiresias: Yes, if the truth has anything of strength.
Oedipus: It has, but not for you; it has no strength
for you because you are blind in mind and ears
as well as in your eyes.
Teiresias: You are a poor wretch
to taunt me with the very insults which
every one soon will heap upon yourself.
Oedipus: Your life is one long night so that you cannot
hurt me or any other who sees the light.
Teiresias: It is not fate that I should be your ruin,
Apollo is enough; it is his care
to work this out.
Oedipus: Was this your own design
or Creon's?
Teiresias: Creon is no hurt to you,
but you are to yourself.
Oedipus: Wealth, sovereignty and skill outmatching skill
for the contrivance of an envied life!
Great store of jealousy fill your treasury chests,
if my friend Creon, friend from the first and loyal,
thus secretly attacks me, secretly
desires to drive me out and secretly
suborns this juggling, trick devising quack,

this wily beggar who has only eyes
for his own gains, but blindness in his skill.
For, tell me, where have you seen clear, Teiresias,
with your prophetic eyes? When the dark singer,
the Sphinx, was in your country, did you speak
word of deliverance to its citizens?
And yet the riddle's answer was not the province
of a chance comer. It was a prophet's task
and plainly you had no such gift of prophecy
from birds nor otherwise from any God
to glean a word of knowledge. But I came,
Oedipus, who knew nothing, and I stopped her.
I solved the riddle by my wit alone.
Mine was no knowledge got from birds. And now
you would expel me,
because you think that you will find a place
by Creon's throne. I think you will be sorry,
both you and your accomplice, for your plot
to drive me out. And did I not regard you
as an old man, some suffering would have taught you
that what was in your heart was treason.

Chorus: We look at this man's words and yours, my king,
and we find both have spoken them in anger.
We need no angry words but only thought
how we may best hit the God's meaning for us.

Teiresias: If you are king, at least I have the right
no less to speak in my defense against you.
Of that much I am master. I am no slave
of yours, but Loxias',° and so I shall not
enroll myself with Creon for my patron.
Since you have taunted me with being blind,
here is my word for you.
You have your eyes but see not where you are
in sin, nor where you live, nor whom you live with.
Do you know who your parents are? Unknowing
you are an enemy to kith and kin
in death, beneath the earth, and in this life.
A deadly footed, double striking curse,
from father and mother both, shall drive you forth
out of this land, with darkness on your eyes,
that now have such straight vision. Shall there be
a place will not be harbor to your cries,

453 *Loxias'*: Apollo's.

a corner of Cithaeron° will not ring
in echo to your cries, soon, soon,—
when you shall learn the secret of your marriage,
which steered you to a haven in this house,—
haven no haven, after lucky voyage?
And of the multitude of other evils
establishing a grim equality
between you and your children, you know nothing.
So, muddy with contempt my words and Creon's!
Misery shall grind no man as it will you.

Oedipus: Is it endurable that I should hear
such words from him? Go and a curse go with you!
Quick, home with you! Out of my house at once!

Teiresias: I would not have come either had you not called me.

Oedipus: I did not know then you would talk like a fool—
or it would have been long before I called you.

Teiresias: I am a fool then, as it seems to you—
but to the parents who have bred you, wise.

Oedipus: What parents? Stop! Who are they of all the world?

Teiresias: This day will show your birth and will destroy you.

Oedipus: How needlessly your riddles darken everything.

Teiresias: But it's in riddle answering you are strongest.

Oedipus: Yes. Taunt me where you will find me great.

Teiresias: It is this very luck that has destroyed you.

Oedipus: I do not care, if it has saved this city.

Teiresias: Well, I will go. Come, boy, lead me away.

Oedipus: Yes, lead him off. So long as you are here,
you'll be a stumbling block and a vexation;
once gone, you will not trouble me again.

Teiresias: I have said
what I came here to say not fearing your
countenance: there is no way you can hurt me.
I tell you, king, this man, this murderer
(whom you have long declared you are in search of,
indicting him in threatening proclamation
as murderer of Laius)—he is here.
In name he is a stranger among citizens
but soon he will be shown to be a citizen
true native Theban, and he'll have no joy
of the discovery: blindness for sight
and beggary for riches his exchange,
he shall go journeying to a foreign country
tapping his way before him with a stick.

467 *Cithaeron:* a mountain outside Thebes where the child Oedipus had been abandoned to die.

He shall be proved father and brother both
to his own children in his house; to her
that gave him birth, a son and husband both;
a fellow sower in his father's bed
with that same father that he murdered.
Go within, reckon that out, and if you find me
mistaken, say I have no skill in prophecy.

(Exeunt separately Teiresias and Oedipus.)

Strophe

Chorus: Who is the man proclaimed
by Delphi's prophetic rock°
as the bloody handed murderer,
the doer of deeds that none dare name?
Now is the time for him to run
with a stronger foot
than Pegasus°
for the child of Zeus° leaps in arms upon him
with fire and the lightning bolt,
and terribly close on his heels
are the Fates that never miss.

Antistrophe

Lately from snowy Parnassus
clearly the voice flashed forth,
bidding each Theban track him down,
the unknown murderer.
In the savage forests he lurks and in
the caverns like
the mountain bull.
He is sad and lonely, and lonely his feet
that carry him far from the navel of earth;
but its prophecies, ever living,
flutter around his head.

Strophe

The augur has spread confusion,
terrible confusion;
I do not approve what was said

517 *Delphi's prophetic rock:* The shrine at Delphi, thought to stand at the geographical center of the world, featured a holy stone known as the Navel of the Earth. 522 *Pegasus:* in Greek mythology, the winged horse born from the neck of the dying gorgon Medusa. A blow of his hoof caused the stream Hippocrene to spring forth from Mount Helicon; its waters were thought to inspire poets to write. 523 *child of Zeus:* Apollo, armed with the thunderbolts of his father.

nor can I deny it.
I do not know what to say;
I am in a flutter of foreboding;
I never heard in the present
nor past of a quarrel between
the sons of Labdacus and Polybus,°
that I might bring as proof
in attacking the popular fame
of Oedipus, seeking
to take vengeance for undiscovered
death in the line of Labdacus.

Antistrophe

Truly Zeus and Apollo are wise
and in human things all knowing;
but amongst men there is no
distinct judgment, between the prophet
and me—which of us is right.
One man may pass another in wisdom
but I would never agree
with those that find fault with the king
till I should see the word
proved right beyond doubt. For once
in visible form the Sphinx
came on him and all of us
saw his wisdom and in that test
he saved the city. So he will not be condemned by my mind.

(Enter Creon.)

Creon: Citizens, I have come because I heard
deadly words spread about me, that the king
accuses me. I cannot take that from him.
If he believes that in these present troubles
he has been wronged by me in word or deed
I do not want to live on with the burden
of such a scandal on me. The report
injures me doubly and most vitally—
for I'll be called a traitor to my city
and traitor also to my friends and you.

Chorus: Perhaps it was a sudden gust of anger
that forced that insult from him, and no judgment.

546 *sons of Labdacus and Polybus:* The son of Labdacus was Laius, previous king of Thebes. At this moment in the play Oedipus is assumed to be the son of Polybus, king of Corinth.

Creon: But did he say that it was in compliance
with schemes of mine that the seer told him lies?
Chorus: Yes, he said that, but why, I do not know.
Creon: Were his eyes straight in his head? Was his mind right
when he accused me in this fashion?
Chorus: I do not know; I have no eyes to see
what princes do. Here comes the king himself.

(Enter Oedipus.)

Oedipus: You, sir, how is it you come here? Have you so much
brazen-faced daring that you venture in
my house although you are proved manifestly
the murderer of that man, and though you tried,
openly, highway robbery of my crown?
For God's sake, tell me what you saw in me,
what cowardice or what stupidity,
that made you lay a plot like this against me?
Did you imagine I should not observe
the crafty scheme that stole upon me or
seeing it, take no means to counter it?
Was it not stupid of you to make the attempt,
to try to hunt down royal power without
the people at your back or friends? For only
with the people at your back or money can
the hunt end in the capture of a crown.
Creon: Do you know what you're doing? Will you listen
to words to answer yours, and then pass judgment?
Oedipus: You're quick to speak, but I am slow to grasp you,
for I have found you dangerous,—and my foe.
Creon: First of all hear what I shall say to that.
Oedipus: At least don't tell me that you are not guilty.
Creon: If you think obstinacy without wisdom
a valuable possession, you are wrong.
Oedipus: And you are wrong if you believe that one,
a criminal, will not be punished only
because he is my kinsman.
Creon: This is but just—
but tell me, then, of what offense I'm guilty?
Oedipus: Did you or did you not urge me to send
to this prophetic mumbler?
Creon: I did indeed,
and I shall stand by what I told you.
Oedipus: How long ago is it since Laius. . . .
Creon: What about Laius? I don't understand.
Oedipus: Vanished—died—was murdered?

Creon: It is long,
a long, long time to reckon.
Oedipus: Was this prophet
in the profession then?
Creon: He was, and honored
as highly as he is today.
Oedipus: At that time did he say a word about me?
Creon: Never, at least when I was near him.
Oedipus: You never made a search for the dead man?
Creon: We searched, indeed, but never learned of anything.
Oedipus: Why did our wise old friend not say this then?
Creon: I don't know; and when I know nothing, I
usually hold my tongue.
Oedipus: You know this much,
and can declare this much if you are loyal.
Creon: What is it? If I know, I'll not deny it.
Oedipus: That he would not have said that I killed Laius
had he not met you first.
Creon: You know yourself
whether he said this, but I demand that I
should hear as much from you as you from me.
Oedipus: Then hear,—I'll not be proved a murderer.
Creon: Well, then. You're married to my sister.
Oedipus: Yes,
that I am not disposed to deny.
Creon: You rule
this country giving her an equal share
in the government?
Oedipus: Yes, everything she wants
she has from me.
Creon: And I, as thirdsman to you,
am rated as the equal of you two?
Oedipus: Yes, and it's there you've proved yourself false friend.
Creon: Not if you will reflect on it as I do.
Consider, first, if you think any one
would choose to rule and fear rather than rule
and sleep untroubled by a fear if power
were equal in both cases. I, at least,
I was not born with such a frantic yearning
to be a king—but to do what kings do.
And so it is with every one who has learned
wisdom and self-control. As it stands now,
the prizes are all mine—and without fear.
But if I were the king myself, I must
do much that went against the grain.
How should despotic rule seem sweeter to me

than painless power and an assured authority?
I am not so besotted yet that I
want other honors than those that come with profit.
Now every man's my pleasure; every man greets me;
now those who are your suitors fawn on me,—
success for them depends upon my favor.
Why should I let all this go to win that?
My mind would not be traitor if it's wise;
I am no treason lover, of my nature,
nor would I ever dare to join a plot.
Prove what I say. Go to the oracle
at Pytho and inquire about the answers,
if they are as I told you. For the rest,
if you discover I laid any plot
together with the seer, kill me, I say,
not only by your vote but by my own.
But do not charge me on obscure opinion
without some proof to back it. It's not just
lightly to count your knaves as honest men,
nor honest men as knaves. To throw away
an honest friend is, as it were, to throw
your life away, which a man loves the best.
In time you will know all with certainty;
time is the only test of honest men,
one day is space enough to know a rogue.

Chorus: His words are wise, king, if one fears to fall.
Those who are quick of temper are not safe.

Oedipus: When he that plots against me secretly
moves quickly, I must quickly counterplot.
If I wait taking no decisive measure
his business will be done, and mine be spoiled.

Creon: What do you want to do then? Banish me?

Oedipus: No, certainly; kill you, not banish you.

Creon: I do not think that you've your wits about you.

Oedipus: For my own interests, yes.

Creon: But for mine, too,
you should think equally.

Oedipus: You are a rogue.

Creon: Suppose you do not understand?

Oedipus: But yet
I must be ruler.

Creon: Not if you rule badly.

Oedipus: O, city, city!

Creon: I too have some share
in the city; it is not yours alone.

Chorus: Stop, my lords! Here—and in the nick of time
I see Jocasta coming from the house;
with her help lay the quarrel that now stirs you.

(Enter Jocasta.)

Jocasta: For shame! Why have you raised this foolish squabbling
brawl? Are you not ashamed to air your private
griefs when the country's sick? Go in, you, Oedipus,
and you, too, Creon, into the house. Don't magnify
your nothing troubles.
Creon: Sister, Oedipus,
your husband, thinks he has the right to do
terrible wrongs—he has but to choose between
two terrors: banishing or killing me.
Oedipus: He's right, Jocasta; for I find him plotting
with knavish tricks against my person.
Creon: That God may never bless me! May I die
accursed, if I have been guilty of
one tittle of the charge you bring against me!
Jocasta: I beg you, Oedipus, trust him in this,
spare him for the sake of this his oath to God,
for my sake, and the sake of those who stand here.
Chorus: Be gracious, be merciful,
we beg of you.
Oedipus: In what would you have me yield?
Chorus: He has been no silly child in the past.
He is strong in his oath now.
Spare him.
Oedipus: Do you know what you ask?
Chorus: Yes.
Oedipus: Tell me then.
Chorus: He has been your friend before all men's eyes; do not cast him away dishonored on an obscure conjecture.
Oedipus: I would have you know that this request of yours
really requests my death or banishment.
Chorus: May the Sun God, king of Gods, forbid! May I die without God's blessing, without friends' help, if I had any such thought. But my spirit is broken by my unhappiness for my wasting country; and this would but add troubles amongst ourselves to the other troubles.
Oedipus: Well, let him go then—if I must die ten times for it,
or be sent out dishonored into exile.
It is your lips that prayed for him I pitied,
not his; wherever he is, I shall hate him.
Creon: I see you sulk in yielding and you're dangerous
when you are out of temper; natures like yours
are justly heaviest for themselves to bear.

Oedipus: Leave me alone! Take yourself off, I tell you.
Creon: I'll go, you have not known me, but they have,
and they have known my innocence.

(Exit.)

Chorus: Won't you take him inside, lady?
Jocasta: Yes, when I've found out what was the matter.
Chorus: There was some misconceived suspicion of a story, and on the other side the sting of injustice.
Jocasta: So, on both sides?
Chorus: Yes.
Jocasta: What was the story?
Chorus: I think it best, in the interests of the country,
to leave it where it ended.
Oedipus: You see where you have ended, straight of judgment
although you are, by softening my anger.
Chorus: Sir, I have said before and I say again—be sure that I would have been proved a madman, bankrupt in sane council, if I should put you away, you who steered the country I love safely when she was crazed with troubles. God grant that now, too, you may prove a fortunate guide for us.
Jocasta: Tell me, my lord, I beg of you, what was it
that roused your anger so?
Oedipus: Yes, I will tell you.
I honor you more than I honor them.
It was Creon and the plots he laid against me.
Jocasta: Tell me—if you can clearly tell the quarrel—
Oedipus: Creon says
that I'm the murderer of Laius.
Jocasta: Of his own knowledge or on information?
Oedipus: He sent this rascal prophet to me, since
he keeps his own mouth clean of any guilt.
Jocasta: Do not concern yourself about this matter;
listen to me and learn that human beings
have no part in the craft of prophecy.
Of that I'll show you a short proof.
There was an oracle once that came to Laius,—
I will not say that it was Phoebus' own,
but it was from his servants—and it told him
that it was fate that he should die a victim
at the hands of his own son, a son to be born
of Laius and me. But, see now, he,
the king, was killed by foreign highway robbers
at a place where three roads meet—so goes the story;
and for the son—before three days were out

after his birth King Laius pierced his ankles
and by the hands of others cast him forth
upon a pathless hillside. So Apollo
failed to fulfill his oracle to the son,
that he should kill his father, and to Laius
also proved false in that the thing he feared,
death at his son's hands, never came to pass.
So clear in this case were the oracles,
so clear and false. Give them no heed, I say;
what God discovers need of, easily
he shows to us himself.

Oedipus: O dear Jocasta,
as I hear this from you, there comes upon me
a wandering of the soul—I could run mad.

Jocasta: What trouble is it, that you turn again
and speak like this?

Oedipus: I thought I heard you say
that Laius was killed at a crossroads.

Jocasta: Yes, that was how the story went and still
that word goes round.

Oedipus: Where is this place, Jocasta,
where he was murdered?

Jocasta: Phocis is the country
and the road splits there, one of two roads from Delphi,
another comes from Daulia.

Oedipus: How long ago is this?

Jocasta: The news came to the city just before
you became king and all men's eyes looked to you.
What is it, Oedipus, that's in your mind?

Oedipus: What have you designed, O Zeus, to do with me?

Jocasta: What is the thought that troubles your heart?

Oedipus: Don't ask me yet—tell me of Laius—
How did he look? How old or young was he?

Jocasta: He was a tall man and his hair was grizzled
already—nearly white—and in his form
not unlike you.

Oedipus: O God, I think I have
called curses on myself in ignorance.

Jocasta: What do you mean? I am terrified
when I look at you.

Oedipus: I have a deadly fear
that the old seer had eyes. You'll show me more
if you can tell me one more thing.

Jocasta: I will.
I'm frightened,—but if I can understand,
I'll tell you all you ask.

Oedipus: How was his company?
Had he few with him when he went this journey,
or many servants, as would suit a prince?
Jocasta: In all there were but five, and among them
a herald; and one carriage for the king.
Oedipus: It's plain—it's plain—who was it told you this?
Jocasta: The only servant that escaped safe home.
Oedipus: Is he at home now?
Jocasta: No, when he came home again
and saw you king and Laius was dead,
he came to me and touched my hand and begged
that I should send him to the fields to be
my shepherd and so he might see the city
as far off as he might. So I
sent him away. He was an honest man,
as slaves go, and was worthy of far more
than what he asked of me.
Oedipus: O, how I wish that he could come back quickly!
Jocasta: He can. Why is your heart so set on this?
Oedipus: O dear Jocasta, I am full of fears
that I have spoken far too much; and therefore
I wish to see this shepherd.
Jocasta: He will come;
but, Oedipus, I think I'm worthy too
to know what it is that disquiets you.
Oedipus: It shall not be kept from you, since my mind
has gone so far with its forebodings. Whom
should I confide in rather than you, who is there
of more importance to me who have passed
through such a fortune?
Polybus was my father, king of Corinth,
and Merope, the Dorian, my mother.
I was held greatest of the citizens
in Corinth till a curious chance befell me
as I shall tell you—curious, indeed,
but hardly worth the store I set upon it.
There was a dinner and at it a man,
a drunken man, accused me in his drink
of being bastard. I was furious
but held my temper under for that day.
Next day I went and taxed my parents with it;
they took the insult very ill from him,
the drunken fellow who had uttered it.
So I was comforted for their part, but
still this thing rankled always, for the story

crept about widely. And I went at last
to Pytho, though my parents did not know.
But Phoebus sent me home again unhonored
in what I came to learn, but he foretold
other and desperate horrors to befall me,
that I was fated to lie with my mother,
and show to daylight an accursed breed
which men would not endure, and I was doomed
to be murderer of the father that begot me.
When I heard this I fled, and in the days
that followed I would measure from the stars
the whereabouts of Corinth—yes, I fled
to somewhere where I should not see fulfilled
the infamies told in that dreadful oracle.
And as I journeyed I came to the place
where, as you say, this king met with his death.
Jocasta, I will tell you the whole truth.
When I was near the branching of the crossroads,
going on foot, I was encountered by
a herald and a carriage with a man in it,
just as you tell me. He that led the way
and the old man himself wanted to thrust me
out of the road by force. I became angry
and struck the coachman who was pushing me.
When the old man saw this he watched his moment,
and as I passed he struck me from his carriage,
full on the head with his two pointed goad.
But he was paid in full and presently
my stick had struck him backwards from the car
and he rolled out of it. And then I killed them
all. If it happened there was any tie
of kinship twixt this man and Laius,
who is then now more miserable than I,
what man on earth so hated by the Gods,
since neither citizen nor foreigner
may welcome me at home or even greet me,
but drive me out of doors? And it is I,
I and no other have so cursed myself.
And I pollute the bed of him I killed
by the hands that killed him. Was I not born evil?
Am I not utterly unclean? I had to fly
and in my banishment not even see
my kindred nor set foot in my own country,
or otherwise my fate was to be yoked
in marriage with my mother and kill my father,

Polybus who begot me and had reared me.
Would not one rightly judge and say that on me
these things were sent by some malignant God?
O no, no, no—O holy majesty
of God on high, may I not see that day!
May I be gone out of men's sight before
I see the deadly taint of this disaster
come upon me.

Chorus: Sir, we too fear these things. But until you see this man face to face and hear his story, hope.

Oedipus: Yes, I have just this much of hope—to wait until the herdsman comes.

Jocasta: And when he comes, what do you want with him?

Oedipus: I'll tell you; if I find that his story is the same as yours, I at least will be clear of this guilt.

Jocasta: Why, what so particularly did you learn from my story?

Oedipus: You said that he spoke of highway *robbers* who killed Laius. Now if he uses the same number, it was not I who killed him. One man cannot be the same as many. But if he speaks of a man travelling alone, then clearly the burden of the guilt inclines towards me.

Jocasta: Be sure, at least, that this was how he told the story. He cannot unsay it now, for every one in the city heard it—not I alone. But, Oedipus, even if he diverges from what he said then, he shall never prove that the murder of Laius squares rightly with the prophecy—for Loxias declared that the king should be killed by his own son. And that poor creature did not kill him surely,—for he died himself first. So as far as prophecy goes, henceforward I shall not look to the right hand or the left.

Oedipus: Right. But yet, send some one for the peasant to bring him here; do not neglect it.

Jocasta: I will send quickly. Now let me go indoors. I will do nothing except what pleases you.

(Exeunt.)

Strophe

Chorus: May destiny ever find me
pious in word and deed
prescribed by the laws that live on high:
laws begotten in the clear air of heaven,
whose only father is Olympus;
no mortal nature brought them to birth,
no forgetfulness shall lull them to sleep;
for God is great in them and grows not old.

Antistrophe

Insolence breeds the tyrant, insolence
if it is glutted with a surfeit, unseasonable, unprofitable,
climbs to the roof-top and plunges
sheer down to the ruin that must be,
and there its feet are no service.
But I pray that the God may never
abolish the eager ambition that profits the state.
For I shall never cease to hold the God as our protector.

Strophe

If a man walks with haughtiness
of hand or word and gives no heed
to Justice and the shrines of Gods
despises—may an evil doom
smite him for his ill-starred pride of heart!—
if he reaps gains without justice
and will not hold from impiety
and his fingers itch for untouchable things.
When such things are done, what man shall contrive
to shield his soul from the shafts of the God?
When such deeds are held in honor,
why should I honor the Gods in the dance?

Antistrophe

No longer to the holy place,
to the navel of earth I'll go
to worship, nor to Abae
nor to Olympia,
unless the oracles are proved to fit,
for all men's hands to point at.
O Zeus, if you are rightly called
the sovereign lord, all-mastering,
let this not escape you nor your ever-living power!
The oracles concerning Laius
are old and dim and men regard them not.
Apollo is nowhere clear in honor; God's service perishes.

(Enter Jocasta, carrying garlands.)

Jocasta: Princes of the land, I have had the thought to go
to the Gods' temples, bringing in my hand
garlands and gifts of incense, as you see.
For Oedipus excites himself too much
at every sort of trouble, not conjecturing,
like a man of sense, what will be from what was,

but he is always at the speaker's mercy,
when he speaks terrors. I can do no good
by my advice, and so I came as suppliant
to you, Lycaean Apollo, who are nearest.
These are the symbols of my prayer and this
my prayer: grant us escape free of the curse.
Now when we look to him we are all afraid;
he's pilot of our ship and he is frightened.

(Enter Messenger.)

Messenger: Might I learn from you, sirs, where is the house of Oedipus? Or best of all, if you know, where is the king himself?

Chorus: This is his house and he is within doors. This lady is his wife and mother of his children.

Messenger: God bless you, lady, and God bless your household! God bless Oedipus' noble wife!

Jocasta: God bless you, sir, for your kind greeting! What do you want of us that you have come here? What have you to tell us?

Messenger: Good news, lady. Good for your house and for your husband.

Jocasta: What is your news? Who sent you to us?

Messenger: I come from Corinth and the news I bring will give you pleasure. Perhaps a little pain too.

Jocasta: What is this news of double meaning?

Messenger: The people of the Isthmus will choose Oedipus to be their king. That is the rumor there.

Jocasta: But isn't their king still old Polybus?

Messenger: No. He is in his grave. Death has got him.

Jocasta: Is that the truth? Is Oedipus' father dead?

Messenger: May I die myself if it be otherwise!

Jocasta (to a servant): Be quick and run to the King with the news! O oracles of the Gods, where are you now? It was from this man Oedipus fled, lest he should be his murderer! And now he is dead, in the course of nature, and not killed by Oedipus.

(Enter Oedipus.)

Oedipus: Dearest Jocasta, why have you sent for me?

Jocasta: Listen to this man and when you hear reflect what is the outcome of the holy oracles of the Gods.

Oedipus: Who is he? What is his message for me?

Jocasta: He is from Corinth and he tells us that your father Polybus is dead and gone.

Oedipus: What's this you say, sir? Tell me yourself.

Messenger: Since this is the first matter you want clearly told: Polybus has gone down to death. You may be sure of it.

Oedipus: By treachery or sickness?

Messenger: A small thing will put old bodies asleep.
Oedipus: So he died of sickness, it seems,—poor old man!
Messenger: Yes, and of age—the long years he had measured.
Oedipus: Ha! Ha! O dear Jocasta, why should one
look to the Pythian hearth?° Why should one look
to the birds screaming overhead? They prophesied
that I should kill my father! But he's dead,
and hidden deep in earth, and I stand here
who never laid a hand on spear against him,—
unless perhaps he died of longing for me,
and thus I am his murderer. But they,
the oracles, as they stand—he's taken them
away with him, they're dead as he himself is,
and worthless.
Jocasta: That I told you before now.
Oedipus: You did, but I was misled by my fear.
Jocasta: Then lay no more of them to heart, not one.
Oedipus: But surely I must fear my mother's bed?
Jocasta: Why should man fear since chance is all in all
for him, and he can clearly foreknow nothing?
Best to live lightly, as one can, unthinkingly.
As to your mother's marriage bed,—don't fear it.
Before this, in dreams too, as well as oracles,
many a man has lain with his own mother.
But he to whom such things are nothing bears
his life most easily.
Oedipus: All that you say would be said perfectly
if she were dead; but since she lives I must
still fear, although you talk so well, Jocasta.
Jocasta: Still in your father's death there's light of comfort?
Oedipus: Great light of comfort; but I fear the living.
Messenger: Who is the woman that makes you afraid?
Oedipus: Merope, old man, Polybus' wife.
Messenger: What about her frightens the queen and you?
Oedipus: A terrible oracle, stranger, from the Gods.
Messenger: Can it be told? Or does the sacred law
forbid another to have knowledge of it?
Oedipus: O no! Once on a time Loxias said
that I should lie with my own mother and
take on my hands the blood of my own father.
And so for these long years I've lived away
from Corinth; it has been to my great happiness;
but yet it's sweet to see the face of parents.

1027 *Pythian hearth:* the oracle at Delphi.

Messenger: This was the fear which drove you out of Corinth?
Oedipus: Old man, I did not wish to kill my father.
Messenger: Why should I not free you from this fear, sir,
since I have come to you in all goodwill?
Oedipus: You would not find me thankless if you did.
Messenger: Why, it was just for this I brought the news,—
to earn your thanks when you had come safe home.
Oedipus: No, I will never come near my parents.
Messenger: Son,
it's very plain you don't know what you're doing.
Oedipus: What do you mean, old man? For God's sake, tell me.
Messenger: If your homecoming is checked by fears like these.
Oedipus: Yes, I'm afraid that Phoebus may prove right.
Messenger: The murder and the incest?
Oedipus: Yes, old man;
that is my constant terror.
Messenger: Do you know
that all your fears are empty?
Oedipus: How is that,
if they are father and mother and I their son?
Messenger: Because Polybus was no kin to you in blood.
Oedipus: What, was not Polybus my father?
Messenger: No more than I but just so much.
Oedipus: How can
my father be my father as much as one
that's nothing to me?
Messenger: Neither he nor I
begat you.
Oedipus: Why then did he call me son?
Messenger: A gift he took you from these hands of mine.
Oedipus: Did he love so much what he took from another's hand?
Messenger: His childlessness before persuaded him.
Oedipus: Was I a child you bought or found when I
was given to him?
Messenger: On Cithaeron's slopes
in the twisting thickets you were found.
Oedipus: And why
were you a traveller in those parts?
Messenger: I was
in charge of mountain flocks.
Oedipus: You were a shepherd?
A hireling vagrant?
Messenger: Yes, but at least at that time
the man that saved your life, son.
Oedipus: What ailed me when you took me in your arms?

Messenger: In that your ankles should be witnesses.
Oedipus: Why do you speak of that old pain?
Messenger: I loosed you;
the tendons of your feet were pierced and fettered,—
Oedipus: My swaddling clothes brought me a rare disgrace.
Messenger: So that from this you're called your present name.°
Oedipus: Was this my father's doing or my mother's?
For God's sake, tell me.
Messenger: I don't know, but he
who gave you to me has more knowledge than I.
Oedipus: You yourself did not find me then? You took me
from someone else?
Messenger: Yes, from another shepherd.
Oedipus: Who was he? Do you know him well enough
to tell?
Messenger: He was called Laius' man.
Oedipus: You mean the king who reigned here in the old days?
Messenger: Yes, he was that man's shepherd.
Oedipus: Is he alive
still, so that I could see him?
Messenger: You who live here
would know that best.
Oedipus: Do any of you here
know of this shepherd whom he speaks about
in town or in the fields? Tell me. It's time
that this was found out once for all.
Chorus: I think he is none other than the peasant
whom you have sought to see already; but
Jocasta here can tell us best of that.
Oedipus: Jocasta, do you know about this man
whom we have sent for? Is he the man he mentions?
Jocasta: Why ask of whom he spoke? Don't give it heed;
nor try to keep in mind what has been said.
It will be wasted labor.
Oedipus: With such clues
I could not fail to bring my birth to light.
Jocasta: I beg you—do not hunt this out—I beg you,
if you have any care for your own life.
What I am suffering is enough.
Oedipus: Keep up
your heart, Jocasta. Though I'm proved a slave,

1102 *your present name:* Oedipus's name means "swollen foot" or "clubfoot."

thrice slave, and though my mother is thrice slave,
you'll not be shown to be of lowly lineage.
Jocasta: O be persuaded by me, I entreat you;
do not do this.
Oedipus: I will not be persuaded to let be
the chance of finding out the whole thing clearly.
Jocasta: It is because I wish you well that I
give you this counsel—and it's the best counsel.
Oedipus: Then the best counsel vexes me, and has
for some while since.
Jocasta: O Oedipus, God help you!
God keep you from the knowledge of who you are!
Oedipus: Here, some one, go and fetch the shepherd for me;
and let her find her joy in her rich family!
Jocasta: O Oedipus, unhappy Oedipus!
that is all I can call you, and the last thing
that I shall ever call you.

(Exit.)

Chorus: Why has the queen gone, Oedipus, in wild
grief rushing from us? I am afraid that trouble
will break out of this silence.
Oedipus: Break out what will! I at least shall be
willing to see my ancestry, though humble.
Perhaps she is ashamed of my low birth,
for she has all a woman's high-flown pride.
But I account myself a child of Fortune,
beneficent Fortune, and I shall not be
dishonored. She's the mother from whom I spring;
the months, my brothers, marked me, now as small,
and now again as mighty. Such is my breeding,
and I shall never prove so false to it,
as not to find the secret of my birth.

Strophe

Chorus: If I am a prophet and wise of heart
you shall not fail, Cithaeron,
by the limitless sky, you shall not!—
to know at tomorrow's full moon
that Oedipus honors you,
as native to him and mother and nurse at once;
and that you are honored in dancing by us, as finding favor in sight
of our king.
Apollo, to whom we cry, find these things pleasing!

Antistrophe

Who was it bore you, child? One of
the long-lived nymphs who lay with Pan°—
the father who treads the hills?
Or was she a bride of Loxias, your mother? The grassy slopes
are all of them dear to him. Or perhaps Cyllene's king°
or the Bacchants' God° that lives on the tops
of the hills received you a gift from some
one of the Helicon Nymphs, with whom he mostly plays?

(Enter an old man, led by Oedipus' servants.)

Oedipus: If some one like myself who never met him
may make a guess,—I think this is the herdsman,
whom we were seeking. His old age is consonant
with the other. And besides, the men who bring him
I recognize as my own servants. You
perhaps may better me in knowledge since
you've seen the man before.
Chorus: You can be sure
I recognize him. For if Laius
had ever an honest shepherd, this was he.
Oedipus: You, sir, from Corinth, I must ask you first,
is this the man you spoke of?
Messenger: This is he
before your eyes.
Oedipus: Old man, look here at me
and tell me what I ask you. Were you ever
a servant of King Laius?
Herdsman: I was,—
no slave he bought but reared in his own house.
Oedipus: What did you do as work? How did you live?
Herdsman: Most of my life was spent among the flocks.
Oedipus: In what part of the country did you live?
Herdsman: Cithaeron and the places near to it.
Oedipus: And somewhere there perhaps you knew this man?
Herdsman: What was his occupation? Who?
Oedipus: This man here,
have you had any dealings with him?
Herdsman: No—
not such that I can quickly call to mind.

1170 *nymphs who lay with Pan:* In Greek mythology, nymphs are beautiful young immortals associated with features of nature or specific places. Pan is the goat-footed god of wildlife and the flocks. In this passage the chorus speculates that Oedipus is the child of a nymph by some god. 1173 *Cyllene's king:* Hermes, messenger of the gods. 1174 *Bacchants' God:* Dionysus. Bacchants are the same as Maenads, the wine god's priestesses.

Messenger: That is no wonder, master. But I'll make him remember what he does not know. For I know, that he well knows the country of Cithaeron, how he with two flocks, I with one kept company for three years—each year half a year—from spring till autumn time and then when winter came I drove my flocks to our fold home again and he to Laius' steadings. Well—am I right or not in what I said we did?

Herdsman: You're right—although it's a long time ago.

Messenger: Do you remember giving me a child
to bring up as my foster child?

Herdsman: What's this?
Why do you ask this question?

Messenger: Look old man,
here he is—here's the man who was that child!

Herdsman: Death take you! Won't you hold your tongue?

Oedipus: No, no,
do not find fault with him, old man. Your words
are more at fault than his.

Herdsman: O best of masters,
how do I give offense?

Oedipus: When you refuse
to speak about the child of whom he asks you.

Herdsman: He speaks out of his ignorance, without meaning.

Oedipus: If you'll not talk to gratify me, you
will talk with pain to urge you.

Herdsman: O please, sir,
don't hurt an old man, sir.

Oedipus (to the servants): Here, one of you,
twist his hands behind him.

Herdsman: Why, God help me, why?
What do you want to know?

Oedipus: You gave a child
to him,—the child he asked you of?

Herdsman: I did.
I wish I'd died the day I did.

Oedipus: You will
unless you tell me truly.

Herdsman: And I'll die
far worse if I should tell you.

Oedipus: This fellow
is bent on more delays, as it would seem.

Herdsman: O no, no! I have told you that I gave it.

Oedipus: Where did you get this child from? Was it your own
or did you get it from another?

Herdsman: Not
my own at all; I had it from some one.

Oedipus: One of these citizens? or from what house?
Herdsman: O master, please—I beg you, master, please
don't ask me more.
Oedipus: You're a dead man if I
ask you again.
Herdsman: It was one of the children
of Laius.
Oedipus: A slave? Or born in wedlock?
Herdsman: O God, I am on the brink of frightful speech.
Oedipus: And I of frightful hearing. But I must hear.
Herdsman: The child was called his child; but she within,
your wife would tell you best how all this was.
Oedipus: She gave it to you?
Herdsman: Yes, she did, my lord.
Oedipus: To do what with it?
Herdsman: Make away with it.
Oedipus: She was so hard—its mother?
Herdsman: Aye, through fear
of evil oracles.
Oedipus: Which?
Herdsman: They said that he
should kill his parents.
Oedipus: How was it that you
gave it away to this old man?
Herdsman: O master,
I pitied it, and thought that I could send it
off to another country and this man
was from another country. But he saved it
for the most terrible troubles. If you are
the man he says you are, you're bred to misery.
Oedipus: O, O, O, they will all come,
all come out clearly! Light of the sun, let me
look upon you no more after today!
I who first saw the light bred of a match
accursed, and accursed in my living
with them I lived with, cursed in my killing.

(Exeunt all but the Chorus.)

Strophe

Chorus: O generations of men, how I
count you as equal with those who live
not at all!
What man, what man on earth wins more
of happiness than a seeming

and after that turning away?
Oedipus, you are my pattern of this,
Oedipus, you and your fate!
Luckless Oedipus, whom of all men
I envy not at all.

Antistrophe

In as much as he shot his bolt
beyond the others and won the prize
of happiness complete—
O Zeus—and killed and reduced to nought
the hooked taloned maid of the riddling speech,
standing a tower against death for my land:
hence he was called my king and hence
was honored the highest of all
honors; and hence he ruled
in the great city of Thebes.

Strophe

But now whose tale is more miserable?
Who is there lives with a savager fate?
Whose troubles so reverse his life as his?

O Oedipus, the famous prince
for whom a great haven°
the same both as father and son
sufficed for generation,
how, O how, have the furrows ploughed
by your father endured to bear you, poor wretch,
and hold their peace so long?

Antistrophe

Time who sees all has found you out
against your will; judges your marriage accursed,
begetter and begot at one in it.

O child of Laius,
would I had never seen you.
I weep for you and cry
a dirge of lamentation.

To speak directly, I drew my breath
from you at the first and so now I lull
my mouth to sleep with your name.

1282 *a great haven:* the womb of Jocasta.

(Enter a second messenger.)

Second Messenger: O Princes always honored by our country,
what deeds you'll hear of and what horrors see,
what grief you'll feel, if you as true born Thebans
care for the house of Labdacus's sons.
Phasis nor Ister cannot purge this house,
I think, with all their streams, such things
it hides, such evils shortly will bring forth
into the light, whether they will or not;
and troubles hurt the most
when they prove self-inflicted.
Chorus: What we had known before did not fall short
of bitter groaning's worth; what's more to tell?
Second Messenger: Shortest to hear and tell—our glorious queen
Jocasta's dead.
Chorus: Unhappy woman! How?
Second Messenger: By her own hand. The worst of what was done
you cannot know. You did not see the sight.
Yet in so far as I remember it
you'll hear the end of our unlucky queen.
When she came raging into the house she went
straight to her marriage bed, tearing her hair
with both her hands, and crying upon Laius
long dead—Do you remember, Laius,
that night long past which bred a child for us
to send you to your death and leave
a mother making children with her son?
And then she groaned and cursed the bed in which
she brought forth husband by her husband, children
by her own child, an infamous double bond.
How after that she died I do not know,—
for Oedipus distracted us from seeing.
He burst upon us shouting and we looked
to him as he paced frantically around,
begging us always: Give me a sword, I say,
to find this wife no wife, this mother's womb,
this field of double sowing whence I sprang
and where I sowed my children! As he raved
some god showed him the way—none of us there.
Bellowing terribly and led by some
invisible guide he rushed on the two doors,—
wrenching the hollow bolts out of their sockets,
he charged inside. There, there, we saw his wife
hanging, the twisted rope around her neck.

When he saw her, he cried out fearfully
and cut the dangling noose. Then, as she lay,
poor woman, on the ground, what happened after,
was terrible to see. He tore the brooches—
the gold chased brooches fastening her robe—
away from her and lifting them up high
dashed them on his own eyeballs, shrieking out
such things as: they will never see the crime
I have committed or had done upon me!
Dark eyes, now in the days to come look on
forbidden faces, do not recognize
those whom you long for—with such imprecations
he struck his eyes again and yet again
with the brooches. And the bleeding eyeballs gushed
and stained his beard—no sluggish oozing drops
but a black rain and bloody hail poured down.

So it has broken—and not on one head
but troubles mixed for husband and for wife.
The fortune of the days gone by was true
good fortune—but today groans and destruction
and death and shame—of all ills can be named
not one is missing.

Chorus: Is he now in any ease from pain?

Second Messenger: He shouts
for some one to unbar the doors and show him
to all the men of Thebes, his father's killer,
his mother's—no I cannot say the word,
it is unholy—for he'll cast himself,
out of the land, he says, and not remain
to bring a curse upon his house, the curse
he called upon it in his proclamation. But
he wants for strength, aye, and some one to guide him;
his sickness is too great to bear. You, too,
will be shown that. The bolts are opening.
Soon you will see a sight to waken pity
even in the horror of it.

(Enter the blinded Oedipus.)

Chorus: This is a terrible sight for men to see!
I never found a worse!
Poor wretch, what madness came upon you!
What evil spirit leaped upon your life
to your ill-luck—a leap beyond man's strength!
Indeed I pity you, but I cannot

look at you, though there's much I want to ask
and much to learn and much to see.
I shudder at the sight of you.

Oedipus: O, O,
where am I going? Where is my voice
borne on the wind to and fro?
Spirit, how far have you sprung?

Chorus: To a terrible place whereof men's ears
may not hear, nor their eyes behold it.

Oedipus: Darkness!
Horror of darkness enfolding, resistless, unspeakable visitant sped by
an ill wind in haste!
madness and stabbing pain and memory
of evil deeds I have done!

Chorus: In such misfortunes it's no wonder
if double weighs the burden of your grief.

Oedipus: My friend,
you are the only one steadfast, the only one that attends on me;
you still stay nursing the blind man.
Your care is not unnoticed. I can know
your voice, although this darkness is my world.

Chorus: Doer of dreadful deeds, how did you dare
so far to do despite to your own eyes?
what spirit urged you to it?

Oedipus: It was Apollo, friends, Apollo,
that brought this bitter bitterness, my sorrows to completion.
But the hand that struck me
was none but my own.
Why should I see
whose vision showed me nothing sweet to see?

Chorus: These things are as you say.

Oedipus: What can I see to love?
What greeting can touch my ears with joy?
Take me away, and haste—to a place out of the way!
Take me away, my friends, the greatly miserable,
the most accursed, whom God too hates
above all men on earth!

Chorus: Unhappy in your mind and your misfortune,
would I had never known you!

Oedipus: Curse on the man who took
the cruel bonds from off my legs, as I lay in the field.
He stole me from death and saved me,
no kindly service.
Had I died then
I would not be so burdensome to friends.

Chorus: I, too, could have wished it had been so.
Oedipus: Then I would not have come
to kill my father and marry my mother infamously.
Now I am godless and child of impurity,
begetter in the same seed that created my wretched self.
If there is any ill worse than ill,
that is the lot of Oedipus.
Chorus: I cannot say your remedy was good;
you would be better dead than blind and living.
Oedipus: What I have done here was best done—don't tell me
otherwise, do not give me further counsel.
I do not know with what eyes I could look
upon my father when I die and go
under the earth, nor yet my wretched mother—
those two to whom I have done things deserving
worse punishment than hanging. Would the sight
of children, bred as mine are, gladden me?
No, not these eyes, never. And my city,
its towers and sacred places of the Gods,
of these I robbed my miserable self
when I commanded all to drive *him* out,
the criminal since proved by God impure
and of the race of Laius.
To this guilt I bore witness against myself—
with what eyes shall I look upon my people?
No. If there were a means to choke the fountain
of hearing I would not have stayed my hand
from locking up my miserable carcase,
seeing and hearing nothing; it is sweet
to keep our thoughts out of the range of hurt.

Cithaeron, why did you receive me? Why
having received me did you not kill me straight?
And so I had not shown to men my birth.

O Polybus and Corinth and the house,
the old house that I used to call my father's—
what fairness you were nurse to, and what foulness
festered beneath! Now I am found to be
a sinner and a son of sinners. Crossroads,
and hidden glade, oak and the narrow way
at the crossroads, that drank my father's blood
offered you by my hands, do you remember
still what I did as you looked on, and what
I did when I came here? O marriage, marriage!
you bred me and again when you had bred

bred children of your child and showed to men
brides, wives and mothers and the foulest deeds
that can be in this world of ours.

Come—it's unfit to say what is unfit
to do.—I beg of you in God's name hide me
somewhere outside your country, yes, or kill me,
or throw me into the sea, to be forever
out of your sight. Approach and deign to touch me
for all my wretchedness, and do not fear.
No man but I can bear my evil doom.

Chorus: Here Creon comes in fit time to perform
or give advice in what you ask of us.
Creon is left sole ruler in your stead.

Oedipus: Creon! Creon! What shall I say to him?
How can I justly hope that he will trust me?
In what is past I have been proved towards him
an utter liar.

(Enter Creon.)

Creon: Oedipus, I've come
not so that I might laugh at you nor taunt you
with evil of the past. But if you still
are without shame before the face of men
reverence at least the flame that gives all life,
our Lord the Sun, and do not show unveiled
to him pollution such that neither land
nor holy rain nor light of day can welcome.

(To a servant.)

Be quick and take him in. It is most decent
that only kin should see and hear the troubles
of kin.

Oedipus: I beg you, since you've torn me from
my dreadful expectations and have come
in a most noble spirit to a man
that has used you vilely—do a thing for me.
I shall speak for your own good, not for my own.

Creon: What do you need that you would ask of me?

Oedipus: Drive me from here with all the speed you can
to where I may not hear a human voice.

Creon: Be sure, I would have done this had not I
wished first of all to learn from the God the course
of action I should follow.

Oedipus: But his word
has been quite clear to let the parricide,
the sinner, die.
Creon: Yes, that indeed was said.
But in the present need we had best discover
what we should do.
Oedipus: And will you ask about
a man so wretched?
Creon: Now even you will trust
the God.
Oedipus: So. I command you—and will beseech you—
to her that lies inside that house give burial
as you would have it; she is yours and rightly
you will perform the rites for her. For me—
never let this my father's city have me
living a dweller in it. Leave me live
in the mountains where Cithaeron is, that's called
my mountain, which my mother and my father
while they were living would have made my tomb.
So I may die by their decree who sought
indeed to kill me. Yet I know this much:
no sickness and no other thing will kill me.
I would not have been saved from death if not
for some strange evil fate. Well, let my fate
go where it will.
Creon, you need not care
about my sons; they're men and so wherever
they are, they will not lack a livelihood.
But my two girls—so sad and pitiful—
whose table never stood apart from mine,
and everything I touched they always shared—
O Creon, have a thought for them! And most
I wish that you might suffer me to touch them
and sorrow with them.

(Enter Antigone and Ismene, Oedipus' two daughters.)

O my lord! O true noble Creon! Can I
really be touching them, as when I saw?
What shall I say?
Yes, I can hear them sobbing—my two darlings!
and Creon has had pity and has sent me
what I loved most?
Am I right?

Creon: You're right: it was I gave you this
because I knew from old days how you loved them
as I see now.
Oedipus: God bless you for it, Creon,
and may God guard you better on your road
than he did me!
O children,
where are you? Come here, come to my hands,
a brother's hands which turned your father's eyes,
those bright eyes you knew once, to what you see,
a father seeing nothing, knowing nothing,
begetting you from his own source of life.
I weep for you—I cannot see your faces—
I weep when I think of the bitterness
there will be in your lives, how you must live
before the world. At what assemblages
of citizens will you make one? to what
gay company will you go and not come home
in tears instead of sharing in the holiday?
And when you're ripe for marriage, who will he be,
the man who'll risk to take such infamy
as shall cling to my children, to bring hurt
on them and those that marry with them? What
curse is not there? "Your father killed his father
and sowed the seed where he had sprung himself
and begot you out of the womb that held him."
These insults you will hear. Then who will marry you?
No one, my children; clearly you are doomed
to waste away in barrenness unmarried.
Son of Menoeceus, since you are all the father
left these two girls, and we, their parents, both
are dead to them—do not allow them wander
like beggars, poor and husbandless.
They are of your own blood.
And do not make them equal with myself
in wretchedness; for you can see them now
so young, so utterly alone, save for you only.
Touch my hand, noble Creon, and say yes.
If you were older, children, and were wiser,
there's much advice I'd give you. But as it is,
let this be what you pray: give me a life
wherever there is opportunity
to live, and better life than was my father's.
Creon: Your tears have had enough of scope; now go within the house.
Oedipus: I must obey, though bitter of heart.

CHECKLIST: Writing About Greek Drama

- ☐ Identify the play's major characters.
- ☐ In what ways do they seem alien to you?
- ☐ What do you notice about a character's beliefs? About his or her values? How do these differ from your own?
- ☐ In what ways are the play's characters like the people you know?
- ☐ How do these qualities—both the alien and the familiar—influence the characters' motivations and actions?

TOPICS FOR WRITING ON SOPHOCLES

1. Write a brief personality profile (two or three pages) of any major character in *Oedipus the King*. Describe the character's age, social position, family background, personality, and beliefs. What is his or her major motivation in the play? In what ways does the character resemble his or her modern equivalent? In what ways do they differ?
2. Suppose you were to direct and produce a new stage production of *Oedipus the King*. How would you go about it? Would you use masks? How would you render the chorus? Would you set the play in contemporary North America? Justify your decisions by referring to the play itself.
3. Compare the version of *Oedipus the King* given in this book with a different English translation of the play. You might use, for instance, any of the versions by Robert Fagles; by Gilbert Murray, J. T. Sheppard, and H. D. F. Kitto; by Dudley Fitts and Robert Fitzgerald; by Paul Roche (in a Signet paperback); by William Butler Yeats (in his *Collected Plays*); or by Stephen Berg and Diskin Clay (Oxford UP, 1978). Point to significant differences between the two texts. What decisions did the translators have to make? Which version do you prefer? Why?
4. Write an essay explaining how Oedipus exemplifies or refutes Aristotle's definition of a tragic hero.

▶ TERMS FOR *review*

Stagecraft in Ancient Greece

Orchestra ▶ "The place for dancing"; a circular, level performance space at the base of a horseshoe-shaped amphitheater, where twelve, then later (in Sophocles's plays) fifteen masked young male chorus members sang and danced the odes interspersed between dramatic episodes in a play. (Today the term *orchestra* refers to the ground-floor seats in a theater or concert hall.)

Skene ▶ The canvas or wooden stage building in which actors changed masks and costumes when changing roles. Its façade, with double center doors and possibly two side doors, served as the setting for action taking place before a palace, temple, cave, or other interior space.

Deus ex machina ▶ (Latin for "god out of the machine.") Originally, the phrase referred to the Greek playwrights' frequent use of a god, mechanically lowered to the stage from the *skene* roof to resolve the human conflict. Today, *deus ex machina* refers to any forced or improbable device used to resolve a plot.

Masks ▶ (In Latin, *personae.*) Classical Greek theater masks covered an actor's entire head. Large, recognizable masks allowed far-away spectators to distinguish the conventional characters of tragedy and comedy.

Cothurni ▶ High, thick-soled elevator boots worn by tragic actors in late classical times to make them appear taller than ordinary men. (Earlier, in the fifth-century classical Athenian theater, actors wore soft shoes or boots or went barefoot.)

Elements of Classical Tragedy

Hamartia ▶ (Greek for "error.") An offense committed in ignorance of some material fact; a great mistake made as a result of an error by a morally good person.

Tragic flaw ▶ A fatal weakness or moral flaw in the protagonist that brings him or her to a bad end. Sometimes offered as an alternative understanding of *hamartia*, in contrast to the idea that the tragic hero's catastrophe is caused by an error in judgment.

Hubris ▶ Overweening pride, outrageous behavior, or the insolence that leads to ruin, the antithesis of moderation or rectitude.

***Katharsis*, catharsis** ▶ (Often translated from Greek as *purgation* or *purification.*) The feeling of emotional release or calm the spectator feels at the end of tragedy. The term is drawn from Aristotle's definition of tragedy, relating to the final cause or purpose of tragic art. Some feel that through *katharsis*, drama taught the audience compassion for the vulnerabilities of others and schooled it in justice and other civic virtues.

Peripeteia ▶ (Anglicized as *peripety*; Greek for "sudden change.") A reversal of fortune, a sudden change of circumstance affecting the protagonist. According to Aristotle, the play's peripety occurs when a certain result is expected and instead its *opposite* effect is produced. In a tragedy, the reversal takes the protagonist from good fortune to catastrophe.

Recognition ▶ In tragic plotting, the moment of recognition occurs when ignorance gives way to knowledge, illusion to disillusion.

27 THE THEATER OF SHAKESPEARE

What You Will Learn in This Chapter

- To understand *Othello* by William Shakespeare in its biographical, critical, and cultural contexts

***"To be or not to be . . ." Is it Shakespeare?* In 2009 the Shakespeare Birthplace Trust unveiled this newly discovered portrait they believe is William Shakespeare. If authentic—and many scholars disagree—it is the only surviving portrait of the author painted during his lifetime.**

All the world's a stage.

—WILLIAM SHAKESPEARE, *AS YOU LIKE IT* (II, vii, 139)

Compared with the technical resources of a theater of today, those of a London public theater in the time of Queen Elizabeth I seem hopelessly limited. Plays had to be performed by daylight, and scenery had to be kept simple: a table, a chair, a throne, perhaps an artificial tree or two to suggest a forest. But these limitations were, in a sense, advantages. What the theater of today can spell out for us realistically, with massive scenery and electric lighting, Elizabethan playgoers had to imagine and the playwright had to make vivid for them by means of language. Not having a lighting technician to work a panel, Shakespeare had to indicate the dawn by having Horatio, in *Hamlet*, say in a speech rich in metaphor and descriptive detail:

> But look, the morn in russet mantle clad
> Walks o'er the dew of yon high eastward hill.

And yet the theater of Shakespeare was not bare, for the playwright did have *some* valuable technical resources. Costumes could be elaborate, and apparently some costumes conveyed recognized meanings: one theater manager's inventory included "a robe for to go invisible in." There could be musical accompaniment and sound effects such as gunpowder explosions and the beating of a pan to simulate thunder.

The stage itself was remarkably versatile. At its back were doors for exits and entrances and a curtained booth or alcove useful for hiding inside. Above the stage was a higher acting area—perhaps a porch or balcony—useful for a Juliet to stand upon and for a Romeo to raise his eyes to. In the stage floor was a trapdoor leading to a "hell" or cellar, especially useful for ghosts or devils who had to appear or disappear. The stage itself was a rectangular platform that projected into a yard enclosed by three-storied galleries.

The building was round or octagonal. In *Henry V*, Shakespeare calls it a "wooden O." The audience sat in these galleries or else stood in the yard in front of the stage and at its sides. A roof or awning protected the stage and the high-priced gallery seats, but in a sudden rain, the *groundlings*, who paid a penny to stand in the yard, must have been dampened.

Built by the theatrical company to which Shakespeare belonged, the Globe, most celebrated of Elizabethan theaters, was not in the city of London itself but on the south bank of the Thames River. This location had been chosen because earlier, in 1574, public plays had been banished from the city by an ordinance that blamed them for "corruptions of youth and other enormities" (such as providing opportunities for prostitutes and pickpockets).

A playwright had to please all members of the audience, not only the mannered and educated. This obligation may help to explain the wide range

The reconstructed Globe Theatre in today's London—built in 1997 as an exact replica of the original.

of subject matter and tone in an Elizabethan play: passages of subtle poetry, of deep philosophy, of coarse bawdry; scenes of sensational violence and of quiet psychological conflict (not that most members of the audience did not enjoy all these elements). Because he was an actor as well as a playwright, Shakespeare well knew what his company could do and what his audience wanted. In devising a play, he could write a part to take advantage of some actor's specific skills, or he could avoid straining the company's resources (some of his plays have few female parts, perhaps because of a shortage of competent boy actors). The company might offer as many as thirty plays in a season, customarily changing the program daily. The actors thus had to hold many parts in their heads, which may account for Elizabethan playwrights' fondness for blank verse. Lines of fixed length were easier for actors to commit to memory.

WILLIAM SHAKESPEARE

William Shakespeare

William Shakespeare (1564–1616), the supreme writer of English, was born, baptized, and buried in the market town of Stratford-on-Avon, eighty miles from London. Son of a glove maker and merchant who was high bailiff (or mayor) of the town, he probably attended grammar school and learned to read Latin authors in the original. At eighteen, he married Anne Hathaway, twenty-six, by whom he had three children, including twins. By 1592 he had become well known and envied as an actor and playwright in London. From 1594 until he retired, he belonged to the same theatrical company, the Lord Chamberlain's Men (later renamed the King's Men in honor of their patron, James I), for whom he wrote thirty-six plays—some of them, such as Hamlet *and* King Lear, *profound reworkings of old plays. As an actor, Shakespeare is believed to have played supporting roles, such as the ghost of Hamlet's father. The company prospered, moved into the Globe in 1599, and in 1608 bought the fashionable Blackfriars as well; Shakespeare owned an interest in both theaters. When plagues shut down the theaters from 1592 to 1594, Shakespeare turned to story poems; his great* Sonnets *(published only in 1609) probably also date from the 1590s. Plays were regarded as entertainments of little literary merit, like comic books today, and Shakespeare did not bother to supervise their publication. After writing* The Tempest *(1611), the last play entirely from his hand, he retired to Stratford, where since 1597 he had owned the second-largest house in town. Most critics agree that when he wrote* Othello, *about 1604, Shakespeare was at the height of his powers.*

A NOTE ON *OTHELLO*

Othello, the Moor of Venice, here offered for study, may be (if you are fortunate) new to you. It is seldom taught in high school, for it is ablaze with passion and violence. Even if you already know the play, we trust that you (like your instructor and these editors) still have much more to learn from it. Following his usual practice, Shakespeare based the play on a story he had appropriated—from a tale, "Of the Unfaithfulness of Husbands and Wives," by a sixteenth-century Italian writer, Giraldi Cinthio. As he could not help but do, Shakespeare freely transformed his source material. In the original tale, the heroine Disdemona (whose name Shakespeare improved) is beaten to death with a stocking full of sand—a shoddier death than the bard reimagined for her.

Surely no character in literature can touch us more than Desdemona; no character can shock and disgust us more than Iago. Between these two extremes stands Othello, a black man of courage and dignity—and

▼ Iago plots to get the fateful handkerchief, *page* 836

▲ Othello despairs, *page* 858

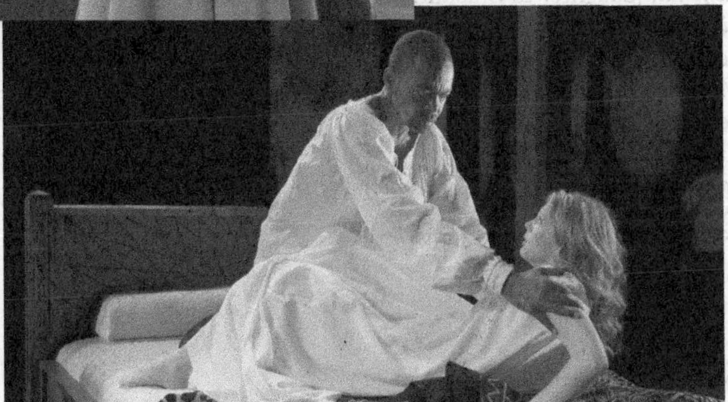

▲ Othello attacks Desdemona in a jealous rage, *page* 878

PRODUCTION PHOTOS

The photos illustrating the play are from the 2008 Utah Shakespeare Festival production of *Othello*. (All photos by Karl Hugh. Copyright Utah Shakespeare Festival 2008.)

Jonathan Earl Peck *Othello*
James Newcomb *Iago*
Lindsey Wochley *Desdemona*
Justin Matthew Gordon *Cassio*
Corliss Preston *Emilia*
Will Zahrn *Brabantio*
Marcella Rose Sciotto *Bianca*
Danny Camiel *Roderigo*
Drew Shirley *Lodovico*
Bernie Balbot *Servant*

Othello, the Moor of Venice

1604?

Edited by David Bevington

THE NAMES OF THE ACTORS

Othello, the Moor
Brabantio, [a senator,] father to Desdemona
Cassio, an honorable lieutenant [to Othello]
Iago, [Othello's ancient,] a villain
Roderigo, a gulled gentleman
Duke of Venice
Senators [of Venice]
Montano, governor of Cyprus
Gentlemen of Cyprus
Lodovico and Gratiano, [kinsmen to Brabantio,] two noble Venetians
Sailors
Clown
Desdemona, [daughter to Brabantio and] wife to Othello
Emilia, wife to Iago
Bianca, a courtesan [and mistress to Cassio]
[*A Messenger*
A Herald
A Musician
Servants, *Attendants*, *Officers*, *Senators*, *Musicians*, *Gentlemen*

SCENE. *Venice; a seaport in Cyprus*]

ACT I

SCENE I [VENICE. A STREET.]

Enter Roderigo and Iago.

Roderigo: Tush, never tell me!° I take it much unkindly
That thou, Iago, who hast had my purse
As if the strings were thine, shouldst know of this.°

NOTE ON THE TEXT:
This text of *Othello* is based on that of the First Folio, or large collection, of Shakespeare's plays (1623). But there are many differences between the Folio text and that of the play's first printing in the Quarto, or small volume, of 1621 (eighteen or nineteen years after the play's first performance). Some readings from the Quarto are included. For the reader's convenience, some material has been added by the editor, David Bevington (some indications of scene, some stage directions). Such additions are enclosed in brackets. Mr. Bevington's text and notes were prepared for his book *The Complete Works of Shakespeare*, updated 4th ed. (New York: Longman, 1997).

1 *never tell me* (An expression of incredulity, like "tell me another one.") 3 *this* i.e., Desdemona's elopement

Iago: 'Sblood,° but you'll not hear me.
If ever I did dream of such a matter,
Abhor me.
Roderigo: Thou toldst me thou didst hold him in thy hate.
Iago: Despise me
If I do not. Three great ones of the city,
In personal suit to make me his lieutenant,
Off-capped to him;° and by the faith of man,
I know my price, I am worth no worse a place.
But he, as loving his own pride and purposes,
Evades them with a bombast circumstance°
Horribly stuffed with epithets of war,°
And, in conclusion,
Nonsuits° my mediators. For, "Certes,"° says he,
"I have already chose my officer."
And what was he?
Forsooth, a great arithmetician,°
One Michael Cassio, a Florentine,
A fellow almost damned in a fair wife,°
That never set a squadron in the field
Nor the division of a battle° knows
More than a spinster°—unless the bookish theoric,°
Wherein the togaed° consuls° can propose°
As masterly as he. Mere prattle without practice
Is all his soldiership. But he, sir, had th' election;
And I, of whom his° eyes had seen the proof
At Rhodes, at Cyprus, and on other grounds
Christened° and heathen, must be beleed and calmed°
By debitor and creditor.° This countercaster,°
He, in good time,° must his lieutenant be,
And I—God bless the mark!°—his Moorship's ancient.°
Roderigo: By heaven, I rather would have been his hangman.°
Iago: Why, there's no remedy. 'Tis the curse of service;

4 *'Sblood* by His (Christ's) blood 11 *him* i.e., Othello 14 *bombast circumstance* wordy evasion. (Bombast is cotton padding.) 15 *epithets of war* military expressions 17 *Nonsuits* rejects the petition of. *Certes* certainly 20 *arithmetician* i.e., a man whose military knowledge is merely theoretical, based on books of tactics 22 *A . . . wife* (Cassio does not seem to be married, but his counterpart in Shakespeare's source does have a woman in his house. See also IV, i, 127.) 24 *division of a battle* disposition of a military unit 25 *a spinster* i.e., a housewife, one whose regular occupation is spinning. *theoric* theory 26 *togaed* wearing the toga. *consuls* counselors, senators. *propose* discuss 29 *his* i.e., Othello's 31 *Christened* Christian. *beleed and calmed* left to leeward without wind, becalmed. (A sailing metaphor.) 32 *debitor and creditor* (A name for a system of bookkeeping, here used as a contemptuous nickname for Cassio.) *countercaster* i.e., bookkeeper, one who tallies with *counters*, or "metal disks." (Said contemptuously.) 33 *in good time* opportunely, i.e., forsooth 34 *God bless the mark* (Perhaps originally a formula to ward off evil; here an expression of impatience.) *ancient* standard-bearer, ensign 35 *his hangman* his executioner.

Preferment° goes by letter and affection,°
And not by old gradation,° where each second
Stood heir to th' first. Now, sir, be judge yourself
Whether I in any just term° am affined°
To love the Moor.
Roderigo: I would not follow him then.
Iago: O sir, content you.°
I follow him to serve my turn upon him.
We cannot all be masters, nor all masters
Cannot be truly° followed. You shall mark
Many a duteous and knee-crooking knave
That, doting on his own obsequious bondage,
Wears out his time, much like his master's ass,
For naught but provender, and when he's old, cashiered.°
Whip me° such honest knaves. Others there are
Who, trimmed in forms and visages of duty,°
Keep yet their hearts attending on themselves,
And, throwing but shows of service on their lords,
Do well thrive by them, and when they have lined their coats,°
Do themselves homage.° These fellows have some soul,
And such a one do I profess myself. For, sir,
It is as sure as you are Roderigo,
Were I the Moor I would not be Iago.°
In following him, I follow but myself—
Heaven is my judge, not I for love and duty,
But seeming so for my peculiar° end.
For when my outward action doth demonstrate
The native° act and figure° of my heart
In compliment extern,° 'tis not long after
But I will wear my heart upon my sleeve
For daws° to peck at. I am not what I am.°
Roderigo: What a full° fortune does the thick-lips° owe°
If he can carry 't thus!°
Iago: Call up her father.
Rouse him, make after him, poison his delight,

37 *Preferment* promotion. *letter and affection* personal influence and favoritism 38 *old gradation* step-by-step seniority, the traditional way 40 *term* respect. *affined* bound 43 *content you* don't you worry about that 46 *truly* faithfully 50 *cashiered* dismissed from service 51 *Whip me* whip, as far as I'm concerned 52 *trimmed . . . duty* dressed up in the mere form and show of dutifulness 55 *lined their coats* i.e., stuffed their purses 56 *Do themselves homage* i.e., attend to self-interest solely 59 *Were . . . Iago* i.e., if I were able to assume command, I certainly would not choose to remain a subordinate, or, I would keep a suspicious eye on a flattering subordinate 62 *peculiar* particular, personal 64 *native* innate. *figure* shape, intent 65 *compliment extern* outward show. (Conforming in this case to the inner workings and intention of the heart.) 67 *daws* small crowlike birds, proverbially stupid and avaricious. *I am not what I am* i.e., I am not one who wears his heart on his sleeve 68 *full* swelling. *thick-lips* (Elizabethans often applied the term "Moor" to blacks.) *owe* own 69 *carry 't thus* carry this off

Brabantio asks, "What is the matter there?" (I, i, 85).

Proclaim him in the streets; incense her kinsmen,
And, though he in a fertile climate dwell,
Plague him with flies.° Though that his joy be joy,°
Yet throw such changes of vexation° on 't
As it may° lose some color.°

Roderigo: Here is her father's house. I'll call aloud.

Iago: Do, with like timorous° accent and dire yell
As when, by night and negligence,° the fire
Is spied in populous cities.

Roderigo: What ho, Brabantio! Signor Brabantio, ho!

Iago: Awake! What ho, Brabantio! Thieves, thieves, thieves!
Look to your house, your daughter, and your bags!
Thieves, thieves!

Brabantio [*enters*] *above* [*at a window*].°

Brabantio: What is the reason of this terrible summons?
What is the matter° there?

Roderigo: Signor, is all your family within?

72–73 *though . . . flies* though he seems prosperous and happy now, vex him with misery 73 *Though . . . be joy* although he seems fortunate and happy. (Repeats the idea of line 72.) 74 *changes of vexation* vexing changes 75 *As it may* that may cause it to. *some color* some of its fresh gloss 77 *timorous* frightening 78 *and negligence* i.e., by negligence 83 s.d. *at a window* (This stage direction, from the Quarto, probably calls for an appearance on the gallery above and rearstage.) 85 *the matter* your business

Iago: Are your doors locked?
Brabantio: Why, wherefore ask you this?
Iago: Zounds,° sir, you're robbed. For shame, put on your gown!
Your heart is burst; you have lost half your soul.
Even now, now, very now, an old black ram
Is tupping° your white ewe. Arise, arise!
Awake the snorting° citizens with the bell,
Or else the devil° will make a grandsire of you.
Arise, I say!
Brabantio: What, have you lost your wits?
Roderigo: Most reverend signor, do you know my voice?
Brabantio: Not I. What are you?
Roderigo: My name is Roderigo.
Brabantio: The worser welcome.
I have charged thee not to haunt about my doors.
In honest plainness thou hast heard me say
My daughter is not for thee; and now, in madness,
Being full of supper and distempering° drafts,
Upon malicious bravery° dost thou come
To start° my quiet.
Roderigo: Sir, sir, sir—
Brabantio: But thou must needs be sure
My spirits and my place° have in° their power
To make this bitter to thee.
Roderigo: Patience, good sir.
Brabantio: What tell'st thou me of robbing? This is Venice;
My house is not a grange.°
Roderigo: Most grave Brabantio,
In simple° and pure soul I come to you.
Iago: Zounds, sir, you are one of those that will not serve God if the devil bid you. Because we come to do you service and you think we are ruffians, you'll have your daughter covered with a Barbary° horse; you'll have your nephews° neigh to you; you'll have coursers° for cousins° and jennets° for germans.°
Brabantio: What profane wretch art thou?
Iago: I am one, sir, that comes to tell you your daughter and the Moor are now making the beast with two backs.

88 *Zounds* by His (Christ's) wounds 91 *tupping* covering, copulating with. (Said of sheep.) 92 *snorting* snoring 93 *the devil* (The devil was conventionally pictured as black.) 102 *distempering* intoxicating 103 *Upon malicious bravery* with hostile intent to defy me 104 *start* startle, disrupt 106 My *spirits and my place* my temperament and my authority of office. *have in* have it in 109 *grange* isolated country house 110 *simple* sincere 113 *Barbary* from northern Africa (and hence associated with Othello). 114 *nephews* i.e., grandsons. *coursers* powerful horses. *cousins* kinsmen. 115 *jennets* small Spanish horses. *germans* near relatives

Brabantio: Thou art a villain.
Iago: You are—a senator.°
Brabantio: This thou shalt answer.° I know thee, Roderigo.
Roderigo: Sir, I will answer anything. But I beseech you,
If't be your pleasure and most wise° consent—
As partly I find it is—that your fair daughter,
At this odd-even° and dull watch o' the night,
Transported with° no worse nor better guard
But with a knave° of common hire, a gondolier,
To the gross clasps of a lascivious Moor—
If this be known to you and your allowance°
We then have done you bold and saucy° wrongs.
But if you know not this, my manners tell me
We have your wrong rebuke. Do not believe
That, from° the sense of all civility,°
I thus would play and trifle with your reverence.°
Your daughter, if you have not given her leave,
I say again, hath made a gross revolt,
Tying her duty, beauty, wit,° and fortunes
In an extravagant° and wheeling° stranger°
Of here and everywhere. Straight° satisfy yourself.
If she be in her chamber or your house,
Let loose on me the justice of the state
For thus deluding you.
Brabantio: Strike on the tinder,° ho!
Give me a taper! Call up all my people!
This accident° is not unlike my dream.
Belief of it oppresses me already.
Light, I say, light! *Exit [above].*
Iago: Farewell, for I must leave you.
It seems not meet° nor wholesome to my place°
To be producted°—as, if I stay, I shall—
Against the Moor. For I do know the state,
However this may gall° him with some check,°

119 *a senator* (Said with mock politeness, as though the word itself were an insult.) 120 *answer* be held accountable for 122 *wise* well-informed 124 *odd-even* between one day and the next, i.e., about midnight 125 *with* by 126 *But with a knave* than by a low fellow, a servant 128 *allowance* permission 129 *saucy* insolent 132 *from* contrary to. *civility* good manners, decency 133 *your reverence* the respect due to you 136 *wit* intelligence 137 *extravagant* expatriate, wandering far from home. *wheeling* roving about, vagabond. *stranger* foreigner 138 *Straight* straightway 141 *tinder* charred linen ignited by a spark from flint and steel, used to light torches or *tapers* (lines 142, 167) 143 *accident* occurrence, event 146 *meet* fitting. *place* position (as ensign) 147 *producted* produced (as a witness) 149 *gall* rub; oppress. *check* rebuke

Cannot with safety cast° him, for he's embarked°
With such loud reason° to the Cyprus wars,
Which even now stands in act,° that, for their souls,°
Another of his fathom° they have none
To lead their business; in which regard,°
Though I do hate him as I do hell pains,
Yet for necessity of present life°
I must show out a flag and sign of love,
Which is indeed but sign. That you shall surely find him,
Lead to the Sagittary° the raisèd search,°
And there will I be with him. So farewell.
Exit.

Enter [below] Brabantio [in his nightgown°] with servants and torches.

Brabantio: It is too true an evil. Gone she is;
And what's to come of my despisèd time°
Is naught but bitterness. Now, Roderigo,
Where didst thou see her?—O unhappy girl!—
With the Moor, sayst thou?—Who would be a father!—
How didst thou know 'twas she?—O, she deceives me
Past thought!—What said she to you?—Get more tapers.
Raise all my kindred.—Are they married, think you?
Roderigo: Truly, I think they are.
Brabantio: O heaven! How got she out? O treason of the blood!
Fathers, from hence trust not your daughters' minds
By what you see them act. Is there not charms°
By which the property° of youth and maidhood
May be abused?° Have you not read, Roderigo,
Of some such thing?
Roderigo: Yes, sir, I have indeed.
Brabantio: Call up my brother.—O, would you had had her!—
Some one way, some another.—Do you know
Where we may apprehend her and the Moor?
Roderigo: I think I can discover° him, if you please
To get good guard and go along with me.
Brabantio: Pray you, lead on. At every house I'll call;

150 *cast* dismiss. *embarked* engaged 151 *loud reason* unanimous shout of confirmation (in the Senate) 152 *stands in act* are going on. *for their souls* to save themselves 153 *fathom* i.e., ability, depth of experience 154 *in which regard* out of regard for which 156 *life* livelihood 159 *Sagittary* (An inn or house where Othello and Desdemona are staying, named for its sign of Sagittarius, or Centaur.) *raisèd search* search party roused out of sleep s.d. *nightgown* dressing gown. (This costuming is specified in the Quarto text.) 162 *time* i.e., remainder of life 172 *charms* spells 173 *property* special quality, nature 174 *abused* deceived 179 *discover* reveal, uncover

I may command° at most.—Get weapons, ho!
And raise some special officers of night.—
On, good Roderigo. I will deserve° your pains.

Exeunt.

SCENE II [VENICE. ANOTHER STREET, BEFORE OTHELLO'S LODGINGS.]

Enter Othello, Iago, attendants with torches.

Iago: Though in the trade of war I have slain men,
Yet do I hold it very stuff ° o' the conscience
To do no contrived° murder. I lack iniquity
Sometimes to do me service. Nine or ten times
I had thought t' have yerked° him° here under the ribs.
Othello: 'Tis better as it is.
Iago: Nay, but he prated,
And spoke such scurvy and provoking terms
Against your honor
That, with the little godliness I have,
I did full hard forbear him.° But, I pray you, sir,
Are you fast married? Be assured of this,
That the magnifico° is much beloved,
And hath in his effect° a voice potential°
As double as the Duke's. He will divorce you,
Or put upon you what restraint or grievance
The law, with all his might to enforce it on,
Will give him cable.°
Othello: Let him do his spite.
My services which I have done the seigniory°
Shall out-tongue his complaints. 'Tis yet to know°—
Which, when I know that boasting is an honor,
I shall promulgate—I fetch my life and being
From men of royal siege,° and my demerits°
May speak unbonneted° to as proud a fortune
As this that I have reached. For know, Iago,
But that I love the gentle Desdemona,

182 *command* demand assistance 184 *deserve* show gratitude for 2 *very stuff* essence, basic material (continuing the metaphor of *trade* from line 1) 3 *contrived* premeditated 5 *yerked* stabbed. *him* i.e., Roderigo 10 *I . . . him* I restrained myself with great difficulty from assaulting him 12 *magnifico* Venetian grandee, i.e., Brabantio 13 *in his effect* at his command. *potential* powerful 17 *cable* i.e., scope 18 *seigniory* Venetian government 19 *yet to know* not yet widely known 22 *siege* i.e., rank. (Literally, a seat used by a person of distinction.) *demerits* deserts 23 *unbonneted* without removing the hat, i.e., on equal terms (?) (Or "with hat off," "in all due modesty.")

I would not my unhousèd° free condition
Put into circumscription and confine°
For the sea's worth.° But look, what lights come yond?

Enter Cassio [and certain officers°] with torches.

Iago: Those are the raisèd father and his friends.
You were best go in.
Othello: Not I. I must be found.
My parts, my title, and my perfect soul°
Shall manifest me rightly. Is it they?
Iago: By Janus,° I think no.
Othello: The servants of the Duke? And my lieutenant?
The goodness of the night upon you, friends!
What is the news?
Cassio: The Duke does greet you, General,
And he requires your haste-post-haste appearance
Even on the instant.
Othello: What is the matter,° think you?
Cassio: Something from Cyprus, as I may divine.°
It is a business of some heat.° The galleys
Have sent a dozen sequent° messengers
This very night at one another's heels,
And many of the consuls,° raised and met,
Are at the Duke's already. You have been hotly called for;
When, being not at your lodging to be found,
The Senate hath sent about° three several° quests
To search you out.
Othello: 'Tis well I am found by you.
I will but spend a word here in the house
And go with you. *[Exit.]*
Cassio: Ancient, what makes° he here?
Iago: Faith, he tonight hath boarded° a land carrack.°
If it prove lawful prize,° he's made forever.
Cassio: I do not understand.
Iago: He's married.
Cassio: To who?

26 *unhousèd* unconfined, undomesticated 27 *circumscription and confine* restriction and confinement 28 *the sea's worth* all the riches at the bottom of the sea. s.d. *officers* (The Quarto text calls for "Cassio with lights, officers with torches.") 31 *My . . . soul* my natural gifts, my position or reputation, and my unflawed conscience 33 *Janus* Roman two-faced god of beginnings 38 *matter* business 39 *divine* guess 40 *heat* urgency 41 *sequent* successive 43 *consuls* senators 46 *about* all over the city. *several* separate 49 *makes* does 50 *boarded* gone aboard and seized as an act of piracy (with sexual suggestion). *carrack* large merchant ship 51 *prize* booty

[*Enter Othello*.]

Iago: Marry,° to—Come, Captain, will you go?
Othello: Have with you.°
Cassio: Here comes another troop to seek for you.

Enter Brabantio, Roderigo, with officers and torches.°

Iago: It is Brabantio. General, be advised.°
He comes to bad intent.
Othello: Holla! Stand there!
Roderigo: Signor, it is the Moor.
Brabantio: Down with him, thief!

[*They draw on both sides*.]

Iago: You, Roderigo! Come, sir, I am for you.
Othello: Keep up° your bright swords, for the dew will rust them.
Good signor, you shall more command with years
Than with your weapons.
Brabantio: O thou foul thief, where hast thou stowed my daughter?
Damned as thou art, thou hast enchanted her!
For I'll refer me° to all things of sense,°
If she in chains of magic were not bound
Whether a maid so tender, fair, and happy,
So opposite to marriage that she shunned
The wealthy curlèd darlings of our nation,
Would ever have, t' incur a general mock,
Run from her guardage° to the sooty bosom
Of such a thing as thou—to fear, not to delight.
Judge me the world if 'tis not gross in sense°
That thou hast practiced on her with foul charms,
Abused her delicate youth with drugs or minerals°
That weaken motion.° I'll have 't disputed on;°
'Tis probable and palpable to thinking.
I therefore apprehend and do attach° thee
For an abuser of the world, a practicer
Of arts inhibited° and out of warrant.°—
Lay hold upon him! If he do resist,
Subdue him at his peril.

53 *Marry* (An oath, originally "by the Virgin Mary"; here used with wordplay on *married*.) 54 *Have with you* i.e., let's go 55 s.d. *officers and torches* (The Quarto text calls for "others with lights and weapons.") 56 *be advised* be on your guard 60 *Keep up* keep in the sheath 65 *refer me* submit my case. *things of sense* commonsense understandings, or, creatures possessing common sense 71 *her guardage* my guardianship of her 73 *gross in sense* obvious 75 *minerals* i.e., poisons 76 *weaken motion* impair the vital faculties. *disputed on* argued in court by professional counsel, debated by experts 78 *attach* arrest 80 *arts inhibited* prohibited arts, black magic. *out of warrant* illegal

Othello: Hold your hands,
Both you of my inclining° and the rest.
Were it my cue to fight, I should have known it
Without a prompter.—Whither will you that I go
To answer this your charge?
Brabantio: To prison, till fit time
Of law and course of direct session°
Call thee to answer.
Othello: What if I do obey?
How may the Duke be therewith satisfied,
Whose messengers are here about my side
Upon some present business of the state
To bring me to him?
Officer: 'Tis true, most worthy signor.
The Duke's in council, and your noble self,
I am sure, is sent for.
Brabantio: How? The Duke in council?
In this time of the night? Bring him away.°
Mine's not an idle° cause. The Duke himself,
Or any of my brothers of the state,
Cannot but feel this wrong as 'twere their own;
For if such actions may have passage free,°
Bondslaves and pagans shall our statesmen be.

Exeunt.

SCENE III [VENICE. A COUNCIL CHAMBER.]

Enter Duke [*and*] *Senators* [*and sit at a table, with lights*], *and Officers.*°
[*The Duke and Senators are reading dispatches.*]

Duke: There is no composition° in these news
That gives them credit.
First Senator: Indeed, they are disproportioned.°
My letters say a hundred and seven galleys.
Duke: And mine, a hundred forty.
Second Senator: And mine, two hundred.
But though they jump° not on a just° account—
As in these cases, where the aim° reports

83 *inclining* following, party 88 *course of direct session* regular or specially convened legal proceedings 96 *away* right along 97 *idle* trifling 100 *have passage free* are allowed to go unchecked s.d. *Enter . . . Officers* (The Quarto text calls for the Duke and senators to "sit at a table with lights and attendants.") 1 *composition* consistency 3 *disproportioned* inconsistent 6 *jump* agree. *just* exact 7 *the aim* conjecture

'Tis oft with difference—yet do they all confirm
A Turkish fleet, and bearing up to Cyprus.
Duke: Nay, it is possible enough to judgment.
I do not so secure me in the error
But the main article I do approve°
In fearful sense.
Sailor (within): What ho, what ho, what ho!

Enter Sailor.

Officer: A messenger from the galleys.
Duke: Now, what's the business?
Sailor: The Turkish preparation° makes for Rhodes.
So was I bid report here to the state
By Signor Angelo.
Duke: How say you by° this change?
First Senator: This cannot be
By no assay° of reason. 'Tis a pageant°
To keep us in false gaze.° When we consider
Th' importancy of Cyprus to the Turk,
And let ourselves again but understand
That, as it more concerns the Turk than Rhodes,
So may he with more facile question bear it,°
For that° it stands not in such warlike brace,°
But altogether lacks th' abilities°
That Rhodes is dressed in°—if we make thought of this,
We must not think the Turk is so unskillful°
To leave that latest° which concerns him first,
Neglecting an attempt of ease and gain
To wake° and wage° a danger profitless.
Duke: Nay, in all confidence, he's not for Rhodes.
Officer: Here is more news.

Enter a Messenger.

Messenger: The Ottomites, reverend and gracious,
Steering with due course toward the isle of Rhodes,
Have there injointed them° with an after° fleet.
First Senator: Ay, so I thought. How many, as you guess?

11–12 *I do not . . . approve* I do not take such (false) comfort in the discrepancies that I fail to perceive the main point, i.e., that the Turkish fleet is threatening 16 *preparation* fleet prepared for battle 19 *by* about 20 *assay* test. *pageant* mere show 21 *in false gaze* looking the wrong way 25 *So may . . . it* so also he (the Turk) can more easily capture it (Cyprus) 26 *For that* since. *brace* state of defense 27 *abilities* means of self-defense 28 *dressed in* equipped with 29 *unskillful* deficient in judgment 30 *latest* last 32 *wake* stir up. *wage* risk 37 *injointed them* joined themselves. *after* second, following

Messenger: Of thirty sail; and now they do restem
Their backward course,° bearing with frank appearance°
Their purposes toward Cyprus. Signor Montano,
Your trusty and most valiant servitor,°
With his free duty° recommends° you thus,
And prays you to believe him.
Duke: 'Tis certain then for Cyprus.
Marcus Luccicos, is not he in town?
First Senator: He's now in Florence.
Duke: Write from us to him, post-post-haste. Dispatch.
First Senator: Here comes Brabantio and the valiant Moor.

Enter Brabantio, Othello, Cassio, Iago, Roderigo, and officers.

Duke: Valiant Othello, we must straight° employ you
Against the general enemy° Ottoman.
[*To Brabantio.*] I did not see you; welcome, gentle° signor.
We lacked your counsel and your help tonight.
Brabantio: So did I yours. Good Your Grace, pardon me;
Neither my place° nor aught I heard of business
Hath raised me from my bed, nor doth the general care
Take hold on me, for my particular° grief
Is of so floodgate° and o'erbearing nature
That it engluts° and swallows other sorrows
And it is still itself.°
Duke: Why, what's the matter?
Brabantio: My daughter! O, my daughter!
Duke and Senators: Dead?
Brabantio: Ay, to me.
She is abused,° stol'n from me, and corrupted
By spells and medicines bought of mountebanks;
For nature so preposterously to err,
Being not deficient,° blind, or lame of sense,°
Sans° witchcraft could not.
Duke: Whoe'er he be that in this foul proceeding
Hath thus beguiled your daughter of herself,
And you of her, the bloody book of law
You shall yourself read in the bitter letter
After your own sense°—yea, though our proper° son

39–40 *restem . . . course* retrace their original course 40 *frank appearance* undisguised intent 42 *servitor* officer under your command 43 *free duty* freely given and loyal service. *recommends* commends himself and reports to 50 *straight* straightway 51 *general enemy* universal enemy to all Christendom 52 *gentle* noble 55 *place* official position 57 *particular* personal 58 *floodgate* i.e., overwhelming (as when floodgates are opened) 59 *engluts* engulfs 60 *is still itself* remains undiminished 62 *abused* deceived 65 *deficient* defective. *lame of sense* deficient in sensory perception 66 *Sans* without 71 *After . . . sense* according to your own interpretation. *our proper* my own

Stood in your action.°
Brabantio: Humbly I thank Your Grace.
Here is the man, this Moor, whom now it seems
Your special mandate for the state affairs
Hath hither brought.
All: We are very sorry for 't.
Duke [*to Othello*]: What, in your own part, can you say to this?
Brabantio: Nothing, but this is so.
Othello: Most potent, grave, and reverend signors,
My very noble and approved° good masters:
That I have ta'en away this old man's daughter,
It is most true; true, I have married her.
The very head and front° of my offending
Hath this extent, no more. Rude° am I in my speech,
And little blessed with the soft phrase of peace;
For since these arms of mine had seven years' pith,°
Till now some nine moons wasted,° they have used
Their dearest° action in the tented field;
And little of this great world can I speak
More than pertains to feats of broils and battle,
And therefore little shall I grace my cause
In speaking for myself. Yet, by your gracious patience,
I will a round° unvarnished tale deliver
Of my whole course of love—what drugs, what charms,
What conjuration, and what mighty magic,
For such proceeding I am charged withal,°
I won his daughter.
Brabantio: A maiden never bold;
Of spirit so still and quiet that her motion
Blushed at herself;° and she, in spite of nature,
Of years,° of country, credit,° everything,
To fall in love with what she feared to look on!
It is a judgment maimed and most imperfect
That will confess° perfection so could err
Against all rules of nature, and must be driven
To find out practices° of cunning hell
Why this should be. I therefore vouch° again

72 *Stood . . . action* were under your accusation 79 *approved* proved, esteemed 82 *head and front* height and breadth, entire extent 83 *Rude* unpolished 85 *since . . . pith* i.e., since I was seven. *pith* strength, vigor 86 *Till . . . wasted* until some nine months ago (since when Othello has evidently not been on active duty, but in Venice) 87 *dearest* most valuable 92 *round* plain 95 *withal* with 97–98 *her . . . herself* i.e., she blushed easily at herself. (*Motion* can suggest the impulse of the soul or of the emotions, or physical movement.) 99 *years* i.e., difference in age. *credit* virtuous reputation 102 *confess* concede (that) 104 *practices* plots 105 *vouch* assert

That with some mixtures powerful o'er the blood,°
Or with some dram conjured to this effect,°
He wrought upon her.
Duke: To vouch this is no proof,
Without more wider° and more overt test°
Than these thin habits° and poor likelihoods°
Of modern seeming° do prefer° against him.
First Senator: But Othello, speak.
Did you by indirect and forcèd courses°
Subdue and poison this young maid's affections?
Or came it by request and such fair question°
As soul to soul affordeth?
Othello: I do beseech you,
Send for the lady to the Sagittary
And let her speak of me before her father.
If you do find me foul in her report,
The trust, the office I do hold of you
Not only take away, but let your sentence
Even fall upon my life.
Duke: Fetch Desdemona hither.
Othello: Ancient, conduct them. You best know the place.

[*Exeunt Iago and attendants*.]

And, till she come, as truly as to heaven
I do confess the vices of my blood,°
So justly° to your grave ears I'll present
How I did thrive in this fair lady's love,
And she in mine.
Duke: Say it, Othello.
Othello: Her father loved me, oft invited me,
Still° questioned me the story of my life
From year to year—the battles, sieges, fortunes
That I have passed.
I ran it through, even from my boyish days
To th' very moment that he bade me tell it,
Wherein I spoke of most disastrous chances,
Of moving accidents° by flood and field,
Of hairbreadth scapes i' th' imminent deadly breach,°

106 *blood* passions 107 *dram . . . effect* dose made by magical spells to have this effect 109 *more wider* fuller. *test* testimony 110 *habits* garments, i.e., appearances. *poor likelihoods* weak inferences 111 *modern seeming* commonplace assumption. *prefer* bring forth 113 *forcèd courses* means used against her will 115 *question* conversation 125 *blood* passions, human nature 126 *justly* truthfully, accurately 131 *Still* continually 137 *moving accident* stirring happenings 138 *imminent . . . breach* death-threatening gaps made in a fortification

Of being taken by the insolent foe
And sold to slavery, of my redemption thence,
And portance° in my travels' history,
Wherein of antres° vast and deserts idle,°
Rough quarries,° rocks, and hills whose heads touch heaven,
It was my hint° to speak—such was my process—
And of the Cannibals that each other eat,
The Anthropophagi,° and men whose heads
Do grow beneath their shoulders. These things to hear
Would Desdemona seriously incline;
But still the house affairs would draw her thence,
Which ever as she could with haste dispatch
She'd come again, and with a greedy ear
Devour up my discourse. Which I, observing,
Took once a pliant° hour, and found good means
To draw from her a prayer of earnest heart
That I would all my pilgrimage dilate,°
Whereof by parcels° she had something heard,
But not intentively.° I did consent,
And often did beguile her of her tears,
When I did speak of some distressful stroke
That my youth suffered. My story being done,
She gave me for my pains a world of sighs.
She swore, in faith, 'twas strange, 'twas passing° strange,
'Twas pitiful, 'twas wondrous pitiful.
She wished she had not heard it, yet she wished
That heaven had made her° such a man. She thanked me,
And bade me, if I had a friend that loved her,
I should but teach him how to tell my story,
And that would woo her. Upon this hint° I spake.
She loved me for the dangers I had passed,
And I loved her that she did pity them.
This only is the witchcraft I have used.
Here comes the lady. Let her witness it.

Enter Desdemona, Iago, [and] attendants.

Duke: I think this tale would win my daughter too.
Good Brabantio,
Take up this mangled matter at the best.°

141 *portance* conduct 142 *antres* caverns. *idle* barren, desolate 143 *Rough quarries* rugged rock formations 144 *hint* occasion, opportunity 146 *Anthropophagi* man-eaters. (A term from Pliny's *Natural History.*) 153 *pliant* well-suiting 155 *dilate* relate in detail 156 *by parcels* piecemeal 157 *intentively* with full attention, continuously 162 *passing* exceedingly 165 *made her* created her to be 168 *hint* opportunity. (Othello does not mean that she was dropping hints.) 175 *Take . . . best* make the best of a bad bargain

Desdemona tells her father, "I do perceive here a divided duty" (I, iii, 183).

Men do their broken weapons rather use
Than their bare hands.
Brabantio: I pray you, hear her speak.
If she confess that she was half the wooer,
Destruction on my head if my bad blame
Light on the man!—Come hither, gentle mistress.
Do you perceive in all this noble company
Where most you owe obedience?
Desdemona: My noble Father,
I do perceive here a divided duty.
To you I am bound for life and education;°
My life and education both do learn° me
How to respect you. You are the lord of duty;°
I am hitherto your daughter. But here's my husband,
And so much duty as my mother showed
To you, preferring you before her father,
So much I challenge° that I may profess
Due to the Moor my lord.
Brabantio: God be with you! I have done.
Please it Your Grace, on to the state affairs.
I had rather to adopt a child than get° it.
Come hither, Moor. [*He joins the hands of Othello and Desdemona.*]
I here do give thee that with all my heart°
Which, but thou hast already, with all my heart°

184 *education* upbringing 185 *learn* teach 186 *of duty* to whom duty is due 190 *challenge* claim 194 *get* beget 196 *with all my heart* wherein my whole affection has been engaged 197 *with all my heart* willingly, gladly

I would keep from thee.—For your sake,° jewel,
I am glad at soul I have no other child,
For thy escape° would teach me tyranny,
To hang clogs° on them.—I have done, my lord.

Duke: Let me speak like yourself,° and lay a sentence°
Which, as a grece° or step, may help these lovers
Into your favor.
When remedies° are past, the griefs are ended
By seeing the worst, which late on hopes depended.°
To mourn a mischief° that is past and gone
Is the next° way to draw new mischief on.
What° cannot be preserved when fortune takes,
Patience her injury a mockery makes.°
The robbed that smiles steals something from the thief;
He robs himself that spends a bootless grief.°

Brabantio: So let the Turk of Cyprus us beguile,
We lose it not, so long as we can smile.
He bears the sentence well that nothing bears
But the free comfort which from thence he hears,
But he bears both the sentence and the sorrow
That, to pay grief, must of poor patience borrow.°
These sentences, to sugar or to gall,
Being strong on both sides, are equivocal.°
But words are words. I never yet did hear
That the bruised heart was piercèd through the ear.°
I humbly beseech you, proceed to th' affairs of state.

Duke: The Turk with a most mighty preparation makes for Cyprus. Othello, the fortitude° of the place is best known to you; and though we have there a substitute° of most allowed° sufficiency, yet opinion, a sovereign mistress of effects, throws a more safer voice on you.° You must therefore be content to slubber° the gloss of your new fortunes with this more stubborn° and boisterous expedition.

198 *For your sake* on your account 200 *escape* elopement 201 *clogs* (Literally, blocks of wood fastened to the legs of criminals or convicts to inhibit escape.) 202 *like yourself* i.e., as you would, in your proper temper. *lay a sentence* apply a maxim 203 *grece* step 205 *remedies* hopes of remedy 206 *which . . . depended* which griefs were sustained until recently by hopeful anticipation 207 *mischief* misfortune, injury 208 *next* nearest 209 *What* whatever 210 *Patience . . . makes* patience laughs at the injury inflicted by fortune (and thus eases the pain) 212 *spends a bootless grief* indulges in unavailing grief 215–218 *He bears . . . borrow* a person well bears out your maxim who can enjoy its platitudinous comfort, free of all genuine sorrow, but anyone whose grief bankrupts his poor patience is left with your saying and his sorrow, too. (*Bears the sentence* also plays on the meaning, "receives judicial sentence.") 219–220 *These . . . equivocal* these fine maxims are equivocal, either sweet or bitter in their application 222 *piercèd . . . ear* i.e., surgically lanced and cured by mere words of advice 225 *fortitude* strength 226 *substitute* deputy. *allowed* acknowledged 226–227 *opinion . . . on you* general opinion, an important determiner of affairs, chooses you as the best man 228 *slubber* soil, sully. 229 *stubborn* harsh, rough

Othello: The tyrant custom, most grave senators,
Hath made the flinty and steel couch of war
My thrice-driven° bed of down. I do agnize°
A natural and prompt alacrity
I find in hardness,° and do undertake
These present wars against the Ottomites.
Most humbly therefore bending to your state,°
I crave fit disposition for my wife,
Due reference of place and exhibition,°
With such accommodation° and besort°
As levels° with her breeding.°
Duke: Why, at her father's.
Brabantio: I will not have it so.
Othello: Nor I.
Desdemona: Nor I. I would not there reside,
To put my father in impatient thoughts
By being in his eye. Most gracious Duke,
To my unfolding° lend your prosperous° ear,
And let me find a charter° in your voice,
T' assist my simpleness.
Duke: What would you, Desdemona?
Desdemona: That I did love the Moor to live with him,
My downright violence and storm of fortunes°
May trumpet to the world. My heart's subdued
Even to the very quality of my lord.°
I saw Othello's visage in his mind,
And to his honors and his valiant parts°
Did I my soul and fortunes consecrate.
So that, dear lords, if I be left behind
A moth° of peace, and he go to the war,
The rites° for why I love him are bereft me,
And I a heavy interim shall support
By his dear° absence. Let me go with him.
Othello: Let her have your voice.°
Vouch with me, heaven, I therefore beg it not
To please the palate of my appetite,

232 *thrice-driven* thrice sifted, winnowed. *agnize* know in myself, acknowledge 234 *hardness* hardship 236 *bending . . . state* bowing or kneeling to your authority 238 *reference . . . exhibition* provision of appropriate place to live and allowance of money 239 *accommodation* suitable provision. *besort* attendance 240 *levels* equals, suits. *breeding* social position, upbringing 245 *unfolding* explanation, proposal. *prosperous* propitious 246 *charter* privilege, authorization 250 My . . . *fortunes* my plain and total breach of social custom, taking my future by storm and disrupting my whole life 251–252 My *heart's . . . lord* my heart is brought wholly into accord with Othello's virtues; I love him for his virtues 254 *parts* qualities 257 *moth* i.e., one who consumes merely 258 *rites* rites of love (with a suggestion, too, of "rights," sharing) 260 *dear* (1) heartfelt (2) costly 261 *voice* consent

Desdemona declares her loyalty to her husband Othello (I, iii, 182–301).

Nor to comply with heat°—the young affects°
In me defunct—and proper° satisfaction,
But to be free° and bounteous to her mind.
And heaven defend° your good souls that you think°
I will your serious and great business scant
When she is with me. No, when light-winged toys
Of feathered Cupid seel° with wanton dullness
My speculative and officed instruments,°
That° my disports° corrupt and taint° my business,
Let huswives make a skillet of my helm,
And all indign° and base adversities
Make head° against my estimation!°

Duke: Be it as you shall privately determine,
Either for her stay or going. Th' affair cries haste,
And speed must answer it.

A Senator: You must away tonight.

Desdemona: Tonight, my lord?

264 *heat* sexual passion. *young affects* passions of youth, desires 265 *proper* personal 266 *free* generous 267 *defend* forbid. *think* should think 270 *seel* i.e., make blind (as in falconry, by sewing up the eyes of the hawk during training) 271 *speculative . . . instruments* eyes and other faculties used in the performance of duty 272 *That* so that. *disports* sexual pastimes. *taint* impair 274 *indign* unworthy, shameful 275 *Make head* raise an army. *estimation* reputation

Duke: This night.
Othello: With all my heart.
Duke: At nine i' the morning here we'll meet again.
Othello, leave some officer behind,
And he shall our commission bring to you,
With such things else of quality and respect°
As doth import° you.
Othello: So please Your Grace, my ancient;
A man he is of honesty and trust.
To his conveyance I assign my wife,
With what else needful Your Good Grace shall think
To be sent after me.
Duke: Let it be so.
Good night to everyone. [*To Brabantio.*] And, noble signor,
If virtue no delighted° beauty lack,
Your son-in-law is far more fair than black.
First Senator: Adieu, brave Moor. Use Desdemona well.
Brabantio: Look to her, Moor, if thou hast eyes to see.
She has deceived her father, and may thee.

Exeunt [Duke, Brabantio, Cassio, Senators, and officers].

Othello: My life upon her faith! Honest Iago,
My Desdemona must I leave to thee.
I prithee, let thy wife attend on her,
And bring them after in the best advantage.°
Come, Desdemona. I have but an hour
Of love, of worldly matters and direction,°
To spend with thee. We must obey the time.°

Exit [with Desdemona].

Roderigo: Iago—
Iago: What sayst thou, noble heart?
Roderigo: What will I do, think'st thou?
Iago: Why, go to bed and sleep.
Roderigo: I will incontinently° drown myself.
Iago: If thou dost, I shall never love thee after. Why, thou silly gentleman?
Roderigo: It is silliness to live when to live is torment; and then have we a prescription° to die when death is our physician.
Iago: O villainous!° I have looked upon the world for four times seven years, and, since I could distinguish betwixt a benefit and an injury,

283 *of quality and respect* of importance and relevance 284 *import* concern 290 *delighted* capable of delighting 298 *in . . . advantage* at the most favorable opportunity 300 *direction* instructions 301 *the time* the urgency of the present crisis 306 *incontinently* immediately, without self-restraint 309 *prescription* (1) right based on long-established custom (2) doctor's prescription 310 *villainous* i.e., what perfect nonsense

I never found man that knew how to love himself. Ere I would say I would drown myself for the love of a guinea hen,° I would change my humanity with a baboon.

Roderigo: What should I do? I confess it is my shame to be so fond,° but it is not in my virtue° to amend it.

Iago: Virtue? A fig!° 'Tis in ourselves that we are thus or thus. Our bodies are our gardens, to the which our wills are gardeners; so that if we will plant nettles or sow lettuce, set hyssop° and weed up thyme, supply it with one gender° of herbs or distract it with° many, either to have it sterile with idleness° or manured with industry—why, the power and corrigible authority° of this lies in our wills. If the beam° of our lives had not one scale of reason to poise° another of sensuality, the blood° and baseness of our natures would conduct us to most preposterous conclusions. But we have reason to cool our raging motions,° our carnal stings, our unbitted° lusts, whereof I take this that you call love to be a sect or scion.°

Roderigo: It cannot be.

Iago: It is merely a lust of the blood and a permission of the will. Come, be a man. Drown thyself? Drown cats and blind puppies. I have professed me thy friend, and I confess me knit to thy deserving with cables of perdurable° toughness. I could never better stead° thee than now. Put money in thy purse. Follow thou the wars; defeat thy favor° with an usurped° beard. I say, put money in thy purse. It cannot be long that Desdemona should continue her love to the Moor—put money in thy purse—nor he his to her. It was a violent commencement in her, and thou shalt see an answerable sequestration°—put but money in thy purse. These Moors are changeable in their wills°—fill thy purse with money. The food that to him now is as luscious as locusts° shall be to him shortly as bitter as coloquintida.° She must change for youth; when she is sated with his body, she will find the error of her choice. She must have change, she must. Therefore put money in thy purse. If thou wilt needs damn thyself, do it a more delicate way than drowning. Make° all the money thou canst. If sanctimony° and a frail vow betwixt an erring° barbarian and a supersubtle Venetian be not too hard for my wits and all the tribe of

313 *guinea hen* (A slang term for a prostitute.) 315 *fond* infatuated 316 *virtue* strength, nature 317 *fig* (To give a fig is to thrust the thumb between the first and second fingers in a vulgar and insulting gesture.) 319 *hyssop* an herb of the mint family 320 *gender* kind. *distract it with* divide it among 321 *idleness* want of cultivation 322 *corrigible authority* power to correct. *beam* balance 323 *poise* counterbalance. *blood* natural passions 325 *motions* appetites 326 *unbitted* unbridled, uncontrolled. 327 *sect or scion* cutting or offshoot 332 *perdurable* very durable. *stead* assist 333–334 *defeat thy favor* disguise your face 334 *usurped* (The suggestion is that Roderigo is not man enough to have a beard of his own.) 337 *an answerable sequestration* a corresponding separation or estrangement 339 *wills* carnal appetites 340 *locusts* fruit of the carob tree (see Matthew 3:4), or perhaps honeysuckle. *coloquintida* colocynth or bitter apple, a purgative 344 *Make* raise, collect 345 *sanctimony* sacred ceremony. *erring* wandering, vagabond, unsteady

hell, thou shalt enjoy her. Therefore make money. A pox of drowning thyself! It is clean out of the way.° Seek thou rather to be hanged in compassing° thy joy than to be drowned and go without her.

Roderigo: Wilt thou be fast° to my hopes if I depend on the issue?°

Iago: Thou art sure of me. Go, make money. I have told thee often, and I retell thee again and again, I hate the Moor. My cause is hearted;° thine hath no less reason. Let us be conjunctive° in our revenge against him. If thou canst cuckold him, thou dost thyself a pleasure, me a sport. There are many events in the womb of time which will be delivered. Traverse,° go, provide thy money. We will have more of this tomorrow. Adieu.

Roderigo: Where shall we meet i' the morning?

Iago: At my lodging.

Roderigo: I'll be with thee betimes.° *[He starts to leave.]*

Iago: Go to, farewell.—Do you hear, Roderigo?

Roderigo: What say you?

Iago: No more of drowning, do you hear?

Roderigo: I am changed.

Iago: Go to, farewell. Put money enough in your purse.

Roderigo: I'll sell all my land. *Exit.*

Iago: Thus do I ever make my fool my purse;
For I mine own gained knowledge should profane
If I would time expend with such a snipe°
But for my sport and profit. I hate the Moor;
And it is thought abroad° that twixt my sheets
He's done my office.° I know not if 't be true;
But I, for mere suspicion in that kind,
Will do as if for surety.° He holds me well;°
The better shall my purpose work on him.
Cassio's a proper° man. Let me see now:
To get his place and to plume up° my will
In double knavery—How, how?—Let's see:
After some time, to abuse° Othello's ear
That he° is too familiar with his wife.
He hath a person and a smooth dispose°
To be suspected, framed to make women false.
The Moor is of a free° and open° nature,

348 *clean . . . way* entirely unsuitable as a course of action 349 *compassing* encompassing, embracing 350 *fast* true. *issue* (successful) outcome 352 *hearted* fixed in the heart, heartfelt 353 *conjunctive* united 356 *Traverse* (A military marching term.) 360 *betimes* early 369 *snipe* woodcock, i.e., fool 371 *it is thought abroad* it is rumored 372 *my office* i.e., my sexual function as husband 374 *do . . . surety* act as if on certain knowledge. *holds me well* regards me favorably 376 *proper* handsome 377 *plume up* put a feather in the cap of, i.e., glorify, gratify 379 *abuse* deceive 380 *he* i.e., Cassio 381 *dispose* disposition 383 *free* frank, generous. *open* unsuspicious

That thinks men honest that but seem to be so,
And will as tenderly° be led by the nose
As asses are.
I have 't. It is engendered. Hell and night
Must bring this monstrous birth to the world's light.

[*Exit.*]

ACT II

SCENE I [A SEAPORT IN CYPRUS. AN OPEN PLACE NEAR THE QUAY.]

Enter Montano and two Gentlemen.

Montano: What from the cape can you discern at sea?
First Gentleman: Nothing at all. It is a high-wrought flood.°
I cannot, twixt the heaven and the main,°
Descry a sail.
Montano: Methinks the wind hath spoke aloud at land;
A fuller blast ne'er shook our battlements.
If it hath ruffianed° so upon the sea,
What ribs of oak, when mountains° melt on them,
Can hold the mortise?° What shall we hear of this?
Second Gentleman: A segregation° of the Turkish fleet.
For do but stand upon the foaming shore,
The chidden° billow seems to pelt the clouds;
The wind-shaked surge, with high and monstrous mane,°
Seems to cast water on the burning Bear°
And quench the guards of th' ever-fixèd pole.
I never did like molestation° view
On the enchafèd° flood.
Montano: If that° the Turkish fleet
Be not ensheltered and embayed,° they are drowned;
It is impossible to bear it out.°

Enter a [Third] Gentleman.

385 *tenderly* readily 2 *high-wrought flood* very agitated sea 3 *main* ocean (also at line 41) 7 *ruffianed* raged 8 *mountains* i.e., of water 9 *hold the mortise* hold their joints together. (A *mortise* is the socket hollowed out in fitting timbers.) 10 *segregation* dispersal 12 *chidden* i.e., rebuked, repelled (by the shore), and thus shot into the air 13 *monstrous mane* (The surf is like the mane of a wild beast.) 14 *the burning Bear* i.e., the constellation Ursa Minor or the Little Bear, which includes the polestar (and hence regarded as the *guards of th' ever-fixèd pole* in the next line; sometimes the term *guards* is applied to the two "pointers" of the Big Bear or Dipper, which may be intended here). 16 *like molestation* comparable disturbance 17 *enchafèd* angry 18 *If that* if 19 *embayed* sheltered by a bay 20 *bear it out* survive, weather the storm

Third Gentleman: News, lads! Our wars are done.
The desperate tempest hath so banged the Turks
That their designment° halts.° A noble ship of Venice
Hath seen a grievous wreck° and sufferance°
On most part of their fleet.
Montano: How? Is this true?
Third Gentleman: The ship is here put in,
A Veronesa;° Michael Cassio,
Lieutenant to the warlike Moor Othello,
Is come on shore; the Moor himself at sea,
And is in full commission here for Cyprus.
Montano: I am glad on 't. 'Tis a worthy governor.
Third Gentleman: But this same Cassio, though he speak of comfort
Touching the Turkish loss, yet he looks sadly°
And prays the Moor be safe, for they were parted
With foul and violent tempest.
Montano: Pray heaven he be,
For I have served him, and the man commands
Like a full° soldier. Let's to the seaside, ho!
As well to see the vessel that's come in
As to throw out our eyes for brave Othello,
Even till we make the main and th' aerial blue°
An indistinct regard.°
Third Gentleman: Come, let's do so,
For every minute is expectancy°
Of more arrivance.°

Enter Cassio.

Cassio: Thanks, you the valiant of this warlike isle,
That so approve° the Moor! O, let the heavens
Give him defense against the elements,
For I have lost him on a dangerous sea.
Montano: Is he well shipped?
Cassio: His bark is stoutly timbered, and his pilot
Of very expert and approved allowance;°
Therefore my hopes, not surfeited to death,°
Stand in bold cure.°

23 *designment* design, enterprise. *halts* is lame 24 *wreck* shipwreck. *sufferance* damage, disaster 28 *Veronesa* i.e., fitted out in Verona for Venetian service, or possibly *Verennessa* (the Folio spelling), i.e., *verrinessa*, a cutter (from *verrinare*, "to cut through") 34 *sadly* gravely 38 *full* perfect 41 *the main . . . blue* the sea and the sky 42 *An indistinct regard* indistinguishable in our view 43 *is expectancy* gives expectation 44 *arrivance* arrival 46 *approve* admire, honor 51 *approved allowance* tested reputation 52 *surfeited to death* i.e., overextended, worn thin through repeated application or delayed fulfillment 53 *in bold cure* in strong hopes of fulfillment

[*A cry*] *within:* "A sail, a sail, a sail!"

Cassio: What noise?
A Gentleman: The town is empty. On the brow o' the sea°
Stand ranks of people, and they cry "A sail!"
Cassio: My hopes do shape him for° the governor.

[*A shot within.*]

Second Gentleman: They do discharge their shot of courtesy;°
Our friends at least.
Cassio: I pray you, sir, go forth,
And give us truth who 'tis that is arrived.
Second Gentleman: I shall. *Exit.*
Montano: But, good Lieutenant, is your general wived?
Cassio: Most fortunately. He hath achieved a maid
That paragons° description and wild fame,°
One that excels the quirks° of blazoning° pens,
And in th' essential vesture of creation
Does tire the enginer.°

Enter [*Second*] *Gentleman.*°

How now? Who has put in?°
Second Gentleman: 'Tis one Iago, ancient to the General.
Cassio: He's had most favorable and happy speed.
Tempests themselves, high seas, and howling winds,
The guttered° rocks and congregated sands—
Traitors ensteeped° to clog the guiltless keel—
As° having sense of beauty, do omit°
Their mortal° natures, letting go safely by
The divine Desdemona.
Montano: What is she?
Cassio: She that I spake of, our great captain's captain,
Left in the conduct of the bold Iago,
Whose footing° here anticipates our thoughts
A sennight's° speed. Great Jove, Othello guard,

55 *brow o' the sea* cliff-edge 57 My . . . *for* I hope it is 58 *discharge . . . courtesy* fire a salute in token of respect and courtesy 64 *paragons* surpasses. *wild fame* extravagant report 65 *quirks* witty conceits. *blazoning* setting forth as though in heraldic language 66–67 *in . . . enginer* in her real, God-given, beauty, (she) defeats any attempt to praise her. *enginer* engineer, i.e., poet, one who devises. s.d. [*Second*] *Gentleman* (So identified in the Quarto text here and in lines 58, 61, 68, and 96; the Folio calls him a gentleman.) 67 *put in* i.e., to harbor 71 *guttered* jagged, trenched 72 *ensteeped* lying under water 73 As as if. *omit* forbear to exercise 74 *mortal* deadly 78 *footing* landing 79 *sennight's* week's

"I thank you, valiant Cassio. / What tidings can you tell me of my lord?" (II, i, 89–90).

And swell his sail with thine own powerful breath,
That he may bless this bay with his tall° ship,
Make love's quick pants in Desdemona's arms,
Give renewed fire to our extincted spirits,
And bring all Cyprus comfort!

Enter Desdemona, Iago, Roderigo, and Emilia.

O, behold,
The riches of the ship is come on shore!
You men of Cyprus, let her have your knees.

[*The gentlemen make curtsy to Desdemona.*]

Hail to thee, lady! And the grace of heaven
Before, behind thee, and on every hand
Enwheel thee round!

Desdemona: I thank you, valiant Cassio.
What tidings can you tell me of my lord?

Cassio: He is not yet arrived, nor know I aught
But that he's well and will be shortly here.

Desdemona: O, but I fear—How lost you company?

Cassio: The great contention of the sea and skies

81 *tall* splendid, gallant

Parted our fellowship.
(Within) "A sail, a sail!" [*A shot.*]
But hark. A sail!
Second Gentleman: They give their greeting to the citadel.
This likewise is a friend.
Cassio: See for the news.

[*Exit Second Gentleman.*]

Good Ancient, you are welcome. [*Kissing Emilia.*] Welcome, mistress.
Let it not gall your patience, good Iago,
That I extend° my manners; 'tis my breeding°
That gives me this bold show of courtesy.
Iago: Sir, would she give you so much of her lips
As of her tongue she oft bestows on me,
You would have enough.
Desdemona: Alas, she has no speech!°
Iago: In faith, too much.
I find it still,° when I have list° to sleep.
Marry, before your ladyship, I grant,
She puts her tongue a little in her heart
And chides with thinking.°
Emilia: You have little cause to say so.
Iago: Come on, come on. You are pictures out of doors,°
Bells° in your parlors, wildcats in your kitchens,°
Saints° in your injuries, devils being offended,
Players° in your huswifery,° and huswives° in your beds.
Desdemona: O, fie upon thee, slanderer!
Iago: Nay, it is true, or else I am a Turk.°
You rise to play, and go to bed to work.
Emilia: You shall not write my praise.
Iago: No, let me not.
Desdemona: What wouldst thou write of me, if thou shouldst praise me?
Iago: O gentle lady, do not put me to 't,
For I am nothing if not critical.°
Desdemona: Come on, essay.°—There's one gone to the harbor?
Iago: Ay, madam.

100 *extend* give scope to. *breeding* training in the niceties of etiquette 105 *she has no speech* i.e., she's not a chatterbox, as you allege 107 *still* always. *list* desire 110 *with thinking* i.e., in her thoughts only 111 *pictures out of doors* i.e., silent and well-behaved in public 112 *Bells* i.e., jangling, noisy, and brazen. *in your kitchens* i.e., in domestic affairs. (Ladies would not do the cooking.) 113 *Saints* martyrs 114 *Players* idlers, triflers, or deceivers. *huswifery* housekeeping. *huswives* hussies (i.e., women are "busy" in bed, or unduly thrifty in dispensing sexual favors) 116 *a Turk* an infidel, not to be believed 121 *critical* censorious 122 *essay* try

Desdemona: I am not merry, but I do beguile
The thing I am° by seeming otherwise.
Come, how wouldst thou praise me?
Iago: I am about it, but indeed my invention
Comes from my pate as birdlime° does from frieze°—
It plucks out brains and all. But my Muse labors,°
And thus she is delivered:
If she be fair and wise, fairness and wit,
The one's for use, the other useth it.°
Desdemona: Well praised! How if she be black° and witty?
Iago: If she be black, and thereto have a wit,
She'll find a white° that shall her blackness fit.°
Desdemona: Worse and worse.
Emilia: How if fair and foolish?
Iago: She never yet was foolish that was fair,
For even her folly° helped her to an heir.°
Desdemona: These are old fond° paradoxes to make fools laugh i' th' alehouse. What miserable praise hast thou for her that's foul and foolish?
Iago: There's none so foul° and foolish thereunto,°
But does foul° pranks which fair and wise ones do.
Desdemona: O heavy ignorance! Thou praisest the worst best. But what praise couldst thou bestow on a deserving woman indeed, one that, in the authority of her merit, did justly put on the vouch° of very malice itself?
Iago: She that was ever fair, and never proud,
Had tongue at will, and yet was never loud,
Never lacked gold and yet went never gay,°
Fled from her wish, and yet said, "Now I may,"°
She that being angered, her revenge being nigh,
Bade her wrong stay° and her displeasure fly,
She that in wisdom never was so frail
To change the cod's head for the salmon's tail,°
She that could think and ne'er disclose her mind,

125 *The thing I am* i.e., my anxious self 128 *birdlime* sticky substance used to catch small birds. *frieze* coarse woolen cloth 129 *labors* (1) exerts herself (2) prepares to deliver a child (with a following pun on *delivered* in line 130) 132 *The one's . . . it* i.e., her cleverness will make use of her beauty 133 *black* dark-complexioned, brunette 135 *a white* a fair person (with word-play on "wight," a person). *fit* (with sexual suggestion of mating) 138 *folly* (with added meaning of "lechery, wantonness"). *to an heir* i.e., to bear a child 139 *fond* foolish 142 *foul* ugly. *thereunto* in addition 143 *foul* sluttish 146 *put . . . vouch* compel the approval 150 *gay* extravagantly clothed 151 *Fled . . . may* avoided temptation where the choice was hers 153 *Bade . . . stay* i.e., resolved to put up with her injury patiently 155 *To . . . tail* i.e., to exchange a lackluster husband for a sexy lover (?) (*Cod's head* is slang for "penis," and *tail*, for "pudendum.")

See suitors following and not look behind,
She was a wight, if ever such wight were—

Desdemona: To do what?

Iago: To suckle fools° and chronicle small beer.°

Desdemona: O most lame and impotent conclusion! Do not learn of him, Emilia, though he be thy husband. How say you, Cassio? Is he not a most profane° and liberal° counselor?

Cassio: He speaks home,° madam. You may relish° him more in° the soldier than in the scholar.

[*Cassio and Desdemona stand together, conversing intimately.*]

Iago [*aside*]: He takes her by the palm. Ay, well said,° whisper. With as little a web as this will I ensnare as great a fly as Cassio. Ay, smile upon her, do; I will gyve° thee in thine own courtship.° You say true;° 'tis so, indeed. If such tricks as these strip you out of your lieutenantry, it had been better you had not kissed your three fingers so oft, which now again you are most apt to play the sir° in. Very good; well kissed! An excellent courtesy! 'Tis so, indeed. Yet again your fingers to your lips? Would they were clyster pipes° for your sake! [*Trumpet within.*] The Moor! I know his trumpet.

Cassio: 'Tis truly so.

Desdemona: Let's meet him and receive him.

Cassio: Lo, where he comes!

Enter Othello and attendants.

Othello: O my fair warrior!

Desdemona: My dear Othello!

Othello: It gives me wonder great as my content
To see you here before me. O my soul's joy,
If after every tempest come such calms,
May the winds blow till they have wakened death,
And let the laboring bark climb hills of seas
Olympus-high, and duck again as low
As hell's from heaven! If it were now to die,
'Twere now to be most happy, for I fear
My soul hath her content so absolute
That not another comfort like to this
Succeeds in unknown fate.°

160 *suckle fools* breastfeed babies. *chronicle small beer* i.e., keep petty household accounts, keep track of trivial matters 163 *profane* irreverent, ribald. *liberal* licentious, free-spoken 164 *home* right to the target. (A term from fencing.) *relish* appreciate. *in* in the character of 166 *well said* well done 168 *gyve* fetter, shackle. *courtship* courtesy, show of courtly manners. *You say true* i.e., that's right, go ahead 171 *the sir* i.e., the fine gentleman 173 *clyster pipes* tubes used for enemas and douches 189 *Succeeds . . . fate* i.e., can follow in the unknown future

Desdemona: The heavens forbid
But that our loves and comforts should increase
Even as our days do grow!
Othello: Amen to that, sweet powers!
I cannot speak enough of this content.
It stops me here; it is too much of joy.
And this, and this, the greatest discords be

[*They kiss.*]°

That e'er our hearts shall make!
Iago [*aside*]: O, you are well tuned now!
But I'll set down° the pegs that make this music,
As honest as I am.°
Othello: Come, let us to the castle.
News, friends! Our wars are done, the Turks are drowned.
How does my old acquaintance of this isle?—
Honey, you shall be well desired° in Cyprus;
I have found great love amongst them. O my sweet,
I prattle out of fashion,° and I dote
In mine own comforts.—I prithee, good Iago,
Go to the bay and disembark my coffers.°
Bring thou the master° to the citadel;
He is a good one, and his worthiness
Does challenge° much respect.—Come, Desdemona.—
Once more, well met at Cyprus!

Exeunt Othello and Desdemona [*and all but Iago and Roderigo*].

Iago [*to an attendant*]: Do thou meet me presently at the harbor. [*To Roderigo.*] Come hither. If thou be'st valiant—as, they say, base men° being in love have then a nobility in their natures more than is native to them—list° me. The Lieutenant tonight watches on the court of guard.° First, I must tell thee this: Desdemona is directly in love with him.
Roderigo: With him? Why, 'tis not possible.
Iago: Lay thy finger thus,° and let thy soul be instructed. Mark me with what violence she first loved the Moor, but° for bragging and telling her fantastical lies. To love him still for prating? Let not thy discreet heart think it. Her eye must be fed; and what delight shall she have to look on the devil? When the blood is made dull with the act of sport,° there

195 s.d. *They kiss* (The direction is from the Quarto.) 198 *set down* loosen (and hence untune the instrument) 199 *As . . . I am* for all my supposed honesty 203 *desired* welcomed 205 *out of fashion* irrelevantly, incoherently (?) 207 *coffers* chests, baggage 208 *master* ship's captain 210 *challenge* lay claim to, deserve 213 *base men* even lowly born men 215 *list* listen to *court of guard* guardhouse. (Cassio is in charge of the watch.) 218 *thus* i.e., on your lips 219 *but* only 222 *the act of sport* sex

should be, again to inflame it and to give satiety a fresh appetite, loveliness in favor,° sympathy° in years, manners, and beauties—all which the Moor is defective in. Now, for want of these required conveniences,° her delicate tenderness will find itself abused,° begin to heave the gorge,° disrelish and abhor the Moor. Very nature° will instruct her in it and compel her to some second choice. Now, sir, this granted—as it is a most pregnant° and unforced position—who stands so eminent in the degree of ° this fortune as Cassio does? A knave very voluble,° no further conscionable° than in putting on the mere form of civil and humane° seeming for the better compassing of his salt° and most hidden loose affection.° Why, none, why, none. A slipper° and subtle knave, a finder out of occasions, that has an eye can stamp° and counterfeit advantages,° though true advantage never present itself; a devilish knave. Besides, the knave is handsome, young, and hath all those requisites in him that folly° and green° minds look after. A pestilent complete knave, and the woman hath found him° already.

Roderigo: I cannot believe that in her. She's full of most blessed condition.°

Iago: Blessed fig's end!° The wine she drinks is made of grapes. If she had been blessed, she would never have loved the Moor. Blessed pudding!° Didst thou not see her paddle with the palm of his hand? Didst not mark that?

Roderigo: Yes, that I did; but that was but courtesy.

Iago: Lechery, by this hand. An index° and obscure° prologue to the history of lust and foul thoughts. They met so near with their lips that their breaths embraced together. Villainous thoughts, Roderigo! When these mutualities° so marshal the way, hard at hand° comes the master and main exercise, th' incorporate° conclusion. Pish! But, sir, be you ruled by me. I have brought you from Venice. Watch you° tonight; for the command, I'll lay 't upon you.° Cassio knows you not. I'll not be far from you. Do you find some occasion to anger Cassio, either by speaking too loud, or tainting° his discipline, or from what other course you please, which the time shall more favorably minister.°

Roderigo: Well.

224 *favor* appearance. *sympathy* correspondence, similarity 225–226 *required conveniences* things conducive to sexual compatibility 226 *abused* cheated, revolted 227 *heave the gorge* experience nausea. *Very nature* her very instincts 229 *pregnant* evident, cogent 230 *in the degree of* as next in line for 231 *voluble* facile, glib. *conscionable* conscientious, conscience-bound 232 *humane* polite, courteous. 233 *salt* licentious. *affection* passion 234 *slipper* slippery 235 *an eye can stamp* an eye that can coin, create. *advantages* favorable opportunities 237 *folly* wantonness. *green* immature 239 *found him* sized him up, perceived his intent 240 *condition* disposition 241 *fig's end* (See Act I, Scene iii, line 317, for the vulgar gesture of the fig.) 242 *pudding* sausage 246 *index* table of contents. *obscure* (i.e., the *lust and foul thoughts* in line 247 are secret, hidden from view) 249 *mutualities* exchanges, intimacies. *hard at hand* closely following 250 *incorporate* carnal 251 *Watch you* stand watch 252 *for the command . . . you* I'll arrange for you to be appointed, given orders 254 *tainting* disparaging 255 *minister* provide

Iago: Sir, he's rash and very sudden in choler,° and haply° may strike at you. Provoke him that he may, for even out of that will I cause these of Cyprus to mutiny,° whose qualification° shall come into no true taste° again but by the displanting of Cassio. So shall you have a shorter journey to your desires by the means I shall then have to prefer° them, and the impediment most profitably removed, without the which there were no expectation of our prosperity.

Roderigo: I will do this, if you can bring it to any opportunity.

Iago: I warrant° thee. Meet me by and by° at the citadel. I must fetch his necessaries ashore. Farewell.

Roderigo: Adieu. *Exit.*

Iago: That Cassio loves her, I do well believe 't;
That she loves him, 'tis apt° and of great credit.°
The Moor, howbeit that I endure him not,
Is of a constant, loving, noble nature,
And I dare think he'll prove to Desdemona
A most dear husband. Now, I do love her too,
Not out of absolute lust—though peradventure
I stand accountant° for as great a sin—
But partly led to diet° my revenge
For that I do suspect the lusty Moor
Hath leaped into my seat, the thought whereof
Doth, like a poisonous mineral, gnaw my innards;
And nothing can or shall content my soul
Till I am evened with him, wife for wife,
Or failing so, yet that I put the Moor
At least into a jealousy so strong
That judgment cannot cure. Which thing to do,
If this poor trash of Venice, whom I trace°
For° his quick hunting, stand the putting on,°
I'll have our Michael Cassio on the hip,°
Abuse° him to the Moor in the rank garb°—
For I fear Cassio with my nightcap° too—
Make the Moor thank me, love me, and reward me
For making him egregiously an ass

257 *choler* wrath. *haply* perhaps 259 *mutiny* riot. *qualification* appeasement. 260 *true taste* i.e., acceptable state 262 *prefer* advance 265 *warrant* assure. *by and by* immediately 269 *apt* probable. *credit* credibility 275 *accountant* accountable 276 *diet* feed 285 *trace* i.e., train, or follow (?), or perhaps *trash*, a hunting term, meaning to put weights on a hunting dog in order to slow him down 286 *For* to make more eager. *stand . . . on* respond properly when I incite him to quarrel 287 *on the hip* at my mercy, where I can throw him. (A wrestling term.) 288 *Abuse* slander. *rank garb* coarse manner, gross fashion 289 *with my nightcap* i.e., as a rival in my bed, as one who gives me cuckold's horns

And practicing upon° his peace and quiet
Even to madness. 'Tis here, but yet confused.
Knavery's plain face is never seen till used. *Exit.*

SCENE II [CYPRUS. A STREET.]

Enter Othello's Herald with a proclamation.

Herald: It is Othello's pleasure, our noble and valiant general, that, upon certain tidings now arrived, importing the mere perdition° of the Turkish fleet, every man put himself into triumph:° some to dance, some to make bonfires, each man to what sport and revels his addiction° leads him. For, besides these beneficial news, it is the celebration of his nuptial. So much was his pleasure should be proclaimed. All offices° are open, and there is full liberty of feasting from this present hour of five till the bell have told eleven. Heaven bless the isle of Cyprus and our noble general Othello!

Exit.

SCENE III [CYPRUS. THE CITADEL.]

Enter Othello, Desdemona, Cassio, and attendants.

Othello: Good Michael, look you to the guard tonight.
Let's teach ourselves that honorable stop°
Not to outsport° discretion.
Cassio: Iago hath direction what to do,
But notwithstanding, with my personal eye
Will I look to 't.
Othello: Iago is most honest.
Michael, good night. Tomorrow with your earliest°
Let me have speech with you. [*To Desdemona.*]
Come, my dear love,
The purchase made, the fruits are to ensue;
That profit's yet to come 'tween me and you.°—
Good night.

Exit [*Othello, with Desdemona and attendants*].

Enter Iago.

292 *practicing upon* plotting against 2 *mere perdition* complete destruction 3 *triumph* public celebration 4 *addiction* inclination 7 *offices* rooms where food and drink are kept
2 *stop* restraint 3 *outsport* celebrate beyond the bounds of 7 *with your earliest* at your earliest convenience 9–10 *The purchase . . . you* i.e., though married, we haven't yet consummated our love

Cassio: Welcome, Iago. We must to the watch.

Iago: Not this hour,° Lieutenant; 'tis not yet ten o' the clock. Our general cast° us thus early for the love of his Desdemona; who° let us not therefore blame. He hath not yet made wanton the night with her, and she is sport for Jove.

Cassio: She's a most exquisite lady.

Iago: And, I'll warrant her, full of game.

Cassio: Indeed, she's a most fresh and delicate creature.

Iago: What an eye she has! Methinks it sounds a parley° to provocation.

Cassio: An inviting eye, and yet methinks right modest.

Iago: And when she speaks, is it not an alarum° to love?

Cassio: She is indeed perfection.

Iago: Well, happiness to their sheets! Come, Lieutenant, I have a stoup° of wine, and here without° are a brace° of Cyprus gallants that would fain have a measure° to the health of black Othello.

Cassio: Not tonight, good Iago. I have very poor and unhappy brains for drinking. I could well wish courtesy would invent some other custom of entertainment.

Iago: O, they are our friends. But one cup! I'll drink for you.°

Cassio: I have drunk but one cup tonight, and that was craftily qualified° too, and behold what innovation° it makes here.° I am unfortunate in the infirmity and dare not task my weakness with any more.

Iago: What, man? 'Tis a night of revels. The gallants desire it.

Cassio: Where are they?

Iago: Here at the door. I pray you, call them in.

Cassio: I'll do 't, but it dislikes me.° *Exit.*

Iago: If I can fasten but one cup upon him,
With that which he hath drunk tonight already,
He'll be as full of quarrel and offense°
As my young mistress' dog. Now, my sick fool Roderigo,
Whom love hath turned almost the wrong side out,
To Desdemona hath tonight caroused°
Potations pottle-deep;° and he's to watch.°
Three lads of Cyprus—noble swelling° spirits,
That hold their honors in a wary distance,°
The very elements° of this warlike isle—

13 *Not this hour* not for an hour yet. *cast* dismissed 14 *who* i.e., Othello 20 *sounds a parley* calls for a conference, issues an invitation 22 *alarum* signal calling men to arms (continuing the military metaphor of *parley*, line 20) 24 *stoup* measure of liquor, two quarts 25 *without* outside. *brace* pair 26 *fain have a measure* gladly drink a toast 30 *for you* in your place. (Iago will do the steady drinking to keep the gallants company while Cassio has only one cup.) 31 *qualified* diluted 32 *innovation* disturbance, insurrection. *here* i.e., in my head 37 *it dislikes me* i.e., I'm reluctant 40 *offense* readiness to take offense 43 *caroused* drunk off 44 *pottle-deep* to the bottom of the tankard. *watch* stand watch 45 *swelling* proud 46 *hold . . . distance* i.e., are extremely sensitive of their honor 47 *very elements* typical sort

Have I tonight flustered with flowing cups,
And they watch° too. Now, 'mongst this flock of drunkards
Am I to put our Cassio in some action
That may offend the isle.—But here they come.

Enter Cassio, Montano, and gentlemen [servants following with wine].

If consequence do but approve my dream,°
My boat sails freely both with wind and stream.°

Cassio: 'Fore God, they have given me a rouse° already.

Montano: Good faith, a little one; not past a pint, as I am a soldier.

Iago: Some wine, ho! [*He sings.*]

"And let me the cannikin° clink, clink,
And let me the cannikin clink.
A soldier's a man,
O, man's life's but a span;°
Why, then, let a soldier drink."

Some wine, boys!

Cassio: 'Fore God, an excellent song.

Iago: I learned it in England, where indeed they are most potent in potting.° Your Dane, your German, and your swag-bellied Hollander—drink, ho!—are nothing to your English.

Cassio: Is your Englishman so exquisite in his drinking?

Iago: Why, he drinks you,° with facility, your Dane° dead drunk; he sweats not° to overthrow your Almain;° he gives your Hollander a vomit ere the next pottle can be filled.

Cassio: To the health of our general!

Montano: I am for it, Lieutenant, and I'll do you justice.°

Iago: O sweet England! [*He sings.*]

"King Stephen was a worthy peer,
His breeches cost him but a crown;
He held them sixpence all too dear,
With that he called the tailor lown.

He was a wight of high renown,
And thou art but of low degree.
'Tis pride that pulls the country down;
Then take thy auld° cloak about thee."

Some wine, ho!

49 *watch* are members of the guard 52 *If . . . dream* if subsequent events will only substantiate my scheme 53 *stream* current 54 *rouse* full draft of liquor 57 *cannikin* small drinking vessel 60 *span* brief span of time. (Compare Psalm 39:6 as rendered in the 1928 Book of Common Prayer: "Thou hast made my days as it were a span long.") 64 *potting* drinking 68 *drinks you* drinks. *your Dane* your typical Dane 69 *sweats not* i.e., need not exert himself. *Almain* German 72 *I'll . . . justice* i.e., I'll drink as much as you. *lown* lout, rascal. *pride* i.e., extravagance in dress 81 *auld* old

Iago persuades Cassio to have a drink, "To the health of our general!" (II, iii, 71).

Cassio: 'Fore God, this is a more exquisite song than the other.

Iago: Will you hear 't again?

Cassio: No, for I hold him to be unworthy of his place that does those things. Well, God's above all; and there be souls must be saved, and there be souls must not be saved.

Iago: It's true, good Lieutenant.

Cassio: For mine own part—no offense to the General, nor any man of quality°—I hope to be saved.

Iago: And so do I too, Lieutenant.

Cassio: Ay, but, by your leave, not before me; the lieutenant is to be saved before the ancient. Let's have no more of this; let's to our affairs.—God forgive us our sins!—Gentlemen, let's look to our business. Do not think, gentlemen, I am drunk. This is my ancient; this is my right hand, and this is my left. I am not drunk now. I can stand well enough, and speak well enough.

Gentlemen: Excellent well.

Cassio: Why, very well then; you must not think then that I am drunk. *Exit.*

90 *quality* rank

Montano: To th' platform, masters. Come, let's set the watch.°

[*Exeunt Gentlemen.*]

Iago: You see this fellow that is gone before.
He's a soldier fit to stand by Caesar
And give direction; and do but see his vice.
'Tis to his virtue a just equinox,°
The one as long as th' other. 'Tis pity of him.
I fear the trust Othello puts him in,
On some odd time of his infirmity,
Will shake this island.
Montano: But is he often thus?
Iago: 'Tis evermore the prologue to his sleep.
He'll watch the horologe a double set,°
If drink rock not his cradle.
Montano: It were well
The General were put in mind of it.
Perhaps he sees it not, or his good nature
Prizes the virtue that appears in Cassio
And looks not on his evils. Is not this true?

Enter Roderigo.

Iago [*aside to him*]: How now, Roderigo?
I pray you, after the Lieutenant; go.

[*Exit Roderigo.*]

Montano: And 'tis great pity that the noble Moor
Should hazard such a place as his own second
With° one of an engraffed° infirmity.
It were an honest action to say so
To the Moor.
Iago: Not I, for this fair island.
I do love Cassio well and would do much
To cure him of this evil. [*Cry within: "Help! Help!"*]
But, hark! What noise?

Enter Cassio, pursuing° Roderigo.

Cassio: Zounds, you rogue! You rascal!
Montano: What's the matter, Lieutenant?
Cassio: A knave teach me my duty?

101 *set the watch* mount the guard 105 *just equinox* exact counterpart. (*Equinox* is an equal length of days and nights.) 111 *watch . . . set* stay awake twice around the clock or *horologe* 120–121 *hazard . . . With* risk giving such an important position as his second in command to 121 *engraffed* engrafted, inveterate s.d. *pursuing* (The Quarto text reads, "driving in.")

I'll beat the knave into a twiggen° bottle.
Roderigo: Beat me?
Cassio: Dost thou prate, rogue? [*He strikes Roderigo.*]
Montano: Nay, good Lieutenant. [*Restraining him.*] I pray you, sir, hold your hand.
Cassio: Let me go, sir, or I'll knock you o'er the mazard.°
Montano: Come, come, you're drunk.
Cassio: Drunk? [*They fight.*]
Iago [*aside to Roderigo*]: Away, I say. Go out and cry a mutiny.°

[*Exit Roderigo.*]

Nay, good Lieutenant—God's will, gentlemen—
Help, ho!—Lieutenant—sir—Montano—sir—
Help, masters!°—Here's a goodly watch indeed!

[*A bell rings.*]°

Who's that which rings the bell?—Diablo,° ho!
The town will rise.° God's will, Lieutenant, hold!
You'll be ashamed forever.

Enter Othello and attendants [*with weapons*].

Othello: What is the matter here?
Montano: Zounds, I bleed still.
I am hurt to th' death. He dies! [*He thrusts at Cassio.*]
Othello: Hold, for your lives!
Iago: Hold, ho! Lieutenant—sir—Montano—gentlemen—
Have you forgot all sense of place and duty?
Hold! The General speaks to you. Hold, for shame!
Othello: Why, how now, ho! From whence ariseth this?
Are we turned Turks, and to ourselves do that
Which heaven hath forbid the Ottomites?°
For Christian shame, put by this barbarous brawl!
He that stirs next to carve for° his own rage
Holds his soul light;° he dies upon his motion.°
Silence that dreadful bell. It frights the isle
From her propriety.° What is the matter, masters?

128 *twiggen* wicker-covered (Cassio vows to assail Roderigo until his skin resembles wickerwork or until he has driven Roderigo through the holes in a wickerwork.) 133 *mazard* i.e., head. (Literally, a drinking vessel.) 136 *mutiny* riot 139 *masters* sirs. s.d. *A bell rings* (This direction is from the Quarto, as are *Exit Roderigo* at line 118, *They fight* at line 135, and *with weapons* at line 142.) 140 *Diablo* the devil 141 *rise* grow riotous 149–150 *to ourselves . . . Ottomites* inflict on ourselves the harm that heaven has prevented the Turks from doing (by destroying their fleet) 152 *carve for* i.e., indulge, satisfy with his sword 153 *Holds . . . light* i.e., places little value on his life. *upon his motion* if he moves 155 *propriety* proper state or condition

Honest Iago, that looks dead with grieving,
Speak. Who began this? On thy love, I charge thee.

Iago: I do not know. Friends all but now, even now,
In quarter° and in terms° like bride and groom
Devesting them° for bed; and then, but now—
As if some planet had unwitted men—
Swords out, and tilting one at others' breasts
In opposition bloody. I cannot speak°
Any beginning to this peevish odds;°
And would in action glorious I had lost
Those legs that brought me to a part of it!

Othello: How comes it, Michael, you are thus forgot?°

Cassio: I pray you, pardon me. I cannot speak.

Othello: Worthy Montano, you were wont be° civil;
The gravity and stillness° of your youth
The world hath noted, and your name is great
In mouths of wisest censure.° What's the matter
That you unlace° your reputation thus
And spend your rich opinion° for the name
Of a night-brawler? Give me answer to it.

Montano: Worthy Othello, I am hurt to danger.
Your officer, Iago, can inform you—
While I spare speech, which something° now offends° me—
Of all that I do know; nor know I aught
By me that's said or done amiss this night,
Unless self-charity be sometimes a vice,
And to defend ourselves it be a sin
When violence assails us.

Othello: Now, by heaven,
My blood° begins my safer guides° to rule,
And passion, having my best judgment collied,°
Essays° to lead the way. Zounds, if I stir,
Or do but lift this arm, the best of you
Shall sink in my rebuke. Give me to know
How this foul rout° began, who set it on;
And he that is approved in° this offense,
Though he had twinned with me, both at a birth,
Shall lose me. What? In a town of ° war

159 *In quarter* in friendly conduct, within bounds. *in terms* on good terms 160 *Devesting them* undressing themselves 163 *speak* explain 164 *peevish odds* childish quarrel 167 *are thus forgot* have forgotten yourself thus 169 *wont be* accustomed to be 170 *stillness* sobriety 172 *censure* judgment 173 *unlace* undo, lay open (as one might loose the strings of a purse containing reputation) 174 *opinion* reputation 178 *something* somewhat. *offends* pains 184 *blood* passion (of anger). *guides* i.e., reason 185 *collied* darkened 186 *Essays* undertakes 189 *rout* riot 190 *approved in* found guilty of 192 *town of* town garrisoned for

Yet wild, the people's hearts brim full of fear,
To manage° private and domestic quarrel?
In night, and on the court and guard of safety?°
'Tis monstrous. Iago, who began 't?
Montano [*to Iago*]: If partially affined,° or leagued in office,°
Thou dost deliver more or less than truth,
Thou art no soldier.
Iago: Touch me not so near.
I had rather have this tongue cut from my mouth
Than it should do offense to Michael Cassio;
Yet, I persuade myself, to speak the truth
Shall nothing wrong him. Thus it is, General.
Montano and myself being in speech,
There comes a fellow crying out for help,
And Cassio following him with determined sword
To execute° upon him. Sir, this gentleman

[*indicating Montano*]

Steps in to Cassio and entreats his pause.°
Myself the crying fellow did pursue,
Lest by his clamor—as it so fell out—
The town might fall in fright. He, swift of foot,
Outran my purpose, and I returned, the rather°
For that I heard the clink and fall of swords
And Cassio high in oath, which till tonight
I ne'er might say before. When I came back—
For this was brief—I found them close together
At blow and thrust, even as again they were
When you yourself did part them.
More of this matter cannot I report.
But men are men; the best sometimes forget.°
Though Cassio did some little wrong to him,
As men in rage strike those that wish them best,°
Yet surely Cassio, I believe, received
From him that fled some strange indignity,
Which patience could not pass.°
Othello: I know, Iago,
Thy honesty and love doth mince this matter,
Making it light to Cassio. Cassio, I love thee,

194 *manage* undertake 195 *on . . . safety* at the main guardhouse or headquarters and on watch 197 *partially affined* made partial by some personal relationship. *leagued in office* in league as fellow officers 207 *execute* give effect to (his anger) 208 *his pause* him to stop 212 *rather* sooner 220 *forget* forget themselves 222 *those . . . best* i.e., even those who are well disposed 225 *pass* pass over, overlook

But nevermore be officer of mine.

Enter Desdemona, attended.

Look if my gentle love be not raised up.
I'll make thee an example.

Desdemona: What is the matter, dear?

Othello: All's well now, sweeting;
Come away to bed. [*To Montano.*] Sir, for your hurts,
Myself will be your surgeon.°—Lead him off.

[*Montano is led off.*]

Iago, look with care about the town
And silence those whom this vile brawl distracted.
Come, Desdemona. 'Tis the soldiers' life
To have their balmy slumbers waked with strife.

Exit [*with all but Iago and Cassio*].

Iago: What, are you hurt, Lieutenant?

Cassio: Ay, past all surgery.

Iago: Marry, God forbid!

Cassio: Reputation, reputation, reputation! O, I have lost my reputation! I have lost the immortal part of myself, and what remains is bestial. My reputation, Iago, my reputation!

Iago: As I am an honest man, I thought you had received some bodily wound; there is more sense in that than in reputation. Reputation is an idle and most false imposition,° oft got without merit and lost without deserving. You have lost no reputation at all, unless you repute yourself such a loser. What, man, there are more ways to recover° the General again. You are but now cast in his mood°—a punishment more in policy° than in malice, even so as one would beat his offenseless dog to affright an imperious lion.° Sue° to him again and he's yours.

Cassio: I will rather sue to be despised than to deceive so good a commander with so slight,° so drunken, and so indiscreet an officer. Drunk? And speak parrot?° And squabble? Swagger? Swear? And discourse fustian with one's own shadow? O thou invisible spirit of wine, if thou hast no name to be known by, let us call thee devil!

233 *be your surgeon* i.e., make sure you receive medical attention 246 *false imposition* thing artificially imposed and of no real value 249 *recover* regain favor with. *cast in his mood* dismissed in a moment of anger 250 *in policy* done for expediency's sake and as a public gesture 250–251 *would . . . lion* i.e., would make an example of a minor offender in order to deter more important and dangerous offenders 251 *Sue* petition 254 *slight* worthless 255 *speak parrot* talk nonsense, rant

Iago advises Cassio to ask Desdemona to plead his cause with Othello (II, iii, 238–297).

Iago: What was he that you followed with your sword? What had he done to you?

Cassio: I know not.

Iago: Is 't possible?

Cassio: I remember a mass of things, but nothing distinctly; a quarrel, but nothing wherefore.° O God, that men should put an enemy in their mouths to steal away their brains! That we should, with joy, pleasance, revel, and applause° transform ourselves into beasts!

Iago: Why, but you are now well enough. How came you thus recovered?

Cassio: It hath pleased the devil drunkenness to give place to the devil wrath. One unperfectness shows me another, to make me frankly despise myself.

Iago: Come, you are too severe a moraler.° As the time, the place, and the condition of this country stands, I could heartily wish this had not befallen; but since it is as it is, mend it for your own good.

263 *wherefore* why 265 *applause* desire for applause 270 *moraler* moralizer

Cassio: I will ask him for my place again; he shall tell me I am a drunkard. Had I as many mouths as Hydra,° such an answer would stop them all. To be now a sensible man, by and by a fool, and presently a beast! O, strange! Every inordinate cup is unblessed, and the ingredient is a devil.

Iago: Come, come, good wine is a good familiar creature, if it be well used. Exclaim no more against it. And, good Lieutenant, I think you think I love you.

Cassio: I have well approved° it, sir. I drunk!

Iago: You or any man living may be drunk at a time,° man. I'll tell you what you shall do. Our general's wife is now the general—I may say so in this respect, for that° he hath devoted and given up himself to the contemplation, mark, and denotement° of her parts° and graces. Confess yourself freely to her; importune her help to put you in your place again. She is of so free,° so kind, so apt, so blessed a disposition, she holds it a vice in her goodness not to do more than she is requested. This broken joint between you and her husband entreat her to splinter;° and, my fortunes against any lay° worth naming, this crack of your love shall grow stronger than it was before.

Cassio: You advise me well.

Iago: I protest,° in the sincerity of love and honest kindness.

Cassio: I think it freely;° and betimes in the morning I will beseech the virtuous Desdemona to undertake for me. I am desperate of my fortunes if they check° me here.

Iago: You are in the right. Good night, Lieutenant. I must to the watch.

Cassio: Good night, honest Iago. *Exit Cassio.*

Iago: And what's he then that says I play the villain,
When this advice is free° I give, and honest,
Probal° to thinking, and indeed the course
To win the Moor again? For 'tis most easy
Th' inclining° Desdemona to subdue°
In any honest suit; she's framed as fruitful°
As the free elements.° And then for her
To win the Moor—were 't to renounce his baptism,
All seals and symbols of redeemèd sin—
His soul is so enfettered to her love
That she may make, unmake, do what she list,

274 *Hydra* the Lernaean Hydra, a monster with many heads and the ability to grow two heads when one was cut off, slain by Hercules as the second of his twelve labors 280 *approved* proved 281 *at a time* at one time or another 283 *in . . . that* in view of this fact, that 284 *mark, and denotement* (Both words mean "observation.") *parts* qualities 286 *free* generous 289 *splinter* bind with splints. *lay* stake, wager 292 *protest* insist, declare 293 *freely* unreservedly 295 *check* repulse 299 *free* (1) free from guile (2) freely given 300 *Probal* probable, reasonable 302 *inclining* favorably disposed. *subdue* persuade 303 *framed as fruitful* created as generous 304 *free elements* i.e., earth, air, fire, and water, unrestrained and spontaneous

Even as her appetite° shall play the god
With his weak function.° How am I then a villain,
To counsel Cassio to this parallel° course
Directly to his good? Divinity of hell!°
When devils will the blackest sins put on,°
They do suggest° at first with heavenly shows,
As I do now. For whiles this honest fool
Plies Desdemona to repair his fortune,
And she for him pleads strongly to the Moor,
I'll pour this pestilence into his ear,
That she repeals him° for her body's lust;
And by how much she strives to do him good,
She shall undo her credit with the Moor.
So will I turn her virtue into pitch,°
And out of her own goodness make the net
That shall enmesh them all.
Enter Roderigo. How now, Roderigo?

Roderigo: I do follow here in the chase, not like a hound that hunts, but one that fills up the cry.° My money is almost spent; I have been tonight exceedingly well cudgeled; and I think the issue will be I shall have so much° experience for my pains, and so, with no money at all and a little more wit, return again to Venice.

Iago: How poor are they that have not patience!
What wound did ever heal but by degrees?
Thou know'st we work by wit, and not by witchcraft,
And wit depends on dilatory time.
Does 't not go well? Cassio hath beaten thee,
And thou, by that small hurt, hast cashiered° Cassio.
Though other things grow fair against the sun,
Yet fruits that blossom first will first be ripe.°
Content thyself awhile. By the Mass, 'tis morning!
Pleasure and action make the hours seem short.
Retire thee; go where thou art billeted.
Away, I say! Thou shalt know more hereafter.
Nay, get thee gone. *Exit Roderigo.*
Two things are to be done.

309 *her appetite* her desire, or, perhaps, his desire for her 310 *function* exercise of faculties (weakened by his fondness for her) 311 *parallel* corresponding to these facts and to his best interests 312 *Divinity of hell* inverted theology of hell (which seduces the soul to its damnation) 313 *put on* further, instigate 314 *suggest* tempt 319 *repeals him* attempts to get him restored 322 *pitch* i.e., (1) foul blackness (2) a snaring substance 326 *fills up the cry* merely takes part as one of the pack 328 *so much* just so much and no more 335 *cashiered* dismissed from service 336–337 *Though . . . ripe* i.e., plans that are well prepared and set expeditiously in motion will soonest ripen into success

My wife must move° for Cassio to her mistress;
I'll set her on;
Myself the while to draw the Moor apart
And bring him jump° when he may Cassio find
Soliciting his wife. Ay, that's the way.
Dull not device° by coldness° and delay. *Exit.*

ACT III

SCENE I [BEFORE THE CHAMBER OF OTHELLO AND DESDEMONA.]

Enter Cassio [and] Musicians.

Cassio: Masters, play here—I will content your pains°—
Something that's brief, and bid "Good morrow, General." [*They play.*]

[*Enter*] *Clown.*

Clown: Why, masters, have your instruments been in Naples, that they speak i' the nose° thus?

A Musician: How, sir, how?

Clown: Are these, I pray you, wind instruments?

A Musician: Ay, marry, are they, sir.

Clown: O, thereby hangs a tail.

A Musician: Whereby hangs a tale, sir?

Clown: Marry, sir, by many a wind instrument° that I know. But, masters, here's money for you. [*He gives money.*] And the General so likes your music that he desires you, for love's sake,° to make no more noise with it.

A Musician: Well, sir, we will not.

Clown: If you have any music that may not° be heard, to 't again; but, as they say, to hear music the General does not greatly care.

A Musician: We have none such, sir.

Clown: Then put up your pipes in your bag, for I'll away.° Go, vanish into air, away!

Exeunt Musicians.

Cassio: Dost thou hear, mine honest friend?

343 *move* plead 342 *jump* precisely 344 *device* plot. *coldness* lack of zeal 1 *content your pains* reward your efforts 3–4 *speak i' the nose* (1) sound nasal (2) sound like one whose nose has been attacked by syphilis. (Naples was popularly supposed to have a high incidence of venereal disease.) 10 *wind instrument* (With a joke on flatulence. The *tail*, line 8, that hangs nearby the *wind instrument* suggests the penis.) 12 *for love's sake* (1) out of friendship and affection (2) for the sake of lovemaking in Othello's marriage 14 *may not* cannot 17 *I'll away* (Possibly a misprint, or a snatch of song?)

Cassio sends a message to Desdemona's gentle-woman (III, i, 21–24).

Clown: No, I hear not your honest friend; I hear you.

Cassio: Prithee, keep up° thy quillets.° There's a poor piece of gold for thee. [*He gives money.*] If the gentle-woman that attends the General's wife be stirring, tell her there's one Cassio entreats her a little favor of speech.° Wilt thou do this?

Clown: She is stirring, sir. If she will stir° hither, I shall seem° to notify unto her.

Cassio: Do, good my friend. *Exit Clown.*

Enter Iago.

In happy time,° Iago.

Iago: You have not been abed, then?

Cassio: Why, no. The day had broke

21 *keep up* do not bring out, do not use. *quillets* quibbles, puns 24 *a little . . . speech* the favor of a brief talk 25 *stir* bestir herself (with a play on *stirring*, "rousing herself from rest"). *seem* deem it good, think fit 27 *In happy time* i.e., well met

Before we parted. I have made bold, Iago,
To send in to your wife. My suit to her
Is that she will to virtuous Desdemona
Procure me some access.

Iago: I'll send her to you presently;
And I'll devise a means to draw the Moor
Out of the way, that your converse and business
May be more free.

Cassio: I humbly thank you for 't. *Exit* [*Iago*].
I never knew
A Florentine° more kind and honest.

Enter Emilia.

Emilia: Good morrow, good Lieutenant. I am sorry
For your displeasure;° but all will sure be well.
The General and his wife are talking of it,
And she speaks for you stoutly.° The Moor replies
That he you hurt is of great fame° in Cyprus
And great affinity,° and that in wholesome wisdom
He might not but refuse you; but he protests° he loves you
And needs no other suitor but his likings
To take the safest occasion by the front°
To bring you in again.

Cassio: Yet I beseech you,
If you think fit, or that it may be done,
Give me advantage of some brief discourse
With Desdemona alone.

Emilia: Pray you, come in.
I will bestow you where you shall have time
To speak your bosom° freely.

Cassio: I am much bound to you. [*Exeunt.*]

SCENE II [THE CITADEL.]

Enter Othello, Iago, and Gentlemen.

Othello [*giving letters*]: These letters give, Iago, to the pilot,
And by him do my duties° to the Senate.
That done, I will be walking on the works;°
Repair° there to me.

39 *Florentine* i.e., even a fellow Florentine. (Iago is a Venetian; Cassio is a Florentine.) 41 *displeasure* fall from favor 43 *stoutly* spiritedly 44 *fame* reputation, importance 45 *affinity* kindred, family connection 46 *protests* insists 48 *occasion . . . front* opportunity by the forelock 54 *bosom* inmost thoughts 2 *do my duties* convey my respects 3 *works* breastworks, fortifications 4 *Repair* return, come

Iago: Well, my good lord, I'll do 't.
Othello: This fortification, gentlemen, shall we see 't?
Gentlemen: We'll wait upon° your lordship. *Exeunt.*

SCENE III [THE GARDEN OF THE CITADEL.]

Enter Desdemona, Cassio, and Emilia.

Desdemona: Be thou assured, good Cassio, I will do
All my abilities in thy behalf.
Emilia: Good madam, do. I warrant it grieves my husband
As if the cause were his.
Desdemona: O, that's an honest fellow. Do not doubt, Cassio,
But I will have my lord and you again
As friendly as you were.
Cassio: Bounteous madam,
Whatever shall become of Michael Cassio,
He's never anything but your true servant.
Desdemona: I know 't. I thank you. You do love my lord;
You have known him long, and be you well assured
He shall in strangeness° stand no farther off
Than in a politic° distance.
Cassio: Ay, but, lady,
That policy may either last so long,
Or feed upon such nice and waterish diet,°
Or breed itself so out of circumstance,°
That, I being absent and my place supplied,°
My general will forget my love and service.
Desdemona: Do not doubt° that. Before Emilia here
I give thee warrant° of thy place. Assure thee,
If I do vow a friendship I'll perform it
To the last article. My lord shall never rest.
I'll watch him tame° and talk him out of patience;°
His bed shall seem a school, his board° a shrift;°
I'll intermingle everything he does
With Cassio's suit. Therefore be merry, Cassio,

6 *wait upon* attend 12 *strangeness* aloofness 13 *politic* required by wise policy 15 *Or . . . diet* or sustain itself at length upon such trivial and meager technicalities 16 *breed . . . circumstance* continually renew itself so out of chance events, or yield so few chances for my being pardoned 17 *supplied* filled by another person 19 *doubt* fear 20 *warrant* guarantee 23 *watch him tame* tame him by keeping him from sleeping. (A term from falconry.) *out of patience* past his endurance 24 *board* dining table. *shrift* confessional

For thy solicitor° shall rather die
Than give thy cause away.°

Enter Othello and Iago [at a distance].

Emilia: Madam, here comes my lord.
Cassio: Madam, I'll take my leave.
Desdemona: Why, stay, and hear me speak.
Cassio: Madam, not now. I am very ill at ease,
Unfit for mine own purposes.
Desdemona: Well, do your discretion.° *Exit Cassio.*
Iago: Ha? I like not that.
Othello: What dost thou say?
Iago: Nothing, my lord; or if—I know not what.
Othello: Was not that Cassio parted from my wife?
Iago: Cassio, my lord? No, sure, I cannot think it,
That he would steal away so guiltylike,
Seeing you coming.
Othello: I do believe 'twas he.
Desdemona: How now, my lord?
I have been talking with a suitor here,
A man that languishes in your displeasure.
Othello: Who is 't you mean?
Desdemona: Why, your lieutenant, Cassio. Good my lord,
If I have any grace or power to move you,
His present reconciliation take;°
For if he be not one that truly loves you,
That errs in ignorance and not in cunning,°
I have no judgment in an honest face.
I prithee, call him back.
Othello: Went he hence now?
Desdemona: Yes, faith, so humbled
That he hath left part of his grief with me
To suffer with him. Good love, call him back.
Othello: Not now, sweet Desdemon. Some other time.
Desdemona: But shall 't be shortly?
Othello: The sooner, sweet, for you.
Desdemona: Shall 't be tonight at supper?
Othello: No, not tonight.
Desdemona: Tomorrow dinner,° then?

27 *solicitor* advocate 28 *away* up 34 *do your discretion* act according to your own discretion 49 *His . . . take* let him be reconciled to you right away 51 *in cunning* wittingly 63 *dinner* (The noontime meal.)

Othello: I shall not dine at home.
I meet the captains at the citadel.
Desdemona: Why, then, tomorrow night, or Tuesday morn,
On Tuesday noon, or night, on Wednesday morn.
I prithee, name the time, but let it not
Exceed three days. In faith, he's penitent;
And yet his trespass, in our common reason°—
Save that, they say, the wars must make example
Out of her best°—is not almost° a fault
T' incur a private check.° When shall he come?
Tell me, Othello. I wonder in my soul
What you would ask me that I should deny,
Or stand so mammering on.° What? Michael Cassio,
That came a-wooing with you, and so many a time,
When I have spoke of you dispraisingly,
Hath ta'en your part—to have so much to do
To bring him in!° By 'r Lady, I could do much—
Othello: Prithee, no more. Let him come when he will;
I will deny thee nothing.
Desdemona: Why, this is not a boon.
'Tis as I should entreat you wear your gloves,
Or feed on nourishing dishes, or keep you warm,
Or sue to you to do a peculiar° profit
To your own person. Nay, when I have a suit
Wherein I mean to touch° your love indeed,
It shall be full of poise° and difficult weight,
And fearful to be granted.
Othello: I will deny thee nothing.
Whereon,° I do beseech thee, grant me this,
To leave me but a little to myself.
Desdemona: Shall I deny you? No. Farewell, my lord.
Othello: Farewell, my Desdemona. I'll come to thee straight.°
Desdemona: Emilia, come.—Be as your fancies° teach you;
Whate'er you be, I am obedient. *Exit [with Emilia.]*
Othello: Excellent wretch!° Perdition catch my soul
But I do love thee! And when I love thee not,

70 *common reason* everyday judgments 71–72 *Save . . . best* were it not that, as the saying goes, military discipline requires making an example of the very best men. (He refers to *wars* as a singular concept.) 72 *not almost* scarcely 73 *private check* even a private reprimand 76 *mammering on* wavering about 80 *bring him in* restore him to favor 86 *peculiar* particular, personal 88 *touch* test 89 *poise* weight, heaviness; or equipoise, delicate balance involving hard choice 92 *Whereon* in return for which 95 *straight* straightway 96 *fancies* inclinations 98 *wretch* (A term of affectionate endearment.)

Chaos is come again.°
Iago: My noble lord—
Othello: What dost thou say, Iago?
Iago: Did Michael Cassio, when you wooed my lady,
Know of your love?
Othello: He did, from first to last. Why dost thou ask?
Iago: But for a satisfaction of my thought;
No further harm.
Othello: Why of thy thought, Iago?
Iago: I did not think he had been acquainted with her.
Othello: O, yes, and went between us very oft.
Iago: Indeed?
Othello: Indeed? Ay, indeed. Discern'st thou aught in that?
Is he not honest?
Iago: Honest, my lord?
Othello: Honest. Ay, honest.
Iago: My lord, for aught I know.
Othello: What dost thou think?
Iago: Think, my lord?
Othello: "Think, my lord?" By heaven, thou echo'st me,
As if there were some monster in thy thought
Too hideous to be shown. Thou dost mean something.
I heard thee say even now, thou lik'st not that,
When Cassio left my wife. What didst not like?
And when I told thee he was of my counsel°
In my whole course of wooing, thou criedst "Indeed?"
And didst contract and purse° thy brow together
As if thou then hadst shut up in thy brain
Some horrible conceit.° If thou dost love me,
Show me thy thought.
Iago: My lord, you know I love you.
Othello: I think thou dost;
And, for° I know thou'rt full of love and honesty,
And weigh'st thy words before thou giv'st them breath,
Therefore these stops° of thine fright me the more;
For such things in a false disloyal knave
Are tricks of custom,° but in a man that's just
They're close dilations,° working from the heart

99–100 *And . . . again* i.e., my love for you will last forever, until the end of time when chaos will return. (But with an unconscious, ironic suggestion that, if anything should induce Othello to cease loving Desdemona, the result would be chaos.) 123 *of my counsel* in my confidence 125 *purse* knit 127 *conceit* fancy 131 *for* because 133 *stops* pauses 135 *of custom* customary 136 *close dilations* secret or involuntary expressions or delays

That passion cannot rule.°
Iago: For° Michael Cassio,
I dare be sworn I think that he is honest.
Othello: I think so too.
Iago: Men should be what they seem;
Or those that be not, would they might seem none!°
Othello: Certain, men should be what they seem.
Iago: Why, then, I think Cassio's an honest man.
Othello: Nay, yet there's more in this.
I prithee, speak to me as to thy thinkings,
As thou dost ruminate, and give thy worst of thoughts
The worst of words.
Iago: Good my lord, pardon me.
Though I am bound to every act of duty,
I am not bound to that° all slaves are free to.°
Utter my thoughts? Why, say they are vile and false,
As where's the palace whereinto foul things
Sometimes intrude not? Who has that breast so pure
But some uncleanly apprehensions
Keep leets and law days,° and in sessions sit
With° meditations lawful?°
Othello: Thou dost conspire against thy friend,° Iago,
If thou but think'st him wronged and mak'st his ear
A stranger to thy thoughts.
Iago: I do beseech you,
Though I perchance am vicious° in my guess—
As I confess it is my nature's plague
To spy into abuses, and oft my jealousy°
Shapes faults that are not—that your wisdom then,°
From one° that so imperfectly conceits,°
Would take no notice, nor build yourself a trouble
Out of his scattering° and unsure observance.
It were not for your quiet nor your good,
Nor for my manhood, honesty, and wisdom,
To let you know my thoughts.
Othello: What dost thou mean?
Iago: Good name in man and woman, dear my lord,

137 *That passion cannot rule* i.e., that are too passionately strong to be restrained (referring to the workings), or that cannot rule its own passions (referring to the heart). *For* as for 140 *none* i.e., not to be men, or not seem to be honest 148 *that* that which. *free to* free with respect to 153 *Keep leets and law days* i.e., hold court, set up their authority in one's heart. (*Leets* are a kind of manor court; *law days* are the days courts sit in session, or those sessions.) 154 *With* along with. *lawful* innocent 155 *thy friend* i.e., Othello 158 *vicious* wrong 160 *jealousy* suspicious nature 161 *then* on that account 162 *one* i.e., myself, Iago. *conceits* judges, conjectures 164 *scattering* random

Is the immediate° jewel of their souls.
Who steals my purse steals trash; 'tis something, nothing;
'Twas mine, 'tis his, and has been slave to thousands;
But he that filches from me my good name
Robs me of that which not enriches him
And makes me poor indeed.

Othello: By heaven, I'll know thy thoughts.

Iago: You cannot, if° my heart were in your hand,
Nor shall not, whilst 'tis in my custody.

Othello: Ha?

Iago: O, beware, my lord, of jealousy.
It is the green-eyed monster which doth mock
The meat it feeds on.° That cuckold lives in bliss
Who, certain of his fate, loves not his wronger;°
But O, what damnèd minutes tells° he o'er
Who dotes, yet doubts, suspects, yet fondly loves!

Othello: O misery!

Iago: Poor and content is rich, and rich enough,°
But riches fineless° is as poor as winter
To him that ever fears he shall be poor.
Good God, the souls of all my tribe defend
From jealousy!

Othello: Why, why is this?
Think'st thou I'd make a life of jealousy,
To follow still the changes of the moon
With fresh suspicions?° No! To be once in doubt
Is once° to be resolved.° Exchange me for a goat
When I shall turn the business of my soul
To such exsufflicate and blown° surmises
Matching thy inference.° 'Tis not to make me jealous
To say my wife is fair, feeds well, loves company,
Is free of speech, sings, plays, and dances well;
Where virtue is, these are more virtuous.
Nor from mine own weak merits will I draw
The smallest fear or doubt of her revolt,°
For she had eyes, and chose me. No, Iago,

169 *immediate* essential, most precious 176 *if* even if 179–180 *doth mock . . . on* mocks and torments the heart of its victim, the man who suffers jealousy 181 *his wronger* i.e., his faithless wife. (The unsuspecting cuckold is spared the misery of loving his wife only to discover she is cheating on him.) 182 *tells* counts 185 *Poor . . . enough* to be content with what little one has is the greatest wealth of all. (Proverbial.) 186 *fineless* boundless 192–193 *To follow . . . suspicions* to be constantly imagining new causes for suspicion, changing incessantly like the moon 194 *once* once and for all. *resolved* free of doubt, having settled the matter 196 *exsufflicate and blown* inflated and blown up, rumored about, or, spat out and flyblown, hence, loathsome, disgusting 197 *inference* description or allegation 202 *doubt . . . revolt* fear of her unfaithfulness

I'll see before I doubt; when I doubt, prove;
And on the proof, there is no more but this—
Away at once with love or jealousy.
Iago: I am glad of this, for now I shall have reason
To show the love and duty that I bear you
With franker spirit. Therefore, as I am bound,
Receive it from me. I speak not yet of proof.
Look to your wife; observe her well with Cassio.
Wear your eyes thus, not° jealous nor secure.°
I would not have your free and noble nature,
Out of self-bounty,° be abused.° Look to 't.
I know our country disposition well;
In Venice they do let God see the pranks
They dare not show their husbands; their best conscience
Is not to leave 't undone, but keep 't unknown.
Othello: Dost thou say so?
Iago: She did deceive her father, marrying you;
And when she seemed to shake and fear your looks,
She loved them most.
Othello: And so she did.
Iago: Why, go to,° then!
She that, so young, could give out such a seeming,°
To seel° her father's eyes up close as oak,°
He thought 'twas witchcraft! But I am much to blame.
I humbly do beseech you of your pardon
For too much loving you.
Othello: I am bound° to thee forever.
Iago: I see this hath a little dashed your spirits.
Othello: Not a jot, not a jot.
Iago: I' faith, I fear it has.
I hope you will consider what is spoke
Comes from my love. But I do see you're moved.
I am to pray you not to strain my speech
To grosser issues° nor to larger reach°
Than to suspicion.
Othello: I will not.
Iago: Should you do so, my lord,
My speech should fall into such vile success°
Which my thoughts aimed not. Cassio's my worthy friend.

212 *not* neither. *secure* free from uncertainty 214 *self-bounty* inherent or natural goodness and generosity. *abused* deceived 222 *go to* (An expression of impatience.) 223 *seeming* false appearance 224 *seel* blind. (A term from falconry.) *oak* (A close-grained wood.) 228 *bound* indebted (but perhaps with ironic sense of "tied") 234 *issues* significances. *reach* meaning, scope 238 *success* effect, result

My lord, I see you're moved.
Othello: No, not much moved.
I do not think but Desdemona's honest.°
Iago: Long live she so! And long live you to think so!
Othello: And yet, how nature erring from itself—
Iago: Ay, there's the point! As—to be bold with you—
Not to affect° many proposèd matches
Of her own clime, complexion, and degree,°
Whereto we see in all things nature tends—
Foh! One may smell in such a will° most rank,
Foul disproportion,° thoughts unnatural.
But pardon me. I do not in position°
Distinctly speak of her, though I may fear
Her will, recoiling° to her better° judgment,
May fall to match you with her country forms°
And happily repent.°
Othello: Farewell, farewell!
If more thou dost perceive, let me know more.
Set on thy wife to observe. Leave me, Iago.
Iago [*going*]: My lord, I take my leave.
Othello: Why did I marry? This honest creature doubtless
Sees and knows more, much more, than he unfolds.
Iago [*returning*]: My Lord, I would I might entreat your honor
To scan° this thing no farther. Leave it to time.
Although 'tis fit that Cassio have his place—
For, sure, he fills it up with great ability—
Yet, if you please to hold him off awhile,
You shall by that perceive him and his means.°
Note if your lady strain his entertainment°
With any strong or vehement importunity;
Much will be seen in that. In the meantime,
Let me be thought too busy° in my fears—
As worthy cause I have to fear I am—
And hold her free,° I do beseech your honor.
Othello: Fear not my government.°
Iago: I once more take my leave. *Exit.*
Othello: This fellow's of exceeding honesty,
And knows all qualities,° with a learnèd spirit,

241 *honest* chaste 245 *affect* prefer, desire 246 *clime . . . degree* country, color, and social position 248 *will* sensuality, appetite 249 *disproportion* abnormality 250 *position* argument, proposition 252 *recoiling* reverting. *better* i.e., more natural and reconsidered 253 *fall . . . forms* undertake to compare you with Venetian norms of handsomeness 254 *happily repent* happily repent her marriage 261 *scan* scrutinize 265 *his means* the method he uses (to regain his post) 266 *strain his entertainment* urge his reinstatement 269 *busy* interfering 271 *hold her free* regard her as innocent 272 *government* self-control, conduct 275 *qualities* natures, types

Of human dealings. If I do prove her haggard,°
Though that her jesses° were my dear heartstrings,
I'd whistle her off and let her down the wind°
To prey at fortune.° Haply, for° I am black
And have not those soft parts of conversation°
That chamberers° have, or for I am declined
Into the vale of years—yet that's not much—
She's gone. I am abused,° and my relief
Must be to loathe her. O curse of marriage,
That we can call these delicate creatures ours
And not their appetites! I had rather be a toad
And live upon the vapor of a dungeon
Than keep a corner in the thing I love
For others' uses. Yet, 'tis the plague of great ones;
Prerogatived° are they less than the base.°
'Tis destiny unshunnable, like death.
Even then this forkèd° plague is fated to us
When we do quicken.° Look where she comes.

Enter Desdemona and Emilia.

If she be false, O, then heaven mocks itself!
I'll not believe 't.
Desdemona: How now, my dear Othello?
Your dinner, and the generous° islanders
By you invited, do attend° your presence.
Othello: I am to blame.
Desdemona: Why do you speak so faintly?
Are you not well?
Othello: I have a pain upon my forehead here.
Desdemona: Faith, that's with watching.° 'Twill away again.

[*She offers her handkerchief.*]

Let me but bind it hard, within this hour
It will be well.
Othello: Your napkin° is too little.

276 *haggard* wild (like a wild female hawk) 277 *jesses* straps fastened around the legs of a trained hawk 278 *I'd . . . wind* i.e., I'd let her go forever. (To release a hawk downwind was to invite it not to return.) 279 *prey at fortune* fend for herself in the wild. *Haply, for* perhaps because 280 *soft . . . conversation* pleasing graces of social behavior 281 *chamberers* gallants 283 *abused* deceived 290 *Prerogatived* privileged (to have honest wives). *the base* ordinary citizens. (Socially prominent men are especially prone to the unavoidable destiny of being cuckolded and to the public shame that goes with it.) 292 *forkèd* (An allusion to the horns of the cuckold.) 293 *quicken* receive life. (Quicken may also mean to swarm with maggots as the body festers, as in IV, ii, 69, in which case lines 292–293 suggest that *even then*, in death, we are cuckolded by *forkèd* worms.) 296 *generous* noble 297 *attend* await 301 *watching* too little sleep 303 *napkin* handkerchief

Let it alone.° Come, I'll go in with you.

[*He puts the handkerchief from him, and it drops.*]

Desdemona: I am very sorry that you are not well.

Exit [*with Othello*].

Emilia [*picking up the handkerchief*]: I am glad I have found this napkin.
This was her first remembrance from the Moor.
My wayward° husband hath a hundred times
Wooed me to steal it, but she so loves the token—
For he conjured her she should ever keep it—
That she reserves it evermore about her
To kiss and talk to. I'll have the work ta'en out,°
And give 't Iago. What he will do with it
Heaven knows, not I;
I nothing but to please his fantasy.°

Enter Iago.

Iago: How now? What do you here alone?
Emilia: Do not you chide. I have a thing for you.
Iago: You have a thing for me? It is a common thing°—
Emilia: Ha?
Iago: To have a foolish wife.
Emilia: O, is that all? What will you give me now
For that same handkerchief?
Iago: What handkerchief?
Emilia: What handkerchief?
Why, that the Moor first gave to Desdemona;
That which so often you did bid me steal.
Iago: Hast stolen it from her?
Emilia: No, faith. She let it drop by negligence,
And to th' advantage° I, being here, took 't up.
Look, here 'tis.
Iago: A good wench! Give it me.
Emilia: What will you do with 't, that you have been so earnest
To have me filch it?
Iago [*snatching it*]: Why, what is that to you?
Emilia: If it be not for some purpose of import,
Give 't me again. Poor lady, she'll run mad
When she shall lack° it.

304 *Let it alone* i.e., never mind 308 *wayward* capricious 312 *work ta'en out* design of the embroidery copied 315 *fantasy* whim 318 *common thing* (With bawdy suggestion; *common* suggests coarseness and availability to all comers, and *thing* is a slang term for the pudendum.) 329 *to th' advantage* taking the opportunity 335 *lack* miss.

Emilia gets the fateful handkerchief for Iago (III, iii, 316–335).

Iago: Be not acknown on 't.°
I have use for it. Go, leave me. *Exit Emilia.*
I will in Cassio's lodging lose° this napkin
And let him find it. Trifles light as air
Are to the jealous confirmations strong
As proofs of Holy Writ. This may do something.
The Moor already changes with my poison.
Dangerous conceits° are in their natures poisons,
Which at the first are scarce found to distaste,°
But with a little act° upon the blood
Burn like the mines of sulfur.

Enter Othello.

I did say so.
Look where he comes! Not poppy nor mandragora°

335 *Be . . . on 't* do not confess knowledge of it 337 *lose* (The Folio spelling, *loose*, is a normal spelling for "lose," but it may also contain the idea of "let go," "release.") 342 *conceits* fancies, ideas 343 *distaste* be distasteful 344 *act* action, working 346 *mandragora* an opiate made of the mandrake root

Nor all the drowsy syrups of the world
Shall ever medicine thee to that sweet sleep
Which thou owedst° yesterday.
Othello: Ha, ha, false to me?
Iago: Why, how now, General? No more of that.
Othello: Avaunt! Begone! Thou hast set me on the rack.
I swear 'tis better to be much abused
Than but to know 't a little.
Iago: How now, my lord?
Othello: What sense had I of her stolen hours of lust?
I saw 't not, thought it not, it harmed not me.
I slept the next night well, fed well, was free° and merry;
I found not Cassio's kisses on her lips.
He that is robbed, not wanting° what is stolen,
Let him not know 't and he's not robbed at all.
Iago: I am sorry to hear this.
Othello: I had been happy if the general camp,
Pioners° and all, had tasted her sweet body,
So° I had nothing known. O, now, forever
Farewell the tranquil mind! Farewell content!
Farewell the plumèd troops and the big° wars
That makes ambition virtue! O, farewell!
Farewell the neighing steed and the shrill trump,
The spirit-stirring drum, th' ear-piercing fife,
The royal banner, and all quality,°
Pride,° pomp, and circumstance° of glorious war!
And O, you mortal engines,° whose rude throats
Th' immortal Jove's dread clamors° counterfeit,
Farewell! Othello's occupation's gone.
Iago: Is 't possible, my lord?
Othello: Villain, be sure thou prove my love a whore!
Be sure of it. Give me the ocular proof,
Or, by the worth of mine eternal soul,
Thou hadst been better have been born a dog
Than answer my waked wrath!
Iago: Is 't come to this?
Othello: Make me to see 't, or at the least so prove it
That the probation° bear no hinge nor loop
To hang a doubt on, or woe upon thy life!

349 *thou owedst* you did own 356 *free* carefree 358 *wanting* missing 362 *Pioners* diggers of mines, the lowest grade of soldiers 363 *So* provided 365 *big* stately 369 *quality* character, essential nature 370 *Pride* rich display. *circumstance* pageantry 371 *mortal engines* i.e., cannon. (*Mortal* means "deadly.") 372 *Jove's dread clamors* i.e., thunder 381 *probation* proof

Iago: My noble lord—
Othello: If thou dost slander her and torture me,
Never pray more; abandon all remorse;°
On horror's head horrors accumulate;°
Do deeds to make heaven weep, all earth amazed;°
For nothing canst thou to damnation add
Greater than that.
Iago: O grace! O heaven forgive me!
Are you a man? Have you a soul or sense?
God b' wi' you; take mine office. O wretched fool,°
That lov'st to make thine honesty a vice!°
O monstrous world! Take note, take note, O world,
To be direct and honest is not safe.
I thank you for this profit,° and from hence°
I'll love no friend, sith° love breeds such offense.°
Othello: Nay, stay. Thou shouldst be° honest.
Iago: I should be wise, for honesty's a fool
And loses that° it works for.
Othello: By the world,
I think my wife be honest and think she is not;
I think that thou art just and think thou art not.
I'll have some proof. My name, that was as fresh
As Dian's° visage, is now begrimed and black
As mine own face. If there be cords, or knives,
Poison, or fire, or suffocating streams,
I'll not endure it. Would I were satisfied!
Iago: I see, sir, you are eaten up with passion.
I do repent me that I put it to you.
You would be satisfied?
Othello: Would? Nay, and I will.
Iago: And may; but how? How satisfied, my lord?
Would you, the supervisor,° grossly gape on?
Behold her topped?
Othello: Death and damnation! O!
Iago: It were a tedious difficulty, I think,
To bring them to that prospect. Damn them then,°
If ever mortal eyes do see them bolster°
More° than their own.° What then? How then?

385 *remorse* pity, penitent hope for salvation 386 *horrors accumulate* add still more horrors 387 *amazed* confounded with horror 391 O *wretched fool* (Iago addresses himself as a fool for having carried honesty too far.) 392 *vice* failing, something overdone 395 *profit* profitable instruction. *hence* henceforth 396 *sith* since. *offense* i.e., harm to the one who offers help and friendship 397 *Thou shouldst be* it appears that you are. (But Iago replies in the sense of "ought to be.") 399 *that* what 403 *Dian's* Diana, goddess of the moon and of chastity 411 *supervisor* onlooker 414 *Damn them then* i.e., they would have to be really incorrigible 415 *bolster* go to bed together, share a bolster 416 *More* other. *own* own eyes

What shall I say? Where's satisfaction?
It is impossible you should see this,
Were they as prime° as goats, as hot as monkeys,
As salt° as wolves in pride,° and fools as gross
As ignorance made drunk. But yet I say,
If imputation and strong circumstances°
Which lead directly to the door of truth
Will give you satisfaction, you might have 't.

Othello: Give me a living reason she's disloyal.

Iago: I do not like the office.
But sith° I am entered in this cause so far,
Pricked° to 't by foolish honesty and love,
I will go on. I lay with Cassio lately,
And being troubled with a raging tooth
I could not sleep. There are a kind of men
So loose of soul that in their sleeps will mutter
Their affairs. One of this kind is Cassio.
In sleep I heard him say, "Sweet Desdemona,
Let us be wary, let us hide our loves!"
And then, sir, would he grip and wring my hand,
Cry "O sweet creature!" and then kiss me hard,
As if he plucked up kisses by the roots
That grew upon my lips; then laid his leg
Over my thigh, and sighed, and kissed, and then
Cried, "Cursèd fate that gave thee to the Moor!"

Othello: O monstrous! Monstrous!

Iago: Nay, this was but his dream.

Othello: But this denoted a foregone conclusion.°
'Tis a shrewd doubt,° though it be but a dream.

Iago: And this may help to thicken other proofs
That do demonstrate thinly.

Othello: I'll tear her all to pieces.

Iago: Nay, but be wise. Yet we see nothing done;
She may be honest yet. Tell me but this:
Have you not sometimes seen a handkerchief
Spotted with strawberries° in your wife's hand?

Othello: I gave her such a one. 'Twas my first gift.

Iago: I know not that; but such a handkerchief—
I am sure it was your wife's—did I today
See Cassio wipe his beard with.

419 *prime* lustful 420 *salt* wanton, sensual. *pride* heat 422 *imputation . . . circumstances* strong circumstantial evidence 427 *sith* since 428 *Pricked* spurred 443 *foregone conclusion* concluded experience or action 444 *shrewd doubt* suspicious circumstance 450 *Spotted with strawberries* embroidered with a strawberry pattern

Othello: If it be that—
Iago: If it be that, or any that was hers,
It speaks against her with the other proofs.
Othello: O, that the slave° had forty thousand lives!
One is too poor, too weak for my revenge.
Now do I see 'tis true. Look here, Iago,
All my fond° love thus do I blow to heaven.
'Tis gone.
Arise, black vengeance, from the hollow hell!
Yield up, O love, thy crown and hearted° throne
To tyrannous hate! Swell, bosom, with thy freight,°
For 'tis of aspics'° tongues!
Iago: Yet be content.°
Othello: O, blood, blood, blood!
Iago: Patience, I say. Your mind perhaps may change.
Othello: Never, Iago. Like to the Pontic Sea,°
Whose icy current and compulsive course
Ne'er feels retiring ebb, but keeps due on
To the Propontic° and the Hellespont,°
Even so my bloody thoughts with violent pace
Shall ne'er look back, ne'er ebb to humble love,
Till that a capable° and wide revenge
Swallow them up. Now, by yond marble° heaven,
[*Kneeling*] In the due reverence of a sacred vow
I here engage my words.
Iago: Do not rise yet.
[*He kneels*.°] Witness, you ever-burning lights above,
You elements that clip° us round about,
Witness that here Iago doth give up
The execution° of his wit,° hands, heart,
To wronged Othello's service. Let him command,
And to obey shall be in me remorse,°
What bloody business ever.° [*They rise*.]
Othello: I greet thy love,
Not with vain thanks, but with acceptance bounteous,
And will upon the instant put thee to 't.°

457 *the slave* i.e., Cassio 460 *fond* foolish (but also suggesting "affectionate") 463 *hearted* fixed in the heart 464 *freight* burden 465 *aspics'* venomous serpents' 466 *content* calm 469 *Pontic Sea* Black Sea 472 *Propontic* Sea of Marmara, between the Black Sea and the Aegean. *Hellespont* Dardanelles, straits where the Sea of Marmara joins with the Aegean 475 *capable* ample, comprehensive 476 *marble* i.e., gleaming like marble and unrelenting 479 s.d. *He kneels* (In the Quarto text, Iago kneels here after Othello has knelt at line 477.) 480 *clip* encompass 482 *execution* exercise, action. *wit* mind 484 *remorse* pity (for Othello's wrongs) 485 *ever* soever 487 *to 't* to the proof

Within these three days let me hear thee say
That Cassio's not alive.

Iago: My friend is dead;
'Tis done at your request. But let her live.

Othello: Damn her, lewd minx!° O, damn her, damn her!
Come, go with me apart. I will withdraw
To furnish me with some swift means of death
For the fair devil. Now art thou my lieutenant.

Iago: I am your own forever. *Exeunt.*

SCENE IV [BEFORE THE CITADEL.]

Enter Desdemona, Emilia, and Clown.

Desdemona: Do you know, sirrah,° where Lieutenant Cassio lies?°

Clown: I dare not say he lies anywhere.

Desdemona: Why, man?

Clown: He's a soldier, and for me to say a soldier lies, 'tis stabbing.

Desdemona: Go to. Where lodges he?

Clown: To tell you where he lodges is to tell you where I lie.

Desdemona: Can anything be made of this?

Clown: I know not where he lodges, and for me to devise a lodging and say he lies here, or he lies there, were to lie in mine own throat.°

Desdemona: Can you inquire him out, and be edified by report?

Clown: I will catechize the world for him; that is, make questions, and by them answer.

Desdemona: Seek him, bid him come hither. Tell him I have moved° my lord on his behalf and hope all will be well.

Clown: To do this is within the compass of man's wit, and therefore I will attempt the doing it. *Exit Clown.*

Desdemona: Where should I lose that handkerchief, Emilia?

Emilia: I know not, madam.

Desdemona: Believe me, I had rather have lost my purse
Full of crusadoes;° and but my noble Moor
Is true of mind and made of no such baseness
As jealous creatures are, it were enough
To put him to ill thinking.

Emilia: Is he not jealous?

Desdemona: Who, he? I think the sun where he was born
Drew all such humors° from him.

491 *minx* wanton 1 *sirrah* (A form of address to an inferior.) *lies* lodges. (But the Clown makes the obvious pun.) 9 *lie . . . throat* (1) lie egregiously and deliberately (2) use the windpipe to speak a lie 13 *moved* petitioned 20 *crusadoes* Portuguese gold coins 25 *humors* (Refers to the four bodily fluids thought to determine temperament.)

Othello's suspicions are building: "This hand of yours requires / A sequester from liberty . . ." (III, iv, 30–41).

Emilia: Look where he comes.

Enter Othello.

Desdemona: I will not leave him now till Cassio
Be called to him.—How is 't with you, my lord?
Othello: Well, my good lady. [*Aside.*] O, hardness to dissemble!—
How do you, Desdemona?
Desdemona: Well, my good lord.
Othello: Give me your hand. [*She gives her hand.*] This hand is moist, my lady.
Desdemona: It yet hath felt no age nor known no sorrow.
Othello: This argues° fruitfulness° and liberal° heart.
Hot, hot, and moist. This hand of yours requires
A sequester° from liberty, fasting and prayer,
Much castigation,° exercise devout;°

32 *argues* gives evidence of. *fruitfulness* generosity, amorousness, and fecundity. *liberal* generous and sexually free 34 *sequester* separation, sequestration 35 *castigation* corrective discipline. *exercise devout* i.e., prayer, religious meditation, etc.

For here's a young and sweating devil here
That commonly rebels. 'Tis a good hand,
A frank° one.
Desdemona: You may indeed say so,
For 'twas that hand that gave away my heart.
Othello: A liberal hand. The hearts of old gave hands,°
But our new heraldry is hands, not hearts.°
Desdemona: I cannot speak of this. Come now, your promise.
Othello: What promise, chuck?°
Desdemona: I have sent to bid Cassio come speak with you.
Othello: I have a salt and sorry rheum° offends me;
Lend me thy handkerchief.
Desdemona: Here, my lord. [*She offers a handkerchief.*]
Othello: That which I gave you.
Desdemona: I have it not about me.
Othello: Not?
Desdemona: No, faith, my lord.
Othello: That's a fault. That handkerchief
Did an Egyptian to my mother give.
She was a charmer,° and could almost read
The thoughts of people. She told her, while she kept it
'Twould make her amiable° and subdue my father
Entirely to her love, but if she lost it
Or made a gift of it, my father's eye
Should hold her loathèd and his spirits should hunt
After new fancies.° She, dying, gave it me,
And bid me, when my fate would have me wived,
To give it her.° I did so; and take heed on 't;
Make it a darling like your precious eye.
To lose 't or give 't away were such perdition°
As nothing else could match.
Desdemona: Is 't possible?
Othello: 'Tis true. There's magic in the web° of it.
A sibyl, that had numbered in the world
The sun to course two hundred compasses,°
In her prophetic fury° sewed the work;°
The worms were hallowed that did breed the silk,

38 *frank* generous, open (with sexual suggestion) 40 *The hearts . . . hands* i.e., in former times, people would give their hearts when they gave their hands to something 41 *But . . . hearts* i.e., in our decadent times, the joining of hands is no longer a badge to signify the giving of hearts 43 *chuck* (A term of endearment.) 45 *salt . . . rheum* distressful head cold or watering of the eyes 53 *charmer* sorceress 55 *amiable* desirable 59 *fancies* loves 61 *her* i.e., to my wife 63 *perdition* loss 65 *web* fabric, weaving 67 *compasses* annual circlings. (The *sibyl*, or prophetess, was two hundred years old.) 68 *prophetic fury* frenzy of prophetic inspiration. *work* embroidered pattern

And it was dyed in mummy° which the skillful
Conserved of ° maidens' hearts.
Desdemona: I' faith! Is 't true?
Othello: Most veritable. Therefore look to 't well.
Desdemona: Then would to God that I had never seen 't!
Othello: Ha? Wherefore?
Desdemona: Why do you speak so startingly and rash?°
Othello: Is 't lost? Is 't gone? Speak, is 't out o' the way?°
Desdemona: Heaven bless us!
Othello: Say you?
Desdemona: It is not lost; but what an if° it were?
Othello: How?
Desdemona: I say it is not lost.
Othello: Fetch 't, let me see 't.
Desdemona: Why, so I can, sir, but I will not now.
This is a trick to put me from my suit.
Pray you, let Cassio be received again.
Othello: Fetch me the handkerchief! My mind misgives.
Desdemona: Come, come,
You'll never meet a more sufficient° man.
Othello: The handkerchief!
Desdemona: I pray, talk° me of Cassio.
Othello: The handkerchief!
Desdemona: A man that all his time°
Hath founded his good fortunes on your love,
Shared dangers with you—
Othello: The handkerchief!
Desdemona: I' faith, you are to blame.
Othello: Zounds! *Exit Othello.*
Emilia: Is not this man jealous?
Desdemona: I ne'er saw this before.
Sure, there's some wonder in this handkerchief.
I am most unhappy in the loss of it.
Emilia: 'Tis not a year or two shows us a man.°
They are all but stomachs, and we all but° food;
They eat us hungerly,° and when they are full
They belch us.

Enter Iago and Cassio.

70 *mummy* medicinal or magical preparation drained from mummified bodies 71 *Conserved of* prepared or preserved out of 75 *startingly and rash* disjointedly and impetuously, excitedly 76 *out o' the way* lost, misplaced 79 *an if* if 87 *sufficient* able, complete 88 *talk* talk to 89 *all his time* throughout his career 99 *'Tis . . . man* i.e., you can't really know a man even in a year or two of experience (?), or, real men come along seldom (?) 100 *but* nothing but 101 *hungerly* hungrily

Look you, Cassio and my husband.
Iago [*to Cassio*]: There is no other way; 'tis she must do 't.
And, lo, the happiness!° Go and importune her.
Desdemona: How now, good Cassio? What's the news with you?
Cassio: Madam, my former suit. I do beseech you
That by your virtuous° means I may again
Exist and be a member of his love
Whom I, with all the office° of my heart,
Entirely honor. I would not be delayed.
If my offense be of such mortal° kind
That nor my service past, nor° present sorrows,
Nor purposed merit in futurity
Can ransom me into his love again,
But to know so must be my benefit;°
So shall I clothe me in a forced content,
And shut myself up in° some other course,
To fortune's alms.°
Desdemona: Alas, thrice-gentle Cassio,
My advocation° is not now in tune.
My lord is not my lord; nor should I know him,
Were he in favor° as in humor° altered.
So help me every spirit sanctified
As I have spoken for you all my best
And stood within the blank° of his displeasure
For my free speech! You must awhile be patient.
What I can do I will, and more I will
Than for myself I dare. Let that suffice you.
Iago: Is my lord angry?
Emilia: He went hence but now,
And certainly in strange unquietness.
Iago: Can he be angry? I have seen the cannon
When it hath blown his ranks into the air,
And like the devil from his very arm
Puffed his own brother—and is he angry?
Something of moment° then. I will go meet him.
There's matter in 't indeed, if he be angry.

104 *the happiness* in happy time, fortunately met 107 *virtuous* efficacious 109 *office* loyal service 111 *mortal* fatal 112 *nor . . . nor* neither . . . nor 115 *But . . . benefit* merely to know that my case is hopeless will have to content me (and will be better than uncertainty) 117 *shut . . . in* confine myself to 118 *To fortune's alms* throwing myself on the mercy of fortune 119 *advocation* advocacy 121 *favor* appearance. *humor* mood 124 *within the blank* within point-blank range. (The *blank* is the center of the target.) 134 *of moment* of immediate importance, momentous

Desdemona: I prithee, do so. *Exit [Iago].*
Something, sure, of state,°
Either from Venice, or some unhatched practice°
Made demonstrable here in Cyprus to him,
Hath puddled° his clear spirit; and in such cases
Men's natures wrangle with inferior things,
Though great ones are their object. 'Tis even so;
For let our finger ache, and it indues°
Our other, healthful members even to a sense
Of pain. Nay, we must think men are not gods,
Nor of them look for such observancy°
As fits the bridal.° Beshrew me° much, Emilia,
I was, unhandsome° warrior as I am,
Arraigning his unkindness with° my soul;
But now I find I had suborned the witness,°
And he's indicted falsely.

Emilia: Pray heaven it be
State matters, as you think, and no conception
Nor no jealous toy° concerning you.

Desdemona: Alas the day! I never gave him cause.

Emilia: But jealous souls will not be answered so;
They are not ever jealous for the cause,
But jealous for° they're jealous. It is a monster
Begot upon itself,° born on itself.

Desdemona: Heaven keep that monster from Othello's mind!

Emilia: Lady, amen.

Desdemona: I will go seek him. Cassio, walk hereabout.
If I do find him fit, I'll move your suit
And seek to effect it to my uttermost.

Cassio: I humbly thank your ladyship.

Exit [Desdemona with Emilia].

Enter Bianca.

Bianca: Save° you, friend Cassio!

Cassio: What make° you from home?
How is 't with you, my most fair Bianca?
I' faith, sweet love, I was coming to your house.

136 *of state* concerning state affairs 137 *unhatched practice* as yet unexecuted or undiscovered plot 139 *puddled* muddied 142 *indues* brings to the same condition 145 *observancy* attentiveness 146 *bridal* wedding (when a bridegroom is newly attentive to his bride). *Beshrew me* (A mild oath.) 147 *unhandsome* insufficient, unskillful 148 *with* before the bar of 149 *suborned the witness* induced the witness to give false testimony 152 *toy* fancy 156 *for* because 157 *Begot upon itself* generated solely from itself 164 *Save* God save. *make* do

Cassio explains to Bianca that he does not know how the handkerchief appeared in his room (III, iv, 171–186).

Bianca: And I was going to your lodging, Cassio.
What, keep a week away? Seven days and nights?
Eightscore-eight° hours? And lovers' absent hours
More tedious than the dial° eightscore times?
O weary reckoning!
Cassio: Pardon me, Bianca.
I have this while with leaden thoughts been pressed;
But I shall, in a more continuate° time,
Strike off this score° of absence. Sweet Bianca,

[*giving her Desdemona's handkerchief*]

Take me this work out.°
Bianca: O Cassio, whence came this?
This is some token from a newer friend.°
To the felt absence now I feel a cause.
Is 't come to this? Well, well.
Cassio: Go to, woman!
Throw your vile guesses in the devil's teeth,
From whence you have them. You are jealous now

169 *Eightscore-eight* one hundred sixty-eight, the number of hours in a week 170 *the dial* a complete revolution of the clock 173 *continuate* uninterrupted 174 *Strike . . . score* settle this account 175 *Take . . . out* copy this embroidery for me 176 *friend* mistress

That this is from some mistress, some remembrance.
No, by my faith, Bianca.
Bianca: Why, whose is it?
Cassio: I know not, neither. I found it in my chamber.
I like the work well. Ere it be demanded°—
As like° enough it will—I would have it copied.
Take it and do 't, and leave me for this time.
Bianca: Leave you? Wherefore?
Cassio: I do attend here on the General,
And think it no addition,° nor my wish,
To have him see me womaned.
Bianca: Why, I pray you?
Cassio: Not that I love you not.
Bianca: But that you do not love me.
I pray you, bring° me on the way a little,
And say if I shall see you soon at night.
Cassio: 'Tis but a little way that I can bring you,
For I attend here; but I'll see you soon.
Bianca: 'Tis very good. I must be circumstanced.°

Exeunt omnes.

ACT IV

SCENE I [BEFORE THE CITADEL.]

Enter Othello and Iago.

Iago: Will you think so?
Othello: Think so, Iago?
Iago: What,
To kiss in private?
Othello: An unauthorized kiss!
Iago: Or to be naked with her friend in bed
An hour or more, not meaning any harm?
Othello: Naked in bed, Iago, and not mean harm?
It is hypocrisy against the devil.
They that mean virtuously and yet do so,
The devil their virtue tempts, and they tempt heaven.
Iago: If they do nothing, 'tis a venial° slip.
But if I give my wife a handkerchief—
Othello: What then?

184 *demanded* inquired for 185 *like* likely 189 *addition* i.e., addition to my reputation 194 *bring* accompany 198 *be circumstanced* be governed by circumstance, yield to your conditions 9 *venial* pardonable

Iago: Why then, 'tis hers, my lord, and being hers,
She may, I think, bestow 't on any man.
Othello: She is protectress of her honor too.
May she give that?
Iago: Her honor is an essence that's not seen;
They have it° very oft that have it not.
But, for the handkerchief—
Othello: By heaven, I would most gladly have forgot it.
Thou saidst—O, it comes o'er my memory
As doth the raven o'er the infectious house,°
Boding to all—he had my handkerchief.
Iago: Ay, what of that?
Othello: That's not so good now.
Iago: What
If I had said I had seen him do you wrong?
Or heard him say—as knaves be such abroad,°
Who having, by their own importunate suit,
Or voluntary dotage° of some mistress,
Convincèd or supplied° them, cannot choose
But they must blab—
Othello: Hath he said anything?
Iago: He hath, my lord; but, be you well assured,
No more than he'll unswear.
Othello: What hath he said?
Iago: Faith, that he did—I know not what he did.
Othello: What? What?
Iago: Lie—
Othello: With her?
Iago: With her, on her; what you will.
Othello: Lie with her? Lie on her? We say "lie on her" when they belie° her. Lie with her? Zounds, that's fulsome.°—Handkerchief—confessions—handkerchief!—To confess and be hanged for his labor—first to be hanged and then to confess.°—I tremble at it. Nature would not invest herself in such shadowing passion without some instruction.° It is not words° that shakes me thus. Pish! Noses, ears, and lips.—Is't possible?—Confess—handkerchief!— O devil!

17 *They have it* i.e., they enjoy a reputation for it 21 *raven . . . house* (Allusion to the belief that the raven hovered over a house of sickness or infection, such as one visited by the plague.) 25 *abroad* around about 27 *voluntary dotage* willing infatuation 28 *Convincèd or supplied* seduced or sexually gratified 36 *belie* slander 36 *fulsome* foul 38 *first . . . to confess* (Othello reverses the proverbial *confess* and *be hanged*; Cassio is to be given no time to confess before he dies.) 39–40 *Nature . . . instruction* i.e., without some foundation in fact, nature would not have dressed herself in such an overwhelming passion that comes over me now and fills my mind with images, or in such a lifelike fantasy as Cassio had in his dream of lying with Desdemona 40 *words* mere words

Falls in a trance.

Iago: Work on,
My medicine, work! Thus credulous fools are caught,
And many worthy and chaste dames even thus,
All guiltless, meet reproach.—What, ho! My lord!
My lord, I say! Othello!

Enter Cassio.

How now, Cassio?
Cassio: What's the matter?
Iago: My lord is fall'n into an epilepsy.
This is his second fit. He had one yesterday.
Cassio: Rub him about the temples.
Iago: No, forbear.
The lethargy° must have his° quiet course.
If not, he foams at mouth, and by and by
Breaks out to savage madness. Look, he stirs.
Do you withdraw yourself a little while.
He will recover straight. When he is gone,
I would on great occasion° speak with you.

[Exit Cassio.]

How is it, General? Have you not hurt your head?
Othello: Dost thou mock me?°
Iago: I mock you not, by heaven.
Would you would bear your fortune like a man!
Othello: A hornèd man's a monster and a beast.
Iago: There's many a beast then in a populous city,
And many a civil° monster.
Othello: Did he confess it?
Iago: Good sir, be a man.
Think every bearded fellow that's but yoked°
May draw with you.° There's millions now alive
That nightly lie in those unproper° beds
Which they dare swear peculiar.° Your case is better.°
O, 'tis the spite of hell, the fiend's arch-mock,
To lip° a wanton in a secure° couch
And to suppose her chaste! No, let me know,

51 *lethargy* coma. *his* its 56 *on great occasion* on a matter of great importance 58 *mock me* (Othello takes Iago's question about hurting his head to be a mocking reference to the cuckold's horns.) 62 *civil* i.e., dwelling in a city 65 *yoked* (1) married (2) put into the yoke of infamy and cuckoldry 66 *draw with you* pull as you do, like oxen who are yoked, i.e., share your fate as cuckold 67 *unproper* not exclusively their own 68 *peculiar* private, their own. *better* i.e., because you know the truth 70 *lip* kiss. *secure* free from suspicion

And knowing what I am,° I know what she shall be.°
Othello: O, thou art wise. 'Tis certain.
Iago: Stand you awhile apart;
Confine yourself but in a patient list.°
Whilst you were here o'erwhelmèd with your grief—
A passion most unsuiting such a man—
Cassio came hither. I shifted him away,°
And laid good 'scuse upon your ecstasy,°
Bade him anon return and here speak with me,
The which he promised. Do but encave° yourself
And mark the fleers,° the gibes, and notable° scorns
That dwell in every region of his face;
For I will make him tell the tale anew,
Where, how, how oft, how long ago, and when
He hath and is again to cope° your wife.
I say, but mark his gesture. Marry, patience!
Or I shall say you're all-in-all in spleen,°
And nothing of a man.
Othello: Dost thou hear, Iago?
I will be found most cunning in my patience;
But—dost thou hear?—most bloody.
Iago: That's not amiss;
But yet keep time° in all. Will you withdraw?

[*Othello stands apart.*]

Now will I question Cassio of Bianca,
A huswife° that by selling her desires
Buys herself bread and clothes. It is a creature
That dotes on Cassio—as 'tis the strumpet's plague
To beguile many and be beguiled by one.
He, when he hears of her, cannot restrain°
From the excess of laughter. Here he comes.

Enter Cassio.

As he shall smile, Othello shall go mad;
And his unbookish° jealousy must conster°
Poor Cassio's smiles, gestures, and light behaviors
Quite in the wrong.—How do you now, Lieutenant?

72 *what I am* i.e., a cuckold. *she shall be* will happen to her 75 *in . . . list* within the bounds of patience 78 *shifted him away* used a dodge to get rid of him 79 *ecstasy* trance 81 *encave* conceal 82 *fleers* sneers. *notable* obvious 86 *cope* encounter with, have sex with 88 *all-in-all in spleen* utterly governed by passionate impulses 92 *keep time* keep yourself steady (as in music) 94 *huswife* hussy 98 *restrain* refrain 101 *unbookish* uninstructed. *conster* construe

Cassio: The worser that you give me the addition°
Whose want° even kills me.
Iago: Ply Desdemona well and you are sure on 't.
[*Speaking lower.*] Now, if this suit lay in Bianca's power,
How quickly should you speed!
Cassio [*laughing*]: Alas, poor caitiff!°
Othello [*aside*]: Look how he laughs already!
Iago: I never knew a woman love man so.
Cassio: Alas, poor rogue! I think, i' faith, she loves me.
Othello: Now he denies it faintly, and laughs it out.
Iago: Do you hear, Cassio?
Othello: Now he importunes him
To tell it o'er. Go to!° Well said,° well said.
Iago: She gives it out that you shall marry her.
Do you intend it?
Cassio: Ha, ha, ha!
Othello: Do you triumph, Roman?° Do you triumph?
Cassio: I marry her? What? A customer?° Prithee, bear some charity to my wit;° do not think it so unwholesome. Ha, ha, ha!
Othello: So, so, so, so! They laugh that win.°
Iago: Faith, the cry° goes that you shall marry her.
Cassio: Prithee, say true.
Iago: I am a very villain else.°
Othello: Have you scored me?° Well.
Cassio: This is the monkey's own giving out. She is persuaded I will marry her out of her own love and flattery,° not out of my promise.
Othello: Iago beckons° me. Now he begins the story.
Cassio: She was here even now; she haunts me in every place. I was the other day talking on the seabank° with certain Venetians, and thither comes the bauble,° and, by this hand,° she falls me thus about my neck—

[*He embraces Iago.*]

Othello: Crying, "O dear Cassio!" as it were; his gesture imports it.
Cassio: So hangs and lolls and weeps upon me, so shakes and pulls me. Ha, ha, ha!
Othello: Now he tells how she plucked him to my chamber. O, I see that nose of yours, but not that dog I shall throw it to.°

104 *addition* title 105 *Whose want* the lack of which 109 *caitiff* wretch 115 *Go to* (An expression of remonstrance.) *Well said* well done 119 *Roman* (The Romans were noted for their *triumphs* or triumphal processions.) 120 *customer* i.e., prostitute 120–121 *bear . . . wit* be more charitable to my judgment 122 *They . . . win* i.e., they that laugh last laugh best 123 *cry* rumor 125 *I . . . else* call me a complete rogue if I'm not telling the truth 126 *scored me* scored off me, beaten me, made up my reckoning, branded me 128 *flattery* self-flattery, self-deception 129 *beckons* signals 131 *seabank* seashore. 132 *bauble* plaything. *by this hand* I make my vow 137 *not . . . to* (Othello imagines himself cutting off Cassio's nose and throwing it to a dog.)

Cassio: Well, I must leave her company.
Iago: Before me,° look where she comes.

Enter Bianca [with Othello's handkerchief].

Cassio: 'Tis such another fitchew!° Marry, a perfumed one.—What do you mean by this haunting of me?
Bianca: Let the devil and his dam° haunt you! What did you mean by that same handkerchief you gave me even now? I was a fine fool to take it. I must take out the work? A likely piece of work,° that you should find it in your chamber and know not who left it there! This is some minx's token, and I must take out the work? There; give it your hobbyhorse.° [*She gives him the handkerchief.*] Wheresoever you had it, I'll take out no work on 't.
Cassio: How now, my sweet Bianca? How now? How now?
Othello: By heaven, that should be° my handkerchief!
Bianca: If you'll come to supper tonight, you may; if you will not, come when you are next prepared for.° *Exit.*
Iago: After her, after her.
Cassio: Faith, I must. She'll rail in the streets else.
Iago: Will you sup there?
Cassio: Faith, I intend so.
Iago: Well, I may chance to see you, for I would very fain speak with you.
Cassio: Prithee, come. Will you?
Iago: Go to.° Say no more. [*Exit Cassio.*]
Othello [*advancing*]: How shall I murder him, Iago?
Iago: Did you perceive how he laughed at his vice?
Othello: O, Iago!
Iago: And did you see the handkerchief?
Othello: Was that mine?
Iago: Yours, by this hand. And to see how he prizes the foolish woman your wife! She gave it him, and he hath given it his whore.
Othello: I would have him nine years a-killing. A fine woman! A fair woman! A sweet woman!
Iago: Nay, you must forget that.
Othello: Ay, let her rot and perish, and be damned tonight, for she shall not live. No, my heart is turned to stone; I strike it, and it hurts my hand. O, the world hath not a sweeter creature! She might lie by an emperor's side and command him tasks.
Iago: Nay, that's not your way.°

139 *Before me* i.e., on my soul 140 *'Tis . . . fitchew* what a polecat she is! Just like all the others. (Polecats were often compared with prostitutes because of their rank smell and presumed lechery.) 142 *dam* mother 144 *A likely . . . work* a fine story 147 *hobbyhorse* harlot 150 *should be* must be 152 *when . . . for* when I'm ready for you (i.e., never) 159 *Go to* (An expression of remonstrance.) 174 *your way* i.e., the way you should think of her

Othello: Hang her! I do but say what she is. So delicate with her needle! An admirable musician! O, she will sing the savageness out of a bear. Of so high and plenteous wit and invention!°
Iago: She's the worse for all this.
Othello: O, a thousand, a thousand times! And then, of so gentle a condition!°
Iago: Ay, too gentle.°
Othello: Nay, that's certain. But yet the pity of it, Iago! O, Iago, the pity of it, Iago!
Iago: If you are so fond° over her iniquity, give her patent° to offend, for if it touch not you it comes near nobody.
Othello: I will chop her into messes.° Cuckold me?
Iago: O, 'tis foul in her.
Othello: With mine officer?
Iago: That's fouler.
Othello: Get me some poison, Iago, this night. I'll not expostulate with her, lest her body and beauty unprovide° my mind again. This night, Iago.
Iago: Do it not with poison. Strangle her in her bed, even the bed she hath contaminated.
Othello: Good, good! The justice of it pleases. Very good.
Iago: And for Cassio, let me be his undertaker.° You shall hear more by midnight.
Othello: Excellent good. [*A trumpet within.*] What trumpet is that same?
Iago: I warrant, something from Venice.

Enter Lodovico, Desdemona, and attendants.

'Tis Lodovico. This comes from the Duke.
See, your wife's with him.
Lodovico: God save you, worthy General!
Othello: With all my heart,° sir.
Lodovico [*giving him a letter*]: The Duke and the senators of Venice greet you.
Othello: I kiss the instrument of their pleasures.

[*He opens the letter, and reads.*]

Desdemona: And what's the news, good cousin Lodovico?
Iago: I am very glad to see you, signor.
Welcome to Cyprus.
Lodovico: I thank you. How does Lieutenant Cassio?
Iago: Lives, sir.
Desdemona: Cousin, there's fall'n between him and my lord

177 *invention* imagination 179 *gentle a condition* wellborn and well-bred 180 *gentle* generous, yielding (to other men) 183 *fond* foolish. *patent* license 185 *messes* portions of meat, i.e., bits 190 *unprovide* weaken, render unfit 194 *be his undertaker* undertake to dispatch him 200 *With all my heart* i.e., I thank you most heartily

An unkind° breach; but you shall make all well.
Othello: Are you sure of that?
Desdemona: My lord?
Othello [*reads*]: "This fail you not to do, as you will—"
Lodovico: He did not call; he's busy in the paper.
Is there division twixt my lord and Cassio?
Desdemona: A most unhappy one. I would do much
T' atone° them, for the love I bear to Cassio.
Othello: Fire and brimstone!
Desdemona: My lord?
Othello: Are you wise?
Desdemona: What, is he angry?
Lodovico: Maybe the letter moved him;
For, as I think, they do command him home,
Deputing Cassio in his government.°
Desdemona: By my troth, I am glad on 't.°
Othello: Indeed?
Desdemona: My lord?
Othello: I am glad to see you mad.°
Desdemona: Why, sweet Othello—
Othello [*striking her*]: Devil!
Desdemona: I have not deserved this.
Lodovico: My lord, this would not be believed in Venice,
Though I should swear I saw 't. 'Tis very much.°
Make her amends; she weeps.
Othello: O devil, devil!
If that the earth could teem° with woman's tears,
Each drop she falls would prove a crocodile.°
Out of my sight!
Desdemona: I will not stay to offend you. [*Going.*]
Lodovico: Truly, an obedient lady.
I do beseech your lordship, call her back.
Othello: Mistress!
Desdemona [*returning*]: My lord?
Othello: What would you with her, sir?°
Lodovico: Who, I, my lord?
Othello: Ay, you did wish that I would make her turn.
Sir, she can turn, and turn, and yet go on

209 *unkind* unnatural, contrary to their natures; hurtful 216 *atone* reconcile 222 *government* office 223 *on 't* of it 226 *I am . . . mad* i.e., I am glad to see that you are insane enough to rejoice in Cassio's promotion (?) (Othello bitterly plays on Desdemona's *I am glad.*) 231 *very much* too much, outrageous 233 *teem* breed, be impregnated 234 *falls . . . crocodile* (Crocodiles were supposed to weep hypocritical tears for their victims.) 240 *What . . . sir* (Othello implies that Desdemona is pliant and will do a *turn*, lines 242–244 for any man.)

And turn again; and she can weep, sir, weep;
And she's obedient,° as you say, obedient,
Very obedient.—Proceed you in your tears.—
Concerning this, sir—O well-painted passion!°—
I am commanded home.—Get you away;
I'll send for you anon.—Sir, I obey the mandate
And will return to Venice.—Hence, avaunt!

[*Exit Desdemona.*]

Cassio shall have my place. And, sir, tonight
I do entreat that we may sup together.
You are welcome, sir, to Cyprus.—Goats and monkeys!° *Exit.*

Lodovico: Is this the noble Moor whom our full Senate
Call all in all sufficient? Is this the nature
Whom passion could not shake? Whose solid virtue
The shot of accident nor dart of chance
Could neither graze nor pierce?

Iago: He is much changed.

Lodovico: Are his wits safe? Is he not light of brain?

Iago: He's that he is. I may not breathe my censure
What he might be. If what he might he is not,
I would to heaven he were!°

Lodovico: What, strike his wife?

Iago: Faith, that was not so well; yet would I knew
That stroke would prove the worst!

Lodovico: Is it his use?°
Or did the letters work upon his blood°
And new-create his fault?

Iago: Alas, alas!
It is not honesty in me to speak
What I have seen and known. You shall observe him,
And his own courses will denote° him so
That I may save my speech. Do but go after,
And mark how he continues.

Lodovico: I am sorry that I am deceived in him. *Exeunt.*

245 *obedient* (With much the same sexual connotation as *turn* in lines 242–244.) 247 *passion* i.e., grief 253 *Goats and monkeys* (See III, iii, 419.) 260–262 *I may . . . were* i.e., I dare not venture an opinion as to whether he's of unsound mind, as you suggest, but, if he isn't, then it might be better to wish he were in fact insane, since only that could excuse his wild behavior 264 *use* custom 265 *blood* passions 269 *courses will denote* actions will reveal

SCENE II [THE CITADEL.]

Enter Othello and Emilia.

Othello: You have seen nothing then?
Emilia: Nor ever heard, nor ever did suspect.
Othello: Yes, you have seen Cassio and she together.
Emilia: But then I saw no harm, and then I heard
Each syllable that breath made up between them.
Othello: What, did they never whisper?
Emilia: Never, my lord.
Othello: Nor send you out o' the way?
Emilia: Never.
Othello: To fetch her fan, her gloves, her mask, nor nothing?
Emilia: Never, my lord.
Othello: That's strange.
Emilia: I durst, my lord, to wager she is honest,
Lay down my soul at stake.° If you think other,
Remove your thought; it doth abuse your bosom.°
If any wretch have put this in your head,
Let heaven requite it with the serpent's curse!°
For if she be not honest, chaste, and true,
There's no man happy; the purest of their wives
Is foul as slander.
Othello: Bid her come hither. Go.

Exit Emilia.

She says enough; yet she's a simple bawd
That cannot say as much.° This° is a subtle whore,
A closet lock and key° of villainous secrets.
And yet she'll kneel and pray; I have seen her do 't.

Enter Desdemona and Emilia.

Desdemona: My lord, what is your will?
Othello: Pray you, chuck, come hither.
Desdemona: What is your pleasure?
Othello: Let me see your eyes.
Look in my face.
Desdemona: What horrible fancy's this?

14 *at stake* as the wager 15 *abuse your bosom* deceive you 17 *the serpent's curse* the curse pronounced by God on the serpent for deceiving Eve, just as some man has done to Othello and Desdemona. (See Genesis 3:14.) 21–22 *she's . . . much* i.e., any procuress or go-between who couldn't make up as plausible a story as Emilia's would have to be pretty stupid 22 *This* i.e., Desdemona 23 *closet lock and key* i.e., concealer

"Ah, Desdemon! Away, away, away!" (IV, ii, 43).

Othello [*to Emilia*]: Some of your function,° mistress.
Leave procreants° alone and shut the door;
Cough or cry "hem" if anybody come.
Your mystery, your mystery!° Nay, dispatch.

Exit Emilia.

Desdemona [*kneeling*]: Upon my knees, what doth your speech import?
I understand a fury in your words,
But not the words.
Othello: Why, what art thou?
Desdemona: Your wife, my lord, your true
And loyal wife.
Othello: Come, swear it, damn thyself,
Lest, being like one of heaven,° the devils themselves
Should fear to seize thee. Therefore be double damned:
Swear thou art honest.
Desdemona: Heaven doth truly know it.
Othello: Heaven truly knows that thou art false as hell.

29 *Some . . . function* i.e., practice your chosen profession, that of bawd (by guarding the door) 30 *procreants* mating couples 32 *mystery* trade, occupation 38 *being . . . heaven* looking like an angel

Desdemona: To whom, my lord? With whom? How am I false?
Othello [*weeping*]: Ah, Desdemon! Away, away, away!
Desdemona: Alas the heavy day! Why do you weep?
Am I the motive° of these tears, my lord?
If haply you my father do suspect
An instrument of this your calling back,
Lay not your blame on me. If you have lost him,
I have lost him too.
Othello: Had it pleased heaven
To try me with affliction, had they° rained
All kinds of sores and shames on my bare head,
Steeped me in poverty to the very lips,
Given to captivity me and my utmost hopes,
I should have found in some place of my soul
A drop of patience. But, alas, to make me
A fixèd figure for the time of scorn°
To point his° slow and moving finger° at!
Yet could I bear that too, well, very well.
But there where I have garnered° up my heart,
Where either I must live or bear no life,
The fountain° from the which my current runs
Or else dries up—to be discarded thence!
Or keep it as a cistern° for foul toads
To knot° and gender° in! Turn thy complexion there,°
Patience, thou young and rose-lipped cherubin—
Ay, there look grim as hell!°
Desdemona: I hope my noble lord esteems me honest.°
Othello: O, ay, as summer flies are in the shambles,°
That quicken° even with blowing.° O thou weed,
Who art so lovely fair and smell'st so sweet
That the sense aches at thee, would thou hadst ne'er been born!
Desdemona: Alas, what ignorant sin° have I committed?
Othello: Was this fair paper, this most goodly book,
Made to write "whore" upon? What committed?
Committed? O thou public commoner!°

45 *motive* cause 50 *they* i.e., heavenly powers 56 *time of scorn* i.e., scornful world 57 *his* its. *slow and moving finger* i.e., hour hand of the clock, moving so slowly it seems hardly to move at all. (Othello envisages himself as being eternally pointed at by the scornful world as the numbers on a clock are pointed at by the hour hand.) 59 *garnered* stored 61 *fountain* spring 63 *cistern* cesspool 64 *knot* couple. *gender* engender. *Turn . . . there* change your color, grow pale, at such a sight 65–66 *Patience . . . hell* (Even Patience, that rose-lipped cherub, will look grim and pale at this spectacle.) 67 *honest* chaste 68 *shambles* slaughterhouse 69 *quicken* come to life. *with blowing* i.e., with the puffing up of something rotten in which maggots are breeding 72 *ignorant sin* sin in ignorance 75 *commoner* prostitute

Othello berates Desdemona as a "strumpet" and "cunning whore" (IV, ii, 73–98).

I should make very forges of my cheeks,
That would to cinders burn up modesty,
Did I but speak thy deeds. What committed?
Heaven stops the nose at it and the moon winks;°
The bawdy° wind, that kisses all it meets,
Is hushed within the hollow mine° of earth
And will not hear 't. What committed?
Impudent strumpet!

Desdemona: By heaven, you do me wrong.

Othello: Are not you a strumpet?

Desdemona: No, as I am a Christian.
If to preserve this vessel° for my lord
From any other foul unlawful touch
Be not to be a strumpet, I am none.

Othello: What, not a whore?

Desdemona: No, as I shall be saved.

Othello: Is 't possible?

Desdemona: O, heaven forgive us!

Othello: I cry you mercy,° then.

79 *winks* closes her eyes. (The moon symbolizes chastity.) 80 *bawdy* kissing one and all 81 *mine* cave (where the winds were thought to dwell) 86 *vessel* body 92 *cry you mercy* beg your pardon

I took you for that cunning whore of Venice
That married with Othello. [*Calling out*.] You, mistress,
That have the office opposite to Saint Peter
And keep the gate of hell!

Enter Emilia.

You, you, ay, you!
We have done our course.° There's money for your pains.
[*He gives money*.]
I pray you, turn the key and keep our counsel.
Exit.

Emilia: Alas, what does this gentleman conceive?°
How do you, madam? How do you, my good lady?
Desdemona: Faith, half asleep.°
Emilia: Good madam, what's the matter with my lord?
Desdemona: With who?
Emilia: Why, with my lord, madam.
Desdemona: Who is thy lord?
Emilia: He that is yours, sweet lady.
Desdemona: I have none. Do not talk to me, Emilia.
I cannot weep, nor answers have I none
But what should go by water.° Prithee, tonight
Lay on my bed my wedding sheets, remember;
And call thy husband hither.
Emilia: Here's a change indeed! *Exit.*
Desdemona: 'Tis meet I should be used so, very meet.°
How have I been behaved, that he might stick°
The small'st opinion° on my least misuse?°

Enter Iago.

Iago: What is your pleasure, madam? How is 't with you?
Desdemona: I cannot tell. Those that do teach young babes
Do it with gentle means and easy tasks.
He might have chid me so, for, in good faith,
I am a child to chiding.
Iago: What is the matter, lady?
Emilia: Alas, Iago, my lord hath so bewhored her,
Thrown such despite and heavy terms upon her,
That true hearts cannot bear it.

97 *course* business (with an indecent suggestion of "trick," turn at sex) 99 *conceive* suppose, think 101 *half asleep* i.e., dazed 108 *go by water* be expressed by tears 112 *meet* fitting 113 *stick* attach 114 *opinion* censure. *least misuse* slightest misconduct

Desdemona: Am I that name, Iago?
Iago: What name, fair lady?
Desdemona: Such as she said my lord did say I was.
Emilia: He called her whore. A beggar in his drink
Could not have laid such terms upon his callet.°
Iago: Why did he so?
Desdemona [*weeping*]*:* I do not know. I am sure I am none such.
Iago: Do not weep, do not weep. Alas the day!
Emilia: Hath she forsook so many noble matches,
Her father and her country and her friends,
To be called whore? Would it not make one weep?
Desdemona: It is my wretched fortune.
Iago: Beshrew° him for 't!
How comes this trick° upon him?
Desdemona: Nay, heaven doth know.
Emilia: I will be hanged if some eternal° villain,
Some busy and insinuating° rogue,
Some cogging,° cozening° slave, to get some office,
Have not devised this slander. I will be hanged else.
Iago: Fie, there is no such man. It is impossible.
Desdemona: If any such there be, heaven pardon him!
Emilia: A halter° pardon him! And hell gnaw his bones!
Why should he call her whore? Who keeps her company?
What place? What time? What form?° What likelihood?
The Moor's abused by some most villainous knave,
Some base notorious knave, some scurvy fellow.
O heaven, that° such companions° thou'dst unfold,°
And put in every honest hand a whip
To lash the rascals naked through the world
Even from the east to th' west!
Iago: Speak within door.°
Emilia: O, fie upon them! Some such squire° he was
That turned your wit the seamy side without°
And made you to suspect me with the Moor.
Iago: You are a fool. Go to.°
Desdemona: Alas, Iago,
What shall I do to win my lord again?
Good friend, go to him; for, by this light of heaven,

128 *callet* whore 135 *Beshrew* curse 136 *trick* strange behavior, delusion 137 *eternal* inveterate 138 *insinuating* ingratiating, fawning, wheedling 139 *cogging* cheating. *cozening* defrauding 143 *halter* hangman's noose 145 *form* appearance, circumstance 148 *that* would that. *companions* fellows. *unfold* expose 151 *within door* i.e., not so loud 152 *squire* fellow 153 *seamy side without* wrong side out 155 *Go to* i.e., that's enough

I know not how I lost him. Here I kneel. [*She kneels.*]
If e'er my will did trespass 'gainst his love,
Either in discourse of thought° or actual deed,
Or that° mine eyes, mine ears, or any sense
Delighted them° in any other form;
Or that I do not yet,° and ever did,
And ever will—though he do shake me off
To beggarly divorcement—love him dearly,
Comfort forswear° me! Unkindness may do much,
And his unkindness may defeat° my life,
But never taint my love. I cannot say "whore."
It does abhor° me now I speak the word;
To do the act that might the addition° earn
Not the world's mass of vanity° could make me.

[*She rises.*]

Iago: I pray you, be content. 'Tis but his humor.°
The business of the state does him offense,
And he does chide with you.
Desdemona: If 'twere no other—
Iago: It is but so, I warrant. [*Trumpets within.*]
Hark, how these instruments summon you to supper!
The messengers of Venice stays the meat.°
Go in, and weep not. All things shall be well.

Exeunt Desdemona and Emilia.

Enter Roderigo.

How now, Roderigo?
Roderigo: I do not find that thou deal'st justly with me.
Iago: What in the contrary?
Roderigo: Every day thou daff'st me° with some device,° Iago, and rather, as it seems to me now, keep'st from me all conveniency° than suppliest me with the least advantage° of hope. I will indeed no longer endure it, nor am I yet persuaded to put up° in peace what already I have foolishly suffered.
Iago: Will you hear me, Roderigo?

160 *discourse of thought* process of thinking 161 *that* if. (Also in line 163.) 162 *Delighted them* took delight 163 *yet* still 166 *Comfort forswear* may heavenly comfort forsake 167 *defeat* destroy 169 *abhor* (1) fill me with abhorrence (2) make me whorelike 170 *addition* title 171 *vanity* showy splendor 172 *humor* mood 178 *stays the meat* are waiting to dine 183 *thou daff'st me* you put me off. *device* excuse, trick 184 *conveniency* advantage, opportunity 185 *advantage* increase 186 *put up* submit to, tolerate

Roderigo starts to suspect Iago's duplicities.

Roderigo: Faith, I have heard too much, for your words and performances are no kin together.

Iago: You charge me most unjustly.

Roderigo: With naught but truth. I have wasted myself out of my means. The jewels you have had from me to deliver° Desdemona would half have corrupted a votarist.° You have told me she hath received them and returned me expectations and comforts of sudden respect° and acquaintance, but I find none.

Iago: Well, go to, very well.

Roderigo: "Very well"! "Go to"! I cannot go to,° man, nor 'tis not very well. By this hand, I think it is scurvy, and begin to find myself fopped° in it.

Iago: Very well.

Roderigo: I tell you 'tis not very well.° I will make myself known to Desdemona. If she will return me my jewels, I will give over my suit and

193 *deliver* deliver to 194 *votarist* nun 195 *sudden respect* immediate consideration 198 *I cannot go to* (Roderigo changes Iago's *go to*, an expression urging patience, to *I cannot go to*, "I have no opportunity for success in wooing.") 200 *fopped* fooled, duped 202 *not very well* (Roderigo changes Iago's *very well*, "all right, then," to *not very well*, "not at all good.")

repent my unlawful solicitation; if not, assure yourself I will seek satisfaction° of you.

Iago: You have said now?°

Roderigo: Ay, and said nothing but what I protest intendment° of doing.

Iago: Why, now I see there's mettle in thee, and even from this instant do build on thee a better opinion than ever before. Give me thy hand, Roderigo. Thou hast taken against me a most just exception; but yet I protest I have dealt most directly in thy affair.

Roderigo: It hath not appeared.

Iago: I grant indeed it hath not appeared, and your suspicion is not without wit and judgment. But, Roderigo, if thou hast that in thee indeed which I have greater reason to believe now than ever—I mean purpose, courage, and valor—this night show it. If thou the next night following enjoy not Desdemona, take me from this world with treachery and devise engines for° my life.

Roderigo: Well, what is it? Is it within reason and compass?

Iago: Sir, there is especial commission come from Venice to depute Cassio in Othello's place.

Roderigo: Is that true? Why, then Othello and Desdemona return again to Venice.

Iago: O, no; he goes into Mauritania and takes away with him the fair Desdemona, unless his abode be lingered here by some accident; wherein none can be so determinate° as the removing of Cassio.

Roderigo: How do you mean, removing of him?

Iago: Why, by making him uncapable of Othello's place—knocking out his brains.

Roderigo: And that you would have me to do?

Iago: Ay, if you dare do yourself a profit and a right. He sups tonight with a harlotry,° and thither will I go to him. He knows not yet of his honorable fortune. If you will watch his going thence, which I will fashion to fall out° between twelve and one, you may take him at your pleasure. I will be near to second your attempt, and he shall fall between us. Come, stand not amazed at it, but go along with me. I will show you such a necessity in his death that you shall think yourself bound to put it on him. It is now high° suppertime, and the night grows to waste.° About it.

Roderigo: I will hear further reason for this.

Iago: And you shall be satisfied. *Exeunt.*

205 *satisfaction* repayment. (The term normally means settling of accounts in a duel.) 206 *You . . . now* have you finished? 207 *intendment* intention 218 *engines for* plots against 226 *determinate* conclusive 232 *harlotry* slut 234 *fall out* occur 238 *high* fully. 239 *grows to waste* wastes away

SCENE III [THE CITADEL.]

Enter Othello, Lodovico, Desdemona, Emilia, and attendants.

Lodovico: I do beseech you, sir, trouble yourself no further.
Othello: O, pardon me; 'twill do me good to walk.
Lodovico: Madam, good night. I humbly thank your ladyship.
Desdemona: Your honor is most welcome.
Othello: Will you walk, sir?
O, Desdemona!
Desdemona: My lord?
Othello: Get you to bed on th' instant. I will be returned
forthwith. Dismiss your attendant there.
Look 't be done.
Desdemona: I will, my lord.

Exit [*Othello, with Lodovico and attendants*].

Emilia: How goes it now? He looks gentler than he did.
Desdemona: He says he will return incontinent,°
And hath commanded me to go to bed,
And bid me to dismiss you.
Emilia: Dismiss me?
Desdemona: It was his bidding. Therefore, good Emilia,
Give me my nightly wearing, and adieu.
We must not now displease him.
Emilia: I would you had never seen him!
Desdemona: So would not I. My love doth so approve him
That even his stubbornness,° his checks,° his frowns—
Prithee, unpin me—have grace and favor in them.

[*Emilia prepares Desdemona for bed.*]

Emilia: I have laid those sheets you bade me on the bed.
Desdemona: All's one.° Good faith, how foolish are our minds!
If I do die before thee, prithee shroud me
In one of these same sheets.
Emilia: Come, come, you talk.°
Desdemona: My mother had a maid called Barbary.
She was in love, and he she loved proved mad°
And did forsake her. She had a song of "Willow."
An old thing 'twas, but it expressed her fortune,
And she died singing it. That song tonight

12 *incontinent* immediately 21 *stubbornness* roughness. *checks* rebukes 24 *All's one* all right. It doesn't really matter 26 *talk* i.e., prattle 28 *mad* wild, i.e., faithless

Will not go from my mind; I have much to do
But to go hang° my head all at one side
And sing it like poor Barbary. Prithee, dispatch.
Emilia: Shall I go fetch your nightgown?°
Desdemona: No, unpin me here.
This Lodovico is a proper° man.
Emilia: A very handsome man.
Desdemona: He speaks well.
Emilia: I know a lady in Venice would have walked barefoot to Palestine for a touch of his nether lip.
Desdemona [*singing*]:
"The poor soul sat sighing by a sycamore tree,
Sing all a green willow;°
Her hand on her bosom, her head on her knee,
Sing willow, willow, willow.
The fresh streams ran by her and murmured her moans;
Sing willow, willow, willow;
Her salt tears fell from her, and softened the stones—"
Lay by these.
[*Singing.*] "Sing willow, willow, willow—"
Prithee, hie thee.° He'll come anon.°
[*Singing.*] "Sing all a green willow must be my garland.
Let nobody blame him; his scorn I approve—"
Nay, that's not next.—Hark! Who is 't that knocks?
Emilia: It's the wind.
Desdemona [*singing*]:
"I called my love false love; but what said he then?
Sing willow, willow, willow;
If I court more women, you'll couch with more men."
So, get thee gone. Good night. Mine eyes do itch;
Doth that bode weeping?
Emilia: 'Tis neither here nor there.
Desdemona: I have heard it said so. O, these men, these men!
Dost thou in conscience think—tell me, Emilia—
That there be women do abuse° their husbands
In such gross kind?
Emilia: There be some such, no question.
Desdemona: Wouldst thou do such a deed for all the world?
Emilia: Why, would not you?
Desdemona: No, by this heavenly light!

32–33 *I . . . hang* I can scarcely keep myself from hanging 35 *nightgown* dressing gown 37 *proper* handsome 43 *willow* (A conventional emblem of disappointed love.) 51 *hie thee* hurry. *anon* right away 63 *abuse* deceive

Emilia prepares Desdemona for bed.

Emilia: Nor I neither by this heavenly light;
I might do 't as well i' the dark.
Desdemona: Wouldst thou do such a deed for all the world?
Emilia: The world's a huge thing. It is a great price
For a small vice.
Desdemona: Good troth, I think thou wouldst not.
Emilia: By my troth, I think I should, and undo 't when I had done. Marry, I would not do such a thing for a joint ring,° nor for measures of lawn,° nor for gowns, petticoats, nor caps, nor any petty exhibition.° But for all the whole world! Uds° pity, who would not make her husband a cuckold to make him a monarch? I should venture purgatory for 't.
Desdemona: Beshrew me if I would do such a wrong
For the whole world.
Emilia: Why, the wrong is but a wrong i' the world, and having the world for your labor, 'tis a wrong in your own world, and you might quickly make it right.
Desdemona: I do not think there is any such woman.
Emilia: Yes, a dozen, and as many
To th' vantage° as would store° the world they played° for.

74 *joint ring* a ring made in separate halves. 75 *lawn* fine linen. *exhibition* gift 76 *Uds* God's 85 *To th' vantage* in addition, to boot. *store* populate. *played* (1) gambled (2) sported sexually

But I do think it is their husbands' faults
If wives do fall. Say that they slack their duties°
And pour our treasures into foreign laps,°
Or else break out in peevish jealousies,
Throwing restraint upon us?° Or say they strike us,
Or scant our former having in despite?°
Why, we have galls,° and though we have some grace,
Yet have we some revenge. Let husbands know
Their wives have sense° like them. They see, and smell,
And have their palates both for sweet and sour,
As husbands have. What is it that they do
When they change us for others? Is it sport?°
I think it is. And doth affection° breed it?
I think it doth. Is 't frailty that thus errs?
It is so, too. And have not we affections,
Desires for sport, and frailty, as men have?
Then let them use us well; else let them know,
The ills we do, their ills instruct us so.

Desdemona: Good night, good night. God me such uses° send
Not to pick bad from bad, but by bad mend!°

Exeunt.

ACT V

SCENE I [A STREET IN CYPRUS.]

Enter Iago and Roderigo.

Iago: Here stand behind this bulk.° Straight will he come.
Wear thy good rapier bare,° and put it home.
Quick, quick! Fear nothing. I'll be at thy elbow.
It makes us or it mars us. Think on that,
And fix most firm thy resolution.

Roderigo: Be near at hand. I may miscarry in 't.

Iago: Here, at thy hand. Be bold, and take thy stand.

87 *duties* marital duties 88 *pour . . . laps* i.e., are unfaithful, give what is rightfully ours (semen) to other women 90 *Throwing . . . us* i.e., jealously restricting our freedom to see other men 91 *scant . . . despite* reduce our allowance to spite us 92 *have galls* i.e., are capable of resenting injury and insult 94 *sense* physical sense 97 *sport* sexual pastime 98 *affection* passion 104 *uses* habit, practice 105 *Not . . . mend* i.e., not to learn bad conduct from others' badness (as Emilia has suggested women learn from men), but to mend my ways by perceiving what badness is, making spiritual benefit out of evil and adversity 1 *bulk* framework projecting from the front of a shop 2 *bare* unsheathed

[*Iago stands aside. Roderigo conceals himself.*]

Roderigo: I have no great devotion to the deed;
And yet he hath given me satisfying reasons.
'Tis but a man gone. Forth, my sword! He dies.

[*He draws.*]

Iago: I have rubbed this young quat° almost to the sense,°
And he grows angry. Now, whether he kill Cassio
Or Cassio him, or each do kill the other,
Every way makes my gain. Live Roderigo,°
He calls me to a restitution large
Of gold and jewels that I bobbed° from him
As gifts to Desdemona.
It must not be. If Cassio do remain,
He hath a daily beauty in his life
That makes me ugly; and besides, the Moor
May unfold° me to him; there stand I in much peril.
No, he must die. Be 't so. I hear him coming.

Enter Cassio.

Roderigo [*coming forth*]: I know his gait, 'tis he.—Villain, thou diest!

[*He attacks Cassio.*]

Cassio: That thrust had been mine enemy indeed,
But that my coat° is better than thou know'st.
I will make proof° of thine.

[*He draws, and wounds Roderigo.*]

Roderigo: O, I am slain! [*He falls.*]

[*Iago, from behind, wounds Cassio in the leg, and exits.*]

Cassio: I am maimed forever. Help, ho! Murder! Murder!

Enter Othello.

Othello: The voice of Cassio! Iago keeps his word.
Roderigo: O, villain that I am!
Othello: It is even so.
Cassio: O, help, ho! Light! A surgeon!
Othello: 'Tis he. O brave Iago, honest and just,

11 *quat* pimple, pustule. *to the sense* to the quick 14 *Live Roderigo* if Roderigo lives 16 *bobbed* swindled 21 *unfold* expose 25 *coat* (Possibly a garment of mail under the outer clothing, or simply a tougher coat than Roderigo expected.) 26 *proof* a test

That hast such noble sense of thy friend's wrong!
Thou teachest me. Minion,° your dear lies dead,
And your unblest fate hies.° Strumpet, I come.
Forth of ° my heart those charms, thine eyes, are blotted;
Thy bed, lust-stained, shall with lust's blood be spotted. *Exit Othello.*

Enter Lodovico and Gratiano.

Cassio: What ho! No watch? No passage?° Murder! Murder!
Gratiano: 'Tis some mischance. The voice is very direful.
Cassio: O, help!
Lodovico: Hark!
Roderigo: O wretched villain!
Lodovico: Two or three groan. 'Tis heavy° night;
These may be counterfeits. Let's think 't unsafe
To come in to° the cry without more help.

[*They remain near the entrance.*]

Roderigo: Nobody come? Then shall I bleed to death.

Enter Iago [*in his shirtsleeves, with a light*].

Lodovico: Hark!
Gratiano: Here's one comes in his shirt, with light and weapons.
Iago: Who's there? Whose noise is this that cries on° murder?
Lodovico: We do not know.
Iago: Did not you hear a cry?
Cassio: Here, here! For heaven's sake, help me!
Iago: What's the matter?

[*He moves toward Cassio.*]

Gratiano [*to Lodovico*]: This is Othello's ancient, as I take it.
Lodovico [*to Gratiano*]: The same indeed, a very valiant fellow.
Iago [*to Cassio*]: What° are you here that cry so grievously?
Cassio: Iago? O, I am spoiled,° undone by villains!
Give me some help.
Iago: O me, Lieutenant! What villains have done this?
Cassio: I think that one of them is hereabout,
And cannot make° away.
Iago: O treacherous villains!

[*To Lodovico and Gratiano.*]

What are you there? Come in, and give some help.

34 *Minion* hussy (i.e., Desdemona) 35 *hies* hastens on 36 *Forth of* from out 38 *passage* people passing by 43 *heavy* thick, dark 45 *come in to* approach 49 *cries on* cries out 54 *What* who (also at lines 60 and 66) 55 *spoiled* ruined, done for 59 *make* get

[*They advance*.]

Roderigo: O, help me there!

Cassio: That's one of them.

Iago: O murderous slave! O villain!

[*He stabs Roderigo*.]

Roderigo: O damned Iago! O inhuman dog!

Iago: Kill men i' the dark?—Where be these bloody thieves?—
How silent is this town!—Ho! Murder, murder!—
[*To Lodovico and Gratiano*.] What may you be? Are you of good or evil?

Lodovico: As you shall prove us, praise° us.

Iago: Signor Lodovico?

Lodovico: He, sir.

Iago: I cry you mercy.° Here's Cassio hurt by villains.

Gratiano: Cassio?

Iago: How is 't, brother?

Cassio: My leg is cut in two.

Iago: Marry, heaven forbid!
Light, gentlemen! I'll bind it with my shirt.

[*He hands them the light, and tends to Cassio's wound*.]

Enter Bianca.

Bianca: What is the matter, ho? Who is 't that cried?

Iago: Who is 't that cried?

Bianca: O my dear Cassio!
My sweet Cassio! O Cassio, Cassio, Cassio!

Iago: O notable strumpet! Cassio, may you suspect
Who they should be that have thus mangled you?

Cassio: No.

Gratiano: I am sorry to find you thus. I have been to seek you.

Iago: Lend me a garter. [*He applies a tourniquet*.] So.—O, for a chair,°
To bear him easily hence!

Bianca: Alas, he faints! O Cassio, Cassio, Cassio!

Iago: Gentlemen all, I do suspect this trash
To be a party in this injury.—
Patience awhile, good Cassio.—Come, come;
Lend me a light. [*He shines the light on Roderigo*.]
Know we this face or no?
Alas, my friend and my dear countryman
Roderigo! No.—Yes, sure.—O heaven! Roderigo!

67 *praise* appraise 70 *I cry you mercy* I beg your pardon 83 *chair* litter

Gratiano: What, of Venice?
Iago: Even he, sir. Did you know him?
Gratiano: Know him? Ay.
Iago: Signor Gratiano? I cry your gentle° pardon.
These bloody accidents° must excuse my manners
That so neglected you.
Gratiano: I am glad to see you.
Iago: How do you, Cassio? O, a chair, a chair!
Gratiano: Roderigo!
Iago: He, he, 'tis he. [*A litter is brought in.*] O, that's well said;° the chair.
Some good man bear him carefully from hence;
I'll fetch the General's surgeon. [*To Bianca.*] For you, mistress,
Save you your labor.°—He that lies slain here, Cassio,
Was my dear friend. What malice° was between you?
Cassio: None in the world, nor do I know the man.
Iago [*to Bianca*]: What, look you pale?—O, bear him out o' th' air.°

[*Cassio and Roderigo are borne off.*]

Stay you,° good gentlemen.—Look you pale, mistress?—
Do you perceive the gastness° of her eye?—
Nay, if you stare,° we shall hear more anon.—
Behold her well; I pray you, look upon her.
Do you see, gentlemen? Nay, guiltiness
Will speak, though tongues were out of use.

[*Enter Emilia.*]

Emilia: 'Las, what's the matter? What's the matter, husband?
Iago: Cassio hath here been set on in the dark
By Roderigo and fellows that are scaped.
He's almost slain, and Roderigo dead.
Emilia: Alas, good gentleman! Alas, good Cassio!
Iago: This is the fruits of whoring. Prithee, Emilia,
Go know° of Cassio where he supped tonight.
[*To Bianca.*] What, do you shake at that?
Bianca: He supped at my house, but I therefore shake not.
Iago: O, did he so? I charge you go with me.
Emilia: O, fie upon thee, strumpet!
Bianca: I am no strumpet, but of life as honest°
As you that thus abuse me.

95 *gentle* noble 96 *accidents* sudden events 100 *well said* well done 103 *Save . . . labor* i.e., never you mind tending Cassio 104 *malice* enmity 106 *bear . . . air* (Fresh air was thought to be dangerous for a wound.) 107 *Stay you* (Lodovico and Gratiano are evidently about to leave.) 108 *gastness* terror 109 *stare* (Iago pretends to interpret Bianca's wild looks as an involuntary confession of guilt.) 119 *know* learn 124 *honest* chaste

Emilia: As I? Faugh! Fie upon thee!
Iago: Kind gentlemen, let's go see poor Cassio dressed.°—
Come, mistress, you must tell's another tale.
Emilia, run you to the citadel
And tell my lord and lady what hath happed.—
Will you go on afore? [*Aside.*] This is the night
That either makes me or fordoes° me quite. *Exeunt.*

SCENE II [A BEDCHAMBER IN THE CITADEL.]

Enter Othello [*with a light*], *and Desdemona in her bed.*°

Othello: It is the cause,° it is the cause, my soul.
Let me not name it to you, you chaste stars!
It is the cause. Yet I'll not shed her blood,
Nor scar that whiter skin of hers than snow,
And smooth as monumental° alabaster.
Yet she must die, else she'll betray more men.
Put out the light, and then put out the light.°
If I quench thee, thou flaming minister,°
I can again thy former light restore,
Should I repent me;° but once put out thy light,
Thou cunning'st pattern° of excelling nature,
I know not where is that Promethean heat°
That can thy light relume.° When I have plucked thy rose,
I cannot give it vital growth again;
It needs must wither. I'll smell thee on the tree.

[*He kisses her.*]

O balmy breath, that dost almost persuade
Justice to break her sword! One more, one more.
Be thus when thou art dead, and I will kill thee,
And love thee after. One more, and that's the last.

[*He kisses her.*]

So sweet was ne'er so fatal. I must weep,
But they are cruel° tears. This sorrow's heavenly;

127 *Cassio dressed* Cassio's wounds dressed 132 *fordoes* undoes, ruins. s.d. *in her bed* (Either the curtains are drawn back to reveal the bed in a recessed area backstage, or the bed is "thrust out" onstage as the scene begins.) 1 *cause* i.e., cause of justice, the offense itself, which Othello must correct as an agent of justice 5 *monumental* i.e., used in making tombs and funeral monuments 7 *the light . . . light* the torch or lamp . . . Desdemona's life 8 *flaming minister* torch or lamp that serves me 10 *repent me* change my mind 11 *Thou . . . pattern* you skillfully wrought perfect example 12 *Promethean heat* divine fire. (Alluding to the theft of fire from heaven by Prometheus.) 13 *relume* rekindle 21 *cruel* unrelenting

Othello asks if Desdemona has confessed all her crimes (V, ii, 31–55).

It strikes where it doth love.° She wakes.
Desdemona: Who's there? Othello?
Othello: Ay, Desdemona.
Desdemona: Will you come to bed, my lord?
Othello: Have you prayed tonight, Desdemon?
Desdemona: Ay, my lord.
Othello: If you bethink yourself of any crime°
Unreconciled as yet to heaven and grace,
Solicit° for it straight.°
Desdemona: Alack, my lord, what may you mean by that?
Othello: Well, do it, and be brief. I will walk by.
I would not kill thy unpreparèd spirit.
No, heaven forfend!° I would not kill thy soul.
Desdemona: Talk you of killing?
Othello: Ay, I do.
Desdemona: Then heaven
Have mercy on me!
Othello: Amen, with all my heart!
Desdemona: If you say so, I hope you will not kill me.

22 *It . . . love* (Compare Hebrews 12:6: "For whom the Lord loveth he chasteneth.") 28 *crime* sin 30 *Solicit* petition, pray. *straight* immediately 34 *forfend* forbid

Othello: Humh!
Desdemona: And yet I fear you; for you're fatal then
When your eyes roll so. Why I should fear I know not,
Since guiltiness I know not; but yet I feel I fear.
Othello: Think on thy sins.
Desdemona: They are loves I bear to you.°
Othello: Ay, and for that thou diest.
Desdemona: That death's unnatural that kills for loving.
Alas, why gnaw you so your nether lip?
Some bloody passion shakes your very frame.
These are portents; but yet I hope, I hope,
They do not point on° me.
Othello: Peace, and be still!
Desdemona: I will so. What's the matter?
Othello: That handkerchief which I so loved and gave thee
Thou gav'st to Cassio.
Desdemona: No, by my life and soul!
Send for the man and ask him.
Othello: Sweet soul, take heed, take heed of perjury.
Thou art on thy deathbed.
Desdemona: Ay, but not yet to die.
Othello: Yes, presently.°
Therefore confess thee freely of thy sin;
For to deny each article with oath
Cannot remove nor choke the strong conception°
That I do groan withal.° Thou art to die.
Desdemona: Then Lord have mercy on me!
Othello: I say, amen.
Desdemona: And have you mercy too! I never did
Offend° you in my life; never loved Cassio
But with such general warranty° of heaven
As I might love. I never gave him token.
Othello: By heaven, I saw my handkerchief in 's hand.
O perjured woman! Thou dost stone° my heart,
And makes me call what I intend to do
A murder, which I thought a sacrifice.
I saw the handkerchief.
Desdemona: He found it, then.
I never gave it him. Send for him hither;
Let him confess a truth.

42 *They are . . . you* i.e., if I sinned, it was in loving you more than my father or more than God 48 *point on* point at, predict what is to happen to 56 *presently* immediately 59 *conception* (1) belief in your guilt (2) plan in my mind 60 *groan withal* (1) groan at in sorrow (2) as in giving birth 63 *Offend* wrong 64 *warranty* sanction 67 *stone* turn to stone, harden

"It is too late" (V, ii, 87).

Othello: He hath confessed.
Desdemona: What, my lord?
Othello: That he hath used thee.
Desdemona: How? Unlawfully?
Othello: Ay.
Desdemona: He will not say so.
Othello: No, his mouth is stopped;
Honest Iago hath ta'en order° for 't.
Desdemona: O, my fear interprets. What, is he dead?
Othello: Had all his hairs been lives, my great revenge
Had stomach for them all.
Desdemona: Alas, he is betrayed and I undone! [*She weeps.*]
Othello: Out, strumpet! Weep'st thou for him to my face?
Desdemona: O, banish me, my lord, but kill me not!
Othello: Down, strumpet!
Desdemona: Kill me tomorrow; let me live tonight!
Othello: Nay, if you strive—
Desdemona: But half an hour!
Othello: Being done,° there is no pause.

76 *ta'en order* taken measures 86 *Being done* i.e., since justice has begun its relentless course

Desdemona: But while I say one prayer!
Othello: It is too late.

Smothers her.

Emilia [*at the door*]: My lord, my lord! What, ho! My lord, my lord!
Othello: What noise is this? Not dead? Not yet quite dead?
I that am cruel am yet merciful;
I would not have thee linger in thy pain.

[*He dispatches her.*]

So, so.
Emilia [*within*]: What, ho! My lord, my lord!
Othello: Who's there?
Emilia [*within*]: O, good my lord, I would speak a word with you!
Othello: Yes, 'tis Emilia.—By and by.—She's dead.
'Tis like° she comes to speak of Cassio's death.—
The noise was here.° Ha! No more moving?
Still as the grave. Shall she come in? Were 't good?—
I think she stirs again. No. What's best to do?
If she come in, she'll sure speak to my wife.
My wife! My wife! What wife? I have no wife.
O, insupportable! O heavy hour!
Methinks it should be now a huge eclipse
Of sun and moon, and that th' affrighted globe
Should yawn° at alteration.°
Emilia [*within*]: I do beseech you
That I may speak with you, O, good my lord!
Othello: I had forgot thee. O, come in, Emilia.—
Soft,° by and by. Let me the curtains draw.—

[*He closes the bed-curtains and opens the door.*]

Where art thou?

Enter Emilia.

What's the matter with thee now?
Emilia: O, my good lord, yonder's foul murders done!
Othello: What, now?
Emilia: But now, my lord.

95 *like* likely that 96 *here* (The Folio's *high* is possible, suggesting that the commotion of the attack on Cassio was loud.) 104 *yawn* gape in amazement, i.e., move in an earthquake. (According to Pliny, earthquakes often happen during eclipses.) *at alteration* at these cataclysmic events in nature, well suited to express the horror of Desdemona's death 107 *Soft* wait a minute 112 *error* aberration, irregularity

Othello: It is the very error° of the moon;
She comes more nearer earth than she was wont,
And makes men mad.
Emilia: Cassio, my lord, hath killed a young Venetian
Called Roderigo.
Othello: Roderigo killed?
And Cassio killed?
Emilia: No, Cassio is not killed.
Othello: Not Cassio killed? Then murder's out of tune,
And sweet revenge grows harsh.
Desdemona: O, falsely, falsely murdered!
Emilia: O Lord, what cry is that?
Othello: That? What?
Emilia: Out° and alas, that was my lady's voice.

[*She opens the bed-curtains.*]

Help, help, ho, help! O lady, speak again!
Sweet Desdemona! O sweet mistress, speak!
Desdemona: A guiltless death I die.
Emilia: O, who hath done this deed?
Desdemona: Nobody; I myself. Farewell.
Commend me to my kind lord. O, farewell! [*She dies.*]
Othello: Why, how should she be murdered?
Emilia: Alas, who knows?
Othello: You heard her say herself it was not I.
Emilia: She said so. I must needs report the truth.
Othello: She's like a liar gone to burning hell!
'Twas I that killed her.
Emilia: O, the more angel she,
And you the blacker devil!
Othello: She turned to folly,° and she was a whore.
Emilia: Thou dost belie° her, and thou art a devil.
Othello: She was false as water.
Emilia: Thou art rash as fire to say
That she was false. O, she was heavenly true!
Othello: Cassio did top her. Ask thy husband else.°
O, I were damned beneath all depth in hell
But that I did proceed upon just grounds
To this extremity. Thy husband knew it all.
Emilia: My husband?

123 *Out* (A cry of dismay, intensifying *alas.*) 136 *folly* i.e., wantonness, fleshly sin
137 *belie* slander 141 *else* i.e., if you don't believe me

Othello: Thy husband.
Emilia: That she was false to wedlock?
Othello: Ay, with Cassio. Nay, had she been true,
If heaven would make me such another world
Of one entire and perfect chrysolite,°
I'd not have sold her for it.
Emilia: My husband?
Othello: Ay, 'twas he that told me on her first.
An honest man he is, and hates the slime
That sticks on filthy deeds.
Emilia: My husband?
Othello: What needs this iterance,° woman? I say thy husband.
Emilia: O mistress, villainy hath made mocks with° love!
My husband say that she was false?
Othello: He, woman;
I say thy husband. Dost understand the word?
My friend, thy husband, honest, honest Iago.
Emilia: If he say so, may his pernicious soul
Rot half a grain a day! He lies to th' heart.
She was too fond of her most filthy bargain.
Othello: Ha? [*He draws.*]
Emilia: Do thy worst!
This deed of thine is no more worthy heaven
Than thou wast worthy her.
Othello: Peace, you were best.°
Emilia: Thou hast not half that power to do me harm
As I have to be hurt.° O gull!° O dolt!
As ignorant as dirt! Thou hast done a deed—
I care not for thy sword; I'll make thee known,
Though I lost twenty lives.—Help! Help, ho, help!
The Moor hath killed my mistress! Murder, murder!

Enter Montano, Gratiano, and Iago.

Montano: What is the matter? How now, General?
Emilia: O, are you come, Iago? You have done well,
That men must lay their murders on your neck.
Gratiano: What is the matter?
Emilia [*to Iago*]*:* Disprove this villain, if thou be'st a man.
He says thou toldst him that his wife was false.
I know thou didst not; thou'rt not such a villain.

150 *chrysolite* precious topaz 157 *iterance* iteration, repetition 158 *made mocks with* derided, made sport of 168 *you were best* it would be best for you 170 *to be hurt* i.e., to endure hurt. *gull* dupe

Speak, for my heart is full.
Iago: I told him what I thought, and told no more
Than what he found himself was apt° and true.
Emilia: But did you ever tell him she was false?
Iago: I did.
Emilia: You told a lie, an odious, damnèd lie!
Upon my soul, a lie, a wicked lie.
She false with Cassio? Did you say with Cassio?
Iago: With Cassio, mistress. Go to, charm° your tongue.
Emilia: I will not charm my tongue; I am bound to speak.
My mistress here lies murdered in her bed—
All: O heavens forfend!
Emilia: And your reports have set the murder on.
Othello: Nay, stare not, masters. It is true indeed.
Gratiano: 'Tis a strange truth.
Montano: O monstrous act!
Emilia: Villainy, villainy, villainy!
I think upon 't—I think I smell 't! O villainy!
I thought so then°—I'll kill myself for grief—
O villainy, villainy!
Iago: What, are you mad? I charge you, get you home.
Emilia: Good gentlemen, let me have leave to speak.
'Tis proper I obey him, but not now.
Perchance, Iago, I will ne'er go home.
Othello: O! O! O! [*Othello falls on the bed.*°]
Emilia: Nay, lay thee down and roar,
For thou hast killed the sweetest innocent
That e'er did lift up eye.°
Othello [*rising*]: O, she was foul!
I scarce did know you, uncle. There lies your niece,
Whose breath indeed these hands have newly stopped.
I know this act shows° horrible and grim.
Gratiano: Poor Desdemon! I am glad thy father's dead.
Thy match was mortal to him, and pure grief
Shore his old thread° in twain. Did he live now,
This sight would make him do a desperate turn,°
Yea, curse his better angel from his side,
And fall to reprobance.°

184 *apt* plausible 190 *charm* keep silent (as though by a magic spell) 199 *then* (Perhaps at III, iii, 331–332, and IV, ii, 137–154.) 205 s.d. *Othello . . . bed* (This direction is from the Quarto, as also *He kisses her* at line 19 and *She dies* at line 129.) 207 *lift up eye* i.e., lift her eyes to heaven 210 *shows* looks 213 *Shore . . . thread* sheared the thread of his old age (as Atropos, one of the three Fates, was thought to do) 214 *turn* deed 216 *reprobance* damnation, i.e., suicide

Othello: 'Tis pitiful. But yet Iago knows
That she with Cassio hath the act of shame
A thousand times committed. Cassio confessed it;
And she did gratify° his amorous works
With that recognizance° and pledge of love
Which I first gave her. I saw it in his hand;
It was a handkerchief, an antique token
My father gave my mother.
Emilia: O God! O heavenly God!
Iago: Zounds, hold your peace.
Emilia: 'Twill out, 'twill out! I peace?
No, I will speak as liberal as the north.°
Let heaven and men and devils, let them all,
All, all, cry shame against me, yet I'll speak.
Iago: Be wise, and get you home.
Emilia: I will not.

[*Iago threatens Emilia.*]

Gratiano: Fie!
Your sword upon a woman?
Emilia: O thou dull Moor! That handkerchief thou speak'st of
I found by fortune and did give my husband;
For often, with a solemn earnestness,
More than indeed belonged° to such a trifle,
He begged of me to steal 't.
Iago: Villainous whore!
Emilia: She give it Cassio? No, alas! I found it,
And I did give 't my husband.
Iago: Filth, thou liest!
Emilia: By heaven, I do not, I do not, gentlemen.
O murderous coxcomb!° What should such a fool
Do with so good a wife?
Othello: Are there no stones° in heaven
But what serves for the thunder?—Precious° villain!

[*He runs at Iago; Montano disarms Othello. Iago, from behind, stabs Emilia.*°]

Gratiano: The woman falls! Sure he hath killed his wife.
Emilia: Ay, ay. O, lay me by my mistress' side.

220 *gratify* reward 221 *recognizance* token 227 *liberal as the north* freely as the north wind (blows) 235 *belonged* was appropriate 240 *coxcomb* fool. (Addressed to Othello.) 242 *stones* bolts, such as those used for thunderbolts 243 *Precious* i.e., arrant, utter. s.d. *He . . . Emilia* (The Quarto text reads, "The Moor runs at Iago. Iago kills his wife." The Quarto also specifies the exit of Iago at line 245 and the death of Emilia at line 260.)

Exit [Iago.]

Gratiano: He's gone, but his wife's killed.
Montano: 'Tis a notorious villain. Take you this weapon,
Which I have here recovered from the Moor.
Come, guard the door without. Let him not pass,
But kill him rather. I'll after that same villain,
For 'tis a damnèd slave.

Exit [with all but Othello and Emilia, who has been laid by Desdemona's side].

Othello: I am not valiant neither,
But every puny whipster° gets my sword.
But why should honor° outlive honesty?°
Let it go all.
Emilia: What did thy song bode, lady?
Hark, canst thou hear me? I will play the swan,
And die in music. [*She sings.*] "Willow, willow, willow."
Moor, she was chaste. She loved thee, cruel Moor.
So come my soul to bliss as I speak true.
So speaking as I think, alas, I die. [*She dies.*]
Othello: I have another weapon in this chamber;
It was a sword of Spain, the ice-brook's temper°—
O, here it is. [*He finds a sword.*] Uncle, I must come forth.
Gratiano [*within*]: If thou attempt it, it will cost thee dear.
Thou hast no weapon, and perforce must suffer.
Othello: Look in upon me then and speak with me,
Or, naked° as I am, I will assault thee.

[*Enter Gratiano.*]

Gratiano: What is the matter?
Othello: Behold, I have a weapon;
A better never did itself sustain
Upon a soldier's thigh. I have seen the day
That, with this little arm and this good sword,
I have made my way through more impediments
Than twenty times your stop.° But O, vain boast!
Who can control his fate? 'Tis not so now.
Be not afraid, though you do see me weaponed;
Here is my journey's end, here is my butt°
And very seamark° of my utmost sail.

253 ***whipster*** contemptible fellow (one who is always ready to whip out his sword) 254 *honor* i.e., the bravery for which one enjoys a soldier's reputation. *honesty* true integrity 262 *the ice-brook's temper* tempered in ice-cold water 267 *naked* unarmed 273 *stop* power (to stop) 276 *butt* goal, limit. (An archery term.) 277 *seamark* beacon (marking his destination or limit)

"O Desdemon! Dead, Desdemon! Dead! O! O!" (V, ii, 290).

[*Gratiano steps back.*]

Do you go back dismayed? 'Tis a lost° fear;
Man but a rush° against Othello's breast
And he retires. Where should Othello go?

[*He turns to Desdemona.*]

Now, how dost thou look now? O ill-starred wench!
Pale as thy smock! When we shall meet at compt,°
This look of thine will hurl my soul from heaven,
And fiends will snatch at it. Cold, cold, my girl?
Even like thy chastity. O cursèd, cursèd slave!°
Whip me, ye devils,
From the possession of this heavenly sight!
Blow me about in winds! Roast me in sulfur!
Wash me in steep-down gulfs of liquid fire!
O Desdemon! Dead, Desdemon! Dead! O! O!

Enter Lodovico, Cassio [carried in a litter°], Montano, and Iago [prisoner], with officers.

Lodovico: Where is this rash and most unfortunate man?

278 *lost* wasted, unneeded 279 *Man . . . rush* wield no more than a reed 282 *compt* account, judgment day 285 *slave* i.e., Othello himself 290 s.d. *in a litter* (The Quarto specifies that Cassio is "in a chair.")

Iago is taken prisoner and his plots are exposed (V, ii, 293–347).

Othello: That's he that was Othello. Here I am.
Lodovico: Where is that viper? Bring the villain forth.

[*Iago is led forward.*]

Othello: I look down towards his feet;° but that's a fable.
If that thou be'st a devil, I cannot kill thee.

[*He wounds Iago.*]

Lodovico: Wrench his sword from him. [*Othello is disarmed.*]
Iago: I bleed, sir, but not killed.
Othello: I am not sorry neither. I'd have thee live,
For in my sense° 'tis happiness to die.
Lodovico: O thou Othello, that was once so good,
Fall'n in the practice° of a cursèd slave,°
What shall be said to thee?
Othello: Why, anything.

294 *towards his feet* i.e., to see if they are cloven, as the devil's are fabled to be 298 *in my sense* to one who feels as I do 300 *in the practice* through the plotting, into the snare. *slave* villain

An honorable murderer, if you will,
For naught I did in hate, but all in honor.
Lodovico: This wretch hath part confessed his villainy.
Did you and he consent° in Cassio's death?
Othello: Ay.
Cassio: Dear General, I never gave you cause.
Othello: I do believe it, and I ask your pardon.
Will you, I pray, demand that demi-devil
Why he hath thus ensnared my soul and body?
Iago: Demand me nothing. What you know, you know.
From this time forth I never will speak word.
Lodovico: What, not to pray?
Gratiano: Torments° will ope your lips.
Othello: Well, thou dost best.
Lodovico: Sir, you shall understand what hath befall'n,
Which, as I think, you know not. Here is a letter
Found in the pocket of the slain Roderigo;
And here another. [*He produces letters.*] The one of them imports
The death of Cassio, to be undertook
By Roderigo.
Othello: O villain!
Cassio: Most heathenish and most gross!°
Lodovico [*showing another paper*]: Now here's another discontented° paper
Found in his pocket too. And this, it seems,
Roderigo meant t' have sent this damnèd villain;
But that belike° Iago in the interim
Came in and satisfied him.°
Othello: O thou pernicious caitiff!—
How came you, Cassio, by that handkerchief
That was my wife's?
Cassio: I found it in my chamber;
And he himself confessed but even now
That there he dropped it for a special purpose
Which wrought to his desire.°
Othello: O fool, fool, fool!
Cassio: There is besides in Roderigo's letter
How he upbraids Iago, that he made him
Brave° me upon the watch, whereon it came°
That I was cast;° and even but now he spake,

305 *consent* agree 314 *Torments* torture 322 *gross* monstrous 323 *discontented* full of discontent 326 *belike* most likely 327 *Came . . . him* interposed and gave him satisfactory explanation 333 *wrought . . . desire* worked out as he wished, fitted in with his plan 336 *Brave* defy. *whereon it came* whereof it came about 337 *cast* dismissed

After long seeming dead, Iago hurt him,
Iago set him on.

Lodovico [*to Othello*]: You must forsake this room and go with us.
Your power and your command is taken off,°
And Cassio rules in Cyprus. For this slave,
If there be any cunning cruelty
That can torment him much and hold him long,°
It shall be his. You shall close prisoner rest°
Till that the nature of your fault be known
To the Venetian state.—Come, bring away.

Othello: Soft you;° a word or two before you go.
I have done the state some service, and they know 't.
No more of that. I pray you, in your letters,
When you shall these unlucky° deeds relate,
Speak of me as I am; nothing extenuate,
Nor set down aught in malice. Then must you speak
Of one that loved not wisely but too well;
Of one not easily jealous but, being wrought,°
Perplexed° in the extreme; of one whose hand,
Like the base Indian,° threw a pearl away
Richer than all his tribe; of one whose subdued° eyes,
Albeit unusèd to the melting mood,
Drop tears as fast as the Arabian trees
Their medicinable gum.° Set you down this;
And say besides that in Aleppo once,
Where a malignant and a turbaned Turk
Beat a Venetian and traduced the state,
I took by th' throat the circumcisèd dog
And smote him, thus. [*He stabs himself.*°]

Lodovico: O bloody period!°

Gratiano: All that is spoke is marred.

Othello: I kissed thee ere I killed thee. No way but this,
Killing myself, to die upon a kiss.

[*He kisses Desdemona and dies.*]

Cassio: This did I fear, but thought he had no weapon;

341 *taken off* taken away 344 *hold him long* keep him alive a long time (during his torture) 345 *rest* remain 348 *Soft you* one moment 351 *unlucky* unfortunate 355 *wrought* worked upon, worked into a frenzy 356 *Perplexed* distraught 357 *Indian* (This reading from the Quarto pictures an ignorant savage who cannot recognize the value of a precious jewel. The Folio reading, *Iudean* or *Judean*, i.e., infidel or disbeliever, may refer to Herod, who slew Miriamne in a fit of jealousy, or to Judas Iscariot, the betrayer of Christ.) 358 *subdued* i.e., overcome by grief 361 *gum* i.e., myrr 366 s.d. *He stabs himself* (This direction is in the Quarto text.) 367 *period* termination, conclusion

For he was great of heart.
Lodovico [*to Iago*]: O Spartan dog,°
More fell° than anguish, hunger, or the sea!
Look on the tragic loading of this bed.
This is thy work. The object poisons sight;
Let it be hid.° Gratiano, keep° the house,

[*The bed curtains are drawn.*]

And seize upon° the fortunes of the Moor,
For they succeed on° you. [*To Cassio.*] To you, Lord Governor,
Remains the censure° of this hellish villain,
The time, the place, the torture. O, enforce it!
Myself will straight aboard, and to the state
This heavy act with heavy heart relate. *Exeunt.*

Questions

ACT I

1. What is Othello's position in society? How is he regarded by those who know him? By his own words, when we first meet him in Scene ii, what traits of character does he manifest?
2. How do you account for Brabantio's dismay on learning of his daughter's marriage, despite the fact that Desdemona has married a man so generally honored and admired?
3. What is Iago's view of human nature? In his fondness for likening men to animals (as in I, i, 49–50; I, i, 90–91; and I, iii, 385–386), what does he tell us about himself?
4. What reasons does Iago give for his hatred of Othello?
5. In Othello's defense before the senators (Scene iii), how does he explain Desdemona's gradual falling in love with him?
6. Is Brabantio's warning to Othello (I, iii, 293–294) an accurate or an inaccurate prophecy?
7. By what strategy does Iago enlist Roderigo in his plot against the Moor? In what lines do we learn Iago's true feelings toward Roderigo?

ACT II

1. What do the Cypriots think of Othello? Do their words (in Scene i) make him seem to us a lesser man or a larger one?
2. What cruelty does Iago display toward Emilia? How well founded is his distrust of his wife's fidelity?
3. In II, iii, 221, Othello speaks of Iago's "honesty and love." How do you account for Othello's being so totally deceived?

372 *Spartan dog* (Spartan dogs were noted for their savagery and silence.) 373 *fell* cruel 376 *Let it be hid* i.e., draw the bed curtains. (No stage direction specifies that the dead are to be carried offstage at the end of the play.) *keep* remain in 377 *seize upon* take legal possession of 378 *succeed on* pass as though by inheritance to 379 *censure* sentencing

4. For what major events does the merrymaking (proclaimed in Scene ii) give opportunity?

ACT III

1. Trace the steps by which Iago rouses Othello to suspicion. Is there anything in Othello's character or circumstances that renders him particularly susceptible to Iago's wiles?
2. In III, iv, 49–98, Emilia knows of Desdemona's distress over the lost handkerchief. At this moment, how do you explain her failure to relieve Desdemona's mind? Is Emilia aware of her husband's villainy?

ACT IV

1. In this act, what circumstantial evidence is added to Othello's case against Desdemona?
2. How plausible do you find Bianca's flinging the handkerchief at Cassio just when Othello is looking on? How important is the handkerchief in this play? What does it represent? What suggestions or hints do you find in it?
3. What prevents Othello from being moved by Desdemona's appeal (IV, ii, 33–92)?
4. When Roderigo grows impatient with Iago (IV, ii, 181–205), how does Iago make use of his fellow plotter's discontent?
5. What does the conversation between Emilia and Desdemona (Scene iii) tell us about the nature of each?
6. In this act, what scenes (or speeches) contain memorable dramatic irony?

ACT V

1. Summarize the events that lead to Iago's unmasking.
2. How does Othello's mistaken belief that Cassio is slain (V, i, 27–34) affect the outcome of the play?
3. What is Iago's motive in stabbing Roderigo?
4. In your interpretation of the play, exactly what impels Othello to kill Desdemona? Jealousy? Desire for revenge? Excess idealism? A wish to be a public avenger who punishes, "else she'll betray more men"?
5. What do you understand by Othello's calling himself "one that loved not wisely but too well" (V, ii, 354)?
6. In your view, does Othello's long speech in V, ii, 348–366 succeed in restoring his original dignity and nobility? Do you agree with Cassio (V, ii, 372) that Othello was "great of heart"?

General Questions

1. What motivates Iago to carry out his schemes? Do you find him a devil incarnate, a madman, or a rational human being?
2. Whom besides Othello does Iago deceive? What is Desdemona's opinion of him? Emilia's? Cassio's (before Iago is found out)? To what do you attribute Iago's success as a deceiver?
3. How essential to the play is the fact that Othello is a black man, a Moor, and not a native of Venice?

4. In the introduction to his edition of the play in *The Complete Signet Classic Shakespeare*, Alvin Kernan remarks:

> *Othello* is probably the most neatly, the most formally constructed of Shakespeare's plays. Every character is, for example, balanced by another similar or contrasting character. Desdemona is balanced by her opposite, Iago; love and concern for others at one end of the scale, hatred and concern for self at the other.

   Besides Desdemona and Iago, what other pairs of characters strike balances?
5. Consider any passage of the play in which there is a shift from verse to prose, or from prose to verse. What is the effect of this shift?
6. Indicate a passage that you consider memorable for its poetry. Does the passage seem introduced for its own sake? Does it in any way advance the action of the play, express theme, or demonstrate character?
7. Does the play contain any tragic *recognition*—as discussed in Chapter 25, a moment of terrible enlightenment, a "realization of the unthinkable"?
8. Does the downfall of Othello proceed from any flaw in his nature, or is his downfall entirely the work of Iago?

WRITING *effectively*

UNDERSTANDING SHAKESPEARE

The basic problem a modern reader faces with Shakespeare is language. Shakespeare's English is now four hundred years old, and it differs in innumerable small ways from contemporary American English. Although Shakespeare's idiom may at first seem daunting, it is easily mastered if you make the effort. To grow comfortable with his language, you must immerse yourself in it. Fortunately, doing so isn't all that hard; you might even find it pleasurable.

- **Let your ears do the work.** There is no substitute for hearing Shakespeare's words in performance. After all, the plays were written to be seen, not to be read silently on the page. After reading the play, listen to or watch a recording of it. It sometimes helps to read along as you listen or watch, hitting the pause button as needed. If you can attend a live performance of any Shakespearean play, do so.
- **But read the text first.** Watching a production is never a full substitute for reading an assigned play. Many productions abridge the play, leaving passages out. Even more important, directors and actors choose a particular interpretation of a play, and their choices might skew your understanding of events and motivation if you are unfamiliar with the original itself.
- **Before you write a paper, read the play again.** The first time through an Elizabethan-era text, you will almost certainly miss many things. As you grow more familiar with Shakespeare's language, you will be able to read it with greater comprehension. If you choose to write about a particular episode or character, carefully study the speeches and dialogue in question (and pay special attention to the footnotes) so that you understand each word.
- **Enjoy yourself.** From Beijing to Berlin, Buenos Aires to Oslo, Shakespeare is almost universally acknowledged as the world's greatest playwright, a master entertainer as well as a consummate artist.

CHECKLIST: Writing About Shakespeare

- ☐ Read closely. Work through passages with difficult language.
- ☐ Pay special attention to footnotes.
- ☐ Read the play more than once if necessary.
- ☐ Watch a DVD or listen to an audio recording after reading a play. Immerse yourself in Shakespeare's language until it becomes familiar.

- ☐ As you view or listen to a play, read along, or revisit the text afterward.
- ☐ Carefully study any speeches and dialogue you choose to write about.
- ☐ Be sure you understand each word of any passage you decide to discuss or quote.

TOPICS FOR WRITING ON SHAKESPEARE

1. Write a defense of Iago.
2. "Never was any play fraught, like this of *Othello*, with improbabilities," wrote Thomas Rymer in a famous attack (*A Short View of Tragedy*, 1692). Consider Rymer's objection to the play, either answering it or finding evidence to back it up.
3. Suppose yourself a casting director assigned to a film version of *Othello*. What well-known actors would you cast in the principal roles? Write a report justifying your choices. Don't merely discuss the stars and their qualifications; discuss (with specific reference to the play) what Shakespeare appears to call for.
4. Emilia's long speech at the end of Act IV (iii, 84–103) has been called a Renaissance plea for women's rights. Do you agree? Write a brief, close analysis of this speech. How timely is it?
5. "The downfall of Oedipus is the work of the gods; the downfall of Othello is self-inflicted." Test this comment with reference to the two plays, and report your findings.

28 THE MODERN THEATER

What You Will Learn in This Chapter

- To identify and define *realism* as a dramatic mode
- To describe the stagecraft developments of modern theater
- To analyze classic works of modern theater

REALISM

The ancient art of the drama experienced a revival in the Renaissance and went through a number of changes over the next several centuries. Elizabethan drama was marked by strong characterization, heightened and intense language, and crowded, sometimes sprawling plots. In the neoclassical period of the seventeenth and eighteenth centuries, greater emphasis was placed upon formality, decorum, and Aristotle's unities of time, place, and action. The early nineteenth century saw the rise of melodrama, with its florid dialogue, plots that relied heavily on often absurd coincidences, and crude stereotypes of good and evil characters. Through all these developments—from kings and generals to lords and ladies of high society to purehearted swashbucklers and craven villains—the one thing that seemed to remain constant was an absence of **realism**—the attempt to reproduce faithfully the surface appearance of life, especially that of ordinary people in everyday situations.

By the end of the nineteenth century, however, realism had become the drama's dominant mode. The writer most responsible for that shift was the Norwegian playwright Henrik Ibsen. From *Pillars of Society* (1877) to *Hedda Gabler* (1890), he wrote a series of prose dramas in which realistically portrayed middle-class characters face conflicts in their lives and relationships. They are often called "problem plays" because of their engagement of social issues, such as women's place in society (*A Doll's House*) and inherited venereal disease (*Ghosts*). In actuality, the social problems in these plays serve as a context for Ibsen's real concern, an examination of the complexities of human personality and psychology, especially those aspects of our natures that are hidden or repressed because of society's expectations.

Conventions of Realism

From Italian playhouses of the sixteenth century, the theater had inherited the **picture-frame stage**: a structure that holds the action within a **proscenium arch**, a gateway standing (as the word *proscenium* indicates) "in front of the scenery." This manner of constructing a playhouse in effect divided the actors from their audience; most commercial theaters even today are so constructed. But as the nineteenth century gave way to the twentieth, actors less often declaimed their passions in oratorical style in front of backdrops painted with waterfalls and volcanoes, while stationed exactly at the center of the stage as if to sing "duets meant to bring forth applause" (as Swedish playwright August Strindberg complained).

In the theater of Realism, a room was represented by a **box set**—three walls that joined in two corners and a ceiling that tilted as if seen in perspective—replacing drapery walls that had billowed and doors that had flapped, not slammed. Instead of posing at stage center and directly facing the audience to deliver key speeches, actors were instructed to speak from wherever the dramatic situation placed them, and now and then even to turn their backs upon the audience. They were to behave as if they were in a room with the fourth wall sliced away, unaware that they had an audience.

To encourage actors further to imitate reality, the influential director Constantin Stanislavsky of the Moscow Art Theater developed his famous system to help actors feel at home inside a playwright's characters. One of Stanislavsky's exercises was to have actors search their memories for personal experiences like those of the characters in the play; another was to have them act out things a character did *not* do in the play but might do in life. The system enabled Stanislavsky to bring authenticity to his productions of Chekhov's plays and of Maxim Gorky's *The Lower Depths* (1902), a play that showed the tenants of a sordid lodging house drinking themselves to death (and hanging themselves) in surroundings of realistic squalor. Stanislavsky's techniques are still used by stage and film actors today.

Lorraine Hansberry's *A Raisin in the Sun* (1959) came a bit later and made history as the first play by a black woman to be produced on Broadway. It explores how we are shaped by our experience in families, how our identities and achievements are influenced by our background and upbringing. First produced at the start of the Civil Rights Movement, *A Raisin in the Sun* depicts troubled relationships between parents and children, brother and sister, husband and wife. Set against the backdrop of a specific era and society, it has a larger, lasting relevance in its portrayal of a family that ultimately holds together.

Following Hansberry's play is one of the pioneering works of Realism, Henrik Ibsen's *A Doll's House*, which also addresses family and marriage, but in a much different way. The play derives a good deal of its power from our ability to identify with its characters and the lives they live, an identification that Ibsen achieves in part by framing the action with the details of daily existence.

Lorraine Hansberry

A Raisin in the Sun 1959

Lorraine Hansberry

Lorraine Hansberry (1930–1965) was born in Chicago. Her father was a banker and real-estate broker, her mother a former schoolteacher; both were active in the struggle for social justice. When Lorraine Hansberry was eight years old, her father bought a home in what she described as a "hellishly hostile 'white neighborhood' in which, literally, howling mobs surrounded our house. . . . My memories . . . include being spat on, cursed and pummeled in the daily trek to and from school." Hansberry's father brought a lawsuit over his right to purchase the house; the case went all the way to the U.S. Supreme Court, which ruled in his favor. Visitors to the family home when Lorraine Hansberry was young included W. E. B. Du Bois, Duke Ellington, Langston Hughes, Paul Robeson, and other prominent black artists and intellectuals. After two years of study at the University of Wisconsin, Hansberry moved to New York City in 1950. She became associate editor of the newspaper Freedom, *published by Paul Robeson, but resigned in 1953 to concentrate on her writing.* A Raisin in the Sun *made history in March 1959 when it became the first play by a black woman to be produced on Broadway. It ran for nineteen months, won the New York Drama Critics Circle Award as Best Play of the Year, and was made into a film in 1961. Her second full-length play,* The Sign in Sidney Brustein's Window, *opened on Broadway in October 1964. By the time of its production, Hansberry was terminally ill; she died of cancer in January 1965, at the age of thirty-four. Posthumously produced works included* To Be Young, Gifted and Black *(1969) and* Les Blancs *(1970). The text of* A Raisin in the Sun *presented here is the most complete version available; it includes two short scenes omitted for reasons of length from the Broadway production and omitted as well from the early published editions.*

CHARACTERS

Ruth Younger
Travis Younger
Walter Lee Younger (Brother)
Beneatha Younger
Lena Younger (Mama)
Joseph Asagai
George Murchison
Mrs. Johnson
Karl Lindner
Bobo
Moving Men

The action of the play is set in Chicago's Southside, sometime between World War II and the present.

ACT I

Scene 1: Friday morning.
Scene 2: The following morning.

ACT II

Scene 1: Later, the same day.
Scene 2: Friday night, a few weeks later.
Scene 3: Moving day, one week later.

ACT III

An hour later.

What happens to a dream deferred?
Does it dry up
Like a raisin in the sun?
Or fester like a sore—
And then run?
Does it stink like rotten meat
Or crust and sugar over—
Like a syrupy sweet?

Maybe it just sags
Like a heavy load.

Or does it explode?

—LANGSTON HUGHES

ACT I

SCENE I

The Younger living room would be a comfortable and well-ordered room if it were not for a number of indestructible contradictions to this state of being. Its furnishings are typical and undistinguished and their primary feature now is that they have clearly had to accommodate the living of too many people for too many years—and they are tired. Still, we can see that at some time, a time probably no longer remembered by the family (except perhaps for Mama), the furnishings of this room were actually selected with care and love and even hope—and brought to this apartment and arranged with taste and pride.

That was a long time ago. Now the once loved pattern of the couch upholstery has to fight to show itself from under acres of crocheted doilies and couch covers which have themselves finally come to be more important than the upholstery. And here a table or a chair has been moved to disguise the worn places in the carpet; but the carpet has fought back by showing its weariness, with depressing uniformity, elsewhere on its surface.

Weariness has, in fact, won in this room. Everything has been polished, washed, sat on, used, scrubbed too often. All pretenses but living itself have long since vanished from the very atmosphere of this room.

Moreover, a section of this room, for it is not really a room unto itself, though the landlord's lease would make it seem so, slopes backward to provide a small kitchen area, where the family prepares the meals that are eaten in the living room proper, which must also serve as dining room. The single window that has been provided for these "two" rooms is located in this kitchen area. The sole natural light the family may enjoy in the course of a day is only that which fights its way through this little window.

At left, a door leads to a bedroom which is shared by Mama and her daughter, Beneatha. At right, opposite, is a second room (which in the beginning of the life of this apartment was probably a breakfast room) which serves as a bedroom for Walter and his wife, Ruth.

TIME. *Sometime between World War II and the present.*

PLACE. *Chicago's Southside.*

AT RISE. *It is morning dark in the living room. Travis is asleep on the make-down bed at center. An alarm clock sounds from within the bedroom at right, and presently Ruth enters from that room and closes the door behind her. She crosses sleepily*

Diana Sands, Ruby Dee, Claudia McNeil, and Sidney Poitier in the original 1959 Broadway production of *A Raisin in the Sun.* The play was made into a film with the same cast in 1961.

toward the window. As she passes her sleeping son she reaches down and shakes him a little. At the window she raises the shade and a dusky Southside morning light comes in feebly. She fills a pot with water and puts it on to boil. She calls to the boy, between yawns, in a slightly muffled voice.

Ruth is about thirty. We can see that she was a pretty girl, even exceptionally so, but now it is apparent that life has been little that she expected, and disappointment has already begun to hang in her face. In a few years, before thirty-five even, she will be known among her people as a "settled woman."

She crosses to her son and gives him a good, final, rousing shake.

Ruth: Come on now, boy, it's seven thirty! *(Her son sits up at last, in a stupor of sleepiness.)* I say hurry up, Travis! You ain't the only person in the world got to use a bathroom!

(The child, a sturdy, handsome little boy of ten or eleven, drags himself out of the bed and almost blindly takes his towels and "today's clothes" from drawers and a closet and goes out to the bathroom, which is in an outside hall and which is shared by another family or families on the same floor. Ruth crosses to the bedroom door at right and opens it and calls in to her husband.)

Sean Combs and Phylicia Rashad in the 2008 film of *A Raisin in the Sun.*

Walter Lee! . . . It's after seven thirty! Lemme see you do some waking up in there now! *(She waits.)* You better get up from there, man! It's after seven thirty I tell you. *(She waits again.)* All right, you just go ahead and lay there and next thing you know Travis be finished and Mr. Johnson'll be in there and you'll be fussing and cussing round here like a madman! And be late too! *(She waits, at the end of patience.)* Walter Lee—it's time for you to GET UP!

(She waits another second and then starts to go into the bedroom, but is apparently satisfied that her husband has begun to get up. She stops, pulls the door to, and returns to the kitchen area. She wipes her face with a moist cloth and runs her fingers through her sleep-disheveled hair in a vain effort and ties an apron around her housecoat. The bedroom door at right opens and her husband stands in the doorway in his pajamas, which are rumpled and mismated. He is a lean, intense young man in his middle thirties, inclined to quick nervous movements and erratic speech habits—and always in his voice there is a quality of indictment.)

Walter: Is he out yet?

Ruth: What you mean *out*? He ain't hardly got in there good yet.

Walter (wandering in, still more oriented to sleep than to a new day): Well, what was you doing all that yelling for if I can't even get in there yet? *(Stopping and thinking.)* Check coming today?

Ruth: They *said* Saturday and this is just Friday and I hopes to God you ain't going to get up here first thing this morning and start talking to me 'bout no money—'cause I 'bout don't want to hear it.

Walter: Something the matter with you this morning?

Ruth: No—I'm just sleepy as the devil. What kind of eggs you want?

Walter: Not scrambled. *(Ruth starts to scramble eggs.)* Paper come? *(Ruth points impatiently to the rolled up* Tribune *on the table, and he gets it and spreads it out and vaguely reads the front page.)* Set off another bomb yesterday.

Ruth (maximum indifference): Did they?

Walter (looking up): What's the matter with you?

Ruth: Ain't nothing the matter with me. And don't keep asking me that this morning.

Walter: Ain't nobody bothering you. *(Reading the news of the day absently again.)* Say Colonel McCormick° is sick.

Ruth (affecting tea-party interest): Is he now? Poor thing.

Walter (sighing and looking at his watch): Oh, me. *(He waits.)* Now what is that boy doing in that bathroom all this time? He just going to have

Colonel McCormick: Robert R. McCormick (1880–1955) was an eccentric but influential newspaper publisher who founded the *Chicago Tribune* in 1914.

to start getting up earlier. I can't be being late to work on account of him fooling around in there.

Ruth (turning on him): Oh, no he ain't going to be getting up no earlier no such thing! It ain't his fault that he can't get to bed no earlier nights 'cause he got a bunch of crazy good-for-nothing clowns sitting up running their mouths in what is supposed to be his bedroom after ten o'clock at night . . .

Walter: That's what you mad about, ain't it? The things I want to talk about with my friends just couldn't be important in your mind, could they?

(He rises and finds a cigarette in her handbag on the table and crosses to the little window and looks out, smoking and deeply enjoying this first one.)

Ruth (almost matter of factly, a complaint too automatic to deserve emphasis): Why you always got to smoke before you eat in the morning?

Walter (at the window): Just look at 'em down there . . . Running and racing to work . . . *(He turns and faces his wife and watches her a moment at the stove, and then, suddenly)* You look young this morning, baby.

Ruth (indifferently): Yeah?

Walter: Just for a second—stirring them eggs. Just for a second it was—you looked real young again. *(He reaches for her; she crosses away. Then, drily)* It's gone now—you look like yourself again!

Ruth: Man, if you don't shut up and leave me alone.

Walter (looking out to the street again): First thing a man ought to learn in life is not to make love to no colored woman first thing in the morning. You all some eeeevil people at eight o'clock in the morning.

(Travis appears in the hall doorway, almost fully dressed and quite wide awake now, his towels and pajamas across his shoulders. He opens the door and signals for his father to make the bathroom in a hurry.)

Travis (watching the bathroom): Daddy, come on!

(Walter gets his bathroom utensils and flies out to the bathroom.)

Ruth: Sit down and have your breakfast, Travis.

Travis: Mama, this is Friday. *(Gleefully)* Check coming tomorrow, huh?

Ruth: You get your mind off money and eat your breakfast.

Travis (eating): This is the morning we supposed to bring the fifty cents to school.

Ruth: Well, I ain't got no fifty cents this morning.

Travis: Teacher say we have to.

Ruth: I don't care what teacher say. I ain't got it. Eat your breakfast, Travis.

Travis: I *am* eating.

Ruth: Hush up now and just eat!

(The boy gives her an exasperated look for her lack of understanding, and eats grudgingly.)

Travis: You think Grandmama would have it?

Ruth: No! And I want you to stop asking your grandmother for money, you hear me?

Travis (outraged): Gaaaleee! I don't ask her, she just gimme it sometimes!

Ruth: Travis Willard Younger—I got too much on me this morning to be—

Travis: Maybe Daddy—

Ruth: Travis!

(The boy hushes abruptly. They are both quiet and tense for several seconds.)

Travis (presently): Could I maybe go carry some groceries in front of the supermarket for a little while after school then?

Ruth: Just hush, I said. *(Travis jabs his spoon into his cereal bowl viciously, and rests his head in anger upon his fists.)* If you through eating, you can get over there and make up your bed.

(The boy obeys stiffly and crosses the room, almost mechanically, to the bed and more or less folds the bedding into a heap, then angrily gets his books and cap.)

Travis (sulking and standing apart from her unnaturally): I'm gone.

Ruth (looking up from the stove to inspect him automatically): Come here. *(He crosses to her and she studies his head.)* If you don't take this comb and fix this here head, you better! *(Travis puts down his books with a great sigh of oppression, and crosses to the mirror. His mother mutters under her breath about his "slubbornness.")* 'Bout to march out of here with that head looking just like chickens slept in it! I just don't know where you get your slubborn ways . . . And get your jacket, too. Looks chilly out this morning.

Travis (with conspicuously brushed hair and jacket): I'm gone.

Ruth: Get carfare and milk money—*(waving one finger)*—and not a single penny for no caps, you hear me?

Travis (with sullen politeness): Yes'm.

(He turns in outrage to leave. His mother watches after him as in his frustration he approaches the door almost comically. When she speaks to him, her voice has become a very gentle tease.)

Ruth (mocking; as she thinks he would say it): Oh, Mama makes me so mad sometimes, I don't know what to do! *(She waits and continues to his back as he stands stock-still in front of the door.)* I wouldn't kiss that woman good-bye for nothing in this world this morning!

(The boy finally turns around and rolls his eyes at her, knowing the mood has changed and he is vindicated; he does not, however, move toward her yet.)

Not for nothing in this world!

(She finally laughs aloud at him and holds out her arms to him and we see that it is a way between them, very old and practiced. He crosses to her and allows her to embrace him warmly but keeps his face fixed with masculine rigidity. She holds him back from her presently and looks at him and runs her fingers over the features of his face. With utter gentleness—)

Now—whose little old angry man are you?

Travis (the masculinity and gruffness start to fade at last): Aw gaalee—Mama . . .

Ruth (mimicking): Aw—gaaaaalleeeee, Mama! *(She pushes him, with rough playfulness and finality, toward the door.)* Get on out of here or you going to be late.

Travis (in the face of love, new aggressiveness): Mama, could I *please* go carry groceries?

Ruth: Honey, it's starting to get so cold evenings.

Walter (coming in from the bathroom and drawing a make-believe gun from a make-believe holster and shooting at his son): What is it he wants to do?

Ruth: Go carry groceries after school at the supermarket.

Walter: Well, let him go . . .

Travis (quickly, to the ally): I *have* to—she won't gimme the fifty cents . . .

Walter (to his wife only): Why not?

Ruth (simply, and with flavor): 'Cause we don't have it.

Walter (to Ruth only): What you tell the boy things like that for? *(Reaching down into his pants with a rather important gesture.)* Here, son—

(He hands the boy the coin, but his eyes are directed to his wife's. Travis takes the money happily.)

Travis: Thanks, Daddy.

(He starts out. Ruth watches both of them with murder in her eyes. Walter stands and stares back at her with defiance, and suddenly reaches into his pocket again on an afterthought.)

Walter (without even looking at his son, still staring hard at his wife): In fact, here's another fifty cents . . . Buy yourself some fruit today—or take a taxicab to school or something!

Travis: Whoopee—

(He leaps up and clasps his father around the middle with his legs, and they face each other in mutual appreciation; slowly Walter Lee peeks around the boy to catch the violent rays from his wife's eyes and draws his head back as if shot.)

Walter: You better get down now—and get to school, man.

Travis (at the door): O.K. Good-bye. *(He exits.)*

Walter (after him, pointing with pride): That's *my* boy. *(She looks at him in disgust and turns back to her work.)* You know what I was thinking 'bout in the bathroom this morning?

Ruth: No.

Walter: How come you always try to be so pleasant!

Ruth: What is there to be pleasant 'bout!

Walter: You want to know what I was thinking 'bout in the bathroom or not!

Ruth: I know what you thinking 'bout.

Walter (ignoring her): 'Bout what me and Willy Harris was talking about last night.

Ruth (immediately—a refrain): Willy Harris is a good-for-nothing loudmouth.

Walter: Anybody who talks to me has got to be a good-for-nothing loudmouth, ain't he? And what you know about who is just a good-for-nothing loudmouth? Charlie Atkins was just a "good-for-nothing loudmouth" too, wasn't he! When he wanted me to go in the dry-cleaning business with him. And now—he's grossing a hundred thousand a year. A hundred thousand dollars a year! You still call *him* a loudmouth!

Ruth (bitterly): Oh, Walter Lee . . .

(She folds her head on her arms over the table.)

Walter (rising and coming to her and standing over her): You tired, ain't you? Tired of everything. Me, the boy, the way we live—this beat-up hole—everything. Ain't you? *(She doesn't look up, doesn't answer.)* So tired—moaning and groaning all the time, but you wouldn't do nothing to help, would you? You couldn't be on my side that long for nothing, could you?

Ruth: Walter, please leave me alone.

Walter: A man needs for a woman to back him up . . .

Ruth: Walter—

Walter: Mama would listen to you. You know she listen to you more than she do me and Bennie. She think more of you. All you have to do is just sit down with her when you drinking your coffee one morning and talking 'bout things like you do and—*(He sits down beside her and demonstrates graphically what he thinks her methods and tone should be.)*—you just sip your coffee, see, and say easy like that you been thinking 'bout that deal Walter Lee is so interested in, 'bout the store and all, and sip some more coffee, like what you saying ain't really that important to you—And the next thing you know, she be listening good and asking you questions and when I come home—I can tell her the details. This ain't no fly-by-night proposition, baby. I mean we figured it out, me and Willy and Bobo.

Ruth (with a frown): Bobo?

Walter: Yeah. You see, this little liquor store we got in mind cost seventy-five thousand and we figured the initial investment on the place be 'bout thirty thousand, see. That be ten thousand each. Course, there's a couple of hundred you got to pay so's you don't spend your life just waiting for them clowns to let your license get approved—

Ruth: You mean graft?

Walter (frowning impatiently): Don't call it that. See there, that just goes to show you what women understand about the world. Baby, don't *nothing* happen for you in this world 'less you pay *somebody* off!

Ruth: Walter, leave me alone! *(She raises her head and stares at him vigorously—then says, more quietly.)* Eat your eggs, they gonna be cold.

Walter (straightening up from her and looking off): That's it. There you are. Man say to his woman: I got me a dream. His woman say: Eat your eggs. *(Sadly, but gaining in power.)* Man say: I got to take hold of this here world, baby! And a woman will say: Eat your eggs and go to work. *(Passionately now.)* Man say: I got to change my life, I'm choking to death, baby! And his woman say—*(In utter anguish as he brings his fists down on his thighs)*—Your eggs is getting cold!

Ruth (softly): Walter, that ain't none of our money.

Walter (not listening at all or even looking at her): This morning, I was lookin' in the mirror and thinking about it . . . I'm thirty-five years old; I been married eleven years and I got a boy who sleeps in the living room—*(very, very quietly)*—and all I got to give him is stories about how rich white people live . . .

Ruth: Eat your eggs, Walter.

Walter (slams the table and jumps up): DAMN MY EGGS—DAMN ALL THE EGGS THAT EVER WAS!

Ruth: Then go to work.

Walter (looking up at her): See—I'm trying to talk to you 'bout myself—*(Shaking his head with the repetition.)*—and all you can say is eat them eggs and go to work.

Ruth (wearily): Honey, you never say nothing new. I listen to you every day, every night and every morning, and you never say nothing new. *(Shrugging.)* So you would rather *be* Mr. Arnold than be his chauffeur. So—I would *rather* be living in Buckingham Palace.

Walter: That is just what is wrong with the colored woman in this world . . . Don't understand about building their men up and making 'em feel like they somebody. Like they can do something.

Ruth (drily, but to hurt): There *are* colored men who do things.

Walter: No thanks to the colored woman.

Ruth: Well, being a colored woman, I guess I can't help myself none.

(She rises and gets the ironing board and sets it up and attacks a huge pile of rough-dried clothes, sprinkling them in preparation for the ironing and then rolling them into tight fat balls.)

Walter (mumbling): We one group of men tied to a race of women with small minds!

(His sister Beneatha enters. She is about twenty, as slim and intense as her brother. She is not as pretty as her sister-in-law, but her lean, almost intellectual face has a handsomeness of its own. She wears a bright-red flannel nightie, and her thick hair stands wildly about her head. Her speech is a mixture of many things; it is different from the rest of the family's insofar as education has permeated her sense of English—and perhaps the Midwest rather than the South has finally—at last—won out in her inflection; but not altogether, because over all of it is a soft slurring and transformed use of vowels which is the decided influence of the Southside. She passes through the room without looking at either Ruth or Walter and goes to the outside door and looks, a little blindly, out to the bathroom. She sees that it has been lost to the Johnsons. She closes the door with a sleepy vengeance and crosses to the table and sits down a little defeated.)

Beneatha: I am going to start timing those people.

Walter: You should get up earlier.

Beneatha (her face in her hands. She is still fighting the urge to go back to bed): Really—would you suggest dawn? Where's the paper?

Walter (pushing the paper across the table to her as he studies her almost clinically, as though he has never seen her before): You a horrible-looking chick at this hour.

Beneatha (drily): Good morning, everybody.

Walter (senselessly): How is school coming?

Beneatha (in the same spirit): Lovely. Lovely. And you know, biology is the greatest. *(Looking up at him.)* I dissected something that looked just like you yesterday.

Walter: I just wondered if you've made up your mind and everything.

Beneatha (gaining in sharpness and impatience): And what did I answer yesterday morning—and the day before that?

Ruth (from the ironing board, like someone disinterested and old): Don't be so nasty, Bennie.

Beneatha (still to her brother): And the day before that and the day before that!

Walter (defensively): I'm interested in you. Something wrong with that? Ain't many girls who decide—

Walter and Beneatha (in unison): —"to be a doctor."

(Silence.)

Walter: Have we figured out yet just exactly how much medical school is going to cost?

Ruth: Walter Lee, why don't you leave that girl alone and get out of here to work?

Beneatha (exits to the bathroom and bangs on the door): Come on out of there, please!

(She comes back into the room.)

Walter (looking at his sister intently): You know the check is coming tomorrow.

Beneatha (turning on him with a sharpness all her own): That money belongs to Mama, Walter, and it's for her to decide how she wants to use it. I don't care if she wants to buy a house or a rocket ship or just nail it up somewhere and look at it. It's hers. Not ours—*hers.*

Walter (bitterly): Now ain't that fine! You just got your mother's interest at heart, ain't you, girl? You such a nice girl—but if Mama got that money she can always take a few thousand and help you through school too—can't she?

Beneatha: I have never asked anyone around here to do anything for me!

Walter: No! And the line between asking and just accepting when the time comes is big and wide—ain't it!

Beneatha (with fury): What do you want from me, Brother—that I quit school or just drop dead, which!

Walter: I don't want nothing but for you to stop acting holy 'round here. Me and Ruth done made some sacrifices for you—why can't you do something for the family?

Ruth: Walter, don't be dragging me in it.

Walter: You are in it—Don't you get up and go work in somebody's kitchen for the last three years to help put clothes on her back?

Ruth: Oh, Walter—that's not fair . . .

Walter: It ain't that nobody expects you to get on your knees and say thank you, Brother; thank you, Ruth; thank you, Mama—and thank you, Travis, for wearing the same pair of shoes for two semesters—

Beneatha (dropping to her knees): Well—I *do*—all right?—thank everybody! And forgive me for ever wanting to be anything at all! *(Pursuing him on her knees across the floor.)* FORGIVE ME, FORGIVE ME, FORGIVE ME!

Ruth: Please stop it! Your mama'll hear you.

Walter: Who the hell told you you had to be a doctor? If you so crazy 'bout messing 'round with sick people—then go be a nurse like other women—or just get married and be quiet . . .

Beneatha: Well—you finally got it said . . . It took you three years but you finally got it said. Walter, give up; leave me alone—it's Mama's money.

Walter: He was my father, too!

Beneatha: So what? He was mine, too—and Travis' grandfather—but the insurance money belongs to Mama. Picking on me is not going to make her give it to you to invest in any liquor stores—*(Underbreath, dropping into a chair.)*—and I for one say, God bless Mama for that!

Walter (to Ruth): See—did you hear? Did you hear!
Ruth: Honey, please go to work.
Walter: Nobody in this house is ever going to understand me.
Beneatha: Because you're a nut.
Walter: Who's a nut?
Beneatha: You—you are a nut. Thee is mad, boy.
Walter (looking at his wife and his sister from the door, very sadly): The world's most backward race of people, and that's a fact.
Beneatha (turning slowly in her chair): And then there are all those prophets who would lead us out of the wilderness—*(Walter slams out of the house.)*—into the swamps!
Ruth: Bennie, why you always gotta be pickin' on your brother? Can't you be a little sweeter sometimes?

(Door opens. Walter walks in. He fumbles with his cap, starts to speak, clears throat, looks everywhere but at Ruth. Finally:)

Walter (to Ruth): I need some money for carfare.
Ruth (looks at him, then warms; teasing, but tenderly): Fifty cents? *(She goes to her bag and gets money.)* Here—take a taxi!

(Walter exits. Mama enters. She is a woman in her early sixties, full-bodied and strong. She is one of those women of a certain grace and beauty who wear it so unobtrusively that it takes a while to notice. Her dark-brown face is surrounded by the total whiteness of her hair, and, being a woman who has adjusted to many things in life and overcome many more, her face is full of strength. She has, we can see, wit and faith of a kind that keep her eyes lit and full of interest and expectancy. She is, in a word, a beautiful woman. Her bearing is perhaps most like the noble bearing of the women of the Hereros of Southwest Africa—rather as if she imagines that as she walks she still bears a basket or a vessel upon her head. Her speech, on the other hand, is as careless as her carriage is precise—she is inclined to slur everything—but her voice is perhaps not so much quiet as simply soft.)

Mama: Who that 'round here slamming doors at this hour?

(She crosses through the room, goes to the window, opens it, and brings in a feeble little plant growing doggedly in a small pot on the windowsill. She feels the dirt and puts it back out.)

Ruth: That was Walter Lee. He and Bennie was at it again.
Mama: My children and they tempers. Lord, if this little old plant don't get more sun than it's been getting it ain't never going to see spring again. *(She turns from the window.)* What's the matter with you this morning, Ruth? You looks right peaked. You aiming to iron all them things? Leave some for me. I'll get to 'em this afternoon. Bennie honey, it's too drafty for you to be sitting 'round half dressed. Where's your robe?

Beneatha: In the cleaners.

Mama: Well, go get mine and put it on.

Beneatha: I'm not cold, Mama, honest.

Mama: I know—but you so thin . . .

Beneatha (irritably): Mama, I'm not cold.

Mama (seeing the make-down bed as Travis has left it): Lord have mercy, look at that poor bed. Bless his heart—he tries, don't he? *(She moves to the bed Travis has sloppily made up.)*

Ruth: No—he don't half try at all 'cause he knows you going to come along behind him and fix everything. That's just how come he don't know how to do nothing right now—you done spoiled that boy so.

Mama (folding bedding): Well—he's a little boy. Ain't supposed to know 'bout housekeeping. My baby, that's what he is. What you fix for his breakfast this morning?

Ruth (angrily): I feed my son, Lena!

Mama: I ain't meddling—*(Underbreath; busy-bodyish)* I just noticed all last week he had cold cereal, and when it starts getting this chilly in the fall a child ought to have some hot grits or something when he goes out in the cold—

Ruth (furious): I gave him hot oats—is that all right!

Mama: I ain't meddling. *(Pause.)* Put a lot of nice butter on it? *(Ruth shoots her an angry look and does not reply.)* He likes lots of butter.

Ruth (exasperated): Lena—

Mama (to Beneatha. Mama is inclined to wander conversationally sometimes): What was you and your brother fussing 'bout this morning?

Beneatha: It's not important, Mama.

(She gets up and goes to look out at the bathroom, which is apparently free, and she picks up her towels and rushes out.)

Mama: What was they fighting about?

Ruth: Now you know as well as I do.

Mama (shaking her head): Brother still worrying hisself sick about that money?

Ruth: You know he is.

Mama: You had breakfast?

Ruth: Some coffee.

Mama: Girl, you better start eating and looking after yourself better. You almost thin as Travis.

Ruth: Lena—

Mama: Un-hunh?

Ruth: What are you going to do with it?

Mama: Now don't you start, child. It's too early in the morning to be talking about money. It ain't Christian.

Ruth: It's just that he got his heart set on that store—

Mama: You mean that liquor store that Willy Harris want him to invest in?

Ruth: Yes—

Mama: We ain't no business people, Ruth. We just plain working folks.

Ruth: Ain't nobody business people till they go into business. Walter Lee say colored people ain't never going to start getting ahead till they start gambling on some different kinds of things in the world—investments and things.

Mama: What done got into you, girl? Walter Lee done finally sold you on investing.

Ruth: No. Mama, something is happening between Walter and me. I don't know what it is—but he needs something—something I can't give him any more. He needs this chance, Lena.

Mama (frowning deeply): But liquor, honey—

Ruth: Well—like Walter say—I spec people going to always be drinking themselves some liquor.

Mama: Well—whether they drinks it or not ain't none of my business. But whether I go into business selling it to 'em *is,* and I don't want that on my ledger this late in life. *(Stopping suddenly and studying her daughter-in-law.)* Ruth Younger, what's the matter with you today? You look like you could fall over right there.

Ruth: I'm tired.

Mama: Then you better stay home from work today.

Ruth: I can't stay home. She'd be calling up the agency and screaming at them, "My girl didn't come in today—send me somebody! My girl didn't come in!" Oh, she just have a fit . . .

Mama: Well, let her have it. I'll just call her up and say you got the flu—

Ruth (laughing): Why the flu?

Mama: 'Cause it sounds respectable to 'em. Something white people get, too. They know 'bout the flu. Otherwise they think you been cut up or something when you tell 'em you sick.

Ruth: I got to go in. We need the money.

Mama: Somebody would of thought my children done all but starved to death the way they talk about money here late. Child, we got a great big old check coming tomorrow.

Ruth (sincerely, but also self-righteously): Now that's your money. It ain't got nothing to do with me. We all feel like that—Walter and Bennie and me—even Travis.

Mama (thoughtfully, and suddenly very far away): Ten thousand dollars—

Ruth: Sure is wonderful.

Mama: Ten thousand dollars.

Ruth: You know what you should do, Miss Lena? You should take yourself a trip somewhere. To Europe or South America or someplace—

Mama (throwing up her hands at the thought): Oh, child!

Ruth: I'm serious. Just pack up and leave! Go on away and enjoy yourself some. Forget about the family and have yourself a ball for once in your life—

Mama (drily): You sound like I'm just about ready to die. Who'd go with me? What I look like wandering 'round Europe by myself?

Ruth: Shoot—these here rich white women do it all the time. They don't think nothing of packing up they suitcases and piling on one of them big steamships and—swoosh!—they gone, child.

Mama: Something always told me I wasn't no rich white woman.

Ruth: Well—what are you going to do with it then?

Mama: I ain't rightly decided. *(Thinking. She speaks now with emphasis.)* Some of it got to be put away for Beneatha and her schoolin'—and ain't nothing going to touch that part of it. Nothing. *(She waits several seconds, trying to make up her mind about something, and looks at Ruth a little tentatively before going on.)* Been thinking that we maybe could meet the notes on a little old two-story somewhere, with a yard where Travis could play in the summertime, if we use part of the insurance for a down payment and everybody kind of pitch in. I could maybe take on a little day work again, few days a week—

Ruth (studying her mother-in-law furtively and concentrating on her ironing, anxious to encourage without seeming to): Well, Lord knows, we've put enough rent into this here rat trap to pay for four houses by now . . .

Mama (looking up at the words "rat trap" and then looking around and leaning back and sighing—in a suddenly reflective mood): "Rat trap"—yes, that's all it is. *(Smiling.)* I remember just as well the day me and Big Walter moved in here. Hadn't been married but two weeks and wasn't planning on living here no more than a year. *(She shakes her head at the dissolved dream.)* We was going to set away, little by little, don't you know, and buy a little place out in Morgan Park. We had even picked out the house. *(Chuckling a little.)* Looks right dumpy today. But Lord, child, you should know all the dreams I had 'bout buying that house and fixing it up and making me a little garden in the back—*(She waits and stops smiling.)* And didn't none of it happen. *(Dropping her hands in a futile gesture.)*

Ruth (keeps her head down, ironing): Yes, life can be a barrel of disappointments, sometimes.

Mama: Honey, Big Walter would come in here some nights back then and slump down on that couch there and just look at the rug, and look at me and look at the rug and then back at me—and I'd know he was down then . . . really down. *(After a second very long and thoughtful pause; she is seeing back to times that only she can see.)* And then, Lord, when I lost that baby—little Claude—I almost thought I was going to lose Big Walter too. Oh, that man grieved hisself! He was one man to love his children.

Ruth: Ain't nothin' can tear at you like losin' your baby.

Mama: I guess that's how come that man finally worked hisself t
like he done. Like he was fighting his own war with this here
that took his baby from him.

Ruth: He sure was a fine man, all right. I always liked Mr. Younger.

Mama: Crazy 'bout his children! God knows there was plenty wrong w Walter Younger—hard-headed, mean, kind of wild with women plenty wrong with him. But he sure loved his children. Alway wanted them to have something—be something. That's where Brother gets all these notions, I reckon. Big Walter used to say, he'd get right wet in the eyes sometimes, lean his head back with the water standing in his eyes and say, "Seem like God didn't see fit to give the black man nothing but dreams—but He did give us children to make them dreams seem worth while." *(She smiles.)* He could talk like that, don't you know.

Ruth: Yes, he sure could. He was a good man, Mr. Younger.

Mama: Yes, a fine man—just couldn't never catch up with his dreams, that's all.

(Beneatha comes in, brushing her hair and looking up to the ceiling, where the sound of a vacuum cleaner has started up.)

Beneatha: What could be so dirty on that woman's rugs that she has to vacuum them every single day?

Ruth: I wish certain young women 'round here who I could name would take inspiration about certain rugs in a certain apartment I could also mention.

Beneatha (shrugging): How much cleaning can a house need, for Christ's sakes.

Mama (not liking the Lord's name used thus): Bennie!

Ruth: Just listen to her—just listen!

Beneatha: Oh, God!

Mama: If you use the Lord's name just one more time—

Beneatha (a bit of a whine): Oh, Mama—

Ruth: Fresh—just fresh as salt, this girl!

Beneatha (drily): Well—if the salt loses its savor°—

Mama: Now that will do. I just ain't going to have you 'round here reciting the scriptures in vain—you hear me?

Beneatha: How did I manage to get on everybody's wrong side by just walking into a room?

Ruth: If you weren't so fresh—

Beneatha: Ruth, I'm twenty years old.

Mama: What time you be home from school today?

if the salt loses its savor: Beneatha's retort is a reference to the verse from Matthew 5:13—"You are the salt of the earth: but if the salt have lost his savor, wherewith shall it be salted? It is thenceforth good for nothing, but to be cast out . . ."

death
world

...usiasm.*) Madeline is going to start my

...*p with the same expression.*)

...f lessons?

...ith

...e you done taken it in your mind to learn to play the

...ust want to, that's all.

...*aling*): Lord, child, don't you know what to do with yourself? ...w long it going to be before you get tired of this now—like you got tired of that little play-acting group you joined last year? (*Looking at Ruth.*) And what was it the year before that?

Ruth: The horseback-riding club for which she bought that fifty-five-dollar riding habit that's been hanging in the closet ever since!

Mama (to Beneatha): Why you got to flit so from one thing to another, baby?

Beneatha (sharply): I just want to learn to play the guitar. Is there anything wrong with that?

Mama: Ain't nobody trying to stop you. I just wonders sometimes why you has to flit so from one thing to another all the time. You ain't never done nothing with all that camera equipment you brought home—

Beneatha: I don't flit! I—I experiment with different forms of expression—

Ruth: Like riding a horse?

Beneatha: —People have to express themselves one way or another.

Mama: What is it you want to express?

Beneatha (angrily): Me! (*Mama and Ruth look at each other and burst into raucous laughter.*) Don't worry—I don't expect you to understand.

Mama (to change the subject): Who you going out with tomorrow night?

Beneatha (with displeasure): George Murchison again.

Mama (pleased): Oh—you getting a little sweet on him?

Ruth: You ask me, this child ain't sweet on nobody but herself—(*Underbreath.*) Express herself! (*They laugh.*)

Beneatha: Oh—I like George all right, Mama. I mean I like him enough to go out with him and stuff, but—

Ruth (for devilment): What does *and stuff* mean?

Beneatha: Mind your own business.

Mama: Stop picking at her now, Ruth. (*She chuckles. A thoughtful pause, and then a suspicious sudden look at her daughter as she turns in her chair for emphasis.*) What DOES it mean?

Beneatha (wearily): Oh, I just mean I couldn't ever really be serious about George. He's—he's so shallow.

Ruth: Shallow—what do you mean he's shallow? He's *rich!*

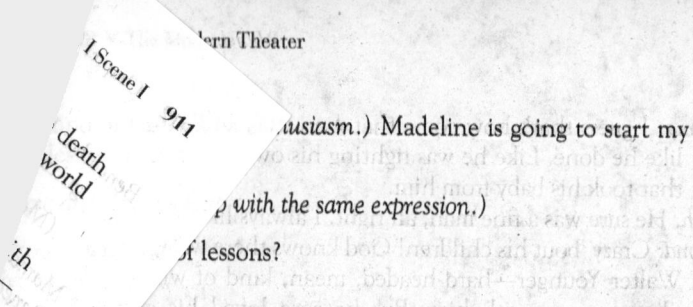

Mama: Hush, Ruth.
Beneatha: I know he's rich. He knows he's rich, too.
Ruth: Well—what other qualities a man got to have to satisfy you, little girl?
Beneatha: You wouldn't even begin to understand. Anybody who married Walter could not possibly understand.
Mama (outraged): What kind of way is that to talk about your brother?
Beneatha: Brother is a flip—let's face it.
Mama (to Ruth, helplessly): What's a flip?
Ruth (glad to add kindling): She's saying he's crazy.
Beneatha: Not crazy. Brother isn't really crazy yet—he—he's an elaborate neurotic.
Mama: Hush your mouth!
Beneatha: As for George. Well. George looks good—he's got a beautiful car and he takes me to nice places and, as my sister-in-law says, he is probably the richest boy I will ever get to know and I even like him sometimes—but if the Youngers are sitting around waiting to see if their little Bennie is going to tie up the family with the Murchisons, they are wasting their time.
Ruth: You mean you wouldn't marry George Murchison if he asked you someday? That pretty, rich thing? Honey, I knew you was odd—
Beneatha: No I would not marry him if all I felt for him was what I feel now. Besides, George's family wouldn't really like it.
Mama: Why not?
Beneatha: Oh, Mama—The Murchisons are honest-to-God-real-*live*-rich colored people, and the only people in the world who are more snobbish than rich white people are rich colored people. I thought everybody knew that. I've met Mrs. Murchison. She's a scene!
Mama: You must not dislike people 'cause they well off, honey.
Beneatha: Why not? It makes just as much sense as disliking people 'cause they are poor, and lots of people do that.
Ruth (a wisdom-of-the-ages manner. To Mama): Well, she'll get over some of this—
Beneatha: Get over it? What are you talking about, Ruth? Listen, I'm going to be a doctor. I'm not worried about who I'm going to marry yet—if I ever get married.
Mama and Ruth: If!
Mama: Now, Bennie—
Beneatha: Oh, I probably will . . . but first I'm going to be a doctor, and George, for one, still thinks that's pretty funny. I couldn't be bothered with that. I am going to be a doctor and everybody around here better understand that!
Mama (kindly): 'Course you going to be a doctor, honey, God willing.
Beneatha (drily): God hasn't got a thing to do with it.
Mama: Beneatha—that just wasn't necessary.

Beneatha: Well—neither is God. I get sick of hearing about God.

Mama: Beneatha!

Beneatha: I mean it! I'm just tired of hearing about God all the time. What has He got to do with anything? Does He pay tuition?

Mama: You 'bout to get your fresh little jaw slapped!

Ruth: That's just what she needs, all right!

Beneatha: Why? Why can't I say what I want to around here, like everybody else?

Mama: It don't sound nice for a young girl to say things like that—you wasn't brought up that way. Me and your father went to trouble to get you and Brother to church every Sunday.

Beneatha: Mama, you don't understand. It's all a matter of ideas, and God is just one idea I don't accept. It's not important. I am not going out and be immoral or commit crimes because I don't believe in God. I don't even think about it. It's just that I get tired of Him getting credit for all the things the human race achieves through its own stubborn effort. There simply is no blasted God—there is only man and it is *he* who makes miracles!

(Mama absorbs this speech, studies her daughter and rises slowly and crosses to Beneatha and slaps her powerfully across the face. After, there is only silence and the daughter drops her eyes from her mother's face, and Mama is very tall before her.)

Mama: Now—you say after me, in my mother's house there is still God. *(There is a long pause and Beneatha stares at the floor wordlessly. Mama repeats the phrase with precision and cool emotion.)* In my mother's house there is still God.

Beneatha: In my mother's house there is still God.

(A long pause.)

Mama (walking away from Beneatha, too disturbed for triumphant posture. Stopping and turning back to her daughter): There are some ideas we ain't going to have in this house. Not long as I am at the head of this family.

Beneatha: Yes, ma'am.

(Mama walks out of the room.)

Ruth (almost gently, with profound understanding): You think you a woman, Bennie—but you still a little girl. What you did was childish—so you got treated like a child.

Beneatha: I see. *(Quietly.)* I also see that everybody thinks it's all right for Mama to be a tyrant. But all the tyranny in the world will never put a God in the heavens!

(She picks up her books and goes out. Pause.)

Ruth (goes to Mama's door): She said she was sorry.

Mama (coming out, going to her plant): They frightens me, Ruth. My children.

Ruth: You got good children, Lena. They just a little off sometimes—but they're good.

Mama: No—there's something come down between me and them that don't let us understand each other and I don't know what it is. One done almost lost his mind thinking 'bout money all the time and the other done commence to talk about things I can't seem to understand in no form or fashion. What is it that's changing, Ruth?

Ruth (soothingly, older than her years): Now . . . you taking it all too seriously. You just got strong-willed children and it takes a strong woman like you to keep 'em in hand.

Mama (looking at her plant and sprinkling a little water on it): They spirited all right, my children. Got to admit they got spirit—Bennie and Walter. Like this little old plant that ain't never had enough sunshine or nothing—and look at it . . .

(She has her back to Ruth, who has had to stop ironing and lean against something and put the back of her hand to her forehead.)

Ruth (trying to keep Mama from noticing): You . . . sure . . . loves that little old thing, don't you? . . .

Mama: Well, I always wanted me a garden like I used to see sometimes at the back of the houses down home. This plant is close as I ever got to having one. *(She looks out of the window as she replaces the plant.)* Lord, ain't nothing as dreary as the view from this window on a dreary day, is there? Why ain't you singing this morning, Ruth? Sing that "No Ways Tired." That song always lifts me up so—*(She turns at last to see that Ruth has slipped quietly to the floor, in a state of semiconsciousness.)* Ruth! Ruth honey—what's the matter with you . . . Ruth!

ACT I

SCENE II

It is the following morning; a Saturday morning, and house cleaning is in progress at the Youngers'. Furniture has been shoved hither and yon and Mama is giving the kitchen-area walls a washing down. Beneatha, in dungrees, with a handkerchief tied around her face, is spraying insecticide into the cracks in the walls. As they work, the radio is on and a Southside disk-jockey program is inappropriately filling the house with a rather exotic saxophone blues. Travis, the sole idle one, is leaning on his arms, looking out of the window.

Travis: Grandmama, that stuff Bennie is using smells awful. Can I go downstairs, please?

Mama: Did you get all them chores done already? I ain't seen you doing much.

Travis: Yes'm—finished early. Where did Mama go this morning?

Mama (looking at Beneatha): She had to go on a little errand.

(The phone rings. Beneatha runs to answer it and reaches it before Walter, who has entered from bedroom.)

Travis: Where?

Mama: To tend to her business.

Beneatha: Haylo . . . *(Disappointed.)* Yes, he is. *(She tosses the phone to Walter, who barely catches it.)* It's Willie Harris again.

Walter (as privately as possible under Mama's gaze): Hello, Willie. Did you get the papers from the lawyer? . . . No, not yet. I told you the mailman doesn't get here till ten-thirty . . . No, I'll come there . . . Yeah! Right away. *(He hangs up and goes for his coat.)*

Beneatha: Brother, where did Ruth go?

Walter (as he exits): How should I know!

Travis: Aw come on, Grandma. Can I go outside?

Mama: Oh, I guess so. You stay right in front of the house, though, and keep a good lookout for the postman.

Travis: Yes'm. *(He darts into bedroom for stickball and bat, reenters, and sees Beneatha on her knees spraying under sofa with behind upraised. He edges closer to the target, takes aim, and lets her have it. She screams.)* Leave them poor little cockroaches alone, they ain't bothering you none! *(He runs as she swings the spraygun at him viciously and playfully.)* Grandma! Grandma!

Mama: Look out there, girl, before you be spilling some of that stuff on that child!

Travis (safely behind the bastion of Mama): That's right—look out, now! *(He exits.)*

Beneatha (drily): I can't imagine that it would hurt him—it has never hurt the roaches.

Mama: Well, little boys' hides ain't as tough as Southside roaches. You better get over there behind the bureau. I seen one marching out of there like Napoleon yesterday.

Beneatha: There's really only one way to get rid of them, Mama—

Mama: How?

Beneatha: Set fire to this building! Mama, where did Ruth go?

Mama (looking at her with meaning): To the doctor, I think.

Beneatha: The doctor? What's the matter? *(They exchange glances.)* You don't think—

Mama (with her sense of drama): Now I ain't saying what I think. But I ain't never been wrong 'bout a woman neither.

(The phone rings.)

Beneatha (at the phone): Hay-lo . . . *(pause, and a moment of recognition)* Well—when did you get back! . . . And how was it? . . . Of course I've missed you—in my way . . . This morning? No . . . house cleaning and all that and Mama hates it if I let people come over when the house is like this . . . You *have?* Well, that's different . . . What is it—Oh, what the hell, come on over . . . Right, see you then. *Arrividerci. (She hangs up.)*

Mama (who has listened vigorously, as is her habit): Who is that you inviting over here with this house looking like this? You ain't got the pride you was born with!

Beneatha: Asagai doesn't care how houses look, Mama—he's an intellectual.

Mama: Who?

Beneatha: Asagai—Joseph Asagai. He's an African boy I met on campus. He's been studying in Canada all summer.

Mama: What's his name?

Beneatha: Asagai, Joseph. Ah-sah-guy . . . He's from Nigeria.

Mama: Oh, that's the little country that was founded by slaves way back . . .

Beneatha: No, Mama—that's Liberia.

Mama: I don't think I never met no African before.

Beneatha: Well, do me a favor and don't ask him a whole lot of ignorant questions about Africans. I mean, do they wear clothes and all that—

Mama: Well, now, I guess if you think we so ignorant 'round here maybe you shouldn't bring your friends here—

Beneatha: It's just that people ask such crazy things. All anyone seems to know about when it comes to Africa is Tarzan—

Mama (indignantly): Why should I know anything about Africa?

Beneatha: Why do you give money at church for the missionary work?

Mama: Well, that's to help save people.

Beneatha: You mean save them from *heathenism*—

Mama (innocently): Yes.

Beneatha: I'm afraid they need more salvation from the British and the French.

(Ruth comes in forlornly and pulls off her coat with dejection. They both turn to look at her.)

Ruth (dispiritedly): Well, I guess from all the happy faces—everybody knows.

Beneatha: You pregnant?

Mama: Lord have mercy, I sure hope it's a little old girl. Travis ought to have a sister.

(Beneatha and Ruth give her a hopeless look for this grandmotherly enthusiasm.)

Beneatha: How far along are you?

Ruth: Two months.
Beneatha: Did you mean to? I mean did you plan it or was it an accident?
Mama: What do you know about planning or not planning?
Beneatha: Oh, Mama.
Ruth (wearily): She's twenty years old, Lena.
Beneatha: Did you plan it, Ruth?
Ruth: Mind your own business.
Beneatha: It is my business—where is he going to live, on the *roof? (There is silence following the remark as the three women react to the sense of it.)* Gee—I didn't mean that, Ruth, honest. Gee, I don't feel like that at all. I—I think it is wonderful.
Ruth (dully): Wonderful.
Beneatha: Yes—really. *(There is a sudden commotion from the street and she goes to the window to look out.)* What on earth is going on out there? These kids. *(There are, as she throws open the window, the shouts of children rising up from the street. She sticks her head out to see better and calls out.)* TRAVIS! TRAVIS! . . . WHAT ARE YOU DOING DOWN THERE? *(She sees.)* Oh Lord, they're chasing a rat!

(Ruth covers her face with hands and turns away.)

Mama (angrily): Tell that youngun to get himself up here, at once!
Beneatha: TRAVIS . . . YOU COME UPSTAIRS . . . AT ONCE!
Ruth (her face twisted): Chasing a rat . . .
Mama (looking at Ruth, worried): Doctor say everything going to be all right?
Ruth (far away): Yes—she says everything is going to be fine . . .
Mama (immediately suspicious): "She"—What doctor you went to?

(Ruth just looks at Mama meaningfully and Mama opens her mouth to speak as Travis bursts in.)

Travis (excited and full of narrative, coming directly to his mother): Mama, you should of seen the rat . . . Big as a cat, honest! *(He shows an exaggerated size with his hands.)* Gaaleee, that rat was really cuttin' and Bubber caught him with his heel and the janitor, Mr. Barnett, got him with a stick—and then they got him in a corner and—BAM! BAM! BAM!—and he was still jumping around and bleeding like everything too—there's rat blood all over the street—

(Ruth reaches out suddenly and grabs her son without even looking at him and clamps her hand over his mouth and holds him to her. Mama crosses to them rapidly and takes the boy from her.)

Mama: You hush up now . . . talking all that terrible stuff . . .

(Travis is staring at his mother with a stunned expression. Beneatha comes quickly and takes him away from his grandmother and ushers him to the door.)

Beneatha: You go back outside and play . . . but not with any rats. *(She pushes him gently out the door with the boy straining to see what is wrong with his mother.)*

Mama (worriedly hovering over Ruth): Ruth honey—what's the matter with you—you sick?

(Ruth has her fists clenched on her thighs and is fighting hard to suppress a scream that seems to be rising in her.)

Beneatha: What's the matter with her, Mama?

Mama (working her fingers in Ruth's shoulders to relax her): She be all right. Women gets right depressed sometimes when they get her way. *(Speaking softly, expertly, rapidly.)* Now you just relax. That's right . . . just lean back, don't think 'bout nothing at all . . . nothing at all—

Ruth: I'm all right . . .

(The glassy-eyed look melts and then she collapses into a fit of heavy sobbing. The bell rings.)

Beneatha: Oh, my God—that must be Asagai.

Mama (to Ruth): Come on now, honey. You need to lie down and rest awhile . . . then have some nice hot food.

(They exit, Ruth's weight on her mother-in-law. Beneatha, herself profoundly disturbed, opens the door to admit a rather dramatic-looking young man with a large package.)

Asagai: Hello, Alaiyo—

Beneatha (holding the door open and regarding him with pleasure): Hello . . . *(Long pause.)* Well—come in. And please excuse everything. My mother was very upset about my letting anyone come here with the place like this.

Asagai (coming into the room): You look disturbed too . . . Is something wrong?

Beneatha (still at the door, absently): Yes . . . we've all got acute ghetto-itis. *(She smiles and comes toward him, finding a cigarette and sitting.)* So—sit down! No! Wait! *(She whips the spray gun off sofa where she had left it and puts the cushions back. At last perches on arm of sofa. He sits.)* So, how was Canada?

Asagai (a sophisticate): Canadian.

Beneatha (looking at him): Asagai, I'm very glad you are back.

Asagai (looking back at her in turn): Are you really?

Beneatha: Yes—very.

Asagai: Why?—you were quite glad when I went away. What happened?

Beneatha: You went away.

Asagai: Ahhhhhhhh.

Beneatha: Before—you wanted to be so serious before there was time.

Asagai: How much time must there be before one knows what one feels?

Beneatha (stalling this particular conversation. Her hands pressed together, in a deliberately childish gesture): What did you bring me?

Asagai (handing her the package): Open it and see.

Beneatha (eagerly opening the package and drawing out some records and the colorful robes of a Nigerian woman): Oh, Asagai! . . . You got them for me! . . . How beautiful . . . and the records too! *(She lifts out the robes and runs to the mirror with them and holds the drapery up in front of herself.)*

Asagai (coming to her at the mirror): I shall have to teach you how to drape it properly. *(He flings the material about her for the moment and stands back to look at her.)* Ah—*Oh-pay-gay-day, oh-gbah-mu-shay. (A Yoruba exclamation for admiration.)* You wear it well . . . very well . . . mutilated hair and all.

Beneatha (turning suddenly): My hair—what's wrong with my hair?

Asagai (shrugging): Were you born with it like that?

Beneatha (reaching up to touch it): No . . . of course not. *(She looks back to the mirror, disturbed.)*

Asagai (smiling): How then?

Beneatha: You know perfectly well how . . . as crinkly as yours . . . that's how.

Asagai: And it is ugly to you that way?

Beneatha (quickly): Oh, no—not ugly . . . *(More slowly, apologetically.)* But it's so hard to manage when it's, well—raw.

Asagai: And so to accommodate that—you mutilate it every week?

Beneatha: It's not mutilation!

Asagai (laughing aloud at her seriousness): Oh . . . please! I am only teasing you because you are so very serious about these things. *(He stands back from her and folds his arms across his chest as he watches her pulling at her hair and frowning in the mirror.)* Do you remember the first time you met me at school? . . . *(He laughs.)* You came up to me and you said—and I thought you were the most serious little thing I had ever seen—you said: *(He imitates her.)* "Mr. Asagai—I want very much to talk with you. About Africa. You see, Mr. Asagai, I am looking for my *identity!*"

(He laughs.)

Beneatha (turning to him, not laughing): Yes—*(Her face is quizzical, profoundly disturbed.)*

Asagai (still teasing and reaching out and taking her face in his hands and turning her profile to him): Well . . . it is true that this is not so much a profile of a Hollywood queen as perhaps a queen of the Nile—*(A mock dismissal of the importance of the question.)*But what does it matter? Assimilationism is so popular in your country.

Beneatha (wheeling, passionately, sharply): I am not an assimilationist!

Asagai (the protest hangs in the room for a moment and Asagai studies her, his laughter fading): Such a serious one. *(There is a pause.)* So—you like the robes? You must take excellent care of them—they are from my sister's personal wardrobe.

Beneatha (with incredulity): You—you sent all the way home—for me?

Asagai (with charm): For you—I would do much more . . . Well, that is what I came for. I must go.

Beneatha: Will you call me Monday?

Asagai: Yes . . . We have a great deal to talk about. I mean about identity and time and all that.

Beneatha: Time?

Asagai: Yes. About how much time one needs to know what one feels.

Beneatha: You see! You never understood that there is more than one kind of feeling which can exist between a man and a woman—or, at least, there should be.

Asagai (shaking his head negatively but gently): No. Between a man and a woman there need be only one kind of feeling. I have that for you . . . Now even . . . right this moment . . .

Beneatha: I know—and by itself—it won't do. I can find that anywhere.

Asagai: For a woman it should be enough.

Beneatha: I know—because that's what it says in all the novels that men write. But it isn't. Go ahead and laugh—but I'm not interested in being someone's little episode in America or—*(with feminine vengeance)*—one of them! *(Asagai has burst into laughter again.)* That's funny as hell, huh!

Asagai: It's just that every American girl I have known has said that to me. White—black—in this you are all the same. And the same speech, too!

Beneatha (angrily): Yuk, yuk, yuk!

Asagai: It's how you can be sure that the world's most liberated women are not liberated at all. You all talk about it too much!

(Mama enters and is immediately all social charm because of the presence of a guest.)

Beneatha: Oh—Mama—this is Mr. Asagai.

Mama: How do you do?

Asagai (total politeness to an elder): How do you do, Mrs. Younger. Please forgive me for coming at such an outrageous hour on a Saturday.

Mama: Well, you are quite welcome. I just hope you understand that our house don't always look like this. *(Chatterish.)* You must come again. I would love to hear all about—*(Not sure of the name.)*—your country. I think it's so sad the way our American Negroes don't know nothing about Africa 'cept Tarzan and all that. And all that money they pour into these churches when they ought to be helping you people over there drive out them French and Englishmen done taken away your land.

(The mother flashes a slightly superior look at her daughter upon completion of the recitation.)

Asagai (taken aback by this sudden and acutely unrelated expression of sympathy): Yes . . . yes . . .

Mama (smiling at him suddenly and relaxing and looking him over): How many miles is it from here to where you come from?

Asagai: Many thousands.

Mama (looking at him as she would Walter): I bet you don't half look after yourself, being away from your mama either. I spec you better come 'round here from time to time to get yourself some decent home-cooked meals . . .

Asagai (moved): Thank you. Thank you very much. *(They are all quiet, then:)* Well . . . I must go. I will call you Monday, Alaiyo.

Mama: What's that he call you?

Asagai: Oh—"Alaiyo." I hope you don't mind. It is what you would call a nickname, I think. It is a Yoruba word. I am a Yoruba.

Mama (looking at Beneatha): I—I thought he was from—*(Uncertain.)*

Asagai (understanding): Nigeria is my country. Yoruba is my tribal origin—

Beneatha: You didn't tell us what Alaiyo means . . . for all I know, you might be calling me Little Idiot or something . . .

Asagai: Well . . . let me see . . . I do not know how just to explain it. . . . The sense of a thing can be so different when it changes languages.

Beneatha: You're evading.

Asagai: No—really it is difficult . . . *(Thinking.)* It means . . . it means One for Whom Bread—Food—Is Not Enough. *(He looks at her.)* Is that all right?

Beneatha (understanding, softly): Thank you.

Mama (looking from one to the other and not understanding any of it): Well . . . that's nice . . . You must come see us again—Mr.—

Asagai: Ah-sah-guy . . .

Mama: Yes . . . Do come again.

Asagai: Good-bye. *(He exits.)*

Mama (after him): Lord, that's a pretty thing just went out here! *(Insinuatingly, to her daughter.)* Yes, I guess I see why we done commence to get so interested in Africa 'round here. Missionaries my aunt Jenny! *(She exits.)*

Beneatha: Oh, Mama! . . .

(She picks up the Nigerian dress and holds it up to her in front of the mirror again. She sets the headdress on haphazardly and then notices her hair again and clutches at it and then replaces the headdress and frowns

at herself. Then she starts to wriggle in front of the mirror as she thinks a Nigerian woman might. Travis enters and stands regarding her.)

Travis: What's the matter, girl, you cracking up?

Beneatha: Shut up.

(She pulls the headdress off and looks at herself in the mirror and clutches at her hair again and squinches her eyes as if trying to imagine something. Then, suddenly, she gets her raincoat and kerchief and hurriedly prepares for going out.)

Mama (coming back into the room): She's resting now. Travis, baby, run next door and ask Miss Johnson to please let me have a little kitchen cleanser. This here can is empty as Jacob's kettle.°

Travis: I just came in.

Mama: Do as you told. *(He exits and she looks at her daughter.)* Where you going?

Beneatha (halting at the door): To become a queen of the Nile!

(She exits in a breathless blaze of glory. Ruth appears in the bedroom doorway.)

Mama: Who told you to get up?

Ruth: Ain't nothing wrong with me to be lying in no bed for. Where did Bennie go?

Mama (drumming her fingers): Far as I could make out—to Egypt. *(Ruth just looks at her.)* What time is it getting to?

Ruth: Ten twenty. And the mailman going to ring that bell this morning just like he done every morning for the last umpteen years.

(Travis comes in with the cleanser can.)

Travis: She say to tell you that she don't have much.

Mama (angrily): Lord, some people I could name sure is tight-fisted! *(Directing her grandson.)* Mark two cans of cleanser down on the list there. If she that hard up for kitchen cleanser, I sure don't want to forget to get her none!

Ruth: Lena—maybe the woman is just short on cleanser—

Mama (not listening): Much baking powder as she done borrowed from me all these years, she could of done gone into the baking business!

(The bell sounds suddenly and sharply and all three are stunned—serious and silent—mid-speech. In spite of all the other conversations and distractions of the morning, this is what they have been waiting for, even Travis, who looks helplessly from his mother to his grandmother. Ruth is the first to come to life again.)

Ruth (to Travis): Get down them steps, boy!

Jacob's kettle: an allusion to Genesis 25:29-34, where the hungry Esau sells his birthright to his twin brother Jacob in return for all the stew in his pot or "kettle."

(Travis snaps to life and flies out to get the mail.)

Mama (her eyes wide, her hand to her breast): You mean it done really come?

Ruth (excited): Oh, Miss Lena!

Mama (collecting herself): Well . . . I don't know what we all so excited about 'round here for. We known it was coming for months.

Ruth: That's a whole lot different from having it come and being able to hold it in your hands . . . a piece of paper worth ten thousand dollars . . .

(Travis bursts back into the room. He holds the envelope high above his head, like a little dancer, his face is radiant and he is breathless. He moves to his grandmother with sudden slow ceremony and puts the envelope into her hands. She accepts it, and then merely holds it and looks at it.)

Come on! Open it . . . Lord have mercy, I wish Walter Lee was here!

Travis: Open it, Grandmama!

Mama (staring at it): Now you all be quiet. It's just a check.

Ruth: Open it . . .

Mama (still staring at it): Now don't act silly . . . We ain't never been no people to act silly 'bout no money—

Ruth (swiftly): We ain't never had none before—OPEN IT!

(Mama finally makes a good strong tear and pulls out the thin blue slice of paper and inspects it closely. The boy and his mother study it raptly over Mama's shoulders.)

Mama: Travis! *(She is counting off with doubt.)* Is that the right number of zeros?

Travis: Yes'm . . . ten thousand dollars. Gaalee, Grandmama, you rich.

Mama (she holds the check away from her, still looking at it. Slowly her face sobers into a mask of unhappiness): Ten thousand dollars. *(She hands it to Ruth.)* Put it away somewhere, Ruth. *(She does not look at Ruth; her eyes seem to be seeing something somewhere very far off.)* Ten thousand dollars they give you. Ten thousand dollars.

Travis (to his mother, sincerely): What's the matter with Grandmama—don't she want to be rich?

Ruth (distractedly): You go on out and play now, baby. *(Travis exits. Mama starts wiping dishes absently, humming intently to herself. Ruth turns to her, with kind exasperation.)* You've gone and got yourself upset.

Mama (not looking at her): I spec if it wasn't for you all . . . I would just put that money away or give it to the church or something.

Ruth: Now what kind of talk is that. Mr. Younger would just be plain mad if he could hear you talking foolish like that.

Mama (stopping and staring off): Yes . . . he sure would. *(Sighing.)* We got enough to do with that money, all right. *(She halts then, and turns and looks at her daughter-in-law hard; Ruth avoids her eyes and Mama wipes her hands with finality and starts to speak firmly to Ruth.)* Where did you go today, girl?

Ruth: To the doctor.

Mama (impatiently): Now, Ruth . . . you know better than that. Old Doctor Jones is strange enough in his way but there ain't nothing 'bout him make somebody slip and call him "she"—like you done this morning.

Ruth: Well, that's what happened—my tongue slipped.

Mama: You went to see that woman, didn't you?

Ruth (defensively, giving herself away): What woman you talking about?

Mama (angrily): That woman who—

(Walter enters in great excitement.)

Walter: Did it come?

Mama (quietly): Can't you give people a Christian greeting before you start asking about money?

Walter (to Ruth): Did it come? *(Ruth unfolds the check and lays it quietly before him, watching him intently with thoughts of her own. Walter sits down and grasps it close and counts off the zeros.)* Ten thousand dollars—*(He turns suddenly, frantically to his mother and draws some papers out of his breast pocket.)* Mama—look. Old Willy Harris put everything on paper—

Mama: Son—I think you ought to talk to your wife . . . I'll go on out and leave you alone if you want—

Walter: I can talk to her later—Mama, look—

Mama: Son—

Walter: WILL SOMEBODY PLEASE LISTEN TO ME TODAY!

Mama (quietly): I don't 'low no yellin' in this house, Walter Lee, and you know it—*(Walter stares at them in frustration and starts to speak several times.)* And there ain't going to be no investing in no liquor stores.

Walter: But, Mama, you ain't even looked at it.

Mama: I don't aim to have to speak on that again.

(A long pause.)

Walter: You ain't looked at it and you don't aim to have to speak on that again? You ain't even looked at it and *you* have decided—*(Crumpling his papers.)* Well, you tell that to my boy tonight when you put him to sleep on the living-room couch . . . *(Turning to Mama and speaking directly to her.)* Yeah—and tell it to my wife, Mama, tomorrow when she has to go out of here to look after somebody else's kids. And tell it to me, Mama, every time we need a new pair of curtains and I have to watch you go out and work in somebody's kitchen. Yeah, you tell me then! *(Walter starts out.)*

Ruth: Where you going?

Walter: I'm going out!

Ruth: Where?

Walter: Just out of this house somewhere—

Ruth (getting her coat): I'll come too.

Walter: I don't want you to come!

Ruth: I got something to talk to you about, Walter.

Walter: That's too bad.

Mama (still quietly): Walter Lee—*(She waits and he finally turns and looks at her.)* Sit down.

Walter: I'm a grown man, Mama.

Mama: Ain't nobody said you wasn't grown. But you still in my house and my presence. And as long as you are—you'll talk to your wife civil. Now sit down.

Ruth (suddenly): Oh, let him go on out and drink himself to death! He makes me sick to my stomach! *(She flings her coat against him and exits to bedroom.)*

Walter (violently flinging the coat after her): And you turn mine too, baby! *(The door slams behind her.)* That was my biggest mistake—

Mama (still quietly): Walter, what is the matter with you?

Walter: Matter with me? Ain't nothing the matter with *me!*

Mama: Yes there is. Something eating you up like a crazy man. Something more than me not giving you this money. The past few years I been watching it happen to you. You get all nervous acting and kind of wild in the eyes—*(Walter jumps up impatiently at her words.)* I said sit there now, I'm talking to you!

Walter: Mama—I don't need no nagging at me today.

Mama: Seem like you getting to a place where you always tied up in some kind of knot about something. But if anybody ask you 'bout it you just yell at 'em and bust out the house and go out and drink somewheres. Walter Lee, people can't live with that. Ruth's a good, patient girl in her way—but you getting to be too much. Boy, don't make the mistake of driving that girl away from you.

Walter: Why—what she do for me?

Mama: She loves you.

Walter: Mama—I'm going out. I want to go off somewhere and be by myself for a while.

Mama: I'm sorry 'bout your liquor store, son. It just wasn't the thing for us to do. That's what I want to tell you about—

Walter: I got to go out, Mama—*(He rises.)*

Mama: It's dangerous, son.

Walter: What's dangerous?

Mama: When a man goes outside his home to look for peace.

Walter (beseechingly): Then why can't there never be no peace in this house then?

Mama: You done found it in some other house?

Walter: No—there ain't no woman! Why do women always think there's a woman somewhere when a man gets restless. *(Picks up the check.)* Do you know what this money means to me? Do you know what this money can do for us? *(Puts it back.)* Mama—Mama—I want so many things . . .

Mama: Yes, son—

Walter: I want so many things that they are driving me kind of crazy . . . Mama—look at me.

Mama: I'm looking at you. You a good-looking boy. You got a job, a nice wife, a fine boy and—

Walter: A job. *(Looks at her.)* Mama, a job? I open and close car doors all day long. I drive a man around in his limousine and I say, "Yes, sir; no, sir; very good, sir; shall I take the Drive, sir?" Mama, that ain't no kind of job . . . that ain't nothing at all. *(Very quietly.)* Mama, I don't know if I can make you understand.

Mama: Understand what, baby?

Walter (quietly): Sometimes it's like I can see the future stretched out in front of me—just plain as day. The future, Mama. Hanging over there at the edge of my days. Just waiting for me—a big, looming blank space—full of *nothing*. Just waiting for *me*. But it don't have to be. *(Pause. Kneeling beside her chair.)* Mama—sometimes when I'm downtown and I pass them cool, quiet-looking restaurants where them white boys are sitting back and talking 'bout things . . . sitting there turning deals worth millions of dollars . . . sometimes I see guys don't look much older than me—

Mama: Son—how come you talk so much 'bout money?

Walter (with immense passion): Because it is life, Mama!

Mama (quietly): Oh—*(Very quietly.)* So now it's life. Money is life. Once upon a time freedom used to be life—now it's money. I guess the world really do change . . .

Walter: No—it was always money, Mama. We just didn't know about it.

Mama: No . . . something has changed. *(She looks at him.)* You something new, boy. In my time we was worried about not being lynched and getting to the North if we could and how to stay alive and still have a pinch of dignity too . . . Now here come you and Beneatha—talking 'bout things we ain't never even thought about hardly, me and your daddy. You ain't satisfied or proud of nothing we done. I mean that you had a home; that we kept you out of trouble till you was grown; that you don't have to ride to work on the back of nobody's streetcar—You my children—but how different we done become.

Walter (a long beat. He pats her hand and gets up): You just don't understand, Mama, you just don't understand.

Mama: Son—do you know your wife is expecting another baby? *(Walter stands, stunned, and absorbs what his mother has said.)* That's what she wanted to talk to you about. *(Walter sinks down into a chair.)* This ain't for me to be telling—but you ought to know. *(She waits.)* I think Ruth is thinking 'bout getting rid of that child.

Walter (slowly understanding): No—no—Ruth wouldn't do that.

Mama: When the world gets ugly enough—a woman will do anything for her family. *The part that's already living.*

Walter: You don't know Ruth, Mama, if you think she would do that.

(Ruth opens the bedroom door and stands there a little limp.)

Ruth (beaten): Yes I would too, Walter. *(Pause.)* I gave her a five-dollar down payment.

(There is total silence as the man stares at his wife and the mother stares at her son.)

Mama (presently): Well—*(Tightly.)* Well—son, I'm waiting to hear you say something . . . *(She waits.)* I'm waiting to hear how you be your father's son. Be the man he was . . . *(Pause. The silence shouts.)* Your wife say she going to destroy your child. And I'm waiting to hear you talk like him and say we a people who give children life, not who destroys them—*(She rises.)* I'm waiting to see you stand up and look like your daddy and say we done give up one baby to poverty and that we ain't going to give up nary another one . . . I'm waiting.

Walter: Ruth—*(He can say nothing.)*

Mama: If you a son of mine, tell her! *(Walter picks up his keys and his coat and walks out. She continues, bitterly.)* You . . . you are a disgrace to your father's memory. Somebody get me my hat!

ACT II

SCENE I

TIME. *Later the same day*

AT RISE. *Ruth is ironing again. She has the radio going. Presently Beneatha's bedroom door opens and Ruth's mouth falls and she puts down the iron in fascination.*

Ruth: What have we got on tonight!

Beneatha (emerging grandly from the doorway so that we can see her thoroughly robed in the costume Asagai brought): You are looking at what a well-dressed Nigerian woman wears—

(She parades for Ruth, her hair completely hidden by the headdress; she is coquettishly fanning herself with an ornate oriental fan, mistakenly more like Butterfly° than any Nigerian that ever was.)

Butterfly: the lead character of *Madama Butterfly* (1904), Giacomo Puccini's (1858–1924) famous tragic opera about a Japanese woman abandoned by her American husband.

Isn't it beautiful? *(She promenades to the radio and, with an arrogant flourish, turns off the good loud blues that is playing.)* Enough of this assimilationist junk!

(Ruth follows her with her eyes as she goes to the phonograph and puts on a record and turns and waits ceremoniously for the music to come up. Then, with a shout—) OCOMOGOSIAY!

(Ruth jumps. The music comes up, a lovely Nigerian melody. Beneatha listens, enraptured, her eyes far away—"back to the past." She begins to dance. Ruth is dumfounded.)

Ruth: What kind of dance is that?
Beneatha: A folk dance.
Ruth (Pearl Bailey°): What kind of folks do that, honey?
Beneatha: It's from Nigeria. It's a dance of welcome.
Ruth: Who you welcoming?
Beneatha: The men back to the village.
Ruth: Where they been?
Beneatha: How should I know—out hunting or something. Anyway, they are coming back now . . .
Ruth: Well, that's good.
Beneatha (with the record):

Alundi, alundi
Alundi alunya
Jop pu a jeepua
Ang gu soooooooooo

Ai yai yae . . .
Ayehaye—alundi . . .

(Walter comes in during this performance; he has obviously been drinking. He leans against the door heavily and watches his sister, at first with distaste. Then his eyes look off—"back to the past"—as he lifts both his fists to the roof, screaming.)

Walter: YEAH . . . AND ETHIOPIA STRETCH FORTH HER HANDS AGAIN! . . .
Ruth (drily, looking at him): Yes—and Africa sure is claiming her own tonight. *(She gives them both up and starts ironing again.)*
Walter (all in a drunken, dramatic shout): Shut up! . . . I'm digging them drums . . . them drums move me! . . . *(He makes his weaving way to his*

Pearl Bailey: Pearl Mae Bailey (1918–1990) was an American entertainer known for her singing voice and larger-than-life personality.

wife's face and leans in close to her.) In my *heart of hearts—(He thumps his chest.)*—I am much warrior!

Ruth (without even looking up): In your heart of hearts you are much drunkard.

Walter (coming away from her and starting to wander around the room, shouting): Me and Jomo° . . . *(Intently, in his sister's face. She has stopped dancing to watch him in this unknown mood.)* That's my man, Kenyatta. *(Shouting and thumping his chest.)* FLAMING SPEAR! HOT DAMN! *(He is suddenly in possession of an imaginary spear and actively spearing enemies all over the room.)* OCOMOGOSIAY . . .

Beneatha (to encourage Walter, thoroughly caught up with this side of him): OCOMOGOSIAY, FLAMING SPEAR!

Walter: THE LION IS WAKING . . . OWIMOWEH!° *(He pulls his shirt open and leaps up on the table and gestures with his spear.)*

Beneatha: OWIMOWEH!

Walter (on the table, very far gone, his eyes pure glass sheets. He sees what we cannot, that he is a leader of his people, a great chief, a descendant of Chaka,° and that the hour to march has come): Listen, my black brothers—

Beneatha: OCOMOGOSIAY!

Walter: —Do you hear the waters rushing against the shores of the coastlands—

Beneatha: OCOMOGOSIAY!

Walter: —Do you hear the screeching of the cocks in yonder hills beyond where the chiefs meet in council for the coming of the mighty war—

Beneatha: OCOMOGOSIAY!

(And now the lighting shifts subtly to suggest the world of Walter's imagination, and the mood shifts from pure comedy. It is the inner Walter speaking: the Southside chauffeur has assumed an unexpected majesty.)

Walter: —Do you hear the beating of the wings of the birds flying low over the mountains and the low places of our land—

Beneatha: OCOMOGOSIAY!

Walter: —Do you hear the singing of the women, singing the war songs of our fathers to the babies in the great houses? Singing the sweet war songs! *(The doorbell rings.)* OH, DO YOU HEAR, MY BLACK BROTHERS!

Beneatha (completely gone): We hear you, Flaming Spear—

(Ruth shuts off the phonograph and opens the door. George Murchison enters.)

Jomo: Jomo Kenyatta (1893?-1978) was a famous African political leader and the first president of Kenya (1964–1978). *THE LION IS WAKING . . . OWIMOWEH:* Walter is referring to the popular pop song "The Lion Sleeps Tonight," whose chorus keeps repeating "Owimoweh." The song, originally recorded by the South African singer Solomon Linda, has been covered by many artists, and became even more popular when used in Disney's *The Lion King.* *Chaka:* or Shaka (1785?-1828), was a famous Zulu warrior and chieftain.

Walter: Telling us to prepare for the GREATNESS OF THE TIME! *(Lights back to normal. He turns and sees George.)* Black Brother! *(He extends his hand for the fraternal clasp.)*

George: Black Brother, hell!

Ruth (having had enough, and embarrassed for the family): Beneatha, you got company—what's the matter with you? Walter Lee Younger, get down off that table and stop acting like a fool . . .

(Walter comes down off the table suddenly and makes a quick exit to the bathroom.)

Ruth: He's had a little to drink . . . I don't know what her excuse is.

George (to Beneatha): Look honey, we're going *to* the theatre—we're not going to be *in* it . . . so go change, huh?

(Beneatha looks at him and slowly, ceremoniously, lifts her hands and pulls off the headdress. Her hair is close-cropped and unstraightened. George freezes mid-sentence and Ruth's eyes all but fall out of her head.)

George: What in the name of—

Ruth (touching Beneatha's hair): Girl, you done lost your natural mind!? Look at your head!

George: What have you done to your head—I mean your hair!

Beneatha: Nothing—except cut it off.

Ruth: Now that's the truth—it's what ain't been done to it! You expect this boy to go out with you with your head all nappy like that?

Beneatha (looking at George): That's up to George. If he's ashamed of his heritage—

George: Oh, don't be so proud of yourself, Bennie—just because you look eccentric.

Beneatha: How can something that's natural be eccentric?

George: That's what being eccentric means—being natural. Get dressed.

Beneatha: I don't like that, George.

Ruth: Why must you and your brother make an argument out of everything people say?

Beneatha: Because I hate assimilationist Negroes!

Ruth: Will somebody please tell me what assimila-whoever means!

George: Oh, it's just a college girl's way of calling people Uncle Toms—but that isn't what it means at all.

Ruth: Well, what does it mean?

Beneatha (cutting George off and staring at him as she replies to Ruth.) It means someone who is willing to give up his own culture and submerge himself completely in the dominant, and in this case *oppressive*, culture!

George: Oh, dear, dear, dear! Here we go! A lecture on the African past! On our Great West African Heritage! In one second we will hear all about the great Ashanti empires; the great Songhay civilizations;

and the great sculpture of Bénin—and then some poetry in the Bantu—and the whole monologue will end with the word *heritage!* *(Nastily.)* Let's face it, baby, your heritage is nothing but a bunch of raggedy-assed spirituals and some grass huts!

Beneatha: GRASS HUTS! *(Ruth crosses to her and forcibly pushes her toward the bedroom.)* See there . . . you are standing there in your splendid ignorance talking about people who were the first to smelt iron on the face of the earth! *(Ruth is pushing her through the door.)* The Ashanti were performing surgical operations when the English—*(Ruth pulls the door to, with Beneatha on the other side, and smiles graciously at George. Beneatha opens the door and shouts the end of the sentence defiantly at George.)*—were still tatooing themselves with blue dragons! *(She goes back inside.)*

Ruth: Have a seat, George. *(They both sit. Ruth folds her hands rather primly on her lap, determined to demonstrate the civilization of the family.)* Warm, ain't it? I mean for September. *(Pause.)* Just like they always say about Chicago weather: If it's too hot or cold for you, just wait a minute and it'll change. *(She smiles happily at this cliché of clichés.)* Everybody say it's got to do with them bombs and things they keep setting off. *(Pause.)* Would you like a nice cold beer?

George: No, thank you. I don't care for beer. *(He looks at his watch.)* I hope she hurries up.

Ruth: What time is the show?

George: It's an eight-thirty curtain. That's just Chicago, though. In New York standard curtain time is eight forty. *(He is rather proud of this knowledge.)*

Ruth (properly appreciating it): You get to New York a lot?

George (offhand): Few times a year.

Ruth: Oh—that's nice. I've never been to New York.

(Walter enters. We feel he has relieved himself, but the edge of unreality is still with him.)

Walter: New York ain't got nothing Chicago ain't. Just a bunch of hustling people all squeezed up together—being "Eastern." *(He turns his face into a screw of displeasure.)*

George: Oh—you've been?

Walter: Plenty of times.

Ruth (shocked at the lie): Walter Lee Younger!

Walter (staring her down): Plenty! *(Pause.)* What we got to drink in this house? Why don't you offer this man some refreshment. *(To George.)* They don't know how to entertain people in this house, man.

George: Thank you—I don't really care for anything.

Walter (feeling his head; sobriety coming.) Where's Mama?

Ruth: She ain't come back yet.

Walter (looking Murchison over from head to toe, scrutinizing his carefully casual tweed sports jacket over cashmere V-neck sweater over soft eyelet shirt and tie, and soft slacks, finished off with white buckskin shoes): Why all you college boys wear them faggoty-looking white shoes?
Ruth: Walter Lee!

(George Murchison ignores the remark.)

Walter (to Ruth): Well, they look crazy as hell—white shoes, cold as it is.
Ruth (crushed): You have to excuse him—
Walter: No he don't! Excuse me for what? What you always excusing me for! I'll excuse myself when I needs to be excused! *(A pause.)* They look as funny as them black knee socks Beneatha wears out of here all the time.
Ruth: It's the college *style*, Walter.
Walter: Style, hell. She looks like she got burnt legs or something!
Ruth: Oh, Walter—
Walter (an irritable mimic): Oh, Walter! Oh, Walter! *(To Murchison.)* How's your old man making out? I understand you all going to buy that big hotel on the Drive? *(He finds a beer in the refrigerator, wanders over to Murchison, sipping and wiping his lips with the back of his hand, and straddling a chair backwards to talk to the other man.)* Shrewd move. Your old man is all right, man. *(Tapping his head and half winking for emphasis.)* I mean he knows how to operate. I mean he thinks *big*, you know what I mean, I mean for a *home*, you know? But I think he's kind of running out of ideas now. I'd like to talk to him. Listen, man, I got some plans that could turn this city upside down. I mean think like he does. *Big*. Invest big, gamble big, hell, lose *big* if you have to, you know what I mean. It's hard to find a man on this whole Southside who understands my kind of thinking—you dig? *(He scrutinizes Murchison again, drinks his beer, squints his eyes and leans in close, confidential, man to man.)* Me and you ought to sit down and talk sometimes, man. Man, I got me some ideas . . .
Murchison (with boredom): Yeah—sometimes we'll have to do that, Walter.
Walter (understanding the indifference, and offended): Yeah—well, when you get the time, man. I know you a busy little boy.
Ruth: Walter, please—
Walter (bitterly, hurt): I know ain't nothing in this world as busy as you colored college boys with your fraternity pins and white shoes . . .
Ruth (covering her face with humiliation): Oh, Walter Lee—
Walter: I see you all the time—with the books tucked under your arms—going to your *(British A—a mimic.)* "clahsses." And for what! What the hell you learning over there? Filling up your heads—*(counting off on his fingers)*—with the sociology and the psychology—but they

teaching you how to be a man? How to take over and run the world? They teaching you how to run a rubber plantation or a steel mill? Naw—just to talk proper and read books and wear them faggoty-looking white shoes . . .

George *(looking at him with distaste, a little above it all)*: You're all wacked up with bitterness, man.

Walter *(intently, almost quietly, between the teeth, glaring at the boy)*: And you—ain't you bitter, man? Ain't you just about had it yet? Don't you see no stars gleaming that you can't reach out and grab? You happy?—You contented son-of-a-bitch—you happy? You got it made? Bitter? Man, I'm a volcano. Bitter? Here I am a giant—surrounded by ants! Ants who can't even understand what it is the giant is talking about.

Ruth *(passionately and suddenly)*: Oh, Walter—ain't you with nobody!

Walter *(violently)*: No! 'Cause ain't nobody with me! Not even my own mother!

Ruth: Walter, that's a terrible thing to say!

(Beneatha enters, dressed for the evening in a cocktail dress and earrings, hair natural.)

George: Well—hey—*(Crosses to Beneatha; thoughtful, with emphasis, since this is a reversal.)* You look great!

Walter *(seeing his sister's hair for the first time)*: What's the matter with your head?

Beneatha *(tired of the jokes now)*: I cut it off, Brother.

Walter *(coming close to inspect it and walking around her)*: Well, I'll be damned. So that's what they mean by the African bush . . . .

Beneatha: Ha ha. Let's go, George.

George *(looking at her)*: You know something? I like it. It's sharp. I mean it really is. *(Helps her into her wrap.)*

Ruth: Yes—I think so, too. *(She goes to the mirror and starts to clutch at her hair.)*

Walter: Oh no! You leave yours alone, baby. You might turn out to have a pin-shaped head or something!

Beneatha: See you all later.

Ruth: Have a nice time.

George: Thanks. Good night. *(Half out the door, he reopens it. To Walter.)* Good night, Prometheus!°

(Beneatha and George exit.)

Walter *(to Ruth)*: Who is Prometheus?

Ruth: I don't know. Don't worry about it.

Prometheus: in Greek legend, the god who gave the secret of fire to humanity.

Walter (in fury, pointing after George): See there—they get to a point where they can't insult you man to man—they got to go talk about something ain't nobody never heard of!

Ruth: How do you know it was an insult? *(To humor him.)* Maybe Prometheus is a nice fellow.

Walter: Prometheus! I bet there ain't even no such thing! I bet that simple-minded clown—

Ruth: Walter—*(She stops what she is doing and looks at him.)*

Walter (yelling): Don't start!

Ruth: Start what?

Walter: Your nagging! Where was I? Who was I with? How much money did I spend?

Ruth (plaintively): Walter Lee—why don't we just try to talk about it . . .

Walter (not listening): I been out talking with people who understand me. People who care about the things I got on my mind.

Ruth (wearily): I guess that means people like Willy Harris.

Walter: Yes, people like Willy Harris.

Ruth (with a sudden flash of impatience): Why don't you all just hurry up and go into the banking business and stop talking about it!

Walter: Why? You want to know why? 'Cause we all tied up in a race of people that don't know how to do nothing but moan, pray and have babies!

(The line is too bitter even for him and he looks at her and sits down.)

Ruth: Oh, Walter . . . *(Softly.)* Honey, why can't you stop fighting me?

Walter (without thinking): Who's fighting you? Who even cares about you? *(This line begins the retardation of his mood.)*

Ruth: Well—*(She waits a long time, and then with resignation starts to put away her things.)* I guess I might as well go on to bed . . . *(More or less to herself.)* I don't know where we lost it . . . but we have . . . *(Then, to him.)* I—I'm sorry about this new baby, Walter. I guess maybe I better go on and do what I started . . . I guess I just didn't realize how bad things was with us . . . I guess I just didn't really realize—*(She starts out to the bedroom and stops.)* You want some hot milk?

Walter: Hot milk?

Ruth: Yes—hot milk.

Walter: Why hot milk?

Ruth: 'Cause after all that liquor you come home with you ought to have something hot in your stomach.

Walter: I don't want no milk.

Ruth: You want some coffee then?

Walter: No, I don't want no coffee. I don't want nothing hot to drink.*(Almost plaintively.)* Why you always trying to give me something to eat?

Ruth (standing and looking at him helplessly): What else can I give you, Walter Lee Younger?

(She stands and looks at him and presently turns to go out again. He lifts his head and watches her going away from him in a new mood which began to emerge when he asked her "Who even cares about you?")

Walter: It's been rough, ain't it, baby? *(She hears and stops but does not turn around and he continues to her back.)* I guess between two people there ain't never as much understood as folks generally thinks there is. I mean like between me and you— *(She turns to face him.)* How we gets to the place where we scared to talk softness to each other. *(He waits, thinking hard himself.)* Why you think it got to be like that? *(He is thoughtful, almost as a child would be.)* Ruth, what is it gets into people ought to be close?

Ruth: I don't know, honey. I think about it a lot.

Walter: On account of you and me, you mean? The way things are with us. The way something done come down between us.

Ruth: There ain't so much between us, Walter . . . Not when you come to me and try to talk to me. Try to be with me . . . a little even.

Walter (total honesty): Sometimes . . . sometimes . . . I don't even know how to try.

Ruth: Walter—

Walter: Yes?

Ruth (coming to him, gently and with misgiving, but coming to him): Honey . . . life don't have to be like this. I mean sometimes people can do things so that things are better . . . You remember how we used to talk when Travis was born . . . about the way we were going to live . . . the kind of house . . . *(She is stroking his head.)* Well, it's all starting to slip away from us . . .

(He turns her to him and they look at each other and kiss, tenderly and hungrily. The door opens and Mama enters—Walter breaks away and jumps up. A beat.)

Walter: Mama, where have you been?

Mama: My—them steps is longer than they used to be. Whew! *(She sits down and ignores him.)* How you feeling this evening, Ruth?

(Ruth shrugs, disturbed at having been interrupted and watching her husband knowingly.)

Walter: Mama, where have you been all day?

Mama (still ignoring him and leaning on the table and changing to more comfortable shoes): Where's Travis?

Ruth: I let him go out earlier and he ain't come back yet. Boy, is he going to get it!

Walter: Mama!

Mama (as if she has heard him for the first time): Yes, son?

Walter: Where did you go this afternoon?

Mama: I went downtown to tend to some business that I had to tend to.

Walter: What kind of business?

Mama: You know better than to question me like a child, Brother.

Walter (rising and bending over the table): Where were you, Mama? *(Bringing his fists down and shouting.)* Mama, you didn't go do something with that insurance money, something crazy?

(The front door opens slowly, interrupting him, and Travis peeks his head in, less than hopefully.)

Travis (to his mother): Mama, I—

Ruth: "Mama I" nothing! You're going to get it, boy! Get on in that bedroom and get yourself ready!

Travis: But I—

Mama: Why don't you all never let the child explain hisself.

Ruth: Keep out of it now, Lena.

(Mama clamps her lips together, and Ruth advances toward her son menacingly.)

Ruth: A thousand times I have told you not to go off like that—

Mama (holding out her arms to her grandson): Well—at least let me tell him something. I want him to be the first one to hear . . . Come here, Travis. *(The boy obeys, gladly.)* Travis—*(She takes him by the shoulder and looks into his face.)*—you know that money we got in the mail this morning?

Travis: Yes'm—

Mama: Well—what you think your grandmama gone and done with that money?

Travis: I don't know, Grandmama.

Mama (putting her finger on his nose for emphasis): She went out and she bought you a house! *(The explosion comes from Walter at the end of the revelation and he jumps up and turns away from all of them in a fury. Mama continues, to Travis.)* You glad about the house? It's going to be yours when you get to be a man.

Travis: Yeah—I always wanted to live in a house.

Mama: All right, gimme some sugar then—*(Travis puts his arms around her neck as she watches her son over the boy's shoulder. Then, to Travis, after the embrace.)* Now when you say your prayers tonight, you thank God and your grandfather—'cause it was him who give you the house—in his way.

Ruth (taking the boy from Mama and pushing him toward the bedroom): Now you get out of here and get ready for your beating.

Travis: Aw, Mama—

Ruth: Get on in there—*(Closing the door behind him and turning radiantly to her mother-in-law.)* So you went and did it!

Mama (quietly, looking at her son with pain): Yes, I did.

Ruth (raising both arms classically): PRAISE GOD! *(Looks at Walter a moment, who says nothing. She crosses rapidly to her husband.)* Please, honey—let me be glad . . . you be glad too. *(She has laid her hands on his shoulders, but he shakes himself free of her roughly, without turning to face her.)* Oh Walter . . . a home . . . a home. *(She comes back to Mama.)* Well—where is it? How big is it? How much it going to cost?

Mama: Well—

Ruth: When we moving?

Mama (smiling at her): First of the month.

Ruth (throwing back her head with jubilance): Praise God!

Mama (tentatively, still looking at her son's back turned against her and Ruth): It's—it's a nice house too . . . *(She cannot help speaking directly to him. An imploring quality in her voice, her manner, makes her almost like a girl now.)* Three bedrooms—nice big one for you and Ruth . . . Me and Beneatha still have to share our room, but Travis have one of his own—and *(With difficulty.)* I figure if the—new baby—is a boy, we could get one of them double-decker outfits . . . And there's a yard with a little patch of dirt where I could maybe get to grow me a few flowers . . . And a nice big basement . . .

Ruth: Walter honey, be glad—

Mama (still to his back, fingering things on the table): 'Course I don't want to make it sound fancier than it is . . . It's just a plain little old house—but it's made good and solid—and it will be *ours*. Walter Lee—it makes a difference in a man when he can walk on floors that belong to him . . .

Ruth: Where is it?

Mama (frightened at this telling): Well—well—it's out there in Clybourne Park—

(Ruth's radiance fades abruptly, and Walter finally turns slowly to face his mother with incredulity and hostility.)

Ruth: Where?

Mama (matter-of-factly): Four o six Clybourne Street, Clybourne Park.

Ruth: Clybourne Park? Mama, there ain't no colored people living in Clybourne Park.

Mama (almost idiotically): Well, I guess there's going to be some now.

Walter (bitterly): So that's the peace and comfort you went out and bought for us today!

Mama (raising her eyes to meet his finally): Son—I just tried to find the nicest place for the least amount of money for my family.

Ruth (trying to recover from the shock): Well—well—'course I ain't one never been 'fraid of no crackers, mind you—but—well, wasn't there no other houses nowhere?

Mama: Them houses they put up for colored in them areas way out all seem to cost twice as much as other houses. I did the best I could.

Ruth (struck senseless with the news, in its various degrees of goodness and trouble, she sits a moment, her fists propping her chin in thought, and then she starts to rise, bringing her fists down with vigor, the radiance spreading from cheek to cheek again): Well—well!—All I can say is—if this is my time in life—MY TIME—to say good-bye—*(And she builds with momentum as she starts to circle the room with an exuberant, almost tearfully happy release.)*—to these goddamned cracking walls!—*(She pounds the walls.)*—and these marching roaches!—*(She wipes at an imaginary army of marching roaches.)*—and this cramped little closet which ain't now or never was no kitchen! . . . then I say it loud and good, HALLELUJAH! AND GOOD-BYE MISERY . . . I DON'T NEVER WANT TO SEE YOUR UGLY FACE AGAIN! *(She laughs joyously, having practically destroyed the apartment, and flings her arms up and lets them come down happily, slowly, reflectively, over her abdomen, aware for the first time perhaps that the life therein pulses with happiness and not despair.)* Lena?

Mama (moved, watching her happiness): Yes, honey?

Ruth (looking off): Is there—is there a whole lot of sunlight?

Mama (understanding): Yes, child, there's a whole lot of sunlight.

(Long pause.)

Ruth (collecting herself and going to the door of the room Travis is in): Well—I guess I better see 'bout Travis. *(to Mama.)* Lord, I sure don't feel like whipping nobody today! *(She exits.)*

Mama (the mother and son are left alone now and the mother waits a long time, considering deeply, before she speaks): Son—you—you understand what I done, don't you? *(Walter is silent and sullen.)* I—I just seen my family falling apart today . . . just falling to pieces in front of my eyes . . . We couldn't of gone on like we was today. We was going backwards 'stead of forwards—talking 'bout killing babies and wishing each other was dead . . . When it gets like that in life—you just got to do something different, push on out and do something bigger . . . *(She waits.)* I wish you say something, son . . . I wish you'd say how deep inside you think I done the right thing—

Walter (crossing slowly to his bedroom door and finally turning there and speaking measuredly): What you need me to say you done right for? *You* the head of this family. You run our lives like you want to. It was your money and you did what you wanted with it. So what you need for me to say it was all right for? *(Bitterly, to hurt her as deeply as he knows is possible.)* So you butchered up a dream of mine—you—who always talking 'bout your children's dreams . . .

Mama: Walter Lee—

(He just closes the door behind him. Mama sits alone, thinking heavily.)

ACT II

SCENE II

TIME. *Friday night. A few weeks later.*

AT RISE. *Packing crates mark the intention of the family to move. Beneatha and George come in, presumably from an evening out again.*

George: O.K. . . . O.K., whatever you say . . . *(They both sit on the couch. He tries to kiss her. She moves away.)* Look, we've had a nice evening; let's not spoil it, huh? . . .

(He again turns her head and tries to nuzzle in and she turns away from him, not with distaste but with momentary lack of interest; in a mood to pursue what they were talking about.)

Beneatha: I'm *trying* to talk to you.

George: We always talk.

Beneatha: Yes—and I love to talk.

George (exasperated; rising): I know it and I don't mind it sometimes . . . I want you to cut it out, see—The moody stuff, I mean. I don't like it. You're a nice-looking girl . . . all over. That's all you need, honey, forget the atmosphere. Guys aren't going to go for the atmosphere—they're going to go for what they see. Be glad for that. Drop the Garbo° routine. It doesn't go with you. As for myself, I want a nice—*(groping)*—simple *(thoughtfully)*—sophisticated girl . . . not a poet—O.K.?

(He starts to kiss her, she rebuffs him again and he jumps up.)

Beneatha: Why are you angry, George?

George: Because this is stupid! I don't go out with you to discuss the nature of "quiet desperation"° or to hear all about your thoughts—because the world will go on thinking what it thinks regardless—

Beneatha: Then why read books? Why go to school?

George (with artificial patience, counting on his fingers): It's simple. You read books—to learn facts—to get grades—to pass the course—to get a degree. That's all—it has nothing to do with thoughts.

(A long pause.)

Garbo: Greta Garbo (1905–1990) was a glamorous and reclusive movie star of the 1920s and 1930s. *"quiet desperation"*: quotation from Henry David Thoreau's *Walden* (1854): "The mass of men lead lives of quiet desperation."

Beneatha: I see. *(He starts to sit.)* Good night, George.

(George looks at her a little oddly, and starts to exit. He meets Mama coming in.)

George: Oh—hello, Mrs. Younger.
Mama: Hello, George, how you feeling?
George: Fine—fine, how are you?
Mama: Oh, a little tired. You know them steps can get you after a day's work. You all have a nice time tonight?
George: Yes—a fine time. A fine time.
Mama: Well, good night.
George: Good night. *(He exits. Mama closes the door behind her.)*
Mama: Hello, honey. What you sitting like that for?
Beneatha: I'm just sitting.
Mama: Didn't you have a nice time?
Beneatha: No.
Mama: No? What's the matter?
Beneatha: Mama, George is a fool—honest *(She rises.)*
Mama (hustling around unloading the packages she has entered with. She stops): Is he, baby?
Beneatha: Yes. *(Beneatha makes up Travis' bed as she talks.)*
Mama: You sure?
Beneatha: Yes.
Mama: Well—I guess you better not waste your time with no fools.

(Beneatha looks up at her mother, watching her put groceries in the refrigerator. Finally she gathers up her things and starts into the bedroom. At the door she stops and looks back at her mother.)

Beneatha: Mama—
Mama: Yes, baby—
Beneatha: Thank you.
Mama: For what?
Beneatha: For understanding me this time.

(She exits quickly and the mother stands, smiling a little, looking at the place where Beneatha just stood. Ruth enters.)

Ruth: Now don't you fool with any of this stuff, Lena—
Mama: Oh, I just thought I'd sort a few things out. Is Brother here?
Ruth: Yes.
Mama (with concern): Is he—
Ruth (reading her eyes): Yes.

(Mama is silent and someone knocks on the door. Mama and Ruth exchange weary and knowing glances and Ruth opens it to admit the

neighbor, Mrs. Johnson, who is a rather squeaky wide-eyed lady of no particular age, with a newspaper under her arm.)

Mama (changing her expression to acute delight and a ringing cheerful greeting): Oh—hello, there, Johnson.

Johnson (this is a woman who decided long ago to be enthusiastic about EVERYTHING in life and she is inclined to wave her wrist vigorously at the height of her exclamatory comments): Hello there, yourself! H'you this evening, Ruth?

Ruth (not much of a deceptive type): Fine, Mis' Johnson, h'you?

Johnson: Fine. *(Reaching out quickly, playfully, and patting Ruth's stomach.)* Ain't you starting to poke out none yet! *(She mugs with delight at the overfamiliar remark and her eyes dart around looking at the crates and packing preparation; Mama's face is a cold sheet of endurance.)* Oh, ain't we getting ready 'round here, though! Yessir! Lookathere! I'm telling you the Youngers is really getting ready to "move on up a little higher!"—Bless God!

Mama (a little drily, doubting the total sincerity of the Blesser): Bless God.

Johnson: He's good, ain't He?

Mama: Oh yes, He's good.

Johnson: I mean sometimes He works in mysterious ways . . . but He works, don't He!

Mama (the same): Yes, He does.

Johnson: I'm just soooooo happy for y'all. And this here child—*(about Ruth)* looks like she could just pop open with happiness, don't she. Where's all the rest of the family?

Mama: Bennie's gone to bed—

Johnson: Ain't no . . . *(The implication is pregnancy.)* sickness done hit you—I hope . . . ?

Mama: No—she just tired. She was out this evening.

Johnson (all is a coo, an emphatic coo): Aw—ain't that lovely. She still going out with the little Murchison boy?

Mama (drily): Ummmm huh.

Johnson: That's lovely. You sure got lovely children, Younger. Me and Isaiah talks all the time 'bout what fine children you was blessed with. We sure do.

Mama: Ruth, give Mis' Johnson a piece of sweet potato pie and some milk.

Johnson: Oh honey, I can't stay hardly a minute—I just dropped in to see if there was anything I could do. *(Accepting the food easily.)* I guess y'all seen the news what's all over the colored paper this week . . .

Mama: No—didn't get mine yet this week.

Johnson (lifting her head and blinking with the spirit of catastrophe): You mean you ain't read 'bout them colored people that was bombed out their place out there?

(Ruth straightens with concern and takes the paper and reads it. Johnson notices her and feeds commentary.)

Johnson: Ain't it something how bad these here white folks is getting here in Chicago! Lord, getting so you think you right down in Mississippi! *(With a tremendous and rather insincere sense of melodrama.)* 'Course I thinks it's wonderful how our folks keeps on pushing out. You hear some of these Negroes round here talking 'bout how they don't go where they ain't wanted and all that—but not me, honey! *(This is a lie.)* Wilhemenia Othella Johnson goes anywhere, any time she feels like it! *(With head movement for emphasis.)* Yes I do! Why if we left it up to these here crackers, the poor niggers wouldn't have nothing—*(She clasps her hand over her mouth.)* Oh, I always forgets you don't 'low that word in your house.

Mama (quietly, looking at her): No—I don't 'low it.

Johnson (vigorously again): Me neither! I was just telling Isaiah yesterday when he come using it in front of me—I said, "Isaiah, it's just like Mis' Younger says all the time—"

Mama: Don't you want some more pie?

Johnson: No—no thank you; this was lovely. I got to get on over home and have my midnight coffee. I hear some people say it don't let them sleep but I finds I can't close my eyes right lessen I done had that laaaast cup of coffee . . . *(She waits. A beat. Undaunted.)* My Goodnight coffee, I calls it!

Mama (with much eye-rolling and communication between herself and Ruth): Ruth, why don't you give Mis' Johnson some coffee.

(Ruth gives Mama an unpleasant look for her kindness.)

Johnson (accepting the coffee): Where's Brother tonight?

Mama: He's lying down.

Johnson: Mmmmmm, he sure gets his beauty rest, don't he? Good-looking man. Sure is a good-looking man! *(Reaching out to pat Ruth's stomach again.)* I guess that's how come we keep on having babies around here. *(She winks at Mama.)* One thing 'bout Brother, he always know how to have a *good* time. And soooooo ambitious! I bet it was his idea y'all moving out to Clybourne Park. Lord—I bet this time next month y'all's names will have been in the papers plenty—*(Holding up her hands to mark off each word of the headline she can see in front of her.)* "NEGROES INVADE CLYBOURNE PARK—BOMBED!"

Mama (she and Ruth look at the woman in amazement): We ain't exactly moving out there to get bombed.

Johnson: Oh, honey—you know I'm praying to God every day that don't nothing like that happen! But you have to think of life like it is—and these here Chicago peckerwoods is some baaaad peckerwoods.

Mama (wearily): We done thought about all that, Mis' Johnson.

(Beneatha comes out of the bedroom in her robe and passes through to the bathroom. Mrs. Johnson turns.)

Johnson: Hello there, Bennie!

Beneatha (crisply): Hello, Mrs. Johnson.

Johnson: How is school?

Beneatha (crisply): Fine, thank you. *(She goes out.)*

Johnson (insulted): Getting so she don't have much to say to nobody.

Mama: The child was on her way to the bathroom.

Johnson: I know—but sometimes she act like ain't got time to pass the time of day with nobody ain't been to college. Oh—I ain't criticizing her none. It's just—you know how some of our young people gets when they get a little education. *(Mama and Ruth say nothing, just look at her.)* Yes—well. Well, I guess I better get on home. *(Unmoving.)* 'Course I can understand how she must be proud and everything—being the only one in the family to make something of herself. I know just being a chauffeur ain't never satisfied Brother none. He shouldn't feel like that, though. Ain't nothing wrong with being a chauffeur.

Mama: There's plenty wrong with it.

Johnson: What?

Mama: Plenty. My husband always said being any kind of a servant wasn't a fit thing for a man to have to be. He always said a man's hands was made to make things, or to turn the earth with—not to drive nobody's car for 'em—or—*(She looks at her own hands.)* carry they slop jars. And my boy is just like him—he wasn't meant to wait on nobody.

Johnson (rising, somewhat offended): Mmmmmmmmm. The Youngers is too much for me! *(She looks around.)* You sure one proud-acting bunch of colored folks. Well—I always thinks like Booker T. Washington° said that time—"Education has spoiled many a good plow hand"—

Mama: Is that what old Booker T. said?

Johnson: He sure did.

Mama: Well, it sounds just like him. The fool.

Johnson (indignantly): Well—he was one of our great men.

Mama: Who said so?

Johnson (nonplussed): You know, me and you ain't never agreed about some things, Lena Younger. I guess I better be going—

Ruth (quickly): Good night.

Johnson: Good night. Oh—*(Thrusting it at her.)* You can keep the paper! *(With a trill.)* 'Night.

Booker T. Washington: the most influential black educator and leader of his time, Washington (1858–1915) was criticized by W. E. B. Du Bois and others for being too accepting of inequality and injustice.

Mama: I ain't never stop trusting you. Like I ain't never stop loving you.

(She goes out, and Walter sits looking at the money on the table. Finally, in a decisive gesture, he gets up, and, in mingled joy and desperation, picks up the money. At the same moment, Travis enters for bed.)

Travis: What's the matter, Daddy? You drunk?

Walter (sweetly, more sweetly than we have ever known him): No, Daddy ain't drunk. Daddy ain't going to never be drunk again . . .

Travis: Well, good night, Daddy.

(The Father has come from behind the couch and leans over, embracing his son.)

Walter: Son, I feel like talking to you tonight.

Travis: About what?

Walter: Oh, about a lot of things. About you and what kind of man you going to be when you grow up . . . Son—son, what do you want to be when you grow up?

Travis: A bus driver.

Walter (laughing a little): A what? Man, that ain't nothing to want to be!

Travis: Why not?

Walter: 'Cause, man—it ain't big enough—you know what I mean.

Travis: I don't know then. I can't make up my mind. Sometimes Mama asks me that too. And sometimes when I tell her I just want to be like you—she says she don't want me to be like that and sometimes she says she does . . .

Walter (gathering him up in his arms): You know what, Travis? In seven years you going to be seventeen years old. And things is going to be very different with us in seven years, Travis . . . One day when you are seventeen I'll come home—home from my office downtown somewhere—

Travis: You don't work in no office, Daddy.

Walter: No—but after tonight. After what your daddy gonna do tonight, there's going to be offices—a whole lot of offices . . .

Travis: What you gonna do tonight, Daddy?

Walter: You wouldn't understand yet, son, but your daddy's gonna make a transaction . . . a business transaction that's going to change our lives . . . That's how come one day when you 'bout seventeen years old I'll come home and I'll be pretty tired, you know what I mean, after a day of conferences and secretaries getting things wrong the way they do . . . 'cause an executive's life is hell, man—*(The more he talks the farther away he gets.)* And I'll pull the car up on the driveway . . . just a plain black Chrysler, I think, with white walls—no—black tires. More elegant. Rich people don't have to be flashy . . . though I'll have to get something a little sportier for Ruth—maybe a Cadillac convertible to do her shopping in . . . And I'll come up the steps to the house and the gardener will be clipping away at the hedges and he'll say, "Good evening, Mr. Younger." And I'll say, "Hello, Jefferson, how are you this evening?" And I'll go inside and Ruth will come downstairs and meet me at the door and we'll kiss each other and she'll take my arm and we'll go up to your room to see you sitting on the floor with the catalogues of all the great schools in America around you . . . All the great schools in the world! And—and I'll say, all right son—it's your seventeenth birthday, what is it you've decided? . . . Just tell me where you want to go to school and you'll go. Just tell me, what it is you want to be—and you'll be it . . . Whatever you want to be—Yessir! *(He holds his arms open for Travis.)* You just name it, son . . . *(Travis leaps into them.)* and I hand you the world!

(Walter's voice has risen in pitch and hysterical promise and on the last line he lifts Travis high.)

ACT II

SCENE III

TIME. *Saturday, moving day, one week later.*

Before the curtain rises, Ruth's voice, a strident, dramatic church alto, cuts through the silence.

It is, in the darkness, a triumphant surge, a penetrating statement of expectation: "Oh, Lord, I don't feel no ways tired! Children, oh, glory hallelujah!"

As the curtain rises we see that Ruth is alone in the living room, finishing up the family's packing. It is moving day. She is nailing crates and tying cartons. Beneatha enters, carrying a guitar case, and watches her exuberant sister-in-law.

Ruth: Hey!
Beneatha (putting away the case): Hi.
Ruth (pointing at a package): Honey—look in that package there and see what I found on sale this morning at the South Center. *(Ruth gets up and moves to the package and draws out some curtains.)* Lookahere—hand-turned hems!
Beneatha: How do you know the window size out there?
Ruth (who hadn't thought of that): Oh—Well, they bound to fit something in the whole house. Anyhow, they was too good a bargain to pass up. *(Ruth slaps her head, suddenly remembering something.)* Oh, Bennie—I meant to put a special note on that carton over there. That's your mama's good china and she wants 'em to be very careful with it.
Beneatha: I'll do it.

(Beneatha finds a piece of paper and starts to draw large letters on it.)

Ruth: You know what I'm going to do soon as I get in that new house?

Beneatha: What?

Ruth: Honey—I'm going to run me a tub of water up to here .... *(With her fingers practically up to her nostrils.)* And I'm going to get in it—and I am going to sit . . . and sit . . . and sit in that hot water and the first person who knocks to tell me to hurry up and come out—

Beneatha: Gets shot at sunrise.

Ruth (laughing happily): You said it, sister! *(Noticing how large Beneatha is absent-mindedly making the note.)* Honey, they ain't going to read that from no airplane.

Beneatha (laughing herself): I guess I always think things have more emphasis if they are big, somehow.

Ruth (looking up at her and smiling): You and your brother seem to have that as a philosophy of life. Lord, that man—done changed so 'round here. You know—you know what we did last night? Me and Walter Lee?

Beneatha: What?

Ruth (smiling to herself): We went to the movies. *(Looking at Beneatha to see if she understands.)* We went to the movies. You know the last time me and Walter went to the movies together?

Beneatha: No.

Ruth: Me neither. That's how long it been. *(Smiling again.)* But we went last night. The picture wasn't much good, but that didn't seem to matter. We went—and we held hands.

Beneatha: Oh, Lord!

Ruth: We held hands—and you know what?

Beneatha: What?

Ruth: When we come out of the show it was late and dark and all the stores and things was closed up . . . and it was kind of chilly and there wasn't many people on the streets . . . and we was still holding hands, me and Walter.

Beneatha: You're killing me.

(Walter enters with a large package. His happiness is deep in him; he cannot keep still with his new-found exuberance. He is singing and wiggling and snapping his fingers. He puts his package in a corner and puts a phonograph record, which he has brought in with him, on the record player. As the music, soulful and sensuous, comes up he dances over to Ruth and tries to get her to dance with him. She gives in at last to his raunchiness and in a fit of giggling allows herself to be drawn into his mood. They dip and she melts into his arms in a classic, body-melding "slow drag.")

Beneatha (regarding them a long time as they dance, then drawing in her breath for a deeply exaggerated comment which she does not particularly mean): Talk about—olddddddddddd-fashionedddddd—Negroes!

Walter (stopping momentarily): What kind of Negroes? *(He says this in fun. He is not angry with her today, nor with anyone. He starts to dance with his wife again.)*

Beneatha: Old-fashioned.

Walter (as he dances with Ruth): You know, when these New Negroes have their convention—*(Pointing at his sister.)*—that is going to be the chairman of the Committee on Unending Agitation. *(He goes on dancing, then stops.)* Race, race, race! . . . Girl, I do believe you are the first person in the history of the entire human race to successfully brainwash yourself. *(Beneatha breaks up and he goes on dancing. He stops again, enjoying his tease.)* Damn, even the N double A C P takes a holiday sometimes! *(Beneatha and Ruth laugh. He dances with Ruth some more and starts to laugh and stops and pantomimes someone over an operating table.)* I can just see that chick someday looking down at some poor cat on an operating table and before she starts to slice him, she says . . . *(Pulling his sleeves back maliciously.)* "By the way, what are your views on civil rights down there? . . ."

(He laughs at her again and starts to dance happily. The bell sounds.)

Beneatha: Sticks and stones may break my bones but . . . words will never hurt me!

(Beneatha goes to the door and opens it as Walter and Ruth go on with the clowning. Beneatha is somewhat surprised to see a quiet-looking middle-aged white man in a business suit holding his hat and a briefcase in his hand and consulting a small piece of paper.)

Man: Uh—how do you do, miss. I am looking for a Mrs.—*(He looks at the slip of paper.)* Mrs. Lena Younger? *(He stops short, struck dumb at the sight of the oblivious Walter and Ruth.)*

Beneatha (smoothing her hair with slight embarrassment): Oh—yes, that's my mother. Excuse me. *(She closes the door and turns to quiet the other two.)* Ruth! Brother! *(Enunciating precisely but soundlessly: "There's a white man at the door!" They stop dancing, Ruth cuts off the phonograph, Beneatha opens the door. The man casts a curious quick glance at all of them.)* Uh—come in please.

Man (coming in): Thank you.

Beneatha: My mother isn't here just now. Is it business?

Man: Yes . . . well, of a sort.

Walter (freely, the Man of the House): Have a seat. I'm Mrs. Younger's son. I look after most of her business matters.

(Ruth and Beneatha exchange amused glances.)

Man (regarding Walter, and sitting): Well—My name is Karl Lindner . . .

Walter (stretching out his hand): Walter Younger. This is my wife—*(Ruth nods politely.)*—and my sister.

Lindner: How do you do.

Walter (amiably, as he sits himself easily on a chair, leaning forward on his knees with interest and looking expectantly into the newcomer's face): What can we do for you, Mr. Lindner!

Lindner (some minor shuffling of the hat and briefcase on his knees): Well—I am a representative of the Clybourne Park Improvement Association—

Walter (pointing): Why don't you sit your things on the floor?

Lindner: Oh—yes. Thank you. *(He slides the briefcase and hat under the chair.)* And as I was saying—I am from the Clybourne Park Improvement Association and we have had it brought to our attention at the last meeting that you people—or at least your mother—has bought a piece of residential property at—*(He digs for the slip of paper again.)*—four o six Clybourne Street . . .

Walter: That's right. Care for something to drink? Ruth, get Mr. Lindner a beer.

Lindner (upset for some reason): Oh—no, really. I mean thank you very much, but no thank you.

Ruth (innocently): Some coffee?

Lindner: Thank you, nothing at all. *(Beneatha is watching the man carefully.)* Well, I don't know how much you folks know about our organization. *(He is a gentle man; thoughtful and somewhat labored in his manner.)* It is one of these community organizations set up to look after—oh, you know, things like block upkeep and special projects and we also have what we call our New Neighbors Orientation Committee . . .

Beneatha (drily): Yes—and what do they do?

Lindner (turning a little to her and then returning the main force to Walter): Well—it's what you might call a sort of welcoming committee, I guess. I mean they, we—I'm the chairman of the committee—go around and see the new people who move into the neighborhood and sort of give them the lowdown on the way we do things out in Clybourne Park.

Beneatha (with appreciation of the two meanings, which escape Ruth and Walter.) Un-huh.

Lindner: And we also have the category of what the association calls—*(He looks elsewhere.)*—uh—special community problems . . .

Beneatha: Yes—and what are some of those?

Walter: Girl, let the man talk.

Lindner (with understated relief): Thank you. I would sort of like to explain this thing in my own way. I mean I want to explain to you in a certain way.

Walter: Go ahead.

Lindner: Yes. Well. I'm going to try to get right to the point. I'm sure we'll all appreciate that in the long run.

Beneatha: Yes.

Walter: Be still now!

Lindner: Well—

Ruth (still innocently): Would you like another chair—you don't look comfortable.

Lindner (more frustrated than annoyed): No, thank you very much. Please. Well—to get right to the point I—(*A great breath, and he is off at last.*) I am sure you people must be aware of some of the incidents which have happened in various parts of the city when colored people have moved into certain areas—

(*Beneatha exhales heavily and starts tossing a piece of fruit up and down in the air.*)

Well—because we have what I think is going to be a unique type of organization in American community life—not only do we deplore that kind of thing—but we are trying to do something about it.

(*Beneatha stops tossing and turns with a new and quizzical interest to the man.*)

We feel—(*Gaining confidence in his mission because of the interest in the faces of the people he is talking to.*)—we feel that most of the trouble in this world, when you come right down to it—(*He hits his knee for emphasis.*)—most of the trouble exists because people just don't sit down and talk to each other.

Ruth (nodding as she might in church, pleased with the remark): You can say that again, mister.

Lindner (more encouraged by such affirmation): That we don't try hard enough in this world to understand the other fellow's problem. The other guy's point of view.

Ruth: Now that's right.

(*Beneatha and Walter merely watch and listen with genuine interest.*)

Lindner: Yes—that's the way we feel out in Clybourne Park. And that's why I was elected to come here this afternoon and talk to you people. Friendly like, you know, the way people should talk to each other and see if we couldn't find some way to work this thing out. As I say, the whole business is a matter of *caring* about the other fellow. Anybody can see that you are a nice family of folks, hard-working and honest I'm sure.

(*Beneatha frowns slightly, quizzically, her head tilted regarding him.*)

Today everybody knows what it means to be on the outside of *something.* And of course, there is always somebody who is out to take advantage of people who don't always understand.

Walter: What do you mean?

Lindner: Well—you see our community is made up of people who've worked hard as the dickens for years to build up that little community. They're not rich and fancy people; just hard-working, honest people who don't really have much but those little homes and a dream of the kind of community they want to raise their children in. Now, I don't say we are perfect and there is a lot wrong in some of the things they want. But you've got to admit that a man, right or wrong, has the right to want to have the neighborhood he lives in a certain kind of way. And at the moment the overwhelming majority of our people out there feel that people get along better, take more of a common interest in the life of the community, when they share a common background. I want you to believe me when I tell you that race prejudice simply doesn't enter into it. It is a matter of the people of Clybourne Park believing, rightly or wrongly, as I say, that for the happiness of all concerned that our Negro families are happier when they live in their *own* communities.

Beneatha (with a grand and bitter gesture): This, friends, is the Welcoming Committee!

Walter (dumfounded, looking at Lindner): Is this what you came marching all the way over here to tell us?

Lindner: Well, now we've been having a fine conversation. I hope you'll hear me all the way through.

Walter (tightly): Go ahead, man.

Lindner: You see—in the face of all the things I have said, we are prepared to make your family a very generous offer. . . .

Beneatha: Thirty pieces and not a coin less!°

Walter: Yeah?

Lindner (putting on his glasses and drawing a form out of the briefcase): Our association is prepared, through the collective effort of our people, to buy the house from you at a financial gain to your family.

Ruth: Lord have mercy, ain't this the living gall!

Walter: All right, you through?

Lindner: Well, I want to give you the exact terms of the financial arrangement—

Walter: We don't want to hear no exact terms of no arrangements. I want to know if you got any more to tell us 'bout getting together?

Linder (taking off his glasses): Well—I don't suppose that you feel . . .

Thirty pieces and not a coin less: reference to Judas's betrayal of Jesus for thirty pieces of silver (Matthew 26: 14–16).

Walter: Never mind how I feel—you got any more to say 'bout how people ought to sit down and talk to each other? . . . Get out of my house, man. *(He turns his back and walks to the door.)*

Lindner (looking around at the hostile faces and reaching and assembling his hat and briefcase): Well—I don't understand why you people are reacting this way. What do you think you are going to gain by moving into a neighborhood where you just aren't wanted and where some elements—well—people can get awful worked up when they feel that their whole way of life and everything they've ever worked for is threatened.

Walter: Get out.

Lindner (at the door, holding a small card): Well—I'm sorry it went like this.

Walter: Get out.

Lindner (almost sadly regarding Walter): You just can't force people to change their hearts, son.

(He turns and put his card on a table and exits. Walter pushes the door to with stinging hatred, and stands looking at it. Ruth just sits and Beneatha just stands. They say nothing. Mama and Travis enter.)

Mama: Well—this all the packing got done since I left out of here this morning? I testify before God that my children got all the energy of the *dead!* What time the moving men due?

Beneatha: Four o'clock. You had a caller, Mama. *(She is smiling, teasingly.)*

Mama: Sure enough—who?

Beneatha (her arms folded saucily): The Welcoming Committee.

(Walter and Ruth giggle.)

Mama (innocently): Who?

Beneatha: The Welcoming Committee. They said they're sure going to be glad to see you when you get there.

Walter (devilishly): Yeah, they said they can't hardly wait to see your face. *(Laughter.)*

Mama (sensing their facetiousness): What's the matter with you all?

Walter: Ain't nothing the matter with us. We just telling you 'bout the gentleman who came to see you this afternoon. From the Clybourne Park Improvement Association.

Mama: What he want?

Ruth (in the same mood as Beneatha and Walter): To welcome you, honey.

Walter: He said they can't hardly wait. He said the one thing they don't have, that they just *dying* to have out there, is a fine family of fine colored people! *(To Ruth and Beneatha.)* Ain't that right!

Ruth (mockingly): Yeah! He left his card—

Beneatha (handing card to Mama): In case—

(Mama reads and throws it on the floor—understanding and looking off as she draws her chair up to the table on which she has put her plant and some sticks and some cord.)

Mama: Father, give us strength. *(Knowingly—and without fun.)* Did he threaten us?

Beneatha: Oh—Mama—they don't do it like that any more. He talked Brotherhood. He said everybody ought to learn how to sit down and hate each other with good Christian fellowship.

(She and Walter shake hands to ridicule the remark.)

Mama (sadly): Lord, protect us . . .

Ruth: You should hear the money those folks raised to buy the house from us. All we paid and then some.

Beneatha: What they think we going to do—eat 'em?

Ruth: No, honey, marry 'em.

Mama (shaking her head): Lord, Lord, Lord . . .

Ruth: Well—that's the way the crackers crumble. *(A beat.)* Joke.

Beneatha (laughingly noticing what her mother is doing): Mama, what are you doing?

Mama: Fixing my plant so it won't get hurt none on the way . . .

Beneatha: Mama, you going to take *that* to the new house?

Mama: Un-huh—

Beneatha: That raggedy-looking old thing?

Mama (stopping and looking at her): It expresses ME!

Ruth (with delight, to Beneatha): So there, Miss Thing!

(Walter comes to Mama suddenly and bends down behind her and squeezes her in his arms with all his strength. She is overwhelmed by the suddenness of it and, though delighted, her manner is like that of Ruth and Travis.)

Mama: Look out now, boy! You make me mess up my thing here!

Walter (his face lit, he slips down on his knees beside her, his arms still about her): Mama . . . you know what it means to climb up in the chariot?

Mama (gruffly, very happy): Get on away from me now . . .

Ruth (near the gift-wrapped package, trying to catch Walter's eye): Psst—

Walter: What the old song say, Mama . . .

Ruth: Walter—Now? *(She is pointing at the package.)*

Walter (speaking the lines, sweetly, playfully, in his mother's face):

I got wings! . . . you got wings! . . .
All God's Children got wings . . .

Mama: Boy—get out of my face and do some work . . .

Walter:

When I get to heaven gonna put on my wings,
Gonna fly all over God's heaven . . .

Beneatha (teasingly, from across the room): Everybody talking 'bout heaven ain't going there!

Walter (to Ruth, who is carrying the box across to them): I don't know, you think we ought to give her that . . . Seems to me she ain't been very appreciative around here.

Mama (eying the box, which is obviously a gift): What is that?

Walter (taking it from Ruth and putting it on the table in front of Mama): Well—what you all think? Should we give it to her?

Ruth: Oh—she was pretty good today.

Mama: I'll good you—*(She turns her eyes to the box again.)*

Beneatha: Open it, Mama.

(She stands up, looks at it, turns and looks at all of them, and then presses her hands together and does not open the package.)

Walter (sweetly): Open it, Mama. It's for you. *(Mama looks in his eyes. It is the first present in her life without its being Christmas. Slowly she opens her package and lifts out, one by one, a brand-new sparkling set of gardening tools. Walter continues, prodding.)* Ruth made up the note—read it . . .

Mama (picking up the card and adjusting her glasses): "To our own Mrs. Miniver°—Love from Brother, Ruth and Beneatha." Ain't that lovely . . .

Travis (tugging at his father's sleeve): Daddy, can I give her mine now?

Walter: All right, son. *(Travis flies to get his gift.)*

Mama: Now I don't have to use my knives and forks no more . . .

Walter: Travis didn't want to go in with the rest of us, Mama. He got his own. *(Somewhat amused.)* We don't know what it is . . .

Travis (racing back in the room with a large hatbox and putting it in front of his grandmother): Here!

Mama: Lord have mercy, baby. You done gone and bought your grandmother a hat?

Travis (very proud): Open it!

(She does and lifts out an elaborate, but very elaborate, wide gardening hat, and all the adults break up at the sight of it.)

Ruth: Travis, honey, what is that?

Travis (who thinks it is beautiful and appropriate): It's a gardening hat! Like the ladies always have on in the magazines when they work in their gardens.

Beneatha (giggling fiercely): Travis—we were trying to make Mama Mrs. Miniver—not Scarlett O'Hara!°

Mrs. Miniver: As portrayed by Greer Garson in the Academy Award-winning World War II film, Mrs. Miniver is a British housewife who loves her family and gardening, and is called to show great courage, strength, and perseverance in the face of German bombardments. *Scarlett O'Hara:* the young, flamboyant, and histrionic heroine of *Gone with the Wind* (1936) by Margaret Mitchell—made into a blockbuster movie in 1939 by David O. Selznick. The Southern belle Scarlett O'Hara is a sharp contrast to the down-to-earth, sensible Mrs. Miniver.

Mama (indignantly): What's the matter with you all! This here is a beautiful hat! *(Absurdly.)* I always wanted me one just like it!

(She pops it on her head to prove it to her grandson, and the hat is ludicrous and considerably oversized.)

Ruth: Hot dog! Go, Mama!

Walter (doubled over with laughter): I'm sorry, Mama—but you look like you ready to go out and chop you some cotton sure enough!

(They all laugh except Mama, out of deference to Travis' feelings.)

Mama (gathering the boy up to her): Bless your heart—this is the prettiest hat I ever owned—*(Walter, Ruth, and Beneatha chime in—noisily, festively and insincerely congratulating Travis on his gift.)* What are we all standing around here for? We ain't finished packin' yet. Bennie, you ain't packed one book.

(The bell rings.)

Beneatha: That couldn't be the movers . . . it's not hardly two o'clock yet—

(Beneatha goes into her room. Mama starts for door.)

Walter (turning, stiffening): Wait—wait—I'll get it. *(He stands and looks at the door.)*

Mama: You expecting company, son?

Walter (just looking at the door): Yeah—yeah . . .

(Mama looks at Ruth, and they exchange innocent and unfrightened glances.)

Mama (not understanding): Well, let them in, son.

Beneatha (from her room): We need some more string.

Mama: Travis—you run to the hardware and get me some string cord.

(Mama goes out and Walter turns and looks at Ruth. Travis goes to a dish for money.)

Ruth: Why don't you answer the door, man?

Walter (suddenly bounding across the floor to embrace her): 'Cause sometimes it hard to let the future begin! *(Stooping down in her face.)*

I got wings! You got wings!
All God's children got wings!

(He crosses to the door and throws it open. Standing there is a very slight little man in a not too prosperous business suit and with haunted frightened eyes and a hat pulled down tightly, brim up, around his forehead. Travis passes between the men and exits. Walter leans deep in the man's face, still in his jubilance.)

When I get to heaven gonna put on my wings,
Gonna fly all over God's heaven . . .

(The little man just stares at him.)

Heaven—

(Suddenly he stops and looks past the little man into the empty hallway.)

Where's Willy, man?

Bobo: He ain't with me.

Walter (not disturbed): Oh—come on in. You know my wife.

Bobo (dumbly, taking off his hat): Yes—h'you, Miss Ruth.

Ruth (quietly, a mood apart from her husband already, seeing Bobo): Hello, Bobo.

Walter: You right on time today . . . Right on time. That's the way! *(He slaps Bobo on his back.)* Sit down . . . lemme hear.

(Ruth stands stiffly and quietly in back of them, as though somehow she senses death, her eyes fixed on her husband.)

Bobo (his frightened eyes on the floor, his hat in his hands): Could I please get a drink of water, before I tell you about it, Walter Lee?

(Walter does not take his eyes off the man. Ruth goes blindly to the tap and gets a glass of water and brings it to Bobo.)

Walter: There ain't nothing wrong, is there?

Bobo: Lemme tell you—

Walter: Man—didn't nothing go wrong?

Bobo: Lemme tell you—Walter Lee. *(Looking at Ruth and talking to her more than to Walter.)* You know how it was. I got to tell you how it was. I mean first I got to tell you how it was all the way . . . I mean about the money I put in, Walter Lee . . .

Walter (with taut agitation now): What about the money you put in?

Bobo: Well—it wasn't much as we told you—me and Willy—*(He stops.)* I'm sorry, Walter. I got a bad feeling about it. I got a real bad feeling about it . . .

Walter: Man, what you telling me about all this for? . . . Tell me what happened in Springfield . . .

Bobo: Springfield.

Ruth (like a dead woman): What was supposed to happen in Springfield?

Bobo (to her): This deal that me and Walter went into with Willy—Me and Willy was going to go down to Springfield and spread some money 'round so's we wouldn't have to wait so long for the liquor license . . . That's what we were going to do. Everybody said that was the way you had to do, you understand, Miss Ruth?

Walter: Man—what happened down there?

Bobo (a pitiful man, near tears): I'm trying to tell you, Walter.

Walter (screaming at him suddenly): THEN TELL ME, GODDAMMIT . . . WHAT'S THE MATTER WITH YOU?

Bobo: Man . . . I didn't go to no Springfield, yesterday.

Walter (halted, life hanging in the moment): Why not?

Bobo (the long way, the hard way to tell): 'Cause I didn't have no reasons to . . .

Walter: Man, what are you talking about!

Bobo: I'm talking about the fact that when I got to the train station yesterday morning—eight o'clock like we planned . . . Man—*Willy didn't never show up.*

Walter: Why . . . where was he . . . where is he?

Bobo: That's what I'm trying to tell you . . . I don't know . . . I waited six hours . . . I called his house . . . and I waited . . . six hours . . . I waited in that train station six hours . . . *(Breaking into tears.)* That was all the extra money I had in the world . . . *(Looking up at Walter with tears running down his face.)* Man, *Willy is gone.*

Walter: Gone, what you mean Willy is gone? Gone where? You mean he went by himself. You mean he went off to Springfield by himself—to take care of getting the license—*(Turns and looks anxiously at Ruth.)* You mean maybe he didn't want too many people in on the business down there? *(Looks to Ruth again, as before.)* You know Willy got his own ways. *(Looks back to Bobo.)* Maybe you was late yesterday and he just went on down there without you. Maybe—maybe—he's been callin' you at home tryin' to tell you what happened or something. Maybe—maybe—he just got sick. He's somewhere—he's got to be somewhere. We just got to find him—me and you got to find him. *(Grabs Bobo senselessly by the collar and starts to shake him.)* We got to!

Bobo (in sudden angry, frightened agony): What's the matter with you, Walter! *When a cat take off with your money he don't leave you no road maps!*

Walter (turning madly, as though he is looking for Willy in every room): Willy! . . . Willy . . . don't do it . . . Please don't do it . . . Man, not with that money . . . Man, please, not with that money . . . Oh, God . . . Don't let it be true . . . *(He is wandering around, crying out for Willy and looking for him or perhaps for help from God.)* Man . . . I trusted you . . . Man, I put my life in your hands . . .

(He starts to crumple down on the floor as Ruth just covers her face in horror. Mama opens the door and comes into the room, with Beneatha behind her.)

Man . . . *(He starts to pound the floor with his fists, sobbing wildly.)* THAT MONEY IS MADE OUT OF MY FATHER'S FLESH—

Bobo (standing over him helplessly): I'm sorry, Walter . . . *(Only Walter's sobs reply. Bobo puts on his hat.)* I had my life staked on this deal, too . . . *(He exits.)*

Mama (to Walter): Son—*(She goes to him, bends down to him, talks to his bent head.)* Son . . . Is it gone? Son, I gave you sixty-five hundred dollars. Is it gone? All of it? Beneatha's money too?

Walter (lifting his head slowly): Mama . . . I never . . . went to the bank at all . . .

Mama (not wanting to believe him): You mean . . . Your sister's school money . . . you used that too . . . Walter? . . .

Walter: Yessss! All of it . . . It's all gone. . . .

(There is total silence. Ruth stands with her face covered with her hands; Beneatha leans forlornly against a wall, fingering a piece of red ribbon from the mother's gift. Mama stops and looks at her son without recognition and then, quite without thinking about it, starts to beat him senselessly in the face. Beneatha goes to them and stops it.)

Beneatha: Mama!

(Mama stops and looks at both of her children and rises slowly and wanders vaguely, aimlessly away from them.)

Mama: I seen . . . him . . . night after night . . . come in . . . and look at that rug . . . and then look at me . . . the red showing in his eyes . . . the veins moving in his head . . . I seen him grow thin and old before he was forty . . . working and working and working like somebody's old horse . . . killing himself . . . and you—you give it all away in a day—*(She raises her arms to strike him again.)*

Beneatha: Mama—

Mama: Oh, God . . . *(She looks up to Him.)* Look down here—and show me the strength.

Beneatha: Mama—

Mama (folding over): Strength . . .

Beneatha (plaintively): Mama . . .

Mama: Strength!

ACT III

TIME. *An hour later*

At curtain, there is a sullen light of gloom in the living room, gray light not unlike that which began the first scene of Act One. At left we can see Walter within his room, alone with himself. He is stretched out on the bed, his shirt out and open, his arms under his head. He does not smoke, he does not cry out, he merely lies there, looking up at the ceiling, much as if he were alone in the world.

In the living room Beneatha sits at the table, still surrounded by the now almost ominous packing crates. She sits looking off. We feel that this is a mood struck perhaps an hour before, and it lingers now, full of the empty sound of profound disappointment. We see on a line from her brother's bedroom the sameness of their attitudes. Presently the bell rings and Beneatha rises without ambition or interest in answering. It is Asagai, smiling broadly, striding into the room with energy and happy expectation and conversation.

Asagai: I came over . . . I had some free time. I thought I might help with the packing. Ah, I like the look of packing crates! A household in preparation for a journey! It depresses some people . . . but for me . . . it is another feeling. Something full of the flow of life, do you understand? Movement, progress . . . It makes me think of Africa.

Beneatha: Africa!

Asagai: What kind of a mood is this? Have I told you how deeply you move me?

Beneatha: He gave away the money, Asagai . . .

Asagai: Who gave away what money?

Beneatha: The insurance money. My brother gave it away.

Asagai: Gave it away?

Beneatha: He made an investment! With a man even Travis wouldn't have trusted with his most worn-out marbles.

Asagai: And it's gone?

Beneatha: Gone!

Asagai: I'm very sorry . . . And you, now?

Beneatha: Me? . . . Me? . . . Me, I'm nothing . . . Me. When I was very small . . . we used to take our sleds out in the wintertime and the only hills we had were the ice-covered stone steps of some houses down the street. And we used to fill them in with snow and make them smooth and slide down them all day . . . and it was very dangerous, you know . . . far too steep . . . and sure enough one day a kid named Rufus came down too fast and hit the sidewalk and we saw his face just split open right there in front of us . . . And I remember standing there looking at his bloody open face thinking that was the end of Rufus. But the ambulance came and they took him to the hospital and they fixed the broken bones and they sewed it all up . . . and the next time I saw Rufus he just had a little line down the middle of his face . . . I never got over that . . .

Asagai: What?

Beneatha: That that was what one person could do for another, fix him up—sew up the problem, make him all right again. That was the most marvelous thing in the world . . . I wanted to do that. I always thought it was the one concrete thing in the world that a human being could do. Fix up the sick, you know—and make them whole again. This was truly being God . . .

Asagai: You wanted to be God?

Beneatha: No—I wanted to cure. It used to be so important to me. I wanted to cure. It used to matter. I used to care. I mean about people and how their bodies hurt . . .

Asagai: And you've stopped caring?

Beneatha: Yes—I think so.

Asagai: Why?

Beneatha (bitterly): Because it doesn't seem deep enough, close enough to what ails mankind! It was a child's way of seeing things—or an idealist's.

Asagai: Children see things very well sometimes—and idealists even better.

Beneatha: I know that's what you think. Because you are still where I left off. You with all your talk and dreams about Africa! You still think you can patch up the world. Cure the Great Sore of Colonialism—*(Loftily, mocking it.)* with the Penicillin of Independence—!

Asagai: Yes!

Beneatha: Independence *and then what?* What about all the crooks and thieves and just plain idiots who will come into power and steal and plunder the same as before—only now they will be black and do it in the name of the new Independence—WHAT ABOUT THEM?!

Asagai: That will be the problem for another time. First we must get there.

Beneatha: And where does it end?

Asagai: End? Who even spoke of an end? To life? To living?

Beneatha: An end to misery! To stupidity! Don't you see there isn't any real progress, Asagai, there is only one large circle that we march in, around and around, each of us with our own little picture in front of us—our own little mirage that we think is the future.

Asagai: That is the mistake.

Beneatha: What?

Asagai: What you just said about the circle. It isn't a circle—it is simply a long line—as in geometry, you know, one that reaches into infinity. And because we cannot see the end—we also cannot see how it changes. And it is very odd but those who see the changes—who dream, who will not give up—are called idealists . . . and those who see only the circle we call *them* the "realists"!

Beneatha: Asagai, while I was sleeping in that bed in there, people went out and took the future right out of my hands! And nobody asked me, nobody consulted me—they just went out and changed my life!

Asagai: Was it your money?

Beneatha: What?

Asagai: Was it your money he gave away?

Beneatha: It belonged to all of us.

Asagai: But did you earn it? Would you have had it at all if your father had not died?

Beneatha: No.

Asagai: Then isn't there something wrong in a house—in a world—where all dreams, good or bad, must depend on the death of a man? I never thought to see *you* like this, Alaiyo. You! Your brother made a mistake and you are grateful to him so that now you can give up the ailing human race on account of it! You talk about what good is struggle; what good is anything! Where are we all going and why are we bothering?

Beneatha: AND YOU CANNOT ANSWER IT!

Asagai (shouting over her): I LIVE THE ANSWER! (Pause.) In my village at home it is the exceptional man who can even read a newspaper . . . or who ever sees a book at all. I will go home and much of what I will have to say will seem strange to the people of my village. But I will teach and work and things will happen, slowly and swiftly. At times it will seem that nothing changes at all . . . and then again the sudden dramatic events which make history leap into the future. And then quiet again. Retrogression even. Guns, murder, revolution. And I even will have moments when I wonder if the quiet was not better than all that death and hatred. But I will look about my village at the illiteracy and disease and ignorance and I will not wonder long. And perhaps . . . perhaps I will be a great man . . . I mean perhaps I will hold on to the substance of truth and find my way always with the right course . . . and perhaps for it I will be butchered in my bed some night by the servants of empire . . .

Beneatha: The martyr!

Asagai (he smiles): . . . or perhaps I shall live to be a very old man, respected and esteemed in my new nation . . . And perhaps I shall hold office and this is what I'm trying to tell you, Alaiyo: Perhaps the things I believe now for my country will be wrong and outmoded, and I will not understand and do terrible things to have things my way or merely to keep my power. Don't you see that there will be young men and women—not British soldiers then, but my own black countrymen—to step out of the shadows some evening and slit my then useless throat? Don't you see they have always been there . . . that they always will be. And that such a thing as my own death will be an advance? They who might kill me even . . . actually replenish all that I was.

Beneatha: Oh, Asagai, I know all that.

Asagai: Good! Then stop moaning and groaning and tell me what you plan to do.

Beneatha: Do?

Asagai: I have a bit of a suggestion.

Beneatha: What?

Asagai (rather quietly for him): That when it is all over—that you come home with me—

Beneatha (staring at him and crossing away with exasperation): Oh—Asagai—at this moment you decide to be romantic!

Asagai (quickly understanding the misunderstanding): My dear, young creature of the New World—I do not mean across the city—I mean across the ocean: home—to Africa.

Beneatha (slowly understanding and turning to him with murmured amazement): To Africa?

Asagai: Yes! . . . *(Smiling and lifting his arms playfully.)* Three hundred years later the African Prince rose up out of the seas and swept the maiden back across the middle passage over which her ancestors had come—

Beneatha (unable to play): To—to Nigeria?

Asagai: Nigeria. Home. *(Coming to her with genuine romantic flippancy.)* I will show you our mountains and our stars; and give you cool drinks from gourds and teach you the old songs and the ways of our people—and, in time, we will pretend that—*(Very softly.)*—you have only been away for a day. Say that you'll come—*(He swings her around and takes her full in his arms in a kiss which proceeds to passion.)*

Beneatha (pulling away suddenly): You're getting me all mixed up—

Asagai: Why?

Beneatha: Too many things—too many things have happened today. I must sit down and think. I don't know what I feel about anything right this minute. *(She promptly sits down and props her chin on her fist.)*

Asagai (charmed): All right, I shall leave you. No—don't get up. *(Touching her, gently, sweetly.)* Just sit awhile and think . . . Never be afraid to sit awhile and think. *(He goes to door and looks at her.)* How often I have looked at you and said, "Ah—so this is what the New World hath finally wrought . . ."

(He exits. Beneatha sits on alone. Presently Walter enters from his room and starts to rummage through things, feverishly looking for something. She looks up and turns in her seat.)

Beneatha (hissingly): Yes—just look at what the New World hath wrought! . . . Just look! *(She gestures with bitter disgust.)* There he is! *Monsieur le petit bourgeois noir*°—himself! There he is—Symbol of a Rising Class! Entrepreneur! Titan of the system!

(Walter ignores her completely and continues frantically and destructively looking for something and hurling things to floor and tearing things out of

Monsieur le petit bourgeois noir: French for "Mr. Black Middle Class."

their place in his search. Beneatha ignores the eccentricity of his actions and goes on with the monologue of insult.)

Did you dream of yachts on Lake Michigan, Brother? Did you see yourself on that Great Day sitting down at the Conference Table, surrounded by all the mighty bald-headed men in America? All halted, waiting, breathless, waiting for your pronouncements on industry? Waiting for you—Chairman of the Board!

(Walter finds what he is looking for—a small piece of white paper—and pushes it in his pocket and puts on his coat and rushes out without ever having looked at her. She shouts after him.)

I look at you and I see the final triumph of stupidity in the world!

(The door slams and she returns to just sitting again. Ruth comes quickly out of Mama's room.)

Ruth: Who was that?
Beneatha: Your husband.
Ruth: Where did he go?
Beneatha: Who knows—maybe he has an appointment at U.S. Steel.
Ruth (anxiously, with frightened eyes): You didn't say nothing bad to him, did you?
Beneatha: Bad? Say anything bad to him? No—I told him he was a sweet boy and full of dreams and everything is strictly peachy keen, as the ofay° kids say!

(Mama enters from her bedroom. She is lost, vague, trying to catch hold, to make some sense of her former command of the world, but it still eludes her. A sense of waste overwhelms her gait; a measure of apology rides on her shoulders. She goes to her plant, which has remained on the table, looks at it, picks it up and takes it to the windowsill and sits it outside, and she stands and looks at it a long moment. Then she closes the window, straightens her body with effort and turns around to her children.)

Mama: Well—ain't it a mess in here, though? *(A false cheerfulness, a beginning of something.)* I guess we all better stop moping around and get some work done. All this unpacking and everything we got to do. *(Ruth raises her head slowly in response to the sense of the line; and Beneatha in similar manner turns very slowly to look at her mother.)* One of you all better call the moving people and tell 'em not to come.
Ruth: Tell 'em not to come?

ofay: Pig Latin for "foe."

Mama: Of course, baby. Ain't no need in 'em coming all the way here and having to go back. They charges for that too. *(She sits down, fingers to her brow, thinking.)* Lord, ever since I was a little girl, I always remembers people saying, "Lena—Lena Eggleston, you aims too high all the time. You needs to slow down and see life a little more like it is. Just slow down some." That's what they always used to say down home—"Lord, that Lena Eggleston is a high-minded thing. She'll get her due one day!"

Ruth: No, Lena . . .

Mama: Me and Big Walter just didn't never learn right.

Ruth: Lena, no! We gotta go. Bennie—tell her . . . *(She rises and crosses to Beneatha with her arms outstretched. Beneatha doesn't respond.)* Tell her we can still move . . . the notes ain't but a hundred and twenty-five a month. We got four grown people in this house—we can work . . .

Mama (to herself): Just aimed too high all the time—

Ruth (turning and going to Mama fast—the words pouring out with urgency and desperation): Lena—I'll work . . . I'll work twenty hours a day in all the kitchens in Chicago . . . I'll strap my baby on my back if I have to and scrub all the floors in America and wash all the sheets in America if I have to—but we got to MOVE! We got to get OUT OF HERE!!

(Mama reaches out absently and pats Ruth's hand.)

Mama: No—I sees things differently now. Been thinking 'bout some of the things we could do to fix this place up some. I seen a second-hand bureau over on Maxwell Street just the other day that could fit right there. *(She points to where the new furniture might go. Ruth wanders away from her.)* Would need some new handles on it and then a little varnish and it look like something brand-new. And—we can put up them new curtains in the kitchen . . . Why this place be looking fine. Cheer us all up so that we forget trouble ever come . . . *(To Ruth.)* And you could get some nice screens to put up in your room 'round the baby's bassinet . . . *(She looks at both of them, pleadingly.)* Sometimes you just got to know when to give up some things . . . and hold on to what you got . . .

(Walter enters from the outside, looking spent and leaning against the door, his coat hanging from him.)

Mama: Where you been, son?

Walter (breathing hard): Made a call.

Mama: To who, son?

Walter: To The Man. *(He heads for his room.)*

Mama: What man, baby?

Walter (stops in the door): The Man, Mama. Don't you know who The Man is?

Ruth: Walter Lee?

Walter: The Man. Like the guys in the streets say—The Man. Captain Boss—Mistuh Charley . . . Old Cap'n Please Mr. Bossman . . .

Beneatha (suddenly): Lindner!

Walter: That's right! That's good. I told him to come right over.

Beneatha (fiercely, understanding): For what? What do you want to see him for!

Walter (looking at his sister): We going to do business with him.

Mama: What you talking 'bout, son?

Walter: Talking 'bout life, Mama. You all always telling me to see life like it is. Well—I laid in there on my back today . . . and I figured it out. Life just like it is. Who gets and who don't get. *(He sits down with his coat on and laughs.)* Mama, you know it's all divided up. Life is. Sure enough. Between the takers and the "tooken." *(He laughs.)* I've figured it out finally. *(He looks around at them.)* Yeah. Some of us always getting "tooken." *(He laughs.)* People like Willy Harris, they don't never get "tooken." And you know why the rest of us do? 'Cause we all mixed up. Mixed up bad. We get to looking 'round for the right and the wrong; and we worry about it and cry about it and stay up nights trying to figure out 'bout the wrong and the right of things all the time . . . And all the time, man, them takers is out there operating, just taking and taking. Willy Harris? Shoot—Willy Harris don't even count. He don't even count in the big scheme of things. But I'll say one thing for old Willy Harris . . . he's taught me something. He's taught me to keep my eye on what counts in this world. Yeah—*(Shouting out a little.)* Thanks, Willy!

Ruth: What did you call that man for, Walter Lee?

Walter: Called him to tell him to come on over to the show. Gonna put on a show for the man. Just what he wants to see. You see, Mama, the man came here today and he told us that them people out there where you want us to move—well they so upset they willing to pay us *not* to move! *(He laughs again.)* And—and oh, Mama—you would of been proud of the way me and Ruth and Bennie acted. We told him to get out . . . Lord have mercy! We told the man to get out! Oh, we was some proud folks this afternoon, yeah. *(He lights a cigarette.)* We were still full of that old-time stuff . . .

Ruth (coming toward him slowly): You talking 'bout taking them people's money to keep us from moving in that house?

Walter: I ain't just talking 'bout it, baby—I'm telling you that's what's going to happen!

Beneatha: Oh, God! Where is the bottom! Where is the real honest-to-God bottom so he can't go any farther!

Walter: See—that's the old stuff. You and that boy that was here today. You all want everybody to carry a flag and a spear and sing some marching songs, huh? You wanna spend your life looking into things and trying to find the right and the wrong part, huh? Yeah. You know what's going to happen to that boy someday—he'll find himself sitting in a dungeon, locked in forever—and the takers will have the key! Forget it, baby! There ain't no causes—there ain't nothing but taking in this world, and he who takes most is smartest—and it don't make a damn bit of difference *how*.

Mama: You making something inside me cry, son. Some awful pain inside me.

Walter: Don't cry, Mama. Understand. That white man is going to walk in that door able to write checks for more money than we ever had. It's important to him and I'm going to help him . . . I'm going to put on the show, Mama.

Mama: Son—I come from five generations of people who was slaves and sharecroppers—but ain't nobody in my family never let nobody pay 'em no money that was a way of telling us we wasn't fit to walk the earth. We ain't never been that poor. *(Raising her eyes and looking at him.)* We ain't never been that—dead inside.

Beneatha: Well—we are dead now. All the talk about dreams and sunlight that goes on in this house. It's all dead now.

Walter: What's the matter with you all! I didn't make this world! It was give to me this way! Hell, yes, I want me some yachts someday! Yes, I want to hang some real pearls 'round my wife's neck. Ain't she supposed to wear no pearls? Somebody tell me—tell me, who decides which women is suppose to wear pearls in this world. I tell you I am a *man*—and I think my wife should wear some pearls in this world!

(This last line hangs a good while and Walter begins to move about the room. The word "Man" has penetrated his consciousness; he mumbles it to himself repeatedly between strange agitated pauses as he moves about.)

Mama: Baby, how you going to feel on the inside?

Walter: Fine! . . . Going to feel fine . . . a man . . .

Mama: You won't have nothing left then, Walter Lee.

Walter (coming to her): I'm going to feel fine, Mama. I'm going to look that son-of-a-bitch in the eyes and say—*(He falters.)*—and say, "All right, Mr. Lindner—*(He falters even more.)*—that's *your* neighborhood out there! You got the right to keep it like you want! You got the right to have it like you want! Just write the check and—the house is yours." And—and I am going to say—*(His voice almost breaks.)* "And you—you people just put the money in my hand and you won't have to live next to this bunch of stinking niggers! . . . " *(He straightens up and moves away from his mother, walking around the room.)* And maybe—maybe I'll just get down on my black knees . . . *(He does so; Ruth and Bennie and Mama watch him in frozen horror.)* "Captain, Mistuh, Bossman—*(Groveling and grinning and wringing his hands in profoundly anguished imitation of the slow-witted movie stereotype.)* A-hee-hee-hee! Oh, yassuh boss! Yasssssuh! Great white—*(Voice breaking, he forces himself to go on.)*—Father, just gi' ussen de money, fo' God's sake, and we's—we's ain't gwine come out deh and dirty up yo' white folks neighborhood . . ." *(He breaks down completely.)* And I'll feel fine! Fine! FINE! *(He gets up and goes into the bedroom.)*

Beneatha: That is not a man. That is nothing but a toothless rat.

Mama: Yes—death done come in this here house. *(She is nodding, slowly, reflectively.)* Done come walking in my house on the lips of my children. You what supposed to be my beginning again. You—what supposed to be my harvest. *(To Beneatha.)* You—you mourning your brother?

Beneatha: He's no brother of mine.

Mama: What you say?

Beneatha: I said that that individual in that room is no brother of mine.

Mama: That's what I thought you said. You feeling like you better than he is today? *(Beneatha does not answer.)* Yes? What you tell him a minute ago? That he wasn't a man? Yes? You give him up for me? You done wrote his epitaph too—like the rest of the world? Well, who give you the privilege?

Beneatha: Be on my side for once! You saw what he just did, Mama! You saw him—down on his knees. Wasn't it you who taught me to despise any man who would do that? Do what he's going to do?

Mama: Yes—I taught you that. Me and your daddy. But I thought I taught you something else too . . . I thought I taught you to love him.

Beneatha: Love him? There is nothing left to love.

Mama: There is *always* something left to love. And if you ain't learned that, you ain't learned nothing. *(Looking at her.)* Have you cried for that boy today? I don't mean for yourself and for the family 'cause we lost the money. I mean for him: what he been through and what it done to him. Child, when do you think is the time to love somebody the most? When they done good and made things easy for everybody? Well then, you ain't through learning—because that ain't the time at all. It's when he's at his lowest and can't believe in hisself 'cause the world done whipped him so! When you starts measuring somebody, measure him right, child, measure him right. Make sure you done taken into account what hills and valleys he come through before he got to wherever he is.

(Travis bursts into the room at the end of the speech, leaving the door open.)

Travis: Grandmama—the moving men are downstairs! The truck just pulled up.

Mama (turning and looking at him): Are they, baby? They downstairs?

(She sighs and sits. Lindner appears in the doorway. He peers in and knocks lightly, to gain attention, and comes in. All turn to look at him.)

Lindner (hat and briefcase in hand): Uh—hello . . .

(Ruth crosses mechanically to the bedroom door and opens it and lets it swing open freely and slowly as the lights come up on Walter within, still in his coat, sitting at the far corner of the room. He looks up and out through the room to Lindner.)

Ruth: He's here.

(A long minute passes and Walter slowly gets up.)

Lindner (coming to the table with efficiency, putting his briefcase on the table and starting to unfold papers and unscrew fountain pens): Well, I certainly was glad to hear from you people.

(Walter has begun the trek out of the room, slowly and awkwardly, rather like a small boy, passing the back of his sleeve across his mouth from time to time.)

Life can really be so much simpler than people let it be most of the time. Well—with whom do I negotiate? You, Mrs. Younger, or your son here?

(Mama sits with her hands folded on her lap and her eyes closed as Walter advances. Travis goes closer to Lindner and looks at the papers curiously.)

Just some official papers, sonny.

Ruth: Travis, you go downstairs—

Mama (opening her eyes and looking into Walter's): No. Travis, you stay right here. And you make him understand what you doing, Walter Lee. You teach him good. Like Willy Harris taught you. You show where our five generations done come to. *(Walter looks from her to the boy, who grins at him innocently.)* Go ahead, son—*(She folds her hands and closes her eyes.)* Go ahead.

Walter (at last crosses to Lindner, who is reviewing the contract): Well, Mr. Lindner. *(Beneatha turns away.)* We called you—*(There is a profound, simple groping quality in his speech.)*—because, well, me and my family *(He looks around and shifts from one foot to the other.)* Well—we are very plain people. . . .

Lindner: Yes—

Walter: I mean—I have worked as a chauffeur most of my life—and my wife here, she does domestic work in people's kitchens. So does my mother. I mean—we are plain people . . .

Lindner: Yes, Mr. Younger—

Walter (really like a small boy, looking down at his shoes and then up at the man): And—uh—well, my father, well, he was a laborer most of his life . . .

Lindner (absolutely confused): Uh, yes—yes, I understand. *(He turns back to the contract.)*

Walter (a beat; staring at him): And my father—*(With sudden intensity.)* My father almost *beat a man to death* once because this man called him a bad name or something, you know what I mean?

Lindner (looking up, frozen): No, no, I'm afraid I don't—

Walter (a beat. The tension hangs; then Walter steps back from it): Yeah. Well—what I mean is that we come from people who had a lot of *pride.* I mean—we are very proud people. And that's my sister over there and she's going to be a doctor—and we are very proud—

Lindner: Well—I am sure that is very nice, but—

Walter: What I am telling you is that we called you over here to tell you that we are very proud and that this—*(Signaling to Travis.)* Travis, come here. *(Travis crosses and Walter draws him before him facing the man.)* This is my son, and he makes the sixth generation of our family in this country. And we have all thought about your offer—

Lindner: Well, good . . . good—

Walter: And we have decided to move into our house because my father—my father—he earned it for us brick by brick. *(Mama has her eyes closed and is rocking back and forth as though she were in church, with her head nodding the Amen yes.)*

We don't want to make no trouble for nobody or fight no causes, and we will try to be good neighbors. And that's *all* we got to say about that. *(He looks the man absolutely in the eyes.)* We don't want your money. *(He turns and walks away.)*

Lindner (looking around at all of them): I take it then—that you have decided to occupy . . .

Beneatha: That's what the man said.

Lindner (to Mama in her reverie): Then I would like to appeal to you, Mrs. Younger. You are older and wiser and understand things better I am sure . . .

Mama: I am afraid you don't understand. My son said we was going to move and there ain't nothing left for me to say. *(Briskly.)* You know how these young folks is nowadays, mister. Can't do a thing with 'em! *(As he opens his mouth, she rises.)* Good-bye.

Lindner (folding up his materials): Well—if you are that final about it . . . there is nothing left for me to say. *(He finishes, almost ignored by the family, who are concentrating on Walter Lee. At the door Lindner halts and looks around.)* I sure hope you people know what you're getting into. *(He shakes his head and exits.)*

Ruth (looking around and coming to life): Well, for God's sake—if the moving men are here—LET'S GET THE HELL OUT OF HERE!

Mama (into action): Ain't it the truth! Look at all this here mess. Ruth, put Travis' good jacket on him . . . Walter Lee, fix your tie and tuck your shirt in; you look like somebody's hoodlum! Lord have mercy, where is my plant? *(She flies to get it amid the general bustling of the family, who are deliberately trying to ignore the nobility of the past moment.)* You all start on down . . . Travis child, don't go empty-handed . . . Ruth, where did I put that box with my skillets in it? I want to be in charge of it myself . . . I'm going to make us the biggest dinner we ever ate tonight . . . Beneatha, what's the matter with them stockings? Pull them things up, girl . . .

(The family starts to file out as two moving men appear and begin to carry out the heavier pieces of furniture, bumping into the family as they move about.)

Beneatha: Mama, Asagai asked me to marry him today and go to Africa—

Mama (in the middle of her getting-ready activity): He did? You ain't old enough to marry nobody—*(Seeing the moving men lifting one of her chairs precariously.)* Darling, that ain't no bale of cotton, please handle it so we can sit in it again! I had that chair twenty-five years . . .

(The movers sigh with exasperation and go on with their work.)

Beneatha (girlishly and unreasonably trying to pursue the conversation): To go to Africa, Mama—be a doctor in Africa . . .

Mama (distracted): Yes, baby—

Walter: Africa! What he want you to go to Africa for?

Beneatha: To practice there . . .

Walter: Girl, if you don't get all them silly ideas out your head! You better marry yourself a man with some loot . . .

Beneatha (angrily, precisely as in the first scene of the play): What have you got to do with who I marry!

Walter: Plenty. Now I think George Murchison—

Beneatha: George Murchison! I wouldn't marry him if he was Adam and I was Eve!

(Walter and Beneatha go out yelling at each other vigorously and the anger is loud and real till their voices diminish. Ruth stands at the door and turns to Mama and smiles knowingly.)

Mama (fixing her hat at last): Yeah—they something all right, my children . . .

Ruth: Yeah—they're something. Let's go, Lena.

Mama (stalling, starting to look around at the house): Yes—I'm coming. Ruth—

Ruth: Yes?

Mama (quietly, woman to woman): He finally come into his manhood today, didn't he? Kind of like a rainbow after the rain . . .

Ruth (biting her lip lest her own pride explode in front of Mama): Yes, Lena.

(Walter's voice calls for them raucously.)

Walter (off stage): Y'all come on! These people charges by the hour, you know!

Mama (waving Ruth out vaguely): All right, honey—go on down. I be down directly.

(Ruth hesitates, then exits. Mama stands, at last alone in the living room, her plant on the table before her as the lights start to come down. She looks around at all the walls and ceilings and suddenly, despite herself, while the children call below, a great heaving thing rises in her and she puts her fist to her mouth to stifle it, takes a final desperate look, pulls her coat about her, pats her hat and goes out. The lights dim down. The door opens and she comes back in, grabs her plant, and goes out for the last time.)

CURTAIN

Questions

1. In the opening scene of the play, what factors account for the irritation and hostility that the family members show toward one another?
2. What values do the members of the family associate with Mama's late husband? In what ways do they try to live up to those values in their own lives?
3. How would you characterize the relationship between Walter and his sister, Beneatha? Do they seem to have a genuine affection for one another?
4. Mama maintains that everything she does is for her family. Do her actions support this claim, in your opinion, or not?
5. Why does Asagai call Beneatha "Alaiyo: One for Whom Bread—Food—Is Not Enough"? (Act I, Scene II.) Why is she flattered by this description?
6. Do Walter and Ruth respect one another? Cite specific details from the play to back up your conclusions.
7. What does Mama mean when she says in Act II, Scene III, about her flower: "It expresses ME!"?
8. Even though the future of the Younger family in their new neighborhood is uncertain, to say the least, does the play have a happy ending? Explain.

Henrik Ibsen

A Doll's House

1879

Translated by R. Farquharson Sharp
Revised by Viktoria Michelsen

Henrik Ibsen

Henrik Ibsen (1828–1906) was born in Skien, a seaport in Norway. When he was six, his father's business losses suddenly reduced his wealthy family to poverty. After a brief attempt to study medicine, young Ibsen worked as a stage manager in provincial Bergen; then, becoming known as a playwright, he moved to Oslo as artistic director of the National Theater—practical experiences that gained him firm grounding in his craft. Discouraged when his theater failed and the king turned down his plea for a grant to enable him to write, Ibsen left Norway and for twenty-seven years lived in Italy and Germany. There, in his middle years (1879–1891), he wrote most of his famed plays about small-town life, among them A Doll's House, Ghosts, An Enemy of the People, The Wild Duck, *and* Hedda Gabler. *Introducing social problems to the stage, these plays aroused storms of controversy. Although best known as a Realist, Ibsen early in his career wrote poetic dramas based on Norwegian history and folklore: the tragedy* Brand *(1866) and the powerful, wildly fantastic* Peer Gynt *(1867). He ended as a Symbolist in* John Gabriel Borkman *(1896) and* When We Dead Awaken *(1899), both encompassing huge mountains that heaven-assaulting heroes try to climb. Late in life Ibsen returned to Oslo, honored at last both at home and abroad.*

CHARACTERS

Torvald Helmer, a lawyer
Nora, his wife
Doctor Rank
Mrs. Kristine Linde
Nils Krogstad
The Helmers' three young children
Anne Marie, their nursemaid
Helene, the maid
A Porter

The action takes place in the Helmers' apartment.

ACT I

The scene is a room furnished comfortably and tastefully, but not extravagantly. At the back wall, a door to the right leads to the entrance hall. Another to the left leads to Helmer's study. Between the doors there is a piano. In the middle of the left-hand wall is a door, and beyond it a window. Near the window are a round table, armchairs, and a small sofa. In the right-hand wall, at the farther end, is another door, and on the same side, nearer the footlights, a stove, two easy chairs and a rocking chair. Between the stove and the door there is a small table. There are engravings on the walls, a cabinet with china and other small objects, and a small bookcase with expensively bound books. The floors are carpeted, and a fire burns in the stove. It is winter.

A bell rings in the hall. A moment later, we hear the door being opened. Enter Nora, humming a tune and in high spirits. She is wearing a hat and coat and carries a number of packages, which she puts down on the table to the right. She leaves the outer door open behind her. Through the door we see a porter who is carrying a Christmas tree and a basket, which he gives to the maid, who has opened the door.

Nora: Hide the Christmas tree carefully, Helene. Make sure the children don't see it till it's decorated this evening. (*To the Porter, taking out her purse.*) How much?

Porter: Fifty ore.

The 1896 production of *A Doll's House* at the Empire Theatre in New York.

Nora: Here's a krone. No, keep the change.

(The Porter thanks her and goes out. Nora shuts the door. She is laughing to herself as she takes off her hat and coat. She takes a bag of macaroons from her pocket and eats one or two, then goes cautiously to the door of her husband's study and listens.)

Yes, he's there. *(Still humming, she goes to the table on the right.)*

Helmer (calls out from his study): Is that my little lark twittering out there?
Nora (busy opening some of the packages): Yes, it is!
Helmer: Is it my little squirrel bustling around?
Nora: Yes!
Helmer: When did my squirrel come home?
Nora: Just now. *(Puts the bag of macaroons into her pocket and wipes her mouth.)* Come in here, Torvald, and see what I bought.
Helmer: I'm very busy right now. *(A little later, he opens the door and looks into the room, pen in hand.)* Bought, did you say? All these things? Has my little spendthrift been wasting money again?
Nora: Yes, but, Torvald, this year we really can let ourselves go a little. This is the first Christmas that we don't have to watch every penny.

The 2009 adaptation of *A Doll's House* at the Donmar Warehouse in London, starring Gillian Anderson and Toby Stephens.

Helmer: Still, you know, we can't spend money recklessly.

Nora: Yes, Torvald, but we can be a little more reckless now, can't we? Just a tiny little bit! You're going to have a big salary and you'll be making lots and lots of money.

Helmer: Yes, after the New Year. But it'll still be a whole three months before the money starts coming in.

Nora: Pooh! We can borrow till then.

Helmer: Nora! *(Goes up to her and takes her playfully by the ear.)* The same little featherbrain! Just suppose that I borrowed a thousand kroner today, and you spent it all on Christmas, and then on New Year's Eve a roof tile fell on my head and killed me, and—

Nora (putting her hand over his mouth): Oh! Don't say such horrible things.

Helmer: Still, suppose that happened. What then?

Nora: If that happened, I don't suppose I'd care whether I owed anyone money or not.

Helmer: Yes, but what about the people who'd lent it to us?

Nora: Them? Who'd care about them? I wouldn't even know who they were.

Helmer: That's just like a woman! But seriously, Nora, you know how I feel about that. No debt, no borrowing. There can't be any freedom or beauty in a home life that depends on borrowing and debt. We two have managed to stay on the straight road so far, and we'll go on the same way for the short time that we still have to be careful.

Nora (moving towards the stove): As you wish, Torvald.

Helmer (following her): Now, now, my little skylark mustn't let her wings droop. What's the matter? Is my little squirrel sulking? *(Taking out his purse.)* Nora, what do you think I've got here?

Nora (turning round quickly): Money!

Helmer: There you are. *(Gives her some money.)* Do you think I don't know how much you need for the house at Christmastime?

Nora (counting): Ten, twenty, thirty, forty! Thank you, thank you, Torvald. That'll keep me going for a long time.

Helmer: It's going to have to.

Nora: Yes, yes, it will. But come here and let me show you what I bought. And all so cheap! Look, here's a new suit for Ivar, and a sword. And a horse and a trumpet for Bob. And a doll and doll's bed for Emmy. They're not the best, but she'll break them soon enough anyway. And here's dress material and handkerchiefs for the maids. Old Anne Marie really should have something nicer.

Helmer: And what's in this package?

Nora (crying out): No, no! You can't see that till this evening.

Helmer: If you say so. But now tell me, you extravagant little thing, what would you like for yourself?

Nora: For myself? Oh, I'm sure I don't want anything.

Helmer: But you must. Tell me something that you'd especially like to have—within reasonable limits.

Nora: No, I really can't think of anything. Unless, Torvald . . .

Helmer: Well?

Nora (playing with his coat buttons, and without raising her eyes to his): If you really want to give me something, you might . . . you might . . .

Helmer: Well, out with it!

Nora (speaking quickly): You might give me money, Torvald. Only just as much as you can afford. And then one of these days I'll buy something with it.

Helmer: But, Nora—

Nora: Oh, do! Dear Torvald, please, please do! Then I'll wrap it up in beautiful gold paper and hang it on the Christmas tree. Wouldn't that be fun?

Helmer: What do they call those little creatures that are always wasting money?

Nora: Spendthrifts. I know. Let's do as I suggest, Torvald, and then I'll have time to think about what I need most. That's a very sensible plan, isn't it?

Helmer (smiling): Yes, it is. That is, if you really did save some of the money I give you, and then really buy something for yourself. But if you spend it all on the housekeeping and all kinds of unnecessary things, then I just have to open my wallet all over again.

Nora: Oh, but, Torvald—

Helmer: You can't deny it, my dear little Nora. (*Puts his arm around her waist.*) She's a sweet little spendthrift, but she uses up a lot of money. One would hardly believe how expensive such little creatures are!

Nora: That's a terrible thing to say. I really do save all I can.

Helmer (laughing): That's true. All you can. But you can't save anything!

Nora (smiling quietly and happily): You have no idea how many bills skylarks and squirrels have, Torvald.

Helmer: You're an odd little soul. Just like your father. You always find some new way of wheedling money out of me, and, as soon as you've got it, it seems to melt in your hands. You never know where it's gone. Still, one has to take you as you are. It's in the blood. Because, you know, it's true that you can inherit these things, Nora.

Nora: Ah, I wish I'd inherited a lot of Papa's traits.

Helmer: And I wouldn't want you to be anything but just what you are, my sweet little skylark. But, you know, it seems to me that you look rather—how can I put it—rather uneasy today.

Nora: Do I?

Helmer: You do, really. Look straight at me.

Nora (looks at him): Well?

Helmer (wagging his finger at her): Has little Miss Sweet Tooth been breaking our rules in town today?

Nora: No, what makes you think that?

Helmer: Has she paid a visit to the bakery?

Nora: No, I assure you, Torvald—

Helmer: Not been nibbling pastries?

Nora: No, certainly not.

Helmer: Not even taken a bite of a macaroon or two?

Nora: No, Torvald, I assure you, really—

Helmer: Come on, you know I was only kidding.

Nora (going to the table on the right): I wouldn't dream of going against your wishes.

Helmer: No, I'm sure of that. Besides, you gave me your word. (*Going up to her.*) Keep your little Christmas secrets to yourself, my darling. They'll all be revealed tonight when the Christmas tree is lit, no doubt.

Nora: Did you remember to invite Doctor Rank?

Helmer: No. But there's no need. It goes without saying that he'll have dinner with us. All the same, I'll ask him when he comes over this morning. I've ordered some good wine. Nora, you have no idea how much I'm looking forward to this evening.

Nora: So am I! And how the children will enjoy themselves, Torvald!

Helmer: It's great to feel that you have a completely secure position and a big enough income. It's a delightful thought, isn't it?

Nora: It's wonderful!

Helmer: Do you remember last Christmas? For three whole weeks you hid yourself away every evening until long after midnight, making ornaments for the Christmas tree and all the other fine things that were going to be a surprise for us. It was the most boring three weeks I ever spent!

Nora: I wasn't bored.

Helmer (smiling): But there was precious little to show for it, Nora.

Nora: Oh, you're not going to tease me about that again. How could I help it that the cat went in and tore everything to pieces?

Helmer: Of course you couldn't, poor little girl. You had the best of intentions to make us all happy, and that's the main thing. But it's a good thing that our hard times are over.

Nora: Yes, it really is wonderful.

Helmer: This time I don't have to sit here and be bored all by myself, and you don't have to ruin your dear eyes and your pretty little hands—

Nora (clapping her hands): No, Torvald, I don't have to any more, do I! It's wonderfully lovely to hear you say so! *(Taking his arm.)* Now let me tell you how I've been thinking we should arrange things, Torvald. As soon as Christmas is over—*(A bell rings in the hall.)* There's the bell. *(She tidies the room a little.)* There's somebody at the door. What a nuisance!

Helmer: If someone's visiting, remember I'm not home.

Maid (in the doorway): A lady to see you, ma'am. A stranger.

Nora: Ask her to come in.

Maid (to Helmer): The doctor's here too, sir.

Helmer: Did he go straight into my study?

Maid: Yes, sir.

(Helmer goes into his study. The maid ushers in Mrs. Linde, who is in traveling clothes, and shuts the door.)

Mrs. Linde (in a dejected and timid voice): Hello, Nora.

Nora (doubtfully): Hello.

Mrs. Linde: You don't recognize me, I suppose.

Nora: No, I don't know . . . Yes, of course, I think so—*(Suddenly.)* Yes! Kristine! Is it really you?

Mrs. Linde: Yes, it is.

Nora: Kristine! Imagine my not recognizing you! And yet how could I—*(In a gentle voice.)* You've changed, Kristine!

Mrs. Linde: Yes, I certainly have. In nine, ten long years—

Nora: Is it that long since we've seen each other? I suppose it is. The last eight years have been a happy time for me, you know. And so now you've come to town, and you've taken this long trip in the winter. That was brave of you.

Mrs. Linde: I arrived by steamer this morning.

Nora: To have some fun at Christmastime, of course. How delightful! We'll have such fun together! But take off your things. You're not cold, I hope. *(Helps her.)* Now we'll sit down by the stove and be cozy. No, take this armchair. I'll sit here in the rocking chair. *(Takes her hands.)* Now you look like your old self again. It was only that first moment. You are a little paler, Kristine, and maybe a little thinner.

Mrs. Linde: And much, much older, Nora.

Nora: Maybe a little older. Very, very little. Surely not very much. *(Stops suddenly and speaks seriously.)* What a thoughtless thing I am, chattering away like this. My poor, dear Kristine, please forgive me.

Mrs. Linde: What do you mean, Nora?

Nora (gently): Poor Kristine, you're a widow.

Mrs. Linde: Yes. For three years now.

Nora: Yes, I knew. I saw it in the papers. I swear to you, Kristine, I kept meaning to write to you at the time, but I always put it off and something always came up.

Mrs. Linde: I understand completely, dear.

Nora: It was very bad of me, Kristine. Poor thing, how you must have suffered. And he left you nothing?

Mrs. Linde: No.

Nora: And no children?

Mrs. Linde: No.

Nora: Nothing at all, then?

Mrs. Linde: Not even any sorrow or grief to live on.

Nora (looking at her in disbelief): But, Kristine, is that possible?

Mrs. Linde (smiles sadly and strokes Nora's hair): It happens sometimes, Nora.

Nora: So you're completely alone. How terribly sad that must be. I have three beautiful children. You can't see them just now, because they're out with their nursemaid. But now you must tell me all about it.

Mrs. Linde: No, no, I want to hear about you.

Nora: No, you go first. I mustn't be selfish today. Today I should think only about you. But there is one thing I have to tell you. Do you know we've just had a fabulous piece of good luck?

Mrs. Linde: No, what is it?

Nora: Just imagine, my husband's been appointed manager of the bank!

Mrs. Linde: Your husband? That is good luck!

Nora: Yes, it's tremendous! A lawyer's life is so uncertain, especially if he won't take any cases that are the slightest bit shady, and of course Torvald has never been willing to do that, and I completely agree with him. You can imagine how delighted we are! He starts his job in the bank at New Year's, and then he'll have a big salary and lots of commissions. From now on we can live very differently. We can do just what we want. I feel so relieved and so happy, Kristine! It'll be wonderful to have heaps of money and not have to worry about anything, won't it?

Mrs. Linde: Yes. Anyway, I think it would be delightful to have what you need.

Nora: No, not only what you need, but heaps and heaps of money.

Mrs. Linde (smiling): Nora, Nora, haven't you learned any sense yet? Back in school you were a terrible spendthrift.

Nora (laughing): Yes, that's what Torvald says now. *(Wags her finger at her.)* But "Nora, Nora" isn't as silly as you think. We haven't been in a position for me to waste money. We've both had to work.

Mrs. Linde: You too?

Nora: Oh, yes, odds and ends, needlework, crocheting, embroidery, and that kind of thing. *(Dropping her voice.)* And other things too. You know Torvald left his government job when we got married? There was no chance of promotion, and he had to try to earn more money than he was making there. But in that first year he overworked himself terribly. You see, he had to make money any way he could, and he worked all hours, but he couldn't take it, and he got very sick, and the doctors said he had to go south, to a warmer climate.

Mrs. Linde: You spent a whole year in Italy, didn't you?

Nora: Yes. It wasn't easy to get away, I can tell you that. It was just after Ivar was born, but obviously we had to go. It was a wonderful, beautiful trip, and it saved Torvald's life. But it cost a tremendous amount of money, Kristine.

Mrs. Linde: I would imagine so.

Nora: It cost about four thousand, eight hundred kroner. That's a lot, isn't it?

Mrs. Linde: Yes, it is, and when you have an emergency like that it's lucky to have the money.

Nora: Well, the fact is, we got it from Papa.

Mrs. Linde: Oh, I see. It was just about that time that he died, wasn't it?

Nora: Yes, and, just think of it, I couldn't even go and take care of him. I was expecting little Ivar any day and I had my poor sick Torvald to look after. My dear, kind father. I never saw him again, Kristine. That was the worst experience I've gone through since we got married.

Mrs. Linde: I know how fond of him you were. And then you went off to Italy?

Nora: Yes. You see, we had money then, and the doctors insisted that we go, so we left a month later.

Mrs. Linde: And your husband came back completely recovered?

Nora: The picture of health!

Mrs. Linde: But . . . the doctor?

Nora: What doctor?

Mrs. Linde: Didn't your maid say that the gentleman who arrived here with me was the doctor?

Nora: Yes, that was Doctor Rank, but he doesn't come here professionally. He's our dearest friend, and he drops in at least once every day. No, Torvald hasn't been sick for an hour since then, and our children are strong and healthy, and so am I. *(Jumps up and claps her hands.)* Kristine! Kristine! It's good to be alive and happy! But how awful of me. I'm talking about nothing but myself. *(Sits on a nearby stool and rests her arms on her knees.)* Please don't be mad at me. Tell me, is it really true that you didn't love your husband? Why did you marry him?

Mrs. Linde: My mother was still alive then, and she was bedridden and helpless, and I had to provide for my two younger brothers, so I didn't think I had any right to turn him down.

Nora: No, maybe you did the right thing. So he was rich then?

Mrs. Linde: I believe he was quite well off. But his business wasn't very solid, and when he died, it all went to pieces and there was nothing left.

Nora: And then?

Mrs. Linde: Well, I had to turn my hand to anything I could find. First a small shop, then a small school, and so on. The last three years have seemed like one long workday, with no rest. Now it's over, Nora. My poor mother's gone and doesn't need me any more, and the boys don't need me, either. They've got jobs now and can manage for themselves.

Nora: What a relief it must be if—

Mrs. Linde: No, not at all. All I feel is an unbearable emptiness. No one to live for anymore. *(Gets up restlessly.)* That's why I couldn't stand it any longer in my little backwater. I hope it'll be easier to find something here that'll keep me busy and occupy my mind. If I could be lucky enough to find some regular work, office work of some kind—

Nora: But, Kristine, that's so awfully tiring, and you look tired out now. It'd be much better for you if you could get away to a resort.

Mrs. Linde (walking to the window): I don't have a father to give me money for a trip, Nora.

Nora (rising): Oh, don't be mad at me!

Mrs. Linde (going up to her): It's you who mustn't be mad at me, dear. The worst thing about a situation like mine is that it makes you so bitter. No one to work for, and yet you have to always be on the lookout for opportunities. You have to live, and so you grow selfish. When you told me about your good luck—you'll find this hard to believe—I was delighted less for you than for myself.

Nora: What do you mean? Oh, I understand. You mean that maybe Torvald could find you a job.

Mrs. Linde: Yes, that's what I was thinking.

Nora: He must, Kristine. Just leave it to me. I'll broach the subject very cleverly. I'll think of something that'll put him in a really good mood. It'll make me so happy to be of some use to you.

Mrs. Linde: How kind you are, Nora, to be so eager to help me! It's doubly kind of you, since you know so little of the burdens and troubles of life.

Nora: Me? I know so little of them?

Mrs. Linde (smiling): My dear! Small household cares and that sort of thing! You're a child, Nora.

Nora (tosses her head and crosses the stage): You shouldn't act so superior.

Mrs. Linde: No?

Nora: You're just like the others. They all think I'm incapable of anything really serious—

Mrs. Linde: Come on—

Nora: —that I haven't had to deal with any real problems in my life.

Mrs. Linde: But, my dear Nora, you've just told me all your troubles.

Nora: Pooh! That was nothing. *(Lowering her voice.)* I haven't told you the important thing.

Mrs. Linde: The important thing? What do you mean?

Nora: You really look down on me, Kristine, but you shouldn't. Aren't you proud of having worked so hard and so long for your mother?

Mrs. Linde: Believe me, I don't look down on anyone. But it's true, I'm proud and I'm glad that I had the privilege of making my mother's last days almost worry-free.

Nora: And you're proud of what you did for your brothers?

Mrs. Linde: I think I have the right to be.

Nora: I think so, too. But now, listen to this. I have something to be proud of and happy about too.

Mrs. Linde: I'm sure you do. But what do you mean?

Nora: Keep your voice down. If Torvald were to overhear! He can't find out, not under any circumstances. No one in the world must know, Kristine, except you.

Mrs. Linde: But what is it?

Nora: Come here. *(Pulls her down on the sofa beside her.)* Now I'll show you that I too have something to be proud and happy about. I'm the one who saved Torvald's life.

Mrs. Linde: Saved? How?

Nora: I told you about our trip to Italy. Torvald would never have recovered if he hadn't gone there—

Mrs. Linde: Yes, but your father gave you the money you needed.

Nora (smiling): Yes, that's what Torvald thinks, along with everybody else, but—

Mrs. Linde: But—

Nora: Papa didn't give us a penny. I was the one who raised the money.

Mrs. Linde: You? That huge amount?

Nora: That's right, four thousand, eight hundred kroner. What do you think of that?

Mrs. Linde: But, Nora, how could you possibly? Did you win the lottery?

Nora (disdainfully): The lottery? That wouldn't have been any accomplishment.

Mrs. Linde: But where did you get it from, then?

Nora (humming and smiling with an air of mystery): Hm, hm! Ha!

Mrs. Linde: Because you couldn't have borrowed it.

Nora: Couldn't I? Why not?

Mrs. Linde: No, a wife can't borrow money without her husband's consent.

Nora (tossing her head): Oh, if it's a wife with a head for business, a wife who has the brains to be a little clever—

Mrs. Linde: I don't understand this at all, Nora.

Nora: There's no reason why you should. I never said I'd borrowed the money. Maybe I got it some other way. *(Lies back on the sofa.)* Maybe I got it from an admirer. When a woman's as pretty as I am—

Mrs. Linde: You're crazy.

Nora: Now, you know you're dying of curiosity, Kristine.

Mrs. Linde: Listen to me, Nora dear. Have you done something rash?

Nora (sits up straight): Is it rash to save your husband's life?

Mrs. Linde: I think it's rash, without his knowledge, to—

Nora: But it was absolutely necessary that he not know! My goodness, can't you understand that? It was necessary he have no idea how sick he was. The doctors came to *me* and said his life was in danger and the only thing that could save him was to live in the south. Don't you think I tried first to get him to do it as if it was for me? I told him how much I would love to travel abroad like other young wives. I tried tears and pleading with him. I told him he should remember the condition I was in, and that he should be kind and indulgent to me. I even hinted that he might take out a loan. That almost made him mad, Kristine. He said I was thoughtless, and that it was his duty as my husband not to indulge me in my "whims and caprices," as I believe he called them. All right, I thought, you need to be saved. And that was how I came to think up a way out of the mess—

Mrs. Linde: And your husband never found out from your father that the money hadn't come from him?

Nora: No, never. Papa died just then. I'd meant to let him in on the secret and beg him never to reveal it. But he was so sick. Unfortunately, there never was any need to tell him.

Mrs. Linde: And since then you've never told your secret to your husband?

Nora: Good heavens, no! How could you think I would? A man with such strong opinions about these things! Besides, how painful and humiliating it would be for Torvald, with his masculine pride, to know that he owed me anything! It would completely upset the balance of our relationship. Our beautiful happy home would never be the same.

Mrs. Linde: Are you never going to tell him about it?

Nora (meditatively, and with a half smile): Yes, someday, maybe, in many years, when I'm not as pretty as I am now. Don't laugh at me! I mean, of course, when Torvald is no longer as devoted to me as he is now, when he's grown tired of my dancing and dressing up and reciting. Then it may be a good thing to have something in reserve—*(Breaking off.)* What nonsense! That time will never come. Now, what do you think of my great secret, Kristine? Do you still think I'm useless? And the fact is, this whole situation has caused me a lot of worry. It hasn't been easy for me to make my payments on time. I can tell you that there's something in business that's called quarterly interest, and something else called installment payments, and it's always so terribly difficult to keep up with them. I've had to save a little here and there, wherever I could, you understand. I haven't been able to put much aside from my housekeeping money, because Torvald has to live well. And I couldn't let my children be shabbily dressed. I feel I have to spend everything he gives me for them, the sweet little darlings!

Mrs. Linde: So it's all had to come out of your own allowance, poor Nora?

Nora: Of course. Besides, I was the one responsible for it. Whenever Torvald has given me money for new dresses and things like that, I've never spent more than half of it. I've always bought the simplest and cheapest things. Thank heaven, any clothes look good on me, and so Torvald's never noticed anything. But it was often very hard on me, Kristine, because it is delightful to be really well dressed, isn't it?

Mrs. Linde: I suppose so.

Nora: Well, then I've found other ways of earning money. Last winter I was lucky enough to get a lot of copying to do, so I locked myself up and sat writing every evening until late into the night. A lot of the time I was desperately tired, but all the same it was a tremendous pleasure to sit there working and earning money. It was like being a man.

Mrs. Linde: How much have you been able to pay off that way?

Nora: I can't tell you exactly. You see, it's very hard to keep a strict account of a business matter like that. I only know that I've paid out every penny I could scrape together. Many a time I was at my wits' end. *(Smiles.)* Then I used to sit here and imagine that a rich old gentleman had fallen in love with me—

Mrs. Linde: What! Who was it?

Nora: Oh, be quiet! That he had died, and that when his will was opened it said, in great big letters: "The lovely Mrs. Nora Helmer is to have everything I own paid over to her immediately in cash."

Mrs. Linde: But, my dear Nora, who could the man be?

Nora: Good gracious, can't you understand? There wasn't any old gentleman. It was only something that I used to sit here and imagine, when I couldn't think of any way of getting money. But it's all right now.

The tiresome old gent can stay right where he is, as far as I'm concerned. I don't care about him or his will either, because now I'm worry-free. *(Jumps up.)* My goodness, it's delightful to think of, Kristine! Worry-free! To be able to have no worries, no worries at all! To be able to play and romp with the children! To be able to keep the house beautifully and have everything just the way Torvald likes it! And, just think of it, soon the spring will come and the big blue sky! Maybe we can take a little trip. Maybe I can see the sea again! Oh, it's a wonderful thing to be alive and happy.

(A bell rings in the hall.)

Mrs. Linde (rising): There's the bell. Perhaps I should be going.

Nora: No, don't go. No one will come in here. It's sure to be for Torvald.

Servant (at the hall door): Excuse me, ma'am. There's a gentleman to see the master, and as the doctor is still with him—

Nora: Who is it?

Krogstad (at the door): It's me, Mrs. Helmer.

(Mrs. Linde starts, trembles, and turns toward the window.)

Nora (takes a step toward him, and speaks in a strained, low voice): You? What is it? What do you want to see my husband for?

Krogstad: Bank business, in a way. I have a small position in the bank, and I hear your husband is going to be our boss now—

Nora: Then it's—

Krogstad: Nothing but dry business matters, Mrs. Helmer, that's all.

Nora: Then please go into the study.

(She bows indifferently to him and shuts the door into the hall, then comes back and makes up the fire in the stove.)

Mrs. Linde: Nora, who was that man?

Nora: A lawyer. His name is Krogstad.

Mrs. Linde: Then it really was him.

Nora: Do you know the man?

Mrs. Linde: I used to, many years ago. At one time he was a law clerk in our town.

Nora: That's right, he was.

Mrs. Linde: How much he's changed.

Nora: He had a very unhappy marriage.

Mrs. Linde: He's a widower now, isn't he?

Nora: With several children. There, now it's really caught. *(Shuts the door of the stove and moves the rocking chair aside.)*

Mrs. Linde: They say he's mixed up in a lot of questionable business.

Nora: Really? Maybe he is. I don't know anything about it. But let's not talk about business. It's so tiresome.

Doctor Rank (comes out of Helmer's study. Before he shuts the door he calls to Helmer): No, my dear fellow, I won't disturb you. I'd rather go in and talk to your wife for a little while.

(Shuts the door and sees Mrs. Linde.)

I beg your pardon. I'm afraid I'm in the way here too.

Nora: No, not at all. *(Introducing him:)* Doctor Rank, Mrs. Linde.

Rank: I've often heard that name in this house. I think I passed you on the stairs when I arrived, Mrs. Linde?

Mrs. Linde: Yes, I take stairs very slowly. I can't manage them very well.

Rank: Oh, some small internal problem?

Mrs. Linde: No, it's just that I've been overworking myself.

Rank: Is that all? Then I suppose you've come to town to get some rest by sampling our social life.

Mrs. Linde: I've come to look for work.

Rank: Is that a good cure for overwork?

Mrs. Linde: One has to live, Doctor Rank.

Rank: Yes, that seems to be the general opinion.

Nora: Now, now, Doctor Rank, you know you want to live.

Rank: Of course I do. However miserable I may feel, I want to prolong the agony for as long as possible. All my patients are the same way. And so are those who are morally sick. In fact, one of them, and a bad case too, is at this very moment inside with Helmer—

Mrs. Linde (sadly): Ah!

Nora: Who are you talking about?

Rank: A lawyer by the name of Krogstad, a fellow you don't know at all. He's a completely worthless creature, Mrs. Helmer. But even he started out by saying, as if it were a matter of the utmost importance, that he has to live.

Nora: Did he? What did he want to talk to Torvald about?

Rank: I have no idea. All I heard was that it was something about the bank.

Nora: I didn't know this—what's his name—Krogstad had anything to do with the bank.

Rank: Yes, he has some kind of a position there. *(To Mrs. Linde)* I don't know whether you find the same thing in your part of the world, that there are certain people who go around zealously looking to sniff out moral corruption, and, as soon as they find some, they put the person involved in some cushy job where they can keep an eye on him. Meanwhile, the morally healthy ones are left out in the cold.

Mrs. Linde: Still, I think it's the sick who are most in need of being taken care of.

Rank (shrugging his shoulders): Well, there you have it. That's the attitude that's turning society into a hospital.

(Nora, who has been absorbed in her thoughts, breaks out into smothered laughter and claps her hands.)

Rank: Why are you laughing at that? Do you have any idea what society really is?

Nora: What do I care about your boring society? I'm laughing at something else, something very funny. Tell me, Doctor Rank, are all the people who work in the bank dependent on Torvald now?

Rank: That's what's so funny?

Nora (smiling and humming): That's my business! *(Walking around the room.)* It's just wonderful to think that we have—that Torvald has—so much power over so many people. *(Takes the bag out of her pocket.)* Doctor Rank, what do you say to a macaroon?

Rank: Macaroons? I thought they were forbidden here.

Nora: Yes, but these are some Kristine gave me.

Mrs. Linde: What! Me?

Nora: Oh, well, don't be upset! How could you know that Torvald had forbidden them? I have to tell you, he's afraid they'll ruin my teeth. But so what? Once in a while, that's all right, isn't it, Doctor Rank? With your permission! *(Puts a macaroon into his mouth.)* You have to have one too, Kristine. And I'll have one, just a little one—or no more than two. *(Walking around.)* I am tremendously happy. There's just one thing in the world now that I would dearly love to do.

Rank: Well, what is it?

Nora: It's something I would dearly love to say, if Torvald could hear me.

Rank: Well, why can't you say it?

Nora: No, I don't dare. It's too shocking.

Mrs. Linde: Shocking?

Rank: Well then, I'd advise you not to say it. Still, in front of us you might risk it. What is it you'd so much like to say if Torvald could hear you?

Nora: I would just love to say—"Well, I'll be damned!"

Rank: Are you crazy?

Mrs. Linde: Nora, dear!

Rank: Here he is. Say it!

Nora (hiding the bag): Shh, shh, shh!

(Helmer comes out of his room, with his coat over his arm and his hat in his hand.)

Nora: Well, Torvald dear, did you get rid of him?

Helmer: Yes, he just left.

Nora: Let me introduce you. This is Kristine. She's just arrived in town.

Helmer: Kristine? I'm sorry, but I don't know any—

Nora: Mrs. Linde, dear, Kristine Linde.

Helmer: Oh, of course. A school friend of my wife's, I believe?

Mrs. Linde: Yes, we knew each other back then.

Nora: And just think, she's come all this way in order to see you.

Helmer: What do you mean?

Mrs. Linde: No, really, I—

Nora: Kristine is extremely good at bookkeeping, and she's very eager to work for some talented man, so she can perfect her skills—

Helmer: Very sensible, Mrs. Linde.

Nora: And when she heard that you'd been named manager of the bank—the news was sent by telegraph, you know—she traveled here as quickly as she could. Torvald, I'm sure you'll be able to do something for Kristine, for my sake, won't you?

Helmer: Well, it's not completely out of the question. I expect that you're a widow, Mrs. Linde?

Mrs. Linde: Yes.

Helmer: And you've had some bookkeeping experience?

Mrs. Linde: Yes, a fair amount.

Helmer: Ah! Well, there's a very good chance that I'll be able to find something for you—

Nora (clapping her hands): What did I tell you? What did I tell you?

Helmer: You've just come at a lucky moment, Mrs. Linde.

Mrs. Linde: How can I thank you?

Helmer: There's no need. *(Puts on his coat.)* But now you must excuse me—

Rank: Wait a minute. I'll come with you. *(Brings his fur coat from the hall and warms it at the fire.)*

Nora: Don't be long, Torvald dear.

Helmer: About an hour, that's all.

Nora: Are you leaving too, Kristine?

Mrs. Linde (putting on her cloak): Yes, I have to go and look for a place to stay.

Helmer: Oh, well then, we can walk down the street together.

Nora (helping her): It's too bad we're so short of space here. I'm afraid it's impossible for us—

Mrs. Linde: Please don't even think of it! Goodbye, Nora dear, and many thanks.

Nora: Goodbye for now. Of course you'll come back this evening. And you too, Dr. Rank. What do you say? If you're feeling up to it? Oh, you have to be! Wrap yourself up warmly.

(They go to the door all talking together. Children's voices are heard on the staircase.)

Nora: There they are! There they are!

(She runs to open the door. The nursemaid comes in with the children.)

Come in! Come in! *(Stoops and kisses them.)* Oh, you sweet blessings! Look at them, Kristine! Aren't they darlings?

Rank: Let's not stand here in the draft.

Helmer: Come along, Mrs. Linde. Only a mother will be able to stand it in here now!

(Rank, Helmer, and Mrs. Linde go downstairs. The Nursemaid comes forward with the children. Nora shuts the hall door.)

Nora: How fresh and healthy you look! Cheeks as red as apples and roses. *(The children all talk at once while she speaks to them.)* Did you have a lot of fun? That's wonderful! What, you pulled Emmy and Bob on the sled? Both at once? That was really something. You *are* a clever boy, Ivar. Let me take her for a little, Anne Marie. My sweet little baby doll! *(Takes the baby from the maid and dances her up and down.)* Yes, yes, mother will dance with Bob too. What! Have you been throwing snowballs? I wish I'd been there too! No, no, I'll take their things off, Anne Marie, please let me do it, it's such fun. Go inside now, you look half frozen. There's some hot coffee for you on the stove.

(The Nursemaid goes into the room on the left. Nora takes off the children's things and throws them around, while they all talk to her at once.)

Nora: Really! Did a big dog run after you? But it didn't bite you? No, dogs don't bite nice little dolly children. You mustn't look at the packages, Ivar. What are they? Oh, I'll bet you'd like to know. No, no, it's something boring! Come on, let's play a game! What should we play? Hide and seek? Yes, we'll play hide and seek. Bob will hide first. You want me to hide? All right, I'll hide first.

(She and the children laugh and shout, and romp in and out of the room. At last Nora hides under the table. The children rush in and out looking for her, but they don't see her. They hear her smothered laughter, run to the table, lift up the cloth and find her. Shouts of laughter. She crawls forward and pretends to scare them. More laughter. Meanwhile there has been a knock at the hall door, but none of them has noticed it. The door is opened halfway and Krogstad appears. He waits for a little while. The game goes on.)

Krogstad: Excuse me, Mrs. Helmer.

Nora (with a stifled cry, turns round and gets up onto her knees): Oh! What do you want?

Krogstad: Excuse me, the outside door was open. I suppose someone forgot to shut it.

Nora (rising): My husband is out, Mr. Krogstad.

Krogstad: I know that.

Nora: What do you want here, then?

Krogstad: A word with you.

Nora: With me? *(To the children, gently.)* Go inside to Anne Marie. What? No, the strange man won't hurt Mother. When he's gone we'll play another game. *(She takes the children into the room on the left, and shuts the door after them.)* You want to speak to me?

Krogstad: Yes, I do.

Nora: Today? It isn't the first of the month yet.

Krogstad: No, it's Christmas Eve, and it's up to you what kind of Christmas you're going to have.

Nora: What do you mean? Today it's absolutely impossible for me—

Krogstad: We won't talk about that until later on. This is something else. I presume you can spare me a moment?

Nora: Yes, yes, I can. Although . . .

Krogstad: Good. I was in Olsen's restaurant and I saw your husband going down the street—

Nora: Yes?

Krogstad: With a lady.

Nora: So?

Krogstad: May I be so bold as to ask if it was a Mrs. Linde?

Nora: It was.

Krogstad: Just arrived in town?

Nora: Yes, today.

Krogstad: She's a very good friend of yours, isn't she?

Nora: She is. But I don't see—

Krogstad: I knew her too, once upon a time.

Nora: I'm aware of that.

Krogstad: Are you? So you know all about it. I thought so. Then I can ask you, without beating around the bush. Is Mrs. Linde going to work in the bank?

Nora: What right do you have to question me, Mr. Krogstad? You're one of my husband's employees. But since you ask, I'll tell you. Yes, Mrs. Linde is going to work in the bank. And I'm the one who spoke up for her, Mr. Krogstad. So now you know.

Krogstad: So I was right, then.

Nora (walking up and down the stage): Sometimes one has a tiny little bit of influence, I should hope. Just because I'm a woman, it doesn't necessarily follow that—You know, when somebody's in a subordinate position, Mr. Krogstad, they should really be careful to avoid offending anyone who—who—

Krogstad: Who has influence?

Nora: Exactly.

Krogstad (changing his tone): Mrs. Helmer, may I ask you to use *your* influence on my behalf?

Nora: What? What do you mean?

Krogstad: Will you be kind enough to see to it that I'm allowed to keep my subordinate position in the bank?

Nora: What do you mean by that? Who's threatening to take your job away from you?

Krogstad: Oh, there's no need to keep up the pretence of ignorance. I can understand that your friend isn't very anxious to expose herself to the chance of rubbing shoulders with me. And now I realize exactly who I have to thank for pushing me out.

Nora: But I swear to you—

Krogstad: Yes, yes. But, to get right to the point, there's still time to prevent it, and I would advise you to use your influence to do so.

Nora: But, Mr. Krogstad, I have no influence.

Krogstad: Oh no? Didn't you yourself just say—

Nora: Well, obviously, I didn't mean for you to take it that way. Me? What would make you think I have that kind of influence with my husband?

Krogstad: Oh, I've known your husband since our school days. I don't suppose he's any more unpersuadable than other husbands.

Nora: If you're going to talk disrespectfully about my husband, I'll have to ask you to leave my house.

Krogstad: Bold talk, Mrs. Helmer.

Nora: I'm not afraid of you anymore. When the New Year comes, I'll soon be free of the whole thing.

Krogstad (controlling himself): Listen to me, Mrs. Helmer. If I have to, I'm ready to fight for my little job in the bank as if I were fighting for my life.

Nora: So it seems.

Krogstad: It's not just for the sake of the money. In fact, that matters the least to me. There's another reason. Well, I might as well tell you. Here's my situation. I suppose, like everybody else, you know that many years ago I did something pretty foolish.

Nora: I think I heard something about it.

Krogstad: It never got as far as the courtroom, but every door seemed closed to me after that. So I got involved in the business that you know about. I had to do something, and, honestly, I think there are many worse than me. But now I have to get myself free of all that. My sons are growing up. For their sake I have to try to win back as much respect as I can in this town. The job in the bank was like the first step up for me, and now your husband is going to kick me downstairs back into the mud.

Nora: But you have to believe me, Mr. Krogstad, it's not in my power to help you at all.

Krogstad: Then it's because you don't want to. But I have ways of making you.

Nora: You don't mean you'll tell my husband I owe you money?

Krogstad: Hm! And what if I did tell him?

Nora: That would be a terrible thing for you to do. *(Sobbing.)* To think he would learn my secret, which has been my pride and joy, in such an ugly, clumsy way—that he would learn it from you! And it would put me in a horribly uncomfortable position—

Krogstad: Just uncomfortable?

Nora (impetuously): Well, go ahead and do it, then! And it'll be so much the worse for you. My husband will see for himself how vile you are, and then you'll lose your job for sure.

Krogstad: I asked you if it's just an uncomfortable situation at home that you're afraid of.

Nora: If my husband does find out about it, of course he'll immediately pay you what I still owe, and then we'll be through with you once and for all.

Krogstad (coming a step closer): Listen to me, Mrs. Helmer. Either you have a very bad memory or you don't know much about business. I can see I'm going to have to remind you of a few details.

Nora: What do you mean?

Krogstad: When your husband was sick, you came to me to borrow four thousand, eight hundred kroner.

Nora: I didn't know anyone else to go to.

Krogstad: I promised to get you that amount—

Nora: Yes, and you did so.

Krogstad: I promised to get you that amount, on certain conditions. You were so preoccupied with your husband's illness, and you were so anxious to get the money for your trip, that you seem to have paid no attention to the conditions of our bargain. So it won't be out of place for me to remind you of them. Now, I promised to get the money on the security of a note which I drew up.

Nora: Yes, and which I signed.

Krogstad: Good. But underneath your signature there were a few lines naming your father as a co-signer who guaranteed the repayment of the loan. Your father was supposed to sign that part.

Nora: Supposed to? He did sign it.

Krogstad: I had left the date blank. That was because your father was supposed to fill in the date when he signed the paper. Do you remember that?

Nora: Yes, I think I remember. . . .

Krogstad: Then I gave you the note to mail to your father. Isn't that so?

Nora: Yes.

Krogstad: And obviously you mailed it right away, because five or six days later you brought me the note with your father's signature. And then I gave you the money.

Nora: Well, haven't I been paying it back regularly?

Krogstad: Fairly regularly, yes. But, to get back to the point, that must have been a very difficult time for you, Mrs. Helmer.

Nora: Yes, it was.

Krogstad: Your father was very sick, wasn't he?

Nora: He was very near the end.

Krogstad: And he died soon after?

Nora: Yes.

Krogstad: Tell me, Mrs. Helmer, can you by any chance remember what day your father died? On what day of the month, I mean.

Nora: Papa died on the 29th of September.

Krogstad: That's right. I looked it up myself. And, since that is the case, there's something extremely peculiar *(taking a piece of paper from his pocket)* that I can't account for.

Nora: Peculiar in what way? I don't know—

Krogstad: The peculiar thing, Mrs. Helmer, is the fact that your father signed this note three days after he died.

Nora: What do you mean? I don't understand—

Krogstad: Your father died on the 29th of September. But, look here. Your father dated his signature the 2nd of October. It is mighty peculiar, isn't it? *(Nora is silent.)* Can you explain it to me? *(Nora is still silent.)* And what's just as peculiar is that the words "October 2," as well as the year, are not in your father's handwriting, but in someone else's, which I think I recognize. Well, of course it can all be explained. Your father might have forgotten to date his signature, and someone else might have filled in the date before they knew that he had died. There's no harm in that. It all depends on the signature, and that's genuine, isn't it, Mrs. Helmer? It was your father himself who signed his name here?

Nora (after a short pause, lifts her head up and looks defiantly at him): No, it wasn't. I'm the one who wrote Papa's name.

Krogstad: Are you aware that you're making a very serious confession?

Nora: How so? You'll get your money soon.

Krogstad: Let me ask you something. Why didn't you send the paper to your father?

Nora: It was out of the question. Papa was too sick. If I had asked him to sign something, I'd have had to tell him what the money was for, and when he was so sick himself I couldn't tell him that my husband's life was in danger. It was out of the question.

Krogstad: It would have been better for you if you'd given up your trip abroad.

Nora: No, that was impossible. That trip was to save my husband's life. I couldn't give that up.

Krogstad: But didn't it ever occur to you that you were committing a fraud against me?

Nora: I couldn't take that into account. I didn't trouble myself about you at all. I couldn't stand you, because you put so many heartless difficulties in my way, even though you knew how seriously ill my husband was.

Krogstad: Mrs. Helmer, you evidently don't realize clearly what you're guilty of. But, believe me, my one mistake, which cost me my whole reputation, was nothing more and nothing worse than what you did.

Nora: You? You expect me to believe that you were brave enough to take a risk to save your wife's life?

Krogstad: The law doesn't care about motives.

Nora: Then the law must be very stupid.

Krogstad: Stupid or not, it's the law that's going to judge you, if I produce this paper in court.

Nora: I don't believe it. Isn't a daughter allowed to spare her dying father anxiety and concern? Isn't a wife allowed to save her husband's life? I don't know much about the law, but I'm sure there must be provisions for things like that. Don't you know anything about such provisions? You seem like a very poor excuse for a lawyer, Mr. Krogstad.

Krogstad: That's as may be. But business, the kind of business you and I have done together—do you think I don't know about that? Fine. Do what you want. But I can assure you of this. If I lose everything all over again, this time you're going down with me. *(He bows, and goes out through the hall.)*

Nora (appears buried in thought for a short time, then tosses her head): Nonsense! He's just trying to scare me! I'm not as naive as he thinks I am. *(Begins to busy herself putting the children's things in order.)* And yet . . . ? No, it's impossible! I did it for love.

Children (in the doorway on the left): Mother, the strange man is gone. He went out through the gate.

Nora: Yes, dears, I know. But don't tell anyone about the strange man. Do you hear me? Not even Papa.

Children: No, Mother. But will you come and play with us again?

Nora: No, no, not just now.

Children: But, Mother, you promised us.

Nora: Yes, but I can't right now. Go inside. I have too much to do. Go inside, my sweet little darlings.

(She gets them into the room bit by bit and shuts the door on them. Then she sits down on the sofa, takes up a piece of needlework and sews a few stitches, but soon stops.)

No! *(Throws down the work, gets up, goes to the hall door and calls out.)* Helene! Bring the tree in. *(Goes to the table on the left, opens a drawer, and stops again.)* No, no! It's completely impossible!

Maid (coming in with the tree): Where should I put it, ma'am?

Nora: Here, in the middle of the floor.
Maid: Do you need anything else?
Nora: No, thank you. I have everything I want.

(Exit Maid.)

Nora (begins decorating the tree): A candle here, and flowers here. That horrible man! It's all nonsense, there's nothing wrong. The tree is going to be magnificent! I'll do everything I can think of to make you happy, Torvald! I'll sing for you, dance for you—

(Helmer comes in with some papers under his arm.)

Oh! You're back already?
Helmer: Yes. Has anyone been here?
Nora: Here? No.
Helmer: That's strange. I saw Krogstad going out the gate.
Nora: You did? Oh yes, I forgot, Krogstad was here for a moment.
Helmer: Nora, I can tell from the way you're acting that he was here begging you to put in a good word for him.
Nora: Yes, he was.
Helmer: And you were supposed to pretend it was all your idea and not tell me that he'd been here to see you. Didn't he beg you to do that too?
Nora: Yes, Torvald, but—
Helmer: Nora, Nora, to think that you'd be a party to that sort of thing! To have any kind of conversation with a man like that, and promise him anything at all? And to lie to me in the bargain?
Nora: Lie?
Helmer: Didn't you tell me no one had been here? *(Shakes his finger at her.)* My little songbird must never do that again. A songbird must have a clean beak to chirp with. No false notes! *(Puts his arm round her waist.)* That's true, isn't it? Yes, I'm sure it is. *(Lets her go.)* We won't mention this again. *(Sits down by the stove.)* How warm and cozy it is here! *(Turns over his papers.)*
Nora (after a short pause, during which she busies herself with the Christmas tree): Torvald!
Helmer: Yes?
Nora: I'm really looking forward to the masquerade ball at the Stenborgs' the day after tomorrow.
Helmer: And I'm really curious to see what you're going to surprise me with.
Nora: Oh, it was very silly of me to want to do that.
Helmer: What do you mean?
Nora: I can't come up with anything good. Everything I think of seems so stupid and pointless.
Helmer: So my little Nora finally admits that?

Nora (standing behind his chair with her arms on the back of it): Are you very busy, Torvald?

Helmer: Well . . .

Nora: What are all those papers?

Helmer: Bank business.

Nora: Already?

Helmer: I've gotten the authority from the retiring manager to reorganize the work procedures and make the necessary personnel changes. I need to take care of it during Christmas week, so as to have everything in place for the new year.

Nora: Then that was why this poor Krogstad—

Helmer: Hm!

Nora (leans against the back of his chair and strokes his hair): If you weren't so busy, I would have asked you for a huge favor, Torvald.

Helmer: What favor? Tell me.

Nora: No one has such good taste as you. And I really want to look nice at the fancy-dress ball. Torvald, couldn't you take me in hand and decide what I should go as and what kind of costume I should wear?

Helmer: Aha! So my obstinate little woman has to get someone to come to her rescue?

Nora: Yes, Torvald, I can't get along at all without your help.

Helmer: All right, I'll think it over. I'm sure we'll come up with something.

Nora: That's so nice of you. *(Goes to the Christmas tree. A short pause.)* How pretty the red flowers look. But, tell me, was it really something very bad that this Krogstad was guilty of?

Helmer: He forged someone's name. Do you have any idea what that means?

Nora: Isn't it possible that he was forced to do it by necessity?

Helmer: Yes. Or, the way it is in so many cases, by foolishness. I'm not so heartless that I'd absolutely condemn a man because of one mistake like that.

Nora: No, you wouldn't, would you, Torvald?

Helmer: Many a man has been able to rehabilitate himself, if he's openly admitted his guilt and taken his punishment.

Nora: Punishment?

Helmer: But Krogstad didn't do that. He wriggled out of it with lies and trickery, and that's what completely undermined his moral character.

Nora: But do you think that that would—

Helmer: Just think how a guilty man like that has to lie and act like a hypocrite with everyone, how he has to wear a mask in front of the people closest to him, even with his own wife and children. And the children. That's the most terrible part of it all, Nora.

Nora: How so?

Helmer: Because an atmosphere of lies infects and poisons the whole life of a home. Every breath the children take in a house like that is full of the germs of moral corruption.

Nora (coming closer to him): Are you sure of that?

Helmer: My dear, I've seen it many times in my legal career. Almost everyone who's gone wrong at a young age had a dishonest mother.

Nora: Why only the mother?

Helmer: It usually seems to be the mother's influence, though naturally a bad father would have the same result. Every lawyer knows this. This Krogstad, now, has been systematically poisoning his own children with lies and deceit. That's why I say he's lost all moral character. *(Holds out his hands to her.)* And that's why my sweet little Nora must promise me not to plead his cause. Give me your hand on it. Come now, what's this? Give me your hand. There, that's settled. Believe me, it would be impossible for me to work with him. It literally makes me feel physically ill to be around people like that.

Nora (takes her hand out of his and goes to the opposite side of the Christmas tree): How hot it is in here! And I have so much to do.

Helmer (getting up and putting his papers in order): Yes, and I have to try to read through some of these before dinner. And I have to think about your costume, too. And it's just possible I'll have something wrapped in gold paper to hang up on the tree. *(Puts his hand on her head.)* My precious little songbird! *(He goes into his study and closes the door behind him.)*

Nora (after a pause, whispers): No, no, it's not true. It's impossible. It has to be impossible.

(The nursemaid opens the door on the left.)

Nursemaid: The little ones are begging so hard to be allowed to come in to see Mama.

Nora: No, no, no! Don't let them come in to me! You stay with them, Anne Marie.

Nursemaid: Very well, ma'am. *(Shuts the door.)*

Nora (pale with terror): Corrupt my little children? Poison my home? *(A short pause. Then she tosses her head.)* It's not true. It can't possibly be true.

ACT II

The same scene. The Christmas tree is in the corner by the piano, stripped of its ornaments and with burnt-down candle-ends on its disheveled branches. Nora's coat and hat are lying on the sofa. She is alone in the room, walking around uneasily. She stops by the sofa and picks up her coat.

Nora (drops her coat): Someone's coming! *(Goes to the door and listens.)* No, there's no one there. Of course, no one will come today. It's Christmas Day. And not tomorrow either. But maybe . . . *(opens the door and looks out)* No, nothing in the mailbox. It's empty. *(Comes forward.)* What nonsense! Of course he can't be serious about it. A thing like that couldn't happen. It's impossible. I have three little children.

(Enter the nursemaid Anne Marie from the room on the left, carrying a big cardboard box.)

Nursemaid: I finally found the box with the costume.

Nora: Thank you. Put it on the table.

Nursemaid (doing so): But it really needs to be mended.

Nora: I'd like to tear it into a hundred thousand pieces.

Nursemaid: What an idea! It can easily be fixed up. All you need is a little patience.

Nora: Yes, I'll go get Mrs. Linde to come and help me with it.

Nursemaid: What, going out again? In this horrible weather? You'll catch cold, Miss Nora, and make yourself sick.

Nora: Well, worse things than that might happen. How are the children?

Nursemaid: The poor little ones are playing with their Christmas presents, but—

Nora: Do they ask for me much?

Nursemaid: You see, they're so used to having their Mama with them.

Nora: Yes, but, Anne Marie, I won't be able to spend as much time with them now as I did before.

Nursemaid: Oh well, young children quickly get used to anything.

Nora: Do you think so? Do you think they'd forget their mother if she went away for good?

Nursemaid: Good heavens! Went away for good?

Nora: Anne Marie, I want you to tell me something I've often wondered about. How could you have the heart to let your own child be raised by strangers?

Nursemaid: I had to, if I wanted to be little Nora's nursemaid.

Nora: Yes, but how could you agree to it?

Nursemaid: What, when I was going to get such a good situation out of it? A poor girl who's gotten herself in trouble should be glad to. Besides, that worthless man didn't do a single thing for me.

Nora: But I suppose your daughter has completely forgotten you.

Nursemaid: No, she hasn't, not at all. She wrote to me when she was confirmed, and again when she got married.

Nora (putting her arms round her neck): Dear old Anne Marie, you were such a good mother to me when I was little.

Nursemaid: Poor little Nora, you had no other mother but me.

Nora: And if my little ones had no other mother, I'm sure that you would—What nonsense I'm talking! *(Opens the box.)* Go in and see to them. Now I have to . . . You'll see how lovely I'll look tomorrow.

Nursemaid: I'm sure there'll be no one at the ball as lovely as you, Miss Nora.

(Goes into the room on the left.)

Nora (begins to unpack the box, but soon pushes it away from her): If only I dared to go out. If only no one would come. If only I could be sure nothing would happen here in the meantime. What nonsense! No one's going to come. I just have to stop thinking about it. This muff needs to be brushed. What beautiful, beautiful gloves! Stop thinking about it, stop thinking about it! One, two, three, four, five, six—*(Screams.)* Aaah! Somebody *is* coming—*(Makes a movement towards the door, but stands in hesitation.)*

(Enter Mrs. Linde from the hall, where she has taken off her coat and hat.)

Nora: Oh, it's you, Kristine. There's no one else out in the hall, is there? How good of you to come!

Mrs. Linde: I heard you came by asking for me.

Nora: Yes, I was passing by. As a matter of fact, it's something you could help me with. Let's sit down here on the sofa. Listen, tomorrow evening there's going to be a fancy-dress ball at the Stenborgs'—they live upstairs from us—and Torvald wants me to go as a Neapolitan fisher-girl and dance the tarantella. I learned it when we were at Capri.

Mrs. Linde: I see. You're going to give them the whole show.

Nora: Yes, Torvald wants me to. Look, here's the dress. Torvald had it made for me there, but now it's all so torn, and I don't have any idea—

Mrs. Linde: We can easily fix that. Some of the trim has just come loose here and there. Do you have a needle and thread? That's all we need.

Nora: This is so nice of you.

Mrs. Linde (sewing): So you're going to be dressed up tomorrow, Nora. I'll tell you what. I'll stop by for a moment so I can see you in your finery. Oh, meanwhile I've completely forgotten to thank you for a delightful evening last night.

Nora (gets up, and crosses the stage): Well, I didn't think last night was as pleasant as usual. You should have come to town a little earlier, Kristine. Torvald really knows how to make a home pleasant and attractive.

Mrs. Linde: And so do you, if you ask me. You're not your father's daughter for nothing. But tell me, is Doctor Rank always as depressed as he was yesterday?

Nora: No, yesterday it was especially noticeable. But you have to understand that he has a very serious disease. He has tuberculosis of the spine, poor creature. His father was a horrible man who always had mistresses, and that's why his son has been sickly since childhood, if you know what I mean.

Mrs. Linde (dropping her sewing): But, my dear Nora, how do you know anything about such things?

Nora (walking around the room): Pooh! When you have three children, you get visits now and then from—from married women, who know something about medical matters, and they talk about one thing and another.

Mrs. Linde (goes on sewing. A short silence): Does Doctor Rank come here every day?

Nora: Every day, like clockwork. He's Torvald's best friend, and a great friend of mine too. He's just like one of the family.

Mrs. Linde: But tell me, is he really sincere? I mean, isn't he the kind of man who tends to play up to people?

Nora: No, not at all. What makes you think that?

Mrs. Linde: When you introduced him to me yesterday, he told me he'd often heard my name mentioned in this house, but later I could see that your husband didn't have the slightest idea who I was. So how could Doctor Rank—?

Nora: That's true, Kristine. Torvald is so ridiculously fond of me that he wants me completely to himself, as he says. At first he used to seem almost jealous if I even mentioned any of my friends back home, so naturally I stopped talking about them to him. But I often talk about things like that with Doctor Rank, because he likes hearing about them.

Mrs. Linde: Listen to me, Nora. You're still like a child in a lot of ways, and I'm older than you and more experienced. So pay attention. You'd better stop all this with Doctor Rank.

Nora: Stop all what?

Mrs. Linde: Two things, I think. Yesterday you talked some nonsense about a rich admirer who was going to leave you his money—

Nora: An admirer who doesn't exist, unfortunately! But so what?

Mrs. Linde: Is Doctor Rank a wealthy man?

Nora: Yes, he is.

Mrs. Linde: And he has no dependents?

Nora: No, no one. But—

Mrs. Linde: And he comes here every day?

Nora: Yes, I told you he does.

Mrs. Linde: But how can such a well-bred man be so tactless?

Nora: I don't understand what you mean.

Mrs. Linde: Don't try to play dumb, Nora. Do you think I didn't guess who lent you the four thousand, eight hundred kroner?

Nora: Are you out of your mind? How can you even think that? A friend of ours, who comes here every day! Don't you realize what an incredibly awkward position that would put me in?

Mrs. Linde: Then he's really not the one?

Nora: Absolutely not. It would never have come into my head for one second. Besides, he had nothing to lend back then. He inherited his money later on.

Mrs. Linde: Well, I think that was lucky for you, my dear Nora.

Nora: No, it would never have crossed my mind to ask Doctor Rank. Although I'm sure that if I had asked him—

Mrs. Linde: But of course you won't.

Nora: Of course not. I have no reason to think I could possibly need to. But I'm absolutely certain that if I told Doctor Rank—

Mrs. Linde: Behind your husband's back?

Nora: I have to finish up with the other one, and that'll be behind his back too. I've got to wash my hands of him.

Mrs. Linde: Yes, that's what I told you yesterday, but—

Nora (walking up and down): A man can take care of these things so much more easily than a woman.

Mrs. Linde: If he's your husband, yes.

Nora: Nonsense! *(Standing still.)* When you pay off a debt you get your note back, don't you?

Mrs. Linde: Yes, of course.

Nora: And you can tear it into a hundred thousand pieces and burn up the filthy, nasty piece of paper!

Mrs. Linde (stares at her, puts down her sewing and gets up slowly): Nora, you're hiding something from me.

Nora: You can tell by looking at me?

Mrs. Linde: Something's happened to you since yesterday morning. Nora, what is it?

Nora (going nearer to her): Kristine! *(Listens.)* Shh! I hear Torvald. He's come home. Would you mind going in to the children's room for a little while? Torvald can't stand to see all this sewing going on. You can get Anne Marie to help you.

Mrs. Linde (gathering some of the things together): All right, but I'm not leaving this house until we've talked this thing through.

(She goes into the room on the left, as Helmer comes in from the hall.)

Nora (going up to Helmer): I've missed you so much, Torvald dear.

Helmer: Was that the seamstress?

Nora: No, it was Kristine. She's helping me fix up my dress. You'll see how nice I'm going to look.

Helmer: Wasn't that a good idea of mine, now?

Nora: Wonderful! But don't you think it's nice of me, too, to do what you said?

Helmer: Nice, because you do what your husband tells you to? Go on, you silly little thing, I am sure you didn't mean it like that. But I'll stay out of your way. I imagine you'll be trying on your dress.

Nora: I suppose you're going to do some work.

Helmer: Yes. (*Shows her a stack of papers.*) Look at that. I've just been at the bank. (*Turns to go into his room.*)

Nora: Torvald.

Helmer: Yes?

Nora: If your little squirrel were to ask you for something in a very, very charming way—

Helmer: Well?

Nora: Would you do it?

Helmer: I'd have to know what it is, first.

Nora: Your squirrel would run around and do all her tricks if you would be really nice and do what she wants.

Helmer: Speak plainly.

Nora: Your skylark would chirp her beautiful song in every room—

Helmer: Well, my skylark does that anyhow.

Nora: I'd be a little elf and dance in the moonlight for you, Torvald.

Helmer: Nora, you can't be referring to what you talked about this morning.

Nora (moving close to him): Yes, Torvald, I'm really begging you—

Helmer: You really have the nerve to bring that up again?

Nora: Yes, dear, you have to do this for me. You have to let Krogstad keep his job in the bank.

Helmer: My dear Nora, his job is the one that I'm giving to Mrs. Linde.

Nora: Yes, you've been awfully sweet about that. But you could just as easily get rid of somebody else instead of Krogstad.

Helmer: This is just unbelievable stubbornness! Because you decided to foolishly promise that you'd speak up for him, you expect me to—

Nora: That's not the reason, Torvald. It's for your own sake. This man writes for the trashiest newspapers, you've told me so yourself. He can do you an incredible amount of harm. I'm scared to death of him—

Helmer: Oh, I see, it's bad memories that are making you afraid.

Nora: What do you mean?

Helmer: Obviously you're thinking about your father.

Nora: Yes. Yes, of course. You remember what those hateful creatures wrote in the papers about Papa, and how horribly they slandered him. I believe they'd have gotten him fired if the department hadn't sent you over to look into it, and if you hadn't been so kind and helpful to him.

Helmer: My little Nora, there's an important difference between your father and me. His reputation as a public official was not above suspicion. Mine is, and I hope it will continue to be for as long as I hold my office.

Nora: You never can tell what trouble these men might cause. We could be so well off, so snug and happy here in our peaceful home, without a care in the world, you and I and the children, Torvald! That's why I'm begging you to—

Helmer: And the more you plead for him, the more you make it impossible for me to keep him. They already know at the bank that I'm going to fire Krogstad. Do you think I'm going to let them all say that the new manager has changed his mind because his wife said to—

Nora: And what if they did?

Helmer: Right! What does it matter, as long as this stubborn little creature gets her own way! Do you think I'm going to make myself look ridiculous in front of my whole staff, and let people think that I can be pushed around by all sorts of outside influence? That would soon come back to haunt me, you can be sure! And besides, there's one thing that makes it totally impossible for me to have Krogstad working in the bank as long as I'm the manager.

Nora: What's that?

Helmer: I might have been able to overlook his moral failings, if need be—

Nora: Yes, you could do that, couldn't you?

Helmer: And I hear he's a good worker, too. But I knew him when we were boys. It was one of those rash friendships that so often turn out to be a millstone around the neck later on. I might as well tell you straight out, we were very close friends at one time. But he has no tact and no self-restraint, especially when other people are around. He thinks he has the right to still call me by my first name, and every minute it's Torvald this and Torvald that. I don't mind telling you, I find it extremely annoying. He would make my position at the bank intolerable.

Nora: Torvald, I can't believe you're serious.

Helmer: Oh no? Why not?

Nora: Because it's so petty.

Helmer: What do you mean, petty? You think I'm petty?

Nora: No, just the opposite, dear, and that's why I can't—

Helmer: It's the same thing. You say my attitude's petty, so I must be petty too! Petty! Fine! Well, I'll put a stop to this once and for all. (*Goes to the hall door and calls.*) Helene!

Nora: What are you going to do?

Helmer (looking among his papers): Settle it.

(*Enter Maid.*)

Here, take this letter downstairs right now. Find a messenger and tell him to deliver it, and to be quick about it. The address is on it, and here's the money.

Maid: Yes, sir. *(Exits with the letter.)*

Helmer (putting his papers together): There, Little Pigheaded Miss.

Nora (breathlessly): Torvald, what was that letter?

Helmer: Krogstad's notice.

Nora: Call her back, Torvald! There's still time. Oh, Torvald, call her back! Do it for my sake—for your own sake—for the children's sake! Do you hear me, Torvald? Call her back! You don't know what that letter can do to us.

Helmer: It's too late.

Nora: Yes, it's too late.

Helmer: My dear Nora, I can forgive this anxiety of yours, even though it's insulting to me. It really is. Don't you think it's insulting to suggest that I should be afraid of retaliation from a grubby pen-pusher? But I forgive you anyway, because it's such a beautiful demonstration of how much you love me. *(Takes her in his arms.)* And that is as it should be, my own darling Nora. Come what may, you can rest assured that I'll have both courage and strength if necessary. You'll see that I'm man enough to take everything on myself.

Nora (in a horror-stricken voice): What do you mean by that?

Helmer: Everything, I say.

Nora (recovering herself): You'll never have to do that.

Helmer: That's right, we'll take it on together, Nora, as man and wife. That's just how it should be. *(Caressing her.)* Are you satisfied now? There, there! Don't look at me that way, like a frightened dove! This whole thing is just your imagination running away with you. Now you should go and run through the tarantella and practice your tambourine. I'll go into my study and shut the door so I can't hear anything. You can make all the noise you want. *(Turns back at the door.)* And when Rank comes, tell him where I am.

(Nods to her, takes his papers and goes into his room, and shuts the door behind him.)

Nora (bewildered with anxiety, stands as if rooted to the spot and whispers): He's capable of doing it. He's going to do it. He'll do it in spite of everything. No, not that! Never, never! Anything but that! Oh, for somebody to help me find some way out of this! *(The doorbell rings.)* Doctor Rank! Anything but that—anything, whatever it is!

(She puts her hands over her face, pulls herself together, goes to the door and opens it. Rank is standing in the hall, hanging up his coat. During the following dialogue it starts to grow dark.)

Nora: Hello, Doctor Rank. I recognized your ring. But you'd better not go in and see Torvald just now. I think he's busy with something.

Rank: And you?

Nora (brings him in and shuts the door behind him): Oh, you know perfectly well I always have time for you.

Rank: Thank you. I'll make use of it for as long as I can.

Nora: What does that mean, for as long as you can?

Rank: Why, does that frighten you?

Nora: It was such a strange way of putting it. Is something going to happen?

Rank: Nothing but what I've been expecting for a long time. But I never thought it would happen so soon.

Nora (gripping him by the arm): What have you found out? Doctor Rank, you must tell me.

Rank (sitting down by the stove): I'm done for. And there's nothing I can do about it.

Nora (with a sigh of relief): Oh—you're talking about yourself?

Rank: Who else? And there's no use lying to myself. I'm the sickest patient I have, Mrs. Helmer. Lately I've been adding up my internal account. Bankrupt! In a month I'll probably be rotting in the ground.

Nora: What a horrible thing to say!

Rank: The thing itself is horrible, and the worst of it is all the horrible things I'll have to go through before it's over. I'm going to examine myself just once more. When that's done, I'll be pretty sure when I'm going to start breaking down. There's something I want to say to you. Helmer's sensitive nature makes him completely unable to deal with anything ugly. I don't want him in my sickroom.

Nora: Oh, but, Doctor Rank—

Rank: I won't have him there, period. I'll lock the door to keep him out. As soon as I'm quite sure that the worst has come, I'll send you my card with a black cross on it, and that way you'll know that the final stage of the horror has started.

Nora: You're being really absurd today. And I so much wanted you to be in a good mood.

Rank: With death stalking me? Having to pay this price for another man's sins? Where's the justice in that? In every single family, in one way or another, some such unavoidable retribution is being imposed.

Nora (putting her hands over her ears): Nonsense! Can't you talk about something cheerful?

Rank: Oh, this *is* something cheerful. In fact, it's hilarious. My poor innocent spine has to suffer for my father's youthful self-indulgence.

Nora (sitting at the table on the left): Yes, he did love asparagus and *pâté de foie gras*, didn't he?

Rank: Yes, and truffles.

Nora: Truffles, yes. And oysters too, I suppose?

Rank: Oysters, of course. That goes without saying.

Nora: And oceans of port and champagne. Isn't it sad that all those delightful things should take their revenge on our bones?

Rank: Especially that they should take their revenge on the unlucky bones of people who haven't even had the satisfaction of enjoying them.

Nora: Yes, that's the saddest part of all.

Rank (with a searching look at her): Hm!

Nora (after a short pause): Why did you smile?

Rank: No, it was you who laughed.

Nora: No, it was you who smiled, Doctor Rank!

Rank (rising): You're even more of a tease than I thought you were.

Nora: I am in a crazy mood today.

Rank: Apparently so.

Nora (putting her hands on his shoulders): Dear, dear Doctor Rank, we can't let death take you away from Torvald and me.

Rank: It's a loss that you'll easily recover from. Those who are gone are soon forgotten.

Nora (looking at him anxiously): Do you really believe that?

Rank: People make new friends, and then—

Nora: Who'll make new friends?

Rank: Both you and Helmer, when I'm gone. You yourself are already well on the way to it, I think. What was that Mrs. Linde doing here last night?

Nora: Oho! You're not telling me that you're jealous of poor Kristine, are you?

Rank: Yes, I am. She'll be my successor in this house. When I'm six feet under, this woman will—

Nora: Shh! Don't talk so loud. She's in that room.

Rank: Again today. There, you see.

Nora: She's just come to sew my dress for me. Goodness, how unreasonable you are! *(Sits down on the sofa.)* Be nice now, Doctor Rank, and tomorrow you'll see how beautifully I'll dance, and you can pretend that I'm doing it just for you—and for Torvald too, of course. *(Takes various things out of the box.)* Doctor Rank, come and sit down here, and I'll show you something.

Rank (sitting down): What is it?

Nora: Just look at these!

Rank: Silk stockings.

Nora: Flesh-colored. Aren't they lovely? It's so dark here now, but tomorrow—No, no, no! You're only supposed to look at the feet. Oh well, you have my permission to look at the legs too.

Rank: Hm!

Nora: Why do you look so critical? Don't you think they'll fit me?

Rank: I have no basis for forming an opinion on that subject.

Nora (looks at him for a moment): Shame on you! *(Hits him lightly on the ear with the stockings.)* That's your punishment. *(Folds them up again.)*

Rank: And what other pretty things do I have your permission to look at?

Nora: Not one single thing. That's what you get for being so naughty. *(She looks among the things, humming to herself.)*

Rank (after a short silence): When I'm sitting here, talking to you so intimately this way, I can't imagine for a moment what would have become of me if I'd never come into this house.

Nora (smiling): I believe you really do feel completely at home with us.

Rank (in a lower voice, looking straight in front of him): And to have to leave it all—

Nora: Nonsense, you're not going to leave it.

Rank (as before): And not to be able to leave behind the slightest token of my gratitude, hardly even a fleeting regret. Nothing but an empty place to be filled by the first person who comes along.

Nora: And if I were to ask you now for a—No, never mind!

Rank: For a what?

Nora: For a great proof of your friendship—

Rank: Yes, yes!

Nora: I mean a tremendously huge favor—

Rank: Would you really make me so happy, just this once?

Nora: But you don't know what it is yet.

Rank: No, but tell me.

Nora: I really can't, Doctor Rank. It's too much to ask. It involves advice, and help, and a favor—

Rank: So much the better. I can't imagine what you mean. Tell me what it is. You do trust me, don't you?

Nora: More than anyone. I know that you're my best and truest friend, so I'll tell you what it is. Well, Doctor Rank, it's something you have to help me prevent. You know how devoted Torvald is to me, how deeply he loves me. He wouldn't hesitate for a second to give his life for me.

Rank (leaning towards her): Nora, do you think that he's the only one—

Nora (with a slight start): The only one?

Rank: Who would gladly give his life for you.

Nora (sadly): Oh, is that it?

Rank: I'd made up my mind to tell you before I—I go away, and there'll never be a better opportunity than this. Now you know it, Nora. And now you know that you can trust me more than you can trust anyone else.

Nora (rises, deliberately and quietly): Let me by.

Rank (makes room for her to pass him, but sits still): Nora!

Nora (at the hall door): Helene, bring in the lamp. *(Goes over to the stove.)* Dear Doctor Rank, that was really horrible of you.

Rank: To love you just as much as somebody else does? Is that so horrible?

Nora: No, but to go and tell me like that. There was really no need—

Rank: What do you mean? Did you know—

(Maid enters with lamp, puts it down on the table, and goes out.)

Nora—Mrs. Helmer—tell me, did you have any idea I felt this way?

Nora: Oh, how do I know whether I did or I didn't? I really can't answer that. How could you be so clumsy, Doctor Rank? When we were getting along so nicely.

Rank: Well, at any rate, now you know that I'm yours to command, body and soul. So won't you tell me what it is?

Nora (looking at him): After what just happened?

Rank: I beg you to let me know what it is.

Nora: I can't tell you anything now.

Rank: Yes, yes. Please don't punish me that way. Give me permission to do anything for you that a man can do.

Nora: You can't do anything for me now. Besides, I really don't need any help at all. The whole thing is just my imagination. It really is. It has to be! *(Sits down in the rocking chair, and smiles at him.)* You're a nice man, Doctor Rank. Don't you feel ashamed of yourself, now that the lamp is lit?

Rank: Not a bit. But maybe it would be better if I left—and never came back?

Nora: No, no, you can't do that. You must keep coming here just as you always did. You know very well Torvald can't do without you.

Rank: But what about you?

Nora: Oh, I'm always extremely pleased to see you.

Rank: And that's just what gave me the wrong idea. You're a puzzle to me. I've often felt that you'd almost just as soon be in my company as in Helmer's.

Nora: Yes, you see, there are the people you love the most, and then there are the people whose company you enjoy the most.

Rank: Yes, there's something to that.

Nora: When I lived at home, of course I loved Papa best. But I always thought it was great fun to sneak down to the maids' room, because they never preached at me, and I loved listening to the way they talked to each other.

Rank: I see. So I'm their replacement.

Nora (jumping up and going to him): Oh, dear, sweet Doctor Rank, I didn't mean it that way. But surely you can understand that being with Torvald is a little like being with Papa—

(Enter Maid from the hall.)

Maid: Excuse me, ma'am. *(Whispers and hands her a card.)*

Nora (glancing at the card): Oh! *(Puts it in her pocket.)*

Rank: Is something wrong?

Nora: No, no, not at all. It's just—it's my new dress—

Rank: What? Your dress is lying right there.

Nora: Oh, yes, that one. But this is another one, one that I ordered. I don't want Torvald to find out about it—

Rank: Oh! So that was the big secret.

Nora: Yes, that's it. Why don't you just go inside and see him? He's in his study. Stay with him for as long as—

Rank: Put your mind at ease. I won't let him escape. *(Goes into Helmer's study.)*

Nora (to the maid): And he's waiting in the kitchen?

Maid: Yes, ma'am. He came up the back stairs.

Nora: Didn't you tell him no one was home?

Maid: Yes, but it didn't do any good.

Nora: He won't go away?

Maid: No, he says he won't leave until he sees you, ma'am.

Nora: Well, show him in, but quietly. Helene, I don't want you to say anything about this to anyone. It's a surprise for my husband.

Maid: Yes, ma'am. I understand. *(Exit.)*

Nora: This horrible thing is really going to happen! It's going to happen in spite of me! No, no, no, it can't happen! I can't let it happen!

(She bolts the door of Helmer's study. The maid opens the hall door for Krogstad and closes it behind him. He is wearing a fur coat, high boots, and a fur cap.)

Nora (advancing towards him): Speak quietly. My husband's home.

Krogstad: What do I care about that?

Nora: What do you want from me?

Krogstad: An explanation of something.

Nora: Be quick, then. What is it?

Krogstad: I suppose you're aware that I've been let go.

Nora: I couldn't prevent it, Mr. Krogstad. I fought for you as hard as I could, but it was no use.

Krogstad: Does your husband love you so little, then? He knows what I can expose you to, and he still goes ahead and—

Nora: How can you think that he knows any such thing?

Krogstad: I didn't think so for a moment. It wouldn't be at all like dear old Torvald Helmer to show that kind of courage—

Nora: Mr. Krogstad, a little respect for my husband, please.

Krogstad: Certainly—all the respect he deserves. But since you've kept everything so carefully to yourself, may I be bold enough to assume that you see a little more clearly than you did yesterday just what it is that you've done?

Nora: More than you could ever teach me.

Krogstad: Yes, such a poor excuse for a lawyer as I am.
Nora: What is it you want from me?
Krogstad: Only to see how you're doing, Mrs. Helmer. I've been thinking about you all day. A mere bill collector, a pen-pusher, a—well, a man like me—even he has a little of what people call feelings, you know.
Nora: Why don't you show some, then? Think about my little children.
Krogstad: Have you and your husband thought about mine? But never mind about that. I just wanted to tell you not to take this business too seriously. I won't make any accusations against you. Not for now, anyway.
Nora: No, of course not. I was sure you wouldn't.
Krogstad: The whole thing can be settled amicably. There's no need for anyone to know anything about it. It'll be our little secret, just the three of us.
Nora: My husband must never know anything about it.
Krogstad: How are you going to keep him from finding out? Are you telling me that you can pay off the whole balance?
Nora: No, not just yet.
Krogstad: Or that you have some other way of raising the money soon?
Nora: No way that I plan to make use of.
Krogstad: Well, in any case, it wouldn't be any use to you now even if you did. If you stood in front of me with a stack of bills in each hand, I still wouldn't give you back your note.
Nora: What are you planning to do with it?
Krogstad: I just want to hold onto it, just keep it in my possession. No one who isn't involved in the matter will ever know anything about it. So, if you've been thinking about doing something desperate—
Nora: I have.
Krogstad: If you've been thinking about running away—
Nora: I have.
Krogstad: Or doing something even worse—
Nora: How could you know that?
Krogstad: Stop thinking about it.
Nora: How did you know I'd thought of that?
Krogstad: Most of us think about that at first. I did, too. But I didn't have the courage.
Nora (faintly): Neither do I.
Krogstad (in a tone of relief): No, that's true, isn't it? You don't have the courage either?
Nora: No, I don't. I don't.
Krogstad: Besides, it would have been an incredibly stupid thing to do. Once the first storm at home blows over . . . I have a letter for your husband in my pocket.
Nora: Telling him everything?
Krogstad: As gently as possible.

Nora (quickly): He can't see that letter. Tear it up. I'll find some way of getting money.

Krogstad: Excuse me, Mrs. Helmer, but didn't I just tell you—

Nora: I'm not talking about what I owe you. Tell me how much you want from my husband, and I'll get the money.

Krogstad: I don't want any money from your husband.

Nora: Then what do you want?

Krogstad: I'll tell you what I want. I want a fresh start, Mrs. Helmer, and I want to move up in the world. And your husband's going to help me do it. I've steered clear of anything questionable for the last year and a half. In all that time I've been struggling along, pinching every penny. I was content to work my way up step by step. But now I've been fired, and it's not going to be enough just to get my job back, as if you people were doing me some huge favor. I want to move up, I tell you. I want to get back into the bank again, but with a promotion. Your husband's going to have to find me a position—

Nora: He'll never do it!

Krogstad: Oh yes, he will. I know him. He won't dare object. And as soon as I'm back there with him, then you'll see! Inside of a year I'll be the manager's right-hand man. It'll be Nils Krogstad, not Torvald Helmer, who's running the bank.

Nora: That's never going to happen!

Krogstad: Do you mean that you'll—

Nora: I have enough courage for it now.

Krogstad: Oh, you can't scare me. An elegant, spoiled lady like you—

Nora: You'll see, you'll see.

Krogstad: Under the ice, maybe? Down in the cold, coal-black water? And then floating up to the surface in the spring, all horrible and unrecognizable, with your hair fallen out—

Nora: You can't scare me.

Krogstad: And you can't scare me. People don't do that kind of thing, Mrs. Helmer. Besides, what good would it do? I'd still have him completely in my power.

Nora: Even then? When I'm no longer—

Krogstad: Have you forgotten that your reputation is completely in my hands? *(Nora stands speechless, looking at him.)* Well, now I've warned you. Don't do anything foolish. I'll be expecting an answer from Helmer after he reads my letter. And remember, it's your husband himself who's forced me to act this way again. I'll never forgive him for that. Goodbye, Mrs. Helmer. *(Exits through the hall.)*

Nora (goes to the hall door, opens it slightly and listens.): He's leaving. He isn't putting the letter in the box. Oh no, no! He couldn't! *(Opens the door little by little.)* What? He's standing out there. He's not going downstairs. He's hesitating? Is he?

(A letter drops into the box. Then Krogstad's footsteps are heard, until they die away as he goes downstairs. Nora utters a stifled cry, and runs across the room to the table by the sofa. A short pause.)

Nora: In the mailbox. *(Steals across to the hall door.)* It's there! Torvald, Torvald, there's no hope for us now!

(Mrs. Linde comes in from the room on the left, carrying the dress.)

Mrs. Linde: There, I can't find anything more to mend. Would you like to try it on?

Nora (in a hoarse whisper): Kristine, come here.

Mrs. Linde (throwing the dress down on the sofa): What's the matter with you? You look so agitated!

Nora: Come here. Do you see that letter? There, look. You can see it through the glass in the mailbox.

Mrs. Linde: Yes, I see it.

Nora: That letter is from Krogstad.

Mrs. Linde: Nora! It was Krogstad who lent you the money!

Nora: Yes, and now Torvald will know all about it.

Mrs. Linde: Believe me, Nora, that's the best thing for both of you.

Nora: You don't know the whole story. I forged a name.

Mrs. Linde: My God!

Nora: There's something I want to say to you, Kristine. I need you to be my witness.

Mrs. Linde: Your witness? What do you mean? What am I supposed to—

Nora: If I should go out of my mind—and it could easily happen—

Mrs. Linde: Nora!

Nora: Or if anything else should happen to me—anything, for instance, that might keep me from being here—

Mrs. Linde: Nora! Nora! What's the matter with you?

Nora: And if it turned out that somebody wanted to take all the responsibility, all the blame, you understand what I mean—

Mrs. Linde: Yes, yes, but how can you imagine—

Nora: Then you must be my witness that it's not true, Kristine. I'm not out of my mind at all. I'm perfectly rational right now, and I'm telling you that no one else ever knew anything about it. I did the whole thing all by myself. Remember that.

Mrs. Linde: I will. But I don't understand all this.

Nora: How could you understand it? Or the miracle that's going to happen!

Mrs. Linde: A miracle?

Nora: Yes, a miracle! But it's so terrible, Kristine. I can't let it happen, not for the whole world.

Mrs. Linde: I'll go and see Krogstad right this minute.

Nora: No, don't. He'll do something to hurt you too.

Mrs. Linde: There was a time when he would have gladly done anything for my sake.

Nora: What?

Mrs. Linde: Where does he live?

Nora: How should I know? Yes *(feeling in her pocket)*, here's his card. But the letter, the letter—

Helmer (calls from his room, knocking at the door): Nora!

Nora (cries out anxiously): What is it? What do you want?

Helmer: Don't be so afraid. We're not coming in. You've locked the door. Are you trying on your dress?

Nora: Yes, that's it. Oh, it's going to look so nice, Torvald.

Mrs. Linde (who has read the card): Look, he lives right around the corner.

Nora: But it's no use. It's all over. The letter's lying right there in the box.

Mrs. Linde: And your husband has the key?

Nora: Yes, always.

Mrs. Linde: Krogstad can ask for his letter back unread. He'll have to make up some reason—

Nora: But now is just about the time that Torvald usually—

Mrs. Linde: You have to prevent him. Go in and talk to him. I'll be back as soon as I can.

(She hurries out through the hall door.)

Nora (goes to Helmer's door, opens it and peeps in): Torvald!

Helmer (from the inner room): Well? May I finally come back into my own room? Come along, Rank, now you'll see—*(Stopping in the doorway.)* But what's this?

Nora: What's what, dear?

Helmer: Rank led me to expect an amazing transformation.

Rank (in the doorway): So I understood, but apparently I was mistaken.

Nora: Yes, nobody gets to admire me in my dress until tomorrow.

Helmer: But, my dear Nora, you look exhausted. Have you been practicing too much?

Nora: No, I haven't been practicing at all.

Helmer: But you'll have to—

Nora: Yes, of course I will, Torvald. But I can't get anywhere without you helping me. I've completely forgotten the whole thing.

Helmer: Oh, we'll soon get you back up to form again.

Nora: Yes, help me, Torvald. Promise that you will! I'm so nervous about it—all those people. I need you to devote yourself completely to me this evening. Not even the tiniest little bit of business. You can't even pick up a pen. Do you promise, Torvald dear?

Helmer: I promise. This evening I will be wholly and absolutely at your service, you helpless little creature. But first I'm just going to—*(Goes towards the hall door.)*

Nora: Just going to what?
Helmer: To see if there's any mail.
Nora: No, no! Don't do that, Torvald!
Helmer: Why not?
Nora: Torvald, please don't. There's nothing there.
Helmer: Well, let me look. *(Turns to go to the mailbox. Nora, at the piano, plays the first bars of the tarantella. Helmer stops in the doorway.)* Aha!
Nora: I can't dance tomorrow if I don't practice with you.
Helmer (going up to her): Are you really so worried about it, dear?
Nora: Yes, terribly worried about it. Let me practice right now. We have time before dinner. Sit down and play for me, Torvald dear. Criticize me and correct me, the way you always do.
Helmer: With great pleasure, if you want me to. *(Sits down at the piano.)*
Nora (takes a tambourine and a long multicolored shawl out of the box. She hastily drapes the shawl around her. Then she bounds to the front of the stage and calls out): Now play for me! I'm going to dance!

(Helmer plays and Nora dances. Rank stands by the piano behind Helmer and watches.)

Helmer (as he plays): Slower, slower!
Nora: I can't do it any other way.
Helmer: Not so violently, Nora!
Nora: This is the way.
Helmer (stops playing): No, no, that's not right at all.
Nora (laughing and swinging the tambourine): Didn't I tell you so?
Rank: Let me play for her.
Helmer (getting up): Good idea. I can correct her better that way.

(Rank sits down at the piano and plays. Nora dances more and more wildly. Helmer has taken up a position beside the stove, and as she dances, he gives her frequent instructions. She doesn't seem to hear him. Her hair comes undone and falls over her shoulders. She pays no attention to it, but goes on dancing. Enter Mrs. Linde.)

Mrs. Linde (standing as if spellbound in the doorway): Oh!
Nora (as she dances): What fun, Kristine!
Helmer: My dear darling Nora, you're dancing as if your life depended on it.
Nora: It does.
Helmer: Stop, Rank. This is insane! I said stop!

(Rank stops playing, and Nora suddenly stands still. Helmer goes up to her.)

I never would have believed it. You've forgotten everything I taught you.

Nora (throwing the tambourine aside): There, you see.
Helmer: You're going to need a lot of coaching.

Nora: Yes, you see how much I need it. You have to coach me right up to the last minute. Promise me you will, Torvald!

Helmer: You can depend on me.

Nora: You can't think about anything but me, today or tomorrow. Don't open a single letter. Don't even open the mailbox—

Helmer: You're still afraid of that man—

Nora: Yes, yes, I am.

Helmer: Nora, I can tell from your face that there's a letter from him in the box.

Nora: I don't know. I think there is. But you can't read anything like that now. Nothing nasty must come between us until this is all over.

Rank (whispers to Helmer): Don't contradict her.

Helmer (taking her in his arms): The child shall have her way. But tomorrow night, after you've danced—

Nora: Then you'll be free.

(The Maid appears in the doorway to the right.)

Maid: Dinner is served, ma'am.

Nora: We'll have champagne, Helene.

Maid: Yes, ma'am. *(Exit.)*

Helmer: Oh, are we having a banquet?

Nora: Yes, a banquet. Champagne till dawn! *(Calls out.)* And a few macaroons, Helene. Lots of them, just this once!

Helmer: Come on, stop acting so wild and nervous. Be my own little skylark again.

Nora: Yes, dear, I will. But go inside now, and you too, Doctor Rank. Kristine, please help me do up my hair.

Rank (whispers to Helmer as they go out): There isn't anything—she's not expecting—?

Helmer: No, nothing like that. It's just this childish nervousness I was telling you about. *(They go into the right-hand room.)*

Nora: Well?

Mrs. Linde: Out of town.

Nora: I could tell from your face.

Mrs. Linde: He'll be back tomorrow evening. I wrote him a note.

Nora: You should have left it alone. Don't try to prevent anything. After all, it's exciting to be waiting for a miracle to happen.

Mrs. Linde: What is it that you're waiting for?

Nora: Oh, you wouldn't understand. Go inside with them, I'll be there in a moment.

(Mrs. Linde goes into the dining room. Nora stands still for a little while, as if to compose herself. Then she looks at her watch.)

Five o'clock. Seven hours till midnight, and another twenty-four hours till the next midnight. And then the tarantella will be over. Twenty-four plus seven? Thirty-one hours to live.

Helmer (from the doorway on the right): Where's my little skylark?

Nora (going to him with her arms outstretched): Here she is!

ACT III

The same scene. The table has been placed in the middle of the stage, with chairs around it. A lamp is burning on the table. The door into the hall stands open. Dance music is heard in the room above. Mrs. Linde is sitting at the table idly turning over the pages of a book. She tries to read, but she seems unable to concentrate. Every now and then she listens intently for a sound at the outer door.

Mrs. Linde (looking at her watch): Not yet—and the time's nearly up. If only he doesn't—*(Listens again.)* Ah, there he is. *(Goes into the hall and opens the outer door carefully. Light footsteps are heard on the stairs. She whispers.)* Come in. There's no one else here.

Krogstad (in the doorway): I found a note from you at home. What does this mean?

Mrs. Linde: It's absolutely necessary that I have a talk with you.

Krogstad: Really? And is it absolutely necessary that we have it here?

Mrs. Linde: It's impossible where I live. There's no private entrance to my apartment. Come in. We're all alone. The maid's asleep, and the Helmers are upstairs at a dance.

Krogstad (coming into the room): Are the Helmers really at a dance tonight?

Mrs. Linde: Yes. Why shouldn't they be?

Krogstad: Certainly—why not?

Mrs. Linde: Now, Nils, let's have a talk.

Krogstad: What can we two have to talk about?

Mrs. Linde: Quite a lot.

Krogstad: I wouldn't have thought so.

Mrs. Linde: Of course not. You've never really understood me.

Krogstad: What was there to understand, except what the whole world could see—a heartless woman drops a man when a better catch comes along?

Mrs. Linde: Do you think I'm really that heartless? And that I broke it off with you so lightly?

Krogstad: Didn't you?

Mrs. Linde: Nils, did you really think that?

Krogstad: If not, why did you write what you did to me?

Mrs. Linde: What else could I do? Since I had to break it off with you, I had an obligation to stamp out your feelings for me.

Krogstad (wringing his hands): So that was it. And all this just for the sake of money!

Mrs. Linde: Don't forget that I had an invalid mother and two little brothers. We couldn't wait for you, Nils. Success seemed a long way off for you back then.

Krogstad: That may be so, but you had no right to cast me aside for anyone else's sake.

Mrs. Linde: I don't know if I did or not. Many times I've asked myself if I had the right.

Krogstad (more gently): When I lost you, it was as if the earth crumbled under my feet. Look at me now—a shipwrecked man clinging to a bit of wreckage.

Mrs. Linde: But help may be on the way.

Krogstad: It *was* on the way, till you came along and blocked it.

Mrs. Linde: Without knowing it, Nils. It wasn't till today that I found out I'd be taking your job.

Krogstad: I believe you, if you say so. But now that you know it, are you going to step aside?

Mrs. Linde: No, because it wouldn't do you any good.

Krogstad: Good? I would quit whether it did any good or not.

Mrs. Linde: I've learned to be practical. Life and hard, bitter necessity have taught me that.

Krogstad: And life has taught me not to believe in fine speeches.

Mrs. Linde: Then life has taught you something very sensible. But surely you believe in actions?

Krogstad: What do you mean by that?

Mrs. Linde: You said you were like a shipwrecked man clinging to a piece of wreckage.

Krogstad: I had good reason to say so.

Mrs. Linde: Well, I'm like a shipwrecked woman clinging to a piece of wreckage, with no one to mourn for and no one to care for.

Krogstad: That was your own choice.

Mrs. Linde: I had no other choice—then.

Krogstad: Well, what about now?

Mrs. Linde: Nils, how would it be if we two shipwrecked people could reach out to each other?

Krogstad: What are you saying?

Mrs. Linde: Two people on the same piece of wreckage would stand a better chance than each one on their own.

Krogstad: Kristine, I . . .

Mrs. Linde: Why do you think I came to town?

Krogstad: You can't mean that you were thinking about me?

Mrs. Linde: Life is unendurable without work. I've worked all my life, for as long as I can remember, and it's been my greatest and my only pleasure. But now that I'm completely alone in the world, my life is so terribly empty and I feel so abandoned. There isn't the slightest pleasure in working only for yourself. Nils, give me someone and something to work for.

Krogstad: I don't trust this. It's just some romantic female impulse, a high-minded urge for self-sacrifice.

Mrs. Linde: Have you ever known me to be like that?

Krogstad: Could you really do it? Tell me, do you know all about my past?

Mrs. Linde: Yes.

Krogstad: And you know what they think of me around here?

Mrs. Linde: Didn't you imply that with me you might have been a very different person?

Krogstad: I'm sure I would have.

Mrs. Linde: Is it too late now?

Krogstad: Kristine, are you serious about all this? Yes, I'm sure you are. I can see it in your face. Do you really have the courage, then—

Mrs. Linde: I want to be a mother to someone, and your children need a mother. We two need each other. Nils, I have faith in your true nature. I can face anything together with you.

Krogstad (grasps her hands): Thank you, thank you, Kristine! Now I can find a way to clear myself in the eyes of the world. Ah, but I forgot—

Mrs. Linde (listening): Shh! The tarantella! You have to go!

Krogstad: Why? What's the matter?

Mrs. Linde: Do you hear them up there? They'll probably come home as soon as this dance is over.

Krogstad: Yes, yes, I'll go. But it won't make any difference. You don't know what I've done about my situation with the Helmers.

Mrs. Linde: Yes, I know all about that.

Krogstad: And in spite of that you still have the courage to—

Mrs. Linde: I understand completely what despair can drive a man like you to do.

Krogstad: If only I could undo it!

Mrs. Linde: You can't. Your letter's lying in the mailbox now.

Krogstad: Are you sure?

Mrs. Linde: Quite sure, but—

Krogstad (with a searching look at her): Is that what this is all about? That you want to save your friend, no matter what you have to do? Tell me the truth. Is that it?

Mrs. Linde: Nils, when a woman has sold herself for someone else's sake, she doesn't do it a second time.

Krogstad: I'll ask for my letter back.

Mrs. Linde: No, no.

Krogstad: Yes, of course I will. I'll wait here until Helmer comes home. I'll tell him he has to give me back my letter, that it's only about my being fired, that I don't want him to read it—

Mrs. Linde: No, Nils, don't ask for it back.

Krogstad: But wasn't that the reason why you asked me to meet you here?

Mrs. Linde: In my first moment of panic, it was. But twenty-four hours have gone by since then, and in the meantime I've seen some incredible things in this house. Helmer has to know all about it. This terrible secret has to come out. They have to have a complete understanding between them. It's time for all this lying and pretending to stop.

Krogstad: All right then, if you think it's worth the risk. But there's at least one thing I can do, and do right away—

Mrs. Linde (listening): You have to leave this instant! The dance is over. They could walk in here any minute.

Krogstad: I'll wait for you downstairs.

Mrs. Linde: Yes, please do. I want you to walk me home.

Krogstad: I've never been so happy in my entire life!

(Goes out through the outer door. The door between the room and the hall remains open.)

Mrs. Linde (straightening up the room and getting her hat and coat ready): How different things will be! Someone to work for and live for, a home to bring happiness into. I'm certainly going to try. I wish they'd hurry up and come home—*(Listens.)* Ah, here they are now. I'd better put on my things.

(Picks up her hat and coat. Helmer's and Nora's voices are heard outside. A key is turned, and Helmer brings Nora into the hall almost by force. She is in an Italian peasant costume with a large black shawl wrapped around her. He is in formal wear and a black domino—a hooded cloak with an eye-mask—which is open.)

Nora (hanging back in the doorway and struggling with him): No, no, no! Don't bring me inside. I want to go back upstairs. I don't want to leave so early.

Helmer: But, my dearest Nora—

Nora: Please, Torvald dear, please, please, only one more hour.

Helmer: Not one more minute, my sweet Nora. You know this is what we agreed on. Come inside. You'll catch cold standing out there.

(He brings her gently into the room, in spite of her resistance.)

Mrs. Linde: Good evening.

Nora: Kristine!

Helmer: What are you doing here so late, Mrs. Linde?

Mrs. Linde: You must excuse me. I was so anxious to see Nora in her dress.

Nora: Have you been sitting here waiting for me?

Mrs. Linde: Yes, unfortunately I came too late, you'd already gone upstairs. And I didn't want to go away again without seeing you.

Helmer (taking off Nora's shawl): Yes, take a good look at her. I think she's worth looking at. Isn't she charming, Mrs. Linde?

Mrs. Linde: Yes, indeed she is.

Helmer: Doesn't she look especially pretty? Everyone thought so at the dance. But this sweet little person is extremely stubborn. What are we going to do with her? Believe it or not, I almost had to drag her away by force.

Nora: Torvald, you'll be sorry you didn't let me stay, even if only for half an hour.

Helmer: Listen to her, Mrs. Linde! She danced her tarantella and it was a huge success, as it deserved to be, though maybe her performance was a tiny bit too realistic, a little more so than it might have been by strict artistic standards. But never mind about that! The main thing is, she was a success, a tremendous success. Do you think I was going to let her stay there after that, and spoil the effect? Not a chance! I took my charming little Capri girl—my capricious little Capri girl, I should say—I took her by the arm, one quick circle around the room, a curtsey to one and all, and, as they say in novels, the beautiful vision vanished. An exit should always make an effect, Mrs. Linde, but I can't make Nora understand that. Whew, this room is hot!

(Throws his domino on a chair and opens the door to his study.)

Why is it so dark in here? Oh, of course. Excuse me.

(He goes in and lights some candles.)

Nora (in a hurried, breathless whisper): Well?

Mrs. Linde (in a low voice): I talked to him.

Nora: And?

Mrs. Linde: Nora, you have to tell your husband the whole story.

Nora (in an expressionless voice): I knew it.

Mrs. Linde: You have nothing to fear from Krogstad, but you still have to tell him.

Nora: I'm not going to.

Mrs. Linde: Then the letter will.

Nora: Thank you, Kristine. Now I know what I have to do. Shh!

Helmer (coming in again): Well, Mrs. Linde, have you been admiring her?

Mrs. Linde: Yes, I have, and now I'll say goodnight.

Helmer: What, already? Is this your knitting?

Mrs. Linde (taking it): Yes, thank you, I'd almost forgotten it.

Helmer: So you knit?

Mrs. Linde: Yes, of course.

Helmer: You know, you ought to embroider.

Mrs. Linde: Really? Why?

Helmer: It's much more graceful-looking. Here, let me show you. You hold the embroidery this way in your left hand, and use the needle with your right, like this, with a long, easy sweep. Do you see?

Mrs. Linde: Yes, I suppose—

Helmer: But knitting, that can never be anything but awkward. Here, look. The arms close together, the knitting needles going up and down. It's sort of Chinese looking. That was really excellent champagne they gave us.

Mrs. Linde: Well, good night, Nora, and don't be stubborn anymore.

Helmer: That's right, Mrs. Linde.

Mrs. Linde: Good night, Mr. Helmer.

Helmer (seeing her to the door): Good night, good night. I hope you get home safely. I'd be very happy to—but you only have a short way to go. Good night, good night.

(She goes out. He closes the door behind her, and comes in again.)

Ah, rid of her at last! What a bore that woman is.

Nora: Aren't you tired, Torvald?

Helmer: No, not at all.

Nora: You're not sleepy?

Helmer: Not a bit. As a matter of fact, I feel very lively. And what about you? You really look tired *and* sleepy.

Nora: Yes, I am very tired. I want to go to sleep right away.

Helmer: So, you see how right I was not to let you stay there any longer.

Nora: You're always right, Torvald.

Helmer (kissing her on the forehead): Now my little skylark is talking sense. Did you notice what a good mood Rank was in this evening?

Nora: Really? Was he? I didn't talk to him at all.

Helmer: And I only talked to him for a little while, but it's a long time since I've seen him so cheerful. *(Looks at her for a while and then moves closer to her.)* It's delightful to be home again by ourselves, to be alone with you, you fascinating, charming little darling!

Nora: Don't look at me like that, Torvald.

Helmer: Why shouldn't I look at my dearest treasure? At all the beauty that is mine, all my very own?

Nora (going to the other side of the table): I wish you wouldn't talk that way to me tonight.

Helmer (following her): You've still got the tarantella in your blood, I see. And it makes you more captivating than ever. Listen, the guests are starting to leave now. *(In a lower voice.)* Nora, soon the whole house will be quiet.

Nora: Yes, I hope so.

Helmer: Yes, my own darling Nora. Do you know why, when we're out at a party like this, why I hardly talk to you, and keep away from you, and only steal a glance at you now and then? Do you know why I do that? It's because I'm pretending to myself that we're secretly in love, and we're secretly engaged, and no one suspects that there's anything between us.

Nora: Yes, yes, I know you're thinking about me every moment.

Helmer: And when we're leaving, and I'm putting the shawl over your beautiful young shoulders, on your lovely neck, then I imagine that you're my young bride and that we've just come from our wedding and I'm bringing you home for the first time, to be alone with you for the first time, all alone with my shy little darling! This whole night I've been longing for you alone. My blood was on fire watching you move when you danced the tarantella. I couldn't stand it any longer, and that's why I brought you home so early—

Nora: Stop it, Torvald! Let me go. I won't—

Helmer: What? You're not serious, Nora! You won't? You won't? I'm your husband—

(There is a knock at the outer door.)

Nora (starting): Did you hear—

Helmer (going into the hall): Who is it?

Rank (outside): It's me. May I come in for a moment?

Helmer (in an irritated whisper): What does he want now? *(Aloud.)* Wait a minute! *(Unlocks the door.)* Come in. It's good of you not to pass by our door without saying hello.

Rank: I thought I heard your voice, and I felt like dropping by. *(With a quick look around.)* Ah, yes, these dear familiar rooms. You two are very happy and cozy in here.

Helmer: You seemed to be making yourself pretty happy upstairs too.

Rank: Very much so. Why shouldn't I? Why shouldn't we enjoy everything in this world? At least as much as we can, for as long as we can. The wine was first-rate—

Helmer: Especially the champagne.

Rank: So you noticed that too? It's almost unbelievable how much of it I managed to put away!

Nora: Torvald drank a lot of champagne tonight too.

Rank: Did he?

Nora: Yes, and it always makes him so merry.

Rank: Well, why shouldn't a person have a merry evening after a well-spent day?

Helmer: Well-spent? I'm afraid I can't take credit for that.

Rank (clapping him on the back): But I can, you know!

Nora: Doctor Rank, you must have been busy with some scientific investigation today.

Rank: Exactly.

Helmer: Listen to this! Little Nora talking about scientific investigations!
Nora: And may I congratulate you on the result?
Rank: Indeed you may.
Nora: Was it favorable, then?
Rank: The best possible result, for both doctor and patient—certainty.
Nora (quickly and searchingly): Certainty?
Rank: Absolute certainty. So wasn't I entitled to make a merry evening of it after that?
Nora: Yes, you certainly were, Doctor Rank.
Helmer: I think so too, as long as you don't have to pay for it in the morning.
Rank: Oh well, you can't have anything in this life without paying for it.
Nora: Doctor Rank, are you fond of fancy-dress balls?
Rank: Yes, if there are a lot of pretty costumes.
Nora: Tell me, what should the two of us wear to the next one?
Helmer: Little featherbrain! You're thinking of the next one already?
Rank: The two of us? Yes, I can tell you. You'll go as a good-luck charm—
Helmer: Yes, but what would be the costume for that?
Rank: She just needs to dress the way she always does.
Helmer: That was very nicely put. But aren't you going to tell us what you'll be?
Rank: Yes, my dear friend, I've already made up my mind about that.
Helmer: Well?
Rank: At the next fancy-dress ball I'm going to be invisible.
Helmer: That's a good one!
Rank: There's a big black cap . . . Haven't you ever heard of the cap that makes you invisible? Once you put it on, no one can see you anymore.
Helmer (suppressing a smile): Yes, that's right.
Rank: But I'm clean forgetting what I came for. Helmer, give me a cigar. One of the dark Havanas.
Helmer: With the greatest pleasure. *(Offers him his case.)*
Rank (takes a cigar and cuts off the end): Thanks.
Nora (striking a match): Let me give you a light.
Rank: Thank you. *(She holds the match for him to light his cigar.)* And now goodbye!
Helmer: Goodbye, goodbye, my dear old friend.
Nora: Sleep well, Doctor Rank.
Rank: Thank you for that wish.
Nora: Wish me the same.
Rank: You? Well, if you want me to. Sleep well! And thanks for the light. *(He nods to them both and goes out.)*
Helmer (in a subdued voice): He's had too much to drink.
Nora (absently): Maybe.

(Helmer takes a bunch of keys out of his pocket and goes into the hall.)

Torvald! What are you going to do out there?

Helmer: Empty the mailbox. It's quite full. There won't be any room for the newspaper in the morning.

Nora: Are you going to work tonight?

Helmer: You know I'm not. What's this? Someone's been at the lock.

Nora: At the lock?

Helmer: Yes, it's been tampered with. What does this mean? I never would have thought the maid—Look, here's a broken hairpin. It's one of yours, Nora.

Nora (quickly): Then it must have been the children—

Helmer: Then you'd better break them of those habits. There, I've finally got it open.

(Empties the mailbox and calls out to the kitchen.)

Helene! Helene, put out the light over the front door.

(Comes back into the room and shuts the door into the hall. He holds out his hand full of letters.)

Look at that. Look what a pile of them there are. *(Turning them over.)* What's this?

Nora (at the window): The letter! No! Torvald, no!

Helmer: Two calling cards of Rank's.

Nora: Of Doctor Rank's?

Helmer (looking at them): Yes, Doctor Rank. They were on top. He must have put them in there when he left just now.

Nora: Is there anything written on them?

Helmer: There's a black cross over the name. Look. What a morbid thing to do! It looks as if he's announcing his own death.

Nora: That's exactly what he's doing.

Helmer: What? Do you know anything about it? Has he said anything to you?

Nora: Yes. He told me that when the cards came it would be his farewell to us. He means to close himself off and die.

Helmer: My poor old friend! Of course I knew we wouldn't have him for very long. But this soon! And he goes and hides himself away like a wounded animal.

Nora: If it has to happen, it's better that it be done without a word. Don't you think so, Torvald?

Helmer (walking up and down): He's become so much a part of our lives, I can't imagine him not being with us anymore. With his poor health and his loneliness, he was like a cloudy background to our sunlit happiness. Well, maybe it's all for the best. For him, anyway. *(Standing still.)* And maybe for us too, Nora. Now we have only each other to rely on. *(Puts his arms around her.)* My darling wife, I feel as though

I can't possibly hold you tight enough. You know, Nora, I've often wished you were in some kind of serious danger, so that I could risk everything, even my own life, to save you.

Nora (disengages herself from him, and says firmly and decidedly): Now you must go and read your letters, Torvald.

Helmer: No, no, not tonight. I want to be with you, my darling wife.

Nora: With the thought of your friend's death—

Helmer: You're right, it has affected us both. Something ugly has come between us, the thought of the horrors of death. We have to try to put it out of our minds. Until we do, we'll each go to our own room.

Nora (with her arms around his neck): Good night, Torvald. Good night!

Helmer (kissing her on the forehead): Good night, my little songbird. Sleep well, Nora. Now I'll go read all my mail. *(He takes his letters and goes into his room, shutting the door behind him.)*

Nora (gropes distractedly about, picks up Helmer's domino and wraps it around her, while she says in quick, hoarse, spasmodic whispers): Never to see him again. Never! Never! *(Puts her shawl over her head.)* Never to see my children again either, never again. Never! Never! Oh, the icy, black water, the bottomless depths! If only it were over! He's got it now, now he's reading it. Goodbye, Torvald . . . children!

(She is about to rush out through the hall when Helmer opens his door hurriedly and stands with an open letter in his hand.)

Helmer: Nora!

Nora: Ah!

Helmer: What is this? Do you know what's in this letter?

Nora: Yes, I know. Let me go! Let me get out!

Helmer (holding her back): Where are you going?

Nora (trying to get free): You're not going to save me, Torvald!

Helmer (reeling): It's true? Is this true, what it says here? This is horrible! No, no, it can't possibly be true.

Nora: It is true. I've loved you more than anything else in the world.

Helmer: Don't start with your ridiculous excuses.

Nora (taking a step towards him): Torvald!

Helmer: You little fool, do you know what you've done?

Nora: Let me go. I won't let you suffer for my sake. You're not going to take it on yourself.

Helmer: Stop play-acting. *(Locks the hall door.)* You're going to stay right here and give me an explanation. Do you understand what you've done? Answer me! Do you understand what you've done?

Nora (looks steadily at him and says with a growing look of coldness in her face): Yes, I'm beginning to understand everything now.

Helmer (walking around the room): What a horrible awakening! The woman who was my pride and joy for eight years, a hypocrite, a liar, worse than that, much worse—a criminal! The unspeakable ugliness of it all! The shame of it! The shame!

(Nora is silent and looks steadily at him. He stops in front of her.)

I should have realized that something like this was bound to happen. I should have seen it coming. Your father's shifty nature—be quiet!—your father's shifty nature has come out in you. No religion, no morality, no sense of duty. This is my punishment for closing my eyes to what he did! I did it for your sake, and this is how you pay me back.

Nora: Yes, that's right.

Helmer: Now you've destroyed all my happiness. You've ruined my whole future. It's horrible to think about! I'm in the power of an unscrupulous man. He can do what he wants with me, ask me for anything he wants, give me any orders he wants, and I don't dare say no. And I have to sink to such miserable depths, all because of a featherbrained woman!

Nora: When I'm out of the way, you'll be free.

Helmer: Spare me the speeches. Your father had always plenty of those on hand, too. What good would it do me if you were out of the way, as you say? Not the slightest. He can tell everybody the whole story. And if he does, I could be wrongly suspected of having been in on it with you. People will probably think I was behind it all, that I put you up to it! And I have you to thank for all this, after I've cherished you the whole time we've been married. Do you understand what you've done to me?

Nora (coldly and quietly): Yes.

Helmer: It's so incredible that I can't take it all in. But we have to come to some understanding. Take off that shawl. Take it off, I said. I have to try to appease him some way or another. It has to be hushed up, no matter what it costs. And as for you and me, we have to make it look as if everything is just as it always was, but only for the sake of appearances, obviously. You'll stay here in my house, of course. But I won't let you bring up the children. I can't trust them to you. To think that I have to say these things to someone I've loved so dearly, and that I still—No, that's all over. From this moment on happiness is out of the question. All that matters now is to save the bits and pieces, to keep up the appearance—

(The front doorbell rings.)

Helmer (with a start): What's that? At this hour! Can the worst—Can he—Go and hide yourself, Nora. Say you don't feel well. *(Nora stands motionless. Helmer goes and unlocks the hall door.)*

Maid (half-dressed, comes to the door): A letter for Mrs. Helmer.

Helmer: Give it to me. *(Takes the letter, and shuts the door.)* Yes, it's from him. I'm not giving it to you. I'll read it myself.

Nora: Go ahead, read it.

Helmer (standing by the lamp): I barely have the courage to. It could mean ruin for both of us. No, I have to know. *(Tears open the letter, runs his eye over a few lines, looks at a piece of paper enclosed with it, and gives a shout of joy.)* Nora! *(She looks at him questioningly.)* Nora! No, I'd better read it again. Yes, it's true! I'm saved! Nora, I'm saved!

Nora: And what about me?

Helmer: You too, of course. We're both saved, you and I. Look, he's returned your note. He says he's sorry and he apologizes—that a happy change in his life—what difference does it make what he says! We're saved, Nora! Nobody can hurt you. Oh, Nora, Nora! No, first I have to destroy these horrible things. Let me see. . . . *(Glances at the note.)* No, no, I don't want to look at it. This whole business will be nothing but a bad dream to me.

(Tears up the note and both letters, throws them all into the stove, and watches them burn.)

There, now it doesn't exist anymore. He says that you've known since Christmas Eve. These must have been a horrible three days for you, Nora.

Nora: I fought a hard fight these three days.

Helmer: And suffered agonies, and saw no way out but—No, we won't dwell on any of those horrors. We'll just shout for joy and keep saying, "It's all over! It's all over!" Listen to me, Nora. You don't seem to realize that it's all over. What's this? Such a cold, hard face! My poor little Nora, I understand. You find it hard to believe that I've really forgiven you. But I swear that it's true, Nora. I forgive you for everything. I know that you did it all out of love for me.

Nora: That's true.

Helmer: You've loved me the way a wife ought to love her husband. You just didn't have the awareness to see what was wrong with the means you used. But do you think I love you any less because you don't understand how to deal with these things? No, of course not. I want you to lean on me. I'll advise you and guide you. I wouldn't be a man if this womanly helplessness didn't make you twice as attractive to me. Don't think anymore about the hard things I said when I was so upset at first, when I thought everything was going to crush me. I forgive you, Nora. I swear to you that I forgive you.

Nora: Thank you for your forgiveness. *(She goes out through the door to the right.)*

Helmer: No, don't go—*(Looks in.)* What are you doing in there?

Nora (from within): Taking off my costume.

Helmer (standing at the open door): Yes, do. Try to calm yourself, and ease your mind again, my frightened little songbird. I want you to rest and feel secure. I have wide wings for you to take shelter underneath. *(Walks up and down by the door.)* What a warm and cozy home we have, Nora: Here's a safe haven for you, and I'll protect you like a hunted dove that I've rescued from a hawk's claws. I'll calm your poor pounding heart. It will happen, little by little, Nora, believe me. In the morning you'll see it in a very different light. Soon everything will be exactly the way it was before. Before you know it, you won't need my reassurances that I've forgiven you. You'll know for certain that I have. You can't imagine that I'd ever consider rejecting you, or even blaming you? You have no idea what a man feels in his heart, Nora. A man finds it indescribably sweet and satisfying to know that he's forgiven his wife, freely and with all his heart. It's as if he's made her his own all over again. He's given her a new life, in a way, and she's become both wife and child to him. And from this moment on that's what you'll be to me, my little scared, helpless darling. Don't worry about anything, Nora. Just be honest and open with me, and I'll be your will and your conscience. What's this? You haven't gone to bed yet? Have you changed?

Nora (in everyday dress): Yes, Torvald, I've changed.

Helmer: But why—It's so late.

Nora: I'm not going to sleep tonight.

Helmer: But, my dear Nora—

Nora (looking at her watch): It's not that late. Sit down here, Torvald. You and I have a lot to talk about. *(She sits down at one side of the table.)*

Helmer: Nora, what is this? Why this cold, hard face?

Nora: Sit down. This is going to take a while. I have a lot to say to you.

Helmer (sits down at the opposite side of the table): You're making me nervous, Nora. And I don't understand you.

Nora: No, that's it exactly. You don't understand me, and I've never understood you either, until tonight. No, don't interrupt me. I want you to listen to what I have to say. Torvald, I'm settling accounts with you.

Helmer: What do you mean by that?

Nora (after a short silence): Doesn't anything strike you as odd about the way we're sitting here like this?

Helmer: No, what?

Nora: We've been married for eight years. Doesn't it occur to you that this is the first time the two of us, you and I, husband and wife, have had a serious conversation?

Helmer: What do you mean by serious?

Nora: In the whole eight years—longer than that, for the whole time we've known each other—we've never exchanged one word on any serious subject.

Helmer: Did you expect me to be constantly worrying you with problems that you weren't capable of helping me deal with?

Nora: I'm not talking about business. I mean we've never sat down together seriously to try to get to the bottom of anything.

Helmer: But, dearest Nora, what good would that have done you?

Nora: That's just it. You've never understood me. I've been treated badly, Torvald, first by Papa and then by you.

Helmer: What? The two people who've loved you more than anyone else?

Nora (shaking her head): You've never loved me. You just thought it was pleasant to be in love with me.

Helmer: Nora, what are you saying?

Nora: It's true, Torvald. When I lived at home with Papa, he gave me his opinion about everything, and so I had all the same opinions, and if I didn't, I kept my mouth shut, because he wouldn't have liked it. He used to call me his doll-child, and he played with me the way I played with my dolls. And when I came to live in your house—

Helmer: What kind of way is that to talk about our marriage?

Nora (undisturbed): I mean that I was just passed from Papa's hands to yours. You arranged everything according to your own taste, and so I had all the same tastes as you. Or else I pretended to, I'm not really sure which. Sometimes I think it's one way and sometimes the other. When I look back, it's as if I've been living here like a beggar, from hand to mouth. I've supported myself by performing tricks for you, Torvald. But that's the way you wanted it. You and Papa have committed a terrible sin against me. It's your fault that I've done nothing with my life.

Helmer: This is so unfair and ungrateful of you, Nora! Haven't you been happy here?

Nora: No, I've never really been happy. I thought I was, but it wasn't true.

Helmer: Not—not happy!

Nora: No, just cheerful. You've always been very kind to me. But our home's been nothing but a playroom. I've been your doll-wife, the same way that I was Papa's doll-child. And the children have been my dolls. I thought it was great fun when you played with me, the way they thought it was when I played with them. That's what our marriage has been, Torvald.

Helmer: There's some truth in what you're saying, even though your view of it is exaggerated and overwrought. But things will be different from now on. Playtime is over, and now it's lesson-time.

Nora: Whose lessons? Mine, or the children's?

Helmer: Both yours and the children's, my darling Nora.

Nora: I'm sorry, Torvald, but you're not the man to give me lessons on how to be a proper wife to you.

Helmer: How can you say that?

Nora: And as for me, who am I to be allowed to bring up the children?

Helmer: Nora!

Nora: Didn't you say so yourself a little while ago, that you don't dare trust them to me?

Helmer: That was in a moment of anger! Why can't you let it go?

Nora: Because you were absolutely right. I'm not fit for the job. There's another job I have to take on first. I have to try to educate myself. You're not the man to help me with that. I have to do that for myself. And that's why I'm going to leave you now.

Helmer (jumping up): What are you saying?

Nora: I have to stand completely on my own, if I'm going to understand myself and everything around me. That's why I can't stay here with you any longer.

Helmer: Nora, Nora!

Nora: I'm leaving right now. I'm sure Kristine will put me up for the night—

Helmer: You're out of your mind! I won't let you go! I forbid it!

Nora: It's no use forbidding me anything anymore. I'm taking only what belongs to me. I won't take anything from you, now or later.

Helmer: This is insanity!

Nora: Tomorrow I'm going home. Back to where I came from, I mean. It'll be easier for me to find something to do there.

Helmer: You're a blind, senseless woman!

Nora: Then I'd better try to get some sense, Torvald.

Helmer: But to desert your home, your husband, and your children! And aren't you concerned about what people will say?

Nora: I can't concern myself with that. I only know that this is what I have to do.

Helmer: This is outrageous! You're just going to walk away from your most sacred duties?

Nora: What do you consider to be my most sacred duties?

Helmer: Do you need me to tell you that? Aren't they your duties to your husband and your children?

Nora: I have other duties just as sacred.

Helmer: No, you do not. What could they be?

Nora: Duties to myself.

Helmer: First and foremost, you're a wife and a mother.

Nora: I don't believe that anymore. I believe that first and foremost I'm a human being, just as you are—or, at least, that I have to try to become one. I know very well, Torvald, that most people would agree with you, and that opinions like yours are in books, but I can't be satisfied anymore with what most people say, or with what's in books. I have to think things through for myself and come to understand them.

Helmer: Why can't you understand your place in your own home? Don't you have an infallible guide in matters like that? What about your religion?

Nora: Torvald, I'm afraid I'm not sure what religion is.

Helmer: What are you saying?

Nora: All I know is what Pastor Hansen said when I was confirmed. He told us that religion was this, that, and the other thing. When I'm away from all this and on my own, I'll look into that subject too. I'll see if what he said is true or not, or at least whether it's true for me.

Helmer: This is unheard of, coming from a young woman like you! But if religion doesn't guide you, let me appeal to your conscience. I assume you have some moral sense. Or do you have none? Answer me.

Nora: Torvald, that's not an easy question to answer. I really don't know. It's very confusing to me. I only know that you and I look at it in very different ways. I'm learning too that the law isn't at all what I thought it was, and I can't convince myself that the law is right. A woman has no right to spare her old dying father or to save her husband's life? I can't believe that.

Helmer: You talk like a child. You don't understand anything about the world you live in.

Nora: No, I don't. But I'm going to try. I'm going to see if I can figure out who's right, me or the world.

Helmer: You're sick, Nora. You're delirious. I'm half convinced that you're out of your mind.

Nora: I've never felt so clearheaded and sure of myself as I do tonight.

Helmer: Clearheaded and sure of yourself—and that's the spirit in which you forsake your husband and your children?

Nora: Yes, it is.

Helmer: Then there's only one possible explanation.

Nora: Which is?

Helmer: You don't love me anymore.

Nora: Exactly.

Helmer: Nora! How can you say that?

Nora: It's very painful for me to say it, Torvald, because you've always been so good to me, but I can't help it. I don't love you anymore.

Helmer (regaining his composure): Are you clearheaded and sure of yourself when you say that too?

Nora: Yes, totally clearheaded and sure of myself. That's why I can't stay here.

Helmer: Can you tell me what I did to make you stop loving me?

Nora: Yes, I can. It was tonight, when the miracle didn't happen. That's when I realized you're not the man I thought you were.

Helmer: Can you explain that more clearly? I don't understand you.

Nora: I've been waiting so patiently for the last eight years. Of course I knew that miracles don't happen every day. Then when I found myself in this horrible situation, I was sure that the miracle was about to happen at last. When Krogstad's letter was lying out there, never for a moment did I imagine that you would agree to his conditions. I was absolutely certain that you'd say to him: Go ahead, tell the whole world. And when he had—

Helmer: Yes, what then? After I'd exposed my wife to shame and disgrace?

Nora: When he had, I was absolutely certain you'd come forward and take the whole thing on yourself, and say: I'm the guilty one.

Helmer: Nora—!

Nora: You mean that I would never have let you make such a sacrifice for me? Of course I wouldn't. But who would have believed my word against yours? That was the miracle that I hoped for and dreaded. And it was to keep it from happening that made me want to kill myself.

Helmer: I'd gladly work night and day for you, Nora, and endure sorrow and poverty for your sake. But no man would sacrifice his honor for the one he loves.

Nora: Hundreds of thousands of women have done it.

Helmer: Oh, you think and talk like a thoughtless child.

Nora: Maybe so. But you don't think or talk like the man I want to be with for the rest of my life. As soon as your fear had passed—and it wasn't fear for what threatened me, but for what might happen to you—when the whole thing was past, as far as you were concerned it was just as if nothing at all had happened. I was still your little skylark, your doll, but now you'd handle me twice as gently and carefully as before, because I was so delicate and fragile. *(Getting up.)* Torvald, that's when it dawned on me that for eight years I'd been living here with a stranger and had borne him three children. Oh, I can't bear to think about it! I could tear myself into little pieces!

Helmer (sadly): I see, I see. An abyss has opened up between us. There's no denying it. But, Nora, can't we find some way to close it?

Nora: The way I am now, I'm no wife for you.

Helmer: I can find it in myself to become a different man.

Nora: Maybe so—if your doll is taken away from you.

Helmer: But to be apart!—to be apart from you! No, no, Nora, I can't conceive of it.

Nora (going out to the right): All the more reason why it has to be done.

(She comes back with her coat and hat and a small suitcase which she puts on a chair by the table.)

Helmer: Nora, Nora, not now! Wait till tomorrow.

Nora (putting on her cloak): I can't spend the night in a strange man's room.

Helmer: But couldn't we live here together like brother and sister?

Nora (putting on her hat): You know how long that would last. *(Puts the shawl around her.)* Goodbye, Torvald. I won't look in on the children. I know they're in better hands than mine. The way I am now, I'm no use to them.

Helmer: But someday, Nora, someday?

Nora: How can I tell? I have no idea what's going to become of me.

Helmer: But you're my wife, whatever becomes of you.

Nora: Listen, Torvald. I've heard that when a wife deserts her husband's house, the way I'm doing now, he's free of all legal obligations to her. In any event, I set you free from all your obligations. I don't want you to feel bound in the slightest, any more than I will. There has to be complete freedom on both sides. Look, here's your ring back. Give me mine.

Helmer: That too?

Nora: That too.

Helmer: Here it is.

Nora: Good. Now it's all over. I've left the keys here. The maids know all about how to run the house, much better than I do. Kristine will come by tomorrow after I leave her place and pack up my own things, the ones I brought with me from home. I'd like to have them sent to me.

Helmer: All over! All over! Nora, will you ever think about me again?

Nora: I know I'll often think about you, and the children, and this house.

Helmer: May I write to you, Nora?

Nora: No, never. You mustn't do that.

Helmer: But at least let me send you—

Nora: Nothing, nothing.

Helmer: Let me help you if you're in need.

Nora: No. I can't accept anything from a stranger.

Helmer: Nora . . . can't I ever be anything more than a stranger to you?

Nora (picking up her bag): Ah, Torvald, for that, the most wonderful miracle of all would have to happen.

Helmer: Tell me what that would be!

Nora: We'd both have to change so much that—Oh, Torvald, I've stopped believing in miracles.

Helmer: But I'll believe. Tell me! Change so much that . . . ?

Nora: That our life together would be a true marriage. Goodbye.

(She goes out through the hall.)

Helmer (sinks down into a chair at the door and buries his face in his hands): Nora! Nora! *(Looks around, and stands up.)* Empty. She's gone. *(A hope flashes across his mind.)* The most wonderful miracle of all . . . ?

(The heavy sound of a closing door is heard from below.)

Questions

ACT I

1. From the opening conversation between Helmer and Nora, what are your impressions of him? Of her? Of their marriage?
2. At what moment in the play do you understand why it is called *A Doll's House*?
3. In what ways does Mrs. Linde provide a contrast for Nora?
4. What in Krogstad's first appearance on stage, and in Dr. Rank's remarks about him, indicates that the bank clerk is a menace?
5. Of what illegal deed is Nora guilty? How does she justify it?
6. When the curtain falls on Act I, what problems now confront Nora?

ACT II

1. As Act II opens, what are your feelings on seeing the stripped, ragged Christmas tree? How is it suggestive?
2. What events that soon occur make Nora's situation even more difficult?
3. How does she try to save herself?
4. Why does Nora fling herself into the wild tarantella?

ACT III

1. For what possible reasons does Mrs. Linde pledge herself to Krogstad?
2. How does Dr. Rank's announcement of his impending death affect Nora and Helmer?
3. What is Helmer's reaction to learning the truth about Nora's misdeed? Why does he blame Nora's father? What is revealing (of Helmer's own character) in his remark, "From this moment on happiness is out of the question. All that matters now is to save the bits and pieces, to keep up the appearance—"?
4. When Helmer finds that Krogstad has sent back the note, what is his response? How do you feel toward him?
5. How does the character of Nora develop in this act?
6. How do you interpret her final slamming of the door?

General Questions

1. In what ways do you find Nora a victim? In what ways is she at fault?
2. Try to state the theme of the play. Does it involve women's rights? Self-fulfillment?
3. What dramatic question does the play embody? At what moment can this question first be stated?
4. What is the crisis? In what way is this moment or event a "turning point"? (In what new direction does the action turn?)
5. Eric Bentley, in an essay titled "Ibsen, Pro and Con" (*In Search of Theater* [New York: Knopf, 1953]), criticizes the character of Krogstad, calling him "a mere pawn of the plot." He then adds, "When convenient to Ibsen, he is a blackmailer. When inconvenient, he is converted." Do you agree or disagree?
6. Why is the play considered a work of Realism? Is there anything in it that does not seem realistic?
7. In what respects does *A Doll's House* seem to apply to life today? Is it in any way dated? Could there be a Nora in North America today?

EXPERIMENTAL DRAMA

In the latter part of the twentieth century, experimental drama, greatly influenced by the traditions of earlier Symbolist, Expressionist, and absurdist theater, flourished. For example, David Henry Hwang's work combines realistic elements with ritualistic and symbolic devices drawn from Asian theater (see his one-act play, *The Sound of a Voice*, in Chapter 29). Caryl Churchill's *Top Girls* (1982) presents a dinner party in which a contemporary woman invites legendary women from history to a dinner party in a restaurant. Tony Kushner's *Angels in America* (1992) also mixes realism and fantasy to dramatize the plight of AIDS. Shel Silverstein, popular author of children's poetry, wrote a raucous one-man play, *The Devil and Billy Markham* (1991), entirely in rime, about a series of fantastic adventures in hell featuring a hard-drinking gambler and the Prince of Darkness. Silverstein's play is simultaneously experimental in form but traditional in content with its homage to American ballads and tall tales.

Experimental theater continues to exert a strong influence on contemporary drama. The following play, Milcha Sanchez-Scott's *The Cuban Swimmer*, deftly assimilates several dramatic styles—symbolism, new naturalism, ethnic drama, theater of the absurd—to create a brilliant original work. The play is simultaneously a family drama, a Latin comedy, a religious parable, and a critique of a media-obsessed American culture.

Milcha Sanchez-Scott

The Cuban Swimmer 1984

Milcha Sanchez-Scott

Milcha Sanchez-Scott was born in 1955 on the island of Bali. Her father was Colombian. Her mother was Chinese, Indonesian, and Dutch. Her father's work as an agronomist required constant travel, so when the young Sanchez-Scott reached school age, she was sent to a convent boarding school near London where she first learned English. Colombia, however, remained the family's one permanent home. Every Christmas and summer vacation was spent on a ranch in San Marta, Colombia, where four generations of family lived together. When Sanchez-Scott was fourteen, her family moved to California. After attending the University of San Diego, where she majored in literature and philosophy, she worked at the San Diego Zoo and later at an employment agency in Los Angeles. Her first play, Latina, *premiered in 1980 and won seven Drama-Logue awards.* Dog Lady *and* The Cuban Swimmer *followed in 1984. Sanchez-Scott then went to New York for a year to work with playwright Irene Fornes, in whose theater workshop she developed* Roosters *(1988). A feature-*

film version of Roosters, *starring Edward James Olmos, was released in 1995. Her other plays include* Evening Star *(1989),* El Dorado *(1990), and* The Old Matador *(1995). Sanchez-Scott lives in Los Angeles.*

CHARACTERS

Margarita Suárez, the swimmer
Eduardo Suárez, her father, the coach
Simón Suárez, her brother
Aída Suárez, her mother
Abuela, her grandmother
Voice of Mel Munson
Voice of Mary Beth White
Voice of Radio Operator

SETTING. *The Pacific Ocean between San Pedro and Catalina Island.*

TIME. *Summer.*

Live conga drums can be used to punctuate the action of the play.

SCENE I

Pacific Ocean. Midday. On the horizon, in perspective, a small boat enters upstage left, crosses to upstage right, and exits. Pause. Lower on the horizon, the same boat, in larger perspective, enters upstage right, crosses and exits upstage left. Blackout.

SCENE II

Pacific Ocean. Midday. The swimmer, Margarita Suárez, is swimming. On the boat following behind her are her father, Eduardo Suárez, holding a megaphone, and Simón, her brother, sitting on top of the cabin with his shirt off, punk sunglasses on, binoculars hanging on his chest.

Eduardo (leaning forward, shouting in time to Margarita's swimming): Uno, dos, uno, dos. Y uno, dos° . . . keep your shoulders parallel to the water.

Simón: I'm gonna take these glasses off and look straight into the sun.

Eduardo (through megaphone): Muy bien, muy bien° . . . but punch those arms in, baby.

Simón (looking directly at the sun through binoculars): Come on, come on, zap me. Show me something. *(He looks behind at the shoreline and ahead at the sea.)* Stop! Stop, *Papi*! Stop!

Uno, dos, uno, dos. Y uno, dos: One, two, one, two. And one, two. *Muy bien, muy bien:* Very good, very good.

A 2005 production of *The Cuban Swimmer* at the People's Light and Theatre, Malvern, Pennsylvania.

(Aída Suárez and Abuela, the swimmer's mother and grandmother, enter running from the back of the boat.)

Aída and Abuela: *Qué? Qué es?*°
Aída: Es *un* shark?°
Eduardo: Eh?
Abuela: *Que es un* shark *dicen?*°

(Eduardo blows whistle. Margarita looks up at the boat.)

Simón: No, *Papi*, no shark, no shark. We've reached the halfway mark.
Abuela (looking into the water): *A dónde está?*°
Aída: It's not in the water.
Abuela: Oh, no? Oh, no?
Aída: No! *A poco* do you think they're gonna have signs in the water to say you are halfway to Santa Catalina? No. It's done very scientific. *A ver, hijo,*° explain it to your grandma.
Simón: Well, you see, Abuela—*(He points behind.)* There's San Pedro. *(He points ahead.)* And there's Santa Catalina. Looks halfway to me.

(Abuela shakes her head and is looking back and forth, trying to make the decision, when suddenly the sound of a helicopter is heard.)

Qué? Qué es?: What? What is it? *Es un shark?*: Is it a shark? *Que es un shark dicen?*: Did they say a shark? *A dónde está?*: Where is it? *A ver, hijo*: Look here, son.

Abuela (looking up): Virgencita de la Caridad del Cobre. Qué es eso?°

(Sound of helicopter gets closer. Margarita looks up.)

Margarita: Papi, Papi!

(A small commotion on the boat, with everybody pointing at the helicopter above. Shadows of the helicopter fall on the boat. Simón looks up at it through binoculars.)

Papi—qué es? What is it?

Eduardo (through megaphone): Uh . . . uh . . . uh, *un momentico . . . mi hija.*° . . . Your *papi*'s got everything under control, understand? Uh . . . you just keep stroking. And stay . . . uh . . . close to the boat.

Simón: Wow, *Papi*! We're on TV, man! Holy Christ, we're all over the fucking U.S.A.! It's Mel Munson and Mary Beth White!

Aída: Por Dios!° Simón, don't swear. And put on your shirt.

(Aída fluffs her hair, puts on her sunglasses and waves to the helicopter. Simón leans over the side of the boat and yells to Margarita.)

Simón: Yo, Margo! You're on TV, man.

Eduardo: Leave your sister alone. Turn on the radio.

Margarita: Papi! Qué está pasando?°

Abuela: Que es la televisión dicen? (She shakes her head.) Porque como yo no puedo ver nada sin mis espejuelos.°

(Abuela rummages through the boat, looking for her glasses. Voices of Mel Munson and Mary Beth White are heard over the boat's radio.)

Mel's Voice: As we take a closer look at the gallant crew of *La Havana* . . . and there . . . yes, there she is . . . the little Cuban swimmer from Long Beach, California, nineteen-year-old Margarita Suárez. The unknown swimmer is our Cinderella entry . . . a bundle of tenacity, battling her way through the choppy, murky waters of the cold Pacific to reach the Island of Romance . . . Santa Catalina . . . where should she be the first to arrive, two thousand dollars and a gold cup will be waiting for her.

Aída: Doesn't even cover our expenses.

Abuela: Qué dice?

Eduardo: Shhhh!

Mary Beth's Voice: This is really a family effort, Mel, and—

Mel's Voice: Indeed it is. Her trainer, her coach, her mentor, is her father, Eduardo Suárez. Not a swimmer himself, it says here, Mr. Suárez is head usher of the Holy Name Society and the owner-operator of Suárez Treasures of the Sea and Salvage Yard. I guess it's one of those places—

Virgencita de la Caridad del Cobre. Qué es eso?: Virgin of Charity. What is that? *un momentico . . . mi hija*: just a second, my daughter. *Por Dios!*: For God's Sake! *Papi! Qué está pasando?*: Dad! What's happening? *Que es la televisión dicen? Porque como yo no puedo ver nada sin mis espejuelos*: Did they say television? Because I can't see without my glasses.

Mary Beth's Voice: If I might interject a fact here, Mel, assisting in this swim is Mrs. Suárez, who is a former Miss Cuba.

Mel's Voice: And a beautiful woman in her own right. Let's try and get a closer look.

(Helicopter sound gets louder. Margarita, frightened, looks up again.)

Margarita: Papi!

Eduardo (through megaphone): Mi hija, don't get nervous . . . it's the press. I'm handling it.

Aída: I see how you're handling it.

Eduardo (through megaphone): Do you hear? Everything is under control. Get back into your rhythm. Keep your elbows high and kick and kick and kick and kick . . .

Abuela (finds her glasses and puts them on): Ay sí, es la televisión° . . . (She points to helicopter.) Qué lindo mira° . . . (She fluffs her hair, gives a big wave.) Aló América! Viva mi Margarita, viva todo los Cubanos en los Estados Unidos!°

Aída: Ay por Dios, Cecilia, the man didn't come all this way in his helicopter to look at you jumping up and down, making a fool of yourself.

Abuela: I don't care. I'm proud.

Aída: He can't understand you anyway.

Abuela: Viva . . . (She stops.) Simón, *cómo se dice viva?°*

Simón: Hurray.

Abuela: Hurray for *mi Margarita* y for all the Cubans living *en* the United States, *y un abrazo . . .* Simón, *abrazo . . .*

Simón: A big hug.

Abuela: Sí, a big hug to all my friends in Miami, Long Beach, Union City, except for my son Carlos, who lives in New York in sin! He lives . . . *(She crosses herself.)* in Brooklyn with a Puerto Rican woman in sin! *No decente . . .*

Simón: Decent.

Abuela: Carlos, *no decente.* This family, *decente.*

Aída: Cecilia, *por Dios.*

Mel's Voice: Look at that enthusiasm. The whole family has turned out to cheer little Margarita on to victory! I hope they won't be too disappointed.

Mary Beth's Voice: She seems to be making good time, Mel.

Mel's Voice: Yes, it takes all kinds to make a race. And it's a testimonial to the all-encompassing fairness . . . the greatness of this, the Wrigley Invitational Women's Swim to Catalina, where among all the

Ay sí, es la televisión: Oh yes, it is the television. *Qué lindo mira:* Look how pretty. *Aló América! Viva mi Margarita, viva todo los Cubanos en los Estados Unidos!:* Hello America! Hurray for my Margarita, hurray for all the Cubans in the United States! *cómo se dice viva?:* how do you say "viva" [in English]?

professionals there is still room for the amateurs . . . like these, the simple people we see below us on the ragtag *La Havana*, taking their long-shot chance to victory. *Vaya con Dios!*°

(Helicopter sound fading as family, including Margarita, watch silently. Static as Simón turns radio off. Eduardo walks to bow of boat, looks out on the horizon.)

Eduardo (to himself): Amateurs.
Aída: Eduardo, that person insulted us. Did you hear, Eduardo? That he called us a simple people in a ragtag boat? Did you hear . . . ?
Abuela (clenching her fist at departing helicopter): Mal-Rayo los parta!°
Simón (same gesture): Asshole!

(Aída follows Eduardo as he goes to side of boat and stares at Margarita.)

Aída: This person comes in his helicopter to insult your wife, your family, your daughter . . .
Margarita (pops her head out of the water): Papi?
Aída: Do you hear me, Eduardo? I am not simple.
Abuela: Sí.
Aída: I am complicated.
Abuela: Sí, demasiada complicada.
Aída: Me and my family are not so simple.
Simón: Mom, the guy's an asshole.
Abuela (shaking her fist at helicopter): Asshole!
Aída: If my daughter was simple, she would not be in that water swimming.
Margarita: Simple? *Papi . . .* ?
Aída: Ahora, Eduardo, this is what I want you to do. When we get to Santa Catalina, I want you to call the TV station and demand an apology.
Eduardo: Cállete mujer! Aquí mando yo.° I will decide what is to be done.
Margarita: Papi, tell me what's going on.
Eduardo: Do you understand what I am saying to you, Aída?
Simón (leaning over side of boat, to Margarita): Yo Margo! You know that Mel Munson guy on TV? He called you a simple amateur and said you didn't have a chance.
Abuela (leaning directly behind Simón): Mi hija, insultó a la familia. Desgraciado!
Aída (leaning in behind Abuela): He called us peasants! And your father is not doing anything about it. He just knows how to yell at me.
Eduardo (through megaphone): Shut up! All of you! Do you want to break her concentration? Is that what you are after? Eh?

Vaya con Dios!: Go with God! [God bless you.] *Mal-Rayo los parta!*: To hell with you! *Cállete mujer! Aquí mando yo*: Quiet woman! I'm in charge here.

(Abuela, Aída and Simón shrink back. Eduardo paces before them.)

Swimming is rhythm and concentration. You win a race aquí. (Pointing to his head.) Now . . . (To Simón.) you, take care of the boat, Aída y Mama . . . do something. Anything. Something practical.

(Abuela and Aída get on knees and pray in Spanish.)

Hija, give it everything, eh? . . . por la familia. Uno . . . dos. . . . You must win.

(Simón goes into cabin. The prayers continue as lights change to indicate bright sunlight, later in the afternoon.)

SCENE III

Tableau for a couple of beats. Eduardo on bow with timer in one hand as he counts strokes per minute. Simón is in the cabin steering, wearing his sunglasses, baseball cap on backward. Abuela and Aída are at the side of the boat, heads down, hands folded, still muttering prayers in Spanish.

Aída and Abuela (crossing themselves): En el nombre del Padre, del Hijo y del Espíritu Santo amén.°

Eduardo (through megaphone): You're stroking seventy-two!

Simón (singing): Mama's stroking, Mama's stroking seventy-two. . . .

Eduardo (through megaphone): You comfortable with it?

Simón (singing): Seventy-two, seventy-two, seventy-two for you.

Aída (looking at the heavens): Ay, Eduardo, *ven acá,*° we should be grateful that *Nuestro Señor*° gave us such a beautiful day.

Abuela (crosses herself): Sí, gracias a Dios.°

Eduardo: She's stroking seventy-two, with no problem. *(He throws a kiss to the sky.)* It's a beautiful day to win.

Aída: Qué hermoso!° So clear and bright. Not a cloud in the sky. *Mira! Mira!*° Even rainbows on the water . . . a sign from God.

Simón (singing): Rainbows on the water . . . you in my arms . . .

Abuela and Eduardo (looking the wrong way): Dónde?

Aída (pointing toward Margarita): There, dancing in front of Margarita, leading her on . . .

Eduardo: Rainbows on . . . *Ay coño!* It's an oil slick! You . . . you . . . *(To Simón.)* Stop the boat. *(Runs to bow, yelling.)* Margarita! Margarita!

(On the next stroke, Margarita comes up all covered in black oil.)

En el nombre del Padre, del Hijo y del Espíritu Santo amén: In the name of the Father, the Son, and the Holy Ghost, Amen. *ven acá:* look here. *Nuestro Señor:* Our Father [God]. *Sí, gracias a Dios:* Yes, thanks be to God. *Qué hermoso!:* How beautiful! *Mira!:* Look!

Margarita: Papi! Papi . . . !

(Everybody goes to the side and stares at Margarita, who stares back. Eduardo freezes.)

Aída: Apúrate, Eduardo, move . . . what's wrong with you . . . *no me oíste*,° get my daughter out of the water.

Eduardo (softly): We can't touch her. If we touch her, she's disqualified.

Aída: But I'm her mother.

Eduardo: Not even by her own mother. Especially by her own mother. . . . You always want the rules to be different for you, you always want to be the exception. *(To Simón.)* And you . . . you didn't see it, eh? You were playing again?

Simón: Papi, I was watching . . .

Aída (interrupting): Pues, do something Eduardo. You are the big coach, the monitor.

Simón: Mentor! Mentor!

Eduardo: How can a person think around you? *(He walks off to bow, puts head in hands.)*

Abuela (looking over side): Mira como todos los little birds are dead. *(She crosses herself)*

Aída: Their little wings are glued to their sides.

Simón: Christ, this is like the La Brea tar pits.

Aída: They can't move their little wings.

Abuela: Esa niña tiene que moverse.°

Simón: Yeah, Margo, you gotta move, man.

(Abuela and Simón gesture for Margarita to move. Aída gestures for her to swim.)

Abuela: Anda niña, muévete.°

Aída: Swim, *hija*, swim or the *aceite*° will stick to your wings.

Margarita: Papi?

Abuela (taking megaphone): Your *papi* say "move it!"

(Margarita with difficulty starts moving.)

Abuela, Aída and Simón (laboriously counting): Uno, dos . . . uno, dos . . . anda . . . uno, dos.

Eduardo (running to take megaphone from Abuela): Uno, dos . . .

(Simón races into cabin and starts the engine. Abuela, Aída and Eduardo count together.)

Simón (looking ahead): Papi, it's over there!

Eduardo: Eh?

Apúrate . . . no me oíste: Finish this . . . didn't you hear me? *Esa niña tiene que moverse:* That girl has to move. *Anda niña, muévete:* Come on, girl, move. *aceite:* oil.

Simón (pointing ahead and to the right): It's getting clearer over there.
Eduardo (through megaphone): Now pay attention to me. Go to the right.

(Simón, Abuela, Aída and Eduardo all lean over side. They point ahead and to the right, except Abuela, who points to the left.)

Family (shouting together): Para yá!° *Para yá!*

(Lights go down on boat. A special light on Margarita, swimming through the oil, and on Abuela, watching her.)

Abuela: Sangre de mi sangre,° you will be another to save us. En Bolondron, where your great-grandmother Luz Suárez was born, they say one day it rained blood. All the people, they run into their houses. They cry, they pray, *pero* your great-grandmother Luz she had *cojones* like a man. She run outside. She look straight at the sky. She shake her fist. And she say to the evil one, "*Mira . . . (Beating her chest.) coño, Diablo, aquí estoy si me quieres.*"° And she open her mouth, and she drunk the blood.

BLACKOUT

SCENE IV

Lights up on boat. Aída and Eduardo are on deck watching Margarita swim. We hear the gentle, rhythmic lap, lap, lap of the water, then the sound of inhaling and exhaling as Margarita's breathing becomes louder. Then Margarita's heartbeat is heard, with the lapping of the water and the breathing under it. These sounds continue beneath the dialogue to the end of the scene.

Aída: Dios mío. Look how she moves through the water. . . .
Eduardo: You see, it's very simple. It is a matter of concentration.
Aída: The first time I put her in water she came to life, she grew before my eyes. She moved, she smiled, she loved it more than me. She didn't want my breast any longer. She wanted the water.
Eduardo: And of course, the rhythm. The rhythm takes away the pain and helps the concentration.

(Pause. Aída and Eduardo watch Margarita.)

Aída: Is that my child or a seal. . . .
Eduardo: Ah, a seal, the reason for that is that she's keeping her arms very close to her body. She cups her hands, and then she reaches and digs, reaches and digs.
Aída: To think that a daughter of mine. . . .
Eduardo: It's the training, the hours in the water. I used to tie weights around her little wrists and ankles.

Para yá: Over there. *Sangre de mi sangre:* Blood of my blood. *Mira . . . coño, Diablo, aquí estoy si me quieres:* Look . . . damn it, Devil, here I am if you want me.

Aída: A spirit, an ocean spirit, must have entered my body when I was carrying her.

Eduardo (to Margarita): Your stroke is slowing down.

(Pause. We hear Margarita's heartbeat with the breathing under, faster now.)

Aída: Eduardo, that night, the night on the boat . . .

Eduardo: Ah, the night on the boat again . . . the moon was . . .

Aída: The moon was full. We were coming to America. . . . *Qué romantico.*

(Heartbeat and breathing continue.)

Eduardo: We were cold, afraid, with no money, and on top of everything, you were hysterical, yelling at me, tearing at me with your nails. *(Opens his shirt, points to the base of his neck.)* Look, I still bear the scars . . . telling me that I didn't know what I was doing . . . saying that we were going to die. . . .

Aída: You took me, you stole me from my home . . . you didn't give me a chance to prepare. You just said we have to go now, now! Now, you said. You didn't let me take anything. I left everything behind. . . . I left everything behind.

Eduardo: Saying that I wasn't good enough, that your father didn't raise you so that I could drown you in the sea.

Aída: You didn't let me say even a good-bye. You took me, you stole me, you tore me from my home.

Eduardo: I took you so we could be married.

Aída: That was in Miami. But that night on the boat, Eduardo. . . . We were not married, that night on the boat.

Eduardo: No pasó nada!° Once and for all get it out of your head, it was cold, you hated me, and we were afraid. . . .

Aída: Mentiroso!°

Eduardo: A man can't do it when he is afraid.

Aída: Liar! You did it very well.

Eduardo: I did?

Aída: Sí. Gentle. You were so gentle and then strong . . . my passion for you so deep. Standing next to you . . . I would ache . . . looking at your hands I would forget to breathe, you were irresistible.

Eduardo: I was?

Aída: You took me into your arms, you touched my face with your fingertips . . . you kissed my eyes . . . *la esquina de la boca y*° . . .

Eduardo: Sí, Sí, and then . . .

Aída: I look at your face on top of mine, and I see the lights of Havana in your eyes. That's when you seduced me.

Eduardo: Shhh, they're gonna hear you.

No pasó nada!: Nothing happened! *Mentiroso!*: Liar! *la esquina de la boca y . . .* : the corner of the mouth and . . .

(Lights go down. Special on Aída.)

Aída: That was the night. A woman doesn't forget those things . . . and later that night was the dream . . . the dream of a big country with fields of fertile land and big, giant things growing. And there by a green, slimy pond I found a giant pea pod and when I opened it, it was full of little, tiny baby frogs.

(Aída crosses herself as she watches Margarita. We hear louder breathing and heartbeat.)

Margarita: Santa Teresa. Little Flower of God, pray for me. San Martín de Porres, pray for me. Santa Rosa de Lima, *Virgencita de la Caridad del Cobre*, pray for me. . . . Mother pray for me.

SCENE V

Loud howling of wind is heard, as lights change to indicate unstable weather, fog and mist. Family on deck, braced and huddled against the wind. Simón is at the helm.

Aída: Ay Dios mío, qué viento.°
Eduardo (through megaphone): Don't drift out . . . that wind is pushing you out. *(To Simón.)* You! Slow down. Can't you see your sister is drifting out?
Simón: It's the wind, *Papi*.
Aída: Baby, don't go so far. . . .
Abuela (to heaven): Ay Gran Poder de Dios, quita este maldito viento.°
Simón: Margo! Margo! Stay close to the boat.
Eduardo: Dig in. Dig in hard. . . . Reach down from your guts and dig in.
Abuela (to heaven): Ay Virgen de la Caridad del Cobre, por lo más tú quieres a pararla.
Aída (putting her hand out, reaching for Margarita): Baby, don't go far.

(Abuela crosses herself. Action freezes. Lights get dimmer, special on Margarita. She keeps swimming, stops, starts again, stops, then, finally exhausted, stops altogether. The boat stops moving.)

Eduardo: What's going on here? Why are we stopping?
Simón: Papi, she's not moving! Yo Margo!

(The family all run to the side.)

Eduardo: Hija! . . . Hijita! You're tired, eh?
Aída: Por supuesto she's tired. I like to see you get in the water, waving your arms and legs from San Pedro to Santa Catalina. A person isn't a machine, a person has to rest.

Ay Dios mío, qué viento: Oh my God, what wind. *Ay Gran Poder de Dios, quita este maldito viento:* By the great power of God, keep the cursed winds away.

Simón: Yo, Mama! Cool out, it ain't fucking brain surgery.

Eduardo (to Simón): Shut up, you. *(Louder to Margarita.)* I guess your mother's right for once, huh? . . . I guess you had to stop, eh? . . . Give your brother, the idiot . . . a chance to catch up with you.

Simón (clowning like Mortimer Snerd): Dum dee dum dee dum ooops, ah shucks . . .

Eduardo: I don't think he's Cuban.

Simón (like Ricky Ricardo): Oye, Lucy! I'm home! Ba ba lu!

Eduardo (joins in clowning, grabbing Simón in a headlock): What am I gonna do with this idiot, eh? I don't understand this idiot. He's not like us, Margarita. *(Laughing.)* You think if we put him into your bathing suit with a cap on his head . . . *(He laughs hysterically.)* You think anyone would know . . . huh? Do you think anyone would know? *(Laughs.)*

Simón (vamping): Ay, mi amor. Anybody looking for tits would know.

(Eduardo slaps Simón across the face, knocking him down. Aída runs to Simón's aid. Abuela holds Eduardo back.)

Margarita: Mía culpa!° Mía culpa!

Abuela: Qué dices hija?

Margarita: Papi, it's my fault, it's all my fault. . . . I'm so cold, I can't move. . . . I put my face in the water . . . and I hear them whispering . . . laughing at me. . . .

Aída: Who is laughing at you?

Margarita: The fish are all biting me . . . they hate me . . . they whisper about me. She can't swim, they say. She can't glide. She has no grace. . . . Yellowtails, bonita, tuna, man-o'-war, snub-nose sharks, *los baracudas* . . . they all hate me . . . only the dolphins care . . . and sometimes I hear the whales crying . . . she is lost, she is dead. I'm so numb, I can't feel. *Papi! Papi!* Am I dead?

Eduardo: Vamos, baby, punch those arms in. Come on . . . do you hear me?

Margarita: Papi . . . Papi . . . forgive me. . . .

(All is silent on the boat. Eduardo drops his megaphone, his head bent down in dejection. Abuela, Aída, Simón, all leaning over the side of the boat. Simón slowly walks away.)

Aída: Mi hija, qué tienes?

Simón: Oh, Christ, don't make her say it. Please don't make her say it.

Abuela: Say what? *Qué cosa?*

Simón: She wants to quit, can't you see she's had enough?

Abuela: Mira, para eso. Esta niña is turning blue.

Aída: Oyeme, mi hija. Do you want to come out of the water?

Margarita: Papi?

Simón (to Eduardo): She won't come out until *you* tell her.

Mía culpa!: It's my fault!

Aída: Eduardo . . . answer your daughter.

Eduardo: Le dije to concentrate . . . concentrate on your rhythm. Then the rhythm would carry her . . . ay, it's a beautiful thing, Aída. It's like yoga, like meditation, the mind over matter . . . the mind controlling the body . . . that's how the great things in the world have been done. I wish you . . . I wish my wife could understand.

Margarita: Papi?

Simón (to Margarita): Forget him.

Aída (imploring): Eduardo, *por favor.*

Eduardo (walking in circles): Why didn't you let her concentrate? Don't you understand, the concentration, the rhythm is everything. But no, you wouldn't listen. *(Screaming to the ocean.)* Goddamn Cubans, why, God, why do you make us go everywhere with our families? *(He goes to back of boat.)*

Aída (opening her arms): Mi hija, ven, come to *Mami. (Rocking.)* Your *mami* knows.

(Abuela has taken the training bottle, puts it in a net. She and Simón lower it to Margarita.)

Simón: Take this. Drink it. *(As Margarita drinks, Abuela crosses herself.)*

Abuela: Sangre de mi sangre.

(Music comes up softly. Margarita drinks, gives the bottle back, stretches out her arms, as if on a cross. Floats on her back. She begins a graceful backstroke. Lights fade on boat as special lights come up on Margarita. She stops. Slowly turns over and starts to swim, gradually picking up speed. Suddenly as if in pain she stops, tries again, then stops in pain again. She becomes disoriented and falls to the bottom of the sea. Special on Margarita at the bottom of the sea.)

Margarita: Ya no puedo . . . I can't. . . . A person isn't a machine . . . *es mi culpa* . . . Father forgive me . . . *Papi! Papi!* One, two. *Uno, dos. (Pause.) Papi! A dónde estás? (Pause.)* One, two, one, two. *Papi! Ay, Papi!* Where are you . . . ? Don't leave me. . . . Why don't you answer me? *(Pause. She starts to swim, slowly.) Uno, dos, uno, dos.* Dig in, dig in. *(Stops swimming.) Por favor, Papi! (Starts to swim again.)* One, two, one, two. Kick from your hip, kick from your hip. *(Stops swimming. Starts to cry.)* Oh God, please. . . . *(Pause.)* Hail Mary, full of grace . . . dig in, dig in . . . the Lord is with thee. . . . *(She swims to the rhythm of her Hail Mary.)* Hail Mary, full of grace . . . dig in, dig in . . . the Lord is with thee . . . dig in, dig in. . . . Blessed art thou among women. . . . *Mami,* it hurts. You let go of my hand. I'm lost. . . . And blessed is the fruit of thy womb, now and at the hour of our death. Amen. I don't want to die, I don't want to die.

(Margarita is still swimming. Blackout. She is gone.)

SCENE VI

Lights up on boat, we hear radio static. There is a heavy mist. On deck we see only black outline of Abuela with shawl over her head. We hear the voices of Eduardo, Aída, and Radio Operator.

Eduardo's Voice: La Havana! Coming from San Pedro. Over.

Radio Operator's Voice: Right, DT6-6, you say you've lost a swimmer.

Aída's Voice: Our child, our only daughter . . . listen to me. Her name is Margarita Inez Suárez, she is wearing a black one-piece bathing suit cut high in the legs with a white racing stripe down the sides, a white bathing cap with goggles and her whole body covered with a . . . with a . . .

Eduardo's Voice: With lanolin and paraffin.

Aída's Voice: Sí . . . con lanolin and paraffin.

(More radio static. Special on Simón, on the edge of the boat.)

Simón: Margo! Yo Margo! *(Pause.)* Man don't do this. *(Pause.)* Come on. . . . Come on. . . . *(Pause.)* God, why does everything have to be so hard? *(Pause.)* Stupid. You know you're not supposed to die for this. Stupid. It's his dream and he can't even swim. *(Pause.)* Punch those arms in. Come home. Come home. I'm your little brother. Don't forget what Mama said. You're not supposed to leave me behind. *Vamos*, Margarita, take your little brother, hold his hand tight when you cross the street. He's so little. *(Pause.)* Oh Christ, give us a sign. . . . I know! I know! Margo, I'll send you a message . . . like mental telepathy. I'll hold my breath, close my eyes, and I'll bring you home. *(He takes a deep breath; a few beats.)* This time I'll beep . . . I'll send out sonar signals like a dolphin. *(He imitates dolphin sounds.)*

(The sound of real dolphins takes over from Simón, then fades into sound of Abuela saying the Hail Mary in Spanish, as full lights come up slowly.)

SCENE VII

Eduardo coming out of cabin, sobbing, Aída holding him. Simón anxiously scanning the horizon. Abuela looking calmly ahead.

Eduardo: Es mi culpa, sí, es mi culpa.° *(He hits his chest.)*

Aída: Ya, ya viejo.° . . . it was my sin . . . I left my home.

Eduardo: Forgive me, forgive me. I've lost our daughter, our sister, our granddaughter, *mi carne, mi sangre, mis ilusiones.*° *(To heaven.) Dios mío*, take me . . . take me, I say . . . Goddammit, take me!

Simón: I'm going in.

Es mi culpa, sí, es mi culpa: It's my fault, yes, it's my fault. *Ya, ya viejo:* Yes, yes, old man. *mi carne, mi sangre, mis ilusiones:* my flesh, my blood, my dreams.

Aída and Eduardo: No!

Eduardo (grabbing and holding Simón, speaking to heaven): God, take me, not my children. They are my dreams, my illusions . . . and not this one, this one is my mystery . . . he has my secret dreams. In him are the parts of me I cannot see.

(Eduardo embraces Simón. Radio static becomes louder.)

Aída: I . . . I think I see her.

Simón: No, it's just a seal.

Abuela (looking out with binoculars): Mi nietacita, dónde estás? (She feels her heart.) I don't feel the knife in my heart . . . my little fish is not lost.

(Radio crackles with static. As lights dim on boat, Voices of Mel and Mary Beth are heard over the radio.)

Mel's Voice: Tragedy has marred the face of the Wrigley Invitational Women's Race to Catalina. The Cuban swimmer, little Margarita Suárez, has reportedly been lost at sea. Coast Guard and divers are looking for her as we speak. Yet in spite of this tragedy the race must go on because . . .

Mary Beth's Voice (interrupting loudly): Mel!

Mel's Voice (startled): What!

Mary Beth's Voice: Ah . . . excuse me, Mel . . . we have a winner. We've just received word from Catalina that one of the swimmers is just fifty yards from the breakers . . . it's, oh, it's . . . Margarita Suárez!

(Special on family in cabin listening to radio.)

Mel's Voice: What? I thought she died!

(Special on Margarita, taking off bathing cap, trophy in hand, walking on the water.)

Mary Beth's Voice: Ahh . . . unless . . . unless this is a tragic . . . No . . . there she is, Mel. Margarita Suárez! The only one in the race wearing a black bathing suit cut high in the legs with a racing stripe down the side.

(Family cheering, embracing.)

Simón (screaming): Way to go, Margo!

Mel's Voice: This is indeed a miracle! It's a resurrection! Margarita Suárez, with a flotilla of boats to meet her, is now walking on the waters, through the breakers . . . onto the beach, with crowds of people cheering her on. What a jubilation! This is a miracle!

(Sound of crowds cheering. Lights and cheering sounds fade.)

BLACKOUT

DOCUMENTARY DRAMA

Some playwrights combine experimental and naturalistic elements, creating documentary works that dramatize actual events. British dramatist Michael Frayn presented the European physicists who did the work preceding the atom bomb in *Copenhagen* (1998) and explored the career of director Max Reinhardt in Nazi-era Austria in *Afterlife* (2008). Actress-playwright Anna Deavere Smith created an extremely innovative version of documentary drama in which she performed *all* of the roles herself in bravura one-woman shows. Using the actual words of real people, she constructed performance pieces to explore complex social events such as the race riots in Crown Heights, Brooklyn, in 1991 and in Los Angeles in 1992.

Anna Deavere Smith

Scenes from Twilight: Los Angeles, 1992 — 1994

Anna Deavere Smith

Anna Deavere Smith was born in Baltimore, Maryland, in 1950, the daughter of a businessman and an elementary school principal. She graduated from Beaver College in 1971 and earned a Master of Fine Arts degree from the American Conservatory Theater in 1977. She taught drama at Stanford University from 1990 to 2000 and is presently a professor at both the Tisch School of the Arts at New York University and the NYU School of Law. Over many years Smith has conducted more than two thousand interviews; from them she has fashioned a number of works of "documentary theater," each of which is a stage presentation in which a single performer speaks a series of monologues using the actual words of her interview subjects. The best-known of these are Fires in the Mirror *(1993), drawn from the 1991 race riots in Crown Heights, Brooklyn,* Twilight: Los Angeles, 1992 *(1994), derived from the 1992 riot in that city, and* Let Me Down Easy *(2009), which examines health care issues. Smith has frequently performed these pieces herself, winning rave reviews both for the works and for her extraordinary ability to bring to life characters of both sexes and many ages and races. In its review of* Twilight: Los Angeles, 1992, *the* New York Times *said: "Anna Deavere Smith is the ultimate impressionist: she does people's souls." As an actress, she has also made many appearances on stage and in films, including* Philadelphia *and* The American President, *and has been seen on television in* The West Wing *and* Nurse Jackie. *Included here are three scenes from the more than fifty monologues in* Twilight: Los Angeles, 1992.

CHARACTERS

Angela King, Rodney King's aunt, African American
Mrs. *Young-Soon Han*, former liquor store owner, Korean American, 40s, heavy accent

Twilight Bey, gang truce organizer, African American, early 30s/late 20s, Crips gang.

GENERAL PRODUCTION NOTE

A slide with the following language should begin the show, just after lights down and before any other visual image:

This play is based on interviews conducted by Anna Deavere Smith soon after the race riots in Los Angeles of 1992. All words were spoken by real people and are verbatim from those interviews.

ANGELA KING

Rodney King's Aunt

Here's a Nobody

Returning from white iron-gated doorway. To her stool. Heavy pounding rain outside. Day. On her stool, in her studio. Crying, has been crying, prior to the speech for ten minutes straight.

We weren't raised like this.
We weren't raised with no black and white thing.
We were raised with all kinds of friends.
Mexicans, Indians, blacks, whites, Chinese
Most of our friends were Spanish.
Who'd have thought this would happen to us?
Well, I guess there's a first time for everything you know.

(Blowing her nose, she stops crying. A sense in the rest of the speech that she is recovering from a long cry.)

I guess you want me to tell the story
I don't know if you understand sometimes I'm just not in the mood, you know just not in the mood.

(Slight pause.)

His brother Galen called to say "Cops done beat Glen up!"
Talkin' about Rodney.
I said "What?"
"Police. They got it on tape."
And when I was just turning the channels
I saw this white car.
I heard him holler,
I recognized him layin' there on the ground

that's what got me.
And he looked just like his father too.
Galen was the one used to favor his father.
Now Rodney looks just like him, identical.
I don't know if it's when you lose a life
it comes back in somebody else.
Oh you should have seen him.
It's a hell of a look.
went through three plastic surgeons just to get Rodney to look like
Rodney again.
I tell him he's got a lot
to be thankful for.
A hell of a lot.
He couldn't talk, just der der der
I said, "Goddamn!"

(Angry.)

My brother's son out there was lookin' like hell
that I saw in that bed and I was gonna fight for every bit of
our justice and fairness.
That (Officer) Koon
that's the one in the whole trial,
that man showed no-kind-of-remorse-at-all,
you know that?
He sit there like "it ain't
no big thing
and I
will do it it *again.*"
And he smile at you.
The nerve,
the audacity!
But I didn't give a damn if it was the President's
whatever it was.

(Slight pause, responding to a question.)

You see how everybody rave when something happens with the
President of the United States?
You know, 'cause he's a higher sort?
Okay, here's a nobody.
But the way they beat him.
This is the way I felt towards him.
You understand what I'm sayin' now?
You do? Alright.

(She lights a "More" cigarette, or long brown cigarette.)

MRS. YOUNG-SOON HAN

Former Liquor Store Owner

Swallowing the Bitterness

At a low coffee table. Deep voice.

When I was in Korea,
I used to watch many luxurious Hollywood lifestyle movies.
I never saw any poor man,
any black
maybe one housemaid?
Until last year
I believed America is the best.
I still believe it.
I don't deny that now.
Because I'm victim.
But
as
the year ends in ninety-two,
and we were still in turmoil,
and having all the financial problems,
and mental problems,
then a couple months ago,
I really realized that
Korean immigrants were left out
from this
society and we were nothing.
What is our right?
Is it because we are Korean?
Is it because we have no politicians?
Is it because we don't
speak good English?
Why?
Why do we have to be left out?

(She is hitting her hand on the coffee table.)

We are not qualified to have medical treatment!
We are not qualified to get, uh,
food stamps!

(She hits the table once.)

Anna Deavere Smith as Mrs. Young-Soon Han.

No GR!

(Hits the table once.)

No welfare!

(Hits the table once.)

Anything!
Many Afro-Americans

(Two quick hits.)

who never worked

(One hit.)

they get
at least minimum amount

(One hit.)

of money

(One hit.)

to survive!

(One hit.)

We don't get any!

(Large hit with full hand spread.)

Because we have a *car*!

(One hit.)

and we have a *house*!

(Pause six seconds.)

And we are *high tax payers*!

(One hit.)

(Pause fourteen seconds.)

Where do I finda [sic] justice?
Okay, black people
Probably,
believe they won
by the trial?
Even some complains only half, right
justice was there?
But I watched the television
that Sunday morning
Early morning as they started
I started watch it all day.
They were having party, and then they celebrated *(Pronounced ceLEbreted.)*
all of South Central,
all the churches,
they finally found that justice exists
in this society.
Then where is the victims' rights?
They got their rights
by destroying *innocent Korean merchants* *(Louder.)*
They have a lot of respect, *(Softer.)*
as I do
for Dr. Martin King?
He is the only model for black community.
I don't care Jesse Jackson.
But,
he was the model
of non-violence
Non-violence?
They like to have hiseh [sic] spirits.

What about last year?
They destroyed innocent people!

(Five second pause.)

And I wonder if that is really justice, *(And a very soft "uh" after "justice" like "justicah," but very quick.)*
to get their rights
in this way.

(Thirteen second pause.)

I waseh swallowing the bitternesseh.
Sitting here alone, and watching them.
They became all hilarious.

(Three second pause.)

And uh,
in a way I was happy for them,
and I felt glad for them,
at least they got something back, you know.
Just lets forget Korean victims or other victims
who are destroyed by them.
They have fought
for their rights

(One hit simultaneous with the word "rights.")

over two centuries

(One hit simultaneous with "centuries.")

and I have a lot of sympathy and understanding for them.
Because of their effort, and sacrificing,
other minorities, like Hispanic
or Asians
maybe we have to suffer more
by mainstream,
you know?
That's why I understand.
And then
I like to be part of their
'joyment.
But.
That's why I had mixed feeling
as soon as I heard the verdict.
I wish I could
live together

with eh [sic] blacks
but after the riots
there were too much differences
The fire is still there
how do you call it

(She says a Korean word asking for translation. In Korean, she says "igniting fire.")

igni
igniting fire
It canuh
burst out any time.

TWILIGHT BEY

Organizer, Gang Truce

Limbo

Walking the full stage and around the table from the dinner party.

So a lot of times when I've brought up ideas to my homeboys,
They say
"Twilight
that's before your time
that's something you can't do now."
When I talked about the truce back in 1988,
that was something they considered before its time.
Yet
in 1992,
we made it
realistic.
So to me, it's like I'm stuck in limbo,
like the sun is stuck between night and day,
in the twilight hours,
You know?
I'm in an area not many people exist.
Night time to me
is like a lack of sun.
And I don't affiliate
darkness with anything negative.
I affiliate
darkness of what was first
because it *was first*

Anna Deavere Smith as Twilight Bey.

and then relative to my complexion,
I am a *dark* individual,
and with me stuck in limbo
I see the darkness as myself
I see the light *(he lights a candle)* as knowledge and the wisdom
of the world and understanding others.
And in order for me to be, a to be, a true human being.
I can't forever dwell in darkness.
I can't forever dwell in the idea,
just identifying with people like me, and understanding me and
mine.
So twilight
is
that time
between day and night
limbo
I call it limbo.

(He blows out the candle and walks off the stage.)

Questions

1. Angela King says of her nephew, Rodney, "I tell him he's got a lot / to be thankful for." Is she being deliberately ironic? Is there a larger irony in her comment?
2. Do you find Mrs. Young-Soon Han to be a sympathetic character? Why or why not?
3. Does the speech by Twilight Bey, which concludes the play, seem conciliatory? Does it explain why the play is called *Twilight*?
4. Taking these monologues together, what do you see as the mood that emerges from the text—despair? hopefulness? resignation? Explain.

WRITING *effectively*

THINKING ABOUT DRAMATIC REALISM

When critics use the word *realism* in relation to a play, are they claiming it is true to life? Not necessarily. Realism generally refers to certain dramatic conventions that emerged during the nineteenth century. A realistic play is not necessarily any truer to life than an experimental one, although the conventions of Realist drama have become so familiar to us that other kinds of drama—though no more artificial—can seem mannered and even bizarre to the casual viewer. Remember, though, that all drama—even the theater of Realism—is artifice.

- **Notice the conventions of Realist drama.** Compare, for example, a play by Henrik Ibsen with one by Sophocles. Ibsen's characters speak in prose, not verse. His settings are drawn from contemporary life, not a legendary past. His characters are ordinary middle-class citizens, not kings, queens, and aristocrats.
- **Be aware that the inner lives, memories, and motivations of the characters play a crucial role in the dramatic action.** Ibsen, like other Realist playwrights, seeks to portray the complexity of human psychology—especially motivation—in detailed, subtle ways. In contrast, Shakespeare appears less interested in the reason for Iago's villainy than its consequences. Did Iago have an unhappy childhood or a troubled adolescence? These questions do not greatly matter in Renaissance drama, but to Ibsen they become central. In *A Doll's House*, for example, we can infer that Nora's self-absorption and naiveté result from her father's overprotection.

- **Remember though, Realist drama does not necessarily come any closer than other dramatic styles to getting at the truths of human existence.** *A Doll's House*, for example, does not provide a more profound picture of psychological struggle than *Oedipus the King*. But Ibsen does offer a more detailed view of his protagonist's inner life and her daily routine.

CHECKLIST: Writing About a Realist Play

- ☐ List every detail the play gives about the protagonist's past. How does each detail affect the character's current behavior?
- ☐ What is the protagonist's primary motivation? What are the origins of that motivation?
- ☐ Do the other characters understand the protagonist's deeper motivations?
- ☐ How much of the plot arises from misunderstandings among characters?
- ☐ Do major plot events grow from characters' interactions? Or, do they occur at random?
- ☐ How does the protagonist's psychology determine his or her reactions to events?

TOPICS FOR WRITING ON REALISM

1. *A Raisin in the Sun* takes its title from Langston Hughes's poem "Harlem" (Chapter 23). Read the poem, then write an essay in which you discuss how its theme applies to the members of the Younger family.
2. There is a great deal of conflict among the family members in *A Raisin in the Sun*. Are their arguments caused more by simple differences of opinion or by a failure to understand one another's feelings and desires? Refer as specifically as possible to the words and actions of the characters to back up your conclusions.
3. How relevant is *A Doll's House* today? Do women like Nora still exist? How about men like Torvald? Build an argument, either that the concerns of *A Doll's House* are timeless and universal or that the issues addressed by the play are historical, not contemporary.
4. Placing yourself in the character of Ibsen's Torvald Helmer, write a defense of him and his attitudes as he himself might write it.
5. Choose a character from Milcha Sanchez-Scott's *The Cuban Swimmer* and examine his or her motivations. What makes your character act as he or she does? Present evidence from the play to back up your argument.
6. Describe some of the difficulties of staging *The Cuban Swimmer* as a play. What would be lost or gained by remaking it as a movie?
7. How effective is the technique of *Twilight: Los Angeles, 1992*? Does the lack of interplay between characters make it less dramatic, or is there sufficient drama in what the speakers say and the ways in which they present themselves?

8. Write a paper that compares and contrasts the different points of view of two characters in *Twilight: Los Angeles, 1992*.
9. Imagine you're a casting director. Choose a play from this chapter and cast it with well-known television and movie stars. Explain, in depth, what qualities in the characters you hope to emphasize by your casting choices.
10. Al Capovilla of Folsom Lake Center College has developed an ingenious assignment based on Ibsen's *A Doll's House* that asks students to combine the skills of a literary critic with those of a lawyer. Here is Professor Capovilla's assignment:

> You are the family lawyer for Torvald and Nora Helmer. The couple comes to you with a request. They want you to listen to an account of their domestic problems and recommend whether they should pursue a divorce or try to reconcile.
>
> You listen to both sides of the argument. (You also know everything that is said by every character.)
>
> Now, it is your task to write a short decision. In stating your opinion, provide a clear and organized explanation of your reasoning. Show both sides of the argument. You may employ as evidence anything said or done in the play.
>
> Conclude your paper with your recommendation. What do you advise under the circumstances—divorce or an attempt at reconciliation?

TERMS FOR *review*

Realism ▸ An attempt to reproduce faithfully on the stage the surface appearance of life, especially that of ordinary people in everyday situations. In a historical sense, Realism (usually capitalized) refers to a movement in nineteenth-century European theater. Realist drama customarily focused on the middle class (and occasionally the working class) rather than the aristocracy.

Naturalism ▸ A type of drama in which the characters are presented as products or victims of environment and heredity. Naturalism, considered an extreme form of Realism, customarily depicts the social, psychological, and economic milieu of the primary characters.

Proscenium arch ▸ An architectural picture frame or gateway "standing in front of the scenery" (as the name *proscenium* indicates) that separates the auditorium from the raised stage and the world of the play.

Picture-frame stage ▸ A stage that holds the action within a proscenium arch, with painted scene panels (receding into the middle distance) designed to give the illusion of three-dimensional perspective. Picture-frame stages became the norm throughout Europe and England into the twentieth century.

Box set ▸ A stage set consisting of three walls joined in two corners and a ceiling that tilts, as if seen in perspective, to provide the illusion of scenic realism for interior rooms.

29 PLAYS FOR FURTHER READING

Sharon E. Cooper

Mistaken Identity 2004

The plays of Sharon E. Cooper (b. 1975) have been produced in the United States and abroad. Her work has won awards and been included in several annual editions of The Best Ten-Minute Plays. *Cooper's production credits include the plays* Painting Seventeen, Occupied, Lifeline, The Cooking King, *and* The Match. *Besides writing for theater and film, she works as a teacher and yoga instructor in New York City.* Mistaken Identity *premiered at the Open Space Arts Center in Reistertown, Maryland, in July 2004.*

Sharon E. Cooper

CHARACTERS

Kali Patel, 29. Single lesbian Hindu of Indian heritage; social worker who works as much as possible; lives in Leicester, England.

Steve Dodd, 32. Single straight guy, desperate to marry, raised Baptist but attends church only on Christmas and Easter; studying abroad for his final year.

SETTING. *The Castle, a pub in Kirby Muxlowe in Leicester, England.*

TIME. *The present.*

Lights up on Steve and Kali in a busy pub on their first date. They are in the middle of dinner.

Steve: You must get tired of fish and chips all the time. Why do y'all call them "chips"? When they're french fries, I mean. And you ever notice when people swear, they say, "Excuse my French." Not me. Nope. I have nothing against the French.

Kali: Right, well, I'm not French, Steve, now am I?

Steve: I just didn't want you to think I was prejudiced against the French or *anyone else*. . . . They're like your neighbors, the French. And your neighbors are like my neighbors. And like a good neighbor, State Farm is there. Have you heard that commercial?

Kali: What? No. Steve—

Steve: It's for insurance. Y'all must not play it here. (*Pause.*) So I know that you all do the "arranged marriage thing." Rashid and I had a long talk about it. Of course, Rashid and I wanted you to approve, too, Kali.

Kali: How twenty-first century of you and my brother. Steve . . .

Kali: I'm gay. / Steve: Will you marry me?

Kali: Come again? / Steve: What?

Kali: How could you ask me to . . . / Steve: Well, I can't believe this.

Kali: Bloody hell, stop talking while I'm talking . . . / Steve: This is very strange.

Kali: So—what?

Steve: This new information is, well, new, and changes things, I guess.

Kali: You guess? What the hell is wrong with you? I'm sorry, Steve, you just happened to show up at the end of a very long line of a lot of very bad dates. You know, movies where the bloke negotiates holding your hand while you're just trying to eat popcorn; running across De Montfort University in the pouring rain; dropping a bowling ball on the bloke's pizza.

Steve: You had me until the bowling ball. Kali, this doesn't make sense. I invite you out on a lovely date. We eat fish and chips—when I would rather be eating a burger or lasagna—

Kali: Steve, I'm sorry.

Steve: I figured we would have a nice long traditional wedding with the colorful tents. All of my family would be there. We're more of the Christmas/Easter Christians, so we'd do your religion and I would wear—

Kali (overlapping): You don't know anything about my people. What are you—

Steve (overlapping): Ooohhh, yes, I do. I saw *Monsoon Wedding.* And the director's cut! And I saw *Bend It Like Beckham* like three times. Three times. Unbelievable!

Kali: Yes, this makes loads of sense at the end of the day. I am a lesbian who has to date every Hindu bloke in England until her brother gets so desperate that he sets her up with a cowboy—

Steve: I take offense to that.

Kali (overlapping): But I should feel sorry for *you* because *you* watched *two*, count them, *two* movies about Indian people in your entire life and ordered fish when there are hamburgers on the menu! Forgive *me* for being so insensitive.

Steve: I ordered fish because I wanted you to like me. And I'm sure I've seen other Asian movies. Like all those fighting movies. You know, the ones where women are jumping through the air—

Kali: Aaahhh! Do you see how all of this is a moot point now?

Steve: I'm confused. Let's review.

Kali: Please, no, bloody hell, let's not review. Let's get the waiter. Haven't you had enough?

(She gets up. He follows.)

Steve (overlapping): Why is your brother setting up his *lesbian* sister—

Kali (overlapping): Will you please keep your voice down?

Steve (overlapping): —up on dates for marriage and tricking well-meaning men— specifically me—into proposing to her? I'm here to finish my business degree, but I wasn't born yesterday. So I took a few years off and changed careers a few times, was a fireman—

Kali (overlapping): What does that have to do with anything?

Steve: And I'm thirty-two years old, but that doesn't mean—

Kali: Mate, are you going to keep on and on?

Steve: Why did your brother put me through this? This isn't one of those new reality shows: "Big Brothers Set Up Their Lesbian Sisters." Is there a camera under the table? (*He looks.*) Let's talk about this. (*He sits back down.*) I'm a good listener. Go ahead. (*Pause.*) I'm listening. (*Pause.*) You have to say something if you want this to continue as what we call in America a conversation.

Kali: Are you done?

Steve: Go ahead.

(*She sits.*)

Kali: I guess I was hoping you wouldn't tell Rashid.

Steve: He doesn't know?

Kali: You are finishing your bachelor's degree, is that right?

Steve: If you're so "bloody" smart, I'm wondering why you would tell me, a man that is friends with your brother and sits next to him twice a week in eight A.M. classes—why would you tell *me* you're a lesbian and *not* your brother?

Kali: Maybe for the same reason you would ask a woman you've never met before to marry you.

Steve: Your brother made it sound like it would be easy. I've been looking for that.

Kali (overlapping): Look, you seem very nice, you do.

Steve: I am very nice.

Kali: And at the end of the day, I hope you find someone you like.

Steve: I like how you say "at the end of the day" and I like how you say "bloke" and "mate." It's so endearing. And you're beautiful and small and your hair falls on your back so.

Kali: Steve, being a lesbian is not negotiable. And don't start with how sexy it would be to be with me or to watch me and another woman—

Steve (overlapping): Kali, I didn't say any of that.

Kali: You didn't have to. Up until a few minutes ago, you thought I was a quiet, subservient Asian toy for sale from her brother. Steve, go get a doll. She can travel with you to America whenever you want. In the meantime, I'll continue to be a loud, abrasive (*Whispering.*) lesbian while my brother sets me up with every bloke on the street—and they don't even have to be Hindu anymore! Do you have any idea what that's like? (*Pause.*) How would you know?

Steve: You're right. I wouldn't.

Kali: Steve, why did you want to be with me? I mean, before.

Steve: I figured that we would have visited my family in the winter when it's so cold here. I would have been willing to stay here when I'm done with school and we would get a nice little place by the—

Kali: Steve, we hadn't even shared dessert yet.

Steve: Don't blame me for all of this. Five minutes ago, we were on a date.

Kali: We're just two people in a pub.

Steve: Kali, do you remember the last time someone—man woman, I don't care—had their hand down the small of your back or leaned into you like it didn't matter where you ended and they began?

Kali: Yes, I do remember that. And that was strangely poetic.

Steve: You don't have to sound so surprised. Anyway, I remember that feeling. Three years ago, at a Fourth of July celebration—you know, that's the holiday—

Kali: Yes, Steve, I know the holiday.

Steve: She was the only woman I ever really loved. I knew it was ending. Could taste it. I just held her as the fireworks went off and the dust got in our skin. Figured I would hold on, hoping that would keep me for a while. You know how they say babies will die if they're left alone too long. Always wondered if it's true for bigger people, too. Like how long would we last? . . . She left with her Pilates mat and Snoopy slippers a few days later. I bet it hasn't been three years for you.

Kali: No, it hasn't. But you wouldn't want to hear about that.

Steve: Why not?

Kali: Come on, Steve, I'm not here for your fantasies—

Steve: This thing where you assume you know what I'm thinking—it's gettin' old.

Kali: I'm . . . sorry. I do have a woman in my life, Michele—She's a teacher for people that are deaf. We've been together for seven months. The longest we were away from each other was this one time for three weeks. She was at a retreat where they weren't allowed to talk—you know, total immersion. So she would call and I would say, "Is it beautiful there, love?" and she would hit a couple of buttons. Sometimes she would leave me messages: "beep, beep, beep beep beep beep." It didn't matter that she didn't say anything . . . But I can't take her home for Diwali.

Steve: What's that?

Kali: It's a festival of lights where—

Steve: You mean like Hanukkah.

Kali: No, like Diwali. It's a New Year's celebration where we remember ancestors, family, and friends. And reflect back and look to the future.

Steve: It sounds nice. You know, my mother has been asking me for grandchildren since I turned twenty-seven. Every year at Christmas, it's the same: "I can't wait to hang another stocking for my grandchildren, if I ever get to have them."

Kali: Now, imagine that same conversation, well, not about Christmas, and what if you could never give that to them—could never bring someone home for any holiday for the rest of your life?

Steve: Then why don't you just tell them the truth?

Kali: I can't say, Mum, Daddy, Rashid, I've chosen women over men—it's not a hamburger over fish. You just don't know how they'll react. I'd run the risk of not being allowed to see my nieces. I'm so exhausted from hiding, I can barely breathe.

Steve: So stop hiding.

Kali: Have you been listening to what I've been saying?

Steve: Have you?

Kali: Are you going to tell my brother?

Steve: Do you want me to?

Kali: I don't know.

Steve: I've never thought about that thing that you said.

Kali: Which thing would that be?

Steve: The one where maybe you can't see your nieces 'cause you're gay. That must suck.

Kali: Yes, well, thanks for trying to make me feel better.

Steve: Listen, you get to decide what you tell your family and when. As far as I'm concerned, I'll tell Rashid tomorrow that we're getting married. Or I can tell him you're a lesbian, and if he doesn't let you be with his kids anymore, I'll punch him in the face. That was me kidding.

Kali: You're funny. (*Pause.*) Maybe I told you because somewhere deep down, I do want him to know. But I don't know if I can take the risk.

Steve: You don't have to rush.

Kali: I just wish it could be more simple. Like, why can't what I want be part of the whole picket-fence thing? That's pretty ridiculous, huh?

Steve: We're all looking for that. My grandparents met before World War II, dated for seven days in a row, and my grandfather asked my grandmother to go with him to Louisiana, where he'd be stationed. She said, "Is that a proposal?" And he said, "Of course it is." And they've been together ever since. And I just want that, too. Huh—asking you to marry me on a first date! You must think I'm pretty desperate, huh?

Kali: Not any more than the rest of us . . . Oh, hell, do you want to have some dessert?

Steve: Oh, hell, sure. You know, we're going to share dessert.

Kali: Hey, mate, no one said anything about sharing.

Steve: I would go home with you for Diwali. I mean, as friends. If you ever wanted one around. You're a nice girl, Kali. I mean woman, mate, bloke. I mean—

Kali: Sssshhhh. Let's just get some dessert.

(*Lights fade as they motion for the waiter. Blackout.*)

David Henry Hwang

The Sound of a Voice

1983

David Henry Hwang (b. 1957) grew up in San Gabriel, California, the son of first-generation Chinese immigrants. He was born into a family of musicians: his mother was a concert pianist, his sister plays cello in a string quartet, and he studied the violin. In 1979, as a senior at Stanford University, he directed his first play, F.O.B. *(an acronym for "fresh off the boat"), in a dormitory lounge.* F.O.B. *was later staged at the New York Shakespeare Festival Public Theater and won a 1981 Obie Award.* The Sound of a Voice *was also produced at the Public Theater as part of a double bill with another one-act play by Hwang,* The House of Sleeping Beauties. *Hwang enjoyed his greatest commercial and critical success with* M. Butterfly *(1988), which won the Tony Award for best play. His other plays include* Face Value *(1993),* Golden Child *(1997), and* Yellowface *(2007). While some of his plays are realistic in their approach, Hwang has always been fascinated by the possibilities of symbolic drama. In* The Sound of a Voice, *he creates a timeless, placeless scene in which two characters named Man and Woman act out a story reminiscent of a folk legend or a traditional Japanese* Nō *drama (a type of symbolic aristocratic drama developed in the fourteenth century in which a ghost recounts the struggles of his or her life for a traveler). Hwang's interest in nonrealistic and experimental drama has also led him to explore opera. He has collaborated with composer Philip Glass on three works:* 1000 Airplanes on the Roof *(1988), a science-fiction music drama;* The Voyage *(1992), an allegorical grand opera commissioned by New York's Metropolitan Opera for the 500th anniversary of Christopher Columbus's arrival in America; and* The Sound of a Voice *(2003), a combined staging of the following play with* The House of Sleeping Beauties. *He has also written the books for the shows* Aida *(2000), with music by Elton John and lyrics by Tim Rice, and* Tarzan *(2006), with music and lyrics by Phil Collins. Hwang lives in New York City.*

David Henry Hwang

CHARACTERS

Man, fifties, Japanese
Woman, fifties, Japanese

SETTING. *Woman's house, in a remote corner of the forest.*

SCENE I

Woman pours tea for Man. Man rubs himself, trying to get warm.

Man: You're very kind to take me in.
Woman: This is a remote corner of the world. Guests are rare.

American Repertory Theater's 2003 production of *The Sound of a Voice* in Cambridge, Massachusetts.

Man: The tea—you pour it well.
Woman: No.
Man: The sound it makes—in the cup—very soothing.
Woman: That is the tea's skill, not mine. *(She hands the cup to him.)* May I get you something else? Rice, perhaps?
Man: No.
Woman: And some vegetables?
Man: No, thank you.
Woman: Fish? *(Pause.)* It is at least two days' walk to the nearest village. I saw no horse. You must be very hungry. You would do a great honor to dine with me. Guests are rare.
Man: Thank you.
Woman (Woman gets up, leaves. Man holds the cup in his hands, using it to warm himself. He gets up, walks around the room. It is sparsely furnished, drab, except for one shelf on which stands a vase of brightly colored flowers. The flowers stand out in sharp contrast to the starkness of the room. Slowly, he reaches out towards them. He touches them. Quickly, he takes one of the flowers from the vase, hides it in his clothes. He returns to where he had sat previously. He waits. Woman re-enters. She carries a tray with food.): Please. Eat. It will give me great pleasure.
Man: This—this is magnificent.
Woman: Eat.

Man: Thank you. *(He motions for Woman to join him.)*
Woman: No, thank you.
Man: This is wonderful. The best I've tasted.
Woman: You are reckless in your flattery. But anything you say, I will enjoy hearing. It's not even the words. It's the sound of a voice, the way it moves through the air.
Man: How long has it been since you last had a visitor? *(Pause.)*
Woman: I don't know.
Man: Oh?
Woman: I lose track. Perhaps five months ago, perhaps ten years, perhaps yesterday. I don't consider time when there is no voice in the air. It's pointless. Time begins with the entrance of a visitor, and ends with his exit.
Man: And in between? You don't keep track of the days? You can't help but notice—
Woman: Of course I notice.
Man: Oh.
Woman: I notice, but I don't keep track. *(Pause.)* May I bring out more?
Man: More? No. No. This was wonderful.
Woman: I have more.
Man: Really—the best I've had.
Woman: You must be tired. Did you sleep in the forest last night?
Man: Yes.
Woman: Or did you not sleep at all?
Man: I slept.
Woman: Where?
Man: By a waterfall. The sound of the water put me to sleep. It rumbled like the sounds of a city. You see, I can't sleep in too much silence. It scares me. It makes me feel that I have no control over what is about to happen.
Woman: I feel the same way.
Man: But you live here—alone?
Woman: Yes.
Man: It's so quiet here. How can you sleep?
Woman: Tonight, I'll sleep. I'll lie down in the next room, and hear your breathing through the wall, and fall asleep shamelessly. There will be no silence.
Man: You're very kind to let me stay here.
Woman: This is yours. *(She unrolls a mat; there is a beautiful design of a flower on the mat. The flower looks exactly like the flowers in the vase.)*
Man: Did you make it yourself?
Woman: Yes. There is a place to wash outside.
Man: Thank you.
Woman: Goodnight.
Man: Goodnight. *(Man starts to leave.)*

Woman: May I know your name?

Man: No. I mean, I would rather not say. If I gave you a name, it would only be made-up. Why should I deceive you? You are too kind for that.

Woman: Then what should I call you? Perhaps—"Man Who Fears Silence"?

Man: How about, "Man Who Fears Women"?

Woman: That name is much too common.

Man: And you?

Woman: Yokiko.

Man: That's your name?

Woman: It's what you may call me.

Man: Goodnight, Yokiko. You are very kind.

Woman: You are very smart. Goodnight.

(Man exits. Hanako° goes to the mat. She tidies it, brushes it off. She goes to the vase. She picks up the flowers, studies them. She carries them out of the room with her. Man re-enters. He takes off his outer clothing. He glimpses the spot where the vase used to sit. He reaches into his clothing, pulls out the stolen flower. He studies it. He puts it underneath his head as he lies down to sleep, like a pillow. He starts to fall asleep. Suddenly, a start. He picks up his head. He listens.)

SCENE II

Dawn. Man is getting dressed. Woman enters with food.

Woman: Good morning.

Man: Good morning, Yokiko.

Woman: You weren't planning to leave?

Man: I have quite a distance to travel today.

Woman: Please. *(She offers him food.)*

Man: Thank you.

Woman: May I ask where you're travelling to?

Man: It's far.

Woman: I know this region well.

Man: Oh? Do you leave the house often?

Woman: I used to. I used to travel a great deal. I know the region from those days.

Man: You probably wouldn't know the place I'm headed.

Woman: Why not?

Man: It's new. A new village. It didn't exist in "those days." *(Pause.)*

Woman: I thought you said you wouldn't deceive me.

Hanako: The woman.

Man: I didn't. You don't believe me, do you?
Woman: No.
Man: Then I didn't deceive you. I'm travelling. That much is true.
Woman: Are you in such a hurry?
Man: Travelling is a matter of timing. Catching the light. *(Woman exits; Man finishes eating, puts down his bowl. Woman re-enters with the vase of flowers.)* Where did you find those? They don't grow native around these parts, do they?
Woman: No; they've all been brought in. They were brought in by visitors. Such as yourself. They were left here. In my custody.
Man: But—they look so fresh, so alive.
Woman: I take care of them. They remind me of the people and places outside this house.
Man: May I touch them?
Woman: Certainly.
Man: These have just blossomed.
Woman: No; they were in bloom yesterday. If you'd noticed them before, you would know that.
Man: You must have received these very recently. I would guess—within five days.
Woman: I don't know. But I wouldn't trust your estimate. It's all in the amount of care you show to them. I create a world which is outside the realm of what you know.
Man: What do you do?
Woman: I can't explain. Words are too inefficient. It takes hundreds of words to describe a single act of caring. With hundreds of acts, words become irrelevant. *(Pause.)* But perhaps you can stay.
Man: How long?
Woman: As long as you'd like.
Man: Why?
Woman: To see how I care for them.
Man: I *am* tired.
Woman: Rest.
Man: The light?
Woman: It will return.

SCENE III

Man is carrying chopped wood. He is stripped to the waist. Woman enters.

Woman: You're very kind to do that for me.
Man: I enjoy it, you know. Chopping wood. It's clean. No questions. You take your axe, you stand up the log, you aim—pow!—you either hit it or you don't. Success or failure.
Woman: You seem to have been very successful today.

Man: Why shouldn't I be? It's a beautiful day. I can see to those hills. The trees are cool. The sun is gentle. Ideal. If a man can't be successful on a day like this, he might as well kick the dust up into his own face. *(Man notices Woman staring at him. Man pats his belly, looks at her.)* Protection from falls.

Woman: What? *(Man pinches his belly, showing some fat.)* Oh. Don't be silly. *(Man begins slapping the fat on his belly to a rhythm.)*

Man: Listen—I can make music—see?—that wasn't always possible. But now—that I've developed this—whenever I need entertainment.

Woman: You shouldn't make fun of your body.

Man: Why not? I saw you. You were staring.

Woman: I wasn't making fun. *(Man inflates his cheeks.)* I was just—stop that!

Man: Then why were you staring?

Woman: I was—

Man: Laughing?

Woman: No.

Man: Well?

Woman: I was—Your body. It's . . . strong. *(Pause.)*

Man: People say that. But they don't know. I've heard that age brings wisdom. That's a laugh. The years don't accumulate here. They accumulate here. *(Pause; he pinches his belly.)* But today is a day to be happy, right? The woods. The sun. Blue. It's a happy day. I'm going to chop wood.

Woman: There's nothing left to chop. Look.

Man: Oh. I guess . . . that's it.

Woman: Sit. Here.

Man: But—

Woman: There's nothing left. *(Man sits; Woman stares at his belly.)* Learn to love it.

Man: Don't be ridiculous.

Woman: Touch it.

Man: It's flabby.

Woman: It's strong.

Man: It's weak.

Woman: And smooth.

Man: Do you mind if I put on my shirt?

Woman: Of course not. Shall I get it for you?

Man: No. No. Just sit there. *(Man starts to put on his shirt. He pauses, studies his body.)* You think it's cute, huh?

Woman: I think you should learn to love it. *(Man pats his belly, talks to it.)*

Man (to belly): You're okay, sir. You hang onto my body like a great horseman.

Woman: Not like that.

Man (ibid.°): You're also faithful. You'll never leave me for another man.

Woman: No.

Man: What do you want me to say? *(Woman walks over to Man. She touches his belly with her hand. They look at each other.)*

SCENE IV

Night. Man is alone. Flowers are gone from stand. Mat is unrolled. Man lies on it, sleeping. Suddenly, he starts. He lifts up his head. He listens. Silence. He goes back to sleep. Another start. He lifts up his head, strains to hear. Slowly, we begin to make out the strains of a single shakuhachi° *playing a haunting line. It is very soft. He strains to hear it. The instrument slowly fades out. He waits for it to return, but it does not. He takes out the stolen flower. He stares into it.*

SCENE V

Day. Woman is cleaning, while Man relaxes. She is on her hands and knees, scrubbing. She is dressed in a simple outfit, for working. Her hair is tied back. Man is sweating. He has not, however, removed his shirt.

Man: I heard your playing last night.

Woman: My playing?

Man: Shakuhachi.

Woman: Oh.

Man: You played very softly. I had to strain to hear it. Next time, don't be afraid. Play out. Fully. Clear. It must've been very beautiful, if only I could've heard it clearly. Why don't you play for me sometime?

Woman: I'm very shy about it.

Man: Why?

Woman: I play for my own satisfaction. That's all. It's something I developed on my own. I don't know if it's at all acceptable by outside standards.

Man: Play for me. I'll tell you.

Woman: No; I'm sure you're too knowledgeable in the arts.

Man: Who? Me?

Woman: You being from the city and all.

Man: I'm ignorant, believe me.

Woman: I'd play, and you'd probably bite your cheek.

Man: Ask me a question about music. Any question. I'll answer incorrectly. I guarantee it.

Woman: Look at this.

ibid.: an abbreviation of the Latin word *ibidem*, meaning "in the same place." *shakuhachi:* a Japanese bamboo flute.

Man: What?
Woman: A stain.
Man: Where?
Woman: Here? See? I can't get it out.
Man: Oh. I hadn't noticed it before.
Woman: I notice it every time I clean.
Man: Here. Let me try.
Woman: Thank you.
Man: Ugh. It's tough.
Woman: I know.
Man: How did it get here?
Woman: It's been there as long as I've lived here.
Man: I hardly stand a chance. *(Pause.)* But I'll try. Uh—one—two—three—four! One—two—three—four! See, you set up . . . gotta set up . . . a rhythm—two—three—four. Like fighting! Like battle! One—two—three—four! Used to practice with a rhythm . . . beat . . . battle! Yes! *(The stain starts to fade away.)* Look—it's—yes!—whoo!—there it goes—got the sides—the edges—yes!—fading quick—fading away—ooo—here we come—towards the center—to the heart—two—three—four—slow—slow death—tough—dead! *(Man rolls over in triumphant laughter.)*
Woman: Dead.
Man: I got it! I got it! Whoo! A little rhythm! All it took! Four! Four!
Woman: Thank you.
Man: I didn't think I could do it—but there—it's gone—I did it!
Woman: Yes. You did.
Man: And you—you were great.
Woman: No—I was carried away.
Man: We were a team! You and me!
Woman: I only provided encouragement.
Man: You were great! You were! *(Man grabs Woman. Pause.)*
Woman: It's gone. Thank you. Would you like to hear me play *shakuhachi*?
Man: Yes I would.
Woman: I don't usually play for visitors. It's so . . . I'm not sure. I developed it—all by myself—in times when I was alone. I heard nothing—no human voice. So I learned to play *shakuhachi*. I tried to make these sounds resemble the human voice. The *shakuhachi* became my weapon. To ward off the air. It kept me from choking on many a silent evening.
Man: I'm here. You can hear my voice.
Woman: Speak again.
Man: I will.

SCENE VI

Night. Man is sleeping. Suddenly, a start. He lifts his head up. He listens. Silence. He strains to hear. The shakuhachi *melody rises up once more. This time, however, it becomes louder and more clear than before. He gets up. He cannot tell from what direction the music is coming. He walks around the room, putting his ear to different places in the wall, but he cannot locate the sound. It seems to come from all directions at once, as omnipresent as the air. Slowly, he moves towards the wall with the sliding panel through which the Woman enters and exits. He puts his ear against it, thinking the music may be coming from there. Slowly, he slides the door open just a crack, ever so carefully. He peeks through the crack. As he peeks through, the Upstage wall of the set becomes transparent, and through the scrim, we are able to see what he sees. Woman is Upstage of the scrim. She is tending a room filled with potted and vased flowers of all variety. The lushness and beauty of the room Upstage of the scrim stands out in stark contrast to the barrenness of the main set. She is also transformed. She is a young woman. She is beautiful. She wears a brightly colored kimono. Man observes this scene for a long time. He then slides the door shut. The scrim returns to opaque. The music continues. He returns to his mat. He picks up the stolen flower. It is brown and wilted, dead. He looks at it. The music slowly fades out.*

SCENE VII

Morning. Man is half-dressed. He is practicing sword maneuvers. He practices with the feel of a man whose spirit is willing, but the flesh is inept. He tries to execute deft movements, but is dissatisfied with his efforts. He curses himself, and returns to basic exercises. Suddenly, he feels something buzzing around his neck—a mosquito. He slaps his neck, but misses it. He sees it flying near him. He swipes at it with his sword. He keeps missing. Finally, he thinks he's hit it. He runs over, kneels down to recover the fallen insect. He picks up two halves of a mosquito on two different fingers. Woman enters the room. She looks as she normally does. She is carrying a vase of flowers, which she places on its shelf.

Man: Look.
Woman: I'm sorry?
Man: Look.
Woman: What? *(He brings over the two halves of mosquito to show her.)*
Man: See?
Woman: Oh.
Man: I hit it—chop!
Woman: These are new forms of target practice?
Man: Huh? Well—yes—in a way.
Woman: You seem to do well at it.
Man: Thank you. For last night. I heard your *shakuhachi*. It was very loud, strong—good tone.

Woman: Did you enjoy it? I wanted you to enjoy it. If you wish, I'll play it for you every night.

Man: Every night!

Woman: If you wish.

Man: No—I don't—I don't want you to treat me like a baby.

Woman: What? I'm not.

Man: Oh, yes. Like a baby. Who you must feed in the middle of the night or he cries. Waaah! Waaah!

Woman: Stop that!

Man: You need your sleep.

Woman: I don't mind getting up for you. *(Pause.)* I would enjoy playing for you. Every night. While you sleep. It will make me feel—like I'm shaping your dreams. I go through long stretches when there is no one in my dreams. It's terrible. During those times, I avoid my bed as much as possible. I paint. I weave. I play *shakuhachi*. I sit on mats and rub powder into my face. Anything to keep from facing a bed with no dreams. It is like sleeping on ice.

Man: What do you dream of now?

Woman: Last night—I dreamt of you. I don't remember what happened. But you were very funny. Not in a mocking way. I wasn't laughing at you. But you made me laugh. And you were very warm. I remember that. *(Pause.)* What do you remember about last night?

Man: Just your playing. That's all. I got up, listened to it, and went back to sleep. *(Man gets up, resumes practicing with his sword.)*

Woman: Another mosquito bothering you?

Man: Just practicing. Ah! Weak! Too weak! I tell you, it wasn't always like this. I'm telling you, there were days when I could chop the fruit from a tree without ever taking my eyes off the ground. *(He continues practicing.)* You ever use one of these?

Woman: I've had to pick one up, yes.

Man: Oh?

Woman: You forget—I live alone—out here—there is . . . not much to sustain me but what I manage to learn myself. It wasn't really a matter of choice.

Man: I used to be very good, you know. Perhaps I can give you some pointers.

Woman: I'd really rather not.

Man: C'mon—a woman like you—you're absolutely right. You need to know how to defend yourself.

Woman: As you wish.

Man: Do you have something to practice with?

Woman: Yes. Excuse me. *(She exits. He practices more. She re-enters with two wooden sticks. He takes one of them.)* Will these do?

Man: Nice. Now, show me what you can do.

Woman: I'm sorry?

Man: Run up and hit me.
Woman: Please.
Man: Go on—I'll block it.
Woman: I feel so . . . undignified.
Man: Go on. *(She hits him playfully with stick.)* Not like that!
Woman: I'll try to be gentle.
Man: What?
Woman: I don't want to hurt you.
Man: You won't—Hit me! *(Woman charges at Man, quickly, deftly. She scores a hit.)* Oh!
Woman: Did I hurt you?
Man: No—you were—let's try that again. *(They square off again. Woman rushes forward. She appears to attempt a strike. He blocks that apparent strike, which turns out to be a feint. She scores.)* Huh?
Woman: Did I hurt you? I'm sorry.
Man: No.
Woman: I hurt you.
Man: No.
Woman: Do you wish to hit me?
Man: No.
Woman: Do you want me to try again?
Man: No.
Woman: Thank you.
Man: Just practice there—by yourself—let me see you run through some maneuvers.
Woman: Must I?
Man: Yes! Go! *(She goes to an open area.)* My greatest strength was always as a teacher. *(Woman executes a series of deft movements. Her whole manner is transformed. Man watches with increasing amazement. Her movements end. She regains her submissive manner.)*
Woman: I'm so embarrassed. My skills—they're so—inappropriate. I look like a man.
Man: Where did you learn that?
Woman: There is much time to practice here.
Man: But you—the techniques.
Woman: I don't know what's fashionable in the outside world. *(Pause.)* Are you unhappy?
Man: No.
Woman: Really?
Man: I'm just . . . surprised.
Woman: You think it's unbecoming for a woman.
Man: No, no. Not at all.
Woman: You want to leave.
Man: No!

Woman: All visitors do. I know. I've met many. They say they'll stay. And they do, For a while. Until they see too much. Or they learn something new. There are boundaries outside of which visitors do not want to see me step. Only who knows what those boundaries are? Not I. They change with every visitor. You have to be careful not to cross them, but you never know where they are. And one day, inevitably, you step outside the lines. The visitor knows. You don't. You didn't know that you'd done anything different. You thought it was just another part of you. The visitor sneaks away. The next day, you learn that you had stepped outside his heart. I'm afraid you've seen too much.

Man: There are stories.

Woman: What?

Man: People talk.

Woman: Where? We're two days from the nearest village.

Man: Word travels.

Woman: What are you talking about?

Man: There are stories about you. I heard them. They say that your visitors never leave this house.

Woman: That's what you heard?

Man: They say you imprison them.

Woman: Then you were a fool to come here.

Man: Listen.

Woman: Me? Listen? You. Look! Where are these prisoners? Have you seen any?

Man: They told me you were very beautiful.

Woman: Then they are blind as well as ignorant.

Man: You are.

Woman: What?

Man: Beautiful.

Woman: Stop that! My skin feels like seaweed.

Man: I didn't realize it at first. I must confess—I didn't. But over these few days—your face has changed for me. The shape of it. The feel of it. The color. All changed. I look at you now, and I'm no longer sure you are the same woman who had poured tea for me just a week ago. And because of that I remembered—how little I know about a face that changes in the night. *(Pause.)* Have you heard those stories?

Woman: I don't listen to old wives' tales.

Man: But have you heard them?

Woman: Yes. I've heard them. From other visitors—young—hot-blooded—or old—who came here because they were told great glory was to be had by killing the witch in the woods.

Man: I was told that no man could spend time in this house without falling in love.

Woman: Oh? So why did you come? Did you wager gold that you could come out untouched? The outside world is so flattering to me. And you—are you like the rest? Passion passing through your heart so powerfully that you can't hold onto it?

Man: No! I'm afraid!

Woman: Of what?

Man: Sometimes—when I look into the flowers, I think I hear a voice—from inside—a voice beneath the petals. A human voice.

Woman: What does it say? "Let me out"?

Man: No. Listen. It hums. It hums with the peacefulness of one who is completely imprisoned.

Woman: I understand that if you listen closely enough, you can hear the ocean.

Man: No. Wait. Look at it. See the layers? Each petal—hiding the next. Try and see where they end. You can't. Follow them down, further down, around—and as you come down—faster and faster—the breeze picks up. The breeze becomes a wail. And in that rush of air—in the silent midst of it—you can hear a voice.

Woman (grabs flower from Man): So, you believe I water and prune my lovers? How can you be so foolish? *(She snaps the flower in half, at the stem. She throws it to the ground.)* Do you come only to leave again? To take a chunk of my heart, then leave with your booty on your belt, like a prize? You say that I imprison hearts in these flowers? Well, bits of my heart are trapped with travellers across this land. I can't even keep track. So kill me. If you came here to destroy a witch, kill me now. I can't stand to have it happen again.

Man: I won't leave you.

Woman: I believe you. *(She looks at the flower that she has broken, bends to pick it up. He touches her. They embrace.)*

SCENE VIII

Day. Woman wears a simple undergarment, over which she is donning a brightly colored kimono, the same one we saw her wearing Upstage of the scrim. Man stands apart.

Woman: I can't cry. I don't have the capacity. Right from birth, I didn't cry. My mother and father were shocked. They thought they'd given birth to a ghost, a demon. Sometimes I've thought myself that. When great sadness has welled up inside me, I've prayed for a means to release the pain from my body. But my prayers went unanswered. The grief remained inside me. It would sit like water, still. *(Pause; she models her kimono.)* Do you like it?

Man: Yes, it's beautiful.

Woman: I wanted to wear something special today.
Man: It's beautiful. Excuse me. I must practice.
Woman: Shall I get you something?
Man: No.
Woman: Some tea, maybe?
Man: No. *(Man resumes swordplay.)*
Woman: Perhaps later today—perhaps we can go out—just around here. We can look for flowers.
Man: Alright.
Woman: We don't have to.
Man: No. Let's.
Woman: I just thought if—
Man: Fine. Where do you want to go?
Woman: There are very few recreational activities around here, I know.
Man: Alright. We'll go this afternoon. *(Pause.)*
Woman: Can I get you something?
Man (turning around): What?
Woman: You might be—
Man: I'm not hungry or thirsty or cold or hot.
Woman: Then what are you?
Man: Practicing. *(Man resumes practicing; Woman exits. As soon as she exits, he rests. He sits down. He examines his sword. He runs his finger along the edge of it. He takes the tip, runs it against the soft skin under his chin. He places the sword on the ground with the tip pointed directly upwards. He keeps it from falling by placing the tip under his chin. He experiments with different degrees of pressure. Woman re-enters. She sees him in this precarious position. She jerks his head upward; the sword falls.)*
Woman: Don't do that!
Man: What?
Woman: You can hurt yourself!
Man: I was practicing!
Woman: You were playing!
Man: I was practicing!
Woman: It's dangerous.
Man: What do you take me for—a child?
Woman: Sometimes wise men do childish things.
Man: I knew what I was doing!
Woman: It scares me.
Man: Don't be ridiculous. *(He reaches for the sword again.)*
Woman: Don't! Don't do that!
Man: Get back! *(He places the sword back in its previous position, suspended between the floor and his chin, upright.)*
Woman: But—
Man: Sssssh!

Woman: I wish—

Man: Listen to me! The slightest shock, you know—the slightest shock—surprise—it might make me jerk or—something—and then . . . so you must be perfectly still and quiet.

Woman: But I—

Man: Sssssh! *(Silence.)* I learned this exercise from a friend—I can't even remember his name—good swordsman—many years ago. He called it his meditation position. He said, like this, he could feel the line between this world and the others because he rested on it. If he saw something in another world that he liked better, all he would have to do is let his head drop, and he'd be there. Simple. No fuss. One day, they found him with the tip of his sword run clean out the back of his neck. He was smiling. I guess he saw something he liked. Or else he'd fallen asleep.

Woman: Stop that.

Man: Stop what?

Woman: Tormenting me.

Man: I'm not.

Woman: Take it away!

Man: You don't have to watch, you know.

Woman: Do you want to die that way—an accident?

Man: I was doing this before you came in.

Woman: If you do, all you need to do is tell me.

Man: What?

Woman: I can walk right over. Lean on the back of your head.

Man: Don't try to threaten—

Woman: Or jerk your sword up.

Man: Or scare me. You can't threaten—

Woman: I'm not. But if that's what you want.

Man: You can't threaten me. You wouldn't do it.

Woman: Oh?

Man: Then I'd be gone. You wouldn't let me leave that easily.

Woman: Yes, I would.

Man: You'd be alone.

Woman: No. I'd follow you. Forever. *(Pause.)* Now, let's stop this nonsense.

Man: No! I can do what I want! Don't come any closer!

Woman: Then release your sword.

Man: Come any closer and I'll drop my head.

Woman (Woman slowly approaches Man. She grabs the hilt of the sword. She looks into his eyes. She pulls it out from under his chin.): There will be no more of this. *(She exits with the sword. He starts to follow her, then stops. He touches under his chin. On his finger, he finds a drop of blood.)*

SCENE IX

Night. Man is leaving the house. He is just about out, when he hears a shakuhachi *playing. He looks around, trying to locate the sound. Woman appears in the doorway to the outside.* Shakuhachi *slowly fades out.*

Woman: It's time for you to go?

Man: Yes. I'm sorry.

Woman: You're just going to sneak out? A thief in the night? A frightened child?

Man: I care about you.

Woman: You express it strangely.

Man: I leave in shame because it is proper. *(Pause.)* I came seeking glory.

Woman: To kill me? You can say it. You'll be surprised at how little I blanch. As if you'd said, "I came for a bowl of rice," or "I came seeking love" or "I came to kill you."

Man: Weakness. All weakness. Too weak to kill you. Too weak to kill myself. Too weak to do anything but sneak away in shame. *(Woman brings out Man's sword.)*

Woman: Were you even planning to leave without this? *(He takes sword.)* Why not stay here?

Man: I can't live with someone who's defeated me.

Woman: I never thought of defeating you. I only wanted to take care of you. To make you happy. Because that made me happy and I was no longer alone.

Man: You defeated me.

Woman: Why do you think that way?

Man: I came here with a purpose. The world was clear. You changed the shape of your face, the shape of my heart—rearranged everything—created a world where I could do nothing.

Woman: I only tried to care for you.

Man: I guess that was all it took. *(Pause.)*

Woman: You still think I'm a witch. Just because old women gossip. You are so cruel. Once you arrived, there were only two possibilities: I would die or you would leave. *(Pause.)* If you believe I'm a witch, then kill me. Rid the province of one more evil.

Man: I can't—

Woman: Why not? If you believe that about me, then it's the right thing to do.

Man: You know I can't.

Woman: Then stay.

Man: Don't try and force me.

Woman: I won't force you to do anything. *(Pause.)* All I wanted was an escape—for both of us. The sound of a human voice—the simplest thing to find, and the hardest to hold onto. This house—my loneliness is etched into the walls. Kill me, but don't leave. Even in death, my spirit would rest here and be comforted by your presence.

Man: Force me to stay.
Woman: I won't. *(Man starts to leave.)* Beware.
Man: What?
Woman: The ground on which you walk is weak. It could give way at any moment. The crevice beneath is dark.
Man: Are you talking about death? I'm ready to die.
Woman: Fear for what is worse than death.
Man: What?
Woman: Falling. Falling through the darkness. Waiting to hit the ground. Picking up speed. Waiting for the ground. Falling faster. Falling alone. Waiting. Falling. Waiting. Falling.

(Woman wails and runs out through the door to her room. Man stands, confused, not knowing what to do. He starts to follow her, then hesitates, and rushes out the door to the outside. Silence. Slowly, he re-enters from the outside. He looks for her in the main room. He goes slowly towards the panel to her room. He throws down his sword. He opens the panel. He goes inside. He comes out. He unrolls his mat. He sits on it, cross-legged. He looks out into space. He notices near him a shakuhachi. He picks it up. He begins to blow into it. He tries to make sounds. He continues trying through the end of the play. The Upstage scrim lights up. Upstage, we see the Woman. She is young. She is hanging from a rope suspended from the roof. She has hung herself. Around her are scores of vases with flowers in them whose blossoms have been blown off. Only the stems remain in the vases. Around her swirl the thousands of petals from the flowers. They fill the Upstage scrim area like a blizzard of color. Man continues to attempt to play. Lights fade to black.)

Brighde Mullins

Click

2001

Brighde Mullins

Brighde Mullins (b. 1963) was born into a military family at Camp Lejeune, North Carolina, and was raised in Las Vegas, Nevada. Her plays have been developed and produced in New York, Dallas, Salt Lake City, London, Los Angeles, and San Francisco. Her full-length plays include The Bourgeois Pig; Rare Bird; Those Who Can, Do; Monkey in the Middle; Teach; Fire Eater; Topographical Eden; *and* Increase. Click, *her darkly comic one-act play, was commissioned by the Actors Theatre of Louisville for the 2001 Humana Festival. Her awards include a Guggenheim Fellowship in Playwriting, a United States Artists Fellowship in Literature, a Whiting*

Foundation Award, a Gold Medal from the Pinter Review, and an NEA Fellowship, and her book of poems, Water Stories *(2003), was nominated for a Pushcart Prize. She has taught at Brown University and was the Director of Creative Writing at Harvard (where she was also a Briggs-Copeland Lecturer in Playwriting). Presently Mullins teaches at the University of Southern California, where she directs the Master of Professional Writing Program. She also teaches in the Theatre Department at the University of California, Santa Barbara. Mullins lives in Los Angeles.*

CHARACTERS

Man
Woman

SCENE. *Dark stage. The low hum of a bad phone connection over thousands of miles. The voices of a Man and a Woman are heard; they are in the middle of a conversation.*

Man: —what are you doing?
Woman: Doing?
Man: While you're talking to me. I hear something. What are you doing?
Woman: What does it sound like?
Man: Click—click—click
Woman (in a rush, in one breath): Oh—that click?—it's the window blind in a breeze, a slight breeze, it's me unsnapping my tortoise shell barrette, I clipped and unclipped it, it's my Italian lighter lighting up my last blonde gauloise, it's some cheap Christmas trash racketing its way down the street, it's my birthstone ring hitting the floor, it's a bird's beak tapping, it's Morse code, it's an urgent message we can't decipher but need to know, it's the deadbolt on the back-door, it's the heater clacking into action, it's the clock stuck on One, One, One, it's a glitch on the wires, it's the loose jawbone that clicks in my head from where I took a fall on the ice last winter. It's my nailclipper.
Man: I'm really sick of your metaphors.
Woman: You used to like my turns of phrase.
Man: That was before I started re-hab.
Woman: Recovery takes the Poetry out of Things, huh?
Man: At a nickel a minute from a payphone in a drafty corridor, yeah. I'd say so.

(slight beat)

Yeah. It's all just words.
Woman: That's all we have right now, isn't it? You're two thousand miles away and we're reduced to Words, Right?

Man: Yeah. I guess so.

Woman: So the corridor is drafty.

Man: Yeah.

Woman: What color are the walls?

Man: Green.

Woman: Make me see the green.

Man: Greenish.

Woman: A brown green or a yellow green?

Man: Cocktail olive green. Drab green. Military green.

Woman: Windows?

Man: One up high. Too small for a body to crawl through.

Woman: Describe it.

Man: High. And sideways. And there are tables, and old mouldy armchairs, they give off a smell like sweat and urine—or maybe it's like old cheese—

Woman: Brie?

Man: Cracker Barrel—sharp and sickly—and there are magazines, lots of them. Piles of old *National Geographics*. And God all of this and talking to you and "this is like" and "this is like." "Nothing" is "Like Anything" except that I could use something like a drink.

(sound in: CLICK)

Man: There's that click again. Are you opening a beer?

Woman (momentary pause): I'm opening a SODA.

Man: You're drinking beer! You're drinking beer while I'm calling you from rehab?

Woman: I understand how very difficult this is for you, and I'm talking to you and I'm trying to be supportive. I would never drink a beer while talking to you.

(pause)

It's a lite beer. It's practically a soda.

Man: A *lite* beer? I have to go.

Woman: Wait. That was a Metaphor—

(SOUND IN: Click. Dead Wire)

Hullo? Hey? Hey.

END PLAY

August Wilson

Fences

1985

August Wilson

August Wilson (1945–2005) was born in Pittsburgh, one of six children of a German American father and an African American mother. His parents separated early, and the young Wilson was raised on the Hill, a Pittsburgh ghetto neighborhood. Although he quit school in the ninth grade when a teacher wrongly accused him of submitting a ghost-written paper, Wilson continued his education in local libraries, supporting himself by working as a cook and stock clerk. In 1968 he co-founded a community troupe, the Black Horizons Theater, staging plays by LeRoi Jones and other militants; later he moved from Pittsburgh to Saint Paul, Minnesota, where at last he saw a play of his own performed. Jitney, *his first important work, won him entry to a 1982 playwrights' conference at the Eugene O'Neill Theater Center. There, Lloyd Richards, dean of Yale University School of Drama, took an interest in Wilson's work and offered to produce his plays at Yale.* Ma Rainey's Black Bottom *was the first to reach Broadway (in 1985), where it ran for ten months and received an award from the New York Drama Critics Circle. In 1987* Fences, *starring Mary Alice and James Earl Jones, won another Critics Circle Award, as well as a Tony Award and the Pulitzer Prize for best American play of its year. It set a box office record for a Broadway nonmusical.* Joe Turner's Come and Gone *(1988) also received high acclaim, and* The Piano Lesson *(1990) won Wilson a second Pulitzer Prize. His subsequent plays were* Two Trains Running *(1992),* Seven Guitars *(1995),* King Hedley II *(2000),* Gem of the Ocean *(2003), and* Radio Golf *(2005).*

Wilson's ten plays, each one set in a different decade of the 1900s, constitute his "Century Cycle" that traces the black experience in America throughout the twentieth century. Seamlessly interweaving realistic and mythic approaches, filled with vivid characters, pungent dialogue, and strong dramatic scenes, it is one of the most ambitious projects in the history of the American theater and an epic achievement in our literature. Wilson died of liver cancer in October 2005, a few months after completing the final play in his cycle. Two weeks after his death the Virginia Theater on Broadway was renamed the August Wilson Theater in his honor. A published poet as well as a dramatist, Wilson once told an interviewer, "After writing poetry for twenty-one years, I approach a play the same way. The mental process is poetic: you use metaphor and condense."

For Lloyd Richards, Who Adds to Whatever He Touches

When the sins of our fathers visit us
We do not have to play host.
We can banish them with forgiveness
As God, in His Largeness and Laws.

—AUGUST WILSON

LIST OF CHARACTERS

Troy Maxson
Jim Bono, Troy's friend
Rose, Troy's wife
Lyons, Troy's oldest son by previous marriage
Gabriel, Troy's brother
Cory, Troy and Rose's son
Raynell, Troy's daughter

SETTING. *The setting is the yard which fronts the only entrance to the Maxson household, an ancient two-story brick house set back off a small alley in a big-city neighborhood. The entrance to the house is gained by two or three steps leading to a wooden porch badly in need of paint.*

A relatively recent addition to the house and running its full width, the porch lacks congruence. It is a sturdy porch with a flat roof. One or two chairs of dubious value sit at one end where the kitchen window opens onto the porch. An old-fashioned icebox stands silent guard at the opposite end.

The yard is a small dirt yard, partially fenced, except for the last scene, with a wooden saw horse, a pile of lumber, and other fence-building equipment set off to the side. Opposite is a tree from which hangs a ball made of rags. A baseball bat leans against the tree. Two oil drums serve as garbage receptacles and sit near the house at right to complete the setting.

THE PLAY. *Near the turn of the century, the destitute of Europe sprang on the city with tenacious claws and an honest and solid dream. The city devoured them. They swelled its belly until it burst into a thousand furnaces and sewing machines, a thousand butcher shops and bakers' ovens, a thousand churches and hospitals and funeral parlors and money-lenders. The city grew. It nourished itself and offered each man a partnership limited only by his talent, his guile, and his willingness and capacity for hard work. For the immigrants of Europe, a dream dared and won true.*

The descendants of African slaves were offered no such welcome or participation. They came from places called the Carolinas and the Virginias, Georgia, Alabama, Mississippi, and Tennessee. They came strong, eager, searching. The city rejected them and they fled and settled along the riverbanks and under bridges in shallow, ramshackle houses made of sticks and tarpaper. They collected rags and wood. They sold the use of their muscles and their bodies. They cleaned houses and washed clothes, they shined shoes, and in quiet desperation and vengeful pride, they stole, and lived in pursuit of their own dream. That they could breathe free, finally, and stand to meet life with the force of dignity and whatever eloquence the heart could call upon.

By 1957, the hard-won victories of the European immigrants had solidified the industrial might of America. War had been confronted and won with new energies that used loyalty and patriotism as its fuel. Life was rich, full, and flourishing. The Milwaukee Braves won the World Series, and the hot winds of change that would make the sixties a turbulent, racing, dangerous, and provocative decade had not yet begun to blow full.

ACT I

SCENE I

It is 1957. Troy and Bono enter the yard, engaged in conversation. Troy is fifty-three years old, a large man with thick, heavy hands; it is this largeness that he strives to fill out and make an accommodation with. Together with his blackness, his largeness informs his sensibilities and the choices he has made in his life.

Of the two men, Bono is obviously the follower. His commitment to their friendship of thirty-odd years is rooted in his admiration of Troy's honesty, capacity for hard work, and his strength, which Bono seeks to emulate.

It is Friday night, payday, and the one night of the week the two men engage in a ritual of talk and drink. Troy is usually the most talkative and at times he can be crude and almost vulgar, though he is capable of rising to profound heights of expression. The men carry lunch buckets and wear or carry burlap aprons and are dressed in clothes suitable to their jobs as garbage collectors.

Bono: Troy, you ought to stop that lying!

Troy: I ain't lying! The nigger had a watermelon this big. (*He indicates with his hands.*) Talking about . . . "What watermelon, Mr. Rand?" I liked to fell out! "What watermelon, Mr. Rand?" . . . And it sitting there big as life.

Bono: What did Mr. Rand say?

Troy: Ain't said nothing. Figure if the nigger too dumb to know he carrying a watermelon, he wasn't gonna get much sense out of him. Trying to hide that great big old watermelon under his coat. Afraid to let the white man see him carry it home.

Bono: I'm like you . . . I ain't got no time for them kind of people.

Troy: Now what he look like getting mad cause he see the man from the union talking to Mr. Rand?

Bono: He come to me talking about . . . "Maxson gonna get us fired." I told him to get away from me with that. He walked away from me calling you a troublemaker. What Mr. Rand say?

Troy: Ain't said nothing. He told me to go down the Commissioner's office next Friday. They called me down there to see them.

Bono: Well, as long as you got your complaint filed, they can't fire you. That's what one of them white fellows tell me.

Mary Alice, Ray Aranha, and James Earl Jones in Yale Repertory Theatre's 1985 world premiere of *Fences*.

Troy: I ain't worried about them firing me. They gonna fire me cause I asked a question? That's all I did. I went to Mr. Rand and asked him, "Why? Why you got the white mens driving and the colored lifting?" Told him, "what's the matter, don't I count? You think only white fellows got sense enough to drive a truck. That ain't no paper job! Hell, anybody can drive a truck. How come you got all whites driving and the colored lifting?" He told me "take it to the union." Well, hell, that's what I done! Now they wanna come up with this pack of lies.

Bono: I told Brownie if the man come and ask him any questions . . . just tell the truth! It ain't nothing but something they done trumped up on you cause you filed a complaint on them.

Troy: Brownie don't understand nothing. All I want them to do is change the job description. Give everybody a chance to drive the truck. Brownie can't see that. He ain't got that much sense.

Bono: How you figure he be making out with that gal be up at Taylors' all the time . . . that Alberta gal?

Troy: Same as you and me. Getting just as much as we is. Which is to say nothing.

Bono: It is, huh? I figure you doing a little better than me . . . and I ain't saying what I'm doing.

Troy: Aw, nigger, look here . . . I know you. If you had got anywhere near that gal, twenty minutes later you be looking to tell somebody. And the first one you gonna tell . . . that you gonna want to brag to . . . is gonna be me.

Viola Davis and Denzel Washington in the 2010 Broadway production of *Fences*.

Bono: I ain't saying that. I see where you be eyeing her.

Troy: I eye all the women. I don't miss nothing. Don't never let nobody tell you Troy Maxson don't eye the women.

Bono: You been doing more than eyeing her. You done bought her a drink or two.

Troy: Hell yeah, I bought her a drink! What that mean? I bought you one, too. What that mean cause I buy her a drink? I'm just being polite.

Bono: It's alright to buy her one drink. That's what you call being polite. But when you wanna be buying two or three . . . that's what you call eyeing her.

Troy: Look here, as long as you known me . . . you ever known me to chase after women?

Bono: Hell yeah! Long as I done known you. You forgetting I knew you when.

Troy: Naw, I'm talking about since I been married to Rose?

Bono: Oh, not since you been married to Rose. Now, that's the truth, there. I can say that.

Troy: Alright then! Case closed.

Bono: I see you be walking up around Alberta's house. You supposed to be at Taylors' and you be walking up around there.

Troy: What you watching where I'm walking for? I ain't watching after you.

Bono: I seen you walking around there more than once.

Troy: Hell, you liable to see me walking anywhere! That don't mean nothing cause you see me walking around there.

Bono: Where she come from anyway? She just kinda showed up one day.

Troy: Tallahassee. You can look at her and tell she one of them Florida gals. They got some big healthy women down there. Grow them right up out the ground. Got a little bit of Indian in her. Most of them niggers down in Florida got some Indian in them.

Bono: I don't know about that Indian part. But she damn sure big and healthy. Woman wear some big stockings. Got them great big old legs and hips as wide as the Mississippi River.

Troy: Legs don't mean nothing. You don't do nothing but push them out of the way. But them hips cushion the ride!

Bono: Troy, you ain't got no sense.

Troy: It's the truth! Like you riding on Goodyears!

(Rose enters from the house. She is ten years younger than Troy, her devotion to him stems from her recognition of the possibilities of her life without him: a succession of abusive men and their babies, a life of partying and running the streets, the Church, or aloneness with its attendant pain and frustration. She recognizes Troy's spirit as a fine and illuminating one and she either ignores or forgives his faults, only some of which she recognizes. Though she doesn't drink, her presence is an integral part of the Friday night rituals. She alternates between the porch and the kitchen, where supper preparations are under way.)

Rose: What you all out here getting into?

Troy: What you worried about what we getting into for? This is men talk, woman.

Rose: What I care what you all talking about? Bono, you gonna stay for supper?

Bono: No, I thank you, Rose. But Lucille say she cooking up a pot of pigfeet.

Troy: Pigfeet! Hell, I'm going home with you! Might even stay the night if you got some pigfeet. You got something in there to top them pigfeet, Rose?

Rose: I'm cooking up some chicken. I got some chicken and collard greens.

Troy: Well, go on back in the house and let me and Bono finish what we was talking about. This is men talk. I got some talk for you later. You know what kind of talk I mean. You go on and powder it up.

Rose: Troy Maxson, don't you start that now!

Troy (puts his arm around her): Aw, woman . . . come here. Look here, Bono . . . when I met this woman . . . I got out that place, say, "Hitch up my pony, saddle up my mare . . . there's a woman out there for me somewhere. I looked here. Looked there. Saw Rose and latched on to her." I latched on to her and told her—I'm gonna tell you the truth—I told her, "Baby, I don't wanna marry, I just wanna be your man." Rose told me . . . tell him what you told me, Rose.

Rose: I told him if he wasn't the marrying kind, then move out the way so the marrying kind could find me.

Troy: That's what she told me. "Nigger, you in my way. You blocking the view! Move out the way so I can find me a husband." I thought it over two or three days. Come back—

Rose: Ain't no two or three days nothing. You was back the same night.

Troy: Come back, told her . . . "Okay, baby . . . but I'm gonna buy me a banty rooster and put him out there in the backyard . . . and when he see a stranger come, he'll flap his wings and crow . . ." Look here, Bono, I could watch the front door by myself . . . it was that back door I was worried about.

Rose: Troy, you ought not talk like that. Troy ain't doing nothing but telling a lie.

Troy: Only thing is . . . when we first got married . . . forget the rooster . . . we ain't had no yard!

Bono: I hear you tell it. Me and Lucille was staying down there on Logan Street. Had two rooms with the outhouse in the back. I ain't mind the outhouse none. But when that goddamn wind blow through there in the winter . . . that's what I'm talking about! To this day I wonder why in the hell I ever stayed down there for six long years. But see, I didn't know I could do no better. I thought only white folks had inside toilets and things.

Rose: There's a lot of people don't know they can do no better than they doing now. That's just something you got to learn. A lot of folks still shop at Bella's.

Troy: Ain't nothing wrong with shopping at Bella's. She got fresh food.

Rose: I ain't said nothing about if she got fresh food. I'm talking about what she charge. She charge ten cents more than the A&P.

Troy: The A&P ain't never done nothing for me. I spends my money where I'm treated right. I go down to Bella, say, "I need a loaf of bread, I'll pay you Friday." She give it to me. What sense that make when I got money to go and spend it somewhere else and ignore the person who done right by me? That ain't in the Bible.

Rose: We ain't talking about what's in the Bible. What sense it make to shop there when she overcharge?

Troy: You shop where you want to. I'll do my shopping where the people been good to me.

Rose: Well, I don't think it's right for her to overcharge. That's all I was saying.

Bono: Look here . . . I got to get on. Lucille going be raising all kind of hell.

Troy: Where you going, nigger? We ain't finished this pint. Come here, finish this pint.

Bono: Well, hell, I am . . . if you ever turn the bottle loose.

Troy (hands him the bottle): The only thing I say about the A&P is I'm glad Cory got that job down there. Help him take care of his school clothes and things. Gabe done moved out and things getting tight around here. He got that job . . . He can start to look out for himself.

Rose: Cory done went and got recruited by a college football team.

Troy: I told that boy about that football stuff. The white man ain't gonna let him get nowhere with that football. I told him when he first come to me with it. Now you come telling me he done went and got more tied up in it. He ought to go and get recruited in how to fix cars or something where he can make a living.

Rose: He ain't talking about making no living playing football. It's just something the boys in school do. They gonna send a recruiter by to talk to you. He'll tell you he ain't talking about making no living playing football. It's a honor to be recruited.

Troy: It ain't gonna get him nowhere. Bono'll tell you that.

Bono: If he be like you in the sports . . . he's gonna be alright. Ain't but two men ever played baseball as good as you. That's Babe Ruth and Josh Gibson.° Them's the only two men ever hit more home runs than you.

Troy: What it ever get me? Ain't got a pot to piss in or a window to throw it out of.

Rose: Times have changed since you was playing baseball, Troy. That was before the war. Times have changed a lot since then.

Troy: How in hell they done changed?

Rose: They got lots of colored boys playing ball now. Baseball and football.

Bono: You right about that, Rose. Times have changed, Troy. You just come along too early.

Troy: There ought not never have been no time called too early! Now you take that fellow . . . what's that fellow they had playing right field for the Yankees back then? You know who I'm talking about, Bono. Used to play right field for the Yankees.

Rose: Selkirk?°

Troy: Selkirk! That's it! Man batting .269, understand? .269. What kind of sense that make? I was hitting .432 with thirty-seven home runs! Man batting .269 and playing right field for the Yankees! I saw Josh Gibson's daughter yesterday. She walking around with raggedy shoes on her feet. Now I bet you Selkirk's daughter ain't walking around with raggedy shoes on her feet! I bet you that!

Josh Gibson: legendary catcher in the Negro Leagues whose batting average and home-run totals far outstripped Major League records; he died of a stroke at age 35 in January 1947, three months before Jackie Robinson's debut with the Brooklyn Dodgers. *Selkirk:* Andy Selkirk, Yankee outfielder who hit .269 in 118 games in 1940.

Rose: They got a lot of colored baseball players now. Jackie Robinson° was the first. Folks had to wait for Jackie Robinson.

Troy: I done seen a hundred niggers play baseball better than Jackie Robinson. Hell, I know some teams Jackie Robinson couldn't even make! What you talking about Jackie Robinson. Jackie Robinson wasn't nobody. I'm talking about if you could play ball then they ought to have let you play. Don't care what color you were. Come telling me I come along too early. If you could play . . . then they ought to have let you play.

(Troy takes a long drink from the bottle.)

Rose: You gonna drink yourself to death. You don't need to be drinking like that.

Troy: Death ain't nothing. I done seen him. Done wrassled with him. You can't tell me nothing about death. Death ain't nothing but a fastball on the outside corner. And you know what I'll do to that! Lookee here, Bono . . . am I lying? You get one of them fastballs, about waist high, over the outside corner of the plate where you can get the meat of the bat on it . . . and good god! You can kiss it goodbye. Now, am I lying?

Bono: Naw, you telling the truth there. I seen you do it.

Troy: If I'm lying . . . that 450 feet worth of lying! *(Pause.)* That's all death is to me. A fastball on the outside corner.

Rose: I don't know why you want to get on talking about death.

Troy: Ain't nothing wrong with talking about death. That's part of life. Everybody gonna die. You gonna die, I'm gonna die. Bono's gonna die. Hell, we all gonna die.

Rose: But you ain't got to talk about it. I don't like to talk about it.

Troy: You the one brought it up. Me and Bono was talking about baseball . . . you tell me I'm gonna drink myself to death. Ain't that right, Bono? You know I don't drink this but one night out of the week. That's Friday night. I'm gonna drink just enough to where I can handle it. Then I cuts it loose. I leave it alone. So don't you worry about me drinking myself to death. 'Cause I ain't worried about Death. I done seen him. I done wrestled with him.

Look here, Bono . . . I looked up one day and Death was marching straight at me. Like Soldiers on Parade! The Army of Death was marching straight at me. The middle of July, 1941. It got real cold just like it be winter. It seem like Death himself reached out and touched me on the shoulder. He touch me just like I touch you. I got cold as ice and Death standing there grinning at me.

Rose: Troy, why don't you hush that talk.

Jackie Robinson: the first African American to play in Major League Baseball, joined the Brooklyn Dodgers in 1947.

Troy: I say . . . what you want, Mr. Death? You be wanting me? You done brought your army to be getting me? I looked him dead in the eye. I wasn't fearing nothing. I was ready to tangle. Just like I'm ready to tangle now. The Bible say be ever vigilant. That's why I don't get but so drunk. I got to keep watch.

Rose: Troy was right down there in Mercy Hospital. You remember he had pneumonia? Laying there with a fever talking plumb out of his head.

Troy: Death standing there staring at me . . . carrying that sickle in his hand. Finally he say, "You want bound over for another year?" See, just like that . . . "You want bound over for another year?" I told him, "Bound over hell! Let's settle this now!"

It seem like he kinda fell back when I said that, and all the cold went out of me. I reached down and grabbed that sickle and threw it just as far as I could throw it . . . and me and him commenced to wrestling.

We wrestled for three days and three nights. I can't say where I found the strength from. Everytime it seemed like he was gonna get the best of me, I'd reach way down deep inside myself and find the strength to do him one better.

Rose: Every time Troy tell that story he find different ways to tell it. Different things to make up about it.

Troy: I ain't making up nothing. I'm telling you the facts of what happened. I wrestled with Death for three days and three nights and I'm standing here to tell you about it. *(Pause.)* Alright. At the end of the third night we done weakened each other to where we can't hardly move. Death stood up, throwed on his robe . . . had him a white robe with a hood on it. He throwed on that robe and went off to look for his sickle. Say, "I'll be back." Just like that. "I'll be back." I told him, say, "Yeah, but . . . you gonna have to find me!" I wasn't no fool. I wasn't going looking for him. Death ain't nothing to play with. And I know he's gonna get me. I know I got to join his army . . . his camp followers. But as long as I keep my strength and see him coming . . . as long as I keep up my vigilance . . . he's gonna have to fight to get me. I ain't going easy.

Bono: Well, look here, since you got to keep up your vigilance . . . let me have the bottle.

Troy: Aw hell, I shouldn't have told you that part. I should have left out that part.

Rose: Troy be talking that stuff and half the time don't even know what he be talking about.

Troy: Bono know me better than that.

Bono: That's right. I know you. I know you got some Uncle Remus in your blood. You got more stories than the devil got sinners.

Troy: Aw hell, I done seen him too! Done talked with the devil.

Rose: Troy, don't nobody wanna be hearing all that stuff.

(Lyons enters the yard from the street. Thirty-four years old, Troy's son by a previous marriage, he sports a neatly trimmed goatee, sport coat, white shirt, tieless and buttoned at the collar. Though he fancies himself a musician, he is more caught up in the rituals and "idea" of being a musician than in the actual practice of the music. He has come to borrow money from Troy, and while he knows he will be successful, he is uncertain as to what extent his lifestyle will be held up to scrutiny and ridicule.)

Lyons: Hey, Pop.

Troy: What you come "Hey, Popping" me for?

Lyons: How you doing, Rose? *(He kisses her.)* Mr. Bono. How you doing?

Bono: Hey, Lyons . . . how you been?

Troy: He must have been doing alright. I ain't seen him around here last week.

Rose: Troy, leave your boy alone. He come by to see you and you wanna start all that nonsense.

Troy: I ain't bothering Lyons. *(Offers him the bottle.)* Here . . . get you a drink. We got an understanding. I know why he come by to see me and he know I know.

Lyons: Come on, Pop . . . I just stopped by to say hi . . . see how you was doing.

Troy: You ain't stopped by yesterday.

Rose: You gonna stay for supper, Lyons? I got some chicken cooking in the oven.

Lyons: No, Rose . . . thanks. I was just in the neighborhood and thought I'd stop by for a minute.

Troy: You was in the neighborhood alright, nigger. You telling the truth there. You was in the neighborhood cause it's my payday.

Lyons: Well, hell, since you mentioned it . . . let me have ten dollars.

Troy: I'll be damned! I'll die and go to hell and play blackjack with the devil before I give you ten dollars.

Bono: That's what I wanna know about . . . that devil you done seen.

Lyons: What . . . Pop done seen the devil? You too much, Pops.

Troy: Yeah, I done seen him. Talked to him too!

Rose: You ain't seen no devil. I done told you that man ain't had nothing to do with the devil. Anything you can't understand, you want to call it the devil.

Troy: Look here, Bono . . . I went down to see Hertzberger about some furniture. Got three rooms for two-ninety-eight. That what it say on the radio. "Three rooms . . . two-ninety-eight." Even made up a little song about it. Go down there . . . man tell me I can't get no credit. I'm working every day and can't get no credit. What to do? I got an empty house with some raggedy furniture in it. Cory ain't got no bed. He's sleeping on a pile of rags on the floor. Working every day and can't get no credit. Come back here—Rose'll tell you—madder than hell. Sit down . . . try to figure what I'm gonna do. Come a knock on the door. Ain't been living here but three days. Who know I'm here? Open the door . . . devil standing there bigger than life. White fellow . . . got on good clothes and everything. Standing there with a clipboard in his hand. I ain't had to say nothing. First words come out of his mouth was . . . "I understand you need some furniture and can't get no credit." I liked to fell over. He say "I'll give you all the credit you want, but you got to pay the interest on it." I told him, "Give me three rooms worth and charge whatever you want." Next day a truck pulled up here and two men unloaded them three rooms. Man what drove the truck give me a book. Say send ten dollars, first of every month to the address in the book and every thing will be alright. Say if I miss a payment the devil was coming back and it'll be hell to pay. That was fifteen years ago. To this day . . . the first of the month I send my ten dollars, Rose'll tell you.

Rose: Troy lying.

Troy: I ain't never seen that man since. Now you tell me who else that could have been but the devil? I ain't sold my soul or nothing like that, you understand. Naw, I wouldn't have truck with the devil about nothing like that. I got my furniture and pays my ten dollars the first of the month just like clockwork.

Bono: How long you say you been paying this ten dollars a month?

Troy: Fifteen years!

Bono: Hell, ain't you finished paying for it yet? How much the man done charged you?

Troy: Aw hell, I done paid for it. I done paid for it ten times over! The fact is I'm scared to stop paying it.

Rose: Troy lying. We got that furniture from Mr. Glickman. He ain't paying no ten dollars a month to nobody.

Troy: Aw hell, woman. Bono know I ain't that big a fool.

Lyons: I was just getting ready to say . . . I know where there's a bridge for sale.

Troy: Look here, I'll tell you this . . . it don't matter to me if he was the devil. It don't matter if the devil give credit. Somebody has got to give it.

Rose: It ought to matter. You going around talking about having truck with the devil . . . God's the one you gonna have to answer to. He's the one gonna be at the Judgment.

Lyons: Yeah, well, look here, Pop . . . Let me have that ten dollars. I'll give it back to you. Bonnie got a job working at the hospital.

Troy: What I tell you, Bono? The only time I see this nigger is when he wants something. That's the only time I see him.

Lyons: Come on, Pop, Mr. Bono don't want to hear all that. Let me have the ten dollars. I told you Bonnie working.

Troy: What that mean to me? "Bonnie working." I don't care if she working. Go ask her for the ten dollars if she working. Talking about "Bonnie working." Why ain't you working?

Lyons: Aw, Pop, you know I can't find no decent job. Where am I gonna get a job at? You know I can't get no job.

Troy: I told you I know some people down there. I can get you on the rubbish if you want to work. I told you that the last time you came by here asking me for something.

Lyons: Naw, Pop . . . thanks. That ain't for me. I don't wanna be carrying nobody's rubbish. I don't wanna be punching nobody's time clock.

Troy: What's the matter, you too good to carry people's rubbish? Where you think that ten dollars you talking about come from? I'm just supposed to haul people's rubbish and give my money to you cause you too lazy to work. You too lazy to work and wanna know why you ain't got what I got.

Rose: What hospital Bonnie working at? Mercy?

Lyons: She's down at Passavant working in the laundry.

Troy: I ain't got nothing as it is. I give you that ten dollars and I got to eat beans the rest of the week. Naw . . . you ain't getting no ten dollars here.

Lyons: You ain't got to be eating no beans. I don't know why you wanna say that.

Troy: I ain't got no extra money. Gabe done moved over to Miss Pearl's paying her the rent and things done got tight around here. I can't afford to be giving you every payday.

Lyons: I ain't asked you to give me nothing. I asked you to loan me ten dollars. I know you got ten dollars.

Troy: Yeah, I got it. You know why I got it? Cause I don't throw my money away out there in the streets. You living the fast life . . . wanna be a musician . . . running around in them clubs and things . . . then, you learn to take care of yourself. You ain't gonna find me going and asking nobody for nothing. I done spent too many years without.

Lyons: You and me is two different people, Pop.

Troy: I done learned my mistake and learned to do what's right by it. You still trying to get something for nothing. Life don't owe you nothing. You owe it to yourself. Ask Bono. He'll tell you I'm right.

Lyons: You got your way of dealing with the world . . . I got mine. The only thing that matters to me is the music.

Troy: Yeah, I can see that! It don't matter how you gonna eat . . . where your next dollar is coming from. You telling the truth there.

Lyons: I know I got to eat. But I got to live too. I need something that gonna help me to get out of the bed in the morning. Make me feel like I belong in the world. I don't bother nobody. I just stay with my music cause that's the only way I can find to live in the world. Otherwise there ain't no telling what I might do. Now I don't come criticizing you and how you live. I just come by to ask you for ten dollars. I don't wanna hear all that about how I live.

Troy: Boy, your mama did a hell of a job raising you.

Lyons: You can't change me, Pop. I'm thirty-four years old. If you wanted to change me, you should have been there when I was growing up. I come by to see you . . . ask for ten dollars and you want to talk about how I was raised. You don't know nothing about how I was raised.

Rose: Let the boy have ten dollars, Troy.

Troy (to Lyons): What the hell you looking at me for? I ain't got no ten dollars. You know what I do with my money. *(To Rose.)* Give him ten dollars if you want him to have it.

Rose: I will. Just as soon as you turn it loose.

Troy (handing Rose the money): There it is. Seventy-six dollars and forty-two cents. You see this, Bono? Now, I ain't gonna get but six of that back.

Rose: You ought to stop telling that lie. Here, Lyons. *(She hands him the money.)*

Lyons: Thanks, Rose. Look . . . I got to run . . . I'll see you later.

Troy: Wait a minute. You gonna say, "thanks, Rose" and ain't gonna look to see where she got that ten dollars from? See how they do me, Bono?

Lyons: I know she got it from you, Pop. Thanks. I'll give it back to you.

Troy: There he go telling another lie. Time I see that ten dollars . . . he'll be owing me thirty more.

Lyons: See you, Mr. Bono.

Bono: Take care, Lyons!

Lyons: Thanks, Pop. I'll see you again.

(Lyons exits the yard.)

Troy: I don't know why he don't go and get him a decent job and take care of that woman he got.

Bono: He'll be alright, Troy. The boy is still young.

Troy: The *boy* is thirty-four years old.

Rose: Let's not get off into all that.

Bono: Look here . . . I got to be going. I got to be getting on. Lucille gonna be waiting.

Troy (puts his arm around Rose): See this woman, Bono? I love this woman. I love this woman so much it hurts. I love her so much . . . I done run out of ways of loving her. So I got to go back to basics. Don't you come by my house Monday morning talking about time to go to work . . . 'cause I'm still gonna be stroking!

Rose: Troy! Stop it now!

Bono: I ain't paying him no mind, Rose. That ain't nothing but gin-talk. Go on, Troy. I'll see you Monday.

Troy: Don't you come by my house, nigger! I done told you what I'm gonna be doing.

(The lights go down to black.)

SCENE II

The lights come up on Rose hanging up clothes. She hums and sings softly to herself. It is the following morning.

Rose (sings):

Jesus, be a fence all around me every day
Jesus, I want you to protect me as I travel on my way
Jesus, be a fence all around me every day

(Troy enters from the house.)

Jesus, I want you to protect me
As I travel on my way

(To Troy.) 'Morning. You ready for breakfast? I can fix it soon as I finish hanging up these clothes.

Troy: I got the coffee on. That'll be alright. I'll just drink some of that this morning.

Rose: That 651 hit yesterday. That's the second time this month. Miss Pearl hit for a dollar . . . seem like those that need the least always get lucky. Poor folks can't get nothing.

Troy: Them numbers don't know nobody. I don't know why you fool with them. You and Lyons both.

Rose: It's something to do.

Troy: You ain't doing nothing but throwing your money away.

Rose: Troy, you know I don't play foolishly. I just play a nickel here and a nickel there.

Troy: That's two nickels you done thrown away.

Rose: Now I hit sometimes . . . that makes up for it. It always comes in handy when I do hit. I don't hear you complaining then.

Troy: I ain't complaining now. I just say it's foolish. Trying to guess out of six hundred ways which way the number gonna come. If I had all the money niggers, these Negroes, throw away on numbers for one week—just one week—I'd be a rich man.

Rose: Well, you wishing and calling it foolish ain't gonna stop folks from playing numbers. That's one thing for sure. Besides . . . some good things come from playing numbers. Look where Pope done bought him that restaurant off of numbers.

Troy: I can't stand niggers like that. Man ain't had two dimes to rub together. He walking around with his shoes all run over bumming money for cigarettes. Alright. Got lucky there and hit the numbers . . .

Rose: Troy, I know all about it.

Troy: Had good sense, I'll say that for him. He ain't throwed his money away. I seen niggers hit the numbers and go through two thousand dollars in four days. Man bought him that restaurant down there . . . fixed it up real nice . . . and then didn't want nobody to come in it! A Negro go in there and can't get no kind of service. I seen a white fellow come in there and order a bowl of stew. Pope picked all the meat out of the pot for him. Man ain't had nothing but a bowl of meat! Negro come behind him and ain't got nothing but the potatoes and carrots. Talking about what numbers do for people, you picked a wrong example. Ain't done nothing but make a worser fool out of him than he was before.

Rose: Troy, you ought to stop worrying about what happened at work yesterday.

Troy: I ain't worried. Just told me to be down there at the Commissioner's office on Friday. Everybody think they gonna fire me. I ain't worried about them firing me. You ain't got to worry about that. *(Pause.)* Where's Cory? Cory in the house? *(Calls.)* Cory?

Rose: He gone out.

Troy: Out, huh? He gone out 'cause he know I want him to help me with this fence. I know how he is. That boy scared of work.

(Gabriel enters. He comes halfway down the alley and, hearing Troy's voice, stops.)

Troy (continues): He ain't done a lick of work in his life.

Rose: He had to go to football practice. Coach wanted them to get in a little extra practice before the season start.

Troy: I got his practice . . . running out of here before he get his chores done.

Rose: Troy, what is wrong with you this morning? Don't nothing set right with you. Go on back in there and go to bed . . . get up on the other side.

Troy: Why something got to be wrong with me? I ain't said nothing wrong with me.

Rose: You got something to say about everything. First it's the numbers . . . then it's the way the man runs his restaurant . . . then you done got on Cory. What's it gonna be next? Take a look up there and see if the weather suits you . . . or is it gonna be how you gonna put up the fence with the clothes hanging in the yard?

Troy: You hit the nail on the head then.

Rose: I know you like I know the back of my hand. Go on in there and get you some coffee . . . see if that straighten you up. 'Cause you ain't right this morning.

(Troy starts into the house and sees Gabriel. Gabriel starts singing. Troy's brother, he is seven years younger than Troy. Injured in World War II, he has a metal plate in his head. He carries an old trumpet tied around his waist and believes with every fiber of his being that he is the Archangel Gabriel. He carries a chipped basket with an assortment of discarded fruits and vegetables he has picked up in the Strip District and which he attempts to sell.)

Gabriel (singing):

Yes, ma'am, I got plums
You ask me how I sell them
Oh ten cents apiece
Three for a quarter
Come and buy now
'Cause I'm here today
And tomorrow I'll be gone

(Gabriel enters.)

Hey, Rose!

Rose: How you doing, Gabe?

Gabriel: There's Troy . . . Hey, Troy!

Troy: Hey, Gabe.

(Exit into kitchen.)

Rose (to Gabriel): What you got there?

Gabriel: You know what I got, Rose. I got fruits and vegetables.

Rose (looking in basket): Where's all these plums you talking about?

Gabriel: I ain't got no plums today, Rose. I was just singing that. Have some tomorrow. Put me in a big order for plums. Have enough plums tomorrow for St. Peter and everybody.

(Troy reenters from kitchen, crosses to steps.)

(To Rose.) Troy's mad at me.

Troy: I ain't mad at you. What I got to be mad at you about? You ain't done nothing to me.

Gabriel: I just moved over to Miss Pearl's to keep out from in your way. I ain't mean no harm by it.

Troy: Who said anything about that? I ain't said anything about that.

Gabriel: You ain't mad at me, is you?

Troy: Naw . . . I ain't mad at you, Gabe. If I was mad at you I'd tell you about it.

Gabriel: Got me two rooms. In the basement. Got my own door too. Wanna see my key? *(He holds up a key.)* That's my own key! Ain't nobody else got a key like that. That's my key! My two rooms!

Troy: Well, that's good, Gabe. You got your own key . . . that's good.

Rose: You hungry, Gabe? I was just fixing to cook Troy his breakfast.

Gabriel: I'll take some biscuits. You got some biscuits? Did you know when I was in heaven . . . every morning me and St. Peter would sit down by the gate and eat some big fat biscuits? Oh, yeah! We had us a good time. We'd sit there and eat us them biscuits and then St. Peter would go off to sleep and tell me to wake him up when it's time to open the gates for the judgment.

Rose: Well, come on . . . I'll make up a batch of biscuits.

(Rose exits into the house.)

Gabriel: Troy . . . St. Peter got your name in the book. I seen it. It say . . . Troy Maxson. I say . . . I know him! He got the same name like what I got. That's my brother!

Troy: How many times you gonna tell me that, Gabe?

Gabriel: Ain't got my name in the book. Don't have to have my name. I done died and went to heaven. He got your name though. One morning St. Peter was looking at his book . . . marking it up for the judgment . . . and he let me see your name. Got it in there under M. Got Rose's name . . . I ain't seen it like I seen yours . . . but I know it's in there. He got a great big book. Got everybody's name what was ever been born. That's what he told me. But I seen your name. Seen it with my own eyes.

Troy: Go on in the house there. Rose going to fix you something to eat.

Gabriel: Oh, I ain't hungry. I done had breakfast with Aunt Jemimah. She come by and cooked me up a whole mess of flapjacks. Remember how we used to eat them flapjacks?

Troy: Go on in the house and get you something to eat now.

Gabriel: I got to sell my plums. I done sold some tomatoes. Got me two quarters. Wanna see? *(He shows Troy his quarters.)* I'm gonna save them and buy me a new horn so St. Peter can hear me when it's time to open the gates. *(Gabriel stops suddenly. Listens.)* Hear that? That's the hellhounds. I got to chase them out of here. Go on get out of here! Get out!

(Gabriel exits singing.)

Better get ready for the judgment
Better get ready for the judgment
My Lord is coming down

(Rose enters from the house.)

Troy: He gone off somewhere.

Gabriel (offstage):

Better get ready for the judgment
Better get ready for the judgment morning
Better get ready for the judgment
My God is coming down

Rose: He ain't eating right. Miss Pearl say she can't get him to eat nothing.

Troy: What you want me to do about it, Rose? I done did everything I can for the man. I can't make him get well. Man got half his head blown away . . . what you expect?

Rose: Seem like something ought to be done to help him.

Troy: Man don't bother nobody. He just mixed up from that metal plate he got in his head. Ain't no sense for him to go back into the hospital.

Rose: Least he be eating right. They can help him take care of himself.

Troy: Don't nobody wanna be locked up, Rose. What you wanna lock him up for? Man go over there and fight the war . . . messin' around with them Japs, get half his head blown off . . . and they give him a lousy three thousand dollars. And I had to swoop down on that.

Rose: Is you fixing to go into that again?

Troy: That's the only way I got a roof over my head . . . cause of that metal plate.

Rose: Ain't no sense you blaming yourself for nothing. Gabe wasn't in no condition to manage that money. You done what was right by him. Can't nobody say you ain't done what was right by him. Look how long you took care of him . . . till he wanted to have his own place and moved over there with Miss Pearl.

Troy: That ain't what I'm saying, woman! I'm just stating the facts. If my brother didn't have that metal plate in his head . . . I wouldn't have a pot to piss in or a window to throw it out of. And I'm fifty-three years old. Now see if you can understand that!

(Troy gets up from the porch and starts to exit the yard.)

Rose: Where you going off to? You been running out of here every Saturday for weeks. I thought you was gonna work on this fence?

Troy: I'm gonna walk down to Taylors'. Listen to the ball game. I'll be back in a bit. I'll work on it when I get back.

(He exits the yard. The lights go to black.)

SCENE III

The lights come up on the yard. It is four hours later. Rose is taking down the clothes from the line. Cory enters carrying his football equipment.

Rose: Your daddy like to had a fit with you running out of here this morning without doing your chores.

Cory: I told you I had to go to practice.

Rose: He say you were supposed to help him with this fence.

Cory: He been saying that the last four or five Saturdays, and then he don't never do nothing, but go down to Taylors'. Did you tell him about the recruiter?

Rose: Yeah, I told him.

Cory: What he say?

Rose: He ain't said nothing too much. You get in there and get started on your chores before he gets back. Go on and scrub down them steps before he gets back here hollering and carrying on.

Cory: I'm hungry. What you got to eat, Mama?

Rose: Go on and get started on your chores. I got some meat loaf in there. Go on and make you a sandwich . . . and don't leave no mess in there.

(Cory exits into the house. Rose continues to take down the clothes. Troy enters the yard and sneaks up and grabs her from behind.)

Troy! Go on, now. You liked to scared me to death. What was the score of the game? Lucille had me on the phone and I couldn't keep up with it.

Troy: What I care about the game? Come here, woman. *(He tries to kiss her.)*

Rose: I thought you went down Taylors' to listen to the game. Go on, Troy! You supposed to be putting up this fence.

Troy (attempting to kiss her again): I'll put it up when I finish with what is at hand.

Rose: Go on, Troy. I ain't studying you.

Troy (chasing after her): I'm studying you . . . fixing to do my homework!

Rose: Troy, you better leave me alone.

Troy: Where's Cory? That boy brought his butt home yet?

Rose: He's in the house doing his chores.

Troy (calling): Cory! Get your butt out here, boy!

(Rose exits into the house with the laundry. Troy goes over to the pile of wood, picks up a board, and starts sawing. Cory enters from the house.)

Troy: You just now coming in here from leaving this morning?

Cory: Yeah, I had to go to football practice.

Troy: Yeah, what?

Cory: Yessir.

Troy: I ain't but two seconds off you noway. The garbage sitting in there overflowing . . . you ain't done none of your chores . . . and you come in here talking about "Yeah."

Cory: I was just getting ready to do my chores now, Pop . . .

Troy: Your first chore is to help me with this fence on Saturday. Everything else come after that. Now get that saw and cut them boards.

(Cory takes the saw and begins cutting the boards. Troy continues working. There is a long pause.)

Cory: Hey, Pop . . . why don't you buy a TV?

Troy: What I want with a TV? What I want one of them for?

Cory: Everybody got one. Earl, Ba Bra . . . Jesse!

Troy: I ain't asked you who had one. I say what I want with one?

Cory: So you can watch it. They got lots of things on TV. Baseball games and everything. We could watch the World Series.

Troy: Yeah . . . and how much this TV cost?

Cory: I don't know. They got them on sale for around two hundred dollars.

Troy: Two hundred dollars, huh?

Cory: That ain't that much, Pop.

Troy: Naw, it's just two hundred dollars. See that roof you got over your head at night? Let me tell you something about that roof. It's been over ten years since that roof was last tarred. See now . . . the snow come this winter and sit up there on that roof like it is . . . and it's gonna seep inside. It's just gonna be a little bit . . . ain't gonna hardly notice it. Then the next thing you know, it's gonna be leaking all over the house. Then the wood rot from all that water and you gonna need a whole new roof. Now, how much you think it cost to get that roof tarred?

Cory: I don't know.

Troy: Two hundred and sixty-four dollars . . . cash money. While you thinking about a TV, I got to be thinking about the roof . . . and whatever else go wrong here. Now if you had two hundred dollars, what would you do . . . fix the roof or buy a TV?

Cory: I'd buy a TV. Then when the roof started to leak . . . when it needed fixing . . . I'd fix it.

Troy: Where you gonna get the money from? You done spent it for a TV. You gonna sit up and watch the water run all over your brand new TV.

Cory: Aw, Pop. You got money. I know you do.

Troy: Where I got it at, huh?

Cory: You got it in the bank.

Troy: You wanna see my bankbook? You wanna see that seventy-three dollars and twenty-two cents I got sitting up in there?

Cory: You ain't got to pay for it all at one time. You can put a down payment on it and carry it on home with you.

Troy: Not me. I ain't gonna owe nobody nothing if I can help it. Miss a payment and they come and snatch it right out of your house. Then what you got? Now, soon as I get two hundred dollars clear, then I'll buy a TV. Right now, as soon as I get two hundred and sixty-four dollars, I'm gonna have this roof tarred.

Cory: Aw . . . Pop!

Troy: You go on and get you two hundred dollars and buy one if ya want it. I got better things to do with my money.

Cory: I can't get no two hundred dollars. I ain't never seen two hundred dollars.

Troy: I'll tell you what . . . you get you a hundred dollars and I'll put the other hundred with it.

Cory: Alright, I'm gonna show you.

Troy: You gonna show me how you can cut them boards right now.

(Cory begins to cut the boards. There is a long pause.)

Cory: The Pirates won today. That makes five in a row.

Troy: I ain't thinking about the Pirates. Got an all-white team. Got that boy . . . that Puerto Rican boy . . . Clemente.° Don't even half-play him. That boy could be something if they give him a chance. Play him one day and sit him on the bench the next.

Cory: He gets a lot of chances to play.

Troy: I'm talking about playing regular. Playing every day so you can get your timing. That's what I'm talking about.

Cory: They got some white guys on the team that don't play every day. You can't play everybody at the same time.

Troy: If they got a white fellow sitting on the bench . . . you can bet your last dollar he can't play! The colored guy got to be twice as good before he get on the team. That's why I don't want you to get all tied up in them sports. Man on the team and what it get him? They got colored on the team and don't use them. Same as not having them. All them teams the same.

Cory: The Braves got Hank Aaron and Wes Covington. Hank Aaron hit two home runs today. That makes forty-three.

Troy: Hank Aaron ain't nobody. That's what you supposed to do. That's how you supposed to play the game. Ain't nothing to it. It's just a matter of timing . . . getting the right follow-through. Hell, I can hit forty-three home runs right now!

Cory: Not off no major-league pitching, you couldn't.

Troy: We had better pitching in the Negro leagues. I hit seven home runs off of Satchel Paige.° You can't get no better than that!

Cory: Sandy Koufax.° He's leading the league in strikeouts.

Troy: I ain't thinking of no Sandy Koufax.

Cory: You got Warren Spahn° and Lew Burdette.° I bet you couldn't hit no home runs off of Warren Spahn.

Troy: I'm through with it now. You go on and cut them boards. *(Pause.)* Your mama tell me you done got recruited by a college football team? Is that right?

Cory: Yeah. Coach Zellman say the recruiter gonna be coming by to talk to you. Get you to sign the permission papers.

Clemente: Hall of Fame outfielder Roberto Clemente, a dark-skinned Puerto Rican, played 17 seasons with the Pittsburgh Pirates. *Satchel Paige . . . Sandy Koufax . . . Warren Spahn . . . Lew Burdette:* The great Satchel Paige pitched many years in the Negro Leagues; beginning in 1948, when he was in his forties and long past his prime, he appeared in nearly 200 games in the American League. Star pitchers Sandy Koufax of the Dodgers and Warren Spahn and Lew Burdette of the Braves were all white.

Troy: I thought you supposed to be working down there at the A&P. Ain't you suppose to be working down there after school?

Cory: Mr. Stawicki say he gonna hold my job for me until after the football season. Say starting next week I can work weekends.

Troy: I thought we had an understanding about this football stuff? You suppose to keep up with your chores and hold that job down at the A&P. Ain't been around here all day on a Saturday. Ain't none of your chores done . . . and now you telling me you done quit your job.

Cory: I'm going to be working weekends.

Troy: You damn right you are! And ain't no need for nobody coming around here to talk to me about signing nothing.

Cory: Hey, Pop . . . you can't do that. He's coming all the way from North Carolina.

Troy: I don't care where he coming from. The white man ain't gonna let you get nowhere with that football noway. You go on and get your book-learning so you can work yourself up in that A&P or learn how to fix cars or build houses or something, get you a trade. That way you have something can't nobody take away from you. You go on and learn how to put your hands to some good use. Besides hauling people's garbage.

Cory: I get good grades, Pop. That's why the recruiter wants to talk with you. You got to keep up your grades to get recruited. This way I'll be going to college. I'll get a chance . . .

Troy: First you gonna get your butt down there to the A&P and get your job back.

Cory: Mr. Stawicki done already hired somebody else 'cause I told him I was playing football.

Troy: You a bigger fool than I thought . . . to let somebody take away your job so you can play some football. Where you gonna get your money to take out your girlfriend and whatnot? What kind of foolishness is that to let somebody take away your job?

Cory: I'm still gonna be working weekends.

Troy: Naw . . . naw. You getting your butt out of here and finding you another job.

Cory: Come on, Pop! I got to practice. I can't work after school and play football too. The team needs me. That's what Coach Zellman say . . .

Troy: I don't care what nobody else say. I'm the boss . . . you understand? I'm the boss around here. I do the only saying what counts.

Cory: Come on, Pop!

Troy: I asked you . . . did you understand?

Cory: Yeah . . .

Troy: What?!

Cory: Yessir.

Troy: You go on down there to that A&P and see if you can get your job back. If you can't do both . . . then you quit the football team. You've got to take the crookeds with the straights.
Cory: Yessir. *(Pause.)* Can I ask you a question?
Troy: What the hell you wanna ask me? Mr. Stawicki the one you got the questions for.
Cory: How come you ain't never liked me?
Troy: Liked you? Who the hell say I got to like you? What law is there say I got to like you? Wanna stand up in my face and ask a damn fool-ass question like that. Talking about liking somebody. Come here, boy, when I talk to you.

(Cory comes over to where Troy is working. He stands slouched over and Troy shoves him on his shoulder.)

Straighten up, goddammit! I asked you a question . . . what law is there say I got to like you?
Cory: None.
Troy: Well, alright then! Don't you eat every day? *(Pause.)* Answer me when I talk to you! Don't you eat every day?
Cory: Yeah.
Troy: Nigger, as long as you in my house, you put that sir on the end of it when you talk to me.
Cory: Yes . . . sir.
Troy: You eat every day.
Cory: Yessir!
Troy: Got a roof over your head.
Cory: Yessir!
Troy: Got clothes on your back.
Cory: Yessir.
Troy: Why you think that is?
Cory: Cause of you.
Troy: Aw, hell I know it's cause of me . . . but why do you think that is?
Cory (hesitant): 'Cause you like me.
Troy: Like you? I go out of here every morning . . . bust my butt . . . putting up with them crackers every day . . . cause I like you? You about the biggest fool I ever saw. *(Pause.)* It's my job. It's my responsibility! You understand that? A man got to take care of his family. You live in my house . . . sleep you behind on my bedclothes . . . fill you belly up with my food . . . cause you my son. You my flesh and blood. Not cause I like you! Cause it's my duty to take care of you. I owe a responsibility to you!

Let's get this straight right here . . . before it go along any further . . . I ain't got to like you. Mr. Rand don't give me my money come payday cause he likes me. He gives me cause he owe me. I done give you everything I had to give you. I gave you your life! Me and your mama worked that out between us. And liking your black ass wasn't part of the bargain. Don't you try and go through life worrying about if somebody like you or not. You best be making sure they doing right by you. You understand what I'm saying, boy?

Cory: Yessir.

Troy: Then get the hell out of my face, and get on down to that A&P.

(Rose has been standing behind the screen door for much of the scene. She enters as Cory exits.)

Rose: Why don't you let the boy go ahead and play football, Troy? Ain't no harm in that. He's just trying to be like you with the sports.

Troy: I don't want him to be like me! I want him to move as far away from my life as he can get. You the only decent thing that ever happened to me. I wish him that. But I don't wish him a thing else from my life. I decided seventeen years ago that boy wasn't getting involved in no sports. Not after what they did to me in the sports.

Rose: Troy, why don't you admit you was too old to play in the major leagues? For once . . . why don't you admit that?

Troy: What do you mean too old? Don't come telling me I was too old. I just wasn't the right color. Hell, I'm fifty-three years old and can do better than Selkirk's .269 right now!

Rose: How's was you gonna play ball when you were over forty? Sometimes I can't get no sense out of you.

Troy: I got good sense, woman. I got sense enough not to let my boy get hurt over playing no sports. You been mothering that boy too much. Worried about if people like him.

Rose: Everything that boy do . . . he do for you. He wants you to say "Good job, son." That's all.

Troy: Rose, I ain't got time for that. He's alive. He's healthy. He's got to make his own way. I made mine. Ain't nobody gonna hold his hand when he get out there in that world.

Rose: Times have changed from when you was young, Troy. People change. The world's changing around you and you can't even see it.

Troy (slow, methodical): Woman . . . I do the best I can do. I come in here every Friday. I carry a sack of potatoes and a bucket of lard. You all line up at the door with your hands out. I give you the lint from my pockets. I give you my sweat and my blood. I ain't got no tears. I done spent them. We go upstairs in that room at night . . . and I fall down on you and try to blast a hole into forever. I get up Monday morning . . . find my lunch on the table. I go out. Make my way. Find my strength to carry me through to the next Friday. *(Pause.)* That's all I got, Rose. That's all I got to give. I can't give nothing else.

(Troy exits into the house. The lights go down to black.)

SCENE IV

It is Friday. Two weeks later. Cory starts out of the house with his football equipment. The phone rings.

Cory (calling): I got it! *(He answers the phone and stands in the screen door talking.)* Hello? Hey, Jesse. Naw . . . I was just getting ready to leave now.

Rose (calling): Cory!

Cory: I told you, man, them spikes is all tore up. You can use them if you want, but they ain't no good. Earl got some spikes.

Rose (calling): Cory!

Cory (calling to Rose): Mam? I'm talking to Jesse. *(Into phone.)* When she say that? *(Pause.)* Aw, you lying, man. I'm gonna tell her you said that.

Rose (calling): Cory, don't you go nowhere!

Cory: I got to go to the game, Ma! *(Into the phone.)* Yeah, hey, look, I'll talk to you later. Yeah, I'll meet you over Earl's house. Later. Bye, Ma.

(Cory exits the house and starts out the yard.)

Rose: Cory, where you going off to? You got that stuff all pulled out and thrown all over your room.

Cory (in the yard): I was looking for my spikes. Jesse wanted to borrow my spikes.

Rose: Get up there and get that cleaned up before your daddy get back in here.

Cory: I got to go to the game! I'll clean it up when I get back.

(Cory exits.)

Rose: That's all he need to do is see that room all messed up.

(Rose exits into the house. Troy and Bono enter the yard. Troy is dressed in clothes other than his work clothes.)

Bono: He told him the same thing he told you. Take it to the union.

Troy: Brownie ain't got that much sense. Man wasn't thinking about nothing. He wait until I confront them on it . . . then he wanna come crying seniority. *(Calls.)* Hey, Rose!

Bono: I wish I could have seen Mr. Rand's face when he told you.

Troy: He couldn't get it out of his mouth! Liked to bit his tongue! When they called me down there to the Commissioner's office . . . he thought they was gonna fire me. Like everybody else.

Bono: I didn't think they was gonna fire you. I thought they was gonna put you on the warning paper.

Troy: Hey, Rose! *(To Bono.)* Yeah, Mr. Rand like to bit his tongue.

(Troy breaks the seal on the bottle, takes a drink, and hands it to Bono.)

Bono: I see you run right down to Taylors' and told that Alberta gal.

Troy (calling): Hey, Rose! *(To Bono.)* I told everybody. Hey, Rose! I went down there to cash my check.

Rose (entering from the house): Hush all that hollering, man! I know you out here. What they say down there at the Commissioner's office?

Troy: You supposed to come when I call you, woman. Bono'll tell you that. *(To Bono.)* Don't Lucille come when you call her?

Rose: Man, hush your mouth. I ain't no dog . . . talk about "come when you call me."

Troy (puts his arm around Rose): You hear this, Bono? I had me an old dog used to get uppity like that. You say, "C'mere, Blue!" . . . and he just lay there and look at you. End up getting a stick and chasing him away trying to make him come.

Rose: I ain't studying you and your dog. I remember you used to sing that old song.

Troy (he sings):

Hear it ring! Hear it ring!
I had a dog his name was Blue.

Rose: Don't nobody wanna hear you sing that old song.

Troy (sings):

You know Blue was mighty true.

Rose: Used to have Cory running around here singing that song.

Bono: Hell, I remember that song myself.

Troy (sings):

You know Blue was a good old dog.
Blue treed a possum in a hollow log.

That was my daddy's song. My daddy made up that song.

Rose: I don't care who made it up. Don't nobody wanna hear you sing it.

Troy (makes a song like calling a dog): Come here, woman.

Rose: You come in here carrying on, I reckon they ain't fired you. What they say down there at the Commissioner's office?

Troy: Look here, Rose . . . Mr. Rand called me into his office today when I got back from talking to them people down there . . . it come from up top . . . he called me in and told me they was making me a driver.

Rose: Troy, you kidding!

Troy: No I ain't. Ask Bono.

Rose: Well, that's great, Troy. Now you don't have to hassle them people no more.

(Lyons enters from the street.)

Troy: Aw hell, I wasn't looking to see you today. I thought you was in jail. Got it all over the front page of the *Courier* about them raiding Sefus's place . . . where you be hanging out with all them thugs.

Lyons: Hey, Pop . . . that ain't got nothing to do with me. I don't go down there gambling. I go down there to sit in with the band. I ain't got nothing to do with the gambling part. They got some good music down there.

Troy: They got some rogues . . . is what they got.

Lyons: How you been, Mr. Bono? Hi, Rose.

Bono: I see where you playing down at the Crawford Grill tonight.

Rose: How come you ain't brought Bonnie like I told you? You should have brought Bonnie with you, she ain't been over in a month of Sundays.

Lyons: I was just in the neighborhood . . . thought I'd stop by.

Troy: Here he come . . .

Bono: Your daddy got a promotion on the rubbish. He's gonna be the first colored driver. Ain't got to do nothing but sit up there and read the paper like them white fellows.

Lyons: Hey, Pop . . . if you knew how to read you'd be alright.

Bono: Naw . . . naw . . . you mean if the nigger knew how to *drive* he'd be alright. Been fighting with them people about driving and ain't even got a license. Mr. Rand know you ain't got no driver's license?

Troy: Driving ain't nothing. All you do is point the truck where you want it to go. Driving ain't nothing.

Bono: Do Mr. Rand know you ain't got no driver's license? That's what I'm talking about. I ain't asked if driving was easy. I asked if Mr. Rand know you ain't got no driver's license.

Troy: He ain't got to know. The man ain't got to know my business. Time he find out, I have two or three driver's licenses.

Lyons (going into his pocket): Say, look here, Pop . . .

Troy: I knew it was coming. Didn't I tell you, Bono? I know what kind of "Look here, Pop" that was. The nigger fixing to ask me for some money. It's Friday night. It's my payday. All them rogues down there on the avenue . . . the ones that ain't in jail . . . and Lyons is hopping in his shoes to get down there with them.

Lyons: See, Pop . . . if you give somebody else a chance to talk sometime, you'd see that I was fixing to pay you back your ten dollars like I told you. Here . . . I told you I'd pay you when Bonnie got paid.

Troy: Naw . . . you go ahead and keep that ten dollars. Put it in the bank. The next time you feel like you wanna come by here and ask me for something . . . you go on down there and get that.

Lyons: Here's your ten dollars, Pop. I told you I don't want you to give me nothing. I just wanted to borrow ten dollars.

Troy: Naw . . . you go on and keep that for the next time you want to ask me.

Lyons: Come on, Pop . . . here go your ten dollars.

Rose: Why don't you go on and let the boy pay you back, Troy?

Lyons: Here you go, Rose. If you don't take it I'm gonna have to hear about it for the next six months. *(He hands her the money.)*

Rose: You can hand yours over here too, Troy.
Troy: You see this, Bono. You see how they do me.
Bono: Yeah, Lucille do me the same way.

(Gabriel is heard singing offstage. He enters.)

Gabriel: Better get ready for the Judgment! Better get ready for . . . Hey! . . . Hey! . . . There's Troy's boy!
Lyons: How are you doing, Uncle Gabe?
Gabriel: Lyons . . . The King of the Jungle! Rose . . . hey, Rose. Got a flower for you. *(He takes a rose from his pocket.)* Picked it myself. That's the same rose like you is!
Rose: That's right nice of you, Gabe.
Lyons: What you been doing, Uncle Gabe?
Gabriel: Oh, I been chasing hellhounds and waiting on the time to tell St. Peter to open the gates.
Lyons: You been chasing hellhounds, huh? Well . . . you doing the right thing, Uncle Gabe. Somebody got to chase them.
Gabriel: Oh, yeah . . . I know it. The devil's strong. The devil ain't no pushover. Hellhounds snipping at everybody's heels. But I got my trumpet waiting on the judgment time.
Lyons: Waiting on the Battle of Armageddon, huh?
Gabriel: Ain't gonna be too much of a battle when God get to waving that Judgment sword. But the people's gonna have a hell of a time trying to get into heaven if them gates ain't open.
Lyons (putting his arm around Gabriel): You hear this, Pop. Uncle Gabe, you alright!
Gabriel (laughing with Lyons): Lyons! King of the Jungle.
Rose: You gonna stay for supper, Gabe? Want me to fix you a plate?
Gabriel: I'll take a sandwich, Rose. Don't want no plate. Just wanna eat with my hands. I'll take a sandwich.
Rose: How about you, Lyons? You staying? Got some short ribs cooking.
Lyons: Naw, I won't eat nothing till after we finished playing. *(Pause.)* You ought to come down and listen to me play, Pop.
Troy: I don't like that Chinese music. All that noise.
Rose: Go on in the house and wash up, Gabe . . . I'll fix you a sandwich.
Gabriel (to Lyons, as he exits): Troy's mad at me.
Lyons: What you mad at Uncle Gabe for, Pop?
Rose: He thinks Troy's mad at him cause he moved over to Miss Pearl's.
Troy: I ain't mad at the man. He can live where he want to live at.
Lyons: What he move over there for? Miss Pearl don't like nobody.
Rose: She don't mind him none. She treats him real nice. She just don't allow all that singing.
Troy: She don't mind that rent he be paying . . . that's what she don't mind.
Rose: Troy, I ain't going through that with you no more. He's over there cause he want to have his own place. He can come and go as he please.

Troy: Hell, he could come and go as he please here. I wasn't stopping him. I ain't put no rules on him.

Rose: It ain't the same thing, Troy. And you know it.

(Gabriel comes to the door.)

Now, that's the last I wanna hear about that. I don't wanna hear nothing else about Gabe and Miss Pearl. And next week . . .

Gabriel: I'm ready for my sandwich, Rose.

Rose: And next week . . . when that recruiter come from that school . . . I want you to sign that paper and go on and let Cory play football. Then that'll be the last I have to hear about that.

Troy (to Rose as she exits into the house): I ain't thinking about Cory nothing.

Lyons: What . . . Cory got recruited? What school he going to?

Troy: That boy walking around here smelling his piss . . . thinking he's grown. Thinking he's gonna do what he want, irrespective of what I say. Look here, Bono . . . I left the Commissioner's office and went down to the A&P . . . that boy ain't working down there. He lying to me. Telling me he got his job back . . . telling me he working weekends . . . telling me he working after school . . . Mr. Stawicki tell me he ain't working down there at all!

Lyons: Cory just growing up. He's just busting at the seams trying to fill out your shoes.

Troy: I don't care what he's doing. When he get to the point where he wanna disobey me . . . then it's time for him to move on. Bono'll tell you that. I bet he ain't never disobeyed his daddy without paying the consequences.

Bono: I ain't never had a chance. My daddy came on through . . . but I ain't never knew him to see him . . . or what he had on his mind or where he went. Just moving on through. Searching out the New Land. That's what the old folks used to call it. See a fellow moving around from place to place . . . woman to woman . . . called it searching out the New Land. I can't say if he ever found it. I come along, didn't want no kids. Didn't know if I was gonna be in one place long enough to fix on them right as their daddy. I figured I was going searching too. As it turned out I been hooked up with Lucille near about as long as your daddy been with Rose. Going on sixteen years.

Troy: Sometimes I wish I hadn't known my daddy. He ain't cared nothing about no kids. A kid to him wasn't nothing. All he wanted was for you to learn how to walk so he could start you to working. When it come time for eating . . . he ate first. If there was anything left over, that's what you got. Man would sit down and eat two chickens and give you the wing.

Lyons: You ought to stop that, Pop. Everybody feed their kids. No matter how hard times is . . . everybody care about their kids. Make sure they have something to eat.

Troy: The only thing my daddy cared about was getting them bales of cotton in to Mr. Lubin. That's the only thing that mattered to him. Sometimes I used to wonder why he was living. Wonder why the devil hadn't come and got him. "Get them bales of cotton in to Mr. Lubin" and find out he owe him money . . .

Lyons: He should have just went on and left when he saw he couldn't get nowhere. That's what I would have done.

Troy: How he gonna leave with eleven kids? And where he gonna go? He ain't knew how to do nothing but farm. No, he was trapped and I think he knew it. But I'll say this for him . . . he felt a responsibility toward us. Maybe he ain't treated us the way I felt he should have . . . but without that responsibility he could have walked off and left us . . . made his own way.

Bono: A lot of them did. Back in those days what you talking about . . . they walk out their front door and just take on down one road or another and keep on walking.

Lyons: There you go! That's what I'm talking about.

Bono: Just keep on walking till you come to something else. Ain't you never heard of nobody having the walking blues? Well, that's what you call it when you just take off like that.

Troy: My daddy ain't had them walking blues! What you talking about? He stayed right there with his family. But he was just as evil as he could be. My mama couldn't stand him. Couldn't stand that evilness. She run off when I was about eight. She sneaked off one night after he had gone to sleep. Told me she was coming back for me. I ain't never seen her no more. All his women run off and left him. He wasn't good for nobody.

When my turn come to head out, I was fourteen and got to sniffing around Joe Canewell's daughter. Had us an old mule we called Greyboy. My daddy sent me out to do some plowing and I tied up Greyboy and went to fooling around with Joe Canewell's daughter. We done found us a nice little spot, got real cozy with each other. She about thirteen and we done figured we was grown anyway . . . so we down there enjoying ourselves . . . ain't thinking about nothing. We didn't know Greyboy had got loose and wandered back to the house and my daddy was looking for me. We down there by the creek enjoying ourselves when my daddy come up on us. Surprised us. He had them leather straps off the mule and commenced to whupping me like there was no tomorrow. I jumped up, mad and embarrassed. I was scared of my daddy. When he commenced to whupping on me . . . quite naturally I run to get out of the way. *(Pause.)* Now I thought he was mad cause I ain't done my work. But I see where he was chasing me off so he could have the gal for himself. When I see what the matter of it was, I lost all fear of my daddy. Right there is where I become a man . . . at fourteen years of age. *(Pause.)* Now it was my turn to run him off. I picked up them same reins that he had used on me. I picked up them reins and commenced to whupping on him. The gal jumped up and run off . . . and when my daddy turned to face me, I could see why the devil had never come to get him . . . cause he was the devil himself. I don't know what happened. When I woke up, I was laying right there by the creek, and Blue . . . this old dog we had . . . was licking my face. I thought I was blind. I couldn't see nothing. Both my eyes were swollen shut. I layed there and cried. I didn't know what I was gonna do. The only thing I knew was the time had come for me to leave my daddy's house. And right there the world suddenly got big. And it was a long time before I could cut it down to where I could handle it.

Part of that cutting down was when I got to the place where I could feel him kicking in my blood and knew that the only thing that separated us was the matter of a few years.

(Gabriel enters from the house with a sandwich.)

Lyons: What you got there, Uncle Gabe?

Gabriel: Got me a ham sandwich. Rose gave me a ham sandwich.

Troy: I don't know what happened to him. I done lost touch with everybody except Gabriel. But I hope he's dead. I hope he found some peace.

Lyons: That's a heavy story, Pop. I didn't know you left home when you was fourteen.

Troy: And didn't know nothing. The only part of the world I knew was the forty-two acres of Mr. Lubin's land. That's all I knew about life.

Lyons: Fourteen's kinda young to be out on your own. *(Phone rings.)* I don't even think I was ready to be out on my own at fourteen. I don't know what I would have done.

Troy: I got up from the creek and walked on down to Mobile. I was through with farming. Figured I could do better in the city. So I walked the two hundred miles to Mobile.

Lyons: Wait a minute . . . you ain't walked no two hundred miles, Pop. Ain't nobody gonna walk no two hundred miles. You talking about some walking there.

Bono: That's the only way you got anywhere back in them days.

Lyons: Shhh. Damn if I wouldn't have hitched a ride with somebody!

Troy: Who you gonna hitch it with? They ain't had no cars and things like they got now. We talking about 1918.

Rose (entering): What you all out here getting into?

Troy (to Rose): I'm telling Lyons how good he got it. He don't know nothing about this I'm talking.

Rose: Lyons, that was Bonnie on the phone. She say you supposed to pick her up.

Lyons: Yeah, okay, Rose.

Troy: I walked on down to Mobile and hitched up with some of them fellows that was heading this way. Got up here and found out . . . not only couldn't you get a job . . . you couldn't find no place to live. I thought I was in freedom. Shhh. Colored folks living down there on the riverbanks in whatever kind of shelter they could find for themselves. Right down there under the Brady Street Bridge. Living in shacks made of sticks and tarpaper. Messed around there and went from bad to worse. Started stealing. First it was food. Then I figured, hell, if I steal money I can buy me some food. Buy me some shoes too! One thing led to another. Met your mama. I was young and anxious to be a man. Met your mama and had you. What I do that for? Now I got to worry about feeding you and her. Got to steal three times as much. Went out one day looking for somebody to rob . . . that's what I was, a robber. I'll tell you the truth. I'm ashamed of it today. But it's the truth. Went to rob this fellow . . . pulled out my knife . . . and he pulled out a gun. Shot me in the chest. It felt just like somebody had taken a hot branding iron and laid it on me. When he shot me I jumped at him with my knife. They told me I killed him and they put me in the penitentiary and locked me up for fifteen years. That's where I met Bono. That's where I learned how to play baseball. Got out that place and your mama had taken you and went on to make life without me. Fifteen years was a long time for her to wait. But that fifteen years cured me of that robbing stuff. Rose'll tell you. She asked me when I met her if I had gotten all that foolishness out of my system. And I told her, "Baby, it's you and baseball all what count with me." You hear me, Bono? I meant it too. She say, "Which one comes first?" I told her, "Baby, ain't no doubt it's baseball . . . but you stick and get old with me and we'll both outlive this baseball." Am I right, Rose? And it's true.

Rose: Man, hush your mouth. You ain't said no such thing. Talking about, "Baby you know you'll always be number one with me." That's what you was talking.

Troy: You hear that, Bono. That's why I love her.

Bono: Rose'll keep you straight. You get off the track, she'll straighten you up.

Rose: Lyons, you better get on up and get Bonnie. She waiting on you.

Lyons (gets up to go): Hey, Pop, why don't you come on down to the Grill and hear me play?

Troy: I ain't going down there. I'm too old to be sitting around in them clubs.

Bono: You got to be good to play down at the Grill.

Lyons: Come on, Pop . . .

Troy: I got to get up in the morning.

Lyons: You ain't got to stay long.

Troy: Naw, I'm gonna get my supper and go on to bed.

Lyons: Well, I got to go. I'll see you again.

Troy: Don't you come around my house on my payday.

Rose: Pick up the phone and let somebody know you coming. And bring Bonnie with you. You know I'm always glad to see her.

Lyons: Yeah, I'll do that, Rose. You take care now. See you, Pop. See you, Mr. Bono. See you, Uncle Gabe.

Gabriel: Lyons! King of the Jungle!

(Lyons exits.)

Troy: Is supper ready, woman? Me and you got some business to take care of. I'm gonna tear it up too.

Rose: Troy, I done told you now!

Troy (puts his arm around Bono): Aw hell, woman . . . this is Bono. Bono like family. I done known this nigger since . . . how long I done know you?

Bono: It's been a long time.

Troy: I done know this nigger since Skippy was a pup. Me and him done been through some times.

Bono: You sure right about that.

Troy: Hell, I done know him longer than I known you. And we still standing shoulder to shoulder. Hey, look here, Bono . . . a man can't ask for no more than that. *(Drinks to him.)* I love you, nigger.

Bono: Hell, I love you too . . . but I got to get home see my woman. You got yours in hand. I got to go get mine.

(Bono starts to exit as Cory enters the yard, dressed in his football uniform. He gives Troy a hard, uncompromising look.)

Cory: What you do that for, Pop?

(He throws his helmet down in the direction of Troy.)

Rose: What's the matter? Cory . . . what's the matter?

Cory: Papa done went up to the school and told Coach Zellman I can't play football no more. Wouldn't even let me play the game. Told him to tell the recruiter not to come.

Rose: Troy . . .

Troy: What you Troying me for. Yeah, I did it. And the boy know why I did it.

Cory: Why you wanna do that to me? That was the one chance I had.

Rose: Ain't nothing wrong with Cory playing football, Troy.

Troy: The boy lied to me. I told the nigger if he wanna play football . . . to keep up his chores and hold down that job at the A&P. That was the conditions. Stopped down there to see Mr. Stawicki . . .

Cory: I can't work after school during the football season, Pop! I tried to tell you that Mr. Stawicki's holding my job for me. You don't never want to listen to nobody. And then you wanna go and do this to me!

Troy: I ain't done nothing to you. You done it to yourself.

Cory: Just cause you didn't have a chance! You just scared I'm gonna be better than you, that's all.

Troy: Come here.

Rose: Troy . . .

(Cory reluctantly crosses over to Troy.)

Troy: Alright! See. You done made a mistake.

Cory: I didn't even do nothing!

Troy: I'm gonna tell you what your mistake was. See . . . you swung at the ball and didn't hit it. That's strike one. See, you in the batter's box now. You swung and you missed. That's strike one. Don't you strike out!

(Lights fade to black.)

ACT II

SCENE I

The following morning. Cory is at the tree hitting the ball with the bat. He tries to mimic Troy, but his swing is awkward, less sure. Rose enters from the house.

Rose: Cory, I want you to help me with this cupboard.

Cory: I ain't quitting the team. I don't care what Poppa say.

Rose: I'll talk to him when he gets back. He had to go see about your Uncle Gabe. The police done arrested him. Say he was disturbing the peace. He'll be back directly. Come on in here and help me clean out the top of this cupboard.

(Cory exits into the house. Rose sees Troy and Bono coming down the alley.)

Troy . . . what they say down there?

Troy: Ain't said nothing. I give them fifty dollars and they let him go. I'll talk to you about it. Where's Cory?

Rose: He's in there helping me clean out these cupboards.

Troy: Tell him to get his butt out here.

(Troy and Bono go over to the pile of wood. Bono picks up the saw and begins sawing.)

Troy (to Bono): All they want is the money. That makes six or seven times I done went down there and got him. See me coming they stick out their *hands.*

Bono: Yeah. I know what you mean. That's all they care about . . . that money. They don't care about what's right. *(Pause.)* Nigger, why you got to go and get some hard wood? You ain't doing nothing but building a little old fence. Get you some soft pine wood. That's all you need.

Troy: I know what I'm doing. This is outside wood. You put pine wood inside the house. Pine wood is inside wood. This here is outside wood. Now you tell me where the fence is gonna be?

Bono: You don't need this wood. You can put it up with pine wood and it'll stand as long as you gonna be here looking at it.

Troy: How you know how long I'm gonna be here, nigger? Hell, I might just live forever. Live longer than old man Horsely.

Bono: That's what Magee used to say.

Troy: Magee's a damn fool. Now you tell me who you ever heard of gonna pull their own teeth with a pair of rusty pliers.

Bono: The old folks . . . my granddaddy used to pull his teeth with pliers. They ain't had no dentists for the colored folks back then.

Troy: Get clean pliers! You understand? Clean pliers! Sterilize them! Besides we ain't living back then. All Magee had to do was walk over to Doc Goldblum's.

Bono: I see where you and that Tallahassee gal . . . that Alberta . . . I see where you all done got tight.

Troy: What you mean "got tight"?

Bono: I see where you be laughing and joking with her all the time.

Troy: I laughs and jokes with all of them, Bono. You know me.

Bono: That ain't the kind of laughing and joking I'm talking about.

(Cory enters from the house.)

Cory: How you doing, Mr. Bono?

Troy: Cory? Get that saw from Bono and cut some wood. He talking about the wood's too hard to cut. Stand back there, Jim, and let that young boy show you how it's done.

Bono: He's sure welcome to it.

(Cory takes the saw and begins to cut the wood.)

Whew-e-e! Look at that. Big old strong boy. Look like Joe Louis. Hell, must be getting old the way I'm watching that boy whip through that wood.

Cory: I don't see why Mama want a fence around the yard noways.

Troy: Damn if I know either. What the hell she keeping out with it? She ain't got nothing nobody want.

Bono: Some people build fences to keep people out . . . and other people build fences to keep people in. Rose wants to hold on to you all. She loves you.

Troy: Hell, nigger, I don't need nobody to tell me my wife loves me. Cory . . . go on in the house and see if you can find that other saw.

Cory: Where's it at?

Troy: I said find it! Look for it till you find it!

(Cory exits into the house.)

What's that supposed to mean? Wanna keep us in?

Bono: Troy . . . I done known you seem like damn near my whole life. You and Rose both. I done know both of you all for a long time. I remember when you met Rose. When you was hitting them baseball out the park. A lot of them old gals was after you then. You had the pick of the litter. When you picked Rose, I was happy for you. That was the first time I knew you had any sense. I said . . . My man Troy knows what he's doing . . . I'm gonna follow this nigger . . . he might take me somewhere. I been following you too. I done learned a whole heap of things about life watching you. I done learned how to tell where the shit lies. How to tell it from the alfalfa. You done learned me a lot of things. You showed me how to not make the same mistakes . . . to take life as it comes along and keep putting one foot in front of the other. *(Pause.)* Rose a good woman, Troy.

Troy: Hell, nigger, I know she a good woman. I been married to her for eighteen years. What you got on your mind, Bono?

Bono: I just say she a good woman. Just like I say anything. I ain't got to have nothing on my mind.

Troy: You just gonna say she a good woman and leave it hanging out there like that? Why you telling me she a good woman?

Bono: She loves you, Troy. Rose loves you.

Troy: You saying I don't measure up. That's what you trying to say. I don't measure up cause I'm seeing this other gal. I know what you trying to say.

Bono: I know what Rose means to you, Troy. I'm just trying to say I don't want to see you mess up.

Troy: Yeah, I appreciate that, Bono. If you was messing around on Lucille I'd be telling you the same thing.

Bono: Well, that's all I got to say. I just say that because I love you both.

Troy: Hell, you know me . . . I wasn't out there looking for nothing. You can't find a better woman than Rose. I know that. But seems like this woman just stuck onto me where I can't shake her loose. I done wrestled with it, tried to throw her off me . . . but she just stuck on tighter. Now she's stuck on for good.

Bono: You's in control . . . that's what you tell me all the time. You responsible for what you do.

Troy: I ain't ducking the responsibility of it. As long as it sets right in my heart . . . then I'm okay. Cause that's all I listen to. It'll tell me right from wrong every time. And I ain't talking about doing Rose no bad turn. I love Rose. She done carried me a long ways and I love and respect her for that.

Bono: I know you do. That's why I don't want to see you hurt her. But what you gonna do when she find out? What you got then? If you try and juggle both of them . . . sooner or later you gonna drop one of them. That's common sense.

Troy: Yeah, I hear what you saying, Bono. I been trying to figure a way to work it out.

Bono: Work it out right, Troy. I don't want to be getting all up between you and Rose's business . . . but work it so it come out right.

Troy: Aw hell, I get all up between you and Lucille's business. When you gonna get that woman that refrigerator she been wanting? Don't tell me you ain't got no money now. I know who your banker is. Mellon° don't need that money bad as Lucille want that refrigerator. I'll tell you that.

Bono: Tell you what I'll do . . . when you finish building this fence for Rose . . . I'll buy Lucille that refrigerator.

Troy: You done stuck your foot in your mouth now!

(Troy grabs up a board and begins to saw. Bono starts to walk out the yard.)

Hey, nigger . . . where you going?

Bono: I'm going home. I know you don't expect me to help you now. I'm protecting my money. I wanna see you put that fence up by yourself. That's what I want to see. You'll be here another six months without me.

Troy: Nigger, you ain't right.

Bono: When it comes to my money . . . I'm right as fireworks on the Fourth of July.

Troy: Alright, we gonna see now. You better get out your bankbook.

(Bono exits, and Troy continues to work. Rose enters from the house.)

Rose: What they say down there? What's happening with Gabe?

Troy: I went down there and got him out. Cost me fifty dollars. Say he was disturbing the peace. Judge set up a hearing for him in three weeks. Say to show cause why he shouldn't be re-committed.

Rose: What was he doing that cause them to arrest him?

Troy: Some kids was teasing him and he run them off home. Say he was howling and carrying on. Some folks seen him and called the police. That's all it was.

Rose: Well, what's you say? What'd you tell the judge?

Troy: Told him I'd look after him. It didn't make no sense to recommit the man. He stuck out his big greasy palm and told me to give him fifty dollars and take him on home.

Rose: Where's he at now? Where'd he go off to?

Troy: He's gone on about his business. He don't need nobody to hold his hand.

Mellon: banker and industrialist Andrew Mellon (1855–1937), U.S. Treasury Secretary 1921–32, was active in philanthropic enterprises, especially in his native Pittsburgh.

Rose: Well, I don't know. Seem like that would be the best place for him if they did put him into the hospital. I know what you're gonna say. But that's what I think would be best.

Troy: The man done had his life ruined fighting for what? And they wanna take and lock him up. Let him be free. He don't bother nobody.

Rose: Well, everybody got their own way of looking at it I guess. Come on and get your lunch. I got a bowl of lima beans and some cornbread in the oven. Come on get something to eat. Ain't no sense you fretting over Gabe.

(Rose turns to go into the house.)

Troy: Rose . . . got something to tell you.

Rose: Well, come on . . . wait till I get this food on the table.

Troy: Rose!

(She stops and turns around.)

I don't know how to say this. *(Pause.)* I can't explain it none. It just sort of grows on you till it gets out of hand. It starts out like a little bush . . . and the next thing you know it's a whole forest.

Rose: Troy . . . what is you talking about?

Troy: I'm talking, woman, let me talk. I'm trying to find a way to tell you . . . I'm gonna be a daddy. I'm gonna be somebody's daddy.

Rose: Troy . . . you're not telling me this? You're gonna be . . . what?

Troy: Rose . . . now . . . see . . .

Rose: You telling me you gonna be somebody's daddy? You telling your *wife* this?

(Gabriel enters from the street. He carries a rose in his hand.)

Gabriel: Hey, Troy! Hey, Rose!

Rose: I have to wait eighteen years to hear something like this.

Gabriel: Hey, Rose . . . I got a flower for you. *(He hands it to her.)* That's a rose. Same rose like you is.

Rose: Thanks, Gabe.

Gabriel: Troy, you ain't mad at me is you? Them bad mens come and put me away. You ain't mad at me is you?

Troy: Naw, Gabe, I ain't mad at you.

Rose: Eighteen years and you wanna come with this.

Gabriel (takes a quarter out of his pocket): See what I got? Got a brand new quarter.

Troy: Rose . . . it's just . . .

Rose: Ain't nothing you can say, Troy. Ain't no way of explaining that.

Gabriel: Fellow that give me this quarter had a whole mess of them. I'm gonna keep this quarter till it stop shining.

Rose: Gabe, go on in the house there. I got some watermelon in the Frigidaire. Go on and get you a piece.

Gabriel: Say, Rose . . . you know I was chasing hellhounds and them bad mens come and get me and take me away. Troy helped me. He come down there and told them they better let me go before he beat them up. Yeah, he did!

Rose: You go on and get you a piece of watermelon, Gabe. Them bad mens is gone now.

Gabriel: Okay, Rose . . . gonna get me some watermelon. The kind with the stripes on it.

(Gabriel exits into the house.)

Rose: Why, Troy? Why? After all these years to come dragging this in to me now. It don't make no sense at your age. I could have expected this ten or fifteen years ago, but not now.

Troy: Age ain't got nothing to do with it, Rose.

Rose: I done tried to be everything a wife should be. Everything a wife could be. Been married eighteen years and I got to live to see the day you tell me you been seeing another woman and done fathered a child by her. And you know I ain't never wanted no half nothing in my family. My whole family is half. Everybody got different fathers and mothers . . . my two sisters and my brother. Can't hardly tell who's who. Can't never sit down and talk about Papa and Mama. It's your papa and your mama and my papa and my mama . . .

Troy: Rose . . . stop it now.

Rose: I ain't never wanted that for none of my children. And now you wanna drag your behind in here and tell me something like this.

Troy: You ought to know. It's time for you to know.

Rose: Well, I don't want to know, goddamn it!

Troy: I can't just make it go away. It's done now. I can't wish the circumstance of the thing away.

Rose: And you don't want to either. Maybe you want to wish me and my boy away. Maybe that's what you want? Well, you can't wish us away. I've got eighteen years of my life invested in you. You ought to have stayed upstairs in my bed where you belong.

Troy: Rose . . . now listen to me . . . we can get a handle on this thing. We can talk this out . . . come to an understanding.

Rose: All of a sudden it's "we." Where was "we" at when you was down there rolling around with some godforsaken woman? "We" should have come to an understanding before you started making a damn fool of yourself. You're a day late and a dollar short when it comes to an understanding with me.

Troy: It's just . . . She gives me a different idea . . . a different understanding about myself. I can step out of this house and get away from the pressures and problems . . . be a different man. I ain't got to wonder how I'm gonna pay the bills or get the roof fixed. I can just be a part of myself that I ain't never been.

Rose: What I want to know . . . is do you plan to continue seeing her. That's all you can say to me.

Troy: I can sit up in her house and laugh. Do you understand what I'm saying. I can laugh out loud . . . and it feels good. It reaches all the way down to the bottom of my shoes. (*Pause.*) Rose, I can't give that up.

Rose: Maybe you ought to go on and stay down there with her . . . if she's a better woman than me.

Troy: It ain't about nobody being a better woman or nothing. Rose, you ain't the blame. A man couldn't ask for no woman to be a better wife than you've been. I'm responsible for it. I done locked myself into a pattern trying to take care of you all that I forgot about myself.

Rose: What the hell was I there for? That was my job, not somebody else's.

Troy: Rose, I done tried all my life to live decent . . . to live a clean . . . hard . . . useful life. I tried to be a good husband to you. In every way I knew how. Maybe I come into the world backwards, I don't know. But . . . you born with two strikes on you before you come to the plate. You got to guard it closely . . . always looking for the curve-ball on the inside corner. You can't afford to let none get past you. You can't afford a call strike. If you going down . . . you going down swinging. Everything lined up against you. What you gonna do. I fooled them, Rose. I bunted. When I found you and Cory and a halfway decent job . . . I was safe. Couldn't nothing touch me. I wasn't gonna strike out no more. I wasn't going back to the penitentiary. I wasn't gonna lay in the streets with a bottle of wine. I was safe. I had me a family. A job. I wasn't gonna get that last strike. I was on first looking for one of them boys to knock me in. To get me home.

Rose: You should have stayed in my bed, Troy.

Troy: Then when I saw that gal . . . she firmed up my backbone. And I got to thinking that if I tried . . . I just might be able to steal second. Do you understand after eighteen years I wanted to steal second.

Rose: You should have held me tight. You should have grabbed me and held on.

Troy: I stood on first base for eighteen years and I thought . . . well, goddamn it . . . go on for it!

Rose: We're not talking about baseball! We're talking about you going off to lay in bed with another woman . . . and then bring it home to me. That's what we're talking about. We ain't talking about no baseball.

Troy: Rose, you're not listening to me. I'm trying the best I can to explain it to you. It's not easy for me to admit that I been standing in the same place for eighteen years.

Rose: I been standing with you! I been right here with you, Troy. I got a life too. I gave eighteen years of my life to stand in the same spot with you. Don't you think I ever wanted other things? Don't you think I had dreams and hopes? What about my life? What about me. Don't you think it ever crossed my mind to want to know other men? That I wanted to lay up somewhere and forget about my responsibilities? That I wanted someone to make me laugh so I could feel good? You not the only one who's got wants and needs. But I held on to you, Troy. I took all my feelings, my wants and needs, my dreams . . . and I buried them inside you. I planted a seed and watched and prayed over it. I planted myself inside you and waited to bloom. And it didn't take me no eighteen years to find out the soil was hard and rocky and it wasn't never gonna bloom.

But I held on to you, Troy. I held you tighter. You was my husband. I owed you everything I had. Every part of me I could find to give you. And upstairs in that room . . . with the darkness falling in on me . . . I gave everything I had to try and erase the doubt that you wasn't the finest man in the world. And wherever you was going . . . I wanted to be there with you. Cause you was my husband. Cause that's the only way I was gonna survive as your wife. You always talking about what you give . . . and what you don't have to give. But you take too. You take . . . and don't even know nobody's giving!

(Rose turns to exit into the house; Troy grabs her arm.)

Troy: You say I take and don't give!
Rose: Troy! You're hurting me!
Troy: You say I take and don't give.
Rose: Troy . . . you're hurting my arm! Let go!
Troy: I done give you everything I got. Don't you tell that lie on me.
Rose: Troy!
Troy: Don't you tell that lie on me!

(Cory enters from the house.)

Cory: Mama!
Rose: Troy. You're hurting me.
Troy: Don't you tell me about no taking and giving.

(Cory comes up behind Troy and grabs him. Troy, surprised, is thrown off balance just as Cory throws a glancing blow that catches him on the chest and knocks him down. Troy is stunned, as is Cory.)

Rose: Troy. Troy. No!

(Troy gets to his feet and starts at Cory.)

Troy . . . no. Please! Troy!

(Rose pulls on Troy to hold him back. Troy stops himself.)

Troy (to Cory): Alright. That's strike two. You stay away from around me, boy. Don't you strike out. You living with a full count. Don't you strike out.

(Troy exits out the yard as the lights go down.)

SCENE II

It is six months later, early afternoon. Troy enters from the house and starts to exit the yard. Rose enters from the house.

Rose: Troy, I want to talk to you.

Troy: All of a sudden, after all this time, you want to talk to me, huh? You ain't wanted to talk to me for months. You ain't wanted to talk to me last night. You ain't wanted no part of me then. What you wanna talk to me about now?

Rose: Tomorrow's Friday.

Troy: I know what day tomorrow is. You think I don't know tomorrow's Friday? My whole life I ain't done nothing but look to see Friday coming and you got to tell me it's Friday.

Rose: I want to know if you're coming home.

Troy: I always come home, Rose. You know that. There ain't never been a night I ain't come home.

Rose: That ain't what I mean . . . and you know it. I want to know if you're coming straight home after work.

Troy: I figure I'd cash my check . . . hang out at Taylors' with the boys . . . maybe play a game of checkers . . .

Rose: Troy, I can't live like this. I won't live like this. You livin' on borrowed time with me. It's been going on six months now you ain't been coming home.

Troy: I be here every night. Every night of the year. That's 365 days.

Rose: I want you to come home tomorrow after work.

Troy: Rose . . . I don't mess up my pay. You know that now. I take my pay and I give it to you. I don't have no money but what you give me back. I just want to have a little time to myself . . . a little time to enjoy life.

Rose: What about me? When's my time to enjoy life?

Troy: I don't know what to tell you, Rose. I'm doing the best I can.

Rose: You ain't been home from work but time enough to change your clothes and run out . . . and you wanna call that the best you can do?

Troy: I'm going over to the hospital to see Alberta. She went into the hospital this afternoon. Look like she might have the baby early. I won't be gone long.

Rose: Well, you ought to know. They went over to Miss Pearl's and got Gabe today. She said you told them to go ahead and lock him up.

Troy: I ain't said no such thing. Whoever told you that is telling a lie. Pearl ain't doing nothing but telling a big fat lie.

Rose: She ain't had to tell me. I read it on the papers.

Troy: I ain't told them nothing of the kind.

Rose: I saw it right there on the papers.

Troy: What it say, huh?

Rose: It said you told them to take him.

Troy: Then they screwed that up, just the way they screw up everything. I ain't worried about what they got on the paper.

Rose: Say the government send part of his check to the hospital and the other part to you.

Troy: I ain't got nothing to do with that if that's the way it works. I ain't made up the rules about how it work.

Rose: You did Gabe just like you did Cory. You wouldn't sign the paper for Cory . . . but you signed for Gabe. You signed that paper.

(The telephone is heard ringing inside the house.)

Troy: I told you I ain't signed nothing, woman! The only thing I signed was the release form. Hell, I can't read, I don't know what they had on that paper! I ain't signed nothing about sending Gabe away.

Rose: I said send him to the hospital . . . you said let him be free . . . now you done went down there and signed him to the hospital for half his money. You went back on yourself, Troy. You gonna have to answer for that.

Troy: See now . . . you been over there talking to Miss Pearl. She done got mad cause she ain't getting Gabe's rent money. That's all it is. She's liable to say anything.

Rose: Troy, I seen where you signed the paper.

Troy: You ain't seen nothing I signed. What she doing got papers on my brother anyway? Miss Pearl telling a big fat lie. And I'm gonna tell her about it too! You ain't seen nothing I signed. Say . . . you ain't seen nothing I signed.

(Rose exits into the house to answer the telephone. Presently she returns.)

Rose: Troy . . . that was the hospital. Alberta had the baby.

Troy: What she have? What is it?

Rose: It's a girl.

Troy: I better get on down to the hospital to see her.

Rose: Troy . . .

Troy: Rose . . . I got to go see her now. That's only right . . . what's the matter . . . the baby's alright, ain't it?

Rose: Alberta died having the baby.

Troy: Died . . . you say she's dead? Alberta's dead?

Rose: They said they done all they could. They couldn't do nothing for her.

Troy: The baby? How's the baby?

Rose: They say it's healthy. I wonder who's gonna bury her.
Troy: She had family, Rose. She wasn't living in the world by herself.
Rose: I know she wasn't living in the world by herself.
Troy: Next thing you gonna want to know if she had any insurance.
Rose: Troy, you ain't got to talk like that.
Troy: That's the first thing that jumped out your mouth. "Who's gonna bury her?" Like I'm fixing to take on that task for myself.
Rose: I am your wife. Don't push me away.
Troy: I ain't pushing nobody away. Just give me some space. That's all. Just give me some room to breathe.

(Rose exits into the house. Troy walks about the yard.)

Troy (with a quiet rage that threatens to consume him): Alright . . . Mr. Death. See now . . . I'm gonna tell you what I'm gonna do. I'm gonna take and build me a fence around this yard. See? I'm gonna build me a fence around what belongs to me. And then I want you to stay on the other side. See? You stay over there until you're ready for me. Then you come on. Bring your army. Bring your sickle. Bring your wrestling clothes. I ain't gonna fall down on my vigilance this time. You ain't gonna sneak up on me no more. When you ready for me . . . when the top of your list say Troy Maxson . . . that's when you come around here. You come up and knock on the front door. Ain't nobody else got nothing to do with this. This is between you and me. Man to man. You stay on the other side of that fence until you ready for me. Then you come up and knock on the front door. Anytime you want. I'll be ready for you.

(The lights go down to black.)

SCENE III

The lights come up on the porch. It is late evening three days later. Rose sits listening to the ball game waiting for Troy. The final out of the game is made and Rose switches off the radio. Troy enters the yard carrying an infant wrapped in blankets. He stands back from the house and calls.

Rose enters and stands on the porch. There is a long, awkward silence, the weight of which grows heavier with each passing second.

Troy: Rose . . . I'm standing here with my daughter in my arms. She ain't but a wee bittie little old thing. She don't know nothing about grownups' business. She innocent . . . and she ain't got no mama.
Rose: What you telling me for, Troy?

(She turns and exits into the house.)

Troy: Well . . . I guess we'll just sit out here on the porch.

(He sits down on the porch. There is an awkward indelicateness about the way he handles the baby. His largeness engulfs and seems to swallow it. He speaks loud enough for Rose to hear.)

A man's got to do what's right for him. I ain't sorry for nothing I done. It felt right in my heart. *(To the baby.)* What you smiling at? Your daddy's a big man. Got these great big old hands. But sometimes he's scared. And right now your daddy's scared cause we sitting out here and ain't got no home. Oh, I been homeless before. I ain't had no little baby with me. But I been homeless. You just be out on the road by your lonesome and you see one of them trains coming and you just kinda go like this . . .

(He sings as a lullaby.)

Please, Mr. Engineer let a man ride the line
Please, Mr. Engineer let a man ride the line
I ain't got no ticket please let me ride the blinds

(Rose enters from the house. Troy, hearing her steps behind him, stands and faces her.)

She's my daughter, Rose. My own flesh and blood. I can't deny her no more than I can deny them boys. *(Pause.)* You and them boys is my family. You and them and this child is all I got in the world. So I guess what I'm saying is . . . I'd appreciate it if you'd help me take care of her.

Rose: Okay, Troy . . . you're right. I'll take care of your baby for you . . . cause . . . like you say . . . she's innocent . . . and you can't visit the sins of the father upon the child. A motherless child has got a hard time. *(She takes the baby from him.)* From right now . . . this child got a mother. But you a womanless man.

(Rose turns and exits into the house with the baby. Lights go down to black.)

SCENE IV

It is two months later. Lyons enters the street. He knocks on the door and calls.

Lyons: Hey, Rose! *(Pause.)* Rose!

Rose (from inside the house): Stop that yelling. You gonna wake up Raynell. I just got her to sleep.

Lyons: I just stopped by to pay Papa this twenty dollars I owe him. Where's Papa at?

Rose: He should be here in a minute. I'm getting ready to go down to the church. Sit down and wait on him.

Lyons: I got to go pick up Bonnie over her mother's house.
Rose: Well, sit it down there on the table. He'll get it.
Lyons (enters the house and sets the money on the table): Tell Papa I said thanks. I'll see you again.
Rose: Alright, Lyons. We'll see you.

(Lyons starts to exit as Cory enters.)

Cory: Hey, Lyons.
Lyons: What's happening, Cory? Say man, I'm sorry I missed your graduation. You know I had a gig and couldn't get away. Otherwise, I would have been there, man. So what you doing?
Cory: I'm trying to find a job.
Lyons: Yeah I know how that go, man. It's rough out here. Jobs are scarce.
Cory: Yeah, I know.
Lyons: Look here, I got to run. Talk to Papa . . . he know some people. He'll be able to help get you a job. Talk to him . . . see what he say.
Cory: Yeah . . . alright, Lyons.
Lyons: You take care. I'll talk to you soon. We'll find some time to talk.

(Lyons exits the yard. Cory wanders over to the tree, picks up the bat, and assumes a batting stance. He studies an imaginary pitcher and swings. Dissatisfied with the result, he tries again. Troy enters. They eye each other for a beat. Cory puts the bat down and exits the yard. Troy starts into the house as Rose exits with Raynell. She is carrying a cake.)

Troy: I'm coming in and everybody's going out.
Rose: I'm taking this cake down to the church for the bake sale. Lyons was by to see you. He stopped by to pay you your twenty dollars. It's laying in there on the table.
Troy (going into his pocket): Well . . . here go this money.
Rose: Put it in there on the table, Troy. I'll get it.
Troy: What time you coming back?
Rose: Ain't no use in you studying me. It don't matter what time I come back.
Troy: I just asked you a question, woman. What's the matter . . . can't I ask you a question?
Rose: Troy, I don't want to go into it. Your dinner's in there on the stove. All you got to do is heat it up. And don't you be eating the rest of them cakes in there. I'm coming back for them. We having a bake sale at the church tomorrow.

(Rose exits the yard. Troy sits down on the steps, takes a pint bottle from his pocket, opens it and drinks. He begins to sing.)

Troy:

Hear it ring! Hear it ring!
Had an old dog his name was Blue

You know Blue was mighty true
You know Blue was a good old dog
Blue treed a possum in a hollow log
You know from that he was a good old dog

(Bono enters the yard.)

Bono: Hey, Troy.
Troy: Hey, what's happening, Bono?
Bono: I just thought I'd stop by to see you.
Troy: What you stop by and see me for? You ain't stopped by in a month of Sundays. Hell, I must owe you money or something.
Bono: Since you got your promotion I can't keep up with you. Used to see you every day. Now I don't even know what route you working.
Troy: They keep switching me around. Got me out in Greentree now . . . hauling white folks' garbage.
Bono: Greentree, huh? You lucky, at least you ain't got to be lifting them barrels. Damn if they ain't getting heavier. I'm gonna put in my two years and call it quits.
Troy: I'm thinking about retiring myself.
Bono: You got it easy. You can *drive* for another five years.
Troy: It ain't the same, Bono. It ain't like working the back of the truck. Ain't got nobody to talk to . . . feel like you working by yourself. Naw, I'm thinking about retiring. How's Lucille?
Bono: She alright. Her arthritis get to acting up on her sometime. Saw Rose on my way in. She going down to the church, huh?
Troy: Yeah, she took up going down there. All them preachers looking for somebody to fatten their pockets. *(Pause.)* Got some gin here.
Bono: Naw, thanks. I just stopped by to say hello.
Troy: Hell, nigger . . . you can take a drink. I ain't never known you to say no to a drink. You ain't got to work tomorrow.
Bono: I just stopped by. I'm fixing to go over to Skinner's. We got us a domino game going over his house every Friday.
Troy: Nigger, you can't play no dominoes. I used to whup you four games out of five.
Bono: Well, that learned me. I'm getting better.
Troy: Yeah? Well, that's alright.
Bono: Look here . . . I got to be getting on. Stop by sometime, huh?
Troy: Yeah, I'll do that, Bono. Lucille told Rose you bought her a new refrigerator.
Bono: Yeah, Rose told Lucille you had finally built your fence . . . so I figured we'd call it even.
Troy: I knew you would.

Bono: Yeah . . . okay. I'll be talking to you.
Troy: Yeah, take care, Bono. Good to see you. I'm gonna stop over.
Bono: Yeah. Okay, Troy.

(Bono exits. Troy drinks from the bottle.)

Troy:

Old Blue died and I dug his grave
Let him down with a golden chain
Every night when I hear old Blue bark
I know Blue treed a possum in Noah's Ark.
Hear it ring! Hear it ring!

(Cory enters the yard. They eye each other for a beat. Troy is sitting in the middle of the steps. Cory walks over.)

Cory: I got to get by.
Troy: Say what? What's you say?
Cory: You in my way. I got to get by.
Troy: You got to get by where? This is my house. Bought and paid for. In full. Took me fifteen years. And if you wanna go in my house and I'm sitting on the steps . . . you say excuse me. Like your mama taught you.
Cory: Come on, Pop . . . I got to get by.

(Cory starts to maneuver his way past Troy. Troy grabs his leg and shoves him back.)

Troy: You just gonna walk over top of me?
Cory: I live here too!
Troy (advancing toward him): You just gonna walk over top of me in my own house?
Cory: I ain't scared of you.
Troy: I ain't asked if you was scared of me. I asked you if you was fixing to walk over top of me in my own house? That's the question. You ain't gonna say excuse me? You just gonna walk over top of me?
Cory: If you wanna put it like that.
Troy: How else am I gonna put it?
Cory: I was walking by you to go into the house cause you sitting on the steps drunk, singing to yourself. You can put it like that.
Troy: Without saying excuse me???

(Cory doesn't respond.)

I asked you a question. Without saying excuse me???
Cory: I ain't got to say excuse me to you. You don't count around here no more.

Troy: Oh, I see . . . I don't count around here no more. You ain't got to say excuse me to your daddy. All of a sudden you done got so grown that your daddy don't count around here no more . . . Around here in his own house and yard that he done paid for with the sweat of his brow. You done got so grown to where you gonna take over. You gonna take over my house. Is that right? You gonna wear my pants. You gonna go in there and stretch out on my bed. You ain't got to say excuse me cause I don't count around here no more. Is that right?

Cory: That's right. You always talking this dumb stuff. Now, why don't you just get out my way?

Troy: I guess you got someplace to sleep and something to put in your belly. You got that, huh? You got that? That's what you need. You got that, huh?

Cory: You don't know what I got. You ain't got to worry about what I got.

Troy: You right! You one hundred percent right! I done spent the last seventeen years worrying about what you got. Now it's your turn, see? I'll tell you what to do. You grown . . . we done established that. You a man. Now, let's see you act like one. Turn your behind around and walk out this yard. And when you get out there in the alley . . . you can forget about this house. See? Cause this is my house. You go on and be a man and get your own house. You can forget about this. Cause this is mine. You go on and get yours cause I'm through with doing for you.

Cory: You talking about what you did for me . . . what'd you ever give me?

Troy: Them feet and bones! That pumping heart, nigger! I give you more than anybody else is ever gonna give you.

Cory: You ain't never gave me nothing! You ain't never done nothing but hold me back. Afraid I was gonna be better than you. All you ever did was try and make me scared of you. I used to tremble every time you called my name. Every time I heard your footsteps in the house. Wondering all the time . . . what's Papa gonna say if I do this? . . . What's he gonna say if I do that? . . . What's Papa gonna say if I turn on the radio? And Mama, too . . . she tries . . . but she's scared of you.

Troy: You leave your mama out of this. She ain't got nothing to do with this.

Cory: I don't know how she stand you . . . after what you did to her.

Troy: I told you to leave your mama out of this!

(He advances toward Cory.)

Cory: What you gonna do . . . give me a whupping? You can't whup me no more. You're too old. You just an old man.

Troy (shoves him on his shoulder): Nigger! That's what you are. You just another nigger on the street to me!

Cory: You crazy! You know that?

Troy: Go on now! You got the devil in you. Get on away from me!

Cory: You just a crazy old man . . . talking about I got the devil in me.

Troy: Yeah, I'm crazy! If you don't get on the other side of that yard . . . I'm gonna show you how crazy I am! Go on . . . get the hell out of my yard.

Cory: It ain't your yard. You took Uncle Gabe's money he got from the army to buy this house and then you put him out.

Troy (advances on Cory): Get your black ass out of my yard!

(Troy's advance backs Cory up against the tree. Cory grabs up the bat.)

Cory: I ain't going nowhere! Come on . . . put me out! I ain't scared of you.

Troy: That's my bat!

Cory: Come on!

Troy: Put my bat down!

Cory: Come on, put me out.

(Cory swings at Troy, who backs across the yard.)

What's the matter? You so bad . . . put me out!

(Troy advances toward Cory.)

Cory (backing up): Come on! Come on!

Troy: You're gonna have to use it! You wanna draw that bat back on me . . . you're gonna have to use it.

Cory: Come on! . . . Come on!

(Cory swings the bat at Troy a second time. He misses. Troy continues to advance toward him.)

Troy: You're gonna have to kill me! You wanna draw that bat back on me. You're gonna have to kill me.

(Cory, backed up against the tree, can go no farther. Troy taunts him. He sticks out his head and offers him a target.)

Come on! Come on!

(Cory is unable to swing the bat. Troy grabs it.)

Troy: Then I'll show you.

(Cory and Troy struggle over the bat. The struggle is fierce and fully engaged. Troy ultimately is the stronger, and takes the bat from Cory and stands over him ready to swing. He stops himself.)

Go on and get away from around my house.

(Cory, stung by his defeat, picks himself up, walks slowly out of the yard and up the alley.)

Cory: Tell Mama I'll be back for my things.

Troy: They'll be on the other side of that fence.

(Cory exits.)

Troy: I can't taste nothing. Helluljah! I can't taste nothing no more. *(Troy assumes a batting posture and begins to taunt Death, the fastball on the outside corner.)* Come on! It's between you and me now! Come on! Anytime you want! Come on! I be ready for you . . . but I ain't gonna be easy.

(The lights go down on the scene.)

SCENE V

The time is 1965. The lights come up in the yard. It is the morning of Troy's funeral. A funeral plaque with a light hangs beside the door. There is a small garden plot off to the side. There is noise and activity in the house as Rose, Lyons, and Bono have gathered. The door opens and Raynell, seven years old, enters dressed in a flannel nightgown. She crosses to the garden and pokes around with a stick. Rose calls from the house.

Rose: Raynell!
Raynell: Mam?
Rose: What you doing out there?
Raynell: Nothing.

(Rose comes to the door.)

Rose: Girl, get in here and get dressed. What you doing?
Raynell: Seeing if my garden growed.
Rose: I told you it ain't gonna grow overnight. You got to wait.
Raynell: It don't look like it never gonna grow. Dag!
Rose: I told you a watched pot never boils. Get in here and get dressed.
Raynell: This ain't even no pot, Mama.
Rose: You just have to give it a chance. It'll grow. Now you come on and do what I told you. We got to be getting ready. This ain't no morning to be playing around. You hear me?
Raynell: Yes, Mam.

(Rose exits into the house. Raynell continues to poke at her garden with a stick. Cory enters. He is dressed in a Marine corporal's uniform, and carries a duffel-bag. His posture is that of a military man, and his speech has a clipped sternness.)

Cory (to Raynell): Hi. *(Pause.)* I bet your name is Raynell.
Raynell: Uh huh.
Cory: Is your mama home?

(Raynell runs up on the porch and calls through the screen door.)

Raynell: Mama . . . there's some man out here. Mama?

(Rose comes to the door.)

Rose: Cory? Lord have mercy! Look here, you all!

(Rose and Cory embrace in a tearful reunion as Bono and Lyons enter from the house dressed in funeral clothes.)

Bono: Aw, looka here . . .
Rose: Done got all grown up!
Cory: Don't cry, Mama. What you crying about?
Rose: I'm just so glad you made it.
Cory: Hey Lyons. How you doing, Mr. Bono.

(Lyons goes to embrace Cory.)

Lyons: Look at you, man. Look at you. Don't he look good, Rose. Got them Corporal stripes.
Rose: What took you so long?
Cory: You know how the Marines are, Mama. They got to get all their paperwork straight before they let you do anything.
Rose: Well, I'm sure glad you made it. They let Lyons come. Your Uncle Gabe's still in the hospital. They don't know if they gonna let him out or not. I just talked to them a little while ago.
Lyons: A Corporal in the United States Marines.
Bono: Your daddy knew you had it in you. He used to tell me all the time.
Lyons: Don't he look good, Mr. Bono?
Bono: Yeah, he remind me of Troy when I first met him. *(Pause.)* Say, Rose, Lucille's down at the church with the choir. I'm gonna go down and get the pallbearers lined up. I'll be back to get you all.
Rose: Thanks, Jim.
Cory: See you, Mr. Bono.
Lyons (with his arm around Raynell): Cory . . . look at Raynell. Ain't she precious? She gonna break a whole lot of hearts.
Rose: Raynell, come and say hello to your brother. This is your brother, Cory. You remember Cory.
Raynell: No, Mam.
Cory: She don't remember me, Mama.
Rose: Well, we talk about you. She heard us talk about you. *(To Raynell.)* This is your brother, Cory. Come on and say hello.
Raynell: Hi.
Cory: Hi. So you're Raynell. Mama told me a lot about you.
Rose: You all come on into the house and let me fix you some breakfast. Keep up your strength.
Cory: I ain't hungry, Mama.
Lyons: You can fix me something, Rose. I'll be in there in a minute.

Rose: Cory, you sure you don't want nothing? I know they ain't feeding you right.

Cory: No, Mama . . . thanks. I don't feel like eating. I'll get something later.

Rose: Raynell . . . get on upstairs and get that dress on like I told you.

(Rose and Raynell exit into the house.)

Lyons: So . . . I hear you thinking about getting married.

Cory: Yeah, I done found the right one, Lyons. It's about time.

Lyons: Me and Bonnie been split up about four years now. About the time Papa retired. I guess she just got tired of all them changes I was putting her through. *(Pause.)* I always knew you was gonna make something out yourself. Your head was always in the right direction. So . . . you gonna stay in . . . make it a career . . . put in your twenty years?

Cory: I don't know. I got six already, I think that's enough.

Lyons: Stick with Uncle Sam and retire early. Ain't nothing out here. I guess Rose told you what happened with me. They got me down the workhouse. I thought I was being slick cashing other people's checks.

Cory: How much time you doing?

Lyons: They give me three years. I got that beat now. I ain't got but nine more months. It ain't so bad. You learn to deal with it like anything else. You got to take the crookeds with the straights. That's what Papa used to say. He used to say that when he struck out. I seen him strike out three times in a row . . . and the next time up he hit the ball over the grandstand. Right out there in Homestead Field. He wasn't satisfied hitting in the seats . . . he want to hit it over everything! After the game he had two hundred people standing around waiting to shake his hand. You got to take the crookeds with the straights. Yeah, Papa was something else.

Cory: You still playing?

Lyons: Cory . . . you know I'm gonna do that. There's some fellows down there we got us a band . . . we gonna try and stay together when we get out . . . but yeah, I'm still playing. It still helps me to get out of bed in the morning. As long as it do that I'm gonna be right there playing and trying to make some sense out of it.

Rose (calling): Lyons, I got these eggs in the pan.

Lyons: Let me go on and get these eggs, man. Get ready to go bury Papa. *(Pause.)* How you doing? You doing alright?

(Cory nods. Lyons touches him on the shoulder and they share a moment of silent grief. Lyons exits into the house. Cory wanders about the yard. Raynell enters.)

Raynell: Hi.

Cory: Hi.

Raynell: Did you used to sleep in my room?
Cory: Yeah . . . that used to be my room.
Raynell: That's what Papa call it. "Cory's room." It got your football in the closet.

(Rose comes to the door.)

Rose: Raynell, get in there and get them good shoes on.
Raynell: Mama, can't I wear these? Them other one hurt my feet.
Rose: Well, they just gonna have to hurt your feet for a while. You ain't said they hurt your feet when you went down to the store and got them.
Raynell: They didn't hurt then. My feet done got bigger.
Rose: Don't you give me no backtalk now. You get in there and get them shoes on.

(Raynell exits into the house.)

Ain't too much changed. He still got that piece of rag tied to that tree. He was out here swinging that bat. I was just ready to go back in the house. He swung that bat and then he just fell over. Seem like he swung it and stood there with this grin on his face . . . and then he just fell over. They carried him on down to the hospital, but I knew there wasn't no need . . . why don't you come on in the house?
Cory: Mama . . . I got something to tell you. I don't know how to tell you this . . . but I've got to tell you . . . I'm not going to Papa's funeral.
Rose: Boy, hush your mouth. That's your daddy you talking about. I don't want hear that kind of talk this morning. I done raised you to come to this? You standing there all healthy and grown talking about you ain't going to your daddy's funeral?
Cory: Mama . . . listen . . .
Rose: I don't want to hear it, Cory. You just get that thought out of your head.
Cory: I can't drag Papa with me everywhere I go. I've got to say no to him. One time in my life I've got to say no.
Rose: Don't nobody have to listen to nothing like that. I know you and your daddy ain't seen eye to eye, but I ain't got to listen to that kind of talk this morning. Whatever was between you and your daddy . . . the time has come to put it aside. Just take it and set it over there on the shelf and forget about it. Disrespecting your daddy ain't gonna make you a man, Cory. You got to find a way to come to that on your own. Not going to your daddy's funeral ain't gonna make you a man.
Cory: The whole time I was growing up . . . living in his house . . . Papa was like a shadow that followed you everywhere. It weighed on you and sunk into your flesh. It would wrap around you and lay there until you couldn't tell which one was you anymore. That shadow digging in your flesh. Trying to crawl in. Trying to live through you. Everywhere I looked, Troy Maxson was staring back at me . . . hiding

under the bed . . . in the closet. I'm just saying I've got to find a way to get rid of that shadow, Mama.

Rose: You just like him. You got him in you good.

Cory: Don't tell me that, Mama.

Rose: You Troy Maxson all over again.

Cory: I don't want to be Troy Maxson. I want to be me.

Rose: You can't be nobody but who you are, Cory. That shadow wasn't nothing but you growing into yourself. You either got to grow into it or cut it down to fit you. But that's all you got to make life with. That's all you got to measure yourself against that world out there. Your daddy wanted you to be everything he wasn't . . . and at the same time he tried to make you into everything he was. I don't know if he was right or wrong . . . but I do know he meant to do more good than he meant to do harm. He wasn't always right. Sometimes when he touched he bruised. And sometimes when he took me in his arms he cut.

When I first met your daddy I thought . . . Here is a man I can lay down with and make a baby. That's the first thing I thought when I seen him. I was thirty years old and had done seen my share of men. But when he walked up to me and said, "I can dance a waltz that'll make you dizzy," I thought, Rose Lee, here is a man that you can open yourself up to and be filled to bursting. Here is a man that can fill all them empty spaces you been tipping around the edges of. One of them empty spaces was being somebody's mother.

I married your daddy and settled down to cooking his supper and keeping clean sheets on the bed. When your daddy walked through the house he was so big he filled it up. That was my first mistake. Not to make him leave some room for me. For my part in the matter. But at that time I wanted that. I wanted a house that I could sing in. And that's what your daddy gave me. I didn't know to keep up his strength I had to give up little pieces of mine. I did that. I took on his life as mine and mixed up the pieces so that you couldn't hardly tell which was which anymore. It was my choice. It was my life and I didn't have to live it like that. But that's what life offered me in the way of being a woman and I took it. I grabbed hold of it with both hands.

By the time Raynell came into the house, me and your daddy had done lost touch with one another. I didn't want to make my blessing off of nobody's misfortune . . . but I took on to Raynell like she was all them babies I had wanted and never had.

(The phone rings.)

Like I'd been blessed to relive a part of my life. And if the Lord see fit to keep up my strength . . . I'm gonna do her just like your daddy did you . . . I'm gonna give her the best of what's in me.

Raynell (entering, still with her old shoes): Mama . . . Reverend Tolliver on the phone.

(Rose exits into the house.)

Raynell: Hi.
Cory: Hi.
Raynell: You in the Army or the Marines?
Cory: Marines.
Raynell: Papa said it was the Army. Did you know Blue?
Cory: Blue? Who's Blue?
Raynell: Papa's dog what he sing about all the time.
Cory (singing):

Hear it ring! Hear it ring!
I had a dog his name was Blue
You know Blue was mighty true
You know Blue was a good old dog
Blue treed a possum in a hollow log
You know from that he was a good old dog.
Hear it ring! Hear it ring!

(Raynell joins in singing.)

Cory and Raynell:

Blue treed a possum out on a limb
Blue looked at me and I looked at him
Grabbed that possum and put him in a sack
Blue stayed there till I came back
Old Blue's feets was big and round
Never allowed a possum to touch the ground.

Old Blue died and I dug his grave
I dug his grave with a silver spade
Let him down with a golden chain
And every night I call his name
Go on Blue, you good dog you
Go on Blue, you good dog you.

Raynell:

Blue laid down and died like a man
Blue laid down and died . . .

Both:

Blue laid down and died like a man
Now he's treeing possums in the Promised Land
I'm gonna tell you this to let you know
Blue's gone where the good dogs go
When I hear old Blue bark
When I hear old Blue bark
Blue treed a possum in Noah's Ark
Blue treed a possum in Noah's Ark.

(Rose comes to the screen door.)

Rose: Cory, we gonna be ready to go in a minute.
Cory (to Raynell): You go on in the house and change them shoes like Mama told you so we can go to Papa's funeral.
Raynell: Okay, I'll be back.

(Raynell exits into the house. Cory gets up and crosses over to the tree. Rose stands in the screen door watching him. Gabriel enters from the alley.)

Gabriel (calling): Hey, Rose!
Rose: Gabe?
Gabriel: I'm here, Rose. Hey, Rose, I'm here!

(Rose enters from the house.)

Rose: Lord . . . Look here, Lyons!
Lyons: See, I told you, Rose . . . I told you they'd let him come.
Cory: How you doing, Uncle Gabe?
Lyons: How you doing, Uncle Gabe?
Gabriel: Hey, Rose. It's time. It's time to tell St. Peter to open the gates. Troy, you ready? You ready, Troy. I'm gonna tell St. Peter to open the gates. You get ready now.

(Gabriel, with great fanfare, braces himself to blow. The trumpet is without a mouthpiece. He puts the end of it into his mouth and blows with great force, like a man who has been waiting some twenty-odd years for this single moment. No sound comes out of the trumpet. He braces himself and blows again with the same result. A third time he blows. There is a weight of impossible description that falls away and leaves him bare and exposed to a frightful realization. It is a trauma that a sane and normal mind would be unable to withstand. He begins to dance. A slow, strange dance, eerie and life-giving. A dance of atavistic signature and ritual. Lyons attempts to embrace him. Gabriel pushes Lyons away. He begins to howl in what is an attempt at song, or perhaps a song turning back into itself in an attempt at speech. He finishes his dance and the gates of heaven stand open as wide as God's closet.)

That's the way that go!

BLACKOUT

Gabriel Garcia Márquez at work, c. 1970s.

WRITING

30 WRITING ABOUT LITERATURE

What You Will Learn in This Chapter

- To read actively
- To plan, draft, and revise a literary argument
- To write analysis, explication, comparison and contrast, and response papers

Assigned to write an essay on *Hamlet*, a student might well wonder, "What can I say that hasn't been said a thousand times before?" Often the most difficult aspect of writing about a story, poem, or play is the feeling that we have nothing unique to say.

Remember that, in the study of literature, common sense is never out of place. For most of a class hour, a professor once rhapsodized about the arrangement of the contents of W. H. Auden's *Collected Poems*. Auden, he claimed, was a master of thematic continuity, who had brilliantly placed the poems in the order that they best complemented each other. Near the end of the hour, his theories were punctured—with a great inaudible pop—when a student, timidly raising a hand, pointed out that Auden had arranged the poems in the book not by theme but in alphabetical order according to the first word of each poem. The professor's jaw dropped: "Why didn't you say that sooner?" The student was apologetic: "I—I was afraid I'd sound too *ordinary*."

Don't be afraid to state a conviction, though it seems obvious. Does it matter that you may be repeating something that has been said before? What matters more is that you are actively engaged in thinking about literature. There are excellent old ideas as well as new ones. You have something to say.

READ ACTIVELY

Most people read in a relaxed, almost passive way. They let the story or poem carry them along without asking too many questions. To write about literature well, however, you need to *read actively*, paying special attention to various aspects of the text. Here are some steps to get you started:

- **Preview the text.** To get acquainted with a work of literature before you settle in for a closer reading, skim it for an overview of its content and organization. Pay attention to the title. Take a quick look at all parts of the work. Even a book's cover, preface, introduction, footnotes, and biographical notes about the author can provide you with some context for reading the work itself.

- **Read closely. Look up any unfamiliar words, allusions, or references.** Often the very words you may be tempted to skim over will provide the key to a work's meaning. Thomas Hardy's poem "The Ruined Maid" (Chapter 12) will remain elusive to a reader unfamiliar with the archaic meaning of the word "ruin"—a woman's loss of virginity to a man other than her husband.
- **Take notes. Annotate the text.** Read with a highlighter and pencil at hand, making appropriate annotations to the text. Later, you'll easily be able to review these highlights, and, when you write your paper, quickly refer to supporting evidence.

  - Underline words, phrases, or sentences that seem interesting or important, or that raise questions.
  - Jot down brief notes in the margin ("*key symbol—this foreshadows the ending*," for example, or "*dramatic irony*").
  - Use lines or arrows to indicate passages that seem to speak to each other—for instance, all the places in which you find the same theme or related symbols.

Robert Frost

Nothing Gold Can Stay

Similar lines

Nature's first green is gold, — *How can green=gold?* — *Rhyme + end-stopped lines* — *Spring leaves*
Her hardest hue to hold.
Her early leaf's a flower; — *Spring blossoms (golden?)*
But only so an hour. — *Exaggeration*
Then leaf subsides to leaf. — *To sink to a lower level (everything becomes less beautiful)*
So Eden sank to grief,
So dawn goes down to day.
Nothing gold can stay. — *Nothing good can last* — *Youth, beauty, innocence*

Everybody loses innocence

rhyme pattern aabbccdd

Adam+Eve: Getting kicked out of Eden was as natural as seasons changing?

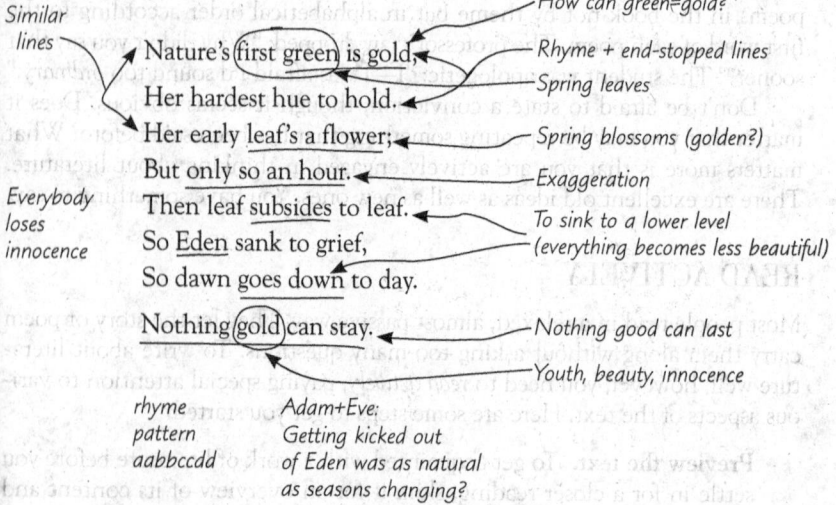

- **Reread as needed.** If a piece is short, read it several times. Often, knowing the ending of a poem or short story will allow you to extract new meaning from its beginning and middle. If the piece is longer, reread the passages you thought important enough to highlight.
- **Read poetry aloud.** There is no better way to understand a poem than to effectively read it aloud. Read slowly, paying attention to punctuation cues. Listen for the audio effects.
- **Read the whole play—not just the dialogue, but also everything in italics, including stage directions and descriptions of settings.** The meaning of a scene, or even of an entire play, may depend on the tone of voice in which an actor is supposed to deliver a significant line or upon the actions described in the stage directions, as in this passage from Susan Glaspell's *Trifles* (Chapter 24).

Mrs. *Peters (to the other woman)*: Oh, her fruit; it did freeze. (*To the County Attorney*) She worried about that when it turned so cold. She said the fire'd go out and her jars would break.

Sheriff: Well, can you beat the women! Held for murder and worryin' about her preserves.

Both men are insulting toward Mrs. Wright.

County *Attorney*: I guess before we're through she may have something more serious than preserves to worry about.

Hale: Well, women are used to worrying over trifles.

He thinks he's being kind.

(*The two women move a little closer together.*)

The women side with each other.

County *Attorney (with the gallantry of a young politician)*: And yet, for all their worries, what would we do without the ladies? (*The women do not unbend. He goes to the sink, takes a dipperful of water from the pail and pouring it into a basin, washes his hands. Starts to wipe them on the roller towel, turns it for a cleaner place.*) Dirty towels! (*Kicks his foot against the pans under the sink.*) Not much of a housekeeper, would you say, ladies?

Courtesy toward women, but condescending

The two women aren't buying it.

Mrs. *Hale (stiffly)*: There's a great deal of work to be done on a farm.

She holds back, but she's mad.

I don't like this guy!

Small, insignificant things or not? Play's title. Significant word? The men miss the "clues"—too trifling.

THINK ABOUT THE READING

Once you have reread the work, you can begin to process your ideas about it. To get started thinking about fiction or drama, try the following steps:

- **Identify the protagonist and the conflict.** Whose story is being told? What does that character desire more than anything else? What stands in the way of that character's achievement of his or her goal? The answers to these questions can give you a better handle on the plot.
- **Consider the point of view.** What does it contribute to the work? How might the tale change if told from another point of view?
- **Think about the setting.** Does it play a significant role in the plot? How does setting affect the tone?
- **Notice key symbols.** If any symbols catch your attention as you go, be sure to highlight each place in which they appear in the text. What do these symbols contribute to the work's meaning? (Remember, not every image is a symbol—only those important recurrent persons, places, or things that seem to suggest more than their literal meaning.)
- **Look for the theme.** Is the work's central meaning stated directly? If not, how does it reveal itself?
- **Think about tone and style.** How would you characterize the style in which the story or play is written? Consider elements such as diction, sentence structure, tone, and organization. How does the work's style contribute to its tone?

You might consider some different approaches when thinking about a poem.

- **Let your emotions guide you into the poem.** Do any images or phrases call up a strong emotional response? If so, try to puzzle out why those passages seem so emotionally loaded. In a word or two, describe the poem's tone.
- **Determine what's literally happening in the poem.** Separating literal language from figurative or symbolic language can be one of the trickiest—and most essential—tasks in poetic interpretation. Begin by working out the literal. Who is speaking the poem? To whom? Under what circumstances? What happens in the poem?
- **Ask what it all adds up to.** Once you've pinned down the literal action of the poem, it's time to take a leap into the figurative. What is the significance of the poem? Address symbolism, any figures of speech, and any language that means one thing literally but suggests something else. In "My Papa's Waltz" (Chapter 11), for example, Theodore Roethke tells a simple story of a father dancing his small son around a kitchen. The language of the poem suggests much more, however, implying that while

the father is rough to the point of violence, the young boy hungers for his attention.

- **Consider the poem's shape on the page, and the way it sounds.** What patterns of sound do you notice? Are the lines long, short, or a mixture of both? How do these elements contribute to the poem's effect?
- **Pay attention to form.** If a poem makes use of rime or regular meter, ask yourself how those elements contribute to its meaning. If it is in a fixed form, such as a sonnet or villanelle, how do the demands of that form serve to set its tone? If the form calls for repetition—of sounds, words, or entire lines—how does that repetition underscore the poem's message? If, on the other hand, the poem is in free verse—without a consistent pattern of rime or regular meter—how does this choice affect the poem's feel?
- **Take note of line breaks.** If the poem is written in free verse, pay special attention to its line breaks. Poets break their lines with care, conscious that readers pause momentarily over the last word in any line, giving that word special emphasis. Notice whether the lines tend to be broken at the ends of whole phrases and sentences or in the middle of phrases. Then ask yourself what effect is created by the poet's choice of line breaks. How does that effect contribute to the poem's meaning?

PLAN YOUR ESSAY

If you have actively reread the work you plan to write about and have made notes or annotations, you are already well on your way to writing your paper. Your mind has already begun to work through some initial impressions and ideas. Now you need to arrange those early notions into an organized and logical essay. Here is some advice on how to manage the writing process:

- **Leave yourself time.** Good writing involves thought and revision. Anyone who has ever been a student knows what it's like to pull an all-nighter, churning out a term paper hours before it is due. Still, the best writing takes time. Your ideas need to marinate. For the sake of your writing—not to mention your sanity—it's far better to get the job started well before your deadline.
- **Choose a subject you care about.** If you have been given a choice of literary works to write about, always choose the play, story, or poem that evokes the strongest emotional response. Your writing will be liveliest if you feel engaged by your subject.
- **Know your purpose.** As you write, keep the assignment in mind. You may have been asked to write a response, in which you describe your reactions to a literary work. Perhaps your purpose is to interpret a work,

analyzing how one or more of its elements contribute to its meaning. You may have been instructed to write an evaluation, in which you judge a work's merits. Whatever the assignment, how you approach your essay will depend in large part on your purpose.

- **Define your topic narrowly.** Worried about having enough to say, students sometimes frame their topic so broadly that they can't do justice to it in the allotted number of pages. Your paper will be stronger if you go more deeply into a well-focused subject than if you choose a gigantic subject and touch on most aspects of it only superficially. A thorough explication of a short story is hardly possible in a 250-word paper, but an explication of a paragraph or two could work in that space. A profound topic ("The Character of Hamlet") might overflow a book, but a more focused one ("Hamlet's View of Acting" or "Hamlet's Puns") could result in a manageable paper.

PREWRITING: GENERATE IDEAS AND ISSUES

Topic in hand, you can begin to get your ideas on the page. To generate new ideas and clarify the thoughts you already have, try one or more of the following useful prewriting techniques as one student did preparing a paper on Robert Frost's poem "Nothing Gold Can Stay."

- **Brainstorm.** Writing quickly, list everything that comes into your mind about your subject. Set a time limit—ten or fifteen minutes—and force yourself to keep adding items to the list, even when you think you have run out of things to say. Sometimes, if you press onward past the point where you feel you are finished, you will surprise yourself with new and fresh ideas.

gold = early leaves/blossoms
or gold = something precious (both?)
early leaf = flower (yellow blossoms)
spring (lasts an hour)
Leaves subside (sink to lower level)
Eden = paradise = perfection = beauty
Loss of innocence?
What about original sin?
Dawn becomes day (dawn is more precious?)
Adam and Eve had to fall? Part of natural order.
seasons/days/people's lives
Title = last line: perfection can't last
spring/summer/autumn
dawn/day
Innocence can't last

- **Cluster.** This prewriting technique works especially well for visual thinkers. In clustering, you build a diagram to help you explore the relationships among your ideas. To get started, write your subject at the center of a sheet of paper. Circle it. Then jot down ideas, linking each to the central circle with lines. As you write down each new idea, draw lines to link it to related old ideas. The result will look something like the following web.

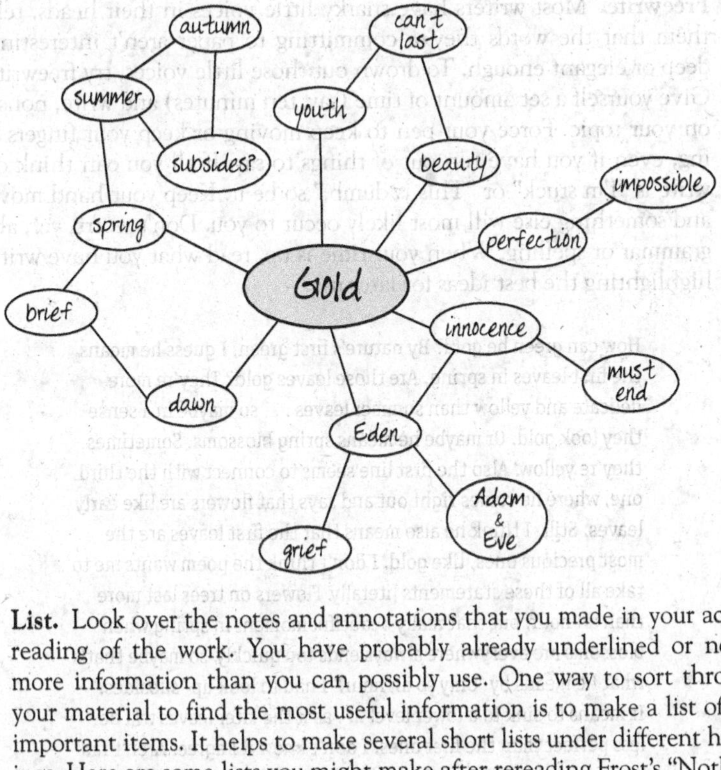

- **List.** Look over the notes and annotations that you made in your active reading of the work. You have probably already underlined or noted more information than you can possibly use. One way to sort through your material to find the most useful information is to make a list of the important items. It helps to make several short lists under different headings. Here are some lists you might make after rereading Frost's "Nothing Gold Can Stay." Don't be afraid to add more comments or questions on the lists to help your thought process.

Images	Colors
leaf ("early leaf")	green
flower	gold ("hardest hue to hold")
dawn	
day	
Eden	
gold	

> <u>Key Actions</u>
> gold is hard to hold
> early leaf lasts only an hour
> leaf subsides to leaf (what does this mean?)
> Eden sinks to grief (paradise is lost)
> dawn goes down to day
> gold can't stay (perfection is impossible?)

- **Freewrite.** Most writers have snarky little voices in their heads, telling them that the words they're committing to paper aren't interesting or deep or elegant enough. To drown out those little voices, try freewriting. Give yourself a set amount of time (say, ten minutes) and write, nonstop, on your topic. Force your pen to keep moving or keep your fingers typing, even if you have run out of things to say. If all you can think of to write is "I'm stuck" or "This is dumb," so be it. Keep your hand moving, and something else will most likely occur to you. Don't worry, yet, about grammar or spelling. When your time is up, read what you have written, highlighting the best ideas for later use.

> How can green be gold? By nature's first green, I guess he means the first leaves in spring. Are those leaves gold? They're more delicate and yellow than summer leaves . . . so maybe in a sense they look gold. Or maybe he means spring blossoms. Sometimes they're yellow. Also the first line seems to connect with the third one, where he comes right out and says that flowers are like early leaves. Still, I think he also means that the first leaves are the most precious ones, like gold. I don't think the poem wants me to take all of these statements literally. Flowers on trees last more than an hour, but that really beautiful moment in spring when blossoms are everywhere always ends too quickly, so maybe that's what he means by "only so an hour." I had to look up "subsides." It means to sink to a lower level . . . as if the later leaves will be less perfect than the first ones. I don't know if I agree. Aren't fall leaves precious? Then he says, "So Eden sank to grief" which seems to be saying that Adam and Eve's fall would have happened no matter what they did, because everything that seems perfect falls apart . . . nothing gold can stay. Is he saying Adam and Eve didn't really have a choice? No matter what, everything gets older, less beautiful, less innocent . . . even people.

- **Journal.** Your instructor might ask you to keep a journal in which you jot down your ideas, feelings, and impressions before they are fully formulated. Sometimes a journal is meant for your eyes only; in other instances your instructor might read it. Either way, it is meant to be informal and immediate, and to provide raw material that you may later choose to refine into a formal essay. Here are some tips for keeping a useful journal:

- Get your ideas down as soon as they occur to you.
- Write quickly.
- Jot down your feelings about and first impressions of the story, poem, or play you are reading.
- Don't worry about grammar, spelling, or punctuation.
- Don't worry about sounding academic.
- Don't worry about whether your ideas are good or bad ones; you can sort that out later.
- Try out invention strategies, such as freewriting, clustering, and outlining.
- Keep writing, even after you think you have run out of things to say. You might surprise yourself.
- Write about what interests you most.
- Write in your journal on a regular basis.

- **Outline.** Some topics by their very nature suggest obvious ways to organize a paper. "An Explication of a Sonnet by Wordsworth" might mean simply working through the poem line by line. If this isn't the case, some kind of outline will probably prove helpful. Your outline needn't be elaborate to be useful. While a long research paper on several literary works might call for a detailed outline, a 500-word analysis of a short story's figures of speech might call for just a simple list of points in the order that makes the most logical sense—not necessarily, of course, the order in which those thoughts first came to mind.

1. Passage of time = fall from innocence
   blossoms
   gold
   dawn
   grief

2. Innocence = perfection
   Adam and Eve
   loss of innocence = inevitable
   real original sin = passing of time
   paradise sinks to grief

3. Grief = knowledge
   experience of sin & suffering
   unavoidable as grow older

DEVELOP YOUR ARGUMENT

Once you have finished a rough outline of your ideas, you need to refine it into a clear and logical shape. You need to state your thesis—your paper's main claim—clearly and then support it with logical and accurate evidence. Here is a practical approach to this crucial stage of the writing process:

- **Consider your purpose.** As you develop your argument, be sure to refer back to the specific assignment; let it guide you. Your instructor might request one of the following kinds of papers:
  - *Response*, in which you explore your reaction to a work of literature.
  - *Evaluation*, in which you assess the literary merits of a work.
  - *Interpretation*, in which you discuss a work's meaning. If your instructor has assigned an interpretation, he or she may have more specifically asked for an *analysis*, *explication*, or *comparison/contrast* essay, among other possibilities.
- **Remember your audience.** Practically speaking, your professor (and sometimes your classmates) will be your paper's primary audience. Some assignments, however, specify a particular audience beyond your professor and classmates. Keep your readers in mind. Be sure to adapt your writing to meet their needs and interests. If, for example, the audience has presumably already read a story under discussion, you won't need to relate the plot in its entirety. Instead, you will be free to bring up only those plot points that serve as evidence for your thesis.
- **Narrow your topic to fit the assignment.** Though you may be tempted to choose a broad topic so that you will have no shortage of things to say, remember that a good paper needs focus. Your choice should be narrow enough for you to do it justice in the space and time allotted.
- **Decide on a thesis.** Just as you need to know your destination before you set out on a trip, you need to decide what point you're traveling toward before you begin your first draft. Start by writing a provisional thesis sentence: a summing up of the main idea or argument your paper will explore. While your thesis doesn't need to be outrageous or deliberately provocative, it does need to take a stand. A clear, decisive statement gives you something to prove and lends vigor to your essay.

WORKING THESIS

The poem argues that, like Adam and Eve, we all lose our innocence, and the passage of time is inevitable.

This first stab at a thesis sentence gave its author a sense of purpose and direction that allowed him to finish his first draft. Later, as he revised his essay, he found he needed to refine his thesis to make more specific and focused assertions.

STRENGTHEN YOUR ARGUMENT: RHETORICAL APPEALS

An argumentative essay states its thesis—its main claim—and tries to influence the reader's opinion. Argumentative essays have something in common with opinion pieces and editorials, as well as with most political speeches. All of these forms are used to try to convince people of something.

After you've formulated a thesis, your task is clear: you need to convince your audience that your thesis is correct. It will help to have an understanding of some key elements of argument as you write to persuade your reader. Effective argumentation requires you to combine logical reasoning with emotional appeals. Remember that you need to speak to both the reader's heart and mind. Additionally, you need to recognize that in any piece you write, your own credibility will be on display through your tone and manner.

Common approaches to effective argumentation—also called **rhetorical appeals**—are traditionally divided into three basic types:

- ***Logos* (logical argumentation).** This approach persuades an audience through logic or reason. *Logos* is the part of an argument that appeals to the head, not the heart. Is the claim of your essay clear? Is the argumentation logical? Is the evidence you offer reasonable? *Logos* is the aspect of the argument a reader can most easily define and analyze. It is essential to get your logical argumentation right in order to convince a reader of your thesis.
- ***Pathos* (emotional persuasion).** This approach evokes emotion or empathy. *Pathos* is the aspect of an argument that appeals to the heart. An argument that uses *pathos* creates an emotional response rather than an intellectual one. Logic alone is often not enough to convince a reader. If you can also make the reader respond with emotion, he or she is more likely to be convinced by your argument.
- ***Ethos* (credibility).** This approach establishes the credibility or character of the writer or speaker. Obviously, readers are more likely to believe the argument of someone who is an established expert on the topic being discussed or someone they believe to be honorable and trustworthy. Credibility can be established through the tone and style of the essay itself, or independently, through the known reputation of the writer.

Logical Argumentation: Evidence and Organization

Logos or logical argumentation requires clear and compelling evidence in support of claims. Here are some pointers on building the logical structure of your argument:

- **State your claims.** Your essay's main claim is your thesis—the central point of your paper. It should be clear, focused, and convincing. Your paper will be more interesting, though, if its main claim is not something entirely obvious. What is a claim? Any time you make a statement you intend to be taken as true, you have made a claim. Some claims are unlikely to be contradicted ("the sky is blue" or "today is Tuesday"), but others are debatable ("every college sophomore dreams of running off to see the world"). The process of supporting your claims will help you clarify and refine your ideas.

- **Offer evidence.** When you offer a debatable claim, you should support it with evidence. When you write about a work of literature, the most convincing evidence generally comes from the text itself. Direct quotations from the poem, play, or story under discussion can provide particularly convincing support for your claims. Be sure to introduce any quotation by putting it in the context of the larger work. It is even more important to follow up each quotation with your own analysis of what it shows about the work.
- **Evaluate how well your evidence supports your claim.** If you were to make the claim that today's weather is absolutely perfect and offer as your evidence the blue sky, your logic would include an unspoken **assumption**, or **warrant**: sunny weather is perfect weather. Not everyone will agree with your example, though. Some folks (perhaps farmers) might prefer rain. In making any argument, including one about literature, you may find that you sometimes need to explain why your evidence is sound. This is especially true when the evidence you provide can lead to conclusions other than the one you are hoping to prove.
- **Refine your thesis as necessary.** If you find the evidence doesn't support certain aspects of your thesis, then refine the thesis. Remember: until you turn in your essay, it is a work in progress. Anything can and should be changed if it doesn't further the development of your paper's main idea.
- **Organize your argument.** Unless you are writing an explication that works its way line by line through an entire literary work, you will need to make crucial decisions about how to shape your essay. Its order should be driven by the logic of your argument, not by the structure of the story, play, or poem you're discussing. In other words, you need not work your way mechanically from start to finish through your source material, touching on every point. Instead, choose only the major points needed to prove your thesis, and present them in whatever order best supports your claim. A rough outline can help you to determine the best order.

Emotional Argumentation

Pathos, or emotional argumentation, requires you to go beyond simply presenting the logical elements of your argument. You also need to create an emotional connection and response in the reader that will lead him or her to support your point of view. Here are some pointers on building the emotional framework for your argument.

- **Create a human connection.** Don't let your entire essay consist of abstract argumentation and support. What emotions can you describe or invoke that will earn the reader's attention and endorsement? How do you use that emotion to support your point of view? Always remember that you are writing for your fellow human beings, not for a computer.

- **Observe and describe emotion.** When you write about a short story, poem, or play, there is almost always emotional content in the text. (Sometimes the emotions are explicit; sometimes they are mostly implied.) Observe how the author evokes and uses that *pathos* to express his or her meaning. Find an emotional element in the work you are discussing and describe it in a way that invites the reader to respond in a manner appropriate to your argument. Don't hesitate to communicate your own emotions, if they are relevant to your argument. Give an example or anecdote that conveys that emotion.
- **Review the role of emotion in your argumentation.** Once you have drafted your essay, review its emotional content. Do you use *pathos* to support any of your points? If so, do you use it effectively? (Unfocused emotion may actually undermine your logical arguments and credibility.) Revise your essay accordingly to strengthen its emotional connection to the reader. Find those points in your essay where you can make an emotional connection to support your reasoning. Find the right example to create emotional support for your argument.

Credibility: Tone and Balance

Ethos, or credibility, is the reader's sense of the author's character and reliability—how trustworthy does the author seem? When weighing the merits of any claim, you probably take into account the credibility of the person making the case. Often this happens almost automatically. An expert on any given topic has a certain brand of authority not available to most of us. Fortunately, there are other ways to establish your own credibility. To strengthen the credibility of your argument, you should also consider the following principles:

- **Keep your tone thoughtful.** Your reader will develop a sense of who you are through your words. If you come across as belligerent, flippant, or disrespectful to those inclined to disagree with your views, you may lose your reader's goodwill. If you seem to exaggerate your evidence, the reader will discount your credibility. Therefore, express your ideas calmly and thoughtfully. A level tone demonstrates that you are interested in thinking through an issue or idea, not in bullying your reader into submission.
- **Take opposing arguments into account.** To make an argument more convincing, demonstrate familiarity with other possible points of view. Doing so indicates that you have taken other claims into account before arriving at your thesis; it reveals your fairness as well as your understanding of your subject matter. In laying out other points of view, though, be sure to

represent them fairly but also to respectfully make clear why your thesis is the soundest claim; you don't want your reader to doubt where you stand.

- **Demonstrate your knowledge.** To gain your reader's trust, it helps to demonstrate a solid understanding of your subject matter. Always check your facts; factual errors can call your knowledge into doubt. It also helps to have a command of the conventions of writing. Errors in punctuation, spelling, or grammar can undermine your credibility.

CHECKLIST: Developing an Argument

- ☐ What is your essay's purpose?
- ☐ Who is your audience?
- ☐ Is your topic narrow enough?
- ☐ Is your thesis interesting and thought-provoking?
- ☐ Is your thesis reasonable? Can you support it with logical evidence?
- ☐ Are there emotional elements or examples you can use to support your thesis?
- ☐ Does everything in your essay support your thesis?
- ☐ Have you considered and refuted alternative views?
- ☐ Is your tone thoughtful?
- ☐ Is your argument sensibly organized? Are similar ideas grouped together? Does one point lead logically to the next?

DRAFT YOUR ARGUMENT

Seated at last, you prepare to write, only to find yourself besieged with petty distractions. All of a sudden you remember a friend you had promised to call, some double-A batteries you were supposed to pick up, a neglected cup of coffee (in another room) growing colder by the minute. If your paper is to be written, you have only one course of action: collar these thoughts and for the moment banish them. Here are a few tips for writing your rough draft:

- **Review your argument.** The shape of your argument, its support, and the evidence you have collected will form the basis of your rough draft.
- **Get your thoughts down.** The best way to draft a paper is to get your ideas down quickly. At this stage, don't fuss over details. The critical, analytical side of your mind can worry about spelling, grammar, and punctuation later. For now, let your creative mind take charge. This part of yourself has the good ideas, insight, and confidence. Forge ahead. Believe in yourself and in your ideas.
- **Write the part you feel most comfortable with first.** There's no need to start at the paper's beginning and work your way methodically through

to the end. Instead, plunge right into the parts of the paper you feel most prepared to write. You can always go back later and fill in the blanks.

- **Leave yourself plenty of space.** As you compose, leave plenty of space between lines and set wide margins. When later thoughts come to you, you will easily be able to go back and squeeze them in.
- **Focus on the argument.** Whenever you bring up a new point, it's good to tie it back to your thesis. If you can't find a way to connect a point to your thesis, it's probably better to leave it out of your paper and come up with a point that advances your central claim.
- **Does your thesis hold up?** If, as you write, you find that most of the evidence you uncover is not helping you prove your paper's thesis, it may be that the thesis needs honing. Adjust it as needed.
- **Be open to new ideas.** Writing rarely proceeds in a straight line. Even after you outline your paper and begin to write and revise, expect to discover new thoughts—perhaps the best thoughts of all. If you do, be sure to invite them in.

SAMPLE STUDENT ROUGH DRAFT: ARGUMENT PAPER

Here is a student's rough draft for an argument essay on "Nothing Gold Can Stay."

On Robert Frost's "Nothing Gold Can Stay"

Most of the lines in the poem "Nothing Gold Can Stay" by Robert Frost focus on the changing of the seasons. The poem's first line says that the first leaves of spring are actually blossoms, and the actual leaves that follow are less precious. Those first blossoms only last a little while. The reader realizes that nature is a metaphor for a person's state of mind. People start off perfectly innocent, but as time passes, they can't help but lose that innocence. The poem argues that, like Adam and Eve, we all lose our innocence, and the passage of time is inevitable.

The poem's first image is of the color found in nature. The early gold of spring blossoms is nature's "hardest hue to hold." The color gold is associated with the mineral gold, a precious commodity. There's a hint that early spring is nature in its perfect state, and perfection is impossible to hold on to. To the poem's speaker, the colors of early spring seem to last only an hour. If you blink, they are gone. Like early spring, innocence can't last.

The line "leaf subsides to leaf" brings us from early spring through summer and fall. The golden blossoms and delicate leaves of spring subside, or sink to a lower level, meaning they become less special and beautiful. There's nothing more special and beautiful than a baby, so people are the same way. In literature, summer often means the prime of your life, and autumn often means the declining years. These times are less beautiful ones. "So dawn goes down to day" is a similar kind of image. Dawns are unbelievably colorful and beautiful but they don't last very long. Day is nice, but not as special as dawn.

The most surprising line in the poem is the one that isn't about nature. Instead it's about human beings. Eden may have been a garden (a part of nature), but it also represents a state of mind. The traditional religious view is that Adam and Eve chose to disobey God and eat from the tree of knowledge. They could have stayed in paradise forever if they had followed God's orders. So it's surprising that Frost writes "So Eden sank to grief" in a poem that is all about how inevitable change is. It seems like he's saying that no matter what Adam and Eve had done, the Garden of Eden wouldn't stay the paradise it started out being. When Adam and Eve ate the apple, they lost their innocence. The apple is supposed to represent knowledge, so they became wiser but less perfect. But the poem implies that no matter what Adam and Eve had done, they would have grown sadder and wiser. That's true for all people. We can't stay young and innocent.

It's almost as if Frost is defying the Bible, suggesting that there is no such thing as sin. We can't help getting older and wiser. It's a natural process. Suffering happens not because we choose to do bad things but because passing time takes our innocence. The real original sin is that time has to pass and we all have to grow wiser and less innocent.

The poem "Nothing Gold Can Stay" makes the point that people can't stay innocent forever. Suffering is the inevitable result of the aging process. Like the first leaves of spring, we are at the best at the very beginning, and it's all downhill from there.

REVISE YOUR ARGUMENT

A writer rarely—if ever—achieves perfection on the first try. For most of us, good writing is largely a matter of revision. Once your first draft is done, you can—and should—turn on your analytical mind. Painstaking revision is more than just tidying up grammar and spelling. It might mean expanding your ideas or sharpening the focus by cutting out any unnecessary thoughts. To achieve effective writing, you must have the courage to be merciless. Tear your rough drafts apart and reassemble their pieces into a stronger order. As you revise, consider the following:

- **Be sure your thesis is clear, decisive, and thought-provoking.** The most basic ingredient in a good essay is a strong thesis—the sentence in which you summarize the claim you are making. Your thesis should say something more than just the obvious; it should be clear and decisive and make a point that requires evidence to persuade your reader to agree. A sharp, bold thesis lends energy to your argument. A revision of the working thesis used in the rough draft above provides a good example.

  WORKING THESIS

  The poem argues that, like Adam and Eve, we all lose our innocence, and the passage of time is inevitable.

  This thesis may not be bold or specific enough to make for an interesting argument. A careful reader would be hard pressed to disagree with the observation that Frost's poem depicts the passage of time or the loss of innocence. In a revision of his thesis, however, the essay's author pushes the claim further, going beyond the obvious to its implications.

  REVISED THESIS

  In "Nothing Gold Can Stay," Frost makes a bold claim: sin, suffering, and loss are inevitable because the passage of time causes everyone to fall from grace.

  Instead of simply asserting that the poem looks with sorrow on the passage of time, the revised thesis raises the issue of why this is so. It makes a more thought-provoking claim about the poem. An arguable thesis can result in a more energetic, purposeful essay. A thesis that is obvious to everyone, on the other hand, leads to a static, dull paper.

- **Ascertain whether the evidence you provide supports your argument.** Does everything within your paper work to support its thesis sentence? While a solid paper might be written about the poetic form of "Nothing Gold Can Stay," the student paper above would not be well served by bringing the subject up unless the author could show how the poem's form contributes to its message that time causes everyone to lose his or her innocence. If you find yourself including information that doesn't serve your argument, consider going back into the poem, story, or play for more useful evidence. On the other hand, if you're beginning to have a sneaking feeling that your thesis itself is shaky, consider reworking *it* so that it more accurately reflects the evidence in the text.

- **Check whether your argument is logical.** Does one point lead naturally to the next? Reread the paper, looking for logical fallacies, moments in which the claims you make are not sufficiently supported by evidence, or the connection between one thought and the next seems less than rational. Classic logical fallacies include making hasty generalizations, confusing cause and effect, or using a non sequitur, a statement that doesn't follow from the statement that precedes it. An example of two seemingly unconnected thoughts may be found in the second paragraph of the draft above:

> To the poem's speaker, the colors of early spring seem to last only an hour. If you blink, they are gone. Like early spring, innocence can't last.

Though there may well be a logical connection between the first two sentences and the third one, the paper doesn't spell that connection out. Asked to clarify the warrant, or assumption, that makes possible the leap from the subject of spring to the subject of innocence, the author revised the passage this way:

> To the poem's speaker, the colors of early spring seem to last only an hour. When poets write of seasons, they often also are commenting on the life cycle. To make a statement that spring can't last more than an hour implies that a person's youth (often symbolically associated with spring) is all too short. Therefore, the poem implies that innocent youth, like spring, lasts for only the briefest time.

The revised version spells out the author's thought process, helping the reader to follow the argument.

- **Supply transitional words and phrases.** To ensure that your reader's journey from one idea to the next is a smooth one, insert transitional words and phrases at the start of new paragraphs or sentences. Phrases such as "in contrast" and "however" signal a U-turn in logic, while those such as "in addition" and "similarly" alert the reader that you are continuing in the same direction you have been traveling. Seemingly inconsequential words and phrases such as "also" and "as well" or "as mentioned above" can smooth the reader's path from one thought to the next, as in the following example:

DRAFT

Though Frost is writing about nature, his real subject is humanity. In literature, spring often represents youth. Summer symbolizes young adulthood, autumn stands for middle age, and winter represents old age. The adult stages of life are, for Frost, less precious than childhood, which passes very quickly. The innocence of childhood is, like those spring leaves, precious as gold.

ADDING TRANSITIONAL WORDS AND PHRASES

Though Frost is writing about nature, his real subject is humanity. As mentioned above, in literature, spring often represents youth. Similarly, summer symbolizes young adulthood, autumn stands for middle age, and winter represents old age. The adult stages of life are, for Frost, less precious than childhood, which passes very quickly. Also, the innocence of childhood is, like those spring leaves, precious as gold.

- **Make sure each paragraph contains a topic sentence.** Each paragraph in your essay should develop a single idea; this idea should be conveyed in a topic sentence. As astute readers often expect to get a sense of a paragraph's purpose from its first few sentences, a topic sentence is often well placed at or near a paragraph's start.
- **Make a good first impression.** Your introductory paragraph may have seemed just fine as you began the writing process. Be sure to reconsider it in light of the entire paper. Does the introduction draw readers in and prepare them for what follows? If not, be sure to rework it, as the author of the rough draft above did. Look at his first paragraph again:

DRAFT OF OPENING PARAGRAPH

Most of the lines in the poem "Nothing Gold Can Stay" by Robert Frost focus on the changing of the seasons. The poem's first line says that the first leaves of spring are actually blossoms, and the actual leaves that follow are less precious. Those first blossoms only last a little while. The reader realizes that nature is a metaphor for a person's state of mind. People start off perfectly innocent, but as time passes, they can't help but lose that happy innocence. The poem argues that, like Adam and Eve, we all lose our innocence, and the passage of time is inevitable.

While serviceable, this paragraph could be more compelling. Its author improved it by adding specifics to bring his ideas to more vivid life. For example, the rather pedestrian sentence "People start off perfectly innocent, but as time passes, they can't help but lose that innocence," became this livelier one: "As babies we are all perfectly innocent, but as time passes, we can't help but lose that innocence." By adding a specific image—the baby—the author gives the reader a visual picture to illustrate the abstract idea of innocence. He also sharpened his thesis sentence, making it less general and more thought-provoking. By varying the length of his sentences, he made the paragraph less monotonous.

REVISED OPENING PARAGRAPH

Most of the lines in Robert Frost's brief poem "Nothing Gold Can Stay" focus on nature: the changing of the seasons and the fading of dawn into day. The poem's opening line asserts that the first blossoms of spring are more precious than the leaves that follow. Likewise, dawn is more special than day. Though Frost's subject seems to be nature, the reader soon realizes that his real subject is human nature. As babies we are all perfectly innocent, but as time passes, we can't help but lose that happy innocence. In "Nothing Gold Can Stay," Frost makes a bold claim: sin, suffering, and loss are inevitable because the passage of time causes everyone to fall from grace.

- **Remember that last impressions count too.** Your paper's conclusion should give the reader some closure, tying up the paper's loose ends without simply (and boringly) restating all that has come before. The author of the rough draft above initially ended his paper with a paragraph that repeated the paper's main ideas without pushing those ideas any further:

DRAFT OF CONCLUSION

The poem "Nothing Gold Can Stay" makes the point that people can't stay innocent forever. Grief is the inevitable result of the aging process. Like the first leaves of spring, we are at the best at the very beginning, and it's all downhill from there.

While revising his paper, the author realized that the ideas in his next-to-last paragraph would serve to sum up the paper. The new final paragraph doesn't simply restate the thesis; it pushes the idea further, in its last two sentences, by exploring the poem's implications.

REVISED CONCLUSION

Some people might view Frost's poem as sacrilegious, because it seems to say that Adam and Eve had no choice; everything in life is doomed to fall. Growing less innocent and more knowing seems less a choice in Frost's view than a natural process like the changing of golden blossoms to green leaves. "Eden sank to grief" not because we choose to do evil things but because time takes away our innocence as we encounter the suffering and loss of human existence. Frost suggests

> that the real original sin is that time has to pass and we all must grow wiser and less innocent.

- **Give your paper a compelling title.** Like the introduction, a title should be inviting to readers, giving them a sense of what's coming. Provide enough specifics to pique your reader's interest. "On Robert Frost's 'Nothing Gold Can Stay'" is a duller, less informative title than "Lost Innocence in Robert Frost's 'Nothing Gold Can Stay,'" which may spark the reader's interest and prepare him or her for what is to come.

CHECKLIST: Revising Your Argument

- ☐ Is your thesis clear? Can it be sharpened?
- ☐ Does all your evidence serve to advance the argument put forth in your thesis?
- ☐ Is your argument logical?
- ☐ Have you made an emotional connection with the reader?
- ☐ Does your presentation seem credible?
- ☐ Do transitional words and phrases signal movement from one idea to the next?
- ☐ Does each paragraph contain a topic sentence?
- ☐ Does your introduction draw the reader in? Does it prepare the reader for what follows?
- ☐ Does your conclusion tie up the paper's loose ends? Does it avoid merely restating what has come before?
- ☐ Is your title compelling?

SOME FINAL ADVICE ON REWRITING

- **Whenever possible, get feedback from a trusted reader.** In every project, there comes a time when the writer has gotten so close to the work that he or she can't see it clearly. A talented roommate or a tutor in the campus writing center can tell you what isn't yet clear on the page, what questions still need answering, or what line of argument isn't yet as persuasive as it could be.
- **Be willing to refine your thesis.** Once you have fleshed out your whole paper, you may find that your original thesis is not borne out by the rest of your argument. If so, you will need to rewrite your thesis so that it more precisely fits the evidence at hand.
- **Be prepared to question your whole approach to a work of literature.** On occasion, you may even need to entertain the notion of throwing

everything you have written into the wastebasket and starting over again. Occasionally having to start from scratch is the lot of any writer.

- **Rework troublesome passages.** Look for skimpy paragraphs of one or two sentences—evidence that your ideas might need more fleshing out. Can you supply more evidence, more explanation, more examples or illustrations?
- **Cut out any unnecessary information.** Everything in your paper should serve to further its thesis. Delete any sentences or paragraphs that detract from your focus.
- **Aim for intelligent clarity when you use literary terminology.** Critical terms can help sharpen your thoughts and make them easier to handle. Nothing is less sophisticated or more opaque, however, than too many technical terms thrown together for grandiose effect: "The mythic *symbolism* of this *archetype* is the *antithesis* of the *dramatic situation*." Choose plain words you're already at ease with. When you use specialized terms, do so to smooth the way for your reader—to make your meaning more precise. It is less cumbersome, for example, to refer to the *tone* of a story than to say, "the way the author makes you feel what she is talking about."
- **Set your paper aside for a while.** Even an hour or two away from your essay can help you return to it with fresh eyes. Remember that the literal meaning of "revision" is "seeing again."
- **Finally, carefully read your paper one last time to edit it.** Now it's time to sweat the small stuff. Check any uncertain spellings, scan for run-on sentences and fragments, pull out a weak word and send in a stronger one. Like soup stains on a job interviewee's tie, finicky errors distract from the overall impression and prejudice your reader against your essay.

Here is the revised version of the student paper we have been examining.

Gabriel 1

Noah Gabriel
Professor James
English 2171
17 October 2019

Lost Innocence in
Robert Frost's "Nothing Gold Can Stay"

Most of the lines in Robert Frost's brief poem "Nothing Gold Can Stay" focus on nature: the changing of the seasons and the fading of dawn into day. The poem's opening line asserts that the first blossoms of spring are more precious than the leaves that follow. Likewise, dawn is more special than day. Though Frost's subject seems to be nature, the reader soon realizes that his real subject is human nature. As babies we are all perfectly innocent, but as time passes, we can't help but lose that happy innocence. In "Nothing Gold Can Stay," Frost makes a bold claim: sin, suffering, and loss are inevitable because the passage of time causes everyone to fall from grace.

Thesis sentence states the main claim

The poem begins with a deceptively simple sentence: "Nature's first green is gold." The subject seems to be the first, delicate leaves of spring which are less green and more golden than summer leaves. However, the poem goes on to say, "Her early leaf's a flower" (3), indicating that Frost is describing the first blossoms of spring. In fact, he's describing both the new leaves and blossoms. Both are as rare and precious as the mineral gold. They are precious because they don't last long; the early gold of spring blossoms is nature's "hardest hue to hold" (2). Early spring is an example of nature in its perfect state, and perfection is impossible to hold on to. To the poem's speaker, in fact, the colors of early spring seem to last only an hour. When poets write of seasons, they often also are commenting on the life cycle. To make a statement that spring can't last more than an hour implies that a person's youth (often symbolically associated with spring) is all too short. Therefore, the poem implies that innocent youth, like spring, lasts for only the briefest time.

Logos: textual evidence backs up thesis

Assumpti[on] (or warra[nt]) is spelled [out]

Claim

Gabriel 2

While Frost takes four lines to describe the decline of the spring blossoms, he picks up the pace when he describes what happens next. The line, "Then leaf subsides to leaf" (5) brings us from early spring through summer and fall, compressing three seasons into a single line. Just as time seems to pass slowly when we are children, and then much more quickly when we grow up, the poem moves quickly once the first golden moment is past. The word "subsides" feels important. The golden blossoms and delicate leaves of spring subside, or sink to a lower level, meaning they become less special and beautiful.

gnificant ord is looked closely

aim

Though Frost is writing about nature, his real subject is humanity. As mentioned above, in literature, spring often represents youth. Similarly, summer symbolizes young adulthood, autumn stands for middle age, and winter represents old age. The adult stages of life are, for Frost, less precious than childhood, which passes very quickly, as we later realize. Also, the innocence of childhood is, like those spring leaves, precious as gold.

hos: edibility writer hanced by elligent neralizations out erature

Frost shifts his view from the cycle of the seasons to the cycle of a single day to make a similar point. Just as spring turns to summer, "So dawn goes down to day" (7). Like spring, dawn is unbelievably colorful and beautiful but doesn't last very long. Like "subsides," the phrase "goes down" implies that full daylight is actually a falling off from dawn. As beautiful as daylight is, it's ordinary, while dawn is special because it is more fleeting.

y phrase nalyzed sely

Among these natural images, one line stands out: "So Eden sank to grief" (6). This line is the only one in the poem that deals directly with human beings. Eden may have been a garden (a part of nature) but it represents a state of mind—perfect innocence. In the traditional religious view, Adam and Eve chose to disobey God by eating an apple from the tree of knowledge. They were presented with a choice: to be obedient and remain in paradise forever, or to disobey God's order. People often speak of that first choice as "original sin." In this religious view, "Eden sank to grief" because the first humans chose to sin.

aim

Gabriel 3

Frost, however, takes a different view. He compares the Fall of Man to the changing of spring to summer, as though it was as inevitable as the passage of time. The poem implies that no matter what Adam and Eve did, they couldn't remain in paradise. Original sin in Frost's view seems less a voluntary moral action than a natural, if unhappy sort of maturation. The innocent perfection of the garden of Eden couldn't possibly last. The apple represents knowledge, so in a symbolic sense God wanted Adam and Eve to stay unknowing, or innocent. But the poem implies that it was inevitable that Adam and Eve would gain knowledge and lose their innocence, becoming wiser but less perfect. They lost Eden and encountered "grief," the knowledge of suffering and loss associated with the human condition. This is certainly true for the rest of us human beings. As much as we might like to, we can't stay young or innocent forever.

Claim

Pathos: appeal to common emotional response

Some people might view Frost's poem as sacrilegious, because it seems to say that Adam and Eve had no choice; everything in life is doomed to fall. Growing less innocent and more knowing seems less a choice in Frost's view than a natural process like the changing of golden blossoms to green leaves. "Eden sank to grief" not because we choose to do evil things but because time takes away our innocence as we encounter the suffering and loss of human existence. Frost suggests that the real original sin is that time has to pass and we all must grow wiser and less innocent.

Ethos: credibility built throug[h] recognition and reconciliatio[n] of different viewpoint

Restatemen[t] of thesis

Gabriel 4

Work Cited

Frost, Robert. "Nothing Gold Can Stay." *Backpack Literature: An Introduction to Fiction, Poetry, Drama, and Writing*, edited by X. J. Kennedy et al., 6th ed., Pearson, 2020. p. 587.

WHAT'S YOUR PURPOSE? COMMON APPROACHES TO WRITING ABOUT LITERATURE

It is crucial to keep your paper's purpose in mind. When you write an academic paper, you are likely to have been given a specific set of marching orders. Maybe you have been asked to write for a particular audience besides the obvious one (your professor, that is). Perhaps you have been asked to describe your personal reaction to a literary work. Maybe your purpose is to interpret a work, analyzing how one or more of its elements contribute to its meaning. You may have been instructed to write an evaluation in which you judge a work's merits. Let the assignment dictate your paper's tone and content. Below are several commonly used approaches to writing about literature.

Explication

Explication is the patient unfolding of meanings in a work of literature. An explication proceeds carefully through a story, passage, or poem, usually interpreting it line by line—perhaps even word by word, dwelling on details a casual reader might miss and illustrating how a work's smaller parts contribute to the whole. Alert and willing to take pains, the writer of such an essay notices anything meaningful that isn't obvious, whether it is a colossal theme suggested by a symbol or a little hint contained in a single word.

To write an honest explication of an entire story takes time and space, and is a better assignment for a long term paper, an honors thesis, or a dissertation than a short essay. A thorough explication of Nathaniel Hawthorne's "Young Goodman Brown," (Chapter 9), for example, would likely run much longer than the rich and intriguing short story itself. Ordinarily, explication is best suited to a short passage or section of a story: a key scene, a critical conversation, a statement of theme, or an opening or closing paragraph.

In drama, explication is best suited to brief passages—a key soliloquy, for example, or a moment of dialogue that lays bare the play's theme. Closely examining a critical moment in a play can shed light on the play in its entirety. To be successful, an explication needs to concentrate on a brief passage, probably not much more than 20 lines long.

Storytellers who are especially fond of language invite closer attention to their words than others might. Edgar Allan Poe, for one, is a poet sensitive to the rhythms of his sentences and a symbolist whose stories abound in potent suggestions. Here is a student's explication of a short but essential passage in "The Tell-Tale Heart." (Chapter 2). The passage occurs in the third paragraph of the story, and to help us follow the explication, the student quotes the passage in full at the paper's beginning.

An unusually well-written essay, "By Lantern Light" cost its author two or three careful revisions. Rather than attempting to say something about *everything* in the passage from Poe, she selects only the details that strike her as most meaningful. In her very first sentence, she briefly shows us how the passage functions in the context of Poe's story: how it clinches our suspicions that the narrator is mad. Notice too that the student who wrote the essay doesn't inch through the passage sentence by sentence, but freely takes up its details in an order that seems appropriate to her argument.

Kim 1

Susan Kim

Professor A. M. Lundy

English 100

20 May 2019

By Lantern Light: An Explication of
a Passage in Poe's "The Tell-Tale Heart"

> And every night, about midnight, I turned the latch of his door and opened it—oh, so gently! And then, when I had made an opening sufficient for my head, I put in a dark lantern, all closed, closed, so that no light shone out, and then I thrust in my head. Oh, you would have laughed to see how cunningly I thrust it in! I moved it slowly—very, very slowly, so that I might not disturb the old man's sleep. It took me an hour to place my whole head within the opening so far that I could see him as he lay upon his bed. Ha!—would a madman have been so wise as this? And then, when my head was well in the room, I undid the lantern cautiously—oh, so cautiously—cautiously (for the hinges creaked)—I undid it just so much that a single thin ray fell upon the vulture eye. And this I did for seven long nights—every night just at midnight—but I found the eye always closed; and so it was impossible to do the work; for it was not the old man who vexed me, but his Evil Eye. (par. 3)

Quotes passage to [be] explicated

Although Edgar Allan Poe has suggested in the first lines of his story "The Tell-Tale Heart" that the person who addresses us is insane, it is only when we come to the speaker's account of his preparations for murdering the old man that we find his madness fully revealed. Even more convincingly

Thesis sentence [...] statement [...] paper's m[...] claim

Kim 2

than his earlier words (for we might possibly think that someone who claims to hear things in heaven and hell is a religious mystic), these preparations reveal him to be mad. What strikes us is that they are so elaborate and meticulous. A significant detail is the exactness of his schedule for spying: "every night just at midnight." The words with which he describes his motions also convey the most extreme care (and I will indicate them by italics): "how wisely I proceeded—with *what caution*," "I turned the latch of his door and opened it—oh, so *gently*!" "how *cunningly* I thrust it [my head] in! I moved it slowly—*very, very slowly*," "I undid the lantern *cautiously*—oh, *so cautiously—cautiously*." Taking a whole hour to intrude his head into the room, he asks, "Ha!—would a madman have been so wise as this?" But of course the word *wise* is unconsciously ironic, for clearly it is not wisdom the speaker displays, but an absurd degree of care, an almost fiendish ingenuity. Such behavior, I understand, is typical of certain mental illnesses. All his careful preparations that he thinks prove him sane only convince us instead that he is mad.

extual idence pports aim

Obviously his behavior is self-defeating. He wants to catch the "vulture eye" open, and yet he takes all these pains not to disturb the old man's sleep. If he behaved logically, he might go barging into the bedroom with his lantern ablaze, shouting at the top of his voice. And yet, if we can see things his way, there *is* a strange logic to his reasoning. He regards the eye as a creature in itself, quite apart from its possessor. "It was not," he says, "the old man who vexed me, but his Evil Eye." Apparently, to be inspired to do his deed, the madman needs to behold the eye—at least, this is my understanding of his remark, "I found the eye always closed; and so it was impossible to do the work." Poe's choice of the word *work*, by the way, is also revealing. Murder is made to seem a duty or a job; and anyone who so regards murder is either extremely cold-blooded, like a hired killer for a gangland assassination, or else deranged. Besides, the word suggests again the curious sense of detachment that the speaker feels toward the owner of the eye.

pic itence on rrator's d logic

Kim 3

In still another of his assumptions, the speaker shows that he is madly logical, or operating on the logic of a dream. There seems to be a dreamlike relationship between his dark lantern "all closed, closed, so that no light shone out," and the sleeping victim. When the madman opens his lantern so that it emits a single ray, he is hoping that the eye in the old man's head will be open too, letting out its corresponding gleam. The latch that he turns so gently, too, seems like the eye, whose lid needs to be opened in order for the murderer to go ahead. It is as though the speaker is *trying* to get the eyelid to lift. By taking such great pains and by going through all this nightly ritual, he is practicing some kind of magic, whose rules are laid down not by our logic, but by the logic of dreams.

Conclusion pushes thesis further, making it more specific

Kim 4

Work Cited

Poe, Edgar Allan. "The Tell-Tale Heart." *Backpack Literature: An Introduction to Fiction, Poetry, Drama, and Writing*, edited by X. J. Kennedy et al., 6th ed., Pearson, 2020, pp. 37–40.

Explication is a particularly useful way to help unravel a poem's complexities. An explication, however, should not be confused with a paraphrase, which puts the poem's literal meaning into plain prose. While an explication might include some paraphrasing, it does more than simply restate. It explains a poem, in great detail, showing how each part contributes to the whole. In writing an explication of a poem, keep the following tips in mind:

- **Start with the poem's first line, and keep working straight through to the end.** As needed, though, you can take up points out of order.
- **Read closely, addressing the poem's details.** You may choose to include allusions, the denotations or connotations of words, the possible

meanings of symbols, the effects of certain sounds and rhythms and formal elements (rime schemes, for instance), the sense of any statements that contain irony, and other particulars.

- **Show how each part of the poem contributes to the meaning of the whole.** Your explication should go beyond dissecting the pieces of a poem; it should also integrate them to cast light on the poem in its entirety.

Here is a successful student-authored explication of Robert Frost's "Design." The assignment was to explain whatever in the poem seemed most essential, in no more than 750 words. This excellent paper finds something worth unfolding in every line of Frost's poem, without seeming mechanical. Although the student proceeds sequentially through the poem from the title to the last line, he takes up some points out of order, when it serves his purpose. In paragraph two, for example, he looks ahead to the poem's ending and briefly states its main theme in order to relate it to the poem's title. In the third paragraph, he explicates the poem's later image of the heal-all, relating it to the first image. He also comments on the poem's form ("Like many other sonnets"), on its similes and puns, and on its denotations and connotations.

Robert Frost (1874–1963)

Design

1922

I found a dimpled spider, fat and white,
On a white heal-all, holding up a moth
Like a white piece of rigid satin cloth—
Assorted characters of death and blight
Mixed ready to begin the morning right,
Like the ingredients of a witches' broth—
A snow-drop spider, a flower like a froth,
And dead wings carried like a paper kite.

What had that flower to do with being white,
The wayside blue and innocent heal-all?
What brought the kindred spider to that height,
Then steered the white moth thither in the night?
What but design of darkness to appall?—
If design govern in a thing so small.

Surprising adjectives
Type of flower
death
Sarcasm?
evil?
Is this flower innocent?
Questions who is the designer? God/nature?
Evil
Small things aren't planned out?

Rhyme Scheme:

abba, abba, acaa, cc A sonnet?

8 6

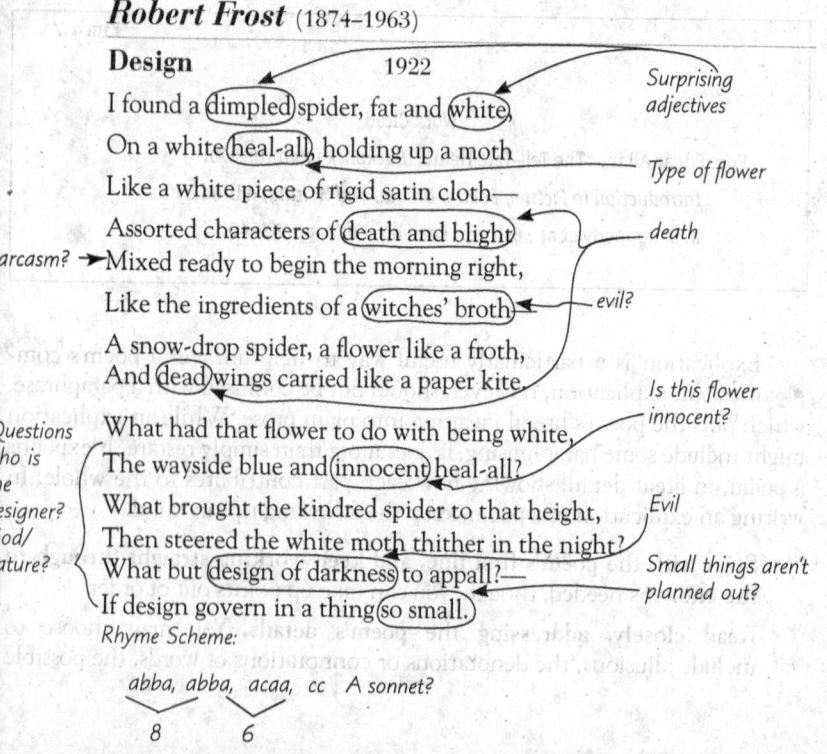

Jasper 1

Ted Jasper
Professor Koss
English 130
21 November 2019

An Unfolding of Robert Frost's "Design"

"I always wanted to be very observing," Robert Frost once told an audience, after reading aloud his poem "Design." Then he added, "But I have always been afraid of my own observations" (qtd. in Cook 126–27). What could Frost have observed that could scare him? Let's examine the poem in question and see what we discover.

Interesting opening. Quotes author

Central question raised

Starting with the title, "Design," any reader of this poem will find it full of meaning. As the *Merriam-Webster Dictionary* defines *design*, the word can denote among other things a plan, purpose, or intention ("Design"). Some arguments for the existence of God (I remember from Sunday School) are based on the "argument from design": that because the world shows a systematic order, there must be a Designer who made it. But the word *design* can also mean "a deliberate undercover project or scheme" such as we attribute to a "designing person" ("Design"). As we shall see, Frost's poem incorporates all of these meanings. His poem raises the old philosophic question of whether there is a Designer, an evil Designer, or no Designer at all.

Defines key word. Sets theme

Topic sentence on significance of title

Like many other sonnets, "Design" is divided into two parts. The first eight lines draw a picture centering on the spider, who at first seems almost jolly. It is *dimpled* and *fat* like a baby, or Santa Claus. The spider stands on a wildflower whose name, heal-all, seems ironic: a *heal-all* is supposed to cure any disease, but this flower has no power to restore life to the dead moth. (Later, in line ten, we learn that the heal-all used to be blue. Presumably, it has died and become bleached-looking.) In the second line we discover, too, that the spider has hold of another creature, a dead moth. We then see the moth described with an odd simile in line three: "Like a white piece of rigid satin cloth." Suddenly, the moth becomes not a creature but a piece of fabric—lifeless and dead—and yet *satin* has connotations of beauty.

Begins line-by-line unfolding of meaning

Discusses images

Jasper 2

:xplores
inguage

Satin is a luxurious material used in rich formal clothing, such as coronation gowns and brides' dresses. Additionally, there is great accuracy in the word: the smooth and slightly plush surface of satin is like the powder-smooth surface of moths' wings. But this "cloth," rigid and white, could be the lining to Dracula's coffin.

efers to
und

In the fifth line an invisible hand enters. The characters are "mixed" like ingredients in an evil potion. Some force doing the mixing is behind the scene. The characters in themselves are innocent enough, but when brought together, their whiteness and look of *rigor mortis* are overwhelming. There is something diabolical in the spider's feast. The "morning right" echoes the word *rite*, a ritual—in this case apparently a Black Mass or a Witches' Sabbath. The simile in line seven ("a flower like a froth") is more ambiguous and harder to describe. Froth is white, foamy, and delicate—something found on a brook in the woods or on a beach after a wave recedes. However, in the natural world, froth also can be ugly: the foam on a polluted stream or a rabid dog's mouth. The dualism in nature—its beauty and its horror—is there in that one simile.

ansition
rds

uotes
ondary
rce

scusses
me

nes key
d

So far, the poem has portrayed a small, frozen scene, with the dimpled killer holding its victim as innocently as a boy holds a kite. Already, Frost has hinted that Nature may be, as Radcliffe Squires suggests, "Nothing but an ash-white plain without love or faith or hope, where ignorant appetites cross by chance" (87). Now, in the last six lines of the sonnet, Frost comes out and directly states his theme. What else could bring these deathly pale, stiff things together "but design of darkness to appall"? The question is clearly rhetorical; we are meant to answer, "Yes, there does seem to be an evil design at work here!" I take the next-to-last line to mean, "What except a design so dark and sinister that we're appalled by it?" "Appall," by the way, is the second pun in the poem: it sounds like *a pall* or shroud. (The derivation of *appall*, according to *Merriam-Webster*, is ultimately from a Latin word meaning "to be pale"—an interesting word choice for a poem full of pale white

Jasper 3

images ["Appall"].) *Steered* carries the suggestion of a steering-wheel or rudder that some pilot had to control. Like the word *brought*, it implies that some invisible force charted the paths of spider, heal-all, and moth, so that they arrived together.

Having suggested that the universe is in the hands of that sinister force (an indifferent God? Fate? the Devil?), Frost adds a note of doubt. The Bible tells us that "His eye is on the sparrow," but at the moment the poet doesn't seem sure. Maybe, he hints, when things in the universe drop below a certain size, they pass completely out of the Designer's notice. When creatures are this little, maybe God doesn't bother to govern them but just lets them run wild. And possibly the same mindless chance is all that governs human lives. And because this is even more senseless than having an angry God intent on punishing us, it is, Frost suggests, the worst suspicion of all.

Answers question raised in introduction

Conclusion

Jasper 4

Works Cited

"Appall." *Merriam-Webster.com*, 2019, www.merriam-webster.com/dictionary/appall.

Cook, Reginald. *Robert Frost: A Living Voice*. U of Massachusetts P, 1974.

"Design." *Merriam-Webster.com*, 2019, www.merriam-webster.com/dictionary/design.

Frost, Robert. "Design." *Collected Poems, Prose, and Plays*, Library of America, 1995, p. 275.

Squires, Radcliffe. *The Major Themes of Robert Frost*. U of Michigan P, 1963.

Analysis

Examining a single component of a piece of literature can afford us a better understanding of the entire work. This is perhaps why in most literature classes students are asked to write at least one **analysis** (from the Greek: "breaking up"), an essay that breaks a work into its elements and, usually, studies one part closely. A topic for an analysis might be "The Character of Alice Walker's Dee," in which the writer would concentrate on showing us Dee's highly individual features and traits of personality, or perhaps "Imagery of Light and Darkness in Frost's 'Design.'"

In this book, you probably already have encountered a few brief analyses: the discussion of connotations in William Blake's "London" (Chapter 13), for instance, or the examination of symbols in T. S. Eliot's "The *Boston Evening Transcript*" (Chapter 20). To write an analysis, remember three key points:

- **Focus on a single, manageable element.** Some possible choices are tone, irony, literal meaning, imagery, theme, and symbolism. If you are writing about poetry, you could also consider sound, rhythm, rime, or form.
- **Show how this element contributes to the meaning of the whole.** While no element of a work exists apart from all the others, by taking a closer look at one particular aspect of the work, you can see the whole more clearly.
- **Support your contentions with specific references to the work you are analyzing.** Quotations can be particularly convincing.

The student papers that follow are examples of brief analyses. The first paper analyzes the imagery of Elizabeth Bishop's poem "The Fish" (Chapter 14). The second paper analyzes Shakespeare's play *Othello* (Chapter 27) in light of Aristotle's famous definition of tragedy (discussed on page 721).

Woods 1

Becki Woods

Professor Bernier

English 220

23 February 2019

Faded Beauty: Bishop's Use of Imagery in "The Fish"

: sentence
s name
uthor and
k

Upon first reading, Elizabeth Bishop's "The Fish" appears to be a simple fishing tale. A close investigation of the imagery in Bishop's highly detailed description, however, reveals a different sort of poem. The real theme of Bishop's poem is a compassion and respect for the fish's lifelong struggle to

Woods 2

survive. By carefully and effectively describing the captured fish, his reaction to being caught, and the symbols of his past struggles to stay alive, Bishop creates, through her images of beauty, victory, and survival, something more than a simple tale.

Thesis sentence

The first four lines of the poem are quite ordinary and factual:

Topic sentence

I caught a tremendous fish
and held him beside the boat
half out of water, with my hook
fast in a corner of his mouth. (1–4)

Except for *tremendous*, Bishop's persona uses no exaggerations—unlike most fishing stories—to set up the situation of catching the fish. The detailed description begins as the speaker recounts the event further, noticing something signally important about the captive fish: "He didn't fight" (5). At this point the poem begins to seem unusual: most fish stories are about how ferociously the prey resists being captured. The speaker also notes that the "battered and venerable / and homely" fish offered no resistance to being caught (8–9). The image of the submissive attitude of the fish is essential to the theme of the poem. It is his "utter passivity [that] makes [the persona's] detailed scrutiny possible" (McNally 192).

Quotation from secondary sources

Once the image of the passive fish has been established, the speaker begins an examination of the fish itself, noting that "Here and there / his brown skin hung in strips / like ancient wallpaper" (9–11). By comparing the fish's skin to wallpaper, the persona creates, as Sybil Estess argues, "implicit suggestions of both artistry and decay" (713). Images of peeling wallpaper are instantly brought to mind. The comparison of the fish's skin and wallpaper, though "helpful in conveying an accurate notion of the fish's color to anyone with memories of Victorian parlors and their yellowed wallpaper . . . is," according to Nancy McNally, "even more useful in evoking the associations of deterioration which usually surround such memories" (192). The fish's faded beauty has been hinted at in the comparison, thereby setting up the detailed imagery that soon follows:

Topic sentence

Essay mo[ves] systemati[cally] through poem, fro[m] start to fi[nish]

Woods 3

He was speckled with barnacles,
fine rosettes of lime,
and infested
with tiny white sea-lice,
and underneath two or three
rags of green weed hung down. (16–21)

extual vidence, nix of long nd short uotations

The persona sees the fish as he is; the infestations and faults are not left out of the description. Yet, at the same time, the fisher "express[es] what [he/she] has sensed of the character of the fish" (Estess 714).

Bishop's persona notices "shapes like full-blown roses / stained and lost through age" on the fish's skin (14–15). The persona's perception of the fish's beauty is revealed along with a recognition of its faded beauty, which is best shown in the description of the fish's being speckled with barnacles and spotted with lime. However, the fisher observes these spots and sees them as rosettes—as objects of beauty, not just ugly brown spots. These images contribute to the persona's recognition of beauty's having become faded beauty.

ansitional rase begins ɔic sentence

The poem next turns to a description of the fish's gills. The imagery in "While his gills were breathing in / the terrible oxygen" (22–23) leads "to the very structure of the creature" that is now dying (Hopkins 201). The descriptions of the fish's interior beauty—"the coarse white flesh / packed in like feathers," the colors "of his shiny entrails," and his "pink swim-bladder / like a big peony"—are reminders of the life that seems about to end (27–28, 31–33).

xtual dence, x of long d short ɔtations

ɔic tence

The composite image of the fish's essential beauty—his being alive—is developed further in the description of the five fish hooks that the captive, living fish carries in his lip:

grim, wet, and weaponlike,
hung five old pieces of fish-line,
. . . .
with all their five big hooks
grown firmly in his mouth. (50–51, 54–55)

Woods 4

As if fascinated by them, the persona, observing how the lines must have been broken during struggles to escape, sees the hooks as "medals with their ribbons / frayed and wavering, / a five-haired beard of wisdom / trailing from his aching jaw" (61–64), and the fisher becomes enthralled by re-created images of the fish's fighting desperately for his life on at least five separate occasions—and winning. Crale Hopkins suggests that "[i]n its capability not only for mere existence, but for action, escaping from previous anglers, the fish shares the speaker's humanity" (202), thus revealing the fisher's deepening understanding of how he or she must now act. The persona has "all along," notes Estess, "describe[d] the fish not just with great detail but with an imaginative empathy for the aquatic creature. In her more-than-objective description, [the fisher] relates what [he/she] has seen to be both the pride and poverty of the fish" (715). It is at this point that the narrator of this fishing tale has a moment of clarity. Realizing the fish's history and the glory the fish has achieved in escaping previous hookings, the speaker sees everything become "rainbow, rainbow, rainbow!" (75)—and then unexpectedly lets the fish go.

Quotations from secondary sources

Bishop's "The Fish" begins by describing an event that might easily be a conventional story's climax: "I caught a tremendous fish" (1). The poem, however, develops into a highly detailed account of a fisher noticing both the age and the faded beauty of the captive and his present beauty and past glory as well. The fishing tale is not simply a recounting of a capture; it is a gradually unfolding epiphany in which the speaker sees the fish in an entirely new light. The intensity of this encounter between an apparently experienced fisher in a rented boat and a battle-hardened fish is delivered through the poet's skillful use of imagery. It is through the description of the capture of an aged fish that Bishop offers her audience her theme of compassion derived from a respect for the struggle for survival.

Conclusion

Restatement of thesis, in light of all that comes before it.

Woods 5

Works Cited

Bishop, Elizabeth. "The Fish." *Backpack Literature: An Introduction to Fiction, Poetry, Drama, and Writing*, edited by X. J. Kennedy et al., 6th ed., Pearson, 2020, pp. 478–80.

Estess, Sybil P. "Elizabeth Bishop: The Delicate Art of Map Making." *Southern Review*, vol. 13, no. 4, Autumn 1977, pp. 705–27.

Hopkins, Crale D. "Inspiration as Theme: Art and Nature in the Poetry of Elizabeth Bishop." *Arizona Quarterly*, vol. 32, 1976, pp. 200–02.

McNally, Nancy L. "Elizabeth Bishop: The Discipline of Description." *Twentieth Century Literature*, vol. 11, no. 4, Jan. 1966, pp. 189–201. *JSTOR*, doi: 10.2307/440842.

Housden 1

Janet Housden

Professor Barth

English 201

3 November 2019

Othello: Tragedy or Soap Opera?

rst aragraph ves name author and ork

When we hear the word "tragedy," we usually think of either a terrible real-life disaster, or a dark and serious drama filled with pain, suffering, and loss that involves the downfall of a powerful person due to some character flaw or error in judgment. William Shakespeare's *Othello* is such a drama. Set in Venice and Cyprus during the Renaissance, the play tells the story of Othello, a Moorish general in the Venetian army, who has just married Desdemona, the daughter of a Venetian nobleman. Through the plotting of a jealous villain, Iago, Othello is deceived into believing that Desdemona has been unfaithful to him. He murders her in revenge, only to discover too late how he has been tricked. Overcome by shame and grief, Othello kills himself.

ey plot formation oids cessive elling

Housden 2

Dealing as it does with jealousy, murder, and suicide, the play is certainly dark, but is *Othello* a true tragedy? In the fourth century BC, the Greek philosopher Aristotle proposed a formal definition of tragedy (Kennedy et al., 721), which only partially fits *Othello*.

The first characteristic of tragedy identified by Aristotle is that the protagonist is a person of outstanding quality and high social position. While Othello is not of royal birth as are many tragic heroes and heroines, he does occupy a sufficiently high position to satisfy this part of Aristotle's definition. Although Othello is a foreigner and a soldier by trade, he has risen to the rank of general and has married into a noble family, which is quite an accomplishment for an outsider. Furthermore, Othello is generally liked and respected by those around him. He is often described by others as being "noble," "brave," and "valiant." By virtue of his high rank and the respect he commands from others, Othello would appear to possess the high stature commonly given to the tragic hero in order to make his eventual fall seem all the more tragic.

While Othello displays the nobility and high status commonly associated with the tragic hero, he also possesses another, less admirable characteristic, the flaw or character defect shared by all heroes of classical tragedy. In Othello's case, it is a stunning gullibility, combined with a violent temper that once awakened overcomes all reason. These flaws permit Othello to be easily deceived and manipulated by the villainous Iago and make him easy prey for the "green-eyed monster" (3.3.179).

It is because of this tragic flaw, according to Aristotle, that the hero is at least partially to blame for his own downfall. While Othello's "free and open nature, / That thinks men honest that but seem to be so" (1.3.383–84) is not a fault in itself, it does allow Iago to convince the Moor of his wife's infidelity without one shred of concrete evidence. Furthermore, once Othello has been convinced of Desdemona's guilt, he makes up his mind to take vengeance, and says that his "bloody thoughts with violent pace / Shall ne'er look back, ne'er ebb to humble love" (3.3.473–74). He thereby

Central question is raised

Thesis statement provides response

Topic sentence on Othello's social positi[on]

Essay systematica[lly] applies Aristotle's definition o[f] tragedy to Othello

Topic sentence o[n] Othello's tragic flaw

Quotes from play [as] evidence t[o] support p[oint]

renders himself deaf to the voice of reason, and ignoring Desdemona's protestations of innocence, brutally murders her, only to discover too late that he has made a terrible mistake. Although he is goaded into his crime by Iago, who is a master at manipulating people, it is Othello's own character flaws that lead to his horrible misjudgment.

opic entence aborates on ea raised previous aragraphs

Aristotle's definition also states that the hero's misfortune is not wholly deserved, that the punishment he receives exceeds his crime. Although it is hard to sympathize with a man as cruel as Othello is to the innocent Desdemona, Othello pays an extremely high price for his sin of gullibility. Othello loses everything—his wife, his position, even his life. Even though it's partially his fault, Othello is not entirely to blame, for without Iago's interference it's highly unlikely that things would turn out as they do. Though it seems incredibly stupid on Othello's part, that a man who has travelled the world and commanded armies should be so easily deceived, there is little evidence that Othello has had much experience with civilian society, and although he is "declined / Into the vale of years" (3.3.281–82) Othello has apparently never been married before. By his own admission, "little of this great world can I speak / More than pertains to feats of broils and battle" (1.3.88–89). Furthermore, Othello has no reason to suspect that "honest Iago" is anything but his loyal friend and supporter.

opic ntence on thello's sfortune

nsitional rds signal ument's ection

While it is understandable that Othello could be fooled into believing Desdemona unfaithful, the question remains whether his fate is deserved. In addition to his mistake of believing Iago's lies, Othello commits a more serious error: he lets himself be blinded by anger. Worse yet, in deciding to take vengeance, he also makes up his mind not be swayed from his course, even by his love for Desdemona. In fact, he refuses to listen to her at all, "lest her body and beauty unprovide my mind again" (4.1.190), therefore denying her the right to defend herself. Because of his rage and unfairness, perhaps Othello deserves his fate more than Aristotle's ideal tragic hero. Othello's punishment does exceed his crime, but just barely.

ic tence orates Othello's fortune

Housden 4

According to Aristotle, the tragic hero's fall gives the protagonist deeper understanding and self-awareness. Othello departs from Aristotle's model in that Othello apparently learns nothing from his mistakes. He never realizes that he is partly at fault. He sees himself only as an innocent victim and blames his misfortune on fate rather than accepting responsibility for his actions. To be sure, he realizes he has been tricked and deeply regrets his mistake, but he seems to feel that he was justified under the circumstances, "For naught I did in hate, but all in honor" (5.2.303). Othello sees himself not as someone whose bad judgment and worse temper have resulted in the death of an innocent party, but as one who has "loved not wisely but too well" (5.2.354). This failure to grasp the true nature of his error indicates that Othello hasn't learned his lesson.

Topic sentence on whether Othello learn[s] from his mistakes

Neither accepting responsibility nor learning from his mistakes, Othello fails to fulfill yet another of Aristotle's requirements. Since the protagonist usually gains some understanding along with his defeat, classical tragedy conveys a sense of human greatness and of life's unrealized potentialities—a quality totally absent from *Othello*. Not only does Othello fail to learn from his mistakes, but he never really realizes what those mistakes are, and it apparently never crosses his mind that things could have turned out any differently. "Who can control his fate?" Othello asks (5.2.274), and this defeatist attitude, combined with his failure to salvage any wisdom from his defeat, separates *Othello* from the tragedy as defined by Aristotle.

Topic sentence elaborating further on whether Othello lea[rns] from his errors

The last part of Aristotle's definition states that viewing the conclusion of a tragedy should result in catharsis for the audience, and that the audience should be left with a feeling of exaltation rather than depression. Unfortunately, the feeling we are left with after viewing *Othello* is neither catharsis nor exaltation but rather a feeling of horror, pity, and disgust at the senseless waste of human lives. The deaths of Desdemona and Othello, as well as those of Emilia and Roderigo, serve no purpose whatsoever. They die not in the service of a great cause but because of lies, treachery, jealousy,

Topic sentence o[n] catharsis

Housden 5

and spite. Their deaths don't even benefit Iago, who is directly or indirectly responsible for all of them. No lesson is learned, no epiphany is reached, and the audience, instead of experiencing catharsis, is left with its negative feeling unresolved.

estatement thesis

Since *Othello* only partially fits Aristotle's definition of tragedy, it is questionable whether or not it should be classified as one. Though it does involve a great man undone by a defect in his own character, the hero gains neither insight nor understanding from his defeat, and so there can be no inspiration or catharsis for the audience, as there would be in a "true" tragedy. *Othello* is tragic only in the everyday sense of the word, the way a plane crash or fire is tragic. At least in terms of Aristotle's classic definition, *Othello* ultimately comes across as more of a melodrama or soap opera than a tragedy.

onclusion

Housden 6

Works Cited

Kennedy, X. J., et al., editors. *Backpack Literature: An Introduction to Fiction, Poetry, Drama, and Writing*. 6th ed., Pearson, 2020, pp. 721–23.

Shakespeare, William. *Othello: The Moor of Venice. Backpack Literature: An Introduction to Fiction, Poetry, Drama, and Writing*, edited by X. J. Kennedy et al., 6th ed., Pearson, 2020, pp. 778–888.

Comparison and Contrast

If you were to write on "The Humor of Alice Walker's 'Everyday Use' and John Updike's 'A & P,'" you would probably employ one or two methods. You might use **comparison**, placing the two stories side by side and pointing out their similarities, or **contrast**, pointing out their differences. Most of the time, in dealing with two pieces of literature, you will find them similar in some ways and different in others, and you'll use both methods. Keep the following points in mind when writing a comparison-contrast paper:

- **Choose works with something significant in common.** This will simplify your task, and also help ensure that your paper hangs together. Before you start writing, ask yourself if the two pieces you've selected throw some light on each other. If the answer is no, rethink your selection.
- **Choose a focus.** Simply ticking off every similarity and difference between two poems or stories would make for a slack and rambling essay. More compelling writing would result from better-focused topics such as "The Experience of Coming of Age in James Joyce's 'Araby' and William Faulkner's 'Barn Burning.'"
- **Don't feel you need to spend equal amounts of time on comparing and contrasting.** If your chosen works are more similar than different, you naturally will spend more space on comparison, and vice versa.
- **Don't devote the first half of your paper to one work and the second half to the other.** This simple structure may weaken your essay if it leads you to keep the two works in total isolation from each other. After all, the point is to see what can be learned by comparison. There is nothing wrong in discussing all of poem A first, then discussing poem B—if in discussing B you keep referring back to A. Another strategy is to do a point-by-point comparison of the two works all the way through your paper—dealing first, perhaps, with their themes, then with their central metaphors, and finally, with their respective merits.
- **Before you start writing, draw up a brief list of points you would like to touch on.** Then address each point, first in one work and then in the other. A sample outline follows for a paper on William Faulkner's "A Rose for Emily" (Chapter 2) and Katherine Mansfield's "Miss Brill" (Chapter 9). The essay's topic is "Adapting to Change: The Characters of Emily Grierson and Miss Brill."

1. Adapting to change (both women)
   Miss Brill more successful
2. Portrait of women
   Miss Emily—unflattering
   Miss Brill—empathetic
3. Imagery
   Miss Emily—morbid
   Miss Brill—cheerful

4. Plot
   Miss Emily
   - loses sanity
   - refuses to adapt

   Miss Brill
   - finds place in society
   - adapts
5. Summary: Miss Brill is more successful

- **Emphasize the points that interest you the most.** This strategy will help keep you from following your outline in a plodding fashion ("Well, now it's time to whip over to Miss Brill again . . .").
- **If the assignment allows, consider applying comparison and contrast in an essay on a single story or play.** You might, for example, analyze the attitudes of the younger and older waiters in Hemingway's "A Clean, Well-Lighted Place" (Chapter 5).

The following student-written paper compares and contrasts the main characters in "A Rose for Emily" and "Miss Brill." Notice how the author focuses the discussion on a single aspect of each woman's personality—the ability to adapt to change and the passage of time. By looking through the lens of three different elements of the short story—diction, imagery, and plot—this clear and systematic essay convincingly argues its thesis.

Ortiz 1

Michelle Ortiz

Professor Gregg

English 200

25 May 2019

Successful Adaptation in
"A Rose for Emily" and "Miss Brill"

In William Faulkner's "A Rose for Emily" and Katherine Mansfield's "Miss Brill," the reader is given a glimpse into the lives of two old women living in different worlds but sharing many similar characteristics. Both Miss Emily and Miss Brill attempt to adapt to a changing environment as they grow older. Through the authors' use of language, imagery, and plot, it becomes clear to the reader that Miss Brill is more successful at adapting to the world around her and finding happiness.

ar
ement of
is

Ortiz 2

In "A Rose for Emily," Faulkner's use of language paints an unflattering picture of Miss Emily. His tone evokes pity and disgust rather than sympathy. The reader identifies with the narrator of the story and shares the townspeople's opinion that Miss Emily is somehow "perverse." In "Miss Brill," however, the reader can identify with the title character. Mansfield's attitude toward the young couple at the end makes the reader hate them for ruining the happiness that Miss Brill has found, however small it may be.

Textual evidence on language supports thesis

The imagery in "A Rose for Emily" keeps the reader from further identifying with Miss Emily by creating several morbid images of her. For example, there are several images of decay throughout the story. The house she lived in is falling apart and described as "filled with dust and shades . . . an eyesore among eyesores." Emily herself is described as being "bloated like a body long submerged in motionless water." Faulkner also uses words like "skeleton," "dank," "decay," and "cold" to reinforce these morbid, deathly images.

Imagery in Faulkner's story suppor[t]s argument

In "Miss Brill," however, Mansfield uses more cheerful imagery. The music and the lively action in the park make Miss Brill feel alive inside. She notices the other old people that are in the park are "still as statues," "odd," and "silent." She says they "looked like they'd just come from dark little rooms or even—even cupboards." Her own room is later described as a "cupboard," but during the action of the story she does not include herself among those other old people. She still feels alive.

Contrasting imagery in Mansfield's story suppor[t]s argument

Through the plots of both stories the reader can also see that Miss Brill is more successful in adapting to her environment. Miss Emily loses her sanity and ends up committing a crime in order to control her environment. Throughout the story, she refuses to adapt to any of the changes going on in the town, such as the taxes or the mailboxes. Miss Brill is able to find her own special place in society where she can be happy and remain sane.

Characters contrasted with examp[les] drawn from plots

Ortiz 3

The final conclusion is stated and the thesis is restated

In "A Rose for Emily" and "Miss Brill" the authors' use of language and the plots of the stories illustrate that Miss Brill is more successful in her story. Instead of hiding herself away she emerges from the "cupboard" to participate in life. She adapts to the world that is changing as she grows older, without losing her sanity or committing crimes, as Miss Emily does. The language of "Miss Brill" allows the reader to sympathize with the main character. The imagery in the story is lighter and less morbid than in "A Rose for Emily." The resulting portrait is of an aging woman who has found creative ways to adjust to her lonely life.

Response Paper

One popular form of writing assignment is the **response paper**, a short essay that expresses your personal reaction to a work of literature. Both instructors and students often find the response paper an ideal introductory writing assignment. It provides you with an opportunity to craft a focused essay about a literary work, but it does not usually require any outside research. What it does require is careful reading, clear thinking, and honest writing.

The purpose of a response paper is to convey your thoughts and feelings about an aspect of a particular literary work. It isn't a book report (summarizing the work's content) or a book review (evaluating the quality of a work). A response paper expresses what you experienced in reading and thinking about the assigned text. Your reaction should reflect your background, values, and attitudes in response to the work, not what the instructor thinks about it. You might consider your response paper a conversation with the work you have just read. What questions does it seem to ask you? What reactions does it elicit? You might also regard your paper as a personal message to your instructor telling him or her what you really think about one of the reading assignments.

Of course, you can't say everything you thought and felt about your reading in a short paper. Focus on an important aspect (such as a main character, setting, or theme) and discuss your reaction to it. Don't gush or meander. Personal writing doesn't mean disorganized writing. Identify your main ideas and present your point of view in a clear and organized way. Once you get started you might surprise yourself by discovering that it's fun to explore your own responses. Stranger things have happened.

Here are some tips for writing a successful response paper of your own:

- **Make quick notes as you read or reread the work.** Don't worry about writing anything organized at this point. Just write a word or two in the margin noting your reactions as you read (e.g., "how unpleasant!" or "very interesting"). These little notes will jog your memory when you go back to write your paper.
- **Consider which aspect of the work affected you the most.** That aspect will probably be a good starting point for your response.
- **Be candid in your writing.** Remember that the literary work is only half of the subject matter of your paper. The other half is your reaction.
- **Try to understand and explain why you have reacted the way you did.** It's not enough just to state your responses. You also want to justify or explain them.
- **Refer to the text in your paper.** Demonstrate to the reader that your response is based on the text. Provide specific textual details and quotations wherever relevant.

The following paper is one student's response to Tim O'Brien's story "The Things They Carried" (Chapter 6).

Martin 1

Ethan Martin

English 99

Professor Merrill

31 March 2019

"Perfect Balance and Perfect Posture": Reflecting on "The Things They Carried"

Reading Tim O'Brien's short story "The Things They Carried" became a very personal experience. It reminded me of my father, who is a Vietnam veteran, and the stories he used to tell me. Growing up, I regularly asked my dad to share stories from his past—especially about his service in the United States Marine Corps. He would rarely talk about his tour during the Vietnam War for more than a few minutes, and what

Martin 2

he shared was usually the same: the monsoon rain could chill to the bone, the mosquitoes would never stop biting, and the M-16 rifles often jammed in a moment of crisis. He dug a new foxhole where he slept every night, he traded the cigarettes from his C-rations for food, and—since he was the radio man of his platoon—the combination of his backpack and radio was very heavy during the long, daily walks through rice paddies and jungles. For these reasons, "The Things They Carried" powerfully affected me.

While reading the story, I felt as if I was "humping" (par. 4) through Vietnam with Lieutenant Jimmy Cross, Rat Kiley, Ted Lavender, and especially Mitchell Sanders—who carries the 26-pound radio and battery. Every day, we carry our backpacks to school. Inside are some objects that we need to use in class: books, paper, and pens. But most of us probably include "unnecessary" items that reveal something about who we are or what we value—photographs, perfume, or good-luck charms. O'Brien uses this device to tell his story. At times he lists the things that the soldiers literally carried, such as weapons, medicine, and flak jackets. These military items weigh between 30 and 70 pounds, depending on one's rank or function in the platoon. The narrator says, "They carried all they could bear, and then some, including a silent awe for the terrible power of the things they carried" (par. 12).

Some of this "terrible power" comes from the sentimental objects the men keep. Although these are relatively light, they weigh down the hearts of the soldiers. Lt. Jimmy Cross carries 10-ounce letters and a pebble from Martha, a girl in his hometown who doesn't love him back. Rat Kiley carries comic books, and Norman Bowker carried a diary. I now own the small, water-logged Bible that my father carried through his tour in Vietnam, which was a gift from his mother. When I open its pages, I can almost hear his voice praying to survive the war.

The price of such survival is costly. O'Brien's platoon carries ghosts, memories, and "the land itself" (par. 39). Their intangible burdens are heavier than what they carry in their backpacks. My father has always said

Martin 3

that, while he was in Vietnam, an inexpressible feeling of death hung heavy in the air, which he could not escape. O'Brien notes that an emotional weight of fear and cowardice "could never be put down, it required perfect balance and perfect posture" (par. 77), and I wonder if this may be part of what my father meant.

Both Tim O'Brien and my father were wounded by shrapnel, and now they both carry a Purple Heart. They carry the weight of survival. They carry memories that I will never know. "The Things They Carried" is not a war story about glory and honor. It is a portrait of the psychological damage that war can bring. It is a story about storytelling and how hard it can be to find the truth. And it is a beautiful account of what the human heart can endure.

Martin 4

Work Cited

O'Brien, Tim. "The Things They Carried." *Backpack Literature: An Introduction to Fiction, Poetry, Drama, and Writing*, edited by X. J. Kennedy et al., 6th ed., Pearson, 2020, pp. 202–16.

THE FORM OF YOUR FINISHED PAPER

If your instructor has not specified the form of your finished paper, follow these commonly accepted guidelines:

- Choose standard letter-size (8 1/2 × 11) white paper.
- Use standard, easy-to-read type fonts, such as Times New Roman or Garamond. Be sure the italic type style contrasts with the regular style.
- Give your name, your instructor's name, the course number, and the date at the top left-hand corner of your first page, starting one inch from the top.
- On all pages, insert a header—your last name and the page number—in the upper right-hand corner, one-half inch from the top.

- Remember to give your paper a title that reflects your thesis.
- Leave an inch or two of margin on all four sides of each page.
- If you include a works-cited section, begin it on a new page.
- Double-space your text, including quotations and notes. Don't forget to double-space the works-cited page also.
- Italicize the titles of longer works—books, full-length plays, periodicals, and book-length poems such as *The Odyssey*. The titles of shorter works—poems, articles, or short stories—should appear in quotation marks.

What's left to do but hand in your paper? By now, you may be glad to see it go. But a good paper is not only worth submitting; it is also worth keeping. If you return to it after a while, you may find to your surprise that it will preserve and even renew what you have learned.

Topics for Writing About Fiction

Topics for Brief Papers (250–500 Words)

1. Explicate the opening paragraph or first few lines of a story. Show how the opening prepares the reader for what will follow. In an essay of this length, you will need to limit your discussion to the most important elements of the passage you explicate; there won't be room to deal with everything. Or, as thoroughly as the word count allows, explicate the final paragraph of a story. What does the ending imply about the fates of the story's characters, and about the story's take on its central theme?
2. Select a story that features a first-person narrator. Write a concise yet thorough analysis of how that character's point of view colors the story.
3. Consider a short story in which the central character has to make a decision or must take some decisive step that will alter the rest of his or her life. Faulkner's "Barn Burning" (Chapter 5) is one such story; another is Updike's "A & P" (Chapter 1). As concisely and as thoroughly as you can, explain the nature of the character's decision, the reasons for it, and its probable consequences (as suggested by what the author tells us).
4. Choose two stories that might be interesting to compare and contrast. Write a brief defense of your choice. How might these two stories illuminate each other?
5. Choose a key passage from a story you admire. As closely as the word count allows, explicate that passage and explain why it strikes you as an important moment in the story. Concentrate on the aspects of the passage that seem most essential.

Topics for More Extended Papers (600–1,000 Words)

1. Write an analysis of a short story, focusing on a single element, such as point of view, theme, symbolism, character, or the author's voice (tone, style, irony).
2. Compare and contrast two stories with protagonists who share an important personality trait. Make character the focus of your essay.
3. Write a thorough explication of a short passage (preferably not more than four sentences) in a story you admire. Pick a crucial moment in the plot, or a passage that reveals the story's theme. You might look to the paper "By Lantern Light" (page 1173) as a model.
4. Write an analysis of a story in which the protagonist experiences an epiphany or revelation of some sort. Describe the nature of this change of heart. How is the reader prepared for it? What are its repercussions in the character's life? Some possible story choices are Alice Walker's "Everyday Use" (Chapter 9), William Faulkner's "Barn Burning," or Raymond Carver's "Cathedral" (Chapter 3).
5. Imagine a reluctant reader, one who would rather play video games than crack a book. Which story in this book would you recommend to him or her? Write an essay to that imagined reader, describing the story's merits.

Topics for Long Papers (1,500 Words or More)

1. Write an analysis of a longer work of fiction. Concentrate on a single element of the story, quoting as necessary to make your point.
2. Read three or four short stories by an author whose work you admire. Concentrating on a single element treated similarly in all of the stories, write an analysis of the author's work as exemplified by your chosen stories.
3. Choose two stories that treat a similar theme. Compare and contrast the stance each story takes toward that theme, marshalling quotations and specifics as necessary to back up your argument.
4. Browse through newspapers and magazines for a story with the elements of good fiction. Now rewrite the story *as* fiction. Then write a one-page accompanying essay explaining the challenges of the task. What did it teach you about the relative natures of journalism and fiction?

Topics for Writing About Poetry

Topics for Brief Papers (250–500 Words)

1. Write a concise *explication* of a short poem of your choice. Concentrate on those facets of the poem that you think most need explaining. (For a sample explication, see page 1177.)
2. Write an *analysis* of a short poem, focusing on how a single key element shapes its meaning. (A sample analysis appears on page 1180.) Some possible topics are:
   - Tone in Edna St. Vincent Millay's "Recuerdo" (Chapter 23)
   - Imagery in Wallace Stevens's Thirteen Ways of Looking at a Blackbird" (Chapter 19)
   - Kinds of irony in Thomas Hardy's "The Workbox" (Chapter 11)

- Theme in W. H. Auden's "Musée des Beaux Arts" (Chapter 23)
- Extended metaphor in Langston Hughes's "The Negro Speaks of Rivers" (Chapter 23). (Explain the one main comparison that the poem makes and show how the whole poem makes it. Other poems that would lend themselves to a paper on extended metaphor include Emily Dickinson's "Because I could not stop for Death" (Chapter 23), and Adrienne Rich's "Aunt Jennifer's Tigers" (Chapter 10.))

(To locate any of these poems, see the Index of Authors and Titles.)

3. Select a poem in which the main speaker is a character who for any reason interests you. You might consider, for instance, T. S. Eliot's "The Love Song of J. Alfred Prufrock" (Chapter 23), or Rhina Espaillat's "Bilingual/Bilingüe" (Chapter 11). Then write a brief profile of this character, drawing only on what the poem tells you (or reveals). What is the character's age? Situation in life? Attitude toward self? Attitude toward others? General personality? Do you find this character admirable?
4. Although both of these poems tell a story, what happens in the poem isn't necessarily obvious: T. S. Eliot's "The Love Song of J. Alfred Prufrock" and Edwin Arlington Robinson's "Luke Havergal" (Chapter 11). Choose one of these poems, and in a paragraph sum up what you think happens in it. Then in a second paragraph, ask yourself: what, *besides* the element of story, did you consider in order to understand the poem?

Topics for More Extended Papers (600–1,000 Words)

1. Perform a line-by-line explication of a brief poem of your choice. Imagine that your audience is unfamiliar with the poem and needs your assistance in interpreting it.
2. Compare and contrast any two poems that treat a similar theme. Let your comparison bring you to an evaluation of the poems. Which is the stronger, more satisfying one?
3. Write a comparison-contrast essay on any two or more poems by a single poet. Look for two poems that share a characteristic thematic concern. Here are some possible topics:
   - Mortality in the work of John Keats
   - Nature in the poems of William Wordsworth
   - How Emily Dickinson's lyric poems resemble hymns
   - E. E. Cummings's approach to the free-verse line
   - Gerard Manley Hopkins's sonic effects

Topics for Long Papers (1,500 Words or More)

1. Review an entire poetry collection by a poet featured in this book. You will need to communicate to your reader a sense of the work's style and thematic preoccupations. Finally, make a value judgment about the work's quality.
2. Read five or six poems by a single author. Start with a poet featured in this book, and then find additional poems at the library or on the Internet. Write an analysis of a single element of that poet's work—for example, theme, imagery, diction, or form.

3. Write a line-by-line explication of a poem rich in matters to explain or of a longer poem that offers ample difficulty. While relatively short, Gerard Manley Hopkins's "The Windhover" (Chapter 23) is a poem that will take a good bit of time to explicate. Even a short, apparently simple poem such as Robert Frost's "Stopping by Woods on a Snowy Evening" (Chapter 23) can provide more than enough material to explicate thoughtfully in a longer paper.
4. Write an analysis of a certain theme (or other element) that you find in the work of two or more poets. It is probable that in your conclusion you will want to set the poets' works side by side, comparing or contrasting them, and perhaps making some evaluation. Here are some sample topics to consider:
   - Langston Hughes, Gwendolyn Brooks, and Dudley Randall as Prophets of Social Change
   - What It Is to Be a Woman: The Special Knowledge of Sylvia Plath, Anne Sexton, and Adrienne Rich
   - The Complex Relations Between Fathers and Children in the Poetry of Robert Hayden, Rhina Espaillat, and Theodore Roethke
   - Making Up New Words for New Meanings: Neologisms in Lewis Carroll and Kay Ryan

Topics for Writing About Drama

Topics for Brief Papers (250–500 words)

1. Analyze a key character from any of the plays in this book. One choice might be Torvald Helmer in *A Doll's House* (Chapter 28). What motivates that character? Point to specific moments in the play to make your case.
2. When the curtain comes down on the conclusion of some plays, the audience is left to decide exactly what finally happened. In a short informal essay, state your interpretation of the conclusion of *A Doll's House* or *A Raisin in the Sun* (Chapter 28). Don't just give a plot summary; tell what you think the conclusion means.
3. Sum up the main suggestions you find in one of these meaningful objects (or actions): the handkerchief in *Othello* (Chapter 27), or the Christmas tree in *A Doll's House* (or Nora's doing a wild tarantella).
4. Attend a play and write a review. In an assignment this brief, you will need to concentrate your remarks on either the performance or the script itself. Be sure to back up your opinions with specific observations.

Topics for More Extended Papers (600–1,000 Words)

1. From a play you have enjoyed, choose a passage that strikes you as difficult, worth reading closely. Try to pick a passage not longer than about 20 lines. Explicate it—give it a close, sentence-by-sentence reading—and explain how this small part of the play relates to the whole. For instance, any of the following passages might be considered memorable (and essential to their plays):
   - Othello's soliloquy beginning "It is the cause, it is the cause, my soul" (*Othello*, 5.2.1–22).
   - Oedipus to Teiresias, speech beginning "Wealth, sovereignty and skill" (*Oedipus the King*, l. 418–76).
   - Nora to Mrs. Linde, speech beginning "Yes, someday, maybe, in many years when I am not as pretty as I am now . . ." (*A Doll's House*, Chapter 28).

2. Analyze the complexities and contradictions to be found in a well-rounded character from a play of your choice. Some good subjects might be Othello or Nora Helmer (in *A Doll's House*).
3. Take just a single line or sentence from a play, one that stands out for some reason as greatly important. Perhaps it states a theme, reveals a character, or serves as a crisis (or turning point). Write an essay demonstrating its importance—how it functions, why it is necessary. Some possible lines include:
   - Iago to Roderigo: "I am not what I am" (*Othello*, 1.1.67).
   - Helmer to Nora: " From this moment on, happiness is out of the question." (*A Doll's House*, Act III).
4. Write an analysis essay in which you single out an element of a play for examination—character, plot, setting, theme, dramatic irony, tone, language, symbolism, conventions, or any other element. Try to relate this element to the play as a whole. Sample topics: "The Function of Teiresias in *Oedipus the King*" or "Imagery of Poison in *Othello*."
5. How would you stage an updated production of a play by Shakespeare, Sophocles, or Ibsen, transplanting it to our time? Choose a play, and describe the challenges and difficulties of this endeavor. How would you overcome them—or, if they cannot be overcome, why not?

Topics for Long Papers (1,500 Words or More)

1. Choose a play you have read and admire from this book, and read a second play by the same author. Compare and contrast the two plays with attention to a single element—a theme they have in common, or a particular kind of imagery, for example.
2. Read *Othello* and view a movie version of the play. You might choose Oliver Parker's 1995 take on the play with Laurence Fishburne and Kenneth Branagh, or even O (2001), an updated version that takes a prep school as its setting and a basketball star as its protagonist. Review the movie. What does it manage to convey of the original? What gets lost in the translation?
3. Choosing any of the works in "Plays for Further Reading" or taking some other modern or contemporary play your instructor suggests, report any difficulties you encountered in reading and responding to it. Explicate any troublesome passages for the benefit of other readers.
4. Attend a play and write an in-depth review, taking into account many elements of the drama: acting, direction, staging, costumes, lighting, and—if the work is relatively new and not a classic—the play itself.

31 WRITING A RESEARCH PAPER

What You Will Learn in This Chapter

- To choose a topic for your research paper
- To find and evaluate sources
- To organize, write, and revise your research paper
- To cite and document your sources using MLA style

Why is it worthwhile to write a research paper? (Apart from the fact that you want a passing grade in the class, that is.) While you can learn much by exploring your own responses to a literary work, there is no substitute for entering into a conversation with others who have studied and thought about your topic. Literary criticism is that conversation. Your reading will expose you to the ideas of others who can shed light on a story, poem, or play. It will introduce you to the wide range of informed opinions that exist about literature, as about almost any subject. Sometimes, too, your research will uncover information about an author's life that leads you to new insights into a literary work. Undertaking a research paper gives you a chance to test your ideas against those of others, and in doing so to clarify your own opinions.

BROWSE THE RESEARCH

The most daunting aspect of the research paper may well be the mountains of information available on almost any literary subject. It can be hard to know where to begin. Sifting through books and articles is part of the research process. Unfortunately, the first material you uncover in the library or on the Internet is rarely the evidence you need to develop or support your thesis. Keep looking until you uncover helpful sources.

Another common pitfall in the process is the creeping feeling that your idea has already been examined a dozen times over. But take heart: like Odysseus, tie yourself to the mast so that when you hear the siren voices of published professors, you can listen without abandoning your own point of view. Your idea may have been treated, but not yet by you. Your particular take on a topic is bound to be different from someone else's. After all, thousands of books have been written on Shakespeare's plays, but people still find new things to say about them.

CHOOSE A TOPIC: FORMULATE YOUR ARGUMENT

- **Find a topic that interests you.** A crucial first step in writing a research paper is coming up with a topic that interests you. If you start with a topic that bores you, the process will be a chore and yield dull results. But if you begin with a topic that intrigues you, developing a compelling research question becomes easier, and seeking its answer will prove to be a more engaging process. The paper that results will inevitably be stronger and more interesting.
- **Find a way to get started.** Browsing through online journal articles and blogs, or skimming through books of literary criticism in the library, can help to spark an idea or two. Prewriting techniques such as brainstorming, freewriting, listing, and clustering can also help you to generate ideas on a specific work of literature. If you take notes and jot down ideas as they occur to you, when you start the formal writing process you will discover you have already begun.
- **Keep your purpose and audience in mind.** Refer often to the assignment, and approach your essay accordingly. Think of your audience as well—is it your professor, your classmates, or some hypothetical reader? As you plan your essay, keep your audience's expectations and needs in mind.
- **Identify an argument—your thesis—that you hope to support with research, and look for material that will help you demonstrate its plausibility.** Your thesis is a work in progress. Do not be afraid to let it evolve as you research your topic and reflect on your findings. Remember: the ideal research paper is based on your own observations and interpretations of a literary text.

BEGIN YOUR RESEARCH

Writing a research paper on literature calls for two kinds of sources. First, there are your primary sources—the literary works that are the central subject of your paper. Then there are your secondary sources—the critical or biographical books, articles, web and database resources that discuss the author or work you are examining. In writing a research paper, your task is to use both kinds of sources to develop a sustained and logical discussion of a specific topic.

Reliable Web Sources

As you begin your research, your first impulse may be to search online for websites and blogs that discuss your topic. If so, proceed with care. Websites may be written and published by anybody for any purpose, with no oversight. Even the online reference site *Wikipedia*, for example, is an amalgamation of voluntary contributors and is rife with small factual errors and contributor biases. Carefully analyze any material you gather from a general online search and compare it with other reputable sources of information. To garner the best sources possible, take these steps:

- **Begin your search at a reliable website.** To avoid sloppy and inaccurate sites, begin your search with one of the following excellent guides through cyberspace:
  - *Library of Congress's Alcove 9.* Fortunately, you don't have to trek to Washington to visit this venerable institution's annotated collection of reference websites in the humanities and social sciences. For your purpose—writing a literary research paper—access the Subject Index, click on "Literatures in English," and then click "Literary Criticism." This will take you to a list of metapages and websites with collections of reliable critical and biographical materials on authors and their works. (A metapage provides links to other websites.)
  - *ipl2.* The aggregation of two popular research websites, *Internet Public Library* and *Librarians' Internet Index*, *ipl2* is hosted and maintained by Drexel University's College of Science and Technology and a consortium of other universities. This site lets you search for literary criticism by author, work, country of origin, or literary period.
  - *Library Spot.* This is a portal to more than 5,000 libraries around the world, and to periodicals, online texts, reference works, and links to metapages and websites on any topic including literary criticism. This carefully maintained site is published by StartSpot Mediaworks, Inc., in the Northwestern University/Evanston Research Park in Evanston, Illinois.
  - *Voice of the Shuttle.* Research links in more than twenty-five categories in the humanities and social sciences, including online texts, libraries, academic websites, and metapages, may be found at this site. It was developed and is maintained by Dr. Alan Liu in the English Department of the University of California, Santa Barbara.

Print Resources

Don't overlook books and print journals. Until quite recently, most literary material existed solely in print—and only some of these resources have been transferred into digital formats. When you are hunting down secondary sources, a good place to begin is your campus library. Plan to spend some time thumbing through scholarly books and journals, looking for passages that you find particularly interesting or that pertain to your topic. Begin your search with the online catalog to get a sense of where you might find the books and journals you need.

To choose from the many books available on your library's shelves and through interlibrary loan, you might turn to book reviews for a sense of which volumes would best suit your purpose. *Book Review Digest* contains the full texts of many book reviews and excerpts of others. The *Digest* may be found in printed form in the reference section of your campus library, which may also provide access to the online version. Whether you are using the online or print version, you will need the author's name, title, and date of first publication of any book for which you hope to find a review.

Also helpful is the multivolume *Dictionary of Literary Biography*. This useful series of more than 360 volumes has entries on most well-known authors and presents excerpts of the best scholarship with complete citations. You may be able to research your entire paper from this comprehensive source alone. Many schools have either a print version of this reference work or subscribe to its online database.

Scholarly journals are another excellent resource for articles on your topic. Indexes to magazines and journals may be found in your library's reference section or on your library's website.

Online Databases

Most college libraries subscribe to specialized online database services covering all academic subjects—treasure troves of reliable sources. If you find yourself unsure of how to use your library's database system, ask the reference librarian to help you get started. Or explore the section on databases or research tools on your library's website to see what your school has available on literature. Many college library home pages provide students with access to subscription databases, which means that if you really can't bear to leave your comfy desk at home, you can still pay a virtual visit. The following databases are particularly useful for literary research:

- *Literature Resource Center* (Thomson Gale) provides biographies, bibliographies, and critical analyses of more than 120,000 authors and their work. This information is culled from journal articles and reference works.
- *MLA International Bibliography*, the Modern Language Association's database, is an excellent way to search for books and full-text articles on literary topics.
- *Google Scholar* provides one of the simplest ways to broadly search for a topic across a vast array of publicly available scholarly articles, theses, books, and other research documents. Some documents may require a university login to access.
- *JSTOR*, a nonprofit organization, indexes articles or abstracts from an archive of journals in more than fifty disciplines.
- *Literature Online (LION)* provides a vast searchable database of critical articles and reference works as well as full texts of more than 300,000 works of prose, poetry, and drama.

- *Project Muse*, a collaboration between publishers and libraries, offers access to more than 400 journals in the humanities, arts, and social sciences.
- *EBSCO*, a multisubject resource, covers literature and the humanities, as well as the social sciences, the medical sciences, linguistics, and other fields.

CHECKLIST: Finding Reliable Sources

- ☐ Locate reputable websites by starting at a reputable website designed for that purpose.
- ☐ Visit your campus library. Ask the reference librarian for advice.
- ☐ Check the library catalog for books and journals on your topic.
- ☐ Look into the online databases subscribed to by your library.

Visual Images

The web is an excellent source of visual images. If a picture, chart, or graph will enhance your argument, you may find the perfect one via an image search on Google, PicSearch, or other search engines. The digital collections at the Library of Congress website offer a wealth of images documenting American political, social, and cultural history—including portraits, prints, photographs, letters, and original manuscripts. Remember, though, that not all images are available for use by the general public. If there is an image you want to use, check for a copyright notice to see if its originator allows it to be reproduced. If so, you may include the photograph, provided you credit your source as you would if you were quoting text.

One note on images: use them carefully. Choose visuals that provide supporting evidence for the point you are trying to make or that enhance your reader's understanding of the work. Label your images with captions. Your goal should be to make your argument more convincing. In the example included here, a reproduction of Brueghel's painting helps to advance the author's argument and provide insight into Auden's poem.

Lombardo 4

Fig. 1. *Landscape with the Fall of Icarus* by Pieter Brueghel the Elder (c. 1558, Musées Royaux des Beaux-Arts de Belgique, Brussels)

W. H. Auden's poem "Musée des Beaux Arts" refers to a specific painting to prove its point that the most honest depictions of death take into account the way life simply goes on even after the most tragic of events. In line 14, Auden turns specifically to Pieter Brueghel the Elder's masterwork *The Fall of Icarus* (see Fig. 1), pointing to the painting's understated depiction of tragedy. In this painting, the death of Icarus does not take place on center stage. A plowman and his horse take up the painting's foreground, while the leg of Icarus falling into the sea takes up a tiny portion of the painting's lower-right corner. A viewer who fails to take the painting's title into account might not even notice Icarus at all.

CHECKLIST: Using Visual Images

- ☐ Use images as evidence to support your argument.
- ☐ Use images to enhance communication and understanding.
- ☐ Refer to the images in your text.
- ☐ Label each image with a figure number—"Fig. 1" in the example above—and provide a title or caption.
- ☐ Check copyrights.
- ☐ Include sources in a works-cited list.

EVALUATE YOUR SOURCES

Trustworthy Resources Build Your Paper's Credibility

It's an old saying, but a useful one: don't believe everything you read. The fact that a book or an article is printed and published doesn't necessarily mean it is accurate or unbiased. Likewise, the highest-ranking results of your web search may not be the most reliable or credible. Resources fall into two categories: scholarly and popular. Scholarly articles and books are written by and for faculty, scholars, and researchers and they feature original research, scholarly or academic language, and full citations for sources. Popular articles and books are written by journalists or professional writers for a general audience. These articles tend to be shorter, use simpler language, and rarely provide full citations of their sources. How can you ensure that the resource you are considering is a scholarly one?

Begin your search in a place that has taken some of the work out of quality control—your school library. Books and articles you find there are regarded by librarians as having some obvious merit. If your search takes you beyond the library and online, though, you will need to be discerning when choosing resources. As you weigh the value of each document, take the following into account:

- **Look closely at information provided about the author.** Is he or she known for expertise in the field? What are the author's academic or association credentials? Is there any reason to believe that the author is biased in any way? For example, a biography of an author written by that author's son or daughter might not be as unbiased as one written by a scholar with no personal connections. If the document appears online, is the web entry unsigned and anonymous? If the website is sponsored by an organization, is it a reputable one?
- **Determine the publisher's reliability.** Books, articles, and blogs published by an advocacy group might be expected to take a particular—possibly biased—slant on an issue. Be aware also that some books are published by vanity presses, companies that are paid by an author to publish his or her books. As a result, vanity press-published books generally aren't subject to the same rigorous quality control as those put out by more reputable publishing houses.

  A word of warning: individual student pages posted on university sites have not necessarily been reviewed by that university and are not reliable sources of information. Also, postings on *Wikipedia* are not subject to a scholarly review process and have been found to contain inaccuracies. It's safer to use a published encyclopedia.
- **Always check for a publication date.** If a document lists an edition number, check to see whether you are using the latest edition of the material. If the article appears on a website or blog, when was it last updated? In

some cases you may want to base your essay on the most current information or theories, so you will want to steer toward the most recently published material.

- **For periodicals, decide whether a publication is an academic journal or a popular magazine.** What type of reputation does it have? Obviously, you do not want to use a magazine that periodically reports on Elvis sightings and alien births. And even articles on writers in magazines such as *Time* and *People* are likely to be too brief and superficial for purposes of serious research. Instead, choose scholarly journals designed to enhance the study of literature.
- **Consult experts.** Cornell University Library has two good online documents with guidance for analyzing sources, titled "Critically Analyzing Information Sources" and "Distinguishing Scholarly from Non-Scholarly Periodicals." Your school's research librarian or library website may have similar resources.

CHECKLIST: Evaluating Your Sources

- ☐ Who wrote it? What are the author's credentials?
- ☐ Is he or she an expert in the field?
- ☐ Does he or she appear to be unbiased toward the subject matter?
- ☐ Does the content seem consistent with demonstrated scholarship?
- ☐ Is the publisher reputable? Is it an advocacy group or a vanity press?
- ☐ Is the source an online journal or magazine? Is it scholarly or popular?
- ☐ When was the source published? Do later editions exist? If so, would a later edition be more useful?

ORGANIZE YOUR RESEARCH

- **Get your thoughts down on note cards or the equivalent on your laptop.** Once you have amassed your secondary sources, it will be time to begin reading in earnest. As you do so, be sure to take notes on any passage that pertains to your topic. A convenient way to organize your many thoughts is to write them down on index cards, which are easy to shuffle and rearrange. If you prefer to use your computer to take notes, you might consider using digital note-card software like *SimpleNote* or *EverNote*. For longer papers, it may be worthwhile to look into more sophisticated programs like *Scrivener*, which give you additional tools for planning and structuring your research and writing. Whatever approach you use, keep to a single fact or opinion on each card. This will make it easier for you to shuffle the deck and re-envision the order in which you deliver information to your reader.

- **Keep careful track of the sources of quotations and paraphrases.** As you take notes, make it unmistakably clear which thoughts and phrases are yours and which derive from others. (Remember, *quotation* means using the exact words of your source and placing the entire passage in quotation marks and citing the author. *Paraphrase* means expressing the ideas of your source in your own words, again citing the author.) Bear in mind the cautionary tale of a well-known historian, Doris Kearns Goodwin. She was charged with plagiarizing sections of two of her famous books when her words were found to be jarringly similar to those published in other books. Because she had not clearly indicated on her note cards which ideas and passages were hers and which came from other sources, Goodwin was forced to admit to plagiarism. Her reputation suffered enormously from these charges, but you can learn from her mistakes and save your own reputation—and your grades.
- **Keep track of the sources of ideas and concepts.** When an idea is inspired by or directly taken from someone else's writing, be sure to jot down the source on that same card or in your computer file. Your deck of cards or computer list will function as a working bibliography, which later will help you put together a works-cited list. To save yourself work, keep a separate list of the sources you're using. Then, as you make the note, you need write only the material's author or title and page reference on the card in order to identify your source. It's also useful to classify the note in a way that will help you to organize your material, making it easy, for example, to separate cards that deal with a story's theme from cards that deal with point of view or symbolism. Another helpful tip is to use an online bibliography manager like *EasyBib*, *Mendeley*, *RefWorks*, or *Zotero*. Many of these services will let you create an account to store your list of sources online and will also generate correctly formatted bibliographies for free.
- **Make notes of your own thoughts and reactions to your research.** When a critical article sparks your own original idea, be sure to capture that thought in your notes and mark it as your own. As you plan your paper, these notes may form the outline for your arguments.
- **Make photocopies or printouts to simplify the process and ensure accuracy.** Scholars once had to spend long hours copying out prose passages by hand. Luckily, for a small investment you can simply photocopy or print your sources to ensure accuracy in quoting and citing your sources. If you do photocopy material from a source, you should make it a habit to copy the publication page from the front of the book. This will ensure you always have the full title and citation information for your bibliography. Some instructors will require you to hand in photocopies of your original sources with the final paper, along with printouts of articles downloaded from an Internet database. Even if this is not the case, photocopying your sources and holding onto your printouts can help you to reproduce quotations accurately in your essay—and accuracy is crucial.

ORGANIZE YOUR PAPER

With your thesis in mind and your notes spread before you, draw up an outline—a rough map of how best to argue your thesis and present your material. Determine what main points you need to make, and look for quotations that support those points. Even if you generally prefer to navigate the paper-writing process without a map, you will find that an outline makes the research-paper writing process considerably smoother. When organizing information from many different sources, it pays to plan ahead.

MAINTAIN ACADEMIC INTEGRITY

What Is Plagiarism?

Simply put, plagiarism is the use of another person's words, ideas, research, or arguments without giving proper credit to their source. In Western academic settings, plagiarism is viewed as a serious type of theft or forgery. By claiming someone else's ideas and language as your own, you rob them of the rightful recognition of their intellectual labor. On the other hand, if you responsibly recognize and respond to the scholarly work of others with proper citations, your own writing will convey more authority and competence.

Papers for Sale Are Papers That "F"ail

Do not be seduced by the apparent ease of cheating by computer. Your Internet searches may turn up several sites that offer term papers to download. Most of these sites charge money for what they offer, but a few do not, happy to strike a blow against the "oppressive" insistence of English teachers that students learn to think and write.

Plagiarized term papers are an old game: the fraternity file and the "research assistance" service have been around far longer than the computer. It may seem easy enough to download a paper, put your name at the head of it, and turn it in for an easy grade. As any writing instructor can tell you, though, such papers usually stick out like a sore thumb. The style will be wrong, the work will not be consistent with other work by the same student in any number of ways, and the teacher will sometimes even have seen the same phony paper before. The ease with which electronic texts are reproduced makes this last possibility increasingly likely.

The odds of being caught and facing the unpleasant consequences are reasonably high. It is far better to take the grade you have earned for your own effort, no matter how mediocre, than to try to pass off someone else's work as your own. Even if, somehow, your instructor does not recognize your submission as a plagiarized paper, you have diminished your character through dishonesty and lost an opportunity to learn something on your own.

A Warning Against Internet Plagiarism

Plagiarism detection services are often a professor's ally in the battle against academic dishonesty. Questionable research papers can be sent to these services (such as Turnitin.com and EVE2), which perform complex searches of the Internet and of a growing database of purchased term papers. The research paper will be returned to the professor with plagiarized sections annotated and the sources documented. The end result will certainly be a failing grade on the essay, possibly a failing grade for the course, and, depending on the policies of your university, expulsion.

ACKNOWLEDGE ALL SOURCES

The brand of straight-out dishonesty described above is one type of plagiarism. There is, however, another, subtler kind: when students incorporate somebody else's words *or* ideas into their papers without giving proper credit. To avoid this second—sometimes quite accidental—variety of plagiarism, familiarize yourself with the conventions for acknowledging sources. First and foremost, remember to give credit to any writer who supplies you with ideas, information, or specific words and phrases.

Using Quotations

- **Acknowledge your source when you quote a writer's words or phrases.** When you use someone else's words or phrases, you should reproduce his or her exact words in quotation marks, and be sure to properly credit the source.

> Already, Frost has hinted that Nature may be, as Radcliffe Squires suggests, "Nothing but an ash-white plain without love or faith or hope, where ignorant appetites cross by chance" (87).

- **If you quote more than four lines, set your quotation off from the body of the paper.** Start a new line; indent one inch and type the quotation, double-spaced. (You do not need to use quotation marks, as the format tells the reader the passage is a quotation.)

> Samuel Maio made an astute observation about the nature of Weldon Kees's distinctive tone:
>
> > Kees has therefore combined a personal subject matter with an impersonal voice—that is, one that is consistent in its tone evenly recording the speaker's thoughts without showing any emotional intensity which might lie behind those thoughts. (136)

Citing Ideas

- **Acknowledge your source when you mention a critic's ideas.** Even if you are not quoting exact words or phrases, be sure to acknowledge the source of any original ideas or concepts you have used.

  Another explanation is suggested by Daniel Hoffman, a critic who has discussed the story: the killer hears the sound of his *own* heart (227).

- **Acknowledge your source when you paraphrase a writer's words.** To paraphrase a critic, you should do more than just rearrange his or her words: you should translate them into your own original sentences—again, always being sure to credit the original source. As an example, suppose you wish to refer to an insight of Randall Jarrell, who commented as follows on the images of spider, flower, and moth in Robert Frost's poem "Design":

  RANDALL JARRELL'S ORIGINAL TEXT

  Notice how the *heal-all*, because of its name, is the one flower in all the world picked to be the altar for this Devil's Mass; notice how *holding up* the moth brings something ritual and hieratic, a ghostly, ghastly formality, to this priest and its sacrificial victim.[1]

It would be too close to the original to write, without quotation marks, these sentences:

PLAGIARIZED REWORDING

Frost picks the *heal-all* as the one flower in all the world to be the altar for this Devil's Mass. There is a ghostly, ghastly formality to the spider *holding up* the moth, like a priest holding a sacrificial victim.

This rewording, although not exactly in Jarrell's language, manages to steal his memorable phrases without giving him credit. Nor is it sufficient just to include Jarrell's essay in the works-cited list at the end of your paper. If you do, you are still a crook; you merely point to the scene of the crime. Instead, think through Jarrell's words to the point he is making, so that it can be restated in your own original way. If you want to keep any of his striking phrases (and why not?), put them exactly as he wrote them in quotation marks:

[1] *Poetry and the Age* (Alfred A. Knopf, 1953) p. 42.

APPROPRIATE PARAPHRASE, ACKNOWLEDGES SOURCE

> As Randall Jarrell points out, Frost portrays the spider as a kind of priest in a Mass, or Black Mass, elevating the moth like an object for sacrifice, with "a ghostly, ghastly formality" (42).

Note also that this improved passage gives Jarrell the credit not just for his words but for his insight into the poem. Both the idea and the words in which it was originally expressed are the properties of their originator. Finally, notice the page reference that follows the quotation (this system of documenting your sources is detailed in the next section).

DOCUMENT SOURCES USING MLA STYLE

You must document everything you take from a source. When you quote from other writers, when you borrow their information, when you summarize or paraphrase their ideas, make sure you give them proper credit. Identify the writer by name and cite the book, magazine, newspaper, pamphlet, website, or other source you have used.

The conventions that govern the proper way to document sources are available in the *MLA Handbook*, Eighth Edition (2016). The following brief list of pointers is not meant to take the place of the *MLA Handbook* itself, but to give you a basic sense of the rules for documentation.

Keep a List of Sources

Keep a working list of your research sources—all the references from which you might quote, summarize, paraphrase, or take information. When your paper is in finished form, it will end with a neat copy of the works you actually used (once called a "Bibliography," now titled "Works Cited").

Use Parenthetical References

In the body of your paper, every time you refer to a source, you need to provide information to help a reader locate it in your works-cited list. You can usually give just the author's name and a page citation in parentheses. For example, if you are writing a paper on Weldon Kees's sonnet "For My Daughter" (Chapter 11) and want to include an observation you found on page 136 of Samuel Maio's book *Creating Another Self*, write:

> One critic has observed that the distinctive tone of "For My Daughter" depends on Kees's combination of "personal subject matter with an impersonal voice" (Maio 136).

If you mention the author's name in your sentence, you need give only the page number in your reference:

> As Samuel Maio has observed, Kees creates a distinctive tone in this sonnet by combining a "personal subject with an impersonal voice" (136).

If you have two books or magazine articles by Samuel Maio in your works-cited list, how will the reader tell them apart? In your text, refer to the title of each book or article by condensing it into a word or two. Condensed book titles are italicized, and condensed article titles are still placed within quotation marks.

> One critic has observed that the distinctive tone of "For My Daughter" depends on Kees's combination of "personal subject matter with an impersonal voice" (Maio, *Creating* 136).

Create a Works-Cited List

- **Provide a full citation for each source on your works-cited page.** At the end of your paper, in your list of works cited, your reader will find a full description of your source—for the above examples, a critical book:

  > Maio, Samuel. *Creating Another Self: Voices in Modern American Personal Poetry*. 2nd ed., Thomas Jefferson UP, 2005.

- **Put your works-cited list in proper form.** The *MLA Handbook* provides detailed instructions for citing a myriad of different types of sources, from books to *YouTube* videos. To format your list:

  1. Start a new page for the works-cited list, and continue the page numbering from the body of your paper.
  2. Center the title, "Works Cited," one inch from the top of the page.
  3. Double-space between all lines (including after title and between entries).
  4. Type each entry beginning at the left-hand margin. If an entry runs longer than a single line, indent the following lines one-half inch from the left-hand margin.
  5. Alphabetize each entry according to the author's last name.

Cite Sources in MLA Style

Each entry in your list should contain all relevant information, as available, that helps your reader locate your source.

Core Elements of Each Entry

1. **Author's full name** as it appears on the title page or section of the work, last name first, followed by a period.
   (a) If the author has a different role than writing the work, identify that role (e.g. "editor" or "translator").
   (b) If the work is published without the author's name, skip this element.
2. **Title of source** (include the subtitle, if there is one, separated from the title by a colon), followed by a period.
   (a) Italicize titles of major works such as books, plays, websites, paintings, photographs, television shows, albums, etc.
   (b) Use quotation marks for titles of shorter works such as poems, short stories, newspaper or journal articles, episodes in television series, song titles, etc.
3. **Title of container,** italicized, and followed by comma. The MLA has coined the term "container" as a descriptor for the place where your source is "held," some examples being the:
   - magazine or newspaper that published source article
   - website that published source article
   - television series of which source episode is part
   - dictionary that contains source definition
   - anthology that printed source poem
   - website that published source blog or comment
4. **Other contributors,** followed by a comma. These are individuals involved in creating the source or its container, if relevant. Precede the names of contributors with a description of their role, e.g.:
   - translated by
   - performance by
   - edited by
5. **Version**, followed by a comma. Oftentimes works are updated or published in different forms. Be sure to identify the specific version you used. Some examples:
   - Book editions are cited as: 2nd ed, rev. ed., updated ed., or expanded ed.
   - Film versions might be cited as: uncut version or director's cut version.

6. **Number**, followed by comma. If your source's container uses a numbering system, be sure to cite the numbers. Some examples:
   - Academic journals often use volumes and numbers, i.e. vol. 7, no. 2.
   - Television series often number episodes, i.e. season 4, episode 7.
   - Books can be issued in multi-volume sets, i.e. vol. 3.
7. **Publisher**, followed by comma. Publishers are generally found on the copyright section of your book or website, but there are circumstances in which publisher information is unavailable.

   (a) **Use the full name of the publisher.** Eliminate articles (*A*, *An*, *The*) and business abbreviations (*Co.*, *Corp.*, *Inc.*, *Ltd.*). Abbreviate the names of university presses, by using the letters *U* (for University) and *P* (for Press).

Publisher's Name	Proper Citation
Harvard University Press	Harvard UP
University of Chicago Press	U of Chicago P
Alfred A. Knopf, Inc.	Alfred A. Knopf

   (b) **You can omit the publisher's name in circumstances where it does not add additional information), e.g.:**
   - periodical or newspaper
   - work published by the author
   - website whose name is the same as the publisher
8. **Publication date**, followed by comma. Many sources have more than one publication date, particularly when works are published in multiple media. The *MLA Handbook* suggests citing the date that is most relevant to your use of the source.
9. **Location**, followed by period. MLA uses the word "location" to designate whatever specific information will help your reader pinpoint your source most easily, e.g.:
   - page numbers (abbreviated as *p*. for a single page or *pp*. for a range of pages)
   - web addresses such as URLs, DOIs (digital object identifiers), or permalinks
   - disc numbers
   - physical locations—the name of the museum where you viewed a piece of art, or the location where you heard an author give a speech, etc.

Each of your entries should end with a period, no matter what element it concludes with. Remember, if the information is not available, you can safely leave it out of your citation. You should focus on providing all the relevant information in a clear manner. Don't worry if you are unsure exactly how properly to cite your source: the 8th edition of the MLA *Handbook* reassures us "there is often more than one way to document a source" (4).

Example Citations

Using the practice template created by the MLA, let's consider how the citation for a standard book entry is developed:

Maio, Samuel. *Creating Another Self: Voice in Modern American Personal Poetry.* 2nd ed., Thomas Jefferson UP, 2005.

AUTHOR/ TITLE

1. Author.	Maio, Samuel.
2. Title of source.	*Creating Another Self: Voice in Modern American Personal Poetry.*

CONTAINER 1

3. Title of container,	
4. Other contributors,	
5. Version,	2nd ed.,
6. Number,	
7. Publisher,	Thomas Jefferson UP,
8. Publication date,	2005,
9. Location.	

Here is the development of a citation for an article found on the web:

"The Poet at Work." *Emily Dickinson Museum*, Trustees of Amherst College, www.emilydickinsonmuseum.org/poet_at_work.

AUTHOR / TITLE

1. Author.	(No author cited)
2. Title of source.	"The Poet at Work."

CONTAINER 1

3. Title of container,	*Emily Dickinson Museum,*
4. Other contributors,	
5. Version,	
6. Number,	
7. Publisher,	Trustees of Amherst College,
8. Publication date,	
9. Location.	www.emilydickinsonmuseum.org/poet_at_work.

Two "Containers"

Sometimes you will find a source (e.g. a journal article) that is included in a "container" (the journal), which you accessed from a second, larger "container" (e.g. an online database). As another example, your source might be a TV episode, which is part of a TV series (the first container), which you streamed from *Netflix* (the second, larger container). When you have multiple containers, use the same procedures to provide complete information for each one. Study the MLA's template below to work through the citation for a print article that was accessed in an online database.

Nelson, Raymond. "The Fitful Life of Weldon Kees." *American Literary History,* vol. 1, no. 4, Winter 1989, pp. 816–52. *JSTOR*, www.jstor.org/stable/489775.

AUTHOR / TITLE

1. Author.	Nelson, Raymond.
2. Title of source.	"The Fitful Life of Weldon Kees."

CONTAINER 1

3. Title of container,	*American Literary History,*
4. Other contributors,	
5. Version,	
6. Number,	vol. 1, no. 4,
7. Publisher,	
8. Publication date,	Winter 1989,
9. Location.	pp. 816–52.

CONTAINER 2

3. Title of container,	*JSTOR,*
4. Other contributors,	
5. Version,	
6. Number,	
7. Publisher,	
8. Publication date,	
9. Location.	www.jstor.org/stable/489775.

Optional Elements

You may include any additional elements in your entry that you think are relevant to your use of the source. Place them with the core elements they relate to so the inclusion makes sense for the reader. Some optional elements commonly added include:

- **Date of original publication**, or prior publication dates
- **City of publication**, particularly if the book was published in many countries
- **Other facts about the source**, e.g. it is part of a unique series
- **Added descriptor for an unexpected type of source** (e.g. a personal meeting with an author or an unpublished letter)
- **Date you accessed online resource** will be relevant in some cases

Additional Resources on MLA Style

Refer as necessary to the MLA *Handbook* or to the "Reference Guide for Citations" examples in this book. The MLA also has a website with tips and advice—*style.mla.org*—or you may find it helpful to use an online citation manager such as *EasyBib* or *Zotero* to generate the citation for a source automatically.

CONCLUDING THOUGHTS

A well-crafted research essay is a wondrous thing—as delightful, in its own way, as a well-crafted poem or short story or play. Good essays prompt thought and add to knowledge. Writing a research paper sharpens your own mind and exposes you to the honed insights of other thinkers. Think of anything you write as a piece that could be published for the benefit of other people interested in your topic. After all, such a goal is not as far-fetched as it seems: this textbook, for example, features a number of papers written by students. Why shouldn't yours number among them? Aim high.

REFERENCE GUIDE FOR MLA CITATIONS

Here are examples of the types of citations you are likely to need for most student papers. The formats follow current MLA style for works-cited lists.

PRINT PUBLICATIONS

Books

No Author Listed

The Chicago Manual of Style. 17th ed., U of Chicago P, 2017.

One Author or Editor

Middlebrook, Diane Wood. *Anne Sexton: A Biography.* Houghton Mifflin, 1991.

Monteiro, George, editor. *Conversations with Elizabeth Bishop*. UP of Mississippi, 1996.

Two Authors or Editors

Jarman, Mark, and Robert McDowell. *The Reaper: Essays*. Story Line Press, 1996.

Craig, David, and Janet McCann, editors. *Odd Angles of Heaven: Contemporary Poetry by People of Faith*. Harold Shaw Publishing, 1994.

Three or More Authors

Phillips, Rodney, et al. *The Hand of the Poet*. Rizzoli International Publications, 1997.

Multiple Works by the Same Author

Bawer, Bruce. *The Aspect of Eternity.* Graywolf Press, 1993.

---. "Civilized Pleasures." *The Hudson Review*, vol. 59, no. 1, Spring 2006. *JSTOR*, www.jstor.org/stable/i20464510.

---. *Diminishing Fictions: Essays on the Modern American Novel and Its Critics*. Graywolf Press, 1988.

Corporate Author and Publisher

Reading at Risk: A Survey of Literary Reading in America. National Endowment for the Arts, June 2004.

Author and Editor

Shakespeare, William. *The Sonnets.* Edited by G. Blakemore Evans, Cambridge UP, 1996.

Translator

Dante Alighieri. *Inferno: A New Verse Translation.* Translated by Michael Palma, W. W. Norton, 2002.

Introduction, Preface, Foreword, or Afterword

Lapham, Lewis. Introduction. *Understanding Media: The Extensions of Man,* by Marshall McLuhan, MIT P, 1994, pp. vi–x.

Thwaite, Anthony. Preface. *Contemporary Poets,* edited by Thomas Riggs, 6th ed., St. James Press, 1996, pp. vii–viii.

Work in an Anthology

Rodriguez, Richard. "Aria: A Memoir of a Bilingual Childhood." *The Best American Essays of the Century,* edited by Robert Atwan and Joyce Carol Oates, Houghton Mifflin, 2001, pp. 447–66. Best American Series.

Translation in an Anthology

Neruda, Pablo. "We Are Many." Translated by Alastair Reid. *Literature: An Introduction to Fiction, Poetry, Drama, and Writing,* edited by X. J. Kennedy et al., 14th ed., Pearson, 2020, pp. 648–49.

Revised or Subsequent Edition

Janouch, Gustav. *Conversations with Kafka.* Translated by Goronwy Rees, rev. ed., New Directions Publishing, 1971.

Republished Book

Ellison, Ralph. *Invisible Man*. 1952. Vintage Books, 1995.

Multivolume Work

Wellek, René. *A History of Modern Criticism, 1750–1950*. 8 vols., Yale UP, 1955–92.

One Volume of a Multivolume Work

Wellek, René. *A History of Modern Criticism, 1750–1950*. Vol. 7, Yale UP, 1991. 8 vols.

Book in a Series

Ross, William T. *Weldon Kees*. Twayne Publishing, 1985. Twayne's United States Authors Series, 484.

Signed Article in a Reference Book

Cavoto, Janice E. "Harper Lee's *To Kill a Mockingbird*." *The Oxford Encyclopedia of American Literature*, edited by Jay Parini, vol. 2, Oxford UP, 2004, pp. 418–21.

Unsigned Encyclopedia Article—Standard Reference Book

"James Dickey." *The New Encyclopaedia Britannica: Micropaedia*. 15th ed., 1987.

Dictionary Entry

"Design." *Merriam-Webster's Collegiate Dictionary*. 11th ed., 2003.

Periodicals

Journal

Salter, Mary Jo. "The Heart Is Slow to Learn." *The New Criterion*, vol. 10, no. 8, Apr. 1992, pp. 23–29.

Signed Magazine Article

Gioia, Dana. "Studying with Miss Bishop." *The New Yorker*, 5 Sept. 1986, pp. 90–101.

Unsigned Magazine Article

"The Real Test." *New Republic*, 5 Feb. 2001, p. 7.

Newspaper Article

Lyall, Sarah. "In Poetry, Ted Hughes Breaks His Silence on Sylvia Plath." *The New York Times*, 19 Jan. 1998, natl. ed., pp. A1+.

Signed Book Review

Fugard, Lisa. "Divided We Love," Review of *Unaccustomed Earth*, by Jhumpa Lahiri. *The Los Angeles Times*, 30 Mar. 2008, p. R1.

Unsigned, Untitled Book Review

Review of *Otherwise: New and Selected Poems*, by Jane Kenyon. *Virginia Quarterly Review*, vol. 72, no. 1, Winter 1996, p. 136.

WEB RESOURCES

Website

Liu, Alan, director. *Voice of the Shuttle*. English Dept., U of California Santa Barbara, vos.ucsb.edu.

Document on a Website

"A Hughes Timeline." *PBS*, Public Broadcasting Service, www.pbs.org.wgbh/masterpiece/americancollection/cora/hughes_timeline.html.

"Wallace Stevens." *Poets.org.*, Academy of American Poets, www.poets.org/poetsorg/poet/wallace-stevens.

Online Reference Database

"Brooks, Gwendolyn." *Encyclopaedia Britannica,* www.britannica.com/biography/Gwendolyn-Brooks.

Entire Online Book, Previously Appeared in Print

Jewett, Sarah Orne. *The Country of the Pointed Firs.* 1896. *Project Gutenberg,* 11 July 2008, www.gutenberg.org/files/367/367-h/367-h.htm. Ebook 367.

Article in an Online Newspaper

Atwood, Margaret. "The Writer: A New Canadian Life-Form." *The New York Times on the Web,* 18 May 1997, www.nytimes.com/books/97/05/18/bookend/bookend.html.

Article in an Online Magazine

Garner, Dwight. "Jamaica Kincaid." *Salon,* 13 Jan. 1996, www.salon.com/1996/01/13/kincaid_2/.

Article in an Online Scholarly Journal

Carter, Sarah. "From the Ridiculous to the Sublime: Ovidian and Neoplatonic Registers in *A Midsummer Night's Dream.*" *Early Modern Literary Studies,* vol 12, no. 1, May 2006, pp. 1–31, purl.oclc.org/emls/12-1/cartmnd.htm.

Article from a Scholarly Journal, Part of an Archival Online Database

Finch, Annie. "My Father Dickinson: On Poetic Influence." *The Emily Dickinson Journal,* vol. 17, no. 2, 2008, pp. 24–38. *Project Muse,* www.muse.jhu.edu/journals/emily_dickinson_journal/v017/17.2.finch.html.

Article Accessed via a Library Subscription Service

Seitler, Dana. "Unnatural Selection: Mothers, Eugenic Feminism, and Charlotte Perkins Gilman's Regeneration Narratives." *American Quarterly*, vol. 55, no. 1, Mar. 2003, pp. 61–87. *ProQuest*, search.proquest.com.libproxy1.usc.edu/docview/223310934/5B0B8A7854AE4085PQ/1?accountid=14789

Online Blog

Gioia, Ted. "*White Teeth* by Zadie Smith." *The New Canon: The Best in Fiction Since 1985*, www.thenewcanon.com/white_teeth.html.

Vellala, Rob. "Gilman: No Trouble to Anyone." *The American Literary Blog*, 17 Aug. 2010, americanliteraryblog.blogspot.com/search/label/Charlotte%20Perkins%20Gilman.

Twitter

Tan, Amy (AmyTan). "#TenThingsNotToSayToAWriter My life would make a great story. If you write it, we can split royalties 50–50." *Twitter*, 30 July 2015, 9:19 p.m., twitter.com/AmyTan/status/626970316087132161.

Photograph or Painting Accessed Online

Langston Hughes in 1936. *Wikimedia Commons*, Wikimedia Foundation, commons.wikimedia.org/wiki/Langston_Hughes#/media/File:Langston_Hughes_1936.jpg.

Bruegel, Pieter, *Landscape with the Fall of Icarus*. c.1558. Musées Royaux des Beaux-Arts de Belgique, Brussels. *Ibiblio*, U of North Carolina-Chapel Hill/Center for the Public Domain, www.ibiblio.org/wm/paint/auth/bruegel.

Video Accessed Online

"Ozymandias: Percy Bysshe Shelley." *YouTube*, E-Verse Radio, 13 Mar. 2007, www.youtube.com/watch?v=6xGa-fNSHaM.

Podcast

Writer's Almanac. Narrated by Garrison Keillor, 23 Feb. 2016, www.writersalmanac.org/episodes/20160223.

OTHER MEDIA

Compact Disc (CD)

Shakespeare, William. *The Complete Arkangel Shakespeare: 38 Fully-Dramatized Plays*. Narrated by Eileen Atkins and John Gielgud, read by Imogen Stubbs, Joseph Fiennes, et al., Audio Partners, 2003.

DVD

Hamlet. By William Shakespeare, performance by Laurence Olivier, Eileen Herlie, and Basil Sydney, 1948. Criterion Collection, 2010.

Film

Hamlet. By William Shakespeare, directed by Franco Zeffirelli, performances by Mel Gibson, Glenn Close, Helena Bonham Carter, Alan Bates, and Paul Scofield, Warner Bros., 1991.

Television or Radio Program

Moby Dick. By Herman Melville, directed by Franc Roddam, performances by Patrick Stewart and Gregory Peck, 2 episodes, USA Network, 16-17 Mar. 1998.

Television Series

The Wire. By David Simon, Blown Deadline/HBO, 2002-2008.

Episode of a Television Series

"Old Cases." *The Wire*, by David Simon, season 1, episode 4, Blown Deadline/HBO, 23 June 2002.

Episode of a Television Series Seen on DVD

"Old Cases." *The Wire: The Complete First Season*, by David Simon, episode 4, HBO Video, 2004.

Episode of a Television Series Streamed Online

"Old Cases." *The Wire: The Complete First Season*, by David Simon, episode 4. *Amazon Prime*, www.amazon.com/The-Detail/dp/B00BSEJR9C/ref=sr_1_1?s=instantvideo&ie=UTF8&qid=1459816276&sr=1-1&keywords=the+wire.

Live Performance

Heartbreak House. By George Bernard Shaw, directed by Robin Lefevre, performances by Philip Bosco and Swoosie Kurtz, Roundabout Theater Company, 1 Oct. 2006, New York.

LITERARY CREDITS

FICTION

Achebe, Chinua. "Dead Men's Path," copyright © 1972, 1973 by Chinua Achebe; from GIRLS AT WAR: AND OTHER STORIES by Chinua Achebe. Used by permission of Doubleday, an imprint of the Knopf Doubleday Publishing Group, a division of Random House LLC. All rights reserved.

Alexie, Sherman. "This is What it Means to Say Phoenix, Arizona." Excerpt from THE LONE RANGER AND TONTO FISTFIGHT IN HEAVEN, copyright © 1993, 2005 by Sherman Alexie. Used by permission of Grove/Atlantic, Inc. Any third party use of this material, outside of this publication, is prohibited.

Atwood, Margaret. "Happy Endings" from GOOD BONES AND SIMPLE MURDERS by Margaret Atwood, copyright © 1983, 1992, 1994, by O. W. Toad Ltd. Used by permission of Nan A. Talese, an imprint of the Knopf Doubleday Publishing Group, a division of Random House LLC. All rights reserved.

Bidpai. "The Camel and His Friends." Retold in English by Arundhati Khanwalkar from the PANVHATANTRA. Used by permission.

Boyle, T. Corraghessan. "Greasy Lake," copyright © 1982 by T. Corraghessan Boyle; from GREASY LAKE AND OTHER STORIES by T. Coraghessan Boyle. Used by permission of Viking Books, an imprint of Penguin Publishing Group, a division of Penguin Random House LLC. All rights reserved.

Bradbury, Ray. "A Sound of Thunder." Reprinted by permission of Don Congdon Associates, Inc. Copyright © 1952 by the Crowell Collier Publishing Company, renewed 1980 by Ray Bradbury.

Carver, Raymond. "A Small, Good Thing—Church Little Rock" from CATHEDRAL. Knopf, 1983.

Carver, Raymond. "Cathedral" from CATHEDRAL by Raymond Carver, copyright © 1981, 1982, 1983 by Tess Gallagher. Used by permission of Alfred A. Knopf, an imprint of the Knopf Doubleday Publishing Group, a division of Penguin Random House LLC. All rights reserved.

Chopin, Kate. "The Story of an Hour." Originally published in *Vogue*, December 6, 1894.

Chopin, Kate. From "The Storm" by Kate Chopin from THE COMPLETE WORKS OF KATE CHOPIN. Copyright © 1969, Louisiana State University Press. Used by permission of Louisiana State University Press.

Cisneros, Sandra. "Barbie-Q" from WOMAN HOLLERING CREEK. Copyright © 1991 by Sandra Cisneros. Published by Vintage Books, a division of Penguin Random House, New York and originally in hardcover by Random House. By permission of Susan Bergholz Literary Services, New York, NY and Lamy, NM. All rights reserved.

Faulkner, William. "A Rose for Emily," copyright © 1930 and renewed 1958 by William Faulkner from COLLECTED STORIES OF WILLIAM FAULKNER by William Faulkner. Used by permission of Random House, an imprint and division of Random House LLC. All rights reserved.

Faulkner, William. "Barn Burning," copyright © 1950 by Random House, Inc. Copyright renewed 1977 by Jill Faulkner Summers; from COLLECTED STORIES OF WILLIAM FAULKNER by William Faulkner. Used by permission of Random House, an imprint and division of Random House LLC. All rights reserved.

Gaiman, Neil. "How to Talk to Girls at Parties" from FRAGILE THINGS: SHORT FICTIONS AND WONDERS by Neil Gaiman. Copyright © 2006 by Neil Gaiman. Reprinted by permission of Writers House LLC acting as agent for the author/illustrator.

Gilman, Charlotte Perkins. "The Yellow Wallpaper." Originally published in *The Forerunner*, October 1913.

Grimm, Jacob and Wilhelm Grimm. "Godfather Death," 1812. Translated by Dana Gioia.

Hawthorne, Nathaniel. "Young Goodman Brown," from "YOUNG GOODMAN BROWN, AND OTHER SHORT STORIES," Courier Corporation, 1992. Originally Published 1835.

Hemingway, Ernest. "A Clean Well-Lighted Place." Reprinted with the permission of Scribner Publishing Group, a division of Simon & Schuster, Inc. from THE SHORT STORIES OF ERNEST HEMINGWAY by Earnest Hemingway. Copyright 1933 by Charles Scribner's Sons. Copyright renewed 1961 by Mary Hemingway. All rights reserved.

Hurston, Zora Neale. "Sweat." Originally published in 1926.

Jackson, Shirley. Reprinted by permission of Farrar, Straus and Giroux: "The Lottery" from THE LOTTERY by Shirley Jackson. Copyright © 1948, 1949 by Shirley Jackson. Copyright renewed 1976, 1977 by Laurence Hyman, Barry Hyman, Mrs. Sarah Webster and Mrs. Joanne Schnurer.

Jin, Ha. "Saboteur" from THE BRIDEGROOM: STORIES by Ha Jin, copyright © 2000 by Ha Jin. Used by permission of Pantheon Books, an imprint of the Knopf Doubleday Publishing Group, a division of Penguin Random House LLC. All rights reserved.

Joyce, James. "Araby." Originally Published in DUBLINERS, Grant Richards Ltd. London, 1914.

Kafka, Franz. "Before the Law." Translated by John P. Siscoe. Used by permission.

Kincaid, Jamaica. Reprinted by permission of Farrar, Straus and Giroux: "Girl" from AT THE BOTTOM OF THE RIVER by Jamaica Kincaid. Copyright © 1983 by Jamaica Kincaid.

Kodama, Maria. "The Gospel According to Mark," copyright © 1998 by Maria Kodama; translation copyright © 1998 by Penguin Random House LLC.; from COLLECTED FICTIONS: VOLUME 3 by Jorge Luis Borges, translated by Andrew Hurley. Used by permission of Viking Books, an imprint of Penguin Publishing Group, a division of Penguin Random House LLC. All rights reserved.

Le Guin, Ursula K. "The Ones Who Walk Away from Omelas." Copyright © 1973 by Ursula K. Le Guin. First appeared in "New Dimension 3" in 1973, and then in THE WIND'S TWELVE QUARTERS, published by Harper Collins in 1975. Reprinted by permission of Curtis Brown, Ltd.

London, Jack. "To Build a Fire" by Jack London, *The Century Magazine*, v. 76, August, 1908, 525–534.

Mahfouz, Naguib. "The Lawsuit" from THE TIME AND THE PLACE by Naguib Mahfouz, copyright © 1991 by the American University in Cairo Press. Used by permission of Doubleday, an imprint of the Knopf Doubleday Publishing Group, a division of Penguin Random House LLC. All rights reserved.

Manguel, Alberto. "Arrendondo, Inés: 'The Shunammite.'" Translation by Alberto Manguel. © Alberto Manguel c/o Guillermo Schavelzon & Asociados, Agencia Literaria www.schavelzon.com.

Mansfield, Katherine. "Miss Brill." Originally published in *The Athenaeum*. November, 1920.

Márquez, Gabriel García. All pages from "The Handsomest Drowned Man in the World" from LEAF STORM AND OTHER STORIES by Gabriel García Márquez. © 1971 by Gabriel García Márquez. Reprinted by permission of HarperCollins Publishers.

McInerney, Jay. Excerpt from BRIGHT LIGHTS, BIG CITY. Vintage Books: 1984.

Morrison, Toni "Recitatif." Copyright © 1983 by Toni Morrison Reprinted by permission of ICM Partners.

Mukherjee, Bharati. "Saints." Copyright © 1985 by Bharati Mukherjee. Originally published in *The Three Penny Review*. Reprinted by permission of the author.

Oates, Joyce Carol. "Where Are You Going, Where Have You Been?" from HIGH LONESOME: NEW AND SELECTED STORIES 1955–2006 by Joyce Carol Oates. Copyright © 2006 by the Ontario Review, Inc. Reprinted by permission of HarperCollins Publishers.

O'Brien, Tim. "The Things They Carried" from THE THINGS THEY CARRIED by Tim O'Brien. Copyright 1990 by Tim O'Brien. Reprinted by permission of Houghton Mifflin Harcourt Publishing Company. All rights reserved.

O'Connor, Flannery. "A Good Man Is Hard to Find" from A GOOD MAN IS HARD TO FIND AND OTHER STORIES by Flannery O'Connor. Copyright © 1953 by Flannery O'Connor; renewed 1981 by Regina O'Connor. Reprinted by permission of Houghton Mifflin Harcourt Publishing Company. All rights reserved.

Poe, Edgar Allan. "The Tell-Tale Heart," 1843. *The Pioneer*, Vol. I, No. I, Drew and Scammell, Philadelphia, January, 1843.

Porter, William Sydney (O Henry). "The Gift of the Magi." 1905.

Springsteen, Bruce. Excerpt from "Spirit In The Night." Copyright © 1972 Bruce Springsteen, renewed © 2000 Bruce Springsteen (ASCAP). Reprinted by permission. International copyright secured. All rights reserved.

Steinbeck, John. "The Chrysanthemums" from THE LONG VALLEY by John Steinbeck, copyright © 1938, copyright © renewed 1966 by John Steinbeck. Used by permission of Viking Books, an imprint of Penguin Publishing Group, a division of Penguin Random House LLC. All rights reserved

Tan, Amy. "A Pair of Tickets" from THE JOY LUCK CLUB by Amy Tan, copyright © 1989 by Amy Tan. Used by permission of G. P. Putnam's Sons, an imprint of Penguin Publishing Group, a division of Penguin Random House LLC. All rights reserved.

Tan, Amy. Excerpted from an interview conducted by National Endowment for the Arts for "The Big Read."

"The Parable of the Prodigal Son." The Bible. Authorized King James Version, Oxford UP, 1998 15:11.

Tzu, Chuang. "Independence" (4th cen. BCE). Translated by Herbert Giles.

Updike, John. "A & P" from PIGEON FEATHERS AND OTHER STORIES by John Updike, copyright © 1962, copyright renewed 1900 by John Updike. Used by permission of Alfred A. Knopf, an imprint of the Knopf Doubleday Publishing Group, a division of Random House LLC. All rights reserved.

Vonnegut Jr., Kurt. "Harrison Bergeron," © 1961 by Kurt Vonnegut Jr.; from WELCOME TO THE MONKEY HOUSE by Kurt Vonnegut. Used by permission of Dell Publishing, an imprint of Random House, a division of Random House LLC. All rights reserved.

Walker, Alice. "Everyday Use" from IN LOVE & TROUBLE: Stories of Black Women by Alice Walker. Copyright 1973, and renewed 2001 by Alice Walker. Reprinted by permission of Houghton Mifflin Harcourt Publishing Company. All rights reserved.

Welty, Eudora. "A Worn Path" from A CURTAIN OF GREEN AND OTHER STORIES by Eudora Welty. Copyright 1941 and renewed 1969 by Eudora Welty. Reprinted by permission of Houghton Mifflin Harcourt Publishing Company. All rights reserved.

Wolff, Tobias. "Bullet in the Brain" from THE NIGHT IN QUESTION: STORIES by Tobias Wolff, copyright © 1996 by Tobias Wolff. Used by permission of Alfred A. Knopf, an imprint of the Knopf Doubleday Publishing Group, a division of Penguin Random House LLC. All rights reserved.

Woolf, Virginia. "A Haunted House." From MONDAY OR TUESDAY, Originally Published by Harcourt Brace, 1921.

POETRY

Abeyta, Aaron. "Thirteen ways of looking at a tortilla" by Aaron A. Abeyta, in COLCHA (Boulder: University Press of Colorado, 2011), Editor: Aaron A. Abeyta, 2001. Reprinted with permission.

Addonizio, Kim. "First Poem for You" by Kim Addonizio from THE PHILOSOPHER'S CLUB. Reprinted by permission of BOA Editions.

Alarcón, Francisco X. "The X in My Name" from NO GOLDEN GATE FOR US (Pennywhistle Press, Tesuque, NM, 1993). Copyright 1993. Used by permission of the author.

Alarcón, Francisco X. "Frontera / Border" by Francisco X. Alarcón. Copyright 2003. Used by permission of the author.

Alexie, Sherman. "The Facebook Sonnet." Copyright © 2011 Sherman Alexie. All rights reserved. Used by permission of Nancy Stauffer Associates.

An-hwei Lee, Karen. "Rainfall" from GOD'S ONE HUNDRED PROMISES, originally published by Swan Scythe Press in 2002. Copyright © 2002. Used with permission.

Arnold, Matthew. "Dover Beach," from THE NEW POEMS, 1867.

Auden, W. H. "Musée des Beaux Arts," "The Unknown Citizen," copyright © 1940 and renewed 1968; from W. H. AUDEN COLLECTED POEMS by W. H. Auden. Used by permission of Random House, an imprint and division of Penguin Random House LLC. All rights reserved.

Barber, David. "Aria," from POETRY, March 2013. Copyright © 2013. Used by permission.

Belloc, Hilaire. "The Hippopotamus" from THE BAD CHILD'S BOOK OF BEASTS, 1896.

Bishop, Elizabeth. Reprinted by permission of Farrar, Straus and Giroux, LLC. "The Fish," "One Art," "Sestina" from POEMS by Elizabeth Bishop. Copyright ©2011 by The Alice H. Methfessel Trust. Publisher's note and compilation copyright © 2011 by Farrar, Straus and Giroux.

Blake, William. "London," "The Garden of Love," originally published in SONGS OF EXPERIENCE, 1794.

Blake, William. "The Chimney Sweeper." Originally published in two parts in SONGS OF INNOCENCE, 1789 and SONGS OF EXPERIENCE, 1794.

Blake, William. "The Tyger," from SONGS OF INNOCENCE AND EXPERIENCE, 1789.

Bly, Robert. "Driving to Town Late to Mail a Letter" from SILENCE IN THE SNOWY FIELDS copyright 1962 by Robert Bly. Reprinted by permission of Wesleyan University Press.

Bogan, Louise. "Medusa" from BODY OF THIS DEATH, 1923.

Brontë, Emily. "Love and Friendship" from POEMS. Currer, Ellis, and Acton Bell. London, England: Aylott and Jones. 1846.

Brooks, Gwendolyn: "the mother," "We Real Cool." Reprinted by consent of Brooks Permissions.

Browning, Elizabeth Barrett. "How Do I Love Thee? (Sonnet 43)" from SONNETS FROM THE PORTUGUESE, 1850.

Browning, Robert. "My Last Duchess." Originally published in 1842.

Bukowski, Charles. "Dostoevsky" from BONE PALACE BATTLE. Copyright © 1997 by Linda Lee Bukowski. Reprinted by permission of HarperCollins Publishers.

Buson, Taniguchi. "The piercing chill I feel" from INTRODUCTION TO HAIKU by Harold Gould Henderson, copyright © 1958 by Harold G. Henderson. Used by permission of Doubleday, an imprint of the Knopf Doubleday Publishing Group, a division of Random House LLC. All rights reserved.

Buson, Taniguchi. "Moonrise on mudflats" by Buson Taniguchi, translated by Michael Stillman. Reprinted by permission of Michael Stillman.

Buson, Taniguchi. "On the one-ton temple bell," translated by X. J. Kennedy.

Carroll, Lewis. [Charles Lutwidge Dodgson]. "Jabberwocky" from THROUGH THE LOOKING-GLASS, and WHAT ALICE FOUND THERE. Macmillan, 1871.

Cofer, Judith Ortiz. "Quinceañera" is reprinted with permission from the publisher of SILENT DANCING by Judith Ortiz Cofer (© 1991 Arte Publico Press—University of Houston).

Coleridge, Samuel Taylor. "Christabel," 1816.

Coleridge, Samuel Taylor. "Kubla Khan," 1816.

Collins, Billy. "Introduction to Poetry" from THE APPLE THAT ASTONISHED PARIS. Copyright © 1988, 1996 by Billy Collins. Reprinted with the permission of The Permissions Company, Inc., on behalf of the University of Arkansas Press, www.uapress.com.

Cornford, Frances. "The Watch" from POEMS, 1910.

Cortez, Sarah. "Adam" from VANISHING POINTS: POEMS AND PHOTOGRAPHS OF TEXAS ROADSIDE MEMORIALS. *Texas Review Press*, 2016. Copyright 2016. Used by Permission.

Crabbe, George. "The Parish Register," 1807.

Crane, Stephen. "The Wayfarer" from WAR IS KIND AND OTHER LINES, published May 20, 1899.

Crane, Sephen. "In the Desert" from BLACK RIDERS AND OTHER LINES, 1895.

Cummings, E. E. "anyone lived in a pretty how town." Copyright 1940, © 1968, 1991 by the Trustees for the E. E. Cummings Trust. Used by permission of Liveright Publishing Corporation.

Cummings, E. E. "Buffalo Bill 's." Copyright 1923, 1951, © 1991 by the Trustees for the E. E. Cummings Trust. Copyright © 1976 by George James Firmage, from COMPLETE POEMS: 1904–1962 by E. E. Cummings, edited by George J. Firmage. Used by permission of Liveright Publishing Corporation.

Cummings, E. E. "in Just—." Copyright 1923, 1951, © 1991 by the Trustees for the E. E. Cummings Trust. Copyright © 1976 by George James Firmage. Used by permission of Liveright Publishing Corporation.

Cummings, E. E. "somewhere i have never travelled,gladly beyond." Copyright 1923, 1951, © 1991 by the Trustees for the E. E. Cummings Trust. Copyright © 1976 by George James Firmage, Used by permission of Liveright Publishing Corporation.

Cunningham, J. V. "Friend, on this scaffold Thomas More lies dead" J. V. Cunningham. Reprinted with permission.

Deutsch, Babette. "The Falling Flower" by Arakida Moritake, translated by Babette Deutsch. Copyright 1957. Reprinted by permission of Benjamin Yarmolinsky and the Estate of Babette Deutsch.

Dickinson, Emily. "A Route of Evanescence." From *Atlantic Monthly*, 68, October 1891.

Dickinson, Emily. "Because I could not stop for Death," "The Lightning is a yellow Fork," "My Life had stood – a Loaded Gun," "I felt a Funeral, in my Brain," THE POEMS OF EMILY DICKINSON: VARIORUM EDITION, edited by Ralph W. Franklin, Cambridge, Mass.: The Belknap Press of Harvard University Press, Copyright © 1998 by the President and Fellows of Harvard College. Copyright © 1951, 1955 by the President and Fellows of Harvard College. Copyright © renewed 1979, 1983 by the President and Fellows of Harvard College. Copyright © 1914, 1918, 1919, 1924, 1929, 1930, 1932, 1935, 1937, 1942 by Martha Dickinson Bianchi. Copyright © 1952, 1957, 1958, 1963, 1965 by Mary L. Hampson.

Dickinson, Emily. "Wild Nights – Wild Nights!" THE POEMS OF EMILY DICKINSON, edited by Thomas H. Johnson, Cambridge, Mass.: The Belknap Press of Harvard University Press, Copyright © 1955.

Dinesen, Isak (Karen Blixen). Excerpt from OUT OF AFRICA. Putnam, 1937.

Donne, John. "Batter my heart, three-personed God, for You," "Death be not proud," "The Flea" from SONGS AND SONNETS, 1633.

Donne, John. "Song," 1633

Doolittle, H. (Hilda Doolittle). "Helen" from COLLECTED POEMS, 1912–1944, copyright ©1982 by The Estate of Hilda Doolittle. Reprinted by permission of New Directions Publishing Corp.

Doolittle, Hilda. "Sea Rose" from SEA GARDEN. St. Martin's Press. New York, 1916.

Dowson, Ernest C. "Days of Wine and Roses" from VITAE SUMMA BREVIS. Published in 1896.

Dunbar, Paul Laurence. "We Wear the Mask" from LYRICS OF LOWLY LIFE. Dodd, Mead, and Company, 1896.

Eliot, T. S. "The Boston Evening Transcript," published in *Poetry*, 1915.

Eliot, T. S. "The Love Song of J. Alfred Prufrock" from PRUFROCK AND OTHER OBSERVATIONS. The Egoist Ltd, 1917.

Eliot, T. S. "Preludes" originally published in PRUFROCK AND OTHER OBSERVATIONS, 1917.

Espaillat, Rhina P. "Bilingual/Bilingüe" from WHERE HORIZONS GO by Rhina Espaillat, published by Truman State University Press Copyright ©1998. Reprinted by permission of the author.

Essbaum, Jill. "The Heart" by Jill Alexander Essbaum from HARLOT. Reprinted by permission of Jill Essbaum.

Foley, Adelle. "Learning to Shave (Father teaching son)" by Adelle Foley. Reprinted with permission from Adelle Foley.

Frost, Robert. "The Road Not Taken" from MOUNTAIN INTERVAL. Henry Holt and Company, 1916.

Frost, Robert. "Fire and Ice" from NEW HAMPSHIRE. Henry Holt and Company, 1923.

Frost, Robert. "A Patch of Old Snow" from MOUNTAIN INTERVAL, 1920.

Frost, Robert. "Mending Wall" from NORTH OF BOSTON. David Nutt, 1914.

Frost, Robert. "Design" from AMERICAN POETRY: A MISCELLANY. Copyright 1922. First published by Harcourt Brace.

Frost, Robert. "Out, Out—." Originally published in *McClure's*, July 1916.

Frost, Robert. "Nothing Gold Can Stay" from the book THE POETRY OF ROBERT FROST edited by Edward Connery Lathem. Copyright © 1923, 1928, 1969 by Henry Holt and Company, LLC, copyright © 1936 1942, 1951, 1956 by Robert Frost, copyright © 1964, 1970 by Lesley Frost Ballantine.

Frost, Robert. "Acquainted with the Night," "Stopping by Woods on a Snowy Evening" from the book THE POETRY OF ROBERT FROST edited by Edward Connery Lathem. Copyright © 1923, 1928, 1969 by Henry Holt and Company, LLC, copyright © 1936, 1951, 1956 by Robert Frost, copyright © 1964 by Lesley Frost Ballantine. Reprinted by permission of Henry Holt and Company, LLC. All rights reserved.

Ginsberg, Allen. All lines from "A Supermarket in California" from COLLECTED POEMS 1947–1980 by Allen Ginsberg. Copyright © 1955 by Allen Ginsberg. Reprinted by permission of HarperCollins Publishers.

Gioia, Dana. "Money" from THE GODS OF WINTER. Copyright © 1991 by Dana Gioia. Reprinted with the permission of The Permissions Company, Inc., on behalf of Graywolf Press, www.graywolfpress.org.

Gwynn, R. S. "Shakespearean Sonnet." Copyright © by R. S. Gwynn. Used by permission of R. S. Gwynn.

Haaland, Tami. "Lipstick" from BREATH IN EVERY ROOM by Tami Haaland

Copyright 2001 by Tami Haaland. Reprinted by permission of the author.

Hakuro, Wada. "Even the Croaking of Frogs" by Wada Hakuro, translated by Violet Kazue de Cristoro in MAY SKY: THERE IS ALWAYS TOMORROW. Reprinted by permission of Kimiko de Cristoforo.

Hardy, Thomas. "Neutral Tones" from WESSEX POEMS AND OTHER VERSES, 1898.

Hardy, Thomas. "The Convergence of the Twain," SATIRES OF CIRCUMSTANCE, LYRICS AND REVERIES WITH MISCELLANEOUS PIECES. London: Macmillan, 1915.

Hardy, Thomas. "The Ruined Maid." Written in 1866, first published in POEMS OF THE PAST AND PRESENT, 1901.

Hardy, Thomas. "The Workbox" from SATIRES OF CIRCUMSTANCE, 1914.

Harrington, Sir John. "Of Treason," 1618.

Hayden, Robert. "Those Winter Sundays," Copyright © 1966 by Robert Hayden, from COLLECTED POEMS OF ROBERT HAYDEN by Robert Hayden, edited by Frederick Glaysher. Used by permission of Liveright Publishing Corporation.

Heaney, Seamus. Reprinted by permission of Farrar, Straus and Giroux: "Digging" from OPENED GROUND: SELECTED POEMS 1966–1996 by Seamus Heaney. Copyright © 1998 by Seamus Heaney.

Henley, William Ernest. "Invictus" from BOOK OF VERSES, 1888.

Herbert, George. "Easter Wings," "Redemption," from THE TEMPLE, 1633.

Herrera, Juan Felipe. "El Ángel de la Guarda" from LOTERÍA CARDS AND FORTUNE POEMS: A BOOK OF LIVES, with linocuts by Artemil Rodrígues. Copyright © 1999 by Juan Felipe Herrera. Reprinted with the permission of The Permissions Company, Inc., on behalf of City Lights Books, www.citylights.com.

Herrick, Robert. "To the Virgins, to Make Much of Time," "Upon Julia's Clothes" from HESPERIDES, 1648.

Holden, Karen. "Bats in a Box" first appeared in CONFLUENCE 2010. Copyright © 2010, 2016. Used with permission of the author. All rights reserved.

Hood, Thomas. "Faithless Nelly Gray," 1826.

Hopkins, Gerard Manley. "God's Grandeur." Written in 1877, published in POEMS OF GERARD MANLEY HOPKINS, 1918.

Hopkins, Gerard Manley. "Pied Beauty," "The Windhover" from POEMS OF GERARD MANLEY HOPKINS, 1918.

Hopkins. Gerard Manley. "Spring and Fall." (1844–1889)

Housman, A. E. "Loveliest of trees, the cherry now," "When I was one-and-twenty" from A SHROPSHIRE LAD. Kegan Paul, Trench, Treubner & Company, 1896.

Hughes, Langston. "Theme for English B," "I, Too," "Harlem (2)" from THE COLLECTED POEMS OF LANGSTON HUGHES by Langston Hughes, edited by Arnold Rampersad with David Roessel, Associate Editor, copyright 1994 by the Estate of Langston Hughes. Used by permission of Alfred A. Knopf, an imprint of the Knopf Doubleday Publishing Group, a division of Random House LLC. All rights reserved.

Hughes, Langston. "The Negro Speaks of Rivers" published in *THE CRISIS*, June 1921.

Jeffers, Robinson. Poems from THE COLLECTED POETRY OF ROBINSON JEFFERS, edited by Tim Hunt, Volume 2, 1928–1938. Published by Stanford University Press. Copyright 1938, renewed by Donnan Jeffers and Garth Jeffers. All rights reserved. Used with the permission of Stanford University Press, www.sup.org

Jonson, Ben. "On My First Son," 1616.

Justice, Donald. "On the Death of Friends in Childhood" from COLLECTED POEMS, copyright © 2004 by Donald Justice. Used by permission of Alfred A. Knopf, an imprint of the Knopf Doubleday Publishing Group, a division of Penguin Random House LLC. All rights reserved

Kaufman, Bob. "No More Jazz at Alcatraz" from CRANIAL GUITAR: SELECTED POEMS. Copyright © 1996 by Eileen Kaufman. Reprinted with the permission of The Permissions Company, Inc. on behalf of Coffee House Press, www.coffeehousepress.org.

Keats, John. "Bright star, would I were steadfast as thou art." Originally published in *The Plymouth and Devonport Weekly Journal*, 1838.

Keats, John. "La Belle Dame sans Merci," 1819.

Keats, John. "Ode on a Grecian Urn" from *Annals of the Fine Arts*, Number 15, January 1820.

Keats, John. "When I have fears that I may cease to be" from LIFE, LETTERS, AND LITERARY REMAINS OF JOHN KEATS, 1848.

Kees, Weldon. "For My Daughter." Reprinted from THE COLLECTED POEMS OF

WELDON KEES edited by Donald Justice by permission of the University of Nebraska Press. Copyright renewed 2003 by the University of Nebraska Press.

Kim, Suji Kwock. "Occupation." From NOTES FROM THE DIVIDED COUNTRY: POEMS by Suji Kwock Kim. Copyright © 2003, Louisiana State University Press. Used by permission of Louisiana State University Press.

Kobayashi, Issa. "Cricket" by Kobayashi Issa, trans. Robert Bly. Reprinted by permission of Robert Bly.

Kobayashi, Issa. Cid Corman's translation of the Issa poem, "Only one guy" is reprinted from ONE MAN'S MOON by permission of Gnomon Press.

Komunyakaa, Yusef. "Facing It" from PLEASURE DOME: NEW AND COLLECTED POEMS © 2001 by Yusef Komunyakaa. Reprinted with permission of Wesleyan University Press.

Larios, Julie. "What Bee Did." Originally appeared in *The Cortland Review*. Copyright © 2006. Used with permission of the author.

Larkin, Philip. Reprinted by permission of Farrar, Straus and Giroux: "Poetry of Departures," from THE COMPLETE POEMS OF PHILIP LARKIN by Philip Larkin, edited by Archie Burnett. Copyright © 2012 by The Estate of Philip Larkin.

Lawrence, D. H. "Piano" from NEW POEMS, 1918.

Lazarus, Emma. "The New Colossus," 1883. Posted on the Statue of Liberty, 1903.

Lee, Li-Young. "Night Mirror" from BOOK OF MY NIGHTS. Copyright © 2001 by Li-Young Lee. Reprinted with the permission of The Permissions Company, Inc., on behalf of BOA Editions, Ltd., www.boaeditions.org.

Levertov, Denise. "Ancient Stairway" from THIS GREAT UNKNOWING, copyright © 1999 by The Denise Levertov Literary Trust, Paul A. Lacey and Valerie Trueblood Rapport, Co-Trustees. Reprinted by permission of New Directions Publishing Corp.

Levertov, Denise. "O Taste and See." By Denise Levertov from POEMS 1960–1967, copyright © 1964 by Denise Levertov. Reprinted by permission of New Directions Publishing Corp.

Lim, Shirley Geok-lin. "Learning to love America" from WHAT THE FORTUNE TELLER DIDN'T SAY. Copyright © 1998 by Shirley Geok-lin Lim. Reprinted with the permission of The Permissions Company, Inc., on behalf of West End Press, Albuquerque, New Mexico, www.westendpress.org.

Longfellow, Henry Wadsworth. "Aftermath" from AFTERMATH, 1873.

Lovelace, Richard. "To Lucasta, Going to the Warres" from LUCASTA, 1649.

Machado, Antonio. "Traveler" by Antonio Machado in CAMPOS DE CASTILLA, 1922, translated by Michael Ortiz 2011. Used by permission.

Markham, Edwin. "Outwitted" from THE SHOES OF HAPPINESS AND OTHER POEMS, Doubleday, Page & Company, 1915.

Marlowe, Christopher. "The Tragical History of the Life and Death of Doctor Faustus," 1592.

Marvell, Andrew. "To His Coy Mistress," 1681.

Masefield, John. "Cargoes." From BALLADS. Elkin Mathews, Vigo Street. London, 1903.

Matsou, Basho. "Heat-lightning streak," "In the old stone pool," translated by X. J. Kennedy.

Matsushita, Suiko. "Cosmos in Bloom" by Suiko Matsushita, translated by Violet Kazue de Cristoro in MAY SKY: THERE IS ALWAYS TOMORROW. Reprinted by permission of Kimiko de Cristoforo.

Matthews, Washington. "Last Words of the Prophet" from THE MOUNTAIN CHANT: A NAVAJO CEREMONY. Government Printing Office, Washington, 1887.

McKay, Claude. "If We Must Die." Originally published in *The Liberator*, July 1919.

Menashe, Samuel. "Bread" from COLLECTED POEMS by Samuel Menashe. Copyright 1986 by Samuel Menashe. Reprinted by permission of the author.

Millay, Edna St. Vincent. "Recuerdo" from A FEW FIGS FROM THISTLES: POEMS AND SONNETS. New York and London: Harper, 1922.

Millay, Edna St. Vincent. "Second Fig" from A FEW FIGS FROM THISTLES. Harper and Brothers Publishers. London, 1920.

Millay, Edna St. Vincent. "What lips my lips have kissed, and where, and why" from THE HARP-WEAVER AND OTHER POEMS, 1923.

Milton, John. "Paradise Lost," Samuel Simmons, 1667.

Milton, John. "When I consider how my light is spent" from POEMS, 1673.

Momaday, N. Scott. "Simile" from ANGLE OF GEESE AND OTHER POEMS. Copyright 1974. Used by permission of the author.

Moss, Howard. "Shall I Compare Thee to a Summer's Day" from A SWIM OFF THE ROCKS: LIGHT VERSE by Howard Moss. Reprinted by permission of the Estate of Howard Moss.

Mother Goose. "Pussy Cat, Pussy Cat," published by James William Elliott in NATIONAL NURSERY RHYMES AND NURSERY SONGS, 1870.

Nelson, Marilyn. "A Strange Beautiful Woman" from THE FIELDS OF PRAISE, 1997 Louisiana State University Press. Used by permission of Louisiana State University Press.

Neruda, Pablo. Reprinted by permission of Farrar, Straus and Giroux: "We Are Many," from EXTRAVAGARIA, translated by Alastair Reid. Translation copyright © 1974 by Alastair Reid.

Newton, John. "Amazing Grace" from OLNEY HYMNS, 1779.

Nezhukumatathil, Aimee. "What I Learned from the Incredible Hulk" from MIRACLE FRUIT. Copyright © 2003 by Aimee Nezhukumatathil. Published by Tupelo Press. Reprinted by permission of the author.

Nguyen, Hieu Minh. "Arranged." Copyright © 2014. Used by permission.

Niedecker, Lorine. "Popcorn-can cover" from LORINE NIEDECKER: COLLECTED WORKS, edited by Jenny Penberthy, Copyright © 2002 Regents of the University of California. Permission conveyed through Copyright Clearance Center, Inc.

O'Donnell, Angela Alaimo. "Tattoo" from MOVING HOUSE © 2009 WordTech Communications LLC. Cincinnati, Ohio, USA.

Olds, Sharon. "Rite of Passage" from THE DEATH AND THE LIVING by Sharon Olds, copyright © 1975, 1978, 1979, 1980, 1981, 1982, 1983 by Sharon Olds. Used by permission of Alfred A. Knopf, a division of Penguin Random House LLC. All rights reserved.

Oliver, Mary. "Wild Geese." Excerpts from DREAM WORK, copyright © 1986 by Mary Oliver. Used by permission of Grove/Atlantic, Inc. Any third party use of this material, outside of this publication, is prohibited.

Owen, Wilfred. "Dulce et Decorum Est." Originally published in POEMS, 1920.

Parker, Dorothy. "Resumé," copyright 1926, 1928, renewed 1954, © 1956 by Dorothy Parker from THE PORTABLE DOROTHY PARKER by Dorothy Parker, edited by Marion Meade. Used by permission of Viking Books, an imprint of Penguin Publishing Group, a division of Penguin Random House LLC. All rights reserved.

Plath, Sylvia. "Lady Lazarus" from THE COLLECTED POEMS OF SYLVIA PLATH, edited by Ted Hughes. Copyright © 1960, 1965, 1971, 1981 by the Estate of Sylvia Plath. Reprint by Permission of HarperCollins Publishers.

Plath, Sylvia. "Metaphors" from CROSSING THE WATER by Sylvia Plath. Copyright © 1960 by Ted Hughes. Reprinted by the permission of HarperCollins Publishers.

Po, Li (701–762). "Drinking Alone by Moonlight."

Poe, Edgar Allan. "Annabel Lee" published in Sartain's *Union Magazine*, 1849.

Poe, Edgar Allen: "Ulalume." Originally Published in the *American Whig Review*. December, 1847.

Pope, Alexander. "True Ease in Writing Comes from Art, Not Chance" from "An Essay on Criticism," 1711.

Pound, Ezra. "In a station of the Metro." Originally published in *Poetry*, 1913.

Pound, Ezra. "The River-Merchant's Wife: A Letter," original by Rihaku from PERSONAE, copyright 1926 by Ezra Pound. Reprinted by permission of New Directions Publishing Corp.

Randall, Dudley. "Ballad of Birmingham" from CITIES BURNING with permission of the Dudley Randall Estate.

Randall, Dudley. "Ballad of Birmingham" in ROSES AND REVOLUTIONS: THE SELECTED WRITINGS OF DUDLEY RANDALL. Reprinted by permission of the Dudley Randall Literary Estate.

Reed, Henry. "Naming of Parts." Reprinted with permission from John Tydeman, literary executor of the Estate of Henry Reed.

Rich, Adrienne. "Aunt Jennifer's Tigers." Copyright © 2002, 1951 by Adrienne Rich, from THE FACT OF A DOORFRAME: SELECTED POEMS 1950–2001 by Adrienne Rich. Used by permission of W. W. Norton & Company, Inc.

Robinson, Edwin Arlington. "Luke Havergal." Originally published in THE TORRENT AND THE NIGHT BEFORE, 1896.

Robinson, Edwin Arlington. "Miniver Cheevy" from THE TOWN DOWN THE RIVER, 1910.

Roethke, Theodore. "My Papa's Waltz," copyright © 1942 by Hearst Magazines, Inc., copyright © 1966 and renewed 1994 by Beatrice Lushington.

Roethke, Theodore. "Root Cellar," copyright © 1943 by Modern Poetry Association, Inc; from COLLECTED POEMS by Theodore Roethke. Used by permission of Doubleday, an imprint of the Knopf Doubleday Publishing Group, a division of Penguin Random House LLC. All rights reserved.

Rossetti, Christina. "Song." Originally published GOBLIN MARKET AND OTHER POEMS, 1862.

Rossetti, Christina. "Up-Hill" from GOBLIN MARKET AND OTHER POEMS. Macmillan, 1862.

Ryan, Kay, "Turtle" from FLAMINGO WATCHING, copyright © 1994 by Kay Ryan. Used by permission of Copper Beech Press.

Ryan, Kay. "A Conversation with Kay Ryan" conducted by Dana Gioia.

Ryan, Kay. "Blandeur." Excerpt from SAY UNCLE, copyright © 1991 by Kay Ryan. Used by permission of Grove/Atlantic, Inc. Any third party use of this material, outside of this publication, is prohibited.

Sandburg, Carl. "Grass" from CORNHUSKERS, Originally published by Henry Holt and Company, 1918.

Sandburg, Carl. "Fog" from CHICAGO POEMS, 1916.

Satyamurti, Carole. "I Shall Paint my Nails Red" by Carole Satyamurti from STITCHING IN THE DARK: NEW AND SELECTED POEMS, copyright 2005 by Bloodaxe Books. Reprinted by permission of Bloodaxe Books.

Service, Robert. "The Shooting of Dan McGrew" from THE SONGS OF A SOURDOUGH, 1907.

Shakespeare, William. "My mistress' eyes are nothing like the sun (Sonnet 130)" from SONNETS, 1609; "Sonnet 116" from SONNETS, 1609; "Sonnet 18" from SONNETS, 1609; "When, in disgrace with Fortune and men's eyes (Sonnet 29)" from SONNETS, 1609.

Shelley, Percy Bysshe. "Adonais: An Elegy on the Death of John Keats, Author of Endymion, Hyperion, etc." 1821.

Shelley, Percy Bysshe. "Ode to the West Wind" from PROMETHEUS UNBOUND, A LYRICAL DRAMA IN FOUR ACTS, WITH OTHER POEMS, 1820.

Shelley, Percy Bysshe. "Ozymandias" from ROSALIND AND HELEN, A MODERN ECLOGUE; WITH OTHER POEMS, 1819.

Sitwell, Edith. "Mariner Man," originally published in WHEELS, 1918.

Smith, Stevie. "Not Waving but Drowning" by Stevie Smith, from COLLECTED POEMS OF STEVIE SMITH copyright ©1957 by Stevie Smith. Reprinted by permission of New Directions Publishing Corp.

Snyder, Gary. "Mid-August at Sourdough Mountain" by Gary Snyder from EARTH HOUSE HOLD, copyright ©1969 by Gary Snyder. Reprinted by permission of New Directions Publishing Corp.

Spenser, Edmund. "Epithalamion" from AMORETTI AND EPITHALAMION. Printed by William Ponsonby, 1595.

Stafford, William. "Ask Me" from ASK ME: 100 ESSENTIAL POEMS. Copyright 1977, 2014 by William Stafford and the Estate of William Stafford. Reprinted with the permission of The Permissions Company, Inc. on behalf of Graywolf Press, www.graywolfpress.org.

Stafford, William. A paraphrase of "Ask Me," excerpted from FIFTY CONTEMPORARY POETS: THE CREATIVE PROCESS, edited by Alberta T. Turner (David McKay Company, Inc., 1977), as shown.

Stallings, A. E. "First Love: A Quiz." Copyright © 2006 by A. E. Stallings. Published 2006 by Northwestern University Press. All rights reserved.

Steele, Timothy. "Epitaph" from "An Interlude of Epigrams," from SAPPHICS AND UNCERTAINTIES: POEMS 1970–1986 Copyright © 1986, 1995 by Timothy Steele Reprinted with the permission of The Permissions Company, Inc., on behalf of the University of Arkansas Press, www.uapress.com.

Stephens, James. "The Wind." From COLLECTED POEMS, 1926.

Stevens, Wallace. "Anecdote of the Jar," "The Snow Man," "Thirteen Ways of Looking at a Blackbird" from HARMONIUM. Knopf 1923.

Stevens, Wallace. "Disillusionment of Ten O'Clock" from HARMONIUM, 1915.

Stillman, Michael. Reprinted by permission from Michael Stillman, "In Memoriam John Coltrane." Published by *Occident* Fall 1971. Copyright © 1971 by Michael Stillman.

Tennyson, Lord Alfred. "Break, Break, Break," 1834.

Tennyson, Lord Alfred. "Tears, Idle Tears," "Come Down, O Maid." From THE PRINCESS, 1847.

Tennyson, Lord Alfred. "The Eagle," 1851.

Tennyson, Lord Alfred. "The Splendor Falls on Castle Walls," 1847.

Tennyson, Lord Alfred. "Ulysses," 1842.

Tennyson, Lord Alfred. "Flower in the Crannied Wall," 1863.

The Bible. "The Parable of the Good Seed," Matthew 13:24–30.

The Bible. "Psalm 150." Authorized King James Version, Oxford UP, 1998.

Thiel, Diane. "Memento Mori" by Diane Thiel from ECHOLOCATIONS, Story Line Press, November 1, 2000, edited by Diane Thiel. Copyright © 2000, by Diane Thiel. Used by permission of Diane Thiel.

Thomas, Dylan. "Do not go gentle into that good night" from THE POEMS OF DYLAN THOMAS, copyright © 1952 by Dylan Thomas. Reprinted by permission of New Directions Publishing Corp.

Thomas, Dylan. "Fern Hill" from THE POEMS OF DYLAN THOMAS copyright ©1945 by The Trustees for the Copyrights of Dylan Thomas. Reprinted by permission of New Directions Publishing Corp.

Toomer, Jean. "Reapers" from CANE by Jean Toomer. Copyright 1923 by Boni & Liveright, renewed 1951 by Jean Toomer. Used by permission of Liveright Publishing Corporation.

Trethewey, Natasha. "White Lies" from DOMESTIC WORK. Copyright © 1998, 2000 by Natasha Trethewey. Reprinted with the permission of The Permissions Company, Inc., on behalf of Graywolf Press, www.graywolfpress.org.

Valdés, Gina. "English con Salsa." Published by *The Americas Review*, Houston, Texas. Reprinted by permission of the author.

Videlock, Wendy. "If Not for the Dark" from THE DARK GNU AND OTHER POEMS, Able Muse Press. Copyright © 2013. Used by permission of the author.

Virgilio, Nick. "The Old Neighborhood" by Nick Virgilio from NICK VIRGILIO: A LIFE IN HAIKU, copyright © 2012. Reprinted by permission of Anthony Virgilio.

Walker, Cody. "I'm like" from *Able Muse: A Review of Poetry, Prose, and Art*, Number 22, Winter 2016. Used by permission.

Webster, John. "The Duchess of Malfi," 1623.

Whitman, Walt. "Beat! Beat! Drums!" Originally Published in *Harper's Weekly*, 1861.

Whitman, Walt. "I Hear America Singing," "O Captain! My Captain," "When I Heard the Learn'd Astronomer" from LEAVES OF GRASS, 1867.

Whitman, Walt. "When Lilacs Last in the Dooryard Bloom'd" from SEQUEL TO DRUM-TAPS, 1865

Wilbur, Richard. "Love Calls Us To The Things Of This World" from THINGS OF THIS WORLD by Richard Wilbur. Copyright 1956 and renewed 1984 by Richard Wilbur. Reprinted by permission of Houghton Mifflin Harcourt Publishing Company. All rights reserved.

Williams, William Carlos. "Queen-Anne's-Lace," "The Widow's Lament in Springtime" from SOUR GRAPES. Boston: The Four Seas Company, 1921.

Williams, William Carlos. "The Red Wheelbarrow," "This is Just to Say" by William Carlos Williams, from THE COLLECTED POEMS: VOLUME I, 1909–1939, copyright ©1938 by New Directions Publishing Corp. Reprinted by permission of New Directions Publishing Corp.

Williams, William Carlos. "The Dance (In Brueghel's)" by William Carlos Williams, from THE COLLECTED POEMS: VOLUME II, 1939–1962, copyright ©1944 by William Carlos Williams. Reprinted by permission of New Directions Publishing Corp.

Williams, William Carlos. "El Hombre." Originally published in AL QUE QUIERE!, 1917.

Wordsworth, William. "Composed upon Westminster Bridge, September 3, 1802," "My Heart Leaps Up" also known as "The Rainbow," "The world is too much with us" from POEMS IN TWO VOLUMES, 1807.

Wordsworth, William. "A Slumber Did My Spirit Seal," Originally published in LYRICAL BALLADS, 1800.

Wordsworth, William. "Mutability." From ECCLESIASTICAL SKETCHES, 1822.

Wordsworth, William. From the Preface to LYRICAL BALLADS WITH A FEW OTHER PIECES OF POETRY, 1798.

Wright, Franz. "Alcohol" from ILL LIT: SELECTED AND NEW POEMS. Copyright © 1989 by Franz Wright. Reprinted with the permission of Oberlin College Press.

Yeats, W. B. "Sailing to Byzantium." Reprinted with the permission of Scribner Publishing Group, a division of Simon & Schuster, Inc. from THE COLLECTED WORKS OF W. B. YEATS, VOLUME I: THE POEMS, REVISED by W. B. Yeats, edited by Richard J. Finneran. Copyright © 1928 by The Macmillan Company, renewed © 1956 by Georgie Yeats. All rights reserved.

Yeats, William Butler. "He Wishes for the Cloths of Heaven" from THE WIND AMONG THE REEDS, 1899.

Yeats, William Butler. "The Lake Isle of Innisfree." Originally published in *National Observer*, 1890.

Yeats, William Butler. "The Second Coming" from MICHAEL ROBARTES AND THE DANCER, 1921.

Yeats, William Butler. "When You Are Old," from THE COUNTLESS KATHLEEN AND VARIOUS LEGENDS AND LYRICS, 1892.

Yeats, William Butler. "Who Goes with Fergus?" from THE ROSE, 1892.

DRAMA

Bevington, David. "Othello" from THE COMPLETE WORKS OF SHAKESPEARE, 7th ed., © 2014. Reprinted by permission of Pearson Education, Inc., Upper Saddle River, New Jersey.

Cooper, Sharon, E. "Mistaken Identity." Originally published in published in LAUGH LINES: SHORT COMIC PLAYS, edited by Eric Lane and Nina Shengold, Vintage, 2007. Used by permission. For inquiries regarding production, please contact the playwright directly. secooper1@ yahoo.com. www.sharonecooper.com.

Glaspell, Susan. "Trifles." First performed at the Wharf Theatre in Provincetown, MA. August 8, 1916.

Grene, David. "Oedipus the King" by Sophocles, translated by David Grene from Sophocles I, 3rd edition Copyright © 2013. University of Chicago Press. Used with permission.

Hansberry, Lorraine. Entire play from "A Raisin in the Sun" by Lorraine Hansberry, copyright © 1958 by Robert Nemiroff, as an unpublished work. Copyright © 1959, 1966, 1984 by Robert Nemiroff. Copyright renewed 1986, 1987 by Robert Nemiroff. Used by permission of Random House, an imprint and division of Penguin Random House LLC. All rights reserved.

Hwang, David Henry. "The Sound of a Voice" from FOB AND OTHER PLAYS by David Henry Hwang. Reproduced with permission from the Steven Barclay Agency.

Isben, Henrik. "A Doll's House," translated by R. Farquharson Sharp and Eleanor Marx-Aveling, revised 2008 by Viktoria Michelsen. Copyright © 2008 by Viktoria Michelsen. Reprinted by permission.

Ives, David. "An Interview with David Ives." Reprinted with permission.

Ives, David. "Sure Thing" from ALL IN THE TIMING: FOURTEEN PLAYS BY DAVID IVES, copyright © 1989, 1990, 1992 by David Ives. Used by permission of Vintage Books, an imprint of the Knopf Doubleday Publishing Group, a division of Penguin Random House LLC. All rights reserved.

Marlowe, Christopher. Scene from "Doctor Faustus," (about 1588). Edited by Sylvan Barnet.

Mullins, Brighde. "Click." Humana Festival, Louisville, KY, 2000. Used by permission.

Sanchez-Scott, Milcha. "The Cuban Swimmer" by Milcha Sanchez-Scott from "The Cuban Swimmer." Copyright © 1984, 1988 by Milcha Sanchez-Scott. Used by permission of the William Morris Agency.

Smith, Anna Deveare. Scenes from the play "Twilight: Los Angeles, 1992" (Dramatist's Play Service Edition). Reprinted by permission of Anna Deavere Smith and the Watkins/Loomis Agency.

Wilde, Oscar. Scene, "Lady Bracknell Interviews Her Daughter's Suitor" from "The Importance of Being Earnest." St James's Theatre, London, February 14, 1895.

Wilson, August. Entire play from "Fences," copyright © 1986 by August Wilson. Used by permission of New American Library, an imprint of Penguin Publishing Group, a division of Penguin Random House LLC. All rights reserved.

PHOTO CREDITS

Fiction

1: Jim McHugh/Los Angeles; 2: Jim McHugh/Los Angeles; 8: Chronicle/Alamy Stock Photo; 9: Ms 680/1389 f.24 The Lion, the King of the Animals, from "The Fables of Bidpai," c.1480 (vellum), German School, (15th century)/Musee Conde, Chantilly, France/Bridgeman Images; 13: Ian Woolcock/SuperStock; 18: Art Archive, The aa525683/Superstock; 32: Library of Congress Prints and Photographs Division [LC-USZC4-4907]; 40: Courtesy of American Bookmen. From Dodd, Mead and Co, NY, 1898; 45: AP Images; 52: Apic/RETIRED/Hulton Archive/Getty Images; 72: BALTEL/SIPA/Newscom; 77: Bernard Gotfryd/ Premium Archive/Getty Images; 91: CSU Archives/Everett Collection Inc/Alamy Stock Photo; 107: Agence Opale/Alamy Stock Photo; 126: J.A. Scholten/Missouri History Museum, St.Louis; 131: CSU Archives/Everett Collection Inc/Alamy Stock Photo; 144: Everett Collection Inc/Alamy Stock Photo; 149: WENN Ltd/Alamy Stock Photo; 171: World History Archive/Alamy Stock Photo; 192: Pictorial Press Ltd/Alamy Stock Photo; 197: Shaun Higson/Portraits/Alamy Stock Photo X. J. Kennedy; 206: David Pickoff/AP Images; 220: INTERFOTO/Alamy Stock Photo; 223: World History Archive/Alamy Stock Photo; 225: Jack Mitchell/Archive Photos/Getty Images; 236: Pictorial Press Ltd/Alamy Stock Photo; 245: Library of Congress Prints and Photographs Division [LC-USZ62-49035]; 265: AP Images; 277: Carlo Bavagnoli/The LIFE Picture Collection/Getty Images; 280: Ana Segovia; 289: Everett Collection Historical/Alamy Stock Photo; 294: Steven Senne/AP images; 303: Neal Boenzi/New York Times Co./Hulton Archive/Getty Images; 305: Chris Steele-Perkins/Magnum Photos; 309: Marty Lederhandler/AP Photo; 318: Anthony Pidgeon/Redferns/Getty Images; 328: Jamieson Fry; 337: CSU Archives/Everett Collection Inc/Alamy Stock Photo; 347: J. A. Scholten/Missouri History Museum, St.Louis; 350: Dpa picture alliance/Alamy Stock Photo; 360: Art Collection 3/Alamy Stock Photo; 372: Everett Collection Historical/Alamy Stock Photo; 382: Photo 12/Archives Snark/Alamy Stock Photo; 387: Chronicle/Alamy Stock Photo; 389: World History Archive/Alamy Stock Photo; 393: CSU Archives/Everett Collection Inc/Alamy Stock Photo; 401: Ian Dagnall Computing/Alamy Stock Photo.

Poetry

405: Martin Klimek (CC-BY-4.0). Courtesy of the John D and Catherine T. MacArthur Foundation; 406: Steve Yeater/AP Images; 407: Thomas W. Roster; 459: Dan Streck Photography; 462: Oleg Golovnev/Shutterstock; 607: Aaron A. Abeyta; 611: Scala/Art Resource, NY; 611: Everett Collection; 613: Art Collection 4/Alamy Stock Photo; 614: Everett Collection Inc/Alamy Stock Photo; 615: MAGNOLIA PICTURES/MONTFORT, MICHAEL/Album/Newscom; 619: Lorenzo Dalberto/Alamy Stock Photo; 620: Library of Congress Prints and Photographs Division [LC-USZ62-116342]; 621: Amherst College; 624: Chronicle/Alamy Stock Photo; 628: Everett Collection Historical/Alamy Stock Photo; 630: CSU Archives/Everett Collection Inc/Alamy Stock Photo; 635: Juan Felipe Herrera, "El ángel de la guarda" from LOTERIA CARDS AND FORTUNE POEMS: A BOOK OF LIVES, with linocuts by Artemio Rodrígues. Copyright © 1999 by Juan Felipe Herrera. Reprinted with the permission of The Permissions Company, Inc., on behalf of City Lights Books, www.citylights.com.; 636: Popperfoto/Getty Images; 637: MPI/Archive Photos/Getty Images; 638: Hulton Archive/Getty Images; 640: GL Archive/Alamy Stock Photo 642: Steven Lewis; 644: Copyright Shirley Geok-Lin Lim; 646: Photo Researchers Science History Images/Alamy Stock Photo 647: Pictorial Press Ltd/Alamy Stock Photo

648: Beowulf Sheehan/ZUMAPRESS.com/Newscom; 653: Georgios Kollidas/Alamy Stock Photo; 654: AP Images; 656: Library of Congress Prints and Photographs Division [LC-USZ62-82784]; 658: Fine Art Images/Heritage Image Partnership Ltd/Alamy Stock Photo; 661: Pictorial Press Ltd/Alamy Stock Photo.

Drama

663: Joseph Marzullo/WENN.com/Newscom; 664: Frank Franklin II/AP Images; 665: Timothy Hiatt/Getty Images Entertainment/Getty Images; 669: AP Images; 679: *Trifles* by Susan Glaspell. Original 1916 Performance; Wharf Theater, Provincetown, Massachusetts; 692: *Doctor Faustus*, from the Utah Shakespeare Festival's 2005 production; 698: Elnur/Shutterstock; 701: Geraint Lewis/Alamy Stock Photo; 704: Janette Pellegrini/WireImage/Getty Images; 706: James Leynse Photography; 771: Oli Scarff/Getty Images News/Getty Images; 773: Andrea Pistolesi/The Image Bank/Getty Images; 774: Georgios Kollidas/Alamy Stock Photo; 781: Photo by Karl Hugh. Copyright Utah Shakespeare Festival, 2008.; 794: Photo by Karl Hugh. Copyright Utah Shakespeare Festival, 2008; 797: Photo by Karl Hugh. Copyright Utah Shakespeare Festival, 2008; 804: Photo by Karl Hugh. Copyright Utah Shakespeare Festival, 2008; 814: Photo by Karl Hugh. Copyright Utah Shakespeare Festival, 2008; 820: Photo by Karl Hugh. Copyright Utah Shakespeare Festival, 2008; 824: Photo by Karl Hugh. Copyright Utah Shakespeare Festival, 2008; 836: Photo by Karl Hugh. Copyright Utah Shakespeare Festival, 2008; 842: Photo by Karl Hugh. Copyright Utah Shakespeare Festival, 2008; 847: Photo by Karl Hugh. Copyright Utah Shakespeare Festival, 2008; 858: Photo by Karl Hugh. Copyright Utah Shakespeare Festival, 2008; 860: Photo by Karl Hugh. Copyright Utah Shakespeare Festival, 2008; 864: Photo by Karl Hugh. Copyright Utah Shakespeare Festival, 2008; 868: Photo by Karl Hugh. Copyright Utah Shakespeare Festival, 2008; 875: Photo by Karl Hugh. Copyright Utah Shakespeare Festival, 2008; 878: Photo by Karl Hugh. Copyright Utah Shakespeare Festival, 2008; 884: Photo by Karl Hugh. Copyright Utah Shakespeare Festival, 2008; 885: Photo by Karl Hugh. Copyright Utah Shakespeare Festival, 2008; 895: Everett Collection Historical/Alamy Stock Photo; 897: Everett Collection; 898: AF archive/Alamy Stock Photo; 975: Harvard Theatre Collection; 976: Geraint Lewis/Alamy Stock Photo; 1036: Courtesy of Milcha Sanchez-Scott; 1038: Mark Garvin; 1051: Joe Kohen/WireImage/Getty Images; 1055: Jay Thompson Archives/Center Theatre Group; 1059: Jay Thompson Archives/Center Theatre Group; 1063: Kevin Watkins Photography; 1068: Adam Rountree/Getty Images News/Getty Images; 1069: Suzan Hanson and Herbert Perry in the American Repertory Theater's 2003 world premiere production of the *The Sound of a Voice* in Cambridge, Massachusetts. Photo by Richard Feldman.; 1084: Cam Sanders/Brighde Mullins; 1087: RICH SUGG/KRT/Newscom; 1090: 1987 Ron Scherl/StageImage/The Image Works.

Writing

1145: CSU Archives/Everett Collection Inc/Alamy Stock Photo; 1206: Scala/Art Resource, NY.

INDEX OF AUTHORS AND TITLES

A number in **bold** refers you to the page on which you will find the author's biography.

A & P, 18
ABEYTA, AARON
thirteen ways of looking at a tortilla, 607
ACHEBE, CHINUA, **277**
Dead Men's Path, 277
Acquainted with the Night, 547
Adam, 458
ADDONIZIO, KIM
First Poem for You, 548
AESOP, **7**
Fox and the Grapes, The, 7
Aftermath, 450
ALARCÓN, FRANCISCO X.
Frontera / Border, 567
X in My Name, The, 609
Alcohol, 428
ALEXIE, SHERMAN, **318**
Facebook Sonnet, The, 549
This Is What It Means to Say Phoenix, Arizona, 318
Ancient Stairway, 557
Anecdote of the Jar, 583
Annabel Lee, 531
ANONYMOUS
Bonny Barbara Allan, 541
Carnation Milk, 460
Dog Haiku, 433
Epitaph on a dentist, 550
Last Words of the Prophet, 609
Sir Patrick Spence, 415
anyone lived in a pretty how town, 457
Araby, 382
Aria, 515
ARNOLD, MATTHEW
Dover Beach, 609
Arranged, 470
ARREDONDO, INÉS, **280**
Shunammite, The, 280
Ask Me, 422
ATWOOD, MARGARET, **197**
Happy Endings, 197
AUDEN, W. H.
Musée des Beaux Arts, 611
Unknown Citizen, The, 437
Aunt Jennifer's Tigers, 414
Ballad of Birmingham, 544
BARBER, DAVID
Aria, 515
Barbie-Q, 220
Barn Burning, 176
BASHO, MATSUO
Heat-lightning streak, 483
In the old stone pool, 483
Bats in a Box, 582
Batter my heart, three-personed God, for You, 449
Beat! Beat! Drums!, 533
Because I could not stop for Death, 622
Before the Law, 387
BELLOC, HILAIRE
Hippopotamus, The, 514
BIBLE
Parable of the Good Seed, The, 576
Parable of the Prodigal Son, The, 223
BIDPAI, **9**
Camel and His Friends, The, 9
Bilingual/*Bilingüe*, 427
BISHOP, ELIZABETH
Fish, The, 478
One Art, 611
Sestina, 552
BLAKE, WILLIAM
Chimney Sweeper, The, 441
London, 467
To see a world in a grain of sand, 495
Tyger, The, 613
Blandeur, 455
BLY, ROBERT
Cricket (*translation*), 483
Driving to Town Late to Mail a Letter, 487
BOGAN, LOUISE
Medusa, 590
Bonny Barbara Allan, 541
BORGES, JORGE LUIS, **144**
Gospel According to Mark, The, 144
Boston Evening Transcript, The, 571
BOYLE, T. CORAGHESSAN, **328**
Greasy Lake, 328
BRADBURY, RAY, **337**
Sound of Thunder, A, 337

Bread, 452
Break, Break, Break, 526
Bright Star, would I were steadfast as thou art, 485
BRONTË, EMILY
Love and Friendship, 502
BROOKS, GWENDOLYN
mother, the, 614
We Real Cool, 525
BROWNING, ELIZABETH BARRETT
How Do I Love Thee? Let Me Count the Ways, 615
BROWNING, ROBERT
My Last Duchess, 419
BRUEGHEL, PIETER, 561, 610
Buffalo Bill 's, 560
BUKOWSKI, CHARLES
Dostoevsky, 615
Bullet in the Brain, 72
BUSON, TANIGUCHI
Moonrise on mudflats, 483
On the one-ton temple bell, 483
piercing chill I feel, The, 476

Camel and His Friends, The, 9
Cargoes, 448
Carnation Milk, 460
CARROLL, LEWIS [CHARLES LUTWIDGE DODGSON]
Jabberwocky, 462
CARVER, RAYMOND, **107**
Cathedral, 107
Cathedral, 107
Chimney Sweeper, The, 441
CHOPIN, KATE, **126**, **347**
Storm, The, 126
Story of an Hour, The, 347
Chrysanthemums, The, 236
CHUANG TZU, **11**
Independence, 11
CISNEROS, SANDRA, **220**
Barbie-Q, 220
Clean, Well-Lighted Place, A, 171
Click, 1084
COFER, JUDITH ORTIZ
Quinceañera, 616
COLERIDGE, SAMUEL
Kubla Khan, 617
COLLINS, BILLY
Introduction to Poetry, 619
Composed upon Westminster Bridge, 659
Convergence of the Twain, The, 631
COOPER, SHARON, **1063**
Mistaken Identity, 1063
CORMAN, CID
only one guy (*translation*), 483
CORNFORD, FRANCES
Watch, The, 511
CORTEZ, SARAH
Adam, 458
Cosmos in bloom, 484
CRANE, STEPHEN
Heart, The, 562
Wayfarer, The, 427
CREELEY, ROBERT
Oh No, 436
Cricket, 483
Cuban Swimmer, The, 1036
CUMMINGS, E. E.
anyone lived in a pretty how town, 457
Buffalo Bill 's, 560
in Just-, 566
somewhere I have never travelled,gladly beyond, 620
CUNNINGHAM, J. V.
Friend, on this scaffold Thomas More lies dead, 452

Dance, The, 561
Days of wine and roses, 540
DE CRISTOFORO, VIOLET KAZUE
Cosmos in bloom (*translation*), 484
Even the croaking of frogs (*translation*), 484
Dead Men's Path, 277
Death be not proud, 623
Death Has an Appointment in Samarra, 6
Design, 1176
DEUTSCH, BABETTE
falling flower (*translation*), The, 482
DICKINSON, EMILY
Because I could not stop for Death, 622
I felt a Funeral, in my Brain, 621
Lightning is a yellow Fork, The, 572
My Life had stood – a Loaded Gun, 494
Route of Evanescence, A, 480
Wild Nights – Wild Nights!, 621
Digging, 632
Disillusionment of Ten O'Clock, 469
Do not go gentle into that good night, 550
Doctor Faustus (*scene*), 692
Dog Haiku, 433
Doll's House, A, 973
DONNE, JOHN
Batter my heart, three-personed God, for You, 449
Death be not proud, 623
Flea, The, 623
Song (*Go and catch a falling star*), 540
DOOLITTLE, HILDA. *See* H.D.
Dostoevsky, 615
Dover Beach, 609